RAPTOR CONSERVATION TODAY

Golden Eagle *Aquila ehrysaetos*

The World Working Group on Birds of Prey and Owls (WWGBP)

The WWGBP has been active for over twenty years and today plays an important role in the promotion of raptor conservation and research on an international level.
Its membership list today comprises over 1,000 raptor specialists and enthusiasts in all parts of the world, and anybody with an interest in raptors is welcome to become a member.
For further information contact:

World Working Group on Birds of Prey and owls, 15b Bolton Gardens, LONDON SW5 0AL, England. Tel/Fax: +44 71 370 1896,

Weltarbeitsgruppe für Greifvögel und Eulen e.V., Wangenheimstr. 32, D-14193 BERLIN, Germany. Fax. +49 30 892 80 67, Tel. +49 30 826 34 99 & +49 30 881 85 25, or

Groupe de Travail Mondial sur les Rapaces, 31, avenue du Maine, F-75015 PARIS, France. Fax. +33 1 45 67 47 13, Tel. +33 1 42 22 22 27.

In addition to issuing to all members a newsletter (in English, German and French) twice a year, thereby keeping them informed of current research, forthcoming conferences, status reports, recent publications, etc. one of the Group's major activities is to organise a World Conference every five years as well as other international meetings. Its next meeting, the International Conference on Holarctic Birds of Prey, in Badajoz, Extremadura, Spain is scheduled for 14 - 17 April 1995.

The following scientific publications are still available from WWGBP:

RAPTORS IN THE MODERN WORLD (1989)
Proceedings of the III World Conference on Birds of Prey and Owls.
612 pages, size 15.5 x 23cm, with colour cover, contains 72 original papers in English by 112 authors from 27 countries. Price US $45, £25, DM 75, FF 240, Ptas 5000.

BIRDS OF PREY BULLETIN No. 3 (1986)
211 pages, 31 original papers covering current raptor studies worldwide. This particular issue , however, consists in large part of the Proceedings of the First Western Hemisphere Meeting of the WWGBP held at Sacramento California, in November 1985, during which, for the first time, a comprehensive series of reports was given on the situation of raptors both resident and migratory, in a number of different countries of Central and South America. Price US $15, £9, DM25.

BIRDS OF PREY BULLETIN No. 4 (1991)
302 pages, size 14.5 x 21cm, with colour cover, many black and white photographs, contains 28 papers by 41 authors from 20 countries worldwide on birds of prey and owls covering a wide range of topics concerning the biology, ecology, status and conservation of these birds, Price US $25, £12, DM 35, FF 115, Ptas 2500.

Forthcoming publication:

EAGLE STUDIES (1994)
(Birds of Prey Bulletin No. 5)
This book will contain some 50 original papers on eagles presented at the World Conference in Berlin, during the International Eagle Symposium held in Poland and during an international meeting on the Imperial eagle in Hungary. Many black and white photographs.

RAPTOR CONSERVATION TODAY

Edited by

B.-U. Meyburg & R. D. Chancellor

Line drawings by Friedhelm Weick

Proceedings
of the IV World Conference
on Birds of Prey and Owls

Berlin, Germany, 10-17 May 1992

Organised with the financial support
of the Berlin Senate
and
the Deutsche Forschungsgemeinschaft (DFG)

W.W.G.B.P.
WORLD WORKING GROUP ON
BIRDS OF PREY AND OWLS

Pica
PRESS

Wangenheimstr. 32, D - 14193 Berlin
15b Bolton Gardens, London SW5 0AL
31, Avenue du Maine, F - 75015 Paris

Trade edition published by
Helm Information Ltd
The Banks, Mountfield,
Near Robertsbridge, East Sussex TN32 5JY

ISBN 1-873403-33-X

A CIP catalogue record for this book is available from the British Library.

The Pica Press is an imprint of Helm Information Ltd

Distributed in the United States of America
by
Buteo Books
Route 1, Box 242
Shipman, Virginia 22971 USA

Distributed in Southern Africa
by
Russel Friedman Books CC
PO Box 73
Halfway House, 1685
South Africa

Typeset by Fluke Art,
Bexhill on Sea, East Sussex

Printed and Bound by
Hartnolls Limited, Bodmin, Cornwall

Preface

From the 10th to 17th May 1992, at the Conference Centre of Humboldt University of Berlin, the World Working Group on Birds of Prey and Owls (WWGBP) organised its most outstanding conference to date, assembling as it did 500 participants from all parts of the world. There were, in particular, 47 attending from both North and South America, 15 from countries of the former Soviet Union, together with 25 others from East Europe, 10 from Africa, 5 from Australia and New Zealand, 6 each from Japan and Israel, 10 from other Asian countries and 150 from Western Europe.

This conference was a particularly moving event for many raptor specialists, since for the first time it enabled an important number of ornithologists from the former "Iron Curtain" countries to participate, thanks not only to the recent political changes but also to substantial financial support given by the Berlin Senate and the Deutsche Forschungsgemeinschaft (DFG) (German Research Council). The bearers of names long familiar in the scientific literature appeared as living persons and paved the way for numerous new friendships.

Conferences of this kind take an excessively long time to prepare and the initial steps for this IV World Conference were already taken immediately after publication of the Proceedings of the III World Conference in the summer of 1989. The first requirement was to select the principal themes according to the following criteria: 1. Important and interesting subjects not hitherto treated; 2. Themes of such consequence that they require further airing; and 3. New methods of research and their recent results.

It is clearly not possible for one person alone to draw up such a scientific programme. Accordingly, it was necessary to find for each principal theme personalities willing to act as their conveners and later as referees of the papers, in the same way as for preceding conferences and the proceedings. We were fortunate enough to be able once again to benefit from the collaboration of the world's leading experts. This is a vital factor in ensuring the success of such an undertaking.

Shortly before the date fixed for the conference, grave and entirely unforeseen problems arose. It was only on the occasion of a visit to the Conference Centre in February that we learned quite by chance that it was due to be closed down on 31st March — a fact of which none of the organisers of other conferences for which the Centre had been booked had been advised. All the Centre's staff had been given notice.

We immediately set about trying to prevent this closure by every means possible. At first this seemed quite hopeless, especially with regard to the short time available. We then learned that for several months past there had been discussions held between the Berlin Senate and Humboldt University regarding the future of the Centre but without any definite decision being reached. We therefore tried to prevent the otherwise almost inevitable cancellation of the Conference by writing to the Senate, sending petitions to members of the Chamber of Representatives and to the Mayor of Berlin, and invoking the support of the press.

Selected extracts from this correspondence, along with several newspaper articles, were included as addenda to the Conference Programme, so as to give some idea of the gravity of the situation. On many days we were convinced that there was really no chance of saving the World Conference.

Parallel with the efforts being made to persuade the Senate to reverse its decision to close the Conference Centre, alternative solutions were sought. We wrote to and visited a number of hotels and centres which offered conference halls. It even proved possible to find fine halls conveniently situated in the centre of Berlin, one of which actually had a view of one of the nesting places of a pair of Peregrine Falcons, but it seemed almost impossible to find lodgings for our participants since the most important congress for the city of Berlin during 1992 was due to be held at the same time as ours and rooms had already been booked for 40,000 people, leaving virtually nothing available.

At this point the unhoped-for news reached us that the Senate had agreed to keep the Centre open for a further six months, so that the conferences planned could still be held there.

A number of the staff at the Centre, where participants were also housed and fed, were signed on again. The Centre also engaged temporary workers, and it was thanks to the great efforts made by all those employees to ensure the smooth running of this Conference — the largest so far to be held at the Centre — that things went without a hitch. The personnel of the Centre amply deserved the congratulations and thanks expressed in one of the Resolutions adopted at the closing session.

It was much regretted that the threat of closure hanging over the Conference Centre led to the transfer to Aix-la-Chapelle of the meeting of the European Section of the former International Council for Bird Preservation (ICBP) (now BirdLife International), originally planned to take place at the same venue immediately after ours.

A fresh and very serious problem, which could have posed an equally grave threat to the success of our conference, arose when, very shortly before the opening date, the General Transport Union in Germany started the longest and most severe strike in its history, resulting in a stoppage of all public transport in Berlin and most other regions for nearly two weeks. Only two days before the conference opened it was still almost impossible to reach Berlin by air. Meanwhile we had naturally been inundated with enquiries from all over the world by participants worried about the situation and it was difficult at times to persuade them not to cancel their journey. It was only 48 hours before the conference opening that things returned to normal.

Most of the participants arrived on Saturday, 9th May, and received the conference papers, particularly a detailed programme and a booklet of 74 pages containing abstracts of the 240 presentations. All these abstracts were limited to about 200 words each. This booklet provides an overall view of the present state of research on diurnal and nocturnal birds of prey.

The walls of both lecture-halls of the conference were decorated with numerous drawings and paintings of birds of prey lent by those two fine artists Friedhelm Weick and Bernd Pöppelmann. The Berlin Natural History Museum had loaned very impressive mounted specimens of White-tailed Sea Eagle, Bearded Vulture, Griffon Vulture and Steller's Sea Eagle, which adorned the stage of the main hall. Three specialist booksellers displayed their books in adjoining rooms and suppliers of telemetry and optical equipment also displayed their wares.

In his capacity as Chairman of the International Organising Committee, Dr. Bernd-U. Meyburg opened the conference at 10 a.m. on Sunday, 10th May, with a brief speech of welcome in German, English and French. Dr. Vladimir Galushin from Moscow, one of WWGBP's Vice-Chairmen, and Prof. Heinrich Mendelssohn, born in Berlin and the oldest participant, also both addressed the participants, for whom there was barely room in the hall. A representative of the Brandenburg Ministry of the Environment also gave a brief introductory speech on nature conservation in this part of Germany.

The keynote scientific address was given by Dr. Claus König of the Stuttgart Natural History Museum and Honorary President of the German Society for Nature Protection (Naturschutzbund Deutschland), at the full opening session. His subject was the taxonomic bio-acoustic field studies he has been conducting for many years on nocturnal birds of prey in South America

During the ensuing lunch break we gave a press conference; many representatives of the press were present, and during the days that followed our World Conference was widely reported in the various media.

After the break, the first scientific session was held on Population Studies. This had been convened by Dr. A. Kostrzewa (Germany) and Dr. Vladimir Galushin (Russia) and comprised 33 oral presentations and posters.

After a brief interval a second session was begun, running concurrently with the first. This concerned the Biology and Conservation of the large Falcons in the subgenus *Hierofalco* and had been convened by Dr. T. Cade (USA), Dr. W. Baumgart (Germany) and Dr. C. White (USA). This session was made up of 16 oral and poster presentations and covered the systematics, status, biology and protection of Gyrfalcons and Saker Falcons.

Following this session it was unfortunately necessary for all the sessions to run concurrently until the end of the conference, owing to the great number of oral presentations (about 200). Films and videos were shown on the first evening.

On Monday (11th May) the session on Large Falcons continued until the evening. At the same time there was a workshop on the protection of African birds of prey, followed by a session on Trapping, Marking and Radio-tagging which continued until the next morning (Tuesday). This session, organised by R. Bögel (Germany) and Dr. R. Kenward (Gt. Britain), included 23 papers on these techniques, some of them of great novelty, e.g. satellite telemetry. The evening was devoted to introductory talks, illustrated with slides, on the areas and reserves around Berlin due to be visited on the following day's excursions.

On Tuesday (12th May) Dr. R. W. Risebrough (USA) opened the session he had convened on Environmental Contaminants and Raptors. This comprised 22 papers and lengthy discussion on the effects of PCBs, lead, Dioxin, Fyranen, Fenthion, etc. and their negative impacts on birds' reproduction.

Parallel with this session was that on Rare and Declining Raptors: their Biology and Conservation, organised by Dr. B.-U. Meyburg (Germany) and R. D. Chancellor (Gt. Britain). This ran right through Thursday (14th May) and included 80 scientific papers.

About 300 participants attended a reception given on the Tuesday evening at Berlin Zoo by invitation of its Director Dr. Hans Frädrich. They were taken there by bus, from which they could obtain some views of Berlin by night. Cocktails were served in the tropical house, where the animals were fed late, thus adding an additional interest to the visit.

After these three days of conference, the participants enjoyed a day's relaxation, with excursions to three areas of Mark Brandenburg of particular interest for their birds of prey. The early days of May had been cold and wet, but on the eve of these excursions a sudden change in the weather led to one of the longest and driest spells of fine weather this century in Germany. The excursions on the Wednesday, as well as those at the end of the week, could thus benefit from a blue, cloudless sky and temperatures of 25-30°C. About 200 participants had chosen to visit the Uckermark and four bus-loads accordingly first visited the "Blumberger Mühle" nature reserve. The four buses then separated, under the leadership of Prof. Dr. M. Succow, Dr. E. Henne & Dr. W. Baumgart, Dr. M. Freude and Dr. B.-U. Meyburg respectively. Division into two German-speaking and two English-speaking busloads made communication much easier. As can be expected on such excursions, the number and composition of species varied on the different routes taken. Those in the bus led by Dr. B.-U. Meyburg were given, almost as if "by appointment", fine views of several Lesser Spotted Eagles. At our next "BlackStorkpossible" objective, Kites, Honey Buzzards and Marsh Harriers were on view. The high point was a visit to an observation post nearby for the study of a Sea Eagle's eyrie. From a safe distance the parent birds could be watched flying round and feeding their young. The party then moved on to see an Osprey's nest on an electricity pylon. The final objective was the Woblitz Nature Protection Centre, where Peregrines were being prepared for release from an artificial tree-nest.

Fifty participants had enrolled for an excursion to Havelland where, under the leadership of Dr. H. Litzbarski, they visited the Great Bustard Conservation Centre at Buckow. A further fifty visited the Spreewald where, led by Steffen Butzeck, they could appreciate this strange landscape during a tour of several hours. At certain fishponds Sea Eagles and Ospreys, along with other raptor species, were to be seen in large numbers. Many other participants took advantage of this free day to visit the city centre of Berlin

On 11th May about 35 persons took part in a day-long round tour of Berlin and Potsdam. On 12th and 14th May respectively, around 30 participants took the opportunity to see the nest site of a pair of Peregrines in Berlin, with a subsequent visit to the Tierpark and Zoo. Watched on a closed-circuit TV screen, an impressive glimpse was given of the family life of this city-dwelling pair and their young. Throughout the conference, to the delighted surprise of the participants, various birds of prey, particularly Red Kites, could be seen circling over the Centre. Even a Sea Eagle put in an appearance.

On Thursday, 14th May, the scientific sessions were resumed. Alongside that on Declining Populations were sessions on Reintroductions of Eagles, Vultures and other Raptors and on the Population Ecology of Owls. The session on reintroductions, convened by John Love (Gt. Britain) and Michel Terrasse (France), was composed of 14 presentations. Important and in some cases long-term projects in various parts of the world were reported on. The session on the Population Ecology of Owls was conducted by Dr. E. Korpimäki (Finland) and Dr. H. Pietiäinen (Finland) and comprised 23 papers. This was the first time that a major session devoted exclusively to owls had been held at a world conference.

On the Thursday evening there was a film shown in one hall, whilst a meeting of members of the WWGBP was held in the other. Firstly, the Group's composition and financial position were reported on by the officers and adopted by the members. Nick Mooney (Australia) took the minutes and the proceedings were translated into English and German by an interpreter. Next came the election of the officers, to conduct which the members appointed U. Robitzky. Dr. B.-U. Meyburg and R. D. Chancellor were duly re-elected as Chairman and Secretary/Treasurer respectively, with only one vote against. The following were elected Vice-Chairmen *en bloc*: Dr. Dean Amadon (USA), Dr. David Bird (Canada), Dr. Tom Cade (USA), Dr. Mark Fuller (USA), Dr. Vladimir Galushin (Russia), Michel Terrasse (France) and Dr. Jean-Marc Thiollay (France). There followed a general discussion on the Group's activities and possible venues for the next World Conference, for which South Africa extended an invitation.

On 15th May the session on owl ecology was succeeded by one on Extirpated, Rare or Lesser-Known Owls organised by Dr. R. Clark (USA) and Dr. H. Mikkola (Mozambique) and comprising 11 presentations. Concurrently with this was a session on the Systematics and Taxonomy of Raptors convened by Dr. C. M. White (USA) and Dr. A. Kemp (South Africa) at which 11 papers were presented. Following this came a final session on Tropical Rain Forests and Raptors organised by Dr. J.-M. Thiollay (France). Since this gravely threatened environment, which is constantly diminishing, is particularly rich in raptor species, it was felt that this theme, although already treated at a previous World Conference, should again be taken up. 13 papers were submitted. Even to-day, virtually nothing is known about many of these species.

Following the close of the scientific programme came the adoption of 24 Resolutions, which had previously been drafted by a small Resolutions Committee. Several of these were hotly debated and needed to have their wording revised before adoption. One resolution was rejected. Immediately after the Conference these were printed as a separate leaflet prior to inclusion in the volume of Conference Proceedings. In this form they were sent to the relevant governments, authorities, organisations, etc.

About 150 participants had enrolled for the two-day excursion to Mecklenburg-Vorpommern, a province extremely rich in raptors. Three bus-loads set off early the next morning, taking the motorway to Rostock. One bus turned off at Röbel and visited the legendary Müritz Reserve with its unusually high density of breeding Sea Eagles and Ospreys. At one fishpond there, 25 Sea Eagles were seen in the air together. The other two buses drove to the Mecklenburgische Schweiz, to the study area of the German Lesser Spotted Eagle Project. Here all three eagle species could be seen, including the first adult Lesser Spotted Eagle which had been trapped the previous year and fitted with a transmitter for radio-tracking purposes, as well as the video installation whereby the activities in a Lesser Spotted Eagle's nest are being automatically recorded. A number of participants were thus able to observe not only the female at the nest on the screen but also, at the same time, the male circling above them with an Osprey.

In the evening a dinner was given for all participants at Klink, near Waren. The occasion began with a general talk on the protection of nature and the environment in this new province by Frau Dr. Petra Uhlmann, Environment Minister of Mecklenburg-Vorpommern, who had come specially from Schwerin. This was followed by more specialised talks on the region and on the three eagle species. This excursion was widely reported in the local press.

The next day the party visited other places in the area which they had not seen the day before. Once again the weather was perfect and the participants were amply rewarded by the great number of birds of prey to be seen. That evening they returned by the motorway to the Conference Centre, where most of them stayed the night.

Preparation of the Proceedings began immediately after the close of the Conference. Unfortunately the Deutsche Forschungsgemeinschaft (DFG) (German Research Council) which had given substantial financial support to the conference itself some time afterwards no longer was in a position to also sponsor conference proceedings as before. In order to reduce the financial risk for the WWGBP and also to increase the circulation of the Proceedings it was decided to produce the book in cooperation with a well established British bird book publisher. We are glad that finally we have achieved the goal to have the book appear within about two years after the conference, as last time.

We would like to offer our sincere thanks to all participants in the IV World Conference on Birds of Prey for attending, and especially the authors for providing the material. Sincere appreciation is extended especially to the conveners of the different sessions for their drive and enthusiasm. To them belongs the lion's share of the credit for the success of the conference programme and the wealth of information included in this book. Friedhelm Weick once again gave us a nice collection of previously unpublished drawings for these Proceedings and Hajime Nakagawa not only came all the way from Hokkaido (Japan) to attend the conference, but also made available his dramatic photograph of an adult Steller's Sea Eagle which was finally selected for the front cover from a large number of photos submitted.

On behalf of everyone who attended the conference in Berlin we must especially thank Christiane Meyburg for the endless hours of work in organizing the conference and preparing these Proceedings. She certainly spent more time than anybody else to make this event a great success and without all her support and enthusiasm it would have been impossible to have the conference take place.

Dr. Bernd-U. Meyburg — Chairman

R. D. Chancellor — Hon. Secretary

World Working Group on Birds of Prey and Owls (WWGBP)

Contents

PART 4
TRAPPING, MARKING & RADIO TAGGING

PART 5
BIOLOGY & CONSERVATION OF LARGE FALCONS

PART 6
REINTRODUCTIONS

PART 7
POPULATION ECOLOGY OF OWLS

Keynote Address

Pygmy Owl *Glaucidium passerinum*

Meyburg, B.-U. & R. D. Chancellor eds.1994
Raptor Conservation Today
WWGBP / The Pica Press

Biological Patterns in Owl Taxonomy, with emphasis on Bioacoustical Studies on Neotropical Pygmy (*Glaucidium*) and Screech Owls (*Otus*)

Claus König

Only a few years ago, leading ornithologists argued that the listing of bird species should be complete. But, a short time after, new species of birds were described, and the descriptions of species new to science still continue. What was the reason for this? Well, up to now taxonomy and systematics of birds were based nearly exclusively on morphology and plumage patterns. I don't want to say that these are not important, but we must keep in mind that many plumage patterns are caused by adaptation to ecological conditions. Therefore some parameters more are wanted to complete the mosaic for a realistic, more biological species concept (E. Mayr 1963; J. Haffer 1974, 1987, 1990), leading to new views in systematics. We all know the phenomenon of convergence, which in many cases has misled taxonomists. A good example of this problem is the New World Vultures, which have been placed in the Falconiformes for a long time. The results of recent studies (König 1982) on morphology and behaviour of that group led to the conclusion that the Cathartidae should be included in the Ciconiiformes, removing them from the Falconiformes. Meanwhile molecularbiological investigations on the DNA have confirmed that the New World Vultures are really storks and not related to birds of prey (Sibley & Ahlquist 1990; Wink pers. comm. 1992).

Biological patterns, such as ecology, bioacoustics, behaviour, and molecular biology may give doubtless very important parameters for a clear and reliable species concept and for a systematic arrangement of bird species as well. Biological patterns are also wanted as measures in owl taxonomy. Nearly all species of that probably polyphyletic order are active at dawn or at night. Most of them show a rather large variability of plumage patterns, so that it is quite difficult to distinguish similar forms according to these patterns. On the other hand many species show different morphs in colouration, being often called "phases", which they are not! A phase is something temporary, while a red morph of an owl will never change into a grey one! The colour-morphs in owls are kept for life.

Because of their nocturnal life, owls can afford variability of plumage patterns in the same species, as well as similarity of plumage in two or more taxa. Therefore it seems that plumage patterns are of less importance for mutual recognition of members of the same taxon than are vocalizations in these nocturnal birds. In addition to this, it is important to know that in owls the whole vocabularies are totally inherited (Scherzinger 1978, 1990; König 1991) and show little geographical variation. Real dialects, as we know in most Passeriformes, don't exist! A few species show a larger individual variation, e.g. *Aegolius funereus* (König 1968, 1969), but the scale of variability is nearly identical in the different populations within the range of their distribution.

Tengmalm's Owls from North America show the same individual variability in song-patterns as do birds from Scandinavia or Germany. Living in a more or less boreal climate, where no competing owl species of about the same size lives in sympatry with it, *Aegolius funereus* can afford individual variation of the song, which species competing with equally-sized specimens of other taxa in tropical or subtropical habitats cannot do. These show very little individual variation of vocal patterns. Knowing this, it may be assumed that vocalizations are obviously the most important mechanisms of isolation between owl species. In our example the Boreal Owl of North America is doubtless conspecific with Tengmalm's Owl of Northern Eurasia. As migratory birds the two populations may have contact with each other across the Bering Strait, as there is a similar situation in some other holarctic species, such as *Asio otus, Surnia ulula* and *Strix nebulosa.*

An example for the contrary is the North American Pygmy Owl, known as *Glaucidium gnoma*, which, according to the different patterns of vocalizations, should be split into two species (König 1991): *Glaucidium californicum* (Rocky Mountains, south to Arizona, perhaps northern Mexico) and *Glaucidium gnoma* (Mexico to Panama or even NW South America). While the first seems to be rather closely related to the Eurasian *Glaucidium passerinum*, the latter has to be separated as a different species, because of its totally different voice - in spite of similarity in plumage patterns! I'll come back to that example somewhat later, when I will give some more details stressing my hypothesis on the specific character of vocalizations, based on my own investigations on South American Pygmy and Screech Owls.

Several years ago I began with taxonomical studies on Neotropical *Glaucidium*. Soon I had to realize that polymorphy, individual variation of plumage patterns, and colour-morphs put up enormous difficulties in distinguishing the different taxa. So I began with ecological and bioacoustical studies in the field in South America, in order to find biological patterns as additional help. These investigations are being continued. Beyond that I kept specimens of some species in aviaries for closer observation of their behaviour.

During the research in the field I dropped into a similar problem in Screech Owls (*Otus*), living sympatrically with Pygmy Owls in several regions of tropical and subtropical South America. For the past three years I have been in cooperative contact on these items with J.W. Hardy (Florida Museum of Natural History), J.T. Marshall (National Museum of Natural History, Washington), J. Vielliard (University of Campinas, Brazil), and M. Wink (University of Heidelberg, Germany). With the latter and his staff a close cooperation has begun on the study of blood-samples of owls (PCR, DNA-sequences) in order to get more and very important biological patterns for the taxonomy and systematics of owls. The investigations in the field have been supported by the German Research Council (Deutsche Forschungsgemeinschaft, DFG).

In many owl-lists only three species of *Glaucidium* are mentioned for the whole of South America (e.g. Burton 1973; Eck & Busse 1981): *Glaucidium brasilianum, G. jardinii,* and *G. minutissimum.* In 1989 J. Vielliard described a new species of Pygmy Owl: *Glaucidium hardyi.* The plumage patterns of this taxon closely resemble those of *G. minutissimum*, but both species have totally different voices (Figs. 1 and 2). While real *minutissimum* utter a song of equally spaced double-notes, the Amazonian species utters a trill at intervals (Figs. 3 and 4). According to Vielliard's studies *Glaucidium minutissimum* is only distributed in Eastern Brazil, while in the Amazon region it is replaced by the new taxon (Vielliard 1989; König 1991). In this case the question arises whether the Least Pygmy Owls from Mexico to Panama are *minutissimum*, or if they represent a separate species, which might be called *G. griseiceps*. This name has been used in a subspecific sense and is the oldest name attributed to races of *G. minutissimum* (Ridgway 1873; Sharpe 1875). The Central American birds differ vocally from those of Eastern Brazil, but are very similar in plumage patterns. They utter sequences of normally 3-8 equally spaced notes repeated, alternating with a pause of a few seconds (Figure 5). Further studies, which will include molecular biology (PCR, DNA-sequences), will show if these birds are in reality specifically distinct from *minutissimum.*

Revising Andean *Glaucidium* (König 1991), I found four different types of songs of Pygmy Owls living at higher altitudes. The first may be recorded in montane forests from Venezuela to Ecuador, the second, a different one, in also rather moist cloud forests from Peru to Northern Argentina. In montane forests of the Western Cordillera of Colombia you may record yet another song differing from the two mentioned, as consisting of series of double-notes or "couplets", while in dry regions of Western Peru and SW-Ecuador, from sea-level up to about 3500 m, series of evenly spaced notes given in a very fast sequence (about 7 notes per second) may be heard.

At first one might think of dialects or subspecific patterns. But, comparing ecological facts and studying the distribution of the birds singing in the manner mentioned, you will come to the conclusion: they must be different species! And so it is: The first is *Glaucidium jardinii*, which has two different types or strophes in its song. The male begins its territorial song with several "stuttering" and irregular, short trills, being then followed by another strophe, an evenly spaced series of rapidly sequenced notes (about 4 per second). (Figs. 6 and 7).

The second taxon utters also two different strophes in its territorial song. It begins in general with 2-3 long (each about 1 - 1 1/2 sec. long), melodious, rather flutelike trills, followed by equally spaced notes in rather slow sequence (1 1/2 - 2 per second). With little individual variation this type of song may be recorded in montane forests on the eastern slope of the Andes from Peru to Tucumán in Argentina (Figs. 8 and 9). This owl apparently is not *jardinii*, but a new species, to be separated from the latter, which lives north of the Marañón-depression. The new species is *Glaucidium bolivianum*, described in 1991 (König 1991). Also, according to PCR-studies of the DNA, this taxon has to be treated as a valid species, as it is beyond that ecologically, bioacoustically and biometrically distinct from *G. brasilianum*, as well as it is apart from *G. jardinii* (König 1991). (Figs. 10 and 11).

The third taxon, of Western Colombia, utters long series with double-notes or "couplets". Like the now separated *G. bolivianum*, this species had been merged with *G. jardinii*. But comparing song patterns, the similarity with the Central American *G. gnoma* is striking (Figure 12). I am rather sure that these birds belong to *gnoma*, as well as the Pygmy Owls of the mountains of Costa Rica (*costaricanum*) which now should be considered a race of *G. gnoma* and not of *G. jardinii*, which is distributed in South America only.

The last taxon lives in arid regions, bushy country and rather dry, open forests from sea-level up to about 3500 m on the western slope of the Andes (W-Ecuador to SW-Peru, and probably NW-Chile, north of the Atacama desert), reaching eastwards into the region of the valley of Río Pampas in Central Peru. Specimens of this taxon have been erroneously determined in museum collections as either *Glaucidium brasilianum* or *G. jardinii*. In reality they represent a new species: *Glaucidium peruanum* (König 1991). The song consists of long sequences of equally spaced notes in very rapid succession (about 6-7 notes per second) (Figure 13). Meanwhile I know by DNA-evidence, studied by M. Wink and his staff, that *peruanum* is apart from both the similar in outward appearance *brasilianum*, as well as *bolivianum*, and has to be treated as a valid species.

Of the West-Colombian taxon we could not yet obtain DNA-material, but we hope to get it quite soon, so that we will be able to prove the affinity with *gnoma*.

The splitting into different species is, of course, not only based on voice and ecological circumstances, but also on biometric characteristics and plumage patterns. But the vocalizations as biological patterns, being apparently the most important mechanisms of isolation between owl species, gave the deciding impetus for intensive research for more parameters. The DNA-evidence is under study, and the first results stress the hypothesis, that vocal evidence is a specific pattern in owls.

As I expressed in the introductory part, *Glaucidium gnoma* should be split into two species. If songs are compared of birds from the Rockies with those of southern Mexico, it will be found that there are enormous differences, while the song of *californicum* (of the Rocky Mountains) shows great affinities with the Eurasian *G. passerinum*. The territorial songs of both are single notes uttered at intervals of several seconds (Figs. 14 and 15). Both species may have allospecific rank within a "superspecies" called *Glaucidium passerinum*. *Glaucidium gnoma*, ranging from Mexico to NW-South America, should be separated specifically from the North American form (*G. californicum*) (Amadon and Bull 1988; Hardy *et al.* 1990; König 1991). Its song consists of sequences of double-notes or "couplets", sometimes in an irregular rhythm (Figure 12).

Glaucidium brasilianum is a polymorhic species. But the vocalizations show rather few individual variations. So the distribution of this rather common species reaches from Texas to central Argentina and Uruguay. It is widely distributed in tropical and subtropical South America, avoiding higher mountains and montane forests, as well as the dry western slopes of the Peruvian and Ecuadorian Andes, where it is replaced by other taxa. Its song consists of sequences of single notes at medium speed (about 3 notes per second. (Figure 16).

By patterns of the barring in the tail, which is not very variable in the Austral Pygmy Owl

(*Glaucidium nanum*) of Patagonia, this taxon has been separated from *G. brasilianum* by some authors (Figs. 17 and 18). Many gave it subspecific rank; others assumed that it might be only a morph. Comparing the vocalizations and studying its ecology, differences between *brasilianum* and *nanum* are rather clear, so that it seems more appropriate to give *nanum* specific rank, as an allospecies within the superspecies *G. brasilianum*. Its song is similar to that of *brasilianum*, but with a more rapid succession (about 4-5 notes per second) and more "staccato" patterns. In other vocalizations the differences are much clearer, as in the "chirrups" being uttered by both species (Figs. 19 and 20). Now the results of DNA-studies of birds from Santa Cruz in Argentine Patagonia prove the hypothesis of *nanum* being specifically distinct from *brasilianum*.

If we arrange the different taxa of Pygmy Owls according to ecological factors and bioacoustical patterns, it seems appropriate to build up species-groups, maybe sometimes superspecies with allo- or paraspecies. The plumage patterns and morphological facts don't speak against that. So the actual taxonomical situation might appear as follows:

Group 1: *Glaucidium passerinum* - superspecies, with allospecies *G. passerinum* (Eurasia) and *G. californicum* (Western North America, south to Arizona).

Group 2: *Glaucidium minutissimum, G. griseiceps, G. gnoma. G. griseiceps* and *minutissimum* might build a superspecies *G. minutissimum*.

Group 3: *Glaucidium jardinii, G. bolivianum, G. hardyi. G. jardinii* and *G. bolivianum* eventually represent allospecies within the superspecies *G. jardinii*.

Group 4: *Glaucidium brasilianum, G. nanum, G. peruanum.* All three species might be allospecies within the superspecies *G. brasilianum*, according to DNA-evidence (König, Heidrich & Wink, in prep.).

Glaucidium siju from Cuba might - according to bioacoustical evidence - perhaps belong to the *passerinum*-group. DNA-evidence is urgently needed.

On the map (Figure 21) the distribution of the Neotropical taxa of *Glaucidium* - according above all to vocal evidence - is indicated.

The situation of the different Neotropical taxa united in the genus *Otus* is even more complicated (Hekstra 1982). So I want to show only one example dealing with four species of southern South America: Morphologically all are very similar, one being slightly larger. All have grey, brown and reddish morphs. Three have yellow, one has mainly brown eyes. In each species males and females utter two different types of songs, which we call "A-song" (territorial song) and "B-song" (songs between mates at close range, maybe sometimes also uttered as response to playback) (Marshall, Behrstock & König 1991).

Otus choliba, the Tropical Screech Owl, has a wide distribution in tropical and subtropical South America. The bird has yellow eyes and a "herring-bone"-like plumage pattern on its underside. The two song-types are much more diagnostic for this species than are plumage patterns. The A-song is a short trill followed by 1-3 loud striking notes. The B-song is a low bubbling, resembling the song of *Aegolius funereus* (Figs. 22 and 23).

The two following species may live sympatrically with *Otus choliba* in certain regions of Southern Brazil, Eastern Paraguay and Northeastern Argentina (Misiones): *Otus atricapillus* is a bird of rather dense rainforest at lower altitudes. It normally has brown eyes, but morphs with yellow eyes occur, and not such a regular, herring-bone-like pattern on the underside. Its two songs are very distinctive. The A-song is a long (8 up to about 20 seconds) rapid trill with normally 14 notes per second. In the B-song a "bouncing-ball" character is diagnostic (rhythm like that of a table-tennis ball dropping onto hard ground). (Figs. 24 and 25). The B-song of the female is similar.

Otus sanctaecatarinae is somewhat larger and stouter than the previous species and has yellow, sometimes hazel-brown eyes. The plumage patterns are similar to *atricapillus*, but the ear-tufts are longer. The bird lives generally at higher altitudes in more open forests, even in groups of trees within human populations (Belton 1984). The vocalizations are very diagnostic. The A-song is a rather long trill (about 8-10 seconds), while the B-song has a "reverse bouncing-ball" character (the sound-sequence begins rather fast and gets gradually slower towards the end). Female B-song consists of sequences of very harsh, rather barking sounds, differing from vocalizations of female *Otus atricapillus* (Figs. 26 - 28).

Otus hoyi has been recently described as new species (König & Straneck 1989). It has yellow eyes, short ear-tufts and resembles in plumage patterns a small *Otus sanctaecatarinae*. The song is similar to that of *Otus atricapillus*, but the sequence of sounds is slower (about 11 notes per second), and the B-song has no "bouncing-ball" character. Also the B-song of the female is different from both *atricapillus* and *sanctaecatarinae* (Figs. 29 - 32). According to DNA-evidence *Otus hoyi* is not too closely related to *atricapillus*, but it obviously builds a superspecies together with the latter and *sanctaecatarinae*. The bird lives in montane forests on the eastern slope of the Andes of Northern Argentina and Southern Bolivia. Its distribution is separated from the occurrence of *atricapillus* and *sanctaecatarinae* by the thorny Chaco (about 700 - 800 km), in which the only screech owl seems to be *Otus choliba*. At rather close range in Bolivia, but at much lower altitudes, lives another similar species with also yellow eyes and an A-song very similar to *Otus atricapillus*: *Otus guatemalae*, which is distributed from Cochabamba in Bolivia northwards through Peru to Mexico. This species seems to have some relationship with *Otus atricapillus*.

According to our actual knowledge, the taxa *atricapillus*, *guatemalae*, *hoyi*, and *sanctaecatarinae* are best understood as allo-, resp. paraspecies in a superspecies: *Otus atricapillus*, while the similar *Otus choliba has* to be set apart, as being not related to them, as the DNA-evidence shows (Wink, pers. comm.). (Figure 33).

As in *Glaucidium* so in *Otus* too, the different taxa within every presumed species-group may have evolved from a common ancestral species. Populations of the latter probably got separated from each other for thousands of years during the Pleistocene, when the distribution of forests had been changing several times due to climate conditions.

These mentioned species of *Otus* are only one example for the difficulties in distinguishing the different taxa of this difficult genus. It was J.T. Marshall (1967) who first pointed out the high importance of vocalizations for taxonomy in this group of owls. In this sense, and using some more biological patterns, we try to get through the "taxonomic jungle" still existing in some groups of owls. The DNA-studies of M. Wink and P. Heidrich in Heidelberg will be an essential and decisive contribution to the mentioned investigations. So Wink and myself intend to establish a new systematics of the Strigiformes, based on a more biological species concept, in which bioacoustics and molecular biology will play an important role. Regarding the results of the mentioned investigations on Neotropical *Glaucidium* and *Otus*, such a revision seems quite urgent. So it may be mentioned that the genus *Glaucidium* should perhaps be split into the "true" *Glaucidium* and other groups of species, among them above all some African and Asian taxa.

Also the taxonomy of the African *Otus leucotis* should be discussed, for example, as the "subspecies" *granti* has a voice quite different from typical *leucotis*. Maybe there is a similar situation as in Eastern (*Otus asio*) and Western Screech Owl (*O. kennicotti*) in North America. Also *Strix* needs a worldwide revision, as well as the *Tytonidae* and some more.

The taxonomic and systematic studies on owls of the world can only be managed by team-work. Therefore we ask our colleagues for cooperation in order to provide us material from museum specimens preserved in alcohol, of which we only need a small tissue of breast-muscle. Zoological gardens and similar institutions who keep live owls might give an important contribution to scientific research if they could provide us with 2-3 small drops of blood of some species in question. The blood can be taken without harming the birds in any way, and can be preserved in a special buffer. Beyond that we are interested in recordings of owl-vocalizations, especially when the exact determination and locality are known. Also every observation of lesser known owls is of great interest. Taxonomy is no longer "grandfather's zoology" dealing only with series of stuffed museum specimens, but a modern and exciting field of research, not only for science but also for the conservation of species. If we want to protect a certain taxon, we must know its specific taxonomic patterns, in order to study and arrange the ecological requirements as well as the habitat of the doubtless right species we wish to preserve. Therefore taxonomy has to play an important role within the research of the World Working Group on Birds of Prey and Owls. In this field quite a lot will have to be done in the near future.

Figure 1. *Glaucidium minutissimum* from Eastern Brazil. Photo: R. Harling.

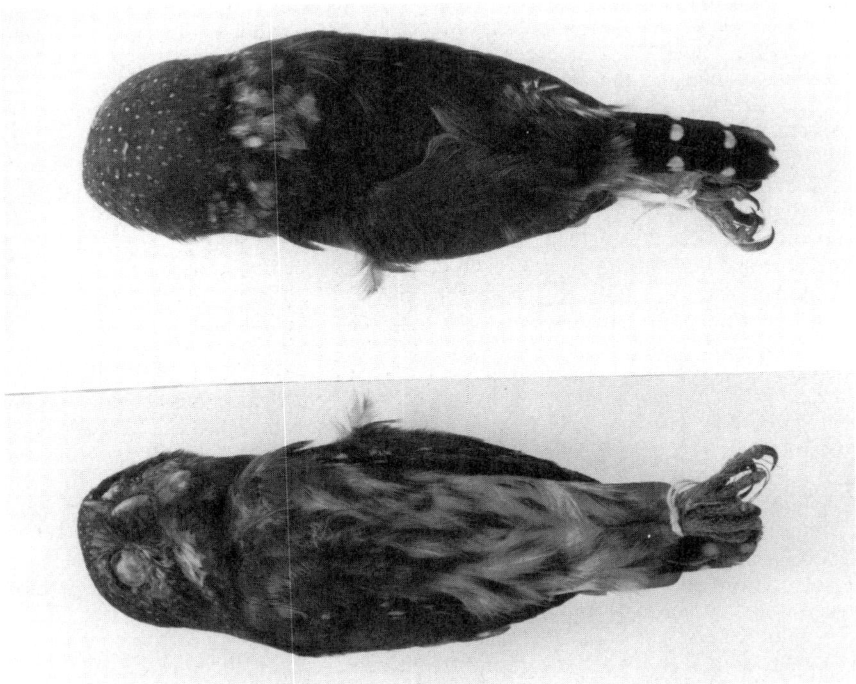

Figure 2. *Glaucidium hardyi* from Eastern Peru. Photo: H. Lumpe.

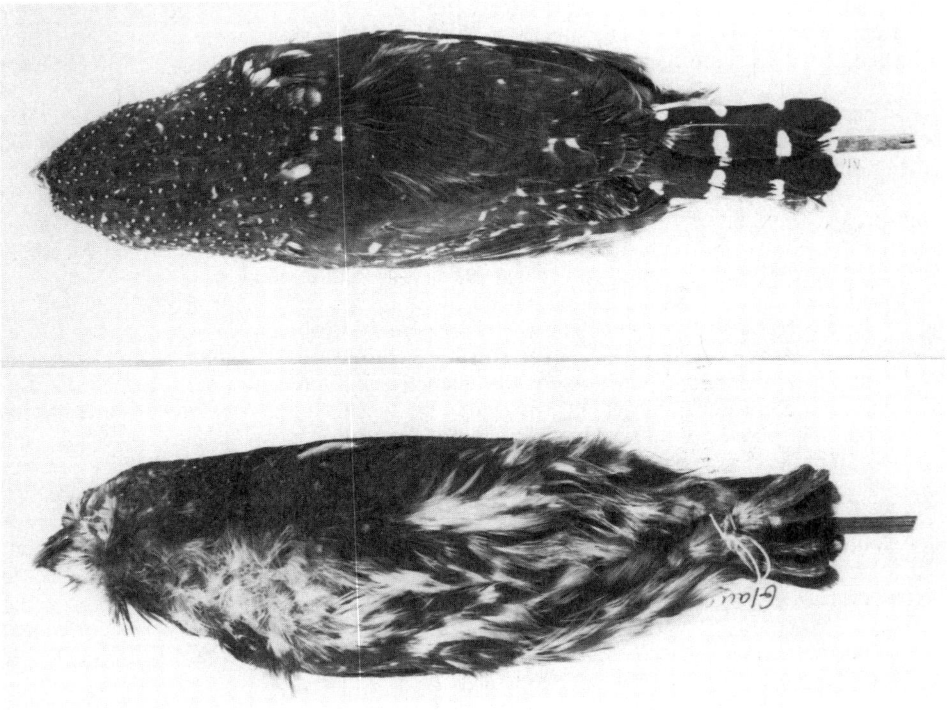

Figure 3. Strophe of song of *Glaucidium minutissimum*. Boissucanga, S. Paulo, Brazil. Rec. J. Vielliard (ARA-Records, Gainesville, Fl.).
All Sonagrams on KAY Elemetrics Sona-Graph, Model 5500. Upper row: waveform display; lower row: spectographic display. If nothing different is mentioned, the frequency range of the machine is put at 4 kHz and the time axis on 2 sec.

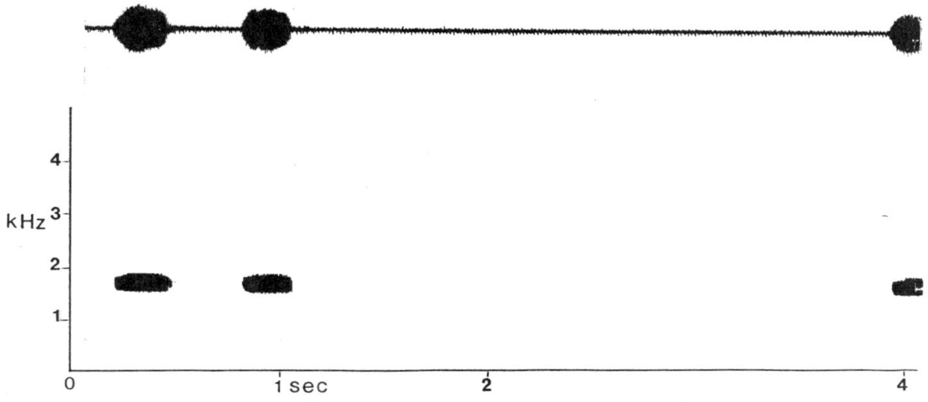

Figure 4. Strophe of song of *Glaucidium hardyi*. Rondónia, Brazil. Rec. J. Vielliard (ARA-Records, Gainesville, Fl.).

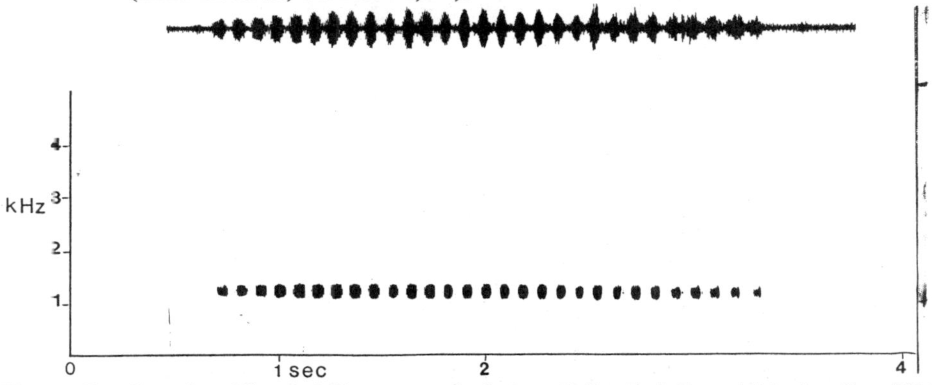

Figure 5. Strophe of Song of *Glaucidium "griseiceps"*. San Luis Potosi, Mexico. Rec. BBC (ARA-Records, Gainesville, Fl.).

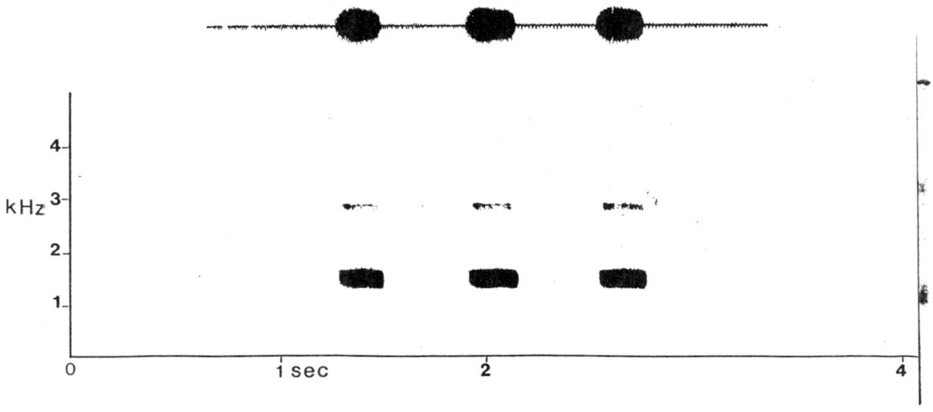

Figure 6. Several strophes of one of the song-types (introductory part) of *Glaucidium jardinii*. Páramo Zumbador, Táchira, Venezuela. Rec. P. Schwartz (ARA-Records, Gainesville, Fl.).

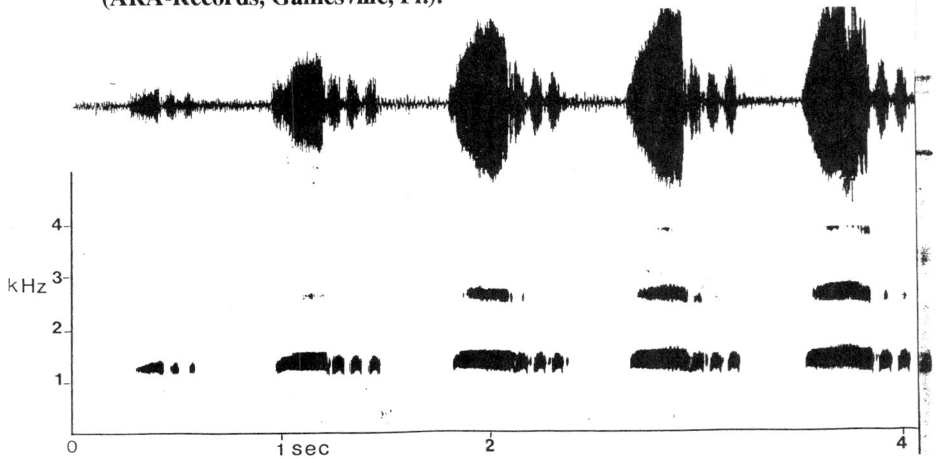

Figure 7. Sequence of the other type of song of *Glaucidium jardinii*. Same individual. Same dates.

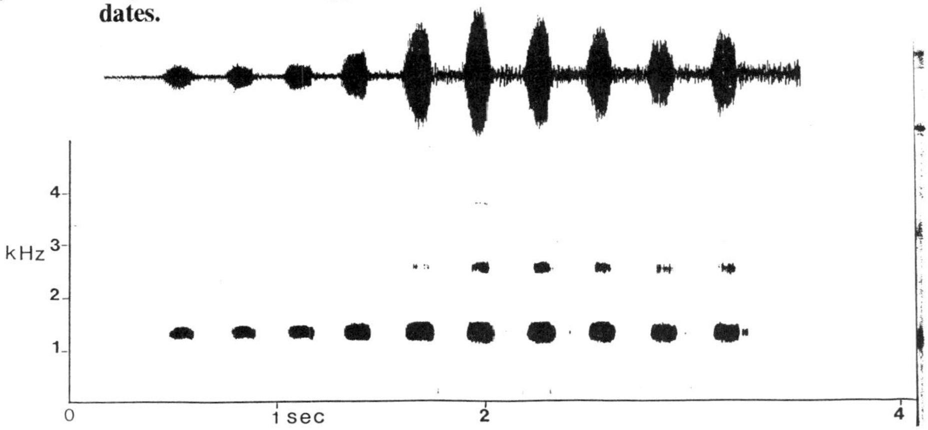

Figure 8. Part of one of the two song-types (introductory part) of *Glaucidium bolivianum*. Salta, Argentina. Rec. C. König.

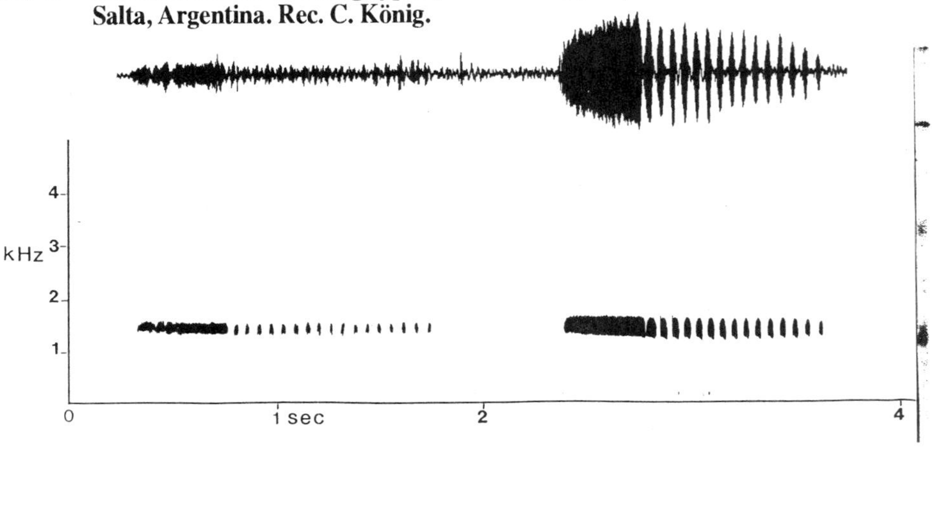

Figure 9. Part of the other song (most common type) of *Glaucidium bolivianum*. Same individual. Same dates.

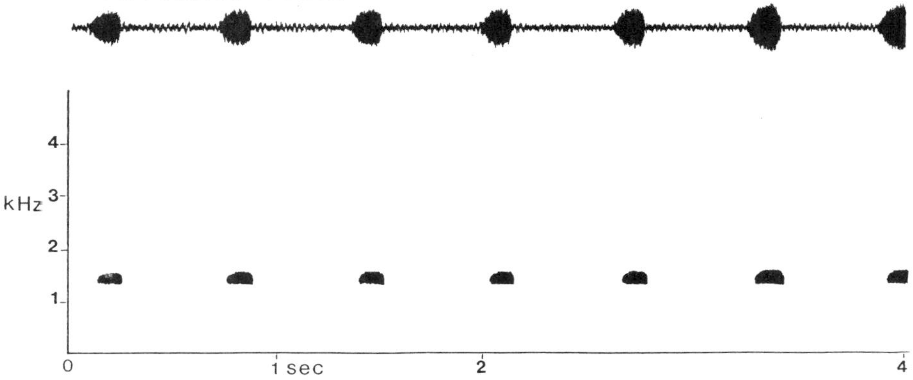

Figure 10. Skin of *Glaucidium bolivianum* from Lambate, La Paz, Bolivia (brown morph). Photo: H. Lumpe.

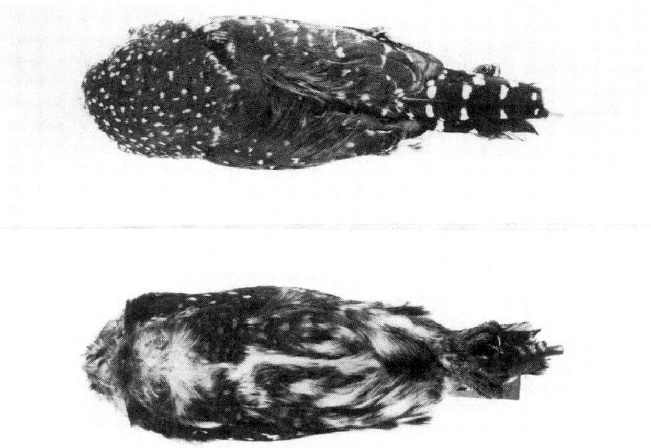

Figure 11. Skins of (from left to right): *Glaucidium bolivianum* (holotype, grey morph) from Salta, Argentina; *Glaucidium brasilianum tucumanum* (grey morph) from Anta, Salta, Argentina; *Glaucidium brasilianum tucumanum* (brownish morph) from Ledesma, Jujuy, Argentina. Photo: M. Harling.

Figure 12. Part of song of *Glaucidium gnoma*. Coahuila, Mexico. Rec. J.T. Marshall (ARA-Records, Gainesville, Fl.).

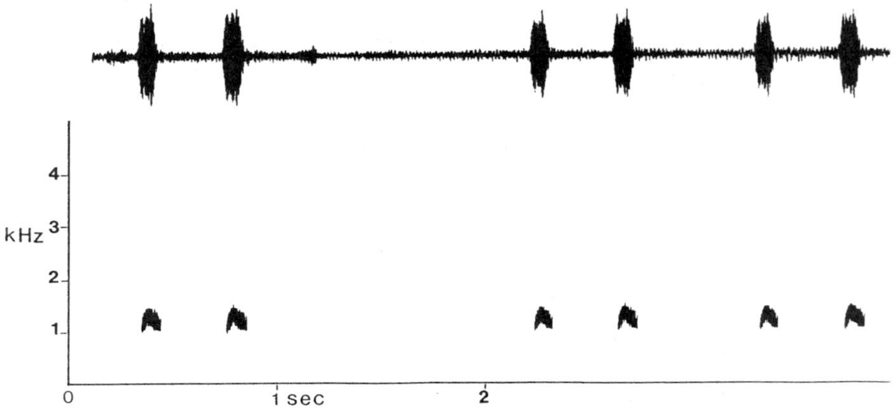

Figure 13. Part of song of *Glaucidium peruanum*. Ancash, Perú. Rec. T. Parker (ARA-Records, Gainesville, Fl.).

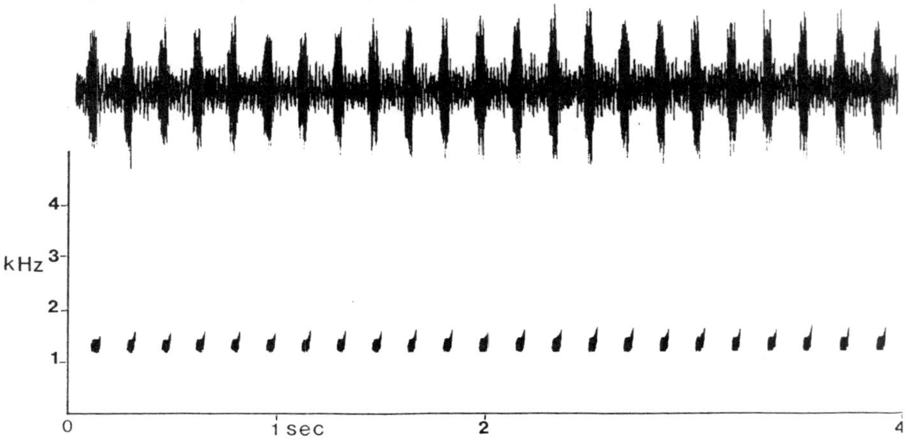

Figure 14. Part of song of *Glaucidium californicum*. California, U.S.A. Rec. J.T. Marshall (ARA-Records, Gainesville, Fl.).

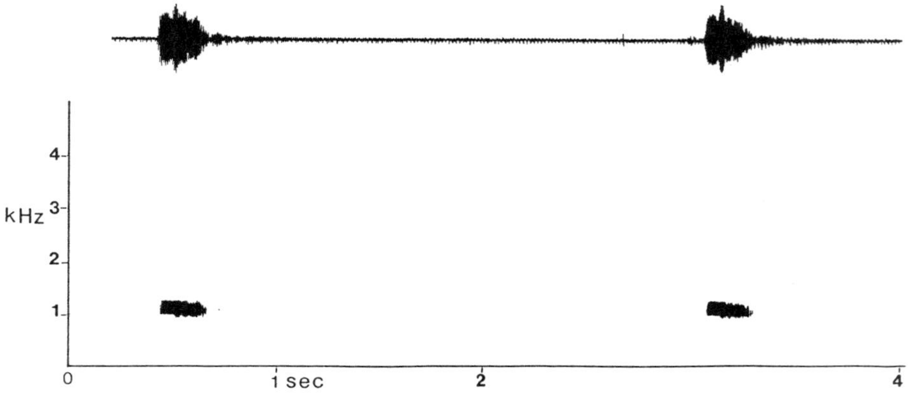

Figure 15. **Part of song of *Glaucidium passerinum*. Schwarzwald, Germany. Rec. C. König.**

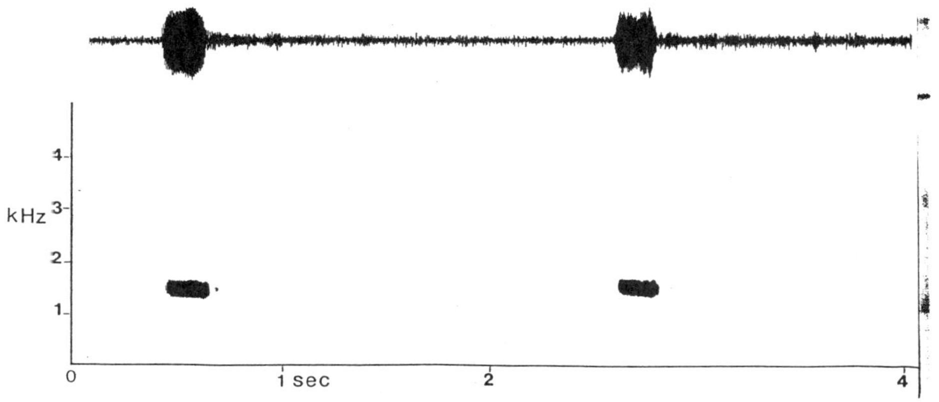

Figure 16. **Part of song of *Glaucidium brasilianum*. Montecarlo, Misiones, Argentina. Rec. C. König.**

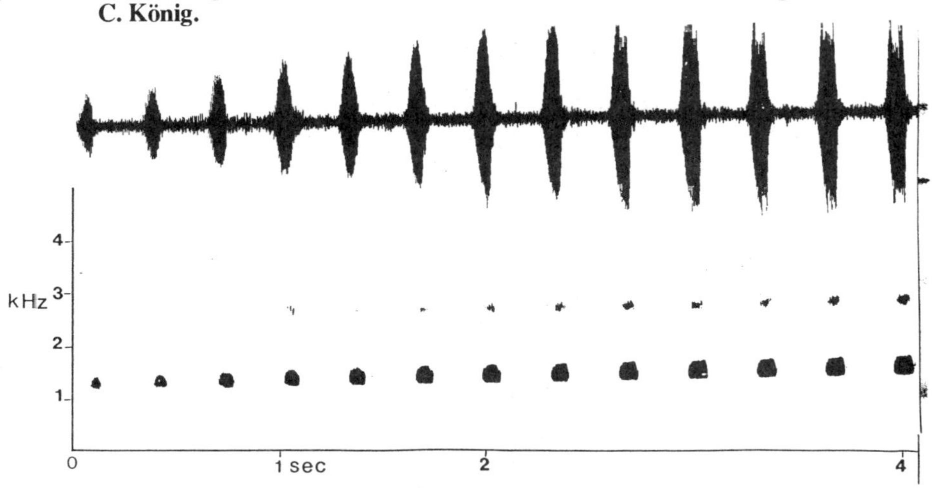

Figure 17. **Tail patterns of (from left to right): *Glaucidium nanum, Glaucidium brasilianum* (red morph), *Glaucidium brasilianum* (grey morph). Photo: C. König.**

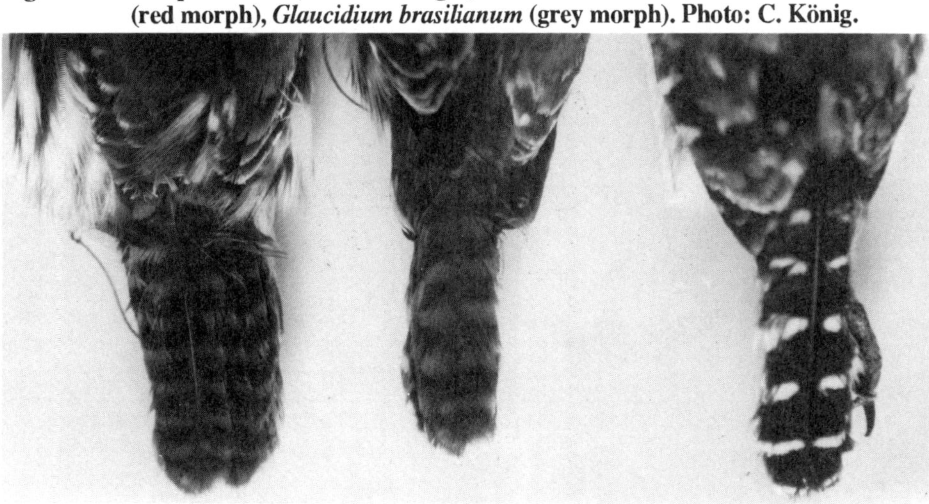

Figure 18. Male of *Glaucidium nanum* at song-perch. Lago Argentino, Santa Cruz, Argentina. Photo: C. König.

Figure 19. "Chirrups" (excited calls) of *Glaucidium nanum*. Lago Roca, Santa Cruz, Argentina. Rec. C. König. This recording and that on Figure 20 are displayed on the Sona-Graph at a frequency range of 8 kHz and a time axis of 1 sec.

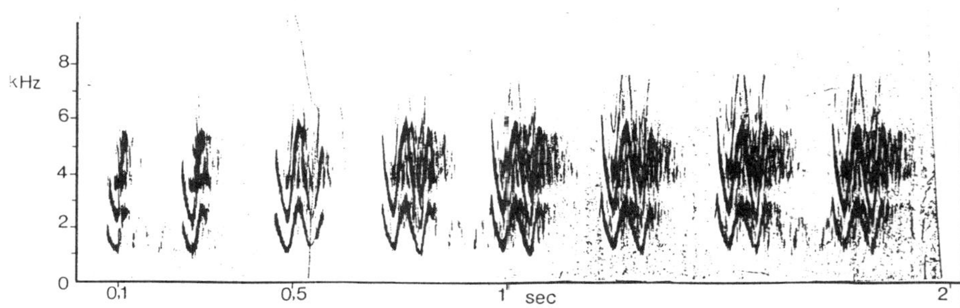

Figure 20. "Chirrups" (excited calls) of *Glaucidium brasilianum*. Salta, Argentina. Rec. C. König. Frequency range and time axis as in Figure 19.

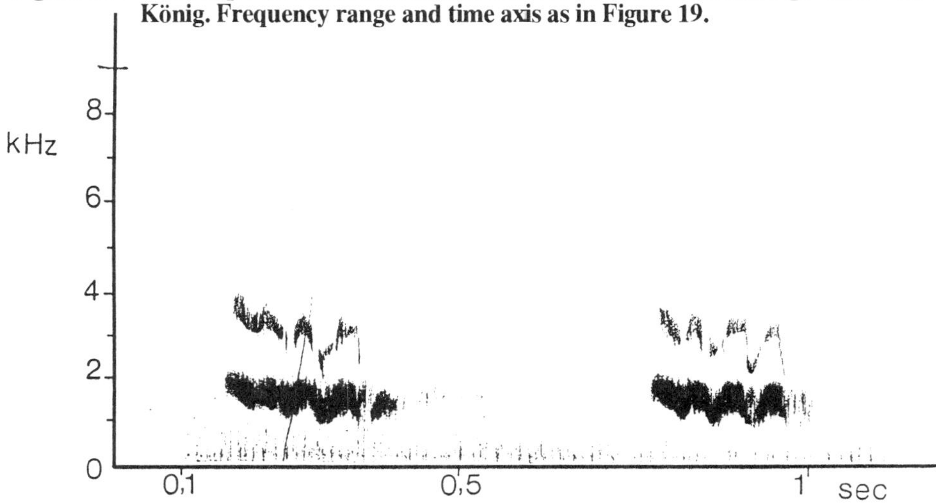

Figure 21. Distribution-map of *Glaucidium*-species (according above all to vocal evidence): A = *Glaucidium jardinii*; B = *Glaucidium bolivianum*; C = *Glaucidium "griseiceps"*; G = *Glaucidium gnoma*; H = *Glaucidium hardyi*; M = *Glaucidium minutissimum*; N = *Glaucidium nanum*; O = *Glaucidium peruanum*; ? = large, brown *Glaucidium* of uncertain status; hatched area = *Glaucidium brasilianum*; black (Cuba) = *Glaucidium siju*.

The North American *Glaucidium californicum* is distributed in coniferous forests of the Rocky Mountains from northern North America to southern Arizona. It seems to be closely related with the Eurasian *Glaucidium passerinum*.

Figure 22. Strophe of A-song of male *Otus choliba*. Iquitos, Perú. Rec. BBC (ARA-Records, Gainesville, Fl.).

This and the following recordings of *Otus* spp. are displayed at a frequency range of 2 kHz and a time axis of 2 sec. on the machine.

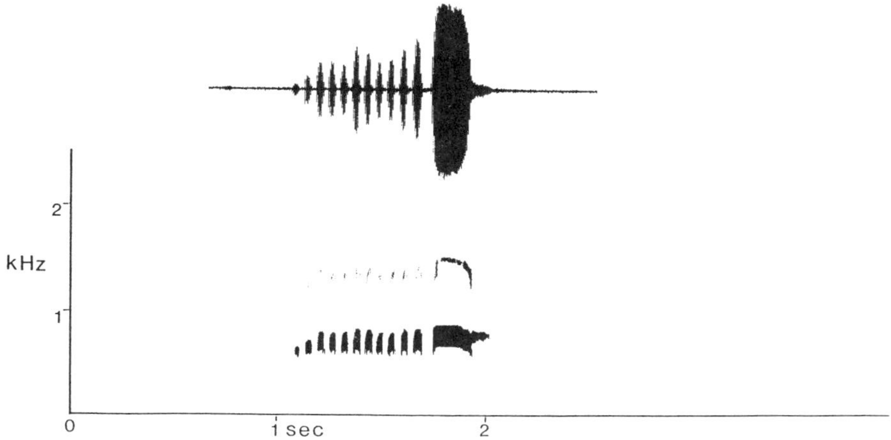

Figure 23. Strophe of B-song of male *Otus choliba*. Same individual, same data.

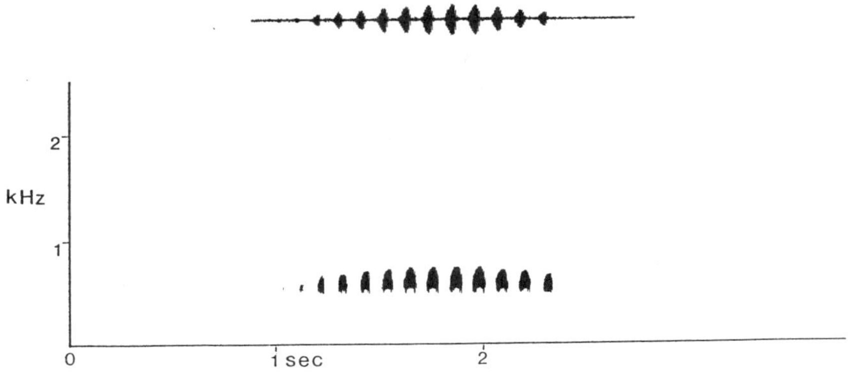

Figure 24. Part of A-song of male *Otus atricapillus*. Iguazú, Misiones, Argentina. Rec. C. König.

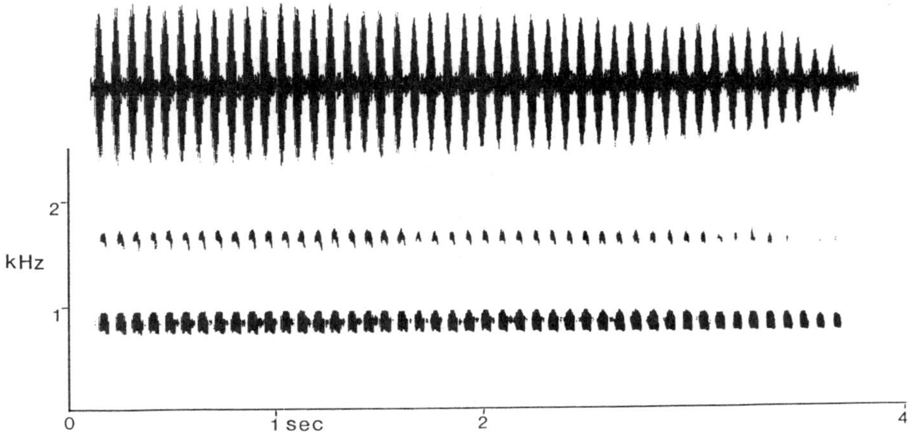

Figure 25. Strophe of B-song ("bouncing ball") of male *Otus atricapillus*. Iguazú, Misiones, Argentina. Rec. M. Castelino.

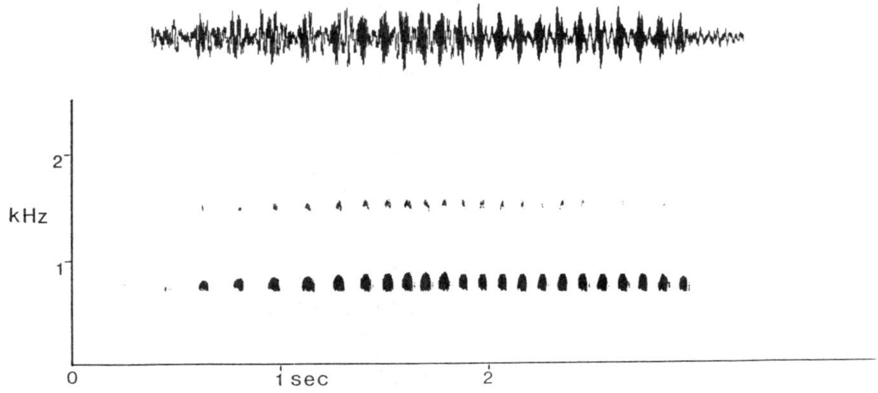

Figure 26. Part of A-song of male *Otus sanctaecatarinae*. Urugua-i Provincial Park, Misiones, Argentina. Rec. C. König.

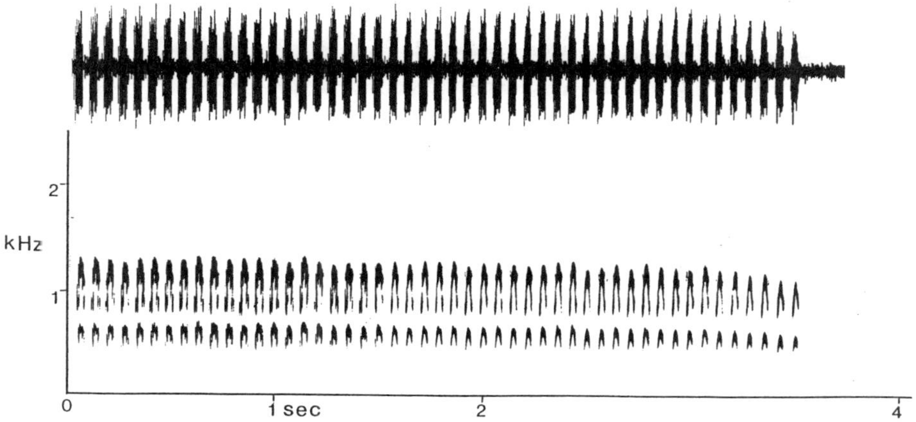

Figure 27. Strophe of B-song ("reverse bouncing ball") of male *Otus sanctaecatarinae*. Rio Grande do Sul, Brazil. Rec. T. Parker.

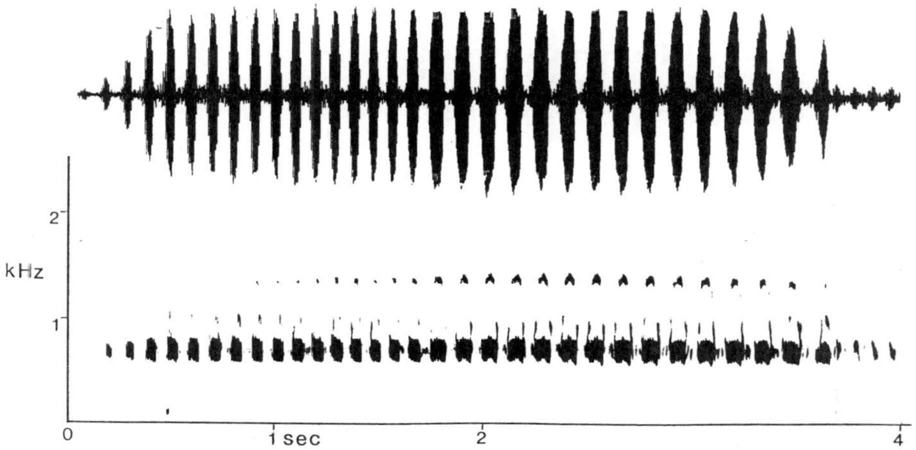

Figure 28. Strophe of B-song of female *Otus sanctaecatarinae*. Rio Grande do Sul. Rec. W. Belton (ARA-Records, Gainesville, Fl.)

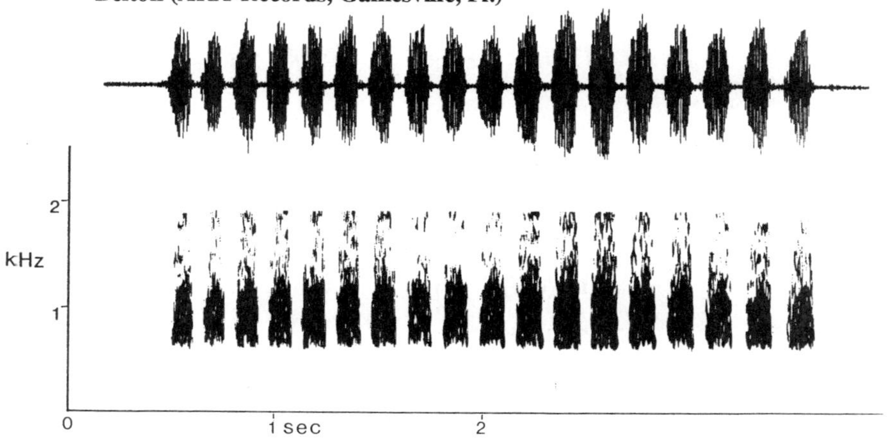

Figure 29. Part of A-song of male *Otus hoyi*. Salta, Argentina. Rec. C. König.

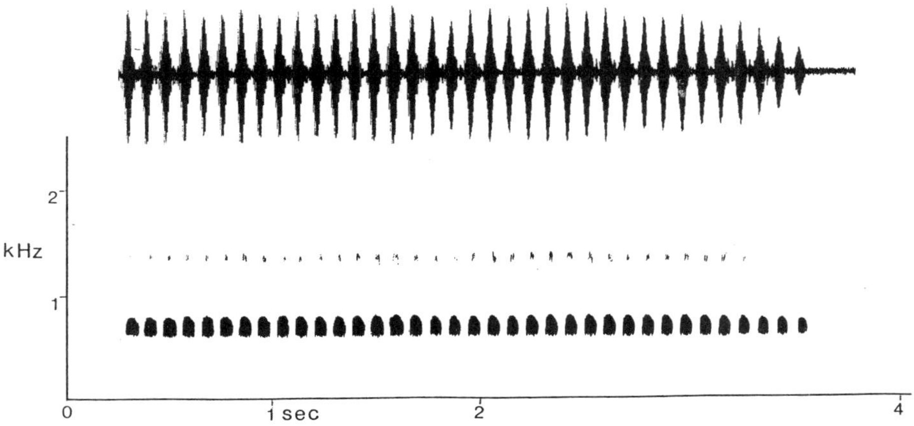

Figure 30. Strophe of B-song of male *Otus hoyi*. Salta, Argentina. Rec. C. König.

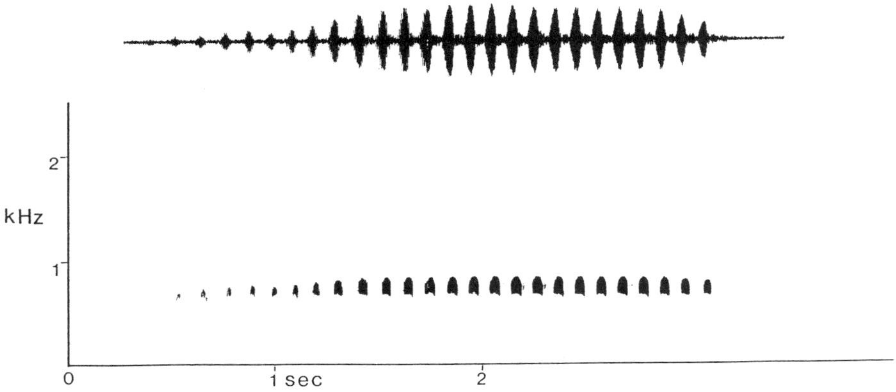

Figure 31. Part of A-song of female *Otus hoyi*. Salta, Argentina. Rec. C. König.

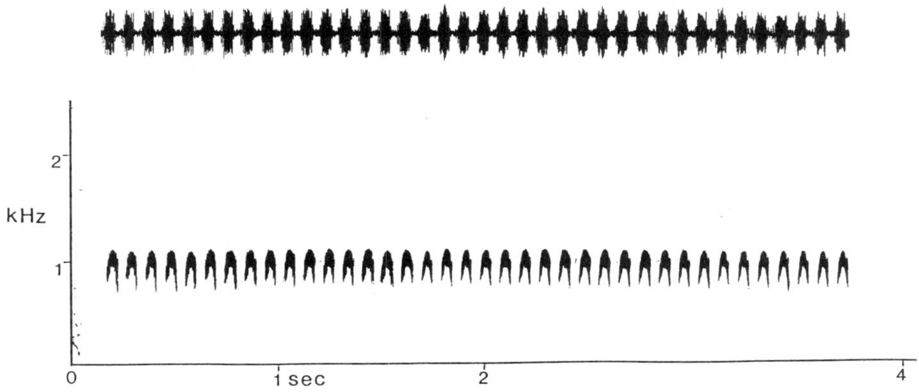

Figure 32. Strophe of B-song of female *Otus hoyi*. Same data.

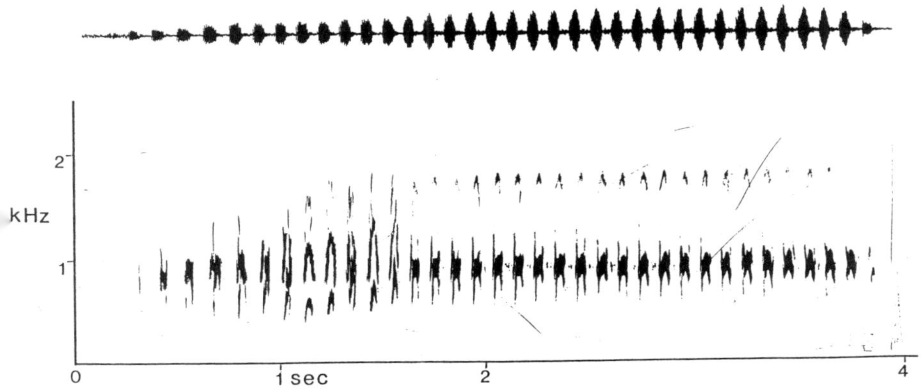

Figure 33. Distribution of ▲ = *Otus atricapillus*,
★ = *Otus sanctaecatarinae*
■ = *Otus hoyi*
○ = *Otus guatemalae*

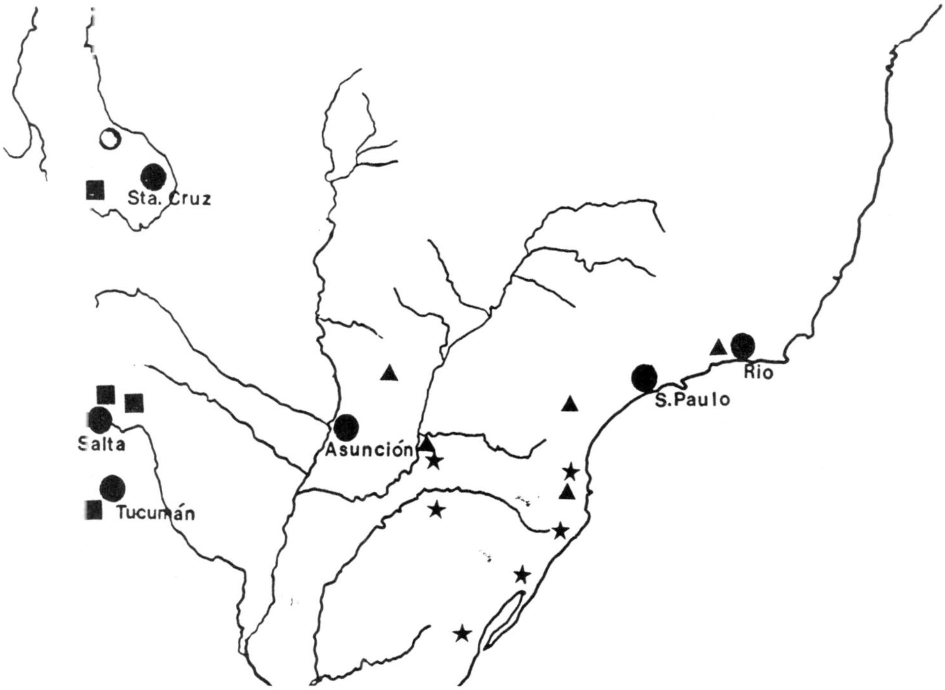

ACKNOWLEDGEMENTS

I owe many thanks to following institutions and persons who either have supported these investigations or helped personally at research. Institutions: Deutsche Forschungsgemeinschaft (DFG), Aerolíneas Argentinas, Gesellschaft für Naturkunde in Württemberg (Stuttgart), Staatl. Museum für Naturkunde (Stuttgart), British Library of Wildlife Sounds (London), Cornell Laboratory of Ornithology (Ithaca), Museo Argentino de Ciencias Naturales "Bernardino Rivadavia" (Buenos Aires), Instituto Miguel Lillo (Tucumán), Museo de Historia Natural de la Universidad de San Marcos (Lima), Museo de La Plata (La Plata), Fundación Vida Silvestre Argentina (Buenos Aires), Administración de Parques Nacionales (Buenos Aires), Dirección Nacional de Fauna Silvestre (Buenos Aires), Dirección Provincial de Fauna Silvestre (Misiones, Salta and Santa Cruz, Argentina), Bundesamt für Ernährung und Forstwirtschaft (Frankfurt a.M.), Institut für Pharmazeutische Biologie der Universität (Heidelberg), Natural History Museum, Bird Division (Tring), Naturhistorisches Museum (Vienna), Senckenberg Museum (Frankfurt a.M.), Zoologische Staatssammlung (Munich), Museum für Naturkunde der Humboldt-Universität (Berlin), Zoologisches Museum der Universität (Hamburg), Museum Alexander Koenig (Bonn) , Florida State Museum of Natural History (Gainesville). - Persons: R. Behrstock, Houston, U.S.A.; R. Buob, Stuttgart, Germany; M. Jannes, Calafate, Argentina; M. Castelino, Iguazú, Argentina; Dr. J. Fjeldså, Copenhagen, Denmark; R. Foerster, Iguazú, Argentina; Dr. M. Fritz, Salta, Argentina; Dr. J.W. Hardy, Gainesville, U.S.A.; P. Heidrich, Heidelberg, Germany; G. Hoy, Salta, Argentina; A. Johnson, La Libertad, Argentina, I. König & C.-G. König, Ludwigsburg, Germany; J. & I. Kuehl, Salta, Argentina; Dr. N. Krabbe, Quito, Ecuador; Dr. J.T. Marshall, Washington, U.S.A.; T.A. Parker III, Baton Rouge, U.S.A.; R. Straneck, Villa General Belgrano, Argentina; Prof. Dr. M. Wink, Heidelberg, Germany.

REFERENCES

AMADON, D. & J. BULL 1988: Hawks and Owls of the World. An annotated list of species.- *Proc. WesternFound. Vertebr. Zool.* 3 (4): 296-273.

BELTON, W. 1984: The Birds of Rio Grande do Sul, Brazil. Part 1. - *Bull. Am. Mus. Nat. Hist. New York*, 178: Art.4: 369-636.

BOCK, W. & J. FARRAND 1980: The number of species and genera of recent birds: A contribution to comparative systematics. - *Amer. Mus. Novitates* 2703: 1-29.

BURTON, J.A. 1973: *Owls of the World.* - Eurobook Peter Lowe, Wallingford.

ECK, S. & H. BUSSE 1981: Eulen. Die rezenten und fossilen Formen. Aves, Strigidae. - NBB, Wittenberg-Lutherstadt.

HAFFER, J. 1974: Avian speciation in tropical South America. *Publ. Nuttall. Orn. Club,* 14: 1-390.

HAFFER, J. 1987: Über Superspezies bei Vögeln. - *Ann. Naturhist. Mus. Wien* 88/89, 1986, B: 147-166.

HAFFER, J. 1990: Geoscientific aspects of allopatric speciation (*in* Peters & Hutterer, (Eds.); *Vertebrates in the Tropics*: 45-60, Bonn.

HARDY, J.W., B. COFFEY & G.B. REYNARD 1989: Voices of New World Owls. - ARA-Records, Gainesville, Florida.

HEKSTRA, G.P. 1982: "I don't give a hoot...". A revision of the American Screech Owls (*Otus, Strigidae*). - Diss. Univ. Amsterdam.

KÖNIG, C. 1968: Lautäusserungen von Rauhfußkauz (*Aegolius funereus*) und Sperlingskauz (*Glaucidium passerinum*). - *Vogelw., Beih.* 1: 115-138.

KÖNIG, C. 1969: Sechsjährige Untersuchungen an einer Population des Rauhfußkauzes (*Aegolius funereus*). - *J. Ornith.* 110 (2): 133-147.

KÖNIG, C. 1982: Zur systematischen Stellung der Neuweltgeier (Cathartidae). - *J. Ornith.* 123 (3): 259-267.

KÖNIG, C. 1991: Zur Taxonomie der Kreischeulen (*Otus spp.*) des südlichen Südamerika. - *J. Ornith.* 132 (2): 209-214.

KÖNIG, C. 1991: Zur Taxonomie und Ökologie der Sperlingskäuze (*Glaucidium spp.*) des Andenraumes. - Ökol. Vögel (Ecol. Birds) 13: 15-76.

KÖNIG, C. & R. STRANECK 1989: Eine neue Eule (Aves: *Strigidae*) aus Nordargentinien. - *Stuttg. Beitr. Naturkde., Ser. A*, 428: 1-20.
MARSHALL, J.T. 1967: Parallel variation in North and Middle American Screech Owls. - *Monogr. Western Found. of Vertebr. Zool.*, 1: 1-72.
MARSHALL, J.T. 1991: Variable Screech Owl (*Otus atricapillus*) and its relatives. *Wilson Bull.* 103 (2): 314-315 (with frontispiece).
MARSHALL, J.T., R. BEHRSTOCK & C. KÖNIG 1991: Review of "Voices of New World Owls" and "Voices of New World Nightjars" of Hardy *et al.* 1989. - *Wilson Bull.* 103 (2): 311-314.
MAYR, E. 1940: Speciation phenomena in birds. - *Amer. Naturalist* 74: 249-278.
MAYR, E. 1963: *Animal Species and Evolution.* - Harvard Univ. Press, Cambridge.
MAYR, E. & L. SORT 1970: Species taxa of North American birds. A contribution to comparative systematics. - *Publ. Nuttall. Orn. Club,* 9: 1-127.
McKITTRICK, M.C. & R.M. ZINK 1988: Species concepts in Ornithology. - *Condor,* 90: 1-14.
RIDGWAY, R. 1873: (*Genus Glaucidium*). - *Proc. Boston Soc. Nat. Hist.,* 16: 91-106.
SCHERZINGER, W. 1978: Vergleich der Stimmeninventare von fünf Arten der Gattung *Glaucidium*. - *J. Ornith.* 119 (4): 475.
SCHERZINGER, W. 1990: Vergleichende Betrachtung der Lautrepertoire innerhalb der Gattung *Athene* (Strigiformes). - Proc. Int. 100. DO-G Meeting, Current Topics on Avian Biology, Bonn 1988: 89-96.
SHARPE, R.B. 1875: Contribution to a History of the Accipitres. The Genus *Glaucidium*. - *Ibis:* 35-59.
SHARPE, R.B. 1875: Catalogue of the Striges, or Nocturnal Birds of Prey, in the Collection of the British Museum (Natural History). - London.
SIBLEY, C. G. & J.E. AHLQUIST 1990: *Phylogeny and Classification of Birds. A study in Molecular Evolution.* - Yale Univ. Press, New Haven and London.
VIELLIARD, J. 1989: Uma nova espécie de *Glaucidium* (Aves, *Strigidae*) da Amazônia. - *Rev. bras. Zool.,* 6 (4): 685-693.
WOLTERS, H.E. 1975-82: *Die Vogelarten der Erde.* - Hamburg and Berlin.

Dr. Claus König
Staatliches Museum für Naturkunde
Rosenstein 1,
Stuttgart 70191
Germany.

Part 1

Population Studies: Aspects of Long-term Changes

Common Buzzard *Buteo buteo*

Conveners:

Dr. A. Kostrzewa & Dr. V. Galushim

Meyburg, B.-U. & R. D. Chancellor eds.1994
Raptor Conservation Today
WWGBP / The Pica Press

Birds of Prey in Georgia in the 20th Century

Alexander Abuladze

Georgia, like all the Caucasus, is one of the most important regions in South-East Europe for birds of prey because of its specific geographical position on the border between Europe and Asia (Fig. 1). In this report an attempt is made to analyse changes in status of birds of prey in Georgia during the last century.

The main method has been comparative analysis of the literature on the Georgian avifauna from the last decades of the previous century to the data collected by the author since 1973. The period of the late 19th to early 20th century has not been selected by chance. The level of ornithological studies was then high and the period could be called the golden age for Georgian birds of prey. Analysis of the ornithological works published during the above-mentioned period indicates a flourishing threat-free situation among practically all species of raptors. According to the literature their numbers were optimal everywhere in Georgia (Bogdanov 1879; Mikhailovski 1880; Radde 1884; Vilkonski 1897; Dinnik 1893; Tsvetkov 1901; Satunin 1907, 1911, 1913; Shavrov 1907; Kobylin 1908; Bankovski 1913; Dombrovski 1913). According to the data at that time, 33 species of birds of prey were recorded in Georgia (Table 1), 23 of them breeding. Some authors recorded four additional breeding species - *Milvus milvus, Aquila clanga, Aquila rapax, Falco cherrug* - but analysis of current data and comparison with data for the beginning of the century by other authors leads to the conclusion that these were errors.

Figure 1. Map of Georgia

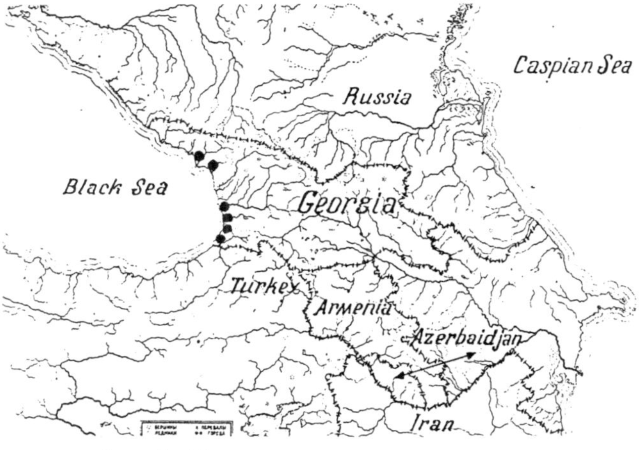

● - most dangerous places for Raptors

Table 1. Comparison of Past and Present Status of Georgian Raptors.

SPECIES	Previous status /1900-20/				Present status /1975-1991/			
	R	B	M	W	R	B	M	W
Pernis apivorus		+	+			+	+	
Milvus milvus		m	+				(?)	
M. migrans		+	+			+	+	+
Haliaeetus albicilla	+							*r*
Gypaetus barbatus	+				+			
Neophron percnopterus		+				+		
Gyps fulvus	+				+			
Aegypius monachus	+				+			
Circaetus gallicus		+				+	+	
Circus aeruginosus		+		+		+	+	+
C. cyaneus		?		+		?	+	+
C. macrourus		?	+	+			+	
C. pygargus			+				+	
Accipiter gentilis	+		+	+	+		+	+
A. nisus	+		+	+	+		+	+
A. brevipes		+	+				+	
Buteo buteo		+	+			+	+	
B. rufinus		+	+	+		+	+	+
B. lagopus				+				+
Aquila pomarina		+	+			+	+	
A. clanga		m	+				+	
A. rapax		m	+	+			+	+
A. heliaca	+				+			
A. chrysaetos	+				+			
Hieraaetus pennatus		+	+			+	+	
Pandion haliaetus	m	+	+			+	+	
Falco naumanni		+	+			+	+	
F. tinnunculus		+	+			+	+	+
F. vespertinus			+				+	
F. columbarius				+				+
F. subbuteo		+	+			+	+	
F. biarmicus					r			
F. cherrug	m			+				r
F. peregrinus	+				r			

R - resident; B - breeding summer visitor; M - passage migrant; W - winter visitor
? - no data; r - rare; m - mistakenly reported

Unfortunately, after the first decades of the 20th century all research work on raptors ceased for over 50 years. The history of Georgian raptors beginning with the 1920s is typical also for other South European populations, when the level of human activities sharply intensified. The most negative factors were;

- nesting habitat destruction and loss, mainly due to the reduction of mountain and lowland forests (since 1930s).
- direct extermination by man and disturbance (1930s-1970s).
- changes in agriculture and forestry (since 1930s);
- pesticides (since 1950s).

It is necessary to note that in Georgia, where the mountainous terrain limits some of the forms of human activity, the lowland landscapes were the most extensively transformed. Development, deforestation and increase in the population had the greatest impact on the raptors. The creation

Table 2. Present Status of Breeding Raptor Populations in Georgia (1975-1991).

SPECIES	NUMBERS /PAIRS/	POPULATION TRENDS	RED DATA BOOK	COMMENTS
Pernis apivorus	50-70 (?)	? (=)		Total number unknown. In E Georgia estimated 35-40.
Milvus migrans	900-1100	>		
Gypaetus barbatus	22-25	=	+	Great Caucasus 19-21 Minor Caucasus 3-4
Neophron percnopterus	about 150	< (=)	R	Some increase in W Georgia No change in E Georgia
Gyps fulvus	about 70	=	R	Now known for Great Caucasus
Aegypius monachus	17-19	= (<)	+	2 colonies in SE Georgia In 1 col. slow decline.
Circaetus gallicus	4-5	=	+	SE Georgia
Circus aeruginosus	25-35	<		Decrease since 1960s.
Accipiter gentilis	220-240	= (>)		Decrease in 1950s=1970s. Slow increase in 1980s.
A. nisus	420-440	=		Decrease in 1950-1970s. Slow increase in 1980s.
Buteo buteo	2100-2200	=		
B. rufinus	under 40	=		Only in E Georgia
Aquila pomarina	80-85	<	R	Decline since 1960s
A. heliaca	8-11	<	+	
A. chrysaetosunder	25	=	+	Data for 1985
Hieraaetus pennatus	about 75	<	R	Decrease since 1960s
Falco naumanni	about 700	= (<)		
F. tinnunculus	over 2300	=		
F. subbuteo	220-225	=		After decrease in 1960s, stabilising
F. biarmicus	1 (2)	?	R	Visual records in 1980s. July 1988 pair with young
F. peregrinus	3-4	? (>)	+	Extirpated in 1960-1970s. After 1985 3-4 pairs in NW
Haliaeetus albicilla			+	Extirpated in 1950s
Accipiter brevipes			R	No data since 1920s
Pandion haliaetus			+	Extirpated in 1930s

< - decrease; > - increase; = no detectable change;

(<), (=), (>) - probable increase, stable or decrease; local appearance

? - no data

– - included in 1st edn. of Red Data Book

R - recommended for 2nd edn. of Red Data Book

of reservoirs, fen farming and intensive grazing added to the negative impact. At the same time organized campaigns were begun to persecute raptors.

As a result, some species have already been extirpated as regular breeders. Thus *Pandion haliaetus* became extinct in the 1930s, *Haliaetus albicilla* in the 1950s. There have been no data about the nesting of *Accipiter brevipes* in Georgia since the 1920s.

In the mid-20th century the status of raptors continued to worsen. However, in Georgia, due to its large areas of mountain and semidesert, where human activity was not promoted, the birds of prey found their refuge. For these reasons a fair amount of the species have survived there, whereas in other regions they have disappeared.

The aggregated data on the present status of raptors in Georgia is given in Table 2. The basis for this information has been the material collected by myself and my assistants since 1975. During this period 33 species of birds of prey have been recorded. In comparison with the past the number of species has not changed, only their composition. I have not recorded *Milvus milvus* during the whole observation period. One new species has been added to the records - *Falco biarmicus*, observed several times in East Georgia in the 1980s. Once, in July 1988, a pair with young was recorded in SE Georgia, near Vashlovani reserve (Abuladze, Eligulashvili & Rostiashvili 1991). As already mentioned, three species no longer breed in Georgia. Still, they have been observed during migration (*P. haliaetus* and *A. brevipes*) or wintering (*H. albicilla*). Seven of the species are resident, 13 are breeding summer visitors, three (*C. pygargus, A. clanga, F. vespertinus*) have been recorded only during migration. Georgia is a very important territory for migrating raptors from northern populations. Many thousands of birds of prey of 21 species have been observed on passage and at stopping-places in the Kolkhida Lowland bottleneck and coastal zone of Adjaria. Four species (*H. albicilla, B. lagopus, F. columbarius, F. cherrug*) have been recorded only during the wintering period. The status of *Circus cyaneus* has not been determined; it is regularly met during the breeding season in S Georgia but I have not succeeded in finding any nest. The species may be just a non-breeding summer visitor.

During my research work, specific attention has been paid to the problems of protection. The factors limiting distribution and population size have been investigated. Data on the causes of death and its extent have been collected. Results are presented on Figures 2,3 & 4. The main cause of death of raptors has been shooting - approximately 73% of recorded cases. More than 80% of deaths occur during the autumn migration, which coincides with the hunting season in Georgia. Hunting is a traditional activity of Georgian men, particularly in the western regions, through which the main migration routes of raptors pass.

In the past, birds of prey had an important place in Georgian folklore. Organised campaigns of annihilation began in Georgia later than in Europe, starting only at the end of the 1930s and lasting up to the end of the 1960s. Since 1983 only three species - *A. gentilis, A. nisus*, and *C. aeruginosus* - could be legally shot during the autumn and winter seasons. As a result, thousands of birds of prey were killed every autumn at places of mass migration, especially in the Black Sea coastal zone, between Sukhumi, Abkhazia and Batumi, Adjaria (border with Turkey). We had a great struggle against upholders of the legal shooting of raptors in Georgia for some years, but in the end our efforts were rewarded. By the nature conservation and hunting laws operating since 1983, all species of birds of prey are under legal protection. Fines have been instituted for the shooting of protected raptors.

In addition, 12 species were included in the 1st edition of the Red Data Book of Georgia, 1982: *H. albicilla, G. barbatus, G. fulvus, A. monachus, C. gallicus, A. rapax, A. heliaca, A. chrysaetos, P. haliaetus, F. cherrug* and *F. peregrinus*. I have recommended the inclusion of three more species - *N. percnopterus, A. brevipes* and *H. pennatus* - in the 2nd edition planned to be published in 1993. Attempts have also been made to include two more - *A. pomarina* and *F. biarmicus*.

Recently the public's attitude towards raptors has improved and their protection intensified. Research on the status of raptors has also improved. A programme of research and monitoring of birds of prey, mainly of rare species, was launched at the Institute of Zoology of the Georgian Academy of Sciences about 15 years ago.

A long-term programme of measures on raptor conservation was developed and transmitted to the authorities. Some years ago attempts were made to organise feeding places for large raptors (Abuladze 1990) and to attract some species to artificial nest sites (Abuladze 1990). Due to our campaign and to the publicity given to conservation activities in the mass media, the number of raptors illegally shot in recent years has been substantially reduced (Figs. 4 & 5.). Unfortunately, at the same time this does not mean that the situation is good. For instance, for some West Georgian, Adjarian and Abkhasian districts illegal shooting of migrating raptors is still known. Sometimes wintering raptors are shot.

Figure 2. Causes of death of raptors in Georgia, 1973 - 1991.

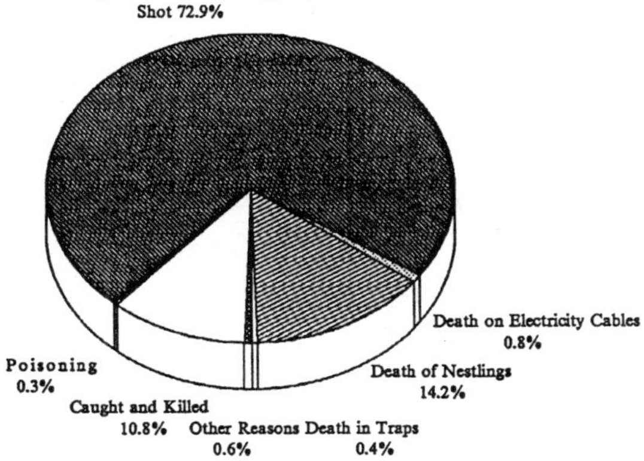

Figure 3. Distribution of registered cases of death of adult raptors in Georgia by seasons, 1973 - 1991 (n = 7692)

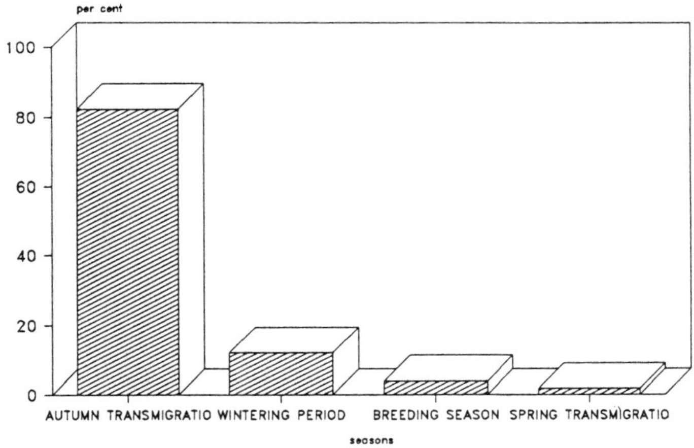

Figure 4. Results of annual counts of shooting on 2 sample plots in SW Georgia.

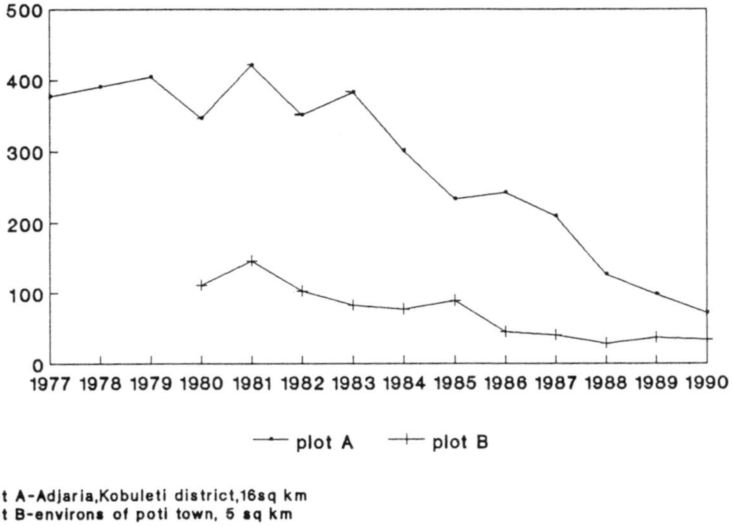

Figure 5. Changes in attitude to raptors by hunters and falconers.

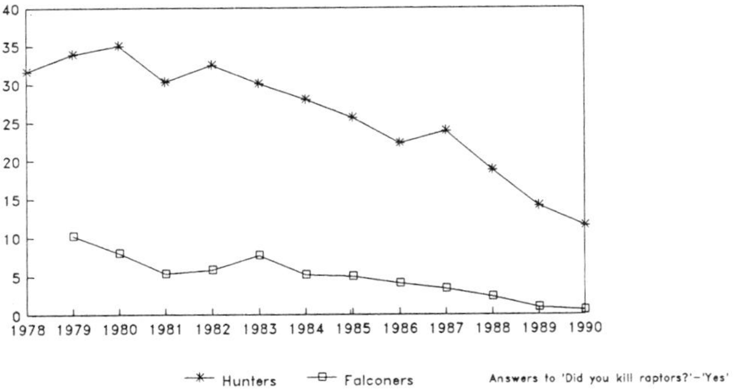

There are some peculiarities regarding the protection of raptors, specific to Georgia. Falconry is very popular. About 3,000 Georgian falconers - Bazieri - often play a very negative role. They trap a great number of hawks and sometimes falcons. Control of their activities is difficult. The small number of professional ornithologists and birdwatchers in Georgia cannot meet the needs of birds of prey protection.

The main threats to Georgian birds of prey to-day are 1. destruction of natural biotopes by industrialisation, mechanization of agriculture and urbanisation; 2) reduction of flood-land, semi-desert and mountain forests; 3) human persecution, 4) lack of food for species with a restricted diet, reducing the numbers of the main prey; 5) recreational pressure, disturbance, caused by tourists and alpinists.

Unfortunately, I cannot look with assurance into the future. The present situation in Georgia, with its political, economic and social cataclysms, is more than unstable. As always during such periods, problems of nature conservation are of no account. All activities related to research and protection of raptors have been stopped. The small group of ornithologists and volunteers has broken up. I still hope that the crisis is not going to be prolonged and that the work started could be soon continued with fruitful results.

REFERENCES

ABULADZE, A. 1990. Organization of feeding-places for large raptors; Attraction of raptors to artificial nest sites. *Study and protection of Birds of Prey* 62-65; 296-229. (in Russian)

ABULADZE, A., V. ELIGULASHVILI & A. ROSTIASHVILI 1991. On the Status of the Lanner in USSR. Proc. of 10th All-Union Ornithological Conf. Vitebsk, Sept. 1991. Part I: 26-28. (in Russian).

BANKOVSKI, V.B. 1913. K ornitofaune Zakavkazia. (in. Russian).

BOGDANOV, M. 1879. Trudy obchestva estestvoispytatelei pri Kazanskom Universitete. (in Russian).

DINNIK, N. 1893. Zapiski Kavkazskogo otdelenia RGO, kn. 15. (in Russian).

DOMBROVSKI, B.A. 1913. Materialy dlya izucheniya ptic Kolkhidy, Adjarya i sopredelnych mest.

KOBYLIN, A.M. 1908. Beträge zur Ornithofauna Kaukasiens. Gouv. Kutais.

MIKHAILOVSKI, I. 1880. Trudy Sankt-Peterburgskogo obshestva estesvoispytatelei, t. 11, 1. (in Russian)

RADDE, G. 1884. Ornitologicheskaya fauna Kavkaza (Ornis Caucasica). (in Russian).

RED DATA BOOK OF GEORGIAN SSR, 1982.

SATUNIN, K.A. 1907. Zapiski Kavkazskogo otdelenia RGO, t. 26, 3. (in Russian).

SATUNIN, K.A. 1911. Zur Ornithologie des Gebietes von Batumi.

SATUNIN, K.A. 1913. Fauna Littoris Orientalis Ponti Euxini. Vertebrata. (in Russian).

SHAVROV, N.N. 1907. Izvestiya Kavkazskogo otdelenya RGO; 19.

TSVETKOV, E.W. 1901. Materialy k poznaniu flory i fauny Rossiikoi Imperii. Bp. 5. (in Russian).

Alexander Abuladze
Institute of Zoology
31 Chavcharadse pr.
Tbilisi, Georgia 380030

Meyburg, B.-U. & R. D. Chancellor eds.1994
Raptor Conservation Today
WWGBP / The Pica Press

Population Trends of the Red Kite *Milvus milvus* in Italy

P. Cortone, A. Minganti, M. Pellegrini, F. Riga, A. Sigismondi and A. Zocchi

ABSTRACT

The Red Kite was a common species in most of Italy in the late 19th century. A sharp decline occurred thereafter, leading to a contraction of its range. The Red Kite can at present be found in southern Italy, Sicily and Sardinia. Its island populations are currently undergoing a dramatic decline. Recovery is being observed in the northern part of the present area of distribution. Shooting and road construction are identified as the main causes of the current decline.

INTRODUCTION

This paper is the result of the effort of a study group to outline the past and present trends of the Red Kite populations in Italy. Besides a review of the literature, data were obtained from members of the Italian Committee for the Protection of Birds of Prey (CIPR) and the Italian League for Protection of Birds (LIPU), dispersed throughout central and southern Italy over a number of years. The regional data were provided by: M. Pellegrini (Abruzzi), G. Battista (Molise), A. Minganti, F. Riga, A. Zocchi (Latium), M. Rocco (Campania), A. Sigismondi (Apulia & Basilicata), P. Cortone (Calabria), A. Campo and M. Sarà (Sicily). The aim of the survey is to identify key areas for the survival of residual populations and introduction of fresh stocks.

METHODS

All available literature regarding the Red Kite in Italy was reviewed in order to define its distribution in the past. It has to be remembered that data up to the 1980s are scarce and general, so that only a rough figure of the situation can be given.

For the last two decades data are more reliable, thanks to field researches carried out by the study group; nevertheless the suitable habitats are not evenly covered, given the huge area and lack of sufficient observers. For some few areas only hypothetical values are therefore given.

RESULTS

Historical background

Map 1 shows the present and past distribution of the Red Kite in Italy. Dates represent the last breeding records found in the literature. From these data it is clear that the Red Kite was once a common species, widespread in suitable habitats from north-western Italy, down the Tyrrhenian side of the peninsula and throughout southern Italy, Sicily and Sardinia (Savi 1827). It was also found in some areas on the Adriatic side, but scarcer and more localized (Gasparini 1894).

At the end of the last century the species was already declining on mainland Italy. Some authors even reported this trend a good deal earlier. The species was extinct in the north by the beginning of the 20th century.

This decline spread southwards, leading to the extinction of the Red Kite population in Tuscany, where it was formerly said to be very common. The last breeding records in this area date from between 1900 and 1930 (Arrigoni degli Oddi 1929).

In central and southern Italy (Southern Latium, Abruzzi, Molise, Gargano promontory, Calabria) it was still a characteristic feature of the countryside until the 1950s. Between the 1960s and '70s the number of breeding pairs suddenly fell and the range of distribution contracted, leading to the disappearance of many marginal pairs.

In those years some small, scattered populations could still be found within the former range; for example, breeding pairs were observed near Varese (Bianchi *et al.* 1973) and Ravenna (Garavini 1950) in the 1950s and '60s, but to-day they are gone.

The Red Kite was still common in Sicily and Sardinia up to the 1970s. A severe decline has been reported in the 1980s for Sicily (Falcone 1985) and some years earlier for Sardinia (Schenk 1976). In Sicily the decline has been the most dramatic ever recorded in Italy. Up to the late 1970s the breeding population was estimated at 100-150 pairs. Only 10-12 are to-day left in the northern part of the island.

Shooting and poaching can be considered the most relevant causes of this decline. Recent comments on the phenomenon in southern and insular Italy suggest that massive funding, from both European and national institutions, is leading to the widespread development of roads, often useless and speculative, in the less developed areas. This in turn allows an ever-increasing section of the public to reach these areas and kill wildlife. In southern Italy the Red Kite is considered a nice bird to have stuffed, and it is killed whenever possible. The species is known to frequent rubbish dumps near villages, and in several instances poachers have been seen hiding near such sites in order to shoot kites. The Red Kite is a resident species in Italy and therefore specially affected by the winter hunting season. Its habit of frequenting rubbish dumps exposes it to the danger of being poisoned, both deliberately and through the presence of toxic waste.

Other evident causes of decrease are poisoned baits, specially in Sardinia, and the environmental changes which have affected most of the nation. One of the limiting factors in Latium is, for example, the shortage of mature woods, which forces the kite to breed on small and insecure trees. In at least one case the chick was found dead after collapse of the nest (Minganti & Panella, 1991). Moreover nests built on small trees are more easily robbed.

A similar decrease affected the wintering population. Historical data on the distribution and numbers of winter communal roosts are very scarce. In south-eastern Sicily at least 50-60 Red Kites were recorded at winter roosts until the 1970s, but not since. In the northern part of the same island two roosts with a total of 150 kites observed up to the late 1970s are nowadays reduced to only 25-50 (M. Sarà, pers. comm.).

Present status

In 1990-92 the total number of breeding pairs in Italy was between 130 and 170.

The bulk of the breeding population (100-130 pairs) is distributed in suitable habitats in central and southern Italy. Two other still used breeding areas are found in Calabria (nearly 10 pairs) and Sicily (10-12 pairs). In Sardinia the figure was 20-30 pairs in 1990 (Schenk, pers. comm.). Records overall suggest a dramatic decline in recent years that has led the species to the brink of extinction. Isolated relic populations exist in Latium (1-3 pairs) and Calabria, where some pairs are said to survive in the extreme south.

DISCUSSION AND CONCLUSIONS

Negative trends

The Red Kite is still decreasing in large portions of the country, especially in the south, where socio-economic conditions have led recently to an increase in road building, with its related problems. Shooting and poaching are widely practised in those areas and controls are

Map 1. Red Kite's breeding populations in Italy.

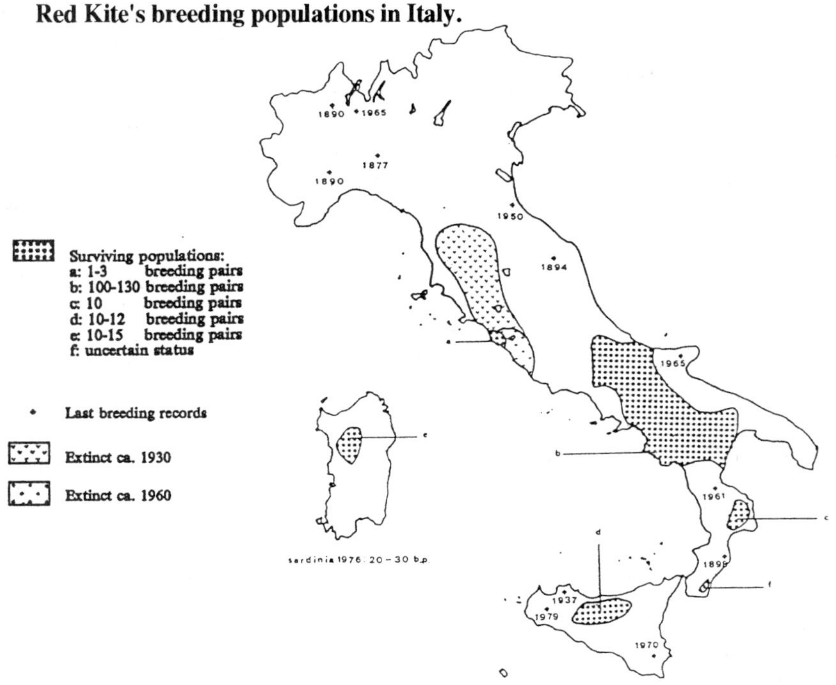

Map 2. Wintering of Red Kite in Italy.

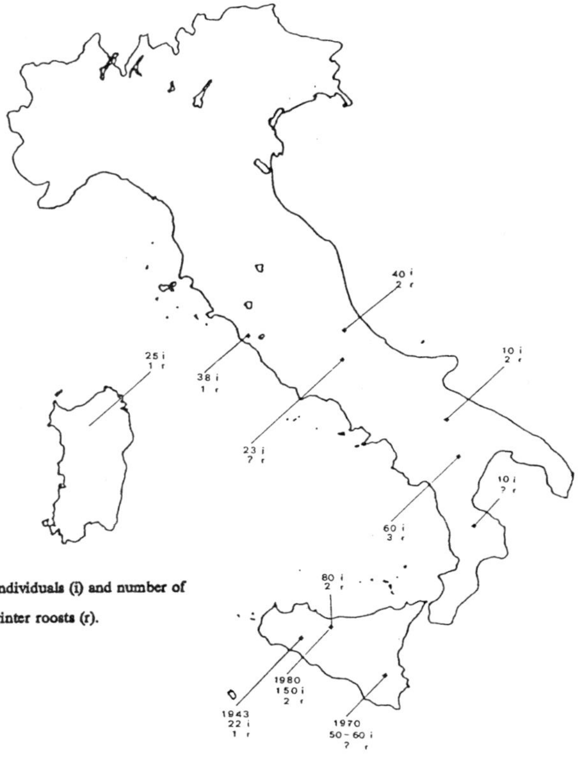

Number of individuals (i) and number of communal winter roosts (r).

very weak. It must not be forgotten that a strong cultural tradition impels hundreds of people to poach Honey Buzzards and other large birds crossing over the Straits of Messina every year during the spring migration.

The general trend seems to be one of severe decline followed in certain areas by a recovery (see following section). This decline occurred first in the north of Italy, steadily spreading in more recent years towards the south. In the extreme south it is still continuing to-day.

Positive trends

In a few areas the Red Kite is slowly recovering after bring brought almost to extinction. Due to the improvement of protected areas (Abruzzi) and to wide information campaigns (Molise) addressed to key groups of the public (mostly hunters) it has recently begun to show signs of increase. The findings of the members of the study group suggest that hunting is the major limiting factor and that an improvement in controls and education is the best means of aiding its recovery. Thus the Red Kite is expanding its distribution in the northern part of its range (Manzi *et al.* 1991). Even the set-aside policy recently applied by the European Community has been claimed as another relevant factor in its recovery.

Conservation and management

From the above picture some useful suggestions can be put forward.

Further research is needed to evaluate the trends of the population on a concrete basis.

The establishing of protected areas and enforcement of controls over hunting and poaching are the top priorities if the species is to be maintained. The Red Kite is nevertheless a difficult species to protect, due to its great mobility.

Feeding places are currently established by CIPR members during winter for counts of wintering kites (which are nevertheless best carried out at the roosting sites) and in order to simplify the search for food and thereby diminish winter mortality caused by hunters (Catullo *et al.* in press). Feeding places are also generally regarded as a useful means of increasing the productivity of breeding pairs and are therefore set out to help the surviving pairs in Latium, Calabria and Sicily.

Education of key groups of the public, such as hunters and farmers, has locally proved to be effective. Efforts to make people aware of the importance of birds of prey are costly but a rewarding element in their conservation.

ACKNOWLEDGEMENTS

We are grateful to all the members of CIPR who contributed information on the past and present distribution and trends of the Red Kite.

REFERENCES

ARRIGONI DEGLI ODDI, E. 1929. *Ornitologia Italiana.* Hoepli, Milan.

BIANCHI, E., L. MARTIRE & A. BIANCHI 1973. *Gli uccelli della provincia di Varese.* Fusi, Pavia.

CATULLO, G., A. MINGANTI, F. NERI, F. RIGA & A. ZOCCHI (in press). Programma di aiuti alimentari per i rapaci del genere *Milvus* sui Monti della Tolfa. *Proc. VI Conv. It. Ornit.*, Torino, 1991.

FALCONE, S. *in* **B. MASSA (Ed.) 1985.** *Atlas Faunae Siciliae:* Aves. Il Naturalista Siciliano XX: 1-242.

GARAVINI, E. 1950. Osservazioni ornitologiche fatte nelle province di Ravenna, Forli, Ferrara: *RIO XX* (II serie): 108-110.

GASPARINI, V. 1894. *Avifauna marchigiana.* Premiata Società Tipografica Cooperativa, Fano.

MANZI, A.,M. PELLEGRINI & M.PELLEGRINI (in press). Primi dati sulla nidificazione del Nibbio reale (*Milvus milvus*) in Abruzzo. *Proc. V Conv. It. Ornit.* Bracciano, 1989.

MINGANTI, A. & M. PANELLA (in press). Sovrapposizione ecologica tra *Milvus milvus* e *Milvus migrans* in Italia Centrale: alimentazione e siti di nidificazione. *Proc. V. Conv. It. Ornit,* Bracciano 1989.

SAVI, P. 1827. *Ornitologia Toscana.* Tip. Nistri, Pisa.

SCHENK, H. 1976. Analisi della situazione faunistica in Sardegna: uccelli e mammiferi. *SOS Fauna*: 465-556, WWF, Camerino.

Pino Cortone
Via Galluppi 10
87100 Cosenza, Italy

Andrea Minganti
Via dei Savorelli 8
00165 Roma, Italy

Masssimo Pellegrini
Via Bovio 437
65100 Pescara, Italy

Francesco Riga
Via Isonzo 3
00053 Civitavecchia, Italy

Antonio Sigismondi
Via Napoli 234
S. Spirito Bari, Italy

Alberto Zocchi
Via Graziano 43
00165 Roma, Italy

Meyburg, B.-U. & R. D. Chancellor eds.1994
Raptor Conservation Today
WWGBP / The Pica Press

Ecological Aspects of Long-term Changes in Population Density of the Kestrel *Falco tinnunculus* around Sofia

Ventzeslav G. Delov and Georgi S. Stoyanov

INTRODUCTION

The Kestrel is very common in Bulgaria. It is a migratory and partly resident species, seen more rarely in winter, mainly in lowlands (Sineonov 1986).

The Sofia Plain is an area of 1180km² with a mean altitude of 550m a.s.l. and surrounded by the Stara Planina, Viskyar, Lulin, Vitosha and Lozensca Planina mountains. The climate is continental temperate, with a relative humidity of 40-78%. The annual rainfall is 6.25ml/m², with highest values in May/June and lowest in December. Snow cover in winter remains on average for up to a few days.

METHODS

During investigations conducted from 1979 to 1991, data on the species' distribution, ecology and factors influencing population size were collected. One-day trips were made during all seasons of the year. The birds were observed using 7x30 and 10x50 binoculars. Prey items were identified by analysis of pellets and by direct observation. Nests below 600m altitude were mapped on a 2km UTM grid.

RESULTS

A notable concentration of the species was observed near fields of alfalfa, where the Common Vole *Microtus arvalis* is most numerous. During the study period 40 pellets were analysed and the following components identified: *Microtus arvalis, Arvicola terrestris, Crocidura leucodon, Lacerta* sp., *Streptopelia turtur* (direct observation), *Motacilla flava, Anthus* sp., *Passer domesticus,* Chrisomelidae, Scaracidae, Curculionidae, Carabidae, *Carabus convexus, Coccinela septenpunctata,* Arachnea, Coleoptera and Orthoptera.

The basic component of the diet was the Common Vole, but the spectrum varied in the different seasons and in different parts of the plain. For example, three pellets found on 4 April 1991 east of Sofia (UTM grid GN 03-6, Fig. 2) contained only insects (*Coleoptera*), probably due to the fact that other species were less active and difficult to catch. In the north-western regions of the plain, where there are nearby areas of karst, apart from the dominant *Microtus*, two *Crocidura leucodon* and pellets containing only *Aczididae* were found (UTM grid FN 74-18, Fig. 2). The percentage of birds in the diet increases in July-August, when House Sparrows are present in the field in great flocks.

According to Baumgart (1971), the Kestrel's habitats in Bulgaria are quite different from those in Germany, since in Bulgaria the species nests mainly on rocks. This was confirmed by our investigations in several rocky areas with a high population density: near the village of Carlucovo (5 June 1990), among rocks near Belogradchik (25 April 1989), around Lacatnic (10 May 1987) and along the Zemen gorge (May-June 1983) an average density of 1.6 pairs per km² was recorded. By comparison, in areas with highest density of breeding birds in the Sofia Plain (UTM grid GN 03-6,11; GN 02-5,9,10), only 0.9 pairs per km² were found in 1979.

Figure 2 gives data about the breeding distribution of the Kestrel in the Sofia Plain. The number of pairs fluctuates from year to year. There are insufficient data for a quantitative evaluation of the whole area (approx. 900km²) for each year, but the average number of pairs is about 70 (0.08 per km²). According to Yancov (1983), in 1982 about 15 breeding pairs became established in Sofia, with a further increase possible (Donchev & Yancov 1989).

The highest density of Kestrels was to the east of Sofia. In an area of 30km² (UTM grid GN 03-2,7,12,1,6,11; GN02-5,10,15,4,9,14,3,8,13) 27 breeding pairs were found during 1979 (0.9 prs/km²), but a sharp decrease in their number has since taken place: 1980 - 25 pairs; 1981 - ?; 1982 - 23 pairs; 1983 - 24 pairs; 1984 - 18 pairs (adverse changes to the habitat, with *ca.* 20% of the wetlands drained and 30% of the alfalfa replaced with maize); 1985 - 12 nests destroyed by electricians, only 6 established in trees; 1986 - 6 pairs (*ca.* 50% of the marshes filled in and 20% of the alfalfa replaced with cereals); 1987 - 7 pairs; 1988 - ?; 1989 - 5 pairs (chlororganic compounds used against the Common Vole); 1990 - 3 pairs (similar measures, 4 young birds found poisoned); 1991 - 5 pairs (a cold spring with heavy rains; one nest abandoned). It is obvious that the main reason for this decrease was the adverse human impact.

Negative factors of prime importance are:

1. Changes in agriculture, in particular from alfalfa to maize and cereals, resulting in deterioration of the food base and hunting conditions. Maize is a particularly unfavourable environment for fledgings; when attempting to alight on a stem they fall to the ground and are unable to resume flight. In 1980 four young from three broods died in this way. The opposite effect was observed in alfalfa in 1984; even young birds unable to fly could make their way through this environment a distance of 150-200m to the base of their nest site, where they were fed by their parents.
2. The filling with garbage of a considerable part of the marshes in the area, about 50% being converted into a rubbish dump, leading to a great increase in the population of Magpie, Hooded Crow and Rook and also to unfavourable environmental conditions for the Kestrel.
3. Destruction of nests by electricians when painting the pylons.
4. Treatment of cultivated land with chlororganic compounds against the Common Vole in 1991. As a result of this campaign, thousands of birds were poisoned. Many dead Rooks were found near Sofia, but only a few Kestrels.

The study area is characterised by wide open areas with a rich food base but few suitable nest sites. The only such sites available are the electricity pylons and shelter belts of trees, situated several km apart. The great density of the Magpie population -- 2.43 pairs per km² (calculated in May 1991 along a 60km route) -- tends to pre-empt all suitable nest sites. Pylons are used for nesting by the Magpie only if other possible sites are absent. In the mountains and foothills there are no Magpie nests on pylons.

Building their nests on pylons, the Magpies create nest sites for the Kestrel but deplete the rich

Figure 1. Different types of electricity pylons around Sofia. The nest sites are marked by arrows.

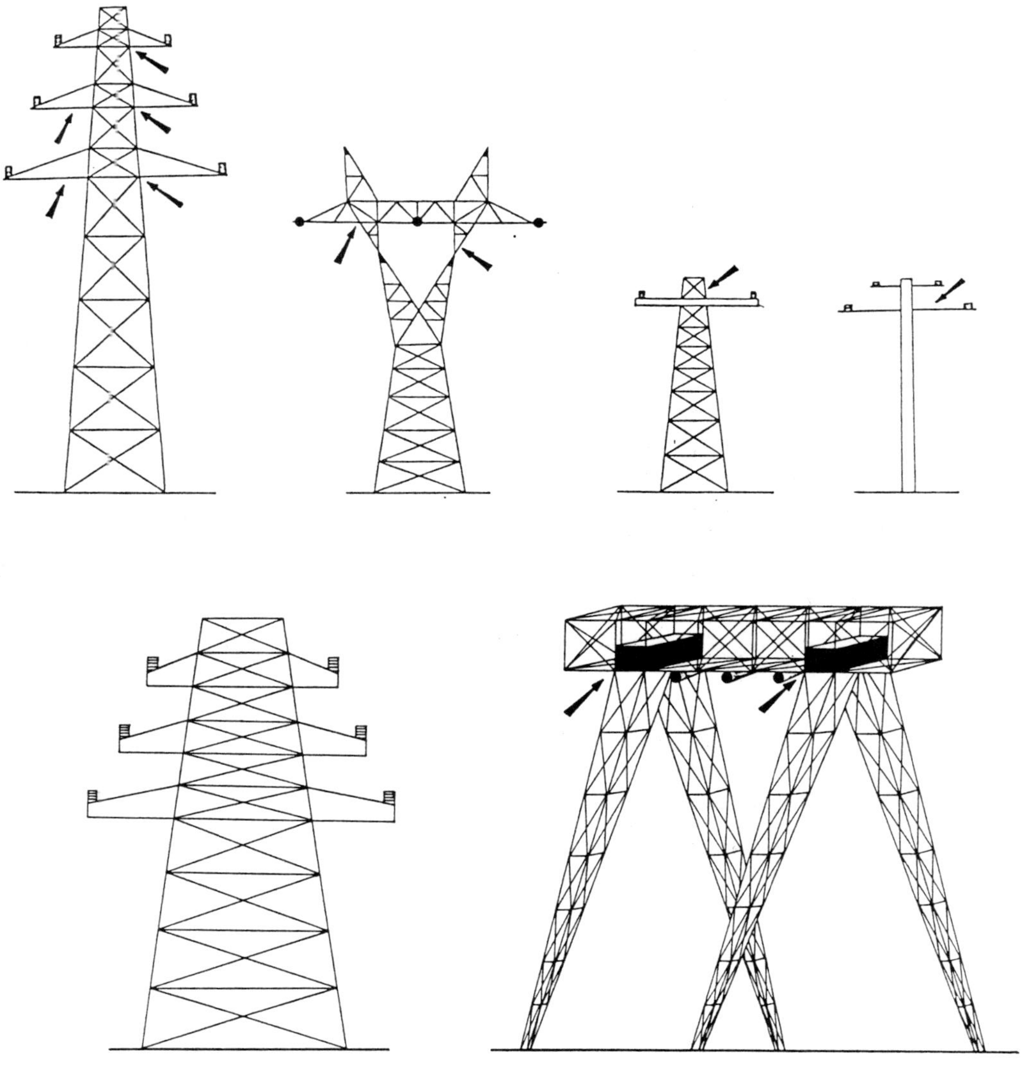

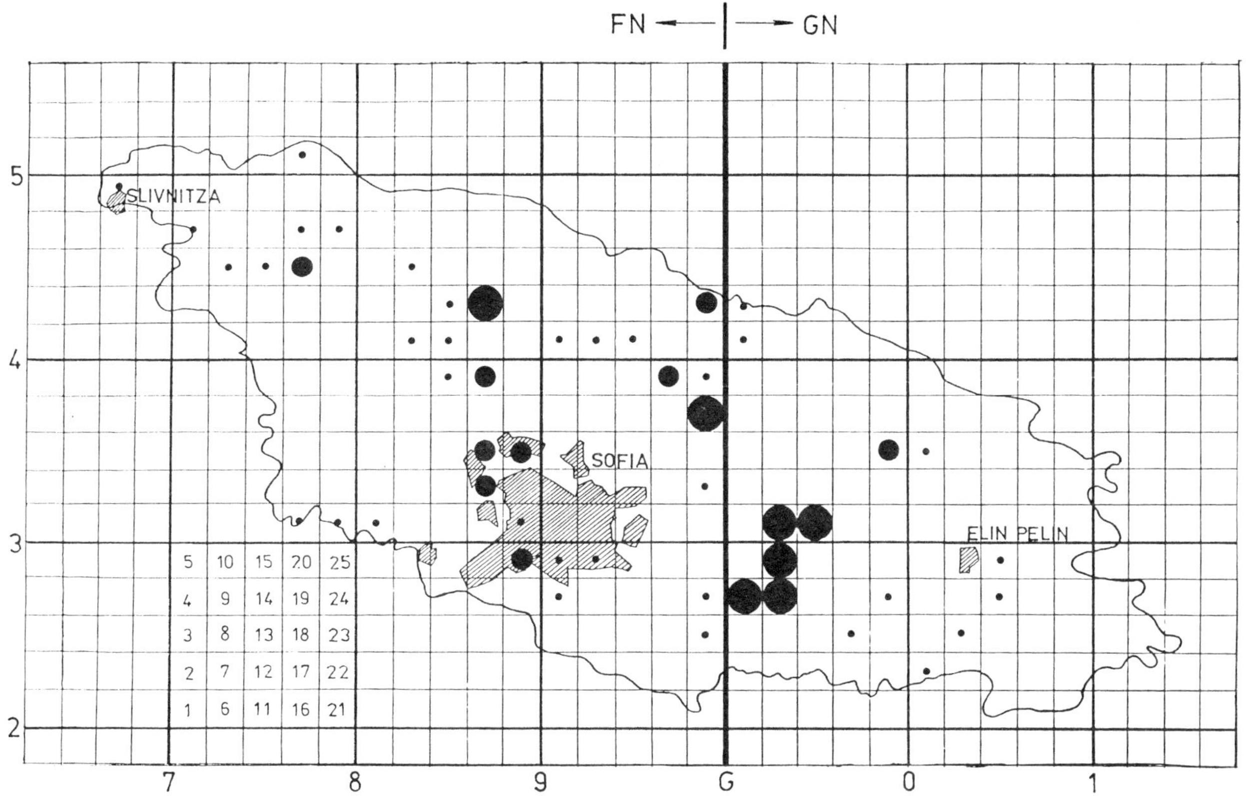

Figure 2. Breeding distribution of the Kestrel in Sofia plain.

- three breeding pairs

- two breeding pairs

- one breeding pair

food base of the agricultural landscape. Pylons about 20m high are mostly preferred by the Kestrel (Fig. 1). Interestingly, during 1973 the nests in the same region were mainly in trees (Nankinov 1981). On the Sofia Plain the following sites were occupied and nests distributed as follows: Holes in rocks - 2; Cliffs of scree - 1; Abandoned quarries - 2; Buildings - 8; Trees - 27 (poplars, 16; willows, 7, false acacias, 4); Metal constructions - 6; Tree hollows - 1; Bridges - 2; Electricity pylons - 23.

Pylon nests have the following advantages over trees: 1. they provide the highest sites in the region; 2. they are more durable, lasting for 5-7 years, whereas those in trees last only 1-4 years; 3. they provide security from natural enemies and humans; during the study period two people were electrocuted in attempts to reach a Kestrel's nest, an Eagle Owl was killed in similar circumstances, and a Goshawk died from collision with a cable whilst attacking young Kestrels.

The breeding cycle starts at the end of February, the earliest courtship flights being recorded on 28 February 1983. Most copulations occur during March and early April. Out of a total of 27 clutches, 2 with 2 eggs, 2 x 3, 12 x 4, 8 x 5, 2 x 6 and 1 x 7 were recorded. In some clutches one or rarely two unhatched eggs were found. According to Styanov (in press) the number of young averages 3-5. On 20 June 1980 a nest with 7 fledglings was found.

The following losses were recorded: 1. a female killed in a swooping attack on a Goshawk; 2. three young killed by a cat; 3 four juveniles poisoned by chlororganic substances in 1990; 4. four fledgings died after falling into maize; 5. two juveniles died from collision with cables (Sileva & Stoyanov, in press); 6. a young bird became entangled in a polyethilene cord in a Hooded Crow's nest (Todorov, pers. comm.): such cords are used for baling straw and taken by the Hooded Crow as nest material; 7. two adult birds caught after entering a building; 8. two adults and one young caught in clapnets for songbirds; 9. seven young taken by children and falconers; 10. two juveniles killed in collision with cars; 11. three adults and one juvenile died from unknown causes.

Interspecific competition affects the Kestrel population only indirectly. On the Sofia Plain nine species of owls have been recorded (Nankinov 1982; Yancov 1983). The Kestrel is known to be a prey of the Eagle Owl, Tawny Owl, Barn Owl and Little Owl (Mikkola 1983). The most dangerous natural enemy is the Eagle Owl, but this species is very rare in the region; in studies of its diet in other parts of the country the Kestrel was represented by only one individual (Boev, in press).

The following cases of interspecific rivalry were recorded: 1. on 10 May 1988 a pair of Kestrels chased away an incubating (?) Long-eared Owl and took over its nest (Stoyanov, in press); 2. on 15 July 1991 a Kestrel lost its prey as a result of a kleptoparasitic attack by a Hobby (Todorov, pers. comm.); 3. on 20 July 1980 three pairs with neighbouring nests simultaneously attacked a Goshawk, one female being wounded and subsequently dying; 4. three young were killed by a cat; 5. in four cases Kestrels chased away Magpies and occupied their nests.

Mobbing of Kestrels was observed by 31 species of birds, the most active being *Parus major* (18 cases), *Pica pica* (16 cases), *Corvus corone* (13 cases), *Passer domesticus* (8 cases) and *Vanellus vanellus* (7 cases). Attacks by the Hooded Crow are the most dangerous.

A marked sensivity to sudden human activity in the Zemen gorge was noted. When building operations started in the gorge of the river Shagava, the number of nesting pairs diminished from 11 to three during the spring of 1990. The only unusual factor was the great noise. In 1991, after completion of the building works, the number of breeding pairs increased.

Apart from the principal ones cited above, two other types of negative factor influence the species. Such secondary negative factors are those which do not provoke permanent changes in the population but only fluctuations, e.g. unfavourable climatic conditions and almost all kinds of human impact which affect a few birds only. Factors of the third type, such as interspecific rivalry, are not a direct result of human activity. The Kestrel has adapted to such factors during the long process of evolution. The numerous Magpie population provides suitable nest sites but on the other hand has a negative influence on the Kestrel's food base.

ACKNOWLEDGEMENTS

Many thanks to Dr. T. Michev for his helpful comments, and to M. Georgieva for help in preparing the manuscript.

REFERENCES

BAUMGART, W. 1971. Beitrag zur Kenntnis der Greifvögel Bulgariens. *Beitr. Vogelk.* 17.

BOEV, Z. (in press). Species composition and metric characteristics of the bird victims of the Eagle Owl. *Hist. Nat. Bulgarica,* Sofia, BAN.

DONCHEV,S. & P.YANCOV 1989. Stages in synantropisation and urbanisation of Bulgarian birds. *Ecology 22,* Sofia, BAN. (in Bulgarian)

MIKKOLA,H. 1983. *The Owls of Europe.* Calton, T. & A. Poyser.

NANKINOV,D. 1981. Some observations on Bulgarian birds of prey. *Bull, Bird Banding* N9. Inst. Bulg. Ring. Centre, Sofia, BAN (in Bulgarian).

NANKINOV,D. 1982. The birds of Sofia. *Bull, Bird Banding* N12. Inst. Bulg. Ring. Centre, Sofia, BAN.

SILEVA,R. & G.STOYANOV (in press). Raptors and owls brought to Sofia Zoological Gardens, 1950-1989. *Bull, Bird Banding.* Inst. Bulg. Ring. Centre, Sofia, BAN.

SIMEONOV,S. 1986. The birds of Pirin Mountain. In *Fauna of SW Bulgaria,* Vol. 1. Sofia, BAN. (in Bulgarian).

STOYANOV,G. (in press). Observations on some Falcons during 1980-1990. *Bull, Bird Banding*. Inst. Bulg. Ring. Centre, Sofia, BAN

YANCOV,P. 1983 The Birds of Sofia. D. Phil.Thesis, Sofia, BAN.

Ventzeslav Delov/Georgi S. Stoyanov
Faculty of Biology
8 Dragan Tzancov St.
1421 Sofia, Bulgaria

Meyburg, B.-U. & R. D. Chancellor eds.1994
Raptor Conservation Today
WWGBP / The Pica Press

Population Limitation in Buzzards *Buteo buteo* and Kestrels *Falco tinnunculus*: the different roles of habitat, food and weather

Achim Kostrzewa and Renate Kostrzewa

ABSTRACT

627 Buzzard nests were studied over 12 years (1980-1991) in a 690km² area and 128 Kestrel nests over 10 years (1982-1991) in a 100km² area near Cologne and Bonn. Vole availability during the breeding season was also monitored.

Habitat use - Both species showed a wide overlap in hunting habitat deriving from the same food preference - mainly voles. Kestrels nest in open farmland or suburban habitats. Buzzards nest in woodland. Thus both species' breeding habitat differs markedly.

Density - Both populations were sedentary. Buzzards were limited by territorial behaviour only during the breeding cycle. Their territories were regularly spaced. Kestrels were mainly limited by winter temperature via reduction of food availability and resulting starvation. Their territories were irregularly spaced.

Reproductive Success - In total 629 young Buzzards fledged from 627 occupied territories (reproductive success = 1.0; fledged young per clutch = 1.33; fledged young per successful pair = 1.7).

Buzzards' reproductive success was mainly influenced by rainfall in May ($r = -0.80$; $P < 0.001$) but not by vole-rank ($r = 0.36$; N.S.). Two more factors of minor importance were identified a) interference by Goshawks and b) grade of territory as a measure for territory quality.

In total 378 young Kestrels fledged from 128 occupied territories (reproductive success = 2.95; fledged young per clutch = 3.6; fledged young per successful pair = 4.2).

Kestrels' reproductive output was affected by two main factors: vole-rank ($r = 0.89$; $P < 0.001$) and temperature in May-June ($r = 0.64$; $P < 0.05$). Vole-rank was also clearly associated with laying date ($r = -0.82$; $P < 0.01$).

It was interesting to see how differently two sympatric raptors reacted to vole availability: the Buzzard obviously did not react in its production of young but the Kestrel's success was strongly affected by vole availability.

INTRODUCTION

Food has been an outstanding limiting factor in the ecology of birds for a long time (Lack 1954), but during the last 20 years ecologists found increasing evidence that raptors' density and breeding success are also affected by other factors than food, as reviewed by Newton (1979). The objective of raptor studies changed over the years as ecologists tried to find out which factors are responsible and how they apply in each case. Most papers deal with multifactorial analyses for single species as for example Sparrowhawks (Newton 1986, 1991), Goshawks (Sulkava *et al.* this volume) or Kestrels (Village 1990). Some researchers try to quantify the amount of each significant limiting factor (e.g. Newton & Marquiss 1986), covering food, weather, intra- and interspecific competition, nest-sites, nesting- and hunting habitat. These factors can be easily studied with relatively large sample sizes. In contrast, others working on the level of individual birds are much more time-consuming and will not be discussed here.

We had the unique opportunity to do research on a raptor community of nine different species (Kostrzewa & Kostrzewa 1988), four of which provided a large enough sample to address ecological questions. Out of these two, the Buzzard and Kestrel used mainly voles as their prey base. In this paper, therefore, we compare the ecology of these two species, which react differently to changes in prey.

STUDY AREA AND METHODS

627 Buzzard nests were studied (by AK and co-workers) over 12 years from 1980 to 1991 in a 690km² area and 128 Kestrel nests (by RK) in a smaller area of 100km² over 10 years, from 1982 to 1991.

The study area is situated near Cologne and Bonn on the west side of the River Rhine (Germany). The Kestrel area is located within the Buzzard study area. Both populations were sedentary. More information about the area and our methods of study have been given in previous papers (see below). For this paper we have updated all information to 1991 which adds three more years (=20-25% of total). To stress the overall success of each species, we use "fledged young per territorial pair" instead of "fledged young per successful pair" (as in Kostrzewa & Kostrzewa 1990, 1991) in all correlations dealing with success.

Methods of nest-habitat evaluation or assessment of competition were given in Kostrzewa (1986, 1989, 1991, in prep.)

RESULTS

The nesting habitat

Buzzards bred in self-constructed stick nests within woodland, whereas Kestrels bred mostly in nest boxes or cavities in buildings like farmhouses or churches in open farmland or suburban habitat. Thus both species' nesting habitat differs strictly in our area. The overlap is in hunting habitat, where both species mainly catch voles.

Spacing and regulation of density

Within woodland Buzzards are regularly spaced out as the G-test according to Brown and Rothery (1978) shows (G=0.77), whereas Kestrels are irregularly scattered over their suitable nesting habitat because they depend on manmade structures which are spaced by chance (G=0.47). We also considered density-dependent-regulation in both species. Buzzards do regulate themselves significantly (Fig. 1), testing density in the previous year versus percent change in the following year (according to Newton & Marquiss 1986). We interpret both findings in Buzzards as a manifestation of territorial behaviour, which can also be observed in the field. In contrast we found neither evidence from observations nor from correlations that Kestrels regulate themselves spatially or temporally by territorial behaviour (Fig. 1).

Figure 1. Comparison of density-dependence in the population fluctuations of Buzzards (r = -0.72; P < 0.05) and Kestrels (r = -0.50; N.S).

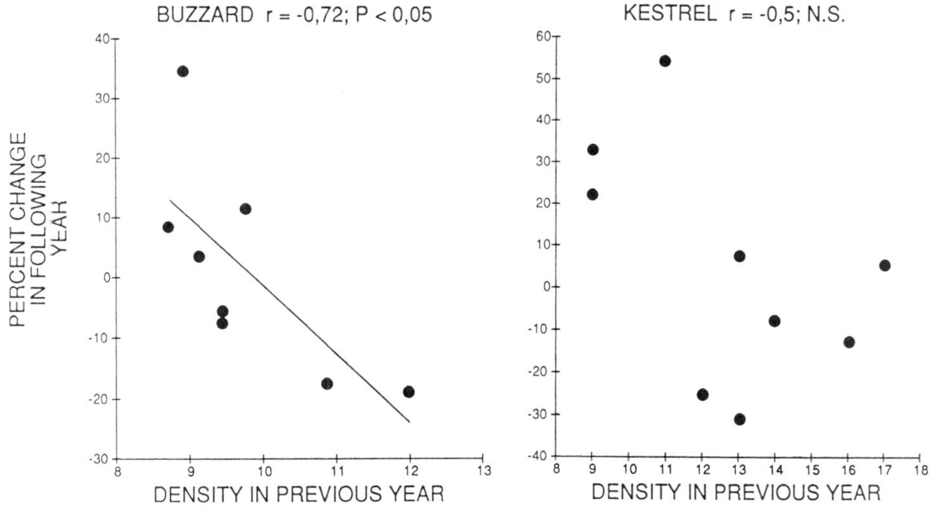

Kestrel

If there is no density-dependent-regulation in Kestrels, what does limit their numbers?

The numbers of territorial and laying pairs (Fig. 2) fluctuate more or less in parallel. There are years with greatly reduced density, such as 1985 and 1987. From observations of starved Kestrels we focussed our interest on two factors: (a) winter temperature and (b) vole numbers during spring and early summer (given here as 1=low, 2=medium and 3=high vole density). Winter temperature is highly significantly correlated with the number of territorial pairs in the following spring (r=0.84; $P < 0.001$), whereas vole rank is not correlated with Kestrel density (r=0.07; N.S.). This does not mean that food could be unimportant for survival, but low winter temperatures mean also more snow cover, which prevents Kestrels from hunting (Kostrzewa 1989).

Therefore we concluded that Kestrel territory numbers were mostly limited by winter temperature.

The next question was: what limits Kestrel's breeding success? Most observers have found voles to be most important, and this was also true in our population. Vole-rank and reproductive success were highly significantly correlated (Fig. 3a). This correlation implicates the finding that most early clutches were observed during years with high vole levels (Fig. 3b)

Findings in other raptors - including Buzzards - indicate that weather could also influence breeding success. The correlation between success and temperature in May and June (i.e. during incubation and the early stages of hatching) was significant (Fig. 4a). The correlation of success versus precipitation during the same period was not significant. This seems easy to explain because more than 95% of our Kestrel pairs breed in sheltered boxes or buildings (Fig. 4b).

Another factor which is now known to affect raptors' breeding success is territory quality. In Kestrels we found frequently used territories being more successful (Fig. 5). At this stage we cannot say exactly why, but habitat analysis is still in progress. Previous results showed contrasting pictures: success was significantly correlated positively with built-up areas and negatively with areas of mixed farmland in 50ha plots around the nest site (Kostrzewa 1989). But we would have expected an opposite result since mixed farmland provides the most vole habitat in the measured plots. Focussing more sharply on meadows and other good vole habitat, correlations were more scattered but still different from those expected. Two explanations seemed to be possible: (a) the Kestrels did not hunt over the measured plots or (b) the nest-habitat analysis itself was inappropriate. From our own observations and the literature (Village 1990) we think that the first hypothesis is correct and that most of the hunting success is outside the measured plot which has a diameter of just 800m. Therefore the plot fits with the description of nesting habitat, but not with hunting habitat and cannot be used to describe territory quality, which is dependent on both. Breeding success itself is closely correlated to vole-rank assessed in the whole study area (Fig. 3).

Figure 2. (a & b) Kestrel population data, (c) vole-rank and (d) winter-temperature for the study area during 1982-1991.

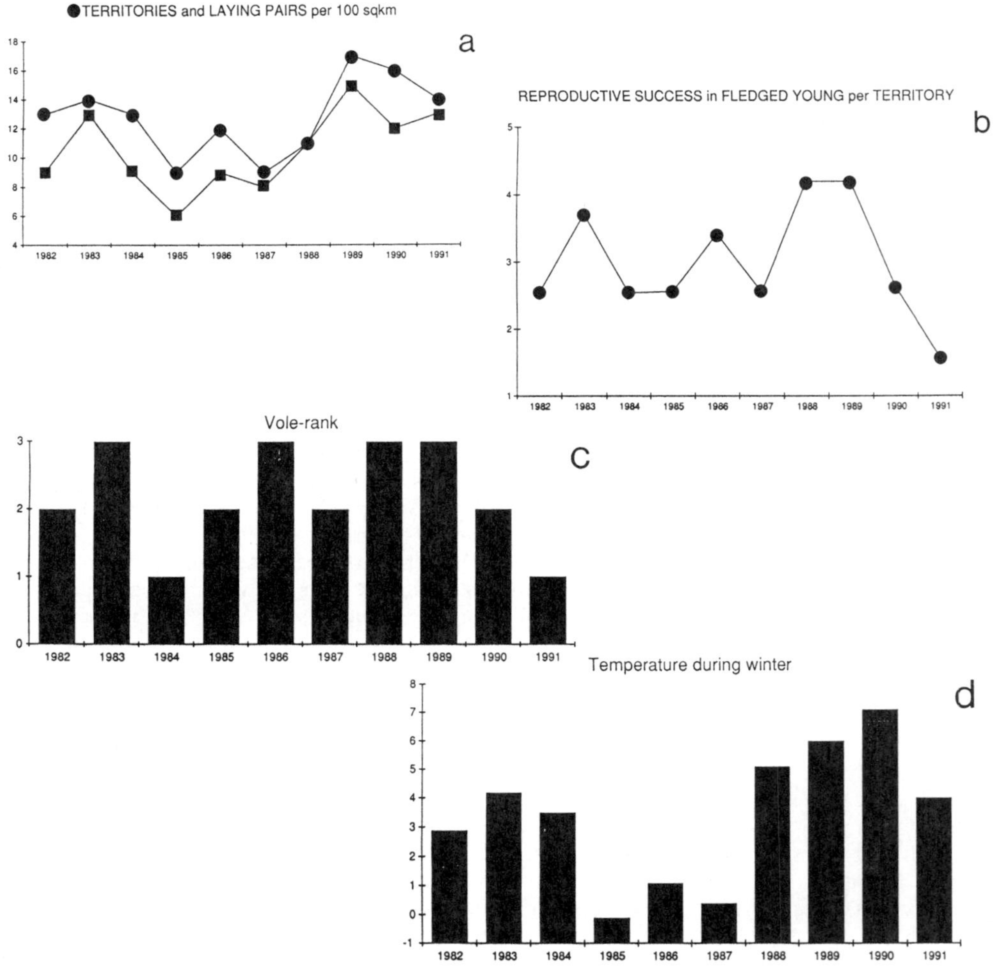

Figure 3. (a) Vole-rank and reproductive success (r = 0.89; P , 0.001) and (b) vole-rank and laying date (r = -0.82; P < 0.01) in Kestrels are highly significantly correlated.

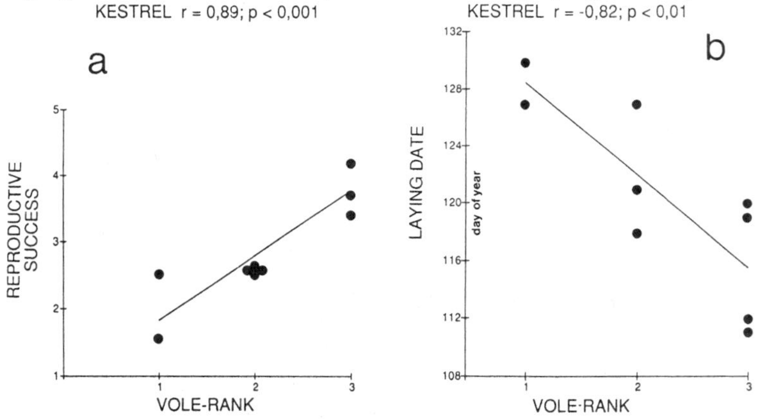

Figure 4. Reproductive success (a) versus temperature in May and June (r = 0.64; P < 0.05) is significantly correlated and (b) versus precipitation in May and June (r = -0.21; N.S.) is not correlated in Kestrels.

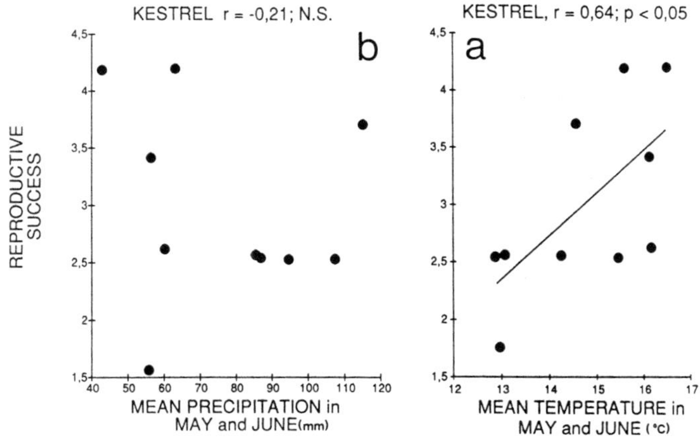

Figure 5. Relationships between frequency of nest success and grade of territory (measured as frequency of occupancy) in Kestrel territories (r = 0.95; P < 0.001; N = 19).

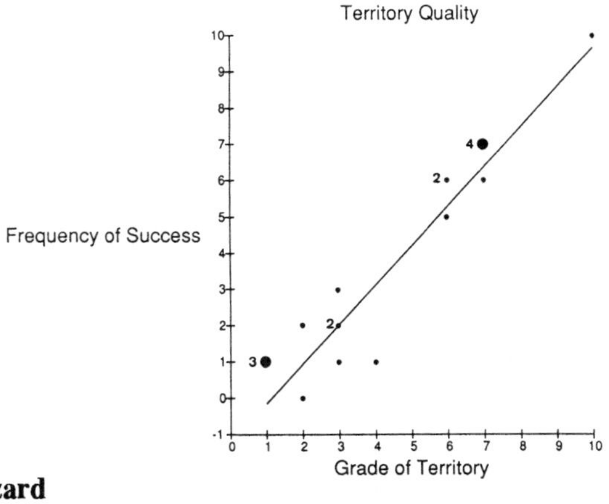

Buzzard

We found no evidence that Buzzard numbers were affected by changes in vole availability (Fig. 6). A high vole rank in 1983 was not accompanied by a change in the number of territories; in 1986 density rose but in 1989 it dropped despite a good vole year (r=0.20; N.S.). Also in winter temperature the correlation to Buzzard territory numbers is nearly nil (r= -0.01, N.S.).

We have therefore concluded that spacing by territorial behaviour is the most important factor for limiting Buzzard numbers in our area. Territory size itself seemed to be adjusted to food supply, because we found different mean nearest-neighbour-distances in two parts of the study area (cf. Kostrzewa 1991, Table 3 for Buzzards).

Buzzards' breeding success should be regulated similarly to that of the Kestrel, because both species depend on the same food resources. But when comparing success to vole rank (Fig. 7) both factors seemed to be not correlated. From observations we concluded that rainfall in May (the stage of incubation and early hatching) was the most important factor as the significant correlation showed (Fig. 8a). To illustrate this very interesting result more clearly we marked the dots in the rainfall correlation with its vole rank and found that a high vole rank is outweighed by high rainfall in May and that a mean breeding success can also be achieved during a dry May with a low vole level (see arrows in Fig. 8a). The same process can be shown between success and vole-rank (Fig. 8b) which gave no significant correlation. Dry years showed generally better success than wet ones.

Figure 6. (a) Density, (b) vole-rank (shown in Fig. 7b: 1981-89) and (c) winter-temperature for the Buzzard over nine years.

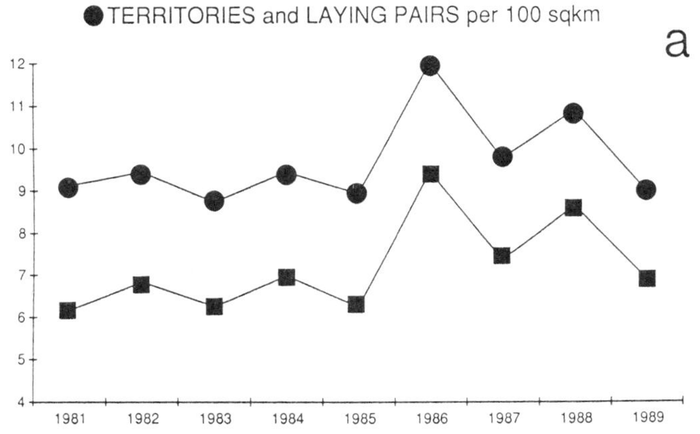

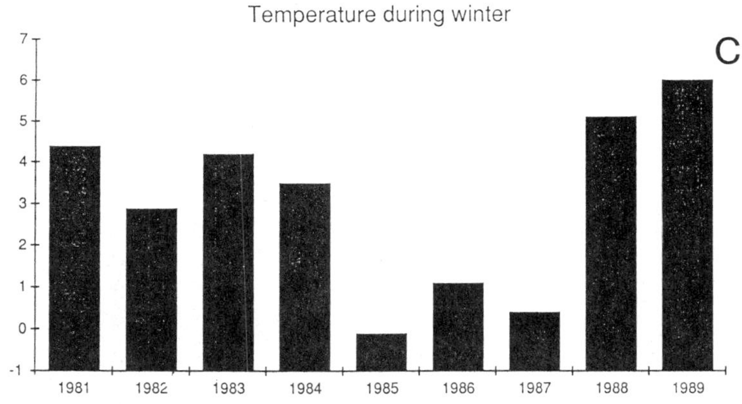

We concluded therefore that the main factor in Buzzards' breeding success was not voles but weather, which can suppress the benefits of a good vole year almost totally for the Buzzards, because they live in unsheltered stick-nests.

The question of territory quality in Buzzards was investigated from the early stages of this study, beginning with 1983 when I started my PhD-work and found evidence for two other factors affecting Buzzards' breeding success in our study population.

One factor was interspecific competition: Buzzard territories close to a Goshawk site were less successful. From 282 nesting records we found a clear correlation between distance to next Goshawk site and the breeding success of individual Buzzard pairs (see Kostrzewa 1991: Fig. 1). Secondly the nest-site itself had influence on the breeding success of its occupant. Sites which were only used once failed more often than sites with a higher degree of use (Fig. 9).

Comparing grade of territory with the frequency of its success, we found a clear positive correlation: sites used more often do have greater success. This was not only true for frequency (Fig. 10) but also for the number of young raised ($r=0.69$; $P<0.001$; $N=119$) which is not shown here. Some habitat features such as the area of open farmland (=hunting habitat) around the nest site were strongly positively correlated with its success (further data on 30 habitat parameters were given in Kostrzewa 1989). The results were consistent with my hypothesis that nest-habitat choice and nest-habitat quality should be positively correlated (Kostrzewa in prep.).

Thus we can conclude that some territories and nest-sites gave a better success than others, but we do not know why. It could be habitat alone, but I believe the quality of individual pairs might also be involved, with the most competent pairs occupying the best territories (Newton 1991).

Figure 7. (a) Reproductive success, (b) vole rank and (c) May rainfall in Buzzards over 12 years.

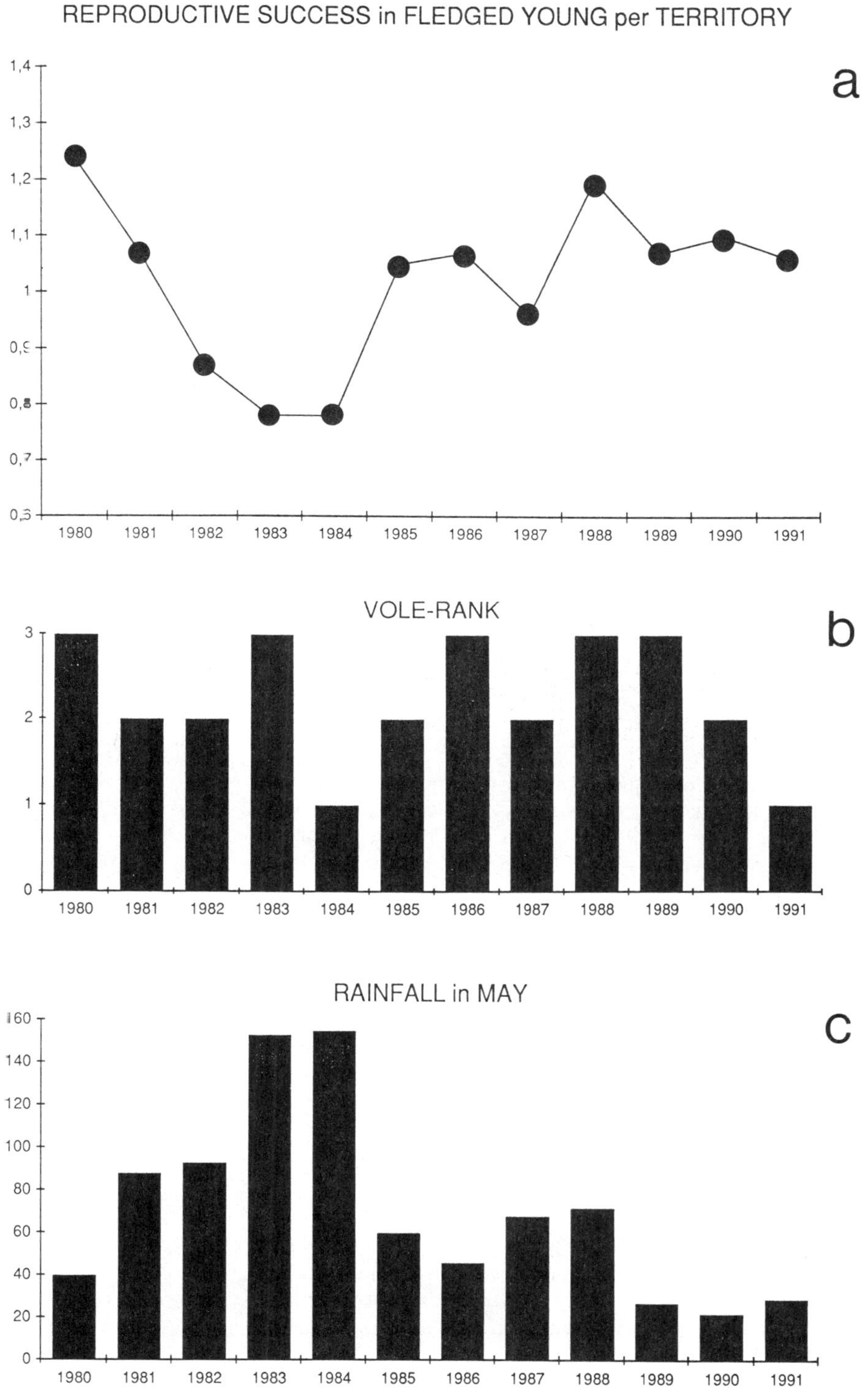

Figure 8. Reproductive success is (a) highly correlated with rainfall in May (r = -0.80; P < 0.001) but (b) not with vole-rank (r = 0.36; N.S.) in Buzzard.

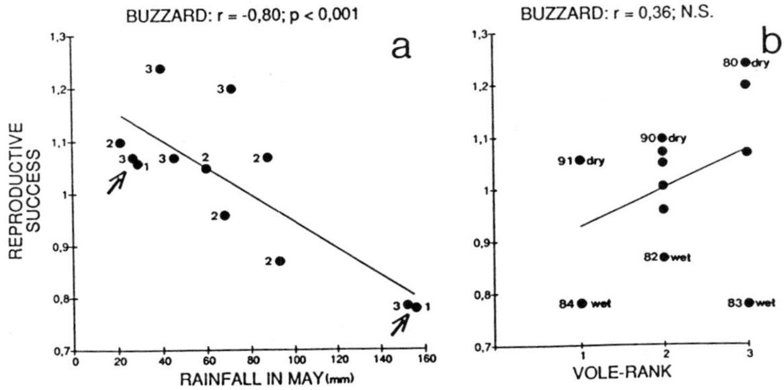

Figure 9. Low grade territories failed more often totally in the Buzzard.

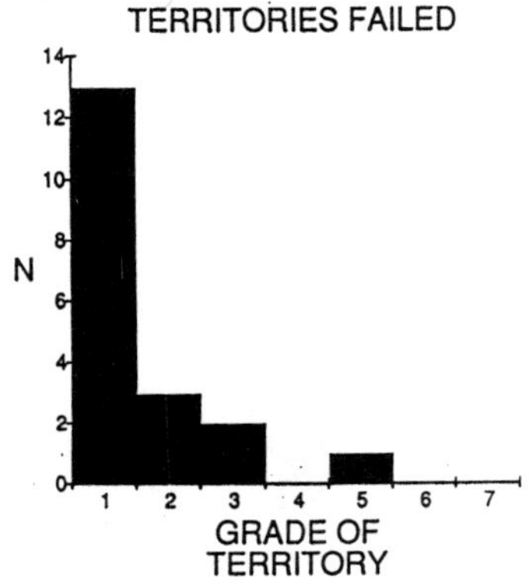

Figure 10. Relationships between frequency of nest success and grade of territory (measured as frequency of occupancy) in Buzzard territories (r = 0.81; P < 0.001; N = 119).

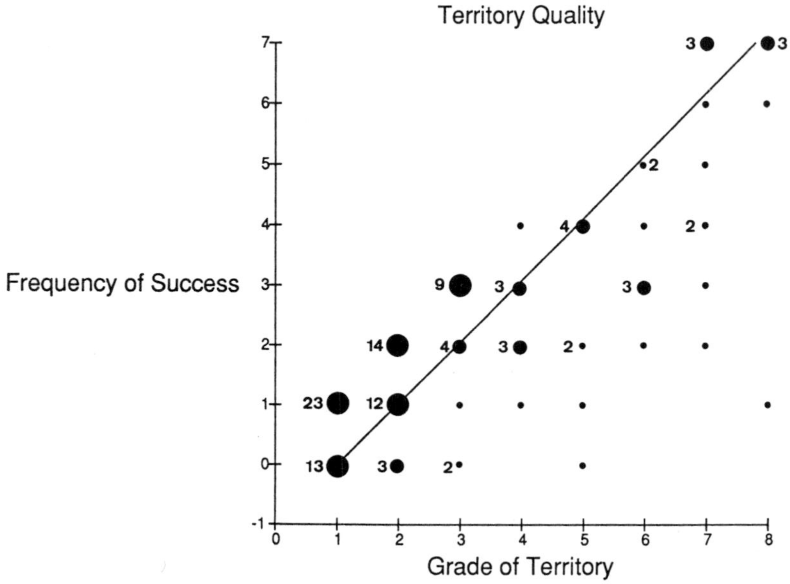

DISCUSSION

In both cases density is not directly dependent on food resources. Buzzards regulate themselves by spacing behaviour. Suitable territories and nest-sites limit the number of pairs in our area (cf. Kostrzewa 1991). A constant number of *ca.* 30% of all territories were non-laying over the years (Fig. 6; cf. Hohmann this volume). These were mostly low grade territories (unpubl. data). This would also highlight the importance of limited nest-sites for Buzzards. Kestrel numbers were mostly limited by starvation because of low winter temperatures causing prolonged snowcover, which prevented Kestrels from hunting efficiently. Buzzards (c. 1000g) weigh up to four times more than Kestrels (c. 250g), so it was to be expected that Kestrels were more affected by food shortage. The population bottleneck for both sedentary species is therefore during winter for the small Kestrels and during spring - while spacing themselves - for Buzzards.

Breeding success in the open nesting Buzzards was affected mainly by weather, especially by rain during the time of hatching in May, which had more effect on the annual variations than voles. Nest habitat also had a significant influence on breeding success (Kostrzewa in prep.) as did interspecific competition (Kostrzewa 1991).

For Kestrels breeding in boxes or cavities, voles were the main factor influencing annual variations in success, but also temperature during hatching had a minor influence. With three more years of data weather has lost its central position in affecting breeding success in Kestrels (cf. Kostrzewa & Kostrzewa 1990). The influence of nest-habitat on success in Kestrels seems to be not measurable, because in most cases hunting-habitat and nesting-habitat were spatially separated (Kostrzewa & Kostrzewa 1993; Village 1990).

We do not know whether our findings on the importance of food availability were typical for Central Europe, since some other studies have found Buzzard density and success more affected by voles (cf. Mebs 1964; Looft & Busche 1981; or Rockenbauch 1975). But these workers never considered factors other than voles and the relationship between voles and abundance or breeding was often not so clear as they thought (see Rockenbauch 1975). Under Central European conditions food and nest-sites might be of equal importance for species density and a Buzzard population, having reached the ceiling of available nesting territories, may cease to fluctuate with vole numbers. Our Kestrels should do the same, but we have good evidence that there are more nest-sites available (Kostrzewa 1989) than the maximum of 17 territorial pairs can occupy. If we have some warm winters during the coming years this population would probably also reach its density limit.

Future studies should therefore take different limiting factors for density and breeding success into consideration. Food should not always be the ultimate factor (as in Lack 1954). It can also act as a proximate factor, especially when prey and predator are more regulated by weather as the real ultimate factor governing animal populations and their behaviour over wide areas.

ACKNOWLEDGEMENTS

The Buzzard study was partly funded by the Graduiertenförderung des Landes Nordrhein-Westfalen (during 1985-86) and by a post-doctoral fellowship and grant from the Deutsche Forschungsgemeinschaft (Ko 943, 1986-89). The Kestrel study has been partly funded by the Deutsche Ornithologen Gesellschaft since 1992. We obtained several smaller grants from the Freunde und Förderer der Universität Köln. We are grateful to all of these.

The field study on Buzzards was performed by F. & R. Borger, W.v. Dewitz, A. & R. Kostrzewa and G. Speer. During more than 10 years of field work at the Department of Zoology, University of Cologne, we were supported by Profs. A. Egelhaaf, H. Engländer and especially by the late U. Lehmann. Dr Ian Newton considerably improved our manuscript.

REFERENCES

BROWN, D. & P. ROTHERY 1978. Randomness and local regularity of points in a plane. *Biometrica* 65: 115-122.

HOHMANN, U. (this volume): Statusspecific habitat use in the Common Buzzard *Buteo buteo*.
KOSTRZEWA, A. 1986. Quantitative Untersuchungen zur Ökologie, Habitatnutzung und Habitattrennung von Mäusebussard *Buteo buteo*, Habicht *Accipiter gentilis* und Wespenbussard *Pernis apivorus* unter Berücksichtigung von Naturschutzmanagement und Landschaftsplanung. Dissertation, Univ. K+ln.
KOSTRZEWA, A. 1989. Nest habitat separation in three European raptors *Accipiter gentilis, Buteo buteo* and *Pernis apivorus* - a multivariate analysis. *In*: B.U. Meyburg & R.D. Chancellor (Eds.) *Raptors in the Modern World.* Proceedings of III World Conference on Birds of Prey: pp. 553-559.
KOSTRZEWA, A. 1991. Interspecific interference competition in three European raptor species. *Ethology, Ecology & Evolution* 3: 127-143.
KOSTRZEWA, A (in prep.): Nest-site occupancy and breeding performance as indicators for nest-habitat quality in three European raptor species.
KOSTRZEWA, A. & R. KOSTRZEWA 1988. Bestandstrends der Greifvögel *Falconiformes* in der Niederrheinischen Bucht. *J. Orn.* 129: 457-461.
KOSTRZEWA, A. & R. KOSTRZEWA 1990. The relationship of spring and summer weather with density and breeding performance of the Buzzard *Buteo buteo*, Goshawk *Accipiter gentilis* and Kestrel *Falco tinnunculus. Ibis* 132: 550-559.
KOSTRZEWA, R. 1989. The biology of the Kestrel *Falco tinnunculus* in different areas in the Federal Republic of Germany and West-Berlin. (in German with summary). Doctoral Thesis, Univ. Cologne.
KOSTRZEWA, R. & A. KOSTRZEWA 1991. Winter weather, spring and summer density, and subsequent breeding success of Eurasian Kestrels, Common Buzzards and Northern Goshawks. *Auk* 108: 342-347.
KOSTRZEWA, R. & A. KOSTRZEWA 1993. *Der Turmfalke (Falco tinnunculus).* Aula-Verlag, Wiesbaden.
LACK, D. 1954. *The Natural Regulation of Animal Numbers.* Univ. Press, Oxford.
LOOFT, V. & G. BUSCHE 1981. *Greifvögel.* Vogelwelt Schleswig-Holsteins. Band 2. Neumünster.
MEBS, T. 1964. Zur Biologie und Populationsdynamik des Mäusebussards *Buteo buteo. J. Orn.* 105: 247-306.
NEWTON, I. 1979. *Population Ecology of Raptors.* Poyser, Berkhamsted.
NEWTON, I. 1986. *The Sparrowhawk.* Poyser, Calton.
NEWTON, I. 1991. Habitat variation and population regulation in Sparrowhawks. *Ibis.* 133 suppl. 1: 76-88.
NEWTON, I. & M. MARQUISS 1986. Population regulation in Sparrowhawks. *J. Anim. Ecol* 55: 463-480.
ROCKENBAUCH, D. 1975. Zwölfjährige Untersuchung zur Ökologie des Mäusebussards *Buteo buteo* auf der Schwäbischen Alb. *J. Orn.* 116: 39-54.
SULKAVA, S., S. HUHTALA & R. TORNBERG (this volume): Regulation of Goshawks *Accipiter gentilis* breeding in Western Finland over the last 30 years.
VILLAGE, A. 1990. *The Kestrel.* Poyser, London.

Drs. A. & R. Kostrzewa
Bonnstr. 63
D-50321 Brühl
Fed. Rep. of Germany

Meyburg, B.-U. & R. D. Chancellor eds.1994
Raptor Conservation Today
WWGBP / The Pica Press

Global Raptor Migration "Bottlenecks" as a Parameter of Long-Term Variations in Raptor Populations

Yossi Leshem

INTRODUCTION

Despite its small size Israel is strategically located at the junction of three continents. As a result, Israel is a "bottleneck", into which all or a large part of the world populations of certain raptor species concentrate, during spring and autumn.

Comparison of our results with data in the relevant literature, proves that our figures for species whose total population, or most of it, passes through "bottleneck" areas provides relatively reliable estimates of minimum population size. The numbers counted during migration are sometimes higher by an order of magnitude than the data from existing studies.

In order to examine long-term regularity in major migrating species' appearance, the weighted average day of arrival was calculated for all the years of the study, as well as the date by which half of the population had passed over Israel, the average peak day, and the average arrival percentage for each species on the peak day. The results show that it is possible to predict the days of appearance of various raptor species with a precision of 1.35 to 3.12 days in autumn and 1.92 to 4.92 days in spring. In many of the species the arrival percentage on the peak day is higher in spring than in autumn.

METHODS

Five different data-gathering methods were used for this research:

1. Ground Observer Network: Dozens of studies have tracked migration with small numbers of observers at 2-3 key observation points. In this study, for the first time ever, ground observers were placed along a broad front: 25 observation points were placed across the country, along 75 kilometres, during several migration seasons. More than 150 experienced birdwatchers logged about 224,000 observation hours.

2. Light Aircraft Tracking: This method proved excellent for locating principal migration routes, their altitudes and counting flocks per time and distance units, and very efficient on "peak" migration days. Additional flights were carried out to confirm the radar distinction ability (see Method 5). Twenty-nine flights totalling 83.40 hours were carried out.

3. Motorised Glider: This method enabled continuous flying, up to 11.5 hours, with the same flock, as well as exact mapping of the migration route, altitude, flock progress rate, climbing and gliding in thermals. One hundred and seventy-three flights totalling about 720 hours were carried out. This was the first time motorised glider migration tracking was used in the Middle East. No study using a motorised glider to systematically follow migrating flocks for such long periods of time had been done up to now, both in the number of flight hours and the number of tracking days.

4. *Unmanned Aircraft (Drones):* This method enabled tracking single flocks for about 150 kilometres with constant documentation of the flock by video camera. Nineteen flights were carried out. To the best of our knowledge, this is the first biological study ever to make use of this military instrument for research.

5. *Radar:* A radar screen at the Ben-Gurion International Airport surveillance radar was permanently available during the migration seasons. This enabled constant tracking during all hours of the day. The cloud radar of the Shaham Company followed migration regularly only during one season. Its use was terminated due to technical problems. A total of 8,125 radar tracking hours was carried out. This is the first time radar was used to follow soaring bird migration in the Middle East in general, and in Israel specifically.

Most migration tracking research has been limited to one method, and only a minority combined two methods simultaneously, such as a combination of radar and ground observers (Evans & Lathbury 1973) or light aircraft and radar (Pennycuick, Alerstam & Larsson 1979). In our study, we have developed for the first time, to the best of our knowledge, research based on a combination of five methods for data gathering from one migration system, with each method complementing, at least partially, the deficiencies of one of the others. At the same time this enabled confirmation of data gathered by one method by one of the other methods. The development of several parallel research methods allowed for integration between the various methods. The radar could, for example, take over from the motorised glider for a short period of time, to enable refuelling and rest; it could then direct the glider to the exact position of the flock it had left to continue tracking.

The statistical analysis in this research is based on nine autumn migration seasons for raptors and four for storks and pelicans. During spring migration raptors were followed in Eilat for six years and storks for four in the western Negev.

RESULTS

Comparison of our results with data in the relevant literature proves that our figures for species whose total population or most of it passes through "bottleneck" areas provide relatively reliable estimates of minimum population size. The numbers counted during migration are sometimes higher by an order of magnitude than data from existing studies (Leshem 1991).

In order to examine long-term regularity in major migrating species' appearance, the weighted average day of arrival was calculated for all the years of the study, as well as the date by which half of the population had passed over Israel, the average peak day and the average arrival percentage for each species on the peak day. The results show that it is possible to predict the appearance days of various raptor species with a precision of 1.35 to 3.12 days in autumn and 1.92 to 4.92 days in spring ($P < 0.001$). The arrival of storks can be predicted with a precision of 3.78 days in autumn and 5.46 days in spring. The rest of the data examined were found to be statistically significant, but for some the time span was broader. The conclusion reached was that it is possible to predict appearance times of the various species.

Comparison of arrival percentages on the peak day for a number of raptor species shows that the passage percentages in autumn for flocking species are greater than for non-flocking species (17.1%-30.1% and 9.0%-15.6% respectively). In spring, the difference between flocking and non-flocking species is even greater: 27.7%-46.0% and 8.3%-12.0% respectively. Intra-specific comparison shows that for many of the species the arrival percentage on the peak day is higher in spring than in autumn. This is probably the adult population, hurrying to return to its breeding grounds in spring, therefore moving in more concentrated waves. Thus an inverse relation between the arrival percentage on the peak day and age of sexual maturity is found: 46% of the Levant Sparrowhawk population, which reaches sexual maturity in its first year, passes over during the peak day compared to 17.7% of the Steppe Eagle population, which reaches sexual maturity at five

Table 1. Summary of Soaring Bird Migration Surveys. Autumn 1982-1990.

	Kfar Kassem - Cross Samaria						Northern Valleys		
Species	1982	1983	1984	1985	1986	1987	1988	1989	1990
C. gallicus	7142	7697	7399	7005	8045	7288	3008	2492	3819
P. haliaetus	48	50	49	61	79	39	52	66	78
A. pomarina	89239	141868	88210	108873	114446	81429	74198	56533	83701
A. nipalensis	296	234	368	411	265	456	224	156	214
A. heliaca	24	9	22	37	13	37	9	18	3
A. clanga	33	41	67	79	74	85	42	50	30
H. pennatus	1176	1267	1127	1498	1973	1304	622	842	811
B. rufinus	18	20	57	32	13	24	43	62	25
B. vulpinus	80	303	139	352	517	461	934	2166	1952
B. buteo	16	13	22	29	30	42	5	6	3
P. apivorus	319660	133621	380576	390612	419164	379672	347397	300972	437432
M. migrans	313	293	447	759	1051	1195	1063	1131	1734
N. percnopterus	301	242	265	474	346	301	124	284	161
G. fulvus	16	52	39	32	73	27	76	39	62
C. aeruginosus	398	476	587	801	1237	1236	751	1534	1516
C. cyaneus	6	6	17	21	21	15	4	1	9
C. pygargus	12	16	20	51	12	34	47	103	55
C. macrourus	21	32	46	57	23	33	12	46	26
C. pyg/macro	340	341	287	469	496	642	215	661	446
Unidentified	2923	2677	2916	3377	3418	1974	1584	2495	1429
A. brevipes	21983	25316	29255	37896	44653	28708	40560	41237	41722
A. nisus	385	513	813	592	1761	1317	620	11508	68
F. peregrinus	15	12	8	20	18	2	15	12	17
F. eleonorae	44	37	15	34	17	22	17	8	15
F. subbuteo	29	29	42	59	55	40		15	19
F. vespertinus	631	1097	1514	2820	5752	1833	2836	4942	4200
Falco sp.	168	197	355	305	294	460		52	200
Total	445317	316459	514662	556756	603846	508676	474458	417073	580617
Double Count/ Eliminated	32378	62714	62207	111294	147440	123112		102818	
Double Count (%)	7.3%	19.8%	12.1%	22.1%	24.4%	21.9		%24.7%	

years of age. In non-flocking species the situation is similar, although in less concentrated waves.

The regularity of passage time period length was examined for each of the species migrating over Israel. Analysis of the data shows that those species flying over in large numbers tend to flock and pass over during the shortest time periods. Thus, 90% of the populations of the five species which flock in autumn pass over during 13-20 days, compared to five non-flocking species which pass over during 24-35 days. The only exception to this rule is the White Pelican *Pelecanus onocrotalus* whose passage time period is long (114 days in autumn), despite its being a true flocker. The reason seems to be that this species flocks during the breeding season as well, populating very broad breeding grounds (between 22-85° longitude), with each breeding colony reaching its nesting site as independent units. Accordingly we find that this is the only flocking species that has no peak days on which more than 10% of the population fly over, and whose weighted average day of arrival is the least statistically significant of all flocking species (12.39 days).

Despite all the above, in non-flocking species, which have a longer passage time period, the weighted average arrival day is very exact, within a span of 1.8 to 2.85 days only, in the four non-flocking species analysed in this study (Booted Eagle *Hieraaetus pennatus* Short-toed Eagle *Circaetus gallicus,* Egyptian Vulture *Neophron percnopterus* and Marsh Harrier *Circus*

Table 2. **Summary of Soaring Bird Migration Surveys, Eilat, Spring 1977, 1983, 1985-1988.**

	1977*	1983**	1985	1986	1987	1988
A. chrysaetos		9			7	
A. nipalensis	19288	23318	75073	22762	17443	10922
A. heliaca	95	25	61	35	47	12
A. pomarina		40	74	58	67	21
A. clanga		11	5	6	4	5
B. vulpinus	315767	109493	225460	465827	380441	429139
B. rufinus		34	105	47	29	28
M. migrans	26770	27039	28834	24728	313363	31774
A. nisus	155	468	138	76	102	52
A. brevipes	5958	2556	905	17034	49836	21380
C. gallicus	220	183	345	151	59	67
H. pennatus	175	147	140	109	105	150
H. fasciatus		4	6	1	5	2
P. haliaetus	122	87	49	64	96	73
N. percnopterus	802	252	541	385	308	263
C. aeruginosus	125	371	242	93	171	71
C. macrourus		52	113	17	88	11
C. pygargus		44	41	13	14	10
P. apivorus	225952	265775	851598	341777	293658	188914
Accipiter sp.	1360		144	42	143	
Buteo/Milvus	149264		6460		3775	
Aquila sp.	9083		1111	17	31	
Falco sp.	8601		83		146	63
Gyps fulvus		3	17		2	4
A. gentilis		1	3		1	
Circus sp.		160	58		30	
F. eleonorae		1	16		9	
F. naumanni		54	13		34	
F. biarmicus		1	7	2	3	
F. peregrinus			4		4	
F. subbuteo		35	20	54		
F. cherrug			2			
Unidentified			2138		203	
Total	763,737	474127	1,193,751	873,388	778,224	688,659

*1977 - Christensen *et al.* (1982)
**1983-1988 - Shirihai, H. (1987)

aeruginosus). These four species also arrive with a high time overlap in autumn and spring, and there is a possibility that what we see here is inter-specific flocking of non-flocking species (they were also observed migrating in common thermals).

The spring migration wave is longer than the autumn one in most birds of prey and storks. In many of the species passage time in spring is almost double that in autumn.

Flocking and non-flocking species passing over Israel were compared according to their wintering grounds and type of food. The data show that all nine flocking species overflying Israel migrate south of the Sahara and some of them reach South Africa. They feed at least partially on exothermic prey. Three of the four commoner non-flocking species: Booted Eagle, Egyptian Vulture and Short-toed Eagle also feed on heterothermic prey and migrate south of the Sahara. Only the Marsh Harrier is an "intermediary species", wintering both north and south of the Sahara, and feeding accordingly on birds and mammals. A number of species feeding on endothermic prey do not flock and accordingly do not migrate south of the Sahara. This phenomenon is paralleled in New World raptors (Mindell 1985).

Comparison of the weighted arrival day of different species according to their chronological order of appearance in autumn shows distinct regularity in the order of arrival according to the type of prey they feed on - from insect eaters to reptiles, fish and finally mammal eaters. During spring migration the picture is reversed, and the first to pass are those feeding on endothermic prey and the last the insect eaters. This phenomenon shows the close relation and dependence between migration times and the availability of prey, whose activity varies with changes in weather, with exotherms disappearing first in autumn and returning first in spring.

ACKNOWLEDGEMENTS

I would like to thank all those people and organisations without whose help this study would not have succeeded: the motorised glider pilots, the many volunteer birdwatchers who participated in this study, the IRIC, the SPNI, the Ministry of Science and Technology, the Israel Airports Authority, the Meteo-tech company, Ester Lachman and Prof. Yoram Yom-Tov, who was my scientific adviser in this study for my Ph.D.

Special thanks are due to the IAF officers and radar operators who helped make this project a classic example of fruitful co-operation between military and civilian elements.

REFERENCES

CHRISTENSEN, S. et al. **1982.** The spring migration of ratpors in southern Israel and Sinai. *Sandgrouse* 3: 1-42.

EVANS, P.R. & G.W. LATHBURY 1973. Raptor migration across the Straits of Gibraltar. *Ibis* 115: 572-585.

LESHEM, Y. 1991. Study and forecast of fall and spring migration of soaring birds over Israel and the effect of climate factors on migration. Ph.D. thesis submitted to the Senate of Tel-Aviv University.

MINDELL, D.P. 1985. Biogeography of New World migrant raptors: a review. *In* Proceedings of the Fourth Hawk Migration Conference, M. Harwood (ed.), 369-385. Rochester, NY: Hawk Migration Association of North America.

PENNYCUICK, C.J., T. ALERSTAM & B. LARSSON, 1979. Soaring migration of the Common Crane *Grus grus* observed by radar and from an aircraft. *Ornis Scand.* 10: 241-251.

SHIRIHAI, H. 1987. Eilat an International Highway for Migrating Raptors. International Birdwatching Center Eilat. pp23-80.Table 1. Summary of Soaring Bird Migration Surveys. Autumn 1982-1990.

Yossi Leshem
Har Gilo Field Study Centre
Doar Na Harei
Jerusalem 91076, Israel

Spectacled Owl *Pulsatrix perspicillata*

Meyburg, B.-U. & R. D. Chancellor eds.1994
Raptor Conservation Today
WWGBP / The Pica Press

Long-term Population Fluctuations of Large Raptors in the Southern Kalahari

Richard Liversidge

The original purpose of this study was to determine the long-term population fluctuations of birds of prey of the Kalahari National Park. Similar work on rodent populations was initially intended to run concurrently.

It soon became apparent that bird of prey numbers fluctuated quite dramatically and somewhat irregularly from year to year. Initially, for the first ten years there seemed to be some correlation with populations and rainfall but as the study continued this relationship disappeared. There was no obvious pattern to the changes in numbers and there were no obvious trends. Even the number of breeding pairs of the resident species fluctuated with no obvious causes.

Thiollay (1978), discussing population influences of West African birds of prey, listed a number of biological reasons for changes. While most of these could be applied to the Kalahari it soon became obvious that the major influence for change in populations was rainfall. It took many years to realise that rainfall was not just the local effect but that heavy rains or drought occurring many hundreds of kilometres away was equally influential in determining the numbers of birds present.

METHODS

The study area was within the Kalahari National Park, where two dry river beds provide the only lines of large trees in an otherwise undulating terrain of red sand dunes covered with sparse grass and shrubs with the occasional tree. This area is some 36,000 km² and adjoins a further 44,000 km² reserve in Botswana. Strip counts covering 11,141km over the period 1973 to 1992 (20 years) were carried out for 18 years by the same observer over the same routes and for the most part at the same times of day.

It is important to stress that the visibility is exceptionally good. The trees are fine-leaved and it is thus possible to see most larger birds with comparative ease. To standardise the results for visits of different duration covering different distances, the numbers of birds per 100km are presented. Identification was mainly through 10x binoculars or in cases of difficulties a telescope with 40x and 80x was used.

RESULTS

The combined counts for the months January through to April are presented in Table 1. These are the late summer rainfall months for the area, when 80 % of the rainfall is recorded. This is the period when 80 % of the birds are to be recorded. The rainfall for the same period is also given in Table 1.

It must be realised that rainfall is irregular in semi-arid regions, and the lower the annual rainfall the less predictable it becomes. The Kalahari National Park has a mean annual rainfall at the southern camp Tweerivieren, of 225mm. This occurs mainly as summer storm rains which according to Leistner (1967) occur on average seven days each year. In the period 1984 to 1989 the number of rain storms varied from 3.3 to 9.3 days each year (Knight 1991).

In the semi-arid region of southern Africa, where the main rainfall occurs in the southern summer, there is a long term periodicity of ten continuous years of above average rainfall followed by ten continuous years of below average rainfall. This study was started in the middle of a so-called wet period and extended after five years into the dry period. Consequently the first ten years of results gave a very reasonable correlation of populations with rainfall. However, now that twenty years have passed and we are back in the wet period, the population correlation with rainfall has disappeared.

In preparation for this paper the rainfall for the same timespan for northern Namibia, northern Botswana and Skukuza in the Kruger National Park, was obtained. This was to see whether good rains in any one of those areas had provided favourable conditions that had prevented the migrants from proceeding further south to the study area. Generally speaking, the rainfall for the other areas followed a similar pattern to that of the Kalahari, so this was considered not to have affected the movements, although for some species at least there are indications of weather from other areas affecting the southern Kalahari populations.

There is no correlation between bird numbers and rainfall for any of the larger birds of prey in the southern Kalahari for the whole twenty-year study.

It must be appreciated that the strategy of the large migratory birds of prey in the southern arid regions of Africa differs a lot from the conventional concept of routine movement back and forth to the same areas. The birds are largely opportunist feeders that take advantage of the massive food resources that arise from good rains in semi-arid regions. Such sources as the flying stages of termites (alates), all stages of locusts, the mass breeding of queleas and the cycles of rodent populations are a constant source of enormous quantities of food. It is believed that the migrants are attracted to areas of heavy rainfall in their search for food and that it is this that determines where they are in their southern winter range.

It can be seen that there is no regular pattern of numbers in the southern Kalahari. Indeed the whole table is very confusing and not helpful in determining the cause and effect of the changes in numbers recorded. This statement not only concerns the migratory species from the north but other raptors as well, that apparently come from the southern areas. Perhaps it should be mentioned that several of the species have both small resident breeding populations as well as summer influxes of migratory individuals of the same species that are derived either from Africa or Europe. Indeed ringing birds in the area has shown that they have been recovered to the north, south, east and west. When some species are considered individually there is some understanding as regards movements.

Secretary Bird *Sagittarius serpentarius*. Changes in numbers are not understood. The general impression is that the numbers do not change very much from year to year. It may be that this species gathers socially in numbers up to 35 at certain water-holes at midday and the observations become distorted through these increased numbers.

White-backed Vulture *Gyps africanus*. It can be seen that the highest numbers are during the locally dry period. It is believed that success of breeding in South Africa has provided the additional birds.

Lappet-faced Vulture *Torgos tracheliotus*. Numbers are highest during the dry periods, this is possibly increased by both east and west populations of this species which at best occur in small numbers.

Black-shouldered Kite *Elanus caeruleus*. Wherever this species occurs the numbers fluctuate without apparent reason. However, a chance visit in late 1991 to the eastern Cape, 1000km from

Table 1. Number of birds observed per 100 kms for months of January to April each year.

	1973	1974	1975	1976	1977	1978	1979	1980	1981	1982	1983	1984	1985	1986	1988	1989	1991	1992
RESIDENT/REGULAR																		
Sagittarius serpentarius	2.3	9.4	10.6	4.1	0.7	1.6	4.1	4.2	8.1	4.3	2.9	10.9	5.0	3.6	1.1	14.0	5.6	3.9
Poliohierax semitorquatus	0.2	3.4	0.3	0.7	0.2	0.0	0.6	0.3	1.0	0.0	0.1	0.0	0.2	0.0	0.0	0.6	0.6	0.7
Polemaetus bellicosus	0.5	0.2	0.5	0.0	1.3	0.3	2.1	0.8	0.3	0.6	0.5	0.0	0.0	0.0	0.2	0.0	0.5	0.3
Melierax canorus	5.8	21.8	8.9	5.4	19.8	8.0	14.3	5.0	4.7	6.0	4.1	0.0	2.3	2.1	3.4	12.3	10.2	6.2
RESIDENT/IRREGULAR																		
Gyps africanus	1.2	1.1	2.2	10.3	42.7	2.6	20.9	5.8	13.8	26.0	16.9	82.4	64.9	0.0	6.4	12.9	4.6	41.6
Torgos tracheliotus	0.9	0.7	0.9	3.1	11.7	0.0	1.2	0.0	2.5	1.8	4.5	6.7	7.5	0.7	0.6	0.0	0.2	2.1
Falco rupicoloides	1.2	4.8	4.1	0.7	1.8	1.6	3.9	4.5	1.9	1.2	1.9	0.0	2.7	2.1	1.6	5.8	2.6	0.8
RESIDENT/MIGRANT																		
Terathopius ecaudatus	1.1	2.9	3.1	4.7	10.1	1.6	11.0	9.3	1.9	2.2	8.0	12.1	3.9	0.7	0.8	1.8	2.2	2.1
Aquila rapax	1.6	0.9	2.5	11.3	12.4	1.3	9.2	8.1	4.9	2.4	2.9	12.7	7.7	0.7	0.4	3.5	1.4	4.4
Elanus caeruleus	0.0	13.9	0.4	3.3	1.6	2.8	0.1	0.3	0.0	0.3	0.2	0.0	6.4	0.0	0.0	12.9	1.4	1.6
Circaetus pectoralis	0.2	0.2	1.7	4.4	0.5	0.8	3.5	1.6	1.0	0.2	0.3	0.0	0.7	0.0	1.1	0.6	2.4	0.0
MIGRANTS																		
Falco biarmicus	1.2	1.5	1.7	5.2	15.1	7.5	9.8	1.3	13.8	1.1	1.1	6.1	1.6	0.0	0.2	4.1	4.5	1.0
Falco rupicolus	0.2	0.2	0.1	0.1	0.2	0.0	0.6	0.0	1.0	0.2	1.0	0.0	0.2	0.0	0.0	0.0	0.2	0.0
Circaetus cinereus	0.0	0.0	0.7	4.0	1.6	1.0	0.1	0.3	0.5	0.1	0.1	0.0	0.0	0.0	0.0	0.6	1.4	0.7
Aquila nipalensis	0.0	0.0	0.3	5.1	1.1	9.8	0.1	0.0	0.0	0.0	0.0	0.0	0.0	0.0	0.3	0.0	0.0	0.0
RAINFALL																		
January to April	155.4	401.9	145.4	491.1	207.1	123.6	100.0	69.0	120.9	14.7	38.3	52.7	81.0	105.7	208.5	305.9	185.5	110.2

the Kalahari, where there was a severe drought, brought home the effect of negative rainfall on the local population. A well-known communal roost there was completely deserted and it is suggested that movements of this species are probably affected by drought to move away from such areas.

Tawny Eagle *Aquila rapax*. There is no doubt that the influx of migratory individuals affects the numbers. This year smallish numbers, mainly resident individuals, were seen. It was established that good rains had fallen in northern Botswana and many Tawny Eagles were seen there, so evidently they did not move as far south as normal. The resident breeding population varies from 0 to 10 pairs, whereas a "good" influx of migrants can exceed 100 birds.

Steppe Eagle *Aquila nipalensis*. In the twenty-year period this species occurred in numbers only in 1976 and 1978. These were exceptionally good years for termite eruptions. This species apparently migrates down the eastern side of Africa arriving in the Kruger Park when queleas start breeding; in good quelea breeding years, when there may be an estimated 15 million nests, the Steppe Eagle may stay in that area.

Martial Eagle *Polemaetus bellicosus*. The resident breeding population from 1988 to 1991 occupied from 2 to 9 nests (pers. comm. J.J. Herholdt). This is within the order of the different numbers seen in different years. These birds move enormous distances and this probably accounts for the variation in numbers. This species is persecuted more that most eagles by the sheep-farming community so that population trends are quite impossible to determine. But there is the belief that the numbers are slowly pickung up again.

Brown Snake Eagle *Circaetus pectoralis*. This appears subject to cycles when it is present for a few years and then disappears for a few years. The area is on the perimeter of its distribution. The bird occurs only as a non-breeding migrant.

Black-breasted Snake Eagle *Circaetus pectoralis*. Numbers are reasonably constant for this resident breeding species.

Bateleur *Terathopius ecaudatus*. A small resident group of breeding birds fluctuates considerably. The numbers are dramatically increased by migrants, the majority of which are juvenile birds. It has been shown (Liversidge, in press) that these birds fly great distances each day and that probably the migratory birds come from central Africa. Brown (1970, 1976) has commented that birds disappear with rains and he regards the dry season as important to the species. It would appear from the numbers and rainfall figures that the Kalahari data support this.

Pale Chanting Goshawk *Melierax canorus*. This is a resident species, although a ringed nestling was recovered nearly 500km to the south-east. The reason for the nearly tenfold change in numbers is not clear.

Lanner *Falco biarmicus*. A ringing recovery from Malawi indicated that the birds come from a considerable distance. Since the study started there has been one breeding record. However, few birds are to be seen during the southern winter period. There is normally a big influx in February, but few birds occurred in 1992 so the migrants did not reach the Park. Again reports from northern Botswana indicated many birds in that area this 1992 season.

Rock Kestrel *Falco rupicolus*. This bird is mainly a local winter non-breeding visitor that occurs in small numbers. There are small variations, with years of absence, which may be a local phenomenon or the result of breeding success elsewhere.

Greater Kestrel *Falco rupicoloides*. A resident breeding species that is quite common in the dunes. Changes in numbers occur with possible cycles of four years but this is not regular. At this stage the causes of the variations in numbers are not understood.

Pygmy Falcon *Poliohierax semitorquatus*. Fairly constant numbers except for one year, 1974, when the numbers peaked. 1974 had heavy floods and this may have brought more birds into this comparatively dryer environment.

CONCLUSIONS

Birds are obviously undertaking long-distance journeys and taking advantage of favourable local conditions over a wide area in their winter or non-breeding quarters. It is evident that the migratory raptors behave differently in the Kalahari or general southern semi-arid regions to those of the west African regions. One gets the impression from Thiollay (1978) that although the movements in West Africa are related to locust abundance they are relatively speaking more regular than those of the Kalahari. In the southern semi-arid, the movements are more determined by locally abundant food resources that result from the unpredictable good rains (Brooke *et al* 1972).

It is shown that the changes that occur from year to year for most species are not related to local rainfall. However, some species are affected by rainfall elsewhere. In the past we have looked at good rains causing such changes but it is now realised that equally important is the effect of drought in distant areas.

It is interesting to me as a worker who knows only this variability in the environment to read Newton's book on population ecology (1979). He writes from a background of relatively stable conditions. Whilst some of his statements on breeding populations are not acceptable locally his basic conclusions about movements are. Thus under "movements" he states that movement patterns can be explained in terms of food supply and then goes on to discuss seasonality, regional variations, annual variations and cyclic prey abundance - all of which fit the Kalahari evidence very well.

It is important to accept that in semi-arid regions the larger birds of prey are dependent upon enormous areas which extend far beyond the boundaries of any nation in central and southern Africa.

It thus becomes imperative for conservation of these birds that international action should be taken and any single country attempting conservation cannot hope to be effective by its own actions.

REFERENCES

BROOKE, R.K., J.H. GROBLER, M.P. STUART IRWIN & P. STEYN 1972. A Study of migratory Eagles *Aquila nipalensis* and *A. pomarina* in Southern Africa with comparative notes on other large raptors. *Occ. Pap. Natn. Mus. Rhod.*, 1972 B5(2):61-114.

BROWN, L.H. 1970. *African Birds of Prey.* London: Collins.

BROWN, L.H. 1976. *Birds of Prey: Their biology and ecology.* London. Collins.

KNIGHT, M.H. 1991. Ecology of the Gemsbok (*Oryx gazella*) and Blue Wildebeest (*Connochaetes taurinus*) in the southern Kalahari. Ph.D. Thesis, University of Pretoria.

LEISTNER, O.A. 1967. The Plant Ecology of the Southern Kalahari. *Bot.Surv.Memoirs* 38. Pretoria.

LIVERSIDGE, R. 1984. Changes in the avian population of the Kalahari National Park. *Proc. 5th Pan-African Orn. Cong.* pp.163-177.

LIVERSIDGE, R. 1989. Factors influencing migration of "Wintering" Raptors in Southern Africa. *In* B.-U. Meyburg & R.D. Chancellor (Eds.) *Raptors in the Modern World.* WWGBP: Berlin, pp 151-158.

NEWTON, I. 1979. *Population Ecology of Raptors.* Poyser.London.

Richard Liversidge
McGregor Museum
Kimberley
South Africa

Bateleur *Terathopius ecaudatus*

Meyburg, B.-U. & R. D. Chancellor eds.1994
Raptor Conservation Today
WWGBP / The Pica Press

Reproductive output of the Kestrel *Falco tinnunculus* in Relation to Small Mammal Dynamics in intensively cultivated Farmland

Jan Plesník and Miroslav Dusík

ABSTRACT

In 1986-1989,a total of 238 pairs of Kestrel *Falco tinnunculus* nested on lowland farmland (100km²) near Hradec Králové, east Bohemia, of them 227 in plastic nest-boxes. The proportion of Common Vole in the diet increased as its abundance increased in the landscape and ranged between 49.2% and 86.7% by number and 36.2% and 84.9% by weight. In a good vole year, clutch size and number of young produced per pair were significantly higher than in a poor vole year, Nevertheless, natality of Kestrels is also affected by factors other than food. The yearly median data on laying the first egg varied over 15 days, from 19 April (good vole year) to 4 May (poor vole year). The values of breeding density (29 to 101 pairs/100km²) surpassed even that of Kestrels in an urban habitat.

INTRODUCTION

Both the breeding biology and diet of the Kestrel *Falco tinnunculus* have been extensively studied but the effects of the population fluctuations of available prey, i.e. small mammals, have been less frequently examined. The importance of voles in the reproductive output of this small falcon has been shown by several investigators in North and West Europe (Cavé 1968; Village 1980, 1990; Korpimäki 1986; Dijkstra 1988; Meijer 1988; Korpimäki & Norrdahl 1991). In Central Europe, where the Common Vole *Microtus arvalis* has been the most abundant member of the small mammal community on farmland, exhibiting sharp fluctuations in numbers, reproductive output of Kestrels has been studied without any exact estimation of small mammal densities.

This paper is part of an extensive study on predation as a regulating factor in small mammal populations, carried out since 1986 in intensively used farmland in eastern Bohemia. In this area plastic nest-boxes of various types have been installed to increase nest-site availability, decreased drastically by human activities since 1977.

Thus the aim of this study is to clarify the effects of population fluctuations in small mammals, especially the Common Vole, on population dynamics (primarily clutch size variation and production of young) of the Kestrel.

MATERIALS AND METHODS

The study was carried out between 1986 and 1989 in Labe basin lowland, east Bohemia (district of Hradec Králové).

The study area is 100km² in size and considered to be typical intensively cultivated farmland.Only small islands of trees and bushes, some windbreaks and two rivers, break the flat cultivations. Numerous railways and roads criss-cross the area. This predominantly cereal growing habitat is a mosaic of arable fields (72.3%) and meadows or pastures (5.0%) surrounded by woodlands (7.5%), water (0.9%) and inhabited areas (7.3%). Orchards and parks cover 6.4% and wetlands have been preserved in only 0.6% of the area.

Plastic nest-boxes have been used to increase the numbers of avian predators. Old plastic canisters, in which agricultural pesticides or other chemicals are stored (25-30 litres capacity) have been installed upside down on woodland edges, solitary trees or in avenues. A female Kestrel will readily accept a nest-box and lay eggs. Nest material (i.e. hay, straw) is regularly replaced after the breeding season every year. Numbers of nest-boxes erected are given in Table 3. See Dusík *et al.* (1986) and Plesník (1990) for additional details on nest-box production and maintenance.

Standard methods were used to study the Kestrels (Brown 1974; Johnson 1978). Territories were mapped by observing courtship displays from early March to late May. We checked all corvid nests, holes in buildings and nest-boxes in the study area from late March to late July each spring. Nests found were visited to obtain data on time of laying the first egg, clutch size and brood size. Brood sizes were estimated by the number of young fledged.

The diet was studied by identification of prey animals in the pellets, in nest-boxes during nesting and analysis of nesting material after fledging of young (total 3,037 prey items).

The small mammal population fluctuations were studied with snap traps in early June (spring catches) and in late September and early October (autumn catches) in 1986-1989 (in all 22,928 trap nights). In these years, 1,724 specimens were captured, of which 83.9% were Common Vole. Two sample quadrats (an alfalfa field, a mown meadow) were used, each one hectrare in size. Thus 242 standard snap traps were distributed over a trapping grid (10x10m) using two traps for each trapping point for six nights. Because of numerous refuges for small mammals on farmland, 200 traps were set in road ditches, railway cuttings, windbreaks, wasteland etc. for 3-6 days. For quadrats, population densities were calculated using standard methods, while the small mammal index was calculated as small mammal number/100 trap-nights for trap-lines.

RESULTS

Figures 1 and 2 show population fluctuations in the Common Vole inhabiting farmland. Density was highest in 1988 (good vole year) and lowest in 1987 (poor year). From the viewpoint of abundance, 1986 and 1989 are considered intermediate vole years.

Figure 1. Small mammal community numbers in various habitats in farmland.

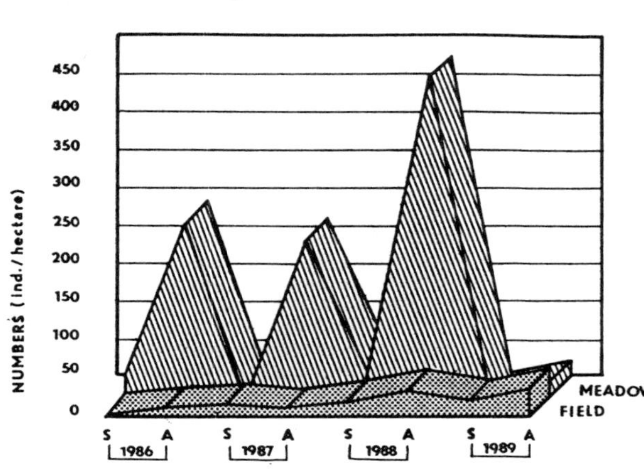

Figure 2. Small mammal numbers in refuges.

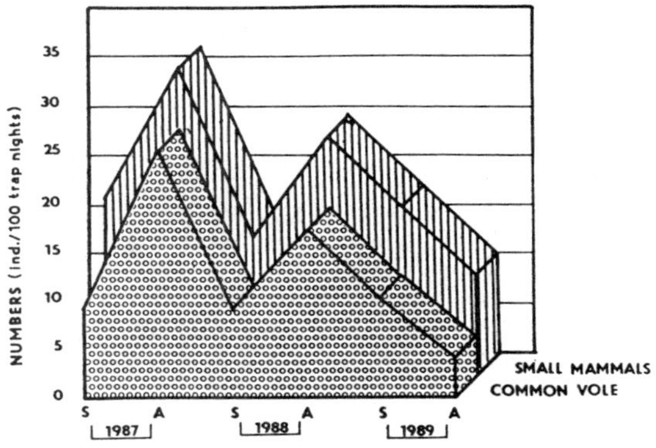

Microtus voles were the most important prey group both by number and by mass in the diet of the Kestrel (Tables 1-2). The proportion of Common Vole in the diet increased in proportion to its abundance. Thus the composition of the Kestrel's diet was dependent on the density of the preferred prey species. By numbers, the proportion of other mammals (shrews, moles, mice), birds and insects seemed to fluctuate inversely with the proportion of voles, since these prey groups were most numerous in the diet in 1987. In addition, the diversity of prey was highest in 1987, and lowest in 1988.

Table 1. Proportions (%) of the most important prey species and groups by number in the diet of the Kestrel in 1986-1989. The diversity of food was measured with Shannon and Weaver's (1949) index (H').

Prey species or groups	1986	1987	1988	1989	1986-1989
Microtus arvalis	80.0	49.2	86.7	76.2	73.6
Microtidae, tot.	80.0	49.6	86.7	76.4	73.7
Mammalia, tot.	84.2	68.7	91.7	85.1	83.1
Aves	10.9	14.5	4.5	8.4	9.1
Reptilia				0.3	0.1
Insecta	4.9	16.8	3.8	6.2	7.7
Prey animals	431	675	832	1009	3037
Nests	15	31	39	47	125
Prey items/nest	28.7	21.8	21.3	23.4	24.3
H'	1.35	3.54	0.96	1.82	1.88

Table 2. Proportions (%) of the most important prey species and groups by weight in the diet of the Kestrel in 1986-1989.

Prey species or groups	1986	1987	1988	1989	1986-1989
Microtus arvalis	72.0	36.2	84.9	68.8	64.6
Microtidae, tot.	72.0	38.2	84.9	69.8	64.8
Mammalia, tot.	77.2	67.6	92.4	83.0	80.4
Aves	22.7	32.3	7.6	16.7	19.4
Reptilia				0.2	0.1
Insecta	0.1	0.1	<0.1	0.1	0.1

Both clutch size and number of young fledged were largest in vole peak years and smallest during vole lows ($t = 4.300$, $df = 110$, $p < 0.01$ for clutch size, $t = 2.345$, $df = 101$, $p < 0.05$ for brood size, Student's t-test, two-tailed). The values in intermediate vole years ranged between poor and good.

In our study, egg-laying commenced earlier in the years with high vole abundance than in intermediate or low vole density years.

Table 3. Some features of Kestrel bionomics in farmland, east Bohemia, 1986-1989.

	1986	1987	1988	1989	1986-1989
Number of breeding pairs	21	46	71	100	238
Number of nest-boxes installed	29	62	99	101	291
% of nest-boxes occupied	72.4	70.8	69.7	92.1	81.8
Median date of laying egg	20.IV	4.V	19.IV	1.V	27.IV
(number of clutches)	(19)	(40)	(67)	(91)	(217)
Clutch size (number of nests)	5.48	4.52	5.98	4.17	4.47
	(21)	(44)	(68)	(91)	(224)
Number of fledged young per laying pair	4.95	3.70	5.25	4.17	4.47
Number of fledged young per successful pair (number of nests)	4.95	4.18	5.58	4.40	4.76
	(21)	(39)	(64)	(91)	(215)
Breeding success (young fledged/eggs laid) (in %)	90.4	81.9	87.7	88.1	87.1

DISCUSSION

Our data on the variation in the Kestrel's diet in relation to the density of its main prey, i.e. *Microtus* voles, are in full agreement with those by Cavé (1968), Korpimäki (1986), Village (1980,1990) and Kostrzewa and Kostrzewa (this volume). Thus *Microtus* voles may be considered the preferred prey in intensively utilised farmland. For clearer knowledge of the most frequent alternate prey, further data from years when voles are scarce are needed. The present results fit with the prediction that the diet of the predator should expand as the abundance of the preferred prey decreases (see also Emlen 1966).

The prey animal chiefly regulating the timing of egg-laying, clutch size and production of young in this raptor in farmland was found to be the Common Vole. Breeding success was lowest in a poor vole year, but higher in intermediate years, probably due to the fact that mortality of eggs and chicks is also affected by factors other than food (e.g. weather, Kostrzewa & Kostrzewa 1990, or predation by martens - but see Cavé 1968).

The total number of Kestrel breeding pairs did not fluctuate closely with *Microtus arvalis* density in the study area, resulting from the continually increased number of plastic nest-boxes installed. Kestrels have preferred these to disused nests of Magpies or wooden nest-boxes. Desertion of the latter for the former, being newly installed, sometimes occurred shortly before egg-laying or even after completion of the clutch (Dusík *et al.* 1986). Results of ringing and wing-tagging show that especially Kestrels hatched in nest-boxes will prefer these. Because plastic nest-boxes have been erected in the area of 536km² (in 1991 1,000 nest-boxes), displacements of Kestrels have been often observed between various sub-areas. In addition, a poor vole year was not so sharply pronounced as extended low densities in some other microtine cycles. As shown from results of snap-trapping in 1991, no Common Vole was captured in alfalfa field in spring as well as in meadow in autumn. For this year, reproductive output was preliminarily measured as follows: total 34 breeding pairs, mean clutch size 4.85 and mean number of young fledged per pair only 1 75 (Plesník & Dusík unpubl.)

Due to the good nest-site availability, increased by artificial nest-boxes, the values of breeding density in the intensively utilised lowland area, ranging between 29 and 101 pairs / $100km^2$ in 1986 - 1989, mostly surpassed those of Kestrels in both urban habitats and farmland (see R. Kostrzewa 1988 and Plesník 1991).

ACKNOWLEDGEMENTS

We are greatly indebted to Bernd-U. Meyburg and Achim Kostrzewa for the opportunity to participate in the conference. We wish to thank all our colleagues and students for their assistance in field work, especially Bohumil Pesek, Martin Fejfar, Vít Hrdousek, Ivan Tláskal and Jirí Zajíc jr. Our thanks are due to Miroslav Dusík jr. and Marcela Plesníková for typing the manuscript and drawing the figures. The text of this paper was greatly improved after comments by Renate and Achim Kostrzewa.

REFERENCES

BROWN, L.H. 1974. Data required for effective study of raptor populations. *In* F.N. Hamerström, B.E. Harrell & R.B. Olendorff (Eds.): *Management of Raptors:* 9-20 Raptor Res. Found. Vermillion, S.D.

CAVÉ, A.J. 1968. The breeding of the Kestrel *Falco tinnunculus* in the reclaimed area of Oostelijk Flevoland. Neth. *J. Zool.* 18: 313-407.

DIJKSTRA, C. 1988. Reproductive tactics in the Kestrel *Falco tinnunculus.* A study in evolutionary biology. Ph. D. thesis. Univ. of Groningen.

DUSÍK, M., J. PLESNÍK, S. ŠIMEK & J. ZAJÍC Jr. 1986. Možnosti usídlování dravců a sov v zemědélskě krajině (Management of raptors in intensively cultivated agricultural habitat). *Buteo* 1: 39-58 (In Czech with English summary).

EMLEN, J.M. 1966. The role of time and energy in food preference. *Am. Nat.* 100: 611-617.

JOHNSON, D.R. 1978. *The Study of Raptor Populations.* Univ. of Idaho Press, Boise City.

KORPIMÄKI, E. 1986. Diet variation, hunting habitat and reproductive output of the Kestrel *Falco tinnunculus* in the light of the optimal diet theory. *Ornis Fenn.* 63: 84-90.

KORPIMÄKI, E. & K. NORRDAHL 1991. Numerical and functional responses of Kestrels, Short-eared Owls, and Long-eared Owls to vole densities. *Ecology* 72: 814-826.

KOSTRZEWA, A. & R. KOSTRZEWA 1990. The relationship of spring and summer weather with density and breeding performance of the Buzzard *Buteo buteo,* Goshawk *Accipiter gentilis* and Kestrel *Falco tinnunculus. Ibis* 132: 550-559.

KOSTRZEWA, R. 1988. Die Dichte des Turmfalken *Falco tinnunculus* in Europa. Übersicht und kritische Betrachtung. *Vogelwarte* 342: 216-224.

MEIJER, T. 1988. Reproductive decisions in the Kestrel *Falco tinnunculus.* A study in physiological ecology. Ph. D. thesis, Univ. of Groningen.

PLESNÍK. 1990. Long-term study of some urban and extra-urban populations of the Kestrel *Falco tinnunculus. in*: K. Štastny & V. Bejcek (Eds.): Bird Census and Atlas studies. *Proc. X1th Conf. on Bird Census and Atlas Work,* Prague: 453-458.

PLESNÍK, J. 1991. Nest-sites and breeding density of the population of the European Kestrel *Falco tinnunculus* in Pardubice. *Acta Soc. Zool. Bohemoslov.* 55: 45-59.

SHANNON, C.E. & W. WEAVER 1949. *The Mathematical Theory of Communication.* Univ. Illinois Press, Urbana.

VILLAGE, A. 1980. The ecology of the Kestrel *Falco tinnunculus* in relation to vole abundance at Eskdalemuir, South Scotland, Ph. D, thesis, Univ. of Edinburgh, U.K.

VILLAGE, a. 1990. *The Kestrel.* T. and A.D. Poyyser, London.

Jan Plesník
Czech Institute for Nature Conservation
Slezská 9
120 29 Prague 2
Czech Republic

Miroslav Dusík
Ekostrix
502 03 Predměřice nad Labem 54
Czech Republic

American Kestrel *Falco sparverius* - male

Meyburg, B.-U. & R. D. Chancellor eds.1994
Raptor Conservation Today
WWGBP / The Pica Press

Regulation of Goshawk *Accipiter gentilis* breeding in Western Finland over the last 30 years

Seppo Sulkava, Kauko Huhtala & Risto Tornberg

ABSTRACT

The Goshawk population is stable in most parts of Finland. The breeding data for this study originate from two main regions in Western Finland in 1961-1991, in total 603 clutches and 861 broods. The laying begins yearly 12.4 - 8.5., regulated most clearly by temperature of February-April. The regional mean clutch sizes are 3.3 - 3.6, and have in 1963-91 been yearly 2.4 - 4.2. The early laid clutches are significantly larger than the later ones. The mean losses in successful broods are 0.52 young. The regional mean brood sizes have been 2.6 - 3.1. In 1967-91 17.0% of breeding attempts failed totally.

The four tetraonid species are the main prey, in spring 50-85 % of the number of prey in Western Finland. The tetraonid populations have a clear and simultaneous fluctuation, 6-7 years between peaks. The yearly changes in the clutch size of the Goshawk follow significantly the fluctuation of the total density of tetraonids. The positive correlation between the brood size in successful Goshawk nests and tetraonid density is significant too. The Red Squirrel is also a common prey of the Goshawk and has pronounced yearly changes in density, but has not any effect on the clutch or brood size.

INTRODUCTION

Breeding in birds of prey is generally regulated by prey availablity, and in some cases also by climatic factors and physiologically by day length (e.g. Hagen 1969; Newton 1979, 1986; Huhtala & Sulkava 1981; Kostrzewa & Kostrzewa 1990, 1991; Dobler 1991). Where conditions have been altered by man, a lack of nest sites, poisons in food, nest robbing and indirect disturbance may be reasons for low breeding success (Fischer 1980; Newton 1986).

The Goshawk suffered a severe decline in the 1960s in Central Europe, but soon after the ban on a number of pesticides the populations increased in many areas, especially in the 1970s (Thissen *et al.* 1981; Storgård & Birkholm-Clausen 1983; Bijlsma 1991). The mainly introduced population in England also increased, especially during the 1980s (Anon. 1989).

Nesting results among the Goshawk population in Finland have remained fairly stable during the last 30 years (Saurola 1985; Korhonen & Saurola 1990), although a decrease was observed in the extreme south of the country during the 1980s (Forsman & Ehrnstén 1985). There are also differences in nesting results between years, but the reasons are mostly natural ones (Sulkava 1964; Wikman & Lindén 1981). Direct human influence on breeding has not been dangerous for the Finnish Goshawk population (Haukioja & Haukioja 1970; Huhtala & Sulkava 1981).

This paper will present:

- some general facts on the breeding and diet of the Goshawk in Finland
- data on regulation of the onset of breeding by environmental factors and
- data on regulation of the clutch and brood sizes of the Goshawk in western Finland.

AREAS STUDIED

The material from western Finland originates from two main areas:

Southern and Central Ostrobothnia (Fig. 1, map). Southern Ostrobothnia is the main area studied by the Suomenselkä Ornithological Society, which has collected annual statistics on breeding in hawks and owls since 1967.

The smaller, and published, sets of material from southern Finland are available from three areas: near the town of Pori on the west coast (Hakila 1968), the inland province of Häme (Sulkava 1964; Kolunen 1987) and the western part of the province of Uusimaa in the extreme south (Wikman & Lindén 1981; Forsman & Ehrnstén 1985).

Figure 1. The areas studied in Western Finland.

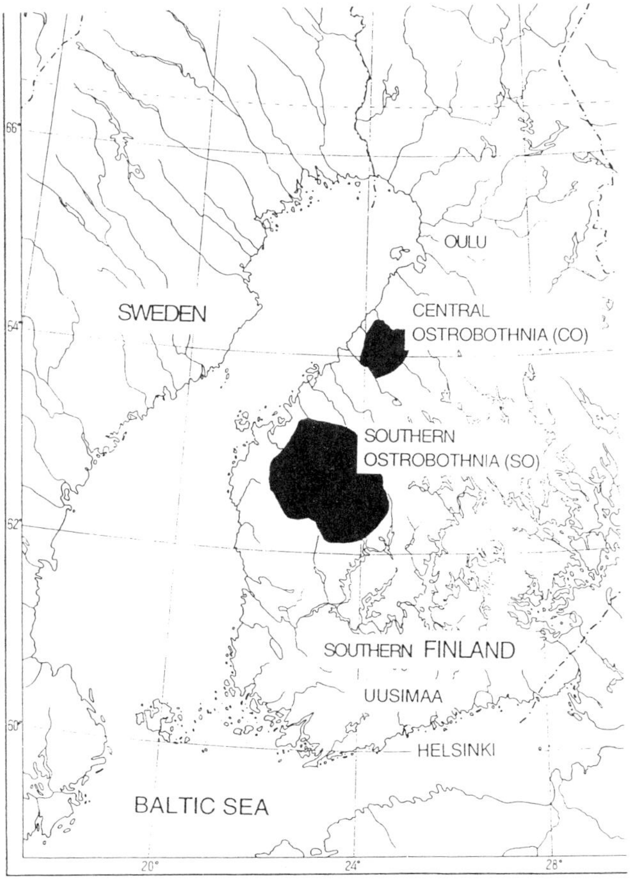

GENERAL FACTS ON BREEDING AND DIET

The nesting season for the Goshawk in western Finland begins with nest-building, mostly in March. The eggs are laid during April. As an example, we show the beginning of nest-building and the onset of egg-laying in Central Ostrobothnia in 1966-77 (Fig. 4). The yearly changes are sometimes relatively large.

Mean clutch and brood sizes in Finland and Central Europe do not show any regular regional differences (Table 1), although the clutch size seems to be a little smaller in Northern Europe than in Central Europe. Relatively small clutch sizes seem to prevail in Southern Finland (and also in more northerly areas, e.g. near Oulu, 3.06, Tornberg & Sulkava 1990), whereas they are large in England.

Table 1. Clutch size and number of young of the Goshawk in some areas of Europe. Uusimaa, Finland (Solonen 1979; Forsman & Ehrnsten 1985); Germany (Fischer 1980; Glutz 1971; Dobler 1991; Möckel *et al.* 1987; Link 1977; Stubbe & Gedeon 1991); England (Anon. 1990).

Region, years	Clutch size Mean	S.E.	N	Large young /successful brood Mean	S.E.	N	Large young /clutch laid Mean	S.E	N
C. Ostrobothnia 1961-76	3.51	0.06	164	2.83	0.11	148	-	-	-
C. Ostrobothnia 1981-90	3.59	0.24	135	3.06	0.19	180	-	-	-
S Ostrobothnia 1971-80	3.44	0.15	122	2.74	0.15	158	2.17	0.17	204
S Ostrobothnia 1981-90	3.28	0.13	182	2.88	0.09	375	2.48	0.16	314
S Finland, Uusimaa 1962-84	3.08	0.13	89	2.63	0.11	135	-	-	-
Germany (publ. 1968-91)	3.64	0.06	132	2.51	-	430	1.73	-	466
England 1980-87	3.96	0.11	47	2.76	0.16	45	2.30	0.20	54

The nesting results of the Goshawk population seem to be the best in Western Finland (Ostrobothnia), however, and the poorest in Central Europe (Germany).The diet of the Goshawk in Finland differs greatly from that in Central Europe, where the main prey groups in the latter region are the Columbidae, Corvidae and Turdidae; the only important group in western Finland is the Tetraonidae (four species), with some squirrels and Corvidae. The tetraonids form the major prey both during nest-building and incubation in spring and during the nestling period in summer (Table 2). The spring food has been studied in both Central and Southern Ostrobothnia, and the percentage of tetraonids is large in both areas.

Table 2. Diet of the Goshawk in Central Europe (Brüll 1964 and Schnurre 1964, from Glutz *et al.* 1971) and in western Finland (Sulkava 1964 and Huhtala 1976).

	Central Europe	Western Finland Spring	Summer
Grouse, Tetraonidae	-	68.1	46.4
Partridge, *Perdix perdix*	6.9	0.5	-
Doves, Columbidae	29.1	1.2	3.1
Crows etc., Corvidae	16.6	3.7	8.8
Thrushes and Starling, Turdidae and *Sturnus*	16.2	2.0	12.1
Rabbits and hares, Leporidae	9.2	0.1	0.3
Material, N	6378	2765	470

The diet during the nestling period has so far only been studied in detail (by accurate methods: direct observation from hides and the cage method) during the 1950s, in Southern Ostrobothnia (Sulkava 1964): The mean proportion of tetraonids in the nestling-time prey in 1954-58 was 53% (according to the prey numbers).

FACTORS REGULATING NESTING REULTS

1. Changing prey availability

The densities of the main forms of prey in Finland, the four tetraonid species, fluctuate markedly and simultaneously (Fig. 2, Rajala & Lindén 1980). The effect of this main food on Goshawk breeding therefore differs from one year to the next.

2. Changing climatic conditions

The temperature in late winter and in spring could be important for breeding in Finland. Very cold weather in late winter may tax the energy reserves needed for breeding, and the rainfall in late spring or early summer could have some effect, as stated by Newton (1986) for the Sparrowhawk in England.

3. Natural enemies

(e.g. the Eagle Owl) and the direct or indirect impact of man could also detract from the nesting result.

REGULATION OF BREEDING UNDER VARYING CLIMATIC AND FEEDING CONDITIONS IN WESTERN FINLAND

Beginning of nest-building in Central Ostrobothnia

The building phase was checked at 3-5 Goshawk nests in one area in Central Ostrobothnia (by K. Huhtala) every weekend from late February onwards in 12 years (1966-77). The first twigs are often brought on the snow, which is often still present when nest building begins. The earliest occasions of beginning to nest were recorded in the last week of February and the latest in the first week of April. Building was often triggered off by the first warm days of the year (= above zero Celsius).

The mean onset of building is positively correlated with the mean temperature in February-March ($r = 0.668$, $P = 0.018$, Fig. 3), in that the building begins about one month later after cold winters than after warm ones.

REGULATION OF LAYING DATE IN CENTRAL OSTROBOTHNIA

The laying date is closely (and significantly) correlated with the date of the beginning of nest-building ($r = 0.753$, $P = 0.005$, Fig. 4), but its yearly variation is smaller (range 16 days, *vs.* 33 days in nest-building).

The midwinter temperature (mean temperature in January and February) also shows a significant correlation with the mean laying date ($r = 0.515$, $P = 0.050$, Fig. 5), which means that cold winters delay laying.

The direct correlation between laying date and mean late winter temperature (mean of February-March, which was stated above to be significantly correlated with the date of nest-building) is also obvious, but not significant ($r = 0.393$, $P = 0.21$), as is the correlation between laying date and the temperature in April (the laying month).

The laying date could also be regulated by the availability of prey (food) as is seen in some owls (e.g. Tengmalm's Owl, Korpimäki 1986).

In the Goshawk, however, it does not correlate significantly with the density of tetraonids or the yearly percentage of tetraonids in the diet. It seems, therefore, that food (prey) does not regulate the laying date of the Goshawk in western Finland, where it is most powerfully regulated by the temperature in late winter (February-March).

Figure 2. Fluctuations in the four tetraonid species, Capercaillie (*Tetrao urogallus*), Black Grouse (*Tetrao tetrix*), Hazel Hen (*Bonasia bonasia*) and Willow Grouse (*Lagopus lagopus*) in western Finland (Southern Ostrobothnia) in 1964-91 according to the Finnish Wildlife Research institute.

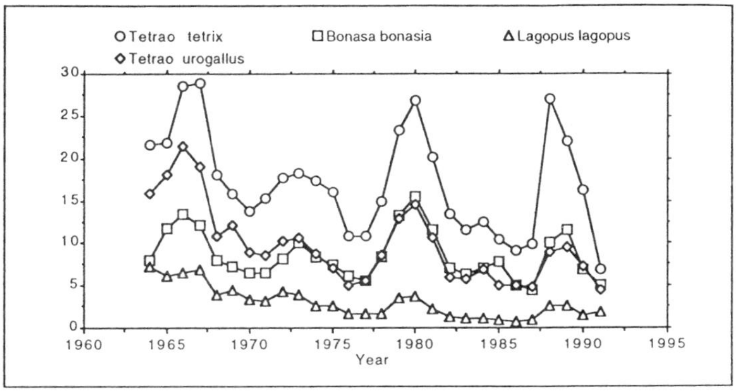

Figure 3. Correlation between the mean date of the beginning of nest building by the Goshawk in March in Central Ostrobothnia in 1966-1977 (18 years) and mean temperature in February-March (r = 0.668, P = 0.018).

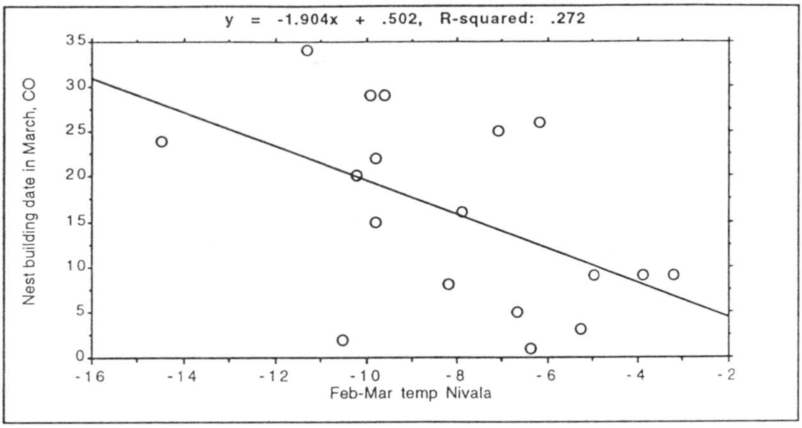

Figure 4. Correlation between the mean date of the beginning of nest building by the Goshawk in Central Ostrobothnia in 1966-77 (17 years) and mean laying date (r = 0.753, P = 0.005).

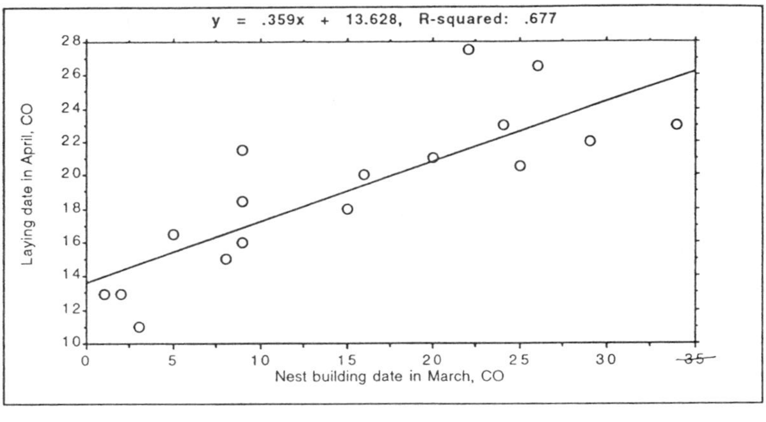

Figure 5. Correlation between midwinter temperature (January and February) and the laying date of the Goshawk (in April) in Central Ostrobothnia in 1963-77 (21 years, r = 0.515, P = 0.050).

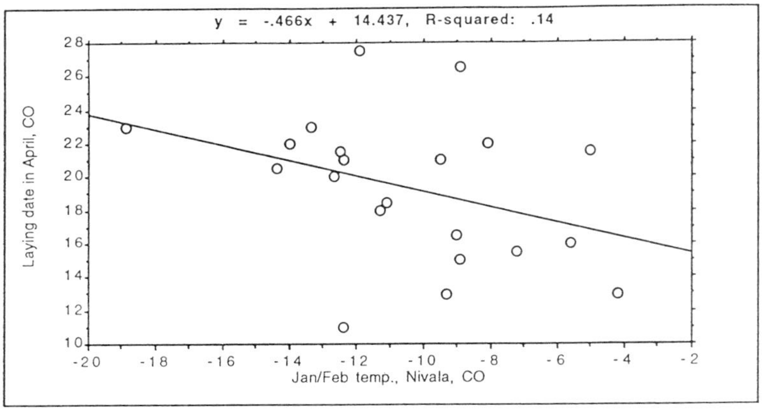

REGULATION OF CLUTCH SIZE

Clutch size and laying date show the normal correlation: i.e. later clutches are highly significantly smaller (yearly means in Central Ostrobothnia 1963-77, r = -0.898, P < 0.001, Fig. 6).

It is well-known that some owls (e.g. Tengmalm's Owl) lay earlier and larger clutches in good vole years, and that changes in food produce corresponding changes in the clutch size in owls (Korpimäki 1981). The Sparrowhawk in Great Britain has been observed to lay significantly earlier and larger clutches with additional feeding (Newton 1986).

In the Goshawk the corresponding changes could be caused by changes in the density of tetraonids, which are their main food in western Finland. This relationship had already been observed in the 1950s in Southern Ostrobothnia (Sulkava 1964), although information on fluctuations of tetraonids was less accurate prior to 1963 (See Rajala 1974).

The correlation between tetraonid density and the clutch size of the Goshawk over the last 30 years is shown below for Southern and Central Ostrobothnia.

In Southern Ostrobothnia clutch size since 1966 has mostly been larger in better tetraonid years (Fig. 7), the correlation being significant (r = 0.421, P = 0.036), although it explains only 18% of the variation in clutch size.

A weak and non-significnat correlation also exists between March and April temperatures and the clutch size of the Goshawk in Southern Ostrobothnia in 1967-91 (r = 0.22 and 0.21), and the correlation with January-February temperatures is still weaker (r = 0.17). The combined correlation of temperatures in different months and the combined effect of temperature and tetraonid density were also checked, but they did not improve the correlations.

In Central Ostrobothnia the positive correlation between clutch size and tetraonid density in the previous August is also significant (Fig. 8, r = 0.429, P = 0.026), the clutch size being larger in better tetraonid years.

Even so, midwinter temperature still has a clear effect on the clutch size, and the correlation between mean January-February temperature and mean clutch size (in 1963-91) is significant (r = 0.424, P = 0.022, Fig. 9). March and April temperatures have corresponding but weaker and non-significant correlations with clutch size.

The yearly relationship between clutch size in the Goshawk and populations of the Mountain Hare and Red Squirrel were also analysed (using population indices from Finnish Wildlife Research Institute), but these prey species had no significant effect on clutch size.

Figure 6. Correlation between the mean clutch size of the Goshawk in Central Ostrobothnia in 1963-1991 (21 years) and the mean date of laying the first egg (r = 0.911).

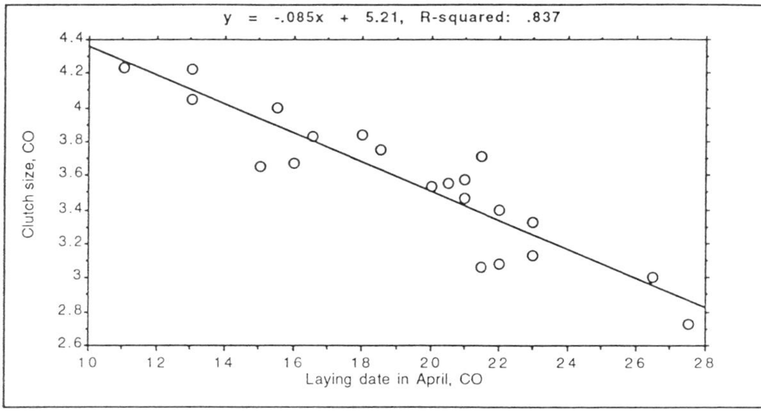

Figure 7. Yearly changes in the clutch size of the Goshawk and the total density of tetraonids (ind./km2, in August of the previous year) in Southern Ostrobothnia in 1967-91 (25 years). (Correlation: r = 0.421, P = 0.036).

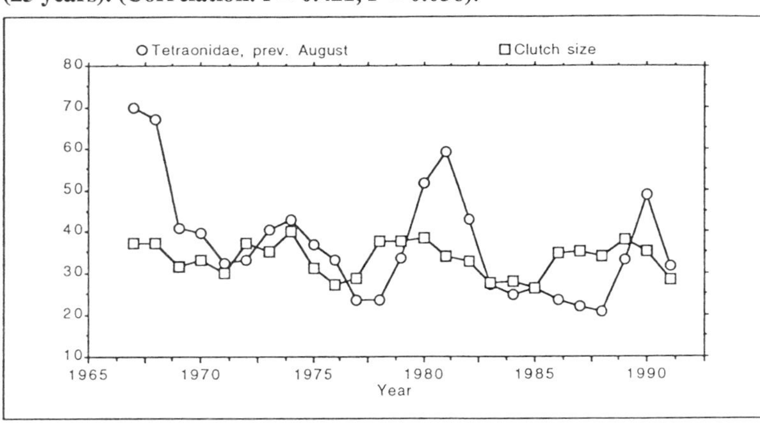

Figure 8. Correlation between the clutch size of the Goshawk and the total density of tetraonids (ind./km2, in August of the previous year) in Central Ostrobothnia in 1964-91 (r = 0.429, P = 0.026).

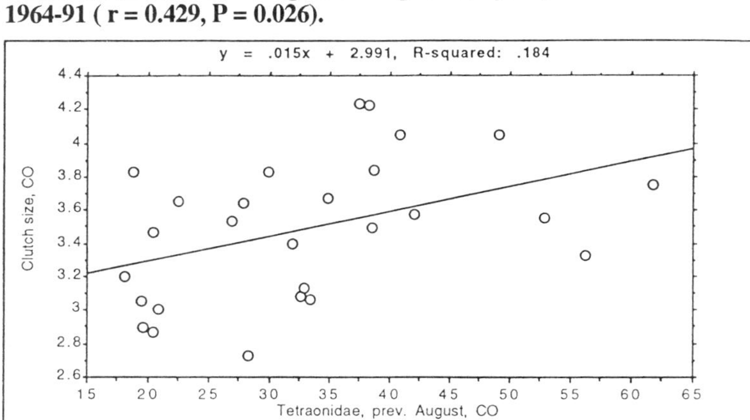

Figure 9. Correlation between the clutch size of the Goshawk and midwinter temperature (mean of January and February) in Central Ostrobothnia in 1963-91 (29 years, r = 0.424, P =0.022).

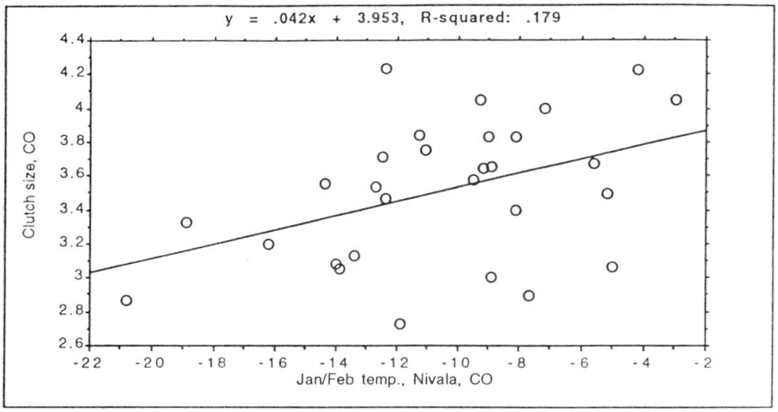

REGULATION OF BROOD SIZE

The tetraonid prey is also very important for the Goshawk and its young in summer (Table 2). The density of tetraonids in the field (adults + their young = availability of food for the young of the Goshawk) could therefore regulate the brood size of the Goshawk in western Finland.

In Southern Ostrobothnia (the area of the Suomenselkä Ornithological Society, Fig. 1) the positive correlation between the yearly changes in brood size (large young) of the Goshawk and total tetraonid density (the next August; years 1967-91) is highly significant (Fig. 10, r = 0.623, P < 0.001), the brood size of the Goshawk being larger in good tetraonid years than in poor ones.

The brood size is, of course, highly significantly correlated with clutch size in spring (r = 0.726, P < 0.001): so that if the clutches are larger, the broods are mostly larger too, and it is therefore also affected by the factors metioned above, as regulating clutch size (e.g. temperature and availability of prey in late winter).

Figure 10. Yearly changes in the brood-size (large young) of the Goshawk and the total density of tetraonids (ind./km2, in August of the same year) in Southern Ostrobothnia in 1967-91 (25 years, correlation: r = 0.623, P =0.001).

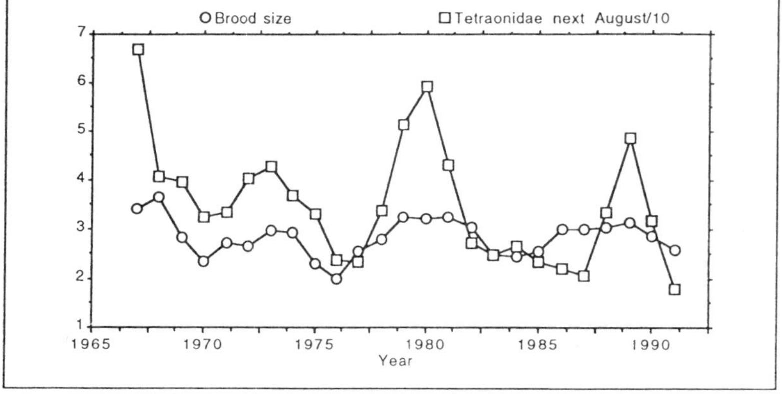

Nestling losses (deaths mostly during the early nestling period; yearly means are 0.4-0.7 young per nest) have only slight and non-significant correlation (r = 0.25) with the density of tetraonids in early summer (in fact in the previous August) before the young of tetraonids appear in late June. In large clutches (4-5 eggs) the last egg often hatches 1-2 days later than the others and this last nestling often disappears soon afterwards (Sulkava 1964), even in good food years. The number of rainy days (over 1 mm) in May and June similarly did not have any correlation with the nestling losses in Southern Ostrobothnia in 1967-91.

It may be concluded from the significances of the correlations for Southern Ostrobothnia that the brood size of the Goshawk is more affected directly by clutch size than indirectly by tetraonid density in summer, and that nestling losses are affected more by clutch size than by prey availability in summer. The clutch size is also regulated by tetraonid density, however, which emerges as the main factor.

In Central Ostrobothnia the effect of the total tetraonid density on the brood size of the Goshawk in 1964-85 is also obvious, but not significant. The correlation is significant (r = 0.377, P = 0.44) only with the main tetraonid species in the diet, the Black Grouse (*Tetrao tetrix*).

CONCLUSIONS

The obvious stability of the Finnish Goshawk population over the last 30 years (Saurola 1985; Korhonen & Saurola 1990) is somewhat difficult to explain, for several reasons:

- nest-robbing and shooting have probably decreased since the 1970s, because the Goshawk has been protected during the nesting season since 1979 (extended to a longer nesting period, April to July, in 1983) and the whole year round since 1989.

- the earlier killing of young and adult Goshawks was obviously not very dangerous to the population, however, because it was mostly only the "surplus" population that was killed and the adult birds became more careful and silent at their nesting sites (Haukioja & Haukioja 1970).

- tetraonids - the main prey - have decreased during the last thirty years, but the Goshawk and its nesting results have generally not (with the exception of a local decrease in the extreme south of Finland, Forsman & Ehrnsten 1985).

- environmental factors, e.g. temperature and availability of food, do not change simultaneously and therefore cause different changes in nesting results and population density.

The future of the Goshawk population in Finland seems to be dependent on the success of the tetraonid populations in the forests. The local decrease in the south of the country during the 1980s mentioned above already suggest that the decrease in tetraonids in Finland may later cause a more general decrease in the Goshawk population. The tetraonids, for their part, are dependent on the forestry measures and hunting practices.

REFERENCES

ANONYMOUS 1989. Goshawk breeding habitat in lowland Britain. *Brit. Birds* 82: 56-67.

ANONYMOUS 1990. Breeding biology of Goshawks in lowland Britain. *Brit. Birds* 83: 527-540.

BIJLSMA, R. 1991. Trends in European Goshawks *Accipiter gentilis:* an overview. *Bird Census News* 4, 2: 3-47.

DOBLER, G. 1991. Klimatische Einflüsse auf Dichte, Brutzeit und Bruterfolg von Habicht *Accipiter gentilis* und Rotmilan *Milvus migrans. Vogelwelt* 112: 152-162.

FISCHER, W. 1980. *Die Habichte.* Neue Brehm-Bücherei 158. Wittenberg-Lutherstadt.

FORSMAN, D. & B. EHRNSTEN 1985. Is the goshawk declining ? (in Finnish with English summary). *Lintumies* 20: 83-88.

GLUTZ, U.N. 1971. *Handbuch der Vögel Mitteleuropas,* Bd. 4. Frankfurt am Main.

HAGEN, Y. 1969. Norwegian studies on the reproduction of birds of prey and owls in relation to micro-rodent population fluctuations. *Fauna* 22: 73-126.

HAUKIOJA, E. & M. HAUKIOJA 1970. Mortality rates of Finnish and Swedish Goshawks (*Accipiter gentilis*). *Finnish Game Research* 31: 13-20.

HUHTALA, K. & S. SULKAVA 1981. Environmental influences on Goshawk breeding in Finland. *In*: R.

Kenward & I. Lindsay (Eds.): *Understanding the Goshawk,* pp. 89-104. Oxford.
KORHONEN, J. & P. SAUROLA 1990. Monitoring common raptors and owls in Finland in 1989. *Lintumies* 25: 113-119 (in Finnish with English summary).
KORPIMÄKI, E. 1981. On the ecology and biology of Tengmalm's Owl (*Aegolius funereus*) in Southern Ostrobothnia and Suomenselkä, western Finland. *Acta Univ. Oul. A* 118. Biol. 13: 1-84.
KORPIMÄKI, E. 1984. Population dynamics of birds of prey in relation to fluctuations in small mammal populations in western Finland. *Ann. Zool. Fenn.* 21: 287-293.
KORPIMÄKI, E. 1986. Timing of breeding of Tengmalm's Owl *Aegolius funereus* in relation to vole dynamics in western Finland. *Ibis* 129: 58-68.
KOSTRZEWA, A. & R. KOSTRZEWA 1990. The relationship of spring and summer weather with density and breeding performanace of the Buzzard *Buteo buteo*, Goshawk *Accipiter gentilis* and Kestrel *Falco tinnunculus. Ibis* 132: 550-559.
KOSTRZEWA, R. & A. KOSTRZEWA 1991. Winter weather, spring and summer density, and subsequent breeding success of Eurasian Kestrels, Common Buzzards and Northern Goshawks. *Auk* 108: 342-347.
LINDÉN, H. & M. WIKMAN 1980. Brood size of the Goshawk in relation to tetraonid densities (in Finnish with English summary). *Suomen Riista* 27: 63-69.
LINK, H. 1986. Untersuchungen am Habicht (*Acciptiter gentilis*). Deutscher Falkenorden. DFO-Schriftenreihe H. 2.
MÖCKEL, R. & G. DIETMAR 1987. Die Reproduktionsrate des Habichts *Accipiter gentilis* (L.) im Westerzgebirge in den Jahren 1974-83. *In*: M. Stubbe (Ed.): *Populationsökologie von Greifvögel- und Eulenarten,* pp. 217-232. Halle (Saale).
NEWTON, I. 1979. *Population Ecology of Raptors.* Poyser Berkhamsted.
NEWTON, I. 1986. *The Sparrowhawk.* Poyser Calton.
RAJALA, P. 1974. The structure and reproduction of Finnish populations of Capercaillie, *Tetrao urogallus*, and Black Grouse, *Lyrurus tetrix*, on the basis of late summer census data from 1963-66. *Finnish Game Res.* 35: 1-51.
RAJALA, P. & H. LINDÉN 1980. Finnish tetraonid populations in 1974-77 and population trends in the period 1964-77 according to the August route-censuses. *Suomen Riista* 28: 15-24 (in Finnish with English summary).
SAUROLA, P. 1985. Finnish birds of prey: status and population changes. *Ornis Fennica* 62: 64-72.
SOLONEN, T. 1979. On the breeding biology of diurnal birds of prey in Uusimaa, S. Finland. *Tringa* 6: 45-48 (in Finnish with English summary).
STORGÅRD, K. & F. BIRKHOLM-CLAUSEN 1986. Duehöge-undersögelsen (*Accipiter gentilis*) i Sydjylland. *Accipiter* 1: 21-32.
STUBBE, M. & K. GEDEON 1991. *Jahresbericht zum Monitoring Greifvögel und Eulen Europas* 3: 1-43. Martin-Luther-Universität, Halle (Saale).
SULKAVA, S. 1964. Zur Nahrungsbiologie des Habichts, *Accipiter gentilis* (L.). *Aquila, Ser.* Zool. 3: 1-103.
THISSEN, J., G. MÜSKENS, & P. OPDAM 1981. Trends in the Dutch Goshawk *Accipiter gentilis* population and their causes. *In* R. Kenward & I. Lindsay (Eds.): *Understanding the Goshawk*, pp. 28-43. Oxford.
TORNBERG, R. & S. SULKAVA 1990. The effect of fluctuations in tetraonid populations on the nutrition and breeding success of the Goshawk in Oulu district in 1965-88. *Suomen Riista* 36: 53-61 (in Finnish with English summary).
WIKMAN, M. & H. LINDÉN, 1981. The influence of food supply on Goshawk population size. *In*: R. Kenward & I. Lindsay (Eds.): *Understanding the Goshawk*, pp. 105-113. Oxford.

Seppo Sulkava/Kauko Huhtala/Risto Tornberg
Department of Zoology
University of Oulu
SF-90570 Oulu, Finland

Meyburg, B.-U. & R. D. Chancellor eds.1994
Raptor Conservation Today
WWGBP / The Pica Press

Population dynamics and lifetime reproductive success in Sparrowhawks *Accipiter nisus* in a Dutch-German study area

Ronald Zollinger & Gerard Müskens

ABSTRACT

This paper deals with a 23-years study of a Dutch-German Sparrowhawk population in a 100 km² forest area. In 1969 the population was nearly extinct due to the adverse effects of organochlorine pesticides. After the ban on organochlorines in 1968/1969 direct mortality decreased immediately, so that a population increase from 2 to 18 breeding pairs could be assessed between 1969 and 1973. Breeding success, however, did not recover before 1976. In 1977 a further population increase occurred, later followed by a stabilisation at approximately 50 breeding pairs. Annual fluctuations in breeding numbers were regulated by weather conditions in the winter. After severe winters yearlings bred in relatively small numbers, after extremely mild winters in relatively large numbers. The number of adult breeders was not affected by weather conditions in the winter.

Lifetime reproductive success (LRS) of 228 females revealed that (a) individual production ranged from 0 to 31 fledglings, (b) birds living from 1976 onwards raised on average twice as many fledglings during their life as those which lived prior to 1976 (6.7 and 3.5 fledglings respectively), (c) most of the variation in LRS is explained by variation in lifespan, and (d) overall, only 6% of all fledglings produced more than 50% of the total offspring. In comparison with Sparrowhawk populations in southern Scotland, females produced on average 20% more fledglings during their lifetime. This is unexpected, since annual survival of the Scottish adult females is about 10% higher. The difference in LRS may be explained by a higher proportion of successful nests and a larger mean brood size in the Dutch-German population.

INTRODUCTION

During the 1960s Sparrowhawk *Accipiter nisus* and other raptor populations in western Europe suffered from the adverse side-effects of organo-chlorine pesticides (Newton 1979, 1986). In the Netherlands during the late 1960s the use of dieldrin and related compounds for seed dressings resulted in mass mortality among birds of prey (Koeman *et al.* 1969). In the early 1970s the Dutch Sparrowhawk population recovered rapidly, after the banning of these compounds in 1968-69 (Opdam 1985; Opdam *et al.* 1987). The use of DDT, however, was not prohibited by the Dutch government until 1973. DDE causes embryo mortality and eggshell thinning resulting in frequent egg breakage (Ratcliffe 1970; Newton & Bogan 1974). Dutch Sparrowhawk populations were contaminated by DDE, which caused a reduction in reproductive output (Koeman *et al.* 1972). The recovery in reproductive output of the Dutch Sparrowhawk population became apparent in the mid-1970s, although DDE residues remained at largely the same level from 1975 up to 1983 (Burgers *et al.* 1986, see also Fuchs & Thissen 1981). Opdam *et al.* (1987) discussed the presumed role of DDE as a main factor suppressing Sparrowhawk populations. They concluded that the onset of recovery must have been caused by decreased adult mortality (after disappearance of dieldrin), whereas DDE retarded only the recovery.

Lifetime Reproductive Success (LRS) is given by the total number of young raised by an individual during lifespan. It combines two key characteristics of individual performance, namely survival and annual breeding success, into a single overall measure of performance (Newton 1985, 1989). Furthermore, it provides a basis for estimating biological fitness (Clutton-Brock 1988; Newton 1989). This paper indicates the trend of a Dutch-German Sparrowhawk population during 1969-1991. The aim is to study the impact of pesticides and weather conditions during the winter. We have further examined the lifetime reproductive success of female Sparrowhawks, based on a sample of 228 individuals, which were identified from year to year by comparing shed feathers. The aims were: (1) to relate lifetime fledgling production by female Sparrowhawks to the birds' features, (2) to assess the impact of pesticides, resulting in suppressed reproductive output until 1977, on the LRS, and (3) to estimate the proportion of individuals that raised young, enabling us to assess the relative contribution from one generation to the next. Finally, differences in life history strategy between the Dutch-German Sparrowhawk population and Sparrowhawk populations in Britain, studied by Newton, will be discussed.

METHODS

Study area

The study was carried out in an extensive partly forested moraine complex area, between the towns of Nijmegen (The Netherlands), and Kleve and Goch (Germany), south of the river Rhine (51° 45' N and 6° E). There is a difference in altitude between the forested moraine (20 - 95 m above sea level) and its cultivated surroundings (10 - 20 m a.s.l.). Two isolated forests are found in the area, one of 40 km^2 on the Dutch side (Rijk van Nijmegen) of the frontier and another one of 60 km^2 on the German side (Reichswald). Conifer woods are prevalent (about 60% of surface) in the area over broad-leaved and mixed woods. Pine (*Pinus sylvestris*) is the most common tree species. Both forests and agricultural land are intensively managed. There are a number of medium-sized villages, mainly on the Dutch side, which are very attractive hunting grounds for the Sparrowhawk, because of the high density of song birds.

Population dynamics and breeding success

In order to find all breeding pairs, the woods were searched systematically every year during springtime for prey remains, droppings, shed feathers and nests. Only breeding pairs in which the female laid at least one egg were counted as breeders. Reliable data concerning non-breeders could not be obtained. Each nest was visited at least thrice during the breeding season in order to collect data on clutch size, brood size at hatching and fledging, and the cause of failure in those cases in which a pair was not successful. From 1978 onwards, the young were ringed when they were between one and three weeks old. Breeding success was measured as the mean number of fledglings in successful nests.

Recognition of individuals and lifetime reproductive success

Sparrowhawks moult each year in summer, overlapping extensively with breeding (Newton 1986). The shed feathers are a useful tool to identify individuals in the field without the need to catch the birds. Opdam and Müskens (1976) proposed the use of shed feathers to identify individual Sparrowhawks. Newton (1986) in Britain and Van Diermen (pers. comm.) in the Netherlands were able to check the method's reliability with known ringed birds. Using shed feathers turned out to be a reliable method.

Shed feathers of each female were collected annually during the breeding season. Since males hunt during the entire breeding season, they moult more slowly than females. So less male than female shed feathers were found.

Age and sex of the bird which shed the feathers are easily distinguished by length (females are larger than males) and by the differences in pattern and colour (Figure 1). The basic pattern - irrespective of age - is one of dark bars alternating with light bars on the inner vane. In yearling plumage the feathers are light reddish brown (greyish on the photograph), unlike the deep brown feathers of adults. Further characteristic details are the marked white patches on the shaft of the central tail feather and the pale edge on the top of the secondary coverts in yearlings' plumage.

After the first year of life, each bird shows a consistent feather pattern each year. This is illustrated by the first and fifth primary of an individual, collected in different years (Figure 2). The equivalent primaries of an individual are very similar in both pattern and length each year.

The equivalent primaries of different individuals differ (a) in number and shape of the dark bars, (b) in the pattern of the light bars, and (c) in length (Figure 3).

A few remarks must be made concerning the method of calculating Lifetime Reproductive Success (LRS). First, LRS could only be calculated for females, because insufficient material (shed feathers) was available to identify males in subsequent years. Secondly, the following selection criteria were used: (1) breeding performance of females had to be known precisely for their entire lifetime, (2) individuals that started breeding after 1989 were excluded (identification took place until 1992), (3) individuals not identified as a breeding bird for two years or more were taken to be dead.

Thirdly, identification of individuals between their yearling and adult plumage is disputable (there are more comparisons possible). For this reason LRS is based only on breeding performance during adulthood. This means that LRS was underestimated for certain individuals (see also discussion).

Figure 1. Shed feathers of yearling and adult female Sparrowhawks. From left to right (yearlings and adults, respectively): fifth primaries, central tailfeathers, secondaries, and two pairs of secondary coverts.

Figure 2. First and fifth primary of the same female showing that equivalent primaries are identical in different years.

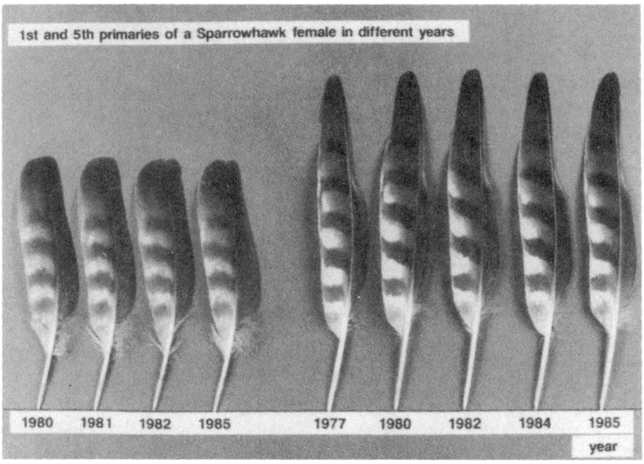

Figure 3. First primaries of eight different females, showing variation in length, shape and pattern in flight feathers between individual birds.

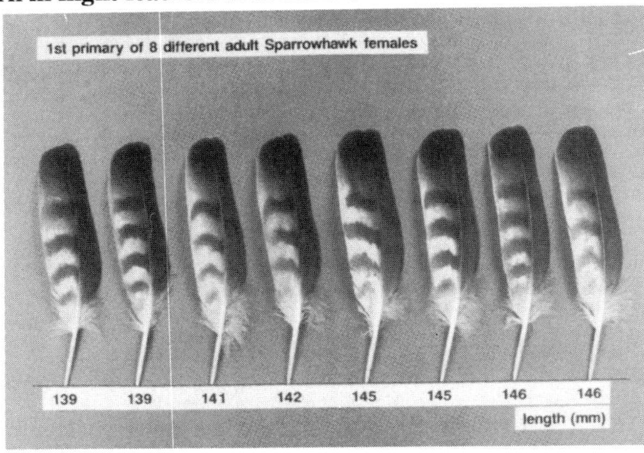

RESULTS

Population trend

The Sparrowhawk became almost extinct in the study area during the 1960s. Only two pairs were known to breed successfully in 1969 (Figure 4). Their territories were in the middle of extensive woodland and were probably not or only marginally affected by pesticides. Figure 4 shows that the population recovered rapidly in the early 1970s to about 20 pairs in the middle of the 1970s. This was followed by a remarkable increase from 1976 to 1977 when the number of breeding pairs almost doubled. Thereafter, the number increased slowly to around 50 breeding pairs per year until 1988. The increase to nearly 100 pairs during the last few years is mainly due to an increase in yearling breeders in the population following extremely mild winters, such as the winters of 1988/1989 and 1989/1990 (Table 1). In Table 1 is shown that the predicted value of yearling breeders is 44% following extremely mild winters. After severe winters, for instance 1978/1979 and 1984/1985, the proportion of yearling breeders was at a very minimum (15%), while the number of adult breeders remained on the same level (see Figure 4). Statistical analyses pointed out that there was no significant relationship between mortality among adult breeders in the population and weather conditions during the preceding winter. Thus, fluctuations in the total number of breeding pairs is related to the proportion of yearling breeders in the population, which is regulated by the weather conditions during the preceding winter.

Table 1. Relationship between the proportion of yearling breeders in the population and weather conditions during the winters 1969-1991. The year 69 is the winter from November 1968 until April 1969, etc. (winters categorized according to IJnsen 1991). Proportion of yearlings are predictions acquired from a regression model.

Category (1-7)	Years	Yearlings (%)	s.e.
Extremely mild	89,90	43,97	3,84
Very mild	75,88	38,10	5,63
Mild	77-78,83	29,81	4,12
Fairly mild	72-74,76,80-81,84	25,93	2,93
Normal	91	32,39	5,11
Cold	69-71,82,86-87	26,53	3,55
Severe	79,85	14,71	3,95

Significance between categories: 1-3*, 1-4, 1-6, 1-7, 7-2, 7-3,7-5, whereby* $p<0.05$; $p<0.01$; $p < 0.005$ (Likelihood-ratio test).

Figure 4. Population trend of Sparrowhawks in study area.

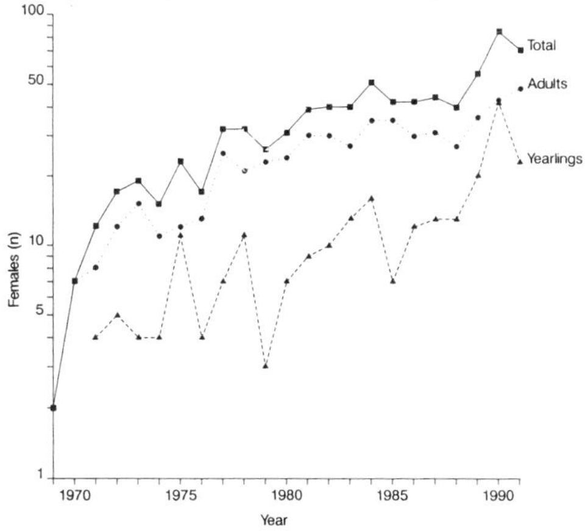

Annual breeding success

Breeding performance of the Sparrowhawks in the study area remained low until 1976. Between 1971 and 1976 the brood size varied between on average 2.4 and 3.3 young (Figure 5A). In the same period the proportion of successful nests varied between 50% and 70% (Figure 5B). Breeding performance reached its lowest level in 1972. The reduced reproductive output during this period was mainly due to eggshell breakage and embryo mortality, resulting in partial or complete losses of clutches. In 1976 breeding performance recovered very suddenly: mean brood size reached over 4 young (Figure 5A), while less than 15% of all nests failed (Figure 5B). From 1976 onwards the proportion of successful nests fluctuated around 80% (Figure 5B), which is similar to a Sparrowhawk population studied in Germany during a 30-year period before organochlorine pesticides came into use (Kramer 1973)

Lifetime reproductive success

Figure 6 shows that adult plumaged females raised 0 to 31 young throughout their life. From the selected 228 individuals 16% failed to raise any young at all. The majority produced 2 to 6 fledglings during their lifespan. On average, lifetime reproductive success amounted to 6.2 fledglings per individual. If these results are compared with a Sparrowhawk population in south Scotland (Newton 1989), it is obvious that both LRS diagrams are highly similar (Figure 6), notwithstanding that female Sparrowhawks in Scotland produced on average 1.13 fewer young during their life. The difference is statistically significant (Student's t-test, $P < 0.0005$).

Much of the variation in lifetime reproductive success can be explained in terms of variation in lifespan (Figure 7). Of the sample of 228 females, lifespan reached up to 11 years old. In the age group with a lifespan of 2 years a relatively large number failed (26 out of 102 (=25%) during 1976-1989, and 9 out of 16 (=56%) during 1969-1976), but those that succeeded in that year class raised up to 7 fledglings. Although lifespan explains 69.2% (total data set) of the variation in lifetime reproductive success, there is still considerable variation within age groups. For instance, in the 5 year age group, one female raised only one young, whereas another female raised 24 fledglings (Figure 7). Part of the variation can be explained by the restrained reproductive success until 1976. Females that lived during 1976-1989 raised on average twice as many fledglings as those that lived during 1969-1976 (6.7 (n=194) and 3.5 (n=34) fledglings, respectively). Annual survival of adult females in the breeding population did not differ between both periods.

The relative contribution of individuals to future generations was not equally distributed. We estimate, on account of ringing recoveries (unpublished data), that at least 75% of the female fledglings died before they could breed in adult plumage. The contribution of the remaining 25% breeders is clearly skewed (Figure 8). Females with a lifespan of 2 years (slightly more than 50% of all females), produced only 22% of all fledglings. A minority (only 25%) of the females reached a lifespan of 4 years or older, but they produced 55% of the total offspring. Overall, only 6% of all fledglings (25% of all breeders) raised more than 50% of the total offspring, which corresponds with Sparrowhawk population studies in Britain (Newton 1985, 1988, 1989).

Figure 5. Breeding success of successful pairs (A) and proportion of successful Sparrowhawk nests (B).

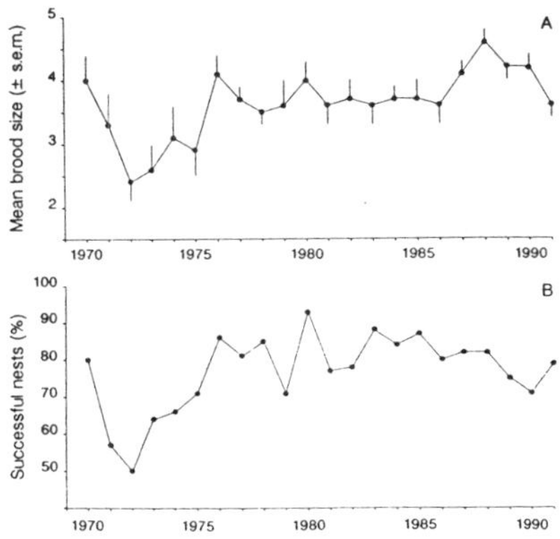

Figure 6. Lifetime fledgling production of female Sparrowhawks in the study area (mean per female = 6.16 young, n = 228), compared with females in southern Scotland (mean per female = 5.03 young, n = 194; after Newton, 1989).

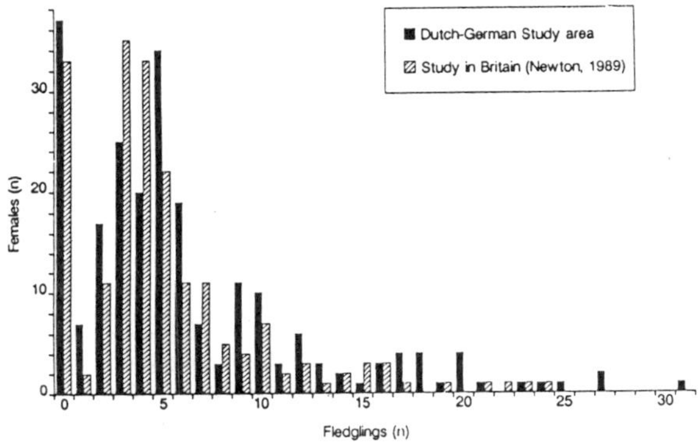

Figure 7. Lifetime fledgling production of adult females in relation to lifespan. Data represent the number of individuals with an equal number of offspring. Relationship between lifetime production (y) and lifespan (x) for period 1969-1976: $y = -2.55 + 1.967x$, $r = 0.716$, $P < 0.025$. For period 1976-1989: $y = -2.853 + 3.042x$, $r = 0.858$, $P < 0.005$. For both periods together: $y = -2.981 + 2.939x$, $r = 0.832$, $P < 0.005$.

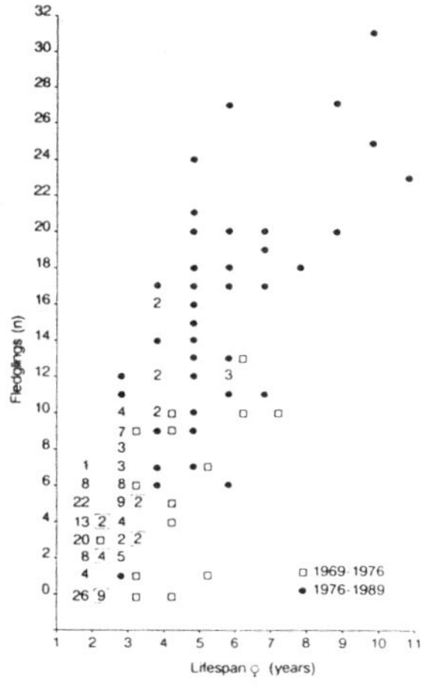

Figure 8. Cumulative presentation of lifetime reproductive success of females in relation to lifespan.

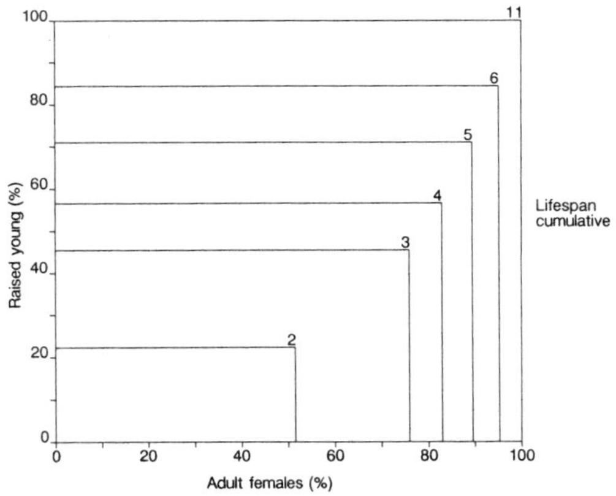

DISCUSSION

The number of Sparrowhawks breeding in the study area increased dramatically during the study period. The population recovery during the early 1970s was probably caused by a decrease in mortality due to disappearance of dieldrin and related compounds from the environment (Opdam *et al.* 1987).

A further increase in nest numbers followed after the breeding performance recovered suddenly in 1976. Burgers *et al.* (1986) showed that the eggshell thickness in Dutch Sparrowhawks (including birds from this study area) increased significantly from 1975 (Ratcliffe index 1.13) to 1977 (1.26), and so passing the presumed critical value of 1.16 for breeding success in 1976. This could explain why the recovery in breeding success from 1976 onwards was so abrupt (see also Opdam *et al.* 1987).

The role of winter weather conditions on population fluctuations is apparent. We found the highest proportion of yearling breeders in the population after extremely mild winters and the lowest proportion after hard winters. In contrast, the number of new adult recruits and the losses among established adult breeders did not show such a relationship. Kramer (1973) recorded that Sparrowhawk nest numbers in the southern Lausitz, Germany, dropped markedly after hard winters, as in 1939/1940, 1941/1942, 1946/1947 and 1962/1963. Unfortunately, he gave no information on the number of yearling and adult breeders in the population. Newton (1986) found in a fairly stable Sparrowhawk population in southern Scotland that both density-dependent factors and weather in early spring regulate the nest numbers. He suggested that: "The weather in early spring intervened to prevent a perfect density-dependent system: cold wet conditions in March-April led to greater decline, or less marked increase, than expected from nest numbers the previous year". We found no such density-dependent relationship for the Dutch-German Sparrowhawk population. The population increase until 1990 may be the reason why a density-dependent relationship could not be determined.

Between 1969 and 1977 females produced on average 3.5 fledglings during their life, or about 0.9 fledgling, when females which died before they could breed are included. Theoretically, each female must produce 2.0 young (by equal proportion of male and female offspring) to maintain population stability. For 1976-1989, replacement was calculated to be on average 1.7 young. One would, however, even expect a replacement greater than 2.0 young, because the population was increasing slightly. First, survival during the pre-breeding period may have been underestimated. Secondly, by using shed feathers to identify individual birds some bias in measuring LRS is introduced, because yearlings which died after their first breeding attempt are not selected. Furthermore, breeding success of the selected individuals in their first year of life could not be included. In some cases we doubted whether shed feathers were from the same individual or not. In these cases the feathers were classified as originating from different individuals. Displacement of individuals was checked, so that females that changed territory were found again. This occurred regularly (mean distance: 2.7 km). Displacements outside the study area might have occurred occasionally, which will have resulted in some underestimation of LRS.

Measurement of the lifetime production of females revealed that (a) females produced between 0 and 31 fledglings during their life, (b) most of the variation in LRS can be explained by variation in lifespan (up to 11 years), and (c) overall, only 6% of all fledglings produced more than 50% of the total offspring.

These results can be compared with Newton's (1985, 1986, 1988, 1989) findings of British Sparrowhawk populations. It appears that LRS in the Dutch-German study area score about 20% higher than in southern Scotland. This difference might be somewhat smaller, because, in contrast with Scottish data, females with lifespan 1-year were not included in our analysis. The larger lifetime production cannot be explained by a higher survival of the Dutch-German Sparrowhawks. The annual survival of adult females in this study of 53% (unpublished 1970-1985 data) is even lower than the 64% survival rate found in southern Scotland (Newton *et al.* 1983). The higher proportion of successful nests (80% against 57%) and the larger mean brood size per successful nest (3.8 against 3.4) we found explain, however, the difference in LRS between both populations to a large extent. It may be that natural circumstances (e.g. food supply) are more favourable in the Dutch-German study area than in southern Scotland. Human settlements and activities may also have increased food supply and consequently breeding performance, but on the other hand, these may have decreased the birds' annual survival (e.g. more window and traffic casualities). The high density of the predator Goshawk *Accipiter gentilis* in the Dutch-German study area (absent in southern Scotland) contributes furthermore to a high mortality among our Sparrowhawks.

Some of the individual variation in LRS can be explained by the restrained reproductive success until 1976. Most of the variation (69%), however, is caused by the variation in lifespan. This corresponds with Sparrowhawk population studies in Britain (Newton 1985, 1988, 1989). The remaining variation might be explained by the age of first breeding, territory quality, quality of the partner or by chance, but these aspects need further examination.

The outcome that only a small proportion of individuals contributes to the next generation to a large extent is a common phenomenon in (long-living) birds, and has been discussed thoroughly elsewhere (Newton 1989).

ACKNOWLEDGMENTS

We wish to thank all friends who helped to collect data in the field, especially Johan Thissen, Paul Opdam, Peter Verschuren, Mark Verschuren and Jan Jacobs. We are also grateful to Johan Thissen, Paul Opdam, and Arie Spaans who gave useful comments on the manuscript. We thank Joop van Osch, Ruud Wegman and Roel van Beek for preparing the photographs and figures.

REFERENCES

BURGERS, J., P. OPDAM, G. MÜSKENS & E. DE RUITER 1986. Residue levels of DDE in eggs of Dutch Sparrowhawks *Accipiter nisus* following the ban on DDT. *Environ. Poll.* Ser B. 11: 29-40.

CLUTTON-BROCK, T.H. (ed.) 1988. *Reproductive Success.* University Press, Chicago.

FUCHS, P. & J.B.M. THISSEN 1981. Die Pestizid- und PCB-Belastung bei Greifvögeln und Eulen in den Niederlanden nach den gesetzlich verordneten Einschränkungen im Gebrauch der chlorierten Kohlenwasserstoffpestizide. *Oekologie der Vögel 3*, Sonderheft, 181-195.

IJNSEN, F. 1991. Karaktergetallen van de winters vanaf 1707. *Zenit* 18: 69-73.

KOEMAN, J.H., J.A.J. VINK & J.J.M. DE GOEIJ 1969. Causes of mortality in birds of prey and owls in The Netherlands in the winter of 1968-1969. *Ardea* 57: 67-76.

KOEMAN, J.H., C.F. VAN BEUSEKOM & J.M.M. DE GOEIJ 1972. Eggshell and population changes in the Sparrowhawk (*Accipiter nisus*). *TNO-Nieuws* 27: 542-550.

KRAMER, K. 1973. *Habicht und Sperber.* Ziemsen, Wittenberg.

NEWTON, I. 1979. *Population Ecology of Raptors.* Poyser, Berkhamsted.

NEWTON, I. 1985. Lifetime reproductive output of female Sparrowhawks. *J. Anim. Ecol.* 54: 241-253.

NEWTON, I. 1986. *The Sparrowhawk.* Poyser, Calton.

NEWTON, I. 1988. Individual performance in Sparrowhawks: the ecology of two sexes. *Proc. Int. Orn.*

Congr. 19: 125-154.

NEWTON, I. (ed.) 1989. *Lifetime Reproduction in Birds.* Academic Press, London.

NEWTON, I. & J. BOGAN 1974. Organochlorine residues, eggshell thinning and hatching success in British Sparrowhawks. *Nature* 249: 582-583.

NEWTON, I., M. MARQUISS & P. ROTHERY 1983. Age structure and survival in a Sparrowhawk population. *J. Anim. Ecol.* 52: 591-602.

OPDAM, P. 1985. *Roofvogels in ons landschap.* Spectrum, Utrecht.

OPDAM, P. & G. MÜSKENS 1976. Use of shed feathers in population studies of Accipiter hawks (Aves, Accipitriformes, Accipitridae). *Beaufortia* 24: 55-62.

OPDAM, P., J. BURGERS & G. MÜSKENS 1987. Population trend, reproduction, and pesticides in Dutch Sparrowhawks following the ban on DDT. *Ardea* 75: 205-212.

RATCLIFFE, D.A. 1970. Changes attributable to pesticides in egg breakage frequency and eggshell thickness in some British birds. *J. appl. Ecol.* 7: 67-107.

Ronald Zollinger/Gerard Müskens
DLO Institute for Forestry and Nature Research
P. O. Box 9201
6800 HB Arnhem
The Netherlands

Sparrowhawk *Accipiter nisus*

Part 2

Rare and Declining Raptors

Osprey *Pandion haliaetus*

Conveners:

Dr. B.-U. Meyburg & R. D. Chancellor

Meyburg, B.-U. & R. D. Chancellor eds.1994
Raptor Conservation Today
WWGBP / The Pica Press

The Java Hawk Eagle *Spizaetus bartelsi*: Results of recent Research on Distribution Status and Ecology

S. van Balen & B.-U. Meyburg

ABSTRACT

This is one of the rarest and least known raptor species in the world. In order to dispel some of the mystery surrounding it, a WWGBP expedition visited Java in 1986, the results of which were published in the proceedings of the last World Conference. Since then, further surveys and research have been continued and are here reported and discussed.

INTRODUCTION

The Java Hawk Eagle *Spizaetus bartelsi* (JHE) was first considered as a race of the more widespread *S. nipalensis* (Finsch 1908), but attained specific (endemic) status after more taxonomic research (Amadon 1953). Due to its dependence on primary rainforest in the lowlands and hills of Java, numbers are extremely low and estimates of 50-60 pairs for the total population were made after a WWBGP expedition in search of remaining subpopulations of the species (Thiollay & Meyburg 1988; Meyburg *et al.* 1989). Subsequent surveys by S. van Balen (van Balen 1991) and the Java Hawk Eagle survey project launched in 1990 yielded more information on the species' distribution and ecology. This paper presents an overview of current information and a discussion the eagle's present known status.

DISTRIBUTIONAL NOTES

A large number of areas were visited during 1990-1993, varying from monsoon to everwet rainforest in the lowlands and hills of west and east Java. In Table 1 all areas visited within the framework of the project are listed and the presence or absence of the Java Hawk Eagle indicated. A number of more recently visited sites have been selected for further discussion below.

Mt Slamet, C Java

A first-year juvenile JHE was photographed by R. Seitre (in litt 1990), in May 1990, at *ca.* 1,500m a.s.l. near the hotsprings above Baturraden, on the south slope of Mt Slamet. The single bird was rather tame and flew around, calling loudly.

A 15,000ha nature reserve at 1,000-3,410m elevation has been proposed by FAO (1982), covering the larger part of the mountain. Mt Slamet belongs to one of the areas for which surveys have been planned in the JHE project.

This observation by Seitre, who also reported that the mountain was still covered by some extensive forest on the southern slopes above 1,000m, raises the hope for a viable population of JHE in at least one of the few possible places in the province of C Java.

Mt Sindoro, C Java

During a short visit in November 1990 to the south-eastern slope of this mountain, above the village of Kledung, it was soon learned that on this and its twin volcano Mt Sumbing probably too little forest was left for a viable population of JHE. Though observations of a Black Eagle *Ictinaetus malayensis* and some other woodland birds indicated a former rich (sub) montane avifauna, the cultivation of the land (tobacco, corn, timberwood monocultures) on the lower slopes of both mountains, and the heavily disturbed parts higher up, very unlikely leave room for many more large-size forest raptors. However, a more profound survey of the area is needed and planned, with regard to the proposal of a 10,000ha large nature reserve on Mt Sumbing (FAO 1982).

Mt Kawi/Arjuno, E Java

A specimen is stored in the American Museum of Natural History, collected earlier this century on Mt Arjuno, but no further data are available. During surveys in 1992-1993, at four different places throughout the mountain complex, Java Hawk Eagles were seen.

Meru Betiri, E Java

Although previous surveys (e.g. Bartels, pers. comm.; Thiollay *et al.* 1988) already showed the presence of JHE, it was felt useful to keep monitoring the local JHE population. During a week's visit in October 1990, JHE was observed on at least three different localities, illustrating the importance of this area.

Meru Betiri National Park might harbour the largest population of JHE on Java on its 50,000ha of largely undisturbed forest. The enclaves of cocoa, coffee, rubber etc., estates and settlements were reported due to be abandoned in the near future, and negligence of the plantations was already noticeable.

DISCUSSION

Conservation

Two of the recently surveyed areas, i.e. Alas Purwo (see van Balen 1991) and Mt Slamet, harbouring populations of JHE in reasonably large stretches of forest, are new additions to the presently known area of distribution of the species. The last mentioned area, which provides habitat for a number of other threatened Javan wildlife as well, i.e. Javan Gibbon, Javan Leaf-Monkey (Seitre *in litt.* 1990), has been proposed as a nature reserve, but further surveys and information are needed to support these plans. Alas Purwo became a national park after having been a game reserve since 1939; its extremely dry conditions, however, might create a less than optimal habitat for JHE.

Of importance are two areas mentioned in an earlier report on the JHE project, i.e. Ijen crater and Lebakharjo (van Balen *op.cit.*). The latter is now much threatened by plans to develop the area, notwithstanding its high conservation value. The former is a 2,560ha reserve at 1,500-2,800m a.s.l. and includes an important sulphur concession. It however doesn't include much JHE habitat: the forest visited during the survey, where JHE was observed, lay just outside the reserve boundaries. The higher parts (> 1,000m) are managed by the Forestry Department as protected forest, without special conservation status; the lower parts belong to a tea estate, and during the survey some 800ha were being cleared for new plantations. The extension of the reserve to these lower zones of the mountain complex should be seriously considered. A 50,000ha reserve is proposed for Mt Kawi and adjacent Mt Kelud, including two localities where JHEs were seen. The proposed nature reserve (see FAO 1982) of 60,000ha north of Ijen (Maelang) would make up a 130,000ha reserve adjacent to Baluran national park in the north-east and Meru Betiri in the south-west, and be of utmost interest. A large portion of Java's endangered wildlife would be safeguarded from further deterioration in such an extensive complex of reserves.

Ecology

At this stage of the project it is unclear what the correlation is between the habitat preferences and distribution of JHE. Certain characters, e.g. high topographic relief in relation to foraging behaviour (cf. Janes 1985) may play a more important role, and without exception the birds were observed in rugged hilly areas. However, in west Java especially there seems to be some dependency on lush rainforest, more pronounced than in east Java.

Population status

With the new data obtained on the species' distribution, it must now be possible to re-evaluate previous population estimates by Meyburg *et al.* 1989, i.e. 50-60 pairs. In Table 1 the areas surveyed of 2,000ha and more (the minimum area to support one pair of JHE, see Thiollay & Meyburg 1988) are listed. Using the same criteria of one pair of JHE per 2-3,000ha, a total number of pairs can be calculated. However, some areas (e.g. Alas Purwo) are only partly suitable, others (e.g. Ijen) only partly cover the available JHE habitat. Table 2 lists the areas with known JHE populations and their estimated numbers of pairs, totalling 52-61 pairs, of which 39-45 are secured in nature reserves. More pairs may be found in areas not yet surveyed, especially the hills and mountains in the surroundings of Bandung, adding an additional 15-20 pairs. Furthermore an unknown proportion of the JHE population consists of immature birds, that are prone to straggle outside the better forest areas, making themselves vulnerable.

Table 1. Distribution of the Java Hawk Eagle across Java (from west to east); climate types from dry (1) to wet (3) (see van Steenis 1972); lw = lowland forest, m = montane forest; + = present, - = absent; * = only superficially surveyed, ** = a few short visits, * = intensively surveyed during several periods of at least 4-5 days. [] = areas without JHE observed; () = areas with JHE reported before World War II; after Bishop 1988, Meyburg *et al.* 1989, van Balen 1989.**

	Climate	Forest Type	Presence	Search Intensity	Area (x1,000ha)
Ujung Kulon	2	lw	-	***	[76]
Mt Aseupan	2	lw	-	***	[2.5]
Mt Halimun	3	lw/m	+	***	40
Mt Salak	3	m	+	***	2.5
Mt Gede/Pangrango	3	m	+	***	14
Cikepuh	2	lw	-	**	[8.5]
Mt Sanggabuana	2	lw	-	*	[2.5]
Mt Patuha	2/3	m	(+)	*	
Mt Tangkuban Perahu	3	m	-	*	
Mt Tilu	3	m	-	*	[8]
Mt Papandayan	3	m	+	***	7
Leuweung Sancang	3	lw	-	**	[2]
Mt Slamet	3	m	+	*	15
Mt Sindoro/Sumbing	3	m	-	*	[10]
Mt Lawu	2	m	-	***	[21]
Mt Kawi/Arjuno	2	m	(+)	***	50
Mt Tengger/Bromo	2/3	m	-	**	[57]
Yang Highlands	2/3	m	(+)	**	14
Lebakharjo	2/3	lw	+	**	16
Meru Betiri	2	lw	+	***	50
Ijen	3	m	+	**	2.5
Baluran	1	lw	+?	***	[25]
Alas Purwo	1	lw	+	***	62

Table 2. Localities with recent observations of Java Hawk Eagle. (* = estimate by Thiollay & Meyburg 1988). ( ) = proposed; NP = national park; nr = nature reserve; pf = protected forest.

	Area (x 1,000ha)	Status	Number of JHE pairs
Mt Halimun	40	NP	10*
Mt Gede/Pangrango/Salak	14	NP/pf	9*
Mt Papandayan	7	nr	2-3
Mt Slamet	15	(nr)	5
Mt Kawi/Kalud	50	(nr)	5-6
Lebakharjo	16	(nr)	5
Meru Betiri	50	NP	11-16*
Ijen	25	nr + ( )	2-3
Alas Purwo	62	NP	4-5

Threats

The destruction and fragmentation of the little remaining rainforest still forms an immediate threat to the survival of the Java Hawk Eagle, and every effort should be undertaken to save what is left. The proposed nature reserves cover a good deal of the present area of distribution and, though not continuous, the vagrant character of JHE juvenile and immatures enhances dispersal amongst the patches and thus gene exchange. The finding of JHE in C Java shows that the western and eastern populations are less isolated than was previously supposed.

Raptors play an increasing role as status symbols, and high prices are paid by bird fanciers. On local bird markets the sight of a chained JHE was not among the extreme rarities. (P. Andrew, *in litt.* 1992). But recently, amendments in 1990 to the environmental laws allow much heavier sanctions against breakers of the law on protected species (which includes all diurnal birds of prey), resulting in a stricter control of the trade at local markets. The use of guns forms another threat. It is encouraging that the Indonesian Government is now working on a total ban on weapons (including air rifles), which will certainly have a positive impact on the JHE's survival.

ACKNOWLEDGEMENTS

The WWGBP surveys were made possible through grants from the American Federation of Aviculture and the Fauna & Flora Preservation Society. Supervision was provided by Prof. S. Somadikarta, Prof. K.H. Voous and Mr H. Bartels. Mr. P. Jepson commented upon earlier drafts of this paper.

REFERENCES

AMADON, D. 1953. Remarks on the Asiatic Hawk-Eagles of the genus *Spizaetus. Ibis.* 95: 492-500.

BALEN, S. van: 1991. The Java Hawk Eagle *Spizaetus bartelsi* WWGBP project report No. 1, March 1990. *Birds of Prey Bull.* 4: 33-40.

BISHOP, K.D. 1988. *In*: C. Robson. Recent Reports *O.B.C. Bulletin* 7: 34-40.

FAO, 1982. National Conservation Plan for Indonesia. Vol. III. Java and Bali, Bogor.

FINSCH, O. 1908. Ein neuer Irrgast f-r Java (*Spizaetus keearti Legge*). *Orn. Mber.*16: 44-45.

JANES, S.W. 1985. Habitat selection in raptorial birds. *In.* M.L. Cody (Ed.) *Habitat selection in birds.* Academic Press: Orlando, etc.

MEYBURG, B.-U., S. van BALEN, J.-M. THIOLLAY & R.D. CHANCELLOR 1989. *Spizaetus bartelsi. In*: B.-U. Meyburg & R.D. Chancellor (Eds.) *Raptors in the Modern World.* WWGBP: Berlin & Paris.

STEENIS, C.G.G.J. van. 1972. *The mountain flora of Java.* Brill, Leiden.

THIOLLAY, J.-M. & B.-U. MEYBURG 1988. Forest fragmentation and the conservation of raptors: a survey on the island of Java. *Biol. Conserv.* 44: 229-250.

Dr. S. van Balen
P.O. Box 47
Bogor 16001
Indonesia

Dr. B.-U. Meyburg
Herbertstrasse 14
D-1000 Berlin 33
Fed. Rep. of Germany

Meyburg, B.-U. & R. D. Chancellor eds.1994
Raptor Conservation Today
WWGBP / The Pica Press

The Pallid Harrier *Circus macrourus* as an Endangered Species in the Palaearctic

A.V. Davygora and V.P. Belik

INTRODUCTION

The following analysis is based on material collected by the authors in 1967-1990 in the steppe regions near the Caucasus and the Urals, down the lower and middle Don and between the Volga and the Don, together with publications and oral reports by fellow ornithologists.

The major part of the population and optimal breeding area for the Pallid Harrier are located in Eastern Europe and Northern Asia, although in some cases the species is reputed to invade North-west and Western Europe too. In the east the breeding area may spread a little further on into Mongolia.

Thus the general status of the Pallid Harrier is determined by its major population within the former USSR — in Russia, Ukraine and Kazakhstan.

RESULTS

Analysis of the collected data proves that the Pallid Harrier has practically vanished from south-east Europe, including the steppe regions in southern Ukraine, from the near Caucasus, down the lower and middle Don, to north-west of the Caspian Sea (Ivanov & Chunikhin 1959; Zubarovsky 1977; Kostin 1983; Melgunov *et al.* 1983, 1984; Vetrov 1986; our data). The species seems to have vanished from these places in the 1960s, apparently after the last stretches of virgin lands there were ploughed up. Now scattered nests have survived only along the northern border of the forest-steppe zone. (Eliseeva 1983; Strigunov 1984, 1987; our data). Separate pairs can spread to the south of the forest zone (Kuznetsov 1986; V.T. Afanasiev, pers.comm.; V.V. Frolov, pers.comm.).

Incidentally, the Pallid Harrier can be seen back in its former long-abandoned breeding areas during migration in places which abound in small rodents, as reported in 1988 from the middle Don (V V. Vetrov, pers. comm.).

Regular breeding invasions outside the original area reported in the early 1950s in Western and North-west Europe (Formozov 1959) are, in our opinion, the result of a disastrous reduction in the number of such rodents as mice in the major part of the Pallid Harrier's breeding area. This is typical of those species whose food supply is unstable over the years.

In Northern Asia the Pallid Harrier breeds in the steppe regions of the near Urals (Davygora & Gavlyk 1980; Davygora 1981, 1985), but its numbers here are not great — 2.2 to 6.2 (on average) breeding pairs per 100 km².

In northern Kazakhstan (Naurzum Reserve) this harrier is now rare and fewer in number than Montagu's, *C. pygargus*. (E.A. Bragin pers.comm.; Pererva 1984). It is breeding in Central Kazakhstan, where its number is also much inferior to that of Montagu's Harrier (Krivicky 1983). The situation is similar in the Irtish region at Pavlodar (Solomatin 1984).

The most recent decades have witnessed a decline in numbers to the south of Western Siberia — in Barabinsk steppe (Danilov 1976; Sagitov 1977). Farther to the east the Pallid Harrier spreads up the Minusinsk depression (Prokofev & Kustov 1988) but is extremely rare south of central Siberia (Kuchin 1976; Tsybulin & Bogomolov 1983; Neifeldt 1986; A.A. Baranov, pers.comm.).

The latest research has shown a greater dependence for breeding on mesophyllic biotopes — steppe brushwood, low-lying marshy lands and water meadows (Davygora 1986). Thus, out of 25 nests that we found in the steppe region of the near Urals, 24 (96%) were located in wetland biotopes along rivers and hollows in the steppe. One nest only (4%) was found away from water.

We have discovered a greater trophic dependence of the Pallid Harrier on birds than was previously considered, particularly when rodents are scarce or unattainable. This dependence, like the swing of a pendulum, increases automatically when rodents become scarce and *vice versa*. In this case it is typical of the Pallid Harrier in the steppe region of the near Uruls to hunt for the young of passerines such as *Alauda arvensis* and *Melanocorypha leucoptera, Motacilla flava, Anthus campestris, Oenanthe oenanthe* and *Oenanthe isabellina*. This is done in an unusual manner, with the harrier like the Hobby forcing its prey to climb high enough for it to be caught in flight (Davygora 1985).

This method is more used during migration and on the wintering grounds than during the breeding season, at which time the prey become more varied at the expense of both sparrows and other larger birds. Thus a sharp increase of birds is reported in the harrier's diet during migration in south-east Kazakhstan (Selevin 1934), including Short-toed Lark *Calandrella cinerea, Alauda arvensis, Sylvia communis* and *Sylvia curruca* as well as *Vanellus vanellus*.

In Askania-Nova Reserve (Southern Ukraine) the Pallid Harrier was reported attacking flocks of doves (species unidentified) in autumn and winter (Sokolov 1928). It was also reported to attack Hooded Crows *Corvus cornix* in the sandy region between the Volga and the Ural (Chevchenko *et al.* 1978).

There are numerous reports from the western coast of the Caspian Sea (in Daghestan on the Samur estuary) on attempts by immature male harriers on migration to catch in flight small birds such as *Galerida cristata, Alauda arvensis, Calandrella cinerea, Anthus* sp. and *Emberiza schoeniclus* (V.T. Butiev, pers.comm.). According to the observers the harriers executed complicated aerial pirouettes in pursuit of their prey 2-5m above the ground. Considering the numerous prey remains of such birds their hunting proved quite successful.

Thus the Pallid Harrier is not the typical mouse-eater it is traditionally believed to be (Dementyev 1951; Cramp & Simmons 1980). Birds are equally an important element in its diet as the above data show.

The wing formation of the Pallid Harrier has some peculiarities due to its need to procure food in flight (Davygora 1986). Objectively speaking, it belongs among those birds of prey that profit by their speed of movement. It has rather short and pointed wings as compared to other harriers, with a high ratio between primaries and secondaries (1.41) and a wedgelike tail. Its high cardiac index (9.09) points to speed in regular flight.

All these features are especially typical of males. Their similarity to bird-eaters is justified by a comparatively high index (0.7) of sexual dimorphism overall, hence morphological features that bring Pallid Harriers and bird-eating falcons together.

DISCUSSION

The above data show that the Pallid Harrier has sharply declined in numbers while its breeding area has undergone great changes in the past 20-30 years. To-day its breeding range comprises three zones — an optimal zone (steppes, forest-steppe and semi-deserts in Eurasia), a zone of sporadic breeding (south of the forest zone in Europe and northern deserts in Kazakhstan), and a zone of incidental breeding invasions (northern and western Europe). The European part of the breeding area has undergone, as was to be expected, some major changes leading to the species' disappearance from the south European steppes and its becoming infrequent in the northern steppe and forest-steppe. Separate pairs may nest to the south of the forest zone.

The Asian part of the breeding area has changed less. It is evident, however, that the species is declining here, whilst its sporadic presence in marginal zones is increasing, especially to the east. At the same time the Pallid Harrier is spreading south to inhabit the reeds by artesian wells in northern deserts east of the Caspian Sea.

The most numerous population is now located in the optimal zone of its Asian breeding area.

The question remains as to why the area of distribution and the number of individuals have grown smaller. This, in our view, can be answered in the following way.

1. Breeding conditions have deteriorated due to anthropogenic influence on their main breeding areas through clearance of the steppe brushwood (in the European part) and by the destruction of the vegetation of mesophyllic biotopes in the steppe hollows, low-lying water meadows and along streams and rivers by grazing cattle (Asian part).

Looking for better breeding places, the Pallid Harrier has to move farther into the forest-steppes and southern forest zones, promoted by a growing (over the last century) variety of open biotopes — forest clearings and clear-felled areas. This is more typical of the European part of the bird's breeding area, where the primary breeding biotopes have almost disappeared.

2. Feeding conditions have deteriorated also, since the number of common Field Mice - the main prey item in the breeding season - has dwindled. This has been brought about by the general degradation of the vegetation and drying up of the hollows and low-lying meadows — the habitual places for this rodent in summer.

3. The virgin terrain has been almost entirely ploughed up, and this has affected hunting conditions for this bird of prey. Cultivation has made it almost impossible for the harrier to hunt over high grass in which rodents become unattainable.

4. Finally, the Pallid Harrier can be over-sensitive to pesticides, due to a possibly greater contamination by them considering their feeding habits (with small rodents prevailing).

A drastic reduction in its habitat and numbers, as these conditions continue to deteriorate, causes great concern over the fate of this species, whose breeding area is almost entirely located within the former USSR. It is essential to devise a package of special measures to restore the population, one of the most essential being to census the present number of breeding pairs and to include it in the Red Data books of Russia, Ukraine and Kazakhstan.

REFERENCES

CHEVCHENKO, V.L. E.I., GAVRILOV, V.A. NAGLOV, A.Y. FEDOSENKO & O.M. TATARINOVA 1978. Ob Ornitofaune Volzhsko-Uralskogo mezhdurechya (Khishchnye ptitsy i sovy), *Tr. In-t zool. AN KazSSR*. T. 38: 99-114.

CRAMP, S. & K.E.L. SIMMONS 1980. *The Birds of the Western Palearctic*. Vol. 2. Oxford Univ. Press.

DANILOV, O.N. 1976. Khishchnye ptitsy i sovy Baraby i Severnoi Kulundy. Novosibirsk. 158 pp.

DAVYGORA, A.V. & E.V. GAVLYUK 1980. K biotopicheskomu raspredeleniyu khishchnykh ptits v usloviyakh stepnyk landshaftov Orenburgskoi oblasti. Oblastnaya konf. molodykh uchenykh VUZov: Tez. dokl. Orenburg: 32-34.

DAVYGORA, A.V. 1981. Khishchnye ptitsy yuga Orenburgskoi oblasti. Ekologiya i okhrana ptits: 8 Vsesoyuz. ornitol. konf.: Tez. dokl. Kichinev: 66-67.

DAVYGORA, A.V. 1985. Vidovoi sostav i chislennost khishchnykh ptits stepei yugo-zapadnogo Preduralya. Nauchnye osnovy okhr. prirody Urala i probl. ekolog. monitoringa: Tez. dokl. obl. konf. molodykh uchenykh i spetsialistov. Sverdlovsk: 15-16.

DAVYGORA, A.V. 1985. K okhotnichemu povedeniyu lunei. *Ornitologiya*. Vyp. 20: 182-183.

DAVYGORA, A.V. 1986. Morfo-ekologicheskii analiz lugovogo i stepnogo lunei v usloviyakh sovmestnogo obitaniya. Izuchenie ptits SSSR, ikh okhrana i rats. ispolzovanie: Tez. dokl. 1-go s'ezda Vsesoyuz. ornitol. obsch-va i 9-i Vsesoyuz. ornitol. konf. Ch. 1: 184-186.

DEMENTYEV, G.P. 1951. Otryad khishchnye ptitsy. *Pticy Sovetskogo Soyuza*. T. 1: 199-221.

ELISEEVA, V.I. 1983. Izmenenie chislennosti khishchnykh ptits v Tsentralno-Chernozemnom zapovednike (TsChZ) za 20 let, Okhrana khishchnykh ptits. M. *Nauka* 45-49.

FORMOZOV, A.N. 1981. O dvizhenii i kolebanii granits rasprostraneniya mlekopitayushchikh i ptits. Problemy ekologii i geografii zhivotnykh. *Nauka*: 134-168.
IVANOV, V.G. & S.P. CHUNIKHIN 1959. K ekologii lunei (rod Circus) v usloviyakh Kabardino-Balkarii. Uch. zap. Kab.-Balk. gos. un-t. Vyp. 5. Seriya skh i biologicheskaya: 177-181.
KOSTIN Y.V. 1983. *Pticy Kryma. Nauka.* 240 pp.
KRIVICKY, I.A. 1983. Dnevnye khishchnye ptitsy stepnykh rayonov Tsentralnogo Kazakhstana. Kharkov, 58 pp.
KUCHIN, A.P. 1976. *Pticy Altaya.* Barnaul: Alt. kn. izd-vo, 231 pp.
KUZNETSOV A.V. 1968. Chislennost gnezdyashchikhsya khishchnykh ptits Kostromskoi nizmennosti Vsesoyuzn. sovesch. po probl. kadastra i ucheta zhivotnogo mira: Tez. dokl. Ch. 2: 324-325.
MELGUNOV, I.L., A.N. KHOKHLOV & A.P. BICHEROV 1983. Luni na Stavropol'e Ekologiya khishchnykh ptits: Mater. 1 sovesch. po ekol. i okhr. khishchnykh ptits. *Nauka* 1983: 83-86.
MELGUNOV, I.L. & A.P BICHEROV 1984. Luni Tsentralnogo Predkavkaz'ya. Fauna Stavropol'ya. - Stavropol: 21-38.
NEIFELDT, I.A. 1986. Iz rezultatov ornitologicheskoi ekspeditsii na Yugo-Vostochnyi Altai. *Tr. Zool. in-t AN SSSR*: 7-43.
PERERVA, V.I. 1984. Ocenka vozdeistviya khishchnykh ptits na ornitofaunu. *Ornitologiya.* Vyp. 19: 68-74.
PROKOFEV, S.M. & Y.I. KUSTOV 1988. Redkie i ischezayushchie vidy ptits Khakasii i ikh okhrana. Redkie nazemnye pozvonochnye Sibiri. Novosibirsk: 180-185.
SAGITOV, R.A. 1977. Osobennosti gnezdovaniya massovykh vidov utok v rayone oz. Malyi Chan (Zap. Sibir), 7 Vsesoyuzn. ornitol. konf.: Tez. dokl. Ch. 1: 315-316.
SELEVIN, V.A. 1934. Nekotorye dannye k vyyasneniyu selskokhozyaistvennogo znacheniya khishchnykh ptits Yugo-Vostochnogo Kazakhstana. *Byull. Sredne-Aziatskii gos. un-t*: 79-90.
SOKOLOV V. 1928. Materialy k izucheniyu ornitofauny pervogo gosudarstvennogo stepnogo zapovednika Chapli. Visti Derzhavny stepovy zapovidnik "Chapli". T. 4: 27-68.
SOLOMATIN A.O. 1984. O gnezdovanii lunei v Pavlodarskom Priirtyshe. Probl. region. ekol. zhivotnykh v tsikle zool. distsiplin pedvu-za: Tez. dok. 3 Vsesoyuz. konf. zoologov ped. in-tov: 155-157.
STRIGUNOV, V.I. 1984. Chislennost i territorialnoe raspredelenie khishchnykh ptits v lesostepi Ukrainy. Probl. region. ekol. zhivotnykh v tsikle zool. distsiplin pedvuza: Tez. dokl. 3 Vsesoyuz konf. zoologov ped. in-tov: 161-162.
STRIGUNOV, V.I. 1987. Khishchnye ptitsy lesostepi basseina Dnepra. Avtoref. diss... kand. biol. nauk. 25 pp.
TSYBULIN, S.M. & I.N. BOGOMOLOV 1983. Chislennost i raspredelenie khishchnykh ptits na Severnom Altae. Ekologiya khishchykh ptits: Mater. 1 sovesch. po ekol. i okhr. khishchnykh ptits. *Nauka:* 152-155.
VETROV, V.V. 1986. Territorialnoe raspredelenie i sovremennoe sostoyanie chislennosti khishchnykh ptits Vorochilovgradskoi oblasti. Izuchenie ptits SSSR, ikh okhrana i rats. ispolzovanie: Tez. dokl. 1-go s'ezda Vsesoyuz. ornitol. obsch-va i 9-i Vsesoyuz. ornitol. konf. Ch. 1: 121-122.
ZUBAROVSKY, V.M. 1977. *Fauna Ukrainy.* T. 5. Pticy. Vyp. 2. Khishchnye ptitsy. Kiev: Naukova jumka.

A.V. Davygora
Orenburg Pedagogical Institute
Orenburg
Russia

V.P. Belik
Rostov Antiplague Institute
Rostov-on-Don
Russia

Meyburg, B.-U. & R. D. Chancellor eds.1994
Raptor Conservation Today
WWGBP / The Pica Press

Breeding Biology, Habitat Selection and Conservation of Montagu's Harrier *Circus pygargus* in the Northern Apennines, Italy

Ugo Faralli

INTRODUCTION

During the 20th century, Montagu's Harrier decreased dramatically as a breeding bird in many European areas because of agricultural and forestry development; in some regions it has totally disappeared (Zijlstra & Hustings 1992).

In Italy this "smart" raptor mainly breeds in plain and cultivated regions of the Po valley (Lombardy, the Veneto, Emilia Romagna), in some plain areas along the Tyrrhenian coast (Toscana, Lazio) and in Sardinia, spreading from sea level to *ca.* 500-600m. a.s.l. (Chiavetta 1981; Martelli & Sandri 1991; Brichetti *et al.* 1992). The Italian breeding population is estimated at about 250 pairs, located along the eastern Po valley and pre-Apennine Adriatic belt (Brichetti *et al.* 1992).

The most frequently used habitats for nest and site selection are cornfields and the edges of wetlands. Unfortunately, in such sites agricultural activity starts almost always when the eggs have not yet hatched or when the nestlings are still unable to fly (Arcá 1991; Pandolfi & Giacchini 1991).

In recent years, some pairs have started breeding along the Apennines, in a particular "Mediterranean" habitat very similar to continental shrublands. In this habitat 8 pairs of Montagu's Harrier have been located and studied from 1986 to 1990. The present paper aims to present new data concerning the species' breeding biology, habitat selection and conservation in the northern Apennines.

STUDY AREA AND METHODS

The study area includes a wide territory which is part of the socalled Sub-Apennine; in particular the high hill area (700-1300m. a.s.l), from the heights of Florence to the banks of Lake Trasimeno, crossing the whole province of Arezzo.

In such area, which spreads over 70km, the vegetation is quite particular: wide broadleaf woodlands, composed of Beech *Fagus silvatica*, Chestnut *Castanea sativa* and some oak species, alternate with small heathlands where the main species are Heather *Erica arborea* and *scoparia* and Broom *Spartium junceum*.

Through the years, this habitat has developed from the frequent annual fires which are a negative factor for nature conservation (as far as woodlands are concerned); but where the soil is calcareous, fire has also had a positive influence, since it has created this rare and threatened heathland habitat. Moreover, the habitat required by Montagu's Harrier has developed following human action impeding the natural evolution of vegetation, contributing, with the fire, to the creation of steppe-grassland.

Besides, these areas also include a natural and discontinuous grass-shrub coverage. Juniper *Juniper communis* and Hawthorn *Crataegus monogyna*, together with groups of scattered trees, give the habitat structure its diversity.

Along this area, from north to south, the breeding sites of eight pairs have been located:-

Site A: Pratomagno
Site B: La Libbia
Site C: Alpe di Poti
Site D: Monte Dogana
Site E: Monte Lignano
Site F: La Foce
Site G: Sant'Egidio

Observations have been carried out at regular intervals, from occupation of the site to the young birds' fledging; of course we tried not to disturb in order not to endanger the clutches.

RESULTS

In this study area we have located eight pairs of Montagu's Harrier. For seven pairs we have precisely located the nest sites; as to the last pair, we have located the breeding area but not the nest. All the nests have been in the heathlands with a north and north-east exposure.

Through the years we have noticed a strong attachment to the breeding site and in two cases (La Libbia and S.Egidio) the same nest (or nevertheless the same spot) has been used two years running. All the nests are on the ground and formed of heather sprigs and small sticks. As far as the choice of site is concerned, we have noticed that Montagu's Harrier prefers areas of tall heather and broom within which it chooses a small spot with shorter vegetation to lay its eggs. In 1990 we collected data concerning distribution of vegetation, height and cover around the nests (Fig. 1).

Figure 1. Distribution of vegetation heigh around the nests.

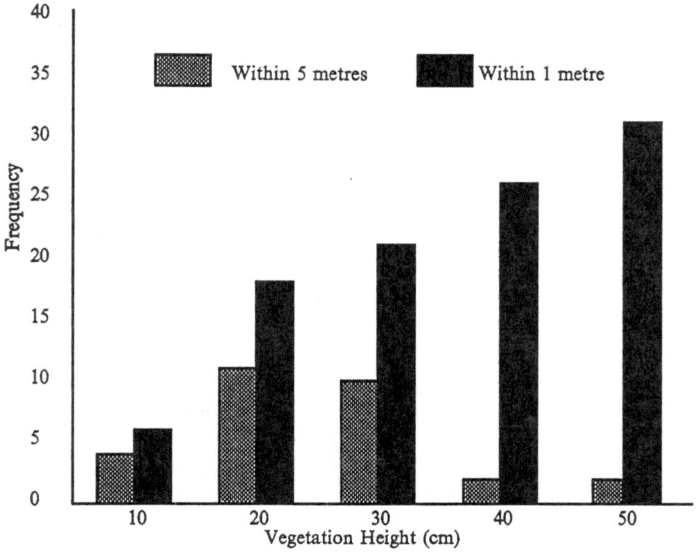

We also noted the height of nest above sea level, number of eggs laid and hatched, number of young and fledged nestlings. Table 1 shows the results concerning the breeding rate of Montagu's Harrier pairs during the period of the observations.

Table 1. Breeding rate of Montagu's Harrier in the Northern Apennines, 1986-1990.

Year	No. of eggs laid	No. of chicks	No. of young fledged	No. of nests
1986	3.25	2.75	1.50	5
1987	3.50	2.83	1.83	6
1988	3.16	1.83	1.16	6
1989	3.43	2.40	1.40	7
1990	3.28	2.00	1.16	7
Average	3.32	2.36	1.41	Total 31

Territory occupation takes place in the second half of April; the males are the first to arrive and start defending their territory, especially from Buzzard *Buteo buteo*, Sparrowhawk *Accipiter nisus* and Carrion Crow *Corvus corone cornix*. The females come to the breeding area some 10-15 days later.

Consequently, in this area nest occupation and incubation take place quite late compared with pairs breeding in plain and cultivated areas (Arcà & Sammuri 1983; Martelli & Sandri 1991); this is very similar to what Pandolfi & Pino d'Astore (1990) found in a pre-Apennine area in Marche region. At this stage in the breeding cycle, we have noticed a strong aerial courtship activity.

In this area we have found nests between 750 and 1,020 m above sea level, generally built along partially eroded slopes: this is the highest among those checked in Italy (Martelli 1987; Martelli & Sandri 1991; Brichetti *et al.* 1992) and one of the highest in the species' total range (Dementiev & Gladkov 1951; Chiscano & Fernandez Cruz 1971; Rufino *et al.* 1985). The top part of this area, covered with smooth turf, exploited as pastureland or completely abandoned, suffers from frequent human disturbance of many kinds (excursions, motorcycle sports and other activities).

Usually, although we do not have extremely precise data, it seems that nests are not built in particularly sloping areas (not more than 20-30%), as verified by Martelli & Sandri (1991). As mentioned above, the chosen areas are covered with dense shrub and high vegetation (even up to 200 cm).

Egg-laying usually takes place in May and can vary according to the year and weather conditions (in some years the first half of May and some years the second). We have also noted the number of eggs laid and hatched. We have observed predation by Fox *Vulpes vulpes* in one case and Carrion Crow in two cases at least. We have noticed a certain delay in egg-laying and a number of eggs have been smaller than in other parts of Italy and Europe (Schipper 1978; Martelli 1984; Pandolfi & Giacchini 1991; Martelli & Sandri 1991). As far as breeding success is concerned, we have observed that only a few pairs and in some particular years have fledged more than one chick. In fact, in most cases only one chick has been able to fledge; this may depend on the degree of prey abundance. We have also several data about hunting and prey. Montagu's Harrier is a good subject for this type of work as it hunts low over open habitat and is easy to observe for relatively long periods (Schipper 1977). We also collected prey remains from certain nests.

According to our observations, in this area the main prey seem to be Field-mouse *Apodemus sylvaticus*. Among birds Skylark *Alauda arvensis*, Corn Bunting *Miliaria calandra* and Cirl Bunting *Emberiza cirlus* and chicks of Pheasant *Phasianus colchicus* are quite frequent, together with some large coleoptera and orthoptera, and Green Lizard *Lacerta viridis* among reptiles.

The vegetation structure may influence prey capture. We observed that in dense and high vegetation Montagu's Harrier hunts especially birds, while in low and open vegetation it hunts mammals and reptiles.

Table 2. Prey remains at two nests (sites B and C) in 1990.

	Number	%		
Mammals	18	38.3		
Birds	15	31.9		
Reptiles	5	10.6		
Insects	9	19.1		
Birds			Mammals	
Alauda arvensis		4	*Apodemus sylvaticus*	15
Phasianus colchicus		4	*Arvicola terrestris*	2
Miliaria calandra		2	*Sorex* spp.	1
Emberiza cirlus		2		
Unidentified		3		
Reptiles			Insects	
Lacerta viridis	4		Orthopera	3
Natrix natrix	1		Coleoptera	3
			Unidentified	3

CONSERVATION

At first we preferred not to spread information on the exact location of this species' nest sites. Then, because of increasing human activity such as tourism, cross-country motorcycling and trekking, together with fires, we decided to inform the public bodies in charge of fauna management.

Consequently, after LIPU action, such sites are now part of more widely protected areas and, with the exception of projects for the reafforestation of some territories, we can say that the Montagu's Harrier population in this area is stable or maybe even increasing.

Summing up, this area differs from the other bordering regions such as Emilia Romagna, Marche and Tuscany, where the protection of Montagu's Harrier nests in cultivated fields may conflict with agricultural interests and involves unskilled people who may spread information on the location of breeding sites (Pandolfi & Giacchini 1991).

ACKNOWLEDGEMENTS

I am very grateful to Loretta Lapini and Guido Tellini for their encouragement and advice on the present work, and to Roberto Bertozzi and Stefano Carresi for field work.

I am very grateful to Marco Lambertini for useful comments and suggestions, to Marco Gustin for his help on references and to Barbara Lombatti for her translation and assistance.

REFERENCES

ARCA', G. 1991. La conservazione dell'Albanella minore (*Circus pygargus*) nelle aree agricole della Maremma tosco-laziale. *In* SROPU (ed.) Atti V Conv. Ital. Ornit., *Ricerche di Biologia della Selvaggina.* Vol. XVII: 287-291.

ARCA', G. & G. SAMMURI 1983. Biologia riproduttiva dell'Albanella minore *Circus pygargus* nella Maremma tosco-laziale, dati preliminari. Atti II Conv. Ital. Ornit. (in press).

BRICHETTI, P., P. DE FRANCESCHI & N. BACCETTI (eds.) 1992. *Fauna d'Italia.* Aves I. Gaviidae-Phasianidae. calderini, Bologna.

BUSCHE, G. 1990. Brutvorkommen der Wiesenweine *Circus pygargus* in Schleswig-Holstein 1981-88. *Corax* 13: 326-331.

CHIAVETTA, M. 1981. *I rapaci d' Italia e d'Europa.* Rizzoli, Milano.

CHISCANO, J.L.P. & M. FERNANDEZ CRUZ 1971. Sobre *Grus grus* y *Circus pygargus* en Extremadura. *Ardeola*, vol. esp.: 509-574.

DEMENTIEV, G.P. & N.A. GLADKOV 1951. (Birds of the Soviet Union).

MARTELLI, D. 1984. L'Albanella minore nell'Appennino bolognese. Grafos, Bologna.

MARTELLI, D. 1987. Dati sull'ecologia dell'Albanella minore (*Circus pygargus*) in Emilia-Romagna. Nota preliminare. *In* N.Baccetti & M. Spagnesi (eds.). *Rapaci Mediterranei III, Ricerche di Biologia della Selvaggina.* Vol.XII : 125-137

MARTELLI, D. & V. SANDRI 1991. Status ed ecologia dell' Albanella minore (*Circus pygargus*) in Emilia Romagna. Analisi conclusiva. In SROPU (ed.) *Atti V Conv. Ital. Ornit., Ricerche di Biologia della Selvaggina.* Vol.XVII: 49-52.

PANDOLFI, M. & P. GIACCHINI 1991. Censimento e successo riproduttivo dell'Albanella minore (*Circus pygargus*) nella fascia pedeappenninica adriatica. Indicazioni per la gestione. *In* M. Spagnesi & S. Toso(eds.). *Atti I I Conv. Naz. Biol. Selvag., Ricerche di biologia Selvaggina.* Vol XIX: 125-134.

PANDOLFI, M. & P.R PINO D'ASTORE 1990. Analysis of breeding behaviour in Montagu's Harrier *Circus pygargus* in a site of Central Italy. *Avocetta* 14: 97-102.

RUFINO, R., A. ARAUJO & M.V. ABREU 1985. Breeding raptors in Portugal: distribution and population estimates. *In* I. Newton & R.D. Chancellor (eds.). *Conservation Studies of Raptors*, ICBP Tech. Publ. 5: 15-28.

SCHIPPER, W.J.A. 1977. Hunting in three European Harriers (*Circus*) during the breeding season. *Ardea* 65: 53-72

SCHIPPER, W.J.A. 1978. A Comparison in breeding ecology in three european harriers *Circus*. *Ardea* 66: 77-102.

ZIJLSTRA, M. & F. HUSTINGS 1992. Teloorgang van de Grauwe Kiekendief *Circus pygargus* als broedvogel in Nederland. *Limosa* 65: 7-18.

Ugo Faralli
LIPU
Nature Conservation Dept.
Vicolo S. Tiburzio 5,
Parma, Italy.

Great Horned Owl *Bubo virginianus* - male & female

Meyburg, B.-U. & R. D. Chancellor eds.1994
Raptor Conservation Today
WWGBP / The Pica Press

The Influence of Tourism on Marsh Harriers *Circus aeruginosus* in the Neusiedlersee-Seewinkel National Park, Austria

Anita Gamauf

ABSTRACT

The impact of human disturbance on Marsh Harriers in the Neusiedlersee-Seewinkel National Park was investigated between March and August 1991. Although the harriers breed mainly in the reed zones undisturbed by humans, problems arise because intensively frequented tourist routes (80% cyclists) lead through the feeding grounds.

Cyclists and pedestrians create a negative factor, especially during the time of highest intake of food by the young, when their presence influences the pattern of hunting time and place. An increase in tourist numbers on particular routes means that the harriers cannot use these areas, including a distance along either side ("avoidance belt"). The more such routes are opened up, the less accessible the regular hunting grounds will become.

INTRODUCTION

In Austria the Marsh Harrier breeds in only a few places (Gamauf 1991) and therefore is included in the Red List (Bauer 1989) as a "potentially endangered" species. The centre of dissemination is the extended area of the planned Neusiedlersee-Seewinkel National Park, which at the same time accommodates one of the largest concentrations of this species in Central Europe (Sezemsky & Ripfel 1985). Disturbances can therefore have a negative impact on the population, also beyond the borders of Austria.

Disturbances in spatial and temporal use of a bird's habitat can locally be the result of mass tourism. Whilst the large reedbeds used as hunting and breeding habitats are disrupted only peripherally, territories further inland are locally exposed to permanent disturbance by humans. Large areas of the Marsh Harrier's habitat in the national park are subjected to the pressure of a fast-rising stream of visitors. Between March and August the number of overnight stays by tourists in the region increases by thirty times, from 8,000 to 238,000, corresponding to the holiday season, especially during June and July, coincident with the harrier's sensitive reproduction cycle (Fig. 1).

Within the scope of a project commissioned by the Neusiedlersee Working Team (AGN), the possible effects of the leisure industry on Marsh Harriers were investigated (Gamauf, in press), in particular the following questions: -

- How do Marsh Harriers react to the presence of human beings ?
- Does tourism influence the space-time system of the harriers?

Figure 1. Breeding cycle of the Marsh Harrier in relation to tourism frequency in the area of the national park Neusiedlersee Seewinkel (for instance "Zitzmannsdorfer Wiesen").

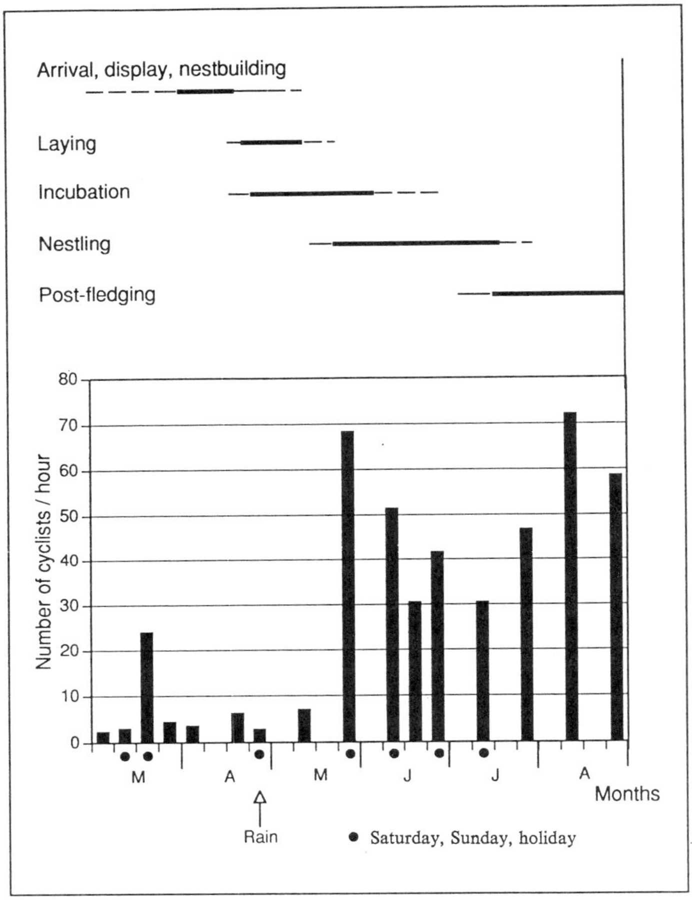

STUDY AREA

The study area, totalling over 70km², lies along the eastern shore of the Neusiedlersee lake and the bordering Seewinkel (Fig. 2). The extended area of the national park is one of the major wetlands of Central Europe. Situated at the western edge of the Little Hungarian Lowland (120m a.s.l.) and at the eastern limit of the Alps, it is notable for its richness of species. It is located only 60km from Vienna with its 1.7 million inhabitants. The resulting stream of visitors creates a series of problems for nature conservation. Swimming and boating activities along the edge of the reedbelt play their part; however, the cyclists (80%) and pedestrians in the reedless areas are the main disturbance factors.

Characteristic for the study areas in the national park are the lake, skirted with its (32%) reed belt of varying width, and the pools. Former pasture land is to-day intensively cultivated as arable land (23%), vineyards (14%) and grassland (31%). Meadows for hay and cattle grazing are predominantly confined to the nature reserve. Conditional on the land use, an extensive network of tracks and paths runs through the research area, and these are widely frequented by tourists. Climatically this region is one of the driest and hottest in Austria, with a rainfall of approximately 600mm per annum and an average annual temperature of 10°C.

Figure 2. Study areas in the national park Neusiedlersee Seewinkel, Austria.

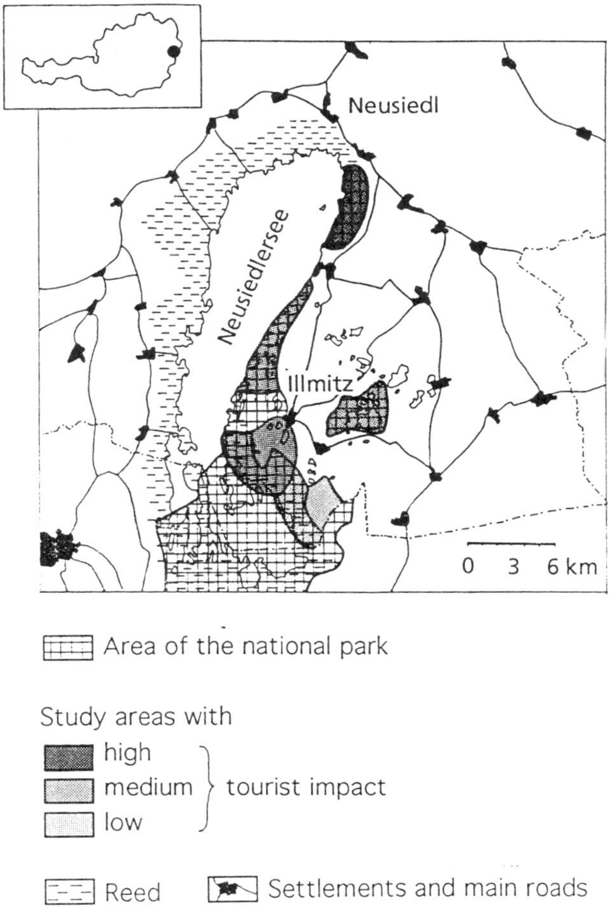

MATERIAL AND METHODS

Investigations were carried out in five sections (See Fig. 2) variously influenced by tourist activities between mid-March and the end of August 1991. At least 61 Marsh Harrier nest sites were known in this area. The non-breeding population was not assessed.

Surveys were conducted in each section regarding the hunting behaviour (e.g. routes taken, habitat use) and the harriers' reaction to humans (e.g. avoidance behaviour, escape distances). The distribution of the birds within the sections, their distances from the paths as well as their habitat use and chosen flying routes were recorded *inter alia*. The number of tourists and the harriers' reaction to them were considered by analogy.

During observation days investigations began before sunrise and ended after sunset. In each section continuous observations for a minimum of six hours were carried out. Particular emphasis was laid on the comparability of data from before the main tourist season (up to mid-May) and from the peak tourist season (mid-May onwards, especially the end of June). Interpreting the results, the behaviour of the Marsh Harriers during the different phases of the breeding cycle was also considered; in all sections, for example, the continually retrograde use of the reed areas during the phases of reproduction (provided they were in the vicinity of roads) was not due to anthropogenic disturbances. For comparison of the results Wilcoxon, Man & Whitney U-test and t-tests were conducted.

RESULTS AND DISCUSSION

Cyclists and pedestrians clearly constitute a disturbance factor as regards escape distances, avoidance behaviour and habitat use by Marsh Harriers. "Disturbance" is defined as an effect factor negatively influencing the birds' behaviour (e.g. escape to other, in part less optimal, habitats, the choice of different hunting routes and the avoidance of certain regions).

1. Avoidance behaviour. (Fig.3)

- Single persons are usually overflown at low heights (8-10m).
- Larger groups of people at greater heights ($\bar{x}$ =35m, n = 64) and with an arching line of flight.
- In the absence of humans, on the other hand, or in undisturbed areas, the harriers fly close to the ground when hunting ($\bar{x}$ = 4m, n =345, $p < 0.0011$).

2. Escape distance.

- The increasing number of visitors results in rising escape distance.
- In areas covered by vegetation and along foot-paths lined with trees and hedges, the escape distances are less ($\bar{x}$ = 50m, n = 61) than in open landscapes (with an average of 90m, n = 178, $p < 0.05$).

3. Distances of harriers from more and less highly frequented tourist routes. (Fig.4)

A. Before main tourist season (up to mid-May):

- On weekdays and during weekends with bad weather (= few visitors), a strip of land 200m wide along the tracks (often more diversified in structure than the surrounding, possibly richer in food) is favoured by the harriers (n = 167). During this period, the paths are used by only 0-5 persons/hour (8 at a maximum).
- During sunny weekends (= many visitors) a corridor of *ca.* 100m width is avoided along the tourist paths (n = 124, $p < 0.05$). Only in early morning, so long as no human disturbances occur, is this area accessible to hunting Marsh Harriers.

B. Main tourist season (mid-May onwards):
Especially from the end of June (start of holiday season), on weekdays as well as at weekends, a corridor approximately 240m wide is avoided (n = 906). During this period some paths are frequented by 50-80 visitors/hour, mostly cyclists. On peak days more than 470 persons/hour may be counted. The network of routes opened up for tourists reduces the habitat available to the harriers; thus 40% of the Zitzmannsdorfer Wiesen are inaccessible to this raptor during the later breeding period, when the young require the maximum amount of food. The birds are accordingly forced to extend and change their feeding range into less optimal habitats.

The results demonstrate the adverse effects of tourism on an endangered species. Only a wider study may confirm whether this causes a genuine loss of fitness, e.g. in the form of reduced breeding success and/or a reduced reproduction rate. For the present study, such data are unfortunately not available because the weather was cold and wet during the breeding period and the cause of many brood failures. Only 27 (44.3%) out of 61 controlled breeding attempts were successful, with only 0.9 fledged young/pair (2.1 young/successful pair). Thus the reproduction rate was lower than that reported from other areas of Europe, where the proportion of successful broods usually ranges between 60% and 80%, whilst the reproduction ranges between 1.6 and 2.8 fledged young/pair (*cf.* Bavoux *et al.* 1989; Bock 1979; Höser *et al* 1979; Missbach 1972; Schipper 1979; Underhill-Day 1984; Witkowski 1989).

Investigations dealing with other bird and mammal species (e.g. Berger 1992; Cederna & Lovarni 1985; Gossow 1992; Ingold 1992; Jenny 1992; Stock 1991; Zehnter & Abs in press) show that increasing recreational activities can play a negative role for wildlife. In spite of this, it is neither necessary nor realistic to ban visitors from nature reserves, since animals can usually adapt to certain tourist routes without unduly detrimental effects.

A clear concept for the guidance of visitors to the national park is needed in order to reduce the conflict between the aims of nature conservation and tourist trade politics.

Figure 3. Behaviour of Marsh Harriers crossing (a) less and (b) frequented tourist ways.

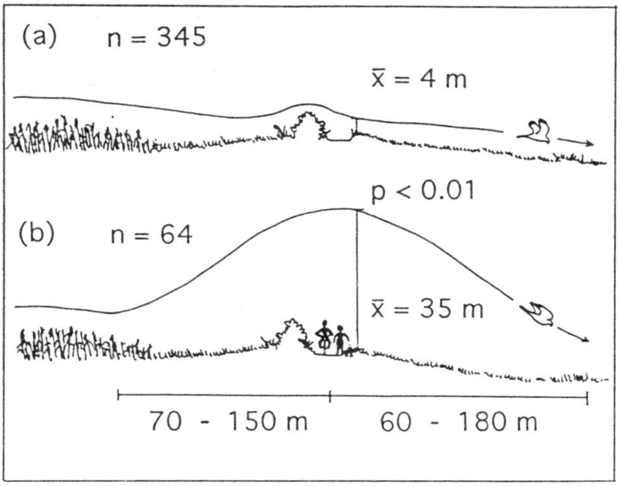

Figure 4. Comparison of Marsh Harrier hunting routes in the vicinity of (a) intense and (b) low frequented ways before and during tourist season.

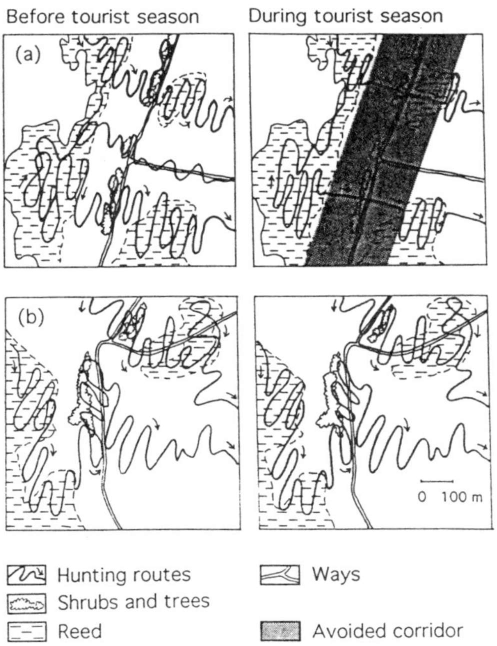

Recommendations for reducing the impact of tourists in sensitive sections of the Neusiedlersee-Seewinkel National Park:

- Tourist routes should not lead through ecologically important areas.
- The opening up of paths and tracks for mass tourism should not be planned for ecologically sensitive areas.
- If necessary, restrictions should be imposed on heavily frequented routes during the breeding season of rare species (at least from the beginning of April to mid-July).
- Ecologically justifiable tourist routes must be controlled, in order to ensure that visitors stay on the paths.

ACKNOWLEDGEMENTS

For critical examinations I wish to thank R.D. Chancellor, H. Gossow, C. Leditznig, R. Parz-Gollner and M. Preleuthner. This study, as part of an interdisciplinary research project of the Arbeitsgemeinschaft Neusiedlersee (AGN) was supported financially by the Government of Burgenland, the Ministry for Science and Research and the Ministry for Environment, Youth and Family.

REFERENCES

BAUER, K. 1989. *Rote Listen der gefährdeten Vögel und Säugetiere Österreichs.* Österr. Ges. f. Vogelkunde. Wien.

BAVOUX, CH., G. BURNELEAU, A. LEROUX & P. NICOLAU-GUILLAUMET 1989. Le Busard des roseaux *Circus a. aeruginosus* en Charente-Maritime (France). *Alauda* 57, 247-262.

BERGER, V. 1992. Herzfrequenzänderungen brütender Waldohreulen (*Asio otus*) auf Grund menschlicher Störungen. *Egretta* 35, 73-79.

BOCK, W. F. 1979. Zur Situation der Rohrweihe (*Circus aeruginosus*) in Schleswig-Holstein. *J. Orn.* 120, 416-430.

CEDERNA, A. & S. LOVARI 1985. The impact of Tourism on Chamois Feeding Activities in an Area of the Abruzzo National Park, Italy. *In*: S. Lovari (Ed.) *The Biology and Management of Mountain Ungulates*, 216-225. Croom Helm, London.

GAMAUF, A. 1991. *Greifvögel in Österreich, Bestand - Bedrohung - Gesetz.* Umweltbundesamt, Wien, pp.131.

GAMNAUF, A. (in press). Einfl-sse der Landwirtschafft und des Tourismus auf das Raum-Zeit-System von Rohrweihen (*Circus aeruginosus*) im Bereich des Nationalparks Neusiedlersee-Seewinkel. BfB-Bericht.

GOSSOW, H. 1992. Alpiner Gelände- und Abenteurersport: Wirkungsnachweis auf Wildtiere ? *In*: W. Pillmann & S. Predl (Eds.) *Strategies for Reducing Environmental Impact of Tourism.* Envirotour Vienna, Nov. 10-12, 1992, 689-704.

HÖSER, N., R. BACHMANN, W. KIRCHHOF & A. WEBER 1979. Der Brutbestand der Greifvögel und Eulen im Altenburger Gebiet. 5. Bericht. *Abh. u. Ber. Naturkundl. Mus. "Mauritanum" Altenburg* 10, 269-277.

INGOLD, P. 1992. Tourismus und Freizeitsport - ein gravierendes Problem für das Wild ? *In*: W. Pillman & S. Predl (Eds.) *Strategies for Reducing Environmental Impact of Tourism.* Envirotour Vienna, Nov. 10-12, 1992, 382-386.

JENNY, D. 1992. Bruterfolg und Bestandsregulation einer alpinen Population des Steinadlers *Aquila chrysaetos*. *Orn. Beob.* 89, 1-43.

MISSBACH, D. 1972. Die Brutplätze der Rohrweihe *Circus aeruginosus* L. im Bezirk Magdeburg. *Apus* 2, 232-245.

SCHIPPER, W. J. A. 1979. A comparison of breeding ecology in three European harriers (*Circus*). *Ardea* 66, 77-102.

SEZEMSKY, R. & J. RIPFEL 1985. Zur Siedlungsdichte der Rohrweihe im Schilfgürtel des Neusiedler Sees. *AGN-Forschungsbericht 1981-1984*, 455-466.

STOCK, M. 1991. Studies on the effects of disturbances on staging Brent Geese: a progress report. *IWRB Goose Res. Group Bull.* 1, 11-18.

UNDERHILL-DAY, J.C. 1984. Population and breeding biology of Marsh Harriers in Britain since 1900. *J. Appl. Ecology* 21, 773-787.

WITKOWSKI, J. 1989. Breeding biology and ecology of the Marsh Harrier *Circus aeruginosus* in the Barycz valley, Poland. *Acta orn.* 25, 223-320.

ZEHNTER, H.C. & M. ABS (in press). Wirken Radfahrer und Fußgänger als Zeitgeber und/oder Störer des diurnen Aktivitätsrhytmusses -berwinternder Reiherenten (*Aythya fuligula*) ? *Dt. zool. Ges.* 84.

Anita Gamauf
Institut für Wildbiologie und Jagdwirtschaft
Peter-Jordan-Strasse 76, Iniversität für Bodenkultur,
1190 Wien, Austria

Meyburg, B.-U. & R. D. Chancellor eds.1994
Raptor Conservation Today
WWGBP / The Pica Press

The Sooty Falcon *Falco concolor* in Saudi Arabia

P. Gaucher, W. D. Daunicht and X. Eichacher

INTRODUCTION

The Sooty Falcon *Falco concolor* shares with the Eleonora's Falcon *Falco eleonorae* the peculiarity of breeding in late summer. This delayed breeding season allows the parents to feed their chicks on the Palearctic migrant birds (Cramp & Simmons 1980). The Red Sea and Arabian Gulf coasts probably form the nucleus of the world Sooty breeding population. The breeding biology of this species has been studied in the Libyan desert (Booth 1961), in Israel (Frumkin 1984, 1986, 1991; Frumkin & Pinshow 1983), in Oman (Walter 1979), in the south (Clapham 1964; von Heuglin 1859) and north (Baha el Din 1984) west coast of the Red Sea. The results presented here deal with a population inhabiting the east coast of the Red Sea in Saudi Arabia.

MATERIAL AND METHODS

An aerial survey was carried out during the breeding season (August) between Jeddah and Jizan along the Red Sea coast. To estimate the breeding populations we flew over all the small islands at altitude of 100m in order to check if they were occupied.

The data presented have been collected between 1st of July to 15th of November during three consecutive years (from 1989 to 1991). The islets were visited three times per month. During these visits, the status of all nests were recorded and the remains of prey were collected. The chicks and in six adult breeding birds were ringed. The adult birds were caught close to the nest with snares or small nets, they were then marked with metallic rings and colored plastic rings such as to identify them without recapturing them. Another means of identification in flight was to cut one primary and to replace it with white pigeon feather, following a standard practice in falconry.

STUDY AREA

From the aerial survey, we identified two main areas where the Sooty Falcons were breeding in significant numbers on islets off the Saudi Red Sea coast, south of Jeddah. The densest population was on three islets north of Al Lith (20°17N-40°05'E) where we recorded the observations presented here. These islets are located approximately 500 to 3000m off shore.

The shore of the islets north of Al Lith is surrounded by mangrove trees and dense bushes of *Salicornia*. The area where *Salicornia* are growing rarely floods. The central part of the islets is baren (Gaucher *et al* 1988).

An other important population is situated on the Farasan Islands (16°70N-42°00'E).

DATE OF ARRIVAL AND DEPARTURE

The earliest observation of birds arriving from their wintering ground situated in southeast Africa and Madagascar was the 30th March 1990. The departure from the breeding islands occurred from the beginning of November and by 5th of November only few individuals remained.

NEST SITE AND NESTING DENSITY

The nests are either located under mangrove trees and/or *Salicornia* bushes providing shade to the incubating bird, as the air temperature averages 38 °C in July August (Siraj, 1984). The same nest sites are used each year. Observations of our ringed adult birds seem to indicate that nesting sites are re-used by the same birds.

Nesting density is directly correlated to the length of a rarely flooded upper narrow band of the vegetation surrounding the islets. The mean distance between nests on the three islands was not significantly different, ranging from 28.5m to 20.7m with the maximum and minimum distances of 65m and 7m respectively. These inter-nests distances presented have been measured in 1989 and 1990 which were regarded as good breeding years (see below),

LAYING DATE, HATCHING DATE AND FLEDGING PERIOD

The date of lying showed a degree of synchronization; 90% of the clutches in 1989-90 were initiated between the 10th and 31st of July and 10% were laid between 1st and the 10th August. The incubation period is 27-29 days (Frumkin, 1991) so the hatching period for 90% of the clutches must have been between 15th and 31st of August and from 31st of August to 10th of September for the remainder. The chicks fledge on average 35 days after hatching, so they left the nest between 19th September and 15 October.

In 1991 the results were quite different since only 15% of the detected clutches were laid during the last two weeks of July, whereas 85% of clutches were laid between 5th and 20th of August. Hatching occurred between the 3rd and the 17th of September. Fledging was recorded up to the second and third week of October.

CLUTCH SIZE AND BREEDING SUCCESS

The clutch size ranges from one to three eggs per nest.

The number of eggs per nest was not significantly different between 1989 and 1990, but is significantly different between 1989 and 1991, 1990 and 1991 (Mann-Whitney test; $t = -2.98$, $p = 0.0047$; $t = -2.8$, $p = 0.0072$).

Table 1: Clutch size of the Sooty Falcon on the islets of Al Lith.

Year	Number of nests with 1 egg	2 eggs	3 eggs	Mean
1989	1	11	14	2.5
1990	4	12	17	2.39
1991	2	16	4	2.09
Total	7	39	35	2.34

Table 2: Results of the breeding season during three consecutive years in Al Lith.

	1989	1990	1991
Number of nests	26	33	22
Number of eggs	65	79	46
Number of eggs/nests	2.53	2.39	2.09
Number of fledglings	59	70	37
Number of fledglings/nests	2.26	2.12	1.68
Breeding success [%] Number of fledglings/Number of eggs	90.7	88.6	80.9
Failures: Dead ckicks	3	1	1
Clear eggs or dead embryos	64	68	68

The number of fledglings per egg laid is not significantly different between the three years. The breeding failures, which are less than 20 %, concerned five chicks of which four died from disease (Trichomoniasis) and one disappeared and twenty unhatched eggs, either infertile or with dead embryo.

HUNTING BEHAVIOUR

Most of the prey are sighted by the Sooty falcons stalking from the top of the mangrove trees. As the continental beach area is without vegetation for several square kilometers around, the trees and shrubs on the islands are a powerful attraction to the migrant birds. The open area across the sea between the sea shore and islands provides a vulnerability which is fully exploited by the falcons. The efficiency of the falcons seems greatly improved by hunting in groups comprising two to five individuals chasing the same prey. The prey can avoid one or two attacks but it is usually caught at the third attempt. Some passerines prefer to sink in the sea rather than to be caught.

DIET OF THE SOOTY FALCON

In Saudi Arabia, outside the breeding season (between April and June), the Sooty Falcons prey mainly on insects such as locusts, crickets and dragonflies but their diet also includes a small number of passerine birds.

During the breeding season preys are almost exclusively small birds, 98% of which are migrants (see Appendix). We have also recorded a rodent and a crab being taken (Gaucher *et al* 1988). Remains collected between 1989 and 1991, have been identified corresponding to a minimum total of 630 different birds. The most common prey was the Marsh Warbler *Acrocephalus palustris* representing 25.6% of all prey. It was followed by the Whitethroat *Sylvia communis* (7.9%), Rufous Bush Robin *Cercotrichas galactotes* (5.7%), Red-backed Shrike *Lanius collurio* (5.2%) and Isabelline Wheatear *Oenanthe isabellina* (5.1%). Part of these identified preys are complete birds either not eaten or lost in the bushes, possibly during the passing of prey from the male to the female.

Figure 1: Prey of Sooty Falcon in Saudi Arabia (1989-1991).

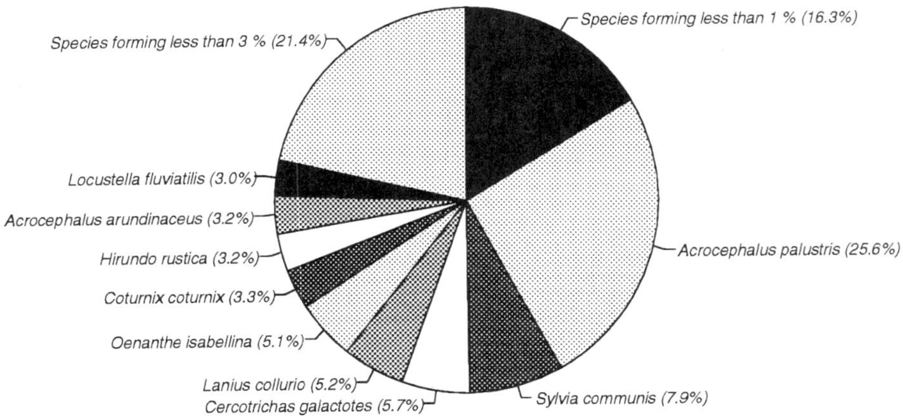

DISCUSSION

Whereas in our study area and in Israel (Frumkin 1991), most of the Falcons departed between 1st and 5th of November, on the islands situated mid distance between Al Lith and the Negev Desert, in the south of Egypt (24°39'N-35°10'E), seventy Sooty Falcons in family groups were still present on 12th and 13th of November (Baha El Din 1984). Stagg (1984) reported also that Sooty Falcons were present on Kutambil island (17°53'N-41°42'E) on south Saudi Red Sea coast between January and July.

The hunting technique we have observed was already described by Walter (1979) and Clapham (1964), but the Sooties in Oman had a greater tendency to stalk by gliding above the islands rather than perching. The former author also noticed that the falcons hunting in group were more efficient whereas Clapham (1964) reported the opposite.

In Walter's study (1979), out of 322 different identified birds, the main prey was the Red-necked Phalarope *Phalaropus lobatus* which represents 25.2% of the total remains of birds, followed by Rufous Bush Chat *Cercotrichas galactotes* (16.5%), Spotted Flycatcher *Muscicapa striata* (12.1%), Common White throat *Sylvia communis* (10.2%), Wilson's Storm Petrel *Oceanites oceaninus* (6.5%), Red-backed Shrike *Lanius collurio* (6.2%).

In Clapham's study (1964) the most common prey was Blue-cheeked Bee-eater *Merops superciliosus* followed by European Bee-eater *M. apiaster,* Hoopoe *Upupa epops* and Golden Oriole *Oriolus oriolus.*

Baha El Din (1984), besides migrant passerine Birds like *Oenanthe sp.*, Bluethroat *Luscinia svecica*, Redstart *Phoenicurus phoenicurus*, *Sylvia sp*, and *Phylloscopus sp.*, reported much larger preys such as Green-backed Heron *Butorides striatus*, Black-headed Gull *Larus ridibundus* and even White-eyed Gull *Larus leucophtalmus*. This last species, bigger than the Sooty, seems unrealistic as a prey.

In the Negev Desert, the majority of identified preys is also migrant birds but mainly aerial feeder birds such as Swallow *Hirundo rustica*, Swift *Apus apus* and European Bee-eater *Merops*

Figure 2: Prey of Sooty Falcon in Oman (Walter, 1979).

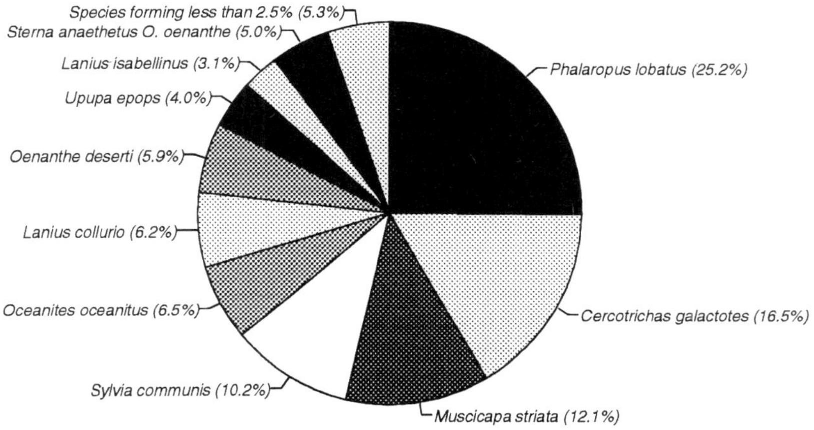

apiaster (Frumkin 1991).

The data gathered on the breeding biology of Sooty Falcon in Saudi Arabia are comparable to the observations reported from similar habitats (Clapham 1964; Walter 1979) but different of those reported from desert habitat (Frumkin 1991)

Table 3: Clutch size of the Sooty Falcon in the different parts of its breeding range.

Study Areas	Number of Nests with 1 egg	2 eggs	3 eggs	4 eggs	Mean	Source
Negev Desert		2	7		2.78	Frumkin, 1991
Libyan Desert			1			Booth, 1961
Oman	1	8	14	1	2.62	Walter, 1979
West Red Sea	2		4	1	2.57	Clapham, 1964
East Red Sea	7	39	35		2.35	This study & Gaucher *et al.*,1988

Because these data have been collected at different years and from different populations, it is no possible to compare them statistically. However, it seems that the birds nesting in the desert (Frumkin 1991) have slightly larger clutches than the birds nesting on the islands.

The average clutch we recorded, was smaller than the average clutches reported from other populations breeding in the similar habitat: Islands in Gulf of Oman (Walter 1979) and Dahlak Archipelago in the Red Sea (Clampham 1964). The reason for this is that our results have been calculated from three years data, including one year with significantly lower production of eggs (see above). The average number of eggs per clutch in our study area during the two years without severe climatic circumstances is 2.52, a number which matches more closely with those of obtained by Clapham (1964) and Walter (1979).

The differences of breeding performances noticed between the two first and the third year could be related to adverse climatic conditions i.e. very strong storms that occurred in July or August 1991 and flooded partially the islets, when the Sooties started laying. Unfortunately, no precise weather data are available. The usual hatching dates were recorded from nests above the flood line, the late clutches could be the replacement clutches.

The breeding success (number of fledging on the number of eggs) with an average of 87.4% can be considered as very high for a raptor (Newton 1979). In Oman, Walter (1979) reported a similar breeding success of 87.1% as fifty-four chicks fledged out of sixty-two eggs. In Israel, (Frumkin 1991) although the observed mean clutch size is the highest of the other study areas (see Table 1), the number of fledglings is the lowest with only two fledglings per nest. The breeding success calculated from a sample (Frumkin & Pinshow 1983) is 62.5% with only five chicks fledging from eight eggs.

The very high breeding success and the relatively high nest density suggests that prey availability is not a limiting factor for the Sooty populations nesting on the islands (Clapham 1964; Walter 1979). In our case, this is supported by the fact that many preys are caught and not eaten and also by the fact that we never found starving chicks, usually observed when preys are lacking (Newton 1979) (see Table 2).

In our study area, the high prey availability is probably related to the islets location on a point where the Asir mountains near to the Red Sea funnelling the flow of migrant birds on the seashore. This hypothesis is supported by the fact that similar islands situated south of the study area do not harbor any important breeding colony.

At this natural funnel, the barrenness of the local environment and the high summer temperatures make the vegetated islands very attractive to paleartic migrant birds. Part of these migrants are very vulnerable and become easy prey when they attempt to cross the sea to reach the vegetated cover of the islets.

A ground survey indicated that such high nest density is encountered only on the islets situated less than 5 km from the shoreline probably because the further islands do not attract so many migrants and so can sustain a lesser number of breeding pairs.

Data from our three years observations suggest that only severe climatic incidents linked with local sea level variations could have a significant influence on the breeding results of the Sooty Falcon.

ACKNOWLEDGEMENTS

We would like to thank His Highness Prince Saud Al Faisal, Managing Director of the National Commission for Wildlife Conservation and Development for his interest and support. We express our gratitude to Dr. A. Abuzinada, Secretary General of National Commission for Wildlife Conservation and Development for his assistance. We extend our thanks to J. Renaud and Dr H. Schulz for their encouragement. A. Khoja, Administrative Director of the National Wildlife Research Center and M. Shobrak have always contributed enthusiastically to this project. Thanks also to the Flight Operation staff especially M. Hinshaw and H. Hemmigsen. Special words of appreciation are due to the following persons who spent time with us on the field,: O. Bouqueau, Dr. S. Chardonnet, Dr. A Greth, B. Pambour, A. Vareille and C. Wilme. We wish to thank also P. McCormick, Dr. P. Seddon, Dr. Y. Van Heezik, Dr S. Newton, Dr S. Ostrovski and also Dr Biquand for corrections and the comments of the manuscript.

REFERENCES

BAHA EL DIN, S. 1984. Notes on the breeding of the Sooty Falcon *Falco concolor* on the islands in the Red Sea, and their prey. *OSME Bull.* 12: 2-3.

BOOTH, B. D. MCD. 1961. Breeding of the Sooty Falcon in the Libyan Desert. *Ibis* 103a: 129-130.
CLANCEY, P.A. 1968.*Falco concolor* in South Africa. *Bull Brit. Ornith. Club* 89: 10-11.
CLAPHAM, C.S. 1964. The bird of Dahlac archipelago. *Ibis* 106: 376-386.
CRAMP, S. & K.E. L. SIMMONS 1980. The birds of the Western Paleartic. Vol. II. Oxford University Press. Oxforc.
FRUMKIN, R. 1984. The Sooty Falcon in Israel. *Israel Land and Nature* 9:138-143.
FRUMKIN, R. 1986. The status of the breeding raptors in Israeli deserts. *Sandgrouse* 8:42-57.
FRUMKIN, R. 1991. Breeding ecology of the Sooty Falcon in Israel. (In press).
FRUMKIN, R. & B. PINSHOW 1983. Notes on the breeding ecology and distribution of the Sooty Falcon *Falco concolor* in Israel. *Ibis* 125: 251-259.
GAUCHER, P., T. PETIT & P. SYMENS 1988. Notes on the breeding of the Sooty Falcon *Falco concolor* in Saudi Arabia. *Alauda* 56(3): 277-283.
HEUGLIN, T. VON 1859. List of birds observed and collected during a voyage in the Red Sea. *Ibis* 1: 337-352.
MOREAU, R.E. 1969. The Sooty Falcon *Falco concolor* Temminck. *Bull. Brit. Ornithol. Club* 89: 62-67.
NEWTON, I. 1979. Population ecology of raptors. Berkhamsted: T. & A.D. Poyser.
SIRAJ, A. 1984. Climatical features of Saudi Arabia. *Fauna of Saudi Arabia.* Vol. 6:32-52.
STAGG, A., J. 1984. Birds of Saudi Arabia. A note on the breed birds of Kutambil Island on the Red Sea Coast of Saudi Arabia. *Fauna of Saudi Arabia.* Vol. 6: 546-548.
WALTER, H. 1979. The Sooty Falcon *Falco concolor* in Oman: Results of a breeding survey. *J. Oman Studies* 5: 9-59.

P. Gaucher/X. Eichacher
National Wildlife Research Center
P. E. Box 1086 Taif
Saudi Arabia

W. D. Daunicht
Institut für Hanstierkunde der Christian Albrechts
Universität Biologùzentrum, Olshausentr. 40
Kiel, Germany

APPENDIX

SOOTY FALCON PREY COLLECTED IN 1989-90-91

Marsh Warbler	*Acrocephalus palustris*	161
Whitethroat	*Sylvia communis*	50
Rufous Warbler	*Cercotrichas galactotes*	36
Red-backed Shrike	*Lanius collurio*	33
Isabelline Wheatear	*Oenanthe isabellina*	32
Quail	*Coturnix coturnix*	21
Swallow	*Hirundo rustica*	20
Great Reed Warbler	*Acrocephalus arundinaceus*	20
River Warbler	*Locustella fluviatilis*	19
Swift	*Apus apus*	15
European Bee-eater	*Merops apiaster*	14
Wryneck	*Jynx torquilla*	12
Basrah Reed Warbler	*Acrocephalus (arundinaceus) griseldis*	11
Reed Warbler	*Acrocephalus scirpaceus*	11
Willow Warbler	*Phylloscopus trochilus*	11

Hoopoe	*Upupa epops*	10
Olivaceous Warbler	*Hippolais pallida*	10
Garden Warbler	*Sylvia borin*	10
Wheatear	*Oenanthe oenanthe*	9
Upcher's Warbler	*Hippolais languida*	8
Black-crowned Lark	*Eremopterix nigriceps*	7
Lesser-Grey Shrike	*Lanius minor*	7
Blue-checked Bee-eater	*Merops superciliosus*	6
Tree Pipit	*Anthus trivialis*	6
White-throated Robin	*Irania gutturalis*	6
Common Sandpiper	*Tringa hypoleucos*	5
Woodchat Shrike	*Lanius senator*	5
Bluethroat	*Luscinia svecica*	5
Stonechat	*Saxicola torquata*	4
Spotted Crake	*Porzana porzana*	4
Laughing Dove	*Streptopelia senegalensis*	3
Turtle Dove	*Streptopelia turtur*	3
Cuckoo	*Cuculus canorus*	3
Hoopoe Lark	*Alaemon alaudipes*	3
Spotted Flycatcher	*Muscicapa striata*	3
Thrush Nightingale	*Luscinia luscinia*	3
Redstart	*Phoenicurus phoenicurus*	3
Barred Warbler	*Sylvia nisoria*	3
African Reed Warbler	*Acrocephalus basticalus*	3
Namaqua Dove	*Oena capensis*	2
Sand Martin	*Riparia riparia*	2
Short-toed Lark	*Calandrella brachydactyla*	2
Blue-headed Wagtail	*Motacilla flava*	2
Desert Wheatear	*Oenanthe deserti*	2
Blackap	*Sylvia atricapilla*	2
Orphean Warbler	*Sylvia hortensis*	2
Little Crake	*Porzana parva*	1
Redshank	*Tringa totanus*	1
Greater Sandplover	*Charadrius leschenaultii*	1
Kentish Plover	*Charadrius alexandrinus*	1
Pratincole	*Glareola pratincola*	1
Alpine Swift	*Apus melba*	1
Water Pipit	*Anthus spinoletta*	1
Masked Shrike	*Lanius nubicus*	1
Great Grey Shrike	*Lanius excubitor*	1
Isabelline Shrike	*Lanius isabellina*	1
Nightingale	*Luscinia megarhynchos*	1
Whinchat	*Saxicola rubetra*	1
Rock Thrush	*Monticola saxatilis*	1
Savi's Warbler	*Locustella luscinoides*	1
Lesser Whitethroat	*Sylvia curraca*	1
Ortolan Bunting	*Emberiza hortulana*	1
Golden Oriole	*Oriolus oriolus*	1
Unidentified		4

Meyburg, B.-U. & R. D. Chancellor eds.1994
Raptor Conservation Today
WWGBP / The Pica Press

Feeding Habits of Montagu's Harrier *Circus pygargus* in Central Italy

Paolo Giacchini and Massimo Pandolfi

INTRODUCTION

The reproductive biology of Montagu's Harrier has been relatively well studied for northern Europe (Robinson 1950; Glutz *et al.* 1971; Schipper 1979), and more recently also in the Mediterranean countries, in particular Italy (Martelli 1984; Martelli & Sandri 1989; Pandolfi & Pino d'Astore 1990a; Pandolfi & Giacchini 1991).

Analyses of the species' diet in its nesting areas have been made in France (Thiollay 1968), the Netherlands and the South of France (Schipper 1973), and Spain (Garzon 1974; Hiraldo *et al.* 1975). However, in Italy there is an almost total lack of any such data, except for reports of some time ago on migrating individuals (Moltoni 1937).

The purpose of the present study is to analyse some aspects of Montagu's Harrier's feeding habits in its central Italian nesting areas. The hunting effort over the course of the day, and the male's behaviour with respect to the various biological phases of the reproductive cycle, are two of these aspects. In addition, the first data are given on the diet, referring only to the role of reptiles, even though in the study area the diet includes other categories such as insects, small birds and micromammals; also factors of selection and seasonal variations in a hilly area of subcolonial utilisation are considered.

MATERIALS AND METHODS

The research was conducted in the province of Pesaro and Urbino (Marches region) during the 1986-1988 breeding seasons in a 60ha hilly area *ca.* 15km from the coast. Observations were made throughout the daylight hours, and in those preceding dawn, using Zeiss 10x40 binoculars, at a distance of not less than 100m from the nest, and for a total of 397h.

The amount of prey could be quantified by direct observation in the field, identifying the reptiles mainly by recognition of the colouring and morphology of the prey carried in his talons by the male for the female, or by both adults for their young. Cases in which the male reached the nesting area with the prey but ate it himself are also included.

ROLE OF THE MALE AT THE NEST

The active role of the male in nest-building or in feeding the chicks was analysed on the basis of the number of flights to the nest, the material brought and the phase of the reproductive cycle in which they occurred. The results are presented in Table 1 and show how the male spends much more time at the nest after the brood has hatched than during incubation or nest-building. Of his visits, 79.4% were in presence of the chicks for whom he was bringing food. This behavioural pattern can be considered a common one in the study area, despite some authors (Perez Chiscano & Fernandez Cruz 1971; Martelli 1984) holding it to be rather anomalous and infrequent.

Out of 62 cases of material being brought by the pair for building or repairing the nest, the male contributed in 3.2%.

Table 1. Visits of the male to the nest during the reproductive cycle.

	without material	with straw	with prey
NEST CONSTRUCTION	1	-	-
INCUBATION	5	1	-
FLEDGING	4	1	22

Table 2. Intervals (in minutes) between two captures of prey during the various parts of the day.

Time of day	Length of interval
5/6	120
6/7	106
7/8	58
8/9	62
9/10	54
10/1	147
11/12	53
12/13	37
13/14	49
14/15	74
15/16	63
16/17	54
17/18	60
18/19	67

During incubation, rapid descents on the nest were noted in which the male assumed the role of caretaker in the brief lapse of time between the food-pass and the return of the female. This behavioural trait is not at all common, since only in exceptional circumstances is the male able to take over incubation (Vincent 1929).

Visits to the nest with food for the young were usually rapid: on six occasions the male remained on the nest for a period of 15-30 seconds and on two occasions for 60-90 seconds. These longer stays might suggest that the male was breaking up the food, as reported by Studinka (1942), but in contrast with the findings of Colling & Brown (1946).

FOOD-PASS

The prey is given to the females or young with the Food-pass, typical for the genus *Circus*. This display, already investigated in detail in previous studies (Pandolfi & Pino d'Astore 1990b), is carried out both in flight (Aerial Food-pass) and on the ground (Ground Food-pass), and fairly

Figure 1. Time frequency of capture of prey.

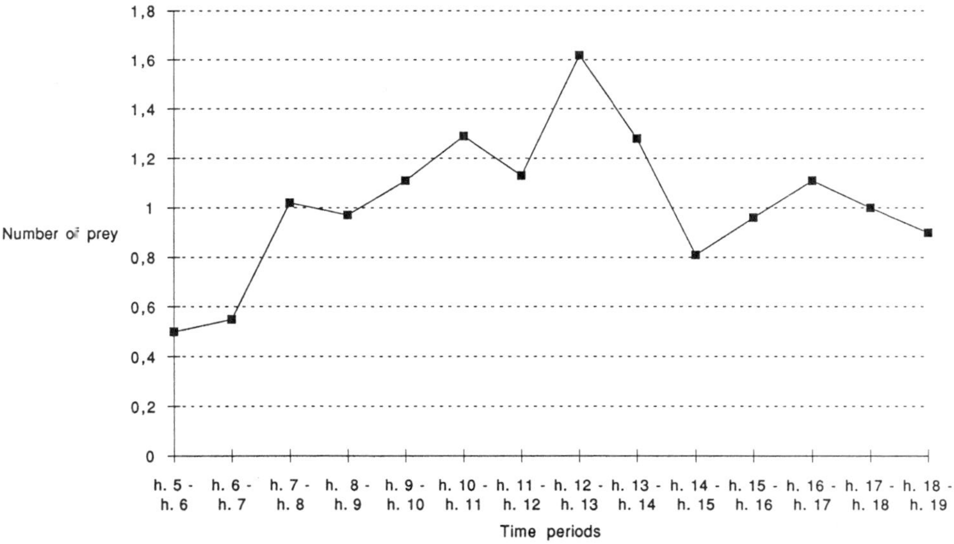

Figure 2. Time frequency of capture of reptiles.

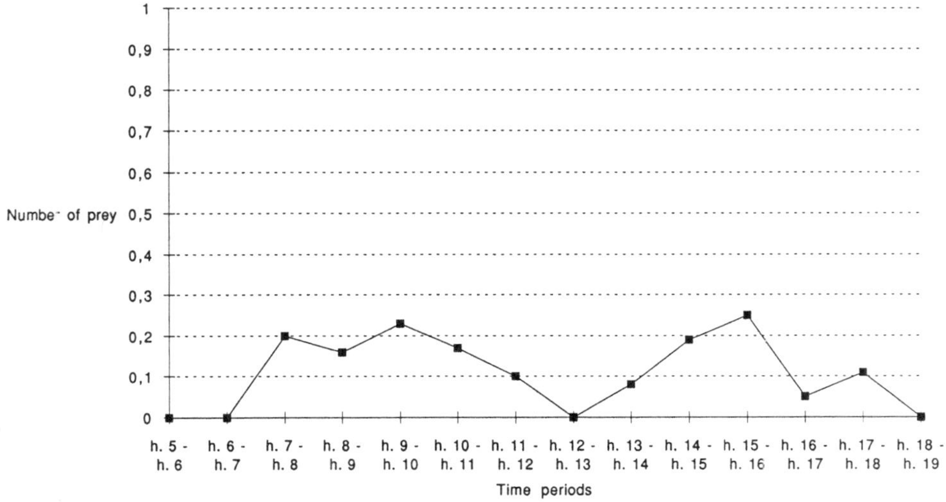

accurate observation can be made, at least as far as certain taxonomic categories are concerned, of the type of prey given. Between male and female, the handing over of prey takes place mainly by an Aerial Food-pass. When the young are fledged, they are almost exclusively fed by the male. The Aerial Food-pass between male and young can be schematically subdivided into three models:

1) the male with prey is approached by one fledgling only, while the others remain still; immediately after the Food-pass, the male returns to hunt while the young bird settles down to feed;

2) the male with prey is approached by several young, but only the first to arrive receives the prey; after the Food-pass the young remain in flight, trying without success to take possession of the food (Pandolfi & Giacchini 1990);

3) the male passes the prey to one of the young, who is at once surrounded by the others, on whom the male performs a series of diving attacks; this behavioural pattern occurred in 18.3% of the cases (N = 71).

In view of what has been reported in previous studies (Pandolfi & Pino d'Astore 1990a), this form of display may be interpreted both as Food-pass training and as a form of protection by the male of the young which received the food, thereby preventing the others from disturbing it and avoiding any loss of food. In fact, this pattern is a modification of the one in which the male assumes the role of protecting the young with the prey from conflict with the other young, and is not just designed to divide the food equally among the fledglings, something which has still to be proved.

TIME OF HUNTING

Fluctuations in hunting intensity during the course of the day and over the whole reproductive cycle are reported in Figure 1 and Table 2, and show the species to be active from dawn to dusk. If, on the one hand, its morphological characteristics allow it to hunt even without upward air-streams, on the other hand with the growing young the amount of food required, therefore of hunting activity, increases. The briefest intervals between successive prey captures, and thus the greatest hunting activity, occurs between 10 a.m. and 2 p.m., with a maximum between 12 a.m. and 1 p.m. These observations are in contrast with those of Thiollay (1968) for France, where the hunting activity may reduce to less than 40% between 11 a.m. and 2.30 p.m. on account of the high temperature. In our study area, a considerable drop in activity was noted after 2 p.m., at which time Thiollay observed a full-scale resumption. No long pauses were revealed during the course of the day, unlike those reported for *Circus aeruginosus* during the mid-day hours (Thiollay 1967).

Table 3. Percentage composition of Montagu's Harrier diet, with particular reference to class of reptiles.

	1987	1988	Σ
Reptiles	24.3	11.2	18.8
Podarcis muralis/ Podarcis sicula	2.9	1.6	
Lacerta viridis	21.4	7.2	
Not identified	-	2.4	
Insects, Birds and Mammals	75.7	88.8	81.2

Table 4. Number of reptiles caught in various weather conditions.

Wind	strong	medium	slight	absent	total	%
Weather						
clear	-	2	2	10	14	48.3
variable	-	-	1	1	2	6.9
cloudy	1	3	2	1	7	24.1
overcast	-	-	2	3	5	17.2
showery	-	1	-	-	1	3.5
total	1	6	7	15	29	
%	3.5	20.7	24.1	51.7		

Despite the fact that hunting may begin early, the frequency of food supply remains low until the atmosphere warms up, and this could depend on the activity of certain prey rather than on the hunting ability of the harrier.

In July and August, the males, which roosted in the same nesting area without forming communal dormitories, left to go hunting after dawn, between 5 a.m. and 5.20 a.m., but never returned with food before 5.41 a.m.

With regard to the evening hours, no food-passes were ever observed shortly before or after sunset, and in any event never after 6.24 p.m., unlike observations in France (Thiollay 1968) and in the Italian Apennines near Bologna (Martelli 1984).

DIET

The present study revealed how throughout the breeding cycle only 3.9% of the food is brought to the nest by the female, whose trophic role in chick-rearing is almost nil, a situation considerably different from that in central European countries (Schipper 1973). On the basis of observations made at the nest site, no prey of any size was noted, e.g. leverets or young pheasants, which are relatively abundant in the study area.

The investigation was mainly directed to the use made of the reptile food resource. Altogether, reptiles amounted to 18.8% (N = 298) (Table 3) of the total prey; the seasonal variation revealed a constant decrease from April (36.4%) to July (13.2%), as was also observed for the Spanish population in similar environmental conditions by Hiraldo *et al.* (1975).

This trend may be explained to some extent by the greater vulnerability of saurians in April, due to their courting activity, and the less dense vegetation cover. In the following months, together with the reduced availability of these reptiles, the fledging of numerous young passerines occurs, which thus constitute a valuable alternative source of food.

Also the hunting of reptiles was analysed over the various parts of the day and in various weather conditions. The most favourable hours proved to be 8 a.m. to 12 a.m., with another peak period from 3 p.m. to 5 p.m. (Fig. 2). In this way, the hottest time of day, when other classes of prey come under pressure, and the beginning and end of day, when the reptiles have still not left, or not yet returned to shelter, are avoided.

With regard to weather, *ca.* 50% of reptiles were caught in conditions of clear sky and absence of wind (Table 4). These findings are in contrast with observations by Schipper (1973) in the Netherlands, where overcast skies and rain seem to be the best conditions for catching reptiles, which appear to be then less mobile.

REFERENCES

COLLING, A.W.& E.B. BROWN 1946. The breeding of Marsh and Montagu's Harriers in North Wales in 1945. *British Birds* 39: 233-243.

GARZON, H.J. 1974. Contribucion al estudio del status, alimentacion y proteccion de las falconiformes en Espana central. *Ardeola* 19: 279-330.

GLUTZ von BLOTZHEIM, U.N., K. BAUER, & E. BEZZEL 1971. *Handbuch der Voegel Mitteleuropas*, 4, Akad. Verlagsgesellscharft, Frankfurt am Main.

HIRALDO, F., F. FERNANDEZ & F. AMORES 1975. Diet of Montagu's Harrier *Circus pygargus* in southwestern Spain. *Donana, Acta Vertebrata* 2 (1): 25-55.

MARTELLI, D. 1984. *L'Albanella minore nell'Appennino bolognese*. Ed. Grafos, Bologna.

MARTELLI, D. & V. SANDRI (in press) - Status ed ecologia riproduttiva dell'Albanella minore *Circus pygargus* in Emilia Romagna. *Analisi conclusiva. V. Conv. Ital. Ornit.*, Bracciano, 1989.

MOLTONI, E. 1937. Osservazioni bromatologiche sugli Uccelli Rapaci italiani. *Riv. Ital. Ornit.* 7: 13-33; 61-119.

PANDOLFI, M. & P. GIACCHINI 1990 - Cleptoparassitismo di juvenes su juvenes in Albanella minore *Circus pygargus. Avocetta,* 14: 74-75.

PANDOLFI, M. & P. GIACCHINI 1991. Distribuzione e successo riproduttivo di Albanella minore *Circus pygargus* nelle Marche. *Riv. Ital. Orn.* 61 (1-2): 25-32.

PANDOLFI, M. & P.R. PINO D'ASTORE 1990a. Analysis of breeding behaviour in Montagu's Harrier *Circus pygargus L.* in a site of Central Italy. *Avocetta* 14: 97-102.

PANDOLFI, M.. & P.R. PINO D'ASTORE 1990b. Food-pass behaviour pattern in *Circus pygargus L. Ethology, Ecology and Evolution,* 2: 321.
PEREZ CHISCANO, J.L. & M. FERNANDEZ CRUZ 1971. Sobre *Grus grus y Circus pygargus* in Extremadura. *Ardeola vol. Especial:* 509-574.
ROBINSON, W. 1950. Montagu's Harrier. *Bird Notes* 24: 103-114.
SCHIPPER, W.J.A. 1973. A comparison of prey selection in sympatric Harriers, *Circus* sp., in Western Europe. *Le Gerfaut,* 63: 17-120.
SCHIPPER, W.J.A. 1979. A comparison of breeding ecology in three European harriers *(Circus). Ardea,* 66: 77-102.
STUDINKA, L. 1942. The habits and plumages of Montagu's Harrier. *Aquila,* 46-9; 247-269.
THIOLLAY, M. 1967. Ecologie d'une population de rapaces diurnes en Lorraine. *La Terre et la Vie,* 21: 116-183.
THIOLLAY, J.M. 1968. La pression de predation estivale du Busard cendré *Circus pygargus L.* sur les populations de *Microtus arvalis* en Vendée. *La Terre et la Vie,* 22: 321-326.
VINCENT, J. 1929. Large clutch of Montagu's Harrier and incubation by cock bird. *British Birds,* 23: 64-65.

Paolo Giacchini and Massimo Pandolfi
Istituto di Scienze Morfologiche - Università di Urbino
Via M. Oddi, 23
61029 Urbino, Italy

Meyburg, B.-U. & R. D. Chancellor eds.1994
Raptor Conservation Today
WWGBP / The Pica Press

Aspects of the Breeding Ecology of the Red-necked Falcon *Falco chicquera horsbrughi* and its Hunting Association with the Gabar Goshawk *Micronisus gabar* in the South-Eastern Kalahari

J. J. Herholdt

SUMMARY

The breeding ecology of the Red-necked Falcon *Falco chicquera* is investigated in the Kalahari Gemsbok National Park. Breeding takes place early, mostly during September, and hatching occurs just before the first summer rains. It is suggested that this timing could be to take advantage of newly-fledged prey species. Nest spacing is in relation to waterholes. High predation rates on eggs and nestlings were observed, as well as a high turnover for males in individual territories. The hunting association with the Gabar Goshawk *Micronisus gabar* is documented.

INTRODUCTION

The Rednecked Falcon *Falco chicquera* occurs in southern Africa mostly in the Kalahari and Namib deserts, along dry watercourses with large trees (Maclean 1958; Brown 1988; Braine 1987). In Zambia (Osborne 1981) and Botswana and Mozambique (Steyn 1982) it is largely confined to areas with Borassus palms. In South Africa the Kalahari Gemsbok National Park supports the only major breeding population. However, it has also been reported sporadically from the western Orange Free State, western Transvaal and northern Kruger National Park (Steyn 1982).

STUDY AREA AND METHODS

The Kalahari Gemsbok National Park is situated in the south-western region of the Kalahari semi-desert, between the dry Auob and Nossob Rivers and the surrounding dune area. These dry river systems have eroded the red sand dunes to expose the underlying limestone plains. The Nossob River, which runs the full length of the Park along its eastern boundary with Botswana, is dominated by stands of *Acacia erioloba* but in the southern part the *Acacia haematoxylon* is more prevalent. Detailed descriptions of the vegetation are provided by Leistner (1967) and Leistner & Werger (1973). Rainfall occurs in summer to early autumn (November to April) with more than 50 % falling between January and April (Nel 1990).

Red-necked Falcons were studied in the northern half of the dry Nossob River and in the surrounding dunes from Kaspersdraai in the south (25°36´S; 20°42´E) to Union's End (24°50´S;20°03´E) in the north, a distance of 167 km. Each nest site located was plotted on a map and examined at least five times during each breeding season. Observations were made between August 1988 and November 1991, covering four breeding seasons. Red-headed Finches *Amadina erythrocephala* were mistnetted during the falcon breeding season of 1988. Observations on the hunting association between the Red-necked Falcons and Gabar Goshawks were also made.

RESULTS

Timing of breeding

Most clutches were laid during August (n=13; 68%) and September (n=6; 32%) and hatched during September (n=9; 69%) and October (n=4; 30,7%) during all four breeding seasons (Fig. 1). Hatching occurred just before the first summer rains, when the Kalahari is at its dryest and cover sparsest. It is also a time when seed-eating birds such as the Red-headed Finch, Scaly-feathered Finch *Sporopipes squamifrons* and Grey-headed Sparrow *Passer griseus* occur in large non-breeding flocks at waterholes to drink (pers.obs.). 1988 immature Red-headed Finch numbers (Fig. 2) peaked at waterholes during August and September (pers. obs. and trapping results 1988) and probably reflects the annual pattern for this winter-breeding species (Maclean 1985).

Although many seed eating species may breed in winter after rains the Red-headed Finch is the only small passerine that regularly breeds mainly in winter. It is suggested that the breeding season of Red-necked Falcon is unusually early in the spring so that advantage can be taken of the new inexperienced Red-headed Finch fledglings which become available when the falcon chicks have just hatched.

Nest placement

All eggs were laid in old Black Crow *Corvus capensis* nests. One nest with three half-grown Red-necked Falcon nestlings was found in an *A. erioloba* tree which also contained the nest of a Greater Kestrel *Falco rupicoloides* with three fully-feathered nestlings. The two nests were approximately four metres apart.

All nests were in *A. erioloba* trees. Mean nest height was 6.8 m (n=14; range 3.8 - 8.9 m; SD = 1.8 m) above ground level. Mean tree height was 9.0 m (n = 13; range 6 - 12.3 m ; SD = 1.9 m).The canopy diameter of nesting trees average 10.0 m (n=13; range 3.7 - 19.4 m; SD = 4.6 m). Nests were placed in forks (n = 8; range 4 - 10; SD = 1.8). Of 16 nests, five (31.3%) were on the southern side of the tree, two (12.5 %) faced south-west, three (18.8 %) west, three (18.8%) east, one (6.3%) north-east and two north (12.5%). Thus 62.5% of all nests were situated on the south, south-west or western side of trees.

The mean distance of nests from the nearest waterpoint was 3.1km (n=16; range 0.2-9.9km; SD= 2.8km) and the mean distance between waterholes in the study area was 10.7 km (n=16; range 3.9 - 22.5 km; SD=5.3 km). Pairs observed in the dune habitat (n=7) were always associated with waterholes, which shows clearly an association with waterpoints, and it is likely that the provision of a local abundance of prey species attracted to the water is the reason. Except in one instance, a new nest was used every year for each nesting attempt by the falcons.

Figure 1. Rainfall and Red-necked Falcon clutches hatching per month.

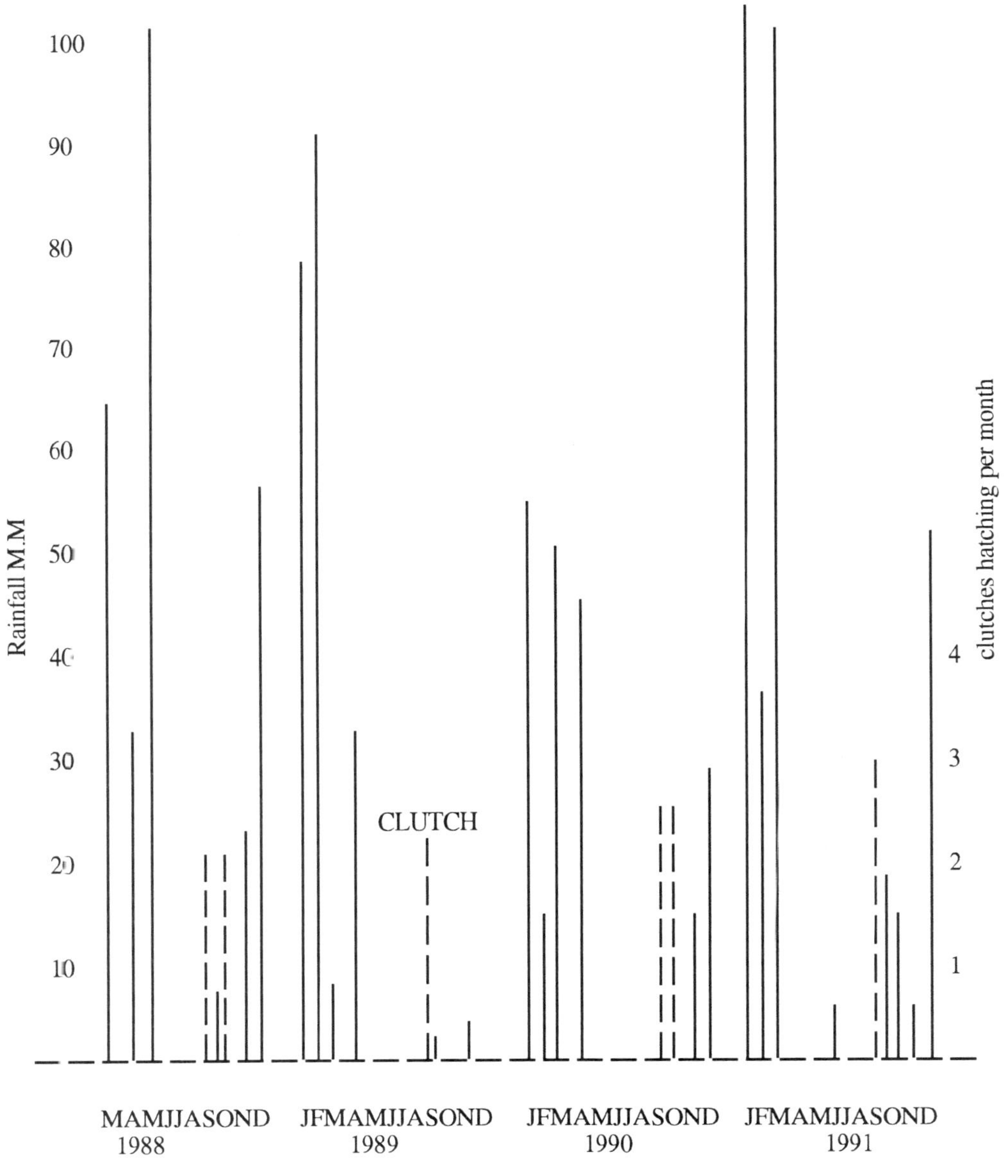

Figure 2. Percentege of immature Red-headed Finches in trap samples for 1988

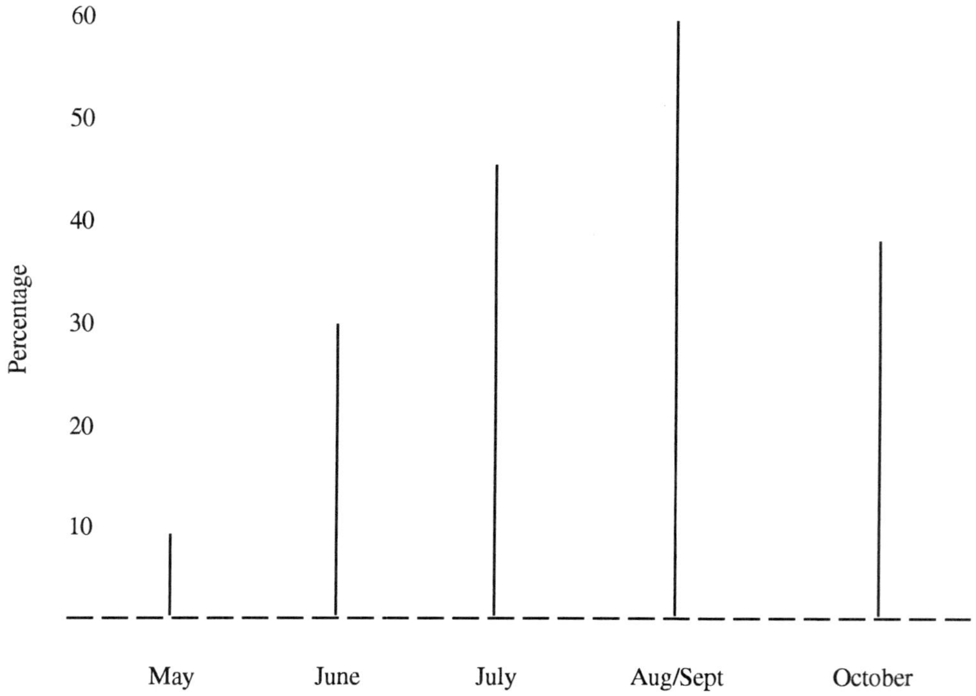

Clutch size

Of 19 clutches examined, six (31.5%) contained four eggs and 13 (68.5%) three eggs, with a mean clutch size of 3.3 eggs.

Breeding success

From 1988 to 1991 a total of 19 breeding attempts were monitored. Of these, 10 were successive attempts by four known pairs. The other (n=7) were for random pairs found along the Nossob River and in the dunes away from the river (n=2). A total of 63 eggs were laid of which 36 hatched (57%) and 21 young (58% of eggs that hatched) fledged successfully. This gives a recruitment of 1.1 young per pair per year (ypp) (Tables 1 & 2).

Of the four known pairs, however, breeding success varied between 0 (n=2 years) and 1.7 ypp (n=3 years), with a mean of 0.9 (Table 1). For the other nine nests found a success rate of 1.3 ypp was observed (Table 1). Although the territories of these pairs were examined each year, the birds or their nests were seldom found.

Table 1. Breeding statistics of individual pairs of Red-necked Falcons in the Kalahari Gemsbok National Park

	1988			1989			1990			1991			
Pair	Egg	Hatch	Rear	Egg	Hatch	Rear	Egg	Hatch	Rear	Egg	Hatch	Rear	YPP
NOS	3	0	0	3	2	2		N/F		4	3	3	1.7
KAN	3	1	0		N/F		3	3	0		N/F		0
RO		N/F		3	1	1	3	0	0	4	4	0	0.3
KO		N/F			N/F		3	3	3	3	0	0	1.5
TOT	6	1	0	6	3	3	9	6	3	11	7	3	0.9
						Random Nests							
MA	4	0	0										
BA	4	3	3										
OK	3	3	3										
BED	3	3	3										
KA							4	4	0				
KAG							3	0	0				
UE							3	3	3				
KW										4	3	0	
LA										3	0	0	
TOT	14	9	9				10	7	3	7	3	0	1.3
Overall TOT	20	10	9	6	3	3	19	13	6	18	10	3	1.1

N/F = nest not found

Table 2. Breeding statistics of Red-necked falcons in the Kalahari Gemsbok National Park

	1988	1989	1990	1991	Total
Total nesting attempts known	6	2	6	5	19
Clutch laid/failed to hatch	2	0	2	2	6
Clutch laid/hatched/fledged	3	2	2	1	8
Clutch hatched/killed by predator	1	0	2	2	5
Young fledged/breeding pair	1.5	1.5	1.0	0.6	1.1

Table 3. Prey pursued by Red-necked Falcons

Species		No
Birds		
Yellow Canary	*Serinus flaviventris*	1
Cape Turtle Dove	*Streptopelia capicola*	2
Namaqua Dove	*Oena capensis*	1
Red-headed Finch	*Amadina erythrocephala*	1
Scaly-feathered Finch	*Sporopipes squamifrons*	2
Grey-headed Sparrow	*Passer qriseus*	1
Lilac-breasted Roller	*Coracias caudata*	1
Mammals		
Striped Mouse	*Rhabdomys pumilio*	2
Termites		
Hodotermes sp.		

Predation on eggs and nestlings

Of 19 clutches laid, the eggs of 31.6% were preyed upon by unknown predators (Table 2). As far as could be ascertained, no clutches were abandoned, although this was possible, as indicated by broken egg-shells in the nests. Of clutches which hatched (Table 2), the young of five broods were killed by predators. On two occasions remains of nestlings were seen hanging from branches around the nests or had fallen to the ground. No predator was ever identified but species such as Honey Badger *Mellivora capensis,* African Wild Cat *Felis lybica* and Pale Chanting Goshawk *Melierax canorus* abound in the area.

Post-fleging dependence

A young male ringed less than a week after fledging was retrapped together with both parents 4 km away from the nest site 64 days later. A young female was retrapped at least 71 days after fledging and two kilometres from the nest site, still with the parents.

Nest site fidelity

Rooikop territory

In the Rooikop territory, a high degree of adult replacement was observed between 1988 and 1990. For example, an adult male (6-59074), captured on 12 November 1988 in this territory, was replaced by another male (6-59093) ringed here six months later on 12 May 1989. It in turn was replaced by male 6-59072, first captured seven months later on 17 December 1989 and recaptured on 14 June 1990. The adult female from this territory (6-63434) was colour-ringed on 24 June 1990 and still occupied the territory 16 months later at the termination of the study.

Nossob territory

Adult male 6-59033 was ringed near Nossob Camp on 14 August 1988 and recaptured there 20 months later on 24 March 1990. The female of this pair (6-59038) was ringed on 8 September 1988 and recaptured 37 months later on 20 October 1991, still in the same territory. The very wary male could not be retrapped , but was most probably the same male.

Kwang territory

The adult female (6-59100) was ringed on 17 September 1989 and subsequently retrapped in the same area four months later on 27 January 1990. This bird was not trapped again.

Marie's Windmill

Adult male 6-59035 was ringed on 16 August 1988 and the adult female 6-59096 on 10 May 1989. Both birds were replaced by a different pair trapped on 18 June 1990 (adult female 6-63427 and 28 June 1990 (adult male 5-84947) respectively. It is not known if the former disappeared from the territory before the new pair arrived, or were ousted from it.

Hunting success

Of 12 observed foraging attempts on various prey species 42 % (n=5) were successful with the majority of items pursued being small birds and mice (Table 3). Termites were also taken occasionally after rains. Two bat (unidentified species) kills were observed during daylight hours, when they were accidentally disturbed from a tree and captured by a female Red-necked Falcon while flying.

Population density

A population survey conducted in the study area along the Nossob River valley yielded a total of 21 pairs with a mean inter-pair distance of 7.2 km (n=19; range 1.9 - 15.5 km ; SD = 3.3 km). A similar survey was conducted in the dunes in the northern third of the park where 7 adjacent pairs were located with a mean inter-pair distance of 15 km (n=4; range 13-18 km; SD=2.2 km). Further south from Kaspersdraai to Twee Rivieren (26°28´S; 20°37'E) 6 pairs were seen with an inter-pair distance of 16.5 km (n=4; range 7,5-28,0 km; SD = 8.8 km), thus giving a minimum of 27 pairs for the whole of the Nossob´s 300 km dry course inside the park. However, the area to the south was not as intensively surveyed as the northern part and may have contained more pairs. No similar data are available for the Auob River.

Hunting association with the Gabar Goshawk

Finch-Davies & Kemp (1980) suggested that the sharp-winged Red-necked Falcon and round-winged Gabar Goshawk *Micronisus gabar* are often closely associated with one another in what may be a mutually beneficial arrangement, in which the goshawks may flush from cover birds which are then preyed upon by the falcon. In turn the latter may force birds into cover were they are more readily captured by the goshawks. This association was also observed in the present study and Red-neked Falcons and Gabar Goshawks often came down to the Balchatri together while I was trapping either species. In addition, 71.4 % of Red-necked Falcon territories (n=21) supported a pair of Gabar Goshawks. These observations prompted an investigation into the interactions of these two bird-eating species.

The following observations of co-operative hunting were documented. During September 1990 a Red-necked Falcon (sex unknown) stooped and knocked a Red-headed Finch to the ground, but before the falcon could return to the kill it was taken by a Gabar Goshawk.

On a second occasion (15 August 1991 at Bitterpan) I observed a Red-necked Falcon and a pair of Gabar Goshawks co-operatively hunting a Yellow Canary *Serinus flaviventris*. The canary, chased by the falcon, dived into an *Acacia mellifera* bush. One Gabar Goshawk immediately followed it into the bush while the other hovered just above. The falcon, however, remained some 15 metres above the bush and as soon as the canary broke cover, unsuccessfully stooped at it. This sequence was repeated once more before the birds disapperared from sight. The eventual outcome is not known.

On a third occasion (2. October 1991), a female Gabar Goshawk and a male Red-necked Falcon were observed chasing a Grey-headed Sparrow. The falcon chased the bird until it dived into the canopy of a tree at which time the goshawk went in after it while the Red-necked Falcon remained some 10 metres above the canopy. As soon as the sparrow broke cover the falcon made an unsuccessful stoop. The sparrow then took cover in the canopy of a nearby tree but was again flushed by the goshawk and soon afterwards captured in an exhausted state by the falcon.

A fourth instance involved a male Red-necked Falcon and a female Gabar Goshawk perched together less than one metre apart on the top of a dry tree. As soon as the goshawk flew off, it was followed by the falcon until it perched some 50 metres off. The goshawk later took off again and was immediately followed by the falcon. This happened three times and strongly suggests that the falcon was actually following the goshawk. This behaviour was again observed at Kameelsleep, where a falcon and a goshawk were seen perched together. As soon as the goshawk flew off (undisturbed) the falcon followed it until they disappeared from sight.

DISCUSSION

As was the case in Osborne´s study (1981) the Red-necked Falcons in the study area occupied a relatively undisturbed and pristine environment, except for the presence of artificial boreholes. No pesticides were ever used in this area.

Eggs were laid mostly during the dryest months of the year and hatched during Septmber and October. At this time the food requirements of falcons feeding young birds were greatest. Large flocks of non-breeding seed-eaters are then present in the study area and gather to drink at the waterholes, providing an abundant source of food for the breeding falcons. Red-headed Finches breed during the winter (Maclean 1985) and large numbers of recently fledged young (Fig. 2) also gather at waterholes to drink, and due to their inexperience may constitute a more easily available food source. Groundcover is less dense during September and October, which may make prey more vulnerable (Osborne 1981).

After the first good summer rains, large numbers of larks, finch-larks and quail move into the area and breed. Since this occurs only 2-3 months after young Red-necked Falcons fledge,these birds may provide a source of inexperienced young prey for the young falcons. Flying termites (*Hodotermes* sp.) are also abundant at this time and are frequently eaten by young falcons on the wing. In his study area, Osborne (1981) speculates that the longer grass during the rainy seasons may make it more difficult for falcons to hunt young seed-eaters. This is probably not a major factor in the Kalahari. The grass, especially on the trampled areas around the boreholes, is never very dense and prey visibbility is generally good.

All breeding attempts were in old Black Crow nests (Maclean 1958; 1985) and except in one instance, a new nest was used each year by the individual pairs of Red-necked Falcons. Osborne (1981) found that a higher frequency of falcon pairs used the same nests in subsequent years, probably besause palm trees provide a more stable breeding platform than old crow nests.

Most nests were situated on the outer lower perimeter of the trees and a significant number of all nests observed (62,5 %) faced south, south-west or west; this is the coolest side of the tree and also shelters nests from the predominant north-easterly winds. Nests were placed closer to the ground in this study as compared with those in the Zambian study (Colebrook-Robjent & Osborne 1975)

Brown (1988) suggested some spatial segregation between the Red-necked Falcon and Greater Kestrel pairs in the Namib. No evidence of this was found in the KGNP where the two species were often seen in close proximity, as is illustrated by the two breeding together in one tree.

Clutch size in this study consisted mostly of three (68.5%) and four (31.5%) eggs and was thus similar to clutch sizes reported by Osborne (1981), Steyn (1982) and Olwagen (1983).

Breeding success averaged 1.1 ypp while in Zambia this figure was 1.3 ypp (Osborne 1981), and 1.5 ypp in a captive study by Olwagen (1983). Of all eggs laid 57 % hatched and thus similar to observations for Zambia, where the hatching rate was 56 % (Osborne 1981). The high percentage of 42.8 % of eggs failing to hatch was due mainly to predation. However, a small percentage may have been infertile. This is similar to the 44 % observed for the Zambian population (Osborne

1981). Of all young that hatched, 41.6 % did not fledge due to predation.

Osborne (1981) cited winds and predation by monkeys and avian predators for mortality of young birds. In the present study there were no monkeys and no evidence of wind destruction, and losses were probably largely due to predation.

The post-fledging periods, of at least 64 and 71 days respectively, are considerably longer than the 24 days mentioned by Osborne (1981). This parental dependence may be variable and governed by environmental factors during the breeding season.

In 10 male pair-years a 40%, and in females a 12.5% (n=8 pair years) turnover was noted. This high turnover in males may be due to mortality and/or movements of the individuals. There is some evidence for a degree of nomadism since in some territories birds breed each year, while in others, pairs were totally absent in following years. It is possible that the population as a whole is subject to annual fluctuations (Pickford *et. al.* 1989), as is the case with Pale Chanting Goshawks and Greater Kestrels in this study area (pers.obs.). Some territories may be marginally suitable for breeding purposes and thus may be occupied only in good years. Osborne (1981) found a high mortality in females in Zambia. Only one killed female was found under a deserted nest during this study.

Also, when breeding these falcons are regularly seen in the breeding territory and in fact hunt mostly in it, but outside the breeding season they move into the dunes and then hunt over a much wider area. This may also be part of the reason why one seldom sees these falcons outside the breeding season.

A hunting success of 42% was observed in the present study, compared with 30.7% in Zambia (Osborne 1981). This could be the result of the more open foraging habitat. Prey consisted mostly of small birds, rodents and termites taken in flight or on the ground. Birds either hunted individually or in pairs. In the latter case one bird flushed the prey and the other attacked it (pers.obs.; G. Malan 1991; Osborne 1981; R. Liversidge pers. comm.). It is also possible that bats are caught more often since on a number of occasions falcons were observed to hunt at dusk (e.g. Bitterpan).However, no actual kills were ever observed as it was too dark. Once some bats were accidentally flushed from a dead tree and two were taken by the Red-necked Falcons soon afterwards, suggesting that they recognized them as prey (Fry 1964).

The inter-pair distance of 7.8 km is similar to the 8.3 km recorded by Brown (1988) in the Namib, but much greater than the 2.05 km reported by Colebrook-Robjent & Osborne (1975) and 2.15 km by Osborne (1984) in Zambia. In the KGNP inter-nest distances are governed by the spacing of waterholes, which influence the choice of a nesting location. Without man-made waterpoints the density and numbers of Red-necked Falcons may change drastically and it may be suggested that few pairs would exist in the Park if waterholes were absent due to the effect on prey availability. The small seedeaters and doves would mostly disappear during the dry season when the falcons breed if there was no surface water. In the dunes pairs were always located close to waterholes and the inter-pair density of 15 km (n=7) largely reflects the spacing of waterholes.

During a survey of the area to the east into Botswana, where there is no surface water for hundreds of kilometres, only a few pairs of Gabar Goshawks were located. Further north-east towards the Mabuasehube Game Reserve some Little Banded Goshawks *Accipiter badius* were observed. No Red-necked Falcons were seen here, suggesting that insectivorous birds and the unstable and seasonal numbers of larks and Scaly-feathered Finch could not support resident falcon pairs in this densely bushed area. The falcons need open areas to hunt (Osborne 1981) such as trampled areas around waterholes. Without waterholes only the seasonal incursions of birds such as larks and quail would occur in the study area after the rains and would probably not support such a large breeding population of falcons as presently occurs in the Park.

How hunting success is influenced by co-operation between the Gabar Goshawk and Red-necked Falcon is still a question to be answered, but it probably benefits both species in the long run, although only one of the two benefits from any particular hunt.

Of the three co-operative attempts observed, two kills resulted. The Red-necked Falcon is an aerial hunter, and while the Gabar Goshawk may also take prey in the air, it is also well adapted for inter-canopy pursuit. Thus, although both species prey largely on the same food types, different hunting techniques probably enable them to obtain adequate food to co-exist in harmony. Further research on this hunting behaviour is needed. This study in general agrees with the findings in Zambia (Osborne 1981) on *Falco chicquera ruficollis.*

ACKNOWLEDGMENTS

I would like to thank the Board of Trustees of National Parks and Mr E.A.N. le Riche for permission to conduct this study. The help of W. Swartz and I. van Wyk in locating the nests is appreciated. Colin Sapsford and Dr. Richard Liversidge kindly commented on a previous draft.

REFERENCES

BRAINE, S.G. 1987. Raptors of the Skeleton Coast Park, SWA/Namibia. *Madoqua* 15: 255 - 262.

BROWN, C.J. 1988. Greater Kestrel and Red-necked Falcon populations in the Ganab region of the central Namib Desert. *Gabar* 3: 21 - 25.

COLEBROOK-ROBJENT, J.F.R. & T.O. OSBORNE 1975. High density of Red-necked Falcon *Falco chicquera* in Zambia. *Bull. Br. Ornith. Club* 94: 172 - 176.

FINCH-DAVIES, C.G. & A.C. KEMP 1980. *The Birds of Prey of Southern Africa.* Johannesburg: Winchester Press.

FRY, C.H. 1964. Red-necked Falcons *Falco chicquera* hunting bats. *Bull.Nigerian Orn. Soc.* 1: 1 - 19.

KEMP, A.C. 1986. The Gabar Goshawk: taxonomy, ecology and further research. *Gabar* 1: 4 - 6.

LEISTNER, O.A. 1967. The plant ecology of the southern Kalahari. *Mem. Bot. Surv. S.A.* 38: 1 - 172.

LEISTNER, O.A. & M.J.A. WERGER 1973. Southern Kalahari phytosociology. *Vegetatio* 28: 353 - 397.

MACLEAN, G.L. 1958. A nest of the Rufous-necked Falcon (*Tinnunculus ruficollis*) in the Namik. *Ostrich* 29: 88 - 89.

MACLEAN, G.L. 1985. *Roberts Birds of Southern Africa.* John Voelcker, Bird Book Fund, Cape Town.

MALAN, G. 1991. Co-operative hunting by Red-necked Falcons. *Gabar* 6: 70 - 71.

NEL, J.A.J. 1990. Foraging and feeding by Bat-eared Foxes *Otocyon megalotis* in the southwestern Kalahari. *Koedoe* 33: 9-16.

OLWAGEN, C.D. 1984. Breeding behaviour of the Red-necked Falcon in captivity. *In* J.M. Mendelsohn & C.W. Sapsford (Eds.) *Proc. 2nd Symp. Afr. Pred. Birds.* Durban: Natal Bird Club.

OSBORNE, T.O. 1984. Red-necked Falcon populations in Zambia. *In* J.M. Mendelsohn & C.W. Sapsford (Eds.) *Proc. 2nd Symp. Afr. Pred. Birds.* Durban: Natal Bird Club.

OSBORNE, T.O. 1981. Ecology of the Red-necked Falcon *Falco chicquera* in Zambia. *Ibis* 123: 289 - 297.

PICKFORD, P., B. PICKFORD & W. TARBOTON 1939. *Southern African Birds of Prey.* Straik Publishers, Cape Town.

STEYN, P. 1982. *Birds of Prey of Southern Africa.* Cape Town: Creda Press.

J.J. Herholdt
Transvaal Natural Conservation
Bird Monitoring Unit
P/Bag X 1088
Lydenburg 1120
Republic of South Africa

Meyburg, B.-U. & R. D. Chancellor eds.1994
Raptor Conservation Today
WWGBP / The Pica Press

Past and present Status of the Lesser Kestrel *Falco naumanni* in Bulgaria

Petar Iankov, Tzeno Petrov, Tanu Michev and Lubomir Profirov

INTRODUCTION

The Lesser Kestrel's status in Bulgaria is not well known despite many fragmentary data in the specialised literature and even in spite of the species being included in the Red Book of Bulgaria (1985) and the newest monograph on the birds of Bulgaria (Simeonov *et al.* 1990). Our present knowledge of the species' distribution and numbers in the country, as well as its vertical distribution, habitat requirements, migration, adverse factors, etc. is rather general and inadequate. This work aims to shed some light on the Lesser Kestrel's status in the past and during recent years, in order to provide for better preservation of a species known to have declined significantly in numbers throughout its range.

MATERIAL AND METHODS

The present work is based on the authors' own research, done mainly from 1969 to 1991, as well as on all information they were able to gather from the literature, personal communications from other ornithologists, skin collections from the Natural History Museums in Sofia and Plovdiv, taxidermic collections, etc. thus covering a period from 1890 till 1991. Status analysis was based on 204 entries about the species, of which 50 refer to the period ending in 1950 (23 on nesting and 27 on migration) and 154 to the period since 1950 (138 on nesting and 16 on migration). A further eight observations were omitted as the data are insufficiently specific. The Lesser Kestrel's distribution, during both the breeding season and on migration, is shown on a standard UTM (10x10km) grid. Exact locations are stored with the BSPB National Bank for ornithological information. All entries dated before 31st March 1916 were set to the Gregorian calendar. Breeding evidence was determined according to criteria set by the European Ornithological Atlas Committee (EOAC) (Sharrock 1976).

RESULTS

Breeding distribution and numbers

Data on the breeding sites of the Lesser Kestrel for the period 1890 to 1950 are shown in Figure 1. This, no doubt, is far from a full and detailed picture because of the sporadic research done in Bulgaria during the above period of time and resulting fragmentary data.

It is hard to-day to make any assessment of the Bulgarian population of that time but we have every reason to believe it was quite numerous, particularly in certain localities and probably at certain periods. Reiser (1894) gives eloquent proof of this by his observation on 21 June, 1893 of a colony of nearly 100 pairs near the town of Karlovo. There were Lesser Kestrel colonies in many other places throughout the country, especially in Southern Bulgaria (Reiser 1894; Arabadzhiev 1962; Bozhkov 1972, etc.) but data on the number of breeding pairs are absent from most of these publications. It is reasonable to assume that the architecture of villages and towns in those days provided suitable nest sites and there arerecords of the species breeding in many human settlements at that time.

Figure 2 shows the breeding distribution of the Lesser Kestrel from 1951 to 1991. A total of 86 breeding sites were recorded, of which 42 were confirmed, 14 probable and 30 possible. They are distributed in 65 of the 10x10km UTM squares (by degrees of breeding evidence in 33, 12 and 20 squares respectively). Thus the species has been recorded in 5.2% of all 1,240 UTM squares of the territory of Bulgaria. For the decade 1980-1990 57 breeding pairs were recorded. This is the minimum of confirmed breeding pairs, and it is possible for their number in the wild to be slightly higher as there might be some unknown breeding localities.

Besides, at many localities the species breeds together with the Kestrel *Falco tinnunculus* on high rock faces and cliffs and it is hard to establish the exact number of pairs of each species.

The size of the colonies found during the last decade does not exceed four pairs. Two known colonies for this period were found in the southernmost border areas of the country, the Eastern Rhodope mountains and the heights of Sakar.

From the available data it is difficult to judge with certainty certain peculiarities of the population dynamics of the Lesser Kestrel in Bulgaria for the past 100 years. It is a well-known fact that the European population has shown significant fluctuations, with peak numbers in the periods 1830-1850, 1885-1915 and 1940-1955 and reduced numbers outside these periods (Gensbol 1987). However, the overall trend towards decrease, both in the numbers of birds and of breeding sites and in the range occupied by the species in the country is indisputable. Evidence of this are the abandoned nesting grounds at a number of places, the reduced number of colonies and of birds per colony, as well as the relatively small number of records of this species despite the increase in ornithological studies in Bulgaria.

Figure 1. Breeding distribution of the Lesser Kestrel during the period 1890-1950 (1 - possible breeding; 2 - probable breeding; 3 - confirmed breeding).

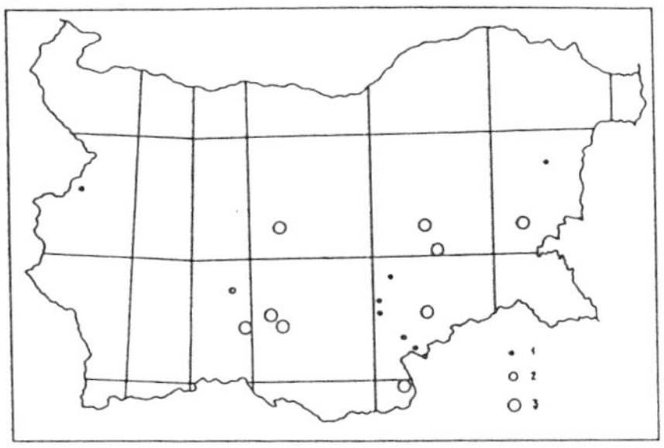

Figure 2. Breeding distribution of the Lesser Kestrel in Bulgaria during the period 1950-1988 (1 - possible breeding; 2 - probable breeding; 3 - confirmed breeding).

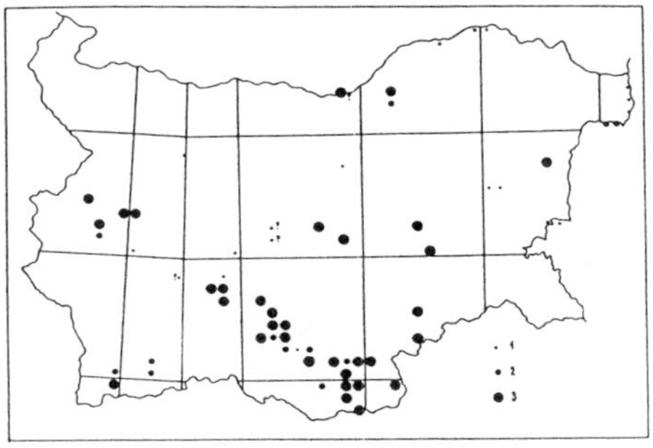

Breeding habitats and periods of breeding

The distribution of the Lesser Kestrel by breeding habitat is shown in Table 1. We should stress that rocky terrain is the major breeding habitat for this species in Bulgaria (52.9% of all known sites), namely mountain slopes, gorges, deep ravines etc. with open areas around them where the birds usually hunt. In human settlements 34 nests (32.1%) were recorded but this figure refers to a large extent to the period before 1960-1965, since when the species has virtually ceased to use buildings, rocks and to a large extent trees within the limits of larger human settlements. At present single pairs still breed in some villages. One cannot overlook the relatively higher percentage of nests in trees (20.7%) a fact considered to be exceptional for the European population of the species as a whole (Cramp & Simmons 1979).

Table 1. Habitat distribution of 106 nests of the Lesser Kestrel for the period 1890-1991.

Type of substrate where the nest is built	Habitat	Number	% of all of pairs	Total nests	%
Rocks (on ledges, in niches, hollows, old nests of other species)	open rocky ground, deep ravines in the wild	49	46.3		
	in human settlements	7	6.6	56	52.9
Buildings (mainly under roofs and in hollows)	in human settlements	24	22.7		
	solitary buildings outside settlements	1	0.9	25	23.6
Trees (in hollows, in old nests of other species etc.)	on banks near water	11	10.4		
	in other places	8	7.5		
	in human settlements	3	2.8	22	20.7
Rock quarries, walls of lime-kilns		3	2.8	3	2.8
	Total:	106	100	106	100

The vertical distribution of the Lesser Kestrel during the breeding season in Europe is known to encompass altitudes of up to 500m a.s.l. (Cramp & Simmons 1979). In Bulgaria there are certain variations. Although it may be assumed that there is a certain preference for breeding at altitudes of between 100 and 200m a.s.l., 11 nests have been recorded at not less than 600m and another three were found at not less than 800m.

In the vicinity of nests the earliest records of Lesser Kestrels were made in mid-March (14 March 1988, pers. comm. of E. and I. Krasteniakovi) and breeding pairs were recorded at the beginning of April (5 April 1986). The latest were observed at the beginning of October (2 October 1960, Boev *et al.* 1964). There was a rather late observation of young kestrels just fledged on 7 September 1959 (Arabadzhiev 1962). Such a late breeding is obviously no exception as there are similar observations of young in down on 9 July 1984 in the Eastern Rhodope mountains (Iankov & Niagolov 1987).

Migration

Figure 3 analyses the available information on seasonal migrations of the Lesser Kestrel. Data shown testify to a comparatively broad front of migration although the birds generally keep to the main flyways. These follow in general 1) Sofia Plain - the river Maritza valley - Sea of Marmara;

2) Sofia Plain - the river Struma valley - the Aegean Sea (the so-called Via Aristotelis flyway); and 3) the Via Pontica flyway along the Black Sea coastline. From our observations it is inferred that Lesser Kestrels do not apparently prefer the latter flyway so much as other soaring migrants. The species migrates over Bulgaria singly or in small flocks consisting of 40 to 50 individuals, as observed by Liedel and Luther (1969) at about 2,000m a.s.l. on Rila mountain on 23 August 1961. The first spring migrants were observed on 14 March 1988 near a nest in north-east Bulgaria (pers. comm. by E. & I. Krasteniakovi). The spring migration lasts until the first ten days of May.

Autumn migration begins at the beginning of August (1 August 1963 - Kalchev 1965), and the last autumn migrant was recorded in Bulgaria on 16 October 1898 (Anon. 1907). The peak was recorded in August: 51 birds for eight observations. In September 14 birds were counted in two observations and only nine Lesser Kestrels were recorded in October during six days in the field.

Figure 3. Distribution of the Lesser Kestrel in Bulgaria during the seasonal migrations (1 - before 1950; 2 - after 1950; 3 - spring migration; 4 - autumn migration).

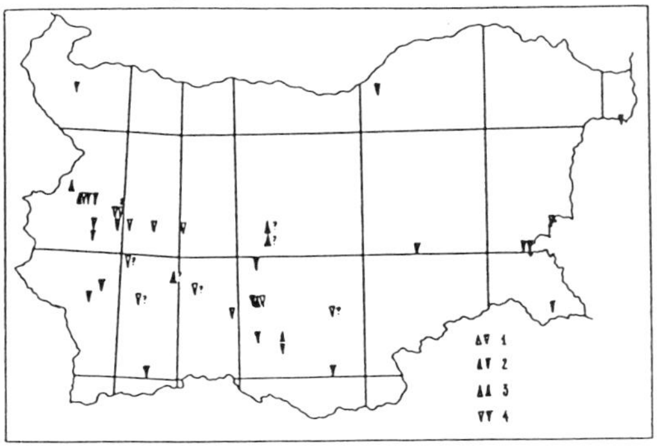

Mortality and threats

For the 100-year period under discussion we have records of 57 deaths of Lesser Kestrels, of which 29 occurred after 1950. Causes of death are as follows: 50 birds shot by hunters (87.7% of all cases), four young taken from the nest (7.0%) and three (5.3%) dead from unknown causes. It seems most likely that the above figure represents a negligible part of all deaths of Lesser Kestrels during the period and, besides, the causes of death mentioned here far from exhaust the whole range of negative factors affecting the species; for instance, among others, the growing use of agricultural chemicals since the end of World War II, the overall increase in environmental pollution, changes in village buildings, etc.

Protection status

The Lesser Kestrel is protected by law. However, analysis of its breeding sites shows that only nine of them (or 10.5% of all known breeding sites for the period 1951-1991) are situated in protected areas. It seems logical to assume that to place as many as possible of the existing breeding sites under legal protection is an indispensable measure to ensure efficient protection more especially in view of the fact that most of the known causes of death are shooting or taking young from nests. Of course, it is necessary to carry out further research into other factors crucial for the species' survival, along with implementation of specific measures for its preservation.

ACKNOWLEDGEMENTS

The authors wish to thank E. & I. Krasteniakovi, Bob Scott from RSPB, J. Bekhuis, I. Vatev, J.L. Roberts, G. Kuzmanov and M. Mikhov for all information they supplied. Special thanks are due to K. Niagolov for his help in our joint field trips.

REFERENCES

ANONYMOUS 1907. Collections du musée d'histoire naturelle. Sofia, State Printers.

ARABADZHIEV, I. 1962. *The Birds of Prey of Bulgaria.* Nauka i iskustvo, Sofia.
BOEV, N., Zh. GEORGIEV & St. DONTCHEV 1964. The birds of Thracia. In *Fauna of Thracia, Part 1.* B.A.S. Publ. Sofia.
BOZHKOV, D. 1972. *Following the Shadows of Kestrels.* Nauka i iskustvo, Sofia.
CRAMP, S. & K.E.L. SIMMONS (Eds.) 1979. *The Birds of the Western Palearctic* Vol. 2, Oxford Univ. Press., Oxford.
GENSBOL, B. 1987. *Collins' Guide to the Birds of Prey of Britain and Europe, North Africa and the Middle East.* Collins, London.
IANKOV, P. & K. NIAGOLOV 1987. Observations on the birds in the Eastern Rhodopes in 1984. *Orn. Inf. Bull.* 21-22: 42-55.
KALCHEV, B. 1965. Notes on the bird fauna of Plovdiv region. *An. Mus. Plovdiv* 4: 259-265.
LIEDEL, K. & D. LUTHER 1969. Beitrag zur Avifauna Bulgariens. *Beitr. Voegelkd.* 14: 406-435.
RED BOOK OF BULGARIA 1985.. Part 2: Animals. B.A.S. Publ. Sofia.
REISER, O. 1894. *Materialen zu einer Ornis Balcanica: II Bulgarien.* Wien.
SHARROCK, J. 1976. *The Atlas of Breeding Birds in Britain and Ireland.* T. & A.D. Poyser Ltd, London.
SIMEONOV, S., T. MICHEV & D. NANKINOV 1990. *Fauna Bulgarica*, vol. 20 *Aves,* Part 1. B.A.S. Publ. Sofia.

P. Iankov, T. Petrov, T. Michev & L. Profirov
Bulgarian Society for the Protection of Birds
8 Dragan Tzankov Street
1421 Sofia, Bulgaria

Lesser Sooty Owl *Tyto multipunctata*

Meyburg, B.-U. & R. D. Chancellor eds.1994
Raptor Conservation Today
WWGBP / The Pica Press

Changes in Status of the Black Vulture *Aegypius monachus* in Bulgaria for the period 1980-1990

Petar Iankov, Khristo Khristov and Stefan Avramov

INTRODUCTION

In spite of some recent publications on the Black Vulture in Bulgaria (Baumgart 1989; Simeonov *et al.* 1990; Nankinov *et al.* 1991) the present status in our country of this globally endangered species, as well as the trends in its population dynamics, are only tentatively known. At the same time the necessity for more and detailed information about the species is obvious. We need, above all, to determine specific preservation measures both in Bulgaria and in this particular part of the Balkan peninsula, as the birds in question are common to Bulgaria and Northern Greece. This information will certainly help action within the framework of the European Black Vulture Conservation Project too.

MATERIAL AND METHODS

This work is based on data gathered intentionally from 1 January 1980 to 31 December 1990 during regular visits to the Eastern Rhodope mountains during all seasons. After 1988 the same region has been visited for about a week at least once monthly. Special attention was paid to places for which there was information about former nests of the Black Vulture, as well as to those areas where there are suitable nesting conditions at present. The species was especially searched for in other parts of the country, too, during repeated visits to suitable places, particularly in the southern and eastern parts of Bulgaria. We also used all available information on this species in the literature, as well as unpublished data kindly placed at our disposal by other persons. Our observations were made considerably easier after the Bulgarian Society for the Protection of Birds built two special sites for feeding vultures in Eastern Rhodope mountains - the so-called "vulture restaurants". A total of 147 observations were made for the above period, detailed data of which are in safe-keeping with BSPB National Bank for ornithological information.

RESULTS

Distribution and general status

Among the information collected there was none to indicate confirmed breeding of the species in Bulgaria for the period of the research. Local people showed us three localities in the Eastern Rhodope mountains in the immediate vicinity of the state border with Greece (Fig. 2), where they claimed there were Black Vultures nests until about 1980-1982. Two of these sites are northern slopes covered with oak forest (*Quercus* sp.) and nests were built on oak trees. During our visits to both sites we found them so radically changed because of felling of the trees that we could not tell for sure if the information about the vulture's nesting there was reliable.

During the period of the study there were only four observations of Black Vultures outside the confines of the Eastern Rhodope mountains (Fig. 1):

Figure 1. Distribution of the Black Vulture in Bulgaria during the period 1980 - 1990 (1 - possible breeding; 2- probable breeding; 3 - observation outside the breeding season: 4 - area of permanent occurrence of the vultures).

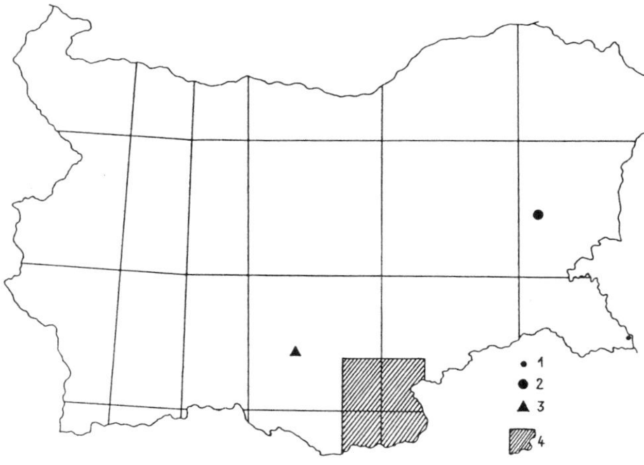

1. On 15th April 1981 two birds were observed at a carcass of a sheep near the village of Yasenovo, district of Burgas, on the Eastern Stara Planina Mountain (UTM NH14) (Lubomir Profirov, pers. comm.);
2. On 25th April 1981 one Black Vulture was observed in flight near the same village of Yasenovo (L. Profirov, pers. comm.);
3. On 11th December 1983 two Black Vultures were seen in agricultural fields near the village of Topolovo, district of Plovdiv (UTM LG34) (Petrov 1990);
4. On 11th July 1989 one bird was observed at some dead pigs near the mouth of the river Silistar, in Strandzha Mountain (UTM NG85) (Boian Milchev, pers. comm.).

While observation No. 3 refers undoubtedly to wanderers, Black Vultures observed during the breeding season in Eastern Stara Planina and Strandzha Mountains could possibly have been birds from nearby breeding sites. Much closer attention should clearly be paid to these places, especially in the region of Strandzha Mountain, where we cannot rule out occupied nests in the border area with Turkey.

Distribution of the Black Vulture over the territory of the Eastern Rhodope mountains is shown in Figure 2, emphasising the two sectors with most observations of the species, although this might be due to the whole range being unevenly covered during the period of study. However, in these two sectors of the mountains Black Vultures can be observed all the year round, indicating that breeding conditions there most closely correspond to the ecological requirements of the species. It seems natural to assume that the probability is highest for the first nest to be built in one of these two sectors in the event of the Black Vulture breeding once again in Bulgaria. Interestingly, both sectors contain considerable areas where only a few ghost villages occur and which are very seldom visited by people. Thus conditions favouring nesting by vultures are present. Unfortunately, the most suitable breeding habitats, namely the forests in the border strip most closely situated to Greek breeding areas, have been subjected to mass felling during the last decade or so. This is most likely one of the most important negative factors preventing the Black Vulture from breeding in the Eastern Rhodope mountains for the last ten years.

Figure 2. Area of permanent occurrence of the Black Vulture in Bulgaria (1 = site of observation; 2 = former breeding site).

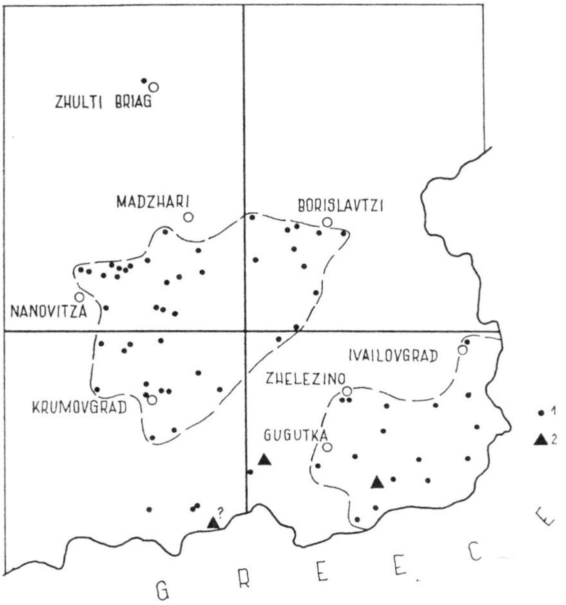

Figure 3 shows the distribution of all 147 observations by years. It can be seen that in spite of certain fluctuations the total number of observations has grown throughout the decade. This corresponds well to the the overall trend of increasing populations of some other vultures and carrion-eating birds in Bulgaria (Raven *Corvus corax*; Griffon Vulture *Gyps fulvus* and others), established since the beginning of the 1970s after these species had nearly become extinct in the 1960s. Among the causes of this increase we should stress the apparent role played by the protective measures undertaken after 1960: a total ban on poisoned baits for controlling terrestrial predators, a ban on shooting all birds of prey (until 1986 all species were banned from shooting with the exception of the Goshawk *Accipiter gentilis,* Sparrowhawk *Accipiter nisus*, Marsh Harrier *Circus aeruginosus* and Rough-legged Buzzard *Buteo lagopus*; after 1986 these four species were also fully protected), and the creation of protected sites in some raptors' habitats. More recently, additional feeding in the Eastern Rhodope mountains has had a very positive effect on raptors in general and vultures in particular, especially for the period from 1989 to 1991, when cattle and sheep numbers sharply decreased following the forced emigration of native Turks to Turkey. There is no clearly shown tendency for increase in numbers on the curve reflecting the maximum numbers of Black Vulture observations made from a single spot, as is obvious for the Griffon Vulture in the Eastern Rhodope mountains (Iankov & Profirov 1991). This is probably due to the fact that the Black Vulture is not as markedly social and gregarious as the Griffon Vulture and searches for food in a solitary manner, the birds thus being more widely dispersed over a larger territory. Our observations since the end of the 1960s have shown that the Black Vulture is much slower in restoring its numbers than the Griffon Vulture, a probable explanation of this being that it was, in general, less numerous than the Griffon and that its breeding habitats - the forests - were subjected to much more severe human pressure than those of the Griffon. Nevertheless a series of observations testify to an overall increase in the Black Vulture's presence in the Bulgarian part of the Eastern Rhodope mountains. Increasingly often one can observe birds staying for the night on trees and rocks at a distance of 40 to 50km from the border with Greece, even without any available food nearby. Black Vultures can be seen the year round in areas where breeding conditions are suitable; in two such places the Working Group on Birds of Prey of BSPB built five artificial nests to attract them to breed. There are single observations of breeding behaviour (mutual preening of two adults). In our opinion all this indicates that it is quite possible to have breeding Black Vultures in our part of the Eastern Rhodope mountains in the near future. Factors favouring such a development are the recent revival of extensive cattle and sheep breeding, the additional feeding and building of artificial nests, the increased numbers of Griffon

Vultures, etc. Of course, it is hardly to be expected this will happen before the population in northern Greece reaches its optimum level.

Figure 3. Dynamics of the numbers of Black Vulture records in Bulgaria for the period 1981-1990 (thick line - total number of records for the year; broken line - maximum number of the Black Vultures seen together).

Mortality and threatening factors

We possess information about four cases of death of Black Vultures for the period of this study, all of which occurred in the Eastern Rhodope mountains. In every case the cause of death was illegal shooting: in 1980 one bird was killed and stuffed; in 1981 two birds were killed for their fatty tissues, used for medication; in 1984 one bird was killed. Along with felling of forests in the border zone, illegal use of poisoned and soporific baits for control of wolves was another major factor threatening the survival of the species in the region. In 1984 we rescued and later freed two Black Vultures taken by local people after consuming soporific baits. In our opinion, this danger will grow in the years to come, along with the liberalisation of private enterprise in stock raising and the presence of wolves in the same regions where vultures occur.

ACKNOWLEDGEMENTS

We cordially thank all who helped us with our studies. Special thanks are due to Lubomir Profirov, Boian Milchev, Plamen Arsov and Dr. Ilia Vatev, who kindly gave us their unpublished observations and information. We are grateful to Evelyn Tewes, Ben Hallmann and Carlota Viada for the useful discussions and exchange of ideas we had on conservation of the species in the Balkan peninsula.

REFERENCES

BAUMGART, W. 1989. Verbreitung und existenzbedingungen von Gänse-,Kutten- und Bartgeier (*Gyps fulvus, Aegypius monachus, Gypaetus barbatus*) in Bulgarien in Vergangenheit und Gegenwart. *Acta ornithoecol.* 2 (1): 15-38.

IANKOV, P. & L. PROFIROV 1991. Contemporary state of the Griffon Vulture (*Gyps fulvus Hablitzl*) population in Bulgaria. *Ecology* 24: 44-52.

NANKINOV, D., G. STOYANOV, G. KOUZMANOV & R. TODOROV 1991. Information sur la situation des rapaces diurnes en Bulgarie. *In Birds of Prey Bulletin* No. 4. WWGBB, Berlin.

PETROV, Tz. 1989. The birds of Dobrostan Hill and its surroundings (Western Rhodopes). Part 1. *Bull. Mus. South Bulgaria* 15: 59-72.

SIMEONOV, S., T. MICHEV & D. NANKINOV 1990. *Fauna Bulgarica.* 20 Aves Part 1. B.A.S. Publ., Sofia.

P. Iankov, K. Khristov & S. Avramov
Bulgarian Society for the Protection of Birds
8 Dragan Tzankov Street
1421 Sofia, Bulgaria

Meyburg, B.-U. & R. D. Chancellor eds.1994
Raptor Conservation Today
WWGBP / The Pica Press

Raptors' Plasticity of Nest Site Selection

Wolfgang Kirmse

The occupation of suitable habitats depends greatly on the capability of raptor species to use different types of nest sites. Species with high plasticity in this respect are able to cover coherently and completely their species area, depending only on food availability. Species which are fixed on one special type of nesting can not cover all areas where they could live, e.g. rock nesters in wooded plains without rocks or tree nesters in steppes bare of trees. In some of these species with fixed and therefore restricted nest site selection there exist subpopulations clumped in remote areas using a quite different nest type, by this being able to occupy vast territories which otherwise could not be used as a breeding area by that species.

According to their different plasticity of nest site selection, raptors may be grouped into the following categories:

1. The majority of raptor species are firmly fixed on a special type of nest site according to a narrow genetical disposition. That group is further labelled as "fixed type"; e.g. Sparrow-hawk is tree nester, Griffon Vulture is rock nester exclusively.

2. A number of species regularly exhibit plasticity of nest site selection. These species use different nest site types within a continuous area and even within the nesting range of one pair, depending on distribution and availability of either nest site type. This group is further labelled as "ubiquists", and their plasticity is due to a wide genetical disposition; e.g. Kestrel or Golden Eagle belong to this group.

3. Only in very few species, originally belonging to the fixed type group, may subpopulations exceptionally originate with very differing nest site selection. These are spatially separated from their conspecifics of the normal fixed nesting type. The differing nest site selection is based on early experience and thus continued by tradition. Members of this group are further labelled as "tradition founders"; e.g. the Peregrine with tree nest and tree hollow tradition and the Red Kite with rock nest tradition, both in few places in the world.

As demonstrated in the classification and in Table 1, plasticity of nest site selection may be based on genetical disposition or on tradition. The deciding difference between both is due to the unequal probability of transition between the nest site types in the tradition founders: unhindered transition from the tradition to the genetically fixed type; no, or extremely exceptional, transition from the inborn type to the tradition type, which latter is normally acquired by early individual experience. This is the only reason why in the tradition founders their extraordinary nest site selection occurs spatially isolated and at only few places on the globe but, where once established, they are clumped together and in good numbers, coherently covering the vacant area - i.e. the deviating type of nesting does not represent a suboptimal ecological situation. Currently the most outstanding example of isolated tradition is the nesting in tree-holes of Peregrines nowadays confined to only one place in the world: South Victoria in Australia. This tradition is another and quite separate line compared to tree-nesting of Peregrines in nests of other birds! Thus ubiquists and tradition founders may be discriminated in the field by the distribution pattern of the different nest sites they use, as schematically shown in Figures 1a and 1b.

Table 1. Groups and examples of nest site selection types in birds of prey.

Group and Species (few examples)	tree nest	tree hollow	pylon nest (tree dummy)	ground	rock	building (rock dummy)
Fixed tree nester:						
Sparrow Hawk *Accipiter nisus*	+					
Honey Buzzard *Pernis apivorus*	+					
Hobby *Falco subbuteo*	+		+			
Ubiquists:						
Kestrel *Falco tinnunculus*	+	+	+	+	+	+
Golden Eagle *Aquila chrysaetos*	+		+		+	
Saker Falcon *Falco cherrug*	+		+		+	+
Fixed rock nester:						
Egyptian Vulture *Neophron percnopterus*					+	
Eleonora's Falcon *Falco eleonorae*				+	+	
Tradition founder:						
Peregrine *Falco peregrinus*	[+]	[+]		+	+	+
Red Kite *Milvus milvus*	+				[+]	

Symbols: + freely accessible nesting type
[+] accessible by tradition only

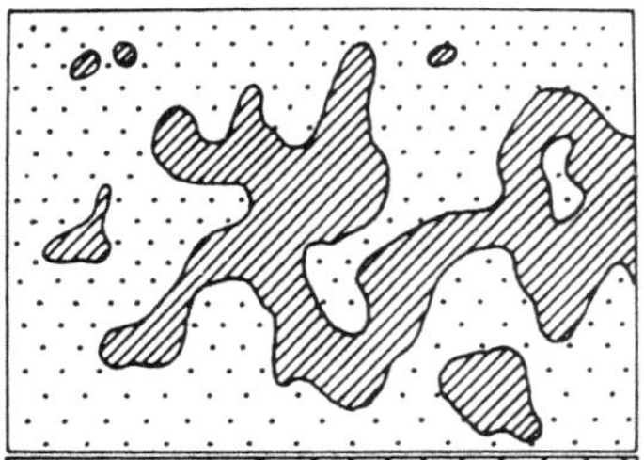

Figure 1a. Mixed distribution pattern of two nesting types of ubiquisits according to regional availability of nest sites.

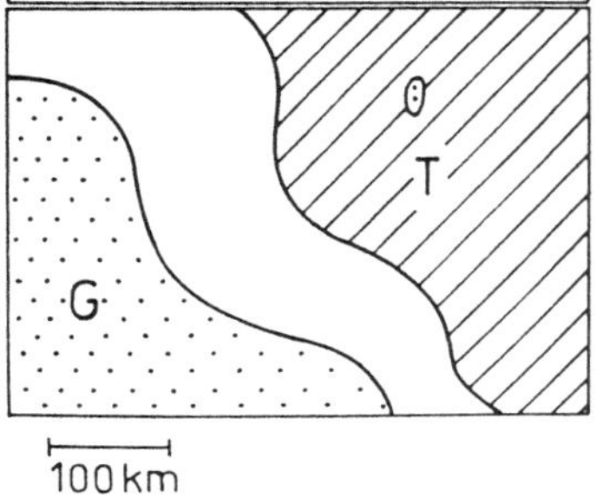

Figure 1b. Disjunct distribution of genetically fixed G and tradition T type of nesting separated by un-occupied territory. A few isolated pairs of G within the area of T occur regularly, but never the reverse.

Tradition founding in the proper and outstanding manner is presently known from few raptor species only: Peregrine, Red Kite, Common Buzzard (rock-nesting); but certainly more examples will be found. Tradition founders can exhibit their capability only in special and remote habitat conditions bare of the inborn nest site type. But in far from all such localities will the tradition of a new nesting type arise. Therefore an established nesting tradition once collapsed may never return spontaneously. Thus, populations representing a special nesting tradition need more attention to prevent their accidental extinction. If they are extinct they essentially need management, using imprinting on nest site type for reintroduction.

In many other species, mainly of the ubiquist group, tradition influences nest site selection, too, but in a less outstanding way. For instance ground nesting of Ospreys, ground nesting and the use of tree-holes in Kestrels, or the new fashion of nesting on power pylons, e.g. by Osprey and different falcon species, mostly occurs locally and clumped. But such local traditions arise in many places, are less extraordinary, and members of those nesting traditions are in continuous contact with their conspecifics of the normal nesting type. Mainly the transition from one type of nesting to the other does not seem to be blocked or hindered in any direction. This latter feature of unequal transition is diagnostic for tradition founders in the proper sense, as explained above.

In conclusion, the formation of tradition influences nest site selection in many species with gradual differences. In the ubiquists and some fixed type nesters it is an additional enlargement of their genetical disposition; in a few fixed type species, here named tradition founders, it is a narrow way to escape the restrictions of their genetically fixed nesting behaviour.

REFERENCES

KIRMSE, W. 1987. Zur Habitatstruktur und brutökologischen Traditionsbildung bei baumbrütenden Wanderfalken *Falco peregrinus. - Populationsökologie Greifvogel- u. Eulenarten* 1: 99-110. Wiss. Beitr. Univ. Halle.

KIRMSE, W. 1989. Zur Fixierung von Nistweisen bei Falken und ihre Bedeutung f-r die Arealbesiedlung. *Mitt. d. DDR-Sektion des IRV 1/Jg*: 31-36.

NEWTON, I. 1979. *Population Ecology of Raptors.* Poyser, Berkhamsted.

WHITE, C.M., S.G. PRUETT-JONES & W.B. EMISON 1981. The status and distribution of the Peregrine Falcon in Victoria, Australia. *Emu* 80: 270-280.

Prof. Wolfgang Kirmse
Am Bogen 43
0-7030 Leipzig
Fed. Rep. of Germany

Short-eared Owl *Asio flammeus*
and Marsh Owl *Asio capensis*

Meyburg, B.-U. & R. D. Chancellor eds.1994
Raptor Conservation Today
WWGBP / The Pica Press

Montagu's Harrier *Circus pygargus* Post-Fledging Activities in Eastern Poland - Preliminary Results.

Ignacy Kitowski

INTRODUCTION

In contrast with the breeding biology, of which detailed studies have been made (Krogulec 1992), the post-fledging ecology Montagu's Harrier in natural habitats is almost completely unstudied.

STUDY AREA AND METHODS

The study was carried out in south-east Poland on calcareous marshes near Chelm (south-east Poland) covered by Saw Sedge (*Cladium mariscus*). The population of Montagu's Harrier consisted of 30-40 pairs. The nests were located exclusively in Saw Sedge. The post-fledging period of 25 juveniles belonging to seven breeding pairs was studied during the summers of 1989-1991. All were wing-tagged with colour plastic strips of Saflag (Kochert *et al.* 1983). Observation started at the end of June shortly before the first flights of the young. The sex of these juveniles was assessed following methods described by Krogulec (1992). Observation covered almost complete days (8-20 h). In 1989 two families were observed daily; in 1990 and 1991 observations were carried out every 1-3 days. All data were recorded on tapes to register data quickly and accurately. Observations were made from stationary points (trees, bushes) at approximately 200 m from the juveniles, using 20 x 60 telescope and 10 x 50 binoculars.

RESULTS AND DISCUSSION

The post-fledging period lasted for 17-28 days (x= 23.7, sd. = 2.9, n = 22). There were no differences between male and female juveniles at age of first flight ($t = 0.63$, $t_{23, 0.05} = 2.07$).

During the first week after fledging, juveniles were clumsy in flight and landing technique, like the young of other harriers (Wiacek 1989). First flights were short, circling and flapping, starting and ending on nest platforms. As the young grew older they used more elaborate flying techniques such as gliding and soaring. For all juveniles studied, all variables in flight skills were significantly correlated with age for the greatest number of individuals, except for the number of flights (NF).

This may be the result of a similar strategy of flight development shown in the post-fledging period of the Black Kite *Milvus migrans* (Bustamante & Hiraldo 1989).

During fieldwork sibling and adult-juvenile aggression was observed. Sibling aggression, measured by the number of dives at other juveniles, was positively correlated with age for all 22 surviving individuals (see below) (r=0.317, p < 0.001, N = 181). Sibling aggression was nearly restricted to the time of presence of food (82%, N=181). As in other raptors (Ceballos & Donazar 1990), maximum aggression occurred during feeds.

Table 1. Duration of post-fledging period in relation to sex in juvenile Montagu's Harriers. All parameters in days. F-female, M-male.

Juveniles	First flight	Leaving breeding area	Duration of PFP
ZC15/89 (F)	35	63	28
ZZ15/89 (F)	35	61	26
ZN15/89 (F)	34	60	26
CZ09/89 (F)	35	61	26
CB09/89 (M)	34	56	22
CN09/89 (F)	35	57	22
CN06/90 (M)	32	56	24
ZN06/90 (M)	32	54	22
BN06/90 (F)	31	57	26
PP08/90 (F)	33	56	23
ZB08/90 (M)	32	55	23
BC08/90 (M)	31	56	25
XP08/90 (F)	32	57	25
BN08/90 (F)	32	53	21
BB06/91 (F)	34	62	28
ZZ06/91 (F)	32	60	28
PPOM/91 (F)	35	60	25
BBOM/91(F)	33	57	24
PP11/91 (M)	34	52	18
ZZ11/91 (M)	34	55	21
OP11/91 (F)	35	52	17
BB11/91 (M)	32	52	20

The above results confirmed previous data, that the post-fledging period in Montagu's Harrier lasts 3-4 weeks (Brown 1976; Newton 1976).

Parental aggression, measured by the number of dives at young, increased slightly in a few families with the age of the juvenile, but the sample size was insufficient to estimate any correlations. Adult aggression mostly took the form of attacks on begging offspring which were flying or perching (60%, N=139). Other forms of aggression were attacks on flying young (20%) and chasing of juveniles from their perch (30%). Parental aggression was not restricted to the time of food presence, but 40% also took place at the time of food transfer or other circumstances connected with the presence of food.

Shortly after the young left the nest, the adults spent much time near the nest. As fledglings grew older, the parents spent less time in their vicinity and this trend was statistically significant in six out of seven families, as in other raptors (Bustamante & Hiraldo 1990; Hiraldo *et al.* 1989). At the end of the post-fledging period, the parents' stay in the vicinity of their young was reduced to the time needed for food transfers. The number of parental flights towards young (NPF) was negatively correlated with age of the youngest juveniles in five out of seven broods.

Juveniles followed parents on hunting forays. There were 24 occasions of adults hunting in the presence of juveniles. On 79% of these the young were able to see the capture of prey. Young unsuccessfully chased mainly passerines - (60%) N=27 (Acrocephalidae, Emberizidae). Some of the young (six out of the 22) pounced on inanimate objects (N=11) such as the tops of branches,

Table 2. Correlation coefficients on juvenile age of the variables MX (maximum flight duration, in seconds), MD (mean flight duration, in seconds), TD (total flight duration, in seconds), NF (number of flights), PS (percentage of time spent circling or soaring out of total time of flights). Sample size in brackets to left of the coefficients.

Juveniles		MX	MD	TD	NF	PS
ZC15/89	(n=21)	0.81**	0.88***	0.80***	0.60**	0.69***
ZZ15/89	(n=19)	0.84***	0.89**	0.85***	0.65**	0.76***
ZN15/89	(n=19)	0.86***	0.87***	0.72***	0.68**	0.65**
CZ09/89	(n=22)	0.56**	0.68***	0.62**	0.44*	0.55**
CB09/89	(n=22)	0.48*	0.70***	0.77***	0.75***	0.52*
CN09/89	(n=22)	0.74***	0.84**	0.75***	0.76***	0.32
CN06/90	(n=8)	0.76*	0.84**	0.81*	0.75*	0.77*
ZN06/90	(n=8)	0.75*	0.89**	0.71*	0.67	0.76*
BN06/90	(n=8)	0.29	0.86**	0.68	0.44	0.72*
PP08/90	(n=8)	0.86**	0.84**	0.84**	0.75*	0.55
ZB08/90	(n=8)	0.75*	0.79*	0.86**	0.78*	0.69
BC08/90	(n=8)	0.66	0.69	0.66	0.54	0.86*
XP08/90	(n=8)	0.80*	0.82	0.68	0.53	0.69
BN08/90	(n=8)	0.68	0.77*	0.89**	0.86**	0.86**
BB06/91	(n=10)	0.83**	0.82**	0.85**	0.59	0.87**
ZZ06/91	(n=9)	0.70*	0.69*	0.66	0.64	0.76*
PPOM	(n=8)	0.72*	0.81*	0.80*	0.61	0.58
BBOM	(n=8)	0.73*	0.88**	0.87**	0.76*	0.57
PP11/91	(n=5)	0.88*	0.82	0.98**	0.76	0.78
ZZ11/91	(n=7)	0.67*	0.95***	0.84*	0.58	0.71
OF11	(n=6)	0.93**	0.91*	0.91*	0.60	0.85*
BE11/91	(n=6)	0.94**	0.95**	0.79	0.42	0.85*
Pooled	(n=248)	0.62***	0.72***	0.70***	0.59***	0.63***

* $p < 0.05$, **$p < 0.01$, ***$p < 0.001$

tops of small trees or elevated sticks. Juveniles were also observed playing with inanimate objects (N = 9).

Three of the 25 colour marked juveniles were killed shortly after the first flights. Two were predated, probably by Red Fox (*Vulpes vulpes*) 35 and 37 days after hatching respectively; the other was certainly killed by its siblings (typical for Cainism: extensive wounds on back of head and internal surface of elbow). This showed that, whilst common in the nesting stage (Krogulec 1992), the phenomenon of Cainism may still exist after the first flights.

Table 3. Relationship between age of youngest juveniles in brood and the variables quantifying some aspects of parental investment. TS - time spent by parents (one or both) in the post-fledging area. NPF - number of flights towards juveniles.

Broods	n	TS	NPF
B15/89	21	-0.820***	-0.919***
B09/89 -	22	-0.537*	-0.884***
B06/90	8	-0.714*	-.0733*
B08/90	11	-0.554	-0.824**
B06/91	8	-0.706*	-0.530
BOM/9	19	-0.732*	-0.679
B11/9	18	-0.871*	-0.989***
Pooled	87	-0.644***	-0.706***

* $p < 0.05$, **$p < 0.01$, ***$p < 0.001$

REFERENCES

BROWN, L. 1976. *British Birds of Prey.* Collins. London

BUSTAMANTE, J. & F. HIRALDO 1989. Post-fledging dependency period and maturation of flights in the Black Kite *Milvus migrans. Bird Study* 36: 199-204.

BUSTAMANTE, J. & F. HIRALDO 1990. Factors influencing family rupture and parent-offspring conflict in the Black Kite (*Milvus migrans*). *Ibis* 132: 58-67.

CEBALLOS, O. & J. DONAZAR 1990. Parent-offspring Conflict during Post-fledging period in Egyptian Vultures *Neophron percnopterus* (Aves, Accipitridae). *Ethology* 85: 225-235.

KOCHERT, M.N., K. STENHOF, & M.Q. MORITSH 1983. Evaluation of patagial markers for raptors and ravens. *Bull Wildlife Society* 11: 271-281.

KROGULEC, J. 1992. Ekologia rozrodu blotniaka lakowego *Circus pygargus* na torfowiskach weglanowych pod Chelmem.Unpbl. Ph.D Thesis. Maria-Curie Sklodowska University, Lublin.

NEWTON, I. 1976. *Population Ecology of Raptors.* T & D. Poyser: Calton.

HIRALDO, F., M. DELIBES & R. ESTRELLA 1989. Some observations of Zone-tailed Hawk *Buteo albonotatus* family during post-fledging period. *Journal of Raptor Research* 23(3): 103-106.

WIACEK J. 1989. Obserwacje nad okresem post -pisklecym u blotniaka stawowego (*Circus aeruginosus*) na torfowiskach weglanowych pod Chelmem. Unpbl, Msc Thesis. University Maria-Curie Sklodowska, Lublin.

Ignacy Kitowski
Dept. Nature Conservation
University Maria Curie-Sklodowska
Akademicka 19, 20-33 Lublin
Poland

Meyburg, B.-U. & R. D. Chancellor eds.1994
Raptor Conservation Today
WWGBP / The Pica Press

Breeding Ecology of Montagu's Harrier *Circus pygargus* on natural and reclaimed Marshes in Poland and France

Jaroslaw Krogulec & Alain B.A. Leroux

Montagu's Harrier is one of the raptors still decreasing in numbers in most European countries. There are now relatively large populations only in France, Spain, Portugal and Poland. Since 1985 we have studied the breeding ecology of this species on marshes with the two highest concentrations of Montagu's Harrier in Europe. One is on natural, calcareous marshes located in south-east Poland (near Lublin, 51° N, 23° 30' E). The other is on reclaimed saltmarshes and wet pastures in western France (near Rochefort/Mer, 46° N, 0° 55' W).

In Poland, where the total population is lower (200-300 and 3000-4000 pairs in France, in Gensbol, 1984), *Circus pygargus* concentrates only on certain marshes suitable for breeding. Surrounding areas, consisting mostly of meadows, pastures and fields, remain unoccupied. In western France the birds are dispersed over a wide area, with some concentration in the most suitable habitats, where they reach the highest density noted for Europe. In one 22ha marsh at Cire in 1990 28 pairs were recorded. On the study area, the Marais de Rochefort, totalling 200km², 54 pairs were noted the same year. On the neighbouring Marais de Brouage on 100km² 43 pairs bred (42-43 censused in 1985-86). The density in these areas reached 2.7 - 4.3 pairs per 10km².

In Poland on 14km² of marshes over the four years (1985-1988) 32-42 pairs were recorded, depending on the year, with a range of action of *ca*.330 km². This gave a density of 1.0 to 1.3 pairs per 10km².

Due to the different distributions of harriers in the two landscapes the comparison of densities is incompatible but give us information about the relative concentration in the two study areas. As Montagu's Harrier is not a typical territorial breeder, comparison between larger study plots should include areas of total home ranges. According to the literature (in Leroux, 1987) the hunting distance of the male usually reaches 5km (exceptionally 10-12km). So for true comparison between different areas we should look at at least 100km².

Taking only density on breeding sites, we can compare concentration of nests in colonies which reach in Cire 12.7 pairs per 10ha. In the largest colony in Poland density reached 1 pair per 10ha. The nearest neighbour distance recorded in France was 20m, in Poland 42m. The mean distance between nearest neighbours was 122m in France and 160m in Poland. In such colonies distances between nests have not exceeded 600m.

Unlike some other raptors, there were no differences in mean near neighbour distances between poor and rich vole years in both countries. Montagu's Harrier is not a territorial bird and breeding dispersion is shaped by pluriannual mean food availability in a large territory and, locally, by suitable undisturbed nest sites at the beginning of the breeding season.

The population number on French marshes fluctuated markedly between years. In poor vole years (1985 & 1991) 22-25 pairs were noted on the Marais de Rochefort. In good vole years (1987 & 1990) 43 to 54 pairs bred there. In poor vole years there was a large proportion of non-breeders (over 50%).

In comparison, the Polish population was more stable: 32 to 42 pairs. The number of pairs has not changed markedly with vole density in individual years.

On marshes in both countries harriers breed in rank vegetation. The height of plants surrounding nests was between 80 and 100cm. At the beginning of the nesting period females choose vegetation tall enough to hide them during incubation. On balance it should not be too high to prevent the female leaving easily upon the approach of a predator or arrival of the male with food. In France in places where natural vegetation still remains Montagu's Harriers choose this first. The increasing area of crops is now used by 15% of pairs. This could be related to loss of natural vegetation at certain sites. Although the same phenomenon has been noted in Poland for the last three years, there has been no change in the area of natural marshes (they are protected).

Montagu's Harrier in certain regions of its range is, like many other raptors, strongly dependent on a diet of microtines. In France during poor vole years, *Microtus* voles were only 5% of the diet (84% was insects). In years of peak density, voles and other small mammals form up to 80% of the adult diet. In Poland dependence on microtines is less marked and their proportion in the diet has not fluctuated markedly between years. As an alternative prey passerines are extensively used. *Microtus* form here 34% of all food and birds 26%. Other prey are insects and reptiles.

The diet components have a considerable impact on the breeding parameters of harriers. In France mean yearly clutch size oscillated between 2.8 and 3.7 (n=115), dependent on the food supply. In Poland clutch size was generally larger (3.9-4.4; n=125) and did not fluctuate significantly between years.

Hatching success was similar in both countries at 73% in Poland and 77% in France. It was again relatively constant on Polish marshes and fluctuated markedly on the Marais de Rochefort (59%-84%).

The final output of reproduction - fledging success - was linked with vole numbers in particular years in both countries, but in France the differences were more extreme. In poor vole years the harriers produced 0.7 fledglings per pair in France and 1.1 in Poland. In years when rodents were abundant they produced 2.3 and 2.2 fledgings per pair. The mean fledging success for France and Poland over the four years (1985-1988) was similar at 1.62 and 1.72 young per breeding pair respectively.

The main reason for losses in both countries was predation, the rates of which were similar on natural marshes (30%) and on French reclaimed marshes (24%). In France additional reasons for losses were of human origin (9%) - cattle, changes in water level and persecution.

To conclude, the differences between both populations studied were linked with latitude and with habitat. Clutch size was larger in Poland as being a more northerly country. This often showed up in the laying of 6-egg clutches, which was never recorded in over 200 nests monitored in France.

Other differences were more related to habitat. In Poland there is a more natural and complex habitat; marshes are surrounded by a mosaic of meadows, pastures and fields which are extensively managed. French marshes, reclaimed from polders, consist more of simple habitat with a poorer spectrum of potential prey and more marked fluctuation in rodents. As a result, Montagu's Harriers in France are more dependent on a single prey - voles.

REFERENCES

GENSBOL B. 1984. *Birds of prey of Britain and Europe*. Ed. Collins, London, 384 p.

LEROUX A.B.A. 1987. Recensements des busards nicheurs, *Circus aeruginosus* et *Circus pygargus*, et zonage de l'espace dans les Marais de l'Ouest de la France. *Acta Oecologica/Oecologia Applicata* 8: 387-402.

Jaroslaw Krogulec
Dept. of Nature Conservation
Curie-Sklodowka University
19 Akademicka Street
20-33 Lublin
Poland

Alain B.A. Leroux
Université de Rennes I
Laboratoire d'Evolution des Systèmes
Naturels et Modifiés
1 Impasse des Alouettes
29000 Quimper, France

Meyburg, B.-U. & R. D. Chancellor eds.1994
Raptor Conservation Today
WWGBP / The Pica Press

The Home Range of the Lanner *Falco biarmicus feldeggi*: influences of territory composition

Giovanni Leonardi

ABSTRACT

Five Lanner nesting sites were studied. Comparison of habitat use with the available prey biomass gave significant results only for high bushes.

Perhaps other prey items such as mammals or reptiles are also important in the trophic biology of the male Lanner.

INTRODUCTION

Since 1989 five Lanner's nest sites were studied in different parts of Eastern Sicily. The physical and biological features of one were analysed.

The Lanner has a variety of hunting techniques that are seemingly related to vegetation cover. Moreover this falcon is largely adapted to open spaces, i.e. low bushes, steppe meadows and cultivated areas.

Cultivated fields supported large amounts of small birds such as sparrows and larks, its possible prey. I conducted a study to determine the effects of the territory composition on the availability of Lanner prey together with the time budget of the male.

STUDY AREA AND METHODS

I censused the total numbers of birds in the study area on 10 occasions by walking across a precise route (Leonardi 1991; Lo Valvo 1988).

The home range sizes were calculated, based on sightings farthest from the nest site, and recorded on a UTM 1:25.000 topographic map (Bechard 1982).

Home range was divided into three main habitat types: high bushes (>2 m.), low bushes (< 1-2 m.) and steppe meadow (Lo Valvo 1986).

The vegetation of the study area consists largely of Olive (*Olea europaea*) grove with some interposed areas of *Opuntia ficus-indica*, whereas steppe meadows are represented by uncultivated fields.

RESULTS AND DISCUSSION

Table 1 shows the results of this study whereas Figure 1 shows the relative foraging use of the males in the different habitats of the five sites.

Figure 1. Foraging use by male Lanner Falcon in different types of habitat.

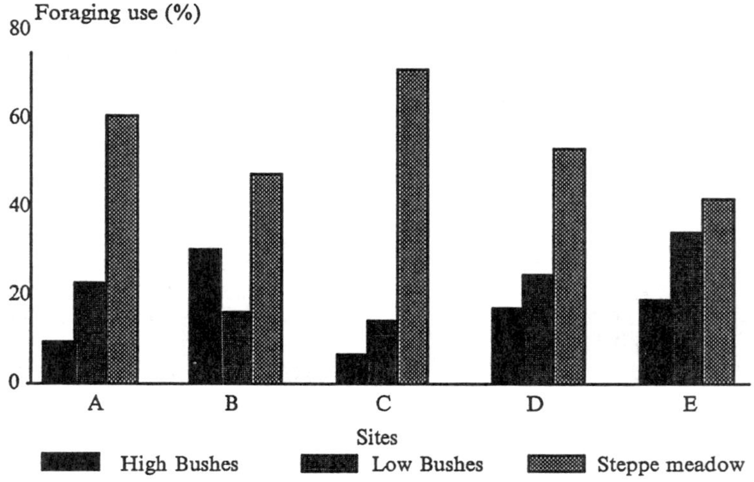

Table 1. Lanner home range structure.

Home range size (Site A)	
Total area	42 ha
1. High bushes	20 ha
2. Low Bushes	12 ha
3. Steppe meadows	10 ha
Climatic characters (Site A)	
Annual rainfall 600-800 mm.	
Annual mean temperature 12-14 ^{0}C	
Bird community	
No. of species	38
No. of ind.	781
No./ha 18.6	
Estimated biomass (gr)	58.070
Estimated biomass (gr./ha.)	382.6
Prey species ($\leqslant$ 100 gr.)	
No. of species	27
No. of probable prey species	14
Estimated biomass (gr.)	11.464
Estimated biomass (gr./hs)	272.9
Prey biomass/Total biomass	0.20
Prey species (1)	7
Prey species (2)	4
Prey species (3)	3
Estimated biomass (gr.) (1)	4790
Estimated biomass (gr.) (2)	2639
Estimated biomass (gr.) (3)	2775
Site A	
Estimated biomass (gr./ha) (1)	239.5
Estimated biomass (gr./ha) (2)	219.9
Estimated biomass (gr./ha) (3)	277.5
Foraging use	12%
Foraging use	24%
Foraging use	64%
Site B	
Estimated biomass (gr./ha)	260.2
Estimated biomass(gr./ha)	195.6
Estimated biomass (gr./ha)	280.4
Foraging use	32%
Foraging use	18%
Foraging use	50%
Site C	
Estimated biomass (gr./ha)	201.4
Estimated biomass (gr./ha)	230.3
Estimated biomass (gr./ha)	330.1
Foraging use	8%
Foraging use	16%
Foraging use	76%
Site D	
Estimated biomass (gr./ha)	230.6
Estimated biomass (gr./ha)	115.2
Estimated biomass (gr./ha)	235.1
Foraging use	17%
Foraging use	28%
Foraging use	55%
Site E	
Estimated biomass (gr./ha)	244.3
Estimated biomass (gr./ha)	220.3
Estimated biomass (gr./ha)	265.2
Foraging use	20%
Foraging use	35%
Foraging use	45%

Much of the males' diet consisted of species with sizes ≤ 100 gr. In fact prey species up to 100 gr. are caught exclusively in pair (Leonardi *et al.* 1992).

The comparison of habitat use with the available prey biomass gave significant (≤ 0.05) Spearman Rank correlation coefficient of 0.9 only for high bushes.

Although the male Lanners spent most of the time in the steppe meadows, there was no correlation with the bird prey abundance (in terms of biomass).

I concluded that the high percentage of high bushes in five Lanner sites supported a good number of potential prey species.

Finally I think that in the steppe meadows there are other important prey items such as mammals, reptiles and invertebrates in additon to birds.

REFERENCES

BECHARD, M.J. 1982. Effects of vegetative cover on foraging site selection by Swainson's Hawk. *Condor* 84: 153-159

LEONARDI, G. (1991). Osservazioni preliminari sull'ecoetologia del Lanario (*Falco biarmicus feldeggi*) in Sicilia. *in* S.R.O.P.U. (Eds) *Atti v Conv. Ital. Orn. in SUPPL. Ric. Biol. Selvaggina XVIII*:147.150.

LEONARDI, G., A. LONGO, & G. CORPINA 1992. The Ecology and Behaviour of the Lanner Falcon. Publ. privately, Catania.

LO VALVO, M. (Ed.) 1986. La fauna del parco della Favorita e del Monte Pellegrino (Palermo). *Nat Sic. 10 suppl.*

Giovanni Leonardi
Via Santangelo Fulci, 28
95127 Catania
Italy

Lanner Falcon *Falco biarmicus*

Meyburg, B.-U. & R. D. Chancellor eds.1994
Raptor Conservation Today
WWGBP / The Pica Press

Relationships between Peregrine and Lanner in the Marches (Central Italy)

Aurelio Manzi and Paolo Perna

ABSTRACT

A study of the populations of Peregrine *Falco peregrinus* and Lanner *Falco biarmicus* has been carried out since 1986 in an area of Central Italy (Marches: latitude between 42.58° & 42.41° N), of particular biogeographic and ecological interest, being one of the northernmost where the two species are sympatric.

Analysis of the breeding sites, classified by a "quality index", has shown competition between the two species, with dominance of the Peregrine. As this is a very populated area, we have also considered the effect of human disturbance on the Peregrine, to which the bird seems to have adapted itself.

INTRODUCTION

Knowledge about the biology of the Peregrine and the Lanner in Mediterranean areas, though recently increasing (Ciaccio *et al.* 1987; Massa *et al.* 1991; Schenk *et al.* 1983; Siracusa *et al.* 1991), is still inadequate. We therefore decided to begin a comparative study of the two species, since this area is among the northernmost where they are sympatric.

In the past six years there has been a large increase of the Peregrine population, with interesting consequences on its relationship with the Lanner.

In order to compare the two species we had somehow to classify the breeding sites. For want of information over a long period of time, we have not been able to use the existing methods (Hickey 1969; Ratcliffe 1980), which considered fidelity to the breeding site. Therefore we worked out an index (Site Quality Index, SQI) that, considering the Peregrine's preference (Hunt 1988; Mearns & Newton 188; Newton 1988), enabled us to distinguish the sites in "quality" classes.

STUDY AREA

The study has been carried out in part of the Central Apennines (Marches). The area, defined with the method proposed by Ratcliffe (1980), is 4,000km² in area.

It is characterised by a series of parallel calcareous chains running NW to SE; the average height being 1,000/1,500m a.s.l., with a maximum of 2,476m. The presence of rivers running from west to east has determined the formation of several gorges that provide the two species with a large number of nesting sites.

The climate ranges from sub-Mediterranean to "axerico temperato" (UNESCO-FAO 1963), with an average annual temperature ranging from 14°C to 11°C with an average annual rainfall from 769mm to over 1,500mm.

The remaining territory of the Marches is hilly, with a widespread human presence.

METHODS

Each year from January to June all pairs were counted regardless of whether they reared young or not, and an index drawn up in order to classify all controlled sites. For this index, three main features of the localities were considered: maximum height of cliffs., complexity of site, and maximum dominance.

For each feature three classes were specified, each with a score from 0 to 2.

The classes for the maximum height of cliffs are: less than 30m (score 0), between 30 and 70m (score 1) and over 70m (score 2).

To quantify the complexity of the site the number of cliffs and the number of different aspects were considered. The localities were divided into three classes: single cliff (0), group of cliffs with just one aspect (1), and group of cliffs with more than one aspect (2).

For dominance (Fig. 1) the angle of view with no intervening obstacle for at least one km was considered (obstacle reliefs 200m lower than the cliff were not included). The three classes are: less than 30° (0), between 30° and 90° (1), and more than 90° (2).

The sum of the scores gives the SQI for each site, so that they can be placed in seven categories, from the least (SQI 0) to the most suitable (SQI 6).

Even though conditioned by a margin of subjectivity the SQI, considering the results, has proved sufficiently correct for the purpose for which it was designed.

Figure 1. Method to determine dominance.

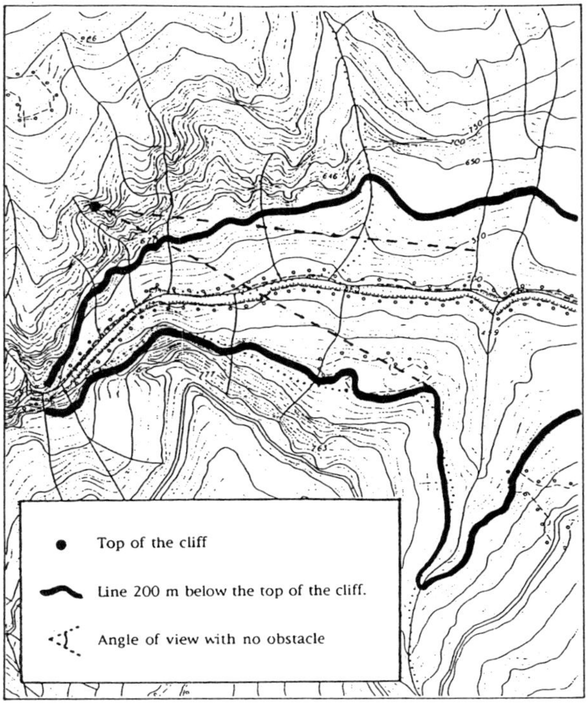

RESULTS

1.STATUS OF THE POPULATIONS

Peregrine

Twenty-four sites have been found,; two of them (8.3%) held by single adult males. This last datum coincides with the European average (Ratcliffe 1984; Mearns & Newton 1988; Boudet & Migot 1989). In the six years only one pair with an immature adult (a female) was observed.

The density was 181.8km²/pair. The average Nearest Neighbour Distance (NND) was 7.97km; the minimum distance between two pairs 2.5km, while between one site held by a pair and another held by a single adult male it was 1.5km.

To show the real average NND between two sites held at the same time, two areas with a high concentration of pairs were chosen. In the first (5 pairs) the average NND was 4.6km, while in the other (7 pairs and a single adult male) the average NND was 4.10km, which reduces to 3.54km if the single-male territory is also considered. In the second area, 350km², there was a density of one breeding pair every 50km².

In the period 1987-1991 the population increased considerably. The number of occupied sites rose from 10 to 22. The increase partly reflects a greater covering of the territory - five sites not controlled in the previous census proved to be positive whereas for seven others it can certainly be stated that they are new colonizations. On the minimum hypothesis, that the five first-mentioned sites were all previously occupied, there should have been a change, in four years, from 15 to 22 pairs, with an increase of 47%.

Lanner

The Lanner population is confined mainly to the eastern (warmer) side of the Apennine chain. To-date six pairs have been found. The average NND is 15.9km; Excluding one more isolated pair, it then reduces to 11.80km. In 1987, four pairs were found; only one of them is still present.

2.BREEDING SITES

Peregrine

The breeding sites are distributed as follows: three below 500m a.s.l. (13.6%), 13 between 500 and 1,000m (59.1%), six above 1,000m (27.3%). The highest site is at an altitude of 1,300m a.s.l.

We found 10 eyries, half on ledges and the other half in holes; no pair has laid in disused eyries, partly because of the absence of the Raven *Corvus corax*, extirpated in the area around the 1950s (Marzi & Perna 1991a), whose nests are the most used by the Peregrine in Europe (Ratcliffe 1980); Fasce & Fasce 1988).

The eyries are on cliffs ranging from 30 to 100m in height. Their aspect is conditioned by the prevalence of cliffs facing north or south.

Lanner

The Lanner also nested on cliffs. In two cases the breeding sites are above 500m a.s.l. (950 and 930m respectively), and in the other four below 500m a.s.l. We found four eyries, all in holes. Only one of the four nesting cliffs exceeds 50m in height; the lowest is only 20m.

DISCUSSION

The observed increase cannot be explained as a natural fluctuation, which should not exceed 10% of the population size (Newton 1988). It is similar to that of some European populations which most suffered the crash of the 1950s-60s, and testifies that in the Marches also the population was well below the carrying capacity of the area.

The causes of the former decline are not clear, but probably due, as in other parts of Italy, to human persecution (Chiavetta 1981). In the Marches there are seven hunters/km² and the shooting season lasts until 10th March, when all pairs (both Peregrine and Lanner) have started breeding. A greater respect for the legal protection and the recent creation of some protected areas could partly explain the recovery.

Food availability is important for the regulation of the Peregrine population (Newton 1979;

Ratcliffe 1980; Thiollay 1982, 1988) and an increase of this is among the causes of the high level reached by the British population (Ratcliffe 1988). But that is not the case in the Marches, where a greater availability of natural prey has not yet been demonstrated, and where pigeon breeding, traditional to the farms, has suffered from the depopulation of the countryside.

Thus it is quite difficult to undersand the strong recovery of this population, though it has probably benefited from a better management of the environment.

Analysing the breeding sites of the new pairs by SQI, the preference for sites of better quality is confirmed; there are three with SQI 6, two with SQI 4 and two with SQI 3.

This tendency has involved relationships of the Peregrine with the Lanner and the Golden Eagle *Aquila chrysaëtos*.

In 1987, the Lanner held four territories, two with SQI 6 and two with SQI 4; at present in all these sites it has been displaced by the Peregrine. It disappeared from three of the sites, while in the fourth it shifted to a small valley (SQI 2), 400m from the Peregrine eyrie. From this, the difference betwen the two species in the features of the breeding sites becomes obvious, as is illustrated by the SQI (Fig. 2).

Figure 2. Percentage of occupation of breeding sites by classes of SQI.

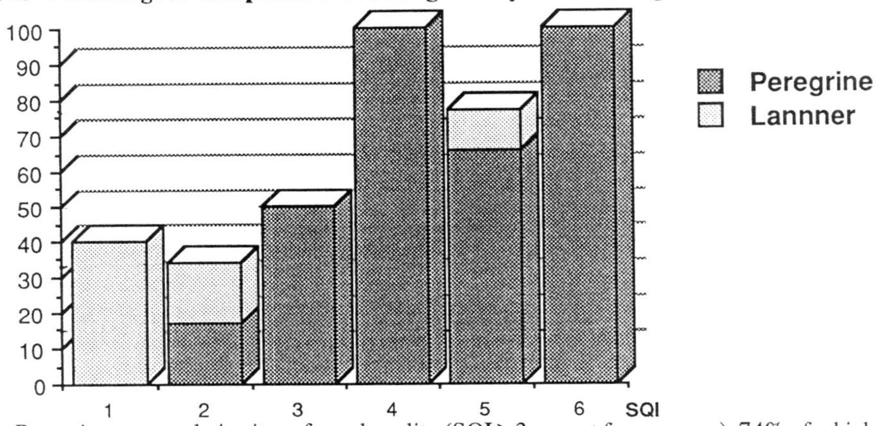

The Peregrine nests only in sites of good quality (SQI ≥ 3 except for one case), 74% of which are occupied by pairs. If we omit the Golden Eagle territories and consider the single male ones, then 92% of the sites are occupied.

Conversely, all Lanner haunts but one have a SQI < 3. What is more interesting is that these low quality sites are chosen because of competition for better quality territories with the Peregrine.

The relationships between the Peregrine and the Golden Eagle are well known and the dominance of the eagle in the choice of the breeding site has been stressed (Thiollay 1967; Ratcliffe 1980; Donazar *et al.* 1989).

In the Marches as well, where there is the Golden Eagle the Peregrine is absent, except for two localities where since 1990 the two species have nested close together - 300m and 600m apart - (Manzi & Perna, 1981b). This is probably due to the high quality of the sites (SQI 6) and to the abundance of prey, mainly Jackdaws *Corvus monedula*, present in large colonies,. Another site where the two species nest together has been found near the study area, in Umbria (Armentano & Magrini, pers. comm.)

Finally, the effects of human disturbance on the Peregrine were weighed (for the Lanner there were not enough sites), considering the presence of roads and villages.

Using the Wilcoxon test, first the mean distance was examined from the nearest road and village to the sites both occupied and unoccupied. In both cases no significant difference was found: the mean distance from the road was 524m for the occupied sites and 420m for the unoccupied ones; the mean distance from the village was 1,308m for the occupied sites and 1,059m for the unoccupied ones. Also the distances from the nearest road and village of old (pre-1987) and new breeding sites were compared. In this case, too, no difference was found: the mean distance from the road was 550m for the old sites and 525m for the new sites, while the mean distance from the village was 1,291m for the old sites and 1,383 for the new.

CONCLUSIONS

Five main points can be stressed:

1 - At the moment the Peregrine population in the Marches is in good health after a period of decline.
2 - In the same area there is a small population of Lanner that is one of the northernmost in the world, and the northernmost in Italy. It is present only on the eastern side of the Apennines, where the climate is warmer.
3 - There is competition between Peregrine and Lanner for breeding sites, with dominance of the Peregrine. The Lanner must breed in sites of lesser quality, where it might be more disturbed.
4 - The Peregrine, as in many other areas, avoids the presence of the Golden Eagle but when the environment is particularly favourable the two species can breed a few hundred metres apart.
5 - The Peregrine does not seem to suffer from the presence of man and some eyries are only a short distance from main roads.

UPDATE

In 1992 seven new pairs of Peregrine have been found. Two of them are present where last year single males were seen, whereas in one site (SQI 1) there has been another case of displacement of Lanner. The quality of the sites held by the Peregrine seems to keep decreasing with the increase of the population.

ACKNOWLEDGEMENTS

We would like to thank J. Angelini, L. Armentano, M. Magrini and M. Pandolfi for their valuable information.

REFERENCES

BOUDET, J.B. & P. MIGOT 1989. La reproduction du Faucon pélerin *Falcon peregrinus* dans le Lot, de 1983 à 1988. *Alauda* 7(1): 75-79.

CHIAVETTA, M. 1981. *I Rapaci d'Italia e d'Europa.* Rizzoli Milano.

CIACCIO A., A. DIMARCA F. LO VALVO & M. SIRACUSA 1987. Primi dati sulla biologia e lo status del Lanario *Falco biarmicus* in Sicilia. *Rapaci mediterranei III* Suppl. Ricerche di Biologia della Selvaggina XII 45-55.

DONAZAR, J.A., O. CEBALLOS & C. FERNANDEZ 1989. Factors influencing the distribution and abundance of seven cliff-nesting raptors: a multivariate study. *In*: B.-U. Meyburg & R.D. Chancellor (Eds.) *Raptors in the Modern World.* WWGBP: Berlin 545-549.

FASCE, P. & L. FASCE 1988. Peregrine in Northern Italy: Numbers, breeding and population dynamics. *In* T.J. Cade,T.J. Enderson, C.G Thelander & C.M. White (Eds.) *Peregrine Falcon Populations.* Boise, The Peregrine Fund, Inc.: 711-718.

HICKEY, J.J. (Ed). 1969. *Peregrine Falcon Populations: their biology and decline.* Madison, Univ. of Wisconsin Press.

HUNT, G.W. 1988. The natural regulation of Peregrine falcon population. *In*: T.J. Cade, J.H. Enderson, C.G. Thelander & C.M. White (Eds.) *Peregrine Falcon Populations.* Boise, The Peregrine Fund, Inc.: 667-676.

MANZI A. & P. PERNA 1991a. L'avifauna nidificante nelle Marche tra '800 e '900. *Proposte e ricerche* 26 (1): 284-298.

MANZI A. & P. PERNA 1991b. Due casi di nidificazione di Pellegrino, *Falco peregrinus,* nelle vicinanze di un nido di Aquila reale, *Aquila chrysaetos. Riv. Ital. Orn.* 61 (1-2): 55-57.

MASSA, B. F. LO VALVO, M. SIRACUSA & A. CIACCIO 1991. Il Lanario *Falco biarmicus feldeggi*

Schlegel) in Italia: status, biologia e tassonomia. *Nauralista Sicil.*, S. IV, XV (1-2): 27-63.

MEARNS, R. & NEWTON I. 1988. Factors affecting breeding success of Peregrine in South Scotland. *Journal of Animal Ecology* 57: 903-916.

NEWTON, I. 1979. *Population Ecology of Raptors.* T & A.D. Poyser, Berkhamsted.

NEWTON, I. 1988. Population regulation in Peregrine: An overview. *In* T.J. Cade, J.H. Enderson, C.G. Thelander & C.M. White (Eds.). *Peregrine Falcon Populations.* Boise, The Pererine Fund, Inc.: 761-770.

RATCLIFFE, D. 1980. *The Peregrine Falcon* T. & A.D. Poyser, Calton.

RATCLIFFE, D. 1984. The Peregrine breeding population of the United Kingdom in 1981. *Bird Study* 31(1): 1-18.

RATCLIFFE, D. 1988. The Peregrine population of Great Britain and Ireland, 1965-1985 *In* T.J. Cade, J.H. Enderson, C.G. Thelander & C.M. White (Eds.) *Peregrine Falcon Populations.* Boise, The Peregrine Fund, Inc.: 147-157.

SCHENK, H., M. CHIAVETTA, S. FALCONE, P. FASCE, B. MASSA, T. MINGOZZI & U. SARACINO, 1983. *Il Falco pellegrino: Indagine in Italia.* L.I.P.U.

SIRACUSA, M., B. MASSA, A. CIACCIO & F. O VALVO 1991. Censimento di Lanario *Falco biarmicus* e Pellegrino *Falco peregrinus* in Sicilia. *In* Atti II Seminario Italiano Censimenti Faunistici dei Vertebrati. *Supplemento alle Ricerche di Biologia della Selvaggina* XVI: 407-409.

THIOLLAY, J.M. 1967. Essai sur les rapaces du Midi de la France: Distribution, ecologie, tentative de dénombrement. *Alauda* 35: 14-150.

THIOLLAY, J.M. 1982. Les resources alimentaires, facteur limitant la reproduction d'une population insulaire de Faucons pélerins, *Falco peregrinus brookei. Alauda* 50(1): 16-44.

THIOLLAY J.M. 1988. Prey availability limiting an island population of Peregrine falcon in Tunisia. *In* T.J. Cade, J.H. Enderson, C.G. Thelander & C.M. White (Eds.). *Peregrine Falcon Populations.* Boise, The Peregrine Fund, Inc.: 701-710.

UNESCO-FAO 1963. Carte bioclimatique de la zone méditerranéenne. Paris: 1-60.

Aurelio Manzi
Dipartimento dí Botanica ed Ecologia
Via Pontoni 5
62032 Camerino (MC) Italy

Paolo Perna
Riserva Naturale "Abbadia di Fiastra"
Abbadia di Fiastra
62010 Urbisaglia (MC) Italy

Meyburg, B.-U. & R. D. Chancellor eds.1994
Raptor Conservation Today
WWGBP / The Pica Press

Status of the Griffon Vulture *Gyps fulvus* in Serbia

Šasa Marinković and Ljiljana Orlandić

ABSTRACT

Prior to 1950, all four species of European vulture used to nest in Serbia. To-day the Griffon Vulture is the last survivor. Its history and distribution in the 19th and first half of the 20th centuries are described from ornithological studies or reports.

This paper analyses population trends among breeding groups of Griffon Vultures in Serbia (size of groups, number of pairs and breeding success) between 1980 and 1991. The population is estimated at about 60 adult birds, but the number of successful pairs is decreasing rapidly and in the last five years has reduced by 44%. The main cause of the population decline and measures now being taken to protect the species are discussed.

INTRODUCTION

The rapid shrinking of the Griffon Vulture's range in the Balkan peninsula began before the 1950s (Matvejev 1963) and has continued up to the present. The species has disappeared from Romania and survives in only one region of Bulgaria (Simeonov *et al.* 1990). To-day in the Balkan peninsula it numbers no more than 700 pairs, taking into consideration a probably isolated population from Crete (Vagliano 1981; Perco *et al.* 1983; Handrinos 1985; Grubač 1991; Marinkovič *et al.* 1985).

HISTORY

In the 19th century and first half of the 20th, Griffon Vultures used to nest on the south slopes of the Panonia basin (Figure 1). Round the rim of Panonia valley are gorges suitable for breeding colonies, such as the Djerdap gorge-Iron Gate and a gorge near Zvornik (Dombrovski 1985; Hodek 1877).

Griffon Vultures needed Panonia valley for food, with its open habitats of steppes and woods and numerous flocks of domestic ungulates (Matvejev & Puncer 1989). Hence the large number of reports and birds collected (Fig. 1) from this region at that time (Marčetič & Medaković 1954; Matvejev 1950).

Panonia valley, as chief place for feeding for the Griffon Vulture, lacks the rocky places necessary for breeding. From these times there are unspecified records of nesting (Fig. 1) in the

Fruška gora, near Djerdap gorge and Deliblato sands. The Griffon Vultures used to breed in empty nests of the Black Vulture or other large tree-nesting birds (Baldamus 1847; Rudolf *et al.* 1878).

Although Lintia (1907) reported that "vultures" (probably Griffon) ceased to breed in 1899 in Djerdap gorge, they still nested there until 1956 (Matvejev 1950; Marinković 1990).

Since the Middle Ages forests in the mountain regions of Serbia have been felled (Fig. 1) for developing upland pasture-grounds. The large numbers of epizoa from this time show a picture of extensive nomadic sheep-raising in the mountains. (Katić 1978). From the beginning of the 20th century we have reports and skins of birds taken from mountain regions and also known nesting places (Fig. 1) in gorges such as Kumanička, Sicevačka and probably Rugovska (Reiser 1939; Deroko 1939; Marčetič & Andrijevič 1960; Matvejev 1950; Marinković 1983).

Figure 1. The distribution of Gyps fulvus in Serbia, 1850-1950. 1. Nesting sites, 2. Reports or birds collected, 3. Recent cattle or sheep-breeding region, 4. Habitat of steppes and woods, (A) Djerdap gorge, (B) Zvornik, (C) Fruška gora, (D) Deliblato sands, (E) Kumanička gorge, (F) Sićevačka gorge, (G) Rugovska gorge.

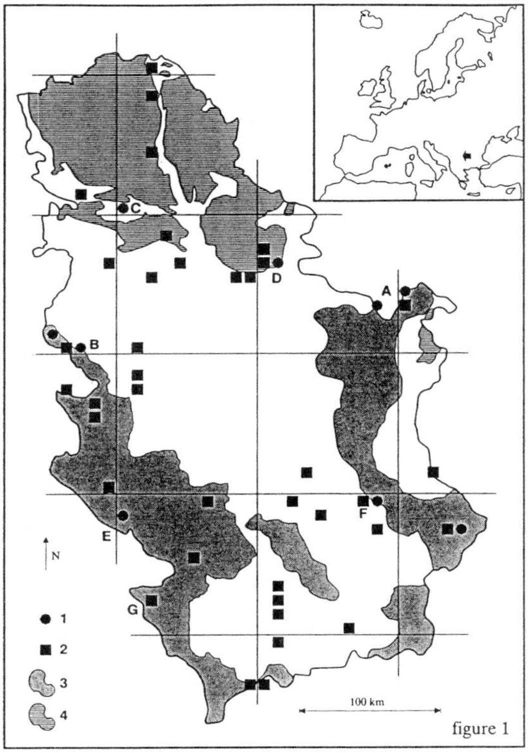

STUDY AREA

The mountainous part of West Serbia lies in the north of the Central Balkan peninsula, stretching from north-west to south-east. The peaks average 1,000m with the highest being 1,600m. To the south lies the Stari Vlah plateau.

The climate is moderate continental and, above 1,000m, approaching subalpine, but in the canyons the influence of sub-Mediterranean elements can be seen. The humidity increases in summer and the average annual precipitation ranges between 500 and 800ml. Down in the valley snow persists for 50 days, whilst on the mountains for over 90 days in an average year. The vultures' nest sites are situated in the gorges of the River Drina, near which passes the major route linking the summer upland pasture-grounds with the wintering grounds in the Panonia valley. Cattle and sheep breeding in West Serbia number 100,000 head.

Table 1. Analysis of population trend of Griffon Vulture in Serbia.

Colony	A	B	C	Σ	Mean No.	Fertility	Average No. of	Average No. of	Mortality in Nests				
Year	1/2	1/2	1/2	1/2	Pair/Year /Colony	Rate Egg/Pair/Year	Chicks Year/Nest	Young Fledged Year/Territory Pair	Poisoning	Drowning	Disturbance	Robbery	Unknown
1980	(9/8)								1*				
1981	?												
1982	(9/7)												
1983	10/8												
1984	(9/9)												
1985	(7/7)	8/5	9/7	24/19	8					1			
1986	10/10	10/7	7/6	27/23	9	0.85	0.96	0.81					1
1987	9/8	10/6	9/6	28/20	9.3	0.71	0.90	0.64					1 + 1*
1988	8/7	6/6	13/7	27/20	9	0.74	0.70	0.52			3* + 1		2
1989	9/7	6/1	9/6	24/14	8	0.58	1.00	0.58					
1990	9/8	6/0	10/8	25/16	8.3	0.64	1.00	0.64					
1991	6/6	2/1	14/6	22/13	7.3	0.59	0.77	0.45	2*			1	
Mean No. Pairs Per Colony	8.7	6.9	10.1	25.7									
No. of Nests Per Colony	13	8	10	31									
Average rate of fertility Per Colony	0.90	0.52	0.63	0.68									
Average Rate of Outlive Young/Colony	0.89	0.76	0.95	0.87									
Average Rate of Occupation Per Colony	67%	86%	101%	85%									
Average No.l of Outlive Young/Year/Territorial Pairs	0.80	0.40	0.60	0.60									

o - data not completely known
* - broken during incubation

METHODS

A review was made of published localities of Griffon Vulture breeding sites (Fig. 1) and unpublished reports were also consulted. Counting began in 1980 at Nesting Site (A) and in 1985 at Nesting Sites (B) and (C).

Observations were made by telescope from a maximum distance of 600m. Counting took place in fine weather. A nest was judged to be active if egg or chick were present.

Counting of birds in the morning flock was done at the time of thermal lifts, between 7.30 and 10.30a.m., comparing the numbers seen with observations at two feeding stations from 1989.

The number of non-breeding pairs was estimated by comparing the number of pairs on the territory and the number of active nests (Newton 1979). In one gorge there are two groups of Griffon Vultures 5km apart and because of this they were taken separately as Nesting Sites (B) and (C), at which we made our census three times per year: pre-laying and laying (15 Jan - 1 Mar), incubation and chicks (1 Apr - 15 May), and fledglings (1 July - 15 Aug). At Nesting Site (A) we made counts only once a year (1980, 1982, 1984, 1985) (Table 1).

We judged the distance between nests and the height of nests by extrapolating the equivalent size of the Griffon Vulture (1m ± 0.1) from telephotographs, while the larger distances were taken from maps.

RESULTS

Griffon Vultures used to nest at two localities in Western Serbia, the direct distance between them being 83km. The nearest known locality where they formerly nested is 160km south-west, in Hercegovina.

Mapping reports in the last 20 years in Serbia (V. Vasić, S. Puzović, B. Grubač, I., Ham, G. Džukić and M. Milenković pers. comm.) give a picture of the area of activity of the Griffon Vulture (Fig. 2). Reports from Mts. Prokletije and Šarplanina refer to birds breeding in neighbouring Albania and Vardar Macedonia. Separate reports are wandering, non-breeding birds.

Characteristics of colony

Griffon Vultures choose limestone gorges for establishing their colony. In the colonies studied the mean height of nest was 850m a.s.l., with highest nest at 1,116m. The mean height from cliff base was 30m. The area covered ranged between 500m and 5,400m (distance between the two nests furthest apart in the colony).

During the study period we discovered 31 nests, of which only six were in isolated positions (Fig. 3). The Griffons preferred to build their nests in small caves, but some selected open ledges exposed to the weather (Fig. 4). Their exposure depended on the orientation of the cliff face, but nests with a northern exposure were noticeably absent (Fig. 5).

Size of colony

The number of adult birds varied between 44 and 56. In the study area the average abundance of birds over the six-year period was 25.7 pairs (Fig. 6). The average number of pairs per separate colony varied between 9.3 and 7.3 (Table 1). The young stayed at their natal sites until the first snows at the end of November.Subadults were recorded sporadically in small numbers and were absent during the winter.

At Feeding Station 1 at Nesting Site (A) the largest number seen was 26 birds (27 Nov, 1991). At Feeding Station 2, between Nesting Sites (B) and (C), the greatest recorded number was 56 birds (16 Aug, 1990).

The reduction in the number of adult birds in 1985 (Fig. 7) resulted from the eviction of the Griffon from Site (A) by Golden Eagles *Aquila chrysaetos*. In 1991 we found four birds killed by poison at Nesting Site (A) (Table 1). There was disturbance since 1988 at Colony (B), because of which some adults transferred to Colony (C) (Figs. 8 & 9).

Breeding success

Breeding success was analysed over six years, 1986-1991 (Table 1). Throughout this period the average rate of fertility was 0.68 (n = 153), and varying between 0.58 to 0.85 per year. The hatching rate was high, averaging 87%, and in some years all young birds successfully fledged (Table 1). In relation to the number of pairs on the territory, the average number of young which successfully fledged was 0.6 per pair.

Capacity of colony

Adult pairs are probably traditionally faithful to long-established sites. During the last seven years nests have been used for four seasons on average. For the last ten years two of them have been used continually. The average rate of occupation per site was 85%. This rate was considerably greater at Nesting Sites (B) and (C), where overpopulation occurred (Table 1), as a consequence of loss of breeding habitat through formation of an artificial lake.

DISCUSSION

The moderate continental climate led this Mediterranean species to nest in limestone gorges for shelter. The rainy season is a bad period for the Griffon Vulture (Leconte 1985). The possibility of flight is reduced, whereby the probability of finding food is reduced. Snow cover reduces the strength of thermals (Pennycuick 1972) in a moderate continental climate and hence the area of activity for finding food is diminished (Houston 1983). In the winter snow camouflages objects and also livestock are enclosed in the valleys. In the Mediterranean region breeding can start one month earlier (Leconte 1985; Sušic 1985). The first known date for egg-laying is 1-2 February (Popović 1971) and the latest is the beginning of April (Lintia 1909).

Food supplies

In the last 20 years sheep-rearing, especially pastorally, has markedly declined, but this has not so far had any major influence on this small breeding group of Griffon Vultures, as can be concluded from the average rate of fertility (0.68) and average of successfully fledged young (0.87) (Table 1). The short supply of food in winter is real, however, as shown by preliminary observations at the feeding stations.

Sheeping-raising in Panonia valley is giving way to agriculture; as a result Panonia valley is losing its value as a feeding point for Vultures (Figs. 1 & 2).

Habitat

The nesting habitat of the Griffon Vulture has been increasingly disturbed during the past decade. The building of large hydroelectric power stations has flooded gorges and destroyed refuges. The high average rate of occupation of nest sites (85%) reflects the reduced capacity of the environment. Further disturbance is manifested by urbanisation of the gorges, road-building and quarrying. Such changes in the habitat impair reproduction and simultaneously increase mortality (electrocution and drowning of young in the artificial lake).

Use of poison

Systematic destruction of the Griffon Vulture in Serbia reached its peak during the period 1946-1955, and caused the disappearance of the species from the sheep-rearing region in East Serbia (Figure 2). This was mainly due to the poisoned baits, using strychnine or cyanide, put out by members of the hunters' association for destroying "pests" (wolf, fox and other carnivores).

Between 1947 and 1952, on Mt. Šarplanina alone, about 340 Griffon Vultures were poisoned (Naumov 1981). Such systematic and legal destruction was stopped by the placing of a ban on the sale and use of these poisons in 1967.

Agricultural poisons, such as the herbicide "furadan" or the insecticide-fungicide "creozan" are, however, on regular sale, and because of this the use of poisoned baits still occurred sporadically during the study period.

Trend

The Griffon Vulture has been declining in Serbia since 1950. According to estimates from 1971 (33 pairs) (Petrović 1974; Popović 1971) and 1982 (32 pairs) (Marinković *et al.* 1985), the trend

Figure 2. The distribution of *Gyps fulvus*, in Serbia 1970-1990.
1. Nesting sites, 2. Observations, (A) Albania, (B) Vardar Macedonia.

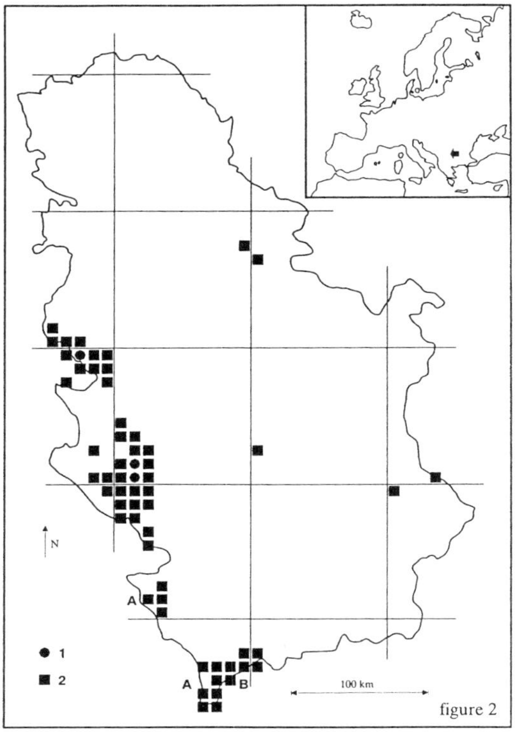

Figure 3. Distance between nests.

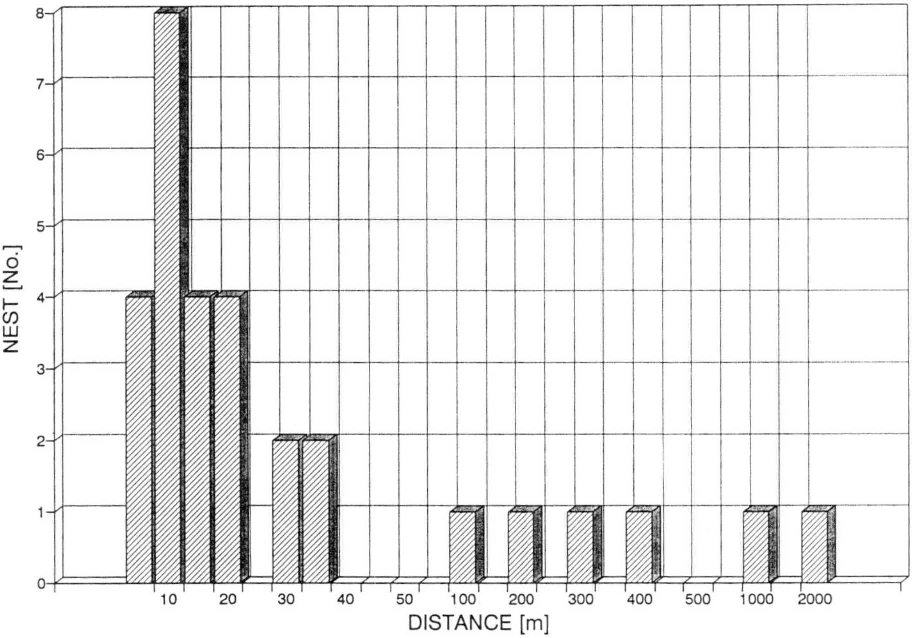

Figure 4. Types of nest.

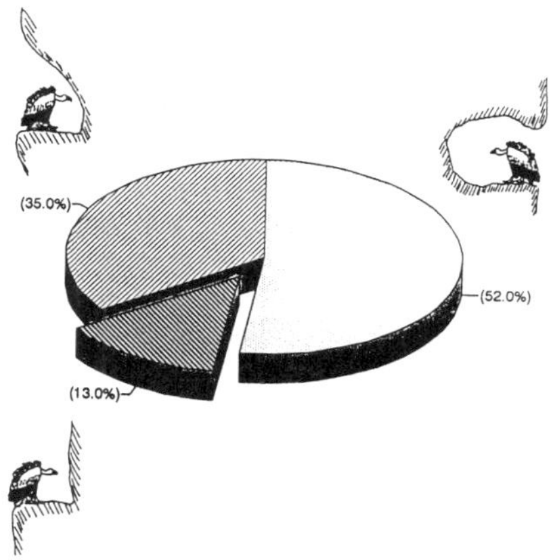

Figure 5. Exposure of nests.

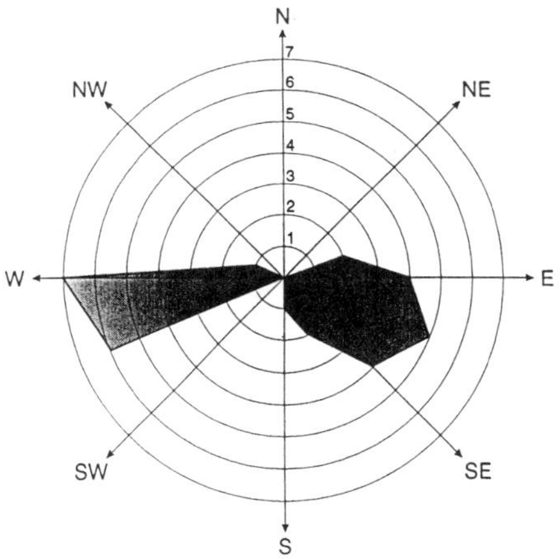

Figure 6. Census of Griffon Vulture in Serbia.

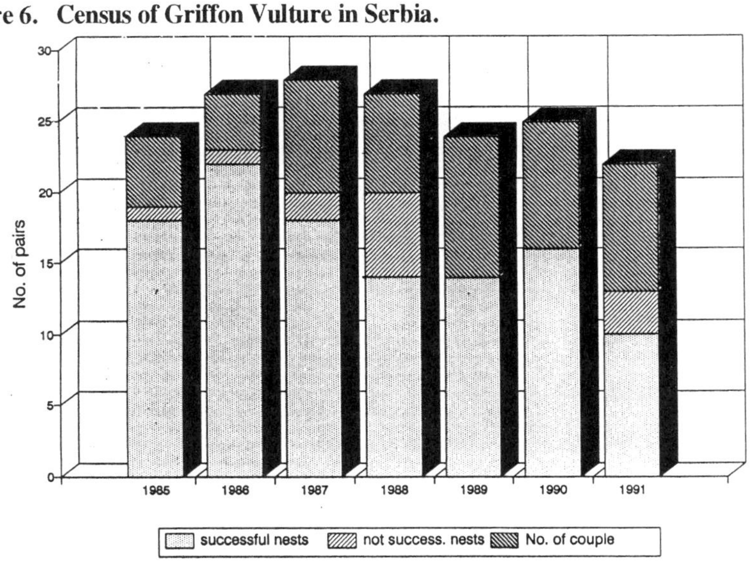

Figure 7. Census of Colony (A)

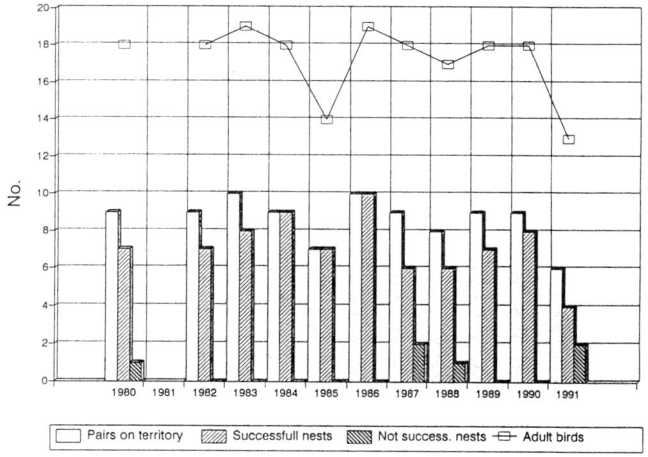

Figure 8. Census of Colony (B)

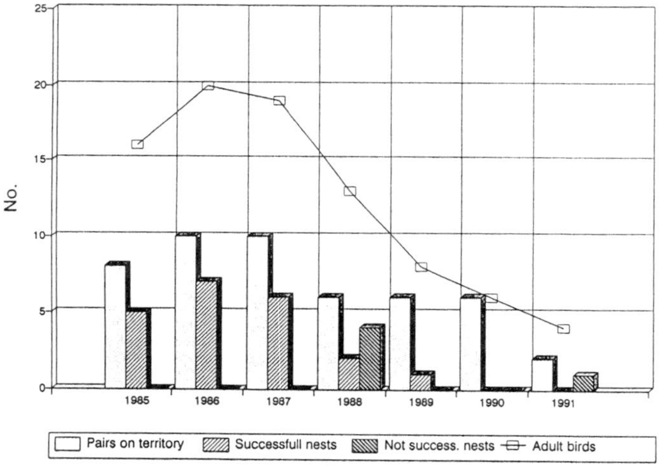

Figure 9. Census of Colony (C)

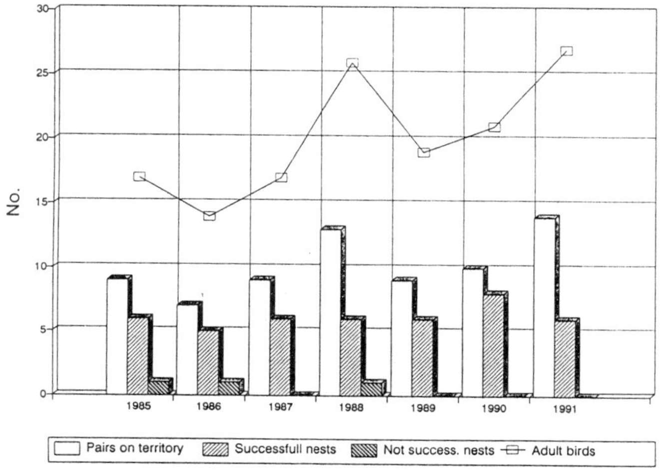

appears to be a steady one. In this work we counted 22 pairs in 1991, indicating a reduction of 33%. The negative trend is obvious in the number of successful nests, in which there has been a reduction in the last six years of 54% (Fig. 6), pointing to the rapid disappearance of the Griffon Vulture from Serbia.

CONSERVATION

Great efforts to protect the Griffon Vulture began in 1971 and led to protection by law in 1976. This protection is only nominal, however, lacking any concrete measures to prevent a further decline of the species.

In 1986 we began a campaign with the local inhabitants to protect the Griffon Vulture. Two feeding stations were opened in 1989. The species is included in the Serbian Red Book of endangered species. In 1991 the whole current breeding habitats of the Griffon Vulture were promoted into ornithological reserves. A citizens' "*Gyps fulvus*" foundation for Griffon Vulture protection and a "Programme of Griffon Vulture Protection" were inaugurated in 1992.

ACKNOWLEDGMENTS

We thank Dr. V. Vasić and S. Puzović (Museum of Natural History, Belgrade) and B. Grubač and M. Milenković (Institute of Biological Research, Belgrade) for additional information. We also thank Dr. G. Sušić for permission to use the library of The Institute of Ornithology, Zagreb. We are grateful to G. Džukić and I. Ham for adivce. Finally we wish to thank our colleagues from the foundation for Griffon Vulture protection "*Gyps fulvus*", Valjevo.

REFERENCES

BALDAMUS, E. 1847. Beitrage zur Naturgeschichte einiger dem S.O.Europa's angehorenden Vögel. *Haumannia* I (1): 28-43.

DEROKO, D.J. 1939. Drina. Društvo Fruške gore. Novi Sad.

DOMBROVSKI, E. 1895. Osnovi ornitofaune severozapadne Srbije. *Glasnik zem. muz. Bosne i Hercegovine* 7:66-68.

GRUBAČ, B. 1991. Situation actuelle des Vautours (Aegypinnae) en Macedonie. I Congreso Internacional sobre Aves Carroneras. Priego (Cuenca) Mayo 1990. Ponencias y conclusiones, ICONA 139-145.

HANDRINOS, G. 1985. The status of Vultures in Greece. ICBP Technical Publication 5, Cambridge: 103-115.

HODEK, E. 1877. Ornitologischer Reisebericht III. *Mittheilungen des Ornithologischen Vereins in Wien* I, 12:83-87.

HOUSTON, D. C. 1983. The Adaptive Radiation of the Griffon Vulture. *Vulture biology and management.* University of California. Berkeley-Los Angeles-London.

KATIC R. V. 1978. Stočarstvo srednjovekovne Srbije. SANU. Monografija 30. Odeljenje za medicinske nauke, Beograd.

LECONTE, M. 1985. Present status of the Griffon Vulture on the northern slopes of the Western Pyrenees. ICBP Technical Publication, 5. Cambridge. 117-127.

LINTIA, D. 1907. Unsere Geierarten in Südungarn. *Aquila* 14, 1-4, 334-336.

LINTIA, D. 1909. Einige Daten über seltener heimische Vögeleier. *Aquila* 16, 1-4, 285-286.

MARČETIĆ, M. & K. MEDAKOVIĆ 1954. Prilog poznavanju ornitofaune Vojvodine, (Falconiformes) grabljivice. Zbornik za prirodne nauke, 7, Matica Srpska. Novi Sad

MARČETIĆ, M. & D.N ANDRIJEVIĆ 1960. Ornitofauna Kosova i Metohije. Rilindia. Priština.

MARINKOVIĆ, S., G. SUŠIC, B. GRUBAČ, B. J ŠOTI & N. SIMONOV 1985. The Griffon Vulture in Yugoslavia. ICBP. Technical Publication 5. Cambridge. 131-135.

MARINKOVIĆ, S. 1983. Prikaz stanja beloglavog supa (*Gyps fulvus* Hablizl, 1783) u Srbiji, Drugi simpozijum o fauni SR Srbije, Zbornik, 159-162. Beograd.

MARINKOVIĆ, S. 1990. Ekologija gneždjenja beloglavog supa (*Gyps fulvus*) u Srbiji. Magistarski rad.

Univerzitet u Beogradu.
MATVEJEV, S. D. 1950. Rasprostranjenje i život ptica u Srbiji (Ornithogeographia serbica), SANU, Monografija, 161. Beograd.
MATVEJEV, S. D. 1963. Višegodišnje i sezonske promene brojnosti ptica grabljivica u Srbiji. *Arhiv biol. nauka*, 15, 127-147.
MATVEJEV, S. D. & PUNCER, I.J. 1989. Karta bioma, Predeli Jugoslavije i njihova zaštita. Pos. izd. Prirodnjacki muzej u Beogradu, 36.
NAUMOV, V. 1981. Akcije smanjivanja broja vukova na Kosovu u razdoblju 1947-1980 godine. Priroda Kosova. 59-72.
NEWTON, I. 1979. *Population Ecology of Raptors.* T & A.D. Poyser. Berkhamsted.
PENNYCUICK, C. J. 1972. Animal Flight. Studies in Biology No 33. London.
PERCO, F., S. TOSO, G. SUŠIĆ, & M. APOLLONIO 1983. Initial data for a study on the status, distribution and ecology of the Griffon Vulture (*Gyps fulvus fulvus* Hablizl 1783) in the Kvarner Archipelago. *Larus* 33-35, 99-134.
PETROVIĆ, S. P. 1974. Prilog poznavanju surog strvinara (*Gyps fulvus f.* Habl.) na teritoriji severozapadne Srbije. Zbornik radova 5, DIM 4-11. Valjevo.
POPOVIC, J. 1971. Ekologija i stanje populacije supa beloglavog - *Gyps fulvus* Habl., kao značajne prirodne retkosti, u stanistima klisure reke Uvac kod Pavlovica broda. Republički zavod SR Srbije. Materijal.
REISER, O. 1939. Materialen zu einer Ornis Balcanica. I Bosnien und Herzegovina. Wien.
RUDOLF von Osterreich, V.HOMEYER & A. BREHM 1878. Zwölf Fruhlingstage an der mittler Donau. *J. Ornit.* 27:1-83.
SIMEONOV, S. D., T.M MIČEV & D.N. NANKINOV 1990. *Fauna na Bulgaria.*
SUŠIĆ, G. 1985. Ekološka uvjetovanost rasprostranjenosti i velicine populacije beloglavih supova, (*Gyps fulvus fulvus* Hablizl 1783) na Kvarnerskim otocima. Magistarski rad, Sveucilište u Zagrebu.
VAGLIANO, C. 1981. Contribution au statut des rapaces diurnes et nocturnes nicheurs en Crête. *In*: Cheylan, G. *Rapaces méditérranéens*, 14-16. Aix-en-Provence.

Marinković Saša/Orlandić Ljiljana
Institute for Biological Research, "Siniša Stankovic"
29. Novembra 142, 11060 Belgrade
Yugoslavia

Meyburg, B.-U. & R. D. Chancellor eds. 1994
Raptor Conservation Today
WWGBP / The Pica Press

Distribution, Migration and Wintering of the Rough-Legged Buzzard *Buteo lagopus* in Bulgaria

Dimitar N. Nankinov

ABSTRACT

The first birds come into Bulgaria at the beginning of October. The autumn migration is most noticeable during November (20.25% of recorded birds), a decline ensues during December, and they are most numerous during January (35.17%). The shift of birds into a northerly direction begins in February, ending on the 14th April. In Bulgaria and the neighbouring countries are found birds ringed in areas from Scandinavia to the Taymir peninsula, but most of them come from breeding territories further to the east. The East-Siberian subspecies *B.l. pallidus* has also been proved to winter in Bulgaria. The Rough-legged Buzzard is not protected yet in Bulgaria and is being hunted everywhere.

INTRODUCTION

The distribution, migration and wintering of the Rough-legged Buzzard in Bulgaria is a matter of some interest, since the southernmost wintering areas of this species in Europe are to be found here and in the neighbouring Balkan countries. Some publications several decades ago reported this bird of the tundra and northern forest zone to be a rare visitor to the Balkan Peninsula (Dementiev 1951). Later, Kishchinski (1982) gave the river Danube as the southern limit of its European wintering grounds. In fact, the bird is a regular visitor to Bulgaria and in some years winters there in sizeable numbers. It is rare in most regions in Greece and a winter visitor mainly to the north-eastern border of that country, along the lower reaches of the river Evros (Handrinos & Demetropoulos 1982). The bird is also a winter visitor to Turkey where the Black Sea coast, Western Anatolia and Central Plateau are visited by small numbers (OST Bird Report 1978).

There is no comprehensive survey of the distribution, migration and wintering of the Rough-legged Buzzard in Bulgaria, and only scant information is to be found in the literature.

In this paper we have used both material collected during fieldwork and all facts known to us that have been published, together with unpublished data. We have in all a corpus of material about 1,052 Rough-legged Buzzards recorded on Bulgarian territory.

DISCUSSION

Judgements as to the species' distribution and numbers in Bulgaria are quite inconsistent: "a regular winter visitor" (Patev 1950); "visits in great numbers in cold winters" (Popov & Stoyanov 1962); "great numbers, especially in cold winters; if the winter is mild it stays north of the Danube and only single birds visit Bulgaria" (Peshev & Boev 1962).

As shown in Figure 1, the plains, valleys, hilly country and the mountain foothills are the haunts in Bulgaria of the Rough-legged Buzzard, which seldom occurs above 1,000m a.s.l.

Figure 1. Distribution of Rough-legged Buzzard in Bulgaria.

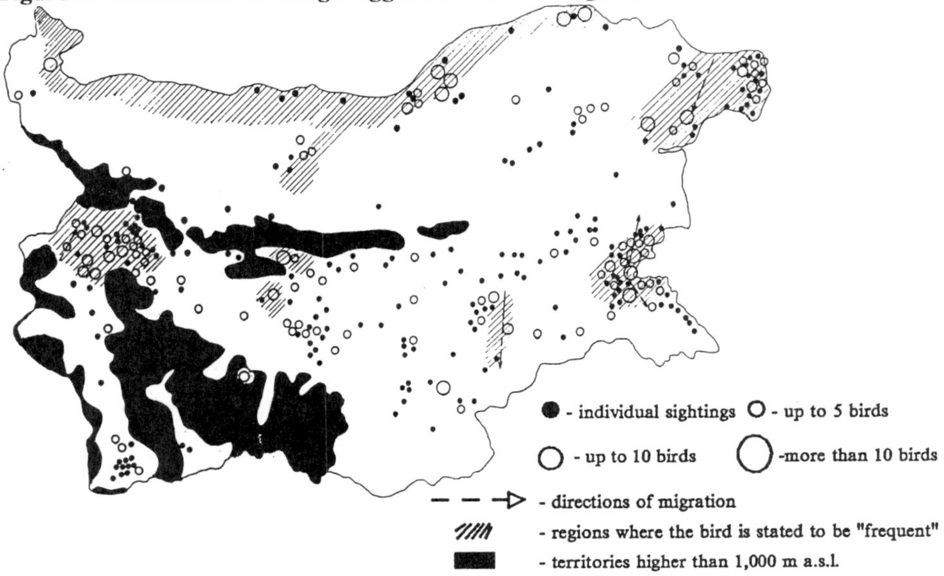

The first birds arrive in October, although Simeonov (1971) records one bird on September 16, 1965, near the village of Mousomishta in the Pirin Mountains. Earliest October appearances were on October 9, 1968, near the city of Rousse (Undjian & Braun 1984); October 10, 1984, near the village of Karloukovo; October 12, 1972, over the Aldomirtsi swamp (Nankinov 1981); and October 21, 1958, near Bourgas (Prostov 1964). In some years the birds arrive at the Black Sea coast much earlier and go farther south, e.g. the young buzzard collected by Count Amede Aleon in Turkey, at Demirci, on September 20/October 3, 1887 (Coll. du Musée d'Hist. Nat., Sophia 1907); on October 13, 1968, one Rough-legged Buzzard reached Lake Tuz in Asian Turkey (OST Bird Report 1972). In October the birds spread all over the country and make up 6.37% of the population recorded in Bulgaria (Fig. 2). We suppose that the October appearances in Bulgaria are not regular every year, and are related to sudden cold spells in Eastern Europe with cool air currents (occasionally the temperature is zero and below), heavy rainfall and occasional snow. The peak of the autumn migration wave is in November when 20.25% of the birds have been recorded with a subsequent decline in December (8.94%). A total of 90 Rough-legged Buzzards were recorded in early November 1975 in north-east Bulgaria alone; of these 70% were concentrated on a 150ha alfalfa field densely populated by Common Voles *Microtus arvalis*. The buzzards are most numerous in January (35.17%). Probably the heavy snowfalls and low temperatures are the reason for the great numbers flying from the northern regions to the Bulgarian wintering areas. The declining numbers in February (20.15%) can be interpreted in conflicting ways. In some years February is the coldest month with heaviest snow cover and the birds migrate further south to Greece and Turkey, where conditions are milder. Usually however, in February the birds begin to return gradually to their nesting areas in the north. Some authors link the slow northward movement with the melting of the snow and the reanimation of rodents (Dementiev 1951). The spring migration is usually in March and April. The birds observed during those months make up 5.99% and 3.14% respectively. The spring migration along the Black Sea coast is prominent. Prostov (1964) writes that the spring passage at Bourgas starts around March 10 and ends around March 20-25 (once on April 7, 1952) and is most intensive between March 14 and 17. We have recorded migrating birds also in West Bulgaria on March 29, 1973, over the village of Rebro (Trun district) and near the town of Breznik. The buzzards stay in Bulgaria till April 14 (Undjian & Braun 1984) though some non-breeders remain even in summer. One bird was seen in July, 1959, in Greece (Bauer *et al.* 1969). The Rough-legged Buzzards may appear on the migration route and wintering grounds even in summer or as a result of a sudden absence of rodents in the breeding areas. After such a depression of rodents some individuals remain on the wintering grounds even during the following summer (Dementiev 1951).

All over Bulgaria the Rough-legged Buzzard population is very variable (Fig. 2), depending on the availability of rodents and the winter conditions. There exists a close relation between an increased buzzard population (winters of 1974, 1977, 1980 and 1983) and abundance of the Common Vole. The Rough-legged Buzzard visits the banks of the Danube and adjacent regions in great numbers (Paspaleva-Antonova 1961), north-east Bulgaria (Petrov & Zlatanov 1955), Pleven, Sofia, Karlovo and Bourgas districts and the valley of the river Toundja (Fig. 1). Those regions coincide largely with the zones where rodents appear in great numbers every three years, and in the Danubian Plain and Dobroudja where they appear every two to six years (Straka & Gerasimov 1977). The Rough-legged Buzzard has not been recorded in many places in the Danubian Plain, where a mass appearance of the Common Vole has not been recorded either. Thus it is established to some degree in all suitable biotopes throughout the country where food is abundant in the shape of colonies of rodents and concentrations of wintering birds. In a cold winter the birds move to the suburbs of cities (Nankinov 1982).

Figure 2. Dynamics in the numbers of the Rough-legged Buzzard in Bulgaria (n = 1052).

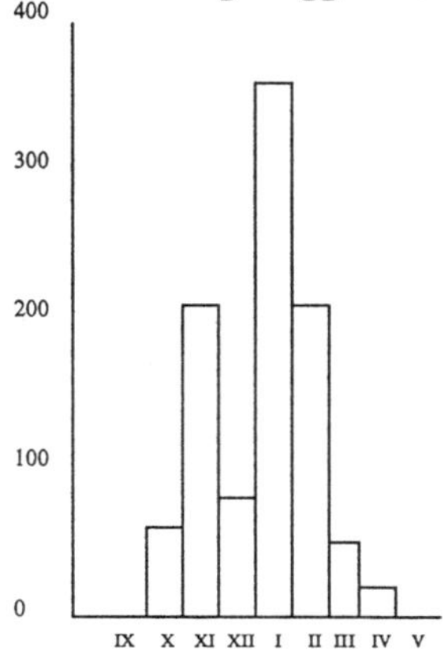

Some authors (Scott 1978) explain the greater Rough-legged Buzzard populations in wintering areas in Western Europe by a redistribution of the species' migration routes in a specific year, in addition to the overpopulation of rodents and the chilly winter. The Western Black Sea coast, via which the bird regularly flies in spring and autumn, is the main route to the Balkan wintering areas.

Ringed birds so far recovered (Plancic 1932; Kroneisl 1948; Nordström 1963; Stromar 1968; Dontschev 1976; Nankinov *et al.* 1986) show that Bulgaria and the neighbouring Balkan countries form the migration route and wintering area of Rough-legged Buzzards that have been hatched in the northern regions of Scandinavia and Russia, as far east as the Taymyr Peninsula (Fig. 3). Birds from Swedish Lapland have been found in Northern Yugoslavia; from Finland in Romanian Dobroudja; from Komi in inland Bulgaria; and from Taymyr along the Bulgarian Black Sea coast. It is interesting that these encounters have been mainly in February and March. A Rough-legged Buzzard ringed in winter in the Balkans has been found nesting in Lapland. The direction of the autumn migration of those birds is from north to south and from north-east to south-west. The distance between the breeding and wintering areas is 2,196-5,000km. The wintering areas of the Scandinavian Rough-legged Buzzard populations are along the Baltic coast and in Central Europe.

Figure 3. Sightings in the Balkans of Rough-legged Buzzard ringed in the northern regions of Euro-Asia.

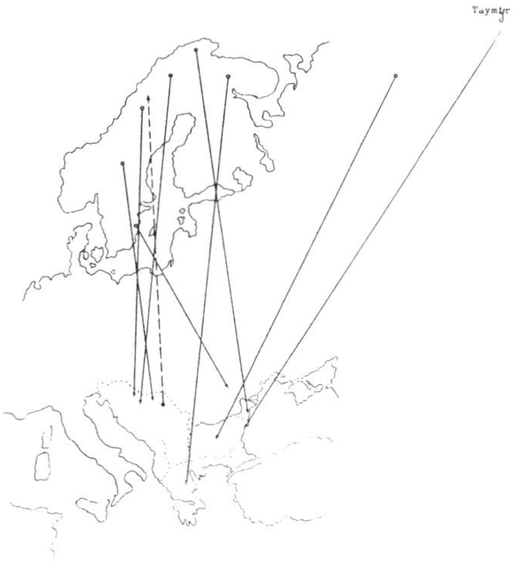

- — — → bird, ringed during winter

In December, January and February the birds do not fly farther south than Czechoslovakia (Glutz *et al.* 1989). According to A. Kishchinski (1982) two populations are found in the Scandinavian Peninsula: a southern (65° N) and a northern (Laplandish) population which flies southwards as late as October and November. The wintering areas of the two populations are in Central Europe, seldom south of the Carpathian Mountains, but individual birds may reach as far as the river Danube. We may assume therefore that the majority of Rough-legged Buzzards wintering in Bulgaria come from nesting areas farther east via Eastern Europe. The species is well represented in the Ukraine and the Crimean Peninsula during migration, and in numbers greater in autumn. The winter migration in Poltava and Kiev regions and in the Crimea starts respectively around September 23, 26 and 28 and the *en masse* flight of parties of 8-12 birds has been recorded in early November near Kharkov and Cherkassy (Zubarovski 1977; Kostin 1983). The wide dispersion and exchange of individuals between the populations of this species is a common phenomenon. Very often birds return to one and the same wintering area. It is believed that attachment to the wintering area is stronger than attachment to the nesting site (Kishchinski 1982).

Most of the Rough-legged Buzzards wintering in Bulgaria belong to the European subspecies *Buteo lagopus*, breeding between the Scandinavian Peninsula and the valley of the river Yenisey. In cold winters, however, east Siberian birds *B.l. pallidus* arrive in Bulgaria and the neighbouring countries. These inhabit regions east of the Yenisey and have brighter plumage (especially on the back and belly), as do some transitional forms between the two subspecies. Rough-legged Buzzards with pale plumage have been observed many times in the proximity of Lake Atanassovsko, near General Toshevo, Varna, Topolovgrad, Yambol and elsewhere. Apart from visual observations a bird ringed in Taymyr (Fig. 4) and recovered near Kavarna, a town in north-east Bulgaria (February 25, 1961) is evidence of the presence of the east Siberian buzzards. Observations of ringed east Siberian Rough-legged Buzzards show that the autumn migration route of many of them is in a south-west direction, to Central Asia, the Caspian Depression, the Southern Ukraine and the Balkans. The passage of the buzzards is clearly visible in the valleys of the rivers Ural and Emba (Korelov 1962), from where some of the east Siberian birds probably move south-west. A Rough-legged Buzzard found in the Northern Black Sea Plain was ringed in North Yakutiya, at the mouth of the river Indigirka (150° E) (Kishchinski 1982). The straight line distance covered by this bird from the nesting site to the wintering area is about 6,200km. Bright-coloured individuals have been observed during passage and wintering in the Volga Region, the Caucasus, along the shore of the Sea of Azov, in the Crimean Peninsula, Romania and other regions in Eastern Europe (Dementiev 1951; Paskonschi & Manolache 1971). To the west they reach as far as Poland, Czechoslovakia, Austria, Hungary (Glutz *et al.* 1989) and Germany (Eck & Feiler 1973). They were also observed in January 1932 near Thessaloniki in Greece (Kattinger 1934).

In the past and to-day Bulgarian ornithological literature describes the nutrition of the Rough-legged Buzzard in terms of generalities, e.g. "it attacks partridge, pheasant, duck, hare etc. and causes serious damage on hunting grounds" (Arabadjiev 1962; Popov & Stoyanov 1962). A. Prostov (1964) was more specific: he found remains of Partridge *Perdix perdix*, Teal *Anas crecca* and Common Vole *Microtus arvalis* in the stomachs of three Rough-legged Buzzards. Simeonov and Petrov (1980), who examined the stomachs of 54 Rough-legged Buzzards, found that 53.09% of the food was birds (18 species altogether), 36.42% was mammals, 5.55% was reptiles, 3.09% amphibians and 1.85% fish. However, visual observations show that the main places where the buzzards remain to winter are closely linked with colonies of the Common Vole. Usually these are alfalfa plots, meadows, rice and cornfields and fallow land where the buzzards fly low, hover like the Kestrel *Falco tinnunculus*, or watch for prey from a post or tree or by the holes of rodents. On arrival the buzzards first swallow the rodents whole. Later, depending on whether still hungry, they skin the voles and eat the flesh. In a colony supplying food for 70 Rough-legged Buzzards we found 20 fresh skins around the holes of rodents. It appears that birds make up the greater portion of the species' diet only in a winter with much snow and frost, usually short and infrequent in Bulgaria. In such weather some buzzards die of starvation since they cannot catch mice. A future survey will give a more exact description. Surveys in other countries show that rodents in general and the Common Vole in particular form the bulk of the Rough-legged Buzzard's diet; in Alaska small rodents vary between 62% and 78% (Springer 1975). Observations at the nest sites in Sweden, together with analysis of prey remains, show that 80-90% of the prey are small rodents (of which the Common Vole constitutes 50%) and birds 10-20%. A pair of Rough-legged Buzzards will fetch about 500 rodents to feed their brood. Only in years when rodents are scarce are birds the main food (70%) (Pasanen 1972). Small mammals account for 88% and birds for 11% in Norway (Ferguson-Lees 1968); in Kazakhstan rodents account for 76.8%, whilst birds and fish are few (Gusev & Chueva, 1951); in the Ukraine the Common Vole makes up 73.3% of the diet (Zubarovski 1977).

Scant information about the food of the Rough-legged Buzzard in Bulgaria is one of the reasons for misinterpretation of the bird's role in the biocoenoses and its severe persecution. No record is kept of the times it is shot. In 1960-1969 alone the Bulgarian Union of Hunters and Anglers was "successful" in the war against raptors: 458,118 accipiters, buteos and falcons (Ruskov & Kolev 1971). Some 50,000 birds were killed every year; in 1960 the number was 80,794. No doubt these figures include great numbers of Rough-legged Buzzard, for the bird visits Bulgaria during the hunting season. Despite the protective measures taken in various countries, 25-30% of Rough-legged Buzzards are shot by the end of the first winter and another 25-30% die from other causes (Kishchinski 1982). A great number were destroyed in the winter 1988/89 when, despite the protests of research workers, rodents were poisoned throughout the country with zinc phosphite, rodentin, azodrin, etc.

The Rough-legged Buzzard is the only raptor excluded from the Bulgarian Protection of Wildlife Act, setting a precedent with disastrous consequences for Bulgarian avifauna in general. Unawareness of nature protection laws and inefficient control have led some hunters to shoot down other protected species together with it, even species in the Bulgarian Red Book. The Rough-legged Buzzard is a bird that Bulgaria needs; its autumn and winter gatherings (together with other raptors) could help detect the Common Vole colonies at an early stage (Nankinov 1978), and location of such colonies in their winter biotopes (meadows) before they spread into cultivated areas makes possible timely and efficient suppression of rodents before their expansion, and the saving of enormous sums of money.

REFERENCES

ARABADJIEV, I. 1962. Hishtnite ptitci v Balgaria. *Nauka i izk.* : 1-176.

BAUER, W., O.V. HELVERSEN, M. HODGE & J. MARTENS 1969. *Catalogus faunae Graeciae Pars 2, Aves.* Thessaloniki: 1-203.

COLLECTIONS DU MUSÉE D'HISTOIRE NATURELLE. Sophia: 1-484.

DEMENTIEV, G. 1951. Otrjad hishtnie ptitsi Accipitres ili Falconiformes. V kn.*Ptitsi Sovetskogo Sojuza* 1: 70-314.

DONTSCHEV, S. 1976. Bulletin der Bulgarischen Ornithozentrale N 4. BAN, Sofia: 1-66.

ECK, S. & A. FEILER 1973. *Buteo lagopus* menzbieri bei Wolmirstedt?. *Zool. Abh. Staatl. Mus. Tierk. Dresden* 32, 17: 267-273.
FERGUSON-LEES, J. 1968. Studies of less familiar birds. 150 Rough-legged Buzzard. *Brit. Birds* 61, 10:456.
GLUTZ von BLOTZHEIM, U., K. BAUER & E. BEZZEL 1989. *Handbuch der Vögel Mitteleuropas.* Band 4. Falconiformes, 2nd Edn. :1-943, Aula-Verlag.
GUSEV, V. & G. CHUEVA 1951. Materiali po pitaniu nekotorih ptits delti reki Ili. *Zool. jurnal*, 30,6.
HANDRINOS, G. & A. DEMETROPOULOS 1982. Rapaces de la Gréce. *Athenes:* 1-199.
KATTINGER, E. 1934. Beiträge zur Vogelkunde Nordgriechenlands. *Verh. Orn. Ges. Bayern* 20: 349-437.
KISHCHINSKI, A. 1982. Zimniak - *Buteo lagopus* (Pontopp.). Migratsii ptits Vost. Evropi i Sev. Azii. *Hishtnie-juravleobraznie. Moskva:* 60-72.
KORELOV, M. 1962. Otriad Hishtnie ptitsi-Falconiformes. V kn. *Ptitsi Kazahstana* 2. Alma-Ata: 488-707.
KOSTIN, Y. 1983 *Ptitsi Krima.* Nauka, Moskva: 1-240.
KRONEISL, R. 1948. Rezultati prstenovanja ptica Ornitoloskog zavoda u Zagrebu u 1947. godini (V izvjestaj). *Larus* 2: 9-21.
NANKINOV, D. 1978. Ptitsite kato biologicheski indikatori. *Orn. inf. bulletin* 4: 1-11.
NANKINOV, D. 1981. Niakoi nabludenia varhu balgarskite dnevni grablivi ptitsi. *Orn. inf. bulletin* 9: 25-35.
NANKINOV, D. 1982. Ptitsite na grad Sofia. *Orn. inf. bulletin* 12: 1-386.
NANKINOV D., M. DJINGOVA & S. SCHIMANOVA 1986. Bird banding. *Bulletin 9, Bulgarian Orn. Centre.* BAS, Sofia: 1-145.
NORDSTRÖM, G. 1963. Einige Ergebnisse der Vogelberingung in Finnland in der Jahren 1913-1962. 1. *Ornis fennica* 40: 82-123.
ORNITHOLOGICAL SOCIETY OF TURKEY 1972, 2. Bird Report: 1-208.
ORNITHOLOGICAL SOCIETY OF TURKEY 1978, 4. Bird Report: 1-216.
PASANEN, S. 1972. Piekanan ravintobiologiasta Metsä-Lapissa. *Suomen riista* 24: 10-18.
PASPALEVA-ANTONOVA, M. 1961. Izuchvania varhu ornitofaunata na Balgarskoto Dunavsko kraibrekie. Kand. dis. BAN, *In-t po zoologia*: 1-145.
PASCONSCHI, S. & L. MANOLACHE 1971. *Buteo lagopus* menzbieri Dementiev, 1951: subspecie nova in Fauna Romaniei. *Rivista muzeelor* 3, 8: 255-256.
PATEV, P. 1950. *Ptitsite v Balgaria.* Sofia, BAN: 1-364
PESHEV, T. & N. BOEV 1962. *Fauna na Balgaria. Kratak opredelitel.* Narodna prosveta, Sofia: 1-520.
PETROV, B. & S. ZLATANOV 1955. Materiali po faunata na ptitsite v Dobrudja. *Spisanie na n. -izsl. in-t pri Min. na zemedelieto* 22, 1: 93-113.
PLANCIC, I. 1932. Markiranje ptica. *Lov-rib. Vjesniku* 3: 1-24. Zagreb.
POPOV, K. & S. STOYANOV 1962. *Pazpoznavane na grablivite ptitsi.* Sofia: 1-70.
PROSTOV, A. 1964. Izuchavane na ornitofaunata v Burgasko. *Izv. na Zool. in-t s muzei pri BAN* 15: 5-68.
RUSKOV, M. & I. KOLEV 1971. Roljata na hishtnitsite v drebnodivechovoto stopanstvo. *Probl. na drebnodiv. lovno stop. v Balgaira*: 132-140.
SCOTT, R. 1978. Rough-legged buzzards in Britain in 1973/74. *Br. Birds* 71, 8: 325-338.
SIMEONOV, S. 1971. Ornitocenologichni prouchvania na Pirin planina. *Kand. dis. Sof. Univ. Biofak*: 1-196.
SIMEONOV, S. & T. PETROV 1980. Prouchvane varhu hranata na krastatia orel (*Aquila heliaca Savigny*), obiknovenia mishelov (*Buteo buteo*) i gashtatia mishelov (*Buteo lagopus Brünnich*) v Balgaria. *Ekologia BAN* 7: 22-32.
SPRINGER, A. 1975. Observations on the summer diet of Rough-legged Hawks from Alaska. *Condor* 77, 3:338-339.
STRAKA, F. & S. GERASIMOV 1977. Numberical Dynamics and Zones of Harmfulness of the Common Vole (*Microtus arvalis* Pall.) in Bulgaria. *Ecology* 3: 79-91.
STROMAR, L. 1968. Prstenovanje ptica u godini 1965. *Larus* 20: 5-27.
UNDJIAN, E. & D. BRAUN 1984. Grablivite ptitsi po r. Dunav (ot svishtov do Silistra). *Orn. inf. bulletin* 15-16: 34-49.
ZUBAROVSKI, V. 1977. *Fauna Ukraini*, tom 5, Ptahi, vip. 2. Hiji ptahi. Kiev: 1-331.

Dimitar N. Nankinov
Institute of Zoology
Bulgarian Academy of Sciences
1000 Sofia, 1 Ruski blvd., Bulgaria

Meyburg, B.-U. & R. D. Chancellor eds.1994
Raptor Conservation Today
WWGBP / The Pica Press

Autumn Migration of Raptors through Sagres (SW Portugal)

Luis Palma and Pedro Rui Beja

INTRODUCTION

The main flight pathways for raptors in Western Europe are probably already well known (Porter & Beaman 1985). However, some inter-linking flyways between these main routes remain to be discovered and described in detail (Porter & Beaman 1985). These studies are important, both to gain a better understanding of migration strategies of raptors and to further identify threats to migrating raptors.

Following preliminary observations suggesting that numbers of migrating soaring birds occur annually in Sagres Peninsula (SW Portugal) (Abreu 1986; L.Palma, unpubl. data), a fall migration count was organized in September/October 1990.

Questions addressed were:

- What are the numbers and species involved, and what is the chronology of their migration?
- What are the patterns of raptor migration and with what weather conditions is the occurrence of large numbers of birds associated?
- Is this a suitable area for further understanding migration strategies and movements of raptors in Iberia?

METHODS

The count was carried out in Sagres (Fig. 1) from 23 September to 13 October. Each day, birds passing by were counted from three to six fixed vantage points and sometimes also a car, usually between one hour after sunrise and the ceasing of migration at mid or late afternoon. Number of birds of each species, flocking patterns and flight behaviour were noted at five minute intervals on registration forms. Weather variables were recorded daily. A total of 47 observers were involved in this count.

Figure 1. Map of the study area, indicating the observation sites and the general ridge orientation of the hills.

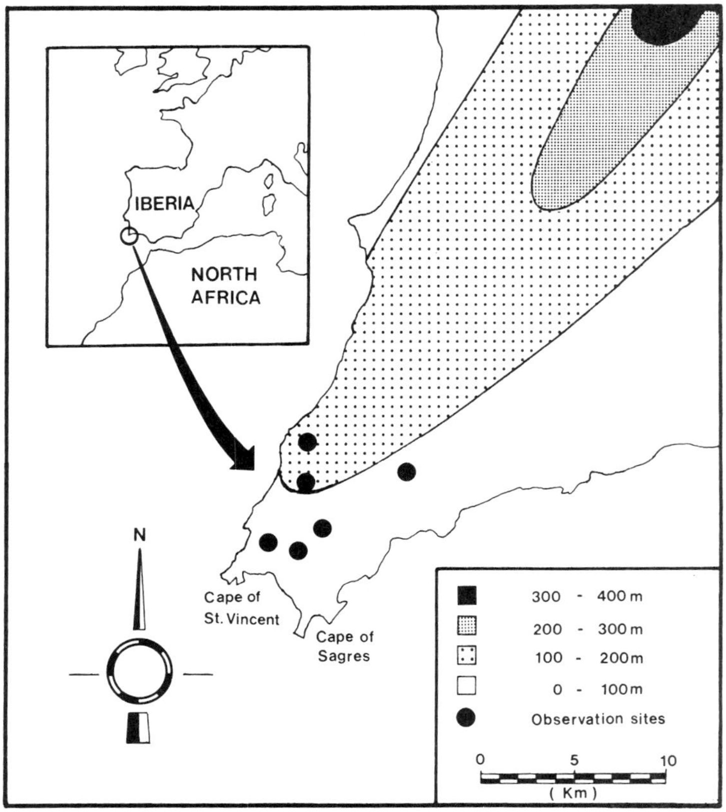

RESULTS

A total of 160 hours were spent counting. Migrants were seen every day, and 2012 raptors of 22 species, 16 storks and 62 large non-soaring migrants were counted (Table 1). Booted Eagles (34.0%) and Sparrowhawks (24.5%) made up the bulk of migrants (Fig. 2). Other migrants were

Figure 2. Proportion of migrant species seen at Sagres, autumn 1990.

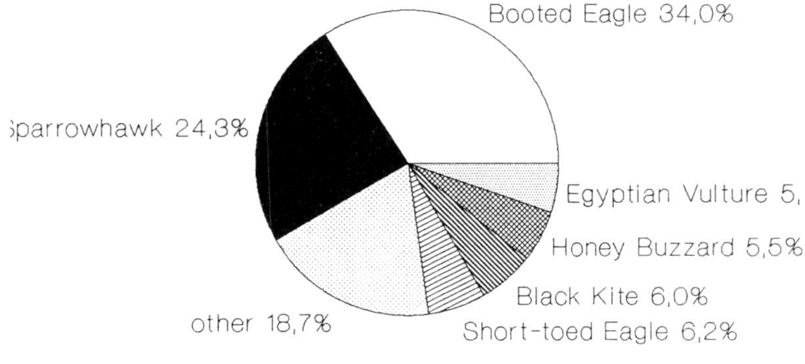

also observed, including numbers of Short-toed Eagles (6.2%), Black Kites (6.0%), Honey Buzzards (5.5%) and Egyptian Vultures (5.2%). A noteworthy feature of the migration was that a large number of species were represented by a very few individuals. These included Long-legged Buzzards (3), a fairly regular early spring vagrant in the area (L.Palma & P.Beja, unpubl. data), Lanners (4) and Eleonora's Falcon (11), probably a former breeder on the Portuguese west coast (Onofre & Palma, in press). Peregrine Falcons and Kestrels were observed every day but were not considered migrants, because several pairs of these two species are resident in the Sagres area. Resident Common Buzzards also occur in Sagres, but it was usually possible to distinguish migrant from non-migrant individuals by differences in behaviour and flight patterns.

Although no particular effort was made for determining the age class of the raptors, scattered observations suggested that juveniles made up the large majority of the migrants. Adults were dominant only in Black Kites and Eleonora's Falcons. Most Short-toed Eagles were light morphs, an inversion of the characteristic ratio in the Portuguese population (L.Palma, unpubl. data).

Figure 3. Chronology of the migration for the most abundant species and for all the migrants together.

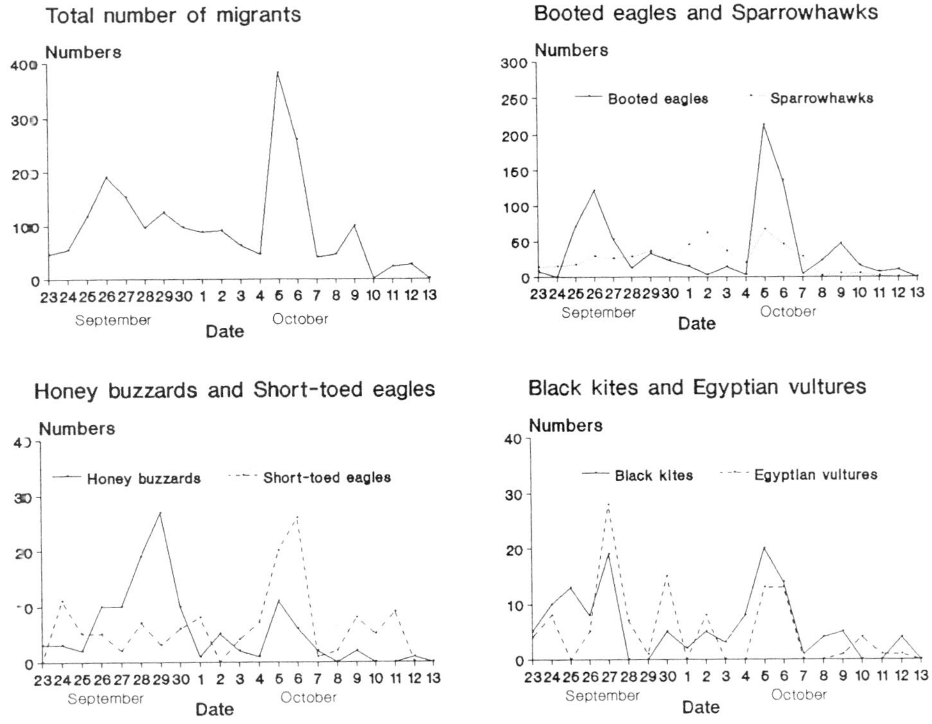

There was a large day-to-day variation in both the species and numbers counted (Fig. 3). These variations were probably related to weather conditions and to the timing of migration for the different species. To test for the effects of wind direction on the numbers of migrants observed every day, we compared the proportion of days with a given prevalent wind direction with the corresponding proportion of migrants counted on those days. No statistically significant differences were found for both the typical soarers altogether (χ^2=2.149, df=2, NS) and for Sparrowhawks (χ^2=0.668, df=2, NS). However, there was a slight non-significant tendency for soarers mostly occurring in days of prevalent easterly winds, and for Sparrowhawks mostly occurring in days of prevalent northerly (tail) winds (Fig. 4). Thermal streets were a common meteorological event in the area, apparently favouring the observation of large numbers of raptors.

Figure 4. Proportion of days with a given prevalent wind direction in relation to the proportion of migrants counted on those days, for all soarers together and for Sparrowhawks.

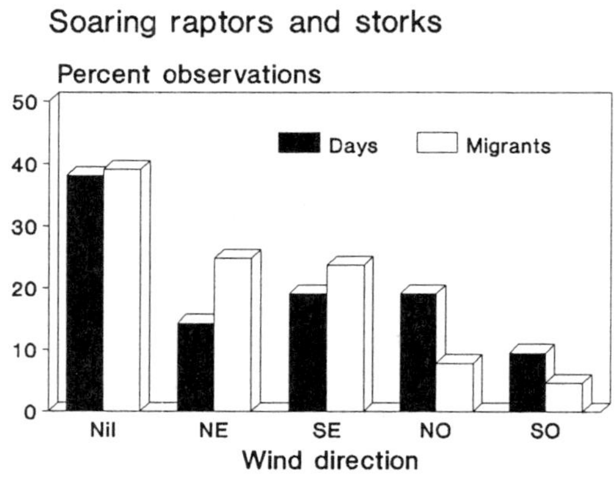

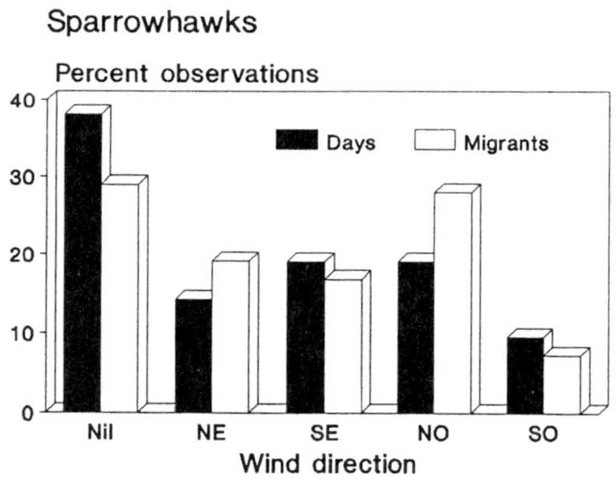

Birds entered the observation area from the north along the west coast cliffs , probably using the associated declivity currents, and from north-east, following the general ridge orientation of the hills located in the near interior (Fig. 1). Local movements were varied, ranging from a direct passage to a prolonged circulation over the area, with small numbers eventually staying overnight. Migrants left Sagres either following a south-east path over land or southwest and south directions over the sea.

Foraging in the area was the rule for Hen Harriers and was frequently observed in Sparrowhawks, Booted Eagles, Black Kites and Egyptian Vultures.

DISCUSSION

During this migration count a large movement of raptors was observed, particularly of Booted Eagles and Sparrowhawks. Although we are confident that the count covered the main stream of migrants, we think that the figures obtained are probably underestimates of the numbers of raptors migrating through Sagres in the autumn of 1990, because some early and late movements are known to occur. Irregular observations carried out in August and September of 1990 and other years indicate that there is some passage of Montagu's Harriers and Black Kites early in the season

Table 1. Migrating raptors, storks, and other large non-soaring migrants seen at Sagres, autumn 1990.

Species		Numbers counted	% of Total
RAPTORS			
Egyptian Vulture	*Neophron percnopterus*	109	5.2
Griffon Vulture	*Gyps fulvus*	6	0.2
Golden Eagle	*Aquila chrysaetos*	1	0.05
Iberian Imperial Eagle	*Aquila adalberti*	2	0.1
Bonelli's Eagle	*Hieraaetus fasciatus*	8	0.4
Booted Eagle	*Hieraaetus pennatus*	814	34.0
Short-toed Eagle	*Circaetus gallicus*	129	6.2
Common Buzzard	*Buteo buteo*	45	2.2
Long-legged Buzzard	*Buteo rufinus*	3	0.1
Honey Buzzard	*Pernis apivorus*	115	5.5
Goshawk	*Accipiter gentilis*	16	0.8
Sparrowhawk	*Accipiter nisus*	507	24.3
Red Kite	*Milvus milvus*	6	0.3
Black Kite	*Milvus migrans*	126	6.0
Black-winged Kite	*Elanus caeruleus*	1	0.05
Marsh Harrier	*Circus aeruginosus*	18	0.9
Hen Harrier	*Circus cyaneus*	76	3.6
Montagu's Harrier	*Circus pygargus*	2	0.1
Lanner	*Falco biarmicus*	4	0.2
Eleonora's Falcon	*Falco eleonorae*	11	0.5
Hobby	*Falco subbuteo*	6	0.3
Lesser Kestrel	*Falco naumanni*	7	0.3
STORKS			
White Stork	*Ciconia ciconia*	5	0.2
Black Stork	*Ciconia nigra*	15	0.5
OTHER LARGE NON-SOARING MIGRANTS			
Grey-Heron	*Ardea cinerea*	41	2.0
Spoonbill	*Platalea leucorodia*	1	0.05
Raven	*Corvus corax*	20	1.0
TOTAL		2090	

(Abreu 1986; L.Palma, unpubl. data) Seemingly, migrants have been observed passing by as late as December. The numbers of Sparrowhawks were also quite probably underestimated because their early morning movements were largely unnoticed in the first half of the count period.

Sagres revealed itself to be a secondary, though relatively important, autumn migration path in Iberia, in particular for juveniles and immatures. However, data from observations made in the same area by Moreau & Monk (1957) and Owen (1958) in late August and September 1956 and 1957 only report on small passages of a few Egyptian Vultures, Montagu's Harriers, Hen Harriers and Black Kites, which together with more recent non-systematic observations (L.Palma, unpubl. data) indicate that migration in quantity may not occur every year.

The origin of raptors migrating through Sagres is not known, though some evidence suggests that at least some birds may not be from Portuguese populations. Short-toed Eagles were predominantly light morphs, a feature not observed in the Portuguese population. Ringing recoveries are scarce, but include a few birds ringed outside Portugal, namely one Griffon Vulture (Spain), one Osprey (Great Britain), one Black Kite (Germany) and one Hobby (France) (Abreu 1986).

As for many other areas (Kerlinger 1989), meteorological conditions may be the reason for oscillations and disparities in numbers observed between days and years at Sagres, pushing birds to or away from this observation point. Although in this study we found no definite relationship between weather and migration, there was some evidence suggesting that the movement of soaring birds through the area may be favoured by easterly winds, whereas birds that rely on powered flight, such as Sparrowhawks, mostly occur in the area during predominant northerly winds. It remains to be ascertained whether this pattern remains constant over the years or whether it was simply a result of a particular set of meteorological conditions during the observation period.

Another point to be determined is the direction in which the birds leave the area. Although some birds were observed flying to the south-east over land, presumably in the direction of Gibraltar, some others were watched flying to the south and south-west, over the sea, apparently trying to cross straight to North Africa Whether or not birds accomplish this long over-sea crossing (at least 400km) is not known, but reports on Griffons found drowned and landing exhausted in fishing boats (Abreu 1986) foster the idea that some birds try to fly directly to Africa. However, preliminary radar observations carried out during this count have shown that sometimes birds leaving in a south-west offshore direction rotate to regain the continent and subsequently follow a south-east overland route.

Migration of raptors through Sagres is most likely a small part of a larger movement of raptors through Portugal that so far has remained unnoticed. The radar observations suggest that other flight paths directly oriented to Gibraltar occur to the north-east of Sagres and that these are alternatives to the coastal route, though they seem not to be mutually exclusive.

Besides the need for a further in-depth characterisation of the migratory movements in Sagres and their interpretation in relation to geography, topography and meteorology, this autumn count raises some interesting ecological and behavioural questions:

- What populations migrate through Sagres? To what extent are there differential migration strategies by age class in these populations?
- What relationships exist between Sagres and other routes in Iberia? Are migrants occurring in Sagres simply being drifted from their main flight pathways or, on the contrary, are they taking a truly alternative route, for example in response to adverse climatic conditions elsewhere?
- Do migrants cross from Sagres to North Africa over the sea, and with what weather conditions are they most likely to do so? Also, what is the fate of migrants that fly over this large body of water?
- How do migrants use the habitats along the coast and the nearby back country? What lessons for conservation and land management can be drawn from that?

ACKNOWLEDGEMENTS

This project was only made possible through the enthusiastic collaboration of almost 50 raptor watchers. Particular thanks are due to Dr. João Carlos Farinha and Dra. Júlia Almeida , who were partially responsible for the organization and logistics of this count, and to Liliana Cosme which provided the radar observations.

This study was supported by the Área de Paisagem Protegida do Sudoeste Alentejano e Costa Vicentina, Serviço National de Parques Reservas e Conservação da Natureza and Câmara Municipal de Vila do Bispo.

REFERENCES

ABREU, M.A. 1986. The migration of raptors through Portugal. *International Seminar on the Protection of Migrant Raptors in the Mediterranean*, Reggio di Calabria, Italy, May 1986.

KERLINGER, P. 1989. *Flight Strategies of Migrating Hawks.* The University of Chicago Press, Chicago. 375 pp.

MOREAU, R.E. & J. MONK 1957. Autumn Migration in South-west Portugal. *Ibis*, 99: 500 - 508.

ONOFRE, N. & L. PALMA in press. Sobre o estatuto de algumas rapinas diurnas localizadas, raras ou acidentais em Portugal. *V Conferência Internacional sobre Rapinas Mediterrânicas*, Évora, September 1986.

OWEN,J 1958. Autumn migration in South-west Portugal, 1957. *Ibis*, 100: 515 - 534.

PORTER,R.F. & M.A.S. BEAMAN 1985. A résumé of raptor migration in Europe and the Middle East. *ICBP Technical Publication*, 5: 237 - 242.

Luis Palma
Universidade do Algarve - UCTRA
Campus de Gambelas
8000 Faro - Portugal
Pedro Rui Beja

Laboratório Marítimo da Guia
Forte de Nª Srª da Guia
2750 Cascais - Portugal

Meyburg, B.-U. & R. D. Chancellor eds.1994
Raptor Conservation Today
WWGBP / The Pica Press

Analysis of Montagu's Harrier *Circus pygargus* Aerial Display during Courtship

Massimo Pandolfi and Alessandra Barocci

INTRODUCTION

The purposes of the present work are to analyse the Montagu's Harrier aerial display patterns during courtship, and to evaluate the intensity and frequency of their daily variations in differing weather conditions.

From this analysis it could also be evaluated which of the aerial displays observed are actually determinant for pair formation, and thus for mating.

MATERIALS AND METHODS

The survey was carried out in the 1988, 1989 and 1990 breeding seasons for a total of 358 hours of observation. Of these, 110h were devoted to the courtship period, with a daily average of 3.5h.

8 x 30 binoculars were used from a roofless fixed observation post, situated at a mean distance of 150-200m. For elaborating the data, entered on appropriate cards, various statistical tests were used: the chi-square test for evaluating significance, Roper's (1984) method for quantifying the intensity of aerial display by means of the local rate (No. of occurrences per type of display observed), and Markov's analysis for establishing whether a sequence was casual or temporal.

RESULTS AND DISCUSSION

Evaluation of aerial display intensity

In central Italy, courtship lasts on average five weeks, from the 5th or 8th of April until the 10th or 15th of May. Eight different types of Montagu's Harrier aerial display are observable in this period, of which seven can be considered to be courting activity (Buxton 1946) (Fig. 1), whereas Flight-drifting (low-level reconnaisance over the nest site) is carried out by single individuals for not more than 7 to 10 days following arrival in the nesting area (Richmond 1959). Since the effective courtship displays are: Sky-dance, Mutual gliding, and Mutual High-circling, the frequency of these was analysed in the various weeks of courtship (Fig. 2).

An increasing trend of activity was evidenced up to the period of mating. The local rate increases continuously up to oviposition and the beginning of incubation (Fig. 3). Subsequently, the "courting" activities and aerial displays in general undergo a sudden reduction, due both to the ending of the period (cf. Hesse in Cramp & Simmons 1980; Delamain 1932), and to the fact that the pair are engaged in autonomous and differentiated activities (the female in incubation. and the male in hunting and food supply). Evidently, once the young are fledged, the aerial display local rate increases with play and training activities, and with the increase in the number of individuals at the site. Only in this period does the local rate assume values analogous with those of the fifth week of courtship (Fig. 4).

Figure 1. Displays observed during courtship.

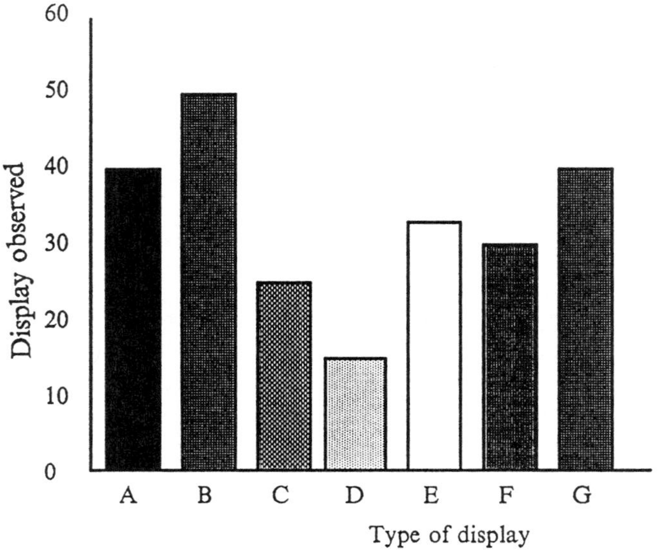

A = Sky dance; B = Flight play C = Mutual gliding
D = Mutual high circling E = Communal soaring
F = Food pass G = Defence of territory

Analysis of pre-mating courtship diplays

From the Markov matrices analysis of display sequences, the basic courtship displays for pair formation were identified, being those prevalently carried out prior to mating: Sky-dance, Flight-play and Food-pass. In 41% of the cases Sky-dance preceded Food-pass, followed by mating, whereas in 15% Sky-dance preceded Flight-play, which led on to the act of mating. In 20%, instead, mating followed directly on from Flight-play, without being preceded by other displays (Delamain 1932).

Sky-dance is a flight display carried out from the first week of courtship and performed at an almost constant rate. Where Sky-dance differs during courtship is in the way it is performed (Table 1). In the first weeks, it is mainly carried out without prey (N = 21; 71%), while after pair formation it occurs more frequently with prey (N= 14; 87%). Generally, the display is performed by the male, although there are also cases when it is done by the female (N = 49; 8%) (Table 2).

Flight-play begins from the first week, but reaches its peak only around the fourth or fifth week of courtship. This is mainly performed by the male on the female (N = 37; 79%).

The Food-pass can be observed from the first week; in these early phases it mainly takes place on the ground (Table 3), whereas subsequently it occurs almost exclusively in flight (Pandolfi & Pino d'Astore 1988). The fundamental role of the Food-pass and, as well, of Flight-play, which is a ritualized form of it (Buxton 1946; Studinka 1942; Glutz *et al.* 1976; Pandolfi & Pino d'Astore 1988), is to reduce aggressivity with the approach of fecundation.

Daily aerial displays in relation to weather conditions

The frequency pattern of aerial displays during the various times of day was found to be identical with that reported by Studinka (1942), the maximum frequency being observed in the middle of the day with a peak at around 1 p.m. (Fig. 5). This pattern is accentuated in fine weather

Figure 2. Quantitative variations in displays during courtship.

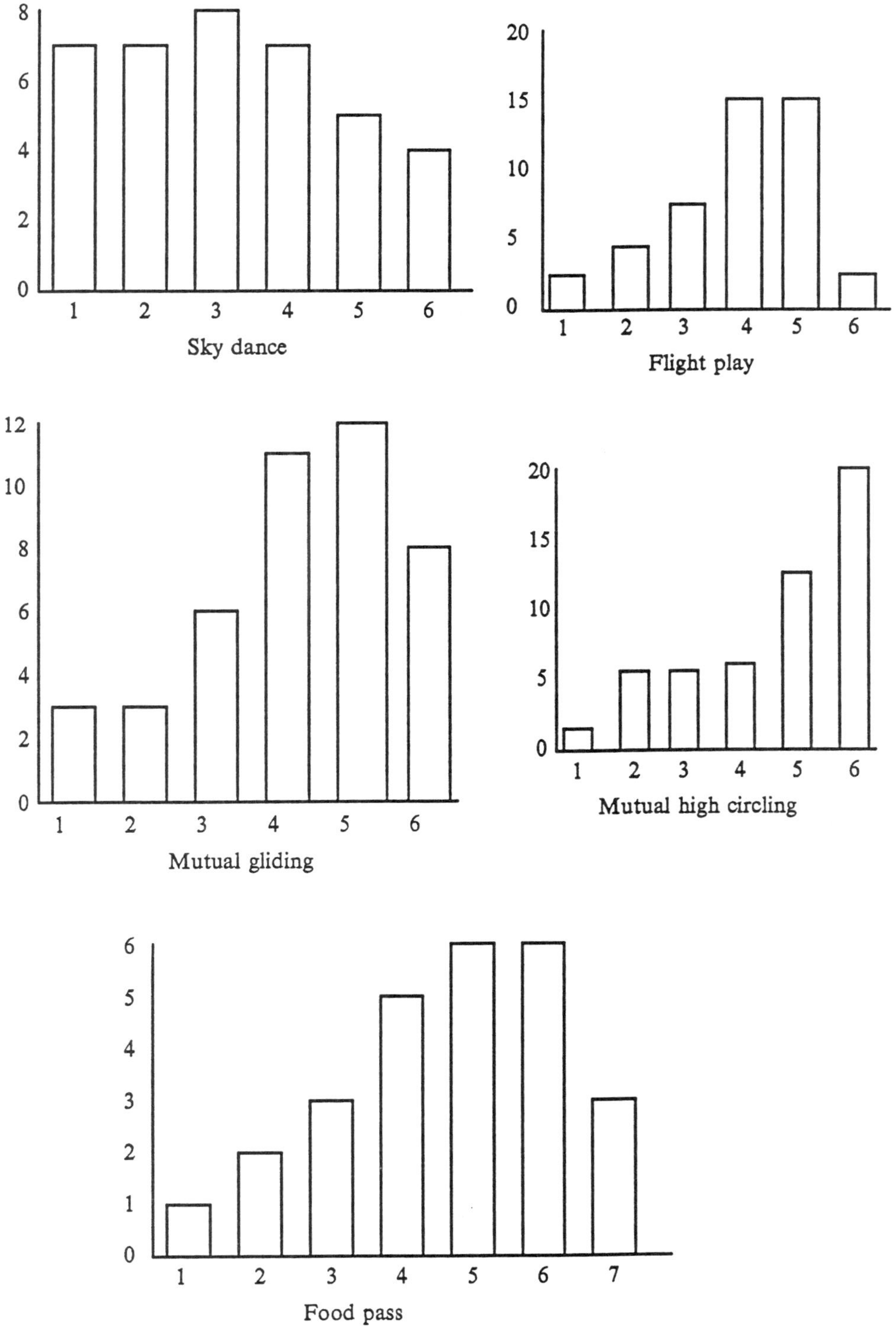

Figure 3. Local rate of the various phases of reproductive cycle.

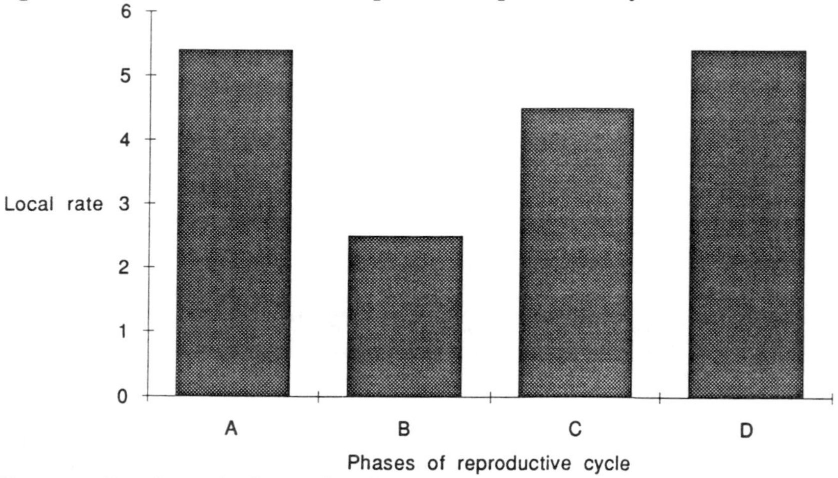

Figure 4. Local rate in the weeks of courtship.

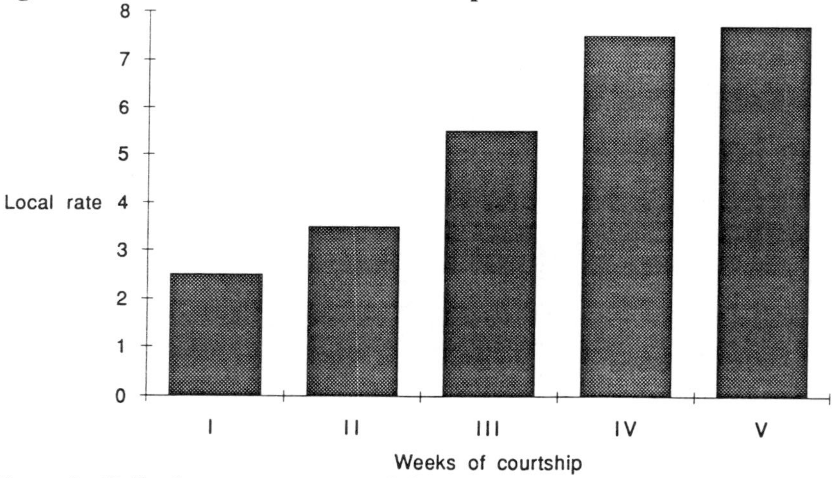

Figure 5. Daily frequency pattern of the various displays during courtship with good weather (- - - - - -) and bad weather (__________).

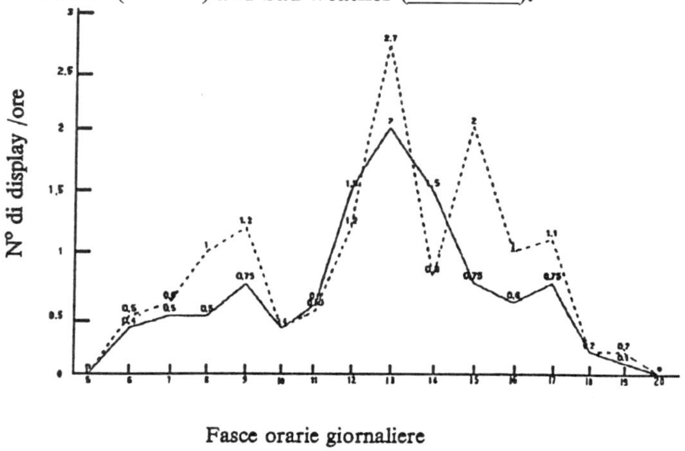

Table 1. Sky-dance distribution in the weeks of courtship (April-May), with distinction between displays with and without prey.

with	without	
	prey	prey
I	2	5
II	2	5
III	5	6
IV	5	2
V	5	-
V	I4	-

Table 2. Sky-dance observed during courtship (April-May).

Sky-dance	with prey	without prey
male	18	19
female	0	4
total	18	23

Table 3. Food-pass during courtship (April-May).

weeks	Ground Food pass	Aerial Food pass
I	3	0
II	4	2
III	4	2
IV	3	4
V	6	7

conditions, whereas in bad weather and with absence of sun, it decreases. This aspect, already noted by Studinka (1942), was analysed here in greater depth, the decrease in the various displays being significantly brought out by the chi-square test. Studinka's observations, several times reiterated (Robinson 1950; Richmond 1959), that aerial activity in general decreases in bad weather can be confirmed by comparing the individual displays in periods of clear and of overcast sky From this analysis it is seen that not all the decreases occurring in bad weather conditions are significant: only for Mutual Gliding (chi-square = 5.76; d.f. = 1; $p < 0.01$) is there any significant reduction. This can be explained by the fact that these displays require strong warm-air currents, which are more intense in good and sunny conditions. Thus, it is not that Montagu's Harriers fly less in bad weather conditions, but that they reduce only those particular displays that cannot be carried out because of the weather.

REFERENCES

BUXTON, A. 1946. - *Fisherman Naturalist.* Collins, London.

CRAMP, S. & K. SIMMONS 1980. *The Birds of the Western Palearctic. Vol. II.* Oxford University Press.

DELAMAIN, J. 1932. *Why Birds Sing.* London.

GLUTZ von BLOTZHEIM, U.N., K.M. BAUER & E. BEZZEL 1971. *Handbuch der Voegel Mitteleuropas. Vol. 4.* Falconiformes, Akademische Verlagsgesellschaft, Frankfurt am Main.
PANDOLFI, M., P.R. PINO D'ASTORE 1988. Aggressivitá intraspecifica ed interspecifica. *Congr. Naz. U.Z.I.*: 19, Camerino.
RICHMOND, W.K. 1959. *British Birds of Prey.* London.
ROBINSON, W. 1950 - Montagu's Harriers. *Bird Notes* 24: 103-114.
ROPER, T.J. 1984. Response of thirsty rats to absence of water. *Anim. Behaviour,* 32: 1225-1235.
STUDINKA, L. 1942. The habits and plumages of Montagu's Harrier. *Aquila*, 46/49: 247-268.

Massimo Pandolfi - Alessandra Barocci
Istituto di Scienze Morfologiche,
Università di Urbino
Via M. Oddi 23
61029 Urbino, Italy

Short-toed Eagle *Circaetus gallicus*

Meyburg, B.-U. & R. D. Chancellor eds.1994
Raptor Conservation Today
WWGBP / The Pica Press

Large-Scale Shooting of Raptors in the Maltese Islands

P. Portelli

INTRODUCTION

The Maltese Archipelago lies 89km south of Sicily and 3340km north of the Libyan coast. The islands have a total area of 342km² and a population of 345,000, of whom 16,000 have a license to hunt birds. 112 out of 367 species of birds recorded in the Maltese Islands are regular migrants, whilst 183 are rare or vagrant visitors. Of these 34 are raptors.

The Maltese Islands have a notable spring and autumn migration of raptors, the most commonly observed species being Marsh Harrier, Honey Buzzard and Kestrel. There is also a significant migration of Hobby, Osprey and Eleonora's Falcon. In some years large numbers of Red-footed Falcons are recorded. Ringing recoveries show that most raptors arrive in the Islands mainly from northern breeding grounds, mainly from north Germany and Scandinavia.

SHOOTING

The popularity of bird hunting results in a density of over 60 hunters per square kilometre of countryside. Hunting is regulated by the 1980 Laws for the Protection of Birds. Amongst other things the law states that it is illegal to shoot birds between 22nd May and 31st August. The law also lists those birds which may be shot or trapped, thereby giving legal protection to most birds including all raptors. In practice the laws are completely ignored by hunters. Enforcement is insignificant as the police do not consider the bird protection laws as a priority.

Raptors are shot mainly for taxidermy. Every hunter tries to get at least one specimen for his private collection. Many specimens are given away as gifts to relatives and friends.

It is estimated that three million birds are shot or trapped every year in Malta. In 1986 Magnin estimated the number of birds shot, concluding that between 3,000 and 5,000 raptors are shot annually. More recent estimates show that nowadays about 8,500 are shot annually.

The estimates given by Magnin and the author are for average years. In some years exceptional numbers are shot, notable occurrences being the estimated shooting of about 6,000 Red-footed Falcons on 25th May 1987 and of about 7,000 Marsh Harriers during March/April 1989.

The increase in the number of raptors shot over the past five years may be explained by the increase in the number of hunters shooting from boats. In the early 1980s it was discovered that more birds could be shot at sea. Over the past 10 years there has been an increase in this practice. A survey carried out in 1988 showed that *ca.* 300 dinghies and high-powered speed-boats were being used by hunters. A similar survey carried out in 1991 showed that the figure had increased to over 600.

The increase in popularity in sea hunting is due to several reasons, mainly:

a) The larger number of birds that may be shot at sea

Table 1. Numbers of raptors shot or trapped annually in Malta.

Species	1986 estimates	1991 estimates
Osprey	25-30	50-60
Black Kite	50-75	50-75
Short-toed Eagle	10-20	10-20
Sparrow Hawk	25-50	25-50
Honey Buzzard	500-1,000	500-1,500
Egyptian Vulture	1-5	1-5
Marsh Harrier	400-800	2,500-3,000
Hen/Pallid Harrier	10-50	10-50
Montagu's Harrier	30-100	100-200
Eleonora's Falcon	25	25
Hobby	500-1,000	500-1,000
Red-footed Falcon	150-300	150-300
Lesser/Kestrel	11,000-1,750	2,000-2,700

b) The total lack of enforcement at sea, due mainly to the fact that the law states that "it is illegal to discharge a firearm whilst afloat within 3km of the foreshore". The army, which is responsible for law enforcement at sea, does not have the necessary craft to chase hunters who are all equipped with high-powered motors. Often hunters just wait for army patrol boats to move away, knowing that as long as they are not seen shooting they will not be prosecuted.

Maltese hunters do not have to pass an examination before being given a hunting licence. It is enough to obtain the signatures of two hunters vouching that the applicant is able to shoot. In spite of the lack of training, most hunters are aware of bird species and are keen to obtain specimens of the rarer ones. Due to the intensive shooting, raptors no longer breed in the Islands. The last pair of Peregrine Falcons were shot from a dinghy in 1982. The Kestrel has not bred since 1972 and the last pair of breeding Barn Owls were shot in 1988.

CONSERVATION

The Malta Ornithological Socity (MOS) is campaigning to stop the killing of birds, especially raptors, in the Islands. MOS initiated a systematic campaign to change public opinion. This has achieved the desired results as far as the non-shooting public is concerned but has not yet managed to bring the situation under control. MOS is now lobbying for more effective legislation, taking advantage of the fact that Malta has applied for membership in the European Community, and pressure is being brought on the government to update and enforce the bird protection legislation, to conform with the standards required by the 1979 EEC Bird Directive.

MOS is proposing that the close season for hunting should start on March 1st, that hunting at sea should be abolished and that it should become illegal to possess a protected species, even if dead or mounted.MOS is also proposing that the income from hunting fees should be used to finance wardens who will be responsible for the enforcement of the bird protection laws.

REFERENCES

MAGNIN, G. 1986. *An Assessment of Illegal Shooting and Catching of Birds in Malta.* ICBP, Cambridge.
MALTA ORNITHOLOGICAL SOCIETY 1987. Birds Eye View No. 10.
MALTA ORNITHOLOGICAL SOCIETY 1990. Bird's Eye View, No. 13.
SULTANA, S. & C. GAUCHI 1982. *A New Guide to the Birds of Malta.*

Paul Portelli
Malta Ornithological Society
P.O. Box 498
Valetta CMR01,
Malta

Meyburg, B.-U. & R. D. Chancellor eds.1994
Raptor Conservation Today
WWGBP / The Pica Press

Time Budget, Organochlorines and Productivity in the Peregrine Falcon *Falco peregrinus* in the Kolyma Lowlands Region (North-Eastern Siberia)

Eugene R. Potapov

ABSTRACT

The Peregrine Falcon was studied in Lower Kolyma, Siberia (1982-1991). Eggshell thickness and time budgets were measured. The thin shell of Siberian Peregrine eggs indicates that the population may have been contaminated by organochlorines. The actual levels of the DDE vary from 6.19 ppm wet weight (181.80 ppm in lipid) in one site to 22.06 ± 2.86 (n = 4) ppm dry weight (383.8 ± 21.93 (n = 4) ppm in lipid) in three sites. There is no significant difference in eggshell thickness between clutches with different fates. Eggs with thick shells may be eaten by the female; on the other hand chicks may hatch from eggs with very thin shells. That suggests that thin eggshells are not the only reason for low reproductive success in the Lower Kolyma.

The duration of male and female hunts was recorded. The duration of single hunts by males dramatically decreased in nests with higher reproductive success. In unsuccessful nests the duration of the hunt could be up to 23 hours. There is a significant difference in the duration of male and female hunts. The time spent hunting by females is less than by males and does not vary significantly with reproductive success. When the brood size is larger than average, both parents may increase their hunting efforts.

MATERIAL AND METHODS

Observations were made in three study areas: in 1982-1983 in the Chukochya river basin (168km²); in 1985 in the Kolyma river basin (40km²); in 1986-1991 in the Konkovaya river basin (1190.22km²). All study areas are located in the Kolyma Lowlands in the typical tundra subzone. All Peregrine Falcons' nests were found (Table 1) in the study areas, checked regularly, and their reproductive success recorded. Eggshell fragments were collected from the nest-sites and their thickness measured with callipers with an accuracy of 0.002mm. Infertile eggs were collected and blown and their eggshell index or Ratcliffe index (Ratcliffe 1980) (weight of shell (mg) divided by length x breadth) estimated. For the eggs collected in 1991 the organochlorine concentrations were measured using gas-liquid chromotography. The analyses were made at the Monks Wood

Experimental station, Institute of Terrestrial Ecology. The organochlorine concentration was measured in five eggs from four clutches.

Measurements of the time budgets were made from a hide located not less than 200m from the nest. Both parents were observed with binoculars and telescopes, and all their movements and activities during not less than 24 hours were recorded. Special attention was paid to the measurement of the duration of a hunting sortie, which proved to be a good parameter for comparing the time budget of pairs with various reproductive success. The duration of a hunting sortie is defined as the time spent by a bird hunting away from a nesting cliff. In total, 15 full daytime budgets from 10 sites were obtained.

RESULTS

The total number of pairs and productivity of Peregrine Falcon is shown in Table 1. The reproductive success was very low (see also Fig. 1).

Table 1. Reproductive success of Peregrine Falcons in Lower Kolyma.

YEAR	1982	1983	1984	1985	1986	1987	1988	1989	1990	1991	1992
Number of pairs under observation	2	3	2	3	4	4	5	6	6	7	8
clutches	2	2	0	0	4	4	5	4	4	7	7
Number of eggs	7	7	0	0	15	16	16	16	15	24	18
Number of chicks hatched	7	0	0	0	3	3	6	6	14	16	13
Number of chicks fledged	?	0	0	0	3	3	2	2	6	13(?)	13
Reproductive success (fledglings per pair)	?	0	0	0	0.75	0.75	0.4	0.3	1	1.86	1.63

The causes of mortality are shown in Figure 2. Besides the ordinary causes such as infertility and accidents (a cliff fall), the most important were cannibalism (chicks eaten by parents) and egg-eating. Only two out of 83 eggs from 23 clutches were recorded as broken. However, most commonly eggs just disappeared. I suggest that the parents ate them. This was observed directly on one occasion, and beak marks on the shell on three other occasions suggested that these eggs were also eaten.

Apparent egg-eating tended to occur in nests where the adults spent long periods hunting. Many chicks also died after hatching. During the first stages of their development the most likely reason for their death was being eaten by their parents. At older stages, some starved to death on the cliff being unable to climb back into their nest. The highest causes of mortality were egg-eating (40.35%) chick-eating (22.81%), infertile eggs (19.30%) and accidents (14.4%). The number of survivors declined steadily through the summer (Figure 3). Both chicks and eggs declined at the same rate during a season; out of 23 clutches (83 eggs) under intensive observation only 31.3% of chicks fledged.

As there is no human population in the region, the likely mortality factors affecting the population are the contamination of adults elsewhere and lack of prey availability.

Figure 4 shows the eggshell thickness with standard deviation measured in different clutches plotted against the number of nestlings. Zero means that the clutch was eaten. The thin shell of Siberian Peregrine eggs indicates that the falcon population has been contaminated by organochlorines similar to British Peregrines in the 1960s (Ratcliffe 1980). The actual levels of pesticides are shown in Table 2.

Table 2. Pesticide levels in Peregrine eggs.

SITE	HCL	HCB	HEOD	DDE	PCBs	Mercury
1	0.01(0.24)	0.02(0.34)	0.07(1.53)	18.47(381.15)	0.83(17.19)	0.33
2	0.13(2.23)	0.01(0.21)	0.07(1.13)	22.16(362.55)	0.41(6.58)	1.35
5	0.03(0.47)	0.06(0.94)	0.04(0.62)	22.44(400.96)	1.48(23.28)	1.20
7	0.01(0.31)	0.03(0.76)	0.08(2.38)	6.19(181.80)	0.29(8.43)	2.79

Comment: HCL is a derivative of lindane; HCB is hexachlorobenzene; HEOD is a derivative from aldrin & dieldrin; DDE is a derivative from DDT; PCBs are polychlorinated biphenyls. Concentration is given in ppm wet weight, figures in brackets are concentrations in lipid.

Figure 1. Reproductive success of Peregrines in the Lower Kolyma region.

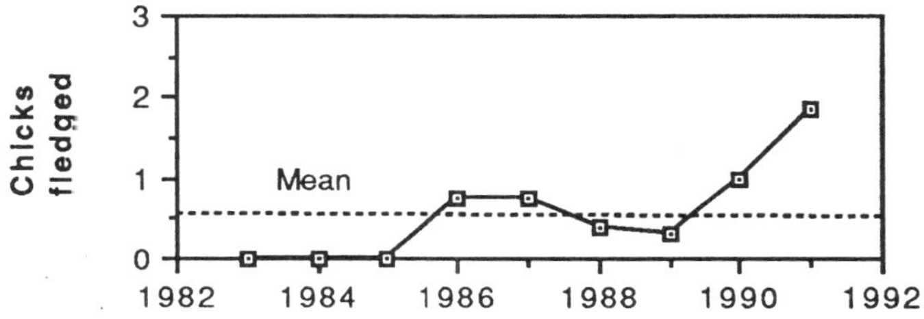

Figure 2A. Causes of mortality in the Peregrine Falcon in the Lower Kolyma region.

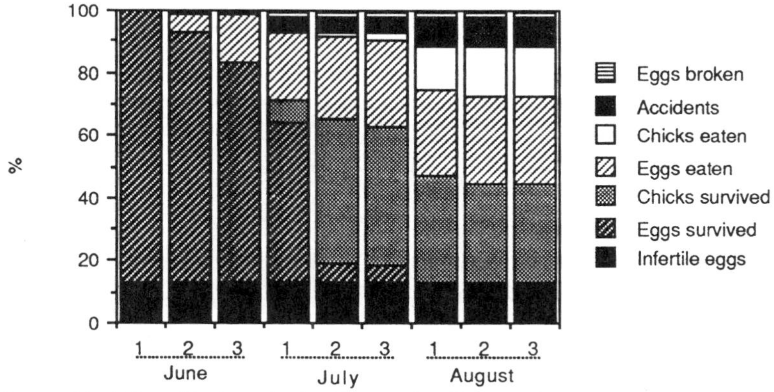

Figure 2B. Mortality/survival of Peregrine Falcons in the Lower Kolyma region.

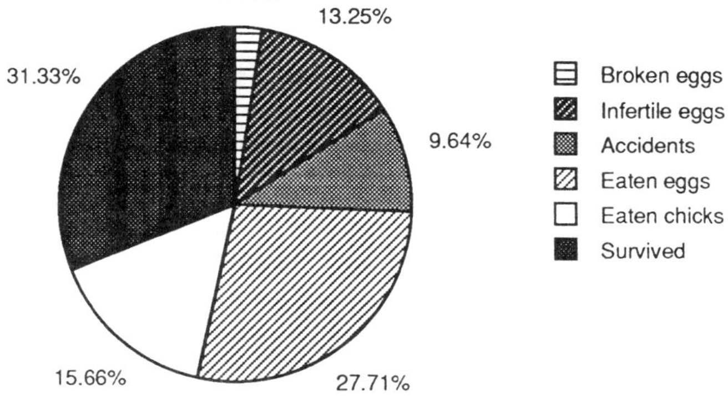

Figure 3. Number of survivors during a summer.

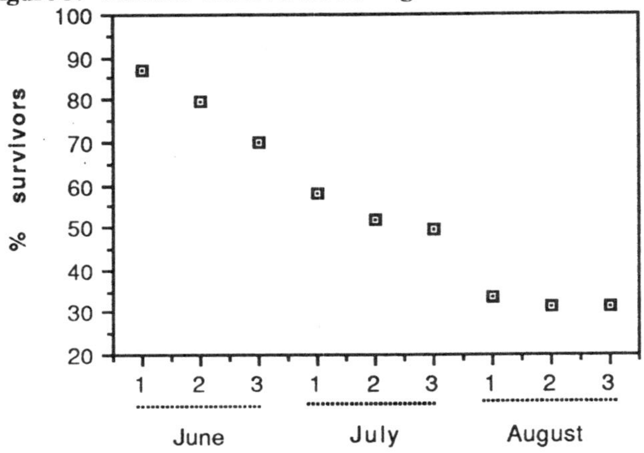

Figure 4. Eggshell thickness in clutches with different fates.

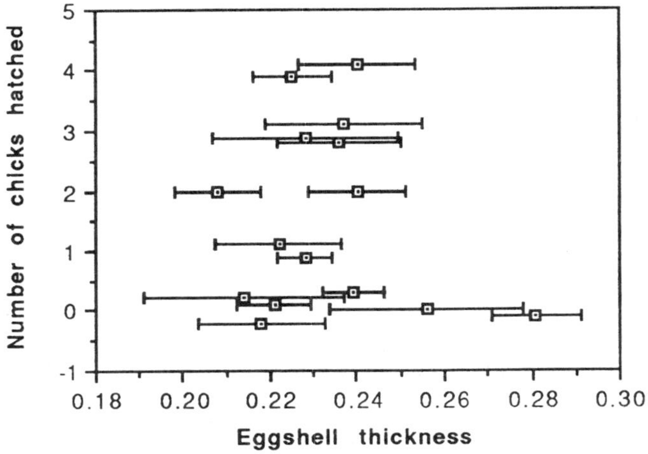

Figure 5. Daily time budget of Peregrines in the Kolyma Lowlands.

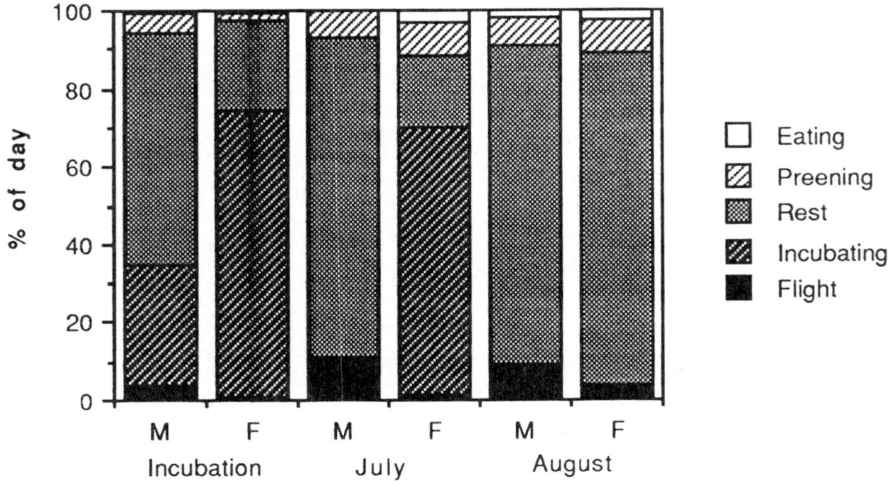

Figure 6A. Reproductive success and duration of a single hunt, Lower Kolyma.

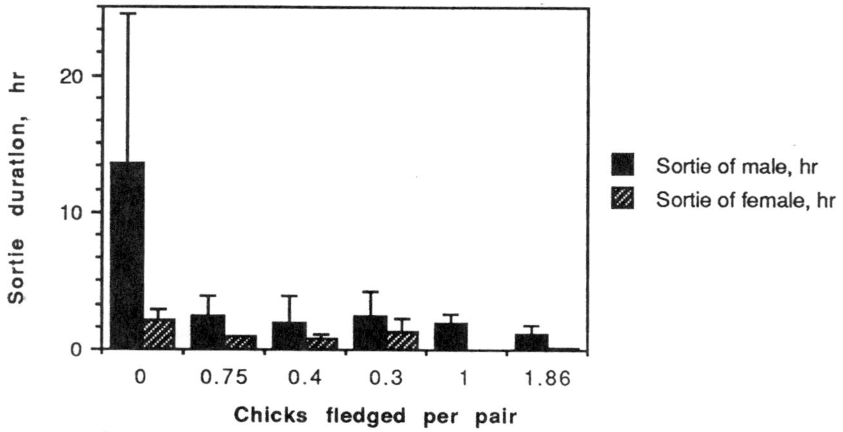

Figure 6B. Duration of a single hunt, Lower Kolyma.

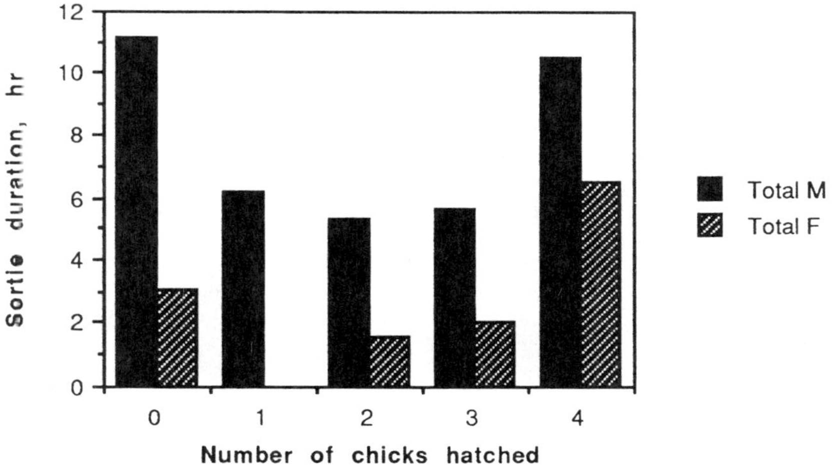

Figure 7. Average number of chicks produced at nest-sites under observation.

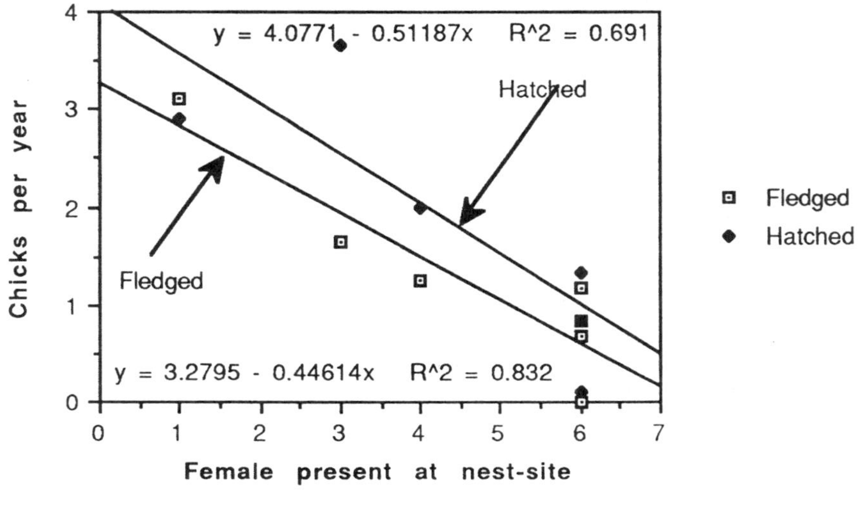

The pesticide levels in the Peregrine eggs may be one of the reasons for low reproductive success. They are known to be the main reason for eggshell thinning in raptors. However, Figure 4 shows that there is no significant difference in eggshell thickness in clutches with different fates. Eggs with very thick shells may be eaten by the female, but on the other hand chicks may hatch from eggs with very thin shells.

The daily time budgets of Peregrines in the Kolyma Lowlands are given in Figure 5. Both parents spend the overwhelming proportion of their time resting or incubating/brooding. These activities have low energy costs (Dol'nik 1982). Flight is an activity of high energy cost, and birds may fly up to 2 hours 43 minutes/day; however, they can significantly reduce the cost by soaring whenever possible. Use of soaring is subject to weather conditions, but can reach up to 40% of the total time spent flying. There is a difference between male and female time budgets. Males tend to spend more time flying, while females spend a larger proportion of their time incubating/ brooding.

The time spent by both parents in flight can be divided into time spent in hunting, in mobbing gulls and skuas and in short flights when the bird changes its position on a cliff. The proportion of time spent in hunting is higher in males than in females and its significance to a family is obvious. Duration of hunting sorties shows a strong correspondence with the reproductive success. Figure 6 represents data on the durations of hunting sorties plotted against numbers of chicks eventually fledged from their nests. The male's hunting period is the most variable parameter in the time budget. The duration of a single hunt by a male is significantly lower in nests with the highest reproductive sucess. In unsuccessful nests the duration of the hunt could be up to 23 hours. In fact, if the male spends more than 7 hours in a single hunt either the clutch or the nestlings will be eaten by the female.

There is a significant difference in the duration of male and female hunts. The time spent hunting by females is less than in males and does not vary significantly with reproductive success. The female seems to have short and constant periods of hunting, and her hunting is not usually connected with transporting prey to the nest. The average duration is 1 hour 13 minutes (n=21), and varies from a few minutes up to 4 hours.

When the brood size is larger than average, both male and female may increase their hunting efforts (Fig. 6). In a case when the pair had 4 chicks (Fig. 6b, right column) both parents had to increase their hunting time. The hunt duration became longer than 7 hours, and eventually the chicks' remains were recovered in the parents' pellets.

The average productivity calculated for the whole period a female was present at a site plotted against the period of her presence is given in Figure 7. This shows that older females tend to produce fewer chicks than younger newcomers to the area. This may be a result of the accumulation of DDT in adults which could affect the parents' hunting success. That is why the correlation coefficient in the regression between the age of a female and her final productivity is higher than that between the number of hatchlings and the female's age.

DISCUSSION

It is well known that organochlorines accumulate in plants and animals, severely affecting animals in the upper end of food chains. The Peregrine Falcon seems to be the species most affected (Cade *et al.* 1968; Cade *et al.* 1988; Ratcliffe 1980; Newton 1979), and in major parts of the world organochlorines were blamed as a main reason for the Peregrine's low reproductive success and survival rate.

Porter & Jenkins (1988) measured eggshell thickness in Peregrine Falcon eggs in California and found a non-significant positive correlation between productivity and eggshell thickness. Fyfe *et al.* (1988) studied the influence of eggshell thickness on the productivity of nests in Merlins and Prairie Falcons in Alberta and showed that in their case eggshell thinning had no bearing on productivity. The data presented in Figure 4 show that eggshell thinning cannot be the only reason for low productivity of the population studied since there was only one recorded case when DDE contamination was a possible direct reason for clutch loss (in 1991 a female was found dead on her eggs, which showed a high concentration of DDE, 3 out of 4 eggs containing embryos). Obviously DDT contamination cannot be a direct reason for mortality in chicks (Fig. 3).

The likely explanation of the low productivity of this Peregrine population in the Kolyma Lowlands region would be that either the organochlorine pesticides accumulate in the adults and somehow reduce their hunting abilities or the unstable and unpredictable availability of food makes it difficult for the parents to feed chicks. The hypothesis of DDT accumulation can be backed by the fact that older females have lower productivity than younger newcomers to the area (Fig. 7). The correlation coefficient is higher in the regression between the number of chicks fledged and the duration of females' presence at a site, than between the number of chicks hatched and the duration of female presence. Therefore the parents' ability to feed a brood limits productivity more than DDE level in eggs.

The question of where the Peregrines pick up the contamination remains unclear. There are two possible ways. The first is via a food chain in the tundra. This is possible because the wading birds which form the main item of the Peregrine's diet spend their winter in regions where the application of DDT may occur. Another possibility is that the Peregrines themselves pick up the contamination during winter, perhaps in South-east Asia or China. However, both may occur together.

ACKNOWLEDGEMENTS

The research was funded in different years by the Leningrad State University (1982-1983), the Institute of Biological Problems of the North (Magadan, Siberia) (1982-1990), the East Palearctic Wetlands Bureau (Magadan, Siberia) (1991), the Soros Scholarship (Soviet-American Foundation "Cultural Initiative") (1989-1990) and Lady Dervorguilla Scholarship from Balliol College (Oxford) (1990-1991). I am particularly grateful to Dr A. Andreev (Magadan) for his support of my research in the tundra. I also wish to acknowledge the help and field assistance given by Valentin Nickolayich Khlestkin, I. Strelkova, E. Khlebosolov, I. Shushkevich and H. Loskutova. The first draft of the paper was commented by Professor Christopher M. Perrins (EGI, Oxford). I am very grateful to Dr. Ian Newton (Monks Wood Experimental station, ITE) who helped with the analyses of organochlorines, and to Derek Ratcliffe for valuable comments on the data.

Participation in the World Conference of Birds of Prey and Owls and presentation of this paper was made possible due to the Oxford University Department of Zoology travel grant and the generosity of Michael Densley, a great lover of birds.

REFERENCES

CADE, T., C. WHITE & J. HAUGH 1968. Peregrines and pesticides in Alaska. *Condor 70:* 170-8.

CADE, T., J. ENDERSON, C. THELANDER & C. WHITE (Eds.) 1988. *Peregrine Falcon Populations.* The Peregrine Fund, Inc.

DOL'NIK, V.R. 1982. Methods of time and energy budget study. *Time and energy budgets of free-living birds* (V.R. Dol'nik, - (Ed.) *Acad. Sci. USSR. Proc. Zool. Inst.* 113:1-156.

FYFE, R., R. RISEBROUGH, J. MONK, W. JARMAN, D. ANDERSON, L. KIFF, J. LINCER, I. NISBET, W. WALKER II & B. WALTON 1988. DDE, Productivity and Eggshell thickness relationships in the genus *Falco. In:* T. Cade, J. Enderson, C. Thelander & C. White (Eds.) *Peregrine Falcon Populations.* The Peregrine Fund, Inc.: 319-335.

NEWTON, I. 1979. *Population Ecology of Raptors.* T.& A. Poyser.

PORTER, R. & M. JENKINS 1988. Pollutants and eggshell thinning in Peregrines and their prey in the Baja California region. *In*: T. Cade, J. Enderson, C. Thelander & C. White (Eds.). *Peregrine Falcon Populations.* The Peregrine Fund, Inc.: 413-21.

RATCLIFFE, D. 1980. *The Peregrine Falcon.* T. & A. Poyser.

Eugene R. Potapov
Edward Grey Institute of Field Ornithology
Dept. of Zoology
South Parks Road
Oxford, OX1 3PS
England

Meyburg, B.-U. & R. D. Chancellor eds.1994
Raptor Conservation Today
WWGBP / The Pica Press

Choice of Prey and Feeding Activity of urban Peregrine Falcons *Falco peregrinus* during the Breeding Season

R. Schneider and I. Wilden

ABSTRACT

From March-July 1991 a pair of Peregrines with two young nesting on a building in Berlin/ Niederschöneweide was observed. All activities related to the nest were recorded continuously by a quick-motion video system. Remains from feeding and plucking were collected around the nest site each day.

Prey amplitude was divided into constant (urban birds: 26.6% Pigeons, 18.7% Starlings) and variable portions (opportunities: spring migration of Thrushes, roosting flights of Black-headed Gulls). There was a preference for large-sized birds. Thus, prey selection seems to be guided by availability and size of birds. The nestlings were nearly exclusively fed by the female. Feeding was observed between about 4.34 a.m. and 6.57 p.m. Mean number of feedings per day was 6.7 with a median interval of 122.5 min. Maxima of feeding activity could be found in the morning and in the afternoon. Due to food storage, climatic factors had only little effect on the daily feeding pattern. Number of feedings and length of intervals were mostly affected by age.

Changes in the feeding pattern are considered as evidence of an arising conflict between growing needs and behavioural development of the young and growing costs for the parents. Food seems not to be a limiting factor in an urban environment.

INTRODUCTION

Man is changing his world and the ecological consequences we can see today are dramatic. Plant and animal species die out and Rathmayer (1990) suggested that in the middle of the next century approximately 30% of recent animal species will be extinct. Unfortunately, the worldwide decline of Peregrine Falcon populations is one of the most famous examples for this work of destruction.

On the other hand, man creates by his work new habitats for animals. Both the diversity of Central European bird life which came about with traditional forms of agriculture up to the 18th

Table 1: Prey taken by the falcons from March 1st until July 10th. 1991 (food items identified from remains of plucking and feeding, n=128)

Species	March			April			May			June			July	Total
	I	II	III	I	II	III	I	II	III	I	II	III	I	
Larus ridibundus	-	-	18.2	16.7	16.7	-	25.0	-	10.0	-	-	-	30.0	8.6
Columba livia	20.0	10.0	5.7	16.7	16.7	-	-	-	40.0	48.3	25.0	37.5	60.0	26.6
Streptopelia decaocto	-	10.0	5.7	-	16.7	-	25.0	-	-	3.4	-	12.5	10.0	5.4
Melopsittacus undulatus	-	-	-	-	-	10.0	-	-	-	-	-	-	-	0.8
Nymphicus hollandicus	-	-	-	-	-	-	-	-	-	-	12.5	-	-	0.8
Apus apus	-	-	-	-	-	-	-	-	20.0	24.2	25.0	12.5	-	9.4
Alauda arvensis	40.0	10.0	5.7	-	-	-	-	-	-	-	-	-	-	3.1
Phylloscopus . sp.	-	-	-	10.0	-	-	-	-	-	-	-	-	-	0.8
Turdus pilaris	-	-	-	-	16.7	-	-	-	-	-	-	-	-	0.8
Turdus iliacus	-	10.0	-	-	-	-	-	-	-	-	-	-	-	0.8
Turdus philomelos	-	10.0	27.2	16.7	-	10.0	-	-	-	3.4	12.5	-	-	8.6
Parus major	-	20.0	-	-	-	-	-	-	-	-	-	-	-	1.6
Parus caeruleus	-	10.0	-	-	-	-	-	-	-	-	-	-	-	0.8
Emberiza schoeniclus	-	-	5.7	-	-	-	-	-	-	-	-	-	-	0.8
Fringilla coelebs	-	-	-	16.7	16.7	-	-	-	-	-	-	-	-	1.5
Chloris chloris	-	-	-	-	-	10.0	-	-	10.0	-	-	-	-	1.5
Pyrrhula pyrrhula	-	-	5.7	-	-	-	-	-	-	-	-	-	-	0.8
C. coccothraustes	-	10.0	-	-	-	-	-	-	-	-	-	-	-	0.8
Loxia curvirostra	-	-	-	-	-	-	-	-	-	-	-	12.5	-	0.8
Passer domesticus	20.0	-	5.7	-	-	10.0	-	-	-	-	-	-	-	2.3
Sturnus vulgaris	20.0	10.0	22.7	33.3	-	40.0	25.0	-	20.0	13.8	12.5	25.0	-	18.7
Garrulus glandarius	-	-	5.7	-	16.7	10.0	25.0	-	-	6.9	-	-	-	4.7

(Numbers in columns: Percentage from the total amount of identified individuals for each decade and the whole collection period) century (Berthold 1990) and the process of urbanization which includes a lot of bird species (Stephan 1987) are examples. Thus, it has been known for a long time that even the Peregrine Falcon is able to live in a manmade environment using buildings as substitutes for cliff nesting sites (Kuhk 1968; Mebs 1968).

Urban spreading observed in several animal species leads us to question the reasons. Maybe there is a simple answer: an animal's specific requirements regarding space, time, metabolism, information, protection and mate should be realized better than elsewhere in an urban environment, or at least well enough to prevent it from seeking an alternative. That is, there should be some advantage. Knowledge about such "advantages" is necessary for each kind of animal protection or reintroduction. The following investigations on Peregine Falcons are within such a framework.

Attention was paid to feeding behaviour, because food is regarded as one of the ultimate factors in habitat selection (Hilden 1965). Information about the feeding of Peregrines is mostly based on prey amplitudes sampled over a long time (reviewed by Brüll 1984; Sömmer 1989). Detailed quantitative studies on actual feeding activity are rare (Thiollay 1982; Haller 1984). Moreover, the mode of prey selection - opportunism or individual specialization - is still discussed (Sömmer 1989). Thus, it seems to be worthwile to present our first results from observations of an urban breeding pair of Peregrines.

METHODS

From March-July 1991 a breeding pair of Peregrine Falcons *Falco p. peregrinus* nesting under the roof of the former broadcasting station Berlin/Niederschöneweide was observed. Two young hatched from a clutch of four eggs and were successfully raised.

From hatching of the first young on April 25th until the young left the nest on May 24th, all activities of the birds in the immediate vicinity of the nest were recorded by a quick-motion video system. Two cameras (a CCD F 12 colour-TV camera and a CCD-100 infra-red camera with infra-red spot) installed 2m in front of the nest allowed continuous monitoring and recording of the activities in an adjacent room. The records were applied to further analyses of parental care. Feedings of the young were scored both for the female and the male. Length of feeding bouts and intervals between feedings were timed.

In addition, remains from plucking and feeding were daily collected around the nest site during the whole breeding and nestling period.

Information about the weather conditions related to Berlin-Tegel (49m a. s. l.) were taken from the offical weather service (DWD 1991).

RESULTS

Altogether 128 identifiable food items were obtained from the collected pluckings. Table 1 shows the resulting composition of the prey amplitude and its seasonal changes. Domestic pigeons and Starlings were caught over the whole observation period, thereby reaching the highest percentages. A second group ranging from a percentage of 8 to 10% involved Songthrushes, Black-headed Gulls and Swifts, which were caught only during distinct periods. Collared Doves at a lowest total percentage of about 5% were taken regularly. All other species were found in smaller quantities, although Skylarks and Jays reached remarkable seasonal peaks.

Table 2. Size preferences in prey selection

classes of catched birds (body weight)	percentage of total prey amplitude
0 - 25 g	5.5 %
26 - 50 g	18.8 %
51 - 100 g	30.5 %
100 - 300 g	45.2 %

The distribution of prey items among different weight classes is significantly different from a random one (chi-squared test, $p<0.001$). Nearly half the birds were heavier than 100g, indicating a clear size preference (Table 2).

The nestlings were fed almost exclusively by the female. Only 2.5% from a total of 202 feedings were directly performed by the male. The first feeding by the male was observed ten days after the beginning of hatching.

Figure 1: Daily feeding pattern (all feeding events summarized within 3-hour intervals over the whole observation period)

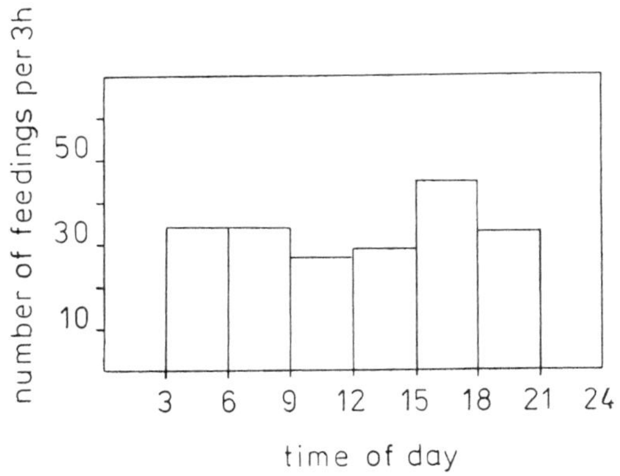

Figure 1 shows the daily feeding pattern. There were on average 6.7 feedings per day, each lasting on average 11.8 min, with a median interval of 122.5 min between them . In the morning, feeding began at about 4.34 a.m. (Central European time). In the evening, last feeding was at about 6.57 p.m. There was only little variation in those times (V=15.2% or 18.4%). On that account, correlations between time of sunrise/sunset and time of first/last feeding didn't reach any significance. But there were two stable peaks of feeding activity in the morning and in the afternoon.

Effects of several climatic factors (daily mean temperature, rainfall, wind force, sunshine) on feeding activity were estimated by calculating coefficients of correlation. Neither times of first feeding nor number of feedings per day, total time spent feeding per day, and daily range of feeding intervals could be found to be affected by climatic conditions. But there was an obvious effect of weather conditions on food delivery (Table 3). On rainy days the use of deposited prey was significantly higher than on days without any rainfall. On the latter days food was mostly handed over from the male to the female at the nest.

Table 3: Use of deposited prey dependent on weather conditions

	rainy days	days without any rainfall
total number of feedings	120	82
number of feedings with deposited prey	80	36
percentage and 5%-confidence interval of feedings with deposited prey	75 (± 10.2)	44 (± 14.1)

Figure 2: Feeding activity (number of feedings per day) during the nestling period.

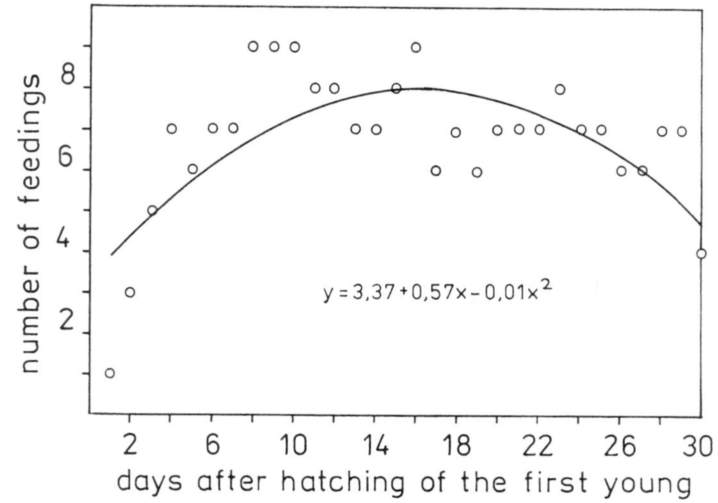

Figure 3: Variability of feeding intervals during the nestling period.

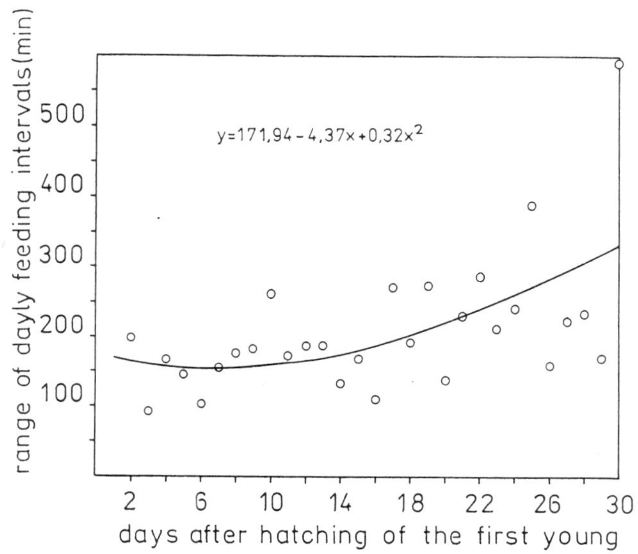

All feeding parameters differed significantly with age of the young (analysis of variance, $p<0.01$). Number of feedings per day as well as daily mean duration of feeding events rose to a maximum level and were lowered again during the second half of the nestling period (correlations of 2nd degree, $r=0.70$ or 0.54). Figure 2 shows age dependent changes of feeding frequency. Feeding intervals were likewise correlated with age (correlation of 2nd degree, $r=0.59$) However, changes in the opposite direction were found with advancing age. Range of feeding intervals, that is the variability of feeding time, increased with advancing maturity in the young too (Figure 3: correlation of 2nd degree, $r=0.56$). Finally, the length of a feeding event depended on the length of the preceding interval (correlation of 2nd degree, $r=0.14$, $p<0.05$).

DISCUSSION

Feeding habits did not differ much from those reported elsewhere (Uttendörfer 1952; Brüll 1984; Sömmer 1989). Despite all the problems connected with sampling methods mentioned by Sömmer (1989), some tendencies in prey selection should be pointed out.

Firstly, there is a group of birds taken throughout the whole observation period: on a considerably high level, domestic pigeons and Starlings, on a lower level Collared Doves. They all belong to the most common urban breeding birds (Degen & Otto 1988), and they spend the winter here. Secondly, a group of birds caught only during distinct periods can be distinguished. These are for instance Swifts, which are highly active in the air during their reproduction period, Thrushes, which have a notable spring migration over Berlin (Reckin 1987), and Black-headed Gulls which are available on roosting-flights outside their breeding period. Maxima of capture are in accordance with the periods of highest mobility in those species (reviewed by Rutschke 1983). That is, availability of prey seems to be a main criterion of prey selection, and this explains local differences in the composition of prey amplitudes mentioned by Sömmer (1989).

A second cue for prey selection seems to be size. A preference for heavy birds is not surprising, because profitability of prey is positively correlated with its size (Tembrock 1983). Thiollay (1982) pointed out that the Peregrine's hunting effort for a small Passerine bird is four times higher than for a pigeon.

The daily pattern of feeding is in accordance with that reported by Haller (1984). There is only one exception: Haller couldn't find any feeding activity before 6.00h. We observed the first feeding at about half past four and take this for an environmental effect (lighting, traffic, human activities). The Peregrine's feeding activity with two peaks in the morning and in the afternoon reflects the general pattern of locomotor activity found in its potential prey species (Aschoff & Wever 1962), the earlier beginning of feeding being due to their advanced activity under urban conditions.

It is amazing that feeding wasn't affected by external (climatic) factors. Vogt (1984) had very good correlations between sunrise or sunset and locomotor activity which we could not find. Maybe it was due to the type of activity measured or to the lighting downtown. We still have to test this.

It is known that weather conditions have little or no effect on the activity of Ospreys (Stinson *et al.* 1987) hunting fish. But the activity of the Peregrine's prey is dependent on weather. This disadvantage was excluded by food storage. We found it to a much larger extent than reported by Haller (1984). It seemed to be due to a good food supply. That it was really good had been reflected by the male's low participation in actual feeding.

Thus, variability of feeding patterns should have been mostly affected by internal factors. The mean duration of a feeding event was dependent on the length of the preceding interval, that is from the degree of hunger of the young. Age was in 2nd degree correlation with all feeding parameters. In that manner, the maximum level of food supply (highest number of feedings per day, brief intervals) corresponded with the period of maximum weight gain per day (weight gain see Heinroth & Heinroth 1925). Moreover, variability of feeding intervals changed over the period. That is, with advanced maturity food supply of the young became not only less frequent but also more unpredictable. It is assumed to be a parental response to growing effort. In addition, it could stimulate the young to become independent or at least to leave the nest.

Altogether, food quantity seems not to limit the Peregrine's living conditions in an urban environment but there are still some questions about the bird's ability to rear more than two young under such circumstances and about food quality. We should try to find the answers.

ACKNOWLEDGEMENTS

This investigation was sponsored by means of the Bundesministerium für Umwelt, Naturschutz und Reaktorsicherheit and the Berlin Government. We are grateful to the AG Greifvogelschutz Berlin/Bernau for co-operation and installation of the equipment. Especially, we thank P. Sömmer for identification of pluckings.

REFERENCES

ASCHOFF, J. & R. WEVER 1962. Beginn und Ende der täglichen Aktivität freilebender Vögel. *J. Orn.* 103: 2-27.

BERTHOLD, P. 1990. Die Vogelwelt Mitteleuropas: Entstehung der Diversität, gegenwärtige Veränderungen und Aspekte der zukünftigen Entwicklung. *Verh. Dtsch. Zool. Ges.* 83: 227-244.

BRÜLL, H. 1984. *Das Leben europäischer Greifvögel.* 4. Aufl. Fischer Verl. Stuttgart, New York.

DEGEN, G. & W. OTTO 1988. Atlas der Brutvögel von Berlin. *Naturschutzarb. Berlin und Brandenburg*, Beiheft 8.

DWD 1991. Amtsblatt des Deutschen Wetterdienstes. Wetterkarten 01.03.-31.07. Zentralamt Offenbach/ Main.

HALLER, M. 1984. Untersuchungen zur Biologie, insbesondere Ernährung des Wanderfalken in der Brut- und Aufzuchtzeit am Beispiel zweier Paare aus dem Schwarzwald. Dipl.-Arb., Forstwiss. Fak., Univ. Freiburg i. B.

HEINROTH, O. & M. HEINROTH 1925. *Die Vögel Mitteleuropas.* II. Bermühler Verlag, Berlin.

HILDEN, O. 1965. Habitat selection in birds. A review. *Ann. Zool. Fenn.* 2: 53-75.

KUHK, R. 1968. Weiteres über Bruten des Wanderfalken (*Falco peregrinus*) an menschlichen Bauten. *Jahrb. Dtsch. Falkenorden*, 65-66.

MEBS, T. 1968. Wanderfalkenbruten an menschlichen Bauwerken. *Jahrb. Dtsch. Falkenorden*, 55-65.

RATHMAYER, W. 1990. Die Aufgaben der Zoologie. Eine Standort- und Wegbestimmung. *Verh. Dtsch. Zool. Ges.* 83: 63-71.

RECKIN, L. 1987. Beringungsergebnisse im Rahmen der Aktion Baltic am Fangplatz Berlin-Wuhlheide 1976-1979. *Pica* No. 13: 42-50.

RUTSCHKE, E. (Hrsg.) **1983.** *Die Vogelwelt Brandenburgs.* Fischer Verlag Jena.

SÖMMER, P. 1989. Die Ernährung des Berliner Wanderfalkenbrutpaares.*Pica* No. 16: 120-128.

STEPHAN, B. 1987. Die Verstädterung der Vögel als Prozeß. *Falke* 34: 106-109.

STINSON, C. H., J. LAUTHNER & R. T. RAY 1987. The effect of weather conditions on the behaviour of ospreys in North Western Washington, USA. *Can. J. Zool.* 65: 2116-2118.

TEMBROCK, G. 1983. *Spezielle Verhaltensbiologie.* Bd. 2. Fischer Verlag, Jena.

THIOLLAY, J. M. 1982. Les ressources alimentaires, facteurs limitant la reproduction d'une population insulaire de faucon pélerins (*Falco peregrinus brookei*). *Alauda* 50: 16-44.

UTTENDÖRFER, O. 1952. *Neue Ergebnisse über die Ernährung der Greifvögel und Eulen.* Verlag Eugen Ulmer, Stuttgart

VOGT, D. 1984. Studien zur Tagesrhythmik mitteleuropäischer felsenbrütender Wanderfalken (*Falco peregrinus*). Ornithol. AG Koblenz u. Umg., Westerwald, Mayen u. Umg. Jahresbericht 1979, Sonderheft 1, 3 überarb. Aufl., Koblenz. 1-38.

Dr. R. Schneider and I. Wilden
Institut für Verhaltensbiologie und Zoologie
Fachbereich Biologie der Humboldt-Universität zu Berlin
Invalidenstr. 43, D-1040 Berlin
Germany

Merlin *Falco columbarius* - adult male

Meyburg, B.-U. & R. D. Chancellor eds.1994
Raptor Conservation Today
WWGBP / The Pica Press

Population Ecology of Peregrine Falcons *Falco peregrinus* in Baden-Württemberg, 1965-1991

P. Wegner

SUMMARY

The population development of Peregrines over a period of 27 years (1965-1991) is discussed. During this time the number of successful pairs in the study area increased ten-fold. Basic parameters of an expanding population (breeding success, age structure, exploring of new habitats, results of ringing experiments) are demonstrated and the results are compared with other European populations. Conservation strategies and the spread of the population into the surrounding regions are illustrated.

DISCUSSION

The Peregrine Falcon *Falco peregrinus* population in Baden-Wüttemberg is one of the best-monitored. Baden-Württemberg is a Federal State in the south of Germany, highly industrialised and densely populated. The Black Forest, Swabian Alps, Rhine and Neckar valleys and Lake Constance are examples of the diversity of its landscapes.

The AGW (Working Group for Protection of the Peregrine) was founded in 1965 and for the past 27 years has carried out a long-term study to which there is no forseeable end, since each year we acquire fresh knowledge and current threats continue to make protection work neccessary (Schilling & Rockenbauch 1985).

The Peregrine population had dramatically crashed from 150 pairs in 1950 to a level of 20-25 pairs, only 15% of its former size, when we started our protection work in 1965. In most of Germany the species had been extirpated with two exceptions: small surviving groups in Baden-Württemberg and in the northern Alps (Fig. 1).

Our own experience indicated that this dramatic decline was the result of human persecution. On the other hand it was becoming apparent that no region of the globe could avoid the negative impact of pesticides on mortality and fertility. We accordingly collected material for pesticide analysis (eggs, dead nestlings and adults, feathers, prey items, etc.).

These revealed that Peregrines in Baden-Württemberg were highly exposed to different pesticides and PCBs (Schilling & König 1980). There were in addition, other, local reasons for the decline, although these were denied by some people, who held that pesticides were solely responsible. Our own experience over more than 20 years has shown that the argument of "pesticides — the only threat" was wrong; their negative impact was accompanied by almost unbelievable human persecution (pigeon breeders, commercial falconry, etc.) combined with the rise and steady growth of a financially attractive market for birds of prey (Brücher & Wegner 1988).

Figure 1. Number of peregrine pairs per year, 1965 -1991.

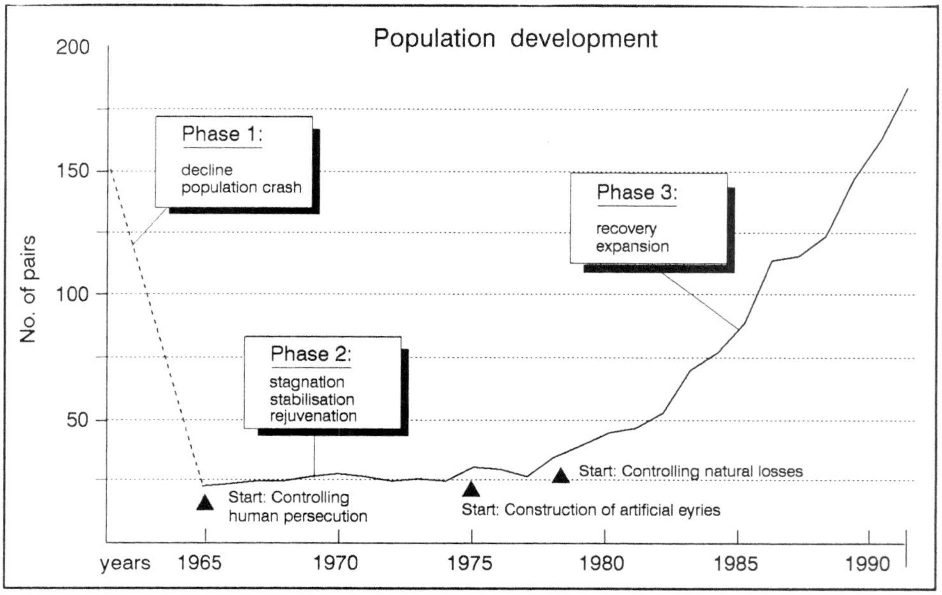

During the first years of our protection work we concentrated on guarding eyries round the clock in order to minimise illegal nest-robbing, trapping amd shooting. For more than ten years there was little change in both the number of breeding pairs and young hatched, but a general rejuvenation of the population. The argument put forward by some, that local residents were being reinforced by immigrants from outside, was incorrect, mainly for three reasons:

1. Estimates of mortality in adult Peregrines were formerly based on ring recoveries and assessed at 25% per year (Mebs 1971). New investigations by Kirmse and Kleinstäuber (1977), our working group and, in particular, Newton and Mearns (1988) clearly indicated that in both declining and expanding populations the mortality of adult females is *ca*. 9% and that of adult males *ca*. 11%.

2. Peregrines show a high degree of philopatry, generally returning to their place of birth or its near neighbourhood. As a result, the rate of geographical dispersion is slow. In Scotland Newton and Mearns (1988) found the average distance between birthplace and first breeding attempt to be *ca*. 20km for males and 68km for females. In Baden-Württenberg these figures are presumed to be lower because of a denser population.

3. At that time the population of surrounding regions was either extinct (north and east) or almost completely extirpated (Switzerland, the French Vosges and parts of the northern Alps).

In 1975 we embarked on what proved to be the most successful programme in the long term: the building of artificial eyries and improvement of existing ones. We even extended this technique to cover the whole region. Thus the colonisation of new areas became possible: higher altitudes in the Black Forest, cliffs lacking suitable nest-holes or ledges, quarries and even buildings.

From 1975 onwards we tried to control losses to martens and ticks (e.g. *Ixodes arboricola*) (see Schilling *et al.* 1981) and, if possible, find solutions to the conflict between Eagle Owls and

Peregrines and, currently, rock climbers.

Stage III saw an expansion of the breeding population to a level never formerly reached, further increased by the exploitation of towns and industrial areas. Parallel with the increasing number of breeding pairs, productivity reached new records: from an average 20-25 fledglings over a long period to more than 300 in 1991 (Fig. 2).

Figure 2. Number of fledged youngs per year, 1965 - 1991.

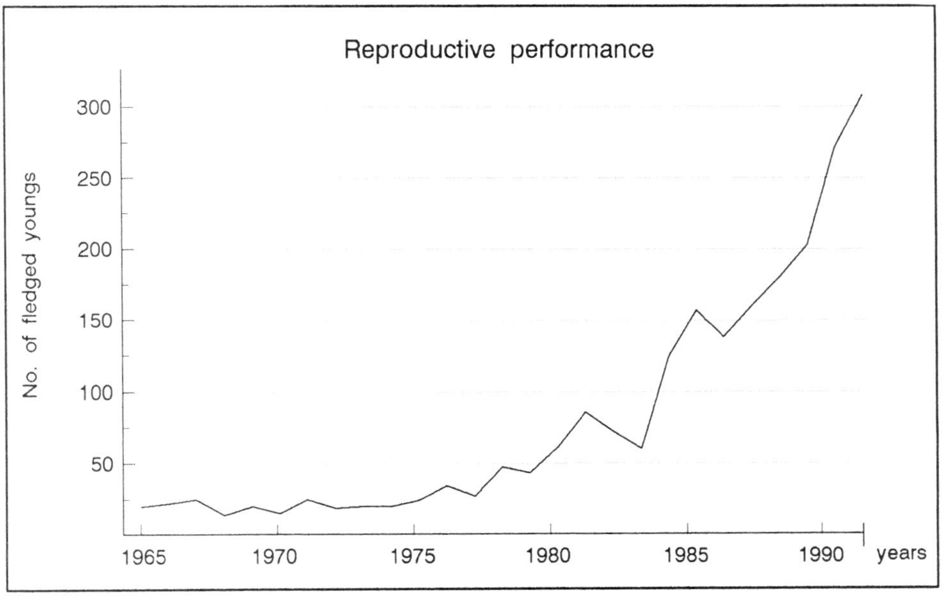

These results were obtained by protection measures alone, without any support from a release programme.

In undisturbed populations the average fledging rate per successful pair is about 2.60. Figure 3 shows clearly that three populations investigated in Western Europe suffered a substantial decrease in productivity in the years 1956-1975, undoubtedly due to the extensive use of pesticides in agriculture.

Several facts need to be mentioned. According to Ratcliffe (1980), in the period 1961-1965 the population in Great Britain achieved only 70% of its normal pre-war level of productivity, but it was in a very weak condition. Between 1966 and 1980 the success rate slowly increased until it reached almost its old level, while during the same period the population size was still only half the norm.

In the French mountains of the Jura both the population and success rate decreased very rapidly during the years 1961-75. Then, in 1974-75 a quite rapid growth began, despite the fact that productivity was low (Monneret 1988). The Peregrine population in Baden-Württemberg suffered relatively less than elsewhere and reached its pre-war level faster (Fig. 4). This was surely due to our combined efforts to combat human and other threats and to our improved and intensified work on artificial eyries (Hepp 1982). For the same reasons the recovery rate was comparatively higher in Baden-Württemberg than in other populations in Central and West Europe.

The recolonisation of cliffs in the former German Democratic Republic has been almost exclusively based on captive-bred falcons released in a programme of the Deutscher Falkenorden (Kleinstäuber 1987). The fitness of these birds is not significantly different from that of wild populations, as is shown by the fact that these captive-bred birds occupied first those same cliffs which had been the last to be abandoned. These cliffs are called "alpha places" on account of their prime attractiveness (Kirmse & Kleinstäuber 1977; Saar *et al.* 1982).

Figure 3. Fledged brood size of the Peregrine (1930 - 1991).

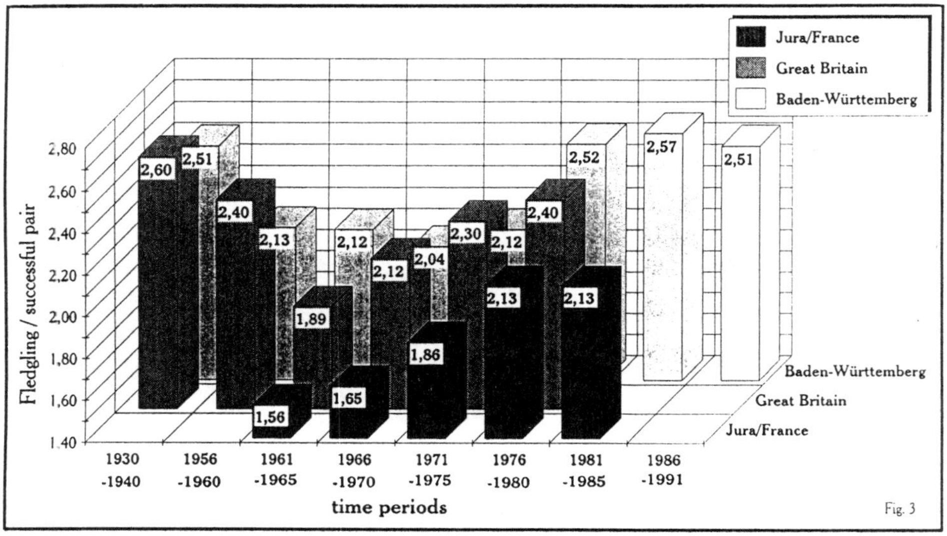

Figure 4. Recovery of Peregrine populations in West and Middle Europe.

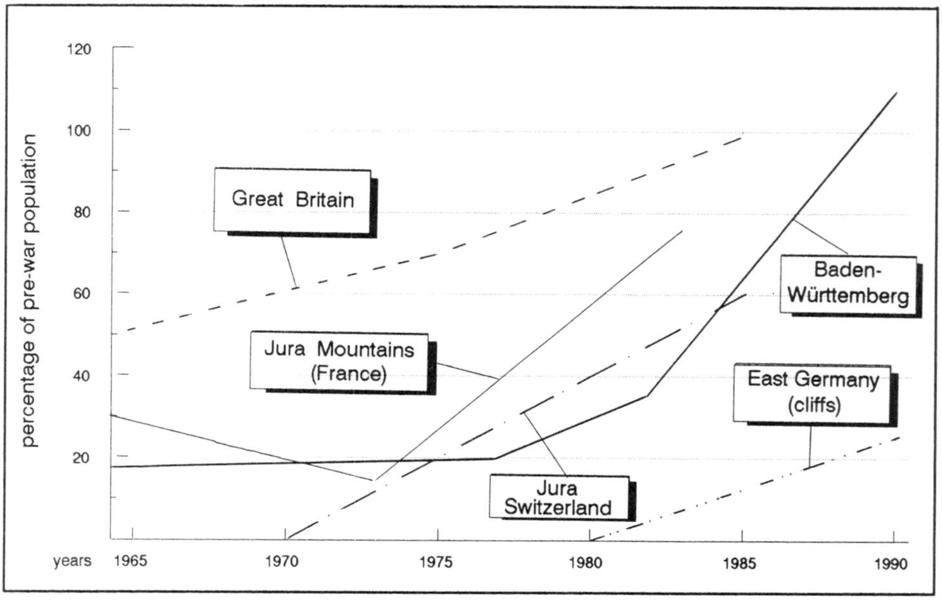

Comparisons of development in breeding pairs and fledglings led to the conclusion that not only new pairs had established themselves but also that the causes of loss could be substantially minimised (Fig. 5).

At the start of our work we had an average success rate of 40% for all broods. This increased to 65% in the years 1990-91, i.e. about 50% more young per pair (successful + unsuccessful) reached the fledging stage than formerly. This is a further important contribution of our protection work.

After the period 1980-85 there was a structural breakthrough, with a steadily increasing part of the population established in quarries and, for the first time, on buildings simultaneously (Fig. 6). Following the first nest on a building we decided, after much discussion, to promote this new trend by providing artificial eyries. This was an immediate success. At present we are trying to establish a completely new population in the industrial belt stretching from Koblenz to Cologne and the Netherlands border. Bearing in mind the normally slow rate of geographical dispersion, we believe that we have here a possibility of reoccupying still abandoned cliff sites from bridgeheads in the lowlands (Wegner 1989). On these cliffs there is an actual need for Peregrines, in order to protect complex habitats for many plants, insects and other fauna. A cooling tower or factory chimney may be a suitable site for an eyrie but provides no chance of promoting a nature reserve.

Despite a steadily increasing breeding success we have been able to maintain a high rate of ringing the young, at over 87% per annum (Fig. 7). We originally used combinations of colour rings from the official Vogelwarte on one leg, and on the other a SOS ring with telephone number in case of emergency. But for some years now both rings are of the same colour, so as to avoid overlap with other ringing programmes.

A 100% ringing value is not possible for several reasons. Some cliffs with nests are too dangerous to climb; at others we arrive too late. But we consider 87% to be a satisfactory figure.

Figure 5. Reproductive performance in Baden-Württemberg.

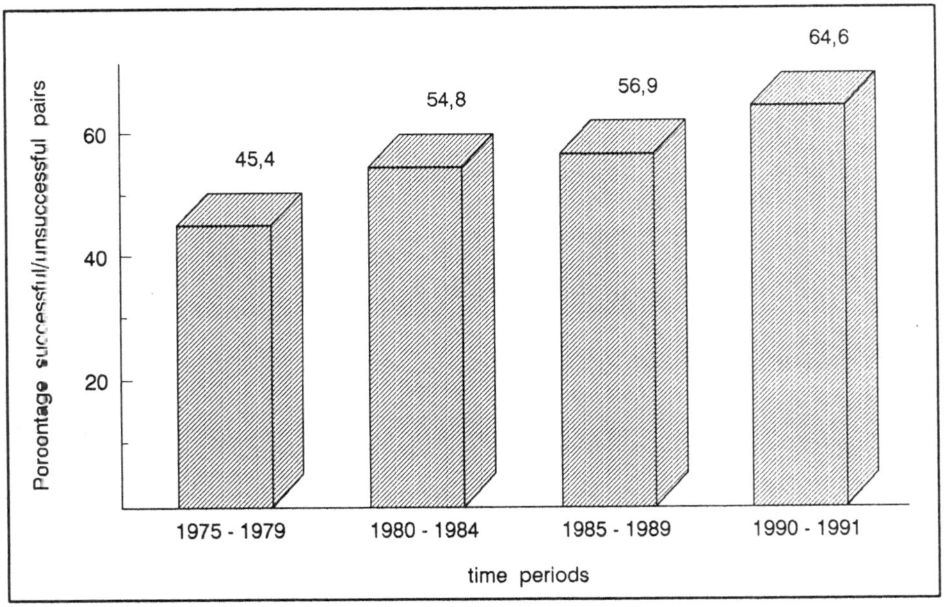

Figure 6. Exploring of new breeding habitats in Baden-Württemberg.

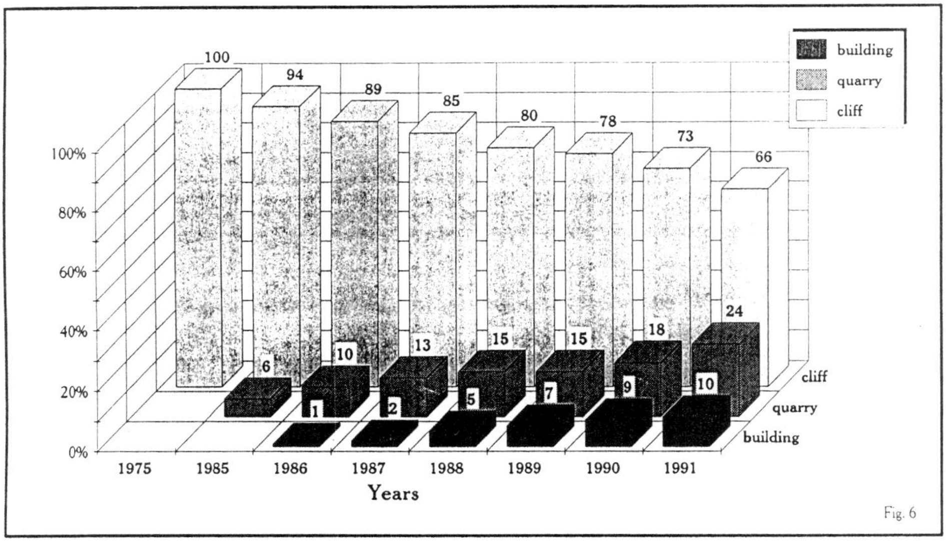

A newly-established population in special deep quarries (i.e. steep-sided holes 100m or more deep in flat country) provided extremely interesting data. There we used a special ringing scheme, with both rings on the same leg. The results agree with the above-mentioned dispersion mechanism. Starting from a founder population, many neighbouring biotopes were explored exclusively by males, which paired with females of other origin, wearing normal ringing patterns or unringed. These males were not detected in the nearby Swabian Alps and nor were any females, which must have moved greater distances. These findings agree with the observations of Newton and Mearns (1988). Generally speaking, the pioneers in still Peregrine-free areas far from the normal distribution centre are females.

Unfortunately we are unable to scan and control all breeding birds, whether ringed or not (Fig. 8). Nevertheless we have done so for roughly 170 birds per year, an average 20% of which are unringed and with only a small fraction wearing rings different from ours; for instance, in 1991 we found only three such females (1 DFO ring and 2 from Switzerland). The number of unringed birds is slightly higher that the 12-14% of fledglings we were unable to ring. This difference may reflect an immigration of falcons from neighbouring countries but, equally, older birds can lose their rings and some may be birds from so far undiscovered eyries.

Up to 1991 we ringed over 2,000 Peregrines and received 170 recoveries. An analysis of these data and of more than 11,000 food items will be published in the near future by Dieter Rockenbauch.

Our work in Baden-Württemberg has been and will continue to be of vital importance for the survival of the Peregrine in Central Europe. No other German state is so densely populated, thus providing a source for recolonisation of other parts of the country. There are already many pairs which wear our rings known in Rheinland-Pfalz, Switzerland, the Vosges, Frankonia, in the Main Valley and along the rivers Mosel and Rhine up to Cologne.

A programme of this scale and quality can be realised only with the help of numerous enthusiasts. Some of the most dedicated among hundreds of fellow-workers are as follows, B. Ficht, V. Hennig, M. Heller, K. Hepp, G. Kersting, H. Loeffler, R. Luehl, H. Nickolaus, D. Rockenbauch, K. Roebel, F. Schilling, H. Walliser, H. Wasser and P. Wegner.

Figure 7. Fledged Peregrines, percentage of colour banding.

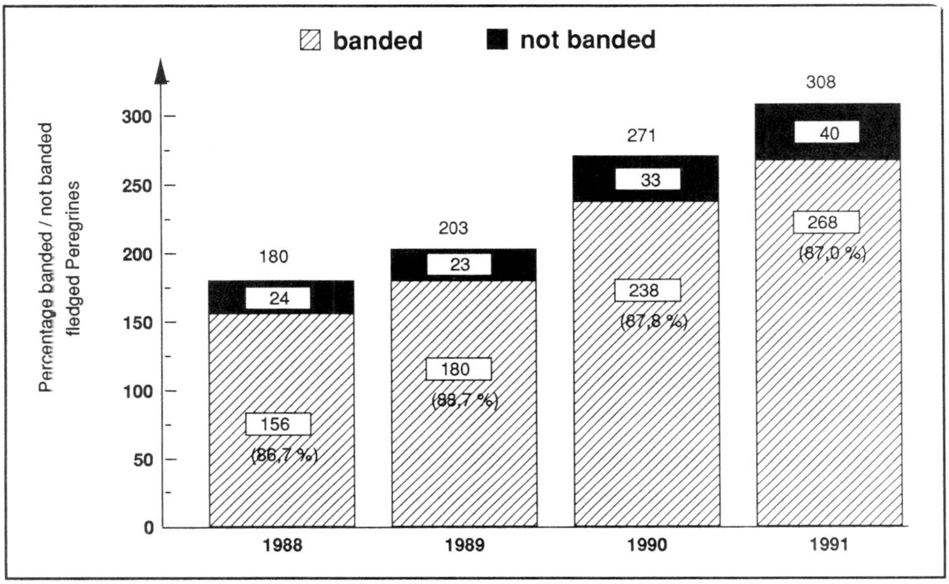

Figure 8. Peregrine Falcon in Baden-Württemberg: Identification of breeding birds by ring-observations.

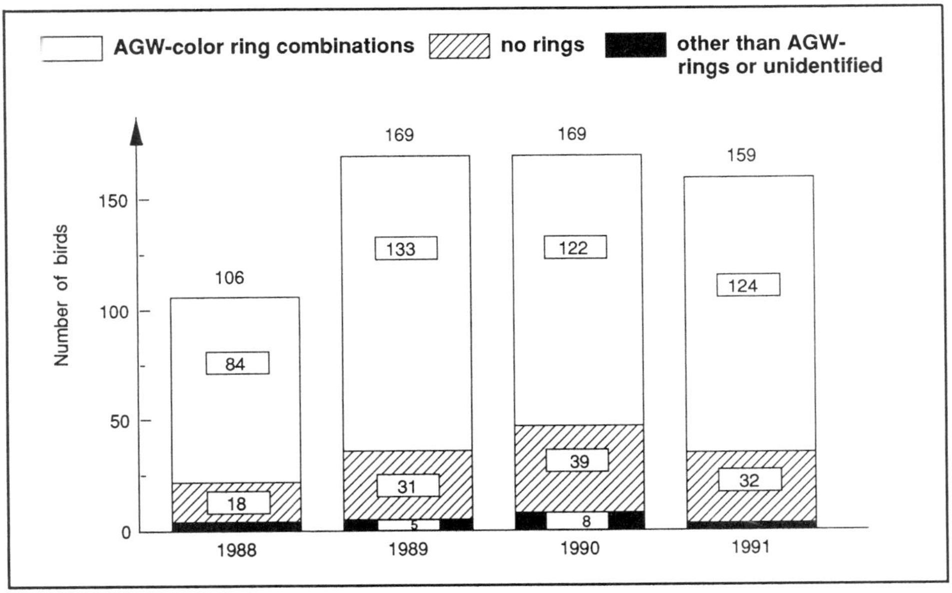

REFERENCES

BRÜCHER, H. & P. WEGNER 1988. Artificial Eyrie Management and the Protection of the Peregrine Falcon in West Germany. *In: Peregrine Falcon Populations. Their Management and Recovery*. Boise: 637-641.

HEPP, K. 1982. Kunsthorstbauten für Wanderfalken in Baden-Württemberg. *Veröff. Naturschutz Landschaftspflege Bad.-Württem.* 55/56: 23-36.

KIRMSE, W. & G. KLEINSTÄUBER 1977. Die Kalkulation der Populationsentwicklung von Wildtierarten, dargestellt am Beispiel der felsbr-tenden Wanderfalken (*Falco p. peregrinus* Gmel.) in der DDR. *Mitt. Zool. Mus. Berlin* 53: 137-148.

KLEINSTÄUBER, G. 1987. Populationsökologische Zusammenhänge bei Erlöschen und beginnendem Neuaufbau des Wanderfalkenbrutbestandes im Mittelgebirgsareal der DDR. *In:Populationsökologie von Greifvögel - und Eulenarten* .Halle. Bd. 1:111-128.

MEBS, T. 1971. Todesursachen und Mortalitätsraten beim Wanderfalken (*Falco peregrinus*) nach den Wiederfunden deutscher und finnischer Ringvögel. *Die Vogelwarte* 26 (1): 98-105.

MONNERET, R.J. 1988. Changes in the Peregrine Falcon Populations of France. *In: Peregrine Falcon Populations: Their Management and Recovery* Boise: 201-213.

NEWTON, I. & R. MEARNS 1988. Population Ecology of Peregrines in South Scotland. *In: Peregrine Falcon Populations. Their Management and Recovery.* Boise: 651-665.

RATCLIFFE, D. 1980. *The Peregrine Falcon*, Poyser, Calton.

SAAR, C., G. TROMMER & W. HAMMER 1982. *Der Wanderfalke*. Deutscher Falkenorden e.V. Bonn.

SCHILLING, F. & C. KÖNIG 1980. Die Biozidbelastung des Wanderfalken (*Falco peregrinus*) in Baden-Württemberg und ihre Auswirkung auf die Populationsentwicklung. *J. Ornithol.* 121: 1-35.

SCHILLING, F., M. BÖTTCHER & G. WALTER 1981. Probleme des Zeckenbefalls bei Nestlingen des Wanderfalken (*Falco peregrinus*). *J. Ornithol.* 122: 359-367.

SCHILLING, F. & D. ROCKENBAUCH 1985. Der Wanderfalke in Baden-Württemberg - gerettet! *Beih. Veröff. Naturschutz Landschaftspflege Bad.*-Württ. 45: 1-81.

WEGNER, P. 1989. Altes und Neues vom Wanderfalken (*Falco peregrinus*) im Rheinland. *Charadrius* 25: 70-84.

Dr. Peter Wegner
Geibelstrasse 3
5090 Leverkusen 1
Fed. Rep. of Germany

Meyburg, B.-U. & R. D. Chancellor eds.1994
Raptor Conservation Today
WWGBP / The Pica Press

The Lesser Kestrel *Falco naumanni*: review of the status of a globally threatened species

Ronald Zollinger & Ward J.M. Hagemeijer

ABSTRACT

A review is presented of the actual breeding numbers, population trends and breeding ranges of the Lesser Kestrel *Falco naumanni* in the (Western) Palearctic. New information is presented especially from the former USSR and reveals that substantial populations exist in this area. Although a decrease occurred also in the European part of the former USSR, it seems that Kazakhstan is one of the last strongholds where Lesser Kestrel populations remain stable. European populations decreased drastically: estimations show that breeding numbers dropped by at least 95% since the 1950s.

Methodological aspects are discussed and recommendations for future studies are given.

INTRODUCTION

The Lesser Kestrel is a small falcon with a Palearctic breeding distribution roughly between 30° and 55° N latitude. It is a migrating species, mainly wintering in Africa, south of the Sahara.

In the western part of the territories of this colonial bird the population size has decreased dramatically during the last three decades. Sharp declines have especially been reported from its European range. The species is known to exhibit fluctuations in population size (Glutz von Blotzheim *et al.* 1971), but the uniformity and extent of its decrease throughout the European range in the last 30 years are alarming.

In the first and second edition (Vincent 1966 resp. King 1981) of the red list of birds of the International Union for the Conservation of Nature and Natural Resources (IUCN), which were compiled by the International Council for Bird Preservation (ICBP), *Falco naumanni* was not listed yet. In their 'Birds to Watch' Collar and Andrew (1988) list 29 species which are globally threatened and regularly occur in Europe. One of these is the Lesser Kestrel. In the most recent ICBP overview of the conservation status of European birds, the Lesser Kestrel falls into priority category 1 (globally threatened) (ICBP, in prep.). In study report 41 of the ICBP 'The conservation of Western Lesser Kestrel Populations' (Biber 1990) a review is given of literature on the species and a conservation plan is put forward.

People became more and more aware that something needed to be done on habitat level, too. The dry grassland bird group of the ICBP suggested that 'a survey programme should be established to determine the European populations of all dry grassland bird species of conservation concern and monitor the effectiveness of conservation measures taken. This is urgently required for the four globally threatened species: *Falco naumanni* (Lesser Kestrel), *Tetrax tetrax* (Little Bustard), *Otis tarda* (Great Bustard) and *Chettusia gregaria* (Sociable Plover)' (Goriup, Batten and Norton 1991).

Data on Lesser Kestrel populations are often fragmentary and anecdotal. This situation was recognized by Biber (1990), and although projects have been carried out to obtain population data of all European birds, the situation has not changed a great deal since then. Still in most countries there has been no census. Furthermore, the knowledge of the ecology of the species was very incomplete. This, together with its threatened status, was the direct incentive for the authors of this paper to set up a study on the Lesser Kestrel in Spain (Bijlsma *et al.* 1988, 1990; Hagememeÿer 1993). Later, Spanish researchers have been working on the species.

During the Canterbury conference on the Biology and Conservation of Small Falcons in 1991, several papers (e.g. Hagemeijer 1993, Negro 1993) and a workshop were dedicated to the Lesser Kestrel. Valuable information was shared between the participants. In the workshop there was a unanimous intention to formulate an approach to assess the probable causes of the decline of the species. However, the discussion did not yet result in specific action.

The aim of this paper is to present new distribution and trend data of Lesser Kestrel populations in Europe and east into Kazakhstan and to match them against the data compiled by Biber (1990). Especially the status of the Lesser Kestrel in countries of the former USSR will be highlighted. The countries dealt with are listed in Table 1. These countries will be indicated as USSR or as Commonwealth of Independent States (CIS) in this paper depending upon the historical aspects. The authors are aware of the fact that this may not always be the most correct approach from a political and geographical point of view.

Table 1. Status of Lesser Kestrel *Falco naumanni* populations in the CIS.
***Population size*: census results are printed bold, estimations are printed in italics.**
***Trend indication*: 0 = stable; -1 = slow decrease; -2 = fast decrease. Information given by: [1] A. Abuladze, [2] V. Ivanovsky, [3] R. Pfeffer, [4] I. Gorban, [5] A. Davygora, * European Ornithological Atlas data.**

	Population size	trend indication	no longer breeding
Armenia[1]	50-100	0/-1	
Azerbaijan[1]	≤ 1000	0/-1	
Byelorussia[2]	**0**		?
Georgia[1]	**650**	-1	
Kazakhstan[3]	≥5 10,000	0	
Ukraine West[4]	**hundreds**	-1/-2	
Moldavia*	**13-130**	?	
Russia:			
Ural South[5]	*hundreds*	?	
Don District*	**6-60**	?	

SOURCES OF INFORMATION

Translation of Russian papers, a questionnaire sent round by the authors and personal contacts led to new insights into the status of the species in especially the CIS. Besides this, the 'European Ornithological Atlas Project' of the European Bird Census Council (EBCC) and the 'Dispersed Bird Species Project' of the ICBP gave rise to new information and to more accurate estimates of the population sizes in several countries in the rest of Europe.

DATA ON RANGE AND POPULATION SIZE

Nowadays, the Lesser Kestrel has a predominantly Mediterranean breeding distribution in Europe and Africa. More to the east it occurs mainly in the steppe and semi-desert zone of the CIS.

CIS

The Lesser Kestrel has been described by Dementiev & Gladkov (1951) as a common species for the USSR, occurring mainly in the Ukraine, Crimea, Caucasus and in Central Asia during the 1950s.

For the whole of the USSR, Zubarovsky (1977) described the breeding range as follows: the northern boundary is located at 49° 50° in the Ukraine (an imaginary line from the city Uzgorod, via Winnicua, Uman, Walki (near Kharkov) to Kupiansk). To the east, this boundary moves to the north, lying at 52°30' (Kuibyshev district), at 56° (Tatar Republic), at 55° (Zauralia Mass) and at 56° (Krasnojarsk). Galushin (1981) suggested that "northern limits are likely to have moved 100-200 km to the south (from former range line across southern Poland to 49° N in the Ukraine, to 55° N in central Siberia)". Galushin (1991, 1993 in press) put the Lesser Kestrel in the category of species with markedly decreasing populations in the European part of the USSR, and noted that the species is close to disappearance.

Below, specific information is given about the actual status and other details of the Lesser Kestrel in the various Republics of the CIS. Per region, historical data will be presented first, followed by recent information (if available).

Moldavia: Data from the late 1980s gathered for the European Ornithological Atlas, show that the Lesser Kestrel was present in 13 out of 20 UTM squares (50x50 km) (65%). The densities are low however: 1-10 pairs per square.

Ukraine: In Figure 1 is a map showing the breeding distribution in the Ukraine, according to Zubarovsky (1977). All breeding places known to have existed in the 18th, 19th and 20th century are included. However, most references are based on data gathered between 1900-1960 (especially in the 1950s). On the map, there are 76 regular and 2 occasional breeding places distinguished. Each dot may represent one breeding pair or a (large) colony. Therefore, the map gives an impression of distribution rather than of quantity.

The biggest colony, consisting of approximately 250 nests, was discovered in the Crimea near the Black Sea on Mt. Opyk in 1951. Of the occasional breeding places in Figure 1, one was based on the fact that some young falconets were found near Kiev in 1916 and were brought to the Zoo.

Figure 1. Distribution of the Lesser Kestrel *Falco naumanni* in the Ukraine (after Zubarovsky 1977).

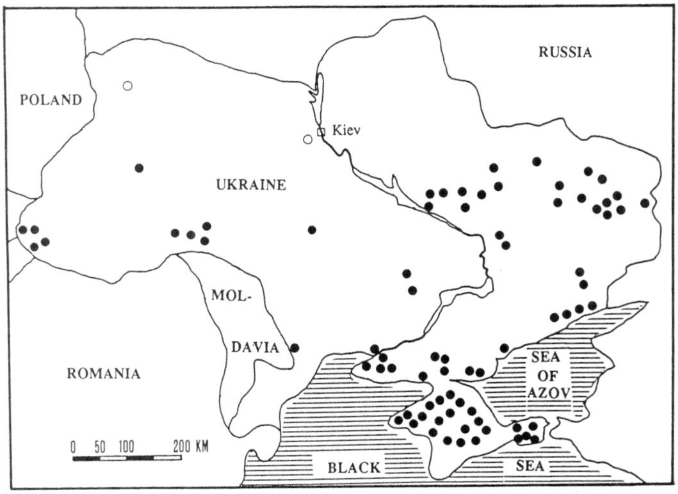

Though the data in Figure 1 are incomplete, one might nevertheless conclude that the Crimea and the eastern part of the Ukraine must have been strongholds for the species, at least until the 1950s. According to Zubarovsky (1977), the species decreased since that time in Zaporoze, the Don district, the E-Dinca district and the Kharkov-Voroshylovgrad region. A strong decrease took place in the steppe and north-eastern part of the Crimea.

Between 1982-1986 a census by means of questionnaires was carried out in 8 regions of 217 quarters each (1 quarter = 25 x 25 km) in the western Ukraine (1/4 of the total Ukraine). The results showed that 199 quarters were occupied (11%). The total population for the western Ukraine is estimated at a few hundred pairs. The species is declining in the Ukraine. (I. Gorban, pers. comm.).

Mostly, breeding pairs were found in trees (30-35% in *Salix*; 65-70% on *Pinus*), rarely on cliffs and buildings. Solitary breeding occurred most often, but sometimes colonies of 5-11 breeding pairs were found.

Data for the European Ornithological Atlas Project were also received from other parts of the Ukraine. The Lesser Kestrel was not on the list. Since recent information points out that the species does occur in the southeastern Ukraine, it is likely that it was not censused.

In the near future the status in the other parts of the Ukraine will be studied in more detail (I. Gorban, pers. comm.).

In spring 1992, some colonies of the Lesser Kestrel were found in the steep sand ridges bordering the Sivash lagoon area (north Crimea, Ukraine) during an expedition of the Working Group International Wader and Waterfowl Research (WIWO). The colonies were small (not larger than ten pairs) but were found in several places. The species was not specifically looked for. Numbers were not high (J. van der Winden, in litt.)

Russia: During the last 5 years (1987-1992) the Lesser Kestrel has been a rare breeder in the Orinburg region (Ural-south) in an area of 30.000 km². The population is estimated at a few hundred pairs. It is not clear whether the population is decreasing, stable or increasing (A. Davygora, pers. comm.). European Ornithogical Atlas data from the area bordering the Ukraine in the east (e.g. Don Region) indicate that *Falco naumanni* occurs in 6 out of 74 censused squares (UTM 50x50 km). The number of breeding pairs does not exceed 10 per 250 km².

Georgia: In 1985, a number of 185 pairs was counted in an area of 1300 km². Extrapolation to an area of 4500 km² resulted in a total estimation of the population of about 700 pairs. Nowadays the population is estimated at 650 breeding pairs. Colonies consist of no more than 11 pairs (formerly 25 pairs). Figure 2 shows that the distribution of the species is restricted to the semi-desert area in the southwestern part of Georgia. Probably the Lesser Kestrel is a rare breeder near Tbilisi, the capital of Georgia. Nests are normally found in trees (old nests of *Pica pica*). (A. v. Abuladze, pers. comm.).

Armenia: The present number of breeding pairs is estimated at a total of 50-100 pairs. There is no reliable information about numbers in the past. The species is known to breed in the outermost northwestern part of Armenia; see Figure 2. (A. v. Abuladze, pers. comm.).

Azerbaijan: The present number of breeding pairs is estimated at several hundreds and less than 1,000 pairs. There is no reliable information about numbers in the past. Figure 2 shows that the breeding distribution stretches from the Mugan Steppe along the Caspian Sea, through the central valley of river Kura to the northwestern part of Azerbaijan, where it is connected with breeding grounds in Georgia and Armenia. (A. v. Abuladze, pers. comm.).

Kazakhstan: According to Gawrin *et al.* (1962) the Lesser Kestrel is breeding in Kazakhstan in steppe, wood-steppe, semi-deserts and deserts. Natural nest sites were used, mainly caves in small rocks and sometimes cliffs along a river. The species was not equally distributed in Kazakhstan, and the number of breeding pairs was fluctuating yearly and from place to place. The number of breeding pairs depended on the availability of food (invertebrates), especially in deserts where the density of the Lesser Kestrel was low. Figure 3 shows that the Lesser Kestrel was a common breeder between 1900 and 1960 in the Mangyshlak mountains (east of the Caspian Sea), along the rivers Emba and Ilek (especially in Shirkala), in the Turgay Steppe, further to the east in the central hills of Kazakhstan, and in the western parts of the Altay mountains (in northwestern Kazakhstan) as far as Zaysan in the east. The Lesser Kestrel was a very common breeder in the Dzhungarskiy Alatau mountains (southeast of Lake Balkhash), in the Kendyktas and Chu-lliyskiy mountains (westwards of Alma-Ata) and in the Talasskiy Alatau and Karatau mountains (northeast of Tashkent). In the Chu-lliyskiye mountains a large colony was observed in subsequent years.

Figure 2. The present distribution of the Lesser Kestrel *Falco naumanni* in the Caucasus. Dots represent colonies of approximately 10 pairs in Georgia. There is no information about the locations of colonies in Armenia and Azerbaijan.

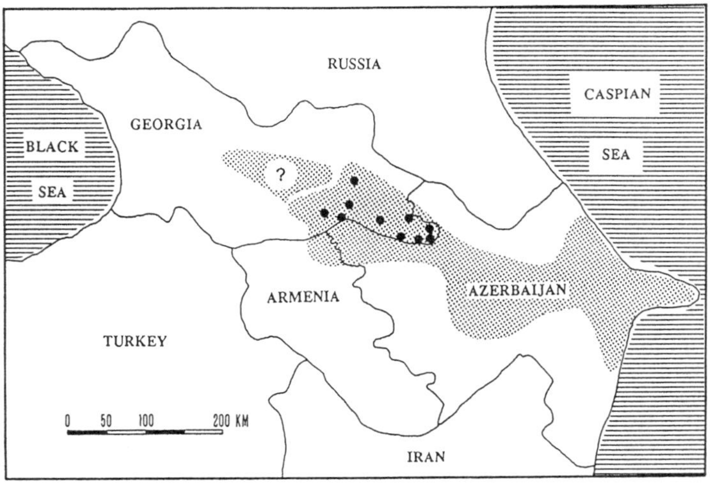

Figure 3. Distribution of the Lesser Kestrel *Falco naumanni* in Kazakhstan between 1990 and 1960 (after Gawrin *et al.* 1962). Dots represent colonies up to 20 pairs or solitary breeding pairs. In the stippled areas the species is common or very common.

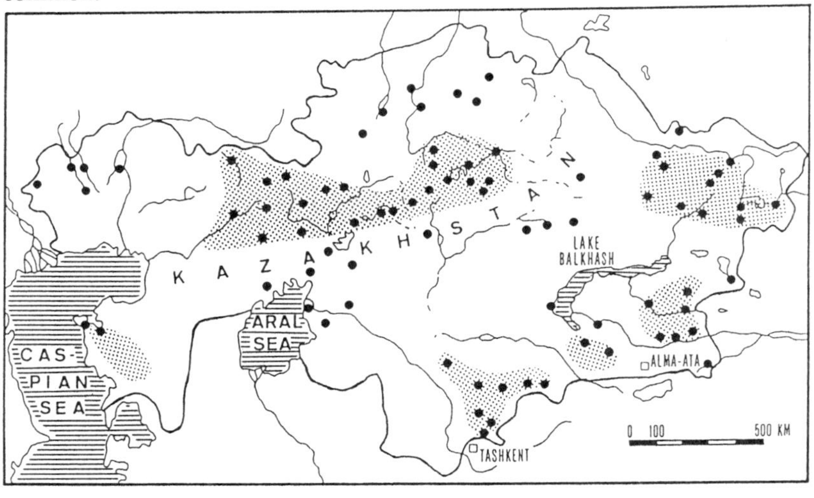

This colony consisted of 60-70 pairs in 1934 and 1937, but in the intermediate year 1936 only 3-4 specimens were reported. Breeding places outside the stippled regions in Figure 3 are in most cases solitary breeding pairs, such as in the western part of Kazakhstan near the places Urda, Uzen and Goryachenskiy, north and eastwards of the Aral Sea, on the western banks of Lake Balkhash, and at several places in central and northern Kazakhstan. Gawrin *et al.* (1962) did not give, however, a precise description of the categories "common and very common breeder" which can be translated in density figures. It is, therefore, impossible to give a reliable estimate of the total number of breeding pairs in these areas. The category "common breeder" can be described as a situation where numerous solitary breeding pairs and colonies up to 10 pairs occurred. Consequently, "very common" means that the density of solitary pairs and colonies was higher and/or the colonies were larger.

The present number of breeding pairs is estimated at several thousands, probably more than 10,000. It is the most common bird of prey in southern Kazakhstan. The population is not decreasing, but stable. It is not threatened by agricultural nor other human activities. The nests are situated in caves on rocky slopes or in graves on the plains. Breeding success is normal for the species: some years 1-3 chicks, in others 4-5 (even 6) chicks. The colonies consist of 10-15 pairs, sometimes 50-100 pairs. The density of the breeding pairs is highest in the south and the east of Kazakhstan. There are also suitable areas where no breeding pairs occur (R. Pfeffer, pers. comm.).

Table 1 sums up data for the countries from the CIS: census results, estimates of the number of breeding pairs, and trends of Lesser Kestrel populations. These data do not cover the whole breeding range in the CIS: only numbers in the western part of the Ukraine are included, for instance.

The Mediterranean area and Central Europe

In Europe and Africa the Lesser Kestrel has mainly a Mediterranean breeding distribution. It breeds in Spain, Portugal, France, Italy, former Yugoslavia, Romania, Bulgaria, Hungary, Greece and Turkey. Breeding is suspected for Albania (Grimmett & Jones 1989). In northern Africa, the species breeds in Morocco, Algeria, Tunisia and in Egypt. In the Near and Middle East, the Lesser Kestrel is a breeder in Syria, the Lebanon and Israel. In Table 2 the number of breeding pairs and trends of the Lesser Kestrel in these countries are given. This table indicates that the most important breeding areas known in the Mediterranean region are situated in Spain and Morocco (in the west), as well as in Greece and Turkey (in the east). Recent data (EBCC/ICBP) suggest that Italy still is an important breeding ground for the species.

Since the 1950s population numbers have decreased rapidly, at least by 95% in the European breeding range. To give some examples: **Austria**, from 280 pairs in 1960 (Cramp & Simmons 1980) to zero in 1984 (Biber 1990); **France**, from *ca.* 100 pairs in the 1950s to 9 pairs in 1987-1989 (Cheylan 1990). Stable in recent years; **Portugal**, from at least 700 pairs in the late 1940s to 100-200 pairs in 1990 (EBCC/IBCC). In Gonzalez & Merino (1990) a number of no more than 150 pairs is mentioned; **Spain**, from more than 100,000 pairs in the early 1960s to approximately 50,000 in the 1970s (Bijleveld 1974; Garzón 1977) and later the number decreased to between 4293 and 5089 pairs in 1988 (Gonzalez & Merino 1990).

A marked decrease in breeding range occurred all over Europe, especially in Poland, Czechoslovakia, and Austria, where the Lesser Kestrel is not breeding any more. In **Poland**, the species was even more common than *F. tinnunculus* near Lublin in 1850. The last breeding record in Poland is from 1968 (Glutz von Blotzheim 1971; Tomialojc 1990). A colony of approximately 300 pairs, breeding in an oak forest, was known between Lednice and Podivín in **Czechoslovakia** from 1889 until 1904-1906. The colony disappeared after the nesting trees had been cut down (Glutz von Blotzheim 1971). Until the second half of this century, the Lesser Kestrel was a rare breeder in Czechoslovakia. The last known breeding place was near Roznava, where a family of Lesser Kestrels was observed on 18 July 1956 (Glutz von Blotzheim 1971; Ferianc 1977). The species is absent in the breeding atlas of Czechoslovakian birds (Stastny 1987).

In its Central European range, the Lesser Kestrel was a regular breeder in southern **Hungary** in the beginning of this century; in the 1960s only a few breeding attempts were reported (Glutz von Blotzheim 1971). However, Márkus (1991) indicated that the species is still breeding in Hungary and estimated the population size at between 1 and 10 pairs. The most recent estimate amounts to 10-20 pairs (EBCC/ICBP). In **Romania** the Lesser Kestrel was reported from 15 out of 110 UTM squares (14%). Only in one square numbers were estimated (10-100). For the whole country the estimate amounts to 50-100. It is striking to see that the trend for Romania was reported to be positive. It is the only country with a positive trend indication (EBCC/ICBP). Glutz von Blotzheim *et al.* (1971) reported a decline in the beginning of this century and disappearance from several areas. The positive trend may refer to the recent situation. For **Bulgaria** a number of 53 pairs was given (Iankov *et al.* in this volume). The estimate in the EBCC/ICBP database amounts to 60-

Table 2: Status of Western Palearctic breeding populations of the Lesser Kestrel *Falco naumanni*:
Figures of Biber (1990) are matched against latest available information. All countries with breeding records of Lesser Kestrels are listed. Latest information based on EBCC/ICBP database. @: Data for Greece new estimate by Hallmann (pers. comm. 1993)
***Population size*: * = census result, ** = estimation, X = no quantitative information available, but species is present, (X) = no recent information available, but species formerly present;**
Trend indication over the period from 1970: -1 = decrease in number of 20-50 %; -2 = decrease > 50 %; - = decrease not quantified; 0 = stable; ? = unknown.

	Biber (1990		Current data	
	Population size	Trend indication (E=extinct)	Population estimate EBCC/ICBP	Trend indication EBCC/ICBP
Albania		E	?	
Algeria	X	?		
Austria		E	0	
Bulgaria	<100**	-1	60-120	-1
Cyprus		E	0	
Czechoslovakia		E	0	
Egypt	X	?		
France	10*	-2	10	-2
Greece	<2000**	-1	1600@	-1
Hungary		E	10-20	0
Iran	X	?		
Iraq	X	?		
Israel	X	-2		
Italy	200-400**	-1	500-1000	-1
Jordan	(X)	?		
Lebanon	(X)	?		
Libya	(X)	?		
Morocco	1000**	-		
Oman	(X)	?		
Poland		E	0	
Portugal	300**	-	100-200	-2
Romania	120-130**	?	50-100	+1
Saudi Arabia	(X)	?		
Spain	4000-5000*(**)	-2	4239-5089	-2
Syria	X	?		
Tunisia	<100**	?		
Turkey	500-2000**	?	500-5000	?
Former USSR	X	?	see table 1	
Yemen	(X)	?		
Former Yugoslavia	10**	-2	55-110	0/-1

120. **Greece** still is an important breeding ground for the species. The European Ornithological Atlas data indicate that 60% of all UTM squares are occupied. This proportion approaches 100% when only the mainland squares are taken into account. The densities reported are low however (1-10 per 250 km²) in most cases). The total population is estimated at 1000-1500 pairs. However, there is reason to believe that the numbers are slightly underestimated. Hallmann (1985) mentioned a number of 2000 for the situation around 1982 and indicated that the species was declining. Later this estimate was thought to be below the actual number (Biber 1990). Especially in the central mainland area, Thessalia and Macedonia, numbers are believed to be higher than reported for the

Atlas. A revised estimate of 1600 pairs is suggested by Hallmann (pers. comm. 1993). The numbers yielded for **Italy** by the European breeding bird projects (500-1000) are remarkably higher than the numbers mentioned in Biber (1990) (200-400).

No proper estimate of the **Turkish** population has been made. The Ornithological Society for the Middle East (OSME) has mapped the known distribution until 1990. Since then, incidental observations suggest that the species concentrates in Anatolia, the central plateau, surrounded by the cities Ankara - Eskisehir - Akselin - Konya - Karaman - Erigli - Nigdi - Kayseri - Kirsehir - Kirikkale. Some regions in this area turned out to have 15 pairs in every village. The total Turkish Lesser Kestrel population may well be larger than 5000 pairs. More research is being carried out to assess the numbers in Turkey (Yarar & Magnin, in litt.).

DISCUSSION

Although valuable new information has become available from the breeding grounds of the Lesser Kestrel the picture of its distribution still is far from complete. Data on population sizes and trends are even more sparsely available. Comparison of the new data regarding its distribution, presented in the two tables, shows that Kazakhstan nowadays probably is the most important stronghold. The dimensions of this country are enormous (2.7 million km²). The regions in which the Lesser Kestrel is indicated still to be a common breeder extend over an area of about 510,000 km². This is about the size of the whole of Spain. Furthermore, the species is believed to be very common in an area of about 110,000 km² in the southeastern Kazakhstan mountains. Colonies of 50 to 100 pairs are still reported. A cautious estimate for Kazakhstan as a whole would be 20,000 pairs.

The awareness that the distribution of the Lesser Kestrel should be further studied was one of the major results of the Canterbury workshop. This most urgently applies to Turkey, the CIS and the countries in the Middle East. A census of the species over a large area brings along specific problems. As an example, the census carried out in Spain in 1988 was very valuable but in our judgment underestimated the real number. There are several reasons for this. Firstly, colonies can be hard to find. During a very intensive study in Extremadura, Spain, in 1987, it took us several weeks to locate most of the colonies in a restricted area around Cáceres (Bijlsma *et al.* 1988, Hagemeijer 1993). New breeding pairs and colonies were found until the end of the breeding season. This shows that colonies and solitary breeding pairs can easily be overlooked. Secondly, to find out the exact number of breeding pairs in a (large) colony is very difficult by observation only. Inspection of nests sometimes yielded a 100% higher number than was estimated by looking at the number of birds flying into a colony (although we observed those colonies for several days before we looked for nest sites). The extent of underestimation varies with the type of colony. The bias will be small in colonies where the entrances of individual nests are separate and easily visible (walls with holes, for example). However, in many cases nests were situated under tiles with shared entrances (in one case a single entrance led to twelve nests). Only by individual colour marking or inspection of individual nests is it possible to assess the exact number of breeding pairs. Of course, this goes beyond the scope of large scale censuses. Thirdly, the proportion of solitary breeding pairs seems to have increased while the total number decreased. These pairs are difficult to detect, which may have resulted in a further underestimation.

A Lesser Kestrel census is being set up for the spring of 1993 in Turkey, stimulated by the national nature conservation agency (DHKD). This census will include a methodological pilot study and hopefully will yield a valuable method for future census work in other areas. Special attention will be paid to a calibration study to correct for the underestimation of colony size. We recommend that this example should be followed elsewhere. The trends of Lesser Kestrel breeding populations clearly show that this species is seriously threatened worldwide. To shed more light on changes in population size, it is necessary to carry out censuses (monitoring with intervals of 5 or 10 years) on important breeding grounds all over its range. Even more regular inventories should be carried out in specific areas, such as Important Bird Areas (Grimmett & Jones 1989), but also in unprotected and not designated areas where the species is still vulnerable. Changes in cultivation or other human activities should be registered in those areas to get an insight into the threats the Lesser Kestrel is exposed to.

Spain, with its recent tradition of attention to the species would be a perfect starting point for this. 1993 is a crucial year in this respect since the Spanish Ornithological Society (SEO) announced it as the year of the Lesser Kestrel.

Other aspects the Canterbury workshop brought up as important subjects to be studied include: problems with the foraging habitat, pesticide contamination affecting reproduction success and food availability, problems with breeding colonies (nesting facilities in general), winter ecology and how to develop and coordinate an international conservation strategy. From this list the winter situation seems to be the most unknown aspect. Knowledge on this might shed light on important parameters including mortality and food availability on the wintering grounds.

ACKNOWLEDGMENTS

We are grateful to many persons who have provided valuable information, especially Alexander v. Abuladze, Vladimir Galushin, Jean-Pierre Biber, Ben Hallman and Jan v.d. Winden. We kindly thank the Executive Committee of the EBCC and Graham Tucker (ICBP), who gave permission to use data from the EBCC/ICBP European Breeding Bird Database. Indirectly we thank all national coordinators of the European Ornithological Atlas Project and the ICBP Dispersed Bird Species Project who provided the data to the above-mentioned database.

We wish to thank Tadeusz Mizera, who was very helpful as interpreter during the Conference and was a great support, translating Polish, Czechoslovakian and Russian papers. We are indebted to Henk Eppenhof for his valuable comments on the wording of our text.

REFERENCES

BIBER, J-P. 1990. *The conservation of Western Lesser Kestrel populations.* ICBP study report No. 41, Cambridge.

BIJLEVELD, M. 1974. *Birds of Prey in Europe.* MacMillan Press Ltd, London.

BIJLSMA, S., E.J.M. HAGEMIJER, G.J.M. VERKLEY & R. ZOLLINGER 1988. Ecological aspects of the Lesser Kestrel *Falco naumanni* in Extremadura (Spain). Rapport 285, Werkgroep Dieroecologie, Universiteit Nijmegen.

BIJLSMA, S., E.J.M. HAGEMIJER, G.J.M. VERKLEY & R. ZOLLINGER 1990. Reproduccion del Cernicalo Primilla en Extremadura, 1987. *In* González, J.L. & M. Merino (Eds.) 1990. *El cernicalo primilla (Falco naumanni) en la Peninsula Iberica. Situación, problemática y aspectos biológicos.* Icona, Madrid.

CHEYLAN, G. 1990. Historique de la régression du Faucon Crécerellette en France. *In*: Biber 1990.

COLLAR, N.J. & P. ANDREW 1988. *Birds to Watch.* The ICBP world checklist of threatened birds. ICBP Techn. Publ. No. 8, Cambridge.

CRAMP, S. & K.E.L. SIMMONS (Eds.) 1980. *Handbook of the Birds of Europe, the Middle East and North Africa.* Vol. 2. Oxford University Press, Oxford.

DEMENTIEV, G.P. & N.A. GLADKOV (Eds) 1951. *The Birds of the Soviet Union.* Vol. 1. Israel Progr. Sci. Translations.

FERIANC, O. 1977. *Birds of Slovakia.* Vol. 1. (in Czechoslovakian).

GALUSHIN, V.M. 1981. Changes in population status and nest range distribution of Falconiforms in the USSR since 1950. *Raptor Research* 15 (1): 4-11.

GALUSHIN, V.M. 1991. Status and protection of birds of prey in the USSR. Populationsökologie Greifvogel- u. Eulenarten 2 (1991): 35-38. Wiss. Beitr. Univ. Halle 1991/ 4 (P45).

GALUSHIN, V.M. 1993 (in press). Recent changes in number and distribution of birds of prey in European Russia and neighbouring countries. *In*: Hagemeijer, E.J.M. & T. Verstrael . *Proceedings of Bird Numbers 1992.* Distribution, Monitoring and Ecological Aspects. SOVON and CBS, Beek-Ubbergen, 1993 *in prep.*

GARZÕN, J. 1977. Birds of prey in Spain, the present situation. Proc. World Conf. Birds of Prey. Vienna, 1975.

GAWRIN, W.F., N.A DOLGUSHIN, M.N. KOPELOW & M.A. KUZMINA 1962. *Birds of Kazakhstan*, Vol.2, Academy of Science of Kazakstan Soviet Republic, Alma-Ata (in Russian).

GLUTZ VON BLOTZHEIM, U.N., K.M. BAUER & E. BEZZEL 1971. *Handbuch der Vögel Mitteleuropas.*

Vol. 4. Akademische Verlagsges., Frankfurt am Main.
GONZÁLEZ, J.L. & M. MERINO (Eds.) 1990. *El cernícalo primilla (Falco naumanni) en la Peninsula Iberica. Situación, problemática y aspectos biológicos*. Icona, Madrid.
GORIUP, P.D., L.A. BATTEN & J.A. NORTON (Eds.) 1991. The conservation of lowland dry grassland birds in Europe. Proc. of an int. sem. held at the Univ. of Reading, 1991. JNCC, Peterborough.
GRIMMETT, R.F.A. & T.A. JONES 1989. *Important Bird Areas in Europe*. ICBP Techn. Publ. No. 9.
HAGEMEIJER, W. 1993. Ecological aspects of the Lesser Kestrel (*Falco naumanni*) in Extremadura, Spain. *In*: M. Nicholls, & R. Clarke (Eds.) 1993. *Biology and Conservation of small Falcons*. Proceedings of The Hawk and Owl Trust Conference, Canterbury, 6th-8th September 1991. Hawk & Owl Trust.
HALLMAUN, B. 1985. Status and conservation problems of birds of prey in Greece.p.55-59 *in*: I. Newton. & R.D. Chancellor, (Eds.) *Conservation Studies on Raptors*: ICBP Techn. Publ. 5.
KING, W.B. 1981. *Endangered Birds of the World*. The ICBP bird red data book. Smithsonian Institution Press, in coop. with ICBP, Washington D.C.
MÁRKUS, F. 1991. Conservation of lowland dry grassland birds in Hungary. *In*: Goriup, Batten & Norton (Eds.).
NEGRO, J.J. 1993. Home range of Lesser Kestrels during the reproductive season. *In*: M.K. Nicholls, & R.R. Clarke (Eds.) 1993. *Biology and Conservation of small Falcons*. Proceedings of The Hawk and Owl Trust Conference, Canterbury, 6th-8th September 1991. Hawk & Owl Trust.
STASTNY, K. (Ed.) 1987. *Breeding Atlas of Czechoslovakian Birds in 1973-77*. Prague (in Czechoslovakian).
TOMIALOJC, L. 1990. *Birds of Poland* (in Polish).
VINCENT, J. 1966. *Red Data Book, Volume 2, Aves*. IUCN, Lausanne.
ZUBAROVSKY, W.M. 1977. *Fauna of Ukraine*. Vol.5 Birds, Chapter 2 Birds of prey. pp. 306-315. Kiev (in Ukrainian).

Ronald Zollinger & Ward J.M. Hagemeijer
c/o SOVON, Rijksstraatweg 178,
6573 DG Beek-Ubbergen,
The Netherlands

Part 3

Tropical Rain Forests and Raptors

Harpy Eagle *Harpia harpyja*

Convener:

Dr. J.-M. Thiollay

Meyburg, B.-U. & R. D. Chancellor eds.1994
Raptor Conservation Today
WWGBP / The Pica Press

A World Review of Tropical Forest Raptors Current trends, Research Objectives and Conservation Strategy

Jean-Marc Thiollay

INTRODUCTORY REVIEW

The total number of diurnal raptor species in the world varies from 292 (Amadon & Bull 1988, Howard & Moore 1991) to 312 (Sibley & Monroe 1990, Clements 1991). Based on the most conservative estimate, 46 % of them (135) are tropical forest species, the richest genera being *Accipiter* (40 species), *Spizaetus* (12 species) and *Leucopternis* (10 species). One third of these tropical forest species (45) may be considered as threatened (appendix) and yet this list does not include some species with limited range or with some subspecies that are endangered. Current status and trends of population dynamics of many species are so little known that more taxa are likely to be added to the red list in the near future. Owls are not considered here because of an even greater lack of knowledge, but their overall situation may be no safer.

The species richness of tropical forests usually decreases from low to higher elevations, from the equator to higher latitudes, from humid evergreen to more seasonal and drier forest types, from well drained soils to seasonally flooded and from high mature to lower more disturbed stands (Thiollay unpublished). So the richest tropical forest type is the undisturbed, wet, evergreen lowland rain forest within 10° of the Equator. We shall mostly refer to this. Other tropical forests include mangrove, swamp, gallery, cloud, montane and monsoon forests. Raptors, like other vertebrate predators, are important in several respects for a general conservation strategy. First, they play the role of "umbrella species" because of their large home ranges. Any area encompassing a viable population of raptors, and even more a complete community of them, would harbour a large set of habitats and sizeable populations of most if not all other species. This is especially true for tropical forests, where many raptors have strikingly low densities or uneven distributions (Thiollay 1989a). Moreover there are some species in every habitat type.

Second, they are "flag" species arousing public interest and supporting wider conservation programmes. The current Philippine Eagle Project is an example of the utilization of a raptor-symbol in a broader habitat conservation and land use management scheme. Third, raptors are often sensitive "bio-indicators" of environmental changes or habitat quality, far beyond their well-known sensitivity to chronic food-chain contamination. For instance, rain forest species in Guiana are highly responsive to relatively moderate levels of disturbance in primary forest such as hunting pressure, selective logging, road construction or moderate fragmentation (Thiollay 1985c, in press & in prep.) Their abundance and community composition can thus be used to monitor forest degradation as well as tropical landscape changes.

At last, the key biological role of predators in primary rain forest begins to be appreciated (Terborgh 1988, Thiollay 1991). By controlling the population level of smaller predators and other prey species, they ease multi-species coexistence and thus help to maintain a high species diversity. The elimination of some predators from isolated forest fragments or secondary vegetation may have unsuspected consequences and could promote the domino-like extinction of seemingly unrelated species.

Unfortunately little can be changed or added to my first review of the world situation of tropical forest raptors written 10 years ago (Thiollay 1985a & b). The deforestation is still continuing unabated, even if locally it tends to be at a slightly lower rate, most probably because of a lack of forest. The areas that are the most affected are still among the richest in species numbers and proportion of endemics: Southeast Asia (from India to Indonesia and the Philippines) and the humid neotropics (especially along the Pacific and Atlantic coasts of South America). Nor has the situation improved on islands such as the Solomons, the Caribbean and Madagascar. There is still no sign of a significant decrease of the rate of logging or shifting cultivation per unit area of remaining tropical forest (Mather 1990, WRI 1990, UNEP 1991). There is no more indication of a compensatory increase in number, size and enforcement of protected areas. Finally, our knowledge of the life history and ecology of the rain forest raptors is slowly and locally improving, but at a pace that probably does not match their rate of extinction.

THREATS TO FOREST RAPTOR POPULATIONS

Most currently identifiable threats to raptors in the tropical forest belt are related to habitat destruction. Other classical threats such as direct killing, trade or pesticide poisoning are of local occurrence and most often of little significance. Moreover they are almost always a consequence of increased human penetration after forest degradation and opening.

Areas undergoing broadscale conversion of their tropical forests at rapid rates and where little forest will be left at the turn of this century are: most forests below 1000 m in India, Bangladesh, Sri Lanka, Thailand, Philippines, South China, Indochina, Malaysia, Madagascar, West Africa, Central America, Pacific coast of Colombia and Ecuador, Atlantic coast of Brazil. The remaining forests of Melanesia, northern Australia, many Indonesian islands and east Africa will also be reduced to tiny patches. The lowest rates of change are expected in the Guianas, Brazil's western Amazonia, Zaire Basin and the mountains of Papua New Guinea.

Three different threats are involved under the general term of habitat loss. They are often concurrent and their detrimental effects are additive:

1/ deforestation, i.e. the conversion of forest to various open habitats, including tree plantations;

2/ disturbance or secondarization of the forest cover, resulting in an important change of the vegetation structure and in an impovershed plant and animal community;

3/ fragmentation of large forest tracts leading to a mosaic of forest patches and open areas.

1. Deforestation

The total destruction of forest and its replacement by cultivated, pasture, urban or even fallow unproductive lands is the most drastic habitat change, usually fatal to most, if not all, forest raptors. The annual rate of tropical forest clearance was 11.3 million ha around 1980, of which 7.5 million ha were closed forests and the remainder were more open woodlands (Lanly 1982). This rate had increased to 17 million ha for the decade 1981-90 (UNEP 1991). Only in the Brazilian Legal Amazon is there any sign of a declining trend, from 8.0 million ha deforested in 1986 to 2.6 in 1989 although this is partly due to changes in measurement methods (Fearnside 1989, UNEP 1991) but also recently to decreasing financial incentives. This continuing world rate of tropical deforestation amounts to at least 1 % of the remaining forest cover per year.

Numerous estimates of potential species loss are being made on theoretical grounds, mostly from island biogeography theory. Yet the prospects and the scale of a mass extinction about to occur remain controversial. However, the most conservative estimates of overall species loss in tropical forests are 0.3 % of all species each year (Wilson 1989) and a total of 12 % of the bird species by the year 2000 (Simberloff 1986). In this general prospect one must remember that raptors, as relatively large species and top predators, are among the most extinction-prone species. Moreover, from a detailed examination of current status of threatened species in the appendix, it is not unreasonable to fear that 12-24 species could disappear within the next one or two decades, i.e., 9-18 % of all the rain forest raptor species. When the immediate threat is the disappearance of sizeable tracts of forest for narrow habitat specialists with limited distribution ranges, there is little hope that any management or the gazetting of necessarily small and isolated forest reserves would reverse the trend in the long term. The successful recovery of the Mauritius Kestrel (*Falco punctatus*) is not a reason for hope. It was probably much helped by the relative adaptability of island species, but it could not be repeated in most continental situations.

2. Forest degradation

In the long term, at least locally, there is some hope of stopping or even reversing tropical deforestation. Yet almost inevitably, the habitat quality will remain, or be further, altered, e.g. the vegetation structure, the community composition and the abundance of some resources needed by food specialists will continue to shift away from the primary forest conditions because of isolation, edge effects or development-oriented management forms involving some human exploitation.

The most widespread and relatively benign tropical forest uses are often favoured by conservationists as the best incentives to promote forest preservation by an economically sustainable or traditional use for indigenous human populations. Unfortunately, they are likely, or are already known, to affect somewhat the maintenance of primary forest raptors. They are, in order of increasing severity for bird populations:

a) Hunting pressure. The traditional hunting by sparsely distributed primitive populations has almost vanished everywhere. Higher human densities, the use of guns or motorboats and some trade for cash have now severe impacts on some large mammals or game birds. Raptors are still only occasionally killed but the domino-like effect of natural community disturbance, probably through prey population decrease, may be detrimental to some raptor species (Thiollay 1985c).

b) Exploitation of minor forest products. Although the overall structure of the forest is little affected, this traditional activity is almost always associated with hunting.

c) Road building. The opening of forest tracts by new roads not only promotes the colonization of road verges by alien species but is always likely to bring disturbance and hunting unless it is strongly controlled.

d) Logging. Even the so-called selective logging, that affects most tropical forests, usually results in unacceptable damage to soil and forest structure, out of proportion with the volume of timber harvested. Commonly, when less than 10 % of the large trees are exploited, 50 % or more of the forest area is heavily damaged and slow to regenerate because of additional wind falls and the growth of a dense secondary vegetation in gaps (Thiollay in press), let alone increased hunting pressure and the settlement of shifting cultivators.

e) The silvicultural management of logged forest to promote a sustainable production of timber further aggravates the disturbance by removing additional, commercially not valuable, tree species and sometimes by introducing new species or by highly favouring a small number of natural species. A step further in the primary forest conversion is traditional agroforestry, most extensively carried out and currently studied in Indonesia (Thiollay in prep.). Although a relatively high variety of large trees are left in these planted and managed forests, the decrease in primary forest bird diversity is striking. At the extreme, industrial tree plantations (Hevea, oilpalm, coffee, cocoa, ...) are extremely poor and retain an insignificant proportion of the natural forest bird density.

The artificial timber plantations (pine, *Eucalyptus, Gmelina*, ...) also fall in this last category, although they are mistakenly called reafforestation.

f) Shifting cultivation is the major cause of deforestation throughout the tropical world, especially because of a break-down of the old agricultural methods. It is now performed intensively, by denser populations over larger continuous areas and with increasingly shorter fallow periods than formerly. It leads at best to a dense secondary forest that bears little resemblance to the primary forest and that retains only a part of its original bird community. Under economic or population pressure, this itinerant cultivation may also be converted into pasture (as in Amazonia, Browder 1988) or into more intensive permanent farming or tree plantation (mainly in Asia). There are an estimated 300 million people involved in shifting cultivation and they are converting the forest at a rate of 100,000 km^2 per year (Mabberley 1992).

Semi-wooded agricultural landscapes or partially open secondary forests resulting from human exploitation have not necessarily a markedly lower raptor species diversity. The problem is that some primary forest species, unable to withstand a high level of disturbance, soon disappear. Conversely other species show a wider range of adaptations, while still others, usually edge or gap specialists, patchily distributed in the primary forest tracts, are favoured by openings and actually increase in logged, secondary or fragmented forests. Additionally, on every continent there is an assemblage of species that readily invade roads or clearings newly opened in continuous undisturbed forest where they are naturally rare or absent. When deforestation creates much larger clearings, then a new set of species typical of open grasslands comes to replace the fast disappearing forest species, thus contributing to a relative maintenance of the overall species richness.

3. Fragmentation

Another serious concern is the increasing patchiness of the remaining forest cover. Even when, at best, patches are protected as primary forest reserves, they tend to be increasingly smaller and more isolated. Both shrinking area and isolation, often occurring simultaneously, are well known to threaten the survival of populations trapped in such reserves (Wilson & Pater 1988). The minimum viable size of isolated populations is still debated and the relative suitability of the surrounding habitats as well as the dispersal ability of the different species are critical parameters. The endless controversies over the inconvenience or benefits of edge effects, corridor design or single large vs several small reserves have still not been tested on raptors and, as usual, they probably depend to a large extent upon local conditions and species' biology.

Before only isolated fragments are left, the forest cover is often punched out into an irregular network of patches interconnected by corridors of variable width, usually on ridges, steep slopes, or in gullies. The effects of such a partial fragmentation are currently studied in Guiana and in the Western Ghats (Thiollay in prep.).

4. Island populations

Endemic species on oceanic islands are a special case. They are often considered as highly vulnerable. However, many of them exhibit life history traits typical of island populations that allow them to survive in conditions where similar species on continents would be in jeopardy. Very small populations may survive and breed successfully even in marginal conditions (e.g., *Chondrohierax uncinatus mirus* on Grenada). They may reach very high densities (e.g., *Buteo platypterus* on little hunted Caribbean islands) and primarily forest species may occupy a wide range of habitats including severely degraded woodlands (e.g., *Accipiter haplochrous* in New Caledonia). All examples above are from recent field studies (Thiollay in prep.). During a long evolution within a limited area, with no genetic exchanges, free from interspecific competition and periodically reduced by random catastrophes, island species seem to have evolved adaptations that facilitate their survival in the face of human-caused habitat destruction and population reduction.

CURRENT STATE OF KNOWLEDGE; RESEARCH AND FUTURE NEEDS

Since the picture I drew ten years ago (Thiollay 1985b), a lot of new information has been accumulated on the distribution and status of the raptors in some areas where they were previously little known, e.g., in Java, the Solomons or New Caledonia, just to name some projects initiated by the World Working Group on Birds of Prey. However relatively little has been added to our knowledge of the life history and ecology of rain forest raptors. Notable exceptions come from Guatemala, French Guiana, Central Amazonia and Madagascar. Only one species, the Red Goshawk in Australia (Baker-Gabb, pers. comm.) has been studied over most of its range. Many species remain virtually unknown and sometimes their current existence or taxonomic position is in doubt. Even more worrying is that we still know almost nothing on the demography and natural population dynamics of any species, except maybe the Crowned Eagle in its marginal habitat of Kenyan highlands. This prevents effective management measures and even the launching of actions.

Several current research programmes on conservation-oriented ecology of tropical forest raptors are in progress. They include most prominently the Maya Project in Guatemala and Belize, where habitat selection, home range use, food habits and breeding success of several species are carefully monitored. Similar studies have also begun in Madagascar. Raptor density and distribution in successive stages of forest degradation, adaptability to forest management (logging, hunting, silviculture, agroforestry, fragmentation) and sensitivity to disturbance are being studied in French Guiana, Sumatra, the Western Ghâts and Andaman Islands (Thiollay 1989a & in prep.). Other monitoring or conservation projects are also actively carried out in Mexico, India, Java and the Philippines, let alone the successful recovery programme of the Mauritius Kestrel.

New advances on the rain forest raptors' ecology will rely on the development and experimentation of specific techniques to ease time-consuming behavioural studies, surveys and monitoring of populations. Promising methods include mid-morning visual censuses from canopy emergent viewpoints, pre-dawn mapping of singing Neotropical forest falcons, broadcast of distressed prey vocalizations to attract some bird predators and indeed a development of radiotelemetry or even satellite tracking of large eagles. Standardization of results is also needed to compare abundance indexes or actual densities obtained by different observers. For instance, the minimum number of individuals recorded during a 4-hour point census above the canopy, beginning one hour after sunrise, in fine weather conditions and limited to 1 km^2 has proven to be a manageable and reliable index of abundance (Thiollay 1989b, Burnham *et al.* 1991). I also increasingly use 1 or 4 sq-km sample quadrats to assess raptor densities, focusing on the identification of territorial pairs and on the distribution of home ranges.

Several research priorities must be outlined. Indeed, classical data of conservation biology are essential, such as area requirements, minimum viable population size, demographic parameters and genetic variability. With the help of radiotracking, it will be possible to find more nests and to gather the first basic data on clutch size, nesting success and breeding intervals. More specifically, we need a detailed assessment of the adaptation, tolerance and vulnerability of every species to habitat changes and to different levels of deforestation or fragmentation. This would allow us to understand the species' adaptability to forest degradation, to predict the composition of raptor communities in new tropical landscapes and to design conservation measures that would reduce the loss of primary forest species. If it is easy to monitor the mere presence of a species in a modified habitat, it is far more difficult to measure its reproductive success or fitness, which is the only way to know the actual value of this new habitat for the long-term maintenance of the species.

Even more urgent is the need to survey the status and distribution of the many endemic raptors known to occur in species-rich, recently little surveyed and rapidly deforested areas including western Colombia and Ecuador, south-eastern Brazil, eastern Indonesia, Andaman and Nicobar, the Philippines, Bismarck and Solomon islands. Among the new projects to be undertaken, such areas should receive top priority.

CONSERVATION STRATEGIES

Time is running short and different objectives must be achieved with equal priority to successfully alleviate the declining trend of tropical forest raptors.

1. Surveys of priority areas

As all too often, it is necessary to focus first on the most threatened species and areas. This strategy was highlighted by Myers (1988 & 1990) who defined hot spots, i.e., areas that feature exceptional concentration of species with high levels of endemism and face the highest threats of destruction. Based only on plant diversity, he defined 14 rain forest hot spots that together cover 310,000 sq-km or 0.2 % of the land surface, with only 3.5 % of their area remaining in primary forest, but that harbour 15 % of the Earth's plant species. They are Madagascar, eastern Tanzania, south-western Ivory Coast, the Atlantic coast of Brazil, western Ecuador, Colombian Choco, uplands of western Amazonia, south-western Sri Lanka, the western Ghats, eastern Himalayas, peninsular Malaysia, northern Borneo, the Philippines and New Caledonia. Together, 92 forest raptor species are found in these areas, i.e., 68 % of all the world's tropical forest raptors.

In Table 1, I emphasize here 4 hot spot areas, including only 2 areas from the above list. They are the most heavily forested countries of Australasia and they have the highest number of endemics and the least known raptor species. They certainly deserve to be designated as priority areas for immediate surveys and conservation actions as far as the forest raptors are concerned.

2. Ecological studies

Again I stress the need to develop new and efficient techniques to survey, study and monitor threatened raptor populations and to accumulate much more life history data than are currently available on most species. This is a fundamental prerequisite to better assess their ecological requirements, demographic trends, sensitivity to habitat alteration and minimum size of viable populations.

3. Habitat management

Indeed the first strategy is to slow down deforestation rates, but the conservation of tropical forests is a far more general problem and we shall focus on measures more specifically directed at raptors.

The maintenance of species strictly associated with primary forest ideally requires the setting aside of large tracts of undisturbed forest. Today 669 areas, totalling 66 million hectares, are under some form of protection within the tropical forest belt (IUCN 1990). However maybe less than half of them are covered with truly primary humid forest and are completely protected. Together only 3.9 % of the world's rain forests are in parks or reserves, whereas the lowest target to prevent extinction of a significant number of species would be the preservation of 10 % of all the tropical moist forest remaining in 1990 (Sayer 1991). Few of these areas reach the minimum size for the long-term maintenance of an entire forest raptor community, estimated to be in the order of 1 million ha or more (Thiollay 1989a).

As options for new protected areas are disappearing almost daily under increasing human pressure, even this modest goal maybe unlikely to be achieved. Moreover legal protection does not always prevent illicit logging, settlement and poaching, let alone the increasing isolation of forest patches as a result of clearance of adjacent forested areas. Thus the importance of unprotected areas will remain critical for the conservation of many species. Education and training of local biologists and reserve managers, with some special focus on raptors, is also necessary.

A significant proportion of broadly-classified forest species are actually gap or edge species, while a number of others, although widespread in undisturbed mature forest, still maintain appreciable population levels in some stages of forest degradation or fragmentation. Hence it is important to devise apppropriate land use policies, management techniques, silvicultural systems, logging methods, agroforestry rules, agricultural practices and landscape design in multiple use areas that are most compatible with the ecological requirements of this category of species tolerant to disturbance. This strategy must be applied not only in the necessary buffer zones around protected reserves but also in the much larger exploited, semi-deforested areas, to mitigate the destructive effect of intensive management and to ensure the conservation of a significant part of

Table 1. Important areas for the conservation of tropical forest raptor diversity. From the conservative taxonomic list of Howard and Moore (1991). Estimated area of moist forest from Collins *et al.* (1991).

Islands	Rain forest area (million ha)	Number of forest raptors		
		Species	Subspecies	Threatened endemic species
Philippines	6.5	15	20	2
Malaysia + Western Indonesia	75.9	19	36	2
Lesser Sundas + Celebes + Moluccas	18.3	21	42	2
New Guinea + Solomons	73.4	22	51	8
Proportion of the world tropical forest total	14.5 %	40 %	45 %	31 %

the original forest biodiversity. Currently, less than 1% of all tropical forest is considered to be sustainably managed (WRI 1990) and the goal of sustainability itself is usually one of timber production. This target of broad-minded conservationists involves silvicultural practices that lead to greatly impoverished forest avifaunas. Other options such as nonwood products or nature tourism must be favoured if most of the richness of tropical forests is to be maintained.

Among the numerous projects currently in progress throughout the world to conserve or sustainably manage tropical forests, only one is specifically aimed at the protection of a threatened raptor (the Philippine Eagle). In forthcoming large-scale programmes initiated by international bodies such as IUCN, WWF, ITTO, FAO, World Bank, etc ... and devoted to the conservation of tropical forests, it would make sense to promote the use of forest raptors as indicators of habitat quality at the landscape level or to assess the minimum size of reserves.

3. Additional guidelines

When dealing with habitat management, one should not forget to control and at least minimize *hunting pressure*. This widespread and traditional activity may have a significant impact, even on non target species such as raptors, through complex interspecific relationships within the tropical forest communities, and it is additive to other forms of disturbance. Education programmes and the development of other cheap protein sources may help to reduce shooting.

Captive breeding, however attractive it may be for some conservationists, must be considered only if enough quality rain forest remains to eventually release the captive-bred individuals. There is no example of a tropical forest raptor vanishing where its natural habitat is still extensive and little disturbed. Nevertheless, ex-situ conservation is also justified when sufficient areas of suitable habitat can be recovered. The readaptation of released, inexperienced raptors into the complex environment of tropical forests may be far more difficult than are similar operations in open temperate habitats.

My last words will be a plea for a renewed interest in the *conservation of subspecies*. This concept was abandoned under the pressure of the fast-growing number of threatened full species to which little or no effort could be devoted. However, subspecies are an integral part of biodiversity. They often have well-differentiated life histories or physiological adaptations and singular interspecific relationships within their own community, whatever their level of morphological differentiation. In this respect also, Indonesia, the Philippines, New Guinea and the Solomons, with their many island forms so little known, should be priority areas.

REFERENCES

AMADON, D. & J. BULL, 1988. Hawks and Owls of the World. An annotated list of species. *Proc. Western Found.* Vert. Zool. 3 (4): 295-357.

BROWDER, J. O. 1988. Public policy and deforestation in the Brazilian Amazon. Pp. 247-297 in "Public policies and the misuse of forest resources". Repetto, R. & M., Gillis, eds. Cambridge University Press, Cambridge.

BURNHAM, W.A. *et al.* **1988-91**. Maya Project. Progress Reports I, II, III, IV. The Peregrine Fund, Boise.

CLEMENTS, J.F. 1991. *Birds of the World.* A checklist, 4th ed. Ibis Publ. Co., Vista.

COLLAR, N.J. & P. ANDREW 1988. *Birds to Watch.* The ICBP World Checklist of Threatened Birds. ICBP Tech. Publ. n° 8.

COLLINS, N.M., J.A. SAYER & T.C. WHITMORE (eds) 1991. *The conservation atlas of tropical forests. Asia and the Pacific.* IUCN & MacMillan Press, London.

FAO 1987. *Yearbook of forest products.* FAO, Rome.

FEARNSIDE, P.M. 1989. Deforestation in Brazilian Amazonia: the rates and causes of forest destruction. *The Ecologist* 19: 214-218.

HOWARD, R. & A. MOORE 1991. *A complete checklist of the birds of the world. 2nd edition.* Academic Press, London.

IUCN (International Union for the Conservation of Nature) 1990. *United Nations list of national parks and protected areas.* IUCN, Gland.

JOHNS, A.D. 1985. Selective logging and wildlife conservation in tropical rain forest: problems and recommendations. *Biological Conservation* 31: 355-375.

LANLY, J.P. 1982. Tropical forest resources. FAO Forestry Paper 30.

MABBERLEY, D.J. 1992. *Tropical rain forest ecology. 2nd edition.* Blackie, Glasgow.

MATHER, A.S. 1990. *Global forest resources.* Belhaven Press, London.

MYERS, N. 1988. Threatened biotas: hot spots in tropical forests. *The Environmentalist* 8 : 187-208.

MYERS, N. 1990. The biodiversity challenge: expanded hot-spots analysis. *The Environmentalist* 10 : 243-256.

SAYER, J. 1991. Conservation and protection of tropical rain forests; the perspective of the World Conservation Union. *Unasylva* 166, 42 : 40-45.

SIBLEY, Ch. G. & B.L. MONROE 1990. *Distribution and taxonomy of birds in the world.* Yale University Press, New Haven.

SIMBERLOFF, D. 1986. Are we on the verge of a mass extinction in tropical rain forests ? Pp. 165-182 in *"Dynamics of extinction"*, Elliot, D.K. (ed.) J. Wiley, New York.

TERBORGH, J. 1988. The big things that run the world. A sequel to E.O. Wilson. *Conservation Biology* 2 : 402-403.

THIOLLAY, J.M. 1985a. Falconiforms of tropical rain forests: a review. ICBP Tech. Publ. 5: 155-165.

THIOLLAY, J.M. 1985b. The tropical rain forest raptors: state of knowledge, world situation and conservation strategy. ICBP Tech. Publ. 5: 223-225.

THIOLLAY, J.M. 1985c. Raptor community structure of a primary rain forest in French Guiana and effect of hunting pressure. *Raptor Research* 18: 117-122.

THIOLLAY, J.M. 1989a. Area requirements for the conservation of rain forest raptors and game birds in French Guiana. *Conservation Biology* 3: 128-137.

THIOLLAY, J.M. 1989b. Censusing of diurnal raptors in a primary rain forest: comparative methods and species detectability. *Journal of Raptor Research* 23: 72-84.

THIOLLAY, J.M. 1991. Tropical rain forest bird communities: emerging patterns and processes of organization. Acta XX Cong. Intern. Ornith., Christchurch.

THIOLLAY, J.M. 1992. Influence of selective logging on birds species diversity in a Guianan rain forest. *Conservation Biology.*

THIOLLAY, J.M. (in prep.). Effects of rain forest disturbance and fragmentation on the raptor community.

Comparative gradient analyzes in French Guiana.
UNEP (United Nations Environment Programme) 1991. *Environmental Data Report. 3rd edition.* Blackwell, Oxford
WILSON, E.O. 1989. Threats to biodiversity. *Scientific American* 261: 60-69.
WILSON, E.O. & F.M. PETER (eds.) 1988. *Biodiversity*. National Academy Press, Washington.
WRI 1990. *World Resources 1990-91*. Oxford University Press, New-York.

Jean-Marc Thiollay,
Laboratoire d'Ecologie, E.N.S.,
46, rue d'Ulm,
75230 Paris
France

APPENDIX

List of tropical forest Falconiformes considered threatened, or at least rare and insufficiently known (?) according to Collar & Andrew 1988, personal experience and an extensive review of adequate literature. The sytematic list follows Amadon & Bull 1988.

ACCIPITRIDAE

Madagascar Cuckoo Hawk, *Aviceda madagascariensis* (Madagascar)
Black Honey Buzzard, *Henicopernis infuscata* (New Britain)
Solomon Sea Eagle, *Haliaeetus sanfordi* (Solomon Islands)
? East African Snake Eagle, *Circaetus fasciolatus* (East Africa)
Kinabalu Serpent Eagle, *Spilornis kinabaluensis* (North Borneo)
? Nicobar Serpent Eagle, *Spilornis minimus* (Nicobar Islands)
? Andaman Serpent Eagle, *Spilornis elgini* (Andaman Islands)
Madagascar Serpent Eagle, *Eutriorchis astur* (Madagascar)
Gray-bel lied Hawk, *Accipiter poliogaster* (South America)
? Blue-and-Gray Sparrowhawk, *Acccipiter luteoschistaceus* (New Britain)
Imitator Sparrowhawk, *Accipiter imitator* (Solomon Islands)
Gray-headed Goshawk, *Accipiter princeps* (New Britain)
Semicollared Hawk, *Accipiter collaris* (N. Andes)
Dwarf Sparrowhawk, *Accipiter nanus* (Sulawesi)
New Britain Collared Sparrowhawk, *Accipiter brachyurus* (New Britain)
? Madagascar Sparrowhawk, *Accipiter madagascariensis* (Madagascar)
Cuban Hawk, *Accipiter gundlachi* (Cuba)
Madagascar Goshawk, *Accipiter henstii* (Madagascar)
? Chestnut-mantled Goshawk, *Accipiter buergersii* (New Guinea)
Red Goshawk, *Accipiter radiatus* (N. Australia)
Plumbeous Hawk, *Leucopternis plumbea* (Choco)
? White-browed Hawk, *Leucopternis kuhli* (W. Amazonia)
White-necked Hawk, *Leucopternis lacernulata* (SE Brazil)
Gray-backed Hawk, *Leucopternis occidentalis* (W. Ecuador)
Mantled Hawk, *Leucopternis polionota* (SE Brazil)
Black Solitary Eagle, *Harpyhaliaetus solitarius* (Tropical America)
Ridgway's Hawk, *Buteo ridgwayi* (Hispaniola)
Hawaiian Hawk, *Buteo solitarius* (Hawaii)
Guiana Crested Eagle, *Morphnus guianensis* (Tropical America)
Harpy Eagle, *Harpia harpyja* (Tropical America)
New Guinea Eagle, *Harpyiopsis novaeguineae* (New Guinea)
Great Philippine Eagle, *Pithecophaga jefferyi* (Philippines)
? Black and White Hawk Eagle, *Spizastur melanoleucus* (Tropical America)
Javan Hawk Eagle, *Spizaetus bartelsi* (Java)
? Celebes Hawk Eagle, *Spizaetus lanceolatus* (Sulawesi)
? Philippines Hawk Eagle, *Spizaetus philippensis* (Philippines)
Wallace's Hawk Eagle, *Spizaetus nanus* (Burma to Sumatra)
? Black and Chestnut Eagle, *Spizaetus isidori* (Andes)

FALCONIDAE

Plumbeous Forest Falcon, *Micrastur plumbeus* (Choco)
Buckley's Forest Falcon, *Micrastur buckleyi* (W. Amazonia)
? Bornean Falconet, *Microhierax latifrons* (N. Borneo)
? Pied Falconet, *Microhierax melanoleucos* (SE Asia)
Mauritius Kestrel, *Falco punctatus* (Mauritius)
? Banded Kestrel, *Falco zoniventris* (Madagascar)
Orange-breasted Falcon, *Falco deiroleucus* (Tropical America)

Meyburg, B.-U. & R. D. Chancellor eds.1994
Raptor Conservation Today
WWGBP / The Pica Press

Threatened Raptors of Australia´s Tropical Forests

David J Baker-Gabb

INTRODUCTION

The continental island of Australia is about 7.7 million km² and about equal in area to the USA, excluding Alaska. It is about 4,000 km from east to west and 3,700 km from Cape York in the tropical north to the south of temperate Tasmania.

Man has occupied Australia for more than 40,000 years. Aboriginal man has very likely played a prominent role in shaping tropical forests through the use of fire (Nix 1972). However, the start of major new disturbance and destruction of the environment coincided with the arrival and occupation of Australia by Europeans 200 years ago. Greatest disturbance in the form of urban development, dryland cash cropping and deforestation has occurred in the temperate south and east, where most of the present human population of 15 million is concentrated.

The human distribution is readily explained by the fact that Australia is the driest continent, excluding Antarctica. Desert and semi-arid areas occupy 70% of Australia (Williams & Lazarides 1985), mainly in the centre and west of the continent. The Australian landscape is subdued, with low mountain ranges in the centre, north-west and one extending for 2,500 km in the east. Forest and woodland occur only in the coastal and subcoastal north, east and south-west. Tropical forest and woodland covers less than 15% of Australia. The climate is predictable in these forested regions but it is irregular throughout most of Australia. Prolonged droughts lasting 3-10 years may be broken by flooding rains. For this reason raptor species of arid and semi-arid regions have had to adapt to an environment that can be vastly different from year to year. Consequently many are resilient to present man-made changes and there is only one threatened raptor from inland Australia. Conversely, those raptor species whose survival is tightly linked with the historically stable forests have not fared so well.

AUSTRALIA'S STABLE ENVIRONMENTS: FORESTS AND ISLANDS

Amongst threatened species world-wide, there is a great predominance of species inhabiting forests and islands (Halliday 1980; King 1981). Whilst this trend does not hold for threatened Australian birds in general (Ford 1989), it certainly does for threatened Australian raptors.

Australia has four species and 11 subspecies of raptor which have been classified as threatened using IUCN definitions (Garnett 1992). Three threatened species are endemic diurnal raptors and one is a large owl, while all but two of the 11 threatened subspecies are owls. Only one of the 15 threatened taxa occurs outside subcoastal, coastal or island forests. The majority (60%) of these forest raptors occur exclusively or partly in the tropics.

The rare Grey Falcon *Falco hypoleacos* is the only threatened raptor from inland Australia. Other taxa which do not occur in the tropics include the Australian subspecies of the rare Sooty Owl *Tyto tenebricosa tenebricosa* and the rare Powerful Owl *Ninox strenua*. The endangered subspecies of the Southern Boobook *Ninox novaeseelandiae undulata* and Wedge-tailed Eagle *Aquila audax fleayi* occur on temperate Norfolk Island and Tasmania respectively. The extinct Southern Boobook *N. n. albaria* occurred on temperate Lord Howe Island.

THE TWO THREATENED DIURNAL SPECIES OF MAINLAND AUSTRALIA'S TROPICAL FORESTS

The Red Goshawk *Erythrotriorchis radiatus* (vulnerable) is restricted to the forests and savannah woodlands of the tropical north, while the Square-tailed Kite *Lophoictinia isura* (rare) is migratory and has a much wider distribution which largely accounts for the different status of the two species. Both raptors are from monotypic genera, have always been considered uncommon, breed at low to very low densities, have low to moderate recruitment rates, and feed mainly on birds (Debus & Czechura 1989; Aumann & Baker-Gabb 1991).

Destruction of forest and woodlands, particularly in eastern Australia, is now the main threat to both species. Illegal egg-collecting and shooting are problems for a few pairs whose nest location has been advertised or those which breed close to human settlement (Debus & Czechura 1989; Aumann & Baker-Gabb 1991). Pesticides are not inhibiting breeding success in remote locations, but they may be a problem in north-east Australia where cropping and the use of pesticides is widespread. Current fire and grazing regimes do not limit the density of prey and the availability of suitable nest trees, but their long-term effects are unknown.

The Red Goshawk and Square-tailed Kite occur in several conservation reserves. Additional conservation measures required for both species include: surveys in north-east Australia to locate and protect nest sites outside reserves, not revealing the location of nest sites in order to protect pairs from egg-collectors, and education of landowners with poultry near known pairs of raptors so that they are not illegally shot. The biology of the Red Goshawk is well known (Debus & Czechura 1988; Aumann and Baker-Gabb 1991), but a comprehensive study of the Square-tailed Kite's status, biology and ecology is required (Garnett 1992).

FIVE THREATENED SUBSPECIES OF LARGE OWL FROM AUSTRALIA'S TROPICAL FORESTS

There are four subspecies of the Masked Owl *Tyto novaehollandiae*. The Tasmanian subspecies *T. n. castanops* is secure, the widespread mainland subspecies *T. n. navaehollandiae* is rare, while *T. n. kimberli* from the north of mainland Australia and *T. n. melvillensis* from Melville and Bathurst Islands are insufficiently known (Garnett 1992). On the mainland *T. n. novaehollandiae* and *T. n. kimberli* appear to occur at low densities (Schodde & Mason 1980; Hollands 1991), though this impression may be deceptive because the Masked Owl is usually silent and may be confused with the more common Barn Owl *Tyto alba*. In the absence of competitors, *T. n. melvellensis* appears to attain higher population densities on Melville and Bathurst Island than do either of the mainland subspecies (Garnett 1992).

All Masked Owl subspecies will use altered habitats and forest margins, particularly for foraging (Schodde & Mason 1980). However, they favour the forest interior for roosting and nest in large hollows in tall, old trees. Such trees can be destroyed by high intensity fires late in the dry season in the tropical north (Garnett 1992). Current forestry management practices may also limit nest site availability in some areas. Conservation measures proposed for threatened subspecies of the Masked Owl include: studies of basic ecology, particularly home range, diet and nest requirements and the effect of current fire, forestry and agricultural practices on nest site availability (Garnett 1992).

There are three subspecies of the Rufous Owl *Ninox rufa*. In north-west Australia *N. r. rufa* is secure, *N. r. queenslandica* of the north-east is rare and *N. r. meesi* of Cape York is insufficiently known (Garnett 1992). All subspecies of Rufous Owl occur at low densities (Schodde & Mason 1980). They roost and nest in rainforest, but often forage in nearby woodlands and wetlands.

Though many pairs of Rufous Owl occur in conservation reserves, some habitat outside reserves is still being cleared for agriculture. Hot fires late in the dry season are the greatest threat because they burn the fringes of rainforest and can destroy nest trees (Garnett 1992). Weed invasion is also a problem in some Rufous Owl habitat. Conservation measures proposed include surveys to obtain a more accurate assessment of the abundance and status of nest sites. Particular attention should be paid to the effects of habitat clearance, invasion of habitat by weeds and the effects of current fire management practices (Garnett 1992).

TWO THREATENED SUBSPECIES FROM TROPICAL CHRISTMAS ISLAND

On Christmas Island the Brown Goshawk *Accipiter fasciatus natalis* and Indonesian Hawk-Owl *Ninox squamipila natalis* occur as vulnerable subspecies of widespread, secure species. There are about 100 pairs of each subspecies (Stokes 1988; Olsen & Stokes 1989). Clearance of forest was the main threat, but this has ceased and much of the island is now national park. Conservation measures proposed include collecting information on the effective population sizes, productivity and recruitment to confirm whether the small populations are viable in the long term.

SUMMARY

Despite the fact that less than 30% of Australia is covered in forest, all but one of its 15 threatened raptors is a forest dweller, and most (73%) are owls. While clearance of forests for agriculture was formerly a major threat, this is no longer the main threat for any taxa. In tropical Australia the main threat now is the loss of large hollow-bearing nesting trees and those which might eventually replace them due to inappropriate fire and forestry management practices. Studies need to be undertaken to provide alternative management strategies and to elucidate the biology of several taxa which are not well known. The most important area for this work to be undertaken is in north-east Australia.

ACKNOWLEDGEMENTS

I thank Stephen Garnett for providing information on threatened raptors prior to its publication, and Nick Mooney for presenting this paper at the Berlin conference.

REFERENCES

AUMANN, T. & D. J. BAKER-GABB 1991. *A Management Plan for the Red Goshawk.* RAOU Report 75.

DEBUS, S. J. S. & G. V. CZECHURA 1988. The Red Goshawk *Erythrotriorchis radiatus*: a review. *Australian Bird Watcher* 12: 175-199.

DEBUS, S. J. S. & G. V. CZECHURA 1989. The Square-tailed Kite *Lophoictinia isura*: a review. *Australian Bird Watcher.*13: 118-123.

FORD, H. A. 1989. *Ecology of Birds: an Australian Perspective.* Surrey Beatty, Sydney.

GARNETT, S. T. 1992. *The Action Plan for Australian Birds.* Australian National Parks and Wildlife Service, Canberra.

HALLIDAY, T. R. 1980. *Vanishing Birds: their Natural History and Conservation.* Penguin, England.

HOLLANDS, D. 1991. *Birds of the Night.* A. H. & A. W. Reed, Sydney

KING, W. B. 1981. *Endangered Birds of the World. The ICBP Bird Red Data Book.* Smithsonian Institution Press, Washington DC.

NIX, H. A. 1972. Environmental control of breeding, post-breeding dispersal and migration of birds in the Australian region. *Proceedings International Ornithological Congress* 16 : 272 - 305.
OLSEN, P. D. & T. STOKES 1989. The state of knowledge of the Christmas Island Hawk-Owl *Ninox squamipila natalis.* In *Raptors in the Modern World* B-U Meyberg & R. D. Chancellor (Eds.) WWGBP, Berlin.
SCHODDE, R. & I. J. MASON. 1980. *Nocturnal Birds of Australia.* Lansdowne, Melbourne.
STOKES, T. 1988. A review of the birds of Christmas Island, Indian Ocean. *Australian National Parks and Wildlife Service Occassional Paper 16.*
WILLIAMS, O. B. & M. LAZARIDES. 1985. Australia. In *Plant Resources of Arid and Semi-arid Lands.* Academic Press, New York.

David J. Baker-Gabb
Wildlife Branch
Department of Conservation and Natural Resources
123 Brown Street
Heidelberg
Victoria 3084
Australia

Meyburg, B.-U. & R. D. Chancellor eds.1994
Raptor Conservation Today
WWGBP / The Pica Press

The Status and Conservation of Birds of Prey in the Sondaic and Wallacean Regions of Indonesia

S. van Balen

ABSTRACT

In the Oriental subregions of the Sundas and Wallacea, which comprise the Malay Peninsula and the larger part of the Indonesian Archipelago, deforestation is proceeding rapidly and at the present rate little will be left within a few decades.

In the area a number of 36 birds of prey *Accipitridae* and *Falconidae* are exclusively dependent on tropical forest. Thirteen amongst these are endemic to one or both of the subregions, four of them being generally consided as globally threatened (*Spilornis kinabaluensis, Accipiter nanus, Spizaetus bartelsi, Spizaetus nanus*), and two near-threatened (*Spizaetus lanceolatus, Microhierax latifrons*) whilst most other seven species are still widely distributed, though information on some is still needed (*Accipiter griseiceps, A. henicogrammus, A. erythrauchen, A. rhodogaster, Spizaetus alboniger*).

In this paper an overview is presented of all raptors of the Indonesian part of the subregions, with special reference to the endemic and resident forest species. A summary is given of our present fragmentary knowledge on their status and distribution and an attempt is made to reassess the conservation status of each species.

INTRODUCTION

An important part of the world's raptors are found as residents in the Sondaic (Malay Peninsula, Sumatra, Borneo, Kalimantan, Java and Bali) and Wallacean (Sulawesi, Moluccas, Lesser Sundas) subregions in the Orient. Forty-three species (two of which are found only in the non-Indonesian, northern part of Borneo - *Spilornis kinabaluensis* and *Microhierax latifrons*) are found in the area, which number is considerably increased during northern and southern winters by migratory species. A few species have both migrant and resident races in the archipelago (e.g., Osprey *Pandion haliaetus*, Oriental Honey-buzzard *Pernis ptilorhynchus*.)

In the past and more recently, reports have been produced on the status of birds, in particular diurnal raptors (e.g. Brown *et al.*, 1978; King 1978, 1979; Meyburg 1986; Collar & Andrew 1988), in which, as a matter of fact, the species discussed did not always cause the same concern, as more information about their status in the wild became available. A number of species are consistently considered as rare and threatened. These are exclusively forest-dwelling species and will receive special attention in this paper. The status of all other species, including non-forest, is also elucidated, in view of the increasing deterioration of the forests and the difficulties in determining the forest dependence of some of them. Even open country species such as Black-shouldered Kite *Elanus caeruleus*, Black Kite *Milvus migrans* and Spotted Kestrel *Falco moluccensis* become increasingly dependent on secure places within protected areas, i.e. forests in most cases. Mangrove forests offer suitable nesting sites for coastal, open country species, such as the Brahminy Kite *Haliastur indus*.

In certain periods a large number of migrants, some just on passage, some wintering, increase the number of birds of prey in the region. It is not clear what the impact may be on the breeding populations, though in some cases the species seem to be segregated by habitat. In the species accounts, the migrants will be mentioned under the supposedly competing resident sibling species or sub-species.

STUDY AREA

Three major islands are included in the Indonesian part of the Sondaic sub-region:

Sumatra: the third largest island of Indonesia, still has large areas of tropical rainforest, but logging activities and forest clearance by smallholders, transmigration projects, etc. are still devastating, especially in the lowlands. The numerous islands along the east and west coasts of the island have a high degree of endemism, expressed in some distinct raptor races. Large nature reserves have been established throughout, amongst which the most important are the national parks Mt Leuser, Way Kambas and Mt Kerinci Seblat.

Borneo: the second largest island, of which the southern two-thirds, Kalimantan, is Indonesian territory. Two endemic raptors, *Spilornis kinabaluensis* and *Microhierax latifrons*, occur in the northern, Malaysian part. Especially the central, hilly part of the island is covered by extensive forest; logging and other destructive activities in most of the rest, especially the lowland parts, will not leave much of the original vegetation. Most important natural areas are the national parks of Kutai, Tanjung Puting and (proposed) Kayan Mentarang.

Java: heavily populated, with only 2% and 30% of the lowland and montane forest respectively left. Natural vegetation survives in the lowlands as patches of tropical rainforest along the south coast, and dry monsoon forest, especially along the north coast of Central and Eastern Java. One endemic species, *Spizaetus bartelsi* and a few endemic races occur on Java. The smaller islands of Madura and Bali, geographically belonging to Java, have impoverished avifaunas, but especially the latter is important for migrating raptors. Important reserves are the national parks of Ujung Kulon, Mt Gede/Cibodas, Meru Betiri and Baluran.

Wallacea is separated as follows:

Sulawesi: still largely covered by forest, though much has disappeared through cultivation (especially in the south and north-east parts) and logging. High degree of endemism, with four endemic Accipiters occurring and an endemic serpent-eagle and hawk-eagle. Numerous associated small islands, of which Peleng, Banggai and the Sula Islands are in particular of importance. The most important reserves are the Lore Lindu and Dumoga Bone national parks, and perhaps Morowali and Mts Peruhumpenai nature reserves.

Lesser Sundas: comprise numerous islands of small to moderate size. Most of the area was once covered by monsoon forest, woodland and grass steppes under the influence of extreme arid climatic conditions. However, much of the natual habitat has been drastically altered by man's agricultural activities. No endemic elements at species level in the raptor fauna, although the Flores Hawk-eagle is a very distinct endemic race, if not a species (P. Andrew, pers. comm.) despite a high degree of endemism in many other species. Important reserves include the Komodo national park near Flores and the Mt Rinjani on Lombok.

Moluccas: a large number of islands once covered with lush forest, which however has largely disappeared under cultivation and logging activities. Two endemic Accipitrines occur on the islands. Major nature reserves include the Manusela national park on Seram and a number of small proposed reserves.

SPECIES ACCOUNT

Data on distribution and status in the subregions have mainly been extracted from standard works and reports published more or less recently, such as Van Marle & Voous (1988: M&V) for Sumatra, Smythies (1981: S) and Holmes & Burton (1987: H&B) for Kalimantan (the Indonesian part of Borneo); McKinnon (1988: M) for Java and Bali; and White & Bruce (1986: W&B) for Wallacea. Furthermore numerous recently published papers and unpublished reports have been consulted. The following paper, however, does not pretend to be exhaustive, as not all recent unpublished reports were available. During 1979-1992 the author visited 19 out of 26 Indonesian provinces included in the study area for special bird surveys. Species order, scientific and English names follow Andrew (1992).

For each species the widely used IUCN/ICBP Red Data Book categories are applied: endangered, vulnerable, rare, indeterminate, insufficiently known and, additionally, no immediate danger.

Pandion haliaetus - Osprey **No immediate danger**

Widespread in coastal areas and along rivers, and presumably resident in part of the area, though breeding data are available only from Lombok (W&B) and Sulawesi (Kukila 1990; Meyburg & van Balen, this volume.) Only two recent records from Kalimantan (Eve & Guigue 1989; van Balen, in prep.) of birds of uncertain status, but apparently more common elsewhere. Two migrant races, *haliaetus* from the north, *cristatus* from the south, increase periodically the resident population *melvillensis*. Taxonomic affinities of these birds need further study, however.

Aviceda jerdoni - Jerdon's Baza **No immediate danger**

An allospecies of the following. Uncommon and sparsely distributed in the western part of the region, where it is found in different, well-marke d races: *jerdoni* (Sumatra), endemic *borneensis* (Kalimantan) and Wallacean endemic *celebensis*. Only few recent records from Sumatra (M&V) and Sulawesi (Van den Berg & Bosman 1986; Rozendaal & Dekker 1989; K.D. Bishop, pers. comm.; Gibbs 1990.), more widely distributed in Kalimantan (H&B). In northern winter the Black Baza *Aviceda leuphotes* visits Sumatra in numbers (M&V) and occasionally reaches Java (van Balen 1984); this, however, is much less a forest species than Jerdon's and interspecific competition seems unlikely. Inconspicuous canopy feeder and consequently overlooked (K.D. Bishop pers. comm.)

Aviceda subcristata - Crested Baza **No immediate danger**

Widespread in the eastern part of the region, not overlapping with the previous species; occurring in five Wallacean endemic races: *timorlaoensis* (Lombok to Timor), *pallida* (Kei), *reinwardtii* (Seram, Ambon), *stresemanni* (Buru) and *rufa* (N. Moluccas). Recent records from Seram (Bowler & Taylor 1989; Andrews 1988; Halmaheira (1983-1992), K.D. Bishop, pers. comm.), Flores and Timor (Gibbs 1990; own obs. 1992).

Pernis ptilorhynchus - Oriental Honey-buzzard **No immediate danger**

Widespread resident in the western part of Indonesia, where the Sondaic endemic *torquatus* occurs on Sumatra and Kalimantan, and *ptilorhynchus* is endemic to Java. In the northern winter the migrant race *orientalis* is a common visitor to Sumatra, Kalimantan, Java and Bali, but only one recent record from Wallacea, in Timor in Jan 1990; (Gibbs 1990).

Pernis celebensis - Barred Honey-buzzard **No immediate danger**

The resident *celebensis* is widespread in Sulawesi and neighbouring islands of Muna and Peleng (a second race, *steerei* is resident in the Philippines). The species was insufficiently known to determine its status in Sulawesi (Meyburg 1986), but a survey in 1987 showed that, after this species was safely distinguished from the very similar Celebes Serpent-eagle, still fair numbers are present in Central Sulawesi, where it was recorded at seven localities between south of Lake Poso and Tinombo, 4-11 Aug 1987 (Kukila 1990; Meyburg & van Balen, this volume.); further recent records, e.g., from Lore Lindu (Gibbs 1990; Watling 1983), five probable records in Jul-Aug 1979 and in 1988 at Soroako in C (Holmes & Wood 1979; Andrews 1988), from Dumoga-Bone: one in Oct 1981, two in Jan 1983 (Rozendaal & Dekker 1989). Often, like other honey-buzzards, seen above open country and along forest edges and presumably secure in most of its range.

Macheiramphus alcinus - Bat Hawk **Insufficiently known**
Widespread but scarce resident in Sumatra, Kalimantan, and in 1981 discovered in Sulawesi (Klapste 1982; one unconfirmed record from the south coast of Java (van Lavieren, pers. comm.). Recent Kalimantan records from Tanjung Puting (Nash & Nash 1988) and Barito Ulu (Wilkinson *et al.* 1991); only recent record from Sumatra at Padang-Sugihan (Nash & Nash 1985). Harrison (in Smythies 1981) considers that the species decreased markedly, perhaps as a result of being hunted by bird cave owners in the 1930s. Though the species is not confined to the vicinity of limestone caves (e.g. P. Andrew, pers. comm.), this could still apply to-day, as raptors near commercial bird (and bat) caves are unscrupulously persecuted.

Elanus caeruleus - Black-shouldered Kite **No immediate danger**
Generally common and widespread in open country, benefits from forest clearance, race sumatranus endemic to Sumatra, *hypoleucus* in the other parts. Numbers in Java appear to have decreased, since only few recent records are available as compared with its former commonness.

Milvus migrans - Black Kite **No immediate danger**
The resident race *affinis* is uncommon and local in open country in Sulawesi, and scattered populations are found in the Lesser Sundas and Timor. Somewhat erratic distribution in Sulawesi where locally common, but has disappeared from former haunts (Kukila 1990). The migrant race *lineatus* is a scarce visitor to Sumatra and Borneo, and an unconfirmed record exists from Bali (Mason & Jarvis 1989).

Haliastur indus - Brahminy Kite **No immediate danger**
Widespread in coastal areas and along major rivers throughout Indonesia in two resident races: *girrenera* in the Moluccas, and *intermedius* in the rest of the area. Though still common and locally abundant in most of its range, the Javan population causes concern, as numbers have shrunk alarmingly since the early 1960s (van Balen *et al.* 1993).

Haliaeetus leucogaster - White-bellied Eagle **No immediate danger**
Widespread and common resident throughout the area.Largely restricted to nature reserves with coastal territories in Java, especially off-shore islands, but more widely occurring in the other areas.

Ichthyophaga humilis - Lesser Fish-eagle **No immediate danger**
Widespread but uncommon resident along forested coasts and rivers in Sumatra, Kalimantan and Sulawesi. Scattered records in Kalimantan (H&B); uncommon in Sumatra (M&V), with recent records, e.g. from Way Kambas (Southampton University Expedition) and Padang-Sugihan (Nash & Nash 1985); uncommon and very local, with few records in Sulawesi, e.g., two records Dumoga-Bone (Rozendaal & Dekker 1989); Lore Lindu (van den Berg & Bosman 1986; Andrews 1988; Gibbs 1990) S Sulawesi (Meyburg & van Balen, this volume) and in 1991 discovered on Taliabu (Sula Islands), the easternmost locality (UEA Expedition, in prep.).

Ichthyophaga ichthyaetus - Grey-headed Fish-eagle **No immediate danger**
Uncommon, but widespread in Sumatra, rare on Java; only few records from Kalimantan (H&B; Wilkinson *et al.* 1991) and only recently confirmed for Sulawesi (King *et al.* 1990).

Circaetus gallicus - Short-toed Eagle **No immediate danger**
Isolated population of cf. *heptneri* occurs widely in open country in the Lesser Sundas, with probable stragglers to Java (van Balen & Compost 1989), whereas migrant cf. *gallicus* is a visitor during raptor migration from Bali (Ash 1984). Recent records from Wallacea: Timor (Andrew 1985; Gibbs 1990), Flores (1992 pers. obs.; Bishop & Coates, in press), Lombok (1990, pers. obs.) and Sumba (Jones & Banjaransari 1990).

Spilornis cheela - Crested Serpent-eagle **No immediate danger**
Widespread and common in woodlands and forest edges in the western half of the Malay archipelago; *malayensis* occurs in north Sumatra, whilst in the other parts eight endemic island races are found: *pallidus* (Borneo), *natunensis* (Belitung), *sipora* (Mentawai), *batu* (south Sumatra,Batu), *asturinus* (Nias), *abbottii* (Simeulue), *bido* (Java, Bali) and *baweanus* (Bawean). Despite habitat destruction and heavy hunting pressure in Java it is still rather commonly seen; the status of most of the other endemics is uncertain.

Spilornis rufipectus - Sulawesi Serpent-eagle **No immediate danger**

Endemic to Sulawesi (*rufipectus*) and Sula islands (*sulaensis*),widespread and common in forests and open woodland. Numerous recent records throughout Sulawesi: at eight localities between 1-7 Aug 1987 throughout S and C Sulawesi (Meyburg & van Balen, this volume), five records in Jul-Aug 1979 at Soroako in C (Holmes & Wood 1979), common in Dumoga Bone (Rozendaal & Dekker 1989), Beteleme (C Sulawesi), Lore Lindu (Watling 1983; Gibbs 1990), Tangkoko (Andrews 1988), etc.; frequently encountered on Taliabu (Sula Islands; UEA 1991). The population is not in direct danger as the species is still widely distributed.

Circus assimilis - Spotted Harrier **No immediate danger**

Local and uncommon resident in open country in Sulawesi, but there are no breeding data (Kukila 1990); recent records from Timor (W&B; Andrews 1988) of presumable migrants from Australia, where it is widespread. In northern winter harriers in small numbers visit Sumatra and Kalimantan, and recently harriers have been recorded in Java as well (D. Watling 1990, pers. comm.). Hitherto the following species have been recorded: *C. aeruginosus, C. cyaneus* (N Borneo only), *C. spilonotus* and *C. melanoleucos*.

Accipiter trivirgatus - Crested Goshawk **No immediate danger**

Widespread in lowland and hill forests in the Greater Sundas; four endemic races: *trivirgatus* (Sumatra), *niasensis* (Nias),*javanicus* (Java) and *microstictus* (Borneo). The species is common throughout its range in suitable habitat; recently its occurrence on Bali was confirmed (van Balen 1991a).

Accipiter griseiceps - Sulawesi Goshawk **Interminate**

Endemic to Sulawesi, where it is widespread in most types of woodland. However, only few recent records are available: one in Jul 1979 at Soroako (Holmes & Wood 1979), two confirmed sightings in Lore Lindu (Watling 1983; Hornbuckle 1988) and two sightings in Aug 1987 (Meyburg & van Balen, this volume) in C Sulawesi, one mistnetted in Dumoga-Bone in Jan 1983 (Rozendaal & Dekker 1989), a pair in July 1985 near Mt Dua Saudara (Kukila 1990) and Tangkoko (Andrews 1988; Entwistle 1988) in N Sulawesi. Considered to be of indeterminate status (Meyburg 1986), but perhaps not in immediate danger, despite the few scattered records.

Accipiter trinotatus - Spot-tailed Goshawk **No immediate danger**

Endemic to Sulawesi, moderately common in suitable habitat in lowland forest and mangroves. Recent records throughout Sulawesi: commonest of four endemic Accipiters in Dumoga-Bone, frequently heard and seen, mistnetted on four occasions (Rozendaal & Dekker 1989): commoner than other Accipiters in Lore Lindu (Watling 1983), observed twice (van den Berg & Bosman 1986). Mentioned as being of indeterminate status (Meyburg 1986), but seems to be out of immediate danger.

Accipiter fasciatus - Brown Goshawk **No immediate danger**

Widespread in woodland and cultivation with scattered trees (W&B) throughout the Lesser Sundas and Moluccas; occurring in seven (Wallacean and single island) endemic races: *tjendanae* (Sumba), *wallacei* (Lombok to Flores), *stresemanni* (small islands south of Sulawesi),*hellmayri* (Alor, Roti, Timor), *savu* (Savu), *didimus* (Buru) and *fasciatus* (Timor). Recent records from Komodo (Madsen 1983), Sumba and Timor (Gibbs 1990), and Buru (P. Jepson pers. comm.).

Accipiter novaehollandiae - Variable Goshawk **No immediate danger**

Occurring in eight races, of which seven endemic to Wallacea: 1. *sylvestris* (Lesser Sundas), 2. *polionotus* (Banda, Tanimbar), 3. *albiventris* (Kai), 4. *obiensis* (Obi), 5. *griseogularis* (Bacan, Halmahera), 6. *mortyi* (Morotai), 7. *hiogaster* (Seram, Ambon), 8. *pallidiceps* (Buru). The species can be placed in three well-marked groups in Wallacea (W&B), sometimes lumped into two species (e.g. Weick 1980): *A. griseogularis* (group 4/5/6) and *A. novaehollandiae* (groups 1/2/3 and 7/8). Scattered records of the species throughout: Seram, occasional in the lowlands (Bowler & Taylor 1989; Andrews 1988), Komodo (pers. obs., 1992), Flores (Gibbs 1990); *griseogularis* as species was considered of indeterminate status, and recent records are available from Halmahera, where a number were collected by Taylor in 1980-1983 (W&B), and where it was not uncommon at Kali Batu Putih in Mar 1989 (Gibbs 1990), and Obi where four were collected by Taylor in 1982-1983 (W&B).

Accipiter henicogrammus - Moluccan (Gray's) Goshawk **Rare**

Wallacean endemic restricted to Halmahera, Bacan and Morotai, where it inhabits forests and forest edges.Uncommon and infrequently seen. Declining in areas of human disturbance (K.D. Bishop. pers. comm.) Recent records from Halmahera, where Taylor (in W&B) collected a number of birds and Gibbs (1990) and Bucket *et a1*. (1987) observed it in Sep 1990.

Accipiter virgatus - Besra **No immediate danger**

Widespread in the submontane forests of the Greater Sundas, where it occurs in four endemic races: *rufotibialis* (only found N Borneo). *vanbemmeli* (Sumatra), *virgatus* (Java, Bali) and *quinquefasciatus* (Flores). Widespread in Sumatra (M&V) and Java (M; own obs.), but no recent records in Wallacea, known from only one old specimen in Flores.

Accipiter nanus - Small Sparrowhawk **Endangered**

Endemic to Sulawesi in mountain forest.Records from Lore Lindu (Watling 1983; K.D. Bishop, pers.comm.) and two probable records of two birds in Dumoga-Bone in Apr 1985 (Rozendaal & Dekker 1989) are the only recent records. In the field the species is extremely difficult to tell with certainty from *A. rhodogaster*, from which it seems to be segregated by altitude. Of indeterminate status according to Meyburg (1986), and considered threatened by Collar & Andrew (1988), which seems to be appropriate in view of the scarcity of recent records, and possible confusion with the other hawk.

Accipiter erythrauchen - Rufous-necked Sparrowhawk **Rare**

Wallacean endemic in lowland forest, occurring in two races: *erythrauchen* (N. Moluccas) and *ceramensis* (Seram, Ambon, Buru).Recent records from Obi, where one specimen was collected by Taylor in 1980-1983 (W&B), Seram, where it is uncommon in submontane forest (Bowler & Taylor 1989), and Halmahera (Buck *et al.* 1987)

Accipiter rhodogaster - Vinous-breastedSparrowhawk **Insufficiently known**

Endemic to Sulawesi and the neighbouring islands in the east, where it is uncommon and sparsely distributed in forest, forest edges, mangroves, etc.; occurs in two races: *rhodogaster* in Sulawesi, and *sulaensis* on Peleng, Banggai and Sula. Only few recent records: probable record of a pair in Lore Lindu (Watling 1983), probable record of a pair in Dumoga-Bone in Jan 1983 (Rozendaal & Dekker 1989) and observed in Sept 1990 (Gibbs 1990); not uncommon in Tangkoko (Gibbs 1990); two definite records for Taliabu in Sep 1991 (UEA). This species is notoriously difficult to distinguish with certainty from the previous species in the field, therefore sight-records of both species should be treated with caution.

Accipiter meyerianus - Meyer's Goshawk **Indeterminate**

Occurring in lowland and hill forest. Only recent records from Seram, where it was uncommon in lowland forest (Bowler & Taylor 1989), but the species is widely but very sparsely distributed through New Guinea and eastward.

In northern winter large numbers of migrant Accipiters are found wintering or on passage in the archipelago.West of Wallace's Line *A. gularis* is dominant, *A. soloensis* is the most common migrant goshawk in the east (W&B), whereas *A. badius* and *A. nisus* seem to have their farthest winter quarters in Sumatra and N Borneo respectively (M & V; S).

Butastur liventer - Rufous-winged Buzzard **No immediate danger**

Only found in Java and Sulawesi in open wooded country. No recent records from Java, where it has always been scarce, but more widespread in small numbers throughout Sulawesi (W&B), with recent records from Dumoga-Bone (Escott & Holmes 1980), in N Lore Lindu (Watling 1983) in C, Rantepao-Palopo (A&H) and Enrekang (Meyburg & van Balen, this volume) in S. In the northern winter *Butastur indicus* and *Buteo buteo* visit the Greater Sundas in small numbers, and the first mentioned is also a common winter visitor to N Wallacea (W&B).

Ictinaetus malayensis - Black Eagle **No immediate danger**

Widespread and moderately common in the hill forests throughout the Greater Sundas, Sulawesi and N Moluccas. A fair number of records from Kalimantan, Sumatra, Java and Sulawesi; few records from the Moluccas, where it was found quite common in Seram (Bowler & Taylor 1989) and on Halmahera (Andrews 1988; Gibbs 1990.). Despite its size, sometimes naive behaviour and habit of roaming the forest edges in search of bird nests, hunting has not decreased numbers notably, even in the overpopulated island of Java.

Aquila gurneyi - Gurney's Eagle **Rare**

Little-known forest dweller, found on Halmahera and neighbouring islands. Only recent certain records are of two individuals seen in Manusela National Park, Seram, in Sep 1987 (Bowler & Taylor 1989), which is a new locality for the species; regularly observed on Hamahera (KD Bishop, pers.comm.; Buck *et al.* 1987; Gibbs 1990).

Hieraaetus fasciatus - Bonelli's Eagle **No immediate danger**

The Wallacean endemic race *renschii* is found in forests up to 2000m in the Lesser Sundas. Recent records from Timor (M&B) and Flores (Gibbs 1990; Verhoeye & King 1990). Vagrants of *H. morphnoides* from Australia and N Guinea are since recently known to visit Wallacea (King 1990).

Hieraaetus kienerii - Rufous-bellied Eagle **No immediate danger**

Scarce but widespread in the area. Reportedly rare in Sumatra (M&V), Borneo (S), Java (M) and Wallacea (W&B), which does not agree with the relatively high number of recent records throughout its range, and perhaps the species is much more common than previously thought. Probably migrant birds from the west increase the local resident populations, as they appear to do in Malaysia (Medway & Wells 1976), and as suggested by some birds in migrant raptor flocks above Bali Straits in Oct 1982 and 1990 (Ash 1984; pers. comm.). Migratory *H. pennatus* have been found on Bali in the northern winter (Ash 1984).

Spizaetus cirrhatus - Changeable Hawk-eagle **No immediate danger**

Widespread in the Greater Sundas, where *limnaaetus* occurs; endemic races *vanheurni* (Simeulue) and *floris* (Sumbawa, Flores). Occurs in two different morphs, widespread throughout forest edges, riverine forest and wooded cultivated areas, apparently not in the forest interior; in Java the species became very scarce outside protected areas.

Spizaetus bartelsi - Javan Hawk-eagle **Endangered**

Javan endemic in primary lowland and hill forest considered globally endangered (Collar & Andrew 1988). Recent surveys pointed out a wider distribution than was previously presumed (Thiollay & Meyburg 1987; Meyburg *et al.* 1989; van Balen 1991b), but the continuing destruction of lowland and hill forest, aggravated by hunting pressure, still puts the species' survival in jeopardy. The present situation of the species is discussed in Van Balen & Meyburg (this volume)

Spizaetus lanceolatus - Sulawesi Hawk **No immediate danger**

Endemic to Sulawesi and Sula Islands, occurring in lowland and mountain forests. A fair number of records throughout Sulawesi: Dumoga-Bone, common (Rozendaal & Dekker 1989); Lore Lindu, probably quite common (Watling 1983; van den Berg & Bosman 1986; Andrews 1988; Gibbs 1990); Tangkoko (Andrews 1988; Gibbs 1990); eleven sightings of adults and immatures during 31 Jul-18 Aug 1987 through S to N Sulawesi (Meyburg & van Balen, this volume); some probable sightings of juvenile birds from Taliabu (UEA). See *Pernis celebensis*. Globally near-threatened (Collar & Andrew 1988) which cannot hold with regard to the number of recent records.

Spizaetus alboniger - Blyth's Hawk-eagle **Indeterminate**

Sondaic endemic occurring mainly in the submontane areas; in Java it is replaced by the allospecies *S. bartelsi*. Recent records of single adults from Riam Kanan? in Aug 1984 (H&B) and Barito Ulu (Wilkinson *et al.* 1991) in S Kalimantan; one bird at the Kutai National Park in Aug 1990 and heard near Long Alango in Feb 1992 (own obs.) in E Kalimantan. No certain recent records from Sumatra, but adults seen in 1974-1985 near Ketambe, Tapanuli, Mt Sibayak, Mt Kerinci and Siberut most likely refer to this species (M&V). Listed as of indeterminate status, but perhaps relatively secure in its (sub) montane forest habitat.

Spizaetus nanus - Wallace's Hawk-eagle **Vulnerable**

Sondaic endemic, occurring in Borneo and Sumatra, where it replaces the previous species in the lowlands; *stresemanni* endemic to Nias Island. Only very few recent records: sight records from Alas Valley, Mt Kerinci, Way Kambas and Siberut need to be confirmed with regard to its resemblance to *S. alboniger* in certain plumage stages (M&V); a subadult seen in Oct 1989 near

Ipuh (Bengkulu) at *ca.* 200m (own obs.)Only recent Kalimantan records from the Kutai National Park, where a pair was regularly seen in Jul/Aug 1990, and two birds in trees along the Samarinda-Bontang road on 27 Jul 1990 (H. Kalisch, J. Meiss & SvB).Because of the ongoing deterioration of its lowland forest habitat and low population densities listed as threatened by Collar & Andrew (1988),but here considered vulnerable, which seems most appropriate with regard to the confusion with other species and in anticipation of more accurate data becoming available on its distribution and status.

Microhierax fringillarius - Black-thighed Falconet **No immediate danger**
Widespread and not uncommon in Sumatra, Kalimantan, Java and Bali in forest edge and open country. The species is absent from many apparently suitable habitats, such as the Kayan Mentarang nature reserve in E Kalimantan, where none was seen during three weeks in Feb 1992 (own obs.) and Tanjung Puting, where only one single bird was observed (Nash & Nash 1988).

Falco moluccensis - Spotted Kestrel **No immediate danger**
Indonesian endemic, widespread in the mid- and eastern half of the archipelago; up to five races described: *moluccensis* (Moluccas), *timorensis* (Timor, Tanimbar), *microbalia* (Lesser Sundas, Sulawesi), *renschii* Sumba) and *javensis* (Java, Bali), but often only the first and third recognised. Recent records of all races are available. In southern and northern winter the migrant allospecies *F. cenchroides* and *F. tinnunculus* are occasional visitors to the eastern half of the archipelago and N Borneo respectively.

Falco severus - Oriental Hobby **No immediate danger**
Extremely rare in Borneo, still to be confirmed in Sumatra, but more common in Java, Sulawesi and part of the Moluccas. Perhaps more widespread than the scarce records suggest, especially in Sulawesi. The following recent records are available: Baluran, Gede/Pangrango (SvB), Krakatau (Zann *et al.* 1990) and Ujung Kulon (Smiet, van Strien & Rijksen, pers. comm.) in Java; Mangkutana, Taripa, Lore Lindu and Malino (Andrews 1988; van den Berg & Bosman 1986; Meyburg & van Balen, this volume) in Sulawesi; Seram (Bowler & Taylor 1989), which confirms an old doubtful record, in the Moluccas. In southern and northern winter the migrant allospecies *F. longipennis* and *F. subbuteo* are rare visitors in Wallacea and Java respectively.

Falco peregrinus - Peregrine Falcon **No immediate danger**
The race *ernesti* is a scarce resident throughout Indonesia, nesting on volcanos and steep cliffs. The N Asian races *calidus* and *japonicus* are winter visitors in small numbers, the latter only found hitherto on Kalimantan, the former more widespread.

DISCUSSION

In the previous sections it was shown that, whilst for a few species the status appears to be less a matter of concern than was thought (e.g.,*Spilornis rufipectus Spizaetus lanceolatus*), others, especially in Java, seem to have declined at least locally. These, interestingly, belong to species of open country and cultivation, which is far from threatened habitat. Whether pesticides, excessive hunting or habitat destruction through the removal of nest trees are the cause for the local decline of *Milvus migrans, Elanus caeruleus, Haliastur indus* and *Spizaetus cirrshatus* remains to be studied. It offers a haunting prospect of the future for the other islands where development proceeds at an increasing rate. The local persecution of bat predating raptors may in particular affect Bat Hawks and to a less extent Peregrine Falcons and sparrowhawks, often found in the neighbourhood of caves (Mees 1950; own obs.). In this respect it is encouraging that since December 1991 the Indonesian Government announced a country-wide ban on air rifles. More surveys are needed in remote areas, especially in the eastern part of the archipelago, where many little known hawks occur, perhaps widespread and secure as species but with threatened local races, whose taxonomic status is often still to be studied. A good example is the Variable Goshawk, not threatened as a species, but with a local race *griseogularis*, Grey-throated Goshawk, with a very restricted distribution.Examples of former races, now considered to be full species, threatened with extinction are *Spizaetis bartelsi* and *Spilornis kinabaluensis*. In recent years a considerable number of surveys have been carried out to little-visited areas. Many of these were or are being organised by English universities (University of E Anglia; Manchester Polytechnic; Southampton, etc.), local universities (outstanding are the National University, University of Indonesia, Gajahmada and Padjadjaran University). Furthermore a survey is currently being carried out under supervision of the WWGBP by the author on the Javan Hawk Eagle, and the ICBP is planning and coordinating surveys to the Moluccas, which will provide valuable new information. In addition to these surveys, field studies are needed in order to assess the adaptability of the forest raptors to the changing conditions of their habitat and to identify which species are exclusively dependent on virgin forest. The identification of a number of raptors causes serious problems. However, no regional field guides handling this adequately as yet exist, despite a major increase of books on Indonesian birds published during the past few years. It is therefore hoped that the forthcoming raptor identification guide by Ferguson-Lees *et al.* will serve serious ornithologists as well as the guide for shorebirds in the same series did and will be an impetus for collecting reliable data on the little-known birds of prey.

CONCLUDING REMARKS

Eleven species of raptor discussed in this paper deserve special attention, as their status causes more or less concern. The availability of more rcent data allows a re-assessment of the conservation status of species treated by Meyburg (1986) and Collar & Andrew (1988). The number insufficiently known to determine to which category they belong has decreased considerably. Birds of endangered, vulnerable, rare and indeterminate (i.e. uncertain which of the former three categories) status include eight species. Only *Spizaetus bartelsi* is considered to be in immediate danger, having regard to the serious situation on Java. All eleven species badly need detailed field studies.

ACKNOWLEDGEMENTS

I would like to express my thanks to the organisers of the conference for financial support to attend the meeting in Berlin. To Paul Andrew, David Bishop and Derek Holmes for critically reviewing the first draft of the manuscript. To the Indonesian Government (represented by LIPI and PHPA) for permitting me to conduct the field surveys.

REFERENCES

ANDREW, P. 1985. Observations on the birds of Kupang Bay, West Timor. Report 2. Unpublished report.

ANDREW, P.1992. *Checklist of the birds of Indonesia.* Kukila.

ANDREWS, T. 1988. Birding in Indonesia. Unpublished MS.

ASH, J.S. 1990. Bird observations on Bali. *Bull. Brit. Orn. Cl.* 104: 24-35.

BALEN, S. van. 1984. Sight records of the Black Baza *Aviceda leuphotes* on Java.*Ardea* 72:234.

BALEN, S. van. 1991a. Faunistic notes from Bali. *Kukila* 5: 125-132.

BALEN, S. van. 1991b. The Java Hawk Eagle *Spizaetus bartelsi* WWGBP Project Report No. 1, March 1990. *Birds of Prey Bull.* 4: 33-40.

BALEN, S. van & A. COMPOST 1989. Overlooked evidence of the Short-toed Eagle *Circaetus gallicus* on Java. *Kukila* 4: 44-46.

BALEN, S. van, I.S. SUWELO, D.S. HADI, D. SOEPOMO, R. MARLON & MUTIARINA 1993. The decline of the Brahminy Kite *Haliastur indus* in Java. *Forktail.* 8: 83-88.

BERG, A.B. van den, & C.A.W. BOSMAN 1986. Supplementary notes on some birds of Lore Lindu Reserve, Central Sulawesi. *Forktail* 1: 7-13

BISHOP, K.D. & B.J. COATES (in press) *Guide to the Birds of Wallacea.*

BOWLER, J. & J. TAYLOR 1989. An annotated Checklist of the birds of Manusela National Park, Seram. (Birds recorded on the Operation Raleigh Expedition). *Kukila* 4: 3-29.

BROWN, L., K. CURRY-LINDAHL, W. KING & A. KEMP 1987. *List of threatened raptor species.* Unpublished MS.

BUCK *et al.* 1987. Birds recorded in Wallacea 19.7.87-22.8.87. Unpublished report.

COLLAR, N.J. & P. ANDREW 1988. Birds to warch. The ICBP World check-list of threatened birds. *ICBP Techn. Publ. 8.*

ENTWISTLE, M. 1988. *Eastern provinces of Indonesia.* Unpublished report.

ESCOTT, C.J. & D.A. HOLMES 1980. The avifauna of Sulawesi, Indonesia: faunistic notes and additions. *Bull. Brit. Orn. Cl.* 100: 189-194

EVE, R. & A.M. GUIGE 1989. Survey of the Mahakam river delta, East Kalimantan. With special reference to its waterbird s. *AWB Publication* 45, Kuala Lumpur.
GIBBS, D. 1990. *Wallacea: A site guide for birdwatchers.* D. Gibbs.
HOLMES, D.A. & K. BURTON 1987. Recent notes on the avifauna of Kalimantan. *Kukila* 3: 2-32.
HOLMES, P. & H. WOOD 1979. Report of the ornithological expedition to Sulawesi, 1979. MS.
HORNBUCKLE, J. 1990. *Birding in Indonesia.* Unpublished report.
JONES, M. & H. BANJARANSARI 1990. *The ecology and conservation of the birds of Sumba and Buru.* Unpublished report.
KING, B. 1990. Little Eagle *Hieraaetus morphnoides* on Halmahera. *Kukila* 5: 77.
KING, B., H. BUCK & D. YONG 1990. Grey-headed Fish-eagle *Ichthyophaga ichthyaetus* sighting on Sulawesi. *Kukila* 5: 75.
KING, W.B. 1978, 1979. *Red Data Book, Vols I & II - Aves.* IUCN, Morges.
KLAPSTE, J. 1982. Bat Hawk on Celebes. *Dutch Birding.* 4: 29-30.
KUKILA 1990. Sulawesi Bird Report. *Kukila* 5: 4-28.
MACKINNON, J. 1988. *Field Guide to the Birds of Java and Bali.* Gajah Mada University Press.
MADSEN, J.J. 1983. *Thailand, Burma, Malaysia, Indonesia.* Unpublished report.
MARLE, J.G. van, & K.H. VOOUS 1988. The Birds of Sumatra. *B.O.U. Check-list* 10.
MASON, V. & F. JARVIS 1989. *Birds of Bali.* Periplus, Berkeley-Singapore.
MEDWAY, LORD, & D.R. WELLS 1976. *The Birds of the Malay Peninsula.* Vol V. Witherby & Penerbit Universiti, Malaya.
MEES, G.F. 1950. Waarnemingen over het vangen van vleermuizen door roofvogels op West-Java. *Ardea* 37: 173-177.
MEYBURG, B.-U. 1986. Threatened and near-threatened diurnal birds of prey of the world. *Birds of Prey Bull* 3 : 1-12.
MEYBURG, B.-U. & S. van BALEN. Raptors on Sulawesi (Indonesia): the influence of rain forest destruction and human density on their populations. This volume.
MEYBURG, B.-U., S. van BALEN, J.-M. THIOLLAY & R.D. CHANCELLOR 1989. Observations on the endangered Java Hawk Eagle *Spizaetus bartelsi.* In Meyburg and Chancellor (eds.): *Raptors in the Modern World*, pp 279-300, Berlin.
NASH, S.V. & A.D. NASH 1985. A Checklist of the forest and forest edge birds of the Padang-Sugihan Wildlife reserve, South Sumatra. *Kukila* 2: 51-59.
NASH, S.V. & A.D. NASH 1988. An annotated checklist of the birds of Tanjung Puting National Park, Central Kalimantan. *Kukila* 3: 93-116.
ROZENDAAL, F.G. & R.W.R.J. DEKKER 1989. Annotated checklist of the birds of the Dumoga-Bone National Park, North Sulawesi. *Kukila* 4: 85-109.
SMYTHIES, B.E. 1981. *The Birds of Borneo.* 3rd Edition. The Sabah Society with the Malayan Nature Society., Kuala Lumpur.
SOUTHAMPTON UNIVERSITY: The Southampton University Expedition to Way Kambas National Park, Lampung Province, Sumatra 1988-1989. Preliminary final Report.
THIOLLAY, J.-M. & B.-U. MEYBURG 1988. Forest fragmentation and the conservation of raptors: a survey on the island of Java. *Biol. Cons.* 44: 229-250.
UNIVERSITY OF EAST ANGLIA. Taliabu Expedition 1991. Preliminary report.
VERHOEYE, J. & B. KING 1990. Notes on three raptor species new to Flores. *Kukila* 5: 65-68.
WATLING, D. 1983. Ornithological notes from Sulawesi. *Emu* 83: 247-261.
WEICK, F. 1980. *Birds of Prey of the World.* Parey, Hamburg, Berlin.
WHITE, C.M.N. & M.D.BRUCE.1986. *The birds of Wallacea.* B.O.U. Check-list 7.
WILKINSON, R., G. DUTSON, B. SHELDON, DARJONO & Y.R. NOOR 1991. The avifauna of the Barito Ulu region, Central Kalimantan. *Kukila* 5: 99-116.
ZANN, R.A., E.B. MALE & DARJONO 1990. Bird colonisation of Anak Krakatau, an emergent volcanic island. *Phil. Trans. R. Soc. Lond.* B 328: 95-121.

Drs. S. van Balen
P.O. Box 47
Bogor 16001
Indonesia

Meyburg, B.-U. & R. D. Chancellor eds.1994
Raptor Conservation Today
WWGBP / The Pica Press

The Ecology of the Madagascar Buzzard *Buteo brachypterus*

Jim Berkelman

The ecology of the Madagascar Buzzard *Buteo brachypterus* was studied from August to December, 1991 in the rainforest of north-eastern Madagascar. It is a medium-sized buzzard with a mottled brown back and white undersides with dark streaking. It is endemic to Madagascar and is common in both wooded and open habitat throughout the island.

The study site was established by the Peregrine Fund of Boise, Idaho, USA on the Masoala Peninsula, which holds the only remaining lowland rainforest in Madagascar. It is currently unprotected, but an area of about 300,000km^2 has been proposed for a national park. It is the wettest place on the island with annual rainfall exceeding 4,000mm. Most of the peninsula is mountainous terrain with elevations from sea level up to 1200m. The coast is a patchwortk of cleared land and secondary growth, and the interior is undisturbed rainforest with very little human activity.

Data were taken on three main aspects of the ecology of the Madagascar Buzzard: nest site characteristics, breeding biology and diet. Nest site characteristics included descriptive and quantitative measurements of the nests, nest trees, and the vegetation surrounding the nest. Breeding biology included behaviours at the nest; dates of egg laying, hatching and fledging; and nesting success. Dietary information was obtained from observations of prey deliveries at the nests.

Nine nests were located by imitating the call of the buzzard and walking in the direction of a response when a response was heard. Elevations ranged from 90m up to 520m (mean = 235m). The three lowest nest sites were at the edge of slash-burn clearings and the others were all in primary forest. Ground slopes at the nest trees ranged from 26° to 51° (mean = 37°). All of the nest sites were on slopes that faced either north, north-west, or west. Reasons for this pattern were unclear as there were no obvious differences in vegetation among slopes facing in different directions.

Nest and nest tree heights were estimated with a clinometer. Nest heights ranged from 14.1 to 20.1m (mean = 18.0m). Nest tree heights ranged from 16.6 to 36.3m (mean = 23.8m). All nine of the nest trees were different species. The nest was at a fork at the top of the main trunk in seven of the nest trees, on a fork in the canopy in one nest tree, and on an epiphyte on the main trunk in one nest tree. The buzzards apparently construct their nests at a fairly specific height and position in the tree, but do not select trees of a specific size or species.

Only one nest was found prior to egg laying and observed for the entire nesting season. An incubation period of 37 days and a nestling period of 48 days were found for that nest and used to estimate laying and hatching dates for the nests found later in the season. Egg laying occurred in late September to early October, hatching in late October to early November, and fledging in mid-to late December. The young fledged in only three of the eight nests observed. One nest fell out of the tree but the cause of the other four nest failures was not determined. Two eggs, of which one never hatched, were found in one of the nests, but clutch size was not determined for the other nests.

Nest attendance by the female decreased from the incubation period (84.7% of observation time) to the early nestling period (52.8%) to the late nestling period (11.5%). The female spent more time at the nest early and late in the day than in the middle of the day at all three periods of the nesting season. The number of prey deliveries per hour was greatest in the middle of the day and least early and late in the day. These results suggest that the adults spend more time hunting in the middle of the day and attending the nest early and late in the day.

A total of 110 prey deliveries were identified. There were 34 birds (31%), 33 lizards (30%), 13 snakes (12%), 11 frogs (10%), 9 chameleons (8%), 4 rats (4%), 3 crabs (3%) and 3 insects (3%). There were also 71 unidentified prey deliveries. Most of the unidentified prey were too small to identify, so arthropods may make up a larger portion of the diet than the data suggest. There was a diurnal pattern in the two most frequent prey items: 71% of the birds were brought to the nest before 1200 and 88% of the lizards were brought to the nest after 1100. If birds are more easily found in the morning and lizards in the afternoon, the buzzard may be switching its prey preference over the course of the day to take advantage of the most abundant prey.

Another field season will be spent studying the Madagascar Buzzard from September 1992 to January 1993. More data on breeding biology and diet will be gathered, and radio-telemetry will be used to study home range size and habitat use. Based on the number seen, the buzzard appears to be thriving both in undisturbed rainforest and in degraded habitats. It would be interesting to look at differences in the buzzard's ecology in different parts of Madagascar, but that is beyond the scope of this study.

Jim Berkelmann
Biology Dept.
Boise State University
Boise, ID 83725
U. S. A.

Meyburg, B.-U. & R. D. Chancellor eds.1994
Raptor Conservation Today
WWGBP / The Pica Press

The Maya Project: Use of Raptors as Tools for Conservation and Ecological Monitoring of Biological Diversity

William A. Burnham,
David F Whitacre & J. Peter Jenny

INTRODUCTION

The Peregrine Fund, founded by Professor Tom J. Cade, is known for its success in restoring the Peregrine Falcon (*Falco peregrinus*) throughout much of the United States. In addition, since the mid-1970s we have cooperated on projects involving more than 40 raptor species in 35 countries. Many factors affect the distribution and abundance of raptors, but increasingly the predominant factor is habitat alteration resulting from humanity's rapidly increasing populations and need for fuel, fibre, food, and minerals. Survival of most species will depend on their abilities to adapt to and persist in highly modified environments, or on mankind's capacity to establish and maintain protected areas of sufficient size and quality to preserve self-sustaining populations. We have found some raptor species to be highly adaptable, but others, such as specialized forest-dwelling eagles, hawk-eagles, and falcons, may not be.

One hundred and eleven of the approximately 296 species of diurnal raptors live in rainforests, and of those, 41 species are listed as threatened in the Red Data Book of the International Council for Bird Preservation while the status of many more is unknown (Thiollay 1990). These facts alone justify actions to preserve this taxon as a significant and disappearing element of the world's biodiversity.

Birds of prey can be effective tools for conservation for several reasons. First, large raptors occur at population densities lower than those of most other tropical forest organisms (Thiollay 1989). Using their spatial requirements for population viability as a yardstick for estimating minimum sizes for effective nature reserves is a first step in providing for whole system viability (Soule & Simberloff 1986).

To conserve raptors and their habitats we must understand their life cycles, their habitat requirements, and the environments in which they live. The research required to gain this knowledge is challenging, and presents opportunities for training of conservationists, students, and resource professionals. Raptor conservation also provides a focus for organizations in developing countries that produce many conservation benefits and assist in building organizational infrastructure.

Apart from these fortuitous benefits of studying and conserving raptors, it may turn out that conservation of this group of organisms is particularly critical to the long-term maintenance of biotic diversity, especially in reserves that are - or will become - habitat islands. For example, there is increasing evidence that vertebrate predators, through their effects on populations of seed consumers and dispersers, may affect seedling establishment patterns, and hence future tree species coemption of the forest (Janzen 1978; Green 1988; Terborgh 1988; Soule & Kohn 1989). If such regulatory roles prove common, maintenance of full complements of raptors and other predators in nature reserves may be an essential ingredient for reserve management schemes. Indeed, presence of intact predator communities is a measurement of the adequacy of conservation efforts, but a disturbing number of nature reserves worldwide fall short of this mark. As D. Janzen (1988) has pointed out, ecological interactions tend to disappear before species. Maintaining complete predator communities in reserves should go a long way toward keeping natural interactions throughout the system.

Finally, raptors are popular, charismatic organisms representing our natural world, and several have become significant "flagships" for conservation, e.g. Peregrine Falcon, Bald Eagle (*Haliaeetus leucocepha.lus*), Philippine Eagle (*Pithecophaga jefferyl*), etc. Being sensitive to environmental contamination and change in quality and quantity of habitat, they are functional indices of environmental health (Peakall & Kiff 1988; Newton 1979; Leck 1979). In addition, the kinds and density of raptor species in a given locality can reflect overall species richness and diversity in that area (Terborgh & Winter 1980; Olendorff *et al.* 1989).

In 1989 and 1990 the governments of Mexico and Guatemala established the Calakmul Biosphere Reserve (723,000 ha) and Maya Biosphere Reserve (1,700,00 ha), respectively (Fig.1).

Figure. 1

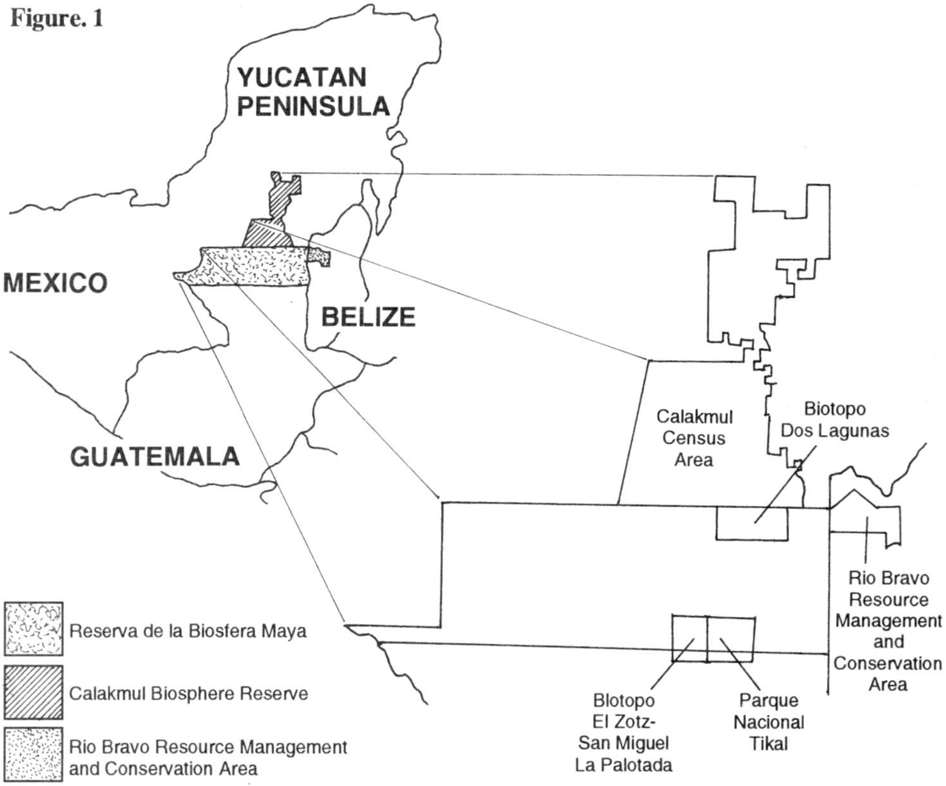

Additionally, Programme for Belize and cooperators established the 102,000 ha Rio Bravo Resource Management and Conservation Area. These adjacent reserves represent the largest protected contiguous lowland tropical forest area in Mesoamerica. Approximately 420 avian species have been identified in the Guatemala portion alone, of which 87 are migrants (Beavers 1991). This is an especially important wintering location for North American migrant passerines. Fifty-three species of raptors occur in the area (42 diurnal and 11 owl species).

In 1987 W. Burnham and P. Jenny selected the combined areas as a focus for the Maya Project, a long-term conservation and community level research programme providing training and education for

Latin Americans while focusing on tropical forest birds of prey. The endeavour is in cooperation with the Comision Nacional del Medio Ambiente, Guatemala; Consejo Nacional de Areas Protegidas, Guatemala; Instituto de Antropología e Historia, Guatemala; Centro de Estudios Conservacionistas, Universidad de San Carlos, Guatemala; Fundacion "Mario Dary Rivera", Guatemala; Guatemala Audubon Society, Guatemala; Secretaria de Desarollo Urbano y Ecologia, Mexico; PRONATURA, Mexico; Ministry of Forestry, Belize; Programme for Belize, Belize; Belize Audubon Society, Belize; and those other organisations listed in this paper.

METHODS

The Maya Project is a highly focused yet multi-faceted conservation approach which employs raptors in an umbrella of protection and as instruments for understanding the environment (Fig.2). The approach is rooted in partnerships with local organisations with crowning goals of (a) conserving biological diversity, (b) building local capacity for conservation, and (c) answering significant scientific questions. Research activities fall into two categories: (1) single species studies, conducted in such a way that community-level questions can ultimately be addressed, and (2) baseline inventory and monitoring efforts.

Figure 2.

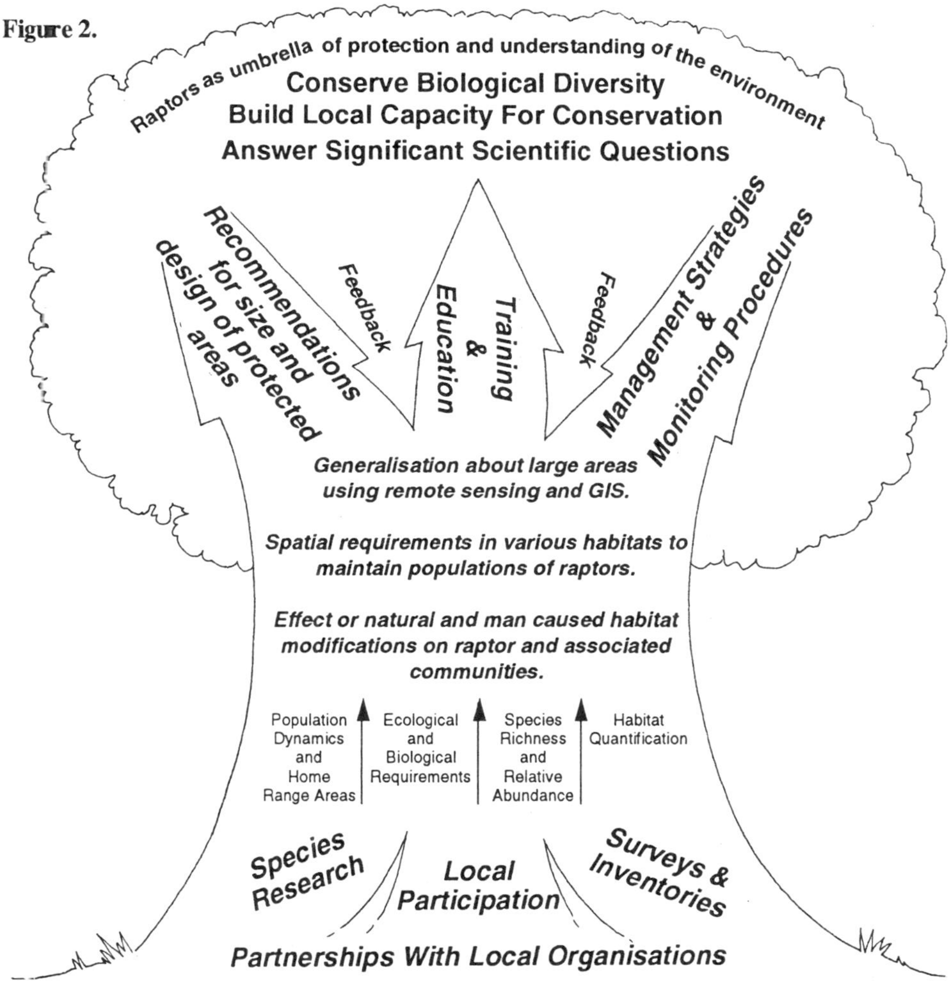

Training and Education

The Maya Project uses the process of conducting research as a vehicle for training and education. Local people with limited formal education but with considerable experience in the forest are being trained in techniques for studying and monitoring forests and wildlife while they participate in data collection, and - in some cases - project design and data analysis and interpretation. Additionally, through scholarships and other education opportunities, students who are willing to pursue resource management careers are enrolled in formal degree programmes at secondary school and university levels. Collaborating organizations receive the benefit not only of more experienced staff, but of field equipment, funding , and a better-informed local constituency.

Species-level Research

Species-level research focuses on population dynamics and ecological requirements such as prey preference, home range area, and population density of selected raptor species. Single-species research is both short-term (two to five years) and long-term (more than five years). These studies provide the detailed biological knowledge that is needed for future management efforts and aids in interpreting data from censusing and monitoring.

Many of the species we are studying have received little or no research attention in the past, and hence much of what we learn is completely new. Information from telemetry studies of density and home range provides estimates of habitat area required for sustainable populations and hence reserve size. A key feature of the single-species studies is that they are accomplished with sufficient standardization of method so that they can eventually be melded to yield a community-level approach.

Inventory and Monitoring

An important goal of the project is to establish a long-term ecological monitoring programme within the Greater Maya Biosphere Reserve Ecosystem (including Calakmul Biosphere Reserve and other portions of the southern Yucatan Peninsula, Belize, and Peten). This part of the project uses repeated censusing of permanent 1km² plots and of certain species groups to reveal possible ecological changes over time and to provide baseline comparisons between communities in different natural and modified habitats.

Habitats which are being or will be compared are various primary forest types along a topographic moisture and drainage gradient, as well as forests subjected to various human uses: selective logging of mahogany (*Swietenia macrophylla*) and cedar (*Cedrela mexicana*), extraction of xate palm (*Chamaedorea* spp.), removal of ramon (*Brosimum alicastrum*), foliage for livestock forage, collection of chicle (*Achras zapote*) sap and allspice (*Pimienta dioica*), fruits, removal of Sabal palm leaves (*Ayabal morrisiana*) for thatch, and conversion of forest to a mosaic of successional stages by slash and burn agriculture. Habitat descriptions have utilized 24 to 31 variables, mostly indicating vegetation structure and floristic and topographic information.

This segment of the project includes refinement and comparison of census techniques described by Turley (1989) and evaluated by Whitacre and Turley (1990), and refined by Whitacre (1991). While censusing efforts centre around raptors, several other bird groups and some mammals have been progressively incorporated into census protocols: tinamous, cracids, doves, psittacines, large woodpeckers, certain passerines, and primates. Our goal is to include species that are readily detected and identified and are likely to provide useful conservation information. For example, parrots and cracids are subject to direct human exploitation, while large woodpeckers may well prove sensitive to logging history.

RESULTS

Training and Education

Over 80 Latin Americans (8, 1988; 11, 1989: 29, 1990; 31, 1991; 35, 1992) have received training to date (Whitacre & Burnham 1991). Six are completing their fifth year with the project and manage survey teams and species investigations, and participate in the training of new personnel. Guatemalans are now project leaders for nine investigations. Cooperating organizations and individuals have received equipment (binoculars, books, projectors, motorcycles, etc.) and financial support. We provided four scholarships for bachelor of science degree candidates in biology at the University of San Carlos, Guatemala, through the Fundacion Juan Mario Dary. Additionally, scholarships for completion of high school degrees exist for some local Guatemalans participating in the field programme. Five master of science students from Boise State University have participated in the project and received support, and volunteers from the United States, Mexico, Guatemala, and Costa Rica have gained experience as part of the field programme.

Species-Level Studies

A number of very poorly-known raptor species are receiving detailed attention for the first time as part of the Maya project. For example, the nests, eggs and young of the Black-and-white Owl (*Ciccaba nigrolineata*), Barred Forest-Falcon (*Micrastur ruficollis*), and Gray-headed Kite (*Leptodon cayanensis*) have been described for the first time. Long-term population dynamics studies are underway on the Barred Forest-Falcon, Ornate Hawk-Eagle (*Spizaetus ornatus*), and Mottled Owl (*C.virgata*). In addition, investigations are being conducted on the Collared Forest-Falcon (*M.semitorquatus*), Black-and-white Owl, American Swallow-tailed Kite (*Elanoides forficatus*), Plumbeous Kite (*Ictinia plumbea*), Laughing Falcon (*Herpetotheres cachinnans*), Orange-breasted Falcon (*F.rufigularis*), White Hawk (*Leucopternis albicollis*), Bicolored Hawk (*Accipiter bicolor*), Black Hawk-Eagle (*Spizaetus tyrannus*), Hook-billed Kite (*Chondroheirax uncinatus*), and Great Black Hawk (*Buteogallus urubitinga*). Incidental information is being collected on other raptor species including the Crane Hawk (*Geranospiza caerulescens*), Gray-headed Kite, Bat Falcon (*Falco deiroleucus*), and Roadside Hawk (*Buteo magnirostris*).

Information on density and home range area, which is particularly valuable for conservation and management efforts, is being collected by the project. The Barred Forest-Falcon has proved to be the most common diurnal raptor in Parque Nacional Tikal. Home range size for breeding Barred Forest-Falcon females was 67 ha (n=3) and 106 ha (n=7) for males (Thorstrom 1990) (all results given utilize the minimum convex polygon method). Among Tikal's raptors, only the Mottled Owl has a higher raptor breeding density, i.e. 15 adults in a 2km² area average home range for males of 24.0 ha (n=4) (Gerhardt & Gerhardt 1990). The largest raptor currently being studied is the Ornate Hawk-Eagle, and in 1990 two females had home ranges of 977 ha and 1,315 ha at 95 days and 45 days respectively, after their young fledged. Additional adult females and males are now being radio-tracked, providing further home-range data. Six young Ornate Hawk-Eagles have been under study via telemetry; these have remained reliant on the adult male for food for over a year. Two yearling birds currently being monitored via telemetry will hopefully reveal much about the interval during which these birds leave to hunt for themselves and achieve full independence (Flatten *et al.* 1990 and Madrid *et al.* 1991). Home range studies continue on these species, as well as on the Collared Forest-Falcon, Laughing Falcon, Bicolored Hawk, and White Hawk.

One type of autecological study is especially germane to conservation questions: studies examining the ecology of a species in both pristine and human-altered habitats. A study currently underway compares the ecology of the Laughing Falcon, a reptile specialist, in primary forest and in slash-and-burn successional mosaic. Results indicate differences in home-range size and diet (Parker 1991).

Bat Falcons bred at the World Centre for Birds of Prey, Boise, Idaho, were released (1989-1990) on Guatemala's Pacific versant by the Fundacion Interamericana de Investigacion Tropical (Vannini 1989 & 1990). These releases serve to test reintroduction procedures and also establish individuals where the species has not been reported breeding for almost twenty years.

Inventory and Monitoring

Evaluation and modification of census methodology continues, and substantial improvements were achieved during the 1991 field season (February - August). We are developing a set of standardized census and habitat description methods which will be highly replicable and practical for use in tropical forests elsewhere. Emphasis is on simple efficient techniques to facilitate use by local personnel with limited equipment or technical training.

Comparison of four raptor census methods has proven point counts from canopy emergent trees to be the most effective method for the bulk of diurnal raptors in closed-canopy forest. An hour of pre-dawn listening reveals the presence of owls and forest-falcons, while two or three problematic species are best revealed by acoustical luring using prey distress calls. Our standardized census protocol combines these three types of censuses at each 1km² census plot. In primary forest, road-based censuses were found to have very limited utility and are not recommended (Whitacre & Turley 1990; Whitacre 1991).

Permanent census plots have been established in the Calakmul Biosphere Reserve, Mexico (10 plots); Rio Bravo Resource Management and Conservation Area, Belize (4); Parque Nacional Tikal, Guatemala, and nearby highly modified-forest areas (24); Biotopo El Zotz-San Miguel La Palotada, Guatemala (10); Biotopo Dos Lagunas, Guatemala (10) (Fig.1). Each plot has been the focus of a quantitative vegetation description and has been censused one to five times annually. The number of plots established and faunal species censused has increased annually.

Principal components analysis ranked primary forest stands at Tikal along a gradient from tall, closed-canopy forest with large vines and little ground cover, to lower forest with more open canopy, many small vines and saplings, and much ground cover, often grasses and sedges. This axis mirrors a topographic moisture and drainage gradient which is probably the predominant influence on Tikal's vegetation; tall, closed, floristically complex forest occupies well-drained terrain, while a lower forest with different tree species composition occupies low, seasonally-flooded sites (*bajos*) (Whitacre *et al.* 1990).

Preliminary results correlate presence of certain raptor species and habitat features. Habitat variables that most often were significantly correlated with abundance of particular raptors were those indicating the forest's position on the gradient from tall, closed-canopy to short, open forest described above (Whitacre *et al.*)

Results to date clearly indicate the value of our census approach for comparing and monitoring the fauna of various habitats and land use categories. Species that occur in greater numbers in human-altered than in pristine forest habitats include the Black-shouldered Kite (*Elanus caeruleus*), Gray Hawk (*Buteo nitidus*), Black Vulture (*Coragyps atratus*), and possibly the Laughing Falcon and Bat Falcon. Species whose numbers were clearly lower in human-altered than in primary forest include the White Hawk and Great Black Hawk. A great many other species also appear to decline or disappear in heavily altered forest, but sample sizes are not yet adequate to permit generalization. Relative abundance of vulture species appears to suggest certain types of human impacts, while presence of rarities such as the Orange-breasted Falcon and large eagles may relate to special ecological conditions or especially pristine environments.

DISCUSSION

The environmental problems we are facing, most of which are associated with rapidly increasing human populations, are staggering, and have no simple solution. National governments are becoming increasingly concerned with and involved in developing solutions. The governments of Guatemala and Mexico, for example, have established the above reserves which, because of their large size, have tremendous importance for conservation. Those countries have taken a further step by establishing the Comision Centro Americana de Ambiente y Desarrollo, a high level multi-national government commission on the environment.

To be realistic, conservation programmes must consider social and economic factors, and they must include local people and organizations in every phase. Typically local people have the greatest understanding of problems and needs, and are a requisite part of any solution. A great deal can be learned from those who spend their lives in the forest. Attempts at preservation of large expanses of land without concern for needs of the local human populace are unlikely to succeed.

As a group, tropical raptors are poorly known. Thiollay (1985 & 1990) reported that nests or eggs of 75 species have been described never, or only once or twice; nor do quantitative survey techniques exist. We are working to change that situation. Future attempts to manage reserves or species must rest on a base of solid biological knowledge, such as that provided by the Maya Project.

Ecological monitoring is an important aspect of the Maya Project. In conjunction with quantitative habitat descriptions and data from remote imagery, census results should allow generalization about large areas, e.g. prediction of avian distributions and species richness. By periodically recensusing permanently located plots, we hope to detect any ecological changes reflected in shifts of abundance of our census species. As more information flows from species-level research and census work in various pristine and human-altered habitats, we should be in a position to develop management strategies, recommendations for size and design of protected areas, and suggestions as to how certain land-use practices may be made more compatible with protection of biodiversity.

In the future, few opportunities for creation of large pristine reserves will exist; the challenge of conservation in the tropics will be largely relegated to the intelligent management of existing reserves, to habitat restoration, and to finding more harmonious ways for mankind to relate to the tropical environment. For all of these activities, effective means of monitoring ecological processes within the forest are extremely important, yet little work has been done along these lines. Indeed, the number of monitoring programs that attempt to track the species composition and relative abundance of "indicator species" or a functional group such as vertebrate predators over time are very limited. With each passing year, the Maya Project has taken on a wider ecological perspective, and monitoring now embraces bird groups ranging from wrens and migrant warblers through raptors. For the future, there is the possibility of monitoring key pollinators and/or establishment of seedlings and other ecological processes.

We are attempting to combine good science and conservation. Specialized organizations like The Peregrine Fund can make multiple, diverse contributions without losing focus or effectiveness. By working closely with local administrators, managers, and field personnel, we can also instill a level of skill and enthusiasm that is difficult for large, generalized organizations to accomplish. As decreasing northern breeding populations of avian Neotropical migrants illustrate, conservation effects, like wildlife, must cross political boundaries. Close cooperation among organizations and individuals nationally and internationally enhances understanding and effectiveness and magnifies results. At the Inter-regional Consultation on People's Participation in Environmentally Sustainable Development meeting in the Philippines, an Australian aborigine woman summarized, "If you have come to help me you can go home again. But if you see my struggle as part of your own survival then perhaps we can work together". (Sharma 1989).

ACKNOWLEDGEMENTS

With great admiration and respect we acknowledge our friends and colleagues in Latin America and the United States who participate in the Maya Project. Individuals who have participated in the Maya Project for three or more years include: Elbert C. Cleaveland, Aquiles Estuardo Hernandez Cordova, Greg S. Draheim, Craig J. Flatten, Richard P. Gerhardt, Miguel Angel Vasquez Marroquin, Julio Alfredo Madrid Montenegro, Cristobal Mateo Morales, Megan Parker, Feliciano Guierrez Ramirez, Jose Dolores Ramos, Russell K. Thorstrom, Charles W. Turley, and Jay P. Vannini. We also recognize and thank many others from Latin America, the United States, and Great Britain who lend advice and many forms of assistance.

Funding for this project has been provided by The John D. and Catherine T. MacArthur Foundation, The Pew Charitable Trusts, Mrs. Evie Donaldson, Mr Robert Berry, Gold Family Charitable Foundation, The Henry M. and Wendy J. Paulson Foundation, Andres and Pilar Sada, Alfred Jurzykowski Foundation, Inc., Frank Weeden Foundation, Dr. Elinor Jenny, The Fanwood Foundation, Crystal Channel Foundation, and The William H. and Mattie Wattis Harris Foundation. We sincerely thank all contributors for their participation.

REFERENCES

BEAVERS, R.A. 1991. *Annotated checklist of birds of Tikal National Park and Peten, Guatemala.* Texas A & M University Press, College Station, Texas. In press.

FLATTEN, C.J., J.A. MADRID M., H.D. MADRID M., S.H. FUNES A., A.E. HERNANDEZ C., & R.R. BOTZOC G. 1990. Biology of the Ornate Hawk-Eagle (*Spizaetus ornatus*). Pages 129-144 in D.F.Whitacre, W.A.Burnham, and J.P.Jenny, editors. *Maya project: progress report III.* The Peregrine Fund Inc.,Boise, Idaho.

GREENE, H.W. 1988. Species richness in tropical predators. Pages 259-280 in F. Almeda and C.M. Pringle, editors. *Tropical rainforest: diversity and conservation.* California Academy of Sciences, San Francisco, California.

JANZEN, D.H. 1978. Complications in interpreting the chemical defenses of trees against the tropical aboreal plant eating vertebrates. Pages 73-84 in G.G.Montgomery, editor. *The ecology of arboreal folivores.* Smithsonian Institution Press, Washington, D.C.

JANZEN, D.H. 1988. Tropical dry forests: the most endangered major tropical ecosystem. Pages 130-138 in E.O.Wilson, editor. *Biodiversity.* Natural Academy Press, Washington, D.C. 521 pp.

LECK, C.F. 1979. Avian extinction in an isolated tropical wet forest preserve, Ecuador. *Auk* 96:343-352.

MADRID, J.A., H.D.MADRID, S.H.FUNES, J.LOPEZ, R.BOTZOC & A. RAMOS. 1991. Reproduction biology and behaviour of the Ornate Hawk-Eagle (*Spizaetus ornatus*) in Tikal National Park. Pages 93-114 in D.F.Whitacre, W.A.Burnham, and J.P.Jenny, editors. *Maya project, progress report IV.* The Peregrine Fund, Inc., Boise, Idaho.

NEWTON, I.1979. *Population ecology of raptors*. Buteo Books, Vermillion, South Dakota. 399pp.
OLENDORFF, R.R., D.D.BIBLES, M.T.DEAN, J.R.HAUGH, & M.N.KOCHERT. 1989. Raptor habitat management under the U.,S.Bureau of Land Management multiple-use mandate. Raptor Research Reports No.8. 80 pp.
PARKER, M. 1991. The breeding biology and diet of Laughing Falcons (*Herpetotheres cachinnans*) in pristine and modified tropical forest habitats. Pages 115-120 in D.F.Whitacre, W.A.Burnham, and J.P.Jenny, editors. *Maya project, progress report IV.* The Peregrine Fund, Inc., Boise, Idaho.
PEAKALL, D.B., & L.KIFF. 1988. DDE contamination in Peregrines and American Kestrels and its effect on reproduction. Pages 337-350 in T.J.Cade, *et al.*, editors. *Peregrine Falcon populations: their management and recovery*. The Peregrine Fund, Inc., Boise, Idaho. 949 pp.
SHARMA, R. 1989. People's participation in sustainable development. *Ecoforum* 14(1):3.
SOULÉ, M.E., & K.A.KOHN. 1989. *Research priorities for conservation biology*. Island Press, Washington, D.C, 97pp.
SOULÉ, M.E., & D.SIMBERLOFF. 1986. What do genetics and ecology tell us about the design of nature reserves? *Biological Conservation* 35:19-40.
TERBORGH, J. 1988. The big things that run the world - a sequel to E.O.Wilson. *Conservation Biology* 2(4):402-403.
TERBORGH, J.W., & B.WINTER. 1980. Some causes of extinction. Pages 119-133 in M.E.Soulé and B.A.Wilcox, editors. *Conservation biology, an evolutionary-ecological perspective.* Sinauer Associates, Sunderland, Massachusetts.
THIOLLAY, J.M. 1985. Falconiforms of tropical rain forest: a review. Pages 155-65 in I.Newton and R.D.Chancellor, editors. *Conservation studies on raptors.* ICBP Technical Publication No.5, Cambridge, England.
THIOLLY, J.M.1989. Area requirements for conservation of rainforest raptors and game birds in French Guiana. *Conservation Biology* 3(2):128-137.
THIOLLAY, J.M.1990. Tropical forest raptors. Page 86 in I.Newton and P. Olsen, editors. *Birds of prey.* Wldon Owen Pty. Limited, McMahons, Australia.
THORSTROM, R.1990. Breeding biology of the Collared Forest-Falcon (*Micrastur semitorquatus*). Pages 149-158 in D.F.Whitacre, W.A.Burnham, and J.P.Jenny, editors. *Maya project: progress report III.* The Peregrine Fund, Inc., Boise, Idaho.
TURLEY, C.W. 1989. Evaluation of raptor survey techniques. Pages 21-32 in W.A.Burnham, J.P.Jenny, and C.W.Turley, editors. *Maya project: progress report II.* The Peregrine Fund, Inc., Boise, Idaho.
VANNINI, J.P. 1989. Reintroduction of Bat Falcons (*Falco rufigularis*) on Guatemala's Pacific versant. Pages 99-104 in W.A.Burnham, J.P.Jenny, and C.W.Turley, editors. *Maya project: progress report II.* The Peregrine Fund, Inc., Boise, Idaho.
VANNINI, J.P. 1990. Reintroduction of Bat Falcons (*Falco rufigularis*), 1990. Pages 173-174 in D.F. Whitacre, W.A.Burnham, and J.P.Jenny, editors. *Maya project progress report III.* The Peregrine Fund, Inc., Boise, Idaho.
WHITACRE, D.F. 1991. Censusing raptors and other birds in tropical forests: further refinements of methodology. Pages 31-42 in D.F.Whitacre, W.A. Burnham and J.P.Jenny, editors *Maya project: progress report IV.* The Peregrine Fund, Inc., Boise, Idaho.
WHITACRE, D.F. & W.A. BURNHAM. 1991. Training of Latin American personnel and graduate students. Pages 15-20 in D.F.Whitacre, W.A.Burnham, and J.P.Jenny, editors. *Maya project: progress report IV.* The Peregrine Fund, Inc., Boise, Idaho.
WHITACRE, D.F. & C.W.TURLEY. 1990. Further comparisons of tropical forest raptor census techniques. Pages 71-92 in D.F.Whitacre, W.A.Burnham, and J.P.Jenny, editors. *Maya project: progress report III.* The Peregrine Fund, Inc., Boise, Idaho.
WHIACRE, D.F., C.W.TURLEY, & E.C. CLEAVELAND. 1990a. Preliminary comparisons of relative abundance of raptors in primary forest and human altered habitats at and near Tikal National Park, Guatemala. Pages 67-70 in D.F.Whitacre, W.A.Burnham, and J.P.Jenny, editors. *Maya project: progress report III.* The Peregrine Fund, Inc., Boise, Idaho.
WHITACRE, D.F., C.W.TURLEY, & E.C.CLEAVELAND. 1990b., Correlations of diurnal raptor abundance with habitat features in Tikal National Park. Pages 53-66 in D.F.Whitacre, W.A.Burnham, and J.P.Jenny, editors. *Maya project: progress report III.* The Peregrine Fund, Inc., Boise, Idaho.

William Burnham
The Peregrine Fund, Inc.
World Center for Birds of Prey
5666 West Flying Hawk Lane
Boise, Idaho 83709

Meyburg, B.-U. & R. D. Chancellor eds.1994
Raptor Conservation Today
WWGBP / The Pica Press

Observations on Greater Yellow-headed Vultures *Cathartes melambrotus* and other *Carthartes* species as Scavengers in Forest in Venezuela

David C. Houston

ABSTRACT

A series of carcasses were provided at a forest site in northern Venezuela to investigate the scavenging efficiency of forest vultures, especially *Cathartes melambrotus,* about which there is almost no published information. Out of 35 carcasses provided, 80% were located by vultures within two days. The first to locate a carcass was invariably either *C. melambrotus* or *C. aura*. Both species used olfaction to locate food and could find carcasses that were completely hidden. It is suggested that *C. melambrotus* may be better adapted for locating food in dense forest due to its low wing loading. A review of the efficiency of forest vultures as scavengers in six different forest sites shows these birds to be the major scavenging animals in neotropical forests, accounting for a substantially greater food consumption than either mammalian or insect scavengers.

INTRODUCTION

The New World Cathartid Vultures are not related to the Old World Vultures, and probably evolved from the same ancestry as the storks. The greatest diversity of species is found in the neotropical forest, where five species coexist: the King Vulture *Sarcoramphus papa*, the Black Vulture *Coragyps atratus*, the Turkey Vulture *Carthartes aura*, the Lesser Yellow-headed Vulture *Carthartes burrovianus* and the Greater Yellow-Headed Vulture *Carthartes melambrotus*. Few studies have been made on this guild of scavenging birds, but for one species, the Greater Yellow-headed, there is virtually no information published. This species was described scientifically only in 1964, despite being one of the largest, commonest and most conspicuous of all birds in South American lowland forest.

The Neotropical forest guild of vultures is unusual in that the location of carcasses is dependent on olfactory detection. The Turkey Vulture is known to have a highly developed sense of smell (Stager 1964), on which it depends to locate its food in forest (Houston 1986). Of the other two members of the genus *Cathartes* it is known that the Lesser Yellow-headed can also locate carcasses by olfaction (Houston 1988) but it is not known if the Greater Yellow-headed has this ability. This paper considers how Greater Yellow-headed Vultures locate food, their position in the feeding sequence of vulture species, and the ecological separation of the three members of the genus Cathartes. It is based on field work carried out in an area of lowland forest along the roadside near El Callao in northern Venezuela in 1989.

METHODS

A series of 32 carcasses were provided on the forest floor to act as 'bait' to attract vultures. Domestic chickens were used, these being of approximately the same body weight as sloths, monkeys and the other common mammal species whose carcasses are the natural food supply for vultures in neotropical forests (Houston 1985). The methods outlined in Houston (1986) were followed except that carcasses were one day old when taken into the forest and were not placed along trails, but at a distance of about 100 paces into the forest. Carcasses were about 500m apart and, to prevent birds becoming accustomed to food being provided in one area, the same site was never used twice. Half of the carcasses were placed straight on the forest floor and half were covered by dried leaves until invisible. Some of the latter were of white-feathered chickens, but all exposed birds had cryptic brown feathers. Carcasses were usually watched for an hour or more after placement to try to observe the first species to arrive. They were then visited at regular intervals throughout daylight hours, at least every 2 ½ hours, by a slow and careful approach to record any birds feeding or in close proximity to the carcass. Carcasses were watched until they had been completely consumed.

RESULTS

Greater Yellow-headed and Turkey Vultures were always the first species to locate a carcass (Table 1). If we assume that all vulture species were equally likely to locate a carcass, then the probability that any one species would arrive first would be determined by its relative abundance in the area. Table 1 also shows the total numbers of each species recorded throughout the whole feeding sequence so that, assuming that this represents their relative abundance in the area, we can calculate the expected number of occasions on which each species should arrive first. Greater Yellow-headed Vultures and Turkey Vultures combined were significantly more likely to locate carcasses than other species (X = 58, p 0.001) while Black Vultures were more numerous later in the feeding sequence.

Table 1. Vulture species recorded at carcasses

	Turkey vulture	Greater Yellow-headed vulture	Black vulture	King vulture
First species to locate carcass	11	13	0	2
Total number of birds seen at carcass during the feeding sequence	27	19	118	2

Neither Turkey nor Yellow-headed Vultures had any difficulty in locating carcasses hidden under leaves on the forest floor. If we use only the number of carcasses where the first bird to arrive was actually seen to locate the food and observed eating, for Yellow-headed Vultures 3 of the 7 carcasses found by this species were hidden, and for the Turkey Vulture 4 out of the 6. Even carcasses left uncovered were almost certainly invisible to a bird searching from above the forest canopy.

This small trial in Venezuela comfirms the major role that vultures play as scavengers in Neotropical forests. 29 of the 35 carcasses available were located and totally consumed within two days. The other carcasses all vanished, presumably taken by mammalian scavengers. Two were taken during the day, probably by dogs from local villages, the others disappeared overnight. A series of bait trails has now been run in which carcassses have been monitored to record which scavenging species arrive and how much food they consume. These studies, carried out at seven different sites in four different countries, have shown that in forests with relatively undisturbed mammal populations vultures locate 70 - 99% of all carcasses available and are the major scavengers (Table 2).Areas mentioned in Table 2 where only a low proportion of carcasses were located are all heavily disturbed forests with greatly reduced mammal populations, and it is known that these also have very low densities of searching vultures (Houston 1987; Kirk 1988).

Table 2. Proportion of carcasses located by Turkey or Greater Yellow-headed Vultures in forested neotropical sites

	n	%	
Barro Colorado, Panama	74	96%	(Houston, 1986)
Gamboa, Panama	8	25%	(Houston, 1987)
Manaus, Brazil	40	0%	(Houston, 1987)
Masaguarel, Venezuela	46	98%	(Houston. 1987)
Masaguarel, Venezuela	88	89%	(Kirk, 1988)
nr. Ell Callao, Venezuela	35	83%	this study
Amacayacu Nat. Pk., Colombia	40	66%	(Bernal, 1991)

DISCUSSION

The Greater Yellow-headed Vulture clearly has the ability to locate carcasses by smell, because those made invisible by a covering of leaves were located as frequently as those that were fully visible. This is also known to be the case for the Turkey Vulture (Stager 1964) and Lesser Yellow-headed (Houston 1986). These three species are very similar, closely related, and it is not surprising that they share good olfactory abilities on which they rely to locate carcasses. The other two small cathartid vultures, the Black und the King Vultures, however, have no functional sense of smell and depend on *Cathartes* species to be led to food (Stager 1964; Houston 1984). They fly at a considerably higher altitude over the forest, from where they can observe the low altitude flight paths of the *Cathartes* species and follow them down to any sources of food (Houston 1988). It is well known that they arrive later in the feeding sequence, are usually dominant over the *Cathartes* species, and take different food items from the carcass (Houston 1988; Kirk 1988).

The small cathartid vultures differ considerably in their wing loadings (Table 3). The Black, and presumably also the King Vultures for which there are no data, have high wing loadings and need strong upcurrents to soar, usually using thermal uplift to reach the high altitudes from which they search. The three *Cathartes* species can use much weaker lift, but differ considerably in their wing shape and mass. Among Turkey Vultures the migrant race has higher wing loadings than the resident race, and the latter is probably better adapted to using the weak lift available at a low altitude over the forest canopy. The two Yellow-headed species are able to exploit weaker aources of lift than any other species, the Lesser Yellow-headed doing this over open wetland habitats, and the Greater Yellow-headed from small patches of lift at emergent trees projecting from the forest canopy. Within their respective habitats, the three *Cathartes* species fulfil very similar roles: locating sources of carrion first, and leading in other species in the guild. The ecological separation

Table 3. Mean weight and wing loadings from small cathartid vultures

	n	Weight kg	Wing area m^2	Wing loading N/m^2
Black Vulture[1]	64	1.63	0.37	43.6
Migrant Turkey[1] Vulture	140	1.42	0.49	28.2
Resident Turkey[1] Vulture	60	1.22	0.47	25.1
Lesser Yellow-headed[1] Vulture	4	0.95	0.42	22.3
Greater Yellow-headed Vulture	2	1.165[2]	0.48[3]	23.8

Source 1. Kirk 1988
2. Karr *et al*, 1990
3. Estimate from museum wing measurements, assuming the same ratio of wing length: wing areas as the other cathartid species

of these *Cathartes* species is probably dependent on slightly different sources of lift available in different habitats, each species being better adapted to one type of soaring behaviour over its preferred habitat. The two Yellow-headed species are both found in restricted habitats, flat grass and wetlands for the Lesser Yellow-headed, and mature lowland forest for the Greater Yellow-headed. The Turkey Vulture is a more generalist species and has a slightly higher wing loading. It is probably slightly less efficient at exploiting the very weak regions of low altitude lift that the Yellow-headed species use. Turkey Vultures are found in the same habitats as the two Yellow-headed species, but they also extend into savannas and higher altitude areas and, in the case of the migrant race, also occupy diverse habitats in North America. The slightly higher wing loading probably makes them more successful at using a wide variety of different flying conditions.

ACKNOWLEDGMENTS

I am extremely grateful to Dr. Stefan Gorzula for all his help is arranging and to the Carnegie Trust for the Universities of Scotland for their help with the funding of this study.

REFERENCES

BERNAL, L.G.G. 1991. Contribucion al conocimiento etologico y ecolocicq de las catartidas del Parque Nacional Natural Amacayacu, Amazonas, Colombia. Thesis, Universidad Nacional de Colombia.
HOUSTON, D.C. 1984. Does the King Vulture *Sarcoramphus papa* use a sense of smell to locate food?. *Ibis* 126: 76-69.
HOUSTON; D.C. 1985. Evolutionary ecology of Afrotropical and Neotropical vultures in forests. *In* Foster, M. (ed.) *Neotropical Ornithology*. American Ornithologists' Union Ornithological Monographs No. 36.
HOUSTON, D.C. 1986. Scavenging efficiency of Turkey Vultures in tropical forest. *Condor* 88: 318 - 323.
HOUSTON, D.C. 1987. The effect of reduced mammal numbers on *Cathartes* vultures in Neotropical forests. *Biol. Cons.* 41: 91 - 98.
HOUSTON, D.C. 1988. Competition for food between Neotropical vultures in forest. *Ibis* 130: 402 - 417.
KARR, J.R., S.K. ROBINSON, J.G. BLAKE & R.O. BIERREGAARD 1990. Birds of four neotropical forests. In *Four Neotropical Forests* (Ed. A.H. Gentry), Yale University Press, New Haven & London.
KIRK, D.A. 1988. Ecological separation of small cathartid vultures in South America. Ph.D. thesis. University of Glasgow.
STAGER, K.E. 1964. The role of olfaction in food location by the Turkey Vulture. Los Angeles County Museum Contributions in Science 81.

Dr. David E. Houston
Department of Zoology
University of Glasgow
Glasgow G12 8QQ, Scotland

Meyburg, B.-U. & R. D. Chancellor eds.1994
Raptor Conservation Today
WWGBP / The Pica Press

Raptors on Sulawesi (Indonesia): The influence of rain forest destruction and human density on their populations

B.-U. Meyburg & B. van Balen

SUMMARY

Six of the 22 raptor species of Sulawesi, with a land surface of 189 000 km², are endemic. Since many of them inhabit the rain forest and this habitat is rapidly diminishing under the spread of human settlement, it was feared that some of the endemic species might be threatened with extinction.

The authors traversed the island from south to north and over a stretch of 2,500 km concentrated on counting raptors. In all, 254 individuals belonging to at least 15 species were observed, averaging one raptor everey 18 km or every 32 minutes. The species seen most frequently were Brahminy Kite *Haliastur indus*, Celebes Serpent Eagle *Spilornis rufipectus*, Barred Honey Buzzard *Pernis celebensis,* Spotted Harrier *Circus assimilis* and Molucca Kestrel *Falco moluccensis*.

The status of individual species is discussed. The northern and southern peninsulas in particular have become heavily populated, so that here the raptor density is noticeably thinner than in the central part of tjhe island, but wherever there is still virgin forest the vulnerable species, e.g. the Sulawesi Hawk Eagle *Spizaetus lanceolatus*, are regularly met with.

Some population changes cannot be attributed to forest clearance or human population increase. Thus the formerly very frequent and adaptable Black Kite *Milvus migrans* is rare to-day as is the Rufous-winged Buzzard *Butastur liventer*.

INTRODUCTION

Sulawesi (formerly Celebes), with a land surface of 189,000 km², is the third largest of the Greater Sunda Islands and, for example, over half the size of Italy. A part of Wallacea, the island is zoogeographically of great interest, particularly on account of its high number of endemic mammal (62%) and bird species (27%). (White & Bruce 1986; Whitten *et al.* 1987). This high degree of endemism is also true for the birds of prey, with no fewer than six of the 21-22 resident species confined to the island.

Since many raptors are inhabitants of the rain-forest — a form of habitat which is rapidly shrinking in Indonesia, as elsewhere — it was feared that several of the endemic species were under threat. Thus Brown (1976) cited both of the island's eagles (*Spizaetus lanceolatus* and *Spilornis rufipectus*) as possibly endangered, and Meyburg (1986) considered it a matter of urgency that six species should be investigated, since not only the status but also the biology and distribution of this island's raptors are very little known.

It accordingly seemed worthwhile to seize the opportunity to traverse the island in order to assess as far as possible the frequency and distribution of the raptor fauna, compare this with the data in the literature, and draw conclusions as to the evolution and adaptability of the various species to the increasing human colonization and clearing of the forest. This appeared all the more urgent in view of Indonesia's immense programme of transmigration, whereby since 1905 at least 2.5 million people from the densely populated islands (Java, Madura, Bali and Lombok) have been resettled on those less heavily populated, including Sulawesi.

Our earlier researches into Indonesian raptors on Java (Thiollay & Meyburg 1988; Meyburg *et al.* 1989; van Balen 1991) had already indicated that dense human settlement can lead to a virtually complete disappearance of birds of prey due to destruction of the rain-forest, whilst on the other hand high numbers of raptors can still be found in extensive, undisturbed forested areas, as in a few reserves.

METHODS

In August 1987 the authors traversed the island from south to north in a Toyota Landcruiser. This had recently become possible but was still difficult. Starting from Ujung Pandang, the route passed through Parepare, Makale, Palopo, Wotu, Pindolo, Lake Poso, Poso, Palu, Tomalu, Moutong, Gorontalo and Maelang to Manado (Fig. 1). Along the way, the following reserves and National Parks were also visited: Bantimurung, Perumpenai, Lore Lindu, Dumoga Bone and Gunung Ambang.

Figure 1. Map of Sulawesi with localities visited

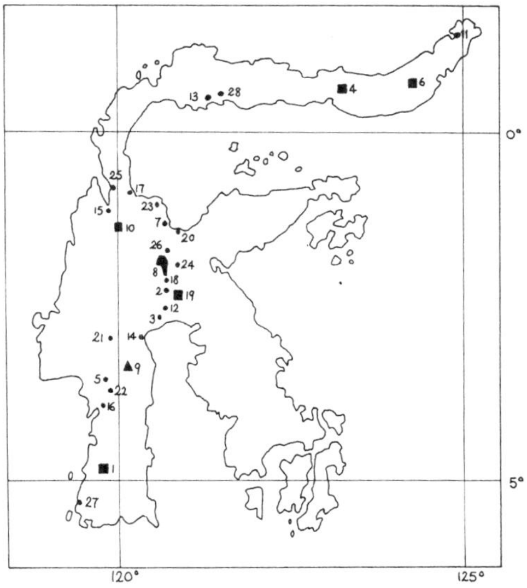

1. Bantimurung nature reserve
2. Batasposo
3. Bonebone
4. Dumoga Bone national park
5. Enrekang
6. Gunung Ambang nature reserve
7. Kasiguncu
8. Lake Poso
9. Latimojkong Mts
10. Lore Lindu national park
11. Manado
12. Mangkutana
13. Moutong
14. Palopo
15. Palu
16. Parepare
17. Parigi
18. Pendolo
19. Perumpenai nature reserve
20. Poso
21. Rantepao
22. Rappang
23. Sausu
24. Taripa
25. Tentena
27. Ujung Pandang
28. Wonggarasi

In order to obtain as accurate a view as possible of the distribution and density of the raptors, a very slow speed was maintained, so that — as confirmed by the first author's experience of making roadside counts on extensive trips in many different countries (e.g. Meyburg 1973) — a major part of the visible birds of prey could be recorded. In this way both authors could concentrate entirely on the lookout for raptors, whilst a native driver drove the vehicle. During the whole trip from Ujung Pandang to Manado, covering 2,497 km in 98.5 hours and 17 days of observation, at an average speed of only 25 km per hour, all sightings of raptors were recorded. At suitable vantage points stops were made and also several excursions into the forest were undertaken on foot. The total duration of these stops and excursions on foot amounted to 28 hrs 22 minutes. Whilst the first author concentrated on birds of prey, his co-author also listed other bird species at these vantage points and made tape recordings of their calls (Kukila 1993).

In order to save time, all observations were dictated into a tape recorder, noting the time, mileage, behaviour, biotope, weather conditions etc.

RESULTS

In all, 254 individuals of at least 15 species were observed (Table 1), averaging throughout the trip one raptor every 18 km or every 42.5 minutes. During stops we saw on average one raptor every 20 minutes. Travelling and stops taken together led to an average of one raptor seen every 32 minutes.

Table 1. Raptors counted on Sulawesi (roadside counts and observations from vantage points).

Species	Total number observed (both methods)	Average distance per individual (roadside counts)	Average time per individual (roadside counts)	Average time per individual (vantage points)
Haliastur indus	87	28,7	1h56mn	1h04mn
Spilornis rufipectus	27	92,5	6h34mn	3h12mn
Pernis celebensis	25	99,9	6h34mn	3h50mn
Circus assimilis	20	124,8	8h57mn	4h16mn
Falco moluccensis	19	131,4	7h34mn	6h24mn
Ictinaetus malayensis	17	146,9	12h18mn	4h16mn
Haliaeetus leucogaster	13	192,1	19h41mn	4h48mn
Spizaetus lanceolatus	8	312,1	24h37mn	9h36mn
Pandion haliaetus	7	356,7	32h48mn	9h36mn
Milvus migrans	4	624,3	24h37mn	-
Butastur liventer	4	624,3	32h48mn	38h22mn
Elanus caeruleus	3	832,3	98h25mn	19h11mn
Falco severus	2	1248,5	98h25mn	38h22mn
Accipiter griseiceps	2	1248,5	-	19h11mn
Ichthyophaga humilis	1	2497	-	38h22mn
Accipiter spp.	3	832,3	-	12h47mn
Unidentified	12	208,1	19h41mn	5h29mn

Twelve sightings could not be positively identified. Nor were the following observed with certainty: *Accipiter rhodogaster, A. nanus, A. trinotatus, Falco peregrinus, Hieraaetus kienerii, Macheiramphus alcinus* and *Aviceda jerdoni.*

Since two of the Accipiter species are barely distinguishable and three Accipiters could not be determined, the number of species observed was in reality perhaps higher. All three Accipiters not seen with certainty are particularly difficult to identify by means of roadside counts. This also applied to two other species not observed (Peregrine *Falco peregrinus* and Jerdon's Baza *Aviceda jerdoni*). The Bat Hawk *Macheiramphus alcinus* was previously recorded only once on Sulawesi (Klapste 1982) and so far there are only four authentic records of the Rufous-bellied Eagle *Hieraaetus kienerii* and very few isolated sightings (White & Bruce 1986; Watling 1983).

The human settlement is not evenly distributed but concentrated in the south-west peninsula and the north-eastern tip (Minahassa) of Sulawesi. There was a clear correlation between the density of the human population, which averages between 100 and 300+ inhabitants per km² on the south-west peninsula, and the density of birds of prey. In areas with a high human density (over 50 per km²), roadside counts produced an average of one raptor per 29.5 km and observation from vantage points gave one every 27 minutes. In less inhabited regions one raptor was seen every 15 km and every 20 minutes from vantage points. About 40% of the roadside counts were conducted in densely settled areas but gave only 25% of the total number of birds recorded.

Less significant is the difference in species richness. Taking only the commoner species, the absence of *Pernis* in densely populated areas was particularly striking, whereas *Spizaetus* was still present.

Osprey *Pandion haliaetus*

Prevost (1983) and Poole (1989) reported the breeding of the Australasian subspecies *P. h. cristatus* on Sulawesi, and this we could confirm. All seven birds seen were in the bay of Tomini. One pair (without nest) was seen 6 km south of the village of Kasimbar and a second pair at a nest in a tall dead tree 67 km east of Moutong. The eyrie was only *ca.* 200 m distant from a Wonggarasi village and was kept under observation for 30 minutes. Both adults spent the whole of this time on the nest, with one of them mainly feeding.

Barred Honey Buzzard *Pernis celebensis*

This was the third most ferquently seen species, and in certain places can clearly reach a high density. Thus on 5 August we located at least two territorial pairs and one individual in Central Sulawesi about 50 km south of Lake Poso in an area of 2 km². *Pernis* is especially to be met with in those parts of the island where forest and open grassland alternate. Human changes to the landscape, often to a massive extent, must have benefited this species, which only occurs in another race on the island of Luzon (Philippines). However, excessive deforestation and dense human settlement as in the south-west peninsula and the far north-east, has led to its disappearance from such regions. Of the commoner species, it was the only one we failed to see in places with over 50 humans per km².

Sulawesi Hawk Eagle *Spizaetus lanceolatus*

Brown (1976) and Meyburg (1986) considered it possible that this rain-forest dweller could be threatened by habitat destruction. At least for the present, this is not the case. Although, for lack of time, it was not possible to undertake long excursions on foot, so that observations had preponderantly to be made from the road, which only rarely ran close to the rain-forest, we saw a comparatively large number of these birds, surprisingly as many from the moving car as during stops. These were almost exclusively juveniles, which in part first attracted our attention by their constant begging calls. These young birds were for the most part seen at the forest edge and could only fly short distances; they were clearly still in the early post-fledging stage.

We got the overall impression that in fact each area of forest harboured the bird, so that the population is not to be feared for, so long as sufficient forest remains.

Since the exhaustive discussion of mimicry by Meyer and Wigglesworth (1898), the similarity of plumage between *S. lanceolatus* and *Pernis celebensis* and the difficulty of identifying them in the field has been constantly stressed (Watling 1983). In our opinion this poses no particular problem if one has had experience of other *Pernis* and *Spizaetus* species. *P. celebensis* has the typical *Pernis* mode of flight (very deep wing beats), longer wings and neck, different vocalisation and is quite variable in plumage.

Black-winged Kite *Elanus caeruleus*

Whereas White & Bruce (1987) cite the occurrence of this species at altitudes of 1,100 m, the three specimens we saw were only a little above sea level. We encountered all three on the northern peninsula: one bird on 12 July only a few km from the coast (40-50 m a.s.l.) hovering over a recently clear-felled area *ca.* 50 km east of Moutong. On the same day a second bird, likewise near the coast, *ca.* 26 km east of Marisa. The third Black-winged Kite was seen on the following day over an area of alang-alang grass near Kwandang.

Black Kite *Milvus migrans*

Heinrich (in Stresemann 1940) termed this species "the commonest raptor of Celebes", which Coomans de Ruiter (1947) also still maintained for the south-west coast from Ujung Pandang to Parepare. According to White & Bruce (1986), too, it was "common in towns and harbours and in open country to 1,100 m". Watling (1983) reported the species as common in the Lore Lindu reserve, but Van den Berg & Bosman (1986) did not see it there.

Since the Black Kite, from our observations, came tenth in degree of frequency, it has clearly suffered a severe decline. Three out of our four sightings were in the environs of Ujung Pandang and Parepare (31 July and 1 August); the fourth was in Dumoga-Bone National Park.

Brahminy Kite *Haliastur indus*

This species was by far the most frequently seen raptor (87 sightings). It has adapted to almost all habitats on Sulawesi but is most often to be seen near water. Not one juvenile was seen, so that at this time of year the young birds have evidently left the island, apart perhaps from a few unidentified raptors seen during the trip and which could have been young Brahminy Kites. This could indicate a very short period during which immatures wear their typical plumage after fledging, all having shed their initial feathers to be replaced by adult plumage in their first year. Other possibilities include the actual absence of immatures, due to a previous poor breeding season in the entire kite population. The long periods of extreme drought during recent years may hit this open area species more than forest dwelling species, such as the Sulawesi Hawk Eagle, of which a considerable number of immatures were seen.

White-bellied Sea Eagle *Haliaeetus leucogaster*

We met with this eagle most often at the northern end of Lake Poso. Here, on 5 August, within three hours, we saw seven White-bellied Sea Eagles, including two immatures which chased each other in play for 15 minutes. Four adults were perched together on a tree at the water's edge. Six others were spotted along the coast of the northern peninsula, five of them on the south side, one on the north, about level with Gorontalo. With the exception of one subadult, all were adult birds. At Molantado, on the northern coast of this peninsula, there was a very bulky but clearly unoccupied nest in a fairly isolated tree, only a few hundred metres from a village, which could only belong to *Haliaetus leucogaster*. One bird, 8 km east of Palasa, flew in from the sea with a *ca.* 1 m long seasnake in its talons. Another similarly swooped down to the water some 80 m from the shore but only brushed this with its claws. This hunting attempt was unsuccessful, however.

Lesser Fishing Eagle *Ichthyophaga humilis*

This species is also classified under the name *I. nana,* but Mees (1967) has shown "that this name was antedated by *humilis*".

Whereas Coomans de Ruiter (1947) described it as not uncommon in the south of the island, White & Bruce (1986) regarded it as infrequent.

We had only one sighting of an adult bird on 5 August 1987, 8 km south of Taripa (*ca.* 18 km east of Lake Poso). Whilst according to Brown and Amadon (1968) this species is seldom to be seen soaring, we nevertheless first noticed it circling low down but gradually gaining height until it eventually disappeared in a steady glide to the north-east. Its manner of flight differed in no way from that of other large eagles.

Sulawesi Serpent Eagle *Spilornis rufipectus*

The supposition that this species was threatened (Brown 1976; Meyburg 1986) proved unfounded. Indeed, this raptor ranked second in the number of sightings (27). It showed a considerable ecological adaptability and is to be met with equally in the tropical rain-forest and in rice-fields near villages. It occurs most readily in a not too densely populated landscape, where open water and forest alternate in a mosaic. So long as the forest does not completely disappear, the species can maintain a relatively high population level. Whether a not excessive human settlement can in fact be an advantage for this species will be shown only from further in-depth research into its population dynamics.

Spotted Harrier *Circus assimilis*

From our observations this raptor ranked fourth in frequency, whereas White & Bruce (1987) described it as "seemingly not numerous". We encountered it in both south and north peninsulas and in the central part of the island. This species undoubtedly benefits from the increasing deforestation. We often saw the birds flying quite low over habitations. It showed little shyness when we prepared to photograph it.

According to White & Bruce (1987) there are no breeding data for Sulawesi. We located an occupied nest on 18 August, at the border of the Dumoga-Bone National Park. This was about 12-15 m high in a not very tall tree within a group of only five trees in the middle of cultivation and 80 m away from a road. The nest itself was decidedly small and flimsy, with the brooding female plainly visible. The male, which was perched in a neighbouring tree, twice within 10 minutes brought a dead twig to the nest in its bill.

Sulawesi Goshawk *Accipiter griseiceps*

"The most remarkable feature of the *Accipiter* fauna of Sulawesi is the wealth of apecies on a relatively small island" (van Merle & Voous 1946). This is in contrast to Borneo, Sumatra and Java. All five Accipters observed were during stops at the forest edge or during excursions on foot. Since these took up only a little of our total observation time, it is not surprising that the number of individuals seen was so small. Only *A. griseiceps* could be identified with certainty.

A thorough study needs to be made of this species-rich *Accipiter* fauna.

Rufous-winged Buzzard *Butastur liventer*

Only rarely met with, mostly over ricefields at the forest edge. Coomans de Ruiter (1947) described it as very common, even occurring in towns, so that a severe decline must have recently taken place, for reasons unknown to us.

Black Eagle *Ictinaetus malayensis*

This species is also highly tolerant of the shrinking of the forest. Wherever there are still patches of forest it exploits the surrounding open areas and at any rate is not dependent on large areas of undisturbed rain-forest.

Spotted Kestrel *Falco moluccensis*

Like other Kestrels, this bird profits from the deforestation, so long as this does not exceed a certain limit. It avoids areas of pristine rain-forest. Human colonization of the island has probably helped this falcon's colonization also.

Oriental Hobby *Falco severus*

Two individuals were seen. The first, on 3 August, was perched at the top of a dead tree at the edge of the rain-forest *ca.* 18 km north of Wutu, 175 m a.s.l. and watched for an hour. It was not at all shy, even when we approached within 30 m of it. Its plumage was in the intermediate stage between young and adult. Breast and belly were in part spotted on a beige background, partly a spotless reddish-brown. Apart from one short flight round, it sat very still the whole time, often briefly closing its eyes. Only once did it call a hurried *gick, gick, gick, gick, gick.*

The second falcon, which was in full adult plumage, was seen on 5 August 22 km south-west of Taripa at 950 m a.s.l. in a lush landscape where open grassland alternated with forest, and also watched for an hour. This bird also spent most of the time perched in a dead tree, making only one brief flight round. Seen from above, in flight it appeared almost black and reminiscent of a swift or swallow, or even a small Peregrine. Its flight was mainly a glide, with barely any wing-beats.

DISCUSSION

Data on the previous and present extent of the rain-forest are relatively scanty. Information on the relative numbers of birds of prey in earlier times is dependent almost solely on the accounts of Heinrich (*in* Stresemann 1940) and Coomans de Ruiter (1947). When these are compared with our own findings, it is clear that two species in particular (*Milvus migrans* and *Butastur liventer*) have severely declined, yet neither is a rain-forest species. We can find no explanation for this plainly drastic decline. On the other hand two species have increased (*Circus assimilis* and *Ictinaetus malayensis*). Both of these must have benefited from the forest clearance. For the true forest-dwellers, especially *Spizaetus lanceolatus*, the situation seems to be the same as in Java. The species subsist in all intact areas of rain-forest, but to-day the minimum area necessary for the survival of a viable population cannot be guaranteed.

It would certainly appear that at present no raptor species on the island is under immediate threat, especially none of the endemics; however, in view of the increase in the human population, the future outlook may well be bleak. Further study of the raptorial fauna of the island is therefore urgently needed and the system of reserves must at all costs be expanded.

REFERENCES

AMADON, D. 1974. Taxonomic notes on the Serpent-eagles of the genus *Spilornis*. *Bull. Brit. Orn. Cl.* 94: 159-163

BALEN, S. van 1991. The Java Hawk Eagle *Spizaetus bartelsi*: WWGBP Project Report No. 1, March 1990. *Birds of Prey Bull.* 4: 33-40.

BALEN, S. van 1994. The status and conservation of birds of prey in the Sondaic and Wallacean Region of Indoniesia. This volume.

BERG, A.B. van den & C.A.W. BOSMAN 1986. Supplementary notes on some birds of Lore Lindu Reserve, Central Sulawesi. *Forktail* 1: 7-13

BROWN, L. 1976. *Eagles of the World.* Newton Abbot: David & Charles.

BROWN & AMADON 1968. *Eagles, Hawks and Falcons of the World.* 2 Vols. Feltham: Hamlyn

COOMANS DE RUITER,L. 1947. Roofvogelwaarnemingen in Zuid-Celebes. *Limosa* 20: 213-229

KLAPSTE, J. 1982. Bat Hawk on Celebes in December 1981. *Dutch Birding* 4: 29-30

KUKILA. 1993. Sulawesi Bird Report. *Kukila* 5: 4-26

MARLE J. G. van & K.H. VOOUS 1946. The endemic Sparrow Hawks of Celebes. *Limosa* 19: 15-23

MACKINNON, J. 1979. A glimmer of hope for Sulawesi. *Oryx* 15: 55-59

MACKINNON, J. & M. B. ARTHA 1982. A National Conservation Plan for Indonesia. Vol. VI: Sulawesi. Bogor: FAO & PPA (Field Report 35)

MEES, G. F. 1967. Zur Nomenklatur einiger Raubvögel und Eulen. *Zool. Meded.* 42: 143-146

MEYBURG, B.-U. 1973. Observations sur l'abondance relative des rapaces (*Falconiformes*) dans le nord et l'ouest de l'Espagne. *Ardeola* 19: 129-150

MEYBURG, B.-U. 1986. Threatened and near-threatened Diurnal Birds of Prey of the World. *Birds of Prey*

Bull. 3: 1-12
MEYBURG, B.-U., S. van BALEN, J.-M. THIOLLAY& R. D. CHANCELLOR 1989. Observations on the endangered Java Hawk Eagle *Spizaetus bartelsi*. Pp. 279-299 *in* Meyburg, B.-U. & R. D. Chancellor (eds.): *Raptors in the modern world.* Berlin, London & Paris: World Working Group on Birds of Prey.
MEYER, A.B. & L.W. WIGGLESWORTH 1898. *The birds of Celebes and neighbouring islands.* 2 Vols. Berlin: Friedländer.
POOL, A. F. 1989. *Ospreys. A natural and unnatural history.* Cambridge: Cambridge University Press
STRESEMANN, E. 1940. Die Vögel von Celebes. III. J. *Orn.* 88: 389-487
STRESEMANN, E. 1940. Zur Kenntnis der Wespenbussarde (*Pernis*). *Arch. f. Naturgesch.* (n.F.) 9: 137-193
STRESEMANN, E. 1959. Die Gliederung der Schlangenadler-Gattung *Spilornis. Vierteljahrschr. Naturforsch. Ges. Zürich* 104: 208-213
PREVOST, Y.A. 1983. Osprey distribution and subspecies taxonomy. Pp. 157-174 in: Bird, D.M. (ed.): *Biology and management of Bald Eagles and Ospreys.* Ste. Anne de Bellevue: Harpell Press
THIOLLAY, J.-M. & B.-U. MEYBURG 1988. Forest fragmentation and the conservation of raptors: A survey on the island of Java. *Biol. Conserv.* 44: 229-250
WATLING, D. 1983. Ornithological notes from Sulawesi. *Emu* 83: 247-261
WHITE, C.M.N. & M. D. BRUCE. 1986. *The Birds of Wallacea.* An annotated check-list. London: British Orn. Union.
WHITTEN, A. J. 1987. Indonesia's Transmigration Program and its role in the loss of Tropical Rain Forests. *Conservation Biol.* 1: 239-246
WHITTEN, A. J., M. MUSTAFA & G. S. HENDERSON. 1987. *The Ecology of Sulawesi.* Yogyakarta: Gadjah Mada Univ. Press

Dr. Bernd-U. Meyburg
Wangenheimstr. 32
D-14193 Berlin
Germany

S. van Balen
P.O.Box 310
Bogor 16003
Indonesia

Meyburg, B.-U. & R. D. Chancellor eds.1994
Raptor Conservation Today
WWGBP / The Pica Press

Socio-economic Incentives for the Conservation of the Rainforest Habitat of the Philippine Eagle *Pithecophaga jefferyi*

Dennis Joseph I. Salvador

ABSTRACT

The Philippine Eagle *Pithecophaga jefferyi* is rapidly slipping from endangerment to extinction. Habitat loss is considered to be the primary factor impacting Philippine Eagle populations. Population status of the species is described. The factors contributing to the loss of its rainforest habitat are also explored. But despite current efforts to save the species using conventional management techniques, its population continues to decline. An alternative approach using socio-economic incentives as a tool for habitat management is presented. Information on how funding for the study was obtained, the project area, the species' status, planning, social preparation, training, organisation, production, forest enhancement and protection measures, and phase-out activities are also presented. The impacts of the study on the community in terms of social acceptability, attitudes, income levels and organisation are discussed. The resultant effect on the target species and its habitat is shown in this paper. Evaluation of the project, its potential and recommendations for replication are also presented.

INTRODUCTION

The Philippine Eagle *Pithecophaga jefferyi* is a giant forest raptor endemic to the Philippines. With a wingspan of nearly two metres and a height of about one metre, it is considered to be one of the largest eagles in the world. It also has the dubious distinction of being one of the world's rarest eagles.

First collected in 1896 by John Whitehead, it has since been described by Gonzales (1968), Lovejoy (1973) and Rabor (1965). Even then the paucity of sightings led investigators during the early 1970s to estimate the total population to be between 36 and 60 individuals (Alvarez 1970; Gonzales 1973; Rabor 1971). But Kennedy (1981) revised the estimate to be 300-500 individuals. By the end of the decade, Krupa (1989) figured its population to have declined to between 89 and 222 individuals.

Despite efforts to save the species, Philippine Eagle populations continue to decline. Habitat loss is considered to be the primary factor impacting Philippine Eagle populations. By the

Department of Environment and Natural Resources' own account (1987), our rainforest is being diminished at the rate of 190,000ha annually. USAID (1989) estimates that we now have only 700,000ha of old growth dipterocarp forest remaining. And these will disappear within seven years. Indiscriminate logging practices and slash-and-burn agriculture are considered the primary causes of deforestation, further aggravated by corruption, inadequate law enforcement and an ambiguous state policy towards rainforest conservation (Porter 1988). In addition, there are now some 17 million people in the uplands, considered to be the country's poorest of the poor, threatening to wipe out what is left of the forest cover. And under conditions of large-scale poverty, there is no doubt that human needs will take precedence over conservation of our natural resources base for the long term.

Obviously, responses to the problems of habitat loss and species extinction in the Philippines must address simultaneously the tangled web of development issues. A new approach to endangered species management was needed. Conventional wildlife management techniques were largely limited to education, biological surveys, delineation of sanctuaries and laying down rules and regulations (Kennedy 1985; Lechoncito 1984; Sinha 1984). But after all this, what next? It is inconceivable that the average marginal-$income family would discontinue its efforts to survive.

This paper presents the results of a study conducted to determine the viability of providing socio-economic incentives to indigenous upland communities as an approach to habitat management. It aims to find out how such a programme would affect the target species and its habitat. By providing upland communities with sustainable livelihood alternatives, we hypothesised that pressures on the habitat could be eased, the communities' basic needs would be met and permanent survey plots for long-term monitoring could be established.

METHODS

Funding

Right at the outset we realised that the study was not going to be easy. Funding agencies were reluctant to part with precious resources to an organisation which had clearly no track record on social development work. To hurdle this obstacle, the services of two development-oriented NGOs were sought. They provided the guidance needed for the social development aspects of the study. In addition, potential donors could not understand how saving the eagle and its habitat could benefit man. We then packaged our proposal to highlight the species' significance, i.e. its position in the food chain made it an ideal indicator of the health of the forest ecosystem. We also argued that the diminishment of the natural resources base is leading not only to the loss of the target species but also to the Filipino people's capability to survive in the long term. This finally convinced Canada Fund, which decided to underwrite the project. We launched it on 17 May 1990.

Project Area

The study was conducted in Salaysay, Marilog District, in Davao City. This site was selected for the challenge it posed: inaccessibility, absence of basic government services, extreme poverty, and severe habitat degradation due to illegal harvesting of forest products. And because of human disturbance, the eagle had not been sighted here since 1988. We reasoned that if the study succeeded under these conditions, we might be able to replicate it in other areas.

Status of Species

Scientifically acceptable surveys of Philippine Eagle populations have not been conducted, primarily because of financial constraints and secondly because of lack of expertise on raptor survey techniques. Nevertheless, we have developed a method to overcome this obstacle.

We first visited remote areas throughout Mindanao island and conducted an extensive awareness campaign. Included in this was a call to the public to report sightings of the birds. Cash incentives were offered to those who found occupied nests. In this way many of our eagle nests were found. Thereafter, each nest was protected through our adopt-a-nest programme wherein the field trustee was paid when the eagles produced an egg, when this hatched and finally when the eaglet fledged. Still, pressures on the eagle's habitat continued to persist. Today we can only account for 17 individuals associated with wild nests throughout the island.

The Salaysay nest was found in the manner outlined above in April 1986, among the branches of a lauan tree *Shorea almon* at about 1,070m a.s.l. (Bonnit *et.al.* 1986). Although the eagles were not seen at that time, enough evidence such as castings, moulted feathers and vocalisation was obtained. In addition, forest dwellers reportedly observed breeding activities during the past breeding season. Our team suspected that the eaglet may have fledged but this was never confirmed.

In December 1986 another team returned to investigate reports of breeding. This time the eagles were seen and nesting activities were noted (Bonnit *et al.* 1986). However, after the egg was laid, we heard no more from the nest finder. Further investigation showed that the egg had failed to hatch (Garcia 1987). Human disturbance may have accounted for the abandonment of the egg and, indeed, 44 occupied houses were recorded within a 3.5km radius of the nest.

The eagles were seen again in May 1988 but it was not known whether they had bred as the nest was never located (Garcia 1988). By this time the old nest tree had been cut down and the area burned for agricultural use. Although the nest site was originally covered by our adopt-a-nest programme, severe funding shortages in 1987 prevented us from monitoring the area as much as we would have liked. As a result the field trustee, unsure of further rewards for his efforts, abandoned his role in the face of community pressure to convert the land.

Follow-up search efforts in June of the same year failed to locate the eagles (Salvador & Cereno 1988). Since then the birds have not been seen, even by local residents.

Socio-Economic Project

The continuing threat to the Philippine Eagle imposed by a rapidly growing upland population called for drastic measures. An innovative programme addressing the needs of the species as well as that of humans had to be designed. And for habitat management to work it must be undertaken in the context of socio-economic realities.

As an initial step, the community was consulted on the aims of the study and asked to participate in the planning progress. Because of the diverse geographic, edaphic and socio-cultural variations in upland areas, we thought it best not to present the programme in a definite form or "package". Rather, a participatory approach to project design and implementation was encouraged. Resources appraisal and a socio-metric survey were conducted to serve as baseline data. Based on this information, our team and the community jointly drafted a programme consistent with available resources and perceived needs. The resulting plan covered the following concerns: social preparation; training; implementation of livelihood; co-operative formation; reforestation and phase-out.

A project officer was assigned to the target community and charged with facilitating the development process. The immediate preparatory task required use of community organising techniques. Particular emphasis was laid on evaluation of attitudes and assessment of cultural practices.

This phase was followed by education and training. During the course of the study period, training was conducted on participatory research, general conservation, wildlife identification, sloping agricultural land technology, organic farming, cash crop production, principles of co-operative management, business planning, fiscal management and project management. In addition, community members were sent on field trips to observe the operation of different farms in southern Mindanao.

Having organised and trained the community, we proceeded to implement the livelihood scheme. All inputs were provided on credit at an interest rate of 6% per cropping. The idea was to make the farmers feel that the assistance provided was not a dole, and that they were obliged to work if they wanted to increase their incomes.

A grouping system was institutionalised to ensure continued performance. Each member of a 5-man group was responsible to and for each other's performance. The group, in turn, was accountable to the community and to us.

Corn was planted as a monocrop during the first season, selected on account of the farmers' familiarity with it and its relatively rapid growth (90-105 days). This choice was also determined by the need to raise income levels as quickly as possible. The aim was to divert their attention from harvesting forest products. At the same time, as part of their loan, their food requirements were provided during the period between planting and harvesting.

During the second season, however, mixed patterns replaced monocropping. The farmers were also weaned off their traditional reliance on inorganic fertilisers and pesticides in favour of organic substitutes and biological control measures.

Apart from farming, a co-operative store was established to provide for their basic needs. We loaned them 1/3rd of the amount they needed for capitalisation, while the rest was borne by the community through membership contributions. This co-operative institutionalised the community organisation.

Incorporated into the study were habitat enhancement and protection measures. This was part of the bargain. In return for our assistance, the community was obliged to conduct reforestation and patrol the forest area. Communal and individual tree nurseries were established, and fruit trees were planted along the borders of their farm lots, while dipterocarp species were planted along the forest edges. Patrols were also regularly conducted.

Phase-out involved the turning over of the project officer's duties and functions to the co-operative organisation and capable community leaders. Today, monitoring and inspection are conducted by the community's volunteer extension workers. We still visit the study area, however, to check if programmed activities have been sustained and, more importantly, to boost the community's morale.

RESULTS AND DISCUSSION

Our initial assessment of the community showed a group of people beset by grinding proverty. The average monthly income was $14 a month or $168 per annum. Crop production was a meagre 3 cavans (45 kilos/cavan) per season. In addition, they neither had the means nor control over the factors of production. This accounted for their tendency to go for short-term exploitation of natural resources. Practically everyone in the community knew of the destructive consequences of their activities, but acknowledged it as a necessary sacrifice to sustain their daily needs. Already the effects of forest denudation were being felt. We were also concerned by the fact that the Philippine Eagle, whose nest was first discovered in 1986, had not been sighted since 1988.

Our proposal of assistance was welcomed by the community with some reservations. This was because past governmental development assistance programmes had ended in neglect and never really benefited the community. Another reason was persistent rumours that we were out to grab their land. This was solved by tracing and confronting their source. But only after the community was directly involved in the planning process did the project gain widespread social acceptability. They found that with their available resources, their own goals and perceptions agreed with our proposed management techniques and strategies for upland development.

Because the community as a whole aspired to a better future, we had little difficulty in preparing them socially. Through our seminars, they found that their own resignation to their plight was the only real obstacle to development. They also realised that their adoption of lowland farming systems and cultural practices had led to disruption of their own way of life, originally attuned to the needs of the environment. They resolved to uphold the old ways. To reinforce this further, we gave the *datu* or tribal chieftain a major role in policy formulation and decision-making. His participation made it easier to implement the project plans since his word was practically law.

Education and training did not deal wholly on the theoretical but also with the practical aspects of the programme. This allowed them to relate concepts and practice. The field trips to model farm sites also confirmed the practicability of the proposed technology. The enthusiasm with which they welcomed these ideas made it possible for us to accelerate the project schedule.

The results of the first cropping have motivated the community further. Despite the onslaught of a freak typhoon, yields had increased dramatically to an average of 35 cavans per farmer. Some lost all their crops but these losses were covered by insurance. Net income was seen to increase by 30%, whilst loan repayment was at a satisfactory 85%. Bad debts were attributed to those who left their farms and joined the gold rush in an adjoining province. They were quickly replaced by applicants on the waiting list.

By the second cropping, yields had increased substantially so that farmers had quadrupled their pre-project monthly income. A 80% collection rate on their loans was also achieved. The remaining 20% was attributed to the drought and post-harvest losses.

The most remarkable performance was that of the co-operative store. By the end of the study, this had grown by 400% from the initial capitalization of 260. It has now extended its services from provision of basic commodities to trading and credit assistance to its members.

It is difficult to assess the reforestation component of the project. For one thing, it takes a long time for dipterocarps and fruit trees to grow. It is, at this point, enough to know that the community is maintaining these seedlings and is planning to grow more. But the success of the habitat protection measures may be gauged more objectively. By the second month of project implementation, the community had stopped all illegal logging, harvesting of forest products and slash-and-burn farming. Since then this tract of forest has remained undisturbed. The crowning success is perhaps the sighting of the Philippine Eagle in the study area in September 1991.

The project is now in the hands of the community. Loan applications for farming inputs are all handled by the co-operative, which has its own duly elected screening committee. The co-operative has been registered with the Securities and Exchange Commission and, with its track record, is now eligible for assistance from formal loan institutions. It is noteworthy that they have evolved their own plans in pursuit of project objectives. When we left them, they had already submitted plans for a spring water development project to a funding agency. They were also exploring the possibility of an ecotourism project in the future.

CONCLUSION

It is still too soon to assess accurately the value of socio-economic incentives as a tool for habitat management. Nevertheless, the results clearly show the potential. Within 18 months we were able to meet our project objectives. This allowed us to establish the area as a permanent survey plot. We now restrict ourselves to advising the community and monitoring the resident eagles and their habitat.

Observers were heartened by the success of this pilot project. In 1991, Conservation International provided us with funds to initiate a similar programme on a 5-year time scale in Mt. Kitanglad National Park in Bukidnon. Del Monte Philippines, a private agribusiness firm, has agreed to assist this project in 1992 by sponsoring one of the communities in this 32,000ha park. The Catholic Relief Service has also agreed to help us on a 3-year project in an eagle habitat located in Davao City, beginning in 1992. These projects are expected to provide us with more information for long-term evaluation of socio-economic incentives for rainforest conservation. But more importantly they will allow for the immediate protection of Philippine Eagle populations in the wild and, at the same time, provide for the needs of local inhabitants.

We learned several lessons from this study, and wildlife managers who wish to undertake a similar scheme would be well advised to consider the following points: creation of an institutional mechanism which will perceive, respond and catalyse the process instead of presenting a definite package for upland development; direct involvement of the target community should be encouraged in all phases of the project's implementation; and finally, a mechanism to ensure sustainability for the long term should be institutionalised. The strategy for upland development as suggested here was conceived out of our own experience and realistic perceptions of the problems that lead to the loss of our rainforest.

Deforestation is a time fuse lit by mankind. Unless drastic measures are employed in conjunction with technological solutions, the threat of extinction will persist. In the Third World, where the human population exerts tremendous pressure on the rainforest, such approaches may be the only solution. The loss of our rainforest will not only mean the extinction of a host of biologically important species but, in a very real sense, the dreams and aspirations of millions of marginal-income families as well. While organisations worldwide are already doing their share to save our rainforest, it is only through concerted action that we can achieve results.

ACKNOWLEDGEMENTS

This study was funded by a grant from the Canada Fund, a development assistance unit of the Canadian Embassy in the Philippines. We thank the Institute for Small Farms and Industry and the Settlements and Livelihood Foundation for their assistance and guidance; Drs. James Grier and William Burnham for their support and encouragement; Joyce for inspiring us to write about it; Joji and Lorenzo for their patience and dedication; Lito Cereño for his efforts in the field; Del Monte Phils., Conservation International and the Catholic Relief Service for sharing our vision and deciding to replicate this project; the MacArthur Foundation and Caltext Philippines for sponsoring my participation in this Conference; and, finally, the PECPF staff for dedicating their lives to the preservation of the Philippine Eagle and its habitat.

REFERENCES

ALVAREZ, J.B. Jr. 1970. A report on the 1969 Status of the Monkey-Eating Eagle of the Philippines. *Proceedings IUCN 11th Technical Meeting*. New Delhi, India, 2:68-73.

BONNIT, C., A. KACHENJUNGA & D. TADENA 1986: Philippine Eagle Conservation Program Field Report. Davao City, Philippines. Unpublished.

GARCIA, E. 1987. Philippine Eagle Conservation Program Foundation Field Report. Davao City, Philippines. Unpublished.

GARCIA, E. 1988. Philippine Eagle Conservation Program Foundation Field Report. Davao City, Philippines. Unpublished.

GONZALES, R.B. 1968. A Study of the Breeding Biology and Ecology of the Monkey-Eating Eagle. Siliman University Press. Dumaguete City, Philippines. 15(4): 461-491.

GONZALES, R.B. 1971. Report on the 1969 Status of the Monkey-Eating Eagle on Mindanao Island, Philippines. *ICBP Bull* 11: 154-168.

KENNEDY, R.S. 1981. Saving the Philippine Eagle. *Nat. Geog.* 159(6): 847-856.

KENNEDY, R.S. 1985. Conservation Research on the Philippine Eagle. Nat. *Geog. Soc. Research Report* 18: 401-413.

KRUPA, R.E. 1989. Social and Biological Implications for Endangered Species Management: The Philippine Eagle *Pithecophaga jefferyi*. Pp. 301-314 *in* Meyburg and Chancellor (Eds.) *Raptors in the Modern World.* WWGBP. Berlin, London & Paris.

LECHONCITO, J.L. 1984. Status and Implications of Managing Wildlife Resources and Reserves in the Philippines. *First ASEAN Forestry Congress Proceedings*. Book III (7): 892-897. Manila.

LOVEJOY, T.E. 1973. The Blue-Eyed Eagle of the Philippines. Frontiers. *Acad. Nat. Science of Philadelphia* 38(1): 2-7.

PORTER, G. & D.J. GANAPIN Jr. 1988. Resources, Population and the Philippines' Future. *World Resources Inst. Paper* No. 4: 1-53.

RABOR, D.E. 1965. Preliminary Report on the Life History and Biology of the Monkey-Eating Eagle of the Philippines. Unpublished.

RABOR, D.E. 1971. The Present Status of the Monkey-Eating Eagle of the Philippines. *Philippine Geographic Journal* 15: 90-103.

SALVADOR, D.I. & A. CERE!O. 1988. Philippine Eagle Conservation Program Foundation Field Report. Davao City, Philippines. Unpublished.

SINHA, C.C. 1984. Principles and Application of Wildlife Population Dynamics: Research Status in the Philippines. *First ASEAN Forestry Congress Proceedings* III (7): 915-929. Manila.

USAID, 1989. Sustainable Natural Resources Assessment Philippines. USAID Project No. 398-0249. Manila, Philippines.

Dennis Joseph I. Salvador
Philippine Eagle Conservation Program Foundation Inc.
2F UCPB Building, Magsaysay St.
Davao City, Philippines 8000

Meyburg, B.-U. & R. D. Chancellor eds.1994
Raptor Conservation Today
WWGBP / The Pica Press

Raptor Studies in Madagascar's Rain Forest

R. T. Watson and R. Lewis

The Peregrine Fund's Madagascar Project comprises two major components: 1) studies and management of the endangered Madagascar Fish Eagle *Haliaeetus vociferoides* along Madagascar's west coast, and 2) studies of tropical rain forest raptors on the Masoala Peninsula in northeastern Madagascar. The objective of the rain forest raptor studies is to develop the use of raptors as tools and indicators for resource management, monitoring and conservation, and to answer significant scientific questions about the biology and ecology of raptors. Studies are of two broad types: i) autecological studies that provide an understanding of spatial, habitat, and other resource requirements, and ii) raptor community monitoring that provides an understanding of species composition and relative abundance in relation to rain forest degradation from virtually pristine through degraded and second growth *(savoka)*. The rationale for using raptors as a conservation tool, the methods used and progress to date will be presented.

INTRODUCTION

Madagascar

Madagascar, the fourth largest island in the world (587,044 km^2), is unusual for the high degree of endemism that exists among its flora and fauna (Guillaumet 1984). Once attached to Africa, Madagascar has been separated for about 160 million years (Rabinowitz *et al.* 1983), an isolation that has contributed to the evolution of many species unique to the island. Many of the endemic species are dependent on forests that, until recently, covered extensive parts of the island. Now less than 20% of the island is forested and only 4.4% is primary growth (FAO 1981) suitable for survival of the majority of endemic species. Slash and burn cultivation of "dry-land" rice, annual grassland burning and charcoal production are the main causes of deforestation countrywide (Jolly & Jolly 1984). Political and social isolation from the West during the 1960s and '70s contributed to environmental degradation through impoverishment of economic and human resources.

Recognizing these problems, in 1988 Madagascar developed its *Environmental Action Plan* with four major goals: develop human resources, conserve biodiversity, develop sustainable resource use and improve standard of living. The Peregrine Fund's unique organisational abilities and highly focused approach will contribute significantly to this. We will assist development of human resources, at the same time helping to conserve biodiversity and contribute to sustainable resource use as follows.

Focus on raptors

As predators, raptors may be some of the most biologically significant and sensitive indicators of the health of the forest (Robinson & Wilcove 1989). Predators are believed to be key elements in the maintenance of equilibria in tropical communities where predation pressure is one of the fundamental determinants of population structure, life history traits and demography (Taylor 1984; Wilcove 1985; Smythe 1987; Greene 1988; Terborgh 1988). Tropical raptors usually exist at low density and are widely dispersed, have low reproductive rates and are sensitive to disturbance and habitat fragmentation. Maintaining viable populations of raptors should insure the survival of the entire ecosystem and provide the justification for the size and location of parks and reserves (Thiollay 1989). Their place at the top of the food chain makes the study of raptor ecology suitable for understanding the forest ecosystem and all that affects it, which makes these birds ideal subjects for training field biologists, resource personnel and students. As spectacular examples of the diversity of fauna, we have found that raptors provide excellent tools for instruction of the public and for generating public support for forest conservation. For example, the direct and indirect impact of deforestation on the Madagascar Fish Eagle is similar to the impact on humans and provides a sobering illustration of the future for humans in Madagascar. Not only do Fish Eagles lose essential nesting habitat as deforestation occurs along lakes, rivers and coastlines, but deforestation in watersheds hundreds of kilometres away leads to high sediment loads and degradation of the rivers and lakes on which the species depends for food.

Fourteen raptor species inhabit Madagascar, eight are endemic, all are seen rarely, and ***three are considered among tha most endangered raptors in the world*** (Langrand & Meyburg 1984). The Madagascar Fish Eagle has been reduced to fewer than 50 known pairs, and its range is limited to the central- to north-west coast where it does not benefit from habitat protection (Langrand 1987; Langrand & Meyburg 1989). The Madagascar Serpent Eagle *Eutriorchis astur* and the Madagascar Red Owl *Tyto soumagnei* inhabit eastern rain forests. The latter has not been seen for over 30 years (Jenkins 1987) but there is recent evidence that the Serpent Eagle may still exist (Langrand, *pers. comm.*; Safford & Duckworth 1990; Sheldon & Duckworth 1990). If these two species still exist, they benefit from some protection because parts of their former range are within reserves. Nothing is known of their ecological requirements, to determine whether existing reserves are large enough to maintain viable populations. The status of the remaining forest species is: Banded Kestrel *Falco zoniventris* - very rare; Madagascar Cuckoo Falcon *Aviceda madagascariensis* - not known; Bat Hawk *Machaeramphus alcinus* - seen rarely; Madagascar Sparrowhawk *Accipiter madagascariensis* - seen rarely and poorly known; Henst's Goshawk *Accipiter henstii* - very rare.

GOALS AND OBJECTIVES

The Peregrine Fund Programme in Madagascar

Working in co-operation with local organisations and individuals we can apply much of what we have learned in Central America and around the world. Using a similar plan and focusing on raptors, we can achieve the following programme:

1) Support and provide training for Malagasy conservation personnel and students:

Education in conservation biology, wildland management, and related areas are essential for scientists and natural resource managers (Ehrenfield 1989). We are providing a hands-on training programme modelled on our Central American Maya Project, that includes:

(i) field training of local NGO or government agency (e.g. *Direction des Eaux et Forêts*) personnel with limited formal education to collect information and monitor resources;

(ii) undergraduate and technical training in co-operation with the University system of Madagascar. Trained personnel will contribute to the training of others and/or fill low- to high-level governmental and non-governmental posts as the present staff retires and conservation efforts are expanded;

(iii) awareness education of the local populace in co-operation with the zoo (*Parc Botanique et Zoologique de Tsimbazaza*), parks (e.g. forest stations such as Ivalouine or the new Ranomafana National Park), NGOs (e.g. WWF, Conservation International, Madagascar Faunal Group and others), and focal communities near target conservation areas (currently Masoala Peninsula and Lake Ankerika complex).

2) Conservation of tropical forest and other ecosystems:

We are providing the expertise and supervision to train Malagasy biologists, students and conservation personnel, as well as resources necessary to initiate and continue the project:

Environmental monitoring involves measuring ecological parameters to detect change, establish its direction and measure its extent or intensity, in order to determine compliance with an *a priori* standard, or deviation from an expected norm. Monitoring in forest conservation areas aims to serve as an early warning of significant change. In complex habitats or extensive sites, the behaviour and responses of a single component of the ecosystem must serve as an indicator of the community as a whole. The presence of group of species commonly found together has considerable value for assessing habitat or environmental quality when their indicator value is known (Goldsmith 1991).

Raptors are one such group which may be used to derive quantitative measures, such as diversity (distribution of numbers or biomass between species), or production (a dynamic measure defined in total biomass per unit time) that indicate ecosystem type, quality and change. Such parameters are the nearest approach to the ideal single key measure for monitoring. For most groups of organisms, such measurements are demanding of human resources. We are developing methods to make these measurements on tropical forest raptors in Central America that are low-cost, low-technology and reliable. Census methods include acoustic luring with recorded vocalisations, point counts from emergent trees or other prominent vantage points, and foot surveys (Whitacre *et al.* 1991). Results provide a description of habitat and species composition, and raptor species distribution and relative abundance. As the area and types of habitat surveyed (primary and modified forest) are expanded, we will learn what species can be expected and at what relative abundance under various habitat and environmental conditions. We are testing the same methods in the eastern rain forests of Madagascar, will modify them as necessary, and apply them in conjunction with Integrated Conservation and Development Programmes (ICDP) being tested in Madagascar.

ICDPs are based on the premise that conservation of biodiversity arises from the ability of sustainable development successfully to relieve human pressure on natural areas. In contrast, success at sustainable development is not dependent on conservation of biodiversity, and implementation of development techniques does not necessarily lessen human impacts on natural areas if these techniques also increase human population size (Kremen *in press*). Continuous monitoring of both the development and conservation aspects of ICDP is needed to evaluate and test the hypotheses. Monitoring provides feedback that allows changes to be made in ICDP methods to cope better with dynamic changes in the human population and its resource use, as well as changes caused by human disturbance in the natural processes of the conservation area.

3) Develop use of resource requirements of raptors as indices for reserve design and management:

From autecological studies we are collecting biological and ecological information on forest raptors, including home range and territory size, habitat utilization, reproductive rates, turnover rates and behaviour (e.g. Berkelmann, *this volume*). We will determine population dynamics and resource requirements for species' survival and the effects of ecosystem changes on species and their associated community.

From species-specific studies we can estimate the number of breeding pairs and the area and quality of forest needed to sustain populations of raptors. Thus size of parks or reserves can be, in part, based on and justified by these data, with raptors serving as the standard for the entire ecosystem. Recommendations will be made to the *Direction des Eaux et Forêts* as data become available to determine whether the size, locality and quality of existing and planned reserves are sufficient to sustain viable raptor populations.

Using data from species-specific studies and community monitoring we can define ways in which forests can be managed to preserve raptor populations and their associated biotic communites. As larger areas of forest are protected more stringently, demands for some economic gain will increase. As we learn more about tropical raptors, recommendations will be developed on how forests can be managed for gain while preserving bio-diversity. Information will be published as data become available and we will work directly with local government and non-government agencies to develop sustainable resource utilisation, using raptors as a monitoring tool.

4) Identify priority areas:

We are identifying ecologically unique or special areas (high species diversity, high population density, or areas that support species with very limited distribution) of critical importance for protection. Predators are excellent indicators: typically, when predators are present in high densities this indicates that unique environmental conditions exist. Surveys for raptors and habitats will detect such areas for conservation. We will work with the USAID-funded Biodiversity Planning Service systematically to survey Madagascar for raptors and make recommendations to *Direction des Eaux et Forêts* as data become available.

5) Conserve biodiversity by preventing the extinction of raptor species:

We are providing expertise and supervision to train Malagasy personnel, as well as resources necessary to initiate and continue an endangered species management programmme, including techniques such as the captive breeding and release that we have successfully used with 21 other species of eagles, hawks, falcons and owls. This will be accomplished in co-operation with the *Direction des Eaux et Forêts* and *Association Nationale pour la Gestion des Aires Protégées (ANGAP)* for those species threatened with extinction, initially the Madagascar Fish Eagle.

METHODS AND PROGRESS

Train Malagasy personnel

The success of any conservation programme is dependent on human resources that allow long-term sustainability. The aim of The Peregrine Fund programme is to develop the local human resources accordingly. Malagasy personnel are receiving training as the project progresses and form a core team of field biologists capable of collecting the data needed, as well as of training other field biologists. Three Malagasy have been trained in the first year, five will be trained in the second, and eight in the third to fifth years. In addition, two students from the University of Antananarivo are participating in the training and studies, so that these future administrators will have an understanding of the need and value of ecological monitoring.

Rain forest conservation and raptor research on Masoala Peninsula

The Masoala Peninsula, on the north-east coast of Madagascar, supports the last remaining coastal rain forest, as well as untouched montane and sclerophyllus rain forest and fringing coral reefs. Masoala is currently not protected. About half of the peninsula remains in a pristine state because topography limits its agricultural value, but there are increasing signs of subsistence level exploitation from villages that fringe the coast and rivers of the peninsula. Much of the flatter eastern area is already dominated by slash and burn cultivation. As the human population doubles in the next 20 years, demands on this area will increase. A 300,000ha reserve is planned for the peninsula, and the peninsula is the object of one of the "Integrated Conservation and Development Programs" funded by U.S. Agency for International Development.

Working in co-operation with Missouri Botanical Garden and collaborating with The Xerces Society and Center for Conservation Biology, the Peregrine Fund's goals are to (1) survey for raptors on the Masoala Peninsula; (2) develop low-technology methods to use raptors as indicators of forest health; and (3) establish criteria needed for monitoring and management of protected forests.

Raptor community and habitat surveys

Working from our small field station, about 6km south of the village of Ambanizana at the mouth of the Andranobe River, we marked routes along water courses and ridges to penetrate the forest inland and ascend mountains to an altitude of just over 700m. From these routes we conducted raptor surveys, using point observations from emergent trees, acoustic luring and listening surveys (Whitacre *et al.* 1991). Each trail was surveyed a minimum of three times during the breeding season (September to February). Surveys lasted from one hour before dawn for five hours to optimize our ability to detect nocturnal, crepuscular and diurnal species. Point counts were also tested throughout the day from sunrise at 05h00 to dusk at 18h00.

1) Raptor census:

The Peregrine Fund developed the following raptor census protocol in Central America (Whitacre *et al.* 1991): Raptors are surveyed using a one-hour pre-dawn listening census, a four-hour visual (point count) census from a canopy emergent viewpoint, and an acoustic luring census along a 1km transect starting at the point count site. Point counts consistently view an arc of 120 degrees, the orientation of which is designated for each viewpoint to allow a 1km uninterrupted view. All raptors sighted within 1km (area of 1,047 km^2) are recorded in five minute intervals (a perching bird being recorded every five minutes), and their position in the survey are described, using a grid system. No two observation arcs overlap. To improve statistical independence of counts, points are spaced to maximize distance between them, within the constraints of accessibility. The number of observation points used are limited by the number of personnel available, accessibility and time available during the breeding period. Ten points have been set up and used repeatedly on Masoala, and another ten will be established in the next season's work.

Initial results from January and February 1992 (Table 1) show that observations made in the early morning reveal highest numbers of species (6), but a lower rate of observation of individuals (0.67 birds per hour). When this season's data collection is complete in May 1992, results will be used to modify methods to maximize counts of species and individuals.

2) Vegetation analysis:

The use of raptors for environmental monitoring is dependent on understanding the relation between raptor population and community parameters and habitat modification. Quantitative analysis of habitat (mainly vegetation physiognomy) has been developed by The Peregrine Fund (Whitacre *et al.* 1991) as follows. To maximize capture of heterogeneity within the vegetation of the point count arc, data are collected along a 1km linear transect centred through the arc from the observation point to the arc's perimeter. Data are collected using two methods, (i) point-quarter sampling at 20 sites located at 80 and 100m, 180 and 200m etc. from the observation point, and (ii) 1.5m x 20m transect sampling between point-quarter sites.

Point-quarter sampling measures canopy density, ground aspect and slope, density of grasses/sedges within 3m of point, mean canopy height in 5m classes, canopy height above the point, height of tallest tree within 30m, human disturbances in four classes, nature of human disturbance, diameter at breast height (dbh) and distance from point of nearest tree of > 10cm dbh in each quarter around the point, tree species name, and topographic positions (flat, slope, hilltop, hill foot, valley).

Transect sampling measures ground cover density from 25 presence/absence samples, number of tree-fall gaps intersected, length and width of tree-fall gaps, number and height of woody plants in 5dbh classes up to > 10cm dbh, number of vines in 5 dbh classes, and number of dead, hanging vegetation in 5 dbh classes.

Multivariate analysis will be applied to all data collected in both pristine and modified forest over the three-year study period to indentify key features of the raptor community that are suitable parameters for monitoring ecological change. Criteria for monitoring and management of protected forests will be based on natural variance of this parameter found in pristine forest and established after the first three-year period, but as long-term data are collected and analyzed, criteria will be reviewed and changed if necessary.

Table 1. Number of individuals of each species seen in three time periods during the day during January and February 1992.

Species	Time of day		
	05h00 - 10h00	10h00 - 14h00	14h00 - 18h00
Buteo brachypterus	29	25	15
Polyboroides radiatus	6	12	2
Accipiter francesii	2	0	1
Falco newtoni	0	0	1
Falco zoniventris	1	0	0
Falco concolor	1	2	0
Asio madagascariensis	1	0	0
Number of observation hours	60	30	32
Number of birds seen per hour	0.67	1.30	0.59

Species Specific Studies

The Madagascar Buzzard *Buteo brachypterus* was chosen as the first species to study because it is one of the larger, more common species inhabiting rain forest and other habitats in Madagascar (Berkelman, *this volume*). Studies will provide information on spatial and habitat resources needed by this species, that can be used as a first step towards developing the use of raptors as indices for reserve design and management.

IDENTIFICATION OF CRITICAL SITES

1) Ambatovaky

Ambatovaky Special Reserve (49°04' - 49°25'E and 16°57' - 16°36'S) is the largest Special Reserve in the country, consisting of 60,050ha primary lowland rain forest, moist montane forest and some slash-and-burn cultivation. It is of special value because it is the only area to have recent (1989) tangible evidence of the endangered Madagascar Serpent Eagle (Langrand *pers. comm.*) in the form of a fresh skull of the species. Ambatovaky is also known to sustain six threatened and five near-threatened bird species, and about 50 endemic forest dependent birds, making it one of the most important rain forests in Madagascar. Although a Réserve Spéciale, Ambatovaky's protected status is not enforced. Much of the southern boundary has been cleared for tavy (slash and burn cultivation); Iampirano village is within the reserve, and in this area tavy extends up to 8km inside the reserve (Raxworthy *et al.* 1990). Ambatovaky may benefit from an integrated development and conservation programme such as those now funded by USAID. The Peregrine Fund has the knowledge and expertise to collect baseline data, evaluate and monitor a programme for conservation of biodiversity. We are planning to work as partners with a development organisation to plan and carry out a conservation programme that incorporates local inhabitants.

2) Lake Ankerika Complex

The Antsalova district on the west coast of Madagascar, due west of the capital, Antananarivo, was identified in 1970 at the International Conference on the conservation of Nature (Resolution

No. 8, Langrand & Meyburg 1984) as an area in need of protection because of its importance for many water birds including the endangered Madagascar Fish Eagle and Madagascar Teal *Anas bernieri*. Despite efforts to include it as a world Heritage Area under the UNESCO programme, it is not listed as such (Thorsell, *pers. comm.*) and currently is not protected. We will work with the UNDP in Madagascar to develop sustainable protection of this area.

SUPPORT FOR SPECIES SURVIVAL

Madagascar Fish Eagle

The Madagascar Fish Eagle (also known as the Madagascar Sea Eagle) is listed as an endangered species (Collar & Stuart 1985), and is considered one of the rarest birds of prey in the world (Meyburg 1986). A population survey in 1985 estimated the entire breeding population to be 45 to 50 pairs, patchily distributed along the central- to north-west coast of Madagascar (Langrand & Meyburg 1989). None of the known pairs are nesting in protected areas. Causes of population decline are thought to be deforestation, silting of water, and shooting, the latter largely due to unawareness of the species' plight. The small population size and clumped distribution of the species has left it vulnerable to extinction from random catastrophic events, such as hurricane or serious disease epidemic.

One goal of The Peregrine Fund's project is to prevent the extinction of the Madagascar Fish Eagle by increasing the species' distribution and abundance, ensuring that a significant number of birds nest in protected areas and increasing public understanding about the need to protect the species and conserve its nesting and foraging habitat. The first objective will be achieved through species management, such as captive breeding and release techniques; the second will be achieved by working with the UN Development Programme to establish a protected area in the Antsalova region incorporating the Lake Ankerika complex. Objective three will be achieved through public education.

Little is known about the species' ecology. Before appropriate management can be planned, we need a basic understanding of its behaviour, breeding biology, population dynamics and factors affecting these. We can then identify ways to increase the species' distribution and abundance. While management can be based on some minimal information about behaviour and breeding biology, understanding its effects requires more detailed, long-term information. We will census the species' population to determine if it has changed in the seven years since the last estimate. In doing so, we will establish baseline data using standardized methods that will be used to monitor the population and evaluate the success of our management programme. Research was begun in 1991 and will provide the data needed by the end of 1992.

CONCLUSION

The Peregrine Fund's programme in Madagascar started in 1991 to contribute to Madagascar's *Environmental Action Plan* by using birds of prey as a focus for conservation. We are developing local human resources by training Malagasy personnel. We are conducting species specific studies that will help develop the use of raptors as indicators for reserve design and management. We are doing raptor community and habitat surveys on Masoala Peninsula to develop use of raptor community and population parameters for monitoring conservation management. We are doing studies to design and initiate an endangered raptor management programme, focusing first on the Madagascar Fish Eagle.

ACKNOWLEDGEMENTS

The successful start of this project in March 1991 was ensured by substantial co-operation with three Malagasy government Ministries (Water and Forests, Higher Education, and Research). Essential support and co-operation was gained from other NGOs, including World Wide Fund for Nature - Madagascar, and Missouri Botanical Garden. Equally important was the development of co-operation and collaboration with local inhabitants of Masoala. Field personnel from the U.S. included Dr. Richard Watson (Project Director), Richard Lewis (In-country Project Manager) and Jim Berkelman. Malagasy trainees included Victor Baba, Fortunat Toto and Fortuné Toto. Students supported include Suzanne Razafindramanana and Lily Arison Rene de Roland. Local assistance was provided by Georges Modeste and many inhabitants of Ambanizana and

Maraontsetra. Financial support is provided by The John D. and Catherine T. MacArthur Foundation, Environment Now, and the Liz Claiborne and Art Ortenberg Foundation.

REFERENCES

BERKELMAN, J. Autecology of the Madagascar Buzzard *Buteo brachypterus*. This volume.

COLLAR, N. J. & S. N. STUART 1985. *Threatened Birds of Africa and Related Islands*. The ICBP/IUCN Red Data Book, Part 1. ICBP/IUCN Cambridge, U.K.

EHRENFELD, D. 1989. Research priorities in conservation biology, excerpts from the "Executive Summary". *Conservation Biology*, Vol. 3(2):113-115.

FAO 1981. Tropical forest resources assessment project (GEMS): tropical Africa, tropical Asia, tropical America. (4 vols.) FAO/UNEP, Rome

GOLDSMITH, F. B. 1991. (ed) *Monitoring for Conservation and Ecology*. Chapman and Hall, London.

GREENE, H. W. 1988. Species richness in tropical predators. Pages 259-274. *In* F. Almeda and C. Pringle (Eds.), 1988. *Tropical Rain Forests: Diversity and Conservation*. California Academy of Sciences, San Francisco.

GUILLAUMET, J.-L. 1984. The vegetation: an extraordinary diversity. pp. 27-54. *In* Jolly *et al.* (Eds.), *Madagascar*. Pergamon Press, NY.

JENKINS, M. D. 1987. *Madagascar: an environmental profile*. IUCN Publication, Gland, Switzerland and Cambridge.

JOLLY, A. & R. JOLLY. 1984. Malagasy economics and conservation: a tragedy without villains, pp 211-217. *In* Jolly *et al.* (Eds.). *Madagascar*. Pergamon Press, NY.

KREMEN, C. *In press*. Ecological monitoring: a vital need in integrated conservation development programs in the tropics. *Conservation Biology*.

LANGRAND, O. 1987. Distribution, status, and conservation of the Madagascar Fish Eagle, *Haliaeetus vociferiodes* Desmus 1845. *Biol. Conserv.* 42: 73-77.

LANGRAND, O. & B-U. MEYBURG 1984. Birds of prey and owls in Madagascar: their distribution, status, and conservation. *In* J. M. Mendelsohn & C. W. Sapsford (Eds.): *Proc. Symp. African Predatory Birds*, Natal Bird Club, Durban.

LANGRAND, O. & B-U. MEYBURG 1989. Range, status and biology of the Madagascar Sea Eagle, *Haliaeetus vociferoides*. *In* R. D. Chancellor & B-U. Meyburg (Eds.): *Raptors in the Modern World*. WWGBP: Berlin, London & Paris.

MEYBURG, B-U. 1986. Threatened and near-threatened diurnal birds of prey of the world. *Birds of Prey Bull.* 3: 1-12.

RABINOWITZ, P. D., M. F. COFFIN & D. FALVEY 1983. The separation of Madagascar and Africa. *Science* 220: 67-69.

RAXWORTHY, C. (ED.) 1990. Expediton to Ambatovaky Special Reserve 1990, Preliminary Report. MERG, The Conservation Foundation, London.

ROBINSON, S. K. & D. S. WILCOVE 1989. Conserving tropical raptors and game birds. *Conservation Biology*, Vol 3(2): 192-193.

SAFFORD, R. & W. DUCKWORTH (Eds.) 1990. A wildlife survey of Marojejy Nature Reserve, Madagascar. ICBP, Cambridge, U. K.

SHELDON, B. C. & J. W. DUCKWORTH 1990. The rediscovery of the Madagascar Serpent Eagle *Eutriorchis astur*. *Bull. Brit. Orn. Club.* 110: 126-130.

SMYTH, N. 1987. The importance of mammals in Neotropical forest management. Pages 79-98. *In* J. Figueroa, V. Wadsworth & S. Branham (Eds.) 1987. *Management of the Forests of Tropical America*. Institute of Tropical Forestry. Southern Forest Experiment Station. U.S.D.A. Forest Service.

TAYLOR. R. J. 1984. *Predation*. Chapman and Hall, New York. 166pp.

TERBORGH, J. 1988. The big things that run the world - a sequel to E. O. Wilson. *Conservation Biology*, Vol. 2 (4): 402-403.

THIOLLAY, J.M. 1989. Area requirements for the conservation of rainforest raptors and game birds in French Guiana. *Conservation Biology*, Vol. 3 (2):128-137.

WHITACRE, D., W. A. BURNHAM & J. P. JENNY 1991. Maya Project: use of raptors and other fauna as environmental indices for design and management of protected areas and for building local capacity for conservation in Latin America. Progress Report IV. The Peregrine Fund, Boise. 185pp.

WILCOVE, D. S. 1985. Nest predation in forest tracts and the decline of migratory songbirds. *Ecology* 66:1211-1214.

Richard T. Watson
The Peregrine Fund
World Center for Birds of Prey
5666 West Flying Hawk Lane
Boise, Idaho 83709, USA

Richard Lewis
The Peregrine Fund Project
in Madagascar
B. P. 4113, Antananario 101
Madagascar

Meyburg, B.-U. & R. D. Chancellor eds.1994
Raptor Conservation Today
WWGBP / The Pica Press

Status, Distribution, Current Research and Conservation of Forest Birds of Prey in Cuba

Carlos Wotzkow

INTRODUCTION

Cuba's forest raptors (Falconiformes and Strigiformes) are characterised by 1. A numerical imbalance between the resident subspecies (13) and the migratory (3); 2. Grades of endemism low in the higher taxonomic categories; 3. Very low population densities in general; and 4. A continuous tendency towards loss of diversity in all remaining forest areas in the Cuban archipelago. These four basic characteristics are directly related to the geographic situation of Cuba and its adjacent keys, the culture of its inhabitants and an inadequate environmental policy, maintained by all governments since the times of the island's discovery.

The majority of the Cuban raptors apparently derive from a small group of ancestral immigrants, which reached the island by chance or by different routes in different geological eras, and generated a rapid process of speciation, culminating in the present great subspecific diversity.

MATERIALS AND METHODS

All human activities expressed as factors degrading the ecology of the areas here referred to have been personally verified by the author over the past twelve years (1979-1992). The information on introduced species was obtained from personnel connected with the National Enterprise for the Protection of Flora and Fauna of the Ministry of Agriculture.

All names of raptors in this paper follow the Scientific and Common terminology of the sixth AOU Check List, with the exception of those where the Cuban term is added to specify reference to an endemic subspecies.

Relative Abundance and Ecological Density (Table 1) are based, both for calculation and denomination, on Johnson 1978.

STATUS AND DISTRIBUTION

Surveys for the analysis of the relative abundance and ecological density of some of these birds have only localised value. On the other hand, those conducted at the beginning of the 1980s cannot be considered up-to-date, due to the accelerating human exploitation to be seen in almost all localities. For some species the situation is desperate. Since 1930 there have been no confirmed reports of the continued existence of the Cuban Hook-billed Kite *Chondrohierax uncinatus*, although some investigators have reported it from the vicinity of Duaba Arriba in 1974, and in San Alejo in 1981, both localities in Guantanamo Province (Giraldo Alayon, pers. comm.).

During the last five years 120 days were spent in an attempt to relocate this species and 420km of forest trails in the Cuchillas de Moa (Holguin Province) and the Cuchillas de Toa (Guantanamo Province) were repeatedly explored, together with 328km of riverine woods along the Jaguani, Toa and Duaba river basins, but with no results. J. C. Gundlach himself, accustomed to describe the ecological aspects of the birds he collected, listed only 10 individuals from only six localities (Gundlach 1893). There is no doubt that to this naturalist the Cuban Hook-billed Kite was already an extremely rare bird. However, lack of institutional support and of resources to continue the search preclude any positive assertion that it is extinct.

Table 1. Relative Abundance (RA) and Ecological Density (ED) of some Cuban forest raptors in localities with continuous human transformation.

Subspecies	Locality	RA (km)	ED (ha)	Year of analysis
Accipiter g. gundlachi	Ciénaga de Zapata	0.30	0.0015	1985
Accipiter g. wileyi	Sierra Maestra	0.21	0.0035	1986
Buteo j. solitudinis	Cordillera Guaniguanico	0.12	0.0003	1985
Buteo p. cubanensis	Cuchillas de Toa	1.10	0.0014	1988
Falco s. sparveroides	Ciénaga de Zapata	0.36	0.176	1985
Glaucidium s. siju	Ciénaga de Zapata	5.0	0.008	1989
Gymnoglaux l. lawrenci	Cuchillas de Toa	0.28	0.050	1988
Gymnoglaux l. exsul	Ciénaga de Zapata	10.0	0.028	1989

The Cuban Sharp-shinned Hawk *Accipiter striatus* finds itself in much the same situation. There are barely a dozen reports of sightings during the past 28 years, and these, including my own, are not wholly reliable, due to the similarity of the Cuban subspecies to the *velox* race, a winter visitor. Its main population is centred on the Sierra del Rosario (Pinar del Río Province), although it also occurs in the submontane forests of the Escambray mountains (Las Villas and Sancti Spiritus Provinces), the Sierra Maestra (Granma and Santiago de Cuba Provinces) and the Cuchillas del Toa.

The best assessment of the status and distribution of Gundlach's Hawk *Accipiter gundlachi* has been published recently (Wotzkow 1991a); it is highly endangered, although relatively well distributed in two large population centres.

The distribution of the Cuban Broad-winged Hawk *Buteo platypterus cubanensis* is the same as at the beginning of the 1980s, as reported by Wotzkow (1985); however, its numbers are decreasing alarmingly in many localities, mainly due to degradation of the natural habitat. The Red-tailed Hawk *Buteo jamaicensis* is, on the other hand, widely distributed throughout the island, present even in small isolated groves, but much hunted by farmers. Between 1982 and 1983 these birds were practically exterminated from the mountain complex of Jaruco (Havana Province), yet in 1991 its status was found to be comparable with that of 1980-81; this could be attributed only to immigrations from North America, from where individuals have already been reported (Wotzkow 1985). However, to judge from the numerous known captures of this species throughout the island, it is doubtful whether its re-establishment is wholly due to the breeding success of neighbouring populations and their subsequent colonisation of vacant ecosystems.

The most abundant and most widely distributed Cuban raptor is the Cuban Kestrel *Falco sparverius sparveroides*. It may be found anywhere, from the densest rain forest to the most intensively cultivated plains. Its habit of using the old nests of woodpeckers, combined with the abundance and diversity of the latter, seems to be the main reason for its high numbers and wide distribution.

Among the owls, one of the least studied is the Burrowing Owl *Speotyto cunicularia*. Its status is completely unknown, and it only occurs in small patches of palm *Saval parviflora* forest mixed with semi-deciduous elements on sandy soil in the southern portion of the extensive rainy plain of Pinar del Rio Province and the surrounding woods of the Ciénaga de Lanier on the Isle of Pines.

The Cuban Bare-legged Owl *Gymnoglaux lawrenci* is widely distributed in the archipelago. In the Ciénaga de Zapata (Matanzas Province) it is relatively abundant in mixed forests of palm and semi-deciduous trees. However, these concentrations are maintained only during the breeding season and depend on the availability of suitable nest sites.

A similar degree of knowledge exists for the Cuban Pygmy Owl *Glaucidium siju*, the distribution of which is continuous throughout the island, where it even inhabits isolated groves surrounded by cultivated fields.

The status of the Stygian Owl *Asio stygius* is unknown. Its distribution is wide, its most important population centres being concentrated in four main areas: the forests of the Sierra del Rosario, the Ciénaga de Zapata, the pine forests of the mountain complex of the Cuchillas de Moa, Toa and Mayarí, and the Isle of Pines, but it has also been reported in other localities of Sierra Maestra, Escambray and the Guanahacabibes peninsula. Judging by the scarcity of individuals in these areas, however, only very few survive from former larger populations.

CURRENT RESEARCH

For reasons unknown, taxonomy has been the principal subject of study on Cuban raptors for the past century. However, although nearly completed, the systematics of the group requires fresh revisions, above all at subspecific level.

The zoogeography of these birds has not as yet been studied, in spite of ample data in numerous publications and MSS. As a result, no coherent distribution map has as yet been drawn. Furthermore, in Cuba research on raptors at a community level is not outstanding. Even more disheartening is the quality of the auto-ecological studies undertaken in recent years, with very few exceptions. Thus the level of knowledge on the ecology of the forest raptors is quite inadequate. Some species have been moderately studied (Gundlach's Hawk, Red-tailed Hawk, Cuban Kestrel, Cuban Pygmy Owl, Cuban Bare-legged Owl) but there are other species about which virtually nothing is known (Cuban Sharp-shinned Hawk, Cuban Hook-billed Kite, Burrowing Owl and Stygian Owl) (Table 2).

During the last three decades collaboration between specialists increased, but their research has been focused on economic interests and not on conservation of the indigenous fauna. Still more revealing is the fact that Cuban raptors have never been included as a subject for research in the programmes of any scientific institution.

Cuban or foreign biologists have not taken raptors into particular consideration, with the exception of check lists covering remote localities: Garrido & Schwartz (1968); Garrido (1973); Estrada & Novo (1984); Silva & Estrada (1982); Acosta & Berovides (1984); Acosta *et al.* (1984); Estrada & Rodriguez (1984); Garrido *et al.* (1986); García *et al.* (1987); Alayón *et al.* (1987); Acosta *et al.* (1988); Kirkconnel & Posada (1988); Posada *et al.* (1989); Torres *et al.* (1988); Torres & Solana (1987) and García *et al.* (1989), to mention only a few. Apart from these, a few studies on the forest raptors of Cuba: Wotzkow (1985); Berovides & Fernandez (1984); Thiollay (1985); Wotzkow (1985); Wotzkow (1986a, 1986b); Wotzkow & Cruz (1987); García *et al.* (1987); Wotzkow & Wiley (1988); and Wotzkow (1991a, 1991b), together with some other research as yet unpublished, constitute the most recent data on the ecology of these birds (Table 2).

CONSERVATION

Conservation policies in Cuba are complex and not clearly defined. As an instrument for legal protection of the environment and the rational use of natural resources, the Law 33/81 was adopted by the National Assembly of Popular Power on the 27th December 1980 (Academia de Ciencias 1983), but the powers contained in Sections III and IV have never been implemented, so that the law is inoperative.

The COMARNA (National Commission for Protection of the Environment and Rational Use of Natural Resources) is, within the Cabinet of Ministers, the instrument through which the government dictates policy in matters of conservation at a national level. The provincial commissions for the environment technically advised by the COMARNA are managed by the local organs of Popular Power, and it is through them that conservation at provincial level should be carried out. However, the National Executive Board of Silviculture of the Ministry of Agriculture(MINAGRI) is also responsible for conservation activities, which it should undertake through its different provincial dependencies and the National Corps of Game-keepers. Within this same Ministry the National Enterprise for the Protection of Flora and Fauna controls 73 reserves (in different IUCN categories). The ACC (Cuban Academy of Sciences), for its part, directs research related to conservation through the Institute of Ecology and Systematics.

Table 2. Present situation of ecological knowledge on Cuban forest raptors: (a) status, (b) distribution, (c) foraging ecology, (d) basic ecology, (e) reproductive ecology, (f) aspects related to general behaviour and, with reference to the migratory species, (g) zones habitually frequented in their temporary distribution, and (h) aspects related to feeding.

SPECIES	BIOLOGICAL ASPECTS KNOWN
	FALCONIFORMES
Chondrohierax u. wilsoni	c
Accipiter g. gundlachi	a,b,c,d,e,f,
Accipiter g. wileyi	a,b,c,f
Accipiter s. fringilloides	-
Accipiter s. velox	g
Buteo j. solitudinis	a,b,c,d,e,f
Buteo p. platypterus	g,h
Buteo p. cubanensis	a,b,c,f
Falco s. sparverius	g,h
Falco s. sparveroides	a,b,c,d,e,f,
	STRIGIFORMES
Speotyto c. floridana	b
Glaucidium s. siju	a,b,c,d,e,f
Glaucidium s. vittatum	-
Gymnoglaux l. lawrenci	b.c.f
Gymnoglaux l. exsul	a,b,d,e,f
Asio s. siguapa	b,c,f

From all the above one would think that conservation in Cuba should function without any problems, but bureaucracy, administrative vices and lack of collaboration between the various institutions gravely impair the efficiency of the system.

The National Institute for Physical Planning (IPF), which authorises or otherwise the use of land, has on the other hand yielded to pressure from development sectors in the government to exploit protected areas for economic benefit. It may be asserted that in 90% of the protected areas many tourists, mining and forest exploitations are now being pursued, in which the conservation element is largely ignored. Thus the official system is daily violated in many ways.

To pinpoint the causes contributing to the dwindling diversity of forest raptor populations, despite such an array of institutions, it is necessary to define the principal and most regular types of human activity in Cuba. Since early days, and particularly since 1959, Cuban wildlife has been submitted to intense, irrational exploitation and, frankly, to bad management of the country's natural resources. After 1990 a special situation arose: the deep economic crisis has led the country, so far as natural resources are concerned, back to the state which prevailed in the days of colonisation. One example of this is the massive consumption of natural fuels (wood and coal), for both domestic and industrial use. Table 3 shows the principal factors and potentially damaging actions affecting the forest ecosystems and the raptors inhabiting them.

Table 3. Degrading factors detrimental to the forest ecosystems and their raptor populations (B) Beneficial effects, (IM) Individual mortality, (TP) Temporary problems (nesting failure, etc.), (DD) Diminution of habitat diversity, (PD) Physiological diminution for reproduction, and (DC) Diminution of essential components of the habitat (e.g. nest sites or food supply).

ACTIONS	(B)	(IM)	(TP)	(DD)	(PD)	(DC)
			EXTRACTION			
a) Commercialisation		x	x	x		x
b) Unselective forest clearance		x	x	x		x
c) Illegal hunting		x	x	x		
d) Depredation and vandalism		x	x	x		x
e) Erroneous research		x	x			
			CONVERSION			
f) Physical alterations of the habitat	x	x	x	x		x
			RECREATION			
g) Camping		x	x			
			CONTAMINATION			
h) Chemicals			x[1]	x	x	
i) Noise pollution			x[1]			
j) Introduction of exotic species		x	x	x		x

[1]In these two examples the temporary problems could only occur if the contamination directly affected breeding adults.

EXTRACTION

A. *Commercialisation*

Cuba exploits for export a considerable number of animals. FAUNICUBA and other such enterprises are directly in charge of the extraction of molluscs, fish, reptiles and birds which form the basic food of many birds of prey. One notorious example is the commercialisation of the Polymita Snail, endemic to the forests of eastern Cuba, and it is quite probable that the disappearance of the Cuban Hook-billed Kite is directly related to the scarcity of this food source. The Polymita travels all over the world in the form of necklaces, earrings, brooches, paperweights, etc. which INTUR (National Institute for Tourism) sells to foreign tourists.

Even within the Cuban Academy of Sciences there is the EMIDICT (Enterprise for the Import and Distribution of Science and Technique) which for many years has promoted the export of live specimens of our indigenous fauna. In the same way, a Cuban-Spanish enterprise of recent creation, INGECO S.A. (Enterprise of Engineering and Ecology) also exports commercial products, the raw material of which is drawn from the Cuban fauna.

Although the direct commercialisation of raptors is not extensive, there unfortunately exists a black market in which they are becoming increasingly involved. Devotees of Afro-Cuban folklore and illegal cock fighters make use of the bones, feathers, fat, eggs and claws of birds of prey, so that dozens of raptors are shot and sold.

B. *Non-selective tree-felling*

The "Plan Turquino", a project created and implemented by the government, has accelerated destruction of many forested areas throughout the country. Its aim is to foster agricultural self-sufficiency among more isolated sections of the population. However, the methods most used (non-selective felling, slash and burn, bull-dozers etc.) threaten the eventual disappearance of important biotopes, leading in turn to a declining rainfall, increased erosion and the loss of biological diversity.

C. *Illegal hunting*

In Cuba, illegal hunting is the general rule for two reasons: 1) lack of adequate scientific bases for the hunting law in force, and 2) uncontrolled and continuous violation of this law. The lack is due to the scarcity of population studies on the species listed in the law, and the violations stem from officially unauthorised and indiscriminate hunting within protected areas, even during close seasons. These violations are committed extensively throughout the country, occasionally even by the very people responsible for conservation within the areas in question. Examples of such activity are the extermination of the Red-tailed Hawk by farmers in the vicinity of Jaruco, and the indiscriminate killing of raptors to the north of Cayo Coco (Ciego de Avila Province) carried out by the wardens of the Enterprise for the Protection of Flora and Fauna. In both cases it was claimed that this was done purely to "protect" domestic fowl and pigeons.

The trapping of live raptors for falconry has been confirmed in several localities. In 19 checks carried out by the author the birds died, due to inability to provide the necessary quantity or quality of food or to faulty handling, whilst a few escaped during the training period.

D. *Depredation and vandalism*

This category includes the empirical use of many faunistic resources, as well as their destruction without purpose, or motivated by prejudice and ignorance. Among the most general practices are: 1) the habitual taking of eggs for use in religious rites; 2) the taking of chicks for partial or total use in fetishist rites and initiations; and 3) the habit, rooted in many sectors of society, of eating the adult birds.

E. *Harmful research practices*

Amongst the ornithologists and other students of the country's fauna examples abound in which the wrongful methods employed directly or indirectly affect a considerable number of forest raptors. Thus careless inspection of nests often leads to predation by rodents, mustelines and snakes, with loss of eggs or chicks. Or modifications are made to the surroundings of the nest to facilitate photography or periodic inspection. It can happen that the canopy above a nest has been completely stripped of leaves in order to obtain a better light, and birds frequently abandon their nests due to an excessive number of visitors.

HABITAT CHANGE

The intensive effort at present being made to increase agricultural output is rapidly changing the physiognomy of many natural areas.

Drainage of the Laguna de Ariguanabo, the importance of which as a natural refuge for birds has been recognised since the last century, has caused the migratory or resident raptors using this lake and its adjacent forests to be mere records of the past.

The "Plan Turquino", already referred to, is, among national projects, the most harmful one to the forested mountain slopes in the Cuchillas de Moa and Toa, Sierra Maestra, Escambray and the mountains of Guaniguanico (Pina del Río Province). The system has led to wide-scale shifting agriculture, with the usual devastating effects of impoverished soil, erosion, tree-felling and abandonment of unproductive lots.

The destruction of many small patches of woodland within the cultivated areas destroys the local insect fauna and eliminates these "islands" as refuges for *Buteo jamaicensis, Accipiter gundlachi, Falco sparverius, Glaucidium siju* and *Gymnoglaux lawrenci*.

The construction or widening of roads and trails within the forest is another prejudicial factor. In the Ciénaga de Zapata electrification along these routes has caused an increase in the mortality of such species as Gundlach's Hawk, Stygian Owl, kestrels etc. — birds which generally fly below the canopy and collide with the electric cables. In areas like Cayo Coco, the number of raptors killed by vehicles is also notorious. The actual figures are not known, but many ecosystems remain virtually empty of raptors as a result.

RECREATION

So-called "Popular Camping" has increased in recent years. It is a practice in which nearly all the detrimental factors mentioned above are to be found. The low cultural level of those working in conservation only compounds all the errors possible in the management of a forest ecosystem. The hiring of airguns, authorisation of bonfires and unlimited hiking within protected areas all impair the biological diversity in general and forest raptors in particular.

POLLUTION

A. *Chemicals*

The most general form of environmental contamination derives from spraying with organochlorinated products and chemical fertilisers over a wide variety of crops. In many localities these substances leach into the river network; in others the wind favours their dispersal. Most prejudicial is the lack of state control over the adverse effects. The rice fields of Pina del Río, Matanzas, Camaguey and Granma are the most notable centres of such contamination. The results of any research corroborating the levels of toxicity are not made public, and this is in fact one of the worst facets of the Cuban Academy of Sciences' environmental policy.

B. *Noise pollution*

Low-level flying over the forest canopy and the detonation of explosives in military manoeuvres or mining work are the two most common elements of noise pollution. The use of large helicopters in low-level flights causes further damage. The Ciénaga de Zapata, Sierra Maestra and the Cuchillas de Moa, Toa and Baracoa, are areas where tourist flights, forest patrols and the dropping of newspapers affect the forest ecosystem almost daily.

C. *Introduction of exotic species*

The present Government of Cuba has completely ignored the danger inherent in the introduction of exotic species, especially in the ecosystems of the islands, and the archipelago has become one of the most notorious examples in the world for arbitrary introductions.

In the last century the White-tailed Deer *Odocoileus virginianus* and the mongoose *Herpestes auropunctatus* were introduced, the former to increase the variety of game species and the latter to act as a biological control against rodents. The effects, familiar to the management of COMARNA, MINAGRI, ACC and Popular Power, have been disastrous, yet far from embarking on the eradication of these two animals, destroyers of the forest and of ground-nesting bird populations, other species have continued to be introduced without scruple.

The 1980s marked the beginning of what will soon become an ecological crisis by reason of the introduction of dozens of species of a markedly destructive nature. Thus several monkey species (*Macaca* spp.) were released on Cayo Rosario (Special Municipality of the Isle of Pines) to be later used for medical research. These have depredated the vegetation and fauna of this key, have dispersed to other nearby keys and amply confirm the disastrous character of the so-called "controlled introduction policy". Likewise, a nostalgia for "safaris" has promoted the introduction, even within protected areas, of such game species as *Tavassu tajacu, Hidrochoerus hidrocharis, Sus scropha, Cervus canadensis, Dama dama, Cervus elaphus, Guis musimon* and various other species of antelope and birds, mainly from South America. Because of this, the future of the ecosystems is in danger and the situation of the indigenous species becomes ever more insecure. Cuba became a signatory to CITES in 1990 and efforts are being made to prevent the country from running out of crocodiles, flamingos and many other species, but export on a tourist level continues, at least institutionally.

To illustrate the ecological disaster threatening Cuba, one cannot do better than quote Antonio Iraizoz, a journalist genuinely concerned over the conservation of Cuban wildlife, who wrote: "Let us not keep on destroying trees, because if we continue to do so there will not remain a single piece of wood on which to hang ourselves!" (Iraizoz 1949).

REFERENCES

ACADEMIA DE CIENCIAS DE CUBA 1983. Ley No. 33/81 de protección del medio ambiente y del uso racional de los recursos naturales. Glosario. Editore de la ACC, La Habana, 32 pp.

ACOSTA CRUZ, M. & V. BEROVIDES 1984. Ornitoceno sis de los cayos Coco y Romano, Archipiélago de Sabana-Camagüey, Cuba. *Poeyana* 274: 1-10.

ACOSTA CRUZ, M., M.E. IBARRA & T. PATERSON 1984. Caracterización y actividad de la ornitocenosis del Jardín Bot-nico Nacional. *Rev. Jardín Bot. Nacl.* 5 (2): 99-132.

ACOSTA CRUZ, M., M.E. IBARRA & E.F. FERNANDEZ ROMERO 1988. Aspectos ecológicos de la avifauna de Cayo Matías (grupo insular de los Canarreos, Cuba). *Poeyana* 360: 1-11.

ALAYON, G.G. 1987. Lista de las aves observadas en la Reserva Natural de Cupeyal, Provincia de Guantánamo, Cuba. *Misc. Zool.* 31: 1-2.

ALAYON, G.G., A.R. ESTRADA & A.T. LEYVA 1987. Lista de las aves observadas en la Reserva de la Biosfera "Cuchillas del Toa", Privincia de Holguín y Guant-namo, Cuba. *Garciana* 6: 1-3.

BEROVIDES ALVAREZ, V. & J.F. FERNÁNDEZ 1984. Polimorfismo genético del Cernícalo (*Falco sparverius sparveroides*). *Poeyana* 283: 1-11

ESTRADA, A.R. & J. NOVO RODRÍGUEZ 1984. Reptiles y aves de Cayo Inés de Soto, Archipiélago de los Colorados, Pinar del Río, Cuba. *Misc. Zool.* 23:;1.

GARCÍA, M.E., M. GONZÁLES ALONSO & D. RODRÍGUEZ 1987. Ecological evaluation on bird community in semideciduous wood in Zapata Peninsula, Cuba. *Cienc. Biol. Acad. Cienci Cuba* 18: 93-101.

GARCÍA, M.E., J. DE LA CRUZ & A. RAMS 1989. Algunes aspectos ecol¦gicos de la ornitofauna de "La Zoilita", Sierradel Cristal. *Garciana* 16: 1-2.

GARRIDO, O.H. 1973. Amphibians, reptiles and birds of Sabana-Camagüey Archipelago, Cuba. *Torreia* 27 (Nov. Ser.): 1-72.

GARRIDO, O.H. & F. GARCÍA MONTANA 1975. *Catálogo de las aves de Cuba.* Acad. Cienc. de Cuba, La Habana. 143 pp.

GARRIDO, O.H. & A. SCHWARTZ 1968. Anfibios, reptiles y aves de Guanahacabibes, Cuba. *Poeyana Inst. Biol. Habana Ser. A.* 53: 1-68.

GARRIDO, O.H., A.R. ESTRADA & A. LLANES 1986. Anfibios, reptiles y aves de Cayo Guajaba, Archipiélago de Sabana-Camagüey, Cuba. *Poeyana* 328: 1-34.

GUNDLACH, J. 1893. *Ornitología Cubana.* Imprenta La Moderna, La Habana. 328 pp.

IRAIZOZ, A. 1949. *Sinfonía del Terruno.* Imp. Molina, La Habana.

KIRKCONNEL, A. & R.M. POSADA 1988. Adiciones a la fauna de Cayo Romano, Cuba. *Misc. Zool.* 37: 4.

POSADA RODRÍGUEZ, R.M., A. KIRKCONNEL, F. DE ARAZOZA & A. LLANES 1989. Ornitocenosis

de los cayos Campos, Avalos y Cantiles, Archipiélago de los Canarreos, Cuba. *Poeyana* 365: 1-9.
RAMS, A. & C. WOTZKOW 1987. Primer reporte de *Falco peregrinus tundrius* (White 1968) para Cuba. *Garciana* 7: 4.
REYNARD, G.B., O.H. GARRIDO & G.G. ALAYON 1987. Nesting, voice, status and relationships of the endemic Cuban Gundlach's Hawk (*Accipiter gundlachi*). *Wilson Bull.* 99: 73-77.
SILVA RODRÍGUEZ, A. & A.R. ESTRADA 1982. Vertebrados de las Estación Ecol!gica Sierra del Rosario. *Misc. Zool.* 15: 1-2.
THIOLLAY, J.-M. 1985. Falconiformes of tropical rainforests: a review. *ICBP Tech. Publ.* 5: 155-165.
TORRES LEYVA, A. & E. SOLANA OSORIO 1987. Lista de las aves observadas en el Municipio de Holguín. *Garciana* 2: 1-2.
TORRES LEYVA, A., C. WOTZKOW & A. RAMS 1988. Algunas consideraciones sobre la biología del gavil-n colilargo *Accipiter gundlachi wileyi* en las provincias orientales. *Garciana* 10: 1-2.
WOTZKOW, C. 1983. Ahorran energía las aves? *Juv. Tec.* 185: 48-49.
WOTZKOW, C. 1985. Status and distribution of Falconiformes in Cuba. *ICBP Tech. Publ.* 2: 1-10.
WOTZKOW, C. 1986. Ecological observations of Gundlach's Hawk *Accipiter gundlachi* in Cuba. *Birds of Prey Bull.* 3: 111-114.
WOTZKOW, C. 1986b. Algunas consideraciones sobre el estado poblacional y la biología del auro tiñosa (Aves: Cathartidae) en Cuba. *V Conf. Cientif. de Ciancias Naturales.* Fac. Biol., Univ. de La Habana, 140-141.
WOTZKOW, C. 1988. Nueva subespecie de gavilán colilargo en la región oriental de Cuba. *Garciana* 9: 2-3.
WOTZKOW, C. 1991. New subspecies of Gundlach's Hawk *Accipiter gundlachi* (Lawrence) for Cuba. *Birds of Prey Bull.* 4: 271-292.
WOTZKOW, C. & J. DE LA CRUZ LORENZO 1987. Nesting success of the American Kestrel (*Falco sparverius sparveroides* Vigors) in the Boca de la Jaula, Tapaste, Havana Province. *Raptor Res. Report* 6: 43-46.
WOTZKOW, C. & O.H. GARRIDO 1991. On the nidification of the Sharp-shinned Hawk *Accipiter striatus fringilloides* (Aves: Accipitridae). *Birds of Prey Bull.* 4: 97-99.
WOTZKOW C. & J.W. WILEY 1988. Turkey Vulture surveys in Cuba. *J. Raptor Res.* 22: 1-5.

Carlos Wotzkow
c/o Fam. Oggier
Marktgasse 13
3177 Laupen B E
Switzerland

Everglade Kite *Rostrhamus sociabilis*

Part 4

Trapping, Marking and Radio-tagging Techniques

White-headed Vulture *Trigonoceps occipitalis* and
European Black Vulture *Aegypius monachus*

Conveners:

R. Bögel & Dr. R. Kenward

Meyburg, B.-U. & R. D. Chancellor eds.1994
Raptor Conservation Today
WWGBP / The Pica Press

The Systematic Study of Radio-Tagged Raptors: I. Survival, Home-range and Habitat-use.

R.E. Kenward and S.S. Walls

SUMMARY

Studies which use radio-tagging frequently fail to provide worthwhile quantitative data, often because there is inadequate planning of data collection and analysis. We review techniques for obtaining and handling data on survival and movements of radio-tagged raptors, using examples from recent studies of Northern Goshawks (*Accipiter gentilis*) and Common Buzzards (*Buteo buteo*).

Survival monitoring requires (i) unbiased tagging of many individuals, (ii) long detection range, with aircraft always necessary (and able to compensate to some extent for low tag output), and (iii) reliable tags. Data from studies of 350 radio-tagged Goshawks and 60 Buzzards are used to show recent improvements in tag reliability and tagging techniques. Harness-mounted back-packs appear safe for long-life radio tagging of broadwinged species (buzzards, eagles), if fitted (i) very carefully and (ii) at times when birds can habituate without risk, ideally just before fledging. Survival of these raptors was higher than expected in the first year, indicating that healthy populations have a large non-breeding component.

Analysis of location data is best based on large samples of birds. Tracking effort can be reduced by analysing at an early stage to minimise the numbers of fixes/bird. RANGES IV software is used to demonstrate this process and to test for evidence of territoriality of Goshawks in an area with released pheasants. Goshawk data are used to illustrate new tests of habitat use, and there are suggestions for how radio-tagging can determine parameters of individual performance (PIPs) for use in future conservation programmes.

INTRODUCTION

Raptors have now been studied by radio-tagging for three decades, starting with work on eagles in North America (Southern 1964). Much of the early work was essentially qualitative, describing behaviour in small numbers of birds. Such descriptions can still be useful, for example if radio-tagging helps to record breeding and foraging habits of species which live so sparsely or in such impenetrable habitats (*eg* rainforests) that they remain unstudied. Such work is enjoyable, combining the use of sophisticated technology with the ability to find and observe birds that are not accessible to other ornithologists. However, if the studies remain essentially descriptive, they are in danger of becoming a bird-watching indulgence, without contributing the quantitative data which should be used, for example, in conservation programmes. In an early review of publications on radio-tagging, Lance & Watson (1980) concluded that the technique "seldom exploited its full potential . . . due less to drawbacks in the equipment than to how the technique has tended to be used". A decade later, many studies still fail to achieve their full potential because of problems with the collection and analysis of data, especially location data (Harris *et al.* 1990).

In the early years, radio tags and attachment techniques were often unreliable and each person was obliged to develop new field techniques. Analyses typically involved polygons drawn on transparent plastic, and the weighing of paper cut-outs unless a planimeter was available. By 1992, however, the availability of reliable tags, and of information on field-techniques suitable for computerised display and analysis (Macdonald & Amlaner 1980; Kenward 1987; Garrott & White 1990), provide little further excuse for not gathering worthwhile quantitative data. In this and our subsequent paper (Walls & Kenward, this volume), we briefly review recent advances in the collection and analysis of data from radio-tagging, and end with some suggestions to help future projects bring results in line with expectations.

SURVIVAL AND PRODUCTIVITY

Data on survival and productivity of raptors have been especially important for monitoring effects of environmental contamination (Newton 1979), or for making predictions about other population changes (Mueller, Berger & Allez 1977). Understanding how survival and breeding are affected by environmental parameters is also important for population models to predict the effects of habitat modification or climate change. Data on productivity can be gathered by visiting nests, at which time the young can also be ringed for subsequent estimation of survival and dispersal rates. However, the rarity of many raptors means that relatively few are ringed, and it can therefore take many years to accumulate enough ring recoveries for survival analyses, even if all the records for a country are added together.

In the whole of Britain and Ireland, for example, only 5 of 19 diurnal raptor and owl species have provided more than 30 ring recoveries in each of the last three years, with only Sparrowhawk, Kestrel, Barn Owl and Tawny Owl providing enough data to consider a study of variation in first-year survival rates (Table 1).

Table 1 The mean numbers of raptors ringed, and recovered, in Britain and Ireland each year, 1988-1990 (data from Mead and Clark 1989, 1990, 1991).

Species	N ringed	N recovered
Hen Harrier *Circus cyaneus*	338	17
Sparrowhawk *Accipiter nisus*	1892	188
Common Buzzard *Buteo buteo*	298	17
European Kestrel *Falco tinnunculus*	1956	134
Merlin *Falco columbarius*	741	42
Peregrine Falcon *Falco peregrinus*	337	26
Barn Owl *Tyto alba*	1093	156
Tawny Owl *Strix aluco*	1147	71
Total*	8678	(8%) 692

*Also includes: Red Kite *Milvus milvus* (46,3), White-tailed Eagle *Haliaeëtus albicilla* (5,1), Marsh Harrier *Circus æruginosus* (50,0), Montagu's Harrier *Circus pygargus* (21,0), Northern Goshawk *Accipiter gentilis* (171,6), Golden Eagle *Aquila chrysaëtos* (45,1), Osprey *Pandion haliaetus* (59,4), Hobby *Falco subbuteo* (36,2), Little Owl *Athene noctua* (195,9), Long-eared Owl *Asio otus* (134,8), Short-eared Owl *Asio flammeus* (114,7).

Despite the exceptional ringing effort in Britain, where the British Trust for Ornithology now supervises the ringing of more than 800,000 birds each year, there are inadequate data to study annual variations in the survival rates of large raptors. Another problem is the possibility of recovery bias in favour of ringed raptors which hit human constructions or are killed deliberately. Since young and inexperienced raptors are not only more frequently trapped or shot at game farms than adults (Marcström & Kenward 1981), but may also be more prone to accidents, ring recovery may be more likely from juveniles than from adults, which die in the wilder areas. Such bias could lead to over-estimation of first-year mortality rates, which were at or above 60% in 17 of 26 analyses for 13 species of diurnal raptor (Newton 1979). A similar bias would result from ring loss by older birds, which has occurred among German and Swedish Goshawks (Ziesemer 1981; unpublished data).

Radio-tagging provides an alternative to ringing for gathering data on survival. Its potential was realised during the 1970s for release schemes, for example of Peregrines in North America and Goshawks in Britain (Sherrod *et al.* 1981; Kenward, Marquiss & Newton 1981), and more recently for the study of wild raptors. Between 1980 and 1987 in Sweden, 352 Goshawks were radio-tagged in a 650 km² area on the Baltic island of Gotland, an average of 50/year of which about 30/year were young hawks at nests (Marcström, Kenward & Karlbom 1990). Similarly, in 1990-91 we have radio-tagged 58 young Buzzards at nests in 150 km² of Dorset in southern Britain. In the Goshawk study, tags weighing 14g transmitted for 9-10 months, and could be detected up to 20 km away (although detection was at 2-6 km during most tracking). The Buzzard tags made in 1991 weigh 25g, have an expected life of about four years, and can be detected at 40 km, a more than fourfold improvement in performance. This means that when contact is lost with dispersing birds, an area of about 10 000 km² can now be searched with a light aircraft in two hours (Figure 1), which is about half the time it took to search the 3 000 km² island of Gotland. Tracking techniques and tag reliability have improved to the extent that only 4 of 51 Buzzards tagged in 1990 and 1991 remained lost in the following April (Table 2).

Figure 1 Movements of juvenile Buzzards radio-tagged in Dorset, southern England, showing aircraft flight paths in searches for lost birds on 21.09.90 (1½ hours), 13.12.90 (2½ hours covering all of SW Britain) and 15.01.91 (2 hours).

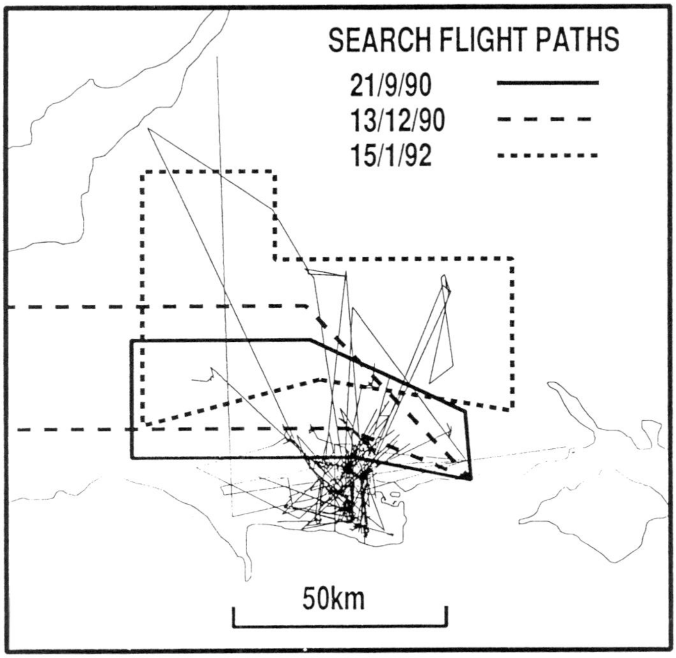

Table 2 The fate of long-life radio tags during the first and last two years of the Goshawk study on Gotland, and of the first two years of the Buzzard study in Dorset.

Years	N Tagged	Known to fail	Shed	Lost	Tracking completed†
1980-1	69	6	4	38	22 (32%)
1983-4	78	0	16	18	44 (56%)
1990-1	51	0‡	1	4*	46 (90%)

† Tracking was completed for birds that died or whose tags lasted at least to the next spring.
‡ Two faulty tags give intermittent signals, but can still be monitored.
* Three of the four lost birds are known emigrants, the other probably emigrated

There are, however, complications when using radio-tagging to monitor survival. An essential consideration, for reasons of animal welfare as well as scientific rigour, is that the tagging should not itself influence survival. The only satisfactory technique for long-term tagging of raptors is the use of back-packs on body harnesses, but this technique itself has been shown to bias behaviour and fitness in a number of bird studies (review by White and Garrott 1990). No such effects have been reported for tail-mounted tags, but these are shed at the next moult, and the antennas on leg tags seldom survive more than a few months. During 1990 and 1991, we have monitored the survival of 35 Buzzards with harnesses and 22 which were equipped initially with 12g leg-tags and later with 15g tail-mounts. We used a harness design of Dunstan (1972), with Teflon ribbon (recommended by M. Fuller), in which a 1/4" strap round the body behind the wings was joined to a 10% larger neck loop by a short strap of 3/8" Teflon along the keel. The tail-mounts were similar to those which had no detectable adverse effect on Goshawks (Kenward 1985).

The mortality of birds with tail-mounts has been 38% (SE=16%) to the end of their first March (after which the tags moulted or exhausted their cells), compared with 27% (SE=8%) for birds with harnesses. Mortality of Buzzards with harnesses was still 27% after a year, which is half the 51-57% first-year mortality estimated for Buzzards by ringing (Mebs 1964; Olsson 1958). Moreover, mortality of only about 10% in the first year has been recorded by Chandler *et al.* (this volume) for Bald Eagles *(Haliaeëtus leucocephalus)* with similar harnesses, and by Nygård, Envik and Kenward (unpubl.) for Sea Eagles *(Haliaeëtus albicilla)*. It therefore seems safe to mount back-packs on nestling broadwinged raptors, which have plenty of time to adjust to the harness before they become independent, and can then have their survival and behaviour monitored for several years.

This is an encouraging finding, but does not necessarily mean that it is safe to put harnesses on all raptors, without at least a pilot study to compare with a safer technique, such as tail-mounting.

Moreover, it is essential that harnesses are very carefully fitted. In Buzzards, variation of only five percent above or below the ideal size of harness loops was found to cause loss of feathers or even chafing of skin on the back. Those who are not familiar with mounting harnesses on raptors must have someone with experience to help them get started.

With equal ability to tag all nestlings, or birds in release projects, it is possible to avoid the marking bias which may occur if birds are trapped. There may, for example, be selection of the better adults if trapping is at nests, or of the hungrier individuals elsewhere. In the Goshawk study, it was possible to catch almost all the birds. Of 187 individuals targeted for capture in the post-fledging period, to attach tail-mounts when their feathers were full grown, only 18 (10%) were not caught (in most cases because trapping was not attempted at some nests where birds were already equipped with leg-mount tags). In contrast, of 31 Buzzards targeted for tail-mounts at the same stage, 15 (48%) could not be caught (χ^2=28.2, P<0.001), despite trapping for up to two weeks near some nests. Since trapping was easiest with the hungriest broods of Buzzards (with feather fret marks) and youngest birds in a brood, we were probably selecting the weaker ones for tail-mounts. This would explain why these had higher mortality and more tendency to disperse than Buzzards with back-packs.

A complication in estimating survival with radio tags, shown in Table 2, is that contact may be lost with a high proportion of tags. If such birds were omitted from the analysis, survival estimates would be biased downwards, because some individuals might have lived for many months before being lost. The solution to this problem is to estimate overall survival as the product of survival in many consecutive small intervals, using only the birds that died or survived through an interval to estimate survival in that interval. The survival of lost birds is then included for all intervals before the one in which they are lost, at which point they are omitted (censored) from further estimates. This approach, which also makes provision for tagged animals to enter the population at different times, is described thoroughly by Pollock *et al.* (1989), with another useful recent review in White & Garrott (1990).

There remains, however, the problem of what happens to censored individuals. If some are lost because of a traumatic death which also destroys the tag (*eg* impact from a vehicle or lead shot), then censoring overestimates the true survival. There is a way round this problem if there are (i) resightings and recoveries of animals from which signals were lost, and (ii) if tags that were known to fail without prejudice to survival can be separated from tags lost inexplicably. This is done in Table 2: birds whose tags were heard to be failing (eg the signal became slow or erratic before contact was lost), or which shed tail-mounts, are separated, in columns two and three respectively, from tags whose signal was lost without explanation. Among all the juvenile Goshawks, the former category included 70 birds which moulted their tags, or for which signal changes indicated that tags were failing; 17 (24%) of these were later recaptured or found dead. There were also 68 tags that were lost without explanation; 16 (24%) of these were recorded again well after the loss. There was thus no evidence of a reduced recovery rate for hawks that were lost inexplicably. They must therefore have been lost mainly because of undetected failures, and not because hawks and their tags were destroyed at the same time. The observed survival rates (with unexplained tag losses censored) could therefore be considered representative of the tagged cohort.

In the case of the Buzzards, only four were lost. Since three were known emigrants, and the fourth disappeared (during a conference) in the peak period for emigration, it can reasonably be assumed that these were alive at the time of signal loss. The survival rate, with these four birds censored, can again be considered representative.

In comparing radio-tagging with ringing for estimating survival, a final concern is the cost. For a fair comparison, the precision of the two techniques should be similar. The precision of a survival estimate with 50 radio-tagged birds is about the same as from 100 ring recoveries: the standard error is 4%. To have 50 radio-tagged raptors at the end of the year, with a 30% annual mortality, requires the marking of 70. For 100 recoveries, with an 8% recovery rate (Table 1), 1250 must be ringed. Except for raptors with very dispersed breeding sites, such as eagles, a skilled operator can track 35 birds annually for sedentary species, and this is comfortably above the 20 individuals/cohort considered by Pollock *et al.* (1989) to be the minimum for inter-cohort comparisons. Movements and survival can be recorded with a minimum of about two days of tracking per month for most of the year, increasing to two days per week for a month during autumn and spring when there are many dispersal movements. That totals 80 man-days over two years. With optimism, a team of two people might hope to find and ring or radio-tag six large raptors a day; they would need 393 workdays for ringing 1180 (= 1250 - 70) birds, or at least 313 more than for radio-tagging and tracking 70. Although more miles would be driven during radio tracking than during the ringing, with extra funds required for radio equipment (*ca.* £·6 000 for tags) and hire of aircraft (in the order of 2-10 hours per year), labour costs would make radio -tagging the less expensive technique for projects in which ringing could not be done by volunteers.

Since the ringing of 1250 birds would require many years of work in one area, or spreading the work over a wide area if the species were common, radio-tagging may often be the more practical technique for gaining data rapidly on rare species, or for building models based on annual variation in weather and food supplies, which can be defined locally but not so precisely over a whole country. In Goshawks, too, ringing data from the same area were biased in favour of hawks killed at farms, and against recording natural deaths at the right time of year (Kenward, Marcström & Karlbom in press). Radio-tagging also provided data not available from ringing, for example by allowing dead hawks to be recovered quickly enough for a thorough *post mortem* examination, and by helping to find nests. The latter saved time which would otherwise have been needed for visual searches, and helped to detect nests in unusual sites. On Gotland, at least two nests were found in pinewoods which would normally have been considered too young. Radio tags can thus aid rational habitat management, in this case by removing the misconception that the Goshawks nest only in old-growth stands. Moreover, in population modelling it is important to record birds whose breeding fails so early that their attempt might not otherwise have been detected.

Perhaps as a result of the bias in ringing, or increased tolerance of raptors and reductions in pollution, the population models obtained by radio-tagging may look rather different from those based on ringing records from earlier this century. Just as the first year mortality of Buzzards was half that estimated previously by ringing, so too the mortality of Goshawks, at 50% for males and 35% for females, was much lower on Gotland than in Fennoscandian ringing studies. Without human intervention, the juvenile mortality of medium-sized raptors may well lie between 20 and 30%. If so, then healthy populations of these species must have many more non-breeding adults than was previously realised. One implication for future conservation is that monitoring nests may give relatively late detection of environmental threats that do not affect reproductive success, because a large proportion of the population may have been lost before numbers of breeding pairs are reduced.

HOME RANGE AND HABITAT USE

Although radio-tagging has not yet been used widely for monitoring survival of wild raptors, many projects have used radio tags for short term studies of ranging behaviour and habitat use. Just as radio-tagging can minimise bias in carefully planned studies of survival and productivity, so too it enables locations and behaviour to be sampled systematically and not just when individuals happen to be most easily detected. The avoidance of bias is not merely of academic interest if, for example, visual sightings focus attention on the immediate surroundings of nests whereas the birds also need preservation of separate hunting areas where they are less easily seen. In creating reserves, there is a need for measurement both of range size and shape, because the latter shows which habitats are most abundant in the area covered by each bird and how much overlap occurs between individuals. Measures of range structure may be required too, for instance to see whether an apparently large range is composed of a small core area in which the bird does most of its foraging and a much greater area used only occasionally, and whether there is a single core or many separate patches, and what the spacing of range centres indicates about the social status of individuals.

One difficulty with estimating the size, shape and structure of home ranges is that there are at least six different analysis techniques, with further variations on each main theme. To be brief, these are summarised in Table 3, with more thorough reviews by Harris *et al.* (1990) and Kenward (1992).

Table 3 Some features of six different home range analysis techniques.

	Grid cells	Normal ellipsoids	Concave polygons	Convex polygons	Contour methods	Cluster analysis
Home range outlines conform well to all recorded fixes	Yes	No	Yes	Yes	No	Yes
Home range outlines conform well to multi-nuclear cores	Yes	No	No	No	Yes	Yes
A single home range centre is estimated	No	Yes	No	Yes	Yes	No
Home range structure statistics (patchiness or fix dispersion)	Yes	Yes	No	No	Yes	Yes
Home range size stabilises with fewer than 100 fixes	No	Yes	?	Yes	Yes	Yes

The grid cell approach (Siniff & Tester 1965) is used relatively infrequently, mainly because it usually requires more than 150 fixes, and sometimes 200-300, to obtain a record of home range size which increases little if more fixes are added. Although ranges are still sometimes plotted as circles or ellipses (Jennrich & Turner 1969; Koeppl, Slade & Hoffman 1975), the estimation assumes that animals distribute their movements about a single range centre, with activity reducing smoothly away from the centre. However, animals often lack a single range centre, at least outside the breeding season, and seldom conform to a statistically normal distribution of locations, so that circular or elliptical outlines usually conform poorly to the fixes (Macdonald, Ball & Hough 1980). Few studies have used concave (minimum area) polygons (Voight & Tinline 1980; Clutton-Brock; Guinness & Albon 1982), at least partly because it is hard to agree on rules for constructing them; their lack of core outlines or structure statistics is a further disadvantage.

Convex polygons are simple to plot and have therefore been used very widely, and thus have the advantage of compatibility with previous studies. They define a convenient limit to the area which may be visited by an animal, and thus to the habitat types and neighbours it can encounter, but their size is strongly influenced by outlying locations. These may be peeled away, by excluding fixes furthest from a range centre, but this is not appropriate for multinuclear or curved ranges. The techniques used for plotting contours of location density can handle multinuclear ranges, are ideal for defining range centres, and provide a very good visual representation of range cores. Harmonic mean contouring (Dixon & Chapman 1980) is used most frequently, but can produce very variable results without the location-centering procedure from Spencer & Barrett (1984). Contouring based on kernel estimators (Worton 1989) is more rigorous. Even so, the density estimation is a smoothing process, so that even the core isolines do not always conform well to the fixes, tending to "balloon" into areas not visited by the animal. This can be avoided by using cluster analysis to define range cores and putting a tight outline round the resulting group of locations (Kenward 1987).

Now that the different estimation techniques are starting to be tested on different data sets, it is becoming apparent that each of the last three methods can be useful, for providing different information. Convex polygons, including cores obtained by peeling, are useful for comparing range areas with previous studies (tests should be based on geometric means, by taking logarithms of the areas), and for defining available habitats, or neighbours with which the animal may interact. The contouring approach is good for visual display and for defining a range centre, whereas cluster analysis appears to be best for defining range cores and resulting structure statistics.

Range cores estimated with the last three approaches can be seen in Figure 2. The data came from five male Goshawks which were radio-tracked in October 1976, at an estate in Sweden where 5 000 pheasants were released each summer and fed at 12 sites with thick cover. The convex polygons containing 100% of the fixes all overlap in the area containing 10 of the 12 feeding sites, and extensive overlap in this northern area remains for (a) the peeled polygons (excluding locations furthest from the location where density was highest) and (b) the harmonic mean contours for the densest 50% of locations. In both cases the two adult male ranges (solid black lines) overlapped extensively at all core sizes, although in cluster analysis (c) the overlaps were much less marked even for the 75% outlines. It is clear that the Goshawks were not being territorial in the sense of excluding each other from hunting areas, so that predation could not be reduced by leaving resident adults to keep others away, although cluster analysis suggested that their foraging was more independent than indicated by the other techniques. Our second paper (Walls & Kenward, this volume) provides further analysis of their sociality.

If location analyses are to provide useful quantitative results, studies need careful planning. Just as conclusions about predation should not be based on observing a single raptor, which may be specialising in a particular prey, nor should assessments of range size and habitat-use come from tracking one animal. Since the movements of each individual are likely to be influenced by its past experience, leading to favoured hunting sites, roosts and routes between them, its location records are not really statistically independent even if they are taken at long enough intervals to avoid serial correlation (*eg* as tested by Swihart & Slade 1985). Comparisons between different categories of animal (*eg* age and sex classes), in different areas, seasons and experimental treatments (*eg* release techniques), should therefore be based on numbers of range records, not numbers of individual locations.

The number of range records can be maximised if data can be obtained from many individuals at a time, by sampling each animal at intervals rather than monitoring single animals continuously. Continuous monitoring of single animals can provide useful insights at the very start of a study,

Figure 2 **Ranges of 5 wintering male Goshawks overlapped extensively where pheasants were released, even when single peeled polygon outlines (a) or harmonic mean density contours (b) contained only 25-50% of the radio fixes, but not when cluster analysis (c) was used to separate foraging areas.**

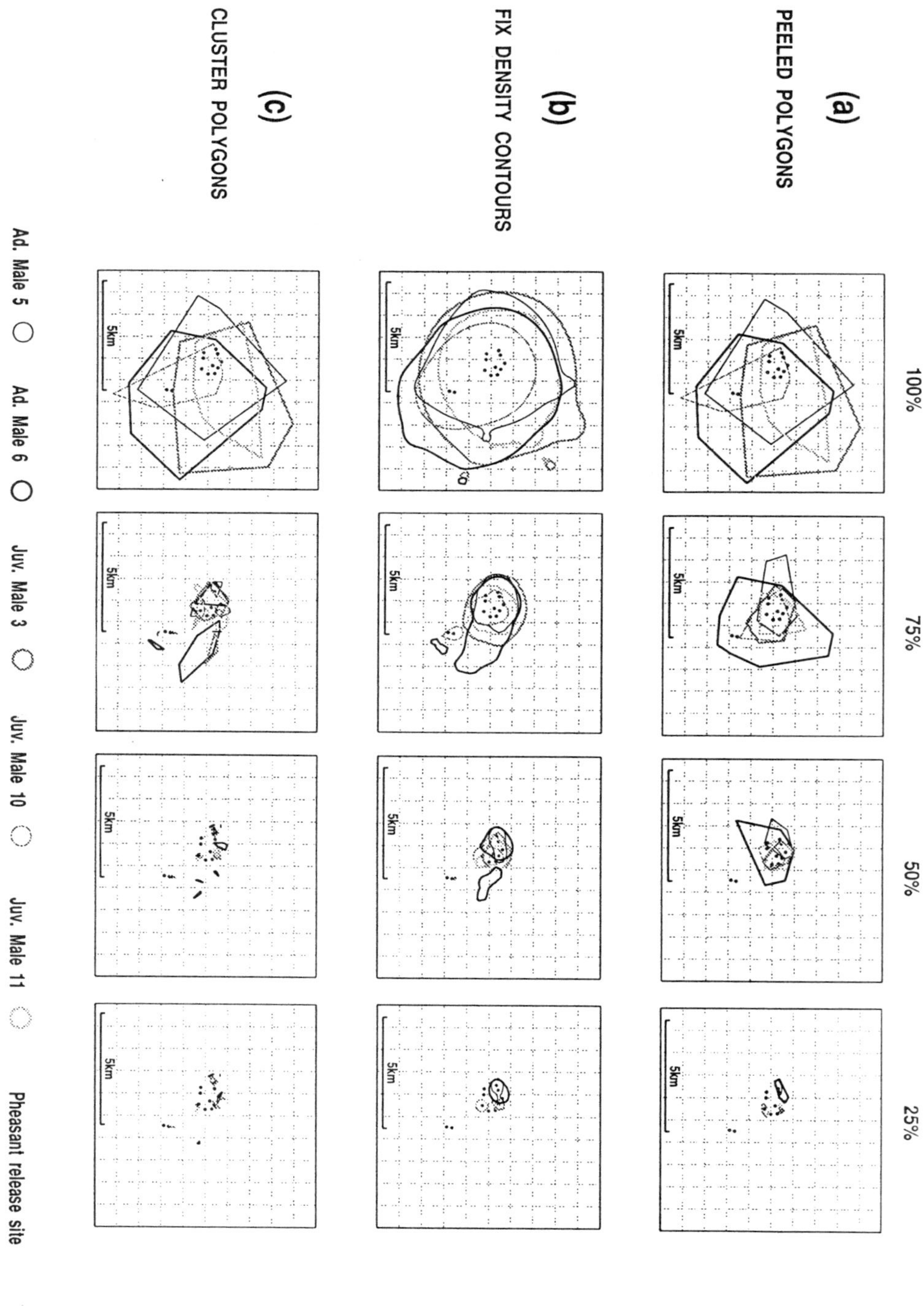

and is sometimes necessary for recording movements or other behaviour in detail, or because very large species are too far apart for an observer to move quickly between them. For systematic sampling, however, a much better approach is to locate a number of individuals in rapid succession, and repeat this at regular intervals. By sampling at regular intervals along a time base, the area containing, say, the densest 80% of the locations is also the area in which the animal spent 80% of its time. By checking all the individuals at a similar time, there is minimum variation in weather and time of day, and data are also most suitable for analysis of sociality. It does require more travel, but we have both used interval sampling to track reasonable samples of large raptors at the same time: REK tracked six Goshawks in October 1976 to record kills as well as locations, and SSW tracked 16 Buzzards in October 1991. Much effort is needed to obtain such records, which makes it desirable to collect no more locations than are needed to define each range. Recording each range rapidly may also be useful for comparing records from consecutive periods, for instance at different points during the breeding season. Even when ranges must be recorded by continuous monitoring, the number of separate records can be maximised by minimising the number of locations in each range. The number required will be least if the locations are not serially correlated, which in principle means that an animal has had time to move across its range between locations (Swihart & Slade 1985). In practice, it seems adequate to record locations at 2-4 hour intervals three times a day. Using this approach, Figure 3 shows that minimum polygon ranges of Common Buzzards *(Buteo buteo)* increased little in size after the first 20 fixes were added. In fact, 30-35 fixes taken over 10-15 days have provided similar sampling saturation for convex polygon ranges of several bird and mammal species (Kenward 1987), although around 60 fixes may be needed for range areas to reach an asymptote with harmonic mean contouring (Harris *et al.* 1990).

Figure 3. Convex polygons round all the fixes increased little in size after the first 20 fixes were collected for 11 Buzzards in October 1990. Plots from RANGES IV are (a) for the individual birds, and (b) for the means, with bars showing maximum to minimum values.

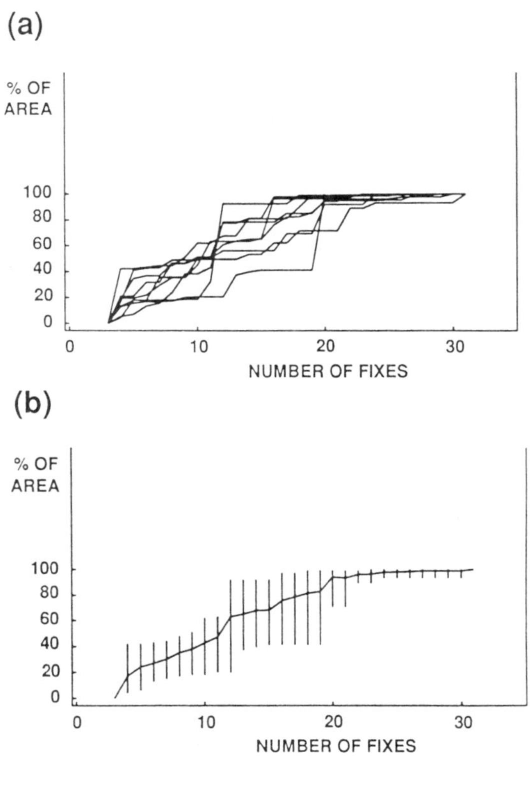

Software which automates incremental analyses and provides multi-range plots is a great help for deciding how many fixes are needed for a standard range record: there is little point in collecting 150 fixes for each home range if 30 will suffice. Such software should if possible be obtained before starting fieldwork because, as noted by Harris *et al.* (1990) "it is important to test the radio-tracking regime before launching into the detailed study". The analysis in Figure 3, and the others in our papers, all used the RANGES IV suite (from ITE Furzebrook, Wareham BH20 5AS, Great Britain), which was designed to handle radio location data from pilot study through to comprehensive analyses of very large data sets.

The range-as-sample approach can be extended to habitat analyses. In fact, if this is not done, statistical testing may be invalid. For example, one should not pool locations from different individuals for χ^2 tests of habitat preference. The final example in this paper shows how such data should be tested.

In habitat analyses it is necessary not only to determine what is available (A) in an area, but also what is used (U) by each animal, where

U is defined as (observations in habitat i)/(observations in all habitats), and

A is defined as (area of habitat i)/(area of all habitats).

Expressing U as a single value for each animal avoids any assumption of independence between locations. However, there is still the problem that all the A_i values, and the U_i for each individual lack independence because they sum to 1. This means that strong avoidance of one habitat can lead to apparent preference for all others. The solution is to investigate habitat use by comparing pairs of habitats. This gives a single comparison if there are only two habitats (because one must be preferred if the other is avoided), and a matrix of $(n\text{-}1)!$ comparisons if there are n habitats.

Testing can be done with a parametric or a non-parametric approach. The parametric approach is based on compositional analysis (Aebischer, Robertson & Kenward, in press), using a logratio transformation, $\ln(U_i/A_i)$, for all the habitats used by each animal. The resulting values are positive if the habitat is used more than expected from its availability, negative if used less than expected, and 0 if use and availability are equal. To compare the use of habitats i and j, the difference $\ln(U_i/A_i) - \ln(U_j/A_j)$ is found for each animal: habitat i is prefered to habitat j if the mean of this difference is significantly greater than 0. If there are more than two habitats, a likelihood ratio test can be applied to the matrix of difference scores to discover whether overall habitat use differs from random.

The main disadvantage of this approach is that it requires the distribution of difference scores to be statistically normal. This would not be the case, for example, if there were divergent strategies between animals, with some favouring habitat i whereas others favour j. If there are enough animals, evidence of divergence can be sought with a test for extreme reactions (*eg* Moses 1952). Alternatively, a non-parametric approach can be used. For example, Kenward (1992) uses Ivlev's index $(U_i\text{-}A_i)/(U_i\text{+}A_i)$ for each animal, because this gives scores from -1 to +1 without the problem of estimating $\ln(U_i/A_i)$ when U_i is 0, and a signed-rank test is used to compare pairs of preference scores. This is done in Table 4 for data from seven Goshawks wintering in a Swedish study area.

In this case there was no sign of a divergence in habitat preferences, although this might have arisen if there had been tracking during breeding: some adults would probably have shown a strong preference for nest areas deep in the woods. As it was, woodland within 200m of an edge ranked most preferred by each bird, and open country ranked less preferred than deep woodland for only two of them (AM9, AF15). Comparing Ivlev indices between pairs of habits, woodland edge was preferred significantly more than deep woodland or open country (Wilcoxon signed-rank matched-pair tests, two-tailed $P = 0.018$ in each case), but there was no significant tendency to avoid deep woodland more than open country in winter (P=0.107). Fortunately, the results are the same as in a previous paper (Kenward & Widèn (1989), which used X^2 tests.

The next decade will see data from radio-tagging used for combined analyses of how range structure and habitat use relates to survival, dispersal and productivity. We are already combining demographic data from Buzzards with habitat analyses based on a landcover map from satellite data. Software advances will make it possible to investigate many parameters of individual performance (PIPs), such as range structure, habitat use and sociality, and to use these in conservation studies. In theory at least, PIPs which predict dispersal, death or breeding failure (Predictors of Impending Peril!) could be used for rapid assessment of an area's suitability for restocking, by releasing very few radio-tagged raptors. For example, if animals in a healthy population prove unsuccessful when they have large range cores, the recording of large range cores for all the individuals released at a new site would cast early doubts on its suitability.

Table 4 Habitat use, availability and Ivlev index scores for seven Goshawks in Sweden.

Fixes in	JM4	AM6	AM8	AM9	JF10	AF11	AF14	
Open country	58	32	38	14	22	4	5	
Woodland edge	203	92	162	139	70	70	81	
Deep woodland	4	2	3	13	1	1	12	
Utilisation *(U)*								Availability (A)
Open country	0.22	0.25	0.19	0.08	0.24	0.06	0.05	0.46
Woodland edge	0.76	0.73	0.80	0.84	0.75	0.93	0.83	0.26
Deep woodland	0.02	0.02	0.01	0.08	0.01	0.01	0.12	0.28
(U-A)/(U+A)								
Open country	-0.4	-0.3	-0.4	-0.7	-0.3	-0.8	-0.8	
Woodland edge	+0.5	+0.5	+0.5	+0.5	+0.5	+0.6	+0.5	
Deep woodland	-0.9	-0.9	-0.9	-0.6	-0.9	-0.9	-0.4	

CONCLUSIONS

Radio-tagging is a simple concept, looks easy and can give exciting results. However, it is a tool which is easy to abuse, particularly by underestimating the skill required. Results presented in this paper, especially in Table 2, represent nearly 20 years spent developing equipment and techniques. Starting projects with the expectation of immediate success can easily lead to frustration and wastage of scarce conservation resources. Would you give a scalpel to a paramedic and expect effective brain surgery?

Although field skills cannot be quickly transferred, it is possible to make recommendations for new projects, as follows:

(i) Be sure that the study species can be caught for tagging and licences are available.

(ii) In projects using harnesses, a pilot study must include training from someone experienced in the technique; it should test safety in species which lack a previous test.

(iii) Location studies should start by obtaining software to develop sampling techniques.

(iv) Sample sizes should be adequate for the investigation concerned, aiming for cohorts of at least 20 in survival studies and never less than five per category in location studies.

(v) It is wise to arrange *post mortem* services in advance and to overestimate travel costs.

ACKNOWLEDGEMENTS

Data on Goshawks were collected in collaboration with V. Marcström and M. Karlbom, with funding from the Swedish Sportsmens Association. Both projects were also funded by the Natural Environment Research Council, with further support for the Buzzard study from Biotrack, the Nature Conservancy Council and the Royal Society for the Protection of Birds. We are deeply grateful to these funding agencies, and to the many landowners and others who provided permissions and assistance in Britain and Sweden. An early manuscript was improved by comments from M.G. Morris.

REFERENCES

AEBISCHER, N.J., P.A. ROBERTSON & R.E. KENWARD in press. Compositional analysis of habitat utilization form animal radiotelemetry data. *Ecology*

AMLANER, C.J. & D.W. MACDONALD 1980. *A Handbook on Biotelemetry and Radio Tracking.* Pergamon Press, Oxford.

CHANDLER, S.K., J.D. FRASER, D.A. BUEHLER, & K.D. JANIS (this volume). Using geographic information systems to analyse Bald Eagle habitat use in Chesapeake Bay, U.S.A.

CLUTTON-BROCK, T.H., F.E. GUINESS & S.D. ALBON 1982. *Red deer: behaviour and ecology of two sexes.* Edinburgh University Press, Edinburgh

DIXON, K.R. & J.A. CHAPMAN 1980. Harmonic mean measure of animal activity areas. *Ecology 61*: 1040-1044

DUNSTAN, T.C. 1972. A harness for radio-tagging raptorial birds. *Inland Bird Banding News* 44: 4-8.

HARRIS, S., W.J. CRESSWELL, P.G. FORDE, W.J. TREWELLA, T. WOOLLARD & S. WRAY 1990. Home-range analysis using radio-tracking data - a review of problems and techniques particularly as applied to the study of mammals. *Mamm. Rev.* 20: 97-123

JENNRICH, R.J. & F.B. TURNER 1969. Measurement of non-circular home range. *J. Theor. Biol.* 22: 227-237

KENWARD, R.E. 1985. Raptor radio tracking and radio telemetry. pp. 409-420 in I. Newton & R.D. Chancellor (eds) *Conservation studies of raptors.* ICBP Technical Bulletin 5.

KENWARD, R.E. 1987. *Wildlife Radio Tagging - Equipment, Field Techniques and Data Analysis.* Academic Press, London.

KENWARD, R.E. 1992. Quantity verses quality: programming for collection and analysis of radio tag data. *In* I.G. Priede, & S.M. Swift (eds) *Wildlife telemetry: remote monitoring and tracking of animals.* Ellis Horwood, Chichester, UK.

KENWARD, R.E., V. MARCSTRÖM & M. KARLBOM (in press). Causes of death in radio-tagged northern goshawks. *In* J.E. Cooper, T.R. Hahn & P.T. Redig (eds) *Raptor Biomedicine.* University Press, Minnesota, U.S.A.

KENWARD, R.E., M. MARQUISS & I. NEWTON 1981. What happens to goshawks trained for falconry. *J. Wildl. Manage.* 45: 802-806.

KENWARD, R.E. & P. WIDÈN 1989. Do Goshawks need forests? Some conservation lessons from radio tracking. pp. 561-567 *in* B.-U. Meyburg, & R.D. Chancellor (eds) *Raptors in the Modern World.* World Working Group on Birds of Prey, Lentz Druck, Berlin.

KOEPPL, J.W., N.A. SLADE & R.S. HOFFMANN 1975. A bivariate home range model with possible application to ethological data analysis. *J. Mamm.* 56: 81-90

LANCE, A.N. & A. WATSON 1980. A comment on the use of radio tracking in ecological research. pp. 335-359 in C.J. Amlaner & D.W. Macdonald (eds.) *A Handbook on Biotelemetry and Radio Tracking.* Pergamon Press, Oxford

MACDONALD, D.W., F.G. BALL & N.G. HOUGH 1980. The evaluation of home range size and configuration using radio tracking data. pp.405-424 *in* C.J. Amlaner & D.W. Macdonald (eds.) *A Handbook on Biotelemetry and Radio Tracking.* Pergamon Press, Oxford

MARCSTRÖM, V. & R.E. KENWARD 1981. Movements of wintering goshawk in Sweden. *Swedish Game Research* 12:1-35.

MARCSTRÖM, V., R.E. KENWARD & M. KARLBOM 1990. *Düvhöken och dess plats i naturen.* Trycksaker, Norrköping, Sweden.

MEAD, C.J. & J.A. CLARK 1989. Report on Bird Ringing for 1988. *Ringing Migration* 10: 158-196.

MEAD, C.J. & J.A. CLARK 1990. Report on Bird Ringing for 1989. *Ringing Migration* 11: 137-176.

MEAD, C.J. & J.A. CLARK 1991. Report on Bird Ringing for Britain and Ireland for 1990. *Ringing Migration* 12: 139-176.

MEBS, T. 1964. Zur Biologie und Populationsdynamik des Mäusebussards (*Buteo buteo*). *J. Orn.* 105: 247-306.

MOSES, L.E. 1952. A two sample test. *Psychometrika* 17: 239-247

MUELLER, H.C., D.D. BERGER & G. ALLEZ 1977. The periodic invasions of goshawks. *Auk* 94: 652-663

NEWTON, I. 1979. *Population Ecology of Raptors.* Poyser, Berkhamsted.

OLSSON, V. 1958. Dispersal, migration, longevity and death causes of *Strix aluco, Buteo buteo, Ardea*

cinerea and *Larus argentatus*. *Acta vertebratica* 1: 91-189.

POLLOCK, K.H., S.R. WINTERSTEIN, C.M. BUNCK & P.D. CURTIS 1989. Survival analysis in telemetry studies: the staggered entry design. *J. Wildl. Manage.* 53: 7-15.

SHERROD, S.K., W.R. HEINRICH, W.A. BURNHAM, J.H. BARCLAY & T.J. CADE 1981. *Hacking: a method for releasing peregrine falcons and other birds of prey.* The Peregrine Fund, Ithaca.

SINIFF, D.B. & J.R. TESTER 1965. Computer analysis of animal movement data obtained by telemetry. *BioScience* 15: 104-108

SOUTHERN, W.E. 1964. Additional observations on winter Bald Eagle populations; including remarks on biotelemetry techniques and immature plumages. *Wilson Bull.* 76: 121-37

SPENCER, W.D. & R.H. BARRETT 1984. An evaluation of the harmonic mean measure for defining carnivore activity areas. *Acta Zool. Fenn.* 171: 255-259

SWIHART, R.K. & N.A. SLADE 1985. Testing for independence of observations in animal movements. *Ecology* 66: 1176-1184

VOIGHT, D.R. & R.R. TINLINE 1980. Strategies for analyzing radio tracking data. pp. 387-404 in C.J. Amlaner & D.W. Macdonald (eds.) *A Handbook on Biotelemetry and Radio Tracking*. Pergamon Press, Oxford

WALLS, S.S. & R.E. KENWARD (this volume). The systematic study of radio-tagged raptors: II. Sociality and dispersal.

WHITE, G.C. & R.A. GARROTT 1990. *Analysis of wildlife radio-tracking data.* Academic press, New York

WORTON, B.J. 1989. Kernel methods for estimating the utilization distribution in home-range studies. *Ecology 70*: 164-168

ZIESEMER, F. 1981. Habichte (*Accipiter gentilis*) verlieren Ringe. *Corax* 8: 211-212.

R.E. Kenward
Institute of Terrestrial Ecology
Furzebrook Research Station
Wareham, Dorset BH20 5AS
Great Britain.

S.S. Walls
Biotrack, Stoborough Croft
Grange Road
Wareham, Dorset BH20 5AS
Great Britain.

African Harrier Hawk *Polyboroides typus*

Meyburg, B.-U. & R. D. Chancellor eds.1994
Raptor Conservation Today
WWGBP / The Pica Press

The Systematic Study of Radio-tagged Raptors: II. Sociality and Dispersal.

S.S. Walls and R.E. Kenward

SUMMARY

The advantages of using radio-tracking for studying sociality and seasonal movements are put into context with previous techniques. Both phenomena are best studied with interval sampling. Analyses of static and dynamic interactions are dicussed, followed by a description of field techniques developed to collect data on survival, dispersal and other movements. Finally, four examples use data from Northern Goshawk (*Accipiter gentilis*) and Common Buzzard (*Buteo buteo*) studies to illustrate how the methods can be applied and their importance for conservation.

INTRODUCTION

Kenward & Walls (this volume) discussed the advantages of radio-tracking over ringing in the study of raptor survival and showed how home range data can be analysed. This paper will look at the study of sociality in more detail, and describe how the mechanics of dispersal can be investigated. It starts, however, by discussing analysis of the data before describing its collection, to stress the need for planning.

Radio-tagging is an ideal technique for tracking animals continuously. Whilst this may be informative in the initial stages of a study, objective analysis can then be difficult (Macdonald, Ball & Hough 1980). When studying sociality, intermittent sampling has the following advantages over continuous monitoring: (i) independence of fixes can be maximised, (ii) more individuals can be studied simultaneously (see Kenward & Walls this volume), (iii) locations relative to other animals, which may not be seen when tracking only one animal, can be recorded for interaction analysis and (iv) disturbance by the observer can be reduced.

Ringing provides some essential information on the abundance and gross movements of many birds. However, there can be problems with bias in ringing studies, especially in the case of threatened species such as raptors, and ring recovery can be slow (Newton 1979; Kenward 1992). Whilst ringing is still essential, this paper will demonstrate how some questions may be answered more efficiently.

Macdonald, Ball & Hough (1980) point out that the overlap in ranges of individuals, described by whichever model, gives an incomplete picture of the interaction between them. Many animals may use the same place but at different times. This is most easily seen across species, (for example lions and wildebeest may occupy the same ranges but will only interact very briefly). A good intraspecific example comes from Davies & Houston (1983) who showed how two Pied Wagtails *(Motacilla alba)* patrolled the same stretch of river bank but at different times. This was partly territorial and partly due to the renewal of their food. Macdonald, Ball & Hough (1980) therefore stressed the difference between static and dynamic interactions. A static interaction is the spatial overlap of one animal's home range on another's (as above). Conversely, a dynamic interaction is the relationship between movements of two or more animals, depending on whether they avoid or attract each other. In essence, a time dimension has been added.

The evaluation of the distance between animals at any given time can be complicated. Macdonald, Ball & Hough (1980) used the Ornstein-Uhlenbeck (O-U) diffusion process to simulate marginal distribution of the distances between two animals, and then tested whether the observed distances differed significantly from the prediction. Not only is this a complicated procedure, but it also has some dubious theoretical assumptions, which were questioned by the authors themselves. For example the O-U model assumes that an animal tends towards the centre of its range, which is often not true, as for example if a bird that nests on the edge of its range commutes long distances each day to a distant food source. Moreover, in testing for significant differences between each pair of animals, it assumes that the set of locations for each animal are independent data, yet again a dubious assumption. There are similar problems with all parametric home-range models. To check for dynamic interactions without any modelling, or assumptions of independence within the data set from each animal, the following method can be used (Kenward 1992, Kenward in press):

First the mean distance (D_o) between fixes observed in the same sampling round is calculated:

$$D_O = \frac{1}{n}\sum_{j=1}^{n}\sqrt{(x_{1j}-x_{2j})^2+(y_{1j}-y_{2j})^2}$$

where n is the number of fix pairs and (x_{1j},y_{1j}) are the coordinates of animal 1 at time j. Thus $x_{1,j}-x_{2j}$ is the distance along the x-axis between individuals 1 and 2 at time j.

The expected mean distance (D_e), if locations are used at random with respect to the other animal, can be found by calculating the mean distance between each fix from one individual and all fixes from the other individual:

$$D_E = \frac{1}{n^2}\sum_{j=1}^{n}\sum_{k=1}^{n}\sqrt{(x_{1j}-x_{2k})^2+(y_{1j}-y_{2k})^2}$$

where j and k are times, such that $x_{1,1}-x_{2,10}$ is the distance along the x-axis between individual 1 in its first position and individual 2 in its tenth.

The observed and expected distances are compared using Ivlev's index to give a coefficient of sociality:

$$S_c = (D_e-D_o)/(D_e+D_o)$$

which is symmetrical about 0, the result obtained if the animals move independently. Results from this index tend towards -1 if the observed distance is much greater than the expected distance, suggesting avoidance. A tendency towards +1 will result from the observed distances being closer than expected, suggesting some attraction. Since each pair of animals produces a single measure, there is no need to make any assumptions about independence within each set of fixes. Results are most consistent if D_o and D_e are the geometric means.

Although the calculations are straightforward, care must be exercised when collecting and analysing these data. When looking for dynamic interactions, animals must be found during every sampling period. If only those distances between fixes taken within a given time period are used, there is a tendency to discard long distances because these tend to occur when there is a delay in finding one individual. This will result in a bias towards attraction, since only those fixes collected at the "same time" are used.

Dispersal in the Common Buzzard has previously been recorded by observation (Olsson 1958) as well as by ringing and wing-tagging (Picozzi & Wier 1976; Tubbs 1974). The data consist of observing general movement during certain seasons, or an absence of a wing-tagged bird. Ringing provides a natal area and a final position, usually for a dead specimen. Nothing can be said as to what has happened in between. Moreover, first year recoveries are a biased sample: they represent unsuccessful birds, which died. Thus Picozzi & Weir (1976) found that 69% of Buzzard recoveries were a result of shooting or poisoning, but is there really so much human impact on Buzzards? Picozzi & Weir (1976) also noted that only first year birds were found more than 100 km from their nest and most adult recoveries are found within 50 km. Was this because unsuccessful, dispersing birds were over-represented in the recoveries, or because juveniles really travelled further than adults? Continuos movement records, from radio-tracking, can answer these questions.

FIELD TECHNIQUES

Our present field techniques are described, both to show how a regime has been developed to permit quantitative analyses and to give some idea of the manpower involved. Although details are specific to Buzzards, the general procedures can be applied to all raptors.

After tagging birds shortly before or after fledging, all were monitored for survival twice a week for at least four weeks. The reason for this frequency was to try and identify causes of death, before the carcass decayed, during a period of presumed high mortality (Newton 1979). Deaths are likely because of the inexperience of the young, but there is also the possibility of adverse effects from harness tags. During this period in 1991 some broods were visited once a day. All members of the brood were found on each occasion, so dynamic interactions could be analysed. Birds were visited only once a day so that broods could be monitored at 13 nests. With a day in between, locations were likely to be independent.

Throughout the winter, birds were checked once a week for survival and location. In late October, after most dispersal, the local birds were found three times a day for a period of ten days to establish range characteristics. The stability of winter ranges, extrapolated from the ten-day track and weekly checks over two years, means that future mortality checks could be reduced to once a month. Lost birds were best sought for by air shortly after the dispersal period. At the end of February, checks were increased to twice a week to detect any returning dispersers, and because all birds tended to move about more in spring.

Initially it took 1.5-2 days to check every Buzzard through the dispersal period. Once they had settled down it was possible in one day, for those within 50 km. During the spring time, as the Buzzards started to move about more, monitoring took 1.5-2 days but was quite variable.

EXAMPLE 1: SOCIALITY OF WINTERING GOSHAWKS.

Between August 1976 and March 1977, 14 Goshawks were trapped and tagged on the Frötuna estate in central Sweden. Ten of the hawks were tracked for a period of at least ten days, the time in which range size reached a maximum for two Goshawks released in Britain (Kenward 1982).

Five males tracked during this period overlapped each other extensively, particularly around some Pheasant *(Phasianus colchicus)* feeding areas. The average percentage overlaps for each pair, calculated by three methods for the outlines which contained 100% and 50% of the locations, are shown in Table 1 (see also Fig.2 and discussion in Kenward & Walls, this volume). The static interaction is high, even when only the most dense 50% of fixes are used, except when using cluster analysis. These overlaps tell us nothing of any temporal separation that may be expected from the territorial behaviour most raptors exhibit around their nest (Newton 1979).

The dynamic interactions shown in the last column are consistently neutral, indicating that the hawks neither avoided nor attracted each other. There appears to be no relationship between the

Figure 1 The ranges of six young Goshawks, in two broods, around their nests. The harmonic mean contours are for 25%, 50%, 75% and 100% cores.

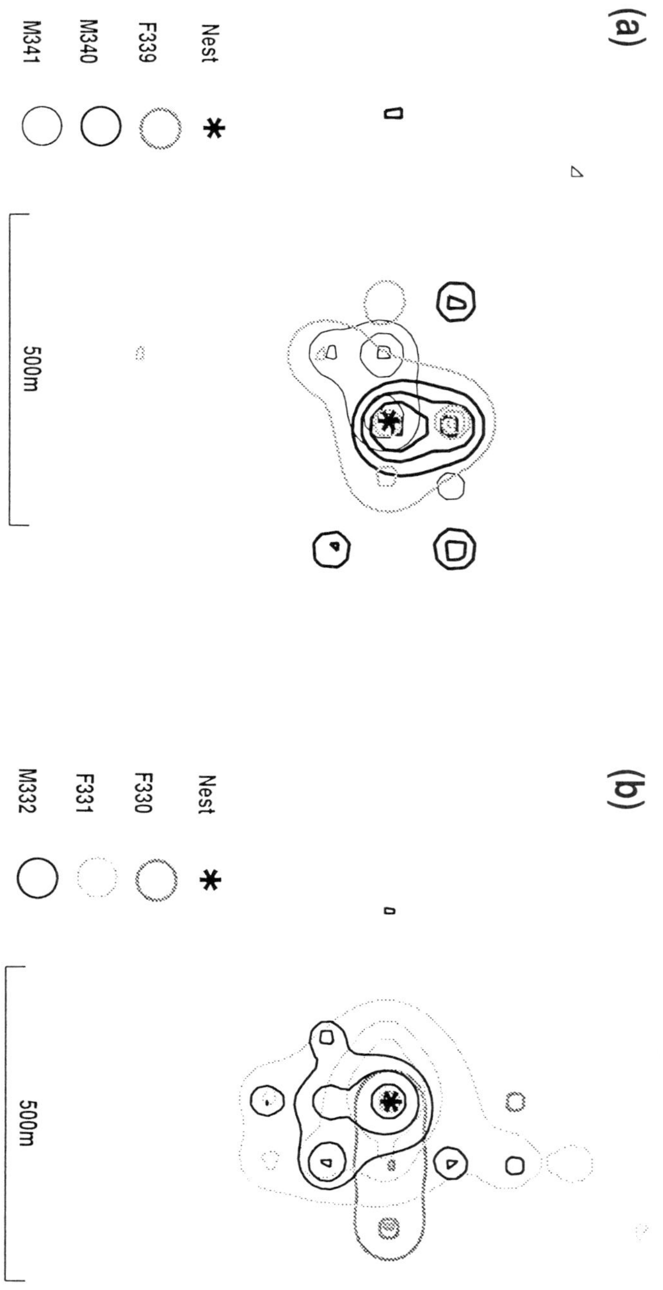

(a)

RANGE OVERLAP % Core %	F339 M340	M340 M341	M341 F339
100%	54.7	58.9	31.3
75%	50.6	25.2	32.0
50%	36.6	0.5	17.7
25%	0	0	0
DYNAMIC INTERACTION	+0.31	+0.03	+0.07

(b)

RANGE OVERLAP % Core %	F330 F331	F331 M332	M332 F330
100%	46.5	36.2	62.4
75%	28.8	27.8	54.9
50%	26.5	30.7	49.7
25%	1.5	48.1	28.8
DYNAMIC INTERACTION	+0.46	+0.01	+0.64

Figure 2 The ranges of six young Buzzards, in two broods, around their nest. The harmonic mean contours are for 25%, 50%, 75% and 100% cores.

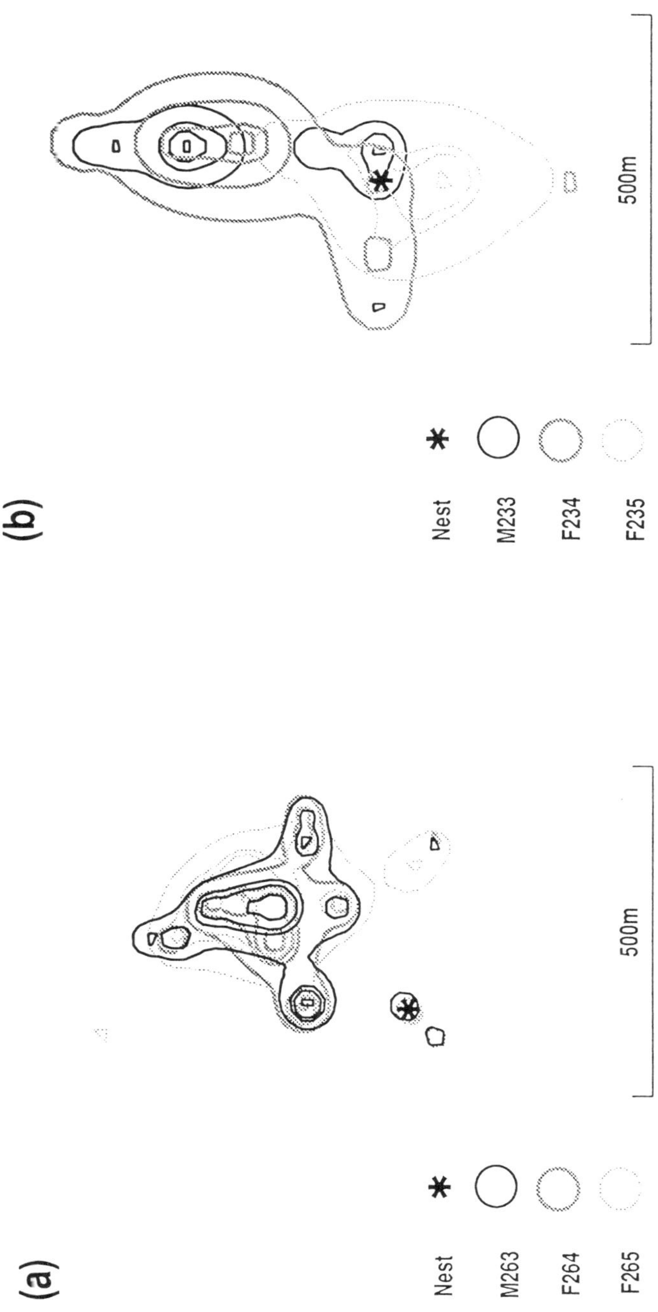

(a)

RANGE OVERLAP % — Core %	M263 F264	F264 F265	F265 M263
100%	86.1	76.4	74.1
75%	70.8	62.9	58.0
50%	63.0	58.1	55.0
25%	1.7	14.5	0
DYNAMIC INTERACTION	+0.98	+0.93	+0.91

(b)

RANGE OVERLAP % — Core %	M233 F234	F234 F235	M233 F235
100%	61.3	26.8	37.2
75%	44.9	15.7	3.3
50%	52.7	0	0
25%	0	0	0
DYNAMIC INTERACTION	+0.67	+0.21	+0.08

amount of static overlap and the index of dynamic interaction *(S_c)*. Hawks JM3 and YM5 overlapped quite extensively throughout all cores (even the 50% cluster) and yet their S_c score shows that they tended, if anything, to avoid each other. The static overlap is therefore due to another factor besides sociality, most likely the abundance of pheasants which provide a suitable food source. However, there is no consistent evidence that the hawks avoided each other, and therefore no hint of territoriality.

Table 1 The average overlap of five male Goshawks compared with the coefficient of sociality. The percentage overlap is shown for outlines containing all the radio locations and the densest 50%, calculated (a) as polygons peeled towards the harmonic mean centre (b) by cluster analysis and (c) by harmonic mean contouring.

Hawks Core%	(a) Peeled polygons 100	(a) Peeled polygons 50	(b) Cluster analysis 100	(b) Cluster analysis 50	(c) Contours (H_c) 100	(c) Contours (H_c) 50	S_c
YM6 & JM3	61	62	61	5	81	53	+0.02
YM6 &YM5	67	52	67	1	78	67	-0.02
YM6 & JM10	62	60	62	0	74	26	+0.08
YM6 & JM11	54	63	54	0	80	47	0.00
JM3 & YM5	64	38	64	43	83	63	-0.03
JM3 & JM10	37	57	37	31	69	50	+0.01
JM3 & JM11	73	82	73	9	79	81	+0.03
YM5 & JM10	58	12	58	10	76	22	+0.01
YM5 & JM11	62	35	62	19	81	51	+0.12
JM10 & JM11	27	54	27	17	68	67	-0.01
Average	57	52	57	14	77	53	+0.002

EXAMPLE 2: SOCIALITY OF POST-FLEDGING GOSHAWKS.

Radio tags were fitted to a total of 187 young Goshawks, from 130 broods found on Gotland (Sweden), between 1980 and 1984. Figure 1 shows the ranges of two broods aged between 65 and 90 days around their nest. The harmonic mean contours represent 100%, 75%, 50% and 25% cores. Fixes found within 50m of the nest were excluded, but the nest is still within the 50% contour of every range. This could be due to a resource, such as food which is dropped at the nest by the parent, providing the necessary focus.

In the first nest, two birds (F339 & M340) are cohesive, but both static and dynamic interaction analyses showed that the other bird (M341) moved independently. In the second brood, M332 had little contact with F331, but was often together with F330, which was sometimes with F331. These results show that some of the birds were associating with each other away from the nest, whereas others were not. Only two nests have been used here, to simplify the explanation. The variability between nests shows that interpretation of such small samples is impossible. However when more nests were examined, with at least two pairs of observations before 65 days, S_c averaged +0.59 for 13 male-female sets, +0.73 for 7 female-female sets and +0.69 for 10 male-male sets. As the young hawks got older, however, they became less cohesive (Mann-Whitney U-tests, $P<0.025$) and male-male sets became less cohesive than female-female sets ($P<0.009$) but males showed no tendency to avoid females (Kenward, Marcström & Karlbom in press).

EXAMPLE 3: SOCIALITY OF POST-FLEDGING BUZZARDS.

In 1990 and 1991, radio-tags were fitted to 58 young Common Buzzards from 38 broods found in a 7km x 20km strip of E.Dorset, England. In 1991, 14 young Buzzards, 65-90 days old, were located once a day for ten days. The resulting harmonic mean contours of two broods' ranges are shown in Figure 2. Unlike Goshawks, activity is not centred around the nest, which lies on or beyond the 75% contours. However core overlaps were very extensive, especially at nest (a).

The coefficients of sociality between individuals at nest (a) are very high suggesting a very strong cohesion between all of them. In this particular case there also seems to be some correlation between the static and dynamic overlap except when using the 25% cores. The second brood had two cohesive hawks (M233 & F234) and a third (F235) which was fairly neutral. Again there was some correlation between core overlap and the dynamic interaction coefficients, but not at 100%. As in the Goshawks, having only two nests makes interpretation impossible.

EXAMPLE 4: BUZZARD DISPERSAL

The value of radiotracking many individuals is also shown by results from the 58 Buzzards tagged in Southern England. Of 46 Buzzards that survived the postfledging period, and whose radios were still working, two thirds dispersed to set up a winter range elsewhere. The dispersal period was short: 18 of 30 dispersers left within three weeks from mid-August to mid-September. This one-way dispersal occurred at the same time as exploratory journeys which took several individuals up to 20 km from the nest. This may be the "local wanderings" described by Picozzi & Weir (1976). but it is far easier to quantify these movements when the positions of all birds are definitely known, rather than having to rely on sighting an individual or assuming it to have gone.

During the spring of 1991, those birds that had remained within a kilometre of their nest suddenly became far more exploratory. One was found over 40 km away despite the average winter range being only 1.4 km in diameter. Simultaneously, five out of eight of those that had dispersed, and spent the winter within a similarly small range, returned to their natal area. Two others returned later. One of these hawks had disappeared without trace during the dispersal period, despite two aerial searches covering more than 100 km from its nest. The hawk not found back at its nest site had not dispersed far and could have returned within an hour, missing detection by the twice-weekly check. Unfortunately only one of those birds had a back-pack tag and could therefore be tracked beyond the spring. This bird then disappeared until spring 1992, when it returned once again. A similar pattern is now emerging among the 1991 cohort. It seems, therefore, that philopatry may explain why first year birds were found further from their natal area.

It may be that these are not representative years but, having followed 23 individuals throughout each year, comparisons are possible between years. If further tracking proves Buzzards to be truly philopatric, and they end up breeding near their natal area, then they may be better aided in returning to distant unpopulated areas by re-introduction programmes than by a *laissez-faire* approach based mainly on protecting established populations.

ACKNOWLEDGEMENTS

Data on Goshawks were collected in collaboration with V. Marcström and M. Karlbom, with funding from the Swedish Sportsmen's association. All projects were also funded by the Natural Environment Research Council. Biotrack provided much support for the Buzzard work, which was also financially aided by the RSPB and NCC, and Tony Tyack collected some of the data. Early manuscripts were improved by comments from M.G. Morris and I. Moy.

REFERENCES

BROWN, L.E. 1962. Home range in small mammal comunities. In B.Glass (ed.) *Survey of Biological Process* 4:131-179. London, Accademic Press.

DAVIES, N.B. & A.I. HOUSTON 1983. Time allocation between territories and flocks and owner-sattelite conflict in foraging the pied wagtail, *Motacilla alba. J. Anim. Ecol.* 52:621-634
DUNN, J.E. & P. GIPSON 1977. Analysis of radio telemetry data in studies of home range. *Biometrics* 33:85-101.
HAYNE, D.W. 1949. Calculation of size of home range. *J. Mammal.* 30:1-18.
KENWARD, R.E. 1977. Predation on released pheasants by goshawks in central Sweden. *Viltrevy* 10:79-112.
KENWARD, R.E. 1982. Goshawk hunting behaviour and range size as a function of food and habitat availability. *J. Anim. Ecol.* 51:69-80.
KENWARD, R.E. 1987. *Wildlife Radio Tagging*. London, Academic press.
KENWARD, R.E. 1992. Modelling raptor populations: to ring or to radio-tag? *In* J.D. LeBreton (ed) *The use of marked individuals in the study of bird population dynamics:models,methods and software*. Birkhauser, Basle, Switzerland.
KENWARD, R.E. (in press) Quantity verses quality: programming for collection and analysis of radio tag data. In I. G. Priede & S. M. Swift (eds) *Wildlife telemetry: remote monitoring and tracking of animals*. Ellis Horwood, Chichester, UK.
KENWARD, R.E. (in press). Post-fledging behaviour in goshawks II. Sex differences in sociality and nest switching. *Anim.Behav.*
MACDONALD, D.W., F.G. BALL & N.G. HOUGH. 1980. The evaluation of home range size and configuration using radio tracking data. pp 405-424 *in* C.J.Amlaner & D.W.Macdonald (eds.), *A Handbook on Biotelemetry and Radio Tracking*. Pergamon Press, Oxford.
MARQUISS, M. & I. NEWTON. 1982. Habitat preference in male & female sparrowhawks *(Accipiter nisus). Ibis* 124:324-328.
MAZURKIEWICZ. M. 1969. Shape, size & distribution of home ranges of *Clethrionomys glareolus. Acta Theriol*, 16:23-60
NEWTON, I. 1979. *Population Ecology of Raptors*. Berkhamsted, Poyser.
NIELSEN, B.P. 1977. Migratory habits and dispersal of Danish Buzzards *(Buteo buteo). Dansk. Orn. Foren. Tidsskr.* 71:1-9.
OLSSON, V. 1958. Dispersal, migration, longevity and death causes of *Strix aluco, Buteo buteo, Ardea cinerea* and *Larus argentatus. Acta Vertebratica* 1:91-189.
PICOZZI, N. & D.N. WEIR 1976. Dispersal and causes of death in Buzzards. *Br. Birds* 69:193-201.
RANDOLPH, S.E. 1977. Changing spatial relationships in a population of *Apodemus sylvaticus,* with the onset of breeding. *J .Anim. Ecol.* 46:653-676.
SINIFF, D.B. & C.R. JESSON 1969. A simulation model of animal movement patterns. pp 185-219 *in* J.B.Cragg (ed.) *Advances in Ecological Research* 6. London, Academic Press.
STORM, G.L. 1965. Movements and activities of foxes as determined by radio tracking. *J. Wildl. Mgmt.* 29:1-13.
TESTER, J.R. & D.B. SINIFF 1965. Aspects of animal movement and home range data obtained by telemetry. *Trans. XXXth N. Am. Wildl. Nat. Res. Conf.* 352-379.
TUBBS, C.R. 1974. *The Buzzard*. Chapman & Hall, London.

S.S. Walls
Biotrack, Stoborough Croft
Grange Road
Wareham, Dorset BH20 5AJ
Great Britain

R.E. Kenward
Institute of Terrestrial Ecology
Furzebrook Research Station
Wareham, Dorset BH20 5AS
Great Britain.

Meyburg, B.-U. & R. D. Chancellor eds.1994
Raptor Conservation Today
WWGBP / The Pica Press

Measuring Locations and Flight Altitudes of Griffon Vultures *Gyps fulvus* by an Automatic Telemetry System*

Ralf Bögel

INTRODUCTION

Conventionally radio-tracking and habitat use has been restricted to a two dimension analysis: radiolocations and home ranges are plotted as polygons, isopleths, clusters or assemblies of grid cells (Kenward 1987; White & Garrott 1990). In spite of that, birds use their habitats three dimensionally and therefore require specially designed transmitters and adapted methods of data recording. Kenward *et al.* (1982) used thermistors for recording the cooling effect of the air during flight as an indicator for flight activity. However, this didn't incorporate the measuring of the altitude. At the 4th European Conference on Wildlife Telemetry in 1991, a prototype transmitter design for birds was introduced featuring a barometric altitude meter (Bögel & Burchard 1992). In the meantime, the transmitter design has been improved in terms of altitude range. In addition, temperature coding has been adapted for an automatic recording device. Data recording is done by a Doppler-telemetry system (Schober *et al.* in press) which improves the accuracy of radio locations compared to a former type of an Automatic Direction Finding (ADF) system (Bögel 1991). The studies are part of a project on home range size and flight biology of a small colony of Griffon Vultures at the northern slope of the European Alps (Bögel *et al.* 1990), that descend for food to a feeding station at the Salzburg Zoo (Mäck & Bögel 1989). The main motives for applying this new technology to Griffon Vultures have been:

i) Griffons have proved to fly at altitudes of 10'000 m and more. Like other soaring gliders, they have a pronounced ability for a three dimensional habitat use.

ii) According to visual observations, vultures can even fly during snowfall or rain, indicating that they have different strategies for an effective exploitation of different air currents. Observations of Pennycuick (1972, 1973) confirm this hypothesis.

iii) It has been argued that flight activities of vultures are depending on thermal updrafts and thus climate changes could have caused the extinction of Bearded Vultures in the Alps (Haller 1983).

iv) Flying at high altitudes may be important for vultures in terms of thermoregulation. The data presented here should quantify the effects and the benefits that Griffons can get out of different weather and wind conditions.

* *financed by the BFANL and the StMLU Bayern.*

METHODS

An air pressure sensor is used for a pulse-interval-modulation (PIM) and thus different pulse intervals indicate different air pressures (Fig.1). Time intervals ranging from 200...1100 ms correspond to air pressures of 350...1000 mb or altitudes ranging from 8000...0 m. A calibration at the laboratory and a regression function (see Fig. 1) is used for determining the air pressure at flight altitude from the pulse interval reading of the telemetry receiver. Then, by recording of air pressure and temperature references (P_o,t_o) at a known altitude (a_o), the bird's altitude can be calculated as follows:

$$a_{(T)} = a_o + \frac{5\,023\,200 + 18\,400 * t_o}{59{,}8 + \dfrac{273{,}15}{\log (P_{(T)} / P_o)}}$$

$a_{(T)}$: flight altitude $P_{(T)}$: air pressure in flight altitude ao: ground level P_o: reference air pressure (ground level) t_o: reference temperature (ground level)

For maximum precision and the elimination of thermal drift effects in the electronic circuits, it is useful to measure the temperature of the tag (see Fig. 1). This is realized by another PIM (Fig. 2). Identification of the transmitted parameter is done by a pulse duration modulation (PDM), resulting in 10 ms pulses for temperature readings and 20 msec pulses for air pressure recordings. If the temperature gradient of the atmosphere is constant, the remaining errors have an extent of max. +/- 80 m (see Fig. 1). Fig. 3 shows a tag for Griffon Vultures designed as a back pack harness using silicone ropes and a weak link with a 2 year lifespan (the same as the batteries). The dimensions are 80x35x28 mm, the weight is 100 g = 2% of body weight. The maximum range is approximately 20 km but could reach up to 50 km for birds at great altitudes. It is interesting to note, that within a few days the tag is completely covered by feathers. If the harness is adjusted carefully, no behavioural effects can be observed. However, the tags might have some impact on the energy budget during flight (Pennycuick *et al.* 1989). For data sampling during field work, a conventional receiver with pulse duration and pulse period option is used (B+R Ing. GmbH, type 235090). For quick results, altitudes are then determined graphically (Fig. 4). An example is given for a pulse period reading of 830 ms and a reference air pressure of 970 mb at 440 m, resulting in a corresponding flight altitude of 2200 m. However, for simultaneous tracking and altitude measuring of several individuals in a mountainous research area, an ADF-Doppler system has been developed (Schober *et al.* in press). It handles the whole data sampling, both automatically and with a high chronological and spatial resolution. In order to minimize error sources, the system was designed as a Doppler Direction Finder (Burchard 1989). An integrated radio data link provides a direct data access. Due to bi-directional data communication the whole system is completely remote controlled by the central personal computer (Fig. 5). This means that all parameters of the receivers (channel selection, frequency fine tune, gain, etc.) can be adjusted according to the actual situation and data can be checked immediately for their plausibility. Retry options are running in such cases as: i) no radio contact is obtained ii) bearings indicate more than one intersection iii) meterings are not likely or con-tradictory iv) changes of receiver parameters are required.

Figure 1: Air pressure - time interval calibration, regression function and evaluation of accuracy.

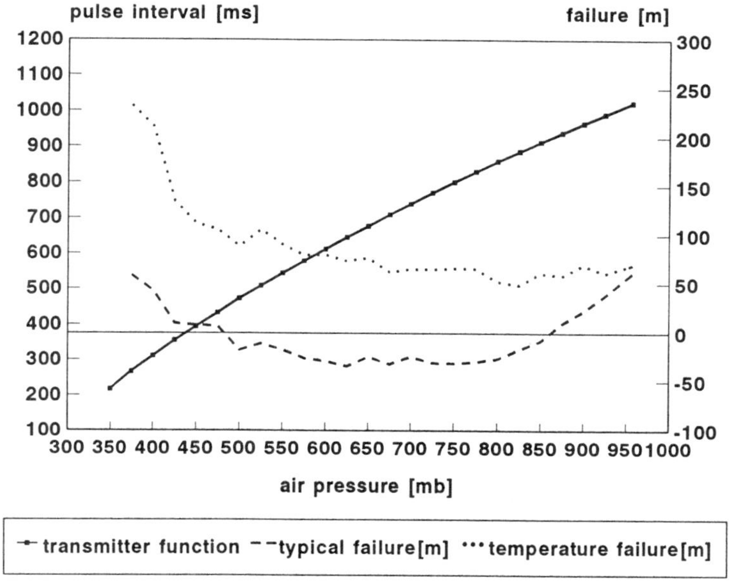

regression: P(T) = (0,764 T + 148,25 + e↑ (0,00124 T + 5,619))/2

Figure 2: Temperature - time interval calibration and regression function.

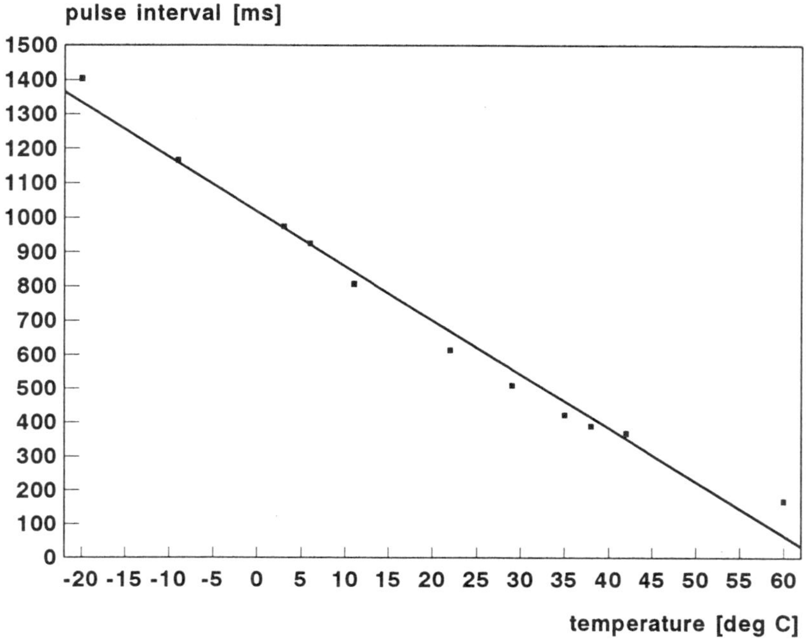

temp(T) = - 0,0631 T + 64,1

Figure 3: Back pack harness with telemetry transmitter featuring a barometric altitude meter.

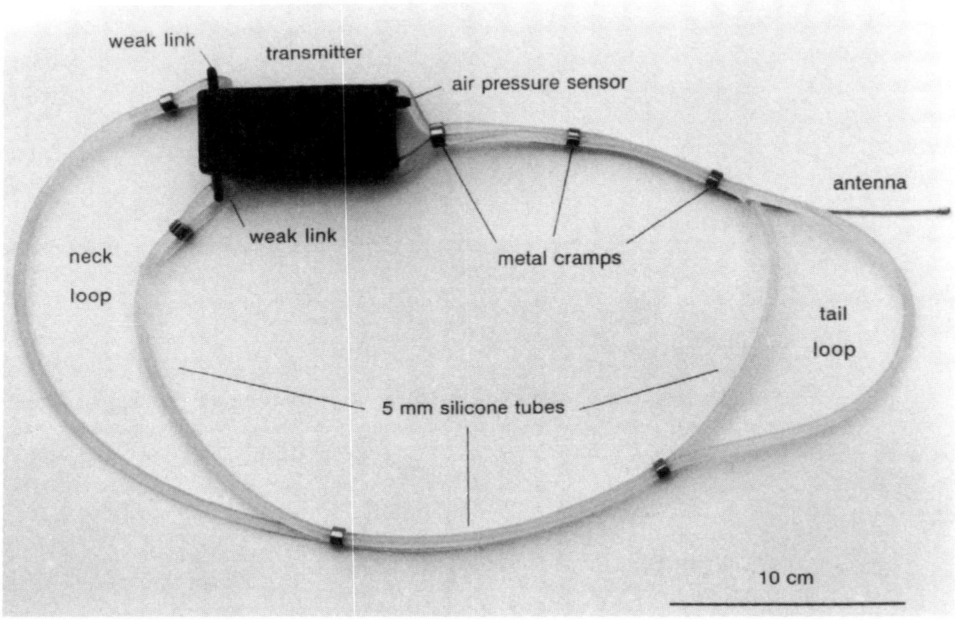

Figure 4: Pulse interval - flight altitude diagram used for field work.

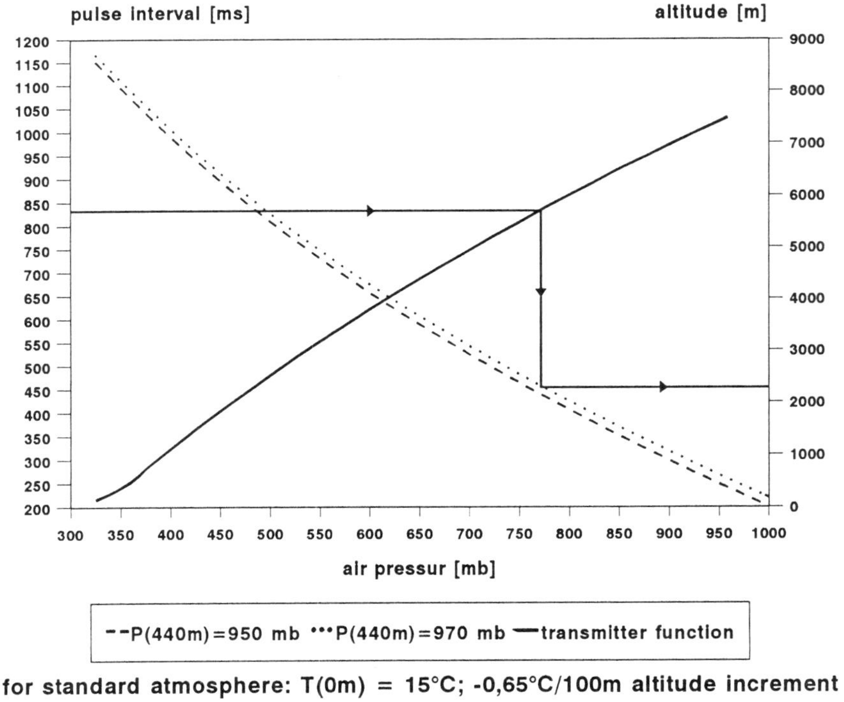

Figure 5: Block diagram of the ADF-telemetry system.

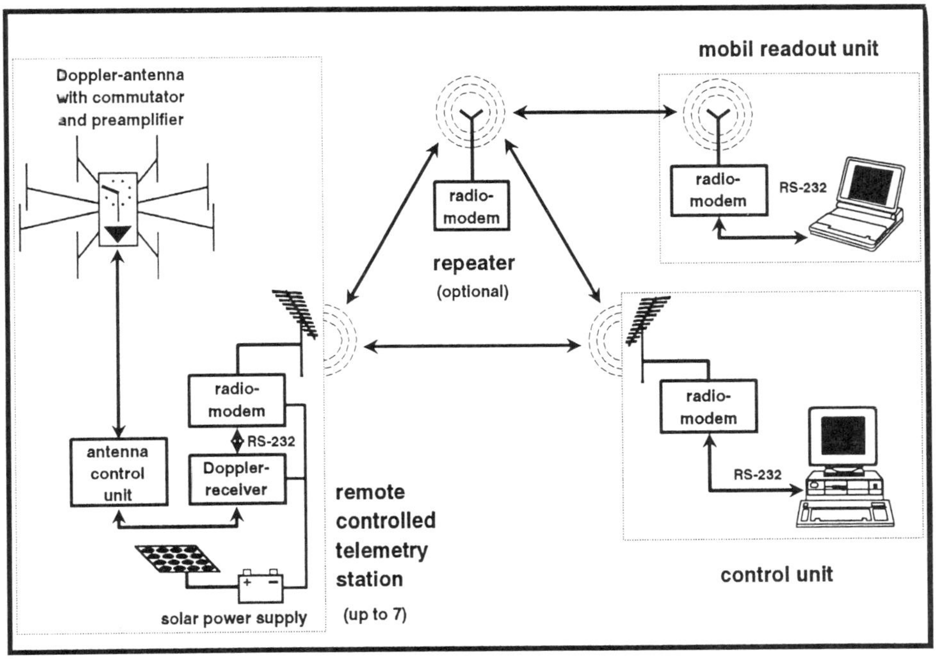

Figure 6: Translocation from the roosting cliff to the zoo. (numbers indicate radio locations and chronology)

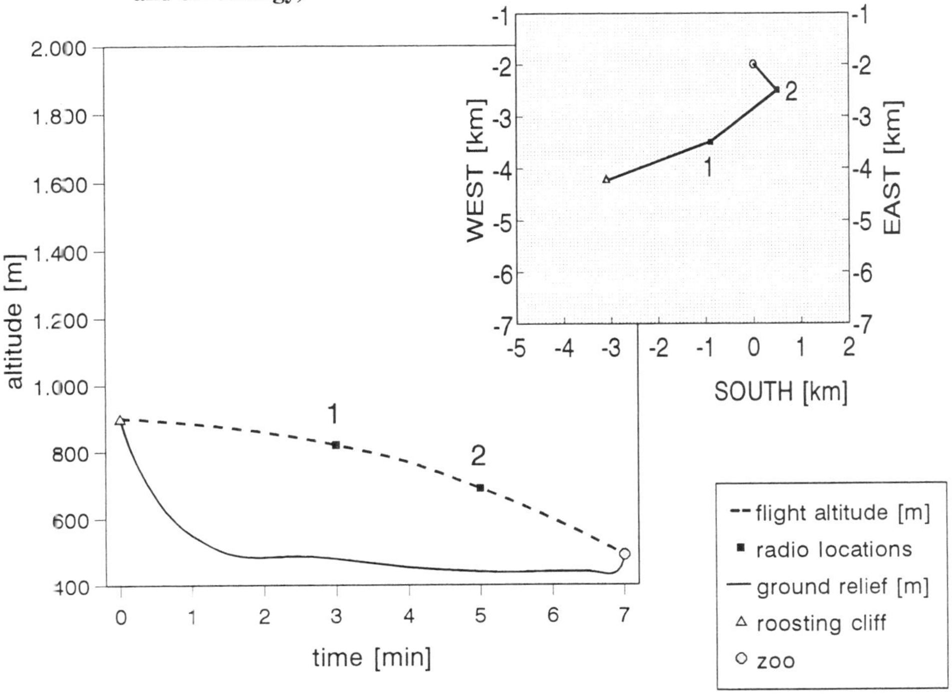

Figure 7: Translocation from the zoo to the roosting cliff: thermal updrafts with NW-winds at 6 m/s. (numbers indicate radio locations and chronology)

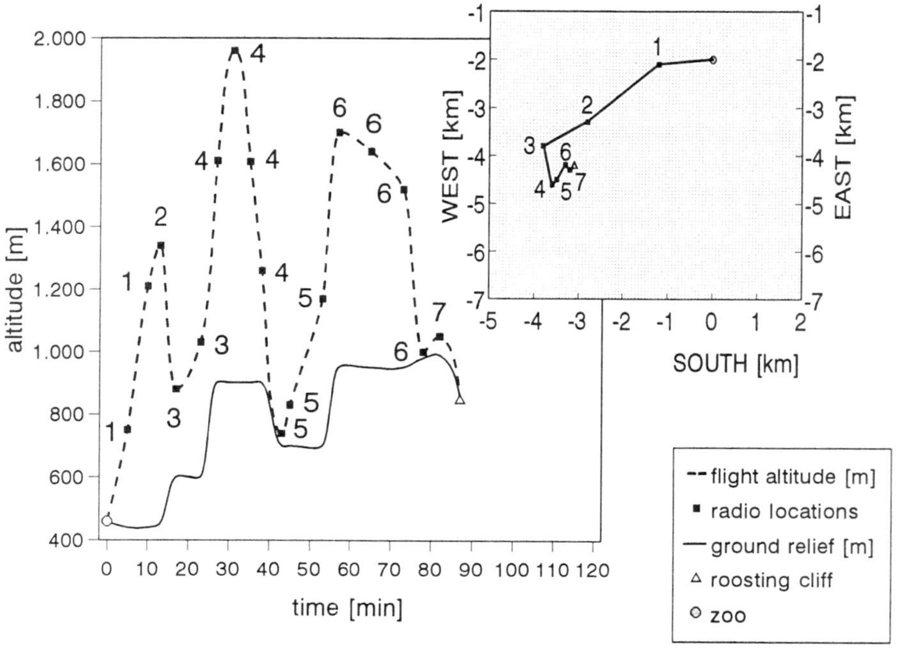

Figure 8: Translocation from the zoo to the roosting cliff: thermal updrafts with W-winds at 3 m/s. (numbers indicate radio locations and chronology)

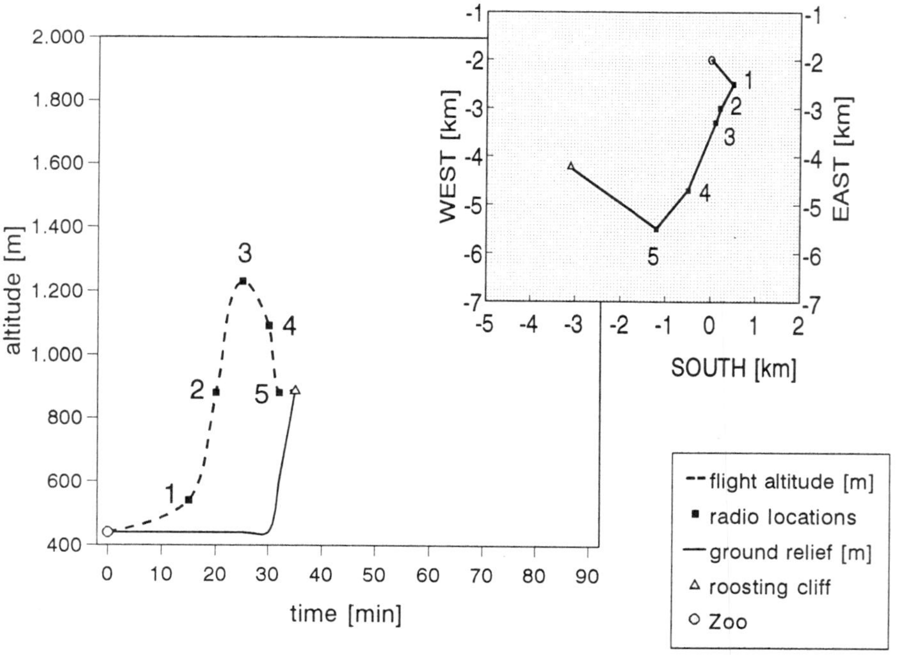

Figure 9: Translocation from the zoo to the roosting cliff: weather cloudy with ESE-winds at 4-5 m/s. (numbers indicate radio locations and chronology)

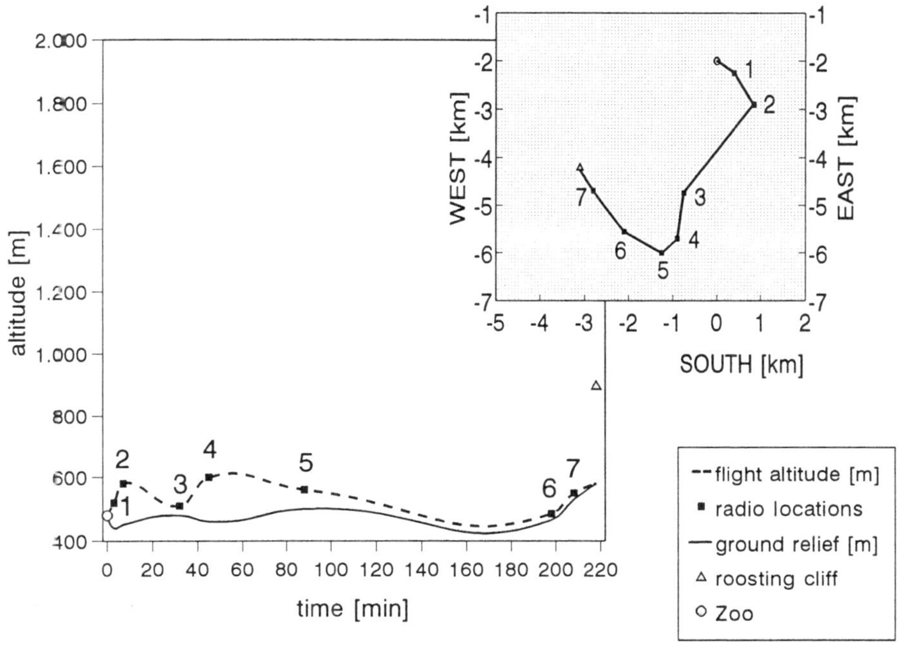

Figure 10: Translocation from the zoo to the roosting cliff: snowfall with W-winds at 7-8 m/ s. (numbers indicate radio locations and chronology)

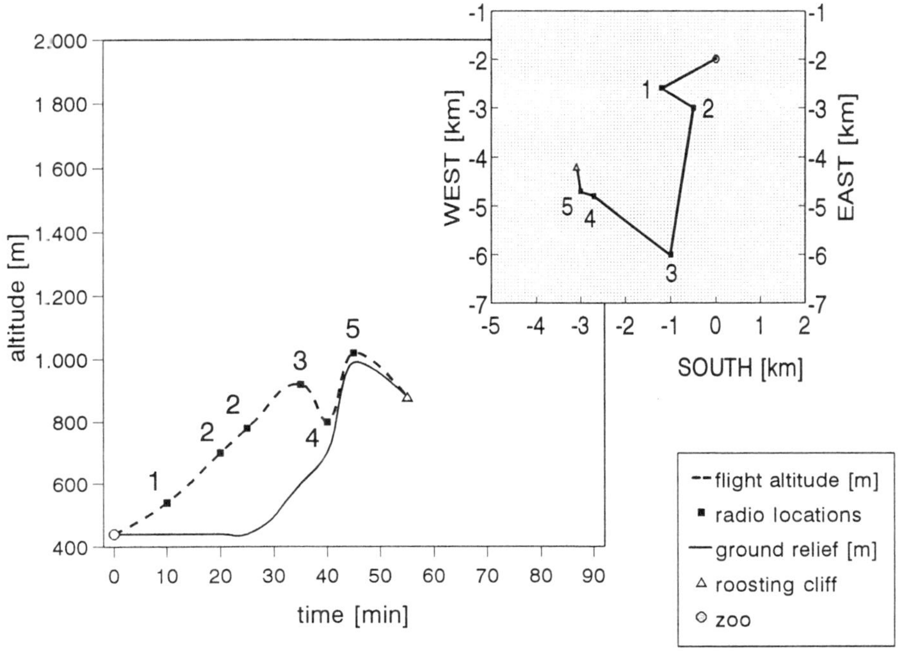

RESULTS AND DISCUSSION

The following examples represent the flight behaviour for various translocations under different weather conditions. Figures 6-10 show tracks and flight profiles as separate graphs. Fig. 6 is typical of all translocations from the roosting cliffs on the Untersberg mountain to the zoo. According to the gliding ratio of 15:1 (Pennycuick 1972), a difference in altitudes of 260 metres would be sufficient for pure gliding. As the zoo is located 500 metres lower, this type of translocation occurs stereotypically under all weather conditions: the vultures choose a direct track. This is different for the translocations in the other direction: in these cases, tracks and altitude profiles differ significantly with different weather and wind directions. Fig. 7 shows the flight behaviour for good weather conditions with NW-winds at 6 m/s and good thermal updrafts. The vulture gains altitude rather effectively over a forested area west of the zoo (points 1-2), then loses height during the translocation to point 3. Approaching the northern slope of the Untersberg mountain, the Griffon gets lifted very quickly by the relief updrafts. At point 4 the vulture changes to relief flight, probably in search for food. Before it is landing at the roosting cliff, it is regaining height without much effort (points 5 to 6), suggesting that its change to relief flight had not been forced by the wind conditions. Fig. 8 demonstrates that for weak W-winds at 3 m/s but fine weather with some thermal updrafts, a quick translocation is possible by gaining altitude over the western slope of a chain of hills southeast of the zoo (points 1 to 3), followed by a short cross-wind translocation with few changes in altitude (point 5 to the roosting cliff). Fig. 9 shows what happens if flight conditions are really bad: the vulture takes a flight track similar to that of Fig. 8, but is trying to be successful by crossing and circling over the eastern slope of the same hills (SE-winds at 4-5 m/s). This is not very efficient and even after a long period of trying and exhausting wing flapping, the Griffon does not succeed in reaching the roosting cliff but is perching below in the mountain forest 600 m a.s.l. Fig. 10 demonstrates that certain wind conditions can totally replace thermal updrafts: even in this bad weather condition with snowfall, the vulture is quite effectively gaining altitude by circling in the strong westerly winds (points 1 to 3), then crossing westwards in close relief flight to the roosting cliff (lee-area of the Untersberg mountain!). It is interesting to note that the time for this translocation is not noticeably longer than in cases with good weather conditions. Temperature decrease during the translocations ranged from 4 to 24 degrees C, varying with air temperature, velocity and altitude difference. If plumage temperatures were close to or exceeded body temperature (vultures inactive on the ground and exposed to full sunshine), the cooling down effect due to flight activities was greatest. Therefore flight behaviour can be interprated as mechanism for thermoregulation.

CONCLUSIONS

The flight behaviour of Griffon vultures indicates that the birds use adapted strategies for specific wind and weather conditions. They obviously seem to know from the start how to act most effectively in a certain situation. Only in cases with bad flight conditions, a trial-and-error strategy can be observed. In addition, the flight behaviour has a clear impact on thermoregulation. For an evaluation of the best strategy for a specific condition, it would be necessary to measure the corresponding energy requirements. As energy budgets of flight mechanics can only be quantified for constant flight conditions (Pennycuick 1990), this would only be possible by simultaneously recording of ECG and / or Oxygen consumption. However, on free-ranging animals this won't be practicable due to the risk of injuries that might be caused by implanted sensors. The data presented here are still preliminary. Data recording by the Doppler-ADF-system will deliver more detailed results due to an increased chronological and spatial resolution. Moreover, it will provide a sample size that is adequate for a statistical analysis.

REFERENCES

BÖGEL, R. 1991. Automatic Radio Tracking. Parc National du Mercantour (Ed.): Acte du Colloque Internationale "Suivi des Vertèbres Terrestres par Radiotélénetrie", Monaco, 1988. pp. 115-124.

BÖGEL, R., U. MÄCK, & W. d'OLEIRE-OLTMANNS 1990. Radiotelemetrische Untersuchungen an Gänse- und Bartgeiern (*Gyps fulvus, Gypaetus barbatus*) in den Alpen. *In* R. Van Den Elzen & K.-L. Schuchmann (Eds.): *Proc. Int. 100. DO-G Meeting, Current Topics of Avian Biology*, Bonn 1988, pp. 201-210.

BÖGEL, R. & D. BURCHARD 1992. An Air Pressure Transducer for Telemetering Flight Altitudes of Birds. *In* I.G. Priede & S.M. Swift (Eds.): *Wildlife Telemetry.* Ellis Horwood, Chichester, U.K. pp. 708

BURCHARD, D. 1989. Direction Finding in Wildlife Research by Doppler Effect. *In* C. J. Jr. Amlaner (Ed.): *BIOTELEMETRY X,* pp. 169-178. University of Arcansas Press, Fayetteville, USA.

HALLER, H. 1983. Die Thermikabhängigkeit des Bartgeiers *Gypaetus barbatus* als mögliche Mitursache für sein Aussterben in den Alpen. *Der orn. Beob.* 80, 263-272.

KENWARD, R.E., G.J.M. HIRONS & F. ZIESEMER 1982. Devices for Telemetering the Behaviour of Free-Living Birds. *Symp. Zool. Soc. London*, 49: 427-432.

KENWARD, R.E. 1987. *Wildlife Radio Tagging.* Academic Press, London, pp. 222.

MÄCK, U. & R. BÖGEL 1990. Untersuchungen zur Ethologie und Raumnutzung von Gänse- und Bartgeier. Nationalpark Berchtesgaden, Doktorberg 6, 8240 Berchtesgaden, Germany: Forschungsbericht Nr. 18, pp 147.

PENNYCUICK, C.J. 1972. Soaring Behaviour and Performance of some East African Birds observed from a Motorglider. *Ibis,* 114:178-217.

PENNYCUICK, C.J. 1973. The Soaring Flight of Vultures. *SAM*, 229(6):102-109.

PENNYCUICK, C.J., M.R. FULLER & L. McALLISTER 1989. Climbing Performance of Harris' Hawks *Parabuteo unicinctus* with Added Load: Implications for Muscle Mechanics and for Radiotracking. *J. exp. Biol.,* 142: 17-29.

PENNYCUICK, C.J. 1990. *Bird Flight Performance.* Oxford Press, Oxford, New York, pp.153.

SCHOBER, F., R. BÖGEL, W.M. BUGNAR, D. BURCHARD, G. FLUCH & N. ROHDE in press. An Automatic Direction Finding and Location System Based on Doppler Effect. *Proceedings of the XIIth International Symposium on Biotelemetry,* August / September 1992, Ancona, Italy.

WHITE, G.C. & R.A. GARROT 1990. *Analysis of Wildlife Radio-Tracking Data.* Academic Press, San Diego, California, USA, pp.383.

Ralf Bögel
Berchtesgaden National Park
Doktorberg 6
W-8240 Berchtesgaden
Germany

Goshawk *Accipiter gentilis* - juvenile

Meyburg, B.-U. & R. D. Chancellor eds.1994
Raptor Conservation Today
WWGBP / The Pica Press

A Honeycomb Repeater Radiotelemetry System and Migration Dataloggers for Raptor Research

Aleksander Bosak

Radiotelemetric technique in phenology and migration studies gives us a chance to acquire qualitatively new knowledge of the biology of birds of prey. However, the conventional techniques of radio and satellite tracking are not flexible/adaptable enough for such studies. Radiotracking is suitable for studying birds within the limits of restricted research areas but of little use for studying migrations. The drawbacks of satellite tracking, given the global character of migration studies, is the high cost, limitation in size of the birds tracked, etc.

The system here under consideration is composed of simple, autonomous and cheap devices for automatic presence-absence recording of radiotagged birds in the area controlled by such a device. They are, in fact, dataloggers, consisting of telemetry receiver, timer and processor with memory.

The processor switches on when a radio signal from a radio-marked animal is detected in the receiver: the individual code is identified and registered in the memory together with the precise time on the reference clock. To avoid overloading of the memory, only changes in the radio-signal are recorded. Recording may take place at certain time intervals.

The antennas of recorders may be directional or omnidirectional depending on the conditions of the experiment.

A single device may provide virtually complete recording of radio-marked birds at 10 to 50km distance when recorders are properly installed in a narrow or bottleneck place on the migration route, with power outputs comparable to those of conventional tracking transmitters. Operational time of these transmitters (with cell power supply) is considerably longer than that of conventional radiotracking units, as the pulse repetition rate may be one pulse per minute or even lower.

These recorders should be installed on hills, cliffs, tree-tops, skyscrapers, chimneys, etc. The instruments are airtight and many of them are supplied with solar cells.

It is desirable to camouflage the units and antennas. The automatic recorders can be installed for one or several seasons.

Information is read out from all the devices installed in the area after the end of the observation period. This general data bank is then used for drawing maps of the birds' route, indicating areas, time and activity patterns of flight.

The automatic recorders may also be part of a retransmitting system, described below, serving as a signal recording station.

Employment of low-powered retransmitters may considerably increase the efficiency of radiotelemetric survey of birds of prey. Successful radiotracking by means of conventional facilities depends greatly on the relief of the terrain. Blind spots between hills or mountains can be much larger than controlled areas. Besides, the region under study often consists of a few areas dozens of miles apart (sites of roosting, feeding, nesting etc.). In such cases the direct receiving of signals is generally impossible, even with uprated radiomarks.

The retransmitting systems differ from direct position-finding systems (radiotracking and triangulation) in their ability to transmit information from the object regardless of the possibility of direct radio contact between the object and the recording station. This enables us to record even low-powered radio tags from birds in valleys, hollows, mountain gorges etc. dozens of miles away from the signal recording station.

Long range of the system is obtained by a long distance between retransmitter and receiver, with directional transmitting and receiving antennas of great amplification. Retransmitters may differ in the constructions of non-scanning receiving antennas and have a range of 0.5km² (a small gorge) to 1,000km².

The principal type of retransmitter we are developing is a construction without mechanical traversing units, supplied with solar cells and storage batteries. It is made up of compact, airtight units, various in shape and weighing 0.3-2.5kg.

Several small solar panels fixed over the top of a tree are employed if there is not enough light for the continuous work of the instrument on tree-trunks or branches suitable for installing retransmitters. Retransmitters on cliffs and other open places may have a specially designed shape with a surface sufficient for carrying solar cells of the required capacity.

Retransmitting antennas are made of thin, strong and corrosion-proof wire, and connected to the main unit by a thin cable. The antennas may also be fixed directly to the frame of the retransmitter. A properly installed device is hard to spot, but additional camouflage is desirable. In any case, wind loading should be taken into consideration. Retransmitting, non-scanning receiving antennas may be omnidirectional or directional for controlling an elliptic area with the defined direction as the longitudinal axis. An object cannot be located within this circle or ellipse. In any case, the distance between object and retransmitter can be estimated from the strength of the signal. In general, it is more efficient to use several retransmitters than to employ radio triangulation techniques for tracking birds with large home ranges of complex shape or relief and remote feeding, nesting and other areas, even if the accuracy of locating the bird is low with the proposed network of retransmitting units.

Location accuracy of radiotransmitters can be increased if the controlled area is divided by installing a number of retransmitters with adjacent or partially overlapping receiving zones. The transmitting power of such a device (let it be called "microtransmitter") can be 10-100 times lower than the above, and placing in the terrain is not so critical. These tiny and very economical transceivers could be used, not only for radiotracking but also as remote transducers of various ecological parameters.

The system may be used as follows: data from these tiny hydro-meteorological stations improve our understanding of the birds' flight biology if the abiotic parameters are constantly monitored by transducers. This is especially useful for high mountains and other extreme conditions.

Continuous recording of physiological parameters by means of retransmitters requires high power consumption as well as the transmission of acoustic signals, but this is possible for the majority of retransmitter designs.

Transmitting of high quality acoustic signals deserves a separate network of specially designed retransmitters with increased power consumption; they would be highly informative for ethological research.

The importance of ethological and physiological data on the nesting and breeding biology of rare and endangered species for artificial rearing justifies not only the employment of a single transmitter but also a separate retransmitter communication line for each nest separately. Employment of a retransmitter network in reserves may also be important in terms of species conservation projects.

Two-way retransmitting systems enable us to affect and control the behaviour of the birds studied and/or other animals by experimental acoustic signals, etc.

Preliminary testing of experimental models of the above instruments is encouraging and we hope that the spectrum of application and possibilities of existing conventional ground-based methods of biotelemetry can be considerably extended through the wide use of simple cheap instruments similar to those described in this paper. It is evident that combining ground-based retransmitters with satellites for transmitting biological information has great potentialities.

Aleksander Bosak
P.O. Box 12
Kiev 254123
Ukraine

Meyburg, B.-U. & R. D. Chancellor eds.1994
Raptor Conservation Today
WWGBP / The Pica Press

Using a Geographic Information System to Analyse Bald Eagle *Haliaeetus leueocaphalus* Habitat on the Chesapeake Bay, Maryland

Sheri K. Chandler, James D. Fraser, David A. Buehler,
Denis J. Dean & Janis K. D. Seegar

INTRODUCTION

A Geographic Information System (GIS) is a computer based system that can store and manipulate spatial information (Aronoff 1991). GIS technology is useful for wildlife studies because it enables us to organise, synthesise, and analyse the data we collect about a species and helps us to understand spatial and nonspatial relationships. We used this technology to study several aspects of habitat use by the endangered Bald Eagle *Haliaeetus leucocephalus* on the Chesapeake Bay.

The Chesapeake Bay is one of the most important Bald Eagle habitats in eastern North America. The Bay supports more than 200 breeding pairs of Bald Eagles and hundreds of immature eagles. The Bay also provides habitat for eagles migrating along the east coast of the United States (Buehler *et al.* 1991a).

Unfortunately, the amount of eagle habitat on the Chesapeake Bay is decreasing rapidly. A report to the Chesapeake Bay Executive Council (Gray *et al.* 1988) predicted a 73% increase in the amount of developed land in the Bay watershed in Virginia and an 80% increase in Maryland between 1978 and 2020.

In order to understand the impact of this shoreline development on Bald Eagles, we studied eagle use of the shoreline during 1985-1991. We radio-tagged and monitored nonbreeding eagles on the northern Chesapeake Bay to identify used shoreline. We used the ARC/INFO GIS (Environmental Systems Research Istitute, Inc. 1988) to analyse habitat use in light of availability and to conduct other spatial calculations. In this paper, we discuss some of the benefits and drawbacks we have experienced with this technology.

STUDY AREA

The study area extended from the William Preston Lane, Jr. Memorial Bridge south of Baltimore, MD, to the Conowingo Dam on the Susquehanna River. The area contained 3,426km^2 and included approximately 2,500km of bay, river and creek shoreline. It also included part of metropolitan Baltimore and the U.S. Army Aberdeen Proving Ground, a military installation (Figure 1).

The shoreline habitat varied greatly. Near Baltimore it was dominated by residential and commercial buildings, roads and parking lots. On Aberdeen Proving Ground, north of Baltimore, the shoreline cover consisted of oak-sweetgum *(Quercus* spp. *-Liquidambar styraciflua)* forests mixed with large marshes. The shoreline of the Susquehanna River, at the north end of the study area, was dominated by oak-hickory *(Carva* spp.)-sweetgum forests. The eastern shore of the study area had small oak-sweetgum woodlots interspersed among large agricultural fields.

Figure 1. U.S. Geological Survey Land Use and Land Cover (LULC) developed areas on the northern Chesapeake Bay (Anderson *et al.* 1976) are shaded. The 614km of shoreline surveyed for eagles is delineated by a bold line.

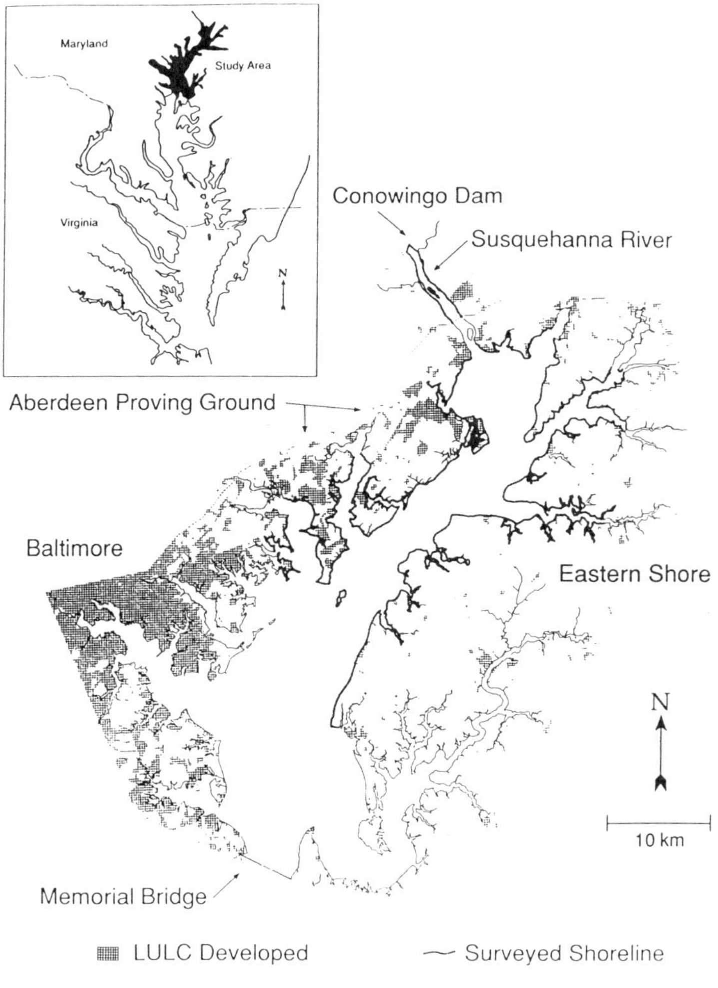

METHODS

Capture and Telemetry

We captured 49 eaglets in nests, and trapped 24 free-flying birds using padded leg hold traps (Young 1983) and floating noose-fish (Cain & Hodges 1989). We attached 65-g radio transmitters with solar-charged, nickel-cadmium batteries (Telemetry Systems, Inc., Mequon, WI) to all eagles. Radios were mounted on the birds in a back-pack configuration using dark brown, teflon ribbon (Bally Ribbon Mills, Bally, PA).

We tracked 73 radio-tagged eagles from a fixed-wing aircraft with strut-mounted H-antennas. We attempted to visually locate the birds on the study area 2-3 times a week during 1985-1988. Visual locations were necessary to obtain the level of accuracy required for our analyses. When $\geq$ 10 radioed birds were present on the study area during a flight, we randomly selected 10 for visual relocation.

We also conducted surveys of Bald Eagles along 614km of the study area shoreline from fixed-wing aircraft (Figure 1). Surveys were flown 50m from the shoreline and 50m above the water at approximately 150km per hr. The surveys began about 30 minutes after sunrise and lasted about 2.5 hours.

Eagle locations were plotted on 1:24,000 U.S. Geological Survey (U.S.G.S.) topographical maps. The Universal Transverse Mercator (UTM) co-ordinates of the locations were determined and manually entered into our ARC/INFO computer data base.

Analyses

We used ARC/INFO software on a MicroVAX II that was linked with an IBM mainframe computer and a Calcomp 1044 plotter. The analyses we describe in this paper involve habitat use versus availability, distance measurements and habitat area determination.

Habitat Use Versus Availability

Wildlife managers and researchers often need to ascertain how a raptor utilises available habitats. When an animal's home range extends over a large area, the difficulty of classifying habitats and their use increases. The first methodology described here involved determining which habitat types eagles used and comparing the frequency of eagle locations in each type with the proportion of the study area with that habitat type.

Our objective for this GIS analysis was to determine if eagle distribution was independent of the distribution of human developments. Eagle location data and the Land Use and Land Cover (LULC) data base from the U.S. Geological Survey (Anderson *et al.* 1976) were used to perform this analysis (these digital representations were referred to as "coverages"). The LULC coverage divided the study area into polygons which were categorised based on the predominant land characteristics (developed, forested, farmland, wetland and other). The minimum polygon size was 4.0ha. Land use was classified as developed if there were $\geq$ 4 buildings within the minimum cell size (Figure 1). The coverage was created in 1976.

The eagle location data were overlaid on the LULC coverage. The ARC/INFO Identity command was used to calculate the number of eagle locations in each habitat type, and the relative abundance of each habitat type. These data were output to our mainframe computer. The number of eagle locations in each habitat type then was compared to the proportion of the study area with that habitat type to determine if the eagles used the habitats in proportion to their availability.

Distance Measurements

For raptor studies, it is often necessary to know the distance from some point to an object or edge. GISs are well suited to such analyses. In this analysis, we determined the distance from the shoreline to all buildings within 500m of the shore. We also calculated building density. The objective was to assess the effects of building density and distance from the shore on Bald Eagle use of the shoreline.

We created an ARC/INFO coverage of the locations of all buildings (houses, marinas, farms, commercial buildings, industrial buildings and military buildings) within 500m of the shoreline.

Table 1. Land Use Land Cover (LULC) classification at radio-tagged Bald Eagle locations and abundance (km^2) in each LULC classification on the study area (obs, exp under the hypotheses of homogenous proportions, and associated cell χ^2 values), northern Chesapeake Bay, Maryland, 1985-88.

	LULC Classification														
	Developed			**Farmland**			**Forested**			**Wetland**			**Other**		
	Obs	Exp	Cell x^2	Obs	Exp	Cell x^2	Obs	Exp	Cell x^2	Obs	Exp	Cell x^2	Obs	Exp	Cell x^2
Eagle Locations[a]	55	153.3	63.0	338	480.0	42.0	562	402.9	62.9	161	72.1	109.7	1	8.8	6.9
Northern Chesapeake Bay[a]	400	301.7	32.0	1,087	945.0	21.3	634	793.1	31.9	53	141.9	55.7	25	17.2	3.5

[a] LULC classification at eagle locations differed from abundance in LULC classifications on the northern Chesapeake Bay (χ^2 428.9, 4 df, $P < 0.001$). (Adapted from Buehler *et al.* 1991b).

The buildings were digitized from 1:24,000 U.S.G.S. topographical maps (Buehler *et al.* 1991b). Because some of the maps were outdated (1953-85), we used 1985 1:12,500 colour aerial photographs to update the building locations.

Using Advanced Revelation computer software, we divided the shoreline coverage digitized from 1:24,000 topographical maps into 250m sections. We then calculated the distance from the shoreline to the closest building for each section and the density of buildings within 500m of each section. We used ARC/INFO to overlay the eagle locations onto the sectioned shoreline and considered a section used if we located ≥ 1 eagle within 50m of that section (Buehler *et al.* 1991b).

Figure 2. Shoreline on the northern Chesapeake Bay, Maryland, showing sampled sections (dark outline) and forested areas based on aerial photographs (shaded). The shoreline and forested areas are poorly aligned. The forest should meet the shoreline on the west and is overlapping approximately 50m on the eastern shore of the peninsula. Shown at 1:12,500 scale.

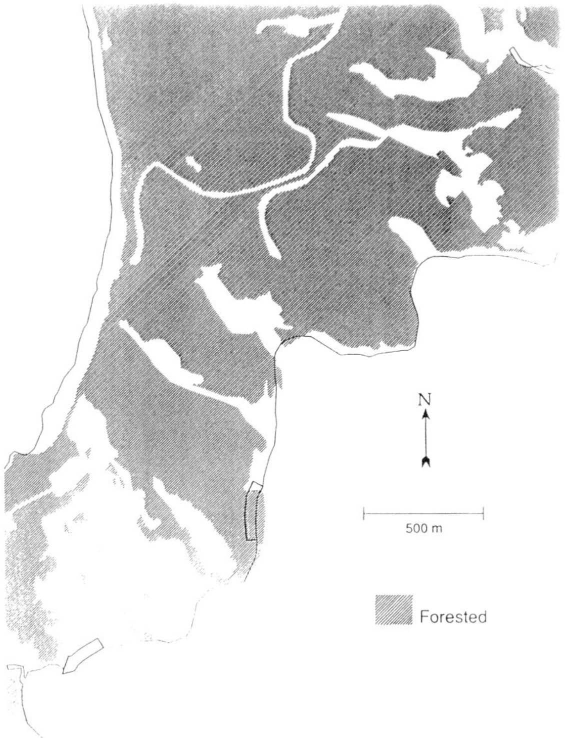

Habitat Area Determination

Ascertaining the amount of area dominated by different habitats can be an important part of raptor studies. In our study, we determined the area (m^2) of forest within shoreline sections 250m long and 50m wide (Figure 2). Our objective in this analysis was to determine if eagle use of shoreline perching areas was related to the percentage of area covered by forest. We used the coverage of the study area shoreline, the eagle locations coverage and a coverage of forested areas along the shoreline. The forest coverage was digitized from 1985, 1:12,500 colour aerial photographs. We randomly selected a sample of 115 shoreline sections used by eagles and 112 unused sections.

Initially, we ocularly estimated the percentage of forest covering each section using the 1:12,500 colour aerial photographs. Each section's boundary was traced onto transparencies and overlaid on the photos. A 1mm dot grid was then used to estimate the percentage of forest on each section.

To produce similar forest cover estimates using ARC/INFO, we used the Buffer function to create a 250 x 50m shoreline area for each selected section. We used the ARC/INFO Intersect command to superimpose the coverage containing the buffered shoreline sections onto the coverage with forested areas (Figure 2). The resulting coverage identified the amount of forested and nonforested area within each selected shoreline section. We then calculated the percentage of each section covered by forest.

RESULTS AND DISCUSSION

Habitat Use Versus Availability

The study area contained 2,199 km^2 of terrestrial area. The LULC data base classified 400km^2 (18.2%) of this area as developed, 1,087km^2 as farmland (49.4%), 634km^2 as forest (28.8%), 53km^2 as wetland (2.4%) and 25km^2 as other (1.1%) (Buehler *et al* 1991b).

Eagle distribution was not independent of development. Eagles used developed land less than expected and forested land more than expected under a model of independence. Only 55 of 1,117 (4.9%) radio-tagged eagle locations occurred on LULC developed areas, although 18.2% of the study area was developed ($\chi^2 = 428.9$, 4 df, $P < 0.001$; Table 1). Most of the locations on developed land (44 of 55, 80.0%) were on Aberdeen Proving Ground, where human activity was low relative to other developed areas, and few buildings occurred. Of the 1,117 eagle locations, only 11 (1.0%) occurred in a nonmilitary-developed area, even though developed areas other than military accounted for 14.8% of all terrestrial area (Buehler *et al.* 1991b).

Distance Measurements

There were 5,120 buildings within 500m of the shoreline we surveyed. Of the 2,532 surveyed sections, 1,673 (66.1%) had buildings within 500m of the shore. The average density of these buildings was 0.09 + 0.003 (SE) buildings per ha. The density of buildings within 100m of the shore was greater than within 500m (Wilcoxon signed rank, x = 1.24 + 0.05 buildings/ha, $P < 0.001$); 245 developed sections had 21 buildings per ha.

Eagles were located less often on shoreline with buildings than would be expected if eagles selected shoreline sections independent of development (Buehler *et al.* 1991b). Sections with 0.01-0.99 buildings per ha within 100m of the shore (94 of 455, 20.7%) were used more frequently than sections with 21 building per ha (17 of 245, 6.95%). We observed eagles on 565 of 1,832 sections (30.8%) with no buildings within 100m of the shore ($\chi^2 = 73.4$, 2 df, $P < 0.001$) (Buehler *et al.* 1991b).

Eagle use of shoreline sections was inversely related to the density of shoreline development (logistic regression, ß = -4.57, SE = 0.97, $\chi^2 = 22.1$, P c 0.001) and directly related to the distance of the development from shore (logistic regression, = 0.001, SE = 0.001, $\chi^2 = 5.3$, $P = 0.02$) (Buehler *et al.* 1991b).

Comparison of Results from Aerial Photo Data and LULC Data

Comparing the locations of houses from aerial photographs and maps with the LULC area classification data, we found that only 143 of the 245 (58.4%) sections with ≥ 1 building per ha within 100m as calculated from aerial photos, were classified as developed in the U.S.G.S. LULC data base (Buehler *et al.* 1991b). This was probably because of additional development since 1976 when the LULC data were collected.

Eagles almost never used shoreline sections with ≥ 1 buildings per ha. This is consistent with the lack of radio-tagged eagle use of sections considered developed (≥ 4 buildings/4 ha) by the LULC data. Radio-tagged eagles used areas identified as forest by the LULC data more frequently than expected based on availability, whereas eagle use of developed and agricultural land was used less than expected based on availability (Buehler *et al.* 1991b). Thus the LULC data base can be used to locate areas which are **not** eagle habitat.

However, eagles did **not** use some of the areas classed as forested in the LULC data base. This was apparently because some areas had been developed since 1976 when the data base was created. Thus LULC forested areas must be examined by some other means to determine which forested sections are likely to be used. Recent aerial photographs or topographical maps provide more up-to-date information on the locations of houses and the configuration of forested areas than the 1976 LULC data.

Habitat Area Determination

Using the aerial photo estimates, we found the percentage of forest cover on sections used by eagles was greater ($\bar{x} = 51.5\%$) than that on unused sections ($\bar{x} = 41.1\%$, Wilcoxon rank-sum, n = 115 and 112 sections, respectively, $P = 0.022$). The same comparison performed using the ARC/INFO estimates also resulted in significant differences between the used and unused sections (Wilcoxon rank-sum, n = 115 and 112 sections, respectively, $\bar{x} = 40.5\%$ vs. 27.9%, respectively, $P = 0.004$). Thus, the ARC/INFO and the dot grid methods appeared to perform similarly when testing for differences in the percentage of forest on shoreline used or unused by eagles.

Unfortunately, when the estimates from both methods were directly compared, discrepancies became apparent. The percentage of forest cover estimates produced by the two techniques were significantly different ($P < 0.0001$; Table 2). Estimates for 21 of 227 sections were ≥ 40 percentage points different. Six of those 21 estimates were ≥ 67 percentage points different. The ARC/INFO method predicted less forest cover than the aerial photo method for 148 of 227 sections, whereas the aerial photo method predicted less forest cover for 33 sections.

Examination of a plot of both the study area shoreline and the forest polygons revealed errors in the alignment of the coverages of 40m or more in some areas, principally on the northern end of the study area (Figure 2). Because the coverages were digitized from different sources (i.e. aerial photographs and topographical maps) at different scales, the forest polygons and shoreline did not precisely match in shape. Therefore these coverages do not have the mutual consistency needed for the determination of the area of shoreline with forest. However, we believe this methodology could be used effectively with coverages created from the same source material.

Table 2. Percentage of forest on northern Chesapeake Bay, Maryland shoreline sections calculated using 1985 aerial photographs and ARC/INFO Geographic Information System coverages created from 1985 aerial photographs and 1970-1985 U.S.G.S. topographical maps.

	Percentage of forest (%)			
Method	n	x	SE	Range
Aerial photo[a]	227	34.3	2.37	0-100
ARC/INFO[a]	227	46.4	2.20	0-100

[a] Percentage of forest on sections differed between methods, based on Wilcoxon signed rank, $\bar{x}$ difference = 12.1%, $P < 0.0001$.

CONCLUSIONS

Telemetry techniques can allow an unbiased approach to habitat studies. Combining telemetry with GIS technology facilitated spatial analysis of the eagle locations and habitat data. The GIS enabled us to efficiently analyse the relationship between eagle use of the shoreline and human development.

The alternative to using GIS techniques is to use maps and overlays. For example, one alternative for our distance measurements analysis would have been counting the buildings and measuring distances to shore by hand. However, this would have been prohibitively time consuming due to the 5,120 buildings on the study area. Furthermore, maps and overlays are much more cumbersome to use. They also are not as easily updated and in many cases must be replaced after several uses. With a GIS, a map becomes an inexpensive output product that can be generated quickly and customized for a special application (Aronoff 1991).

As in all methodologies, there also are disadvantages associated with GIS technology. The cost associated with data base creation can be extremely high. For example, the cost of data base creation can be 75% or more of the total cost of implementing a GIS (Aronoff 1991). If coverages of the study area are not readily available they must be digitized or entered into the GIS programme manually from an external data source. This can be time consuming and expensive, depending on the size and complexity of the area.

If the needed coverages are available, expenses are considerably reduced. However, one should ascertain that available coverages are appropriate for the planned analysis before they are purchased.

Data bases become less accurate over time due to land changes, especially human development. The ability to update a coverage should be considered when it is intended to be used over a period of years. The maintenance required to keep a data base current also can be costly.

When more than one coverage must be used, consistency between the coverages should be assessed. This will avoid problems such as the ones we experienced with the shoreline forest analysis where the coverages were not appropriately consistent for the analysis we attempted. Our data were not only collected from different sources, but also at different times and at different scales.

Accuracy levels of data should be requested from the creator of all acquired data and compared across data sources. Even if the data base completely reflects the characteristics of the data source used to build the coverage, the original data source, for example a topographical map, may not reflect reality. It is wise to ground truth data before conducting analyses.

GIS technology is a powerful tool that can increase the speed and accuracy with which spatial data can be analysed. It enables researchers and managers to synthesise data from several sources to solve problems more effectively. Acquiring the necessary hardware, software and coverages can be expensive, but GIS technology can greatly increase the ability of researchers to analyse telemetry and other geographic data.

ACKNOWLEDGEMENTS

Our work was supported by the U.S. Army Chemical Research, Development and Engineering Center. We thank E. Adams, P. Andrews, L. Arnold, B. Buehler, C. Campbell, J. Cazell, J. Coleman, A. Davidson, A. Delong, D. Delong Jr., S. Eisner, K. Hegstad, W. Iko, E. Kascenska, D. Liedlich, D. Mackler, K. McCabe, J. McConnaughey, M. Moss, M. Ogle, M. Roeder, J. Seegar, L. Serlin, K. Stout and T. Weller, for assisting with data collection and/or data computerisation. A. B. Jones III assisted with Advanced Revelation and ARC/INFO analyses. We thank M. Fuller, J. Ondek, W. Seegar, and F. Ward for their help. M. Causey, K. Cline, C. Koppie, and T. Steffer climbed nest trees as part of the National Wildlife Federation's Chesapeake Bay Banding Project and cooperated with radio-tagging of nestlings. R. L. Kirkpatrick and D. F. Stauffer provided valuable comments on earlier versions of this text. We thank the many landowners on the Chesapeake Bay for allowing us access to their land.

REFERENCES

ANDERSON, J. R., E. E. HARDY, J. T. ROACH & R. E. WITMER 1976. A land use and land cover classification system for use with remote sensor data. *U.S. Geol. Surv. Prof. Pap. 964*. 28pp.

ARONOFF, S. 1989. *Geographic Information Systems: A Management Perspective*. W.D.L. Publ, Ontario, Canada. 294pp.

BUEHLER, D. A., T. J. MERSMANN, J. D. FRASER & J. K. D. SEEGAR 1991a. Differences in distribution of breeding, nonbreeding and migrant bald eagles on the northern Chesapeake Bay. *Condor*

93:399-408.
BUEHLER, D. A., T. J. MERSMANN, J. D. FRASER & J. K. D. SEEGAR 1991b. Effects of human activity on bald eagle distribution on the northern Chesapeake Bay. *J. Wildl. Manage.* 55:282-290.
CAIN, S. L. & J. I. HODGES 1989. A floating-fish snare for capturing bald eagles. *J. Raptor Res.* 23:10-13.
ENVIRONMENTAL SYSTEMS RESEARCH INSTITUTE, INC. 1989. ARC/INFO User's Guide, Volume 2, Command References. ESRI Inst., Inc., Redlands, C.A.
GRAY, R. J., J. C. BREEDEN, J. B. EDWARDS, M. P. ERKILETIAN, J. P. BLASE COOKE, O. J. LIGHTHIZER, M. J. FORRESTER JR., I. HAND, J. D. HIMES, A. R. MCNEAL, C. S. SPOONER & W. T. MURPHY JR. 1988. Population growth and development in the Chesapeake Bay watershed to the year 2020. U.S. Environ. Prot. Agency, Chesapeake Bay Liaison Off, Annapolis, MD. 73pp.
YOUNG, L. S. 1983. Movements of bald eagles associated with autumn concentrations in Glacier National Park. M.S. Thesis, Univ. Montana, Missoula. 102pp.

Sheri K. Chandler, James D. Fraser & David A. Buehler
Dept. of Fisheries & Wildlife Sciences,
Denis J. Dean
Dept. of Forestry,
Virginia Polytechnic Institute and State University,
Blacksburg, Virginia 24061
U.S.A.

Janis K. D. Seegar
Chemical Research, Development and Engineering Center,
U.S. Army, Aberdeen Proving Ground,
Maryland 21010-5423
U.S.A.

Bald Eagle *Haliaeetus leueocephalus*

Meyburg, B.-U. & R. D. Chancellor eds.1994
Raptor Conservation Today
WWGBP / The Pica Press

Tracking Local and Seasonal Movements of Wintering Bald Eagles *Haliaeetus leucocephalus* from Arizona and Michigan with Satellite Telemetry

T.G. Grubb, W.W. Bowerman & P.H. Howey

ABSTRACT

In 1990, two wintering, 3rd-year female Bald Eagles were captured in Arizona and Michigan, and fitted with 95g, backpack, satellite transmitters and conventional 8g, tailmount transmitters. The Arizona eagle ranged over 40,387km² between 24 January - 26 March (35ºN) and used at least 23 different roost locations in the Ponderosa Pine forests of north-central Arizona. From 3 - 27 March, the Michigan eagle covered ≥ 21,768km² between Lakes Michigan and Huron (45ºN). Both birds migrated over 400km about 27 March, the Michigan eagle to remain north of Lake Superior (50ºN) within a 55,160km² summer range. The Arizona eagle migrated 3,020km in 37 days (15 days migrating ≥ 100km north interspersed with 22 days of local or non-northward movements) to a 56,022km² summer range along Great Slave Lake, North-west Territories, Canada (65ºN). Both transmitters expired in June. Eight grand checks of the Arizona PTT yielded a mean error distance of 24.4km (s.d. = 24.2). Advantages and limitations of satellite telemetry for large raptor study are also considered.

INTRODUCTION

Satellite telemetry for wildlife tracking has been developing since its first experimental application on Elk (*Cervus elaphus)* in 1970 (Craighead *et al.* 1972). Most early efforts were necessarily associated with larger terrestrial and marine mammals (Fancy *et al.* 1988) because of the size of transmitter units. It was not until the mid-1980s that technology permitted effective deployment on several large avian species, including Mute, Trumpeter and Tundra Swans *Cygnus olor, C. buccinator, C. columbianus*, Antarctic Giant-Petrel *Macronectes giganteus*, and Bald Eagle *Haliaeetus leucocephalus* (Strikwerda *et al.* 1985, 1986; Howey 1992). Since then,

Wandering Albatross *Diomedea exulans* (Jouventin & Weimerskirch 1990), Golden Eagle *Aquila chrysaetos*, (McIntyre *et al.* 1991) and Gyrfalcon *Falco rusticolus* (Seegar *et al.* 1990) have also been successfully satellite instrumented and tracked.

As part of the field testing and developmental application of a new generation of avian-borne, satellite trannsmitters by Microwave Telemetry, Inc. (MTI)[1], and in association with continuing, independent Bald Eagle research by the USDA Forest Service in Arizona and Michigan State University in the Great Lakes, we radio-equipped two immature, migrant eagles during the winter of 1990. Daily, night roost locations were the primary goal of the Arizona study, while both projects shared common objectives of determining local movement, winter and summer ranges, migratory paths and source breeding populations. Simultaneous monitoring of two eagles of the same age and sex also permitted intraspecific comparison between two widely separated regions of this species' geographic range.

METHODS

Satellite telemetry currently uses the Argos Data Collection and Location System, which is a co-operative international project of the Centre National d'Etudes Spatiales of France, the National Oceanic and Atmospheric Administration (NOAA), and the National Aeronautics and Space Administration (NASA). This system includes equipment on two Tiros-N satellites (currently NOAA-11 and NOAA-12), and a network of satellite tracking stations and communications links that transfer satellite data to processing centres in Landover, Maryland, and Toulouse, France. These centres distribute results to users via telephone modem/computer, diskette and/or print-out. The near-polar, sun-synchronous orbits of Tiros-N satellites permit coverage of a specific geographic area at approximately the same time each day. Location of a transmitter, called a platform transmitter terminal (PTT), is estimated from the Doppler shift in its carrier frequency (401.650 MHz). For normal processing, Argos requires four transmissions, or messages, during an overpass to calculate location, but special processing for wildlife research estimates locations from as few as two Doppler measurements. Argos grades locations according to precision (i.e. 68% of a series of locations expected within the given distance) with location quality indices (LQ): LQ3 - 150m, LQ2 - 350m, LQ1 - 1km, and LQ0 - undetermined/animal tracking. Within LQ0, Argos also provides an interpretative index, which helps in assessing estimated locations by explaining why normal processing failed (summarized from Harris *et al.* 1990).

During the winter of 1990, in Coconino County, Arizona, we captured a 3rd-year (McCollough 1989) female Bald Eagle with a rocket net (Grubb 1988) on 24 January; and on 3 March, in Manistee County, Michigan, using a bownet (Bloom 1987), we captured a second, seasonal migrant of the same age class and sex. Both birds were fitted with experimental, MTI PTT100 series, satellite transmitters. Each unit weight 95g and measured 9.4 x 3.3 x 3.0cm, with a 17.8cm antenna protruding posteriorly at a 45º angle. The PTT's were attached as backpacks with teflon ribbon and sewn with biodegradable cotton thread. Transmitter life can be varied with timer setup, as well as battery power: the Arizona unit was set on an 8 hours on/16 off schedule with a 28-week life expectancy, while the Michigan unit was set on 4/44 for a potential life of 112 weeks. Both transmitters were active 1200-1600 with the Arizona unit continuing 1600-1800 to facilitate night roost location. All times are local: for Arizona, Mountain Standard Time (MST), and for Michigan, Eastern Standard Time (EST). Both eagles were also fitted with conventional (165 MHz) 8g, tailmounted transmitters for initial ground tracking, but due to logistical and budgetary constraints we were limited to following only the Arizona bird on its winter range.

Data on our eagles gathered by ARGOS in France were transferred to MTI in Maryland via telephone modem/computer. Locations were then telephoned to the field, sometimes within as little as 30 minutes after a satellite pass, and later followed with a hard copy and/or diskette. Date, time, grade of fix (LQ), number of messages, latitude, longitude and bird identification were then compiled in a Lotus 1-2-3[1] spreadsheet (Lotus Development Corp. 1986). Local date and time were calculated and, with the aid of maps, spurious data were eliminated. Next any remaining

[1] *The use of trade and company names is for the benefit of the reader; such use does not constitute an official endorsement or approval of any service or product by the U.S. Dept. of Agriculture or Michigan State University to the exclusion of others that may be suitable.*

unreplicated, distant, outlying fixes were culled. We excluded any fixes with <4 messages from the Arizona PTT, but because of limited data we had to include 2-message locations for the Michigan bird. Data were plotted by hand on United States Geological Survey (USGS) 1:500,000 Base Maps, and Defense Mapping Agency (DMA) Aerospace Center 1:5,000,000 Global Navigation and Planning Charts.

Software programme Home Range[1] (Ackerman *et al*. 1989) was used to calculate areas of minimum convex polygons (100%, 95% and 75%) and mean distances from locations to the arithmetic centre, and to plot chronological movements. (Chronological = date/time ordered locations, which may not be consecutive; consecutive = next day locations.) All locations were included in winter and summer range calculations, but calculations on the Arizona eagle's migration were made using only one fix per day, subjectively determinated by a consideration of the LQ, number of messages and time of day (later being more likely representative of the day's net movement). Daily movements during migration were categorised as migratory if ≥ 100km northerly, and local if <100km northerly or non-northerly. For winter roost locations in Arizona we used only fixes after 1700 MST.

RESULTS

Table 1. Satellite telemetry coverage of two Bald Eagles captured as winter migrants in Arizona and Michigan in 1990.

Period	State or Province	Dates	Days	Fix[1] Days	Fixes	Fixes/Days
Eagle captured in Arizona (PTT 8 h on/16 h off):						
Winter	Arizona	24 Jan-26 Mar	62	41	63	1.5
Migration		27 Mar-02 May	37	37	95	2.6
Summer	NW Terr.	03 May-08 Jun	37	22	47	2.1
Totals		24 Jan-08 Jun	136	100	205	2.1
Eagle captured in Michigan (PTT 4 h on/44 h off):						
Winter	Michigan	03 Mar-28 Mar	26	8	5	0.6
Migration	-	29 Mar	1	1	2	2.0
Summer	Ontario	30 Mar-29 Jun	92	15	20	1.3
Totals		03 Mar-29 Jun	119	24	27	1.1

[1] *Number of days with usable, satellite-derived fixes (locations).*

We tracked the Bald Eagle captured in Arizona for 136 days, 24 January - 8 June, and the eagle from Michigan for 119 days, 3 March - 29 June (Table 1). The first PTT operated to full term but the second ceased functioning prematurely. Mean number of fixes per day ranged between 0.6 - 2.6, was highest during migration, and increased with latitude. The 8/16 PTT deployed in Arizona provided more fixes/day (2.1 versus 1.1) and better coverage (74% of 136 possible fix-days versus 20% of 119) than the 4/44 unit used in Michigan. Eleven ground checks of the Arizona PTT before and after deployment yielded a mean error distance of 50.7km (s.d. = 58.3, Table 2). Two-message fixes had the largest error distance and were the least reliable. Without them, the mean error distance was 24.4km (s.d. = 24.2).

Table 2. Ground verifications of satellite location data for a PTT before and after being deployed on a wintering Bald Eagle in Arizona, 1990. Actual transmitter location while in hand, or as determined by conventional triangulation and visual confirmation, follow below the satellite data.

Date	Time[1]	Location Quality	Number Messages	Latitude (N)	Longitude (W)	Distance (km)
19 Jan	1948	0	5	35.259	111.793	
	1948			35.250	111.750	4.5
20 Jan	1400	0	6	35.262	111.789	
	1400			35.250	111.750	3.4
	1921	0	2	34.977	114.477	
	1921			35.250	111.750	202.2
21 Jan	1349	0	6	35.224	111.951	
	1349			35.250	111.750	19.0
22 Jan	1341	0	3	35.384	111.349	
	1341			35.250	111.750	35.4
24 Jan	1935	0	9	35.094	112.350	
	1900			35.083	112.875	47.0
30 Jan	1900	0	4	35.018	111.474	
	2203			35.025	111.467	4.3
31 Jan	1833	0	2	35.904	110.509	
	2127			35.058	111.497	115.5
06 Feb	1244	0	7	35.592	111.030	
	1620			35.025	111.467	74.4
24 Feb	1427	1	4	35.504	113.053	
	1345			35.450	113.111	7.4
26 Feb	2026	0	2	34.317	111.233	
	1950			34.892	111.431	44.8

[1] *Mountain Standard Time*

Between January and March the Arizona eagle ranged over 40,000km² in north-central Arizona (35°N), while the Michigan eagle covered about 22,000km² between Lakes Michigan and Huron in March (45°N, Table 3). The Arizona bird wandered widely across its winter range (Fig. 1). The chronological plot shows roughly four cycles of movements between north-west and south-east areas of heavier activity. The Michigan eagle appeared to move more progressively (Fig. 2), but data are too limited to be conclusive. The winter range in Arizona was approximately twice the area estimated for Michigan.

Table 3. Winter and summer range estimates from Program Home Range (Ackerman *et al.* 1989) for two Bald Eagles equipped with satellite transmitters in Arizona and Michigan in 1990.

Date	Days	State or Province	Area (km²) of Percent Minimum 100%	Convex 95%	Polygons 75%	Distance Centre[1] (km)
Eagle captured in Arizona:						
24 Jan-26 Mar	62	Arizona	40,387	26,431	16,526	77.8
03 May-08 Jun	37	NW Terr.	56,022	47,280	33,713	100.4
Eagle captured in Michigan:						
03 Mar-28 Mar	26	Michigan	21,768	11,106	3,618	103.9
30 Mar-29 Jun	92	Ontario	55,160	53,946	25,276	127.4

[1] *Mean distance from fixes in 100% polygon (n = 62, 47, 9, 28) to arithmetic centre of plot.*

The eagle wintering in Arizona used at least 23 different night roost locations between January and March; 21 of these were new, i.e. previously unrecorded (Grubb *et al.* 1989). The same roost was used a second night twice in the 18 pairs of consecutive nights for which location data were available. These were the only roosts occupied more than once during the period. The mean distance between night roosts was 50.7km (s.d. = 38.7, range 0-144km). There were 19 pairs of afternoon (mean time = 1430) and evening (mean time = 1926) fixes, with an average separation of 61.8km (s.d. = 42.1, range 0-177km). No winter same-day fixes were recorded in Michigan, and comparable consecutive night distances could not be calculated from the 4/44 PTT operation pattern.

The Arizona and Michigan eagles began their northward, spring migration with flights of 410 and 435km respectively, within two days of each other (27 and 29 March). The Michigan bird reached its summering grounds north of Lake Superior in Ontario, Canada (50°N), after only one apparent day of migration across the lake (Fig. 3). The Arizona eagle continued northward, covering 3,032km (direct distance) in 37 days, essentially following the Rocky Mountains to north of Great Slave Lake in the North-west Territories, Canada (65°N, Fig 4). Fifteen days of migratory movements were interspersed with 22 days of local movements, totalling an additional 1,509km (Table 4). Migratory moves lasted 1-4 days and local moves 4-7 days (Fig. 5). Local meandering accounted for 33.2% of the total distance covered (4,541km) and 59.5% of the total time spent en route. Migratory flights averaged three times the length of local movements ($t = 4.00$, $P = 0.001$) and were 10% less variable.

From 3 May - 8 June the Arizona eagle ranged over 56,022km², while the Michigan bird covered 55,160km² from 30 March - 29 June (Table 3). The summer ranges of both eagles were larger than winter and showed greater spread, as indicated by the mean distance to arithmetic centres. Chronological movements of the Arizona bird (Fig. 1) indicated heavier use in the south-east portion of its range near Great Slave Lake, and one long, meandering sojourn off to the north-west. Twenty-four pairs of same day fixes yielded a mean flight distance of 64.8km (s.d. = 54.9, range 11-232), which was comparable to the 62.8km average for winter in Arizona (s.d. = 43.0, range 0-123, n = 22 pairs; $t = 0.13$, $P = 0.895$). The six pairs of consecutive evening fixes (mean time = 1930) had a mean separation of 98.1km (s.d. = 47.4, range 23-102), approximately twice the winter figure ($t = 2.39$, $P = 0.026$). The Michigan eagle wandered back and forth across its summer range in a northwest-southeast pattern with no definitive area of consistent use (Fig. 2). Length of within day movements (mean = 96.3km, s.d. = 40.3, range 26-154, n = 5 pairs) appeared greater than that for the Arizona eagle, but results were not significant ($t = 1.17$, $P = 0.250$).

Table 4. Migratory (100km northward) and local (<100km northward or non-northward) movements during the migration of a Bald Eagle tracked via satellite telemetry from Arizona to the North-west Territories, Canada, in 1990.

Type of Movement	Total Distance (km)	Days	Mean Distance /Day	Std.Dev.	Coeff. Var.	Range (km)
Migratory	3,032	15	202.1	118.7	59%	96-435
Local	1,509	22	68.6	47.3	69%	13-160
Total	4,541	37	122.7	106.5	87%	13-435

DISCUSSION

Until this study the origins of Bald Eagles wintering in Arizona and Michigan were uncertain. Presumably both marked birds returned to their natal areas to summer. The wide-ranging movements across their summer ranges are not surprising for immature non-breeders (Gerrard *et al.* 1980). Weather (Richardson 1978), prey availability (Fretwell 1980), and social interactions (Newton 1979) influence movements on both summer and winter ranges, as well as affect the pattern, distance and duration of migration. The differential migration of these two satellite-tracked eagles gives intraspecific verification of the established tendency for avian species, or individuals within a species, breeding at higher latitudes to migrate further south for the winter (Welty 1975; Newton 1979).

The route followed by the Arizona eagle appears typical. It closely approximates flight paths of 14 Bald Eagles from wintering areas across the intermountain states moving to summer locations in northern Alberta and the North-west Territories (Young 1983). Also, the remains of another, conventionally marked, eagle from the Arizona study were recovered in south-western Montana in November 1990, not far from the satellite track. Our daily migation distances are consistent with the findings of Harmata (1984), who found daily migratory flights ranged from 33-435km and averaged 180km (n = 10), for four wintering eagles tracked 1,968-2,077km from Colorado to northern Saskatchewan.

Through our culling procedures, we tried to be conservative in using the satellite data for determining local and seasonal movements, and home ranges. Coverage of the Arizona eagle was sufficient to provide reliable results, but the smaller number of fix days and total fixes, as well as a lack of consecutive and same day data for the Michigan bird, must qualify resultant estimates. The 4/44 operational period was limiting, and we suspect the PTT was not functioning properly. In addition, winter coverage was brief. The chronological movement pattern in Michigan could reflect gradual northward migration rather than winter range movements. The associated area estimates are conservative at best and, because of the small sample size, inconclusive. Even so, the large winter range is likely related to physiographic features and a tendency to wander back and forth between the Great Lakes. Winter meandering in Arizona is explained by an ephemeral prey source, mostly large ungulate carrion, and shifts between higher elevation ponderosa pine (*Pinus ponderosa*) forest and lower pinon (*P. edulis*) - juniper (*Juniperus sp.*) grassland. The extensive summer wandering of both birds may relate to abundant prey and territorial exclusion by breeding adults.

Our winter range sizes are much larger than any previously determined. Young (1983) reported a mean of 761km² (range 4-2,471, n = 7) and Harmata (1984), 311km² (range 61-795, n = 12). Based solely on roosting locations, previous work in Arizona (Grubb *et al.* 1989), estimated a mean minimum winter range of 401km² (range 292-593, n = 4). However, with conventional telemetry, the birds were out of range 51% of the time. Satellite telemetry offers better coverage and greater continuity, especially for long-distance and peripheral movements or when continuous tracking is not otherwise possible.

Although from a small sample, our ground verification results provide a good indication of the

Figure 1. Winter and summer ranges in Arizona and the North-west Territories, Canada, shown as 100% minimum convex polygons with chronological movements, derived from satellite data from a Bald Eagle captured in Arizona in winter, 1990.

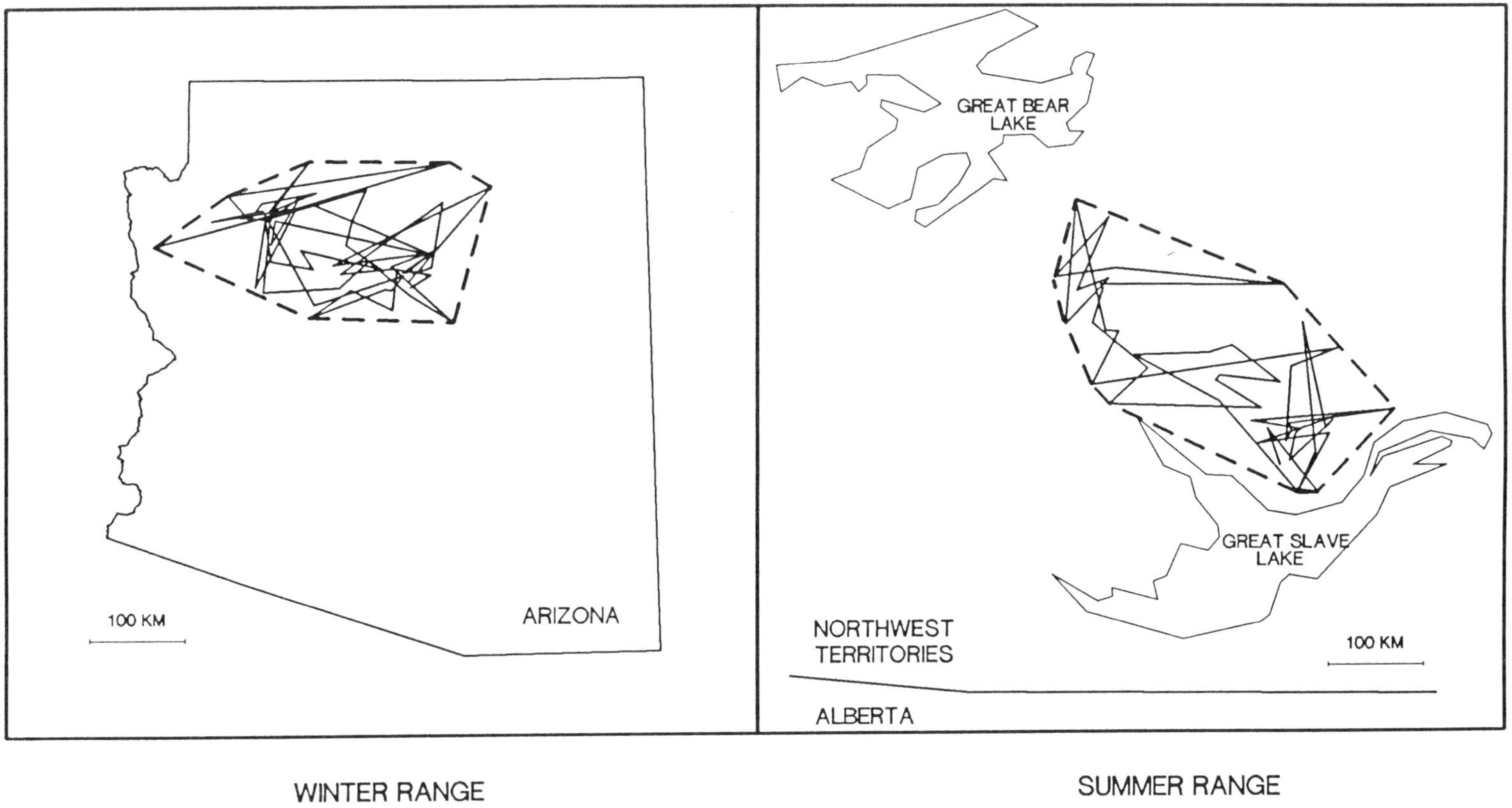

Figure 2. Winter and summer ranges across Michigan and in Ontario, Canada, shown as 100% minimum convex polygons with chronological movements, derived from satellite data from a Bald Eagle captured in Michigan in winter, 1990.

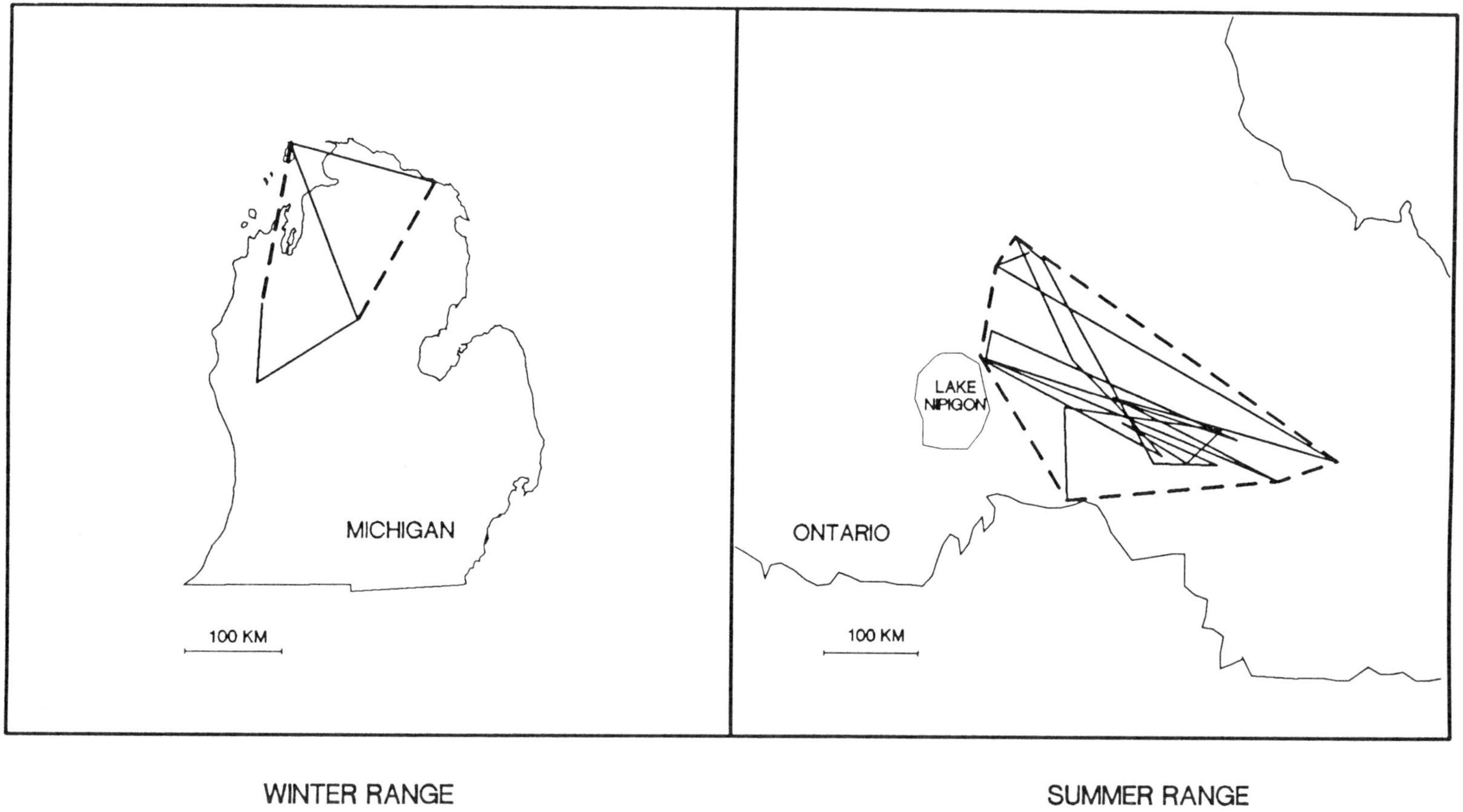

Figure 3. Migration route between winter and summer ranges for a Bald Eagle captured in Michigan in winter, 1990, as determined by satellite telemetry.

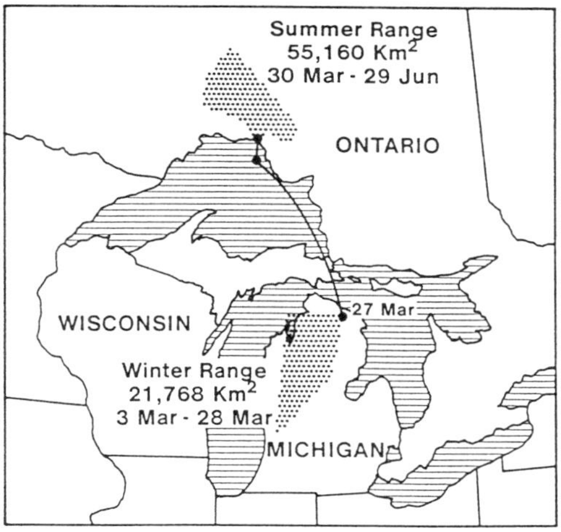

Figure 4. Migration route between winter and summer ranges for a Bald Eagle captured in Arizona in winter, 1990, as determined by satellite telemetry.

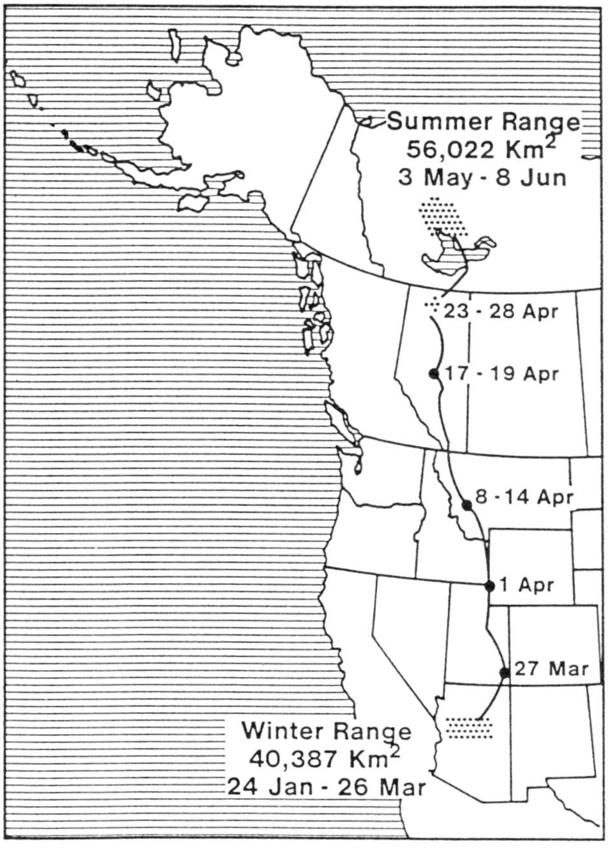

Figure 5. Pattern of local and migratory movements during northward migration of a 3rd-year, female Bald Eagle captured in Arizona in winter, 1990.

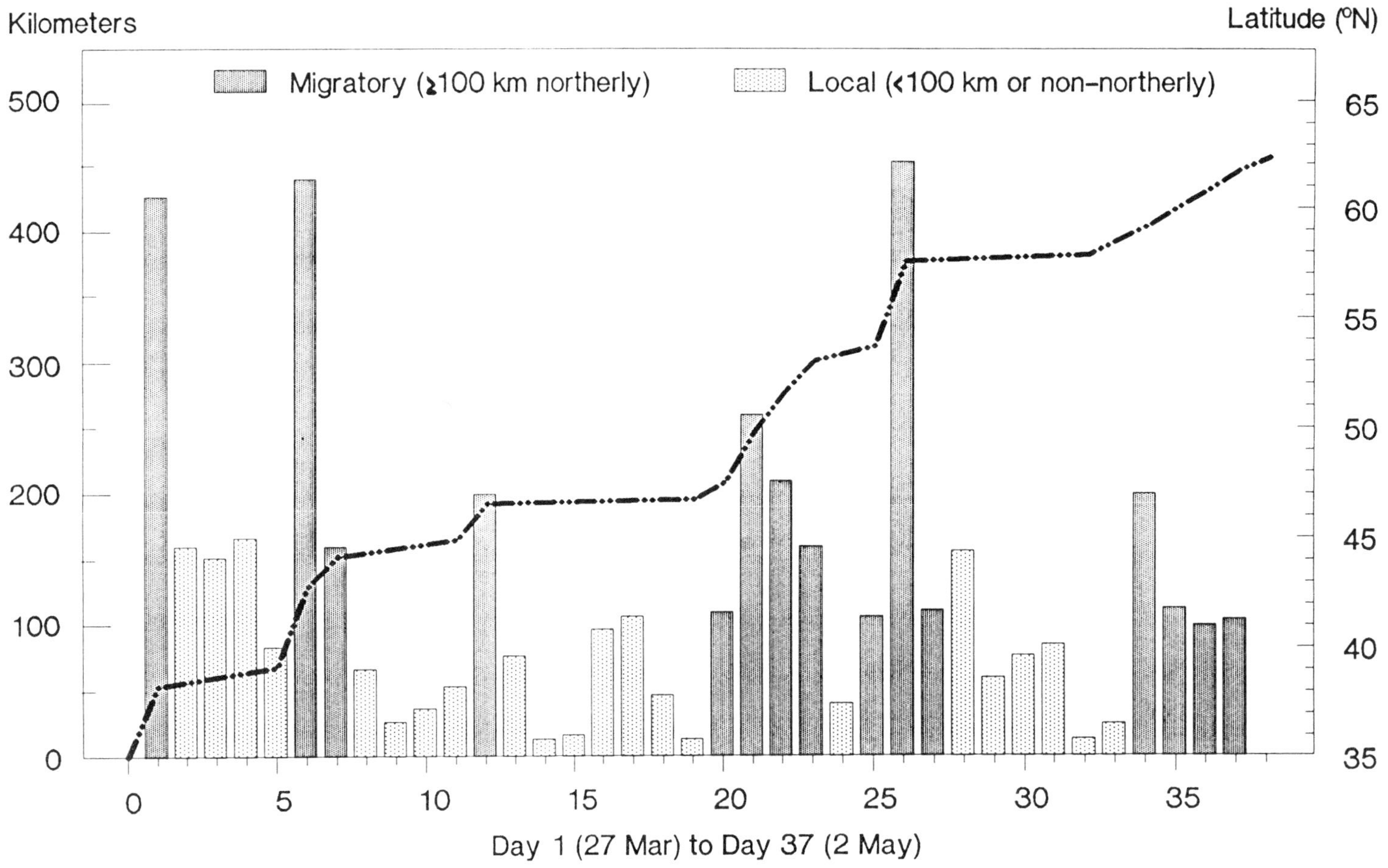

variability in accuracy for wildlife tracking via satellite. Attachment of a small conventional transmitter remains mandatory for conventional triangulation, exact location and visual contact. These were necessary elements of the Arizona study. The greatest advantage of satellite tracking in this case is the constant, remote surveillance, which accommodates the inevitable breaks in field tracking due to weather, logistics, administration, etc. A second advantage is being able to get a satellite fix less than an hour old via telephone on the way to the field (or even from the field in some situations). This significantly increases the efficiency of relocation and ground tracking. A conventional transmitter is not needed for home range and migration tracking; for this work, satellite telemetry is unsurpassed in efficiency and effectiveness.

We found, as already indicated, a 4/44 PTT operational cycle provided too few data for certainty in determining the validity of individual fixes, necessary for accurate home range and daily movement determination. The 8/16 cycle was excellent for assessing within day movements, but it tended to provide more data than necessary, which confounded the process of eliminating erroneous or superfluous locations. Better, more diagnostic programmes are improving output, but at the time of this analysis the culling process was tedious and time consuming and, unfortunately, fairly subjective. Although aided by a series of diagnostic keys, the user ultimately assesses the validity of any given fix. Thus a thorough knowledge of the target species and attendant conditions are prerequisite. Although daily locations are sacrificed, experience has shown an 8/40 cycle to be most efficient and effective. PTT's provide better tracking data when kept on as long as possible, and 8/40 gives a 1-year life expectancy. Typical of satellite telemetry, we received more and better fixes as our birds moved north and also during migration, when they were more often airborne and therefore more visible to the satellite.

We believe satellite telemetry is an invaluable technique for tracking the movements of large birds of prey; however, there are several limiting considerations. The questionable accuracy of wildlife-type fixes and the difficulties of data compilation have been mentioned. The number and timing of fixes within the PTT operational period varies from day to day. Quality of fix is affected by several satellite parameters and by the orientation, location and movement of the transmitter on the ground. There are often gaps in the data, resulting from days when no fixes were possible. PTT's are at present larger and less streamlined than conventional transmitters, and require antennas that protrude at a 45° angle rather than contour down the back and tail. Thus satellite units should be used with discretion and attached with great care. They have shorter life cycles than comparable-sized conventional transmitters, but solar-powered units are becoming available to improve longevity. Satellite telemetry is initially expensive: PTT 100 series units cost about $2,900 each, and data processing/tracking approximately another $1,500. However, this technique is more than cost effective when compared to conventional long distance tracking, which involves tracking equipment, field personnel, vehicle and aircraft expenses, and is subject to myriad logistical, administrative, weather and telemetry related limitations.

ACKNOWLEDGEMENTS

A.J. Bath and M.L. Nixon provided technical and field assistance in capturing and radio-marking the eagles in Michigan and Arizona respectively. In Arizona, Nixon also contributed significantly to ground tracking on the winter range, and J.K. Aitkin assisted in collating and entering data for analysis. In Michigan, R. Radtke and D. Elsing procured original seed funding for satellite telemetry; S.A. Hogle, M.J. Keck and D. Pinzino provided additional field assistance; and G.A. Dawson and J.P. Giesy supplied logistical and administrative support. D.E. Berry developed the computer maps with range/movement plots. This research was co-operatively funded by the USDA Forest Service -- Rocky Mountain Forest and Range Experiment Station and Hiawatha National Forest, Michigan State University, Microwave Telemetry, Inc. and Consumers Power Company.

REFERENCES

ACKERMAN, B.B., F.A. LEBAN, E.O. GARTON & M.D. SAMUEL 1989. *User's manual for program Home Range, 2nd edn.* Tech. Rep. 15, For., Wildl. and Rang. Exper. Sta., Univ. of Idaho, Moscow. 81pp.

BLOOM, P.H. 1987. Capturing and handling raptors. Pages 99-123 *in* B.A. Giron Pendleton, B.A. Millsap, K.W. Cline & D.M. Bird, (Eds.) *Natl. Wildl. Fed. Raptor Manage. Tech. Man.*

CRAIGHEAD, F.C., Jr., J.J. CRAIGHEAD, C.E. COTE & H.K. BUECHNER 1972. Satellite and ground radio tracking of elk. Pages 99-111 *in* S.R. Galler, K. Schmidt-Koenig, G.J. Jacobs & R.E. Belleville (Eds.) *Animal Orientation and Navigation -- a symposium.* NASA Spec. Publ. 262. 606pp.

FANCY, S.G., L.F. PANK, D.C. DOUGLAS, C.H. CURBY, G.W. GARNER, S.C. AMSTRUP & W.L. REGELIN 1988. *Satellite Telemetry: a new tool for wildlife research and management.* USDI Fish Wildl. Serv. Resourc. Publ. 172. 54pp.

FRETWELL, S. 1980. Evolution of migration in relation to factors regulating bird numbers. Pages 517-527 *in* A. Keast & E.S. Morton (Eds.). *Migrant birds in the neotropics - ecology, behavior, distribution, and conservation.* Symposium of Natl. Zool. Park, Smithsonian Institution Press.

GERRARD, J.M., P.N. GERRARD & D.W.A. WHITFIELD 1980. Behaviour in a nonbreeding Bald Eagle. *Canadian Field-Nat,* 94:391-397.

GRUBB, T.G. 1988. A portable rocket-net system for capturing wildlife. USDA For. Serv., Rocky Mount. For. Rang. Exper. Sta. Res. Note RM-484. 8pp.

GRUBB, T.G., S.J. NAGILLER, W.L. EAKLE & G.A. GOODWIN 1989. Winter roosting patterns of Bald Eagles in north-central Arizona. *Southwestern Nat.* 34:453-459.

HARMATA, A.R. 1984. Bald Eagles of the San Luis Valley, Colorado: their winter ecology and spring migration. Unpubl. Ph.D. dissert., Montana St. Univ., Bozeman. 222p.

HARRIS, R.B., S.G. FANCY, D.C. DOUGLAS, G.W. GARNER, S.C. AMSTRUP, T.R. MCCABE & L.F. PANK 1990. Tracking wildlife by satellite: current systems and performance. USDI Fish Wildl. Serv. Fish Wildl Rep. 30.

HOWEY, P.W. (in press). Tracking birds by satellite. Wildlife Telemetry: Proc. of 4th Intl. Conf. on Wildl. Telemetry.

JOUVENTIN, P. & H. WEIMERSKIRCH 1990. Satellite tracking of Wandering Albatrosses. *Nature* 343:746-748.

LOTUS DEVELOPMENT CORP. 1986. Lotus 1-2-3. Release 2.01. Cambridge, MD.

MCCOLLOUGH, M.A. 1989. Molting sequence and aging of Bald Eagles. *Wilson Bull.* 101: 1-10.

MCINTYRE, C.L., R.E. AMBROSE & P.W. HOWEY 1991. Using satellite radio telemetry to track local and long distance movements of an Alaskan Golden Eagle. Abstr. and unpubl. pap., Raptor Res. Found. annual meeting, Tulsa, OK.

NEWTON, I. 1979. *Population Ecology of Raptors.* Buteo Books, Vermillion, SD. 399p.

RICHARDSON, W.J. 1978. Timing and amount of bird migration in relation to weather: a review. *Oikos* 30:224-272.

SEEGAR, W.S., P.W. HOWEY, M.R. FULLER, W.W. BOWERMAN & T.G. GRUBB 1990. Using satellite to study bird movements. Abstr. and unpubl. pap., Raptor Res. Found. annual meeting, Allentown, PA.

STRICKWERDA, T.E., H.D. BLACK, N. LEVANON & P.W. HOWEY 1985. The bird-borne transmitter. Johns Hopkins APL Tech. Dig. 6:60-67.

STRICKWERDA, T.E., M.R. FULLER, W.S. SEEGAR, P.W. HOWEY & H.D. BLACK 1986. Bird-borne satellite transmitter and location program. John Hopkins APL Tech. Dig. 7:203-208.

WELTY, J.C. 1975. *The Life of Birds.* W.B. Saunders Co., Philadelphia, PA. 623p.

YOUNG, L.S. 1983. Movements of Bald Eagles associated with autumn concentrations in Glacier National Park. Unpubl. M.S. thesis, Univ. Montana, Missoula. 99p.

T.G. Grubb
USDA Forest Service
Rocky Mountain Forest and Range
Experiment Station
2560 S. Pine Knoll Dr.
Flagstaff, AZ
USA 86001

W.W. Bowerman
Dept. of Fisheries and Wildlife
Pesticide Research Center
Institute for Environmental Toxicology
Michigan State University
East Lansing, MI
USA 48824

P.W. Howey
Microwave Telemetry, Inc.
8945 Guilford Rd.
Columbia, MD
USA 21046

Meyburg, B.-U. & R. D. Chancellor eds.1994
Raptor Conservation Today
WWGBP / The Pica Press

Status Specific Habitat Use in the Common Buzzard *Buteo buteo*

Ulf Hohmann

ABSTRACT

A population of Common Buzzards *Buteo buteo* was studied in 1991 in a lowland area in Central Europe with respect to habitat utilization, social status and intraspecific interactions. The population consisted of adult paired birds, subadults, immatures, juveniles and transients (mostly of unknown age, here dismigrants and migrants). 36 birds were colour-marked or radio-tagged, in order to allow studies on population composition and -phenology.

In birds of different social status different habitat use was discovered. Pairs were resident and did reproduce in the area, therefore investing much energy to maintain high quality habitats. Paired Buzzards appeared to be socially dominant towards unpaired birds and transients. This dominance hierarchy could be the reason why unpaired birds and transients had to use habitats of lower quality.

INTRODUCTION

Ornithology in general and research on birds of prey in particular mostly over-estimate the breeding stock within a given population.

Non-breeders, however, make up considerable quantities in populations of longliving raptors: For the Common Buzzard in Germany up to approx. 38% of all individuals are younger than two years (a calculation based on age specific mortality rates given by Mebs 1964).

Moreover, in addition up to 50% of fully matured and paired Buzzards lay no eggs in years with poor food supply (Hohmann 1992). One has to assume that in general 25% to 30% of potential breeders do not actually reproduce (Newton *et al.*1982; Picozzi & Weir 1974; Wittenberg 1974).

In view of this situation it appears logical that patterns of habitat-utilization are not necessarily identical for all members of a population. Habitat requirements of immature and subadult singles will substantially differ from those of paired and breeding birds, e.g. areas with unstable food resources and a lack of nesting sites are hardly acceptable for breeders but still valuable for non-breeders.

The study presented below deals with the following topics:

1. Actual composition of the individuals of a small but precisely observed population with respect to social status.
2. Utilization distribution and habitat use of individuals of different social status and its intrapopulation mechanisms.

Special consideration was given to intraspecific aspects like territoriality (territory defined as "defended area", according to Tinbergen 1957) or social dominance hierarchy according to the fundamental studies of Picozzi & Weir (1974) or Weir & Picozzi (1975, 1983). The term "dismigration or dismigrants" will be used referring to Berndt & Winkel (1983) as an "abbreviated term for dispersion-migration; it includes dispersal and spacing" and excludes here any kind of longway flights towards special destinations further away.

STUDY AREA

The study, including trapping and marking, took place between February and December 1991 in an area of 70 km², of lowland grassland, typical of the western parts of Schleswig-Holstein, Germany, located circa 54° 22 N and 9° 19 W at an elevation of nearly NN (Figure 1). It is a landscape with only few small woods and copses, with almost the entire area being used as pasture for dairy-farming:

Potential nesting-places for Buzzards are rare but optimal feeding grounds are abundant.

For the study three different types of habitats were distinguished:

Type 1: Nesting, resting or sleeping habitats: woods or smaller copses.

Type 2: Optimal hunting habitats: pastures with high perching points and/or located close to type 1.

Type 3: Less suitable hunting habitats: pastures without or with only lower perching points and/or located far from type 1.

Figure 1. The study area (black) was located in the north of Germany.

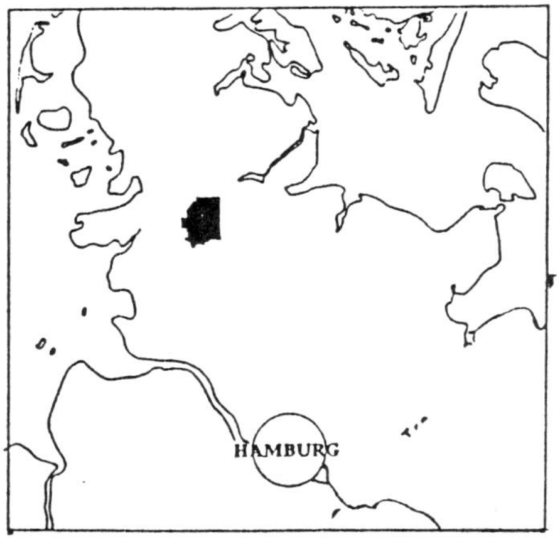

METHODS

In winter, due to the shortage of alternative prey caused by snow cover, Buzzards were easily attracted to carrion-baited Goshawk traps and similar falling-lid traps (Kenward & Marcstrom 1983). During summer and autumn, with food being abundant, Goshawk traps and falling-lid traps apparently were too conspicuous and did not work any more. It was then possible to overcome the Buzzards' suspicion by using bow nets, which were hidden by a cover of cut off surrounding vegetation like grass (Bub 1974).

A total of 46 Common Buzzards were individually marked or recognized, 33 of them were trapped, 14 with Goshawk- or falling-lid traps, 15 with bow nets, and 4 birds with other traps.

Nine of these birds were equipped with tail-mounted transmitters (GFT, Kiel), the remaining birds were marked with patagial fixed wingtags or special tailtags (see Hohmann 1992). In addition

9 birds were individually recognized by their characteristic plumage or peculiarities of voice (hoarse). Seven nestlings were wing-tagged but only 4 of them reached the post-fledgling phase (Table 1).

Table 1. Trapping success, including recaptures and non-target species

Total of birds trapped	45
Recaptures	- 9
Rough-legged *B. Buteo lagopus*	- 2
Marsh Harrier *Circus aeruginosus*	- 1
Additional marked fledglings	+ 4
Buzzards recognized by plumage or voice	+ 9
Individually marked Common Buzzards	**46**

Due to the open landscape it was generally possible to discover all birds visually with binoculars. Transmitter-equipped birds allowed the study of long distance movements and observations during days of poor visibility or in cover.

After a bird was located, its position was plotted on a map in a 125-m-square-grid. Square grid coordinates were entered into a computer, and grid-cell and minimum convex polygon analyses were carried out (I.A. Todd in prep., "Wildtrak" Non parametric home range analyses for Macintosh Computers, see also Doncaster 1990). The grid cell method facilitated non-parametric quantitative estimates of habitat utilization in the Buzzards' home range, for example the use of core areas (the degree of differentiation is restricted by the grid cell size).

In addition to the location any social behaviour of the observed individuals was recorded (after Weir & Picozzi 1975). Normally one bird was observed for 15 min., but occasionally observations of individual birds were extended over several hours.

In addition to the marked Buzzards between July and November also all other Buzzards - mostly transients - were recorded. A short description of plumage patterns and behaviour of these unmarked Buzzards was prepared, in order to minimize bias resulting from difficulties in identification or differences in detectability of unmarked and marked Buzzards. This method allows to obtain comparable estimates of numbers of both groups. Thus in total 65 purely visual censuses - not using transmitters - were carried out within this period. Although I did not knowingly collect data on any unmarked Buzzard more than once, it is probable that some individuals were used more than once during the study.

Age classes of trapped individuals were differentiated by moult patterns of the primaries. A normal sequential and symmetric way usually identifies first year birds in their first moult. A completely asymmetric and transilient order is typical of adult birds. Subadults probably moult with an intermediate pattern (Piechocki 1963; Bährmann 1969; Hohmann in prep.).

Age class or status specific aggressiveness towards conspecifics is here called "social dominance", defined as proportion of successful interactions to all antagonistic interactions of one group observed. It became apparent that dominance differed with status of the counterpart or target (e.g. territory holders to strange intruders or territorial neighbours).

RESULTS

Composition of the population

A total of 317 Buzzards was recorded in the study area. 85% of all records fall within the period between July and November, when total censuses were carried out. Most of these birds were transients, which were not properly individually recognized.

As mentioned before 46 Buzzards were individually known.

Three groups of social status were assigned to these birds (Table 2):

A. Paired birds: long term residents, usually territorial all over the year.

B. Unpaired birds: residents for some weeks up to several months; none was present for the entire study period; only a minority was territorial.

C. Transients: short-term residents; generally present for one day; not territorial.

Table 2. Distribution of age and status of individually marked Buzzards.

1): yearling included

2): all marked Buzzards which are recorded in the area only for some days.

Age	adult	subadult	immature	juv.	unknown
	29	1	7	5	4
Status	paired	unpaired[1]	transient[2]		unknown
	25	13	5		3
	territorial ~92%	territorial ~31%			
	resident ~92%	resident ~23%			

Despite the much higher total numbers of non-marked transients, the number of transients observed during separate census days was in general 4 times lower than that of the resident birds (Residents/census day: $\bar{x} = 13.0 \pm 3.2$; Transients/ census day: $\bar{x} = 2.9 \pm 2.6$; n = 65 censuses). Their occurrence varied 3.7 times more than that of the local birds and did not correlate with the locals (SPEARMAN-R-coefficient: -0.06, $p > 0.25$, n = 65 censuses). Only in July and at the end of September transient Buzzards reached numbers comparable to the local Buzzards' population.

Within the groups of local Buzzards (Groups A + B) more directly comparable figures of occurrence per day were available because many of the resident birds were individually marked. The vast majority, approx. 80%, were paired birds, while only about 20% were unpaired.

In general: The more resident and the more territorial a group (paired: unpaired: transient) the higher its proportion present at a time in the area.

Social dominance hierarchy

Paired Buzzards were by far the dominant group and transients the most submissive group. This was shown by the outcome of antagonistic interactions between individuals of all social status groups (Figure 2)

Paired Buzzards seldom interacted with other pairs, even paired neighbours, due to the respected territory border of other pairs (only 5% of all interactions of paired Buzzards) .

Interactions of paired birds with unpaired territorial neighbours occurred more frequently and were usually won by the paired Buzzards (35% of all interactions of paired Buzzards).

It could be the other way round if a paired male encountered an unpaired bigger female. (The term "paired" does not mean that the mates were together, so that there was no immediate numerical superiority).

Transients obviously "did not know" the boundary line of the territories of the birds of the territorial population. They therefore often moved into territories of local Buzzards, provoking interactions, which mostly ended in dominating behaviour by the territory owners (up to overt hostility) (see Weir & Picozzi 1975). However, in territories of unpaired birds transient intruders seemed more likely to be tolerated (Figure 3).

Unpaired Buzzards appeared to be intermediate dominant depending on whether territorial or

Figure 2. Interactions dominated by paired, unpaired and transient Buzzards (ordinate) towards other paired, unpaired and transient Buzzards (abscissa). Amount of each interaction unit (status x1 with status x2) set 100%.

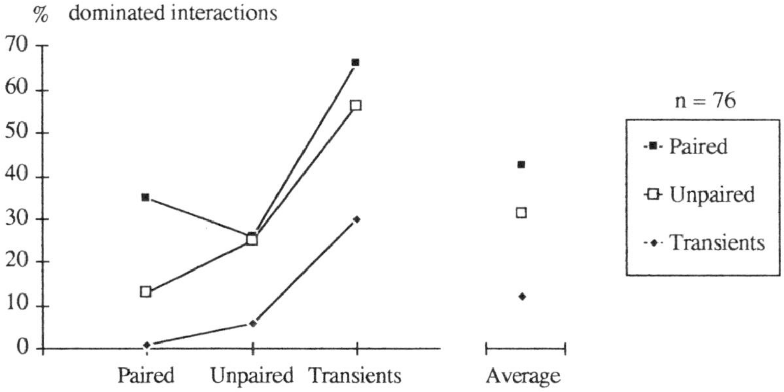

not. E.g. one radio-tagged unpaired Buzzard defended an area of approx. 100 ha but tended to extraterritorial excursions where it behaved like any other nonterritorial conspecific.

As a rule: The closer the status positions of two birds within the hierarchy the more likely an intrusion was tolerated. There is evidence that dominating paired Buzzards were able to move into other territories without being attacked except when moving into territories of other pairs.

Paired Buzzards were dominated by unpaired owners in only 3 of 14 cases of observed intrusions, whereas 7 unpaired intruders were not even tolerated once by paired owners.

Figure 3. Space utilization of transients compared with the core areas of local territorial Buzzards.

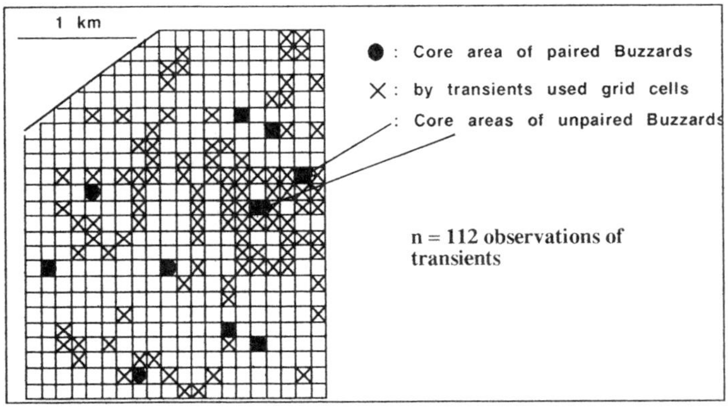

Habitat utilization

Paired Buzzards occupied high quality habitats, with (hunting) territories of type 2 being located in close vicinity to habitats of type 1 providing shelter. Their home ranges thus were equipped with the major logistic elements needed for feeding, roosting and nesting.

The few unpaired but territorial Buzzards set up their territories in areas of type 3, usually with no direct access to shelter. They therefore had to move at dusk to distant roost places, which were usually occupied by pairs. At dawn they left these extraterritorial overnight roosts usually long before sunrise. When an early departure was not possible (after heavy rain, I observed that a subadult had to dry its feathers in the morning sun) such birds had to face hostile pursuits by territory owners.

The differences in quality of habitats used by the social groups are also reflected in the supply of home ranges with perches. In all territories of unpaired Buzzards (n = 4) fencing posts of only 1 m height were the only perches available. In contrast every territory claimed by pairs (n = 8) included posts of up to 4 m height, dead tall trees or pylons of 6 to 8 m height. For pronounced sit and wait hunters like Buzzards it has to be considered a real disadvantage, if no high perching points are available (Fitch *et al.* 1946; Janes 1985).

Transients as well as some local immatures and juveniles established no territories at all. Habitat characteristics of these non-territorial birds were similar to those areas used by territorial unpaired birds: they provided no shelter and no higher perches. The grid cell analysis supports what was expected by regarding the social dominance hierarchy: Transients were driven away more effectively from core areas used mainly by paired Buzzards (defined as areas which contain more than 50% of fixes of a bird) than from core areas used by unpaired Buzzards (Figure 3).

Due to the lack of territorial behaviour in non-territorials, and due to their lower social dominance, they appear restless and show patterns of unsettled space utilization. In terms of home range analysis this means that the total of used grid cells was smaller (actual used space) compared to the larger polygones (distance between fringe locations) even at small sample sizes (Table 3).

Table 3. Space utilization of three radio-tagged unpaired Buzzards associated with territoriality.

MCP: Minimum convex polygone

	territorial	semi-territorial	non-territorial
Fixes	99	60	23
MCP (ha)	164	321	1016
Grid cells (ha)	92	98	27

DISCUSSION

Habitat selection has been regarded as a function of environmental conditions (supply) and species-specific needs (demand) (Berndt & Winkel 1983) effected by overlying interspecific competition. Intraspecific mechanisms, except referring to sexual size dimorphism, have been considered to have less importance in habitat utilization of nongregarious or nonsocial animals, as are most raptors (see Janes 1985), e.g. the Common Buzzard.

This study, however, presents evidence that the differences in habitat utilization in the Common Buzzard were strongly associated with social dominance patterns.

1. Paired adult individuals are potential breeders of the area, probably for their entire life time (Mebs 1964). Requirements for successful reproduction are unlimited access to wooded areas for nesting and longterm stable hunting areas providing enough food for the adults over the entire year and for the offspring during each breeding season. Paired adults - having more at stake - invest much energy, through high aggressiveness and maintenance of social dominance to establish and hold territories incorporating the best possible habitat features.

2. Younger (or adult but unpaired) individuals, which could not breed at present, have no need to invest the same amount of energy as paired birds into aggressiveness and maintenance of social dominance. However, areas providing enough food for a limited time seemed to be still valuable for them, despite their lack of shelter and high perching points. The costs of establishing a territory for several months in such a habitat are therefore still worthwhile.

3. Transients like vagabonding (wandering) Buzzards, dismigrants or immigrants only had a

low local interest, as they stayed in the area only for hours or days at least in 1991. Pronounced aggressiveness or the establishing and maintenance of a territory and social dominance would therefore be a waste of energy for these birds.

The observed status-specific social dominance in Buzzards represents status-specific interests, with the interests being combined from actual and future needs of the individuals. In areas with limited availability of high quality habitats one has to expect that the social status group with highest interests will exclusively and successfully make a claim of these habitats, due to their readiness to invest more energy than others (Patterson 1980).

Younger individuals as well as strangers often seemed to be reluctant to use conspicuous perches. Travellers were frequently observed sitting directly in front of a high perch without using it. Unpaired Buzzards, even when strong enough to win direct interactions with weaker paired adults (i.e. female to male), never showed any kind of conspicuous display. Paired birds showed display flights or joined mutual soaring parties while unpaired neighbours were hardly ever seen soaring high in the air. Direct physical superiority as well as experience or age seemed to be of less importance. As soon as an individual changes its status (even if by chance), it also changes its behaviour (see McCrary *et al.* 1992).

Other studies on Common Buzzards support the conclusions here presented: Sylven (1978) observed single and paired individuals defending fixed areas in winter in southern Sweden. An exclusion of wintering migrants from otherwise suitable habitats by intraspecific territoriality seemed to be obvious as well.

Newton *et al.* (1982) found that paired Buzzards in Wales claimed all areas which included sheltered habitat, while unpaired birds stayed in treeless, open areas. Weir & Picozzi (1983) studied space utilization of marked unpaired Buzzards in Scotland. These birds selected similar open habitats. The authors emphasize that good habitats with shelter were used by unpaired Buzzards only when paired territory owners disappeared. It is interesting in this context that Scottish unpaired Buzzards only claimed small territories (35 ha) only for some weeks outside the breeding season. Unpaired Buzzards in my study area maintained summer territories over several months. Their territory size was similar to the space claimed by paired Buzzards in the study area (approx. 100-150 ha).

At the site here examined, paired Buzzards were bounded by the restricted nesting habitats available. Huge areas were left over for other population groups like unpaired or transient Buzzards. These areas (type 3) obviously allow unpaired birds to establish bigger and longer lasting territories than for example in Scotland.

Lowlands, flat valleys, plains and similar habitats with few nesting sites should generally be regarded as habitats providing suitable conditions for single and migrant Buzzards due to the restricted distribution of socially dominant pairs. The social mechanisms emphasized here could be, in addition to an advantageous food supply, a further explanation for the sometimes large numbers of Buzzards in some open areas.

In winter 1991/92 none of the immigrants tended to stay for a longer period of time or even establish new territories. No remarkable influx of Scandinavian migrants occurred during autumn due to small numbers of rodents in the study area. On the other hand, it is known that during favourable previous years the winter population could surpass the summer population by far (approx. 100 to 150 Ind./100 km^2 in summer to 1000 Ind/100 km^2 in some winters) (Looft & Busche 1990). It is possible that under these conditions the order of habitat use characteristics in the Common Buzzard depending on status and dominance will change.

ACKNOWLEDGEMENTS

This study was supported by the University of Kiel, Institut fur Haustierkunde, Germany, especially by Prof. Dr. W. Schultz. I am greatly indepted to V. Looft and K. Müller-Groeling for their helpful advice and ideas. Special thanks to S. Eggers, J. Jacobsen, J. Kaiser, R. Kruse and D. Wirsig for their time spent handling the trapped Buzzards or banding the chicks high in the tree tops. I further wish to thank H. D. Martens and M. Stock for their support concerning computer software or trap supply. I thank H. Schulz from the Institute for Grassland Conservation and Research, Bergenhusen, Germany, for his critical review of the manuscript.

REFERENCES

BÄHRMANN, U. 1969. Einiges über die Flügel- und Schwanzmauser des Mäusebussards. *Beitr. Vogelkde* 14, 330-333.

BERNDT, R. & W. WINKE 1983. Öko-ornithologisches Glossarium. *Die Vogelwelt, Beiheft 3*. Duncker & Humblot/ Berlin

BUB, H. 1974. *Vogelfang und Vogelberingung*. Part 3. Die neue Brehm-Bücherei, Wittenberg.

DONCASTER, C.P. 1990. Non-parametric estimates of interaction from radiotracking data. *J. theor. Biol.* 143,431-443.

FITCH, H.S., F. SWENSON & D.F. TILLOTSON 1946. Behavior and food habits of the Red-tailed Hawk *Buteo jamaicensis* . *Condor* 48, 205-237.

HINDE, R.A. 1956. The biological significance of the territories of birds. *Ibis* 98,340-369.

HOHMANN, U. 1992. Untersuchungen zur raumzeitlichen Habitatnutzung des Mäusebussards *Buteo buteo* in der Eider-Treene-Sorge-Niederung. Unpublished MSThesis at the Univ. Kiel, Institut für Haustierkunde, Germany

JANES, S.W. 1985. Habitat selection in raptorial birds. *In*: M. L. Cody (Ed.): *Habitat selection in birds* Acadamic Press, Inc., London.

KENWARD, R.E. & V. MARCSTROM 1983. The price of success in Goshawk trapping. *Raptor Research* 17(3), 84-91.

LOOFT, V. & G. BUSCHE 1990. *Vogelwelt Schleswig-Holsteins, Greifvögel.* Karl Wachholtz Verlag, Neumünster.

McCRARY, M.D., P.H. BLOOM & M.J. GIBSON 1992. Observations on the behavior of surplus adults in a Red-shouldered Hawk *Buteo lineatus* population. *The J. of Raptor Research* 26, 10-12.

MEBS, T. 1964. Über Wanderung und bestandsgestaltende Faktoren beim Mäusebussard *Buteo buteo* nach deutschen Ringfunden. *Die Vogelwarte* 22, 180-194.

NEWTON, I., P.E. DAVIS & J.E. DAVIS 1982. Ravens and Buzzards in relation to sheepfarming and forestry in Wales. *J. appl. Ecol.* 19, 681-706.

PATTERSON, I. J. 1980. Territorial behavior and the limitation of population density. *Ardea* 68, 53-62.

PIECHOCKI, R. 1963. Vorläufiges über Mauser der Handschwingen beim Mäusebussard *Buteo buteo J. Orn.* 104, 182-184.

PICOZZI, N. & D. WEIR 1974. Breeding biology of the Buzzard *Buteo buteo* in Speyside. *British Birds* 67,199-210.

SYLVEN, M. 1978. Interspecific relation between sympatrically wintering Common Buzzards *Buteo buteo* and Rough-legged Buzzards *Buteo lagopus*. *Ornis Scand.* 9, 197-206.

TINBERGEN, N. 1957. The function of territory. *Ibis* (4)1, 14-27.

WITTENBERG, J. 1972. Der Brutbestand von Mäusebussard *Buteo buteo*, Rotmilan *Milvus milvus* und Habicht *Accipiter gentilis* 1958 und 1970 bei Braunschweig und das Problem der Vergleichbarkeit. *Die Vogelwelt* 93, 227-23S.

WEIR, D. & N. PICOZZI 1975. Aspects of social behaviour in the Buzzard *Buteo buteo* . *Brit. Birds* 68, 12S-141.

WEIR,-D. & N. PICOZZI 1983. Dispersion of Buzzards *Buteo buteo* in Speyside. *Brit. Birds* 76, 68-78.

Ulf Hohmann
Schloß Nienover
3417 Bodenfelde
Germany

Meyburg, B.-U. & R. D. Chancellor eds.1994
Raptor Conservation Today
WWGBP / The Pica Press

Distance Immobilisation by Telinject of Griffon Vultures *Gyps fulvus* with the drug Ketamine-Xylazine*

Rainer Revers and Ralf Bögel

INTRODUCTION

During a study on home range size and flight biology of a small colony of Griffon Vultures in the European Alps (Mäck & Bögel 1990; d'Oleire-Oltmenns *et al.* 1989; Bögel see these proceedings), birds have to be captured and radio-tagged. This colony, which decends from the Salzburg Zoo, still depends in its food requirements on a feeding station at the zoo. As these birds can behave quite tamely at the zoo, it was easy to capture them years ago by baiting them with meat and catching them manually in an inattentive moment. Unfortunately, Griffons not only learn very quickly, but there also seems to be a kind of intraspecific communication within the colony: within a few attempts all birds seem to be informed quite well about your capturing intentions, even if they have not been present themselves. Other commonly used capturing methods (Bloom 1987) like baited snare traps or exclosure traps for large raptors are not suitable due to the feeding behaviour of the vultures. Snare loops are too dangerous because Griffons feed in groups, acting very aggressively with their necks low above the ground. Exclosure traps are designed for solitary birds and therefore are impractible as too many birds are standing around the carcass. An application of canon nets is critical in terms of handling a couple of birds si-moultaneously. Furthermore, Griffons act extremely timid if anything is changed at the feeding place. Oral drugs are hardly applicable in the appropriate dose, poorly tolerated, and therefore can be dangerous (Day *et al.* 1980; Ebedes 1973).

METHODS

Distance application of drugs by gun is a method which is commonly used on mammals (Day *et al.* 1980). In spite of that, very few studies are published on applying this method to birds (Rietschel & Wiesener 1982). Even on the immobilization of birds by injecting drugs few data are available (Allen & Oosterhuis 1986; Van Heerden *et al.* 1987; Degernes *et al.* 1988). Therefore experiments were carried out trying to adapt this method for capturing vultures. A mixture of ketamine-xylazine was used (HBM, concentration: 125 mg xylazine + 100 mg ketamine hydrochloride / ml solution). A dose of 0,034-0,044 ml HBM per kg (estimated) body weight has

* *financed by the BFANL and the StMLU Bayern.*

been injected by an 1.4 ml TELINJECT syringe (type S 100 V3) which is divided into a chamber for the drug and another for air pressure (Fig.1). A silicone plug avoids injection of the drug before the needle penetrates the body. Total weight of the syringe is 9 g (incl. drug). Immediately after catching the immobilized bird, Yohinbine is used as antidote in a dosage of 0.1 mg/kg. As Griffons try to escape and hide during induction time, a syringe with integrated telemetry transmitter has been developed for ensuring the localisation of the narcoticized bird (see Fig. 1). The transmitter (Fig. 2) fits into a housing that can be plugged to the rear side of any standard TELINJECT syringe. By this, weight and dimensions of the syringe are increased by 6 grams, resp. 78 millimetres. A specially designed needle has to be used for ensuring that the syringe keeps fixed to the body during flight. A shock absorber compensates for the increased power of hit.

Fig. 1: **TELINJECT syringe type S 100 V3 with and without integrated telemetry transmitter.**

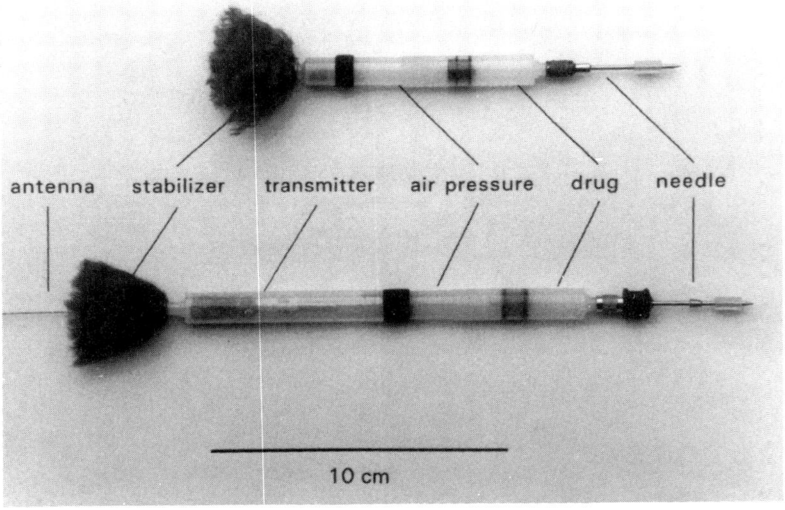

Fig. 2: **Telemetry transmitter (AUSTEC KG 80, modified) with battery (NATIONAL BR 425).**

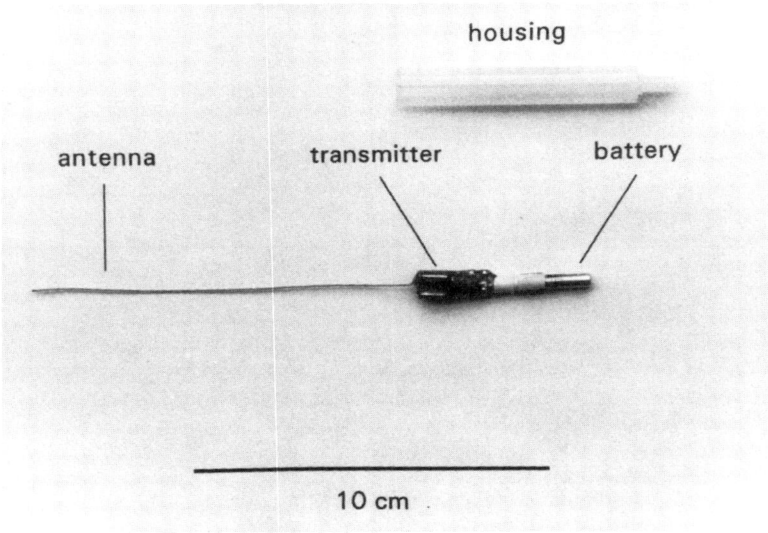

RESULTS AND DISCUSSION

Three of five attempts have been successful. In those cases without success, the syringe was rejected by the plumage before the needle entered the body. The successful applications showed that induction time varies greatly according to the injection point and the tissues which were hit: values ranged from 7 (pectoral muscle) to 20 minutes (shoulder / air sacculus). Time for recovery usually takes 0.5 -1 hour until full body control is regained. The precision of hits varies with distance and air pressure of the gun. For a distance of 10 metres and an air pressure of 4.5 bar, all injection points are covered by the pectoral muscle (Fig. 3). Compared to that, at a distance of 15 metres (pressure 6 bar) there is an increased risk of missing the pectoral muscle and thus of injuring the bird seriously (Fig. 4). Shooting at this distance, we once hit a vulture at the shoulder with the needle penetrating an air sacculus. Anyway, the Griffon completely recovered within two days. Compared to the published results on other vulture species, the ketamine dosage used in this study is 2.5-10 times lower resulting in a prolongation of the induction time by a factor of 1 - 10 (Allen & Oosterhuis 1986; Van Heerden *et al.* 1987). This will mainly be caused by a non-intravenous, but diffuse, injection. For the same reason, the recovery times were prolonged by 1-6 times compared to other studies in which an antidote drug has been applied (Allen & Oosterhuis 1986; Degernes *et al.* 1988). Yohinbine as antagonism drug is recommended as the recovery time is significantly shorter (up to 10 times, see Degernes *et al.* 1988).

Fig. 3: distribution of hits for a distance of 10 metres (air pressure: 4.5 bar) (hits on the left and right side are equally distributed but are all projected to the right side).

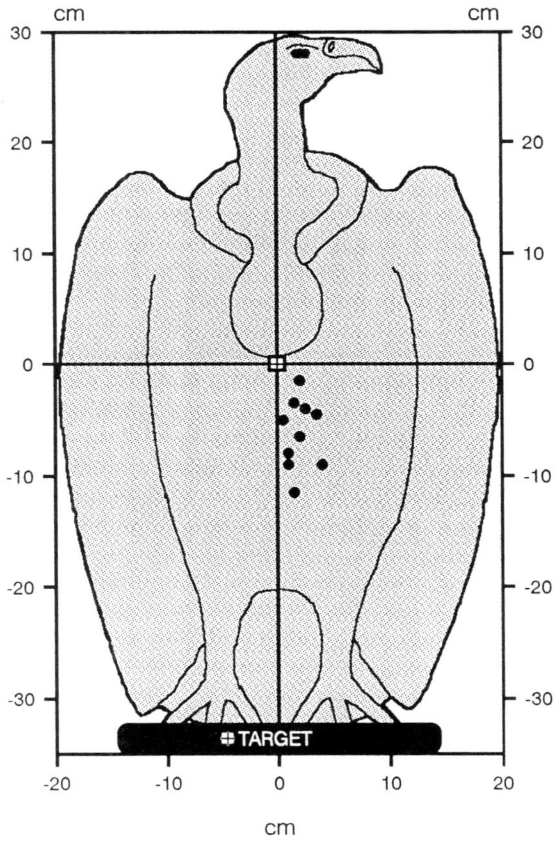

Fig. 4: **distribution of hits for a distance of 15 metres (air pressure: 6:0 bar) (hits on the left and right side are equally distributed but are all projected to the right side).**

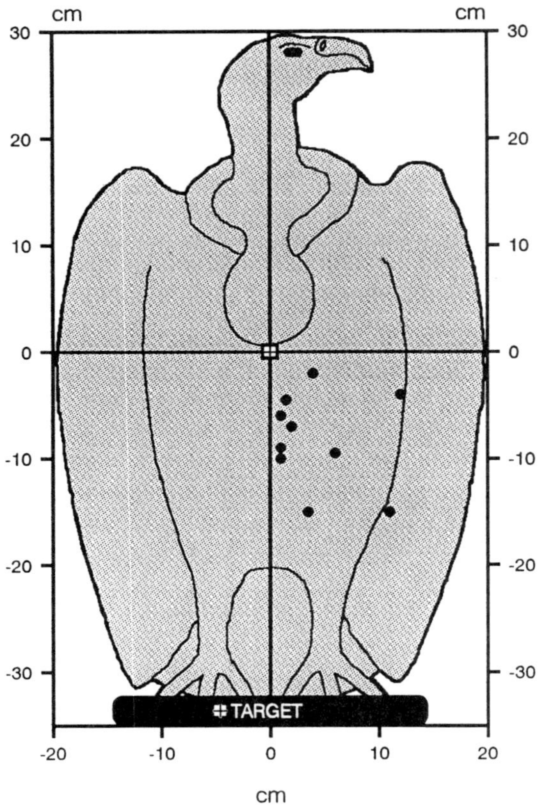

CONCLUSIONS

Distance immobilisation of large birds by TELINJECT gun can be an adequate alternative if other capturing methods fail or if they are too dangerous. The described method cannot guarantee success because there is a certain risk that the syringe gets rejected by the plumage. Shooting from below, for example at a bird perching in a tree, clearly reduces this source of failure, but is not always possible. Applying this method on distances greater than 10 metres greatly increases the risk of injuring the birds. Improvements on the ballistic characteristics of the integrated transmitter syringe might increase the possible spectrum of application. Concer-ning this and the fixation of the transmitter syringe to the body during flight further investiga-tions are required.

REFERENCES

ALLEN, J.L. & J.E. OOSTERHUIS 1986. Effect of Tolazoline on Xylazine-Ketamine-Induced Anesthesia in Turkey Vultures. *JAVMA*, 189(9): 1011-1012.

BLOOM, P.H. 1987. Capturing and handling raptors. *In* B.A.b. Pendleton, B.A. Millsap, K.W. Kline & D.M. Bird (Eds.). *Raptor Management Techniques Manual*, p.p. 99-123. Natl. Wildl. Fed., Washington D.C.

BÖGEL, R. 1993. Measuring Locations and Flight Altitudes of Griffon Vultures *Gyps fulvus* by an Automatic Telemetry System. This volume.

DAY, G.I., S.D. SCHEMNITZ & R.D. TABER 1980. Capturing and Marking Wild Animals. *In*: SD (Ed.):

Wildlife Management Techniques Manual. The Wildlife Society, Washington D.C., USA. pp. 61-88.
DEGERNES, L.A., KREEGER, T.J., R. MANDSAGER, & P.T. REDIG 1988. Ketamine-Xylazine Anesthesia in Red-Tailed Hawks with Antagonism by Yohinbine. *Journal of Wildlife Diseases*, 24(2): 322-326.
EBEDES, H. 1973. The Capture of Free-Living Vultures in the Etosha National Park with Phency-clidine. *Journal of the South-African Wildlife Management Association,* 3(2): 105-107.
MÄCK, U. & R. BÖGEL 1990. Untersuchungen zur Ethologie und Raumnutzung von Gänse- und Bartgeier. Nationalpark Berchtesgaden, Doktorberg 6, 8240 Berchtesgaden, Germany: Forschungsbericht Nr. 18, pp 147.
d'OLEIRE-OLTMANNS, W., U. MÄCK, & R. BÖGEL 1989. Radiotracking of Bearded Vultures *Gypaetus barbatus* and Griffon Vultures *Gyps fulvus* in the Alps. *In*: B.-U. Meyburg & R.D. Chancellor (Eds.): *Raptors in the Modern World*, pp. 345-352. WWGBP Berlin, London, Paris.
VAN HEERDEN, J., J. KOMEN, & E. MYER 1987. The Use of Ketamine Hydrochloride in the Immobilisation of the Cape Vulture *Gyps coprotheres. Journal of the South African Veterinary Association,* September 1987: 143-144.
RIETSCHEL, W. & H. WIESENER 1982. Erfahrungen über die Immobilisation von Vögeln mit dem Blasrohr. Tagungsberichte der Arbeitstagung über Greifvogelmedizin, München, Februar 1982. pp. 95-96.

Rainer Revers
Salzburger Tiergarten Hellbrunn
A-5081 Anif
Austria

Ralf Bögel
Berchtesgaden National Park
Doktorberg 6
W-8240 Berchtesgaden
Germany

Eagle Owl *Bubo bubo*

Meyburg, B.-U. & R. D. Chancellor eds.1994
Raptor Conservation Today
WWGBP / The Pica Press

Wing-marking of Eurasian Griffons *Gyps fulvus* in Croatia - Evaluation and Initial Results

Goran Sušić

ABSTRACT

This paper presents the initial results of a wing-marking programme begun in 1990 and applied to Eurasian Griffon (*Gyps fulvus*) in Croatia. In two years 48 birds were marked, 41 in the nest and 7 birds for experimental releasing. Wing-marking is a method which permits identification of individuals without recapture. Marker detectability, migration routes, immature survival and wing-tag safety were studied.

INTRODUCTION

Wing markers have been used with a wide variety of bird species when it is necessary to identify individuals without recapturing them. They have been used in studies on behaviour, dispersal, nest-site fidelity, age structure, age-dependent mortality, longevity etc. Wild Eurasian Griffons were not wing-tagged in nature until this research. Recently, Tewes has (1991) reported on wing-marked Black Vultures (*Aegypius monachus*) in Mallorca during release by "hacking method". Mendelssohn and Leshem (1983) marked three Eurasian Griffons during their reintroduction project. In 1990 a wing-marking programme started in Croatia as part of a long-term population study of Griffons at five breeding colonies on Kvarner Archipelago, Croatia. There are 95-100 pairs on four islands in the Kvarner Archipelago (about 50 pairs on the Island of Cres), and in Croatia the whole population is estimated at 110-150 pairs.

MATERIAL AND METHODS

All important general considerations in designing and conducting a marking programme, suggestions on how to select the most useful marking technique and descriptions of individual techniques including application, materials, procedure, physiological and behaviourial effects on marked birds, are collected in an extremely useful paper by Young and Kochert (1987). There are two basic types of wing markers: wrap-around and piercing, referring to the way the marker is secured to the wing (Young and Kochert 1987). Both types are attached to the patagial region. Piercing markers are more varied but usually consist of a tag or streamer attached to the wing by a pin or clip that pierces the patagium. There are several different shapes of wing markers, and I decided to use a single tag that wraps around the leading edge of the wing and is secured both above

Figure 1a and b. Griffon equipped with piercing wing marker, used the method developed by Wallace *et al.* (1980). My experience is that the correct position for the piercing fastener is not as shown by Young and Kochert (1987), but at a more distant point (not so close to the body).

Table 1. Re-sightings of Griffons wing-marked on the Island of Cres (Croatia) and re-sighted out of the breeding area.

		1	2	3	4	5	6	7
	Date of marking	16.05.90	16.05.90.	18.05.90.	04.06.90.	24.04.91.	23.04.91.	23.04.91.
1st resight	Date	29.07.90	18.08.90	29.08.90	24.11.90	17-19.08.91.	20.07.91	06.08.91
	Distance	loco	280 km	loco	950 km	227 km	loco	190 km
	Country	Croatia	Austria	Croatia	Bulgaria	Austria	Croatia	Austria
2nd resight	Date	24.07.-14.08.91.	15.08.91.	19.07.91.	04.12.90.	20.08.91.	02.-03.11.91.	
	Distance	330 km	950 km	270 km	950 km	270 km	950 km	
	Country	Austria	Bulgaria	Austria	Bulgaria	Austria	Bulgaria	
3rd resight	Date				02.04.91.			
	Distance				950 km			
	Country				Bulgaria			
4th resight					10.04.91			
					950 km			
					Bulgaria			

Griffons: 1 = Banco, 2 = Mauro, 3 = Indiana Jones, 4 = Mark Spitz, 5 = Hristo, 6 = Jelena, 7 = Stefan

Table 2. Re-sightings of Griffons wing-marked on the Island of Cres (Croatia) and re-sighted inside the breeding area ("local" findings).

Griffons	1	2	3	4	5	6	7	8	9	10	11	12
Date of marking	16.05. 90.	18.05. 90.	18.05. 90.	18.05. 90.	02.06. 90.	22.04. 91.	22.04. 91.	22.04. 91.	22.04. 91.	23.04. 91.	20.06. 91.	23.04. 91.
Date of 1st resight	29.07 90.	22.04. 91.	18.03. 91.	27.07 90.	15-27. 07.90.	19.08. 91.	19.06. 91.	19.06. 91.	19.06. 91.	20.07. 91.	20.07. 91.	20.07. 91.
Date of 2nd resight		06-07. 05.91.	22-23. 04.91.					28.08. 91.	27.07. 91.	20.08. 91.	07.08. 91	15-19. 08.91.
Date of 3rd resight		18-21. 06.91.	24.05. 91.							28.08. 91.	21.10. 91.	
Date of 4th resight		17.08. 91.									15.01. 92.	

Griffons: 1 = Ogi, 2 = Tatanke Iyotake, 3 = Vladek, 4 = Miss Piggy, 5 = Sismis, 6 = George, 7 = Dragica, 8 = Corina, 9 = Mile, 10 = Ante, 11 = Good Boy, 12 = Vesna

Figure 2. Re-sighting locations, possible and probable directions of migrating immature and juvenile Griffons wing-marked in Croatia in 1990/91. Bird "Mauro" is designated with 7 and 7* because seen both in Austria and in Bulgaria. Numbered circles indicate localities of re-sightings of each Griffon. Open circle with no number is breeding (marking) area - Kvarner Archipelago.

■ ■ ➡ arrow = autumn/winter direction

● ● ➡ arrow = spring/summer direction

━━➡ arrow = probable direction during winter months

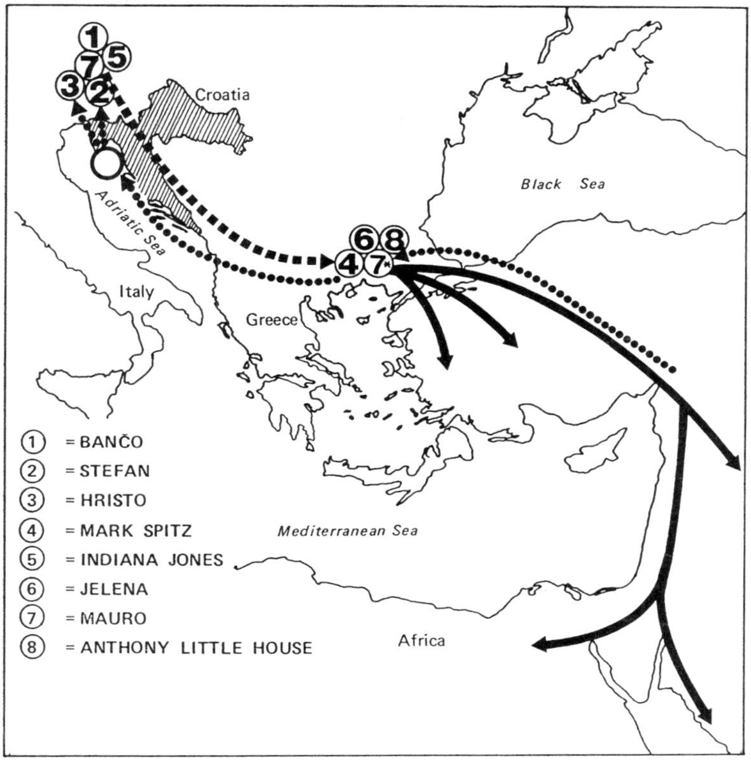

and below the patagium. I used piercing markers, because they can be applied to nestlings and do not involve the leading edge of the wing. The piercing fastener also prevents the marker from rotating around the wing. I used almost the same method of attaching these tags to the wings of vultures as Wallace *et al.* (1980) did with Condors. There is only one difference: in my opinion,the area on the wing for a piercing fastener must not be so close to the bird's body as Young and Kochert (1987) show in their Fig. 8.7. (p.140), but at the more distant position (Fig. 1, a and b). I used a plastic cattle ear button to secure the marker to the patagium (Young & Kochert 1987, p. 138, Fig. 8.5.). Patagial tags were attached to the wings using Allfex ear-tags to anchor the streamer. Vinyl wing-tags (Herculite 80 or similar) have dimensions 155 x 95 mm and each is marked with a number and/or letter with dimensions 95x60 mm. Numbers and letters were cut out of vinyl of the same kind as for wing-tags and vinyl of one colour has been glued on to another. Characters are printed in such a manner as to reduce similarities and/or mistakes during observation. I used only two colours (white with dark-blue characters or dark-blue streamer with white characters), because the more colours used, the greater the chances of observer error. Nestlings were tagged when 70-80 days old to allow sufficient size and feather development for adequate marker retention. Later in the breeding season it could be dangerous for a fledgling to fall in the sea. The markers are easily visible when the birds are perched or on the nest.

RESULTS

In 1990 and 1991 48 Eurasian Griffons were marked in Croatia, 41 in the nest and seven birds (1-7 years old) for experimental releasing. Those seven birds came from Zagreb, where with our help one very old pair (more than twenty years, maybe even thirty years old) produce one fledgling per year. In 1990 only on the colony on the Island of Cres 67% and in 1991 80% of all fledglings were marked.

1. *Marker detectability*

The alphanumerics on wing-tags are easily read at 40m (average person) and even at 50-60 m (sharp-eyed person). With average field glasses at 300 m, with Zeiss Dialyt field glasses at 400 m and with a 20x-25x spotting scope at 1000-1300 m. Wing-tag characters were readable in 91% (43 out of 47 sightings) of re-sightings of flying marked vultures. Eurasian Griffons are slow fliers and tags were easily read on soaring or flapping birds at the Island of Cres. This wing-marking programme was even useful for birds that moved greater distances, and during the first two years there were nine re-sightings in Austria (190-330km) and five in Bulgaria (about 1000km). Each tagged Griffon has a different colour ring combination what ensures that if the wing tag fails, rings continue to allow identification.

2. *Migration*

Initial results indicate two directions of migration: NW (to the Austrian and Italian Alps) and SE (to the Rhodope Mountains in Bulgaria, near the borders with Greece and Turkey - Fig. 2). It seems that the routes, timing and annual circuit are very complex (Sušić 1984). Even one first-year immature travelled a long distance: six months after wing-tagging it has been sighted almost 1,000 km SE from the natal colony. The average distance moved by marked Griffons out of the natal area was 621.7 km in 1990 and 409.2 km in 1991.

3. *Immature survival*

The survival rate for marked immature birds could be high. During the first two years six out of 16 (37.5%) Griffons have been resighted in flight more than one year after marking. It is still too early for definite conclusions, but it seems that mortality during the first year is not over 50% as Houston (1974a) supposed.

4. *Wing-tag safety*

Mundy (1982) thinks that wing-tags are not safe enough for vultures "due to the way the birds fight and tumble at carcasses". To evaluate the patagial tagging system for marking Eurasian Griffons in the wild, I marked two Griffons and observed them in captivity. One of them bore the wing-tag for four years. After its removal there was no visible injury on the patagium. The second bird I marked two years ago, applying the different system of attachment. Up to now no signs of wear or injury on the wing have been recorded. In addition, there was one wild bird recaptured four months after marking, also without any sign of wear or injury . Besides, during the initial period following attachment, I never noticed birds preen or tug at the markers in order to remove them.

DISCUSSION

Until this research, there were no published results on wing-marking programmes applied to wild Eurasian Griffons probably because in some opinions wing-markers are not safe enough for *Gyps* species (Mundy 1982). My experience shows that it is a safe method, if wing-markers are applied on nestlings when 70-80 days old. The correct position for a piercing fastener on the wing has to be more distant than is the area proposed by Young and Kochert (1987). There have been many African vultures marked by numbered P.V.C. coloured rings which could be identified with field glasses from a distance, but results are not so promising. Piper (1990) reported that of 7000 Cape Vultures ringed since 1948, about 5% have subsequently been recovered, re-sighted or recaptured. To study the movements of African Griffons Houston (1974b) marked 162 birds by numbered coloured rings, but only 13 individuals were re-sighted over the following 18 months

(8%). During the first two years of our marking programme six Griffons out of 16 marked (37.5%) have been re-sighted more than one year after marking. So, the rate of re-sighting is much higher in wing-marking than in ringing. This research has proved that the summer population of Griffons in the Austrian and Italian Alps are birds from Croatia, and that in October, after leaving that area, they do not winter in the Croatian islands, but migrate to Bulgaria or even further south. Wing-tags did not appear to reduce the mobility or increase mortality of the birds we studied. One first-year immature travelled a long distance: only six months after wing-tagging it has been re-sighted about 1.000km SE in Bulgaria.

CONCLUSIONS

1 This work is part of a long-term population study of Eurasian Griffons at five breeding colonies on the Kvarner Archipelago, Croatia, where there are 95-100 pairs of on four islands (about 50 pairs on the Island of Cres).

2.In 1990 and 1991 48 Griffons were marked. More than one year after marking 37.5% birds have been re-sighted. Wing-tags did not appear to reduce the mobility or increase mortality of the birds studied.

3.The alphanumerics on wing-tags were easily read with a 20x-25x spotting scope at 1000-1300m in 91% of sightings of flying marked vultures. The rate of re-sighting is much higher in wing-marking than in ringing.

4.Some birds moved great distances and during the first two years there were nine re-sightings in Austria (190-330km from the colony) and five in Bulgaria (about 1,000km).

5.Wing-tagging is a time-consuming, not so simple, and expensive method useful only for long-term studies.

ACKNOWLEDGEMENTS

I express my thanks to Dr. M.P. Wallace (Los Angeles) for practical marking technique advice, and some necessary marking equipment, and to my friends and co-workers as well as many Griffon-watchers who helped in the marking programme: B. Jalžić, R. Dado, M. Stipčević, O. Vukadinovič Z. Ružanović, D. Radovič and V. Bartovsky. I am also grateful to those who spent many patient hours in the Ornithological Station near Vulture Restaurant, waiting for marked Griffons to come to table: O. Vakadinović, D. Lučić, V. Tuti, J. Majcen, Z. Ružanović, M. Stipčević, A. Znaor, C.A. Penić, S. Fiedler, D. Radović, V. Bartovsky, B. Rebrović, M. Zagorac, D. Gatolin, B. Debogovič and those who have sent me data about G.V. they have seen: in Austria R. Bögel, H. Frey and F. Genero, and in Bulgaria S. Avramoff, H. Hristov and P. Jankov. The touristic company "CRESANKA" from Cres was always ready to help in many ways, and I acknowledge its director Stevo Filinič as well as Dolores Mužić, Karin Filinić and Sergjo Negovetić; also Arlen Abramic and her Island Develpment Center from Mali Lošinj. The insurance company "OSIGURANJE HELIOS", general sponsor of the conservation part of the project, enabled me to participate in the Conference.

REFERENCES

HOUSTON, D.C. 1974a. Mortality of the Cape Vulture. *Ostrich* 45 (2): 57-62.

HOUSTON, D.C. 1974b. Food searching in Griffon Vultures. *E. Afr. Wildl.J.* 12: 63-77.

MENDELSSOHN, H. & Y LESHEM 1983. The status and conservation of vultures in Israel. *In*: S.R., Wilbur, & J.A Jackson, (Eds.) *Vulture Biology and Management*. Univ. of California Press, Berkeley; Pp. 86-98

MUNDY, P.J. 1982. *The Comparative Biology of Southern African Vultures.* Vulture Study Group, Johannesburg.

PIPER, S.E. 1990. Dispersal, nomadism and conservation in the Cape Vulture. *Ring* 13, 1-2: 217-218.

SUŠIČ G. 1984. Is the migration of Yugoslav Griffon Vultures, *Gyps fulvus* (Hablizl, 1783) to the Alps exclusively trophically motivated? Proceedings of III Ecological Congress of Yugoslavia: pp. 139-142, Sarajevo.

TEWES, E. 1990. El Voltor (*Aegypius monachus*) a Europa, un pas Endavant en la Seva Recuperacio. *Anuari Ornitol. de les Balears* 90, 5: 2-8.

WALLACE, M.P., P.G. PARKER & S.A TEMPLE 1980. An evaluation of patagial markers for cathartid vultures. *J. Field Ornithol.* 51:309-314.

YOUNG, L.S. & M.N. KOCHERT 1987. Marking techniques. *In*: B.A.G. Pendleton, B.A. Millsap, K.W. Cline & D.M. Bird (Eds.) *Raptor Management Techniques Manual.* National Wildlife Federation. Washington, D.C. pp. 134-151.

Dr. Goran Sušić
Institute of Ornithology
Ilirski trg 9/2
41000 Zagreb, Croatia

Indian Black Vulture *Sarcogyps calvus* and
Lappet-faced Vulture *Torgos tracheliotus*

Meyburg, B.-U. & R. D. Chancellor eds.1994
Raptor Conservation Today
WWGBP / The Pica Press

Patagial Transmitters for Large Vultures and Condors

Michael P. Wallace, Mark Fuller and James Wiley

During a study to develop release techniques for cathartid vultures (Wallace & Temple 1983), 20-gram transmitters were attached to the backs of 15 fledgling Black Vultures *Coragyps atratus* and Turkey Vultures *Cathartes aura*. Seven of these battery- and solar-powered transmitters were attached to scapular feathers by two leather strips glued to their bases. Another transmitter was incorporated into a harness similar to those used on eagles (Kenward 1987).

Large dark scapular feathers covering the solar packages were apparently sufficient to reduce the recharging capacity, causing radios to function intermittently or fail. Also, loss of some transmitters due to pulled feathers and one case of entanglement with the harness in brush encouraged the consideration of alternative methods of attachment.

During the same study, patagial identification tags were being evaluated for use on cathartid vultures (Wallace *et al.* 1980). If a light, aerodynamic radio-transmitter could safely be affixed to the patagium portion of the wing where the identification tags had proved successful, the short contour feathers of the wing might not inhibit solar transmitter function.

This paper outlines the development of patagial transmitters that are now being attached to Andean Condors *Vultur gryphus* and California Condors *Gymnogyps californianus* released to the wild in repopulation programmes in North and South America (Lieberman *et al.* 1991; Wallace & Toone 1992).

METHODS

On July 15, 1979, four Turkey Vultures were released to the wild, each carrying a radio-transmitter on one wing and a patagial tag on the other. The transmitters were solar-powered and the entire package weighed approximately 20g. Each measured 4.5cm x 2cm x 1.5cm tall, with a light 40cm antenna emerging from the centre of one of the narrow ends. It was mounted on the dorsal side of the wing, on the radial-ulna side of the patagium when the wing is folded. Its centre of gravity was over a plastic attachment rivet (See Fig. 1 for position). Using a similar position and attachment technique as vinyl patagial tags successfully in use, the rivet pierced the patagium 1cm from the leading edge (Wallace *et al.* 1980).

One of the birds was imprinted on humans and tame enough to be easily captured and released several times over a two-month period, allowing close inspection of its transmitter while in flight as well as in the hand. The other three vultures had been raised together and held captive for one year prior to release into a rural area near Madison, Wisconsin. These three wilder birds remained in the release vicinity for several weeks, allowing daily observations of the transmitters through

Figure 1.

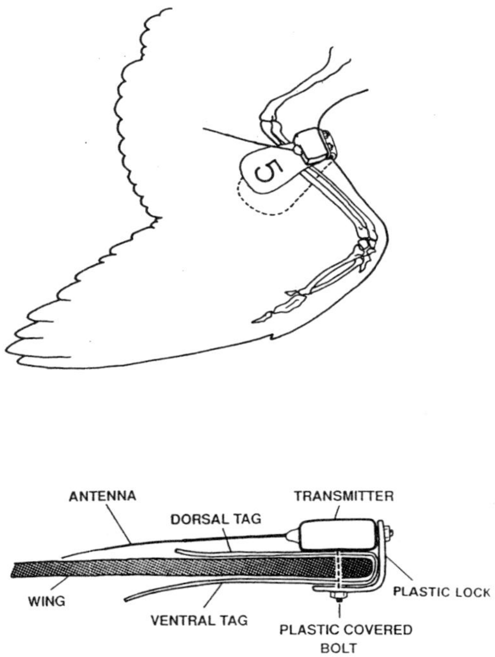

binoculars. They were radio-tracked for several months after release as they explored new foraging areas before migrating south (Wallace & Temple 1983).

In the fall of 1979 a modified version of the Turkey Vulture patagial transmitter was attached initially to both wings of six Andean Condors at the Patuxent Wildlife Research Center in Maryland as a pilot study. These transmitters were different from those of the vultures in that they weighed approximately 40g (less than 5% of the condor's body weight). Instead of the plastic rivet of a modified cattle ear-tag, a plastic-covered 3 mm steel bolt was used to attach the transmitter to the wing. The acrylic rectangular block measured 40 x 45 x 13 mm. With manual restraint the incision in the patagium was made using a leather punch of the largest hole size prior to the insertion of the transmitter bolt. These birds were opportunistically observed through several breeding seasons.

In July 1982, 12 dummy transmitters, similar in design to those used in the pilot study, were attached to six more Andean Condors at Patuxent. They were observed for one month prior to their marking, using an ethogram consisting of 63 behaviour patterns. Four transmitters were replaced on the wings of three of the original six pilot study condors as well. The birds were observed immediately after marking in July and again in November. Observations lasted 15 minutes, during which time one of 63 behaviour categories was assigned to the bird every 15 seconds. Each bird was observed during 6 to 8 bouts of observation at various times of the day over a one-week period in June, July and November. Behaviour categories were compared among months and among birds (previously marked *versus* previously unmarked). Types of behaviour observed too infrequently were pooled into a broader category for statistical analysis. An analysis of variance (general linear model, SAS) was used to determine statistical significance ($P < .01$).

We were particularly interested in how working transmitters might function on free-flying condors in the wild. During a study to develop condor reintroduction techniques conducted in northern Peru, South America, between 1980 and 1984, 12 captive-reared Andean Condors were released to the wild, each carrying a patagial transmitter on one wing and a patagial tag on the other (Wallace & Temple 1987). The transmitters were similar in design to those tested at Patuxent but slightly heavier at 60-70g. Using binoculars and telescopes at distances and sometimes from close blinds, these birds were observed on a daily basis for three months and less frequently (weekly or monthly) for two years thereafter. During 21 recaptures their transmitters and wings were closely inspected. Fifteen of 47 wild condors caught during the same study were similarly fitted. They were observed only from a distance after release. Two of these birds were subsequently killed by goat herders. Their carcasses were recovered in adequate condition for a wing and transmitter assessment. One adult male condor was obtained from the Lima Zoo, tamed and trained to fly loose and return. This bird proved invaluable, since he allowed us close observation while he flew with real and dummy patagial transmitters of different weights. His functional left transmitter was 75g, whlie the right wing dummy package was 100g.

Between 1982 and 1987 11 California Condors were radio-tagged, using patagial transmitters with frequencies of 410 and 411 Mhz (Meretsky & Snyder 1992). These higher frequencies allowed for a shorter, better-reinforced antenna 20cm long. Where the attachment bolt of previous transmitters required assembly of the bolt through a hole in the transmitter during placement on a wing, the California Condor version had the attachment bolt already soldered to a plate within the acrylic base of the transmitter, making it a more complete unit prior to placement. These transmitters weighed between 60g and 80g.

In order to test the efficacy of releasing California Condors within their former range, 13 Andean Condors were released in southern California between 1988 and 1991, carrying a patagial transmitter and tag combination on each wing (Wallace 1990). A one-piece, coloured vinyl tag, displaying identification numbers on both dorsal and ventral portions of the wing, was incorporated into the transmitter package (Fig. 1). The dorsal tag measured 8cm wide and 13.5cm long from the leading edge of the wing. The ventral tag was slightly larger at 9cm wide and 15cm long. A battery-powered transmitter was placed on the right wing and a solar-powered package on the left as backup. Having one battery unit insured a constant signal through the night, while the solar transmitter theoretically would have longer than the 15-month life expectancy of the battery units.

Weighing between 55 and 65 grams with tags attached, these transmitters were lighter than those previously used. To reduce technical complications of working at the higher frequency of 410 and 411 Mhz, we worked within the 164 Mhz band. The antennae were increased from 20cm to 29cm to maintain transmission efficiency for the new lower frequency and their bases were reinforced with graduating sizes of heat-shrink plastic tubing.

During 1991 a three-month study of transmitter balance conducted at the Los Angeles Zoo, eight dummy patagial transmitters were placed on six Andean Condors. All were housed together in a 30 x 14 x 14 m high pen. The dummy transmitters varied in weight, bolt location, antenna length and flexibility (Table 1). The bolt location was either in the centre of the transmitter, 1.7 cm from the front, or offset toward the back, 2.8 cm from the front. All the fake transmitter antennae were 0.20 cm in diameter except for number 7 (0.16 cm) and number 8 (0.13 cm), which were considerably more flexible. These condors were observed opportunistically throughout each day during the study period to detect malposition of any transmitter, a condition correlated with transmitter loss in the field. All six birds could be seen during each observation sample.

Table 1. Dummy transmitters on Andean Condors at the Los Angeles Zoo.

Unit Number	Weight (gm)	Bird (Wing)	Bolt Position	Antenna Length (cm)	Antenna Diameter (cm)
1	54.5	Y-1 (L)	Centre	Short (21.5)	Stiff (.23)
2	54.8	Y-2 (L)	Centre	Short(21.3)	Stiff (.23)
3	56.0	Y-1 (R)	Offset	Long (29)	Flexible (.23)
4	55.0	R-4 (L)	Offset	Long (29)	Flexible(.23)
5	45.6	R-4 (R)	Centre	Long (29)	Flexible (.23)
6	45.0	R-5 (L)	Centre	Long (29)	Flexible (.23)
7	51.6	R-2 (R)	Centre	Long (29)	Flexible (.16)*
8	51.0	R-5 (R)	Centre	Long (29)	Flexible (.13)*

*Denotes increased flexiblity

RESULTS AND DISCUSSION

It became clear during the vulture release experiments in Wisconsin that patagial transmitters were not only feasible, but could also become a viable alternative to other methods of attaching transmitters to large soaring birds. The vultures' reaction to the transmitters, in all four cases, was to treat them in a similar fashion as they did patagial tags (Wallace *et al.* 1980); to be irritated by or merely attentive to the object for the first five to twenty-four hours before appearing to accept it.

The small package adhered well to the wing, with little or no movement on the surface during wing beats, and did not appear to interfere with flight. Attaching the transmitter, however, was cumbersome since it was a two-stage process. The plastic rivet was first pierced through the wing using a tag applicator designed for cattle. Then the transmitter was attached to the top of the plastic tag with pop rivets. Five inspections of the attachment site on the tame, free-flying Turkey Vulture over a three-month period did not reveal any noticeable irritation to the patagium. During the initial two weeks the incision site appeared reddened but soon after the area was smooth, healed and paler in colour, matching the surrounding skin.

Because the project was not designed to track the wilder birds on migration, only relatively short-term data were collected but seemed encouraging, with no loss of transmitters or any obvious negative effects on the birds.

At the Patuxent Wildlife Research Center in Maryland the pilot study on six Andean Condors yielded similar encouraging information. The presence of the transmitters did not appear to inhibit breeding activity or disrupt any other behaviour in general. The intensive study that followed focused more on quantifying individual relations to the transmitters.

On average, during all three observation periods from June through November, the condors could be seen only 17% of the observation time because they were otherwise behind or in their shelter. During the period they could be observed they were inactive (in a fixed *Posture*) an average of 75% of the time. The remaining 25%, during which they were active, could be broken down into components as follows: 14% *Preening*, 5% *Locomotion*, 5% *General Comfort,* 1% *Eating*.

The only observed activity that condors focused directly on the transmitters was *Preening*. Preening accounted for 7% of the time the birds were actually seen during the June observations, 10% during July, and 22% in November. Only 7% of the observed preening time was spent on the transmitter, 1% to 2% of the total time observed. Considered as a percentage of time spent preening, the difference becomes more apparent, changing from 1% of the time preening in June to 17% in July when they were marked, and falling to 5% during November.

The data were examined by categorizing the birds into groups, based on whether they had been newly fittted during the June observation period or whether the transmitters were replacements. To adjust for a general increase in overall activity observed from June to November, specific activities were expressed as proportions of the whole or by using a measure of overall activity as a co-variate in the analyses. The birds showed an increase in preening of the transmitters and the surrounding area immediately after these were attached ($P < 0.01$), but this activity returned to the same pre-tagging level within three months ($P < 0.01$). Individual condors varied significantly ($P < 0.01$) in the amount of preening attention given to newly-attached transmitters, which is not surprising given the high variability in their backgrounds and personalities.

Other than an increase in preening activity after attachment, the Andean Condors appeared to tolerate the patagial mounted transmitters well; however, after several years the patagia at attachment sites of three of the transmitters became distorted when the holes in the wing greatly enlarged, with no infection or trauma evident. Similar occurrences encountered in other studies suggest a possible balance problem with those particular packages.

With the release of Andean Condors in Peru, we could test patagial transmitters on flying birds. While most transmitters remained well positioned on the wing of all birds we released, there were two that tended to roll forward when the birds raised their wings, twisting the patagium at the attachment point. By repositioning where the attachment bolt emerged from the acrylic block (accomplished by drilling a new hole in the transmitter) and placing the centre of gravity at the bolt site, movement of the transmitter on the wing was largely eliminated.

Close inspection of the attachment site on the 15 wild condors was limited to two birds that were captured (13 weeks and 17 weeks after release) and two others that were shot (20 weeks and 43 weeks after release). The attachment sites of these birds appeared in good condition, with no sign of irritation to the area.

All 13 Andean Condors released in Peru were each examined carefully during recapture (Table 2) and one of them, the tame bird, was monitored continuously. Except for some initial redness and scabbing noticeable during the first weeks, the incision site normally healed to a smooth-edged 0.5 cm hole in the patagium of normal skin colour. No transmitters were known to fall off or be pulled out of the wing of any of the released wild birds over the two-year period during which they were intensively monitored.

Table 2. Transmitter attachment site inspection on 11 Andean Condors at various times after release (- day indicates inspection prior to release).

Andean Condor	Inspection Date	Days After Release	Weight (lbs)	Condition of Attachment Site
13-Y	22/7/80	-5	23 lbs	Reddened, no scabbing
	30/11/80	126	15 lbs	Normal colour, no scabbing
17-Y	22/7/80	-5	21 lbs	Reddened, scabbing
	23/8/80	27	15 lbs	Normal colour, no scabbing
	04/9/80	39	16.5 lbs	Normal colour, no scabbing
	06/12/80	132	15lbs	Normal colour, no scabbing
11-Y	22/7/80	-5	21.5 lbs	Reddened, no scabbing
	18/4/81	342	22 lbs	Normal colour, no scabbing
	13/8/81	459	22 lbs	Normal colour, no scabbing
15-Y	10/8/80	-6	19 lbs	Reddened, scabbing
	18/4/81	322	18 lbs	Normal colour, no scabbing
	23/3/82	661	23 lbs	Normal colour, no scabbing
15-Y	10/8/80	-6	24 lbs	Reddened, no scabbing
	18/4/81	322	25 lbs	Normal colour, no scabbing
	13/8/81	439	25.5 lbs	Normal colour, no scabbing
14-Y	10/8/80	-6	24.5 lbs	Reddened, no scabbing
	22/4/81	326	25 lbs	Normal colour, no scabbing
	13/8/81	439	28 lbs	Normal colour, no scabbing
21-0	15/1/81	2	23 lbs	Normal colour, no scabbing
	13/8/81	208	23 lbs	Normal colour, no scabbing
22-0	14/1/81	1	23.5 lbs	Normal colour, no scabbing
	14/6/81	150	15 lbs	Normal colour, no scabbing
23-0	28/1/81	-6	23 lbs	Normal colour, no scabbing
	13/8/81	191	23 lbs	Normal colour, no scabbing
	10/12/81	309	15 lbs	Normal color, no scabbing
	31/3/82	420	23 lbs	Normal colour, no scabbing
24-0	28/1/81	-6	24 lbs	Normal colour, no scabbing
	30/8/81	208	bias reading	No colour, no scabbing
25-0	28/1/81	-6	22.5 lbs	Normal colour, no scabbing
	13/8/81	191	22.5 lbs	Normal colour, no scabbing
	10/12/81	309	16.5 lbs	Normal colour, no scabbing
	02/3/82	391	22.5 lbs	Normal colour, no scabbing

Both the 12 zoo-raised released birds and the 15 wild-caught condors became habituated to the patagial transmitters, substantially within 48 hours and almost completely within the week. After the initial pulling at and intense investigation behaviour shown by some individuals to the tags or transmitters, the condors could be seen mandibulating the antenna or tag during preening bouts as if they were their own feathers. Others seemed to ignore the new appendage from the onset. Certain individuals defensively protected their transmitters from other curious condors.

Weights of 70g and 100g were tested on the trained condor (#10-W) to try to determine the consequences of heavier transmitters. After 46 hours of observing the 100g dummy transmitter (an acrylic block 2.5cm x 7cm x 4.5cm) on condor 10-W over a three-week period, we discontinued the test. Although the bird did not appear to have difficulty flying, the block moved considerably on the wing during flapping flight, no doubt stressing and irritating the patagium at the attachment point. The bolt hole in the patagium remained reddened and had increased to 1cm in diameter. The other wing of this bird carried a 70g functional transmitter for over one year without any signs of hole enlargement.

The long and flexible antenna proved to be too weak at the base for even the infrequent flapping of condors. Even after reinforcing the area with extra layers of heat-shrink tubing, virtually all the antennae were broken at the base within 2.5 years of being on the birds, reducing the functional 200 km transmission range to no more than 3km.

Based on these results, transmitters placed on California Condors between 1982 and 1987 had shorter, stiffer antennae. Only one antenna loss was recorded on any of the 11 wild birds that received transmitters and this was one of the first prototypes (D. Clendennen, pers. comm.). There were, however, three cases of transmitter loss off the wings. It was felt at the time that the nut securing the transmitter to the wing had loosened and the package fell off (F. Grantham, pers. comm.). A drop of fast-drying "super glue" was thereafter used to secure the nut on the bolt. Occasionally, however, the adhesion would be lost over time. By using teflon locking "aircraft" nuts this problem has been eliminated.

It was thought that the technical problems causing some unreliability with these transmitters were related to the high frequency band of 411 Mhz and 412 Mhz. By using the lower frequency of 164 Mhz many of the complications could be avoided. The transmitters used during the test releases of Andean Condors in Southern California mountains in 1988 used this lower frequency. The most efficient antenna for 164 Mhz is longer than that used on the California Condors and more flexible. Several months into the project we began to lose transmitters off the wings of some of the birds and eventually six fell off. These losses seemed correlated with transmitters that tended to be unstable on the wing. Examination of such transmitters that had been on wings varying lengths of time indicated that the units were not tearing out of the wing, but that the attachment bolt was slowly migrating toward the wing's leading edge until the transmitter eventually fell out. The patagia of these birds healed remarkably quickly and within a month of an incident it was often difficult to determine by examining the wing that it had occurred. We appeared, again, to be dealing with a balance problem, causing transmitter movement on the wing with the end result of transmitter loss and trauma to the patagium.

To look more closely at transmitter balance, we attached eight dummy transmitters to the wings of four Andean Condors at the Los Angeles zoo (Table 1). Only two of the eight were seen flipped over out of position. Out of 23 observer days, No. 7 malpositioned 8% of the time and No. 8 30% of the observed time. The centre of gravity on these two dummy transmitters was more toward the antennae than the others, except for Nos. 5 and 6. Having smaller gauge cable made the antennae of Nos. 7 and 8 more flexible than any of the others. No. 8 was the most flexible and most often seen out of position. Due to the particular characteristics of condor wing-beat frequency and amplitude, a flexible antenna tends to increase torque to the transmitter attachment site, which would lead to greater irritation of the patagium.

Based on these and other observations, the modifications we included on 12 transmitters placed on six California Condors released on December 1, 1992, appear to have made a positive difference. The antennae were stiffened and shortened to 20cm. This reduced flexibility and maintained the centre of gravity close to the attachment bolt. Including the patagial tag these transmitters weigh between 50g and 55g. By properly balancing the transmitter and slightly increasing the size of the plastic securing piece along the leading edge of the wing (Fig. 1), there appears to be little movement or malpositioning of the transmitter on the wing.

The use of radio telemetry has allowed researchers new and valuable insight into many areas of study of wild vertebrates. In some cases data on behaviour, movements and life span of wild species would be nearly impossible to obtain otherwise. In release programmes, such as with condors, where successful management necessitates knowledge of the daily positions and movements of each bird, it is a critically important tool. There are, however, moral and practical obligations to ensure that there are no adverse effects of transmitters on the animals being studied. Obviously an impaired individual in a release programme may have a reduced chance of survival and could compromise the ultimate goal of reestablishing a population. An overriding consideration throughout the development of this transmitter design has been the safety and wellbeing of the birds.

At this time it appears that there is a viable patagial transmitter for use on large vultures and condors, but no doubt we will continue to make refinements as the need arises.

ACKNOWLEDGEMENTS

Supporting agencies for various portions of this inquiry were: the U.S.Fish and Wildllife Service, U.S.Forest Service, California State Fish and Game Department, University of Wisconsin, Los Angeles Zoo, San Diego Wild Animal Park, National Audubon Society, National Geographic Society, and the Peruvian Ministerio de Agricultura Departmento de Fauna y Flora. Individuals who have made important contributions to this study are: G. Austin, E. Berg, J. Carpenter, D. Clendennen, B. Cockran, J. Grantham, S. Kasielke, D. Ledig, A. Leete, R. Mesta, J. Ogden, S. Porter, N. Snyder, and special thanks to S. Temple for his guidance and support.

REFERENCES

KENWARD, R.E. 1987. *Wildlife Radio Tagging*. Biological Techniques Series, Academic Press Inc. (London) LTD.

LIEBERMAN, A., J. WILEY, J.V. RODRIQUES & J.M. PAEZ 1991. First experimental reintroduction of captive-reared Andean condors (*Vultur gryphus*), into Columbia, South America. Pages 129-136 in American Zoological Parks and Aquariums Annual Conference Proc. San Diego, California, USA.

MERETSKY V. J. & N.F.R. SNYDER 1992. Range use and movements of California Condors. *Condor* 94(2): 313-333.

WALLACE, M.P., P.G. PARKER & S.A. TEMPLE 1980. An evaluation of patagial markers for cathartid vultures. *J.Field Ornithology* 51: 309-314.

WALLACE, M.P. & S.A. TEMPLE 1983. An evaluation of techniques for releasing hand-reared vultures to the wild. Pages 400-423 *in* S.R. Wilbur and J.A. Jackson (Eds.). *Vulture Biology and Management.* University of California Press, Berkeley and Los Angeles, California, USA.

WALLACE, M.P. & S.A. TEMPLE 1988. A comparison between raptor and vulture hacking techniquess. Pages 75-81 *in* D.K. Garcelon & G.W. Roemer (Eds.). *Proc. of the International Symposium on Raptor Reintroduction* 1985. Institute for Wildlife Studies, Arcata, California.

WALLACE, M.P. 1990. The California Condor: Current Efforts for its Recovery. *Endangered Species Update,* Nov. (8) 1: 32-35. Univ. Michigan, School of Nat. Resources.

WALLACE, M.P. & W. TOONE 1992. Captive management for the long-term survival of the California Condor. Pages 766-774 *in* D.R. McCullough & R.H. Barrett (Eds.). *Proc. Wildlife 2001: Populations, 1991.* Elsevier Applied Science.

Michael P. Wallace,
Los Angeles Zoo,
Dept. of Conservation and Science,
5333 Zoo Drive
Los Angeles
CA90027, USA

Mark R. Fuller
Bureau of Land Management
Division of Wildlife & Fisheries
1849 C.Street North-West
Washington DC 20240
USA.

James Wiley
Grambling Cooperative Wildlife Project
Grambling State University
P.O. Box 4290, Grambling
LA 71245, USA

Part 5

Biology and Conservation of the large Falcons in the subgenus *Hierofalco*

Aplomado Falcon *Falco femoralis*

Conveners:

Dr. T. J. Cade, Dr. W. Baumgart & Dr. C. M. White

Meyburg, B.-U. & R. D. Chancellor eds.1994
Raptor Conservation Today
WWGBP / The Pica Press

Methods and Results of Saker Falcon *Falco cherrug* Management and Conservation in Hungary

J. Bagyura, L. Haraszthy & T. Szitta

ABSTRACT

Following the Second World War increasingly few pairs of Saker Falcon bred in Hungary. All known nests were annually robbed illegally by falconers - often from other countries. Cliff-nesting pairs suffered in particular.

By the beginning of the 1970s a maximum of only 25 pairs were attempting to breed. In 1974 the Hungarian Ornithological Society initiated a conservation project, subsequently receiving support from the WWF. Thanks to the measures taken, the population was stabilised and, by the mid-1980s, had begun to increase. These measures included wardening of nests, construction of artificial nests and the protection and reintroduction in breeding areas of ground-squirrels.

In recent years nest-boxes have been installed on low-voltage electricity pylons and the illegal trade in falcons has been suppressed. By 1992 there were 90 known pairs, whilst the total population stands at around 150 pairs.

INTRODUCTION

Following World War II the Saker Falcon population in Hungary steadily declined and reached its lowest level during the 1970s. This decline was very largely due to nest-robbers from Western Europe. The cliff-nesting Sakers had regularly failed to rear young; there were even some pairs which had had no breeding success for ten successive years. Nests were frequently disturbed by rock climbers and tourists and occasionally even destroyed. We do not know whether poisoning by pesticides also had a negative influence on Saker Falcons and their breeding success, as has been proved with other species. The Saker's feeding habits, chiefly Susliks (ground-squirrels) and pigeons, the majority of which are domestic pigeons, seem to show that the negative factors known to affect the Peregrine left our Saker Falcons unharmed.

The Hungarian Ornithological and Nature Conservation Society (HONS), formerly the Hungarian Ornithological Society, was founded in 1974. One of its priorities from the beginning was to organise the protection of birds of prey threatened with extirpation.

METHODS

An important part of the Hungarian population of Saker Falcons breeds in the hills and mountains (between 300 and 1,000m a.s.l.). The majority of these nest on cliffs, either in small cavities or in old nests of Ravens.

Only a minority occupy tree nests, even at times using old nests of Ravens and of other raptors. At the start of our protection programme, when we still did not have enough experienced collaborators to help with nest wardening, we made many attempts to divert the birds away from known cliff sites by artificial means (e.g. blocking up the cavity, removing the nest, etc.). This was hardly ever successful, since with these birds tree-nesters will switch to a cliff - and vice versa - if there is a change of partners.

In protecting the Saker Falcon population in Hungary, priority has been given to the organisation of nest wardening, in order to thwart robbers. Up to the mid-1980s this was successfully achieved with the active participation of *ca.* 300 members of the Society. On the other hand, the condition of certain cliff nests was also often unsatisfactory; for instance they were liable to flooding, etc. To begin with we blocked up such nests as well, but later on tried to repair them. At the same time it was also necessary to re-establish the population of Susliks, by now largely extirpated.

Parallel with the growth in the population, there was also an increased number of pairs breeding in the lowlands. These would take over the disused nests of Buzzards, various herons, Crows, Cormorants, etc. Since these nests were for the most part in a very parlous condition, they would frequently distintegrate, with the resulting loss of the eggs or chicks. To avoid this we accordingly began to erect artificial nests.

Particularly dangerous for the birds which settle on them are the country-wide chains of high tension pylons, on which many perish by electrocution. Initially this was no major threat to the rare Saker Falcon, but with the increase in the population more birds have been killed. So this was now the second priority in our programme. Crows were taking to building their nests more and more frequently on the electricity pylons, raising a further danger for the Saker Falcons, since these nests were insecure and only occasionally was it possible for the falcons to achieve breeding success in them. In order to solve this latest problem we turned to the setting up of nest boxes.

RESULTS

1. Nest wardening

To the best of our knowledge, there are to-day in Hungary 14 groups of cliffs, quarries, etc. where the Saker Falcon has bred more or less successfully. Since most of these sites are widely known among the public, breeding success can be ensured only by wardening of the nests. In this work we have above all involved young people who, after the end of their studies, can take an active and successful part in our protection work, e.g. foresters, gamekeepers, etc.

During the first years, it sometimes happened that, due to inexperience, we guarded a nest only during the daytime, to find that the chicks had been stolen during the night. More thorough wardening during the past six years has made it impossible for any nest to be robbed. Thanks to this, not only the fledged young but also the adult breeding pairs have significantly benefited.

Since the Saker Falcon frequently has to face various negative factors during the breeding season, e.g. flooding of the nest cavity, predation by Pine Martens, Goshawks, etc. wardening can also go far towards preventing such disasters. By spotting such accidents immediately, we can take preventive measures and ensure the successful fledging of the young to a far greater degree than with nests that are not wardened. For example, during 1986-87 an average of 2.75 young were fledged from wardened nests, in contrast to not more than 1.66 from nests only routinely monitored. The success of wardening is borne out by the fact that during 1986-87 it was possible to ensure breeding success for 12 pairs which had consistently failed during the preceding years. During this one year more young were fledged from regularly guarded nests than were fledged for the whole country between 1960 and 1970. It is unquestionably thanks to this activity that the Hungarian Saker population is now steadily on the increase.

1960-70	20-25 pairs
1978	44 pairs + 6-8 possible
1989	65 pairs
1991	*ca.* 100 pairs

To-day our population has passed the point where it was still necessary to locate every nest and control it by wardening. Among the nests still controlled by us during the past two years, the birds have been even more successful. During 1990 84 young flew from 35 wardened, i.e. controlled, broods, and this figure increased during 1991 to 93 young from 28 nests.

2. Creation of nest sites

During the 1970s the Saker population in Hungary bred mainly on cliffs. In spite of constant failure, several pairs remained firmly attached to their nest hole.

To begin with, we tried to block up these holes in order to compel the birds to choose new nest sites. Later on, when we could organise wardening, we constructed new cliff nest sites ourselves. It often happened that the holes preferred by the Sakers got flooded by rainwater, which washed out the sandy floor, leading in turn to cracked or otherwise damaged eggs. Eggs also got swept out of the holes by heavy rain. Our intervention in these cases was also effective.

3. Erection of artificial nests

With the increase in the population, more and more pairs are breeding in the lowlands, where the tree nests they occupy are often unsuitable, which leads in turn to failure. The falcons prefer nests with decayed interiors, and this means that such nests are in very poor condition; thus they often collapse just when the young falcons are well developed and they fall to their death.

When a pair's territory can be considered quite suitable from other points of view, we can increase productivity by erecting artificial nests. In our experience the falcons readily select one of these nests, which are filled with rotting material. We construct large and very solidly built nests, made to last for a number of years. Generally the material we fill them with is taken from other, disused nests in the vicinity, whereby our birds are doubly ecouraged to adopt them.

During the past ten years we have had a number of old nests blown down by gales with the young lying dead below. In one case, for instance, an old Raven's nest containing five young Sakers collapsed, killing three of them. The two survivors were rescued by our members, who took them home and fed them. On learning of this three days later we immediately erected an artificial nest for them, in which they were duly reared by their parents.

To date we have erected over 100 artificial nests, 42 in 1989-91 alone. Most of these are well adapted to Saker Falcons.

During 1990-91 an average of 30 pairs bred in our artificial nests. In all, it can definitely be concluded that breeding success is dependent above all on the size and condition of the nest.

4. Establishment of Suslik colonies.

According to the literature the Suslik *Citellus citellus* is the Saker Falcon's prinicipal source of food. Researches carried out over the past five years in Hungary have added a large question mark to this assertion, but we can at least confirm that is it certainly the Saker's favourite prey. For the safeguarding of individual pairs the safeguarding of the Suslik colony in their hunting territory is accordingly esential. On the initiative of the HONS the Suslik, formerly regarded as a pest, has now been placed under protection. Understandably, legal protection does not go nearly far enough. In the mountain region, in the wooded and intensively exploited areas and adjacent meadowland, many Suslik colonies have been either extirpated or else severely depleted. The Suslik cannot recolonise these isolated areas on its own, so we have resorted to artificial means. During the first years of our attempts we released young Susliks which had been trapped elsewhere, but within a few days they were all taken by Sakers and Imperial Eagles since they were unable to dig burrows for themselves. From 1986 on, we took to trapping females in spring, before the birth of their young. At this time the females rapidly excavate burrows in which to conceal their young; this ensures their increase and gives them protection through the winter. The success of this method is dependent on the ability to introduce as many female Susliks as possible.

Between 1986 and 1991 we trapped altogether 1,989 Susliks in other parts of Hungary and released them in the mountain areas of Börszöny and the Bükk, where Saker Falcons and Imperial Eagles like to breed. We have in this way met with considerable success, as four self-sustaining colonies have now been re-established, and these areas appear to have retained their full complement of Saker Falcons and Imperial Eagles.

5. Prevention of electrocution

The pylons erected for high-tension cables in Hungary were so designed that the raptors alighting on them were frequently the victims of electrocution.

With the collaboration of "electricity experts" we have devised a plastic insulator which can be incorporated in the structure and prevent electrocution. To illustrate the size of this problem, during one inspection of a 7km stretch of 20 kv high-tension cables in the lowlands we found seven dead Sakers and 40 dead Kestrels.

Raptor mortality is caused above all by the high-tension pylons in the lowlands, on which the birds like to perch. With the co-operation of our friends from the electricity board, nearly all of these have now been fitted with the aforesaid insulator, following which there have have been no more cases of death by electrocution. This has also helped to preserve a large number of Storks, Kestrels and Rollers. In one case regarding a particularly critical 1km stretch where many dead birds were regularly found, we managed to get the whole structure dismantled.

6. Protection of pylon-nesting Saker Falcons

During recent years an increasing number of Hooded Crows have been making their nests on pylons. They build these on the metal cross-beams, but as a rule they only last for one breeding season. This leads to failure for the Sakers that occupy them in the following years.

Apart from this, such nest sites are ideal, guaranteeing inaccessibility both for human and animal predators. The pylons are 43m high and carry a voltage of 10,000 kv.

In 1991 we erected 10 nest boxes on these pylons, three of which were already adopted by Sakers in 1992. In this year we also had to retrieve one rotting nest containing six eggs before it collapsed. A screw had already broken one egg. We packed the nest in a nest box, in which the falcon soon settled back on her eggs. The creation of nest sites on pylons can only be done in close co-operation with sympathetic experts, and has resulted in some notable successes in recent years.

This method has given us high hopes for the future, since it makes it possible to establish pairs of Saker Falcons in areas where they have not bred for many years past or which previously provided no such opportunity, e.g. wide tracts of cultivated and arable land without trees.

7. Threats from animal predators

A. *Goshawk*

During 1986 on two occasions a Goshawk was observed taking young Sakers from the nest. In one case it returned within two days and took a second chick. We had to transfer the third chick to another nest in order to save it from the same fate. In 1989 we had a case of a young, ringed Saker with severe clawmarks, probably caused by attack from a Goshawk.

B. *Marten*

We have also recorded one case of a young bird killed by a Marten. In another case the falcon was seen to grab a Marten as it approached the nest, and drop it 10-15m away; the Marten was unhurt by its fall. In a further instance we believe a Marten to have been responsible for egg-stealing. On one occasion we managed to drive a Marten away from the vicinity of a nest, and we have other instances when a Marten was almost certainly responsible for the death of young falcons.

C. *Ticks*

In cliff nests we have found young birds infested with ticks on five occasions, in one case causing the death of the chicks. We observed that the young thus infested leave the nest prematurely and perish. We have sprayed such nests with an insecticide which causes no harm to the birds.

CONCLUSIONS

1. The decline of the Saker Falcon in Hungary has been halted. For many years the population was drained by "exports" to falconers in Western Europe. Round-the-clock nest wardening has finally brought this human form of predation to an end.

2. Pairs can be coerced into adopting safer nest sites, both in the mountains and the lowlands, by the construction of artificial nests. This method also opens up new territories. Such nests have also been adopted by Sea Eagle, Imperial Eagle, Lesser Spotted Eagle, Honey Buzzard, Goshawk, Buzzard, Red-footed Falcon and Kestrel.

3 By halting the decline of the Suslik colonies and establishing fresh ones it has been possible to create new territories.

4.By insulation of electricity pylons we have been able to eliminate one of the major causes of mortality.

5.Through nest boxes erected on these pylons it has been possible to establish new breeding areas.

6.Between 1975 and 1991 we have succeeded in increasing the population of Saker Falcons fourfold.

J. Bagyura/L. Haraszthy/T. Szitta
Hungarian Ornithological & Nature Conservation Society
Költő u. 21
1121 Budapest
Hungary

Lagger Falcon *Falco jugger* - adult female

Meyburg, B.-U. & R. D. Chancellor eds.1994
Raptor Conservation Today
WWGBP / The Pica Press

Feeding Biology of the Saker Falcon *Falco cherrug* in Hungary

J. Bagyura, L. Haraszthy and T. Szitta

ABSTRACT

The Hungarian Ornithological and Nature Conservation Society operates a special project for protecting the Saker Falcon. This provides opportunities to collect food remains from individual monitored nests, and over the past six years more than 1,000 prey items have been collected.

In Hungary the Saker Falcon breeds in two separate regions, in the low mountains on the one hand, in the plains and lowland forests on the other.

Each region has a very different food spectrum, and comparisons between the two are of considerable interest. The list of different prey is considerably greater in the lowlands. The current literature states that the suslik (ground-squirrel) is the principal food of the Saker Falcon, but our findings show that it constitutes less than 25% of the total.

INTRODUCTION

The feeding biology and diet composition of the Saker Falcon in Hungary has so far been little studied; occasional references to it are to be found in the literature (Boroviczény 1958; Tapfer 1968; Bécsy 1978).

The first publication covering this theme was presented by Jánossy (1983), who collected together the scattered data derived from our 1977-1981 project, as described in this paper. True, we have data from Austria (Bauer 1955; Frey & Senn 1980), and also from northern Jugoslavia (Suetens & van Groenendad 1968), but these refer to analogous populations which, like ours in Hungary, are closely dependent on what their environment is able to provide. Whereas observations in Slovakia (see Svehlik & Šimák 1977) give pigeons as the preferred food of several pairs, the Suslik (Ground-squirrel *Citellus citellus*) is nevertheless regarded there as the principal prey.

Baumgart (1977) considered the distribution of the Suslik and the Saker to be mutually interependent. Unfortunately it is not possible for us to-day to accurately reconstruct the true composition of the bird's diet at a time when the populations of both Saker and Suslik were at a considerable level.

METHODS

Throughout Europe all populations of the Saker Falcon are considered threatened, and from a number of regions it has been extirpated. As a result of protective measures, already initiated in 1975, the Hungarian population had almost quadrupled by 1991. If our efforts to protect this falcon were to succeed, it became a matter of prime importance for us to understand its specific food requirements. Between 1986 and 1991 we accordingly analysed the data from 89 breeding attempts by 43 pairs.

The overwhelming majority of these data (1,940 prey items) were acquired while the young were being ringed and from prey remains collected after fledging. A further 332 prey items were identified by direct observation during round-the-clock nest wardening. These could be only partial, since on the one hand such observations were only occasional, so as to avoid undue disturbance at the nest site, whilst on the other hand prey brought by the adults to the nest was not always clearly identifiable. With small birds, only fragments are visible, whereas a Suslik is generally quite easily recognised; also, since the adults bring larger birds to the nest already plucked, these too can scarcely be identified with any certainty.

Identification of the bone remains collected from individual nests was made with the generous help of Prof. Dénes Jánossy, and we take this opportunity to express our indebtedness to him. One of the basic shortcomings in research of this kind has to be mentioned: since only very few bone remains of small prey survive, these prey are for the most part not detectable.

RESULTS

Highland region

During the study period we compiled data from altogether 56 successful breedings by 21 different pairs and covering 1,236 prey items.

From these data it became clear that, for the Saker Falcons that breed in the mountain regions, the principal prey are pigeons (up to 67%) as against Susliks (up to 22%). We concluded two different reasons for this: on the one hand, over the past thirty years the meadowland in this region has been widely developed for cultivation and buildings (in 1991 *ca.* 51% of the land surface in Hungary was under cultivation), with the consequent loss of habitat suitable for Susliks, so that the falcons have had to turn to new sources of food; on the other hand, there are ever greater numbers of homing pigeons crossing these mountains, many of which fly over our study area in a state of exhaustion and are easily taken by the falcons - a fact amply borne out by the heaps of pigeon rings which we found in the eyries.

Substantial populations of starlings and crows also contribute to the diet in some degree; these manifestly come from nests in the close neighbourhood and from newly-fledged, inexperienced young birds. In contrast with the lowland-dwelling Sakers, the proportion of pheasant and partridge in the prey is small, indicating on the one hand that the Saker does not necessaily have to hunt these larger birds, otherwise not so well suited to their needs, and on the other that our falcons do not hunt over areas developed for agriculture, being spared this necessity by the large numbers of pigeons passing through.

Table 1. Prey of Saker Falcons in the highland region.

Rana sp.	1	*Cornus frugilegus*	29
Perdix perdix	4	*Sturnus vulgaris*	43
Phasianus colchicus	2	Other	30
V. vanellus	16	*C. citellus*	262
Streptopelia sp.	17	*C. cricetus*	16
Columba sp.	812	Other mammals	4
		Total	1236

Significant differences in the consumption of Susliks in an analysis pair by pair reflect the fact that our falcons can only prey on the Suslik where substantial populations of the latter are available. Wherever such a Suslik colony exists, these by far outstrip the number of pigeons taken. Table 2 shows the food composition of a pair of "Suslik specialists" and Table 3 that of a pair of "pigeon specialists". (The data in Table 1 cover both Tables 2 and 4). The category "other birds" in Table

1 refers to the following species: Teal, Greater Spotted Woodpecker, Jackdaw, Jay, Blackbird, Song Thrush, other *Turdus* spp. and Hawfinch.

In addition to collecting prey remains fallen from the nest, we also obtained data from nest wardening. A comparison of the same falcon pair's diet identified by observation and bone analysis respectively leads to further interesting results (Table 4). While it is acknowledged that identification by observation is often impossible, nevertheless the list of items becomes larger and the number of Susliks even inreases. The reason lies in the fact that whilst the young falcons digest the Susliks almost entirely, leaving very few remains, they barely attempt to eat any of the larger pigeon bones, which therefore remain more surely in the nest. The same phenomenon is to be found with all other, smaller prey.

Table 2. Collected prey items of a "Suslik-specialist" pair in the highlands.

V. vanellus	4
L. ridibundus	4
Columba sp.	17
Corvus sp.	13
Turdus sp.	1
Sturnus vulgaris	2
C. citellus	65
C. cricetus	7
Total	113

Table 3. Collected prey items of a "pigeon-specialist" pair in the highlands.

Anas querquedula	1
V. vanellus	2
L. ridibundus	1
Columba sp.	233
Columba palumbus	2
C. oenas	2
C. frugilegus	2
C. monedula	1
G. glandarius	1
Turdus sp.	2
St. vulgaris	7
C. citellus	27
C. cricetus	2
Total	283

2. Lowland region

This category includes all pairs breeding in the Great Plain of Hungary below 250m a.s.l. in small or large patches of woodland, floodplain forest, etc. During the study period we collected data from 33 successful nestings by 22 pairs, including 704 prey items which we analysed. Although we organised the wardening of nests in the lowlands, it was not possible to observe what prey the adults brought without causing undue disturbance, so that we were limited to an analysis of bone remains, the results of which are set out in Table 5. This clearly showed that in the lowlands the consumption of Susliks was substantially higher (30%), whilst that of pigeons was lower (47%). Pheasants and partridges also formed an important part of the diet here: among pheasants we recorded two each fully-grown cocks and hens, 12 poults and 24 indeterminates.

Interestingly, although there are widespread colonies of Rooks on the Great Hungarian Plain, we record only one instance of a Rook being taken by our falcons. Other bird prey consisted of 6 Ring-doves, 7 Thrushes, 1 Crested Lark and 1 other unidentifiable species.

Here in the lowlands we also found "pigeon specialists" in areas where no Susliks were readily available (see Table 6).

CONCLUSIONS

So far as the Hungarian population is concerned, the rather sweeping assertion in the literature that the Saker chiefly preys on Susliks has been only partly confirmed by our researches during the breeding season.

It is very difficult to be sure whether the high level of pigeon consumption first developed during the past thirty years, due to the increasing shortage of Susliks, or whether it has always been an important element in this region.

Table 4. Prey items identified by both observation and bone analysis.

	Observation	Bone analysis		Observation	Bone analysis
Pair A			*St. vulgaris*	-	1
A. querquedula	-	1	Unidentified birds	4	-
V. vanellus	-	2	*Talpa europea*	1	-
Columba sp.	31	233	*Lepus europeus*	3	-
C. palumbus	1	2	*C. citellus*	87	59
C. oenas	1	1	*C. cricetus*	3	5
Streptopelia	5	5	*Microtus* sp.	20	-
C. monedula	-	1	*Mustella* sp.	1	-
G. glandarius	2	1	Pair C		
Turdus sp.	19	-	*Reptile* sp.	1	-
T. merula	2	-	*P. perdix*	-	2
A. trivialis	1	-	*V. vanellus*	-	2
St. vulgaris	2	7	*Columba* sp.	9	189
Passeriformes sp.	3	2	*Streptopelia* sp.	1	3
Lepus europeus	3	-	*Corvus* sp.	-	8
C. citellus	52	27	*P. pica*	-	1
C. cricetus	-	2	*Turdus* sp.	3	-
Microtus sp.	22	-	*T. merula*	1	-
Cockchafer	8	-	*St. vulgaris*	1	5
Pair B			Unidentified birds	3	-
V. vanellus	-	4	*T. europea*	-	1
L. ridibundus	-	4	*Lepus europeus*	1	-
Columba sp.	-	21	*C. citellus*	10	48
Streptopelia	1	-	*C. cricetus*	2	5
Corvus	2	9	*Microtus* sp.	8	-
Turdus sp.	12	1			

Table 5. Collected prey items of lowland-dwelling Saker Falcons.

P. perdix	25
Ph. colchicus	45
V. vanellus	28
Columba sp.	330
Streptopelia	7
Corvus	1
St. vulgaris	25
Other birds	15
C. citellus	210
C. cricetus	13
Other mammals	5
Total	704

Table 6. Collect prey of lowland-dwelling A pigeon, and B Suslik specialist Saker Falcons.

	A	B
P. perdix		1
Ph. colchichus	14	-
V. vanellus		1
Columba	61	-
Streptopelia sp.		1
Galerida cristata	1	-
St. vulgaris	3	1
Talpa europea	1	-
C. citellus	13	35
C. cricetus	5	
Lepus europeus	3	-
Total	101	39

Since the Saker Falcon population in Hungary is continually and significantly increasing (25 pairs in 1975; 100 pairs in 1991), there is presumably a strong bias towards pigeons as more pairs lack available Suslik colonies. Even so, the visual observations made in parallel with the analysis of prey remains testify that the chances of pigeon bones surviving are substantially greater than those of Susliks or other small mammal or bird prey.

Our observations have also shown that the parent birds often remove prey remains from the nest, simply dropping them some distance away.

All the data presented here derive from the breeding season when, for three weeks after the chicks hatch, only the male hunts whilst the female feeds them. After the fourth week both parents go hunting in order to meet the growing demands of the young for food.

Our observations have also established the fact that the partents "store" captured prey temporarily. This occurrence is demonstrated by the fact that, only a few minutes after leaving the nest, the male will return with a fully-plucked pigeon (sometimes no longer fresh).

The analysis of bone remains and visual observations combined, covering 2,272 identifiable prey items, are presented in Table 7. Where identification cannot be positively made by visual observation, these data have naturally been omitted.

Table 7. Total of prey items recorded in the diet of Saker Falcon in Hungary 1936-1991.

Coleoptera	8	*Streptopelia*	31
Reptilia	1	*Corvus*	32
Rana sp.	1	*St. vulgaris*	71
P. perdix	29	Other birds	98
Ph. colchicus	47	*C. citellus*	622
V. vanellus	44	*C. cricetus*	34
Columba	1186	Other mammals	68
		Total	2272

REFERENCES

BAUER, K. 1955. Der Würgfalke (*Falco cherrug Gray*) in Österreich. *J. Orn* 96: 34-42.

BAUMGART, W. 1977. Der gegenwärtige Status des Sakers in Europa. *Falke* 24: 154-158.

BÉCSY, L. 1977. Daten zur Ökologie und Biologie des Würgfalken (*Falco cherrug*). *Aquila* 84: 83-88.

BOROVICZÉNY, A. 1958. Am Würgfalkenhorst. *Aquila* 65: 261-263.

FREY, H. & H. SENN 1980. Zur Ernährung des Würgfalken (*Falco cherrug*) und Wanderfalken (*Falco peregrinus*) in den niederösterreichischen Kalkvoralpen. *Egretta* 23: 31-38.

JÁNOSSY, D. 1983. Beitrage zur Nahrung des Sakerfalken (*Falco cherrug*). *Puszta* (1/10): 5-10.

SUETENS, W. & P. VON GROENENDAEL 1968. Notes sur deux oiseaux de prioe de la Yugoslavie Orientale: Faucon sacre (*Falco cherrug* Gray) et Pygargue à queue blanche (*Haliaetus albicilla* Linné). *Gerfaut* 58: 78-93.

ŠVEHLIK, J. & L. ŠIMÁK 1977. Zur Brutbiologie des Sakerfalken in der Ostslowakei. *Falke* 24: 159-163.

TAPFER, D. 1968. Beobachtungen über das Nistan des Würgfalken im Ost-Bakony-Gebirge. *Mit. Mus. Kom. Veszprém* 7: 427-439.

Jànos Bagyura / László Haraszthy
Hungarian Ornithological & Nature
Conservation Society
Költö u. 21, H-1121 Budapest
Hungary

Tamás Szitta
Bükk National Park
Sánd u. 6
H-3304 Eger
Hungary

Meyburg, B.-U. & R. D. Chancellor eds.1994
Raptor Conservation Today
WWGBP / The Pica Press

Long Term Trends in the Breeding Density and Productivity of Gyrfalcon *Falco rusticolus* in the Yukon Territory, Canada

D.H. Mossop and R.D. Hayes

ABSTRACT

Demography of Gyrfalcon has been studied from 1973-1991 in 15 of the 22 ecoregions of the Yukon Territory. Data are from 2,500 nest site visits and survey by helicopter of 86,624 km². 259 different nesting territories have been identified, monitoring has involved 172. All have been cliff nest sites, secondarily associated with overhangs, tundra communities, and in the southern Yukon with altitudes above 1,500 m. Variation in nesting density between extreme ecoregions was 0.6 to 6.1 pairs per 1,000 km²; within ecoregions nesting density was highly uniform.

Extrapolating these densities yields an estimated breeding population of 750 pairs over the 482,681 km² territory of which about 75% is acceptable breeding habitat (overall average breeding density: 1 pair per 453 km²).

Productivity has varied in a 10-year periodicity from a high of 90% of territories being attended by adults and 70% producing young, to a low of 40% attended by adults and 10% producing young. Brood size at fledge varied in synchrony with other productivity parameters from a low of 2.1 young per successful nest to a high of 3.3. Changes in breeding chronology have not tracked productivity; instead this remained relatively constant over the initial 10 years, then in the last five has shown a steady trend to be earlier. The productivity and estimated non-breeding population is discussed in light of Gyrfalcon breeding strategies to deal with fluctuating prey base.

INTRODUCTION

The Yukon Territory in the extreme northwestern corner of Canada, represents a significant portion of the mountainous western subarctic region of North America (Figure 1). The Gyrfalcon (*Falco rusticolus*) occurs in its grey to dark brown colour phase throughout the region. It is resident year round (Platt 1976). Prior to the mid 1970s no systematic study of the species had been carried out in the Yukon, but about that time, its management began to demand a vastly improved data base. This led to an organized field survey which has lasted over a decade and a half (1974-90), and now gives a valuable picture of the species' ecology in the Yukon and the Canadian Northwest.

The priority was to establish a data base upon which to build management options for the species including harvest of live birds. Surveys in Alaska (Cade 1960; White & Cade 1971;

Roseneau 1972) gave some indication of densities that could be expected in the Pacific Northwest but there was no evidence they were expandable to larger areas. In particular measures of overall abundance, productivity and differences between sub-regions were needed; there was also a need to sort out the difference between short term fluctuations and long term trends.

SURVEY DESIGN

The Yukon survey was designed to systematically catalogue nesting pairs over representative areas of the territory. Sample areas were then monitored annually to follow changes over time. The objective was to produce long term measures of breeding density, productivity and habitat use in representative areas which could then be extrapolated. In fact, the areas of survey tended to be planned opportunistically, often in association with funding made available through development proposals. To counter this, survey technique and data storage were standardized to facilitate territory-wide analysis. A significant proportion of the Yukon land area has now been covered by these surveys (Figure 1).

Figure 1. The Yukon Territory, Canada, showing locations of areas surveyed for breeding Gyrfalcons.

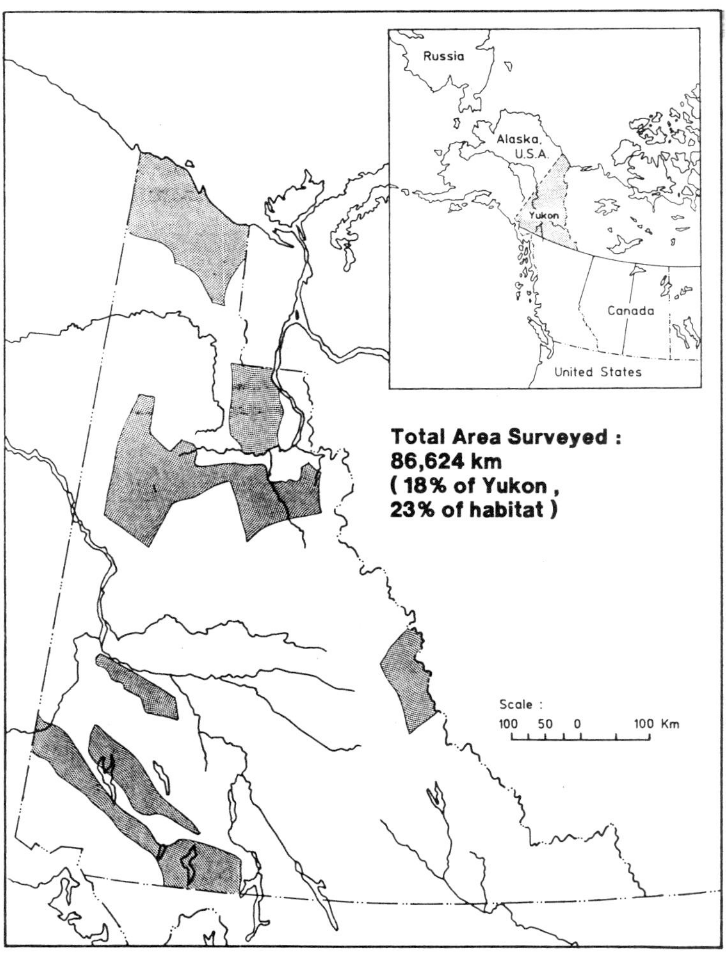

All initial surveys and subsequent monitoring surveys have been conducted by helicopter. A variety of types have been used; the present analysis involves about 2,500 visits to Gyrfalcon nests of which 1,593 have resulted in usable data. Although surveys almost always had additional objectives to Gyrfalcon survey, roughly 2,000 hours of flying time have been spent collecting these data.

The basic survey technique has been a total search of defined study areas. In practice this has involved search of all the cliff faces in the study area. (All known Gyrfalcon nest sites in the Yukon have been associated with cliffs. Because these surveys were also designed to locate other species of nesting raptors, it is unlikely Gyrfalcons using non-cliff nest sites would have been overlooked). The helicopter search pattern varied but normally watercourses were used to break the search blocks into manageable pieces. A carefully followed standard routine was adopted to facilitate observation of all nests and minimize disturbance. During subsequent monitoring surveys a sample area was visited with a similar helicopter search which focused on known nest sites, but also involved search of intervening habitat.

Data collection and handling

Criteria for data collection were standardized (Hayes & Kale 1982). A **"nesting territory"** was a cliff face or series of cliffs where there was evidence the area was or had been defended by one or more adults. In some instances this identification was inferred from the presence of excrement (wash) at the cliff, but in these instances follow-up surveys normally confirmed the identity of the occupying adults and in all cases the observation used as evidence was recorded. The nest location at the territorial site was recorded separately. Information recorded at newly discovered territories included a series of observations of the habitat including cliff size, rock type, altitude, aspect, distance of nest ledge from top, percent of overhang above the nest, distance to water and vegetative cover in the general area. An **"occupied site"** was a nesting territory where there was evidence of the presence of adults in the current year. This normally meant seeing an adult in the vicinity or observing the presence of obviously fresh wash. A **"productive site"** was a territory where there was direct evidence of young being produced in the current year. At these sites, the observations included the number of young and/or eggs in the nest, and an estimate of the age of the young. Ground visits to nests were conducted on a less regular basis. On these visits all young were banded and a sample of prey remains was collected. Over a period of 4 years (1977-80) these visits were prioritized. All data were coded and entered as a SAS (Statistical Analysis Systems - SAS Institute 1985) data set on an IBM mainframe and analysis was via procedures of the SAS programme.

Study areas

Seven intensive search areas have been covered, scattered from the Yukon's north coast to its southern border (Figure 1 and Table 1). In total 86,624 sq. km. of the Yukon's 482,681 sq. km. area have been intensively searched. Between, extensive areas totalling about 20,240 sq. km. have also been covered in survey incidental to other field research. The total area surveyed is approximately 18% of the area of the Yukon.

The Yukon has been subjected to ecoregion analysis since the mid-1970s in an attempt to describe regions with comparable landscape, bedrock, surficial geology, climate, soils and vegetation (Oswald & Senyk 1977). Twenty-two polygons have been recognized averaging 22 thousand sq. km. each. Gyrfalcon survey has been conducted in 15 of the 22 ecoregions:

a) North Slope/Old Crow basin (17,500 sq.km.): This area lies almost exclusively in the Northern Mountains and Coastal Plain ecoregion of Oswald and Senyk (1977). It is mostly treeless tussock tundra with a lush growth of shrub and shrub tundra associated with drainages. Scattered black and white spruce occur on protected sites. It is the area of longest study, survey began in 1973 (Platt & Tull 1977) and monitoring has been systematically conducted annually until 1990. Riverside cliffs and ridge top tors provide abundant nesting habitat for Gyrfalcons throughout.

b) Southern Richardson Mountains (9,070 sq. km.): This study area is part of a southern extension of the Northern Mountains and Coastal Plain ecoregion. It grades from treeless tussock tundra at higher elevations to closed spruce at its lower elevations. The rivers draining to the east and west have well developed cliffs providing ample nesting habitats. The area was subjected to initial search in 1977-78 but monitoring since has been sporadic and incomplete.

c) Nahoni Range (8,000 sq. km.): In the North Ogilvie Mountains ecoregion, this area has extensive areas of treeless tundra and shrub tundra at upper elevations with white spruce in lower and protected areas. An identifiable treeline occurs at about 900m a.s.l. Initial search was in 1979 and monitoring has been incomplete and of an incidental nature since.

d) Ogilvie Mountains (6,166 sq. km.): This study area straddles the South and North Ogilvie Mountain ecoregions. It covers an area of the upper Klondike river of the Yukon river basin and the upper Peel river basin. It is an area of diverse, relatively productive alpine tundra, shrub and open white and black spruce forest. Treeline is about 1,050m a.s.l. The area was initially searched in 1977-78 and was the subject of intensive research into Gyrfalcon breeding strategies over a three year period (Barichello 1983). The area has since been systematically monitored on a periodic basis averaging about every five years.

e) Dawson Range (5,030 sq. km): This area in the Dawson Range ecoregion is mostly treeless shrub tundra with extensive areas of wet treeless habitats occupying flat drainage valleys. Tree line is approximately 1,200m a.s.l. Initial search was in 1980-81 and monitoring has been systematic, averaging about once in five years.

f) Macmillan Pass area (10,595 sq. km.): This sudy area lies mostly in the Logan Mountains ecoregion. The area is mostly wet alpine treeless tundra with some alpine fir and shrub in a relatively extensive subalpine. Treeline is at approximately 1,400m a.s.l. The area was searched initially in 1981 and monitoring has not been carried out in any systematic way.

g) Coast Mountains (10,023 sq. km.): This area lies in the Coast Mountain and Ruby Range ecoregions. Relatively lush alpine tundra predominates with open white spruce forest at lower elevations. Treeline is at about 1,200m a.s.l. and extensive mountain cliff habitat provides an abundance of nesting habitat. The area was searched initially in 1978-80 and monitoring has been systematic, conducted annually since. All measurements of area were made with a digital-reading automatic planimeter from an air photo mosaic at a scale of 1:2,500,000.

Table 1. Breeding Gyrfalcons on seven study areas surveyed in the Yukon Territory, 1973-1991.

Study Area	Area searched (sq. km.)	nesting territories	breeding density (prs/1000 km^2)
N. Slope	17,500	106	6.06
S. Richardson/Werneke	15,947	17	0.58
Ogilvie Mountains	17,302	58	3.35
Dawson Range	5,030	10	1.98
Kluane Range	10,227	6	0.59
Hess/Logan	20,695	7	0.66
Coast Mountains	10,023	36	3.59
TOTAL	86,724	240	2.77

RESULTS

The breeding population

Area of occupied habitat: There is no doubt these highly mobile birds make use of the whole of the Yukon Territory; wherever species lists have been kept the species has eventually been recorded. Breeding birds are, however, not found in all habitats. In an attempt to characterize what constitutes acceptable habitat in the territory, we examined the 227 different nest sites where measurements of physical parameters were recorded. Breeding Gyrfalcons were always associated with cliff faces. This fact was not a surprising conclusion for the Pacific northwest (Cade 1960; Roseneau 1972; Barichello 1983). In over 2,000 visits to Gyrfalcon nests, none were found in situations other than cliff faces. Unfortunately the presence of cliffs is not obviously useful in characterizing acceptable Gyrfalcon breeding habitat on a large scale. Virtually all habitats in the Yukon in all ecoregions probably have cliff faces available within reasonable flight range for a Gyrfalcon. Even though there may be areas of extensive flat country (for example in the Eagle plains of the north central Yukon) where this feature could conceivably limit Gyrfalcon breeding, it is almost impossible to conceive of a method for broad remote habitat characterization using it.

More useful measures, because of the ease with which they could be mapped, were the altitude above sea level and the vegetative community in which nests were located. The nest sites in the southern half of the territory predictably (p=0.05) were found above 1500 m a.s.l. (In the northern half of the territory, no such association was evident). Characterization of the vegetation within 5 km. of nests as forested, open taiga, shrub tundra or tundra likewise showed a strong association with one identifiable feature: tundra. Treeless tundra predominated (67%). Open taiga accounted for 24% and the remaining 9% were classified as shrub tundra. No sites were characterized as being associated with forested habitat. Combining these features and assuming a Gyrfalcon may travel some distance (at least 10 km) from 'acceptable' habitat to use a nest site, the area of the territory which can conceivably be considered Gyrfalcon breeding habitat is about 74% of the Yukon, 356,000 sq. km., — of which 24% was surveyed (Figure 2).

Figure 2. Estimated area of acceptable Gyrfalcon breeding habitat based on elevation and distance from tundra vegetation communities, Yukon Territory.

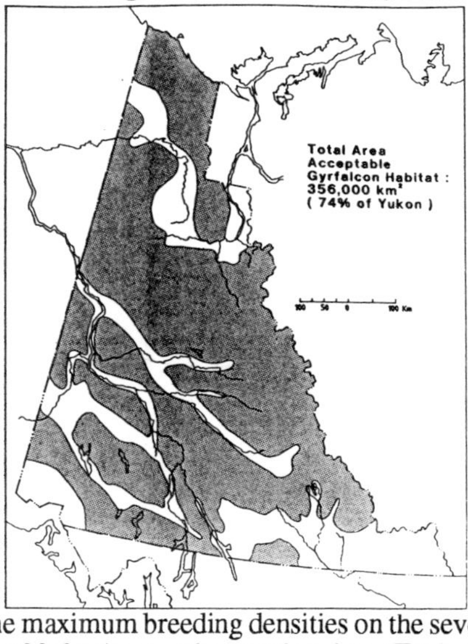

Breeding numbers: The maximum breeding densities on the seven study areas varied greatly from a high of 6.1 to a low of 0.6 pairs, per thousand sq. km. (Table 1). Additionally, an apparent feature of the Yukon Gyrfalcon populations was a remarkably uniform spacing between nest sites which showed a highly significant departure from a random spacing (nearest neighbour spatial relation test, Clark and Evans, 1954, p < .0001 and Table 2).

Table 2. Nearest neighbour measurements, Gyrfalcon breeding territories in the Yukon Territory

	(km)	(s.d)
N. Slope	8.1	2.3
Richardson	18.2	8.6
Ogilvie	11.0	3.9
Dawson	25.6	11.2
Kluane	-	-
Hess	96.7	14.6
Coast Mountains	12.4	3.5

Based on this apparent uniform spacing of the nesting pairs regionally, extrapolation of the territory-wide population was by ecoregion. Pooling ecoregions with equal Gyrfalcon density or obvious climatic and vegetative similarities, seven larger ecological regions emerged (Figure 3). Extrapolating Gyrfalcon breeding density to the acceptable habitat within these areas suggests a total maximum population of about 750 pairs for the whole of the Yukon Territory (Table 3).

Fluctuations in breeding numbers: The number of adult pairs observed has fluctuated significantly on all areas monitored. This variation has followed an apparent 10-year period (Figure 4). The variations recorded were in the order of 25-60% with a suggestion of higher amplitudes in the more northern sections of the territory. Additionally, over the 15 years of this study, the peak population levels have remained remarkably stable. In fact, we feel the apparent fluctuation in adults may be misleading. In the 'down' phases of the cycle adults attending nesting territories are far less faithful to the site; the accurate focus on the actual number of breeding adults is likely limited to the peak populations when most pairs at least attempt to breed and are 'available' for us to count.

Figure 3. Regions of similar Gyrfalcon breeding density within which extrapolations of total breeding populations were made, Yukon Territory, Canada.

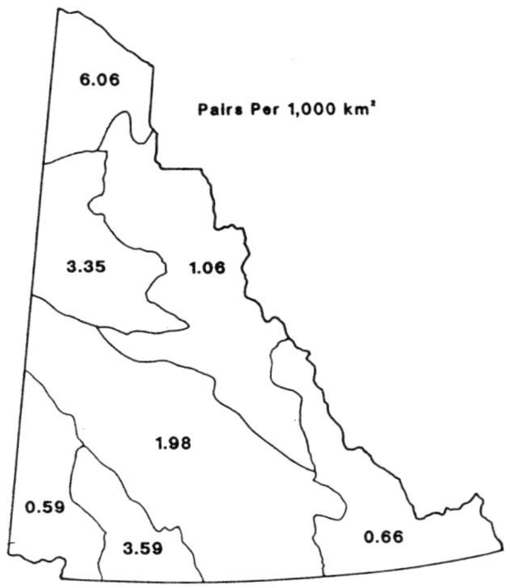

Table 3. Extrapolations of Gyrfalcon breeding numbers by ecoregion areas in the Yukon Territory.

Gyrfalcon 'regions'	Area of Gyrfalcon habitat (km²)	Breeding density (prs/1000 sq. km.)	Total pairs
1.	42,436	0.66	28
2.	25,550	3.59	92
3.	18,906	0.59	11
4.	78,450	1.98	155
5.	85,200	1.06	90
6.	54,903	3.35	184
7.	31,020	6.06	188
			TOTAL 748

Figure 4. Cyclic changes in the number of breeding adults over fifteen years, shown are the proportions of nest sites attended by breeders in years surveyed.

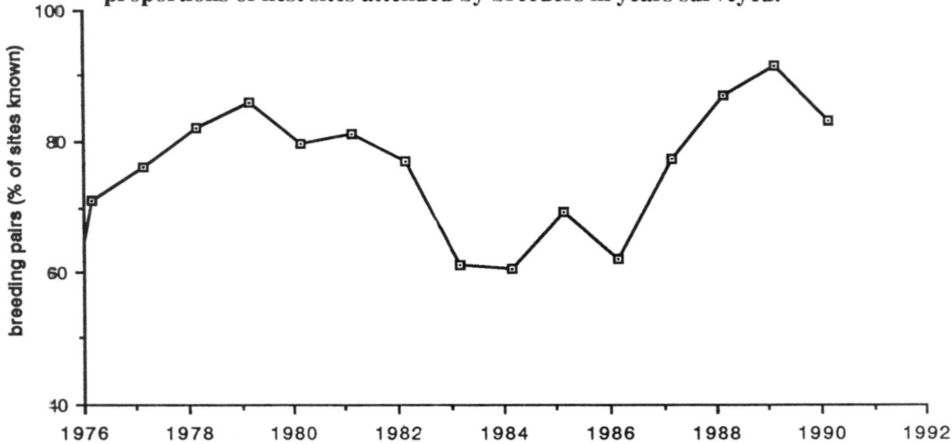

Figure 5. Variations in prodution of young over time, compared to changes in adult numbers counted.

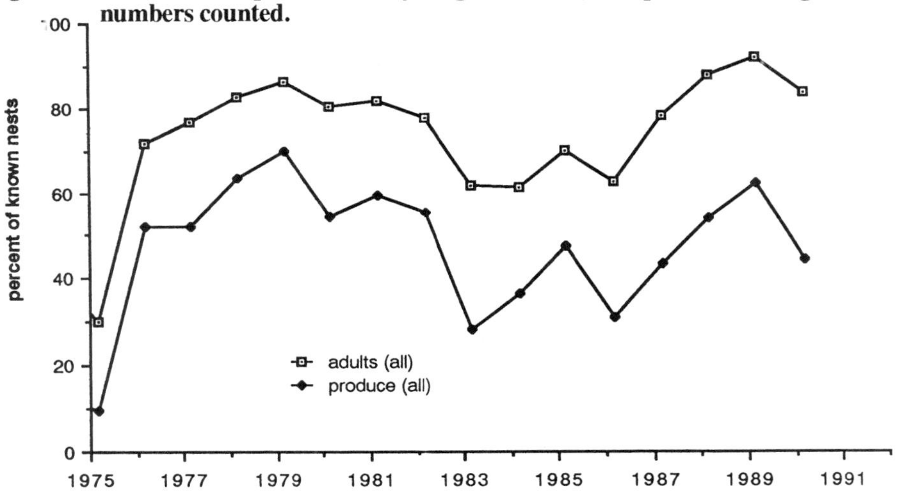

Figure 6. Variation in the number of young produced by successful pairs over time.

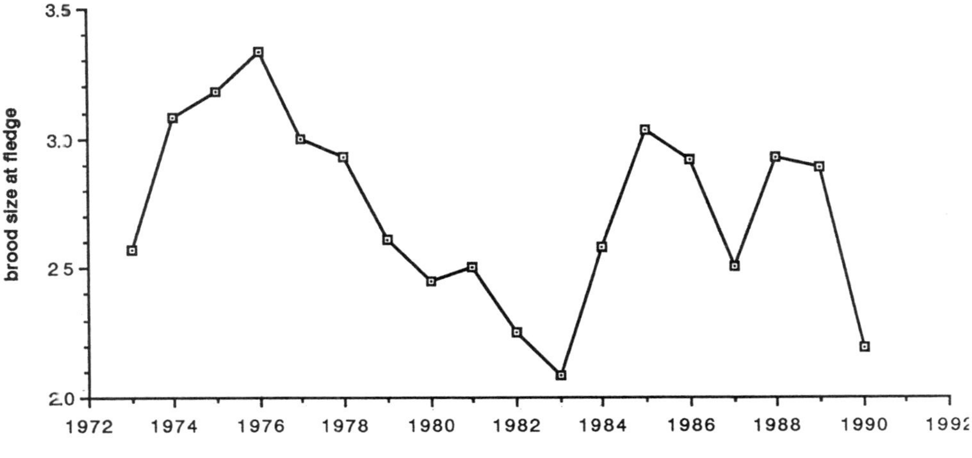

Figure 7. Comparison of the cyclic changes in Gyrfalcon demographics in the northern and southern halves of Yukon, 1976-1990.

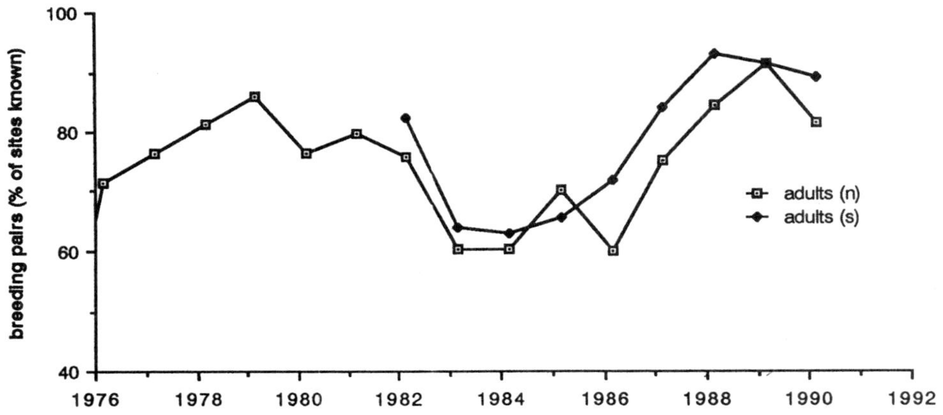

Production of young: The fluctuations we recorded probably relate more to changes in productivity than to changes in the number of adult breeders. The number of young raised to fledging on the various study areas all varied greatly, in a regular cycle approximating a 10-year period that mirrored the cycle observed in adult attendance (Figure 5). In peak years approximately 60% of breeding pairs produced young, in lows as few as 10% did so. In synchrony, the number of young fledged by successful pairs varied significantly ($p = 0.05$) from 3.3 young annually to 2.2 (Figure 6). Moreover the cyclic productivity changes were a territory-wide phenomenon; there were no significant differences between any of the study areas or even between pooled samples from the northern and southern halves of the territory (Figure 7).

Prey abundance: The close links between Gyrfalcon population performance and ptarmigan abundance has been the focus of research in the Yukon (Barichello & Mossop 1983; Mossop 1988). A very close correlation between the classic 10-year cyclic changes in (notably) Willow Ptarmigan (*Lagopus lagopus*) population dynamics and Gyrfalcon population cycles has been documented (Figure 8). Gyrfalcons in the Yukon are apparently totally dependent on ptarmigan in the early breeding season.

Nesting chronology: Hatch dates determined from back-dating from the age of young observed suggests a latitudinal adjustment toward later hatch in the northern study areas: Southern Yukon hatch date: May 16 (S.D. = 10 days); Northern Yukon hatch date: June 1 (S.D. = 14 days). Although significant variation occurred in all years in all populations, overall, hatch dates remained relatively stable at similar latitude in spite of the cyclic phase of the population through the major portion of the study period.

A possible feature is a suggestion of change in the mean hatch date over the last 5 years (Figure 9). The trend may be occurring toward earlier nest initiation/hatch, notably in the southern portions of the territory. Although the overall change involved in still within the long term variation observed ($p = 0.05$) the fact that an increasing change in chronology has been observed in 4 of 5 consecutive years (notably in the southern half of the territory) lends some significance to this observation.

Figure 8. The relationship between Willow Ptarmigan(*Lagopus lagopus*) numbers and Gyrfalcon demographics in the Yukon, 1975-1990.

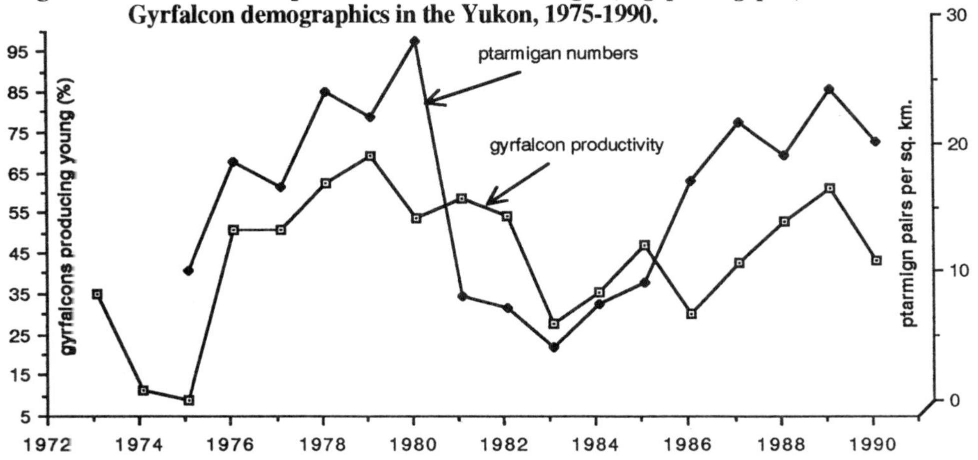

Figure 9. Mean hatch dates of Gyrfalcon in the Yukon, 1973-1990 comparing the northern and southern halves of the territory.

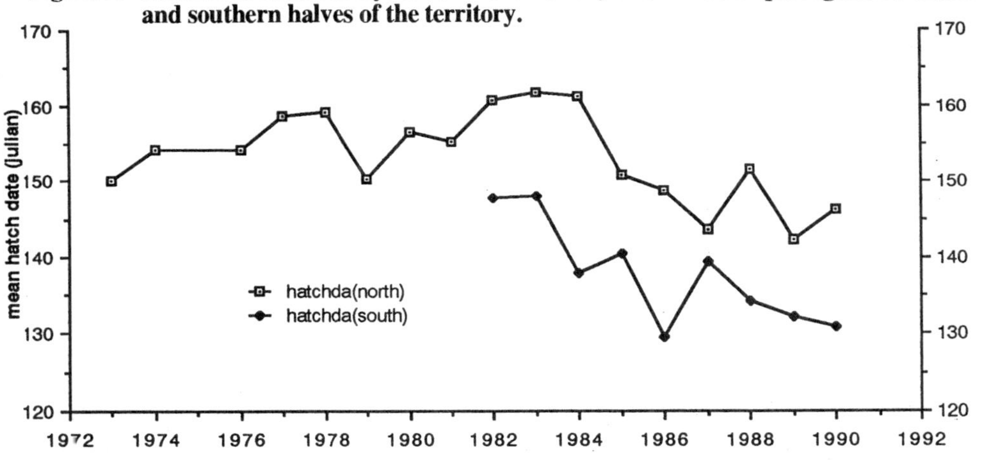

DISCUSSION

Population size and trend: These data are mostly of value in providing evidence for long term stability in the cyclic Gyrfalcon populations of the North American western arctic and western subarctic regions. Population densities over this large area, in the long term, have varied mostly between habitats, presumably reflecting productivity of differing ecoregions. Over at least the last 15 years, the species has been exhibiting remarkably uniform cycles in abundance and reproductive performance, suggesting a tracking of cycling factors in the environment but exhibiting no overall trend. The dynamics of the prime prey species in the Yukon, the three species of ptarmigan, closely resemble the cycles observed and provide the best explanation for all the temporal variation observed in Gyrfalcon demographics.

A breeding population of about 750 pairs in the Yukon is higher than was predicted based on earlier surveys in Alaska (Cade 1960). Fall numbers based on production numbers observed and non-breeding subadults estimated, may average 2,490 to 4,180 birds depending on the stage of the population in its cycle.

A feature of the Gyrfalcon ecology in the Yukon is its apparent simplicity, based as it is on a single critical non-migratory prey. This simplicity may contrast to the larger eastern areas Gyrfalcon inhabit in Northern America (Poole & Bromley 1985). The less complicated community association in the Yukon lends a level of confidence to the extrapolations of numbers and conclusions we have drawn about trend analysis at the population level. The dominant nesting strategy of even spacing over their nesting habitat is key in providing some of the best evidence for a broad estimate of numbers of Gyrafalcon in a relatively large northern area. A clumped nesting strategy may be the norm in other areas of the north, making extrapolation of population size to the rest of the habitat in those areas almost impossible (Poole & Bromley 1985). The area to which our conclusions can safely be extrapolated will wait field testing; we feel confident large areas of the North American 'Pacific Northwest' will follow suit, including large portions of Alaska as well as the North West Territories west of the Mackenzie River.

Breeding strategies to deal with fluctuating prey base: Clearly a predator like the Gyrfalcon, dependent on a prey that undergoes regular 6 to 10 fold changes in abundance, will have to develop profound strategic adaptations to deal with this problem. A simple modelling of the numeric responses observed gives some insight into the mechanism and may have implications for the management of the species. Assuming adult mortality that may be as high at 25% and mortality of fledged young of at least 50% (Newton 1979), at the population level Gyrfalcons are probably not replacing themselves in almost half the breeding seasons over the long term (Mossop & Hayes 1982). It is probably key for managers to understand this strategy by which reproduction effort is so finely tuned to the prey base. Work on the breeding territories has led to a general understanding of the role of courtship and prey abundance during early courting in determining reproductive output (Barichello & Mossop 1983; Bente 1981). Unfortunately the ecology of birds in the downward phases of the cycle, when the breeding territories are far less faithfully attended, is almost totally unknown simply because the birds become 'invisible' to normal study techniques.

From a management perspective the immediate concern must be to understand the vulnerability of the species at all stages in the cycle. There is no known evidence that either juvenile or adult mortality is static throughout the cycle. Nor are there any data on the simple whereabouts of adults (and especially non-breeding sub-adults) during the down turn phases when nesting territories are abandoned. Clearly prey utilization strategies at that time may be far more critical to understand than even those on the breeding grounds. As well, a strong research initiative at least tracking ptarmigan demography is likely an essential companion to any Gyrfalcon population work in the North American Pacific Northwest.

Changing breeding chronology: Enhanced nest success associated with early spring and hence early nest initiation has been observed in Peregrines (Mearns & Newton 1988) and several other raptor species (Newton 1979). In arctic-adapted species like the Gyrfalcon which clearly pursue a breeding strategy in which timing is critical, it would seem logical to predict a very close association between breeding output and chronology. All things being equal, birds subject to equal environment situation should breed roughly at the same time. Our findings of standard nesting periods over time but tending to be earlier in the southern Yukon would seem to bear this out.

Although we were unable to demonstrate statistical significance, there is a suggestion an anomaly may have arisen in the most recent period, 1986-91: nesting chronology seems to have been advancing. The ecology of northern systems has been the subject of much speculation as supposedly highly sensitive to world climate, presumably as a result of atmospheric pollution. Instruments are apparently on the edge of being able to measure the predicted climatic changes which seem to suggest a warming northern climate (Cohen 1990). It may be that birds like the Gyrfalcon, whose reproductive strategies are designed to take advantage of short arctic summers, may be offering a sensitive indication of climate change.

REFERENCES

BARICHELLO, N. 1983. Selection of nest sites by Gyrfalcons (*Falco rusticolus*). Unpubl. MSc. Thesis, Univ. of British Columbia, Vancouver.

BARICHELLO, N. & D. H. MOSSOP 1983. Productivity of gyrfalcons (*Falco rusticulous*) as a response to changes in the ptarmigan (*Lagopus spp.*) abundance over a five year period. Unpubl proceedings 34th Arctic Science Conference, Whitehorse, 1983.

BENTE, P.J. 1981. Nesting behaviour and hunting activities of the Gyrfalcon (*Falco rusticolus*) in south central Alaska. Unpubl. MSc. thesis Univ, of Alaska, Fairbanks.

CADE, T.J. 1960. Ecology of the Peregrine and Gyrfalcon populations in Alaska. *Univ. Calif. Publ. Zool.* 63.

COHEN, S.J. 1990. Bringing the global warming issue closer to home: the challenge of regional impact studies. *Bulletin of the American Meterological Soc.* 71(4): 520-526.

HAYES, R. & W. KALE. 1982. Yukon raptor data storage and retrieval system. Unpubl. Yukon Dept. Ren. Res. Report.

MEARNS, R. & I. NEWTON 1988. Factors affecting breeding success of Peregrines in south Scotland. *J. Animal Ecology* 57: 903-916.

MOSSOP, D. H. 1988. Winter survival and breeding strategies of willow ptarmigan. *In*: A.T. Bergerud and M.W. Gratson (Eds). *Adaptive strategies and population ecology of northern grouse.* Univ. of Minnesota press. Minn. p 330-378.

MOSSOP, D. H. & R. HAYES 1982. The Yukon Territory Gyrfalcon harvest experiment (1974-80). *In*: proceedings of a symposium: raptor management and biology in Alaska and western Canada. W.N. Ladd and P.F Schempf Eds. 263-280.

NEWTON, I. 1979. *Population Ecology of Raptors.* Buteo Books, Vermilion, South Dakota. 399 pp.

OSWALD, E.T. & J.P. SENYK. 1977. *Ecoregions of Yukon Territory.* Can. For. Serv. Rep., Victoria B.C. 115 pp.

PLATT, J.B. & C.E. TULL 1977. A study of wintering and nesting gyrfalcons on the Yukon North Slope during 1975 with emphasis on their behaviour during experimental overflights by helicopter. *Arctic Gas Bio. Rep. Ser.* Vol 35, ch 1.

PLATT, J.B. 1976. Gyrfalcon nest site selection and winter activity in western Canadian Arctic. *Can. Field-naturalist* 90(3): 338-345.

POOLE, K.G. & R.G. BROMLEY 1985. Aspects of the ecology of the gyrfalcon in the central arctic, Northwest Territories, 1983-84. File Rep. Dept. Ren. Res. Govt. NWT no. 52.

ROSENEAU, D.G. 1972. Summer distribution, numbers and food habits of the gyrfalcon (*Falco rusticolus*) on the Seward Peninsula, Alaska. MSc. thesis, Univ. of Alaska, College, Alaska. 124 pp.

SAS INSTITUTE 1985. SAS user's guide: basics, version 5 edition. Cary, NC: SAS Institute Inc. 1290 pp.

WHITE, C.M. & T.J. CADE 1971. Cliff-nesting raptors and ravens along the Colville River in arctic Alaska. *Living Bird* 10:107-150.

D.H. Mossop
R.D. Hayes
Dept, of Renewable Resources
Government of Yukon
P.O. Box 2703
Whitehorse
Yukon Territory
Canada Y1A 2C6

Snowy Owl *Nyctea scandiaca*

Meyburg, B.-U. & R. D. Chancellor eds.1994
Raptor Conservation Today
WWGBP / The Pica Press

Use of the Saker and other Large Falcons in Middle East Falconry

Kenton E. Riddle and J. David Remple

ABSTRACT

The development of specialty veterinary hospitals for falcons in the Arabian peninsula has improved the standard of falconry and vastly improved the health and survival of the birds. To understand the status of large falcons (Saker and Gyrfalcon) used in the Middle East, interviews were conducted with falcon merchants from two principle source countries. Syrian trappers supplied 80 Sakers (60 female, 20 male) compared to 300 previously. Smaller numbers trapped were thought due to a developing export trade from Turkey (150-200). Pakistan marketed approximately 1,700 Sakers (300 males). Annual numbers have remained constant although the numbers of trappers and locations have increased since 1980. Of the 1,700, 300 were marketed in Kuwait and Qatar; 200 in U.A.E.; and 100 each in Saudi Arabia and Bahrain. The remainder were purchased directly in Pakistan by individuals. Saker Falcons admitted by the Dubai Falcon Hospital and the Abu Dhabi Falcon Research Hospital (434 and 956 respectively) reflect the popularity of the sport. Immature-adult ratios (1.1:1 and 1.8:1 respectively) and female-male ratios (1.7:1 and 18.7:1 respectively) differed between the two hospitals. Gyrfalcons have been limited to a few captive-raised individuals and are regarded as useless by most falconers. Practices which affect the status of Sakers are discussed.

INTRODUCTION

Sakers and other large falcon species have been trained in falconry for centuries in the Middle East. Historically, the practice was sustained by the ability to provide supplemental meat for a meagre subsistence diet. Today, falconry is a pervasive cultural thread woven through the Arab fabric, from bedouins acquainted with the austerity of the desert to wealthy urban dwellers seeking communion with the past. Subsistence hunting is no longer required; however, cultural constraints and customs continue to dictate the practice of falconry as a pragmatic sport (Platt & Remple 1988). The practice of modern Arab falconry, including sources of falcons and estimates on numbers employed in the region, have been previously reported (Platt & Remple 1988).

Because the region is removed from usual scientific information networks, there is particular interest in acquiring new and up-to-date information on falconry in Arabia. Interviews were conducted with trappers, dealers and falconers to provide information on the origins and numbers of the large falcons utilised. Annual visits to falcon markets provided information on the arrival, condition and disease status of imported falcons, and trends in numbers and species involved.

The development of two specialty veterinary hospitals (Dubai 1983, Abu Dhabi 1985) for the care of the hunting falcons of the ruling families and citizens of the United Arab Emirates, has upgraded the practice of falconry in the region. They have provided comprehensive medical and surgical care for the falcons, and have served as a base for the exchange of information and ideas. Falconer-veterinarians and staff, themselves master falconers, provided insight into modern western veterinary medicine, falcon husbandry practices, and emphasized the value of preventive medicine. Arab falconers have also been introduced to new concepts in physical conditioning and nutrition, and have been exposed to other falconry practices, equipment and philosophies.

Detailed hospital records were maintained throughout the period. They allowed tabulation of patient population demographics, and diseases and injuries were analysed to determine trends in the health and survivability of the falcons. Evolving attitudes and changes in the use of the resource were also considered. This paper intends an objective discussion on present day use of the large falcons, notably the Saker, Gyrfalcon and Peregrine Falcon in the Arabian Peninsula.

SOURCES AND DISTRIBUTION OF FALCONS

Before the acquisition of oil wealth in the region all falcons were trapped locally. It is now possible for many more falcons to be utilised in hunting, thus a flourishing trade in wild-caught falcons has developed in a number of countries surrounding the Arabian Peninsula. Small numbers of falcons continue to be trapped locally along the coastlines and islands of the Arabian Gulf countries (primarily Peregrines). Additional Peregrines and Sakers are trapped along the northern Saudi Coast of the Red Sea, Eastern Province of Saudi Arabia, and Bahrain (Platt 1988). Additional trapping occurs along the mountain ridges near Taif. Few Peregrines are retained for training in Saudi Arabia.

Large numbers of Sakers (300), and Peregrines (60), were shipped annually from Syria to Gulf countries in the early 1980s (Abu Ali, pers. comm.). Syrian exports presently number 60 Sakers (40 female, 20 male) and 30 Peregrines annually. A larger number are sold to individual falconers and small dealers in Syrian hawk markets. Dealers and trappers implicate a developing export trade in falcons trapped in Turkey as being responsible for a decline in the number of falcons in the Syrian trade. It was estimated that Turkey is now supplying from 150-200 Sakers annually.

The largest number of falcons come from Pakistan, 2,000 annually (Zaman, pers. comm.). Of those 1,700 were Sakers and 300 were Peregrines. Of the 1,700 Sakers less than 300 (18%) were males. Only a "small percentage were adults". "Many of the adult falcons were re-trapped Arab birds", having survived at least six months since release. They were identifiable as re-traps by having old needle holes in their lower eyelids (a custom known as seeling), or by scale wear on their tarsi from Arab jesses. Several falconers reported locating one of their Pakistan-released falcons in the possession of another falconer several years later. Many falcons which were previously identified with permanent implantable microchips by the Dubai Falcon Hospital were later found in hawk markets or were identified as freshly trapped birds from Pakistan.

Trapping locations in Pakistan include areas adjacent to the Afghanistan, China and Indian borders where topographical and prey species features serve to concentrate migrating falcons. Other major trapping areas include the Punjab and coastal margins along the Arabian Sea. "During the past 18 years the numbers of trappers and trapping stations have increased markedly, while the annual harvest has remained constant or increased".

The majority of trapped falcons are marketed to hawk dealers in the Arabian Peninsula, with the remainder being sold in Pakistan. Of the 1,700 Sakers exported from Pakistan, 300 each were destined for Kuwaiti and Qatari markets for redistribution to other Gulf countries. The United Arab Emirates received 200, and Saudi Arabia and Bahrain each received 100. The remaining 700 Sakers were purchased by falconers in markets in Pakistan. Prices have increased by 30-35% over those quoted ten years ago (Platt 1988).

Falcons trapped in Iran, Afghanistan, Egypt, Iraq, Morocco and Libya also contribute to the supply of birds for falconry. Large numbers are thought to come from Iran, while the numbers from Morocco and Iraq are thought to be negligible. Substantial numbers of Peregrines are trapped in Libya and marketed in Egypt and Syria.

Captive-raised falcons are increasingly being offered for sale in Gulf coast countries by private breeders in Europe and America. During the past seven years, captive-raised falcons admitted to the Abu Dhabi Falcon Research Hospital (ADFRH) have accounted for 53 hybrid falcons, 12 Peregrines, 5 Sakers, and 9 Gyrfalcons. Eighteen captive-raised falcons were seen in 1991-92. During the same period (1991-92) the Dubai Falcon Hospital (DFH) admitted 40 captive-raised falcons, most of which were Gyrfalcon hybrids. All of the Gyrfalcons seen in the United Arab Emirates since 1983 have been raised in captivity.

USE AND DISPOSITION

Observations of falconry practices over the past nine years have revealed some basic changes in training techniques and patterns of use. In the early years, falconers preferred the use of hatch year (HY) falcons for hunting flights, limiting the use of captive moulted adults (AHY) to that of "spotter" birds. These experienced falcons were allowed to sight or locate the quarry, then were quickly hooded to allow a hunting falcon to be released. Since physical conditioning for endurance flights was not practiced, captive moulted falcons were weak, and were regarded as inferior to the recently captured juvenile (Rample 1988). Today, most captive falcons retained for moulting are thoroughly and effectively conditioned by endurance training methods which prepare them for use as primary hunters. Among many falconers, some with large collections, these birds are now the preferred hunter. In other collections, many previously moulted birds are given their freedom after one or two years of service. In Abu Dhabi there has been an increase of 220% in the number of falcons retained for moulting. Some individuals have increased the number of moulted birds by more than 350% since 1975 (Allen 1980).

Females, due to their larger size, are preferred over males, especially when hunting the Houbara Bustard. However there is disparity in the use of males and females (females cost from seven to ten times more than males) depending on the availability of appropriate quarry and the relative wealth of the falconers in different countries. Therefore in Qatar, female male ratios are 3:1 (al Timimi, pers. comm.) In Abu Dhabi the ADFRH documents a female male rato of 18:1. By contrast the DFH documents a ratio of 3.5:1. Male Sakers are used much like Peregrines in hunting rabbits and Stone Curlews.

Other differences are noted. Whereas falconers generally prefer the easier trained HY birds over wild-caught adults, up to 5% of newly trapped falcons seen in the ADFRH were AHY birds. In Dubai a smaller number of wild-caught adults is seen and their use has been strongly discouraged.

The use of radio telemetry is widely accepted by Arab falconers. However, its use differs from western falconry, i.e. transmitters are not routinely used during training sessions, flights at released quarry or casual hunting of rabbits and Stone Curlews. As a consequence, birds are frequently lost and, because the use of telemetry in no way insures the recovery of a hunting falcon, many birds are lost during the season. Attrition in this manner may amount to 15%.

Favourite hunting falcons are increasingly being retained for moulting. Moulting facilities are characteristically large, well constructed rooms with open or subdivided housing space having sand floors. They may be cooled and ventilated by elaborate wind towers, large screened windows, or air conditioning. Falcons are most commonly moulted on the block; however, housing designs are changing, and in Dubai the trend is to free loft most birds during the moult. Some collections in the region contain as many as 200 communally moulted Sakers housed in mammoth free-flight enclosures. Most are fed a diet of *coturnix* quail and pigeon.

A number of captive breeding facilities continue to retain favourite or outstanding specimens for breeding.

Arab falconers have historically released large numbers of falcons following the end of the hunting season (Allen 1980; Platt 1988; Remple 1988). They are released in good flesh following 2-4 weeks rest with full rations. Release sites are in the desert, mountains and coastal regions of the Arabian Peninsula or, more commonly, in the Cholistan Desert in Pakistan. Numbers released in the normal migratory range vary from a few birds by some individuals to 60-70% of large collections. Some of the sheikhs and princes keep more than 200 hunting falcons through the hunting season and the annual release of more than a hundred birds is a common tradition (Slaytor, pers. comm.). Individual birds are released from time to time throughout the year as undesirable or unhealthy specimens.

MEDICAL CARE

With the exceptions noted previously, the falcon hospitals in the United Arab Emirates document many similarities in the use of large falcons and the numbers employed. The hospitals attract clientele from virtually all of the countries of the region, but in small numbers from all but the Emirates.

Dubai Falcon Hospital

The Dubai Falcon Hospital (DFH), established in 1983 by H.H. Sheikh Hamdan bin Rashid Al Maktoum, has experienced wide-spread acceptance of modern veterinary medical care and has increased its services and realised many of the stated goals (Remple 1988). The hospital is centrally located within metropolitan Dubai, and is only a short drive from Sharjah. The hospital has a peak capacity of 60 patients. Computerised medical record keeping and the use of microchip implants identified 988 different falcons during the 1991-92 season which generated over 10,000 clinical visits (10 visits per falcon), up from an average of three visits per falcon several years ago. At the same time the patient population has increased considerably. The increase is due to familiarity with and acceptance of the veterinary services provided rather than an increase in the numbers of falcons employed in the region.

The total number of falcons seen over the past two years (1990-91, 1991-92) averaged 889. Saker Falcons averaged 444. Immature/adult ratios were 1.25:1. Female/male ratios were 4.75:1. Peregrine Falcons averaged 368. Immature/adult ratios were 3.5:1. Female-male ratios were 2.7:1. Other falcon species averaged 75.

Abu Dhabi Falcon Research Hospital

The Abu Dhabi Falcon Research Hospital was established in 1985 under the sponsorship of the President of the United Arab Emirates and Ruler of Abu Dhabi, H.H. Sheikh Zayed bin Sultan al Nahyan.

The hospital is located in a sparsely populated area midway between Al Ain and the capital Abu Dhabi, 88km to the west. The hospital has a capacity of 84 in-patients. Medical and surgical services are provided free of charge. A more detailed description of the facility design, operation and admissions summary for the ADFR has been described (Riddle *et al.* 1992).

The ADFRH has experienced an increase in clinical cases from 506 in 1985 to more than 3,000 in 1992. The total number of individual falcons seen over the past two years (1990-91, 1991-92) averaged a minimum of 1,350. Saker Falcons averaged 702. Immature/adult ratios were 1.25:1. Female-male ratios were 18.1.

Peregrine Falcons averaged 553. Immature/adult ratios were 3.1:1. Female-male ratios were 24:1. Other falcon species averaged 81. Hybrids and captive-raised Peregrines and Gyrfalcons averaged 14.

Hospitalised cases amounted to a cumulative 15,208 in-patient days annually (average 41.6 falcons/day).

The ADFRH also provides additional veterinary services during hunting trips in the desert. Two well-equipped field hospitals provide medical and surgical care totalling 200 to 300 cases during each of two periods in the fall and winter months.

Stress is a primary factor in the cause of many diseases encountered in the hunting falcons of the UAE (Remple 1988). Composite stressors (phychological, physical, nutritional and environmental) weaken the immune system, leading to the development of disease. Stress-related diseases include coccidiosis, avian pox, aspergillosis, air sacculitis and associated complications from air sac worms of the genus *Serratospicula.* A falcon wasting disease of unknown etiology (possibly viral) is thought directly related to stress.

Although the use of the weighing balance for managing the weight of hunting falcons is now quite common in the UAE, many birds continue to be flown in lean condition, and most remain subject to prolonged and significant stress. Nevertheless most of the stress-related diseases are treatable by supportive measures. An exception is aspergillosis, in which virtually all of the cases result in death (some cases have been successfully treated by both hospitals). The incidence of aspergillosis varies from 5-10%. Air sacculitis and complications from serratospicula infection respond poorly to treatment. Although mortality is low, chronic respiratory disease results in profound and irreversible dyspnea. Most other frequently encountered diseases present a brighter prognosis. Bumblefoot may be treated conservatively by instituting changes in husbandry practices, while employing topical preparations and protective bandages. In complicated cases surgical procedures and foot casting provide a 90-95% cure rate. Bumblefoot surgery averaged 80 falcons per year in the two hospitals (7%). Mortality as a percentage of all cases was 8.6%. An estimated total mortality of 20% included birds which were deemed hopeless but were released to the wild by owner; treatment or hospitalisation was refused; or the patient was discharged prematurely from hospital by the owner. The severity of such cases assured a terminal outcome.

CONCLUSION

Falconry in the Arabian Peninsula is steeped in tradition but is not resistant to change. Improved falconry standards are evident throughout the region. Improvement has been sorely needed, as man and new-found knowledge emerged from the primitive past. Significant accomplishments are investments in falcon housing and quail production facilities, commitment to captive breeding and the development of new programmes, and the establishment of ultra-modern veterinary hospitals which are committed to research in addition to patient service and client education. The use of the weighing balance, improved falconry equipment, radiotelemetry and endurance conditioning of moulted falcons are additional changes which have conservation dividends. An emerging association with captive-bred falcons and the hunting success obtained by some individuals foretell a greater emphasis on these birds as experience is gained in the future.

Acceptance of modern western veterinary medicine, at first slow, has now proceeded apace with the acceptance of other emerging medical and biological disciplines. It is no longer common to encounter "firing" or "branding" scars on the heads, beaks and limbs of trained falcons, as was practiced only recently in traditional folk medicine. Sal ammoniac is increasingly shunned as a cathartic to condition fat falcons following the moult.

Problems remain with some falconers, due to a lack of dedication or stewardship, and proper concern for the health and needs of their falcons. However some educated and youthful sheikhs and devotees are demonstrating skill and vision in their pursuit of falconry. Peer pressure by role-models such as these are producing encouraging signs.

Saudi Arabia has two large regional falcon hospitals in the planning stages, promising specialty care for hunting falcons in that country (Slaytor, Algalth, pers. comm.).

These are important changes in Arab falconry considering the large numbers of falcons utilised in the Arabian peninsula. Estimates of the total number of falcons utilised are commonly quoted as 3,000, with yearly replacements for dead, lost or released birds estimated at 2,000. Our impression is that those figures should be adjusted upwards based on current information supplied by dealers, knowledgeable falconers and patient demographic data obtained by the falcon hospitals in the UAE and Qatar. A minimum of 2,750 new replacements are supplied each year, principally from Pakistan. An unknown number of falcons are trapped in Saudi Arabia annually, and total numbers maintained in falconry are difficult to assess. An increasing number of falcons are being retained for moulting; indeed, in some countries falcons are no longer released at the end of the season but are moulted by the original falconer or are passed on to others. For this reason it is estimated that total numbers of falcons retained for falconry in the region may number up to 8,600.

The maintenance of large numbers of captive moulted falcons has been brought about by changing attitudes, economic factors, availability of a proper food source and environmentally controlled moulting facilities. The practice has been aided by the adoption of endurance conditioning techniques and comprehensive veterinary care in some countries. The trend will be toward requiring fewer replacement falcons. Already the average age of the hunted falcon has risen, and in some areas the average age is five to seven years (Al Galth, pers. comm.) These are encouraging signs of measures that have direct conservation benefits. The concept of sustainable and wise use of the wildlife resource is being forced in the proper direction, even if the methods and constraints are unique.

Taking into account the number of birds removed annually from the population, 2,750, 30-50% would be retained for replacements, with 25% mortality, and an off-setting figure returned to the wild of 15% lost and 15% released. This would leave a net effect of approximately 25-75% removed from the wild, a figure which is in the range of commonly quoted mortality figures for immature raptors. The result would have a negligible effect on the wild population. Estimates of 20,000-100,000 pairs of producing Saker Falcons in the wild would result in an annual production of 60,000-300,000 young (Cade 1982), a figure that would suggest that Middle East Falconry practices are within the bounds of wise and sustainable use of the resource.

ACKNOWLEDGEMENTS

The authors wish to acknowledge their Highnesses Sheikh Zayed bin Sultan al Nahyan and Sheikh Hamdan bin Rashid al Maktoum, whose concern for the welfare of falcons, wise use of a culturally and biologically important resource and understanding of the need for continuing research have provided the foundation for these hospitals and programmes.

REFERENCES

ALLEN, M.A. 1980 *Falconry in Arabia.* London, Orbis Publishing

CADE, T.J. 1982 *The Falcons of the World.* London, William Collins Sons.

PLATT, J.B. 1988. The genus *Falco* in Arabia. Pp. 307-312 *In*: T.J. Cade (Ed.) *Peregrine Falcon Populations: their Management and Recovery.* Boise, Idaho, The Peregrine Fund Inc.

REMPLE. J.D. 1988. An overview of Arab falconry, its medical lore, and the introduction of avian medicine in the Arabian Gulf. Pp. 825-830 *.In.* T.J. Cade (Ed.) *Peregrine Falcon Populations: their Management and Recovery.* Boise. Idaho, The Peregrine Fund Inc.

RIDDLE, K.E. & J.H. HOOLIHAN 1992. Research hospital for falcons: facility design, operation, and admissions summary. *In*:P. Redig (Ed.) *Raptor Biomedicine.* Minneapolis, Mn. University of Minnesota Press (In press).

Kenton E. Riddle, D.V.M.
Director,
Abu Dhabi Falcon Research Hospital
P.O. Box 77, Abu Dhabi
United Arab Emirates

John D. Remple, D.V.M.
Director,
Dubai Falcon Hospital
P.O. Box 23919, Dubai
United Arab Emirates

Meyburg, B.-U. & R. D. Chancellor eds.1994
Raptor Conservation Today
WWGBP / The Pica Press

Status of Gyrfalcon *Falco rusticolus* Populations in the Northwest Territories, Canada

C. C. Shank and K. G. Poole

ABSTRACT

Gyrfalcon (*Falco rusticolus*) population surveys were conducted during 1982-1991 in 16 areas of the Northwest Territories (NWT), Canada, to document abundance and productivity of breeding populations. Most surveys were conducted by helicopter during the early to mid-nestling period. Fifty-four individual surveys were conducted, totalling 632 hours of helicopter survey time. Some areas were surveyed infrequently to establish nest locations and internest distances, and other areas were monitored more regularly to establish trends. Trends in the size of local breeding populations were assessed by four methods; proportional occupancy, search effort, mean internest distance, and total counts. No trends in breeding numbers or productivity were detected. Gyrfalcon breeding populations in the NWT appeared to neither increase nor decline over the 10 years of the study. Mean internest distances were smaller in regions with higher mean July temperatures and taller willow (*Salix* sp.) growth forms, corresponding to more productive habitats. Breeding population size in the NWT is estimated very roughly at 1300 pairs. Assuming equal numbers of adult breeders and non-breeders, the total adult population size in the NWT is estimated to be in the range of 5000 individuals.

INTRODUCTION

The Gyrfalcon (*Falco rusticolus*) breeds throughout the Northwest Territories (NWT), Canada, in suitable arctic and alpine tundra habitat. Interest in Gyrfalcons in the NWT increased in the 1980s as a result of attempts to develop a commercial harvest for the aboriginal Inuit and the listing of the species on Appendix I of the Convention on the International Trade in Endangered Species (CITES). Little information was available on the population biology of the Gyrfalcon. Therefore, in 1982, the Department of Renewable Resources, Government of the NWT, initiated studies to gather baseline data and establish long-term monitoring of the species.

The purpose of this paper is to summarize information on abundance and productivity of Gyrfalcon breeding populations in the NWT between 1982 and 1991.

Figure 1. Location of Gyrfalcon survey areas within the NWT, 1982-1991.

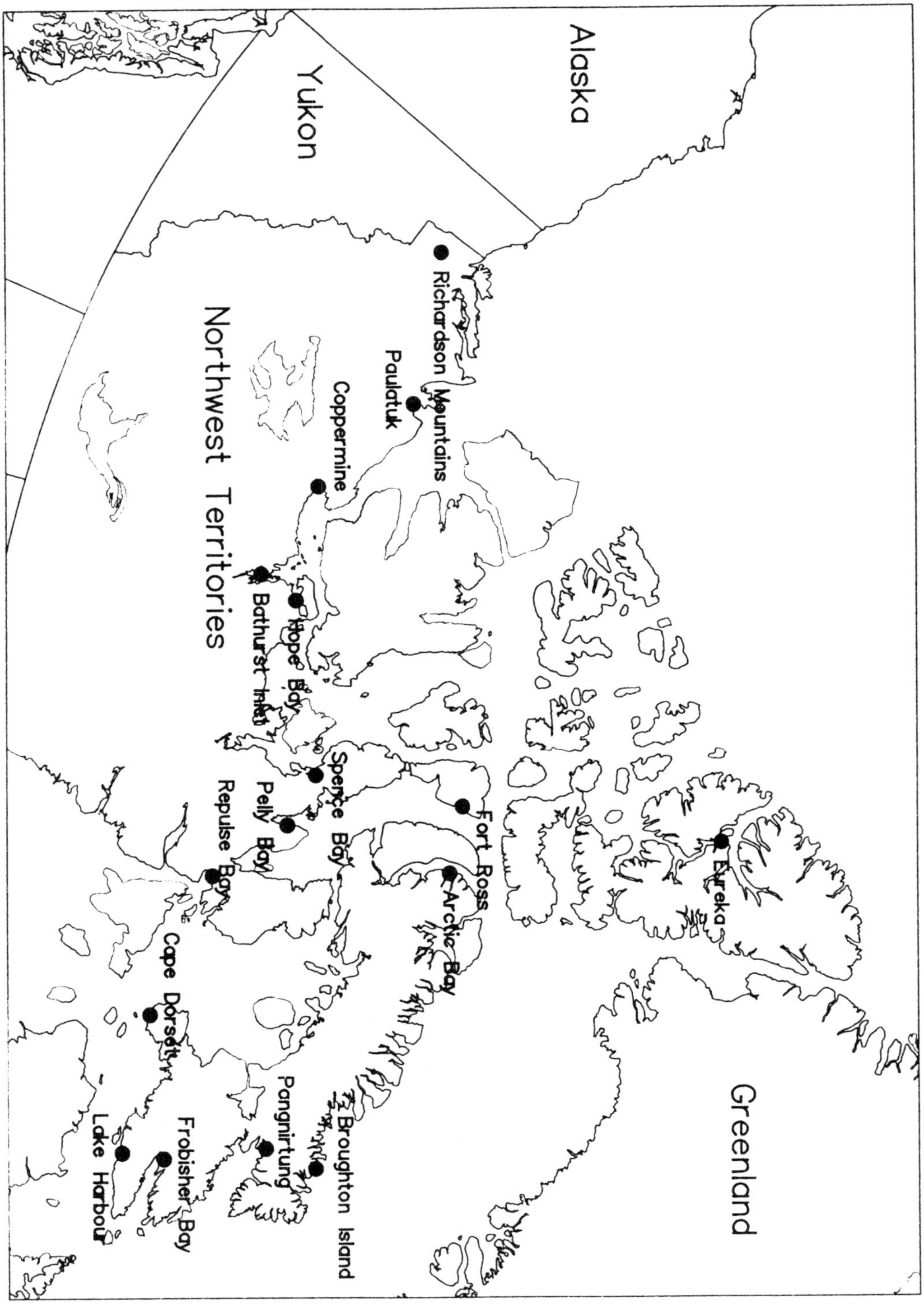

STUDY AREAS

Sixteen areas were surveyed over the course of the study (Figure 1). Because of logistical constraints, most surveys were conducted within about 200 km of a community. Study areas were chosen on the basis of suitable nesting terrain and sighting reports by naturalists and Inuit hunters.

All study areas are characterized as tundra habitat, although they encompass riverine, marine, upland and alpine habitats. For example, the Richardson Mountains study area is, strictly speaking, alpine tundra despite being north of the Arctic Circle. Sparse trees are found in protected river valleys in the Paulatuk (encompassing the Anderson, Horton and Hornaday rivers) and Coppermine study areas.

Mean July temperature (Table 1) is used as an index of climate severity during the breeding season. Habitat productivity is indexed by percent plant cover and as willow (*Salix* sp.) growth form (Table 1).

METHODS

Of the 54 surveys undertaken, 47 were done by helicopter (Bell 206B Jet Ranger) representing a total of 632 hours of survey time (Table 2). The remaining seven surveys were conducted by boat (Table 2). Helicopter surveys were done by slowly (20-60 kph) flying along all suitable nesting cliffs in the study areas. Many of the nests were entered using climbing gear, and the nestlings were banded. We leg-banded 338 (42%) of the 803 nestlings observed. Locations of occupied nests were marked on 1:250,000 topographical maps and were re-visited in subsequent surveys.

Most surveys were conducted in early to mid-July, when Gyrfalcon nestlings were of banding age (3 - 5 weeks old). The Richardson Mountains are characterized by an earlier breeding phenology and were therefore surveyed in late June. Studies of breeding population size are best done in spring by examining the number of pairs initiating courtship, because many pairs fail to produce a brood through to the advanced nestling stage and are therefore uncounted in summer surveys. However, helicopter surveys during egg-laying and incubation can cause nest abandonment (Platt 1976) and ground surveys are practical only for a few of the more accessible study areas.

Definitions used here are appropriate specifically to helicopter surveys of Gyrfalcons. The term "nest" refers to a specific nest site with features allowing it to be recognized in subsequent years. Gyrfalcon nests are generally under overhangs and are heavily marked with "whitewash" and orange nitrophilus lichens. They consist of rocky ledges, or nests built by Common Ravens (*Corvus corax*) or Golden Eagles (*Aquila chrysaetos*). In different years, individual Gyrfalcon pairs use alternative nests often on distinct but nearby cliffs. A "territory" is therefore conceptually defined as the area containing all nests used interchangeably by a pair regardless of whether the identity of the breeders changes from year to year. The term "occupied" refers to the territory when at least one adult was seen in the territory, or to the nest when it contains eggs or young. The term "productive" means that an occupied nest contained live young at the time of the survey.

Trends in the size of raptor breeding populations can be examined in a variety of manners. For intensively studied areas, the total number of pairs nesting within a defined area can be compared among years (the Total Count Method). For less detailed studies in which search effort is not intense or varies from year to year, trends can be sought using three other measures. In the Proportional Occupancy Method the proportion of previously occupied territories which are seen to support a breeding pair is assessed and compared among years. In the Search Effort Method the trend in number of occupied nests relative to the number of helicopter hours used is monitored. The mean distance between nests is compared among years for the Internest Distance Method.

Each of these methods has its pitfalls. The Total Count Method is expensive and one can never be certain that every pair has been counted. One is never sure, therefore, whether to ascribe the discovery of new pairs to an increasing breeding population or to inadequacy of previous surveys. The Proportional Occupancy Method makes assumptions regarding complex behavioural aspects of territory definition and fidelity to territory, and contains a bias toward higher occupancies early in multi-year studies. The Search Effort Method also contains an underlying bias. As the researcher becomes more familiar with the study area, the catalogue of nest sites becomes larger and search routes become more efficient, generally resulting in an increasing number of nests seen per hour

Table 1 Latitude, mean July temperature, vegetative cover class, and willow growth form at each study area.

Area	Latitude (N)	Mean July Temperature (C)[1]	Percent Cover[2]	Willow Form[3]
Richardson Mountains	68	14	>50	1
Paulatuk	69	11	>50	1
Coppermine	68	9	>50	1
Pelly Bay	69	8	25-50	3
Spence Bay	70	7	25-50	3
Repulse Bay	67	7	25-50	2
Lake Harbour	63	7	25-50	1
Frobisher Bay	64	7	25-50	2
Pangnirtung	66	7	25-50	2
Hope Bay	68	6	25-50	2
Bathurst Inlet	67	6	25-50	2
Cape Dorset	64	6	25-50	3
Fort Ross	73	5	<25	3
Broughton Island	68	5	<25	4
Arctic Bay	73	5	<25	4
Eureka	80	5	<25	4

[1] from Figure 2 in Edlund (1987), except for Richardson Mountains and Paulatuk which are taken from Environment Canada (1982).

[2] from Figure 4 in Edlund (1986).

[3] Willow growth forms are defined after Edlund (1986:Figure 5): 1 = erect *Salix* thickets > 1 m tall,; 2 = erect *Salix* thickets < 1 m tall; 3 = *Salix* capable of erect growth; 4 = *Salix arctica* dominance.

Table 2 Number of hours flown by helicopter in surveying for Gyrfalcon nests, 1982-1991. Paulatuk refers to the Anderson, Horton and Hornaday rivers.

AREA	'82	'83	'84	'85	'86	'87	'88	'89	'90	'91	Σ
Richardson Mountains	-	-	-	-	-	13	15	11	-	-	39
Paulatuk	-	-	-	-	-	*	*	*	*	*	-
Coppermine	-	17	15	18	17	12	14	15	13	14	135
Pelly Bay	17	-	-	-	-	-	-	-	-	-	17
Coppermine	26	9	-	-	-	-	-	-	-	-	35
Repulse Bay	14	-	-	-	-	-	-	-	-	-	14
Lake Harbour	11	14	-	6	-	-	-	-	-	-	31
Frobisher Bay	12	8	19	12	13	9	*	*	15	-	88
Pangnirtung	-	-	13	12	14	-	-	-	-	-	39
Hope Bay	30	21	15	12	12	10	11	14	11	16	152
Bathurst Inlet	-	-	-	10	-	-	-	-	-	-	10
Cape Dorset	13	13	-	6	-	-	-	-	-	-	32
Fort Ross	-	7	-	-	-	-	-	-	-	-	7
Broughton Island	-	-	6	-	-	-	-	-	-	-	6
Arctic Bay	-	-	-	-	-	16	-	-	-	-	16
Eureka	-	-	-	-	-	-	11	-	-	-	11
TOTAL	123	89	68	76	56	60	51	40	39	30	632

"*" denotes survey by boat.

flown in succeeding years of a multi-year study. A decline in survey efficiency may be considered evidence for a decline in the number of breeding pairs. Because areas differ in mean internest distance, the internest distance technique can be used only to compare individual areas among years.

Even in intensive studies, it is difficult to determine which nests are alternatives within a territory. We used "average linkage cluster analysis" (SAS Institute, Inc. 1988) as an objective means for differentiating territories and defining alternative nest sites. This allows rapid and automatic determination of territory clusters from location data. Cluster analysis has often been used to determine bird territories from point data (i.e., Scheffer 1987).

Cluster analysis was first done for Hope Bay, our most intensive study area (Poole and Bromley 1988). At a fusion distance of 3.75 km, the technique separated 43 nest sites into 21 territories, compared to 20 empirically known territories. The only disagreement was a case of three nests clustered mathematically into one territory, whereas in actuality there were two territories simultaneously occupied in 3 of 9 years. The two territories are on opposite sides of a large, steep outcrop where the pairs would be effectively isolated from each other. We do not expect this technique to completely mirror a reality as complex as raptor territory occupancy, but we are confident that it is superior to using the nest as the counted unit and that it is accurate enough to allow qualitative conclusions.

We make no statements about density (pairs/unit area) because of practical difficulties created by diversity of Gyrfalcon dispersion. In the Arctic, Gyrfalcon nests are often distributed in a linear fashion as a result of the distribution of both nest sites and prey availability. Nesting cliffs are most commonly a result of erosional processes along rivers and coastlines, where Gyrfalcon prey species are also most common. Gulls (*Larus* sp.), Black Guillemots (*Cepphus grylle*), and ducks are found near coastlines, whereas the shelter of river valleys allows willow growth and the associated occurrence of Ptarmigan (*Lagopus* sp.). In the high Arctic, vegetative cover declines dramatically at 50 - 100 m above sea level, effectively restricting prey to low-lying coastal strips. In lower-latitude alpine areas and low Arctic tundra, nest sites used by Gyrfalcons are more commonly distributed two-dimensionally. This results from prey being more uniformly distributed, which causes nest site availability to become a larger factor in nest distribution. Suitable nest locations tend to be numerous and evenly distributed in mountainous areas and those characterized by igneous intrusions (e.g., diabase dyke swarms). This makes it possible for Gyrfalcons to space themselves widely in two dimensions. One-dimensional measures of dispersion (distance between nests) are not easily comparable with two-dimensional ones (density). We therefore present all data in terms of internest distance although we speak of "density" in a generic sense.

We have attempted to provide a very rough estimate of the number of breeding pairs of Gyrfalcons present in the NWT using the protocol described in Appendix I. Our reasoning rests on the assumption that suitable hunting and nesting habitats must coincide. In many areas with good nesting cliffs (e.g., the Queen Elizabeth Islands), the habitat is too barren to support a Gyrfalcon prey base. Conversely, many areas (e.g., the Keewatin Barrens in the eastern portion of mainland NWT) are characterized by suitable prey but very few nest locations. We calculated average dispersion in good nesting habitat within ecological zones of the NWT, and then discounted this estimate by an intuitive estimate of the ubiquity of nest sites within these zones.

The slopes of linear regressions were tested for statistical significance by use of t-tests. Single classification analysis of variance was used to test for differences in mean brood size among geographic areas characterized by differing willow heights. Chi-square analysis was used to test whether proportions of different brood sizes differed with the amount of vascular plant ground cover in the geographic area. In all cases, the level of statistical significance was set at 0.05.

RESULTS

Stability in Number of Productive Pairs

Total Count-- The Total Count Method was undertaken only for the two most intensively studied areas, Hope Bay and Coppermine (Figure 2). At Hope Bay, the number of productive nests has varied between 9 and 12 between 1983 and 1991 (not all of the study area was searched in 1982). At Coppermine, the number of productive nests has varied more widely (4 - 13). Despite differences among years in number of productive nests, there is no evidence of trend. This suggests long-term stability in the breeding populations.

Proportional Occupancy-- In total, territories were checked 797 times, 430 (54%) were occupied and 340 (43%) were productive (Table 3). Figure 3 shows yearly changes in proportion of territories observed to be productive in three study areas over 10 years. There is no relationship between year and proportional occupancy for Coppermine ($R^2 = 0.17$, df = 7, P = 0.28) or Frobisher Bay ($R^2 = 0.07$, df = 7, P = 0.51). However, the negative trend apparent for Hope Bay is statistically significant ($R^2 = 0.41$, df = 8, P = 0.05).

The very slight negative trend at Hope Bay cannot be considered indicative of a decline in size of the breeding population. In a stable population, we expect proportional occupancy to decline in succeeding years of multi-year studies. This results from two factors. First, all newly discovered territories are necessarily occupied leading to a bias toward higher proportional occupancy early in a long-term study. Secondly, the rough categorization of territories utilized here fails to capture the complexity of actual territorial dynamics. At Hope Bay, the number of territorial pairs has remained constant despite a continuing increase in number of defined territories and identified nest sites, because pairs have shifted the geographic focus of their nesting activities. Through cluster analysis techniques, we interpret this as abandonment of an old territory and creation of a new one, whereas it actually comprises an adjustment of an existing territory. Uncritically considering human-defined raptor territories as fixed entities can lead to misinterpretation of proportional occupancy data.

Search Effort-- The number of nests observed per hour of helicopter search time has not increased or declined through time at Coppermine (P = 0.56) or Hope Bay (P = 0.08) (Figure 4). The absence of a decrease in survey efficiency suggests that there has been no decline in the number of breeding pairs in these two study areas.

Internest Distance-- Mean distance between nests varied from 5 km along a 35 km stretch of the Hornaday River near Paulatuk to 93 km at Arctic Bay (Table 4). The large increases seen at Spence Bay and Cape Dorset result from the small number of helicopter hours used in nest searches in the later years (Table 2). Internest distances from 1982 - 1991 for Hope Bay, Coppermine, and Frobisher Bay (Figure 5) do not show a significant trend in internest distance through time (Coppermine P = 0.69, Hope Bay P = 0.07, Frobisher Bay P = 0.07).

The four methods are not independent representations of population trend. However, conclusions of these four viewpoints are consistent in suggesting that there is no long-term trend in densities or numbers of breeding Gyrfalcons in the NWT.

Stability in Brood Size

Mean brood size for the 10 study years was 2.54 (n = 316) (Table 5). Mean brood size from all surveys combined did not show any trend over the 10 years ($R^2 = 0.01$, P = 0.75). There was no trend in mean brood size at Coppermine ($R^2 = 0.04$, df = 7, P = 0.61), Hope Bay ($R^2 = 0.01$, df = 8, P = 0.84), or Frobisher Bay ($R^2 = 0.25$, df = 6, P = 0.20) (Figure 6). Chi-square analysis shows that in none of the 10 years was the distribution of brood sizes different than expected from the 10 year mean (all P > 0.05). Although brood sizes have varied widely during the course of the study, there are no trends detectable.

Geographical Trends in Internest Distance

Several interrelated environmental factors are associated with differences in mean internest distance. Nests are significantly closer together in areas with higher mean July temperatures (Figure 7) (F = 19.19, df = 49, P < 0.001) and in areas with taller willows (Figure 8)($R^2 = 0.13$, df = 47, P = 0.01). This suggests, as expected, that Gyrfalcon densities are higher in more productive habitats.

Geographical Trends in Brood Size

Brood size did not vary with mean July temperature (Figure 9, $R^2 = 0.03$, df = 43, P = 0.25). Brood sizes of 3 and 4 were observed more commonly in study areas having more than 50% vascular plant cover (Figure 10) but these differences are not statistically significant ($\chi^2 = 4.69$, df

Figure 2. Number of productive Gyrfalcon nests within the Hope Bay and Coppermine study areas, 1982-1991. Survey incomplete for Hope Bay in 1982.

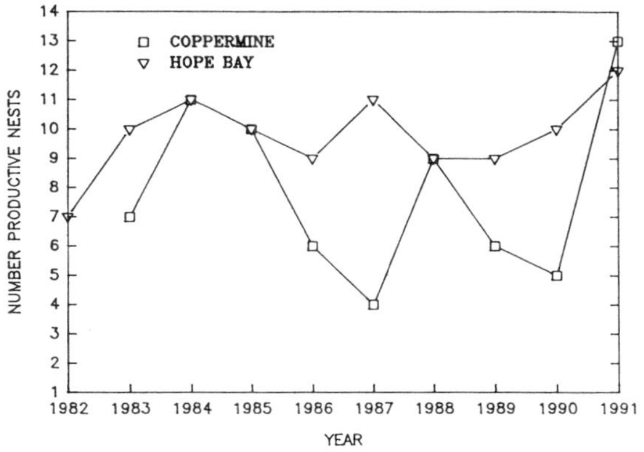

Figure 3. Proportion of known Gyrfalcon territories that were productive each year in the three intensive survey areas.

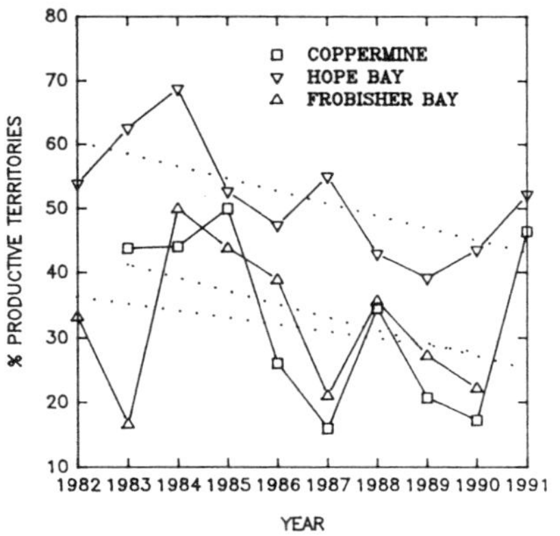

Figure 4. Productive Gyrfalcon nests observed per hour of helicopter survey within the Hope Bay and Coppermine study areas, 1982-1991.

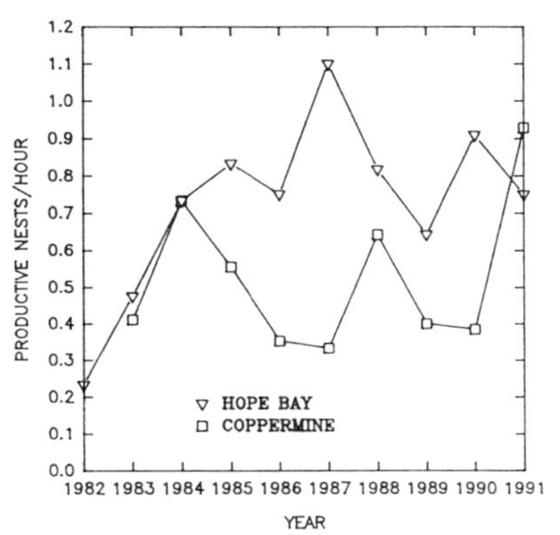

Table 3 Territories checked (C), occupied (O) and productive (P) between 1982 and 1991. Data are only from June/July production surveys. All surveys were conducted by helicopter except for the 1988-1989 Frobisher Bay surveys and all Paulatuk surveys. The Paulatuk surveys refer to the Anderson, Horton and Hornaday rivers. % O/C = the percentage of checked territories which were occupied by Gyrfalcons. % P/C = the percentage of checked territories in which a productive Gyrfalcon nest was observed.

Area	1982 C O P	1983 C O P	1984 C O P	1985 C O P	1986 C O P	1987 C O P	1988 C O P	1989 C O P	1990 C O P	1991 C O P
Rich. Mtns.	-- -- --	-- -- --	-- -- --	-- -- --	-- -- --	10 7 7	16 12 12	18 13 12	-- -- --	-- -- --
Paulatuk	-- -- --	-- -- --	-- -- --	-- -- --	-- -- --	26 19 17	8 8 8	6 5 2	32 23 6	22 20 9
Coppermine	-- -- --	16 9 7	25 13 11	20 10 10	23 8 6	25 5 4	26 11 9	29 6 6	29 6 5	28 16 13
Pelly Bay	1 1 0	-- -- --	-- -- --	-- -- --	-- -- --	-- -- --	-- -- --	-- -- --	-- -- --	-- -- --
Spence Bay	6 4 4	6 3 3	-- -- --	-- -- --	-- -- --	-- -- --	-- -- --	-- -- --	-- -- --	-- -- --
Repulse Bay	2 2 2	-- -- --	-- -- --	-- -- --	-- -- --	-- -- --	-- -- --	-- -- --	-- -- --	-- -- --
Lake Harbour	7 6 5	9 3 2	-- -- --	7 4 3	-- -- --	-- -- --	-- -- --	-- -- --	-- -- --	-- -- --
Frobisher Bay	6 2 2	6 2 1	16 12 8	16 7 5	18 8 7	19 7 4	14 6 5	11 3 3	18 5 4	-- -- --
Pangnirtung	-- -- --	-- -- --	15 11 9	11 8 5	14 7 6	-- -- --	-- -- --	-- -- --	-- -- --	-- -- --
Hope Bay	13 9 7	16 15 10	16 11 11	19 12 10	19 15 9	20 11 11	21 11 9	23 10 9	23 10 10	23 12 12
Bathurst Inlet	-- -- --	-- -- --	-- -- --	6 3 2	-- -- --	-- -- --	-- -- --	-- -- --	-- -- --	-- -- --
Cape Dorset	9 9 8	7 3 3	-- -- --	9 2 2	-- -- --	-- -- --	-- -- --	-- -- --	-- -- --	-- -- --
Fort Ross	-- -- --	1 1 1	-- -- --	-- -- --	-- -- --	-- -- --	-- -- --	-- -- --	-- -- --	-- -- --
Broughton I.	-- -- --	-- -- --	3 2 2	-- -- --	-- -- --	-- -- --	-- -- --	-- -- --	-- -- --	-- -- --
Arctic Bay	-- -- --	-- -- --	-- -- --	-- -- --	-- -- --	2 2 1	-- -- --	-- -- --	-- -- --	-- -- --
Eureka	-- -- --	-- -- --	-- -- --	-- -- --	-- -- --	-- -- --	6 3 1	-- -- --	-- -- --	-- -- --
% O/C	47	59	65	53	51	50	56	43	62	66
% P/C	40	44	55	42	38	43	48	37	45	48

Table 4 Mean internest distance for productive nests, 1982-1991. Number in parentheses = SD. Number in brackets = number of distances = number of nests - 1. Data are presented separately for the rivers (Anderson, Horton, Hornaday) comprising the Paulatuk data set.

	x internest distance in km (SD) [n]									
	1982	1983	1984	1985	1986	1987	1988	1989	1990	1991
Rich. Mtns.	-	-	-	-	-	20 (8.5) [6]	12 (7.7) [12]	12 (6.5) [11]	-	-
Anderson River	-	-	-	-	-	23 (-) [1]	-	-	-	-
Horton River	-	-	-	-	-	15 (9.6) [16]	-	11 (0.9) [3]	9 (6.4) [18]	-
Hornaday River	-	-	-	-	-	-	5* (2.5) [6]	-	23 (21.9) [4]	-
Coppermine	-	29 (13.7) [7]	22 (14.0) (12)	28 (20.7) [9]	28 (19.2) [7]	44 (21.3) [4]	21 (10.8) [10]	32 (16.1) [5]	30 (11.4) [4]	16 (9.7) [15]
Pelly Bay	[0]	-	-	-	-	-	-	-	-	-
Spence Bay	57 (10.1) [3]	91 (-) [1]	-	-	-	-	-	-	-	-
Repulse Bay	61 (-) [1]	-	-	-	-	-	-	-	-	-
Lake Harbour	20 (14.4) [5]	28 (5.0) [2]	-	24 (15.7) [3]	-	-	-	-	-	-
Frobisher Bay	[1]	[1]	31 (12.5) [11]	31 (10.3) [6]	25 (10.7) [7]	33 (20.1) [6]	34 (16.0) [5]	##	45 (24.9) [4]	-
Pangnirtung	-	-	42 (38.3) [9]	33 (34.8) [8]	32 (26.7) [6]	-	-	-	-	-
Hope Bay	16 (9.3) [7]	12 (5.7) [14]	12 (4.5) [10]	14 (9.2) [11]	13 (9.6) [14]	18 (8.9) [10]	18 (9.7) [10]	19 (14.6) [9]	19 (10.5) [9]	15 (9.4) [11]
Bathurst Inlet	-	-	-	25 (8.8) [3]	-	-	-	-	-	-
Cape Dorset	27 (21.2) [6]	45 (27.0) [2]	-	91 (-) [1]	-	-	-	-	-	-
Fort Ross	-	[0]	-	-	-	-	-	-	-	-
Broughton Island	-	-	[0]	-	-	-	-	-	-	-
Arctic Bay	-	-	-	-	-	93 (--) [1]	-	-	-	-
Eureka	-	-	-	-	-	-	56 (13.0) [2]	-	-	-

- Incomplete boat survey, data insufficient.
* - Inclusion of outlier point yields mean of 21, SD = 38.8 and n = 7.

Table 5 Frequencies of Gyrfalcon brood sizes observed at 13 study areas, 1982-1991.

	1982	1983	1984	1985	1986	1987	1988	1989	1990	1991	Total	Mean N
Brood Size	1 2 3 4	1 2 3 4	1 2 3 4	1 2 3 4	1 2 3 4	1 2 3 4	1 2 3 4	1 2 3 4	1 2 3 4	1 2 3 4	1 2 3 4	
Rich. Mtns.						0 1 1 3	0 3 5 4	1 1 7 3			1 5 13 10	3.10 29
Paulatuk						0 1 6 1	1 3 2 0	0 1 1 0	2 1 2 0	1 4 4 0	4 10 15 1	2.43 30
Coppermine		3 1 1 1	1 2 7 1	4 1 2 4	0 2 4 2	0 0 3 2	1 4 3 1	1 2 3 0	0 3 2 0	4 6 2 1	14 21 27 12	2.50 74
Spence Bay	0 0 0 1	0 0 1 2									0 0 1 3	3.75 4
Repulse Bay	0 1 1 0										0 1 1 0	2.50 2
Lake Harbour	0 1 2 0	0 1 0 0		0 1 1 1							0 3 3 1	2.71 7
Frobisher Bay		0 2 0 0	0 3 2 4	2 1 2 0	0 3 3 1	0 2 2 0	2 0 3 0	2 0 1 0	2 1 1 0		8 12 14 5	2.41 39
Pangnirtung		1 5 3 0	1 2 1 1	1 2 1 1							3 9 5 2	2.32 19
Hope Bay	0 5 1 1	1 6 2 1	0 5 3 3	2 7 2 1	1 3 2 2	2 3 5 1	1 2 4 3	2 3 4 1	0 3 6 1	1 4 3 1	10 41 32 15	2.53 98
Bathurst Inlet		0 2 0 0									0 2 0 0	2.00 2
Cape Dorset	2 0 2 0	0 3 0 0		0 1 1 0							2 4 3 0	2.11 9
Broughton Island			0 2 0 0								0 2 0 0	2.00 2
Arctic Bay						0 0 1 0					0 0 1 0	3.00 1
TOTAL	2 7 6 2	4 13 4 4	2 17 15 8	9 15 9 7	2 10 10 6	2 7 18 7	5 12 17 8	6 7 16 4	4 8 11 1	6 14 9 2	42 110 115 49	2.54 316 Σ= 803

Figure 5. Mean internest distance in the three intensive survey areas, 1982-1991.

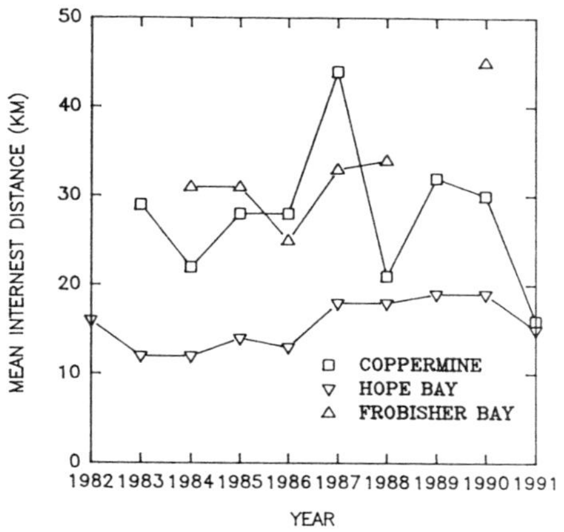

Figure 6. Mean brood size in the three intensive survey areas, 1982-1991.

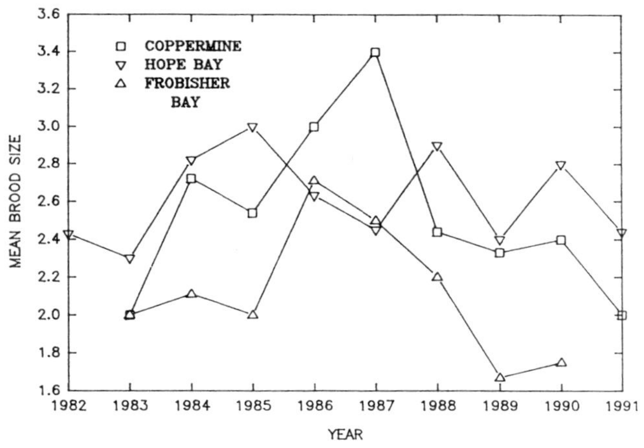

Figure 7. Annual mean internest distance relative to long-term mean July temperature.

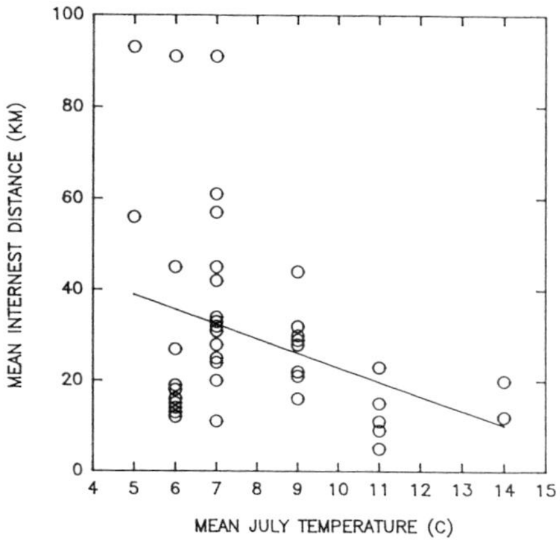

Figure 8. Annual mean internest distance relative to willow height class (Edlund 1986)

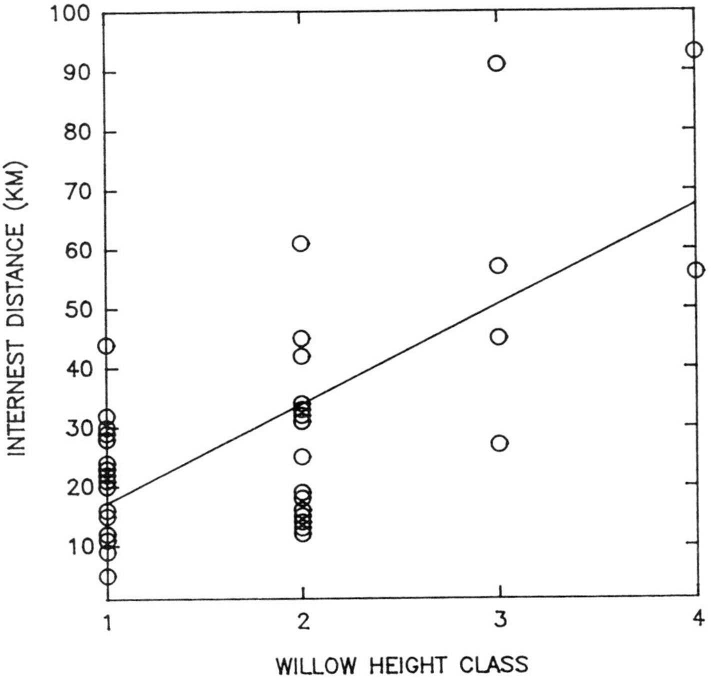

Figure 9. Annual mean brood size relative to long-term mean July temperature.

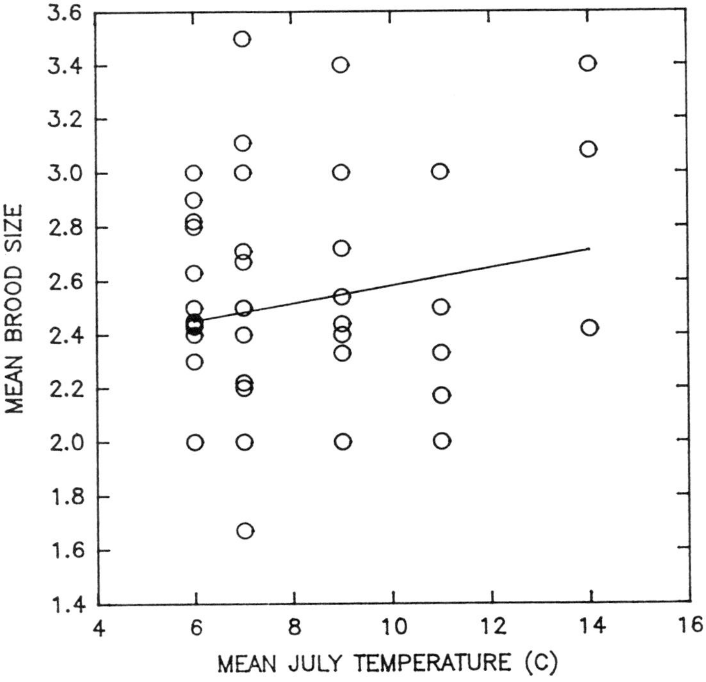

Figure 10. Percentage of total broods with 1, 2, 3 or 4 nestlings in areas of >50% or <50% vascular plant cover. Plant cover from Edlund (1986).

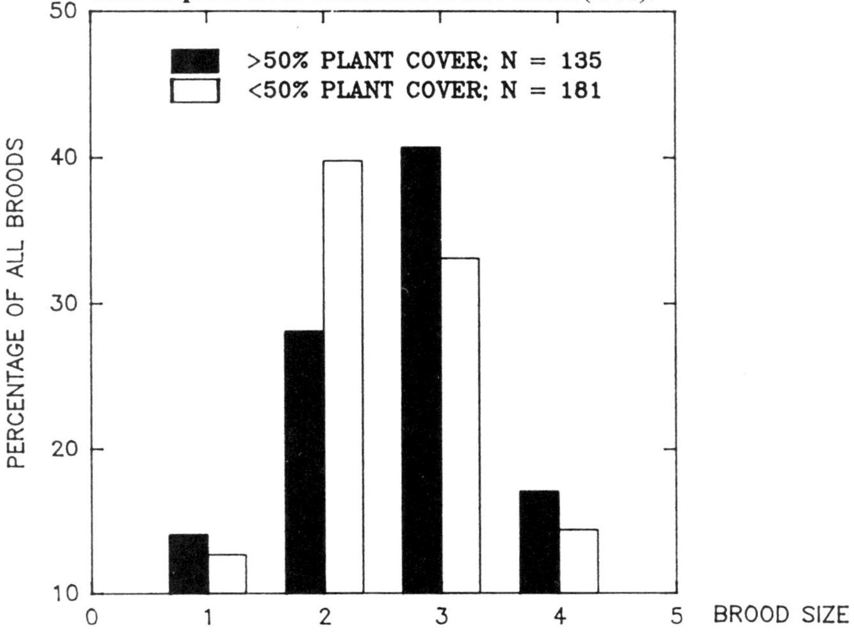

Figure 11. Male Rock Ptarmigan ground counts (1983-1989) and helicopter counts (1987-1991) at the Hope Bay study area.

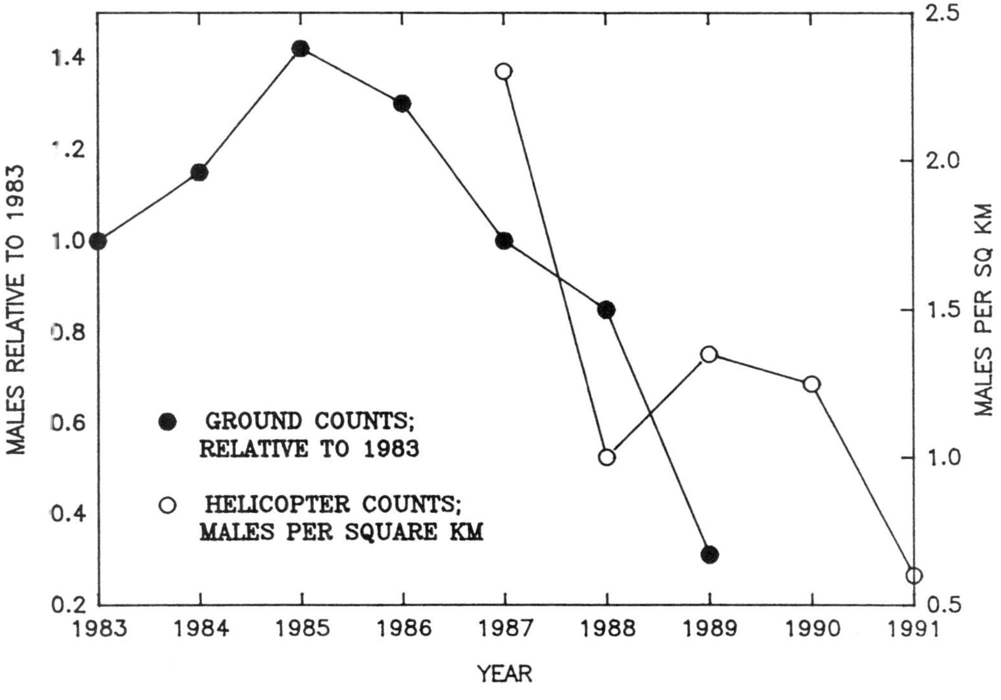

= 3, P = 0.20). Analysis of variance showed no difference in mean brood sizes among areas of differing willow height classes (F = 0.15, df = 45, P = 0.87). Environmental factors do not seem to have as great an influence on brood size as on population density. In general, the large amount of inter-year variability in mean brood size overshadows any geographical trend which might exist.

Effect of Ptarmigan Populations on Gyrfalcon Populations

Parallel data on Ptarmigan and Gyrfalcon numbers are available only for the Hope Bay study area. Rock Ptarmigan (*L. mutus*) numbers peaked in 1985 and declined through 1991 (Figure 11). Correlation coefficients of number of productive Gyrfalcon nests with indices of Ptarmigan numbers are not significant for either the ground counts (R^2 = 0.13, df = 5, P = 0.44) or for the helicopter counts (R^2 = 0.00, df = 3, P = 0.94). At Hope Bay, the number of successfully breeding Gyrfalcons is apparently unaffected by density of Ptarmigan, their primary prey (Poole and Boag 1988).

DISCUSSION

In 1975, Fyfe (1977) stated that too little data were available to assess the current population trend in Gyrfalcons in Canada. Although the four methods we employed to examine trend in breeding populations of Gyrfalcons in the NWT from 1982-1991 are interrelated to varying degrees, we suggest that taken together they indicate that Gyrfalcon populations in the NWT have neither increased nor declined in the past 10 years, although there has been considerable variability in reproductive success among years and among areas.

This long-term stability is not unexpected. Human disturbance and habitat alteration in the Canadian North have been minimal. The NWT covers 3,380,000 km^2, approximately two-thirds of which includes potential Gyrfalcon nesting habitat. Few roads exist (<500 km) within this vast breeding area, and less than 25,000 people live in 32 widely scattered communities. Access to most areas of the Arctic requires aircraft. Pesticides, which have greatly affected some raptor populations (Peakall *et al.* 1990), have likely had little or no impact on Gyrfalcon productivity (Noble and Elliott 1990). Gyrfalcon diet in many areas in the NWT is formed primarily of resident mammalian and resident or short-distance migratory avian prey (Poole and Boag 1988). In addition, available evidence suggests little or no migration in most northern Gyrfalcons (Platt 1976, Poole and Bromley 1988), so that pesticide loads are not increased on the wintering grounds.

Gyrfalcon population densities are governed by the simultaneous presence of suitable nesting locations and sufficient prey biomass. In the presence of suitable nesting habitat, Gyrfalcon breeding populations appear to be denser in regions of higher productivity as indexed by mean July temperature and willow growth form and vascular plant cover.

There was no indication of trend in mean brood size over the 10 years of the study. The variability was very wide from year to year, which masked any underlying tendency for brood size to vary with environmental productivity.

The number of productive Gyrfalcon pairs at Hope Bay has remained remarkably constant despite a continuous decline in Ptarmigan numbers from 1985-1991. We are uncertain as to how widespread this lack of a direct relationship between Gyrfalcon and Ptarmigan numbers is in other areas of the NWT. Gyrfalcon breeding populations are known to fluctuate with Ptarmigan numbers in Iceland (Nielsen 1986). The greater among-year variability in territory occupancy and breeding numbers seen in areas such as Coppermine and Frobisher Bay leads us to suspect that the Hope Bay situation may be a regional or local phenomenon.

Given the circumpolar nature of the Gyrfalcon and its use of generally isolated tundra and alpine habitats, few regional population estimates are possible or available (Cade 1982). The widespread and extensive surveys we conducted over the past decade have offered the opportunity to provide an estimate of the numbers of Gyrfalcons in the NWT. We utilized extrapolated internest distances or densities (*sensu stricti*) from our study areas, and coarsely divided the NWT into roughly similar regions of available Gyrfalcon habitat. Because many of our surveys were conducted in what was believed to be optimal habitat for the region, we have added conservative "fudge factors". We estimate about 1300 breeding pairs of Gyrfalcons for the NWT (Appendix 1). If we assume an equal number of adult non-breeders then the total adult population for the NWT is about 5000 birds.

ACKNOWLEDGEMENTS

We thank the numerous field assistants and Department of Renewable Resources staff who have assisted in the surveys conducted over the past decade. They are too numerous to mention individually, but we would particularly like to acknowledge the contribution of Robert G. Bromley in initiating the study program. That the hundreds of helicopter hours flown were completely free of accidents is a tribute to the many skilled helicopter pilots who flew "low and slow" under often difficult conditions. Funding and logistical support for this research came from the NWT Department of Renewable Resources and the Polar Continental Shelf Project, Department of Energy, Mines and Resources. We thank L.A. Wakelyn for reviewing an earlier draft of this manuscript.

REFERENCES

CADE, T.J. 1982. *The Falcons of the World.* Ithaca, New York. Cornell Univ. Press. 192 pp.

EDLUND, S.A. 1986. Plants: living weather stations. *Geos* 16:9-13.

EDLUND, S.A. 1987. Modern arctic vegetation distribution and its congruence with summer climate patterns. Pp. 84-99, *in*: Impact of climate change on the Canadian Arctic. March 3-5, 1986, Orillia, Ontario. Atmospheric Environment Service, Environment Canada.

ENVIRONMENT CANADA. 1982. Canadian Climate Normals: Temperature and Precipitation 1951 - 1980, The North - Y.T. and N.W.T. Atmospheric Environment Services. 55 pp.

FYFE, R.W., 1977. Status of Canadian raptor populations. Pp. 34-37, *in*: R.D. Chancellor, (Ed.). *World conference on birds of prey, report on proceedings, Vienna, 1975.* ICBP.

NIELSEN, O.K. 1986. Population ecology of the Gyrfalcon in Iceland, with comparative notes on the Merlin and the Raven. Unpubl. Ph.D. thesis, Cornell Univ., Ithaca, New York. 215 pp.

NOBLE, D.G., AND J.E. ELLIOTT. 1990. Levels of contaminants in Canadian raptors, 1966 to 1988; effects and temporal trends. *Can. Field-Nat.* 104:222-243.

PEAKALL, D.B., D.G. NOBLE, J.E. ELLIOTT, J.D. SOMERS, AND G. ERICKSON. 1990. Environmental contaminants in Canadian Peregrine Falcons, *Falco peregrinus:* a toxicological assessment. *Can. Field-Nat.* 104:244-254.

PLATT, J.B. 1976. Gyrfalcon nest site selection and winter activity in the western Canadian arctic. *Can. Field-Nat.* 90:338-345.

POOLE, K.G., AND D.A. BOAG. 1988. Ecology of Gyrfalcons, *Falco rusticolus*, in the central Canadian Arctic: diet and feeding behaviour. *Can. J. Zool.* 66:334-344.

POOLE, K.G., AND R.G. BROMLEY. 1988. Natural history of the Gyrfalcon in the central Canadian Arctic. *Arctic* 41:31-38.

SAS INSTITUTE, INC. 1988. SAS/STAT user guide, release 6.03 edition. SAS Institute, Inc., Cary, North Carolina. 1028 pp.

SCHEFFER, M. 1987. An automated method for estimating the number of bird territories from an observation map. *Ardea* 75:231-236.

C.C. Shank and K.G. Poole
Department of Renewable Resources
Government of the Northwest Territories
Yellowknife, NT
Canada X1A 2L9

APPENDIX 1

ESTIMATING NUMBERS OF GYRFALCONS IN THE NORTHWEST TERRITORIES

QUEEN ELIZABETH ISLANDS

Gyrfalcons will be limited to coastlines and major river valleys. Measured internest distance is about 75 km. There are about 17,000 km of coastline in the Queen Elizabeth Islands if one smooths out major irregularities. Most does not contain reasonable habitat. Assume that density estimates are 5 times average coastal density. Accordingly, we estimate 1 pair for every 375 km of coast or a total estimate for the Queen Elizabeth Islands of 45 pairs.

LOW ARCTIC ISLANDS

Gyrfalcons will be limited to the coastlines and major rivers although not as strictly as in the high arctic islands. Measured internest distance is about 50 km. There are about 26,000 km of low arctic island coastline if one smooths out major irregularities. Most will not contain reasonable habitat. Assume that density estimates are 3 times average coastal density. Accordingly, we estimate about 1 pair per 150 km of coastline or 175 pairs for the Low Arctic Islands.

MAINLAND COAST

Assume that Gyrfalcons will be at high density along a 20 km wide strip of habitat along the coastline. At best, densities approach 1 pair per 175 km^2. There are about 8500 km of arctic mainland coast north of the Arctic circle if major irregularities are smoothed. Assume that measured density is about 5 times average. Accordingly, we estimate 1 pair per 875 km^2 or 195 pairs for the Mainland Coast.

MAINLAND

We know very little about Gyrfalcons densities in the mainland. They tend to occur along rivers and to a lesser extent along lakes. We assume a density of 1 pair per 2000 km^2 over 900,000 km^2 of area north of treeline and not included in the coastal estimate. Accordingly, we very tentatively estimate 450 pairs for the mainland tundra. This is considered the weakest component of the estimate.

MACKENZIE AND RICHARDSON MOUNTAINS

Assume that Gyrfalcons can occur at densities of 1 pair per 350 km^2. Nest sites are not expected to be limiting. With an aerial extent of approximately 150,000 km^2, the NWT portion of the Mackenzie and Richardson mountains probably sustain a population of about 425 pairs.

Accordingly, the estimate of breeding pairs of Gyrfalcons for the entire Northwest Territories is 1300 pairs. Assuming an equal number of adult non-breeders, the total adult population size of the NWT is *ca*. 5000.

Meyburg, B.-U. & R. D. Chancellor eds.1994
Raptor Conservation Today
WWGBP / The Pica Press

Distribution, Abundance, and notes on the Breeding Biology of Gyrfalcons *Falco rusticolus* in Alaska

Ted Swem, Carol McIntyre, Robert J. Ritchie,
Peter J. Bente and David G. Roseneau

INTRODUCTION

There have been several studies of Gyrfalcons (*Falco rusticolus*) in Alaska. Cade (1960) summarized what was known of Gyrfalcon ecology in Alaska, including his own work along the Colville River on the North Slope. White and Cade (1971) further discussed the biology of Gyrfalcons nesting along the Colville River, emphasizing relationships with other cliff-nesting raptors. Roseneau (1972) studied their distribution, numbers, and diet during nesting on the Seward Peninsula in western Alaska. Bente (1981) analyzed Gyrfalcon nesting behaviour and hunting activity in the Alaska Range in south-central Alaska.

More recent observations of Gyrfalcons have expanded our knowledge of their distribution and breeding biology in Alaska. In this paper, we have provided an updated summary of information on the distribution and abundance of Gyrfalcons. Information was collected from published literature, unpublished government agency reports, discussions with field ornithologists and biologists, and field investigations of the authors. Rather than searching for every known nesting location, we focused our attention on areas where Gyrfalcons are known to breed regularly and, therefore, our search may have overlooked areas where Gyrfalcons breed irregularly or at low densities.

We also have reported on variations in productivity and population size in selected areas in northern and central Alaska. These areas (Colville River and Denali National Park & Preserve) have been surveyed regularly by the leading authors. Finally, we have briefly discussed the status of Gyrfalcons in Alaska.

REGIONAL DISTRIBUTION AND ABUNDANCE

Kessel and Gibson (1978) divided Alaska into six biogeographic regions (Figure 1). These regions are useful for characterizing the distribution and abundance of Gyrfalcons in Alaska

Figure 1. Gyrfalcon Nest Sites in Alaska

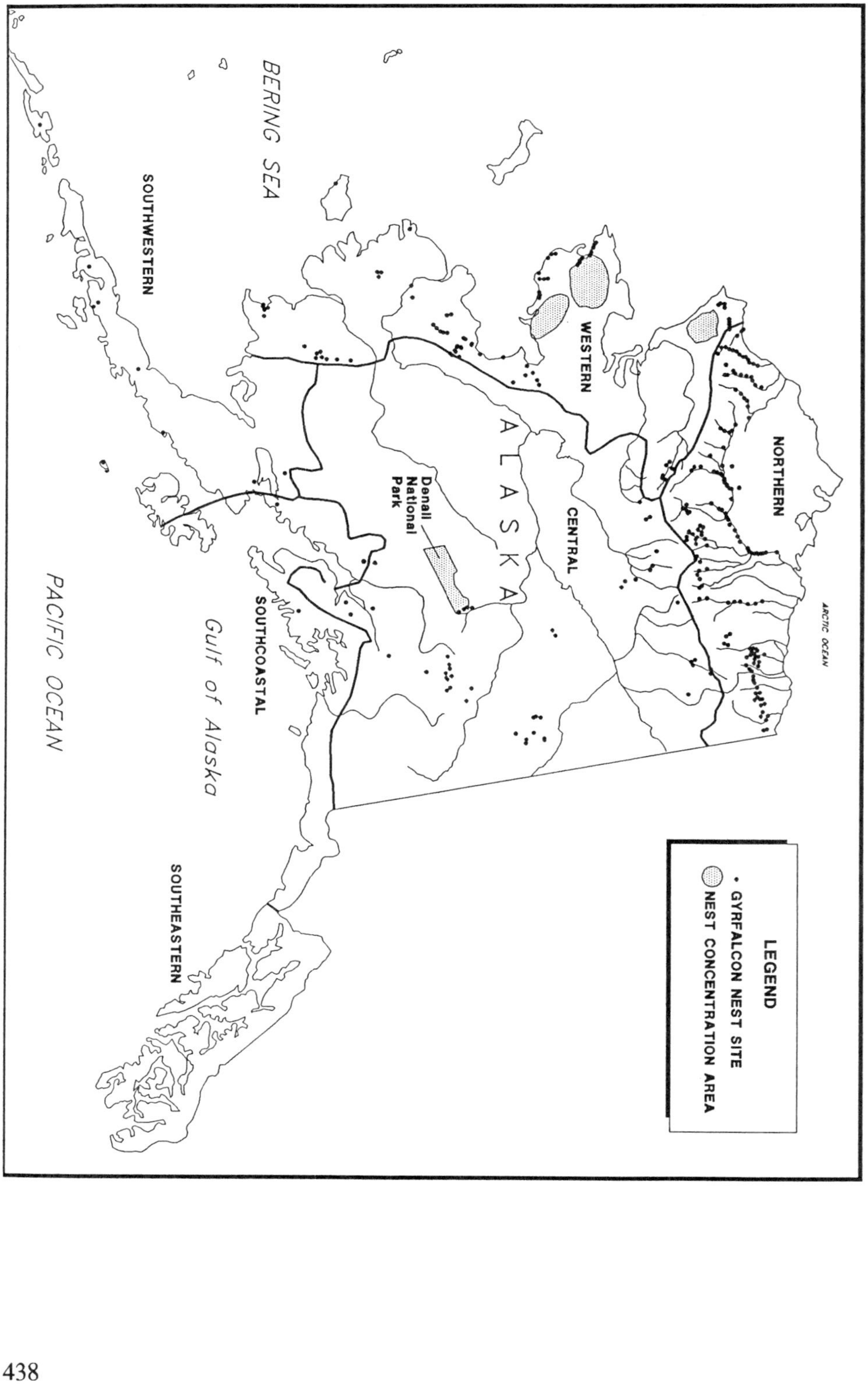

because habitat and prey availability varies greatly among them. Individual nest sites and concentrations of nest sites are shown in Figure 1. A brief description of these regions and a discussion of the distribution of Gyrfalcons in them follows.

Keep in mind that the accuracy of our Gyrfalcon estimates was compromised by several factors, including: survey technique (both aircraft and ground surveys were conducted); survey timing (many surveys were conducted late in the breeding cycle); and intensity. Additionally, pairs with active nests are more easily detected during short visits to territories than non-beeding or failed pairs. As a result, these surveys often underestimated the total number of pairs actually occupying territories.

Northern: This region encompasses the mountains and foothills of the north slope of the Brooks Range and the arctic coastal plain. The foothills and coastal plain are limited in extent in the eastern portion of this region, but are much more expansive in the central and western portions. Arctic and alpine tundra predominate. The climate is cold and relatively dry, being influenced by the Arctic Ocean to the north.

The availability of cliff nesting sites varies within this region. In the mountains of the Brooks Range, cliffs are numerous and are not confined to river and stream drainages. In the northern foothills, isolated outcrops occur, but most cliffs occur along streams and rivers. At the northern edge of the foothills and on the coastal plain, cliffs are almost exclusively formed by stream erosion. In the northern portions of this region, therefore, the distribution of nesting Gyrfalcons tends to be linear Gyrfalcon densities appear to decrease above 1000 m in the Brooks Range, although nests have been found up to 1400 m (Roseneau 1974).

Although Gyrfalcons nest on the south slope of the Brooks Range, most known sites are on the north slope. Concentrations have been found on the northern edge of the mountains, such as in the Arctic National Wildlife Refuge (Arctic Refuge), and along the southern border of the Colville River drainage. A survey in 1989 in the Brooks Range in the Arctic Refuge (the Sadlerochit and Shublik Mountains and the north side of the Franklin, Romanzof, and British Mountains) located 42 occupied territories in an area of about 7600 km^2, for an average of about one pair/181 km^2. It appeared that ptarmigan (*Lagopus* spp.) numbers were high during 1989, so the number of pairs with active nests may have reflected the relative abundance of prey. The density of one pair/181 km^2 compares to one pair/125 km^2 found in the Kilgavik area of the Northwest Territories (Poole 1987), one pair/175 km^2 in the Ogilvie Mountains in the Yukon (Barichello 1983), and one pair/113 km^2 in Iceland (Nielsen 1986). Many areas in the Brooks Range and higher foothills have not been thoroughly surveyed, so our lack of knowledge of these areas does not indicate an absence of Gyrfalcons.

Large numbers of Gyrfalcons nest along the major rivers in this region, including the Colville River (> 30 pairs in some years), the Kokolik River (11 pairs), the Kukpowruk River (12 pairs), and the Utokok drainage (8 pairs). Gyrfalcons will nest in fairly dense clusters along stretches of these rivers where cliffs are abundant: nine pairs in 38 km of the Colville; seven pairs in 40 km of the Kokolik; and nine pairs in 56 km of the Kukpowruk.

The lower foothills and coastal plain have been more thoroughly surveyed (Ritchie 1978a) than the Brooks Range and higher foothills. Suitable nesting sites are scarce in some areas, and the abundance of Gyrfalcons is limited by the number of suitable nesting cliffs. A large area in the central portion of the coastal plain is devoid of cliffs and, consequently, nesting Gyrfalcons.

Since 1981, surveys have been conducted annually on the Colville River along a 345 km section of the river between the mouth of the Etivluk River and Ocean Point. All surveys consisted of at least two boat trips through the study area, one during June, when Gyrfalcon young are 1-5 weeks of age, and a second trip during late July, when Gyrfalcons range in age from nearly fledged to competent flyers. It occasionally was impossible to determine whether territories were occcupied by single Gyrfalcons or by failed or non-breeding pairs, so territories were considered occupied if at least one Gyrfalcon showed an affinity to an area. The number of occupied territories may have been undercounted, as non-breeding and failed pairs can be difficult to detect by June and July. Additionally, many young fledged before the second nest visit and were difficult to count. As a result, production was expressed as the number of young reaching banding age, usually 3-6 weeks of age.

Gyrfalcons occupied 40 distinct territories between 1981 and 1991. The number of territories

Figure 2. Gyrfalcon Population Size and Productivity Colville River, Northern Alaska

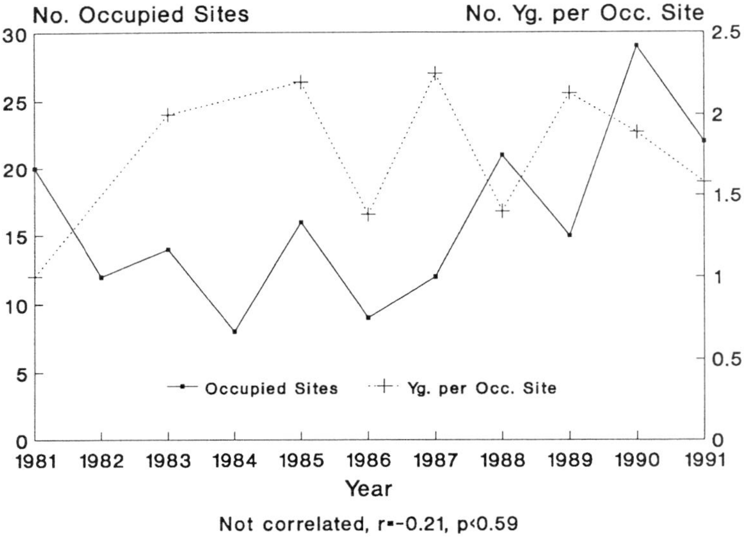

occupied each year ranged from 8 to 29, averaging about 16 (Figure 2). Twenty percent of the territories were occupied only one out of 11 years, and only 40% were occupied during 6 or more of the 11 years. Short distance movement between cliffs or territories is common in Gyrfalcons (Roseneau 1972; Poole 1987), and probably is in response to the changing availability of suitable stick nests.

The number of young reaching banding age varied from about 5 to at least 56. This variation can be partially attributed to a difference in the percent of territorial Gyrfalcons that raised young to banding age, which varied from 33 to 80% (mean of 60.5%).

The number of young produced per occupied site also varied considerably, from about 1.0 to a maximum of 2.3 (Figure 2). An increase in the number of occupied territories did not coincide with an increase in the number of young produced per occupied site. Studies in Iceland (Nielsen 1986) and the Northwest Territories (Poole 1987) showed that the number of ptarmigan in spring was the major factor affecting the number of Gyrfalcons that bred, but spring weather conditions determined the productivity of those that did breed. The lack of a correlation between population size and breeding performance on the Colville (Figure 2) may be explained by a similar phenomenon.

During previous studies (Roseneau 1972; Poole 1987), non-breeding or failed Gyrfalcons were rarely encountered at nesting territories; however, pairs occupying territories but without active nests were regularly seen on the Colville. At 151 sites determined to be occupied during the first visit to a territory, 39 (25.8%) of these sites were occupied by birds that had no active nest. In most cases it was impossible to determine whether these were non-breeders or failed breeders. Pairs that definitely attempted nesting but failed in late June or early July, however, tended to be absent from territoires during a visit in late July; Gyrfalcons were seen during one of 14 (7%) visits to territories where nest attempts had previously failed.

West: This region comprises an area along the western edge of Alaska, from south of the Brooks Range to the north side of the Alaska Peninsula. The region includes mountains up to 1365 m, rolling foothills, and flat, open lowlands. Arctic tundra is the predominant vegetation, although some small stands of boreal forest occur in the eastern portions of the region. The climate is warmer and wetter than the northern region due to the influence of the Chukchi and Bering Seas. Cliffs are relatively abundant in some mountainous areas and in some portions of the Seward Peninsula, but are rare or absent in other large portions of this region.

Several concentrations of Gyrfalcons occur in the western region. Several dozen pairs nest on the Lisburne Peninsula on sea cliffs, river cliffs, and isolated outcrops in the Delong Mountains. Another local population, numbering about 70 pairs, nests on the Seward Peninsula (Roseneau 1972) The density of Gyrfalcons on the Seward Peninsula varies from one pair/176 km^2 in areas where cliffs are abundant to one pair/1000 km^2 where cliffs are few (Roseneau 1972). The average density on the entire 43,500 km^2 peninsula was estimated to be one pair/622 km^2 (Roseneau 1972).

Gyrfalcons also nest along tributaries of the lower Yukon and Kuskokwim Rivers (White and Boyce 1978; Mindell and Dotson 1980). Between one and five pairs nest along several rivers, but the total in this area is no more than a few dozen pairs. Cliffs are rare in the Yukon-Kuskokwim Delta, but Gyrfalcons have been found on the few suitable cliffs. A few nests have been found on a small series of volcanic extrusions in the delta near the coast (B. McCaffery and C. White, pers. comm.), and one was found in the Askinuk Mountains (White and Springer 1965). Several nest sites were reported from the Goodnews Bay area, but it is unknown how many are occupied simultaneously (Bull in Cade 1960).

Gyrfalcons have been seen on several islands in the Bering Sea (Gabrielson and Lincoln 1959). They are most frequently seen during fall and winter, occurring on islands and on the pack ice (Johnson and Herter 1989). There is one reliable nest record from Nunivak Island (Ritchie 1978b).

Southwest: This region is comprised of the Alaska Peninsula and the Aleutian Islands. Tundra predominates. The climate is wet due to the influence of the Pacific Ocean to the south.

Gyrfalcons nest in southwest Alaska, although in small numbers. Ptarmigan and Arctic Ground Squirrels (*Spermophilus parryi*) occur on the Alaska Peninsula and on several of the Aleutian Islands, and nesting sites are common in at least some areas. Although wet summer weather may limit Gyrfalcon reproduction in this region, Gyrfalcons are common during the fall and winter. Apparently a considerable number of Gyrfalcons concentrate along the Alaska Peninsula during October and November, and some may migrate westward through the Aleutians (see discussion of band recoveries, below).

We located only four nest records from the Aleutians, two from Unalaska (D. Gibson, pers. comm.; L. Merrick, pers. comm.) and two from Umnak Island (C. White, pers. comm.). Probably a few dozen pairs nest along the Alaska Peninsula, but survey coverage has been limited. Two nests have been found on Tugidak Island to the west of Kodiak Island.

Central: The central region is the largest region within the state. The region contains numerous mountainous areas, including the Alaska Range, southern slope of the Brooks Range and part of the Wrangell Mountains, as well as large expanses of boreal forest and lowlands. Winters are long and cold and summers tend to be warmer and dryer than in other regions of the state.

Gyrfalcons occur mainly in the mountainous portions of this region. They nest from treeline, which usually occurs at about 700 m, to about 1200 m, although nests have been found as high as 1630 m (Frank Bird, pers. comm.). A large portion of the Alaska Range and Wrangell Mountains lies above the elevational limit of Gyrfalcons.

In the Alaska Range, the most extensive surveys have been conducted in Denali National Park and Freserve (Denali Park). In 1991, 26 pairs of Gyrfalcons occupied territories in a 5,500 km^2 area in Denali Park, for an average density of one pair/212 km^2. This density is only slightly lower than those found in the Arctic Refuge and in portions of the Seward Peninsula. Several pairs are also known to nest east of Denali Park along the Denali Highway, but extensive aerial surveys have not been conducted in this area. Most of the Alaska Range has not been surveyed, so it is unknown if the densities seen in Denali Park and along the Denali Highway are typical for the Alaska Range.

A few Gyrfalcons nest in the Yukon-Tanana Uplands, the White Mountains, the Talkeetna Mountains (T. Sell, pers. comm.), and along the south slope of the Brooks Range. However, much of this country remains unsurveyed.

Early observations of Gyrfalcons in Denali in the north central Alaska Range were recorded by Dixon (1932) and Murie (1963). More recently, observations were made from 1987 to 1991 during Golden Eagle (*Aquila chrysaetos*) surveys. Surveys were conducted from helicopters. A first check of cliffs was made in mid-May when Gyrfalcon nests contain eggs or small young, and a second check was made in late June and early July, when young are generally 4-6 weeks old.

Some territories were also visited on the ground during July. Since counts of fledglings were not possible, production is reported as the number of young reaching banding age, usually 3-6 weeks old.

Thirty-six nests have been found in Denali. Twenty-three (64%) were in nests originally built by Golden Eagles, 10 (28%) nests were on rock ledges with no sticks, and 3 (8%) were in nests built by Northern Ravens (*Corvus corax*). Among years, switching of nests between Gyrfalcons and Golden Eagles was noted 18 times. One renesting effort was observed. Gyrfalcons tended to use sites that have a southerly exposure. Twenty-seven (75%) faced either southeast, south, or southwest. Elevations of nest sites ranged from 750 m to 1350 m (n=36, $\bar{x}$ =1070).

The number of Gyrfalcons found breeding increased during the study period (See Figure 3), a result probably of both an increase in the size of the breeding population and an increase in survey efficiency as the observer became more familiar with the study area. The number of young reaching banding age per occupied territory varied from 0.73 to 1.93. As was found on the Colville River, variation in the number of occupied territories was not correlated with the number of young produced per occupied territory.

Figure 3. Gyrfalcon Population Size and Productivity Denali Park, Central Alaska

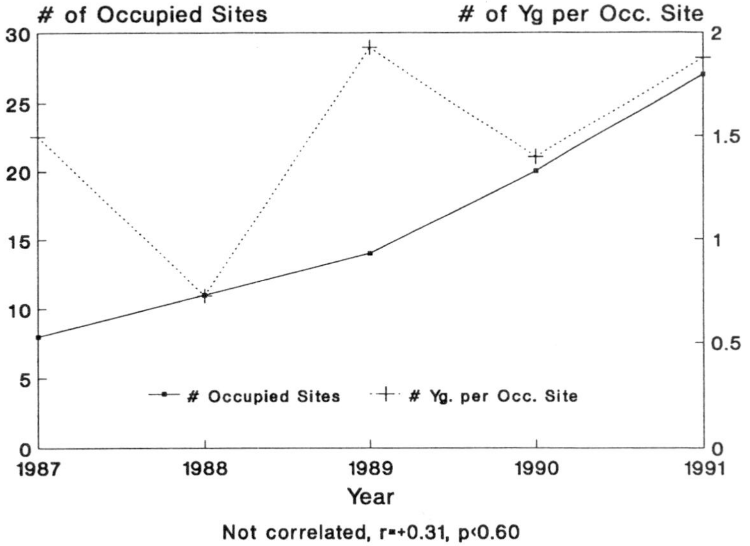

Southcoastal and Southeast: These two regions border the Gulf of Alaska and Pacific Ocean. Most of the region is forested, but some open country occurs in alpine areas, coastal flats, and river deltas. The climate in these regions is more temperate, and coastal areas are extremely wet.

Gyrfalcons are very uncommon nesters throughout the Southcoastal and Southeastern regions. A few nest sites are known from the Chugach Mountains (T. Sell, pers. comm.), but probably no more than a few dozen pairs nest throughout both regions. Gyrfalcons are seen regularly in several coastal areas during the fall and winter, and from 1-3 Gyrfalcons usually winter in Anchorage, feeding on feral rock doves and waterfowl.

Banding Recoveries: To date, 458 Gyrfalcons have been banded in Alaska. Five banded Gyrfalcons have been recovered, providing information about movements within and out of the state: two were recovered within a few months of banding within 50 km of the banding location; one banded as a nestling on the Kivalina River in northwestern Alaska was recovered in December of the same year on the Beaufort Sea coast 40 km northwest of Prudhoe Bay; one banded as a nestling at Summit Lake in the Alaska Range was recovered in winter 1 1/2 years later at Kamloops,

British Columbia; and one banded as a nestling on the Seward Peninsula was recovered in January of its first winter on the Kamchatka Peninsula in Asia. In addition, one banded as a nestling in the Yukon Territory, Canada was recovered near Kotzebue, Alaska, during August of the following year.

SUMMARY AND CONCLUSIONS

In summary, Gyrfalcons are most common in northern Alaska, in portions of the western region, most notably the Seward and Lisburne Peninsulas, and in the Alaska Range. Densities up to about one pair/200 km^2 have been found in each of these areas. However, densities are much lower throughout most of the Gyrfalcon's range in Alaska, and Gyrfalcons are absent as nesters from large areas of the state.

Cade (1960) originally estimated the Alaska population at 200-300 pairs, and Roseneau (1974) later revised that estimate upwards to 300-500 pairs. Since then, it has been found that densities are higher in the northern foothills of the Brooks Range and in the Alaska Range than was previously thought. Based upon current knowledge, we now believe that between 375 and 635 pairs of Gyrfalcons nest in Alaska. This compares to an estimate of 700 to 800 breeding pairs in the neighbouring Yukon Territory (Bromley 1987; Mossop this volume).

Studies aimed at detecting long-term changes in the status of Alaska's Gyrfalcons have not been conducted. However, most of the Gyrfalcon's range in Alaska remains unaltered by man, and no factors significantly affecting their status have been identified. Exposure to organochlorine pesticides was limited, and reproduction was apparently never affected (Cade *et al.* 1971; Walker 1977). Harvest of Gyrfalcons by falconers is restricted to Alaska residents only, and the annual harvest has been fewer than ten nestlings. Exploration and development of petroleum and other resources have intruded into some Gyrfalcon nesting areas, but at least in some cases, this intrusion has benefited Gyrfalcons by providing nesting substrates. Gyrfalcons have been found nesting on a variety of man-made structures, including the trans-Alaska oil pipeline (Ritchie 1991), gold dredges, and sluice boxes (White and Roseneau 1970). Development is often accompanied by new roads, however, increasing access to remote areas. This increases the potential for disturbance of Gyrfalcons during the nesting season. Addionally, increased contact with humans may result in slightly greater mortality from shooting, trapping, collision with automobiles, etc. At this time, however, Gyrfalcon numbers in Alaska are presumably stable, and there have been no imminent threats identified.

ACKNOWLEDGEMENTS

A large number of people contributed to this effort and we greatly appreciate their contributions. So many worked with us in the field that it is impossible to name them. Many others allowed us to use their own observations, including Macgill Adams, Frank Bird, Mike Britten, Chris Dau, Bob Dittrick, Terry Doyle, Dan Gibson, Bob Gill, Jeff Hughes, Brian McCaffery, Lee Merrick, Tim Sell, Shelly Swanson, Bill Taylor, and Ann Wildman. Tom Cade and Clayton White provided suggestions on a draft of this paper. Skip Ambrose initiated a great deal of the field work reported on, and encouraged and supported the writing of this paper.

REFERENCES

BARICHELLO, N. 1983. Selection of nest sites by Gyrfalcons (*Falco rusticolus*). Unpubl. M.S. Thesis, Univ. of British Columbia, Vancouver.

BENTE, P.J. 1981. Nesting behavior and hunting activities of the Gyrfalcon (*Falco rusticolus*) in south central Alaska. Unpubl. M.S. Thesis, Univ. of Alaska, Fairbanks.

BROMLEY, R.G. 1987. Update report on the status of the Gyrfalcon, (*Falco rusticolus*) in Canada. Unpubl. Rep. to COSEWIC, Yellowknife, Northwest Territories.

CADE, T.J. 1960. Ecology of the Peregrine and Gyrfalcon populations in Alaska. *Univ. Calif. Publ. Zool.*

63:151-290.
CADE, T.J., J.L. LINCER, C.M. WHITE, D.G. ROSENEAU & L.G. SWARTZ 1971. DDE residues and eggshell changes in Alaskan falcons and hawks. *Science* 172: 955-957.
DIXON, J.S. 1938. Birds and mammals of Mt. McKinley National Park, Alaska. Fauna of the National Parks of the U.S., Fauna Ser. No. 3. Wash. D.C.
JOHNSON, S.R. & D.R. HERTER 1989. The birds of the Beaufort Sea. BP Exploration (Alaska) Inc., Anchorage.
KESSEL, B. & D.D. GIBSON 1978. Status and distribution of Alaska birds. *Studies in Avian Biol* 1:1-100.
MINDELL, D.P & R.A. DOTSON 1980. Raptor surveys and river profiles in the Kuskokwim, Unalakleet, and Yukon River drainages, Alaska, 1979 and 1980. Unpubl. Rep. to U.S. Bureau of Land Mgmt., Anchorage.
MOSSOP, D.H. & R.D. HAYES 1992. Long term trends in the breeding density and productivity of Gyrfalcons *Falco rusticolus* in the Yukon Territory, Canada. This volume.
MURIE, A. 1963. *The birds of Mount McKinley*. Mt. McKinley Natural History Association. San Francisco
NIELSEN, O.K. 1986. Population ecology of the Gyrfalcon in Iceland, with comparative notes on the Merlin and raven. Unpubl. Ph.D. Thesis, Cornell Univ., Ithaca, N.Y.
POOLE, K.G. 1987. Aspecits of the ecology, food habits, and foraging characteristics of Gyrfalcons in the central Canadian arctic. Unpubl. M..S. Thesis, Univ. of Alberta, Edmonton.
RITCHIE, R.J. 1978A. Inventory and evaluation of, and recommendations for, cliff-nesting raptor habitat in Naval Petroleum Reserve-Alaska (NPR-A). Unpubl. Rep. to U.S. Fish and Wildlife Service, Anchorage.
RITCHIE, R.J. 1978B. Seabirds and their habitats on western Nunivak Island, Alaska. Unpubl. Rep. to U.S. Fish and Wildlife Ser., Anchorage.
RITCHIE, R.J. 1991. Effects of oil development on providing nesting opportunities for Gyrfalcons and Rough-legged Hawks in northern Alaska. *Condor* 93(1):180-183.
ROSENEAU, D.G. 1970. Numbers and productivity of Gyrfalcons on the Seward Peninsula, Alaska. In Alaska Dept. of Fish and Game Bird Segment Report Vol. XI.
ROSENEAU, D.G. 1972. Summer distribution, numbers, and food habits of the Gyrfalcon (*Falco rusticolus*) on the Seward Peninsula, Alaska. Unpubl. M.S. Thesis, Univ. of Alaska, Fairbanks.
ROSENEAU, D.G. 1974. A continuation of studies of raptorial bird nesting sites along proposed pipeline routes in Alaska. Unpubl. Rep. to Northern Engineering Services Co, Ltd, Anchorage.
WALKER, W. 1977. Chlorinated hydrocarbon pollutants in Alaskan Gyrfalcons and their prey. *Auk* 94:442-447.
WHITE, C.M. & D.A. BOYCE 1978. A profile of various rivers and their raptor populations in Western Alaska, 1977. Unpubl. Rep. to U.S. Bureau of Land Mgmt., Anchorage.
WHITE, C.M. & T.J. CADE 1971. Cliff-nesting raptors and ravens along the Colville River in arctic Alaska. *Living Bird* 10:107-150.
WHITE, C.M. & T.J. CADE 1975. Raptor studies along the proposed Susitna powerline corridors, oil pipeline and in the Yukon and Colville River regions of Alaska. Unpubl. Rep. to U.S. Fish and Wildlife Ser., Bureau of Land Mgmt., National Park Ser., Arctic Institute of North America, and American Museum of Natural History.
WHITE, C.M. & D.G. ROSENEAU 1970. Observations on food, nesting, and winter populations of large North American falcons. *Condor* 72(1):113-115.
WHITE, C.M. & H.K. SPRINGER 1965. Notes on the Gyrfalcon in western Alaska. *Auk* 82(1):104-105.

Ted Swem
U.S. Fish and Wildlife Service
1412 Airport Way
Fairbanks, AK 99701, U.S.A.

Carol McIntyre
National Park Sevice
2525 Gambell St.
Anchorage, AK 99503, U.S.A.

Robert J. Ritchie
Alaska Biological Research
P.O. Box 81934
Fairbanks, AK 99708, U.S.A.

Peter J. Bente
U.S. Fish and Wildlife Service
1412 Airport Way
Fairbanks, AK 99701, U.S.A.

David G. Roseneau
BioSystems Alaska
P.O. Box 80810
Fairbanks, AK 99708, U.S.A.

Part 6

Reintroduction of Eagles, Vultures and other Raptors

Bearded Vulture *Gypaetus barbatus*

Conveners:

J. Love & M. Terrasse

Meyburg, B.-U. & R. D. Chancellor eds.1994
Raptor Conservation Today
WWGBP / The Pica Press

Population and Range Restoration of Threatened Raptors in the United Kingdom

I.M. Evans, J.A. Love, C.A. Galbraith & M.W. Pienkowski

ABSTRACT

This paper outlines the experimental reintroduction programmes for the White-tailed Eagle and Red Kite in the UK. Both projects aim to evaluate how self-sustaining nucleus populations can be established which are capable of expanding and recolonising areas of the birds' former ranges which are at present vacant but still remain suitable. The methods of population establishment are outlined within the context of current international guide-lines. The progress made so far is reported and future plans discussed.

INTRODUCTION

The White-tailed Eagle (*Haliaeetus albicilla*) and Red Kite (*Milvus milvus*) are the only species of raptor in the United Kingdom that are threatened on a world scale. Consequently, both are priority species for conservation action in the UK as part of our commitment to maintain and enhance biodiversity through re-creation and protection of typical species assemblages.

An estimated population of 200 pairs of White-tailed Eagles inhabited the north and west coasts of Scotland and Ireland, with a possibly wider distribution earlier (Love 1988; Brown 1976). Red Kites were abundant breeders over most of England, Scotland and Wales. Intense persecution by humans eliminated White-tailed Eagles from their range in the United Kingdom and Republic of Ireland. The last recorded nesting attempt was on the Isle of Skye in 1916 (Baxter & Rintoul 1953). Red Kites also suffered from persecution in the seventeenth, eighteenth and nineteenth centuries. Their range was drastically reduced to a small area of central Wales where a small but expanding population of Red Kites survive today as a result of intensive conservation efforts (Lovegrove 1991).

The world populations of these species (11000 pairs of White-tailed Eagle; 13000 pairs of Red Kite) have also suffered from the effects of persecution, loss of habitat and pollution and are now very fragmented and restricted to relatively small areas of their former range. Within the Western Palearctic, about 80% of White-tailed Eagles breed in Norway, the Baltic coast and the Volga Delta, while 90% of all Red Kites breed in France, Germany and Spain (Gensbol 1989; Evans & Pienkowski 1991; Meyburg *et al.* 1991). Restoration of their former ranges within the UK will make a significant international contribution to safeguarding their future in the most effective way: by widening their existing world ranges, which in turn reduces the vulnerability of their global populations to unforeseen environmental threats.

Natural recolonisation by the White-tailed Eagle and the Red Kite is unlikely to restore their former breeding ranges within the UK in the foreseeable future. Hence, human intervention is essential to initiate re-establishment of population centres which will expand and recolonise naturally large areas of their former ranges which still remain suitable. Pioneering efforts to reintroduce White-tailed Eagles and Red Kites have been undertaken on a small scale in the past without achieving success (Bannerman 1956; Dennis 1968, 1969; Lovegrove 1991; Sandeman 1965). However, the current reintroduction programmes for these species recognise the need for careful consideration and planning which includes a post-release monitoring programme. In addition, strict adherence to international criteria (Green 1979) is essential to maintain standards and to demonstrate that reintroduction is a useful and appropriate conservation technique.

The IUCN criteria have appeared in various forms with slightly different wording. They can, however, be summarised as follows:

1. There should be good historical evidence of former natural occurrence.
2. There should be a clear understanding of why the species was lost to the area. In general, only those species lost though human agency and unlikely to recolonise naturally within a reasonable time scale should be regarded as suitable candidates for reintroduction.
3. The factors causing extinction have been rectified.
4. There should be suitable habitats of sufficient extent to which the species can be reintroduced.
5. The individual organisms taken for reintroduction should be from a population as genetically close as possible to that of the native population.
6. Their loss should not prejudice the population from which they are taken.

The work on White-tailed Eagles was initiated by the Nature Conservancy Council (NCC) but is now operated jointly by its successor in Scotland, Scottish Natural Heritage (SNH) and the Royal Society for the Protection of Birds. The project steering committee includes representatives from the Joint Nature Conservation Committee (JNCC), Institute of Terrestrial Ecology (ITE) and the Scottish Wildlife Trust (SWT). The experimental work on Red Kites is being undertaken by the Joint Nature Conservation Committee and Royal Society for the Protection of Birds. Both projects are long-term operations which are divided into a succession of phases, each of increasing temporal duration (Pienkowski & Love 1991; Pienkowski & Evans 1991). Monitoring each stage carefully provides the means of assessing progress and determining the level of future action required.

METHODS

Procuring release stock

Translocating individuals of a species from one part of their traditional geographic range to another is the basic principle underlying both reintroduction programmes currently underway. The translocated individuals provide the basis for population establishment, broadly emulating natural immigration. Captive breeding and the use of eggs which were unlikely to produce fledged young were also evaluated as alternatives to translocation.

The release stock of White-tailed Eagles was collected under special licence from nests in northern Norway as this is one of the nearest populations to the UK. In addition, the population in this area is relatively large (1200 pairs) and could accommodate the removal of a small number of individuals without any adverse affects. Even so, great efforts were taken to keep nests viable wherever possible by collecting single eaglets from broods of two. The collection of eaglets from the same nests in successive years was avoided in order to maximize genetic diversity in the founder population.

Procuring the entire release stock of Red Kites from within Great Britain was not possible. Even so, a very small number of chicks were obtained from Wales by removing eggs from nests that were likely to fail and these were reared artificially. However the majority of birds released (see Table

2) were donated by Swedish and Spanish conservationists from their much larger populations in Skania, southern Sweden, and Navarra and Aragon in northeast Spain. Recent evidence supports the view that there are unlikely to be any major natural genetic differences between British and Continental populations; which were a continuous population until recently (May *et al.* 1993).

The collection of young Red Kites from Continental nests was based on the experience gained from the White-tailed Eagle project and on information gleaned from work on the translocation of Ospreys in North America (Gillette & Englund 1985; Hammer & Beddow 1984; Rymon 1989; Schaadt & Rymon 1983). The same procedures were used to maintain genetic diversity in the founder population and to maintain viability of the donor nests.

Captive breeding was considered as an option to obtain birds, since it could supplement or even preclude the need for importing wild release stock. With this in mind, four (two males and two females) of the imported wild White-tailed Eagles were retained in 1976 with the view to establish a viable captive breeding stock, since captive breeding of White-tailed Eagles was possible (Fiedler 1970; Fentzloff 1977). However, the potentially lengthy and expensive commitment to captive breeding was abandoned when Norwegian conservationists agreed to guarantee further supplies of wild-bred stock for release in Scotland. The surviving captive eagles were released in 1979 after three and a half years in captivity.

Experimental captive breeding of Red Kites has been carried out in a limited way as part of the release programme. The breeding experiment was set-up in 1989, using rehabilitated birds which cannot be released back into the wild as potential breeding stock. No chicks have yet been reared in captivity but one pair laid eggs in 1992. It is apparent from the progress made so far that the captive-breeding option is unlikely to replace wild stock entirely because of the time scale involved and the relatively large number of rehabilitated birds that are required to establish a viable captive breeding stock. However, the potential of this supplementary technique is demonstrated by the careful deployment of even injured birds.

Pre-release care

White-tailed Eagles were released between 1975-85 from the island of Rum, a National Nature Reserve, situated in the heart of the White-tailed Eagles' former range in the Scottish Hebrides. In 1985, releases of young eagles were suspended to allow a period of assessment as to whether further releases were required. The Red Kite experimental reintroduction programme followed on from this work. However, as the former range of the Red Kite in the UK was much more extensive than the White-tailed Eagle, it was apparent that several population centres would need to be established over a much larger area and in different geographic regions to evaluate if and how population and range recovery could be achieved within a reasonable timescale. For this reason, two experimental release sites (one in the north of Great Britain and another in the south) were established in 1989.

Red Kites start breeding at 2-7 years old in Wales (Newton *et al.* 1989) whereas White-tailed Eagles do not start breeding until at least five years old (Love 1988). In addition, one of the lessons learnt from the White-tailed Eagle programme was that larger numbers of birds should be released over a shorter time period. Taking these aspects into account, it was decided to operate the experimental Red Kite release scheme for an initial period of five years (1989-1993), to evaluate methodology and assess future requirements. The total number of Red Kites released at each site was planned to be similar to the number of White-tailed Eagles released on Rum (see Table 1) but the release period would be much shorter.

The release methods developed were based on the falconry technique of 'hacking' but have been refined to suite the individual requirements of each project. In both schemes, specially constructed aviaries of quarantine standard were built to rear and house the birds through the mandatory 35 day quarantine period. The aviaries were situated in secluded areas offering suitable habitat; the only difference being the relative security afforded to the White-tailed Eagle release site on the Isle of Rum meant that it could be publicized widely. In contrast, the mainland localities of the two Red Kite release sites have been kept confidential to minimize unsanctioned disturbance.

At the White-tailed Eagle release site, a total of four release aviaries were constructed of wire mesh stretched over a timber framework and divided into two compartments, 4m square and 2m high; each containing an open-fronted shelter 1m square and a log perch (Love 1983, 1988). In comparison, two release aviaries were built at each Red Kite release site approximately 1km apart in England and 12km apart in Scotland. Each aviary consisted of three compartments (6m x 2.5m x 2.5m in England; 3.5m x 3m x 2.5m in Scotland) which were provided with a sheltered artificial nest platform and both natural and artificial perches. The top and front were open, but were covered with an outer layer of metal wire and inner layer of plastic wire. The wooden panelled sides proved invaluable in affording shelter from adverse weather and by acting as a screen which reduced human contact considerably, although progress could be monitored through small peepholes in the sides (Evans, Pienkowski & Dennis 1990).

The eaglets and kite chicks were placed in their quarantine aviaries in June, aged 7-8 weeks and 4-6 weeks respectively. By this age they were well feathered and able to maintain body temperature without brooding. Chicks of this age require very little 'hands on' care which reduced the risk of imprinting and conditioning to humans considerably. This was reduced further by rearing the chicks in brood sized groups (up to 4 for Kites and 2 for Eagles), although in cases where eaglets were raised separately, visual contact was maintained with their neighbours through the wire mesh of the aviary walls.

During the rearing period, human contact was limited in both projects to brief visits to provide food and to fit monitoring marks. Experience gained in the White-tailed Eagle work recognised the need to reduce human contact even further for Red Kites. This was achieved by feeding the kite chicks through small feeding hatches. The aviaries were only entered to fit monitoring marks and to return any flightless chicks that had fallen off their nest platform. In addition, a small number of visits were undertaken for detailed veterinary examinations of the Red Kite nestlings and to take blood samples for haematology tests, genetic finger printing studies and sexing.

The diet of the young eagles was designed to be representative of the variety of natural foods available in the area. It comprised fish (mainly mackerel, whiting, dogfish, herring), sea-birds (greater black-backed gull, herring gull and their chicks), hooded crow, carrion (scraps of venison, goat meat and offal), and was provided in excess to permit an average daily food intake of 550-600g (Love & Ball 1979; Love 1979). Red Kites, were given a varied diet of mammals (rabbit, grey squirrel, hare, fox, venison scraps), birds (magpie, carrion crow, jay, rook) and fish (mainly trout). Depending on the age of the Kites, the food was either minced (4-7 weeks), skinned (7-9 weeks) or given whole (after 10 weeks) and supplied daily in excess amounts. Individual consumption rates could not be calculated as the Kites were reared in groups. The first week proved the most critical for both Eagles and Kites as the birds had to adjust after collection to life with no parents, and to new surroundings. During this period it was necessary to ensure that the chicks were feeding themselves and receiving adequate food. Hand-feeding was required in some cases for a short period during the initial few days, but once the birds had settled, this was discontinued (Evans 1991; Love 1983,1988).

Prior to release, the young White-tailed Eagles were fitted with a British Trust for Ornithology metal leg ring. In addition, two Darvic colour rings were also fitted on young birds between 1975 and 1983 for individual recognition. However, this marking technique was not very satisfactory and individually inscribed, coloured patagial tags visible on the upper wing surface were fitted to the Eagles released in 1982-1985. The value of patagial tags as visual markers has already been established by Newton & Davis (1989), and based on this experience all the Red Kites released were fitted with BTO leg rings and wing tags. Radio telemetry was found to be unsuitable for White-tailed Eagles due to the remote mountainous and coastal habitat (Love 1988). In contrast, tail-mounted radio transmitters with a 50km range and 12 month life-span have proved highly successful in monitoring juvenile Red Kites.

Release into the wild

The release methods developed differed slightly as a result of the size difference between the two species. In the larger White-tailed Eagle, the aviaries proved less suitable after fledging (at 10-11 weeks old), as some nervous individuals risked injury from colliding with the aviary walls. For this reason a free-flying leash system was devised in 1976 (Love 1983, 1988) which permitted tethered flight between a wooden shelter and a perching block 5m apart. Immediately prior to release each eagle was fitted with a falconry hood in order to keep it calm for measurement and marking. The hood was then removed and the Eagle was able to fly free from a nearby rock.

The Red Kites were kept in their quarantine aviaries for up to a month after fledging (at 7-8 weeks old). Release simply involved opening a release door at the front of the aviary. During the period of captivity, damage to individual feathers was recorded in a small number of cases but occurred immediately after fledging when the flight feathers were not fully hard penned. Hence, during this stage of development it was most important to ensure that the birds were not disturbed unduly.

In the early years of the White-tailed Eagle release scheme, juvenile eagles were released singly or in pairs from the end of September to May. However, in later years the procedure was modified and releases took place much earlier in August/September and more eagles were released simultaneously (up to six). In the Red Kite project, birds were released at about 12 weeks old in batches of 3-10 individuals per day during July/early August.

Once liberated, both eagles and kites remained together in loose groups in the vicinity of the release area where several food dumps had been established for their use. On Rum, the food dumps were maintained for several months until the eagles had dispersed or proved able to fend for themselves. Some young eagles were seen to kill sea-birds within a month or so after release while many were able to locate natural carrion much earlier, demonstrating that independence could be achieved relatively quickly. The Red Kites returned to food dumps for a relatively shorter period of up to 14 days. During this period their visits became less frequent as their reliance on this food source decreased as they became independent. By the middle of August, food was no longer provided, since the birds had moved away from the release site and began to explore the surrounding countryside in their search for natural foods.

RESULTS

Number released

From 1975 to 1985, a total of 85 White-tailed Eagle chicks were imported from Norway and 82 of these were subsequently released (Table 1). The release programme was stopped in 1985 to assess the performance of the reintroduced population and to determine whether further releases were necessary. Only three died in captivity (representing 4% of the total) during the early stages of the project, one from complications arising from an injury and the others from illness or disease. Although such losses are to be expected through chance events, every effort was made to ensure that such losses were at an absolute minimum.

Table 1. Number of White-tailed Eagles released on Rum in 1975-1985.

Year	No. released
1975	3
1976	9
1977	4
1978	7
1979	6
1980	8
1981	5
1982	10
1983	10
1984	10
1985	10

The Red Kite experimental release programme has received 74 chicks from Sweden, 44 from Spain and 7 from Wales; 69 have been released in northern Britain and 53 in southern Britain between 1989-1992 (Table 2). Future plans include the release of 24 Red Kites in northern Britain and 20 in southern Britain in 1993. Only three imported Red Kites, representing 2.4% of the total, were not released into the wild. One from Sweden was rather weak when taken from its nest and later died in captivity after developing complications. The two other Red Kites originated from Spain; one died from an acute infection of Trichomonas (caught in Spain) and the other (the runt of a brood of three) was severely handicapped and is now confined to an aviary. In addition to these three birds another Spanish bird was released but was rescued five months later following damage to its primary flight feathers rendering it incapable of flight. It is now in captivity and is being used in the Red Kite experimental captive breeding programme.

Table 2. The number and country of origin of Red Kites released annually in 1989-1991.

Release site	Origin	1989	1990	1991	1992	Total
N. Britain	Sweden	6	19	20	24	69
S. Britain	Sweden	4	-	-	-	53
	Spain	-	11	11	20	
	Wales	1	2	4	-	

The sex ratios of the total number of White-tailed Eagles and Red Kites released was approximately 50:50.

Dispersal patterns after release

Monitoring of the White-tailed Eagles after release was very difficult and relied on observations gathered by project staff and from reports solicited from the public. Sightings of newly-released birds were recorded mainly on Rum, its neighbouring islands and adjacent mainland during the autumn and winter months and several localities proved to be particularly attractive, often holding groups of six or more birds (Love 1983). However, some of the records received between September-January included sub-adult birds which had returned temporarily to the release area. Some of the sub-adults were even recorded associating with the captive and recently released eagles at the release site (Love 1983, 1988).

During spring and early summer, the most distant sightings were reported and this coincided with the dispersal of the young eagles from the release area. Consequently, reports from Rum became less frequent. During the initial few years after release, White-tailed Eagles were recorded over a wide area from Shetland in the north to the Antrim coast, Northern Ireland in the south; the Outer Hebrides in the west and central Highlands in the east. Analysis of re-sighting data of individually marked birds released in 1982 revealed that as the birds matured, sightings of them became progressively concentrated to within an area of 80km radius of Rum (Table 3). It is believed that this pattern is probably true for all eagles released, although suitable data are lacking.

Table 3. Number of reported sightings received between 1982-1988 of White-tailed Eagles released on Rum in 1982.

	Number of reports						
Year	1982	1983	1984	1985	1986	1987	1988
Area							
<80km from Rum	13	23	16	7	7	15	105
Western Isles	1	1	0	2	1	1	0
Highland Mainland	0	5	0	0	0	0	0
Orkney	0	3	1	0	0	0	0
Shetland	1	4	3	0	0	0	0
Islay	0	0	1	0	0	0	0
Northern Ireland	0	0	0	4	0	0	0
% < 80km from Rum	87	64	76	54	88	94	100

Monitoring Red Kites in northern and southern Britain has allowed a great deal of information to be collected by radio telemetry on the movements of juvenile birds and details will be published at a later date. The main pattern emerging is that during September and October juvenile birds disperse away from the release area and by November they have all settled on winter ranges. Some disperse over several hundreds of kilometres, often in small groups but also as individuals. A greater proportion of the released population of Swedish origin undertake long distance dispersal (up to 1000km), presumably because they are from a more northern population. Even so, some Spanish and Welsh birds also disperse over large distances (up to 250km) in the autumn, albeit in smaller numbers. Those juveniles which do not disperse, tend to move over much shorter distances (up to 100km) and remain within northern and southern Britain throughout the winter. At this time (November-February), populations become spatially stable and individuals associate in loose groups which roost communally and move around considerably in response to changing food supplies. Those which have dispersed out of northern and southern Britain often overwinter alone.

In spring, populations become spatially unstable as winter ranges break up and new summer ranges are established. Those juveniles which had dispersed from the release areas in the previous summer/autumn return to northern and southern Britain in the following spring. However, their visits can be very brief because by early summer some have already left their summer ranges for their wintering areas outside. This movement continues through to the autumn. In southern Britain a more complex pattern is emerging since, in addition to autumn emigration/spring immigration, there is also spring emigration of overwintering juveniles out of southern Britain. However, the number involved is relatively small.

Movements of adult Red Kites can be recorded only by observation of wing tags, since radio transmitters are lost during the bird's first moult. Even so, details have been obtained on the movements of several individuals. In northern Britain, many adults now have well-established summer and winter ranges often several hundreds of kilometres apart. In southern Britain, adults that have established home ranges move around over relatively shorter distances and as a result winter and summer ranges are closer together and often coincide.

Interchange between adjacent Red Kite populations within Britain has been recorded when one juvenile of Spanish origin overwintered within the Red Kite range in Wales. Further interactions should become more frequent if populations in England and Wales continue to increase. No similar interactions through immigration or emigration are believed to have occurred in White-tailed Eagles between Scotland and Europe.

Survival/Mortality

Population estimates in 1989 suggest that as many as 46-47 of the current stock of eagles had disappeared from Scotland, a figure that is quite feasible when compared to recorded recovery rates for other large raptors (Mead & Clark 1989). However, available data on 30 tagged eagles indicate that as many as 80% survive through their first year of life, a period when a high mortality is expected (Newton 1979). Unfortunately, the present survival rates for White-tailed Eagles cannot be estimated, since the identity of most individuals cannot be ascertained because of tag loss and as a result of difficulties in reading wing tag inscriptions. Population estimates are now limited to observed numbers of known territory holding immature and adult birds, which in 1991 was 22 individuals (Table 4).

All mortality recorded for the 82 released White-tailed Eagles occurred between 1975-1987 and involved eight individuals (10% of the total released). Four died in their first year while another, held captive for two and a half years, died six months after release. The cause of death was ascertained in only two cases and illegal poisoning was involved. Another factor influencing the ability to survive was the time of release, since only 8% of birds released in the autumn were later reported dead compared to 25% of spring releases (Love 1988). In addition to the above mortality, three White-tailed Eagles reared from nests in Scotland between 1985-1992 have also been reported dead; two in their first year of life and the third in its second year. The actual number of deaths is, of course, likely to be higher than recorded as some will not have been detected.

Table 5 summarizes the survival statistics of Red Kites released in Britain. It is estimated that 48 Red Kites released in northern Britain are still alive while in southern Britain 38 individuals survive. This is equivalent to survival rates of 70% and 72%, respectively. All recorded mortality (15 individuals found between 1989-1992) occurred within the first year of life and accounts for about 11% of all birds released. Direct persecution accounts for 47% of all recorded mortality but this must be regarded as an absolute minimum as some suspected cases of persecution could not be evaluated fully because the corpses were too putrefied for analysis. No other mortality factors were identified positively, although circumstances suggest that for 13% of the recorded cases, collision with electricity wires and high speed vehicles were the probable cause of death. Only 13% of recorded mortality was considered to have resulted from natural causes. Comparative figures from Davis & Newton (1981) showed that during the period 1951-1980, 32 Red Kites were reported dead. Human persecution could be attributed to 31% of the recorded mortality, 9% to collision with electric wires/vehicles and 19% to natural causes. In their study, 41% of the corpses were too putrefied for analysis and hence the cause of death remains unknown.

Table 4. Numbers of territorial White-tailed Eagles located, number of territorial pairs and numbers of young fledged.

Year	individuals	pairs	fledged young
1981	1	0	0
1982	3	1	0
1983	6	2	0
1984	11	5	0
1985	14	6	1
1986	14	6	2
1987	19	9	3
1988	18	9	2
1989	22	9	5
1990	21	9	2
1991	22	10	7
1992	c. 20	8	7

Illegally laid poison baits targeted at foxes and crows still pose a serious threat, since White-tailed Eagles and Red Kites feed readily on carrion. Absolute mortality figures from illegal poisoning may be higher than recorded as some incidents will go undetected, although the problem tends to be more acute in dispersing birds. Illegal poisoning also affects the remaining Red Kite population in Wales: for example 19 birds were found poisoned in Wales between 1971-1991 (Cadbury 1991; Fletcher *et al.* 1991). Most of these were adults which had a high potential for survival. Efforts are now underway to alleviate this problem in the UK to reduce this mortality factor in future, although there is some concern over two juvenile Red Kites found poisoned outside the UK. Other mortality factors such as collision with wires and moving vehicles as well as natural causes are not cause for concern at the moment as they involve only a small number of birds.

Breeding of released birds

Released White-tailed Eagles first showed signs of courtship and nest building behaviour in 1982 (see Table 4). In 1983 and 1984, clutches were laid but failed in early May during periods of adverse weather. Successful breeding was achieved in 1985 when one pair reared a single chick. Since this time more eagles have acquired territory and by 1991; 15 territories had been occupied. In most years some territories were held by single unmated birds, three have supported a polygamous trio and at least 13 territories have supported a pair. In 1991, ten territories held pairs, of which successful breeding took place on four where a total of 7 young were reared. A fifth pair helped contribute to another 7 young (four broods) fledged in 1992 (Table 4).

In White-tailed Eagles, there was a wide span of age at which breeding was first attempted. This could be linked to the period spent in captivity, since three birds which spent one year or more in captivity were the oldest to attempt to breed at 8-9 years old and have not yet been successful. The youngest eagles (which were in captivity for 2-4 months) attempted to breed at only 3-4 years old and successfully reared their first chick when 5-6 years old. There is a clear trend for reproductive performance to improve with age and current evidence suggests that most territories currently occupied have not reached their full potential.

In the Red Kite experimental reintroduction project, most of the birds that can be accounted for are still too young to breed, while those approaching breeding age were released in too small numbers for any serious breeding attempts to be undertaken. However, against these odds, the first signs of courtship behaviour by birds in their first year were observed in 1991 in both northern and southern Britain. Two pairs established territories in southern Britain in which nests were built and clutches of eggs laid. Both attempts failed and the adults deserted early in incubation, probably as a result of their inexperience. In 1992, more birds attempted to breed and four pairs successfully reared nine chicks in southern Britain, whilst a single pair raised a single chick in northern Britain.

Table 5. Red Kite release and survival statistics for the period 1989-1991 are summarized for Release Site 1 and Release Site 2 in northern and southern Britain, respectively.

Year of Release		1989	1990	1991	1992	Total
Total imported	Site 1	6	20	20	24	70
	Site 2	5	13	17	20	55
Total released	Site 1	6	19	20	24	69
	Site 2	5	13	15	20	53
Whereabouts Known	Site 1	2	8	15	23	48
	Site 2	-	6	14	18	38
Whereabouts Unknown	Site 1	3	7	3	-	13
	Site 2	4	4	-	-	8
Dead: Poisoned	Site 1	1	2	1	-	4
	Site 2	1	1	-	1	3
Dead: Unknown	Site 1	-	2	2	1	5
	Site 2	-	1	1	1	3
Captivity: Dead	Site 1	1	-	-	-	1
	Site 2	-	-	1	-	1
Captivity: Alive	Site 1	-	-	-	-	-
	Site 2	-	1	1	-	2

CONCLUSIONS

The current White-tailed Eagle and Red Kite reintroduction schemes have both reached the stage where the basis for population establishment has been evaluated in terms of translocation of release stock from suitable donor populations and their successful integration into the wild at their respective release sites. This was achieved without any input from captive breeding and very little input from nest manipulation. The use of wild stock nestlings from healthy donor populations was by far the easiest option to use in this case.

Variations in the release methods used allowed some comparison of the most appropriate techniques to use. The use of release aviaries does not appear to influence behaviour leading to reduced survival or future breeding performance. However, the period in captivity did appear to be significant. It is now recognised that it is important to rear the nestlings in groups of conspecifics (see Bird *et al.* 1985) and to release them soon after fledging. Collecting the nestlings at an age where they could feed themselves and maintain their own body temperature reduced the risk of imprinting/conditioning on their human keepers, although minimum contact was maintained as a further precaution. Releasing White-tailed Eagles and Red Kites in large groups proved to be a satisfactory way of establishing nucleus populations where the majority were less likely to disperse widely, which small groups were prone to do. This could be related to the fact that both species forage and roost gregariously, especially when young, which could be significant in terms of enhancing their survival (Heredia *et al* 1991; Hiraldo *et al.* 1993). In addition, individuals that disperse are more likely to relocate other conspecifics if large groups are released together.

The establishment of nucleus populations by these reintroduction programmes confirms that the countryside is still capable of supporting Red Kites and White-tailed Eagles. In both experimental projects, the breeding performance of successful pairs is at least as good as the donor populations from which they were taken, which lends further support to the suitability of the environment in which they were released. However, both projects have yet to reach the stage where breeding populations are self-sustaining and of sufficient size to allow extensive recolonisation of the former breeding range. For this reason, monitoring the established populations will continue. This is because the number released may not be sufficient and further releases may be necessary at either existing or additional release sites. Furthermore, conditions may change over time which could either adversely affect the outcome of the reintroduction programme or could act favourably and preclude the need for further releases.

There is now sufficient population data from the White-tailed Eagle programme to investigate the viability of the current breeding population and to predict future population levels based on present breeding performance parameters. The results indicate that the current breeding population is still very small and vulnerable to chance events which could result in extinction (Green & Pienkowski unpublished). Consequently, the rate of expansion is still very slow and the analysis recommends that further releases should be undertaken in an effort to raise the current breeding population to a more reliably self-sustainable level. In the Red Kite reintroduction programme, the initial five-year period of experimental releases is scheduled to finish in 1993/4 and a further 44 juvenile birds are planned to be released in northern and southern Britain in 1993. At this stage, the future needs to be assessed and evaluated. Hence, decisions on whether to continue the release programme, the scale and duration on which it should be undertaken and the possibility of establishing other population centres in other parts of Great Britain will rely entirely on the results of this work.

REFERENCES

BANNERMAN, D.A. 1956. *The Birds of the British Isles.* Volume 5. 260-274. Oliver & Boyd, London.

BAXTER, E.V. & L.J. RINTOUL, 1953. *The birds of Scotland.* Volume 1. Edinburgh, Oliver and Boyd.

BIRD, D.M., BURNHAM, W. & R.W. FYFE 1985. A review of cross-fostering in Birds of Prey. *In* I. Newton, & Chancellor, R.D. (eds.), *Conservation Studies on Raptors,* ICBP Technical Publication 5: 433-438.

BROWN, L. 1976. *British Birds of Prey.* Colins, London.

CADBURY, J. 1991. Persecution: Birds of Prey and Owls killed in the UK, 1979-1989. RSPB/NCC, Sandy.

DENNIS, R.H. 1968. Sea eagles. Fair Isle Bird Observatory Report, No. 21, 17-21.

DAVIS, P.E. & I. NEWTON 1981. Population and breeding of Red Kites in Wales over a 30-year period. *Journal of Animal Ecology,* 50, 759-772.

DENNIS, R.H. 1969. Sea eagles. Fair Isle Bird Observatory Report, No. 22, 23-29.

EVANS, I.M. 1991. Reintroduction of the Red Kite to England and Scotland. In: B.-U. Meyburg, R.D. Chancellor, & C. Meyburg (eds.). WWGBP Newletter No. 15. 6-8.

EVANS, I.M. & M.W. PIENKOWSKI 1991. World status of the Red Kite: a background to the experimental reintroduction to England and Scotland. *British Birds,* 84, 171-187.

EVANS, I.M., M.W. PIENKOWSKI & R.H. DENNIS, 1991. Experimental reintroduction of Red Kites: report to 1990. NCC Chief Scientist Directorate commissioned research report no. 1224.

FENTZLOFF, C. 1977. Successful breeding and adoption of sea eagles (*Haliaeetus albicilla*). *In:* Papers on the veterinary medicine and domestic breeding of diurnal birds of prey, ed. by J.E. Cooper and R.E. Kenwood, Oxford, 71-91. British Falconers Club.

FIEDLER, W. 1970. Breeding of white-tailed sea eagles *Haliaeetus albicilla* at Vienna Zoo. *International Zoo Yearbook,* 10, 17-19.

FLETCHER, M.R., K. HUNTER, M.P. QUICK, M.P. & R.C. GRAVE 1991. Pesticide poisoning of

animals 1991: Investigations of suspected incidents in Great Britain. A report of the Environmental Panel of the Advisory Committee on Pesticides. MAFF Publications, London.
GENSBOL, B. (1986). *Collins Guide to Birds of Prey of Britain and Europe with North Africa and the Middle East.* Collins, London.
GILLETTE, L.N. & J.V. ENGLAND 1985. The Hennepin County Park Reserve District's Osprey Reintroduction Project. *Loon,* 57, 52-58.
GREEN, B.H. 1979. Wildlife Introductions to Great Britain. Report by the Working Group on Introductions of the UK Committee for International Nature Conservation. (1979). Nature Conservancy Council, London.
HAMMER, D.A. & T.E. BEDDOW 1984. Hacking young Ospreys to restore Tennessee Valley populations. *In* M.A. Westall (Ed.). *Proceedings of the southeastern U.S. and Caribbean Osprey Symposium.* 66-74. Sanibel, FL: TIOF
HEREDIA, B., J.A. ALONSO, J.A. & F. HIRALDO 1991. Space and habitat use by Red Kites *Milvus milvus* during winter in the Guadalquivir marshes: a comparison between resident and wintering populations. *Ibis,* 133, 374-381.
HIRALDO, F., B. HEREDIA, & J.C. ALONSO 1993. Communal roosting of wintering Red Kites *Milvus milvus* (Aves, Accipitridae): Social feeding strategies for the exploitation of food resources. *Ethology*, 93, 117-124.
LOVE, J.A. & M.E BALL 1979. White-tailed Sea Eagle *Haliaeetus albicilla.* Reintroduction to the Isle of Rhum, Scotland 1975-1977. *Biological Conservation*, 16(1), 23-30.
LOVE, J.A. 1979. Daily food intake of captive White-tailed Eagles. *Bird Study*, 26, 64-66.
LOVE, J.A. 1988. The reintroduction of the White-tailed Sea Eagle to Scotland: 1975-1987. NCC Report No. 12, Peterborough.
LOVE, J.A. 1983. *The Return of the Sea Eagle.* Cambridge University Press, Cambridge.
LOVEGROVE, R. 1991. *The Kite's Tale: The Story of the Red Kite in Wales.* RSPB, Sandy.
MAY, C.A., J.H., WETTON, P.E. DAVIS, J.F.Y. BROOKFIELD & D.T. PARKIN 1993. Single locus profiling reveals loss of variation in inbred populations of the Red Kite (*Milvus milvus*). Proceedings of the Royal Society of London series B, 251, 165-170.
MEAD, C.J. & J.A CLARK 1989. Report on bird ringing for Britain and Ireland for 1988. *Ringing and Migration*, 10, 159-196.
MEYBURG B.-U., T. MIZERA, & TH. NEUMANN 1991. Sea and Spotted Eagle Meeting in Poland. *In*: B.-U. Meyburg R.D. Chancellor, & C. Meyburg (Eds.). WWGBP Newletter No. 15. 10-12.
NEWTON, I. 1979. *Population Ecology of Raptors.* T & A.D. Poyser, Berkhamsted.
NEWTON, I. & P.E. DAVIS, & J.E. DAVIS 1989. Age of first breeding, dispersal and survival of Red Kites *Milvus milvus* in Wales. *Ibis,* 131, 16-21.
PIENKOWSKI, M.W. & J.A. LOVE 1991. The reintroduction of the White-tailed Eagle to Britain. *In:* Stroud, D.A. & Glue, D. (Eds.). *Britain's Birds in 1989/90: the conservation and monitoring review.* British Trust for Ornithology/ Nature Conservancy Council, Thetford. 120-123.
PIENKOWSKI, M.W. & I.M. EVANS 1991. Red Kite reintroduction to Scotland and England. *In*: D.A. Stroud, & D. Glue, *Britain's Birds in 1989/90: the conservation and monitoring review.* British Trust for Ornithology/ Nature Conservancy Council, Thetford. 124-127.
RYMON, L.M. 1979. The restoration of Osprey *Pandion haliaetus* to breeding status in Pennsylvania by hacking (1980-1986). *In*: B.-U. Meyburg, & R.D. Chancellor, (Eds.). *Raptors in the Modern World.* WWGBP: Berlin, London & Paris.
SANDEMAN, P. 1965. Attempted reintroduction of White-tailed Eagle to Scotland. *Scottish Birds,* 3, 411-412.
SCHAADAT, C.P. & L.M. RYMON, 1983. Restoration of Ospreys by hacking. *In*: D. Bird, (Ed.). *Biology and Management of Bald Eagles and Ospreys.* Ste Anne de Bellevue, Quebec, Harper Press.

J. A. Love
Scottish Natural Heritage
Western Isles South Sub-area Office
Tallowqulairn, Stilgarry
South Uist PA81 5rs, Scotland

I. M. Evans/C. A. Galbraith
Vertebrate Ecology & Conservation Branch
Joint Nature Conservation Committee
Monkstone House, City Road
Peterborough PE1 1JY, England

M. W. Pienkowski
Director, Life Sciences
Joint Nature Conservation Committee
Monkstone House, City Road
Peterborough PE1 1JY, England

Meyburg, B.-U. & R. D. Chancellor eds.1994
Raptor Conservation Today
WWGBP / The Pica Press

The Reintroduction of the Bearded Vulture, *Gypaetus barbatus aureus* into the Alps

Hans Frey and Maarten Bijleveld van Lexmond

ABSTRACT

Within the framework of the European Bearded Vulture Project (Frankfurt Zoological Society Nr. 832/78 and WWF Nr. 1657) started in 1978, 35 young captive-born Bearded Vultures *Gypaetus barbatus* have been released by means of the 'hacking' method since 1986. Release took place at Rauris, Austria (17 birds) as from 1986; in the Haute Savoie, France (15 birds) as from 1987; and in the Swiss National Park (3 birds) as from 1991. Three birds were reported dead and two birds had to be taken back into captivity. Young birds from all three release sites - maximum distance 600km - came into contact with each other. Up to now, pair formation has been observed in three cases, and as from 1991 nest-building as well. One additional and final release site is being planned at the French-Italian Nature Reserve of Mercantour-Argentera.

INTRODUCTION

Stemmler (1932) initiated the debate on the reintroduction of the Bearded Vulture into the Alps for the first time since the extermination of the species. His proposal to the Swiss National Park Commission as early as 1922 met, however, with resistance. Impressed by the breeding results of the Zoological Garden of Sophia (Schumann 1928; Peters 1935) Stemmler had already in those days the idea to use captive bred birds for this purpose. Also Heinroth (1927) discussed reintroduction and suggested the creation of feeding places as tourist attractions.

Following an unsuccessful attempt with wild-caught birds from Afghanistan in France (Géroudet 1979), Walter, WWF Austria, inspired by the remarkable and regular breeding successes of the Alpenzoo Innsbruck (Psenner 1976; Thaler & Pechlaner 1978), proposed an internationally co-ordinated reintroduction project, exclusively based on captive breeding. FZG (Frankfurt Zoological Society) and WWF considered this application and agreed to finance the main aspects of the Bearded Vulture project (FZG 832/78; WWF 1657/78). At an international meeting in Morges, Switzerland, in 1978 the basic guidelines and *modus operandi* were elaborated (Bijleveld 1979). Preparations for the first release of captive-born young birds demanded a long period of time. The establishment of a sufficiently large captive population in numerous European zoological gardens alone required nearly ten years and is still continuing (Frey 1988). Intensive public information as well as field research were equally important activities in this phase of the project. Yearly meetings and the Bearded Vulture Bulletin became important instruments of coordination.

RELEASING TECHNIQUE

In 1986 it was decided to carry out a pilot study at the beginning of the release phase. Based on the results of the earlier field studies (Müller & Buchli 1982) Rauris in the Hohen Tauern of Salzburg was selected as the first release site. As recently as the 1980s lone Bearded Vultures of unknown origin had again and again shown up in this region (Hummel 1982; Tratz, 1951, 1963). In line with the project's objective, i.e. the establishment of a breeding population totally independent of human intervention, a release method was chosen close to the natural juvenile development of the Bearded Vulture: hacking back with the use of eyries (Frey 1985). Nestlings are placed in imitation nests in small groups to guarantee social contact. This is done as soon as they are able to feed independently, i.e. at the age of about three months. Only young birds raised by parents or foster-parents of the same species and brought into contact with each other while still in the parental nest, are being used. Bearded Vultures breed from the month of December. Consequently, they reach the right age at about the middle of May. At the release site a team of collaborators takes over the daily care and surveillance of the nestlings. Feeding is carried out avoiding direct contact by throwing food into the nesting niche. Guarding takes place from a far-away observation point. Records are kept of all events and activities in relation to the Bearded Vultures. To ascertain an almost perfect supervising system, small radio-transmitters were fixed onto the backs of the vultures during the pilot release of 1986 (d'Oleíre-Oltmanns *et al.* 1989). The emitted signals were registered with mobile direction finders and two automatic receivers (Sonnblick, Schmittenhöhe).

The applied release technique relies on two basic principles: 1. the imprinted attachment of the young birds to the release site and 2. the supposition that the basic search for food is determined by instinctive behaviour, and that after the ending of ontogenesis, i.e. the completion of the development of in-born instincts such as to search for food and the typical bone breaking behaviour, nothing prevents the released Bearded Vulture from reaching total independence.

RESULTS

Young birds fly from their nest at the age of about four months. From this moment on, food is distributed near the nesting cliff and quickly consumed by the vultures. Already at the age of 4°-5 months additional food from the wild is being taken, especially skeletons of sheep on the nearby alpine pastures. Since from the early age of six months independence from artificially provided food resources is obtained and, at least in part, the birds start to leave the release area, artificial feeding is consequently stopped in the month of August.

As from 1986 releases have taken place at Rauris. Intensive contact occurs at times between birds of different age groups. Older Bearded Vultures accept, in most cases, the presence of younger congeners, and let these accompany them on their extended flights, returning all together to the nesting area. Apart from permanently present older Bearded Vultures, other individuals which fledged from this site also always returned at sporadic and long intervals. Thus, at certain moments, 9-10 different Bearded Vultures were observed in the valley of release in the summer months of 1990 and 1991. Individual marking is obtained by bleaching particular wing and tail feathers. These marks can be well observed on flying birds over large distances, i.e. 2km and over. They remain visible well into the second year and sometimes up to the third year. After that, identification is only possible with the help of colour bandings. These, however, are only visible under very favourable circumstances. Particularly sedentary individuals can later on also be identified through moulting gaps.

Telemetry was abandoned in 1987. The results did not meet expectations, and especially the automatic receivers did not function in those cases where Bearded Vultures disappeared or found themselves at risk.

Due to the increase in captive breeding releases became also possible in the Haute Savoie, France, as from 1987, and in Switzerland (Swiss National Park) as from 1991. A fourth and final release site is being planned in the Maritime Alps, i.e. in the joint Regional/National Park of Argentera (Italy) and Mercantour (France). These release sites are situated approx. 300km apart and cover the entire Alpine range. The fourth release site would also serve to create a link with the nearby natural population of Corsica.

Tables 1-3 give an overview of the number and sex ratio of all hitherto released juvenile Bearded Vultures. In all, 35 Bearded Vultures were released since 1986. After six years the outcome is the following:

1. Released birds found dead

Before being able to leave its nest in Haute Savoie a male died of disease in 1991.

The female "Melusine", released in 1987 in Haute Savoie, was found dead in a state of decomposition in Diemtigtal, Adelboden, Switzerland, on the 30th July 1989. The spot where found was in an avalanche gully at an altitude of 2000m. The stomach contents revealed the hoofs of a newly born chamois, while nearby the remains of some sheep were found. Thus it could be concluded that death took place in May or early June. "Melusine" fell victim to an avalanche.

The third documented case of death concerned the male "Robespierre", released in Haute Savoie in 1989. It collided with a high-tension wire and broke a wing. Subsequently trampled upon by cattle, the bird died shortly after having been recuperated.

2. Birds taken back into captivity

The female "Winnie", released as a latecomer in 1986, was little active and not very independent from the beginning. On the 18th of January 1987 it was found with its feathers frozen with ice but otherwise unhurt, in the Mölltal at a distance of 60km.

"Hubertus", a male released in Rauris in 1990, was unable to fly at the age of five months. It had also to be taken back into captivity.

3. Missing Bearded Vultures

The male "Saturnin" was released in Haute Savoie, France, in June of 1987. Having left the eyrie successfully it disappeared suddenly in mid-July, since when observations of this animal have been lacking.

In Rauris, the male "Heinz", released in 1987, was regularly observed until September. From then on no indications as to its whereabouts exist. Contrary to "Saturnin", this bird was already independent and the time of its disappearance was not unusual. Also other Bearded Vultures left the release area at this age. But of these, however, certified observations from other Alpine regions do exist.

Table 1. Bearded Vultures released at the Rauris Site in the period 1986-1991.

Year of release	Name	Sex	Origin
1986	Hans	M	Wassenaar
	Fritz	F	Innsbruck
	Ellen	F	Innsbruck
	(Winnie	F	Grunau)
1987	Heinz	M	Wassenaar
	Nina	F	La Garenne
1988	Alexa	F	Innsbruck
	Ulli	M	Haringsee [1]
	Paradatsch	F	Grunau
1989	Karl	M (?)	Haringsee
	Joey	M	Haringsee
	Colleen	F	Innsbruck
	Baselisk	F	Haringsee
1990	(Hubertus	M	Haringsee)
	Lotte	F	Haringsee
1991	Nicola	F	Haringsee
	Diana	F	Haringsee

The birds in parentheses were brought back into captivity.

[1]In the context of the Bearded Vulture Project this central breeding station is usually described as the Vienna Breeding Unit.

Table 2. Bearded Vultures released at the site in Haute Savoie, France, in the period 1987-1991.

Year of release	Name	Sex	Origin
1987	Melusine	F (d)	Wassenaar
	Saturnin	M	Innsbruck
	Marie Paradise	F	Innsbruck
1988	Balthazar	?	Wassenaar
	Melkior	?	Innsbruck
1989	Assignat	F	La Garenne
	Danton	M	Wassenaar
	Robespierre	M (d)	Haringsee [1]
	Marie-Antoinette	F	Innsbruck
	Charlotte	F	Grunau
1990	Yvan	F	Haringsee
	Robin	F	Haringsee
1991	Republic	M	Harinngsee
	-	M (d)	Haute-Savoie
1991	Savoie	F	Dortmund

(d) found dead
[1] see caption Table 1.

Table 3. Bearded Vultures at the site in Engadin, Switzerland in 1991.

Year of release	Name	Sex	Origin
1991	Settschient	M	Haringsee [1]
	Moische	F	Haringsee
	Margunet	M	Tierpark Berlin

[1] see caption Table 1.

The distribution of the remaining juvenile Bearded Vultures in the Alpine region is quite remarkable. They occupy by preference the former strongholds of the species in the range of its distribution. However, the availability of food also plays an important role in the choice of a territory, e.g. Alpine meadows with sheep, epidemics among wild animals like chamois (scabies and blindness) and areas rich in avalanches and wild animals. Rich food sources do bind Bearded Vultures sometimes for months on end to a relatively small area, while in other cases reconnaisance flights of over 100km are carried out, which take up a few days and always end in an early return to the point of departure. In only exceptional cases do such excursions lead Bearded Vultures to untypical regions. This happened to the female "Baselisk", observed on the coastal cliffs near Trieste at the age of eight months. Young birds released from all the hitherto used release areas are in contact with each other, thereby covering distances of over 600km.

In 1989 the first pair formation took place in the Hohe Tauern, Austria. The male "Ulli" and the female "Paradatsch", both released in Rauris in 1988, formed a pair in the summer of 1989, the male having taken the initiative. In the autumn the young pair started to show interest in an old Golden Eagle eyrie. They stayed together during 1990 and 1991. Almost daily the pair is to be found in the Krumltal, where it has developed territorial behaviour and only tolerates juvenile congeners in the vicinity of the nesting cliff. In September 1991 the male took possession of a Raven's nest and subsequently the pair constructed on top of this an impressive nest from branches and sheep wool. Pair formation equally took place within the French release area.*

From field experiences with 35 Bearded Vultures during six years the following conclusions can be drawn:

1. The release technique used came up to expectations and prognoses. The released Bearded Vultures distribute themselves over the whole Alpine range. Already at the age of six months they become independent of artificial feeding, and at this point in time the bone breaking behaviour starts to develop. One of the goals of the project was thus reached, being the establishment of a free-living population independent of food provided by man.

2. Behaviour towards humans varies from indifference to curiosity. Tourists on roads are ignored, while persons who find themselves at conspicuous spots in the landscape draw the immediate attention of Bearded Vultures. They overfly them to inspect at sometimes very short distances, a kind of behaviour also known from "wild" Bearded Vultures. This unusual lack of shyness for a bird of prey has, up to now, not been a disadvantage. There were no offences by hunters, proof of the acceptance and understanding on the part of the hunting community in the countries concerned. The short flight distance, on the other hand, facilitates accurate observations, sketching and photography, which in turn allows for a fairly good documentation of the reoccupation of the Alps. Aggressiveness against humans, often demonstrated by hand-reared, falsely imprinted Bearded Vultures, has never been observed.

3 Intentional disturbance or threatening of domestic grazing animals or wild ungulates, including direct attacks, were never observed. Alpine Marmots react to Bearded Vultures as they would to Golden Eagles or Griffon Vultures, i.e. they give the alarm call for aerial enemies in the shape of a long-drawn whistle. They, too, were never attacked by Bearded Vultures.

4. Interactions between Bearded Vultures and Golden Eagles show a great deal of variation. As larger predators are generally absent, Golden Eagles have some importance in providing food. Golden Eagles are extremely tolerant towards Bearded Vultures. Only rarely do attacks occur, for instance, when they try to steal presumed prey from Bearded Vultures such as skins of Alpine Marmots. On the other hand Golden Eagles are successfully attacked and driven away by Bearded Vultures in the vicinity of their nesting cliff. Likewise juvenile Bearded Vultures are defended against Golden Eagles by older individuals. In winters with little snow and therefore few avalanches, Bearded Vultures can be found in the close proximity of Golden Eagle families, making use of the left-overs. Progress of this-long term project has, so far, been encouraging. Losses were only slight in comparison to natural populations. This is probably explained by the fact that optimal biotopes are as yet not occupied by territorial breeding pairs. For that reason, it is difficult at this stage to make prognoses of the future successful development of the overall project.

**Note*: Unfortunately "Ulli" disappeared suddently in the late spring of 1992 and is supposed to have met with accidental death. "Paradatsch" is still present in the Krumltal.

REFERENCES

BIJLEVELD, M. 1979. Preface: Meeting on reintroduction of the Bearded Vulture, *Gypaetus barbatus aureus* (Hablizl 1788), into the Alps. Report of proceedings, Morges, 17-18 Nov. 1978. IUCN, Morges.

D'OLEIRE - OLTMANNS, W., U. MACK & R. BÖGEL 1989. Radiotracking of Bearded Vultures *Gypaetus barbatus* and Griffon Vultures *Gyps fulvus* in the Alps. *In*: Meyburg, B.-U. &; R. Chancellor (Eds.): *Raptors in the Modern World* WWGBP, Berlin, 345-352.

FREY, H. 1985. Die Verwilderung von Bartgeiernestlingen über Horste - Detailvorschlag zur Durchführung. Swiss Wildl. Inf. Service, Univ. Zürich, Bull. Proj. Bearded Vulture 7, 13-18.

FREY, H. 1988. Biologie, Zucht und Wiederansiedlung des Bartgeiers (*Gypaetus barbatus*). *Die Voliere* 11, 45-50.

GÉROUDET, P. 1979. Short history of the project. *In*: I.U.C.N. (Eds.): Meeting on reintroduction of the Bearded Vulture *Gypaetus barbatus aureus* (Hablizl 1788) into the Alps. Report of proceedings, Morges, 17-18 Nov. 1978, 2-6.

HEINROTH, O. 1927. *Die Vögel Mitteleuropas* II. Behrmüller, Berlin - Lichtenfelds.
HUMMEL, D. 1982. Wieder ein Bartgeier (*Gypaetus barbatus*) in den österreichischen Alpen. *Egretta* 25, 49-52.
MÜLLER, H.U. & CH. BUCHLI 1982. *Projekt Bartgeier. Vergleich von fünf potentiellen Wiedereinbrgerungsgebieten im Alpenraum.* Fornat, Zürich. 100 pp.
PETERS, H.B. 1935. Beitrag zur Brutbiologie des Bartgeiers (*Gypaetus barbatus*). *Vögel ferner Länder* 9, 2-5, 41-47, 76-79, 92-96.
PSENNER, H. 1976. Haltung und Zucht des Bartgeiers (*Gypaetus barbatus*). *Zool. Garten N.F.* 46, 293-304.
SCHUMANN, A. 1928. Über die erfolgreiche Zucht von *Gypaetus barbatus* im Königlich Zoologische Garten von Sofia. *Mitt. königl. naturw. Inst. Sofia* 1, 145-155.
STEMMLER, C. 1932. *Die Adler der Schweiz.* Hallberg &; Büchting, Leipzig.
STRAUBINGER, J. 1990. Vogelwelt im östlichen Chiemgau, Grundlagen zur Avifauna des Rupertiwinkels. Abhandlungen der Kreisgruppe Traunstein des Landesbundes für Vogelschutz (LBV) in Bayern e. V., 61.
THALER, E. & H. PECHLANER 1978. Volierenbrut und Handaufzucht beim Bartgeier (*Gypaetus barbatus aureus*): Beobachtungen aus dem Alpenzoo Innsbruck. *Gefied. Welt* 103, 21-25.
TRATZ, P. 1951. Der Bart- oder Lämmergeier ein ständiger Bewohner der salzburgischen Alpen. *Die Vogelwelt* 72, 177-180.
TRATZ, P. 1963. Ergänzendes zum Vorkommen des Europäischen Bartgeiers. *Anz. orn. Ges. Bayern* 6, 470-471.

Dr. M. Bijleveld van Lexmond,
Foundation for the Conservation of the Bearded Vulture (F.C.B.V.)
En Levremont
CH-1143 Apples
Switzerland

Dr. Hans Frey,
Institut für Parasitologie und Allgem. Zoologie
Veterinärmedizinische Universität
Linke Bahngasse 11
1030 Vienna, Austria

Meyburg, B.-U. & R. D. Chancellor eds.1994
Raptor Conservation Today
WWGBP / The Pica Press

The Introduction of Three Native Raptors into the Midwestern United States

Mark S. Martell, Harrison B. Tordoff and Patrick T. Redig

ABSTRACT

Reintroduction of Peregrine Falcons *Falco peregrinus,* Ospreys *Pandion haliaetus* and Burrowing Owls *Athene cunicularia* into appropriate areas of the upper Midwestern US were conducted from 1982 through 1990. All birds were released using hacking techniques and were banded and colour-marked. From 1982-1990, 432 captive-reared Peregrine Falcons were released from 18 hack sites in seven states. Through 1991 we had reports of 75 dead (17%), and knew of 30 territorial pairs of which 22 nested, 17 successfully, fledging 36 young. Between 1984-1990, we assisted Hennepin County Park System in the release of 87 wild-caught Osprey nestlings at six sites in East Central Minnesota. We know of two mortalities, and two males have returned to breed near their release site. From 1986 through 1990 we released 104 wild-trapped nestling Burrowing Owls at two sites in western Minnesota. Through 1991 we knew of eight mortalities (8%), and no birds were seen after the year of release.

The Peregrine and Osprey projects both seem to be successful. The lack of any known returning Burrowing Owls puts that project in doubt. However, assessment and monitoring is problematic in species where basic knowledge about dispersal and natal fidelity are poorly understood.

INTRODUCTION

Current management techniques available for endangered or threatened populations of raptors include reintroduction of individuals to parts of their former range, or the stocking of individuals to supplement declining populations. We report here on two translocations of wild young, and one programme of releasing captive-produced young. All three programmes were begun during the 1980s, and involved releasing raptors into selected areas of the upper Midwestern United States. The programmes, which involved Peregrine Falcons, Ospreys and Burrowing Owls, were run independently of each other, with separate objectives, personnel and budgets.

The Peregrine Falcon release was begun in Minnesota in 1982 and expanded into other Midwestern states beginning in 1986. Overall coordination, including chick acquisition, banding and colour-marking as well as site selection and release advice, was provided by P. Redig and H. Tordoff at the University of Minnesota. Individual hack sites were funded and managed by consortiums of public and private agencies and individuals in each state.

Osprey releases were initiated in 1984 by L. Gillette and J. Voight-Englund in the Hennepin County Park System with the assistance of the authors. The project was expanded in 1985 to include other release sites and organizations, and in 1989 overall coordination was assumed by the authors.

Burrowing Owl releases were begun in 1985 by M. Martell, P. Redig and J. Schladweiler of the Minnesota Department of Natural Resources. The project was expanded in 1986 as part of M. Martell's thesis work at the University of Minnesota under the guidance of F. Cuthbert and H. Tordoff and with the continued assistance of J. Schladweiler, P. Redig and L. Pfanmuller.

The purpose of all three programmes was to have released individuals return and successfully breed in the release area. However, differences in the status and biology of each species required that different goals be set for each. For the Peregrine Falcon, listed as Endangered at both national and state level, a goal of 40 breeding pairs in the upper Midwest was set as the point at which the release programme could be considered a success. It was felt that this would establish a population capable of sustaining itself and allow expansion into available habitat without further releases. The Midwestern releases paralleled and complemented other releases occurring in North America. Thus, our second goal was to contribute to the larger effort of restoring this species continent-wide.

Ospreys, listed as a species of Special Concern in Minnesota, were once a common breeding bird in southern Minnesota but receded northward during the early part of the 20th century in the face of heavy human settlement (Roberts 1932). The goal of the initial release effort was to establish breeding birds in the Hennepin County Park system located on the western edge of the Minneapolis-St. Paul (Twin Cities) Minnesota metropolitan area. That goal was later expanded to 10 breeding pairs in the local metropolitan area.

Burrowing Owls are listed as Endangered in Minnesota, and Endangered or of Special Concern in neighbouring states (Martell 1991). The goal of this project was to develop release techniques which could be used to supplement the dwindling Minnesota population and be used elsewhere where the species was in trouble (Martell 1990).

METHODS

Release Sites

Peregrine Falcon releases were conducted throughout the upper Midwestern states of Minnesota, Wisconsin, Iowa, Illinois, Missouri, Nebraska, Indiana, Ohio and Michigan. A release programme not associated with ours released birds into western Ontario, complementing our efforts. A total of 22 Peregrine Falcon release sites were used and included historically occupied, relatively secluded sites along the shores of Lake Superior and the Mississippi River as well as 15 urban sites in medium to large metropolitan areas including Chicago, Illinois; Detroit, Michigan; Milwaukee, Wisconsin and Minneapolis, Minnesota.

Ospreys were released at five sites in parks and nature preserves located around the edges of the Twin Cities metropolitan area. This densely populated area of over two million people has an extensive system of lakes and large rivers which provide suitable Osprey habitat.

Burrowing Owls were released into historically occupied areas at the edge of their range in western Minnesota. This is a rural, sparsely populated area used for row crops, hay and grazing. The primary release site was a Wildlife Management Area managed for upland game and waterfowl.

Release Techniques

All three species were released using variations of hacking techniques described by Sherrold *et al.* (1982). Peregrine Falcon releases most closely followed these techniques. Young falcons were released from hack boxes located on towers, cliffs and buildings. All released birds were obtained from captive breeding stock.

Osprey release techniques followed those described by Hammer and Hatcher (1983), a modification of the standard raptor hacking technique. All released Osprey were taken from nests located in north-central Minnesota, approximately 250km north of the Twin Cities. The chicks were taken when they were between five and seven weeks of age and placed in hack boxes located on the shoreline of a lake or large river within 24 hours of capture. The hack box was opened and the birds released two to three weeks later.

Burrowing Owls, an underground nesting bird, were released from pens located on grassland sites. The hack site was prepared by mowing a 40 x 22m section of grassland and constructing pens (7.6m x 5.5m x 1.7m) with roof and sides made from cotton mesh netting strung along metal fence poles. Up to four artificial wooden burrows (Collins & Landry 1977; Henderson 1984) were placed inside each pen, buried 1m underground (Martell 1990). All released Burrowing Owls were wild-trapped birds, translocated from South Dakota, a movement of between 450 and 600km (depending on the trapping site) east of their natal nests.

Marking and Ringing

All of the released birds were banded with USFWS aluminium leg bands and colour marked. Peregrine Falcon chicks were colour-marked with a black alpha-numerically coded aluminium leg band. Many of these birds were also temporarily marked by lightly spray-painting their feathers. Ospreys were colour-marked with blue, gold or black anodized aluminium leg bands which were alpha-numerically coded. The chicks were also temporarily marked by lightly spray-painting their feathers. Burrowing Owls were colour-marked with a unique combination of red, yellow and green leg markers. Radio-telemetry was used during the first year of the Peregrine Falcon, and first two years of the Burrowing Owl releases, to monitor the movements and habitat use of the birds.

Artificial Nest Sites

Peregrine Falcon nest boxes have been placed on buildings, bridges, smokestacks and cliffs across the Midwest, to provide suitable nesting sites for returning birds. Twenty-seven artificial Osprey nesting platforms were erected in the Twin Cities area. Artificial burrows (Collins & Landry 1977; Henderson 1984) were placed in grasslands around the release area to attract returning Burrowing Owls.

RESULTS

Peregrine Falcon

Between 1982-1991, 542 captive-bred falcons were released from 22 hack sites in nine states (Redig & Tordoff 1992). The number of birds released each year increased from five in 1982 to 108 in 1991. Overall, 316 (58%) of the birds were released in urban areas. Urban releases became more frequent in the later years of the programme, increasing from 11% of the birds released from 1982-85 to 72% in 1990-91. An additional 36 birds were released along the shore of Lake Superior by Canadian biologists, bringing the total number of Peregrine Falcons released in the area to 578.

The first pair of falcons nested in 1986 along the Mississippi River across from their release site. No young were fledged that year nor in the following two years when nesting was attempted at that site. The first successful modern nesting in the Midwest occurred in 1987 when one young was fledged from a nest box on the Multifoods Tower in Minneapolis. Since that time, the population has grown steadily. In 1991 we knew of 30 territorial pairs in the Midwest, of which 22 nested and 17 pairs successfully fledged 36 young. Urban nesters accounted for 15 of the 22 pairs documented in 1991. Since 1987 we have documented 104 wild-produced young which have successfully fledged in the region. Thus a total of 682 young Peregrine Falcons have been put into the Midwestern population since 1982.

We have documented mortality in 95 (17.5%) of the birds we released. Seventy-four (77.9%) of them were found in their hatching year. Twenty-four (10.6%) of the falcons hacked from non-urban sites were found dead compared with 71 (22.5%) of those hacked from urban sites. Thirty-eight wild adult, nestling and young Peregrine Falcons were found dead during this same period. The leading known causes of mortality and injury to both wild and captive-produced falcons were: collisions with buildings (19% of total), collisions with vehicles (12%), disease/starvation (8%), and natural predation (8%).

Osprey

A total of 93 Osprey chicks have been released between 1984 and 1991 into the Twin Cities area. The releases began in 1984 with 6 birds from two hack sites and were expanded in 1985 with the release of 13 chicks from four sites. The largest number of releases occurred in 1987 and 1988, when 18 birds were released from five sites each year.

The first modern Osprey nesting in this area occurred in 1986, when one of the released males and two females (both unbanded and not from our project) unsuccessfully attempted to nest. They laid six eggs in the same nest, all three birds shared incubation, but no eggs hatched. An unbanded male and female nested at this site in 1987 and again were unsuccessful, but were given a foster chick to raise. In 1988 a male released from our project was present at this site with an unbanded female during courtship but was replaced by another male during incubation. By 1988 there were three nesting pairs in the area, two of which laid eggs, one successfully. In 1989 there were four active pairs, all of which had eggs, two of which successfully fledged young. In the summer of 1991 we knew of four nesting pairs in the release area. Out of these, two males (one released in 1984, the other in 1986) were from the release project. Two other birds, a three-year-old male, and a two-year-old female, have been seen in the vicinity of the hack sites but are not yet part of nesting pairs.

We have recorded mortality in eight of the released birds (8.6%). Six died during fledging; one from a collision, three from natural predation and two from dehydration. We also received two reports of dead birds from Central America; a bird released in 1986 was shot at a fish hatchery in Costa Rica later that fall, and a bird released in 1985 was found dead in Panama in April of 1986.

Burrowing Owls

From 1986 through 1990 we released 104 fledgling Burrowing Owls; 9 in 1986, 17 in 1987, 21 in 1988, 27 in 1989 and 30 in 1990. We documented eight mortalities, all fledglings recovered in the hack site area. We have not found, nor received reports of, any owls after they left the hack site. We located eight wild nesting pairs in Minnesota during this time, with a high of five pairs in 1988.

DISCUSSION

To be successful, a reintroduction should result in the establishment of a self-sustaining population (Griffith *et al.* 1989). Using this definition, it is too early to declare any of the efforts outlined here as successful, although both the Peregrine Falcon and Osprey programmes look very promising. Released Peregrine Falcons are establishing new territories across the Midwest. The number of successful territories in urban areas, probably in response to the lure of new high-rise buildings and dependable food sources, is an unexpected yet positive development. In addition to providing safe nesting sites, added benefits are found from the positive public education opportunities and easy accessibility of birds for research and monitoring.

The released Ospreys now nesting near their former hack site are, we hope, the beginning of a long-term breeding population in the Twin Cities area. While we have not had as high a return rate as reported by L. Rymon in Pennsylvania (in Poole 1989), our results are similar to those reported by other Osprey reintroduction projects (Poole 1989).

The attraction to the area of unmarked Ospreys, most likely young adults looking for a place to breed, has doubled our nesting population. We believe these birds are setting up territories in the Twin Cities in response to the presence of our released birds. This, in addition to the tolerance of nesting pairs to each other and our observations of adults feeding young at the hack boxes, contrasts with the aggressive territorial behaviour of Peregrine Falcons. We have not been forced to abandon Osprey hack sites due the presence of new nesting pairs as we were with Peregrine Falcon release sites.

The Burrowing Owl releases have shown the least success to date. While the released birds have demonstrated foraging competence, burrow finding ability, and dispersal and migration at the end of summer (Martell 1990), none has been encountered after leaving the hack site. The number of owls released to date is relatively low and one might expect a very low band return rate in this species. Nonetheless, the absolute lack of contact with released birds is troublesome. The continued removal of owlets from neighbouring populations must be justified by the benefit of establishing satellite populations. Further studies of Burrowing Owls, which are ongoing, should try to determine natal fidelity, mortality and wintering ground location.

We estimate the cost (1990 U.S.) of the releases as \$200/Burrowing Owl, \$335/Osprey and

$3,000/Peregrine Falcon. The higher cost for the Peregrine Falcon project is primarily due to the expense of buying captive-reared falcons from breeders ($2,000 per bird) and transporting them from various sources across the country. Additionally, Burrowing Owls were released in groups of up to 30 birds, decreasing the number of hack sites, attendants and their associated costs.

The conclusions to be gained from these releases, while tentative, are obvious: reintroductions involving many birds to repopulate large regions, as we and others are attempting to do with the Peregrine Falcon, are proving effective. This strategy is being used with many other species, in many areas of the world (Griffith *et al.* 1989). On a smaller scale, reintroductions to establish satellite populations or expand the range of a species may also be useful. This is essentially what we are attempting to do with Ospreys and Burrowing Owls.Finally, we emphasize the importance of public education and acceptance of a raptor reintroduction. We have made concerted efforts to publicize our programmes and to involve the public, the media and local politicians. This has resulted not only in a favourable climate for the reintroduced birds but has also resulted in a new public awareness and acceptance of all raptors.

REFERENCES

COLLINS, C.T. & R.E. LANDRY 1977. Artificial nest burrows for Burrowing Owls. *M. Am. Bird Bander* 2: 151-154.

GRIFFITH, B., J.M. SCOTT, J.W. CARPENTER & C. REED 1989. Translocation as a species conservation tool: status and strategy. *Science* 245: 477-480.

HAMMER, D.A. & R.M. HATCHER 1983. Restoring Osprey populations by hacking preflighted young. *In* D.M. Bird, N.R. Seymour & J.M. Gerrard (Eds.) *Biology and Management of Bald Eagles and Osprey.* Harpell Press, Ste. Anne de Bellevue, Quebec. 325 pp.

HENDERSON, C.L. 1984. *Woodworking for wildlife: homes for birds and mammals.* MN Dept. of Nat. Res.; St. Paul, MN. 47 pp.

MARTELL, M.S. 1990. Reintroduction of Burrowing Owls into Minnesota: a feasibility study. Unpubl. thesis, Univ. of Minnesota, Mnpls. MN 95 pp.

MARTELL, M.S. 1991. Grassland Owls. Pages 96-104 *in* proc. Midwest raptor management symposium and workshop. Natl. Wildl. Fed., Washington, D.C.

POOLE, A.F. 1989. *Osprey, a natural and unnatural history.* Cambridge University Press, Cambridge. 246pp.

REDIG, P.T. & H.B. TORDOFF 1992. Midwest Peregrine Falcon restoration project report. Unpub. Rept. The Raptor Center at the University of Minnesota, St. Paul, MN. 180pp.

ROBERTS, T.S. 1932. *The Birds of Minnesota* Vol I. Univ. of Minnesota Press, Minneapolis, 690pp.

SHERROD, S.K., W.R. HEINRICH, W.A. BURNHAM, J.H. BARCLAY & T.J. CADE 1982. *Hacking: A method for releasing Peregrine Falcons and other birds of prey.* The Peregrine Fund Inc., Ithaca, New York. 61pp.

Mark S. Martell/Patrick T. Redig
The Raptor Center at
The University of Minnesota
St. Paul
MN 55108, USA

Harrison B. Tordoff
Bell Museum of Natural History
University of Minnesota
Minneapolis
MN 55485, USA

Burrowing Owl *Athene cunicularis*

Meyburg, B.-U. & R. D. Chancellor eds.1994
Raptor Conservation Today
WWGBP / The Pica Press

The Re-introduction of the Red Kite *Milvus milvus* into Scotland

M.J. McGrady, D.C. Orr-Ewing, and T.J. Stowe

The Red Kite *Milvus milvus* is a medium-large bird of prey whose range is primarily European, although some sub-populations are found in Northern Africa and western Asia. Part of the population (mostly in the northern part of the range) is migratory (Cramp *et al.* 1980).

Throughout its range the Red Kite needs woodland in which to nest and roost, but hunts primarily over open fields, moor and unimproved pasture, usually while on the wing. Although the Red Kite will tolerate a variety of habitats, it flourishes in areas characterised by a diverse mosaic of woodland, improved and unimproved pasture, and moorland. Throughout most of its range it is primarily a lowland bird (Cramp *et al.* 1980).

Prey includes small mammals such as voles (*Microtus* sp., *Clethrionomys* sp., *Arvicola* sp.), birds up to the size of Wood Pigeons (*Columba palumbus*), stranded fish, amphibians, reptiles, insects and carrion. It will also pirate food from other birds and rob nests. It will feed on offal and will scavenge garbage from refuse-tips.

During the 20th century, the species' range has contracted in many places, mostly due to human persecution. However, in some countries, such as Sweden, the population is on the increase, due largely to increased protection in good habitat.

The Red Kite in Britain

The fortunes of the Red Kite in Britain have varied throughout the ages, closely connected with the activities of humans. Prior to the development of agricultural methods, the kite was probably limited to areas with naturally occurring open lands, including damp river valleys, swampy land, estuaries and some coastal areas. With the development of agriculture from slash-and-burn to more settled farms, kites found more and more land over which they could hunt.

By the Middle Ages the population was probably at its peak, taking advantage of not only an expansion of its nesting habitat, but also the fact that in England and Wales it was protected by royal decree in recognition of its importance as a street cleaner.

The esteem in which it was held in England and Wales was not matched in Scotland. In 1457, James II of Scotland decreed that the kite, along with other predatory birds, should be destroyed. This and later laws, in 1532, 1566, 1572 and 1598, signalled the beginning of the decline of the Red Kite throughout Britain, placing it among 'vermin' to be controlled (Lovegrove 1990).

In 1879 the Red Kite became extinct as a breeding bird in Scotland. Extinction in England occurred about the same time. By the beginning of the 20th century, the British population was reduced to about six breeding pairs, all confined to the hills of mid-Wales.

Today, the Red Kite remains one of Britains rarest birds. It is one of only three British bird species listed in the World Checklist of Threatened Birds (Collar & Andrew 1988), and is included in the Red Data Book. Its breeding range is still limited to the hills of mid-Wales. However, the location of this present population of, today, 70-80 breeding pairs is due not so much to the fact that mid-Wales is an ideal habitat as to the relative lack of persecution in the area compared to other parts of Britain in the last century.

Still, persecution persists. Egg collecting remains a problem; despite high security, in some years nearly 10% of nests are robbed. Also, birds are poisoned and shot.

The re-introduction in Scotland

As a consequence of persecution, the cold, wet weather and relatively poor habitat, the productivity of the Welsh Red Kite population has been very low. So, although it looks to be relatively secure within Wales, the natural recolonisation of other parts of Britain from this nucleus seems unlikely in the foreseeable future. Recolonisation of the United Kingdom by the continental Red Kite population is also unlikely because Britain does not lie on any direct migration routes of that population.

Given this state of affairs, in 1988 the Royal Society for the Protection of Birds (RSPB) and Joint Nature Conservancy Council (JNCC) examined the possibility of re-introducing the Red Kite into England and Scotland. Before any re-introduction of kites (or any other species) could be supported, certain conditions needed to exist:

1. There should be good historical evidence that the re-introduction was taking place in an area of former natural occurrence.
2. There should be a clear understanding of why the species was lost. In general, only those populations lost through human agency should be considered for re-introduction.
3. Any natural recolonisation of an area by an extant population would be unlikely to occur.
4. The factors causing the extinction should no longer be in force.
5. There should be sufficient suitable habitats to support the re-introduced population.
6. The re-introduced individuals should be from a population as close as possible to the extirpated one.
7. The loss of the individuals from the donor population should not negatively affect that population.

The situation of the Red Kite in Britain in 1988 fitted these conditions.

Attempts at such re-introduction had been made before, in the 1920s and the 1950s (Bannerman 1956; Lovegrove 1990). Both were largely unsuccessful. To avoid any repetition of past mistakes and ensure a high probability of success, detailed research was undertaken. This identified an area for the re-introduction, a likely donor population, and detailed the process itself. The success of the re-introduction of the White-tailed Eagle (*Haliaeetus albicilla*) into Scotland had proved that reintroduction could be accomplished with the resources available to the RSPB and the JNCC. With this as a backdrop, the decision was taken to proceed. The background to the Red Kite projects in England and Scotland has been detailed by Pienkowski and Evans (1991) and by Evans and Pienkowski (1991).

The re-introduction site in Scotland was chosen in the Highlands, in an area characterised by a mosaic of relatively small farms and villages. The land use is primarily agricultural, but no one agricultural product predominates; livestock, cereal and root crops and forestry are all part of the landscape. Large areas are lowlands, but there are upland areas as well. The latter are primarily covered in heather (*Calluna vulgaris*) and grass (e.g. *Molina caerulea*), but also strips of birch (*Betula pendula*) and plantation forestry (mostly Sitka spruce, *Picea sitchensis*). This mosaic provides good habitat for potential prey (both mammalian and avian) for the kites. The main urban area is Inverness, a city of 40,000 people.

The ideal donor population was identified as breeding in the area of Scania in southern Sweden. There the population was and is expanding rapidly, and has grown from 50 pairs in 1980 to 150 in 1986, and to 200 pairs in 1989 (Lovegrove 1990). The landscape of this part of Sweden is very similar to that found in the reintroduction area in the Highlands.

Details of release

Pre-release

In 1989, the Swedish National Environmental Protection Board, WWF-Sweden and Skanes Ornitologiska Forening were approached to provide the birds for re-introduction. In June of that year ten Red Kite chicks were collected under CITES licence and transported to Britain by the Royal Air Force. This was the first flight by the RAF to Sweden since the war because of Sweden's status as a neutral country. In 1989, six kites were released in Scotland, in 1990 19 kites, and in 1991 a further 20.

Upon arrival in Britain, the kites were isolated at the release site in two large quarantine aviaries for the mandatory 35 days. These aviaries were purpose-built, giving the birds adequate shelter from the weather and predators, as well as enough room to exercise their wings during the fledging period.

The release cages were constructed of plywood and wire netting, and contained a variety of perches. Each had a food delivery hatch through which the birds were fed. The approach to the cages was such that the kites could not see the people who fed them and monitored their development, thus avoiding the possibility of their becoming accustomed to or imprinted upon their keepers. Access could be gained by a door, and the wire-mesh front could be opened from behind the cage, out of sight of the fledgling kites.

The kites were fed on a variety of food, primarily rabbits, and fish from a local fish farm. For the first few days food was chopped up before being placed in the cage. By the end of their pre-release time, whole dead rabbits were being placed in the cages. The kites ate about one-third of a rabbit each per day.

Four to five days prior to release, the birds were weighed, measured and ringed with British Trust for Ornithology rings. They were also fitted with coloured, numbered wing tags; different colours denoted the year of release. Birds were also fitted with tail-mounted radio transmitters. The adjustment of the birds to the transmitter was monitored for two days prior to release.

Post-release

Birds were released at approximately 55 to 65 days of age by opening the cage front remotely from the rear of the cage at night. The 'branching out' of the kites into the trees in front of the cages could be monitored from a hill about 600m away.

All the kites left the cages the morning after the cage doors had been opened. They perched in the surrounding trees and made their first longer flights very soon after release. Food was provided on top of the release cages. This ensured that it was visible and orientated the birds to the release site itself. After one week the kites tended to forage mostly by themselves with only occasional visits to the feeding station.

For the first days post-release, the kites would return to the release site to roost at night. Gradually, as they became more excursive, the kites began to roost in neighbouring woodlands. However, they stayed in the relase area for about the first six weeks.

Movements of kites

In the ensuing months attempts were made to follow the movement of all the kites, primarily by searching for the radio-tagged birds by car, using a scanning radio receiver programmed to the frequencies of the kites' transmitters. As winter approached, some of the kites moved farther afield. Those that did so started leaving in the first weeks of September. Their movements were mainly monitored using radio telemetry, but in some cases reports by the public of colour-marked birds were used. Searches for radio-tagged birds were also conducted from a light aircraft, flying at about 5,000ft. This was a much more efficient way of searching for individuals which had moved out of the immediate area, but was limited by the weather, particularly in western parts of the country.

As in the donor population, only a proportion moved away from the release area. Generally, those that moved did so to the south, mostly into Perthshire and southern Scotland. Some moved greater distances than others (See Figs. 1-3) Notable movements include:

- a 1989 release travelled to Orkney before wintering in Lanarkshire in 1989-90, again in 1990-1991, and possibly again in 1991-1992
- a 1990 release moved to Argyll and then was found poisoned on 9 February 1991 in County Longford in the Republic of Ireland
- a 1990 release was found dead on 8 December 1990 at Kilmacthomas, County Waterford, Republic of Ireland
- a 1990 release moved to east Sutherland, wintered in Yorkshire, and returned to the release area in 1991
- a 1991 release left on 6 September 1991. It was recorded in Perthshire, and in late October in County Down, Northern Ireland. A bird marked with yellow wing tags (which could refer to this bird) was seen in County Cork, and County Kerry in the Republic. In December 1991, this bird was found dead in Cornwall. It had been poisoned (Fig. 1, Kite J)
- a 1991 release left the area on 11 September. It was found in Grampian, then in Argyll in October. In November and December this bird was in Morayshire before going missing (Fig. 2, Kite Y)
- a 1990 release spent its first winter in Perthshire and returned to the release area for the summer of 1991. It was located in Perthshire in the autumn of 1991, but since December 1991 has been in Inverness-shire (Fig. 3, Kite T).

Thus far, no known nesting has occurred. In other populations, Red Kites can breed as early as two-three years of age. This statistic suggests that this year, 1992, could be the first year one might expect a breeding attempt. Because this re-introduced population is reproductively inexperienced, it is perhaps overly hopeful that the birds will breed at this relatively young age and more realistic to expect breeding in the years to come.

Figure 1. Red Kite released in 1991. This bird left the release area on 6 September 1991. It was recorded in Perthshire, and in late October in County Down, Northern Ireland. A bird marked with yellow wing tags (which could refer to this bird) was seen in County Cork and County Kerry in the Republic. In December 1991, this bird was found dead in Cornwall. It had been poisoned.

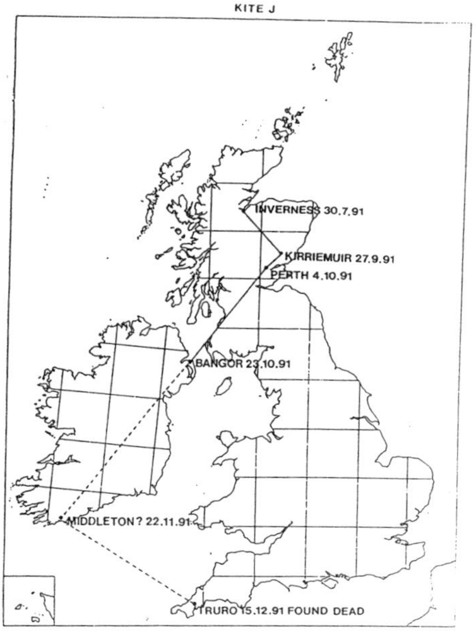

Figure 2. Red Kite released in 1991. This bird left the release area on 11 September. It was found in Grampian, then in Argyll in October. In November and December of 1991 it was in Morayshire before going missing.

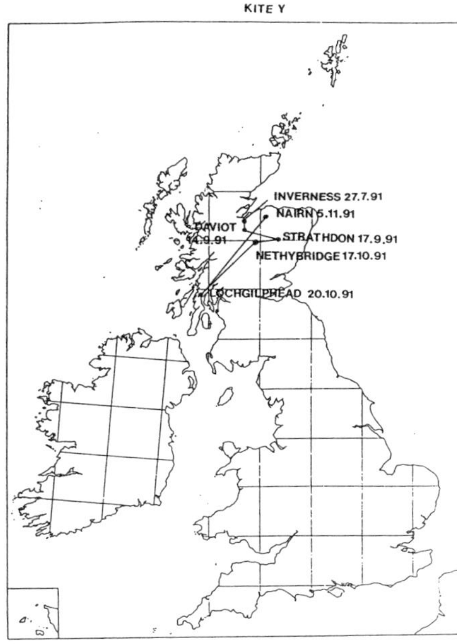

Figure 3. Red Kite released in 1990. It spent its first winter in Perthshire and returned to the release area for the summer of 1991. It was located in Perthshire in the autumn of 1991, but since December 1991 has been in Inverness-shire

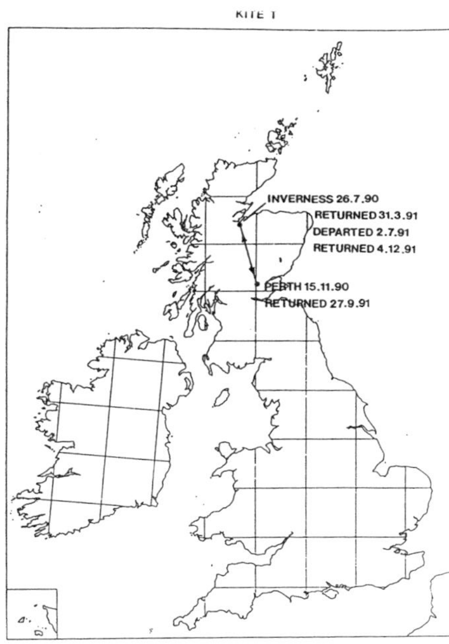

Survival of Red Kites released in Scotland

Table 1 summarises the release and survival of Red Kites in Scotland; at 1st Jan 1992 50% of the birds released in 1989 were known to be alive. We know that at least 73.6% of those released in 1990, and 80% of those released in 1991 have survived. It must be emphasised that these statistics should be taken as minima since a proportion of the released birds are unaccounted for.

The main cause of mortality has been poisoning, accounting for four of the five known deaths. Four out of 45 birds (8.8%) have been poisoned.

Table 1. Red Kite release and survival statistics in Scotland 1989-1991 (at 1.1.92).

	1989	1990	1991
Total Number of Birds Released	6	19	20
Accounted for Alive	3	14	16
Dead (Poisoned)	1(1)	3(2)	1(1)
Unaccounted for	2	2	3

CONCLUSIONS AND FUTURE PROSPECTS

It is still too early to be certain that the re-introduction of Red Kites will result in the first breeding of this species in the wild in Scotland in over 100 years. However, the initial signs point to success. The project has demonstrated that:

1. translocation of Red Kites from a suitable donor population in Sweden is practicable. No obvious detrimental effects (to either donor or introduced population) have resulted.
2. the release methods employed are a practical way of creating a population centre from which breeding may eventually take place.
3. the Highlands of Scotland are capable of supporting the released individuals. It is likely that this same area will be suitable for a breeding population.
4. birds that disperse widely can re-find release areas. It is hoped that in the near future the Red Kite will be re-established as a breeding species from this nucleus of individuals.

Releases of Red Kites in Scotland will continue for at least two more years. This will ensure that a variety of age classes will be represented in the core population. The establishment of a breeding population in Scotland, and good reproductive success within that population may take some years to achieve since Red Kites take several years to reach sexual maturity, and because this nucleus of birds is reproductively inexperienced. It is hoped that a breeding population will finally be established which will produce at least as many fledglings as are being brought in from Sweden at this time (20-25 individuals). Once established, it is expected that production in Scotland will exceed that of the Welsh kite population. This is not an unreasonable expectation since in the release area the weather is drier, the average altitude lower, and the land generally more productive than that in which Welsh kites breed.

ACKNOWLEDGEMENTS

The authors and the RSPB would like to recognise continuing efforts of the Swedish National Environmental Protection Board, WWF-Sweden, Skanes Ornitologiska Forening and the Royal Air Force in making this project a success. In and around the release area, many people including landowners, game-keepers, farmers and fish farmers, have taken an interest in the kites and provide food, a release site and support to the project. We would also like to thank the many people who reported sightings of kites in Britain and Ireland. Those sightings have been extremely useful in helping us to follow the birds after release. Thanks also go to Justin Grant, who commented on an early draft of this paper.

REFERENCES

BANNERMAN, D.A. 1956. *The Birds of the British Isles.* Vol. 5. Oliver and Boyd, London.

COLLAR, N.J. & P. ANDREW 1988. *Birds to Watch:* the ICBP world checklist of threatened birds. Cambridge.

CRAMP, S. & K.E.L. SIMMONS 1980. *Handbook of the Birds of Europe, the Middle East and North Africa: the Birds of the Western Palearctic,* Vol. 2. Oxford University Press.

EVANS, I.M. & M.W. PIENKOWSKI 1991. World status of the Red Kite: a background to the experimental re-introduction to England and Scotland. *British Birds* 84: 171-187.

LOVEGROVE, R. 1990. *The Kite's Tale: the story of the Red Kite in Wales.* Royal Society for the Protection of Birds, Sandy.

PIENKOWSKI, M.W. & I.M. EVANS 1991.1 Red Kite re-introduction to Scotland and England. Pp 124-127 *In* D.A. Stroud & D.Glue (Eds.) *Britain's Birds in 1989-90: the conservation and monitoring review.* British Trust for Ornithology/Nature Conservancy Council, Thetford.

M.J. McGrady
RSPB, 17 Regent Terrace
Edinburgh, Scotland

D.C. Orr-Ewing, T.J. Stowe
Royal Society for the Protection of Birds
Etive House
Beechwood Park
Inverness, IV2 3BW Scotland

Postscript. In 1992 subsequent to the presentation of this paper, a reintroduced pair of Red Kites successfully reared a chick in Scotland.

Meyburg, B.-U. & R. D. Chancellor eds.1994
Raptor Conservation Today
WWGBP / The Pica Press

Reintroduction of the Griffon Vulture *Gyps fulvus* in the Massif Central, France.

M. Terrasse, C. Bagnolini, J. Bonnet, J-L. Pinna and F. Sarrazin

ABSTRACT

Griffon Vultures disappeared from the Causses in the Southern Massif Central around 1945. In 1981, a reintroduction project began in this area. Ten years later, the new colony includes about a hundred individuals. The different steps of its settlement and increase are described. They concern spatial dispersion and foraging zone as well as reproduction and exchanges between the Causses colony and Pyrenean and Iberian populations.

INTRODUCTION

Griffon Vultures (*Gyps fulvus fulvus*) were eliminated from south central France during the first third of the twentieth century because of direct destruction by gun and poison. They were extinct by 1945 (Berthet 1946).

In 1968 a reintroduction project was started (Fonds d'Intervention pour les Rapaces - Parc National des Cevennes) near the last known breeding site (Heim de Balzac 1922) in an area of still good habitat for vultures; cliffs and limestone plateaux, the Causses, where important sheep rearing persists. This project occurred in three successives stages (Brosselin 1971; Terrasse 1980, 1982, 1983, 1990):

— 1968 to 1981 : Preparation of public opinion, education of hunters, obtaining strychnine prohibition and gathering of about 50 captive Griffon Vultures:

— 1981 to 1986: release of captive vultures (at the end of this first stage the colony was about 50 free-flying individuals strong):

— after 1986: free evolution of this population.

The reintroduction method based on releasing adult pairs in order to fix a breeding group fundamentally differs from those usually used in other raptor reintroduction projects like those of the Bearded Vulture, *Gypaetus barbatus*, (Esteve 1986), White-tailed Sea Eagle, *Haliaeetus albicilla,* (Love 1983) and Peregrine Falcon, *Falco peregrinus*, (Cade 1979), in which only immature birds were preliminarily released. In 1970, attempts to release young Griffon Vultures failed because of high juvenile dispersion in this species.

The nearest wild breeding colonies of Béarn and Catalonia are located at least 300 km from the release site.

This study analyses the progressive adaptation of this colony to its new environment, focussing on the exploitation of food resources and basic demographic parameters.

Figure 1. Situation map of the study area.

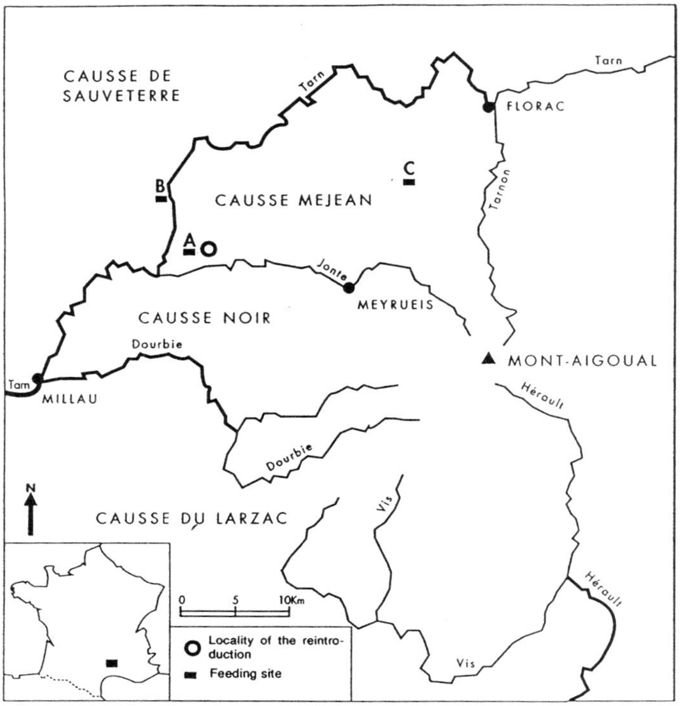

Figure 2. Number of yearly releases (by age classes).

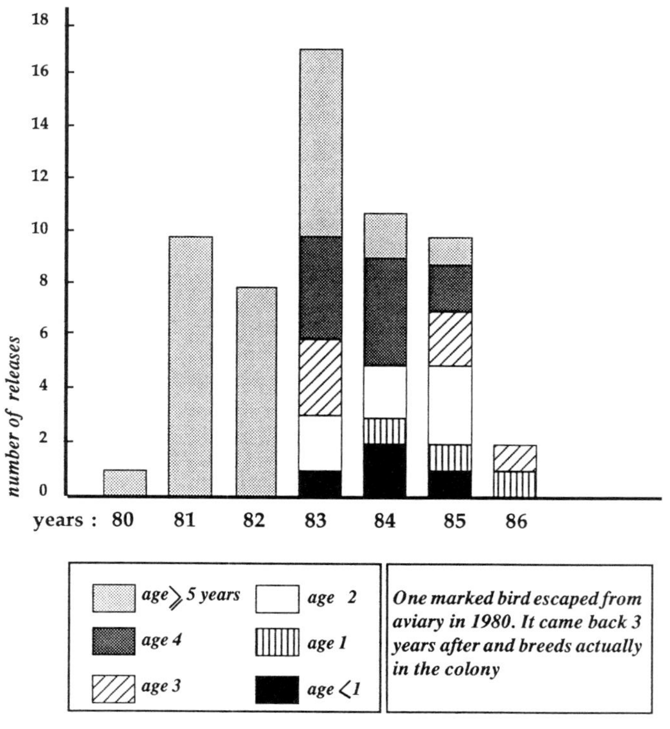

METHOD

Study area

The study area covers all the Grands Causses of South Central France especially in Lozère and Aveyron department (Figure 1) where the Tarn, Jonte and Dourbie rivers flow into deep canyons. The release site is located on the southern rim of the Causse Méjean, where the aviary for captive breeding was built at the top of a cliff overlooking the gorges of the Jonte river.

Vulture group used

From 1970 to 1987, 86 Griffon Vultures had been obtained from different origins:

— 47 came from the wild or from rehabilitation centres (31 from Spain and 16 from France)

— 24 were given or exchanged by zoos,

— 6 were seized from dealers (unknown origin),

— 9 were born in our aviary.

More than one third of these vultures had lived in captivity for a long time (5 to more than 10 years). Moreover, even some of those held in captivity for shorter times were already habituated to man.

Release conditions

To maximize the chances of settling a colony, the first released vultures (in 1981 and 1982) were all paired adults and most of them had bred in an aviary. The first ten adults were released in December at the time of display and mating. Because of unfavourable climatic conditions in winter with few thermal currents, younger individuals which had spent less time in captivity were released only in 1983 (Figure 2).

Monitoring

Since first release all individuals were monitored daily with visual marks or radio transmitters. All released vultures were marked with a metallic ring and one plastic lettered ring or a combination of coloured rings. Because of ring losses and problems with reading letters from distances over 300 m, young vultures are today marked in the nest with DARVIC coloured rings and recapture sessions will occur every year in order to ensure that all adults will be marked. From 1981 to 1983, all released birds wore radio-transmitters (17 gr) fixed to their two central tail feathers. Radio tracking permitted us to retrieve vultures who landed, during their first flights, in anomalous sites like dense bushes on slopes. The maximal theoretical range of the transmitters was about 20 km but the usual recording distance was less than 1 km and the lifespan of the transmitters never exceeded 6 months (4 - 5 months on average). These results, the easy visual monitoring and the increasing trend of released birds to remain around the release site quickly led us to stop radio-tracking after 1983.

The census and observations were essentially made by three persons permanently involved in the project, subsequently helped by several amateur ornithologists. All the following results were derived from marked birds.

Feeding method

Some months before the first releases, feeding site A (Figure 1), close to the aviary, was supplied in order to establish links between corvids and captive vultures as were also sites B and C respectively 5 km and 20 km away from A. These feeding sites were 100 to 400 m^2 fenced areas to keep off foxes and dogs. They were supplied with carcasses mainly coming from farms and sometimes from two nearby slaughter houses. Since 1985, vultures have begun to feed on carcasses laid out by farmers.

Figure 3. Movements and dispersal of Griffon Vultures from December 1981 to December 1984.

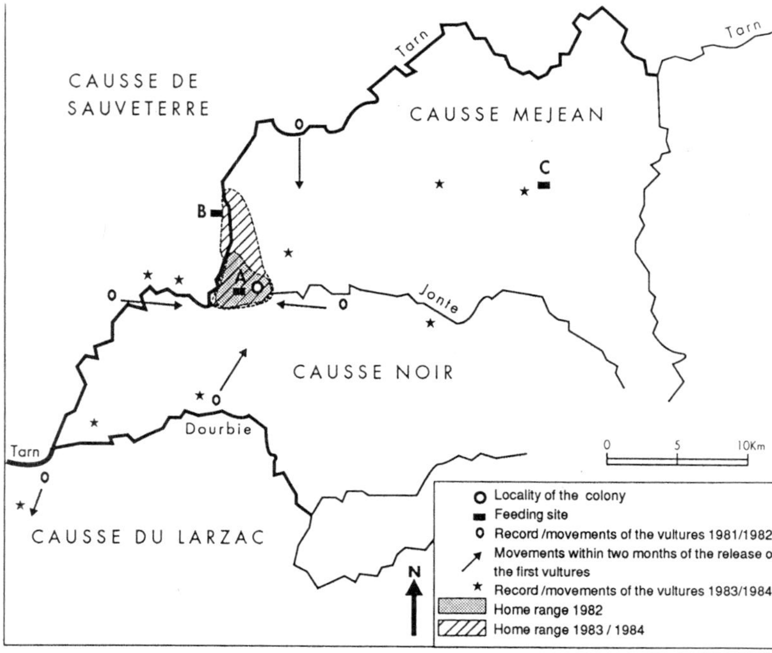

Figure 4. Range and foraging area of Griffon Vulutres in 1985-1986.

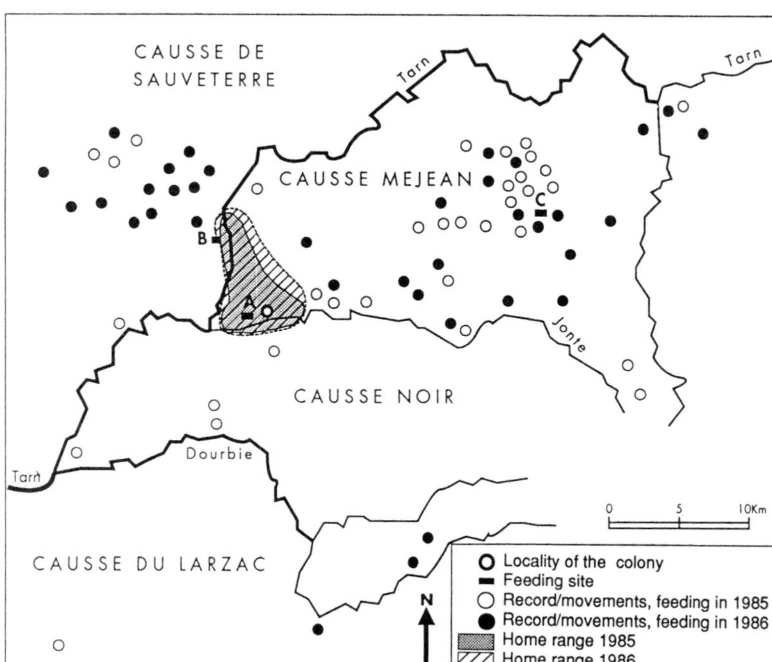

RESULTS

Adaptation of released Griffon Vultures to the wild

The behaviour of the first released adults and of younger released birds must be distinguished (Figure 2).

During the first two to four weeks, the released adults presented poor flight abilities (Bonnet *et al.* 1990). They dispersed and adults of the same pair were sometimes several kilometres apart. They divided their time between long rests and flapping flights. The dispersal area, centred on the canyons of Tarn and Jonte, covered about 500 km² (Figure 3). The correct use of thermal currents began at the end of this period, during which these vultures did not feed. Thus one individual sustained 3 weeks without feeding but another bird died after 40 days. The energy cost of flight learning was certainly high, therefore their ability to endure starvation is remarkable. From 1983, 2-4 years old birds were released. They were in captivity for less than one year and consequently they could fly within less than two weeks. The released fledglings seemed to have the same flying ability as the wild-born fledgings. Among 59 released marked birds, 8 were found dead and 5 were removed from the wild. Furthermore, among 76 marked wild-born individuals, 10 were found dead and 4 were removed from the wild. Electrocution was the main cause of mortality (10 dead marked birds from 1981 to 1991). To date it has killed 15 marked or non-marked Griffon Vultures in the Causses.

Establishment and increase of the colony

* *settling of the breeding group (1981-1983).*

In order to favour the settling of the first released birds, several caves and ledges on the cliff closest to the aviary were cleared and painted with white to mimic occupied sites. This site had harboured the last known colony of Griffon Vultures in the Grands Causses (Heim de Balzac 1922; Rochon-Duvigneaud 1921). In February 1982, three pairs (Table 1) settled in a 500 m portion of that cliff and one pair succeeded in rearing a chick. In 1983, the colony extended along 1200 m of this same cliff.

Table 1. Timing of the settlement of the Griffon Vulture's colony in the Causses.

year	Released birds	Wild born birds	Dead birds	Recaptured birds
1980	1*	0	0	0
1981	10	0	0	0
1982	8	1	3	2
1983	17	1	1	1
1984	11	1	0	2
1985	12**	5	4	0
1986	2	6	0	0
1987	0	12	1	1
1988	0	10★	3	0
1989	0	9	2	1
1990	0	15	5	1
1991	0	17	1	1
Total	61	77	20	9

*This marked Griffon Vulture escaped and came back three years later.
**Two non-marked birds escaped.
★One fledgling was not marked.

Figure 5. Range and foraging area of Griffon Vultures in 1987-1988.

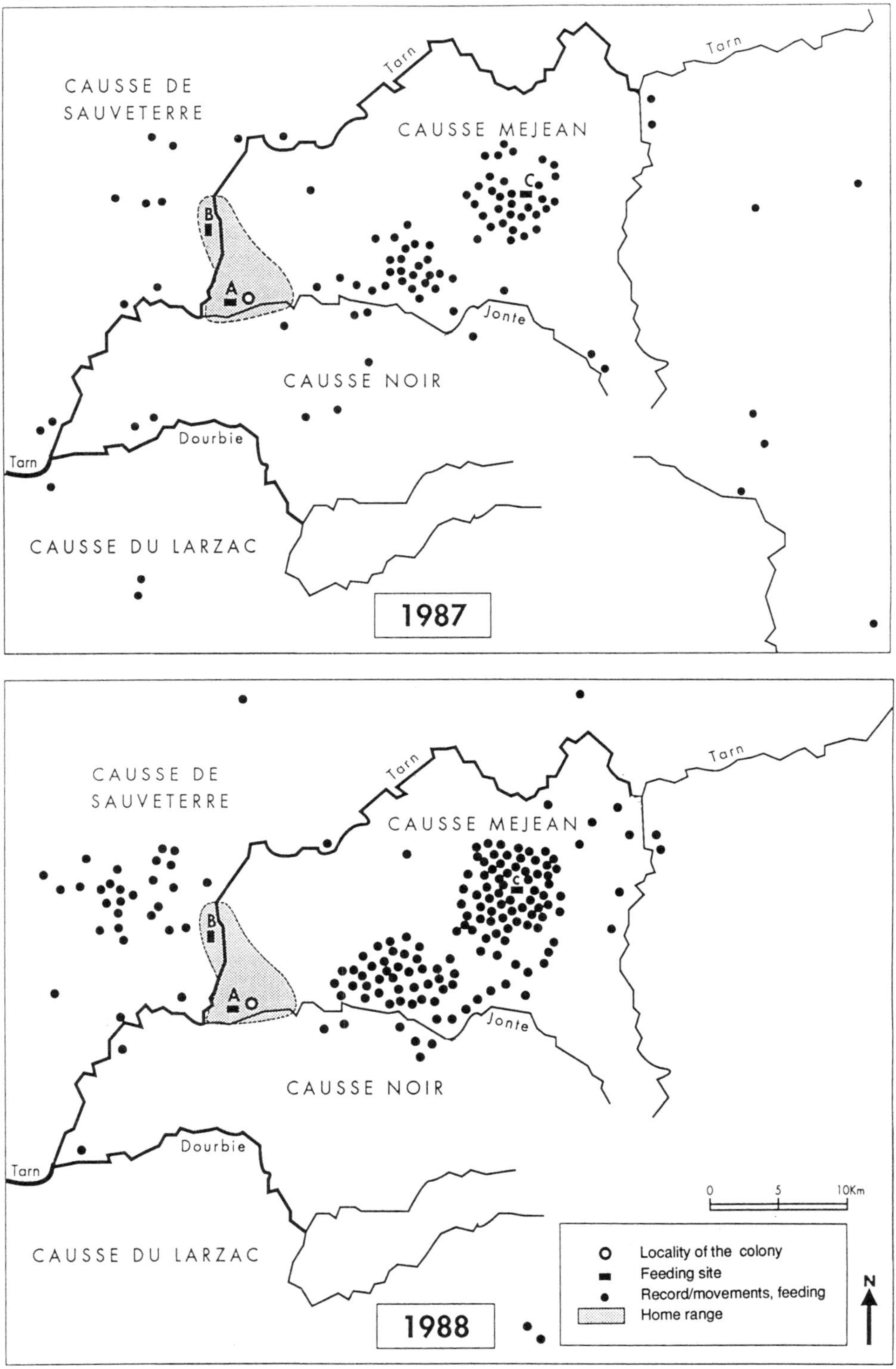

Figure 6. Number of total breeding pairs and nests in Jonte and Tarn canyons.

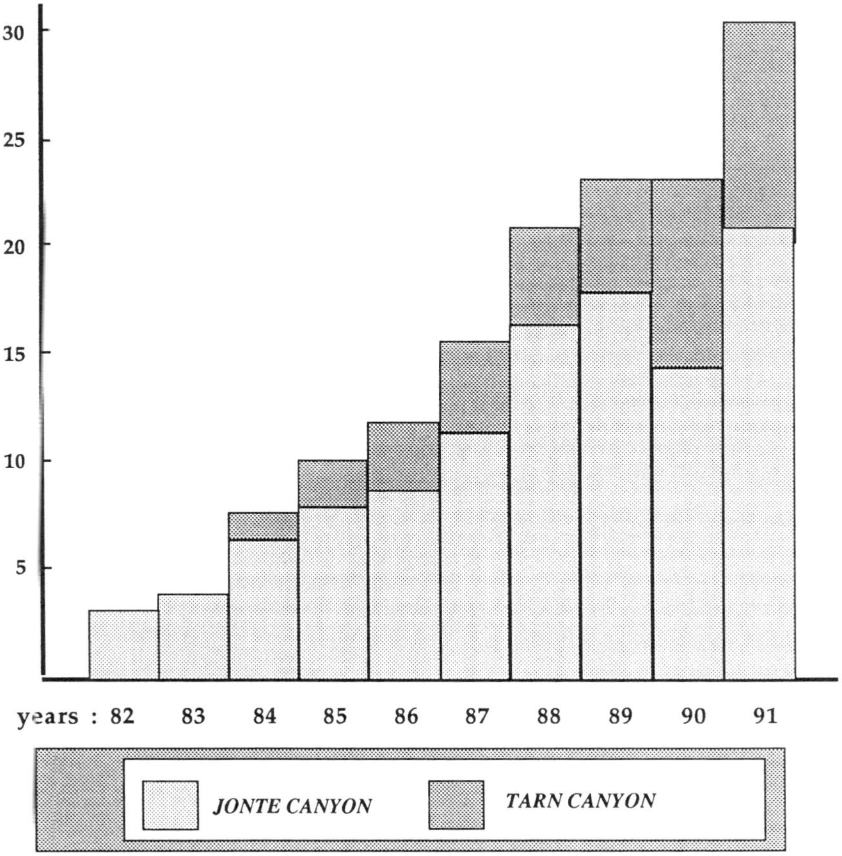

Figure 7. Area (hectares) of the home range.

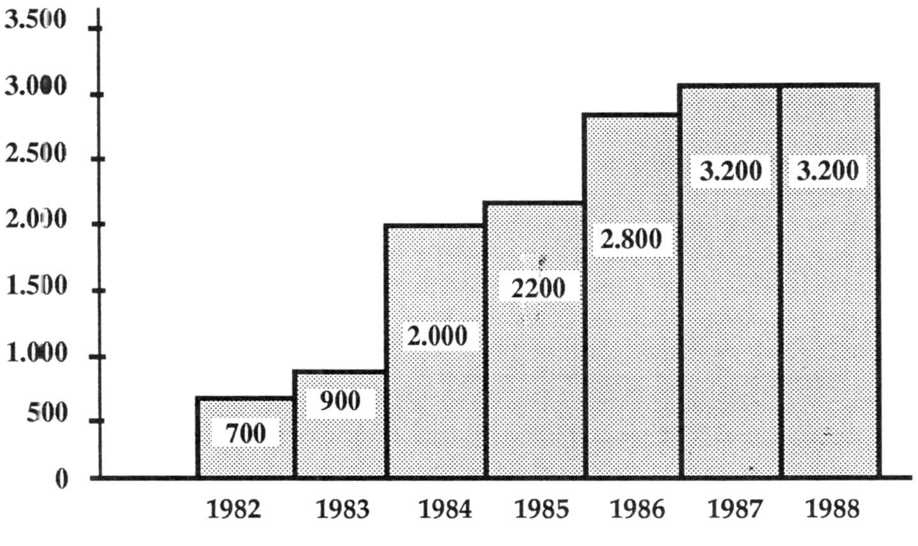

** spatial increase of the colony*

From 1984, the increase in the number of free vultures favoured the split-up of the breeding group. Several pairs settled in the Tarn valley at 3 - 6 km from the first breeding group (Figure 3, 4, 5 and 6). The Tarn cliff chosen by these vultures was precisely one where this species nested a century ago (Solanet 1894). The first successful reproduction occurred in 1985 in this second breeding group. Therefore the cliff length occupied by the overall colony increased from 500 m in 1982 to 4 km in 1991 with a 6.2 km distance between the outermost nests. Here we define the home range as the area that embraces all the activities of the overall colony during the breeding period instead of the activities of one pair (Newton 1979). After a rapid increase, the home range seemed to stabilize in 1987 with an area of 3000 ha. This home range is centred on the release point and the feeding site A (Fig. 7).

Reproduction in the wild

The increase in the number of breeders across years and a faulty ringing system (ring loss, non-marked immigrants...) make good monitoring information more and more difficult to obtain. Therefore the following trends should be interpreted as minimals. Futhermore, a population dynamics study is now in progress and only a few preliminary descriptive data will be given here.

** recruitment*

Among 140 marked individuals, 46 built a nest and were considered as breeders for at least one year (Figure 8). 35 released birds were identifi ed as breeders. Because of no information on the age of most of them we cannot discuss their breeding success according to age. However, one individual released as juvenile in 1984 paired and built a nest when 3 years old but did not lay. Nine wildborn vultures were recruited, 8 when 4 years old and 1 when 5 years old. Therefore it seems that age at first breeding is 4 in our colony instead of 5 or 6 in other natural populations (Terrasse 1977; Elosegui 1989).

The first Griffon Vulture which was born in the wild in 1982 never paired nor reproduced. In 1991, when it was 9 years old, its plumage still exhibited signs of immaturity.

** breeding success*

The temporal evolution of the number of breeding pairs and clutch, hatching and fledging successes (Figure 9) shows the dynamism of this population and is helpful to understand its demographic increase (Figure 10). Because of small population size, the breeding success is not studied in relation to age but is calculated over all breeding pairs (Table 2). However, the production of pairs with one or two wild-born breeders is for the whole period relatively high (0.92 i.e., 12 fledglings for 13 "annual pairs" having at least one wild-born individual). Only one pair is surely composed of two wild-born individuals. These two vultures began to breed when 4 years old. They failed in their first breeding attempt in 1989 but succeeded in 1990 and 1991.

Table 2. Yearly breeding success parameters

Year	Number of clutches	Hatching success	Fledging success	Breeding success
1982	2	0.50	1.00	0.50
1983	4	0.25	1.00	0.25
1984	7	0.29	0.50	0.14
1985	9	0.56	1.00	0.56
1986	12	0.50	1.00	0.50
1987*	12	0.83	1.00	0.83
1988*	15	0.65	0.88	0.53
1989*	20	0.50	0.88	0.40
1990*	24	0.72	0.88	0.62
1991	29	0.72	0.81	0.59

*In order not to artificially maximize breeding success, only early recorded breeding pairs have been taken into account.

Figure 8. Recruitment of released, young and suspected immigrant Griffon Vultures for the first year of breeding.

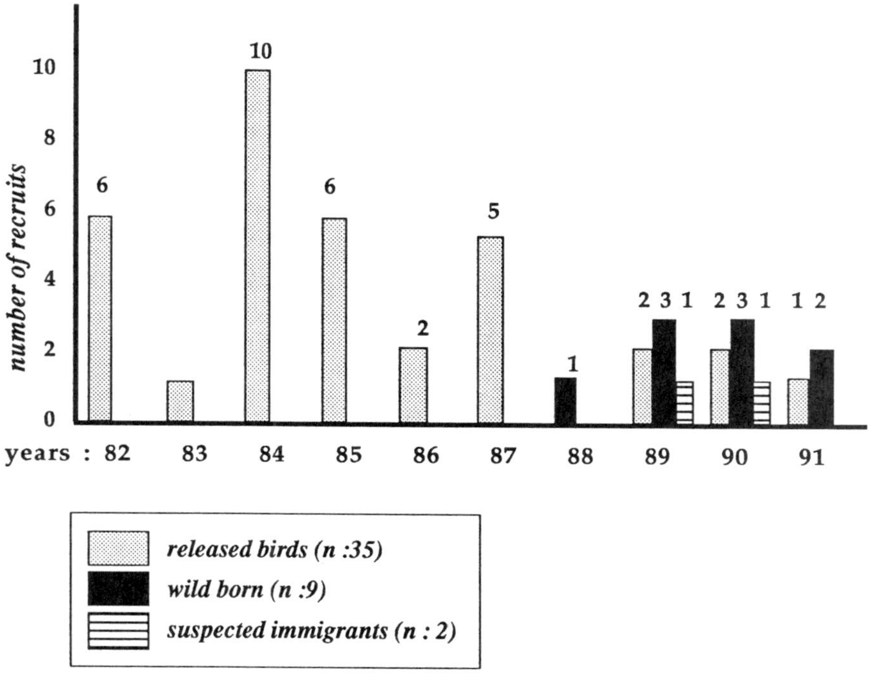

Figure 9. Annual number of clutches, hatchlings and fledglings.

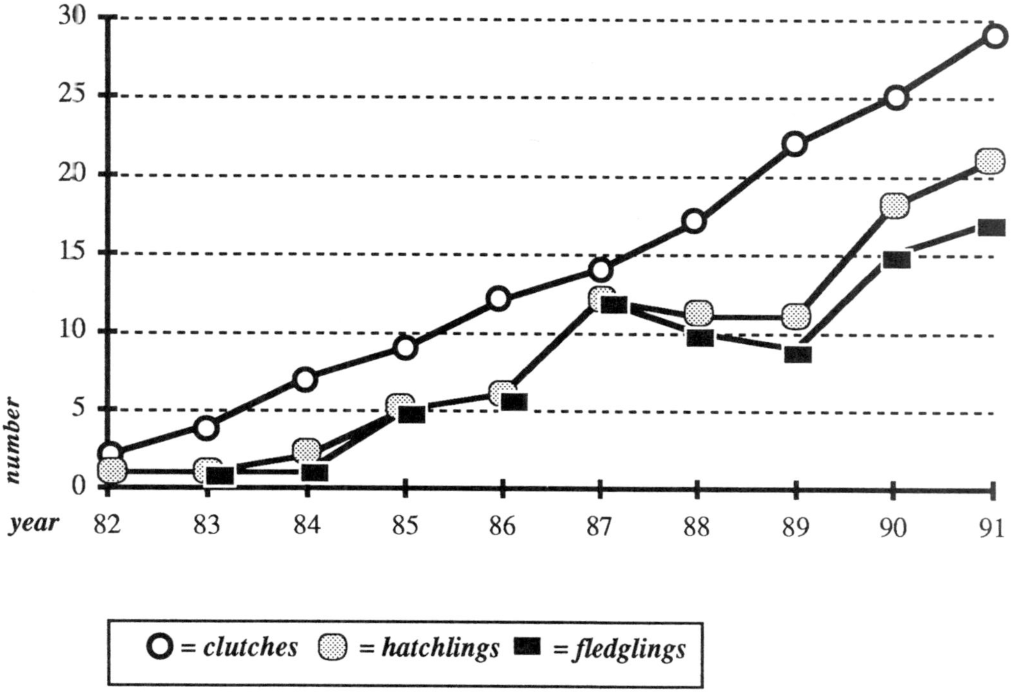

**juvenile mortality*

From 1982 to 1991, 77 Griffon Vultures were born in the wild and 76 of them were ringed. Among these birds, 4 disappeared and 10 died, all of them before the end of their second year (8 as yearlings, 5 before 2 years, 1 before 3 years).

Exchange with other populations

Seasonal movements of Griffon Vultures have been recorded in the Austrian Alps (Perco *et al.* 1983), the Crau (Jaubert & Lapommeraye 1859) and in the Pyrenees (Dendaletche 1970; Elosegui 1987). These vultures forage on areas with high food availability. This could be the case for Crau or Basque country in winter and also for Iberian vultures in the central and Catalonian Pyrenees in summer. In Pyrenean colonies, these movements include only immatures and non breeders and fundamentally differ from those of yearlings in autumn (Elosegui & Elosegui 1977). This behaviour is not a real migration but a juvenile dispersion with a south south-west direction for Pyrenean colonies which lead some individuals to cross the Mediterranean from Gibraltar to Africa (Mauritania and Senegal).

** wandering juveniles in the Causses colony*

Because of the low number of free fledging birds before 1984 (Table 1), the only known case of juvenile dispersion was the disappearance of a yearling in December 1985 and its return to the colony in April 1988. Analyses of juvenile survival and recapture rates are currently being conducted and should confirm this juvenile tendency to move around. Recently, we have received a report on the recovery of a juvenile, born in 1991 and found poisoned in North Senegal, proving that our colony can be involved in the south migration down to sub-Saharan Africa.

** movements of foreign vultures*

In spite of its geographical isolation, the colony of the Causses attracted Iberian and Pyrenean Griffon Vultures. Since 1983, about 9 immigrants settled more or less definitively in the colony (Figures 8 and 10). At least two stayed and one of them paired and reproduced successfully. Five non-marked birds were recaptured in 1988 and 1991 but three of them could have been local birds.

One Griffon Vulture 1 or 2 years old was caught and released at Malaga (Spain) on 14 June 1985. This bird was recaptured in Cuers (Var department) 1159 km away and released in the Causses, where it joined the breeding group of which it is now a member. On the other hand, it is very difficult to know the origin of about 30 vultures observed in France since 1977 (Figure 11). Most of them (especially those observed before the first releases in 1981) probably came from Spanish colonies. These birds usually appear in France after April, in spring and summer, and follow a north-east direction. They come from the eastern Pyrenees and go to the southern Alps following the Rhône valley.

Foraging

Two aims of the project were to settle the colony and to facilitate spatial and feeding emancipation of the breeding group. Thus the feeding places A and B were first established. Feeding site C was later built far away from the colony and the first feeding sites were closed from time to time.

**foraging area*

From 1981 to 1984 the foraging area was equal to the home range (Figure 3). Vultures attracted by the feeding place A did not move away and avoided flying over the Causse. In 1984, the first vultures settled in the Tarn canyon and feeding place B begun to be overflown more regularly. Thus the foraging area expanded to both sides of the valley. It seems that no spontaneous feedings occurred during these first years in spite of the great flying ability of some individuals.

From 1985 to 1988, the foraging area increased (Figures 4 and 5). In 1985, vultures fed at feeding site B and some spontaneous feedings were recorded. When exploring the eastern part of the Causse Méjean, the vultures discovered feeding site C. They landed for the first time in May 1986 and fed there for the first time in April 1987. This event was followed by a more regular exploitation of the food resources of this region (Table 3) and a significant increase of the average

Figure 10. **Number of marked birds entering the population with time.**

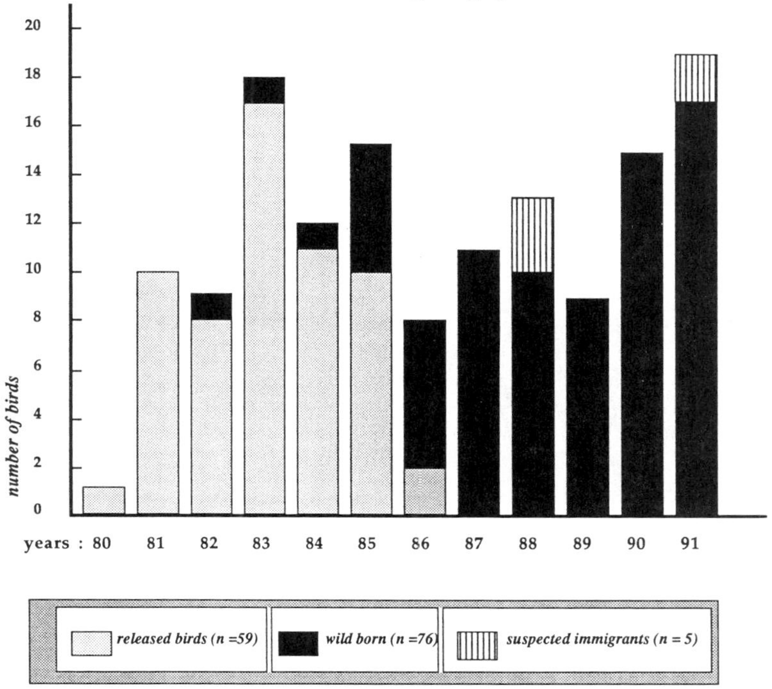

Figure 11. **Records of Griffon Vultures from 1977 to 1989 (outside of the Pyrenean zone).**

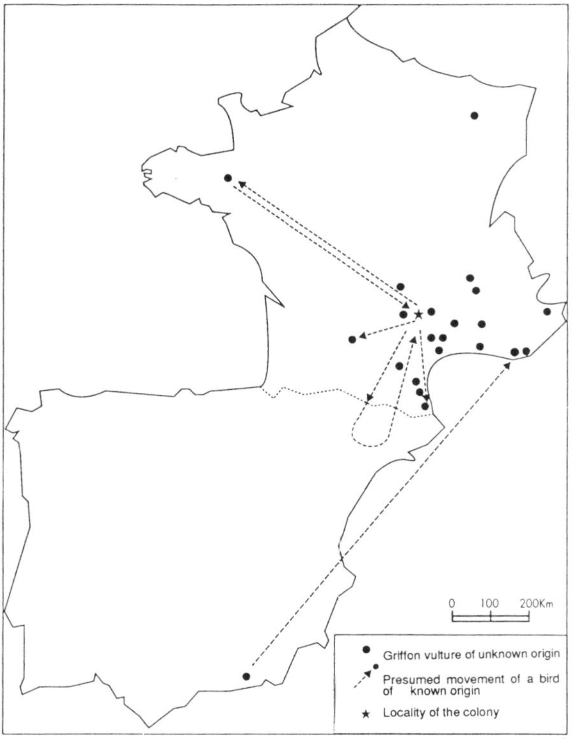

distances between feeding sites. Table 4 and Figures 4 and 5 show the increase of the foraging area and the exploitation of the Causses around the colony. Area measurement only takes into account records of feeding excluding unusually far sightings. They are thus to be considered as minima.

Since 1989 it seems that there was little effort to explore new foraging areas.

Table 3. Distance between observed feeding sites (other than fixed sites A and B) and the release site of the vultures.

Distances (km)	0-5	6-10	11-15	16-20	21-25	Mean Distance	n
1985	5	3	-	-	-	4.6	8
1986	2	3	5	-	1	10.3	11
1987	3	13	8	13	4	12.6	41
1988	11	16	3	28	5	13	63

**foraging method*

The emancipation of released birds and the appearance of wild-born individuals influence the foraging strategy of the whole group. Furthermore, a better flying ability in bad weather conditions allowed Griffon Vultures to forage in winter. The vultures currently forage up to 15 km from the release site.

Table 4. Area (hectares) covered by foraging vultures around the colony.

	1985	1986	1987	1988
Causse Méjean	15.000	17.000	23.800	37.000
Causse de Sauveterre	4.700	8.000	8.300	12.800
Causse Noir (et du Larzac)	3.000	3.400	12.500	6.000
Total	22.700	28.400	44.600	55.800

DISCUSSION

First established in December 1981, the new colony of Griffon Vultures in the Causses is now more than one hundred individuals strong and its increase solely depends on its ability to reproduce and to exploit food resources available on its territory. In studying the number of sheep carcasses produced by local ranching, R.Briquet (1987) showed that four Grands Causses, excepting the south Larzac, on a 200,000 ha area could support a mean population of 700 Griffon Vultures with a monthly fluctuation from 300 in August and September to 1200 in November and December. In order to facilitate the emancipation of the colony and to help foraging on new territories north and south of the current home range, new feeding places are sometimes opened by farmers themselves. This method, associated with the progressive desertion of feeding sites close to the colony, should make the population less dependent on the project team and create closer links with local shepherds. Considering the favourable food resources availability, we can hope for a significant demographic increase during the next years. In spite of a lower breeding success than in the Pyrenees, where an average 0.60 to 0.81 young/pair/year are produced (Elosegui 1989) the turnover of the population with the recruitment of wild-born birds when 4 years old is a good indicator of the vitality of this population.

We saw that this new colony plays an attractive role for even the distant Pyrenean Griffon Vultures. The appearance of Egyptian Vultures *Neophron percnopterus* in 1982 and the settling of the first pair in 1988, albeit without reproduction, are good signs for the return of this species whose nearest nest sites are 80 km away from the Grands Causses.Finally, the reintroduction project of Black Vulture, *Aegypius monachus*, within the framework of the European Black Vulture Conservation Programme scheduled for spring 1992, should complete this scavengers' community.

REFERENCES

BERTHET, G. 1946. Les derniers Vautours fauves du Massif Central. *Rev. Soc. For. Franche-Comté,* 1-6.

BONNET, J., M. TERRASSE, C. BAGNOLINI & J.L. PINNA 1990. Installation et extension d'une colonie de Vautours fauves (*Gyps fulvus fulvus*) réintroduite dans les Grands Causses du Massif Central. *L'Oiseau et la R.F.O.,* V.60 No.3: 181-206.

BRIQUET, R. 1987. Les ressources alimentaires des Vautours fauves dans la région des Grands Causses. Paris, Rapport stage enseignement optionnel de 4ème année-E.N.V.Maisons-Alfort.

BROSSELIN, M. 1971. Réintroduction du Vautour fauve dans les Causses de Lozère et d'Aveyron, *Le Courrier de la Nature,* 18: 74-76.

CADE, T.J. 1979. A perspective of the review of the status of *Falco peregrinus* on the list of endangered species. Unpublished Memor. Cornell University, 1-7.

DENDALETCHE, C. 1970. Observations éthologiques sur quelques grands rapaces des Pyrénées basques. *Bull. Nat. parisiens,* 26: 31-36.

ELOSEGUI, I. 1987. Biologie et éco-éthologie du Vautour fauve. Mémoire de DEA, université de Pau.

ELOSEGUI, I 1989. Vautour fauve (*Gyp s fulvus*), Gypaète barbu (*Gypaetus barbatus*), Percnoptère d'Egypte (*Neophron percnopterus*): Synthèse bibliographique et recherches. *Acta Biologica Montana* 3. Série Document de Travail.

ELOSEGUI, J. & R. ELOSEGUI 1977. Desplazamiento s de buitres comunes (*Gyps fulvus*) pirenaicos, *Munibe*, 29: 97-104.

ESTEVE, R. 1986. La réintroduction du Gypaète barbu dans les Alpes du Nord. *Bièvre*, 8: 35-46.

HEIM DE BALZAC, H. 1922. Excursion ornithologique dans la région des Causses. *Rev. Fr. Orn.*162: 337-341 163: 358-362.

JAUBERT, J.B., & B. LAPOMMERAYE 1859. *Richesses ornithologiques du midi de la France.* Marseille.

LOVE, J. 1983. *The Return of the Sea-eagle.* Cambridge University Press.

NEWTON, I. 1979. *Population Ecology of Raors.* T & A.D.Poyser. Berkhamsted.

PERCO, F., S. TOSO & M. APOLLONIO 1983. Initial data for the study on the status, distribution and ecology of the Griffon Vulture in the Kvarner archipelago. *Larus.* 33-35: 99-134.

ROCHON-DUVIGNEAUD, A. 1921. Les grands rapaces des Gorges du Tarn. *Rev. Fr. Orn.,* 142: 21-25, 143: 33-37.

SOLANET 1894. *Les gorges du Tarn illustrées.* Paris, 154-158.

TERRASSE, J.F. 1977. Maturité sexuelle du Vautour fauve, premières données obtenues dans la nature. *L'O.R.F.O.,* 47(2): 214-218.

TERRASSE, M. 1980. Réintroduction du Vautour fauve dans les Cévennes. *Le Courrier de la Nature*, 70: 32-35.

TERRASSE, M. 1982. Le retour des Bouldras. *Le Courrier de la Nature,* 79: 15-24.

TERRASSE, M. 1983. The project of réintroduction of the Griffon Vulture in the Cévennes, France. *Vulture News,* 4: 7-10.

TERRASSE, M. 1990. Réintroduction du Vautour fauve dans les grands Causses et renforcement de population de Vautour percnoptère. Acte du colloque sur les réintroductions, St-Jean-du-Gard. *Revue d'Ecologie.*

Michel Terrasse
Fonds d'Intervention pour les Rapaces
29 rue du Mont Valérièn
92210 Saint-Cloud
France

Bay Owl *Phodilus badius*

Meyburg, B.-U. & R. D. Chancellor eds.1994
Raptor Conservation Today
WWGBP / The Pica Press

The European Black Vulture *Aegypius monachus* Project in Mallorca

Evelyn Tewes

Status in Europe

Until the middle of the century the Black Vulture (*Aegypius monachus*) was distributed through all north Mediterranean countries. As a result of poisoning and hunting, as well as habitat destruction and food shortage, the population decreased to a mere fraction (see Fig. 1): the species is now extinct in Portugal (Glutz von Blotzheim, Bauer & Bezzel 1971), France (Terrasse 1989), Italy (Bijleveld 1984; Schenk pers. comm. 1990), Cyprus (Cramp & Simmons 1980), Bulgaria (Iankov 1992), Rumania (Glutz von Blotzheim, Bauer & Bezzel 1971), Morocco (Cramp & Simmons 1980), the Crim peninsula (Peklo, pers. comm. 1992) and probably Yugoslavia (Grubac 1990) and Albania. The status in Turkey is not well known, there might be about 100 pairs (Beaman & Porter 1984). Recent decline is supposed (Garzon, pers. comm. 1992). In Greece one colony with 14 breeding pairs is left (Hallman, pers. comm. 1991). The largest European population exists in Spain, which has recovered from about 200 pairs to 774 pairs in 1989 (González, 1990) and is continuously increasing. In Mallorca there now survives the last island population of the Mediterranean with 4 pairs (Tewes 1990).

Figure 1. Present Black Vulture distribution in Europe.

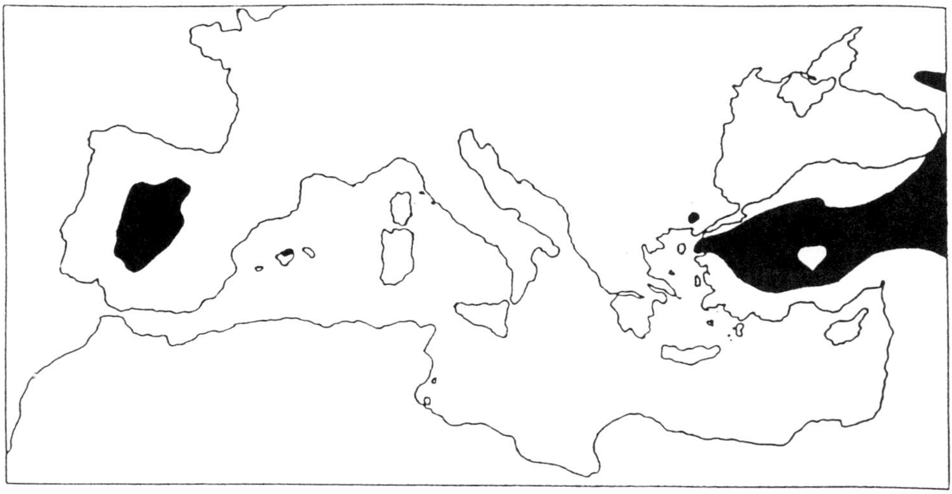

The Black Vulture Conservation Foundation (BVCF)

In view of the alarming situation in Europe, the Black Vulture Conservation Foundation was founded in 1986 with the aim of supporting endangered populations with captive-bred nestlings. At present the Foundation has four projects running (BVCF 1990, 1991, 1992)

1. The breeding project in collaboration with zoos and private breeders,
2. The recovery project in Mallorca, which is well advanced,
3. The recovery project in Greece in preparation,
4. The reintroduction of the species in France, starting this year.

The Mallorcan project

This is where most experience has been obtained. Local and foreign conservationists have been working for the species since the 1960s, when a decline was first noted (Thiollay 1967; Richford, Steward & Houston 1975; Mayol 1975, 1977). In 1983 the first official recovery programme was elaborated by the biologists of the Nature Conservation Section (SECONA) of the Balearic Government (Unid-d de Vida Silvestre, 1983). From 1986 on, a close collaboration started with the Foundation in the recovery programme. This included the restocking of the remaining population, which at that time was about 20-22 birds. Other management measures applied were additional feeding, population control, artificial nest construction, nest guarding in the breeding period and an education programme (Unidád de Vida Silvestre 1987). In 1991 the census showed about 57 birds (Unidád de Vida Silvestre 1991, see Fig. 2). The pre-determined population of over 50 birds had then been reached. It was decided to stop the releases and to wait and see how the doubled population would respond with natural reproduction. The Recovery Programme is now replaced by a Conservation Programme which is continuing with all other management measures.

Figure 2. Black Vulture population development in Mallorca.

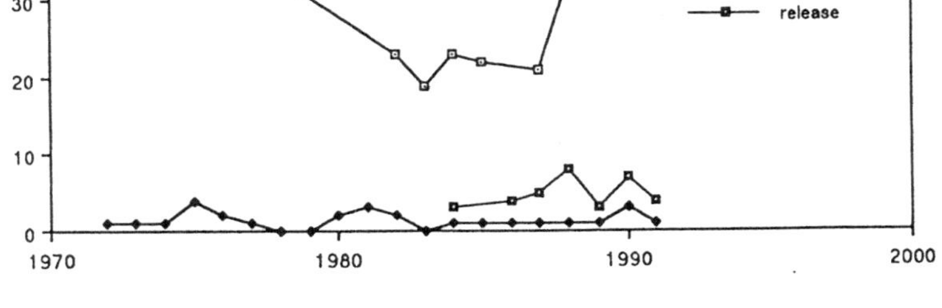

In the release programme three different methods were applied: the first was in 1984 and 1986 and was not successful because the adaptation period of only three days before release was too short. The second ran from 1987-1991. A total of 14 vultures were released from an adaptation cage in the Mallorcan mountain range. The birds had an adaptation period of about four weeks near a feeding place where they had regular contact with the wild Black Vultures. As a third, parallel method, hacking was applied from 1988 to 1990. Eleven captive-bred nestlings from European zoos and one wild-born nestling were released.

A total of 33 Black Vultures have been released in eight years. From the first seven birds in 1984 and '86, two have been found dead, the others disappeared several days or weeks after their release. From the caged birds two disappeared within the first days. From the hacked birds one died five days after its arrival and one has been found dead one year after its release, probably poisoned; both deaths were not due to the release method. Taking into account the observations within the first six months after release, we have a survival rate of 70% of the 33 released birds. The survival rate of the caged birds is 86% and that of the hacked birds is 92%.

All released birds have been marked individually. As marking techniques, plastic coloured rings together with wrap-around patagial wing tags were used in the cage release and coloured rings together with feather bleaching were used in the hacking. The persistence of the wing tags is very variable, between a few days and three years. The feathers bleached with hydrogen were recognizable after 1½-2 years. After moulting or losing the wing tags the birds can be identified by the coloured rings using a 60X telescope up to 300m and with binoculars with 10X magnification up to 75m. Comparing the results of bleached feathers with wing tags, the former have the advantage that they do not inconvenience the birds, cannot be lost and give surer information about the survival of the birds than the wing tags. With the latter you do not know whether the bird died or lost its marks when it disappeared. On the other hand, in some birds with longer-lasting wing tags, the development of the individuals can be followed during a longer period than with the bleaching marks.

The most interesting, as well most laborious, releases have been with the hacking. It was the first time the technique was used with this species. A pilot project started in 1988 with the release of three nestlings, one of which died a few days after. The other two birds developed well, fledged without problems, integrated themselves in the wild population and became independent from our feeding. After this success the hacking continued in 1989 with three and in 1990 with six nestlings. The individual data of the development of all nestlings are shown in Table 1. In 1991 poor breeding success in captivity prevented its continuation. The hacking method was in general applied as in the Reintroduction Project of the Bearded Vulture in the Alps (Frey & Bijleveld 1992). The released birds passed the following phases until they became full members of the population:

1. Parent-or fosterparent raising in a zoo.
2. Transport and introduction to the hacking nest site.
3. Adaptation period.
4. Exercise period.
5. Fledging period.
6. Postfledging period with gradual independence from the release site and integration in the population.

Hand-reared nestlings have not been accepted for hacking because of bad experiences with abnormal behaviour in the Bearded Vulture Project. In 1990 the first foster-parent reared nestling was raised in Zoo de Haye in France together with the true young of the parents. This also proved that cainism does not occur in this species. Both vultures have been successfully released.

In August and September, aged between two and three months, the nestlings were sent to Mallorca, where they needed to spend at least three weeks in an artificial nest before fledging, to become adapted and attached to the place. As the nestling stays without parents, social company is necessary, so at least two nestlings have to be put together. In 1989 the first nestling was left alone for ten days, because the second did not arrive as planned. Its loneliness was evident from its passivity and finally it started to eat less. The moment we obtained a companion bird for it, its behaviour changed completely, it became very active and ate well again. There were up to six nestlings together on the nest platform. Normally they lived together quite peacefully, only competing regularly for the best piece of food. In their social relations different degrees of sympathy could be recognized between individuals, and in one case antipathy.

Between seven and 28 days before fledging, the nestlings started exercising, including wingbeating, jumping and finally short flights on the nest platform.

The nestlings fledged at an age between 97 and 146 days, on average 117 days (see Table 2). One bird that fledged one month older (5 months) than the others (4 months), was introduced to the nest at an advanced age after having had a traumatic history: it was found below the nest in a Spanish colony, hand-reared in a recovery centre and sent to Mallorca already at fledging age (4 months). As the bird was tame, it was not planned to release it. After one week without contact with

Table 1. Individual data of nestlings released by hacking in Mallorca.

Name	Origin	Hatching date (days)	Release date	Age at Release	Fledging date	Age at Fledging	Days in nest
Pep	Son Reus (E)	10.5.1988	6.7	57	4.9	117	60
Gaspard	*De Haye (F)*	*12.5.1988*	*11.9*	*123*	-	-	*6*
Otto	Osnabrück (D)	16.6.1988	26.8	71	29.9	105	34
Colette	De Haye (F)	19.5.1989	19.8	92	8.9	112	20
Suso	Wild colony (E)	1st week of 5.1989	29.8	*ca.*120	24.9	*ca.*146	26
Kalev	Tallinn (USSR)	20.6.1989	1.10	103	19.10	121	18
Mohrli	Grünau (A)	*ca.*6.5.1990	1.8	*ca.*86	2.9	*ca.*118	32
Schönbrunn	Vienna (A)	8.5.1990	1.8	84	3.9	117	33
Valentina	Wassenaar (NL)	8.5.1990	5.8	89	1.9	116	27
Dominique	De Haye (F)	20.5.1990	9.8	81	10.9	114	33
Mulhouse	Mulhouse (F)	30.5.1990	9.8	71	4.9	97	26
Bernardí	La Garenne (CH)	12.5.1990	25.8	105	11.9	122	17

Table 2. Nestlings released by hacking in Mallorca.

	Age at Release (days)	Age at Fledging (days)	Days in Nest
Maximum	*ca.* 120	*ca.* 146	60
Minimum	71	97	17
Average	87	117	30
Considered optimal	80-90		25-35

humans, however, it showed quite normal social behaviour with the other vultures in the cage. At that time a companion for the lonely nestling was urgently needed and this older young was introduced and successfully released.

In the fledging period the birds began with several short, straight flights each day, trying not to lose height. They continued practicing circular flights, gaining height, landing and flying for longer periods every day. After three to ten days they were able to fly well and some days later started to join the wild birds on excursions to neighbouring valleys.

To facilitate the integration of the nestlings into the population, a feeding place was maintained in the release valley. First contacts with the wild birds had already been made when the wild vultures came to feed and rest near the release place, and sometimes also fed on the nest platform with the nestlings. After fledging these fed either on the nest or at the feeding place, in company with the wild vultures.

During the first weeks after fledging the youngsters slept in the release valley; later on they disappeared more and more often for some days from the release place to stay with the wild vultures. In December, two to two and a half months after fledging, they were considered to be integrated in the population. At the beginning of November the youngsters were observed to fly over the whole northern mountain range, Zone 1 of the Black Vulture distribution (see Fig. 3). Later on they used Zone 2 as well and on several occasions have also been seen in the Mallorcan plain, where the population used to feed on rabbits during the summer months.

Figure 3. Distribution in Mallorca.

Zone I: Northern mountain range: breeding and main foranging area.
Zone II: Southern mountain range: regular foraging
Zone III: Mallorcan plain: rare foraging

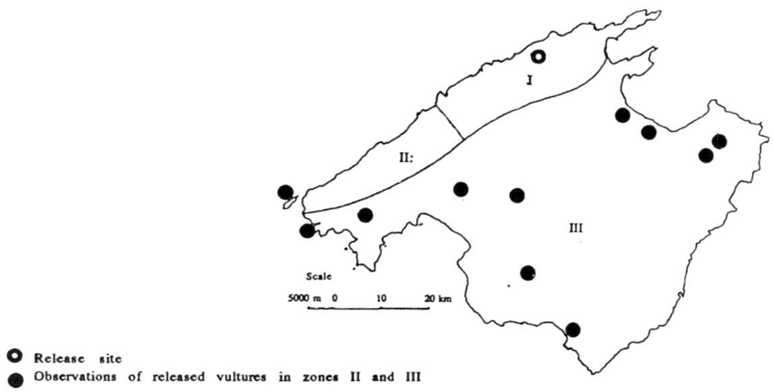

Observation of the nestlings was continuous until they could fly well and started to become independent of the release place. Now the first released nestlings are five years old and from next year on we hope they may start to reproduce. Some of the cage-released birds are already adult. A first sign of the integration of released vultures in the breeding population was observation of a copulation between a subadult vulture with plastic marks and an unmarked bird. The same bird has been observed at a nest but is not yet breeding. Breeding of the released vultures will be proof that the releases have been successful.

ACKNOWLEDGEMENTS

The project has been financed by the Balearic Government, the Frankfurt Zoological Society, WWF Austria, the Austrian Fund for Scientific Investigation (FWF) and the Veterinary University of Vienna. The releases would not have been possible without the help of the zoological gardens and recovery centres of Spain, which donated the captive-bred nestlings and recovered birds.

REFERENCES

BEAMAN, M. & R.F. PORTER 1984. Status of the Birds of Prey in Turkey. *Proc.II. World. Conf. on Birds of Prey.* Thessaloniki.

BIJLEVELD, M. 1974. *Birds of Prey in Europe.* London.

BVCF 1990. Annual Report 1989 (unpubl.).

BVCF 1991. Annual Report 1990 (unpubl.).

BVCF 1992. Annual Report 1991 (unpubl.).

CRAMP, S. & K.E.L. SIMMONS 1980. *Handbook of the Birds of Europe, the Middle East and North Africa,* Vol II, pp 89-95.

FREY, H. & M. BIJLEVELD 1992. The Reintroduction of the Bearded Vulture *Gypaetus barbatus aureus* (Hablizl 1788) into the Alps (this volume).

GLUTZ von BLOTZHEIM, BAUER & BEZZEL 1971. *Handbuch der Vögel Mitteleuropas,* Bd. 4, pp 259-274

GONZÁLEZ, L.M. 1990. Situacíón de las poblaciones de águila imperial y buitre negro en España. *Quercus* 58: 16-22.
GRUBAC, B. 1990. Situation actuelle des Vautours (Aegypinae) en Macedoine. *Proc. I Congreso Internacional sobre Aves Carroñeras*: 139-145.
IANKOV, P. 1992. Changes in Status of the Black Vulture *Aegypius monachus* in Bulgaria during 1980-1990 (this volume).
MAYOL, J. 1975. Un plan para la conservación del Buitre Negro, *Aegypius monachus,* en Mallorca. *Ardeola* 21 (esp): 1017-1028.
MAYOL, J. 1977. Contribución al conocimiento de Buitre Negro (*Aegypius monachus*), en Mallorca. *Bol. Soc. Hist. Nat. Baleares* 22: 150-178.
RICHFORD, A.S., J.G. STEWARD & D.C. HOUSTON 1975. The status of the Black Vulture (*Aegypius monachus*) in Mallorca. *Ardeola* 21 (esp): 225-243.
TERRASSE, J.F. 1989. Le Vautour moine (*Aegypius monachus*) appartient encore a la faune Française. *Alauda* 57,3, pp. 231-232.
TEWES, E. 1990. El Voltor (*Aegypius monachus*) a Europa, un pas endavant en la seva recuperació. *Anuari ornitológic de les Balears* 1990.
THIOLLAY, J.M. 1967. Observations sur le Faucon d'Eleonore (*Falco eleonorae*) et quelques autres rapaces des Baleares. *Nos Oiseaux* 29, pp. 29-40.
UNIDÁD DE VIDA SILVESTRE 1983. Programa de Conservación del Buitre Negro, Mallorca 1983.
UNIDÁD DE VIDA SILVESTRE 1987. Programa de Recuperación del Buitre Negro, Mallorca 1988-90.
UNIDÁD DE VIDA SILVESTRE 1991. Recompte de Voltors 1991.

Evelyn Tewes
Secona
c/ Foners 10, 07006 Palma de Mallorca
Baleares, Spain

Part 7

Population Ecology of Owls

Tengmalm's Owl *Aegolius funereus*

Conveners:

Dr. E. Korpimäki & Dr. H. Pietiäinen

Meyburg, B.-U. & R. D. Chancellor eds.1994
Raptor Conservation Today
WWGBP / The Pica Press

Territorial Behaviour and Habitat Selection by the Scops Owl *Otus scops* in a Karstic Valley (NE Italy)

Paolo Galeotti and Armando Gariboldi

INTRODUCTION

The Scops Owl (*Otus scops*) is a small-sized predator which feeds almost exclusively on invertebrates.

In Italy, it is a summer breeder in the North, arriving in late March-early April and leaving in early September, while it is resident in the South (Fig. 1). Little is known about its status, except for a more or less marked decrease in the mixed farmland of the Po Valley. Furthermore, we have no data on territorial behaviour and habitat selection (Cramp 1985) by this species. We present data collected during a preliminary study of the territorial behaviour and habitat selection by Scops Owls in a karstic valley near Trieste (Northeastern Italy)

STUDY AREA AND METHODS

The Rosandra Valley has a surface area of 460ha, and varies in altitude from 100 to 500m; the vegetation cover is mainly deciduous brushwood (*Ostrya carpinifolia* and *Quercus pubescens*), and the valley is crossed by a small river (which is the only river on the karst plateau.) Habitats included in the valley are shown in detail in Figure 2. The climate of the study area is sub-Mediterranean with rainfall concentrated in spring-autumn and a mean yearly temperature of 12°C.

We censused the Scops Owl population using the playback method for mapping territories (Fallis 1982; Forsman *et al.* 1984; McGarigal & Fraser 1984). We carried out a census at fortnightly intervals, from March to October 1991, eliciting owl calls from 11 spots fixed along a 11.5km transect. We broadcast playbacks of Scops, Tawny and Eagle Owls in succession.

The territories with a minimum of three observations were considered stable and their boundaries were projected using the "minimum convex polygon". Habitat breadth was calculated using the B-Index (Feinsinger *et al.* 1981):

$$B = 1/R \, \Sigma \, p_i^2$$

where
R = number of habitat types
p_i = use-ratio of each habitat

Owl habitat preference was determined considering the area of different habitats in the territories in relation to the total availability of the same habitats in the study area, using Chesson´s (1978) electivity Index (W):

$$W = \frac{p_i/r_i}{\Sigma \, p_i/r_i}$$

where
p_i = use-ratio of each habitat
r_i = availability-ratio of each habitat

Figure 1. Breeding distribution of the Scops Owl in Italy (E= possible breeding; P= probable breeding; C= certain breeding).

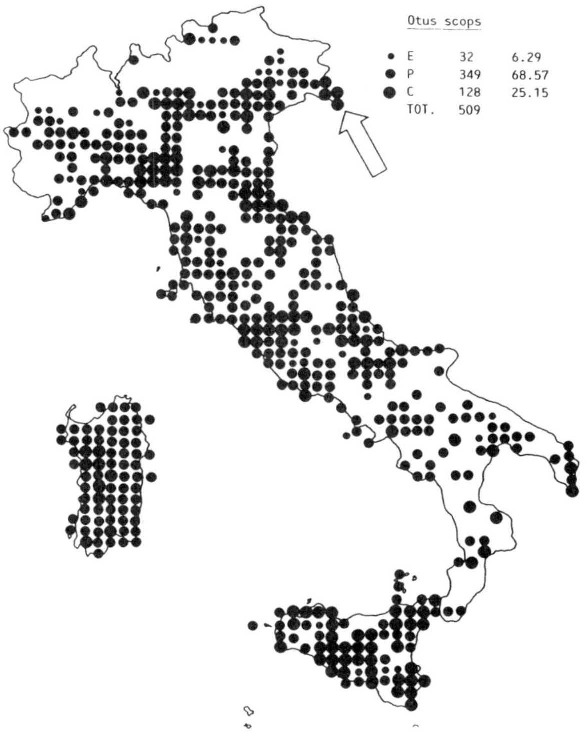

Figure 2. Habitat composition of the study area.

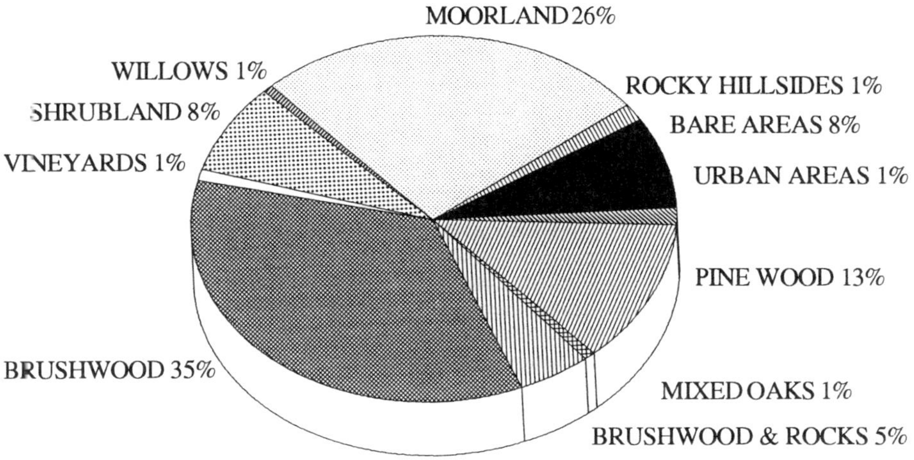

RESULTS

We identified 10 stable territories defended by a pair of Scops Owls and 5 territories with less than 3 contacts defended by a single Scops Owl, with density varying from 2.2 to 3.3 terr/km^2.

We also found 4 Tawny Owl territories and 1 Eagle Owl territory (Fig. 3). All Scops Owl territories had a SW exposure.

Figure 3. Territories of Scops Owls, Tawny Owls und Eagle Owls.

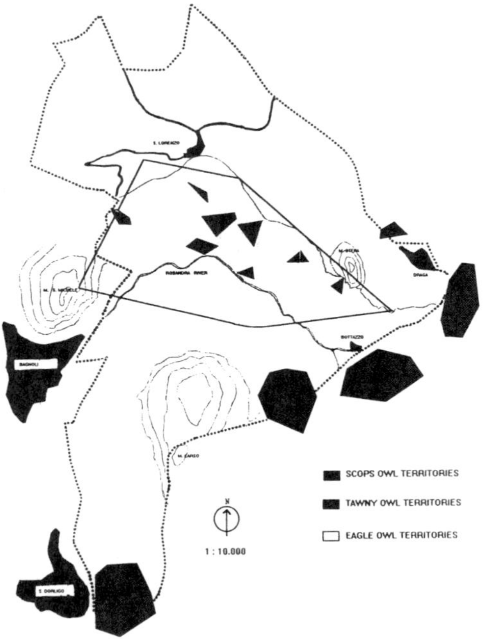

Figure 4. Availability and use of each habitat type by Scops Owls.

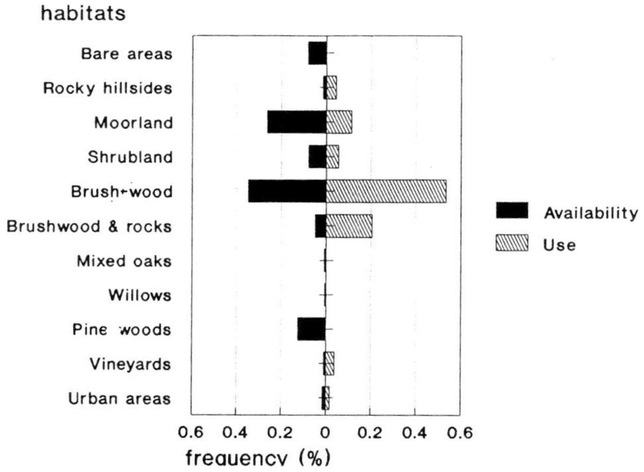

Table 1. Size (ha) of Scops Owl territories (D = mean distance between territories; B = niche-breadth).

Territories	ha	D	B
T1	0.5	204.86	0.26
T2	0.4	169.11 SD	
T3	1.56	12-472 Range	
T4	0.89		
T5	0.79		
T6	0.17		
T7	0.39		
T8	0.47		
T9	0.29		
T10	0.51		
Mean	0.60		
SD	0.38		
Range	0.17-1.56		

Surprisingly, while 9 Scops Owl territories were within the Eagle Owl's territory and were concentrated close to its nest (in which 3 owlets fledged), at a mean altitude of 269.1 ± 80.58m, the Tawny Owl territories were located well outside the breeding range of the Eagle Owl and at a lower altitude (100-150m). The surface area of Scops Owl territories, mean distance between neighbouring territories and habitat breadth are shown in Table 1.

Habitat use by Scops Owls reflects clear preference toward 3 habitat types: rocky hillsides, brushwood with rocks and vineyards. (Table 2). These are the rarest habitats in the Valley (Fig. 4). On the other hand, bare areas, moorland, mixed oaks, willows and pine woods were used less than their availability.

Table 2. Electivity Index values (W; Chesson 1978)

HABITATS	W
BARE AREAS	0.00 -
ROCKY HILLSIDES	0.19 +
MOORLAND	0.03 -
SHRUBLAND	0.05 -
BRUSHWOOD	0.10
BRUSHWOOD & ROCKS	0.29 +
MIXED OAKS	0.00 -
WILLOWS	0.00 -
PINE WOODS	0.00 -
VINEYARDS	0.26 +
URBAN AREAS	0.08

+ indicate preference
- indicate avoidance

DISCUSSION

Our data show that the Scops Owl breeding territories we studied are in general small, but we have no other information on this topic (Cramp 1985). The population density we found is similar to that observed on the Mediterranean island of Port-Cros (France: 1.8-2.3 pairs per km^2; Glutz & Bauer 1980) and higher than that found in central Europe (Czechoslovakia: 0.7 territory per km^2; Randik 1959, in Cramp 1985); on the other hand, in Roumania (Kalabér 1971, in Cramp 1985), southern Tyrol (Austria) and southern France (Glutz & Bauer 1980) Scops Owl densities are on average higher (5 pairs per km^2) than in our study area.

The complementary distribution of Scops and Tawny Owls, and the close vicinity of Scops Owl territories to the Eagle Owl nest, suggest that, apart from feeding habits and habitat requirements, other factors such as microclimate preferences and predation are also involved, the Tawny Owl often preying on the Scops Owl and being preyed on in turn by the Eagle Owl.

REFERENCES

CHESSON, J. 1978. Measuring preference in selective predation. *Ecology* 59: 211-215.

CRAMP, S. 1985. *The Birds of the Western Palearctic*, vol. IV. Oxford University Press.

FALLS, J. B. 1981. Mapping territories with playback: an accurate census method for songbirds. *In:* C. J. Ralph & J. M . Scott (Eds.), *Estimating numbers of terrestrial birds. Studies in Avian biology*, 6. Cooper Ornithol. Soc., pp. 86-91.

FEINSINGER, P., E. E. SPERS & R. W. POOLE 1981. A simple measure of niche breadth. *Ecology*, 62: 27-32.

FORSMAN E., C. MESLOW & A. M. WIGHT 1984. Distribution and biology of the Spotted Owl in Oregon. *Wildl. Monogr.* 87: 1-64.

GLUTZ VON BLOTZHEIM, U. N. & BAUER K. M. 1980. *Handbuch der Vögel Mitteleuropas*, vol 9. Akademische Verlagsgesellschaft, Wiesbaden.

Mc GARIGAL, & FRASER J. D. 1984. The effect of forest stand age on owl distribution in southwestern Virginia. *J. Wildl. Manage.*, 48: 1393-1398.

Paolo Galeotti, Armando Gariboldi
Dipartimento di Biologia Animale
Università di Pavia
Piazza Botta 9
27100 Pavia, Italy

Meyburg, B.-U. & R. D. Chancellor eds.1994
Raptor Conservation Today
WWGBP / The Pica Press

Recruitment in an Eastern Screech Owl *Otus asio* Population: on Components of Fitness and Inheritance

Frederick R. Gehlbach

INTRODUCTION

Since 1967 I have studied the life history and population ecology of Eastern Screech Owls (*Otus asio*) in suburban Waco, Texas, USA, and a nearby rural environment (Gehlbach 1988, 1989). The investigations focussed on comparative aspects related to the cultural versus rural settings. They were intensive in that 20 nest boxes, all natural cavities, and 2km-wide perimeter zones around study plots were used to learn about behaviour, demography, dispersal, life-history strategy, lifetime reproduction, etc. of the owls in 270ha plots at each site. The 1967-1975 period was strictly exploratory, a time to eliminate biases by perfecting techniques, so a confirmatory study could assess four generations of the owls during 1976-1987.

RESULTS

Beginning in 1988, only the suburban population has been monitored, and this account deals entirely with it, employing data on 16 suburban recruits that first nested as yearlings between 1976 and 1991. Overall, 17 of 272 suburban fledglings and one of 58 from the rural population became breeders in suburbia. Two other suburban owlets bred six and 13km from the plot and perimeter zone. The 6 % recovery rate is the highest reported among owls (e.g. Southern 1970; Van Camp & Henny 1975; Korpimäki & Lagerstrom 1988). Besides the recruits, I will note some features of their mothers and environments, pertinent to understanding their recruitment.

Mothers of Recruits

Sixteen owlets that became suburban breeders originated in the initial annual nests of only 10 females (12 % out of 80), all of which were long-lived (2-9 years). One produced four, another three, a third produced two, and the rest one recruit apiece. This strongly skewed distribution (1.43) and the limited number of involved females is evidence that only a few "quality" individuals reproduce successfully. Collectively, the 10 females furnished five recruits at age one, six at two, and five at age three, hence breeding experience did not seem to matter. Also, number of recruits was unrelated to number of lifetime fledglings among the 10 or all 27 long-lived suburban females ($r < 0.37$, ns), contrary to my earlier report on a more limited data-set (Gehlbach 1989).

The recruit-producers used their nest sites as faithfully as all other long-lived females and were similar in other aspects of lifetime reproduction with three important exceptions. They averaged six grams larger ($P= 0.06$), began nesting a week earlier ($P= 0.01$), and were more efficient at fledging offspring from eggs ($P= 0.04$). Perhaps the critical link to recruitment is early nesting by larger females, because such nests generally contain larger clutches with larger eggs that hatch into larger nestlings which grow faster and fledge at larger sizes relative to later nests. Indeed, in a logistic stepwise regression early nesting accounts for more variation (26 %, $P= 0.01$) in recruit-making or not than the total of body mass and fledging efficiency (21 %, $P= 0.05$).

Recruits

Surely recruits come from early nests, because they permit early fledging and thus more time to learn self-sufficiency before dispersal, together with early settlement on home ranges before winter stress. That their mothers nest at larger sizes more efficiently suggests better nutrition, perhaps even better parental care; and, on average, recruits grew 0.3 g/day faster than 30 non-sibling members of their cohorts ($P= 0.07$). Also, they fledged two weeks earlier ($P= 0.01$) with 5g average advantage in body size ($P= 0.05$). In these regards they did not differ from siblings, and none of the owlets differed in hatching order or brood size.

When I regress number of recruits in each of their 10 cohorts on the environmental factors of their fledging years, population density explains 50 % of the variation and is a negative influent ($P= 0.05$) while food supply adds another 41 % to the total explanation and is positive ($P= 0.08$). Neither factor nor any weather parameter explains differences among years in which recruits first nest. Therefore, it is apparent that favourable conditions in the fledging year, not the first breeding year, are important to recruitment and in a density-dependent fashion.

Owlets originating in a sparse population amidst plentiful food are the most probable recruits, because they are less likely to be driven away and more likely to find vacant cavities for roosting and nesting plus sufficient food. Natal-dispersal distance is directly related to population density ($r= 0.65$, $P= 0.01$); and competitive pressure is apparent, as the Eastern Screech Owl is a permanent-resident, polyterritorial species. Natal dispersal averaged 2.7 (median 1.2) km in the suburban population.

Inheritance

Among long-lived suburban females, variation in all reproductive features except first-egg date declined before apparent senescence at five years of age ($P< 0.03$). Can this be due to stabilizing selection? To understand better the selective values of body mass, first-egg date, clutch size, number of fledglings, and production efficiency (fledglings/eggs), repeatability analyses were performed on these features of the 27 long-lived suburban females. Heritabilities of the same attributes among nine female recruits (yearlings) were analysed by regressing them on the yearling characteristics of their mothers.

Body mass has a significantly high repeatability (69 %, $P< 0.001$), nearly matched by its mean heritability (68 %), although all heritability values are insignificant, probably due to the small sample. The body-mass values are close enough to a 60 % estimate of female size attributable to variation other than food supply and mate attentiveness to underscore the importance of inherited size. The remaining four features also have significant ($P< 0.04$) but smaller repeatability and heritability values with number of fledglings being somewhat higher (37 %, 38 % respectively) than the others (19-35 %).

CONCLUSIONS

Recruitment into a breeding population apparently requires selectively advantageous reproductive features that are inherited. In particular, large body mass is selected for, because it also increases the chance of long-term survival (27 long-lived females were larger as yearlings than 19 contemporaries that did not survive beyond one year, P= 0.03). Recruit producing females are larger and more efficient breeders aside from the qualities of their mates. Thus they are able to raise larger offspring earlier, which are more likely to survive their early independence by finding food and housing locally. Long-distance dispersal over potentially inhospitable terrain is avoided.

A low-density population is also important to survival and the local settling of recruits through reduced intraspecific competition for resources; and a plentiful food supply simply augments recruitment, which is fostered primarily by available space in the natal population. Moreover, a low-density population is more likely to promote the genes of recruits which are proportionately more common, hence influential, among fewer nesting individuals.

ACKNOWLEDGEMENTS

This presentation is summarized from sections of three chapters in my manuscript on the life history and population ecology of Eastern Screech Owls. I thank my collaborators and Baylor University for their support, Robert Baldridge for reading this manuscript, and Erkki Korpimäki for inviting my participation in this symposium.

REFERENCES

GEHLBACH, F.R. 1988. Population and environmental features that promote adaptation to urban ecosystems: the case of Eastern Screech Owls (*Otus asio*) in Texas. *Acta XIX Congr. Internatl. Ornithol.* 2: 1809-1813.

GEHLBACH, F.R. 1989. Screech Owl. *In* I. Newton (Ed) *Lifetime Reproduction in Birds*. pp. 315-326 London: Academic Press.

KORPIMÄKI, E. & M. LAGERSTROM 1988. Survival and natal dispersal of fledglings of Tengmalm's Owl in relation to fluctuating food conditions and hatching date. *J. Animal Ecol.* 57: 433-441.

SOUTHERN, H.N. 1970. The natural control of a population of Tawny Owls (*Strix aluco*). *J. Zool. London* 162: 197-285.

VAN CAMP, L.F. & C.J. HENNY 1975. The Screech Owl: its life history and population ecology in northern Ohio. *N. Amer. Fauna* 71.

Frederick R. Gehlbach
Dept. of Biology
Baylor University
Waco, TX 76798
U. S. A.

Scops Owl *Otus scops*

Meyburg, B.-U. & R. D. Chancellor eds.1994
Raptor Conservation Today
WWGBP / The Pica Press

Breeding Biology of the Little Owl *Athene noctua* in France

Jean-Claude Génot

INTRODUCTION

Much work has been devoted to the breeding biology of the Little Owl *Athene noctua* in Europe: Juillard (1984) in Switzerland, Schönn (1986), Exo (1983), Knötzsch (1978) and Ullrich (1973) in Germany and Glue and Scott (1980) in Great Britain. In France, with the exception of a few notes collected by Labitte (1951), no study has yet taken stock of this subject.This communication will present data relating to the Little Owl's nesting sites and breeding in France, collected by inquiry and analysis of the bibliography, from 1895 to 1990 for nesting sites and from 1957 to 1990 for breeding (Hamonville 1895; Pardieu 1927; Pecheyrand 1961; Baudvin 1974; Sardenne 1976; Bergier 1980; Boutinot 1980; Bavoux & Burneleau 1983; Melliger 1987; Pepin 1989; Mandrillon & Renaudier 1989; Aleman & Dalmau 1990 and Joveniaux 1991), as well as the results of a study made by the author from 1984 onwards in the Northern Vosges, a region situated in eastern France, within the framework of the Ecology Laboratory of Dijon University and the Regional Natural Park of the Northern Vosges, with financial aid from the Ministry of Environment.

RESULTS AND DISCUSSION

Nesting sites

In France, the Little Owl lives in extremely varied habitats: traditional orchards, pasture and meadow with pollard willows, cultivated areas, parks, gardens, cliffs, quarries, villages, marshes or the banks of rivers, such as the Loire for example (Pailley *et al.* 1991).

All these habitats frequented by the species nevertheless have points in common:

- the presence of cavities for nesting,
- the existence of roosts for hunting,
- areas of short grass for feeding

The diversity of its habitat explains the great variety of the Little Owl's nesting sites (Table 1).

Trees represent the majority of nesting sites (41.9%), coming before buildings (32.1%) and the other sites (26%). In the Northern Vosges, 25 nests in trees counted by the author are in apple trees (Genot 1990). In the eastern Pyrenees, out of 27 nests in trees, 13 are in willows (Aleman & Dalmau 1990).

Fruit trees, above all apple, and pollarded trees, more particularly willow, offer the most cavities to the Little Owl.This due to the distribution of these two species over the entire French territory but above all to the fact that they offer the Little Owl roomy cavities.The nature of the trees chosen for nesting emphasises the species' anthropophilic character: pruned trees and fruit-producing trees. In spite of the tranquillity it needs in order to breed, the Little Owl willingly nests in inhabited houses (n=34). It installs itself usually under the roof, using a displaced tile or an opening in fibreglass. It can also nest in a hole in a facade or ventilation hole.

Table 1: Nesting sites of the Little Owl in France

NESTING SITES	n	%	NESTING SITES	n	%
TREES	222	41.9	BUILDINGS	170	32.2
FRUIT TREES	99	18.7	Inhabited house	34	
Apple *Malus domestica*	73		Farm	29	
Pear *Pyrus pyraster*	9		Barn	19	
Walnut *Juglans regia*	7		Hut, shed	15	
Cherry *Prunus avium*	6		Church	9	
Undetermined	3		Ruin	8	
Apricot *Prunus armeniaca*	1		Sheep-fold	8	
			Loft	7	
OTHER	67	12.6	Electric transformer	2	
Undetermined	13		Blockhouse	2	
Mulberrv *Morus alba*	9		Football changing-room	1	
Willow *Salix*	9		Garage	1	
Poplar *Populus*	8		Chicken-house	1	
Plane *Platanus acerifolia*	8		Other	34	
Ash *Fraxinus excelsior*	5				
Oak *Quercus*	2		OTHER SITES	138	26.00
Maple *Acer*	2		Nestbox	61	
Sweet chestnut			Piles of stones	19	
Castanea sativa	2		Wall	17	
Conifer	2		Rockface	16	
Tamarisk *Tamarix gallica*	2		Quarry	14	
Weeping willow			Burrow	4	
Salix babylonica	1		Cliff	2	
Horse chestnut			Haystack	1	
Aesculus hippocastanum	1		Bale of straw	1	
Linden *Tilia*	1		Woodpile	1	
Palm	1		Fallen tree	1	
Elm *Ulmus*	1				
			TOTAL	530	100
POLLARD TREES	56	10.6			
Willow *Salix*	38				
Oak *Quercus*	6				
Ash *Fraxinus excelsior*	5				
Poplar *Populus*	3				
Undetermined	3				
Mulberry *Morus alba*	1				

Currently modern houses do not offer as many cavities and openings as traditional houses in mud and wattle, half-timbered, with thatched roof or a tile with an opening into the loft. Certain owners who cohabit with the Little Owl have confirmed its presence in their house for several decades.

The Little Owl lives essentially in rural areas, which leads to occupation of agricultural buildings: farms, barns, sheds, sheep-folds, chicken-houses (n=72). The species may also inhabit churches (n=9), quiet places but often monopolised by the Barn Owl *Tyto alba.*

For the other sites, nestboxes are relatively important (n=62). If the diameter of the entry is 7 cm and the position is suitable, the model is of little significance.

The choice of sites such as piles of stones, walls and rockfaces (n=52) justifies the species' German name: Steinkauz or Stone Owl. The cases of nesting in rabbit burrows or foxholes are exceptional. Unlike trees, buildings and other sites of human origin, rockfaces, cliffs, stony areas or burrows form natural nesting sites.These are principally found in the south of France and correspond to the only cavities available in its original habitats: open country from the Mediterranean basin to central Asia (Mikkola 1983).

Comparison of the type of nesting sites with other authors

TYPE OF NESTING SITES

The Little Owl clearly prefers hollow trees in western Europe (Table 2). But the species does adapt to local conditions for nesting and settles for buildings where there are no hollow trees.The proportion of trees is lower in France, as many regions do not have the pollarded trees or the fruit trees necessary for nesting. Moreover, "stone" sites, such as piles of stones, rockfaces, walls, ruins, are more frequent in the Mediterranean part of the country (Juillard 1985). Finally, the survey takes into account data from ornithologists who have installed Little Owl nestboxes.

Table 2: Comparison of nesting sites in different European countries

Country	Total number of nests	% Trees	% Buildings	% Other	Author
France	530	41.9	32.1	26	Génot present study
Great Britain	526	91.6	6.6	1.8	Glue & Scott (1980)
West Germany	319	66.5	26.6	6.9	Richter (1973) Hegger (1977) Exo (1981) Mildenberger (1984)
East Germamy	316	54.4	27.5	18.1	Schönn (1986)
Switzerland	33	78.8	21.2		Juillard (1980)

HEIGHT OF NESTING CAVITIES FROM THE GROUND

The greatest average height, noted by Juillard (1984), is explained by the taking into account of nestboxes fixed quite high with the help of a ladder.The other average values are between 2.4 and 3 m (Table 3) and correspond to cavities in trees. In the Northern Vosges the average height of 26 cavities situated in fruit trees is 2.62 m.When the Little Owl nests in buildings, cavities are generally higher and may be over 10 m.

Table 3: Comparison of average heights of nesting cavities in different countries

Country	Author	Number of nests studied	Average height in metre
Great Britain	Glue & Scott (1980)	482	3.00
France	Genot	74	2.93
East Germany	Schönn (1986)	62	2.50
Switzerland	Juillard (1984)	59	3.90
West Germany	Exo (1981)	28	2.40

Breeding

MATING

In particular regions, mating can take place from February to May but it is more frequent in March and April. Some dates are known: 07.02.87, 04.03.80, 15.03.80, 20.03.82, 13.05.87, 15.03.88, 19.04.88 and 02.05.89. Mating was observed on 04.07.88 in eastern France: did this precede replacement egg-laying or was it mating in vain (Hainard 1955)?

EGG-LAYING DATE

In the Northern Vosges, the author notes egg-laying frequency of 58% (n=24) between the third decade of April and the first decade of May. Labitte (1951) states that 60% of egg-laying dates (n=23) are in the second decade of April. Egg-laying appears to be later in the south, where the feeding of young in July coincides with the abundance of insects and in particular of orthoptera. In France, the earliest laying of eggs was recorded on 18.01.27 in the department of Allier (Pardieu 1927).

Figure 1: Number and size of 94 clutches in France

CLUTCH SIZE

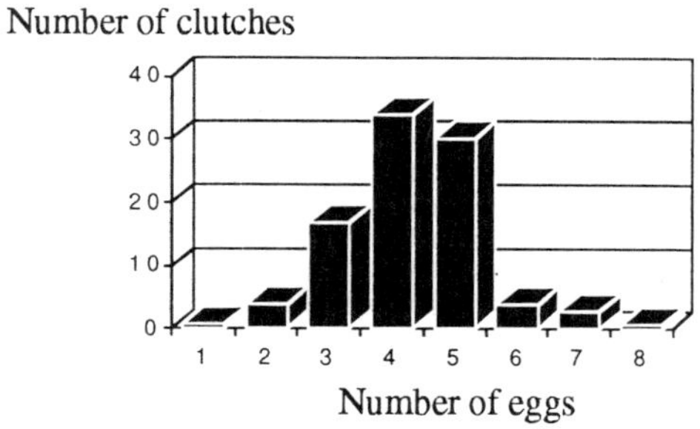

The average is 4.24 eggs per breeding pair (n=94) (Figure 1). It is interesting to compare this result with that of Labitte (1951) which indicates an average clutch size of 3.91 (n=80) for the period 1918-1950. This value, less than that recorded between 1957 and 1990, appears to eliminate contamination by biocides, of less importance before 1950, as the cause of a drop in fertility.

In the Northern Vosges, the average clutch size is 3.96 (n=33) and 3 replacement clutches were recorded out of the total of 33. Replacement clutches are rare and never exceed 10% (Knötzsch 1978 and Furrington 1987).

NUMBER OF FLEDGED YOUNG

The average productivity is 2.96 fledged young per successful breeding pair (n=218) (Figure 2), which places France among the average of European results (Table 6). In the Northern Vosges, the number of fledged young per successful breeding pair is 2.91 (n=22).

Figure 2: Number of fledged young per successful breeding pair (n=218) in France

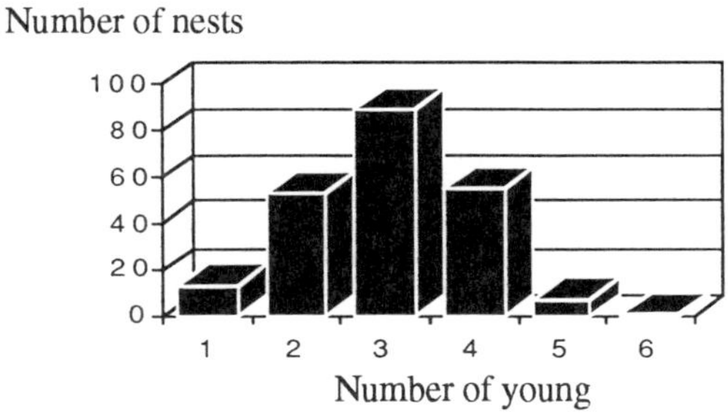

GEOGRAPHICAL AND SEASONAL VARIATIONS IN THE BREEDING RESULTS IN FRANCE

The values of clutch size and number of fledged young per successful breeding pair have been classified according to geographical region (Table 4); those of clutch size, number of hatched young per breeding pair and per successful breeding pair, as well as number of fledged young per successful breeding pair according to climatic region: oceanic, semi-continental and Mediterranean (Table 5).

Table 4: Average and standard deviation of breeding results in France according to geographical region

BP = breeding pair SBP = successful BP	North	South	East	West
Number of eggs/BP				
sample	35	22	26	9
average	4.2	4.7	4.5	3.8
standard deviation	1.0	0.9	1.1	0.7
Number of fledged young /SBP				
sample	119	81	77	32
average	2.8	3.0	3.1	2.6
standard deviation	0.9	0.8	0.9	0.7

The results in Table 4 reveal a significant difference between clutch size in the south and west ($p<0.02$) and between the number of fledged young per successful breeding pair in the east and west ($p<0,02$) and in the south and west ($p<0,03$).

Table 5: Average and standard deviation of breeding results in France according to climatic region.

BP = breeding pair SBP = successful BP	Mediterranean climate	Oceanic climate	Semi-continental climate
Number of eggs/BP			
sample	8	19	34
average	4.7	4.0	4.5
standard deviation	1.1	0.8	1.0
Number of hatched young/BP			
sample	3	19	31
average	3.0	3.3	3.8
standard deviation	1.0	0.8	1.0
Number of hatched young/SBP			
sample	3	6	21
average	3	3	4
standard deviation	1.0	0.8	0.8
Number of fledged young/SBP			
sample	41	61	82
average	3.1	2.5	3.1
standard deviation	0.8	0.9	0.9

The results in Table 5 show a significant difference ($p<0.03$) between the number of hatched young per successful breeding pair in oceanic and semi-continental climates.

As regards the number of fledged young per successful breeding pair, a highly significant difference exists between oceanic and semi-continental climates ($p<0.001$) and between oceanic and Mediterranean climates ($p<0,002$). The synthesis of these comparisons shows better overall productivity (number of fledged young per successful breeding pair) in the east and in the south than in the west, and higher fertility (clutch size) in the south than in the west.

COMPARISON OF BREEDING RESULTS IN FRANCE WITH OTHER COUNTRIES

Table 6 shows that the average clutch size in France (4.24) is between the value indicated in Great Britain (3.59) by Glue and Scott (1980) and those established in Germany by Schönn (1986) (4.11) and Furrington (1987) (4.43), in Hungary (5.00) by Nemeth *in* Schönn (1986) and in Rumania (5.24) by Kohl *in* Schönn *et al.* (1991), confirming the relationship pointed out by Exo (1983) concerning the increase in clutch size from west to east. In the east, this fertility appears to increase with the aridity as in the desert of Turkmenistan (Sopyiev 1982). Table 6 also underlines the difference in average productivity between the Northern Vosges and the rest of France. The value of 1.45 fledged young per breeding pair (n=40) represents the lowest average productivity in Europe. It is lower than values recorded in Switzerland (Juillard 1984 and Baur in Krischer 1990) and in Germany (Schönn 1986 and Kaus 1981), already considered as insufficient for the maintenance of the species by Exo and Hennes (1980). In the rest of France, the average number of fledged young per breeding pair is 2.84 (n=237), one of the best values in Europe.

Table 6: Comparison of breeding results in France with other countries.

Country	E/BP		HY/BP		HY/SBP		FY/BP		FY/SBP		Author
	x	n	x	n	x	n	x	n	x	n	
EAST GERMANY	4.11	126	2.35	111	3.48	75	1.871	67	2.84	10	Schönn (1986) 1960 - 1985
WEST GERMANY											
Franconia							1.961	21	2.93	81	Kaus (1981) 1975 - 1981
North Rhineland, Coesfeld							3.122	94			Rusch (1989) 1982 - 1988
North Rhineland, Kleve	3.61	96	2.52	81	3.24	63	1.89	89	2.75	61	Exo (1987) 1974 - 1984
North Rhineland, Weil	3.87	154					2.041	86			Illner *in* Schönn *et al.* (1991) 1974 - 1982
North Würtemberg, Heilbronn	4.43	112	2.74	120	5.21	74	2.831	70	3.18	98	Furrington (1987) 1973 - 1987
Lake of Constance	4.42	265	3.49	265			2.662	65			Knötzsch *in* Schönn et al. (1991) 1973 - 1988
Würtemberg, Göppingen	4.12	141	2.78	203	3.78	149	2.352	03	3.341	43	Ullrich *in* Schönn *et al.* (1991) 1969 - 1986
Sarr			3.15	99							Schwarzenberg *in* Hahn (1984) 1980 - 1983
SWITZERLAND											
Ajoie	3.12	153	2.22	153	2.78	122	1.821	53			Juillard (1984) 1973 - 1980
Basle	3.78	76	2.98	76	4.72	48	1.78	76	2.83	48	Baur *in* Krischer (1990) 1981 - 1990
GREAT BRITAIN	3.59	268					2.402	41			Glue & Scott (1980) 1939 - 1975
CZECHOSLOVAKIA	3.90	12			2.84	39					Danko (1985a and b, 1986 and 1989) 1982, 1983, 1986 and 1989
HUNGARY	5.00	89									Nemeth *in* Schönn (1986) 1910 - 1976
RUMANIA	5.24	21									Kohl *in* Schönn *et al.* (1991) 1902 - 1975
FRANCE	4.24	94	3.62	53	3.70	30	2.842	37	2.962	18	Génot survey 1957 - 1990
Eure-et-Loir	3.91	80									Labitte (1951) 1918 - 1950
Northern Vosges	3.96	33	3.50	6			1.45	40	2.90	22	Génot study 1984 - 1991

E/BP: number of eggs per breeding pair
HY/BP: number of hatched young per breeding pair
HY/SBP: number of hatched young per successful breeding pair
FY/BP: number of fledged young per breeding pair
FY/SBP: number of fledged young per successful breeding pair

Losses during breeding

The main cause of clutch losses is predation (Table7). This percentage (65.2%, n=69) is due to taking into account the Northern Vosges study results, which highlight important predation by the Stone Marten *Martes foina* with 19 out of 40 clutches destroyed.

Table 7: Losses of clutches and young in nests in France

Cause-Clutch	n	%	Cause-young in nest	n	%
Predation	45	65.2	Undetermined	8	40
Disturbance	10	14.5	Flooding	5	25
Sterility	9	13.0	Cannibalism	3	15
Human destruction	2	2.9	Taking from nest	2	10
Bad weather	2	2.9	Predation	2	10
Undetermined	1	1.5			
TOTAL	69	100	TOTAL	20	100

The predation rate is the highest in Europe, as Juillard (1984) notes only 25.8% (n=31), Glue and Scott (1980) 1 0.8% (n=37) and Schönn (1986) 31 .2% (n=48). Sterility, which represents 13% of egg loss in France, is higher than in Great Britain, with 5.4% (n=37) (Glue & Scott 1980) and in East Germany with 8.3% (n=48) (Schönn 1986) but less than in Switzerland where Juillard (1984) notes 51.6% loss (n=31).

As far as loss of young in the nest is concerned, predation only covers 10% of cases (n=20) whereas it is 15% in Switzerland (n=60), 23.5% in East Germany (n=51) and 33.4% in Great Britain (n=15). Cases of syngenophagy (cannibalism) are rare (15%, n=20) compared with Switzerland where Juillard (1984) records 33.3% (n=60). Exo (1983) reports about ten cases where the youngest chick has disappeared, probably eaten by its elders, whereas Schönn (1986) considered cannibalism as a cause of loss secondary to victims succumbing to illness, lack of food or to the development of cloaca in the nest.

CONCLUSION

In France the Little Owl mainly adopts fruit trees for its nest but may choose buildings when trees are rare. The average productivity, 2.84 fledged young per breeding pair (n=237) is one of the best in Europe. But in the Northern Vosges, this productivity, 1.45 fledged young per breeding pair (n=40), can drop well below the level needed to maintain populations, for reasons which do not appear to be linked only to trophic resources (Génot 1992).The number of fledged young per successful breeding pair increases from west to east and south and clutch size from west to south. The very low productivity in the Northern Vosges is probably linked to the lack of food, to the isolation of pairs and perhaps to a lack of social stimulation by singing birds, as is the case with the quail *Coturnix coturnix* (Guyomarc'h 1991).

ACKNOWLEDGEMENTS

I wish to thank the following for all the information they gave me: J. Alamargot, Y. Aleman, D. Ambroise, C. Ancelet, P. Athanaze, J.-C. Austruy, C. Bavoux, P. Bayle, D. Bersuder, G. Bertran, F. et J.-C. Bertrand, D. Bestel, Y. Bleichner, G. Boisson, F. Boleat, J. Bonnet, J-L. Bourrioux, M. Bouvier, J.-M. Bronner, G. Bultel, F. Burda, la Centrale ornithologique Ar Vran, la Centrale ornithologique picarde, le Centre d'études ornithologiques d'Alsace, le Centre d'études ornithologiques de Bourgogne, le Centre ornithologique Auvergne, le Centre ornithologique Champagne-Ardennes, le Centre ornithologique lorrain, le Centre ornithologique Rhône-Alpes, G. Coppa, F.P.L. Cordier, G. Couloumy, R. Dallard, P. Deschamps, D. Desmots, D. Ducruet, F. Dziezuck, L. Frebet, M. Gallardo, P. Garguil, L. Gelineau, M. Gervais, P. Gradoz, G. Greff, le Groupe ornithologique normand, le Groupe ornithologique savoyard, le Groupe ornithologique Touraine, J.-P. Hiss, Indre Nature, C. Ingouf, F. Jallu, G. Jarry du C.R.B.P.O., M. Juillard, B.Kabouche, B. Kerdelhue, C. Kurtz, F. Kwast, P. Labalette, C. Le Bihan, D. Lecci, P. Lecomte, T. Lefevre, O. Lemoine, F. Lloret, J.-P. Mannechez, P. Mariatte, J.-J. Marquart, N. Martin, D. Martinoles, A. Maurer, T. Michel, C. Nappee, C. Naudi, P. Odez, Mr Ormond, P. Pailley, J.-L. Pernot, I. Picard, M. Pierrat, M. Renner, M. Ribette, B. Ricau, J.-M. Rihoux, G. Ritter, R. Rosoux, P. Rossetti, D. Roux, L. Russias, B. Sonnerat, F. Spill, F. Steimer, J.-C. et F. Sturm, G. Teyssier, P. Transon, J.-M. Triboulot, D. Vein, J.-P Vieron, A. Wernet.

I also wish to thank Yves Muller who was kind enough to carry out the statistical tests.

REFERENCES

ALEMAN, Y. & J.DALMAU 1990. La Chouette chevêche *(Athene noctua)* dans les Pyrénées-Orientales.1. Les sites de nidification. *La Melanocephale* 7 :16-27.

BAUDVIN, H. 1974. Le surmulot *(Rattus norvegicus)* proie de la Chevêche *(Athene noctua). Jean-le-Blanc* 13: 25.

BAVOUX, C. & G.BURNELEAU 1983. Statut des rapaces nocturnes a l'Ile d'Oléron. *Trajhasse. Bull. Groupe Ornithologique Aunis-Saintonge* 13-14: 64-68.

BERGIER, P. 1980. L'avifaune nicheuse des Alpilles. *Bull. Centre de Recherche Ornithologiques de Provence* 3: 27.

BOUTINOT, S. 1980. *Étude écologique de l'avifaune du Vermandois. Structure, dynamique et évolution des populations depuis 1950.* Thèse d'université. Université de Reims. 443 p. (p. 178).

DANKO, S. 1985a. Report on activities of the group for research and protection of birds of prey and owls in Czechoslovakia in 1982. *Bull. World Working Group Birds of Prey* 2: 48.

DANKO, S. 1985b. Report on activities of the group for research and protection of birds of prey and owls in Czechoslovakia in *1983. Bull World Working Group Birds of Prey* 2: 50.

DANKO, S. 1986. Report on activities of the Group for Research and Protection of Birds of Prey and Owls in Czechoslovakia in 1*986.Buteo* 1: *22.*

DANKO, S. 1989. Report on the Activity of the Group for Research and Protection of Birds of Prey and Owls in Czechoslovakia in 1*989.Buteo* 4: 1-2*8.*

EXO, K.-M. 1981. Zur Nistökologie des Steinkauzes *(Athene noctua). Vogelwelt* 102: 161- 180.

EXO, K.-M.1983. Habitat, Siedlungsdichte und Brutbiologie einer niederrheinischen Steinkauzpopulation *(Athene noctua). Ökologie der Vögel* 5 :140.

EXO, K.-M. 1987. *Das Territorialverhalten des Steinkauzes (Athene noctua). Eine verhaltensökologische Studie mit Hilfe der Telemetrie.* Inaugural-Dissertation zur Erlangung des Doktorgrades der Mathematisch Naturwissenschaftlichen Fakultät der Universität zu Köln. 238 p.

EXO, K-M. & R. HENNES 1980. Beitrag zur Populationsökologie des Steinkauzes *(Athene noctua)*-eine Analyse deutscher und niederländischer Ringfunde. *Vogelwarte* 30: 162 - 179.

FURRINGTON, H. 1987. Steinkauz - Bestandsentwicklung auf einer ca .750 km² großen Fläche im Landkreis Heilbronn von 1973 - 1987. *D.B.V. AG zum Schutz bedrohter Eulen. Informationsblatt* 27: 2-4.

GÉNOT, J.-C.1990. Habitat et sites de nidification de la Chouette chevêche, *Athene noctua* SCOP., en bordure des Vosges du Nord. *Ciconia* 14: 85-115.

GÉNOT, J.-C.1992. *Contribution à l'éco-écologie de la Chouette chevêche, Athene noctua, (Scop.) en France.* Thèse de doctorat. Université de Dijon. à paraltre: 245 p.

GLUE, D.E. & D.SCOTT 1980. Breeding biology of the Little Owl. *Brit. Birds* 3: 1 67- 1 80.

GUYOMARC'H, J.-C. 1991. *Biologie et gestion de la Caille des blès Coturnix c. coturnix ou Caille européenne. Bilan sommaire des recherches réalisées entre 1984 et 1990.* Laboratoire d'écologie. Universite de Rennes. Office National de la Chasse .27 p.

HAHN, E. 1984. *Welche der mitteleuropäischen Eulenarten eignet sich als Biomonitor*? Diplomarbeit Universität des Saarlandes. Saarbrücken.249 p.

HAINARD, R. 1955. Accouplement <<inutile>> et attitude de chant chez la Chouette chevêche. *Nos*

Oiseaux 23: 48-49.
HAMONVILLE, D'L. 1895. Les oiseaux de la Lorraine. *Mem.Soc.Zool.France,* 8 :257.
JOVENIAUX, A. 1991. La Chouette chevêche. Biologie, comportement, habitat... *Jura Nature* 47: 10-12.
JUILLARD, M. 1984. *La Chouette chevêche.* Prangins: Nos Oiseaux.243 p.
JUILLARD, M. 1985. A propos des habitats de la Chouette chevêche, *Athene noctua,* dans les régions méditerranéennes. *Nos Oiseaux* 38 :121-132.
KAUS, D. 1981. Steinkauz in Franken. *Vortrag auf der Tagung der A. G. zum Schutz bedrohter Eulen, Giessen* 6-8.
KNOTZSCH, G. 1978. Ansiedlungsversuche und Notizen zur Biologie des Steinkauzes *(Athene noctua). Vogelwelt* 99: 41-54.
KRISCHER, O. 1990. Rückgang der Steinkauzpopulation in der Region *Basel. Mitglieder - Informationen A.G. zum Schutz bedrohter Eulen* 35:3-4.
LABITTE, A. 1951. Notes biologiques sur la Chouette chevêche, *Carine noctua vidalii* A.E. Brehm, 1857. *L'Oiseau et R.F.O.* 21: 120-126.
MANDRILLON, L. & A.RENAUDIER 1989. *Chronique ornithologique départementale Effraie CORA Section Rhone* 7 :12-53.
MELLIGER, I .1987. Steinkauzfamilie in Naturhöhle. *Vögel der Heimat* 57: 116-117.
MIKKOLA, H. *1983. Owls of Europe.* Calton: T & AD Poyser. 397 p.
PARDIEU, Marquis de. 1927. Nidification précoce d'une Chevêche. *R.F.O.* 11: 118.
PAILLEY, M., P. PAILLEY& L.-M. PREAU 1991. Prédation de la Chouette chevêche *(Athene noctua)* sur des populations nicheuses de Sternes pierregarin *(Sterna hirundo)* et de Sternes naines *(S.albifrons)* en Maine-et-Loire. *L'Oiseau et R.F.O.* 61: 337-338.
PECHEYRAND, R. 1961. La Chevêche. In *Chouettes et hiboux.* Paris: Crepin Leblond et Cie.63 p. (p. 41-44).
PEPIN, D. 1989. Dans l'intimité des petites chouettes aux yeux d'or. *L'Oiseau magazine* 16*:* 9-11.
RUSCH, W. 1989. Schleiereulen-und Steinkauzbestandserhebung im Kreis Coesfeld 1988. *Kiebitz* 9: 34-36.
SARDENNE, J. 1976. Les oiseaux nicheurs d'une propriété rurale corrézienne. *Ornithologie en Limousin* 6: 59, annexe 3.
SCHÖNN, S. 1986. Zu Status, Biologie, Ökologie und Schutz des Steinkauzes *(Athene noctua)* in der *D.D.R. Acta ornithoecol.* 1 :103-133.
SCHÖNN, S., W. SCHERZINGER, K.-M. EXO & R. ILLE 1991. *Der Steinkauz.* Wittenberg Lutherstadt: Die Neue Brehm-Bücherei. A Ziemsen Verlag. 237 p.
SOPYIEV, O. 1982. On some adaptations of birds due to the anthropogenic effects on the Kara-Kum desert *Abstracts XVIII Congr. Int. Orn. Moscow* p. 1060-1061.
ULLRICH, B. 1973. Beobachtungen zur Biologie des Steinkauzes *(Athene noctua). Anz. Orn. Ges. Bayern* 12: 163-175.

Jean-Claude Génot
Regional Natural Park of the Northern Vosges
67290 La Petite-Pierre
France

Ecology Laboratory
Dijon University
21034 Dijon Cedex
France

Meyburg, B.-U. & R. D. Chancellor eds.1994
Raptor Conservation Today
WWGBP / The Pica Press

Moult in Tawny Owls *Strix aluco* in Relation to Food Supply and Reproductive Success

S. J. Petty

ABSTRACT

1.The number of flight feathers (rectrices and remiges) moulted annually in Tawny Owls was investigated by dye-marking feathers one year, before moult commenced, and recapturing the owls in the following year. The recaptures of 214 females and 91 males from a forest in northern England were used in the analyses.

2. There was considerable variation in the number of wing feathers moulted annually. Males moulted slightly more feathers than females but the differences were not significant. The median number of primary feathers moulted annually for males and females was 6 and 4 respectively out of a total of 20. For secondary feathers it was 10 and 9 respectively for males and females out of 26.

3. Wing feather moult was significantly related to breeding success. Birds that did not breed moulted most feathers, while those that reared the largest broods moulted fewest.

4. Breeding success of Tawny Owls was significantly related to a three-year cycle of Field Vole abundance. Therefore, because moult was related to breeding success, it was also indirectly related to vole abundance. The result was that Tawny Owls moulted most wing feathers in years of low vole abundance, when most did not breed, and fewest in years of high vole numbers (increasing and decreasing vole year classes) when most pairs bred.

5. Tail feather moult was not related to breeding success, or to any other factor investigated. Most birds replaced all twelve tail feathers biennially. Usually all feathers were replaced in the same year, but in a minority of birds a variable number of feathers were replaced each year, although individual feathers were only replaced every two years.

6. The reasons for the evolution of different moulting strategies for feather tracts are discussed. All body feathers were replaced annually and this may be crucial to prevent heat loss. The moult of wing feathers can be deferred for one, two or even more years. This suggests that in a perch hunter like the Tawny Owl, the condition of wing feathers is less important than tail feathers which are maintained in better condition by a biennial moult. Tail feathers are probably more important for steering Tawny Owls when they drop from perches onto prey.

INTRODUCTION

The replacement of feathers is necessary for both efficient insulation and flight (for reviews see Payne 1972; King 1980). Most passerines undergo a complete annual moult whereas many larger, longer-lived birds replace body feathers annually but may defer the replacement of flight feathers for two or more years. Because additional energy and protein are required for feather growth, most temperate species moult either before or just after breeding, or during a lull in the breeding cycle when energy demands for these purposes are reduced.

The Tawny Owl *Strix aluco* is a sedentary, nocturnal predator of small mammals (Mikkola 1983; Cramp 1985). Its moult is complex and has been described in some detail by Piechocki (1961, 1968), Stresemann & Stresemann (1966), Glutz & Bauer (1980), Hardy *et al.* (1981), Ginn & Melville (1983), Hirons *et al.* (1984) and Cramp (1985). There are considerable differences between most of these accounts.

In this paper I present data from individually known Tawny Owls which were caught during each nesting attempt when their remiges (primary and secondary feathers) and rectrices (tail feathers) were dye-marked at each capture to check the progression of moult. There were significant annual differences in numbers of wing and tail feathers moulted related to reproductive success. The main food of Tawny Owls in the study area was the Field Vole *Microtus agrestis* which exhibited a three-year cycle of abundance (Petty 1987a). In low vole years, few pairs of Tawny Owls even laid, and those that did produced small broods. In both increasing and decreasing vole years a high proportion of Tawny Owls bred and successfully reared chicks (Petty 1989).

STUDY AREA

The study was undertaken in the central part of Kielder Forest, Northumberland in northern England (55°N, 2°W). In the study area the forest comprised largely Sitka Spruce *Picea sitchensis* and Norway Spruce *Picea abies* grown on rotations of 45-55 years. The forest was entirely man-made. Afforestation commenced in 1933, while clear-felling and replanting (restocking) commenced in 1968. By 1991 there was an extensive patchwork of first and second generation tree crops developing, particularly at lower elevations where the initial planting took place.

METHODS

Moult was studied during 1985-1990. In this period the Tawny Owl population increased from 54 to 66 occupied teritories. Most of the Tawny Owls bred in nestboxes (Petty 1987b). Female owls were caught at the nestbox with a hand-held net similar in shape to a butterfly net. Male owls were caught in a trap which was placed over the entrance to the nestbox. The trap was a modification of that described by Saurola (1987). Most breeding females were caught each time they bred during 1985-1991 and males during 1988-1991. Female and male owls were caught when the oldest chick was 5 - 15 days old.

The presence of active flight feather moult (growing feathers) was checked in each owl caught during the incubation and nestling periods. Tawny Owls have 10 primary and 13 secondary feathers in each wing and 12 tail feathers. The first time a bird was caught, part of the white area on the underside of these 58 feathers was permanently dyed yellow with picric acid in a solution of 70% alcohol plus a wetting agent. During subsequent recaptures the position of any new feathers (undyed) was recorded and the feather dyed.

Owls were not always caught every year, but providing they were caught every second year, then feathers moulted in the first or second year could be identified by looking at the white basal area on the underside of the primary and secondary feathers. Feathers replaced on the last moult had a pink/brown wash to this white area while those replaced on the previous moult had faded to white. It was not possible to do the same with tail feathers, so the sample sizes for tail moult analysis were smaller than for primary and secondary feathers.

Two reproductive parameters from the owls were used in the analysis. Brood size was the number of chicks leaving the nest site. Pairs which failed to rear chicks could be classed either as those which laid and then failed during the incubation or the nesting period, or those which failed to lay altogether. The start of incubation was used to measure the timing of breeding (Petty, unpublished).

The analyses treat each annual moult record from an owl independently, although moult data from the same individual but in different years were used.

The population of Field Voles exhibited a pronounced three-year cycle of abundance (Petty 1989; Petty unpublished). Years were classified according to vole populations as low (1986, 1989) increasing (1987, 1990) or decreasing (1985, 1988).

RESULTS

Timing of moult

In 226 owls that were recaptured during the nesting period none out of 62 males was moulting. In 164 females, one bird had six primaries partly-grown, one had two secondaries partly-grown and five had one secondary partly-grown. None had active tail moult. Moult mainly commenced in both sexes once the chicks had left the nest site in May-June, as evidence came from the presence of moulted flight feathers found in the territory. Therefore, most birds caught during a breeding attempt had not started their annual moult.

Number of flight feathers moulted annually

There was considerable variation in the number of flight feathers moulted annually (Table 1). A surprising number (17-19%) of owls replaced no primary feathers at all in a particular year, while very few (1-6%) replaced all 20. Males appeared to moult slightly more primary feathers at each moult than females (Table 1), but there was no significant difference between the sexes in the median number of feathers moulted annually (Mann-Whitney U-test, $z=-1.179$, $p>0.05$).

In contrast to the moult of primary feathers, very few owls failed to moult some secondary feathers, but none moulted all 26 (Table 1). Again males appeared to moult slightly more secondaries than females (Table 1), with no significant difference between the sexes in the median numbers of feathers moulted ($z=-0.903$, $p>0.05$).

The pattern of tail feather moult was quite different to that of wing feathers. Most owls moulted either none or all 12 tail feathers (Table 1). This was because tail feathers were replaced in total every second year in most owls (see later).

What influences the number of flight feathers moulted?

Variation in the annual replacemant of wing feathers was related to breeding success. Birds that failed to lay moulted most primary and secondary feathers, while those rearing the largest broods moulted fewer (Table 2). The number of wing feathers moulted by males and females showed a similar significant relationship with breeding success. However, in males the number of chicks reared (1-4) was progressively associated with a decrease in the number of wing feathers moulted, particularly primaries. In females, however, the number of wing feathers moulted showed less variation with brood size (Table 2 and Figure 1).

Breeding success in Tawny Owls was related to vole abundance (Petty 1987a and 1989), so understandably wing feather moult but not tail moult was also related to vole abundance (Table 3). There were great similarities between the sexes in the numbers of primary, secondary and tail feathers moulted in each vole year class (low, increasing or decreasing). Males moulted slightly more primary and secondary feathers than females (Table 3). In low vole years significantly more primary and secondary feathers were moulted than in other vole year classes. In increasing and decreasing vole years there were no significant differences in the numbers of primary feathers moulted (Table 3), but significantly fewer secondaries were moulted in decreasing than in increasing vole year classes.

The number of primary feathers moulted in a given year was positively related to the number of secondary feathers moulted (males $r=0.72$, $df=90$, $p<0.001$; females $r=0.64$, $df=213$, $p<0.001$). Hence, moulting more primaries did not lead to a decrease in the number of secondaries moulted.

Table 1. The number (%)of flight feathers moulted annually by Tawny Owls in Kielder (1985-1990). Each owl has 12 tail feathers, 20 primary and 26 secondary feathers (both wings).

Number of feathers moulted	Primaries		Secondaries		Tail	
	female	male	female	male	female	male
0	40 (18.7)	15 (16.5)	3 (1.4)	0 (0.0)	38 (23.3)	22 (30.1)
1	25 (11.7)	6 (6.6)	1 (0.5)	0 (0.0)	15 (9.2)	6 (8.2)
2	13 (6.1)	7 (7.7)	7 (3.3)	4 (4.4)	6 (3.7)	8 (11.0)
3	18 (8.4)	2 (2.2)	7 (3.3)	3 (3.3)	14 (8.6)	5 (6.9)
4	12 (5.6)	9 (9.9)	11 (5.1)	5 (5.5)	11 (6.8)	1 (1.4)
5	10 (4.7)	4 (4.4)	12 (5.6)	8 (8.8)	3 (1.8)	1 (1.4)
6	8 (3.7)	6 (6.6)	14 (6.5)	7 (7.7)	2 (1.2)	0 (0.0)
7	8 (3.7)	3 (3.3)	23 (10.7)	5 (5.5)	4 (2.5)	2 (2.7)
8	6 (2.8)	4 (4.4)	14 (6.5)	8 (8.8)	8 (4.9)	1 (1.4)
9	6 (2.8)	5 (5.5)	19 (8.9)	2 (2.2)	10 (6.1)	3 (4.1)
10	12 (5.6)	5 (5.5)	13 (6.1)	4 (4.4)	9 (5.5)	6 (8.2)
11	7 (3.3)	3 (3.3)	10 (4.7)	4 (4.4)	13 (8.0)	3 (4.1)
12	8 (3.7)	1 (1.1)	10 (4.7)	5 (5.5)	30 (18.4)	15 (20.6)
13	3 (1.4)	3 (3.3)	5 (2.3)	3 (3.3)		
14	7 (3.3)	3 (3.3)	12 (5.6)	4 (4.4)		
15	5 (2.3)	0 (0.0)	10 (4.7)	4 (4.4)		
16	9 (4.2)	4 (4.4)	6 (2.8)	4 (4.4)		
17	5 (2.3)	3 (3.3)	10 (4.7)	4 (4.4)		
18	5 (2.3)	3 (3.3)	11 (5.1)	2 (2.2)		
19	4 (1.9)	0 (0.0)	5 (2.3)	4 (4.4)		
20	3 (1.4)	5 (5.5)	7 (3.2)	1 (1.1)		
21			4 (1.9)	6 (6.6)		
22			0 (0.0)	1 (1.1)		
23			0 (0.0)	1 (1.1)		
24			0 (0.0)	1 (1.1)		
25			0 (0.0)	1 (1.1)		
26			0 (0.0)	0 (0.0)		
Number of owls	214 (100)	91 (100)	214 (100)	91 (100)	163 (100)	73 (100)
Median number of feathers moulted	4	6	9	10	4	3

Table 2. The mean number of flight feathers moulted annually in Tawny Owls in relation to sex and brood size, Kielder 1985-90.

Brood size	Primary feathers				Secondary feathers				Tail feathers		
	Mean	n	SE	RT	Mean	n	SE	RT	Mean	n	SE
Female											
NB	13.17	48	0.69	D	15.69	48	0.57	B	6.60	25	1.08
0	8.56	16	1.23	C	11.82	16	1.48	AB	7.36	11	1.56
1	5.06	17	1.28	ABC	9.18	17	1.18	A	5.77	13	1.49
2	5.72	46	0.81	BC	8.33	46	0.63	A	5.63	38	0.80
3	2.54	52	0.42	A	7.85	52	0.53	A	5.04	43	0.65
4-5	3.40	35	0.67	AB	8.71	35	0.73	A	4.94	33	0.76
ANOVA	F=33.24, p<0.001				F=21.86, p<0.001				F=0.77, p>0.05		
Male											
NB	13.67	21	1.00	D	18.00	21	0.90	B	6.18	17	1.34
0	10.86	7	2.25	CD	12.43	7	2.74	AB	10.00	4	1.68
1	9.38	8	2.19	ACD	11.13	8	1.44	A	5.57	7	1.78
2	5.96	23	1.14	ABC	9.09	23	1.13	A	3.44	16	1.00
3	3.04	25	0.58	AB	7.84	25	0.80	A	4.04	23	1.03
4-5	1.43	7	0.54	A	8.57	7	2.17	A	6.00	6	2.42
ANOVA	F=16.40, p<0.001				F=12.05, p<0.001				F=1.60, p>0.05		

Brood size = number of chicks fledging; NB = not breeding; 0 = birds which laid but failed to rear any chicks.

RT = Scheffe range test (95%); similar letter denotes no significant difference.

Table 3. The mean number of flight feathers moulted annually in Tawny Owls in relation to sex and vole year classes, Kielder 1985-90.

Vole year class	Primary feathers				Secondary feathers				Tail feathers		
	Mean	n	SE	RT	Mean	n	SE	RT	Mean	n	SE
Female											
1	12.84	58	0.65	A	14.50	58	0.63	A	5.86	35	0.87
2	3.95	102	0.43	B	9.77	102	0.46	B	5.24	93	0.47
3	4.09	54	0.61	B	6.59	54	0.44	C	6.37	35	0.85
ANOVA	F=79.67, p<0.001				F=46.10, p<0.001				F=0.78, p>0.05		
Male											
1	13.37	30	0.88	A	16.40	30	0.97	A	5.30	23	1.06
2	4.42	37	0.76	B	10.27	37	0.78	B	4.72	36	0.79
3	4.38	24	0.83	B	6.13	24	0.77	C	5.43	14	1.54
ANOVA	F=40.39, p<0.001				F=32.99, p<0.001				F=0.14, p>0.05		

Vole year class: 1 = low, 2 = increasing, 3 = declining
RT = Scheffe range test (95%), similar letter denotes no significant difference.

Table 4. Moult of two female Tawny Owls (ring numbers GJ73197 and GH40939) through their first five and six annual moult cycles. Both owls were ringed as nestlings.

Bird number	Age *	Wing	Primaries										Secondaries													Tail											
			1	2	3	4	5	6	7	8	9	10	1	2	3	4	5	6	7	8	9	10	11	12	13	1	2	3	4	5	6	7	8	9	10	11	12
1	1	L	J	J	J	J	J	J	J	J	J	J	J	J	J	J	J	J	J	J	J	J	J	J	J	J	J	J	J	J	J	J	J	J	J	J	J
1	1	R	J	J	J	J	J	J	J	J	J	J	J	J	J	J	J	J	J	J	J	J	J	J	J												
1	2	L	J	J	J	J	N	N	J	J	J	J	J	J	J	J	J	J	J	J	J	N	N	N	N	N	N	N	N	N	N	N	N	N	N	N	N
1	2	R	J	J	J	J	N	N	J	J	J	J	J	J	J	J	J	J	J	J	J	N	N	N	N												
1	3	L	J	N	N	N	O	O	N	N	N	N	J	N	N	J	N	N	N	N	N	O	O	O	N	O	O	O	O	O	O	N	O	N	N	O	O
1	3	R	J	N	N	N	O	O	N	N	N	N	J	N	N	J	N	N	N	N	N	O	O	N	N												
1	4	L	N	O	O	O	N	N	O	O	O	O	N	O	O	N	O	O	O	O	O	N	N	N	N	N	N	N	N	N	N	O	N	O	O	N	N
1	4	R	N	O	O	O	O	N	O	O	O	O	N	O	O	N	O	O	O	O	O	N	N	O	O												
1	5	L	O	O	O	O	O	O	N	N	N	N	O	O	O	O	N	O	N	N	N	O	O	O	N	O	O	O	O	O	O	N	X	O	N	N	O
1	5	R	O	O	O	O	N	O	N	N	N	N	O	O	O	O	N	O	N	N	N	O	O	N	N												
1	6	L	O	N	N	N	O	N	O	O	O	O	O	N	N	O	O	N	O	O	O	N	N	N	N	N	N	N	N	N	N	N	N	O	O	N	N
1	6	R	O	N	N	N	O	N	O	O	O	O	O	N	N	O	O	N	O	O	O	N	N	O	N												
2	1	L	J	J	J	J	J	J	J	J	J	J	J	J	J	J	J	J	J	J	J	J	J	J	J	J	J	J	J	J	J	J	J	J	J	J	J
2	1	R	J	J	J	J	J	J	J	J	J	J	J	J	J	J	J	J	J	J	J	J	J	J	J												
2	2	L	J	J	J	J	N	N	J	J	J	J	J	J	J	J	J	J	J	J	N	N	J	J	J	N	N	N	N	N	N	N	N	N	N	N	N
2	2	R	J	J	J	J	N	N	J	J	J	J	J	J	J	J	J	J	J	J	N	N	N	J	J												
2	3	L	N	N	N	N	O	O	N	N	J	J	J	N	N	J	N	N	N	N	O	O	N	N	N	O	O	O	O	O	O	O	O	O	O	O	O
2	3	R	N	N	N	N	O	O	N	N	J	J	J	N	N	J	N	N	N	N	O	O	O	N	N												
2	4	L	O	O	O	O	O	O	O	O	N	N	N	O	O	N	O	O	O	O	O	N	O	N	N	N	N	N	N	N	N	N	N	N	N	N	N
2	4	R	O	O	O	O	O	O	O	O	N	N	N	O	O	N	O	O	O	O	O	N	O	O	N												
2	5	L	O	O	O	O	N	O	O	O	O	O	O	O	O	O	N	O	O	O	N	O	O	O	O	O	O	O	O	O	O	O	O	O	O	O	O
2	5	R	O	O	O	O	N	O	O	O	O	N	O	O	O	O	N	O	O	O	N	O	O	O	O												
2	6	L	N	N	N	N	O	N	N	N	N	N	O	N	N	O	O	N	N	N	O	N	N	N	N	N	N	N	N	N	N	N	N	N	N	N	N
2	6	R	N	N	N	N	O	N	N	N	O	O	O	N	N	O	O	N	N	N	O	N	N	N	N												
2	7	L	O	O	O	O	N	O	O	O	O	O	N	O	O	O	N	O	O	O	N	O	O	N	N	O	O	O	O	O	O	O	O	O	O	O	O
2	7	R	O	O	O	O	N	O	O	O	N	O	N	O	O	O	N	O	O	O	N	O	O	O	N												

* Age: 1 = prior to the first adult moult in the second year of life, 2 = after the first adult moult and prior to the second adult moult in the third year of life, etc.
J = juvenile feather; N = new adult feather grown during the last moult; O = old adult feather not replaced at the last moult; X = feather missing.
Primary feathers are numbered outwards from the body, secondary feathers inwards towards the body and tail feathers from left (1) to right (12).

Figure 1. The mean (with 95% confidence limits) number (y axis) of wing feathers moulted annually in relation to breeding success (x axis) by Tawny Owls in Kielder. Breeding success scores are; 0 = eggs laid but no chicks fledged, 1-4 = number of chicks fledging, NB = no breeding attempts. The left-hand figures are for primaries, the centre ones for secondaries and the right-hand ones for tail feathers. The upper graphs are for females and the lower ones for males.

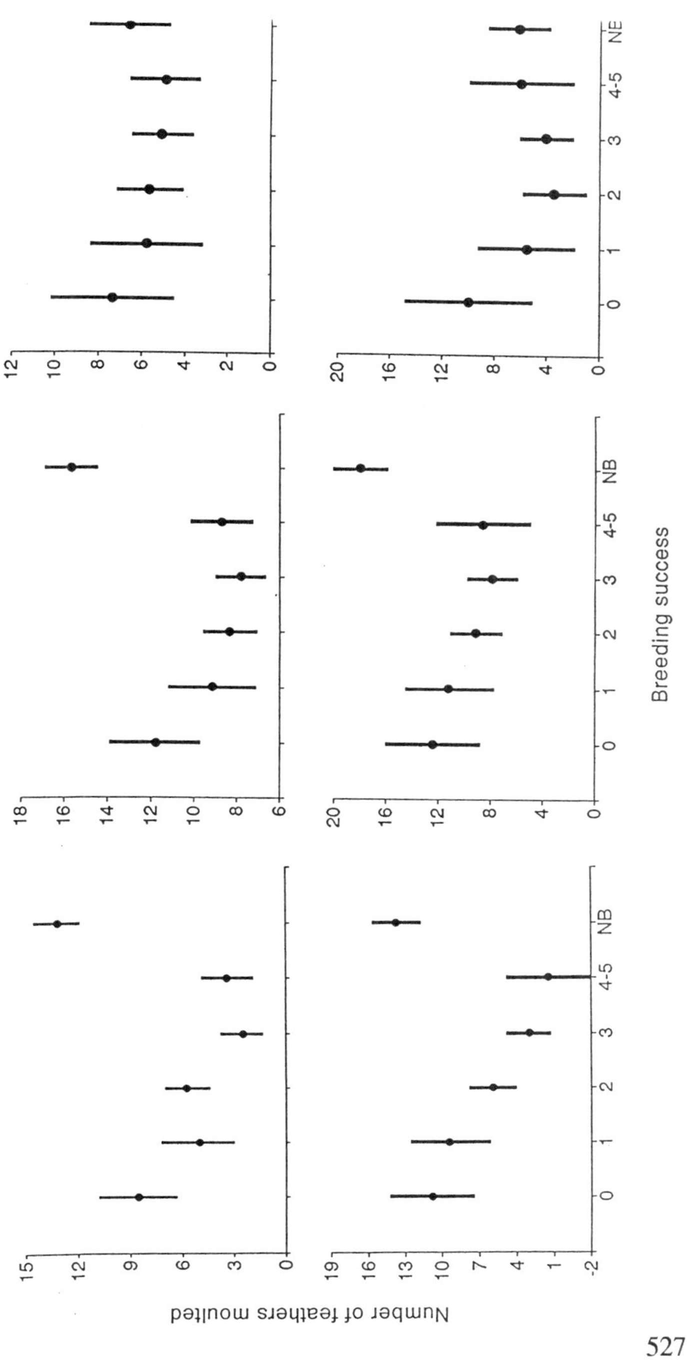

In contrast, there was no relationship between the number of tail feathers moulted and breeding success (Table 2), vole year type (Table 3) or total wing feathers moulted (males r=0.14, df=72, p>0.05), (females P=0.01, df=162, p>0.05). Nor could I find any other factor related to tail feather moult.

All twelve juvenile, tail feathers were replaced on the first adult moult in the second year of life (Table 4). All yearlings (31 females and 30 males) caught prior to their first adult moult had complete juvenile tails. In contrast, all two-year olds (13 females and 18 males) caught before their second adult moult had complete adult tails. All three- and four-year old owls also had complete adult tails.

DISCUSSION

Moult of body feathers

Although this study did not specifically consider the moult of body feathers, the evidence indicates body feathers are replaced annually (Witherby *et al.* 1940; Stresemann & Stresemann 1966, Glutz & Bauer 1980; Cramp 1985).

Tawny Owls are extremely well feathered, even the legs and toes have a dense cover. This is probably an adaptation to conserve heat during periods of inactivity, particularly during cold weather. Therefore it is essential that body feathers should be kept in prime condition. The only way to do this is to replace them annually.

Moult of wing feathers

Most previous reports of wing feather moult in Tawny Owls suggest that all feathers are replaced annually (Piechocki 1968; Hardy *et al.* 1981; Ginn & Melville 1983; Hirons *et al.* 1984), whereas some continental studies suggest that wing feather moult is rarely completed each year (Stresemann & Stresemann 1966; Glutz & Bauer 1980).

My study demonstrates clearly that the number of wing feathers moulted was closely related to breeding success, which in turn was related to food abundance. Tawny Owls fed largely on Field Voles, which had a pronounced three-year cycle of abundance. Most Tawny Owls bred and reared broods in years when vole populations were increasing or decreasing. In these years relatively few primary and secondary feathers were moulted, presumably due to the high energy demands of rearing chicks.

After leaving the nest, young Tawny Owls are dependent on their parents for about three months (Southern *et al.* 1954; Southern 1970; Petty & Thirgood 1989). So juveniles do not become independent until mid to late August, and most adult owls have finished moulting by the end of September (Hirons *et al.* 1984).

Moult requires energy and is often associated with a substantial reduction in locomotory activity (Wijnandts 1984). Tawny Owls with dependent young cannot afford to reduce locomotory activity, and thus moulting is delayed until late August. Once their offspring have dispersed, little time is left for moulting and it may be essential for their own survival to channel surplus energy into replacing body feathers rather than wing feathers.

Primary feathers provide forward propulsion while the secondary feathers provide lift. So, a perch hunter like the Tawny Owl may not be heavily dependent on its wing feathers being in perfect condition for efficient prey capture. Therefore, energy is more appropriately channelled into breeding rather than spent on wing feather replacement. In contrast, Sparrowhawks *Accipiter nisus* are more agile aerial hunters which are dependent on the efficiency of their wing feathers, and replace all their primary and most secondary feathers annually (Newton & Marquiss 1982). Unlike Tawny Owls, female Sparrowhawks commence their wing and tail feather moult during incubation at a time when energy requirements are low. This ensures that enough time is available to replace all wing feathers before the autumn. Failure to do so may reduce hunting efficiency and jeopardise their own survival through the winter.

In my study, most Tawny Owls did not breed every third year when vole populations reached the low point in the cycle. In these years many more primary and secondary feathers were moulted, even though food was scarce. Without the constraints of a family, Tawny Owls could spread their moult over a substantially longer period extending from April/May until September/October. However, even in these years most owls did not undergo a complete moult of primary and secondary feathers.

Virtually all studies of Tawny Owls have shown them dependent on rodents that exhibit pronounced annual population fluctuations (Southern 1970; Delmée *et al.* 1978; Petty 1987a; Petty 1989). Therefore, annual variations in breeding success related to changes in small mammal abundance are likely to have the same influence on moult. Pietiäinen *et al.* (1984) demonstrated a very similar moult strategy in the Ural Owl *Strix uralensis* in Finland to that of Tawny Owls in Kielder. Most wing feathers were moulted when the birds did not breed or failed in a breeding attempt, and least when three or more chicks were reared. It therefore seems unlikely that other wild Tawny Owl populations would show a substantially different pattern of moult to that described.

Few studies apart from Pietiäinen *et al.* and this study on wing feather moult in owls in the genus *Strix* have been based on recaptures of known individuals in the wild. Some previous accounts have relied heavily on captive birds (e.g. Piechocki 1968). Captive birds are not usually stressed by food shortage or breeding, so they should be expected to moult far more heavily each year compared to wild owls. This may account for the differences in some of the published accounts of wing feather moult in Tawny Owls.

Korpimäki (1988) studied the moult of primary feathers in wild male Tengmalm's Owl in Finland and found no relationship between the number of feathers moulted and fledglings reared. So the constraint on wing feather moult imposed by reproduction in *Strix* owls may not apply to more mobile owls such as Tengmalm's.

Moult of tail feathers

All accounts of the moult of tail feathers in Tawny Owls suggest that all twelve feathers are moulted annually (Piechocki 1968; Ginn & Melville 1983; Cramp 1985). However, my study shows that most owls moult their tail feathers biennially. All birds of both sexes completely moulted their tail feathers for the first time at their first adult moult in their second year of life (Table 4). Thereafter, in most birds, feathers were replaced every other year. There were at least two instances where owls retained all tail feathers for an extra year. In other cases one or more feathers were moulted out of sequence with the rest (Table 4). The closely-related Spotted Owl *Strix occidentalis* in North America appears to follow a similar biennial tail moult, but the initial replacement of the juvenile tail occurs at the second adult moult in the third year of life (Forsman 1981; Moen *et al.* 1991).

My analysis also shows that tail moult in Tawny Owls was unrelated to the moult of wing feathers, brood size or food supply. The reason why tail feathers appear to have a predetermined moult sequence in contrast to wing feathers may be related to the value of these different feather groups for hunting. Tail feathers are used mainly for steering and braking. These aspects may be far more crucial to a perch hunter like the Tawny Owl than the need for propulsion and lift. Once prey is located, largely by sound, a silent precise descent to the origin of the sound on the ground is vital for successful prey capture.

ACKNOWLEDGEMENTS

I thank David Anderson for help with the fieldwork, Drs. Erkki Korpimäki, Ian Newton and Phil Ratcliffe for comments on the manuscript, Diane Chadwick for word processing the text and the British Trust for Ornithology for providing licences to dye-mark owls.

REFERENCES

CRAMP, S.(Ed.) 1985. *The Birds of the Western Palearctic*, Volume IV. Oxford University Press, Oxford.

DELMÉE;E., P.DACHY & P.SIMON 1978. Quinze années d'observations sur la reproduction d'une population forestière de chouettes hulottes (*Strix aluco*). *Le Gerfaut* 68:590-650.

FORSMAN, E.D. 1981. Molt of the Spotted Owl. *The Auk* 98: 735-742.

GINN, H.B. & D.S. MELVILLE 1983. Moult in birds. *BTO guide 19*. British Trust for Ornithology, Tring.
GLUTZ VON BLOTZHEIM, U.N. & K.BAUER 1980. *Handbuch der Vögel Mitteleuropas, Volume 9, Columbiformes-Piciformes*. Akademische Verlagsgesellschaft, Wiesbaden.
HARDY, A.R., G.J.M. HIRONS & P.I. STANLEY 1981. The relationship of body weight, fat deposit and moult to the reproductive cycles in wild Tawny Owls and Barn Owls. *In* J.E.Cooper & A.G.Greenwood (Eds.) *Recent Advances in the Study of Raptor Diseases*. 159-163. Chirons Publications, Keithley.
HIRONS, G.J.M., A.R. HARDY & P.I. STANLEY 1984. Body weight, gonad development and moult in the Tawny Owl (*Strix aluco*). *Journal of Zoology, London* 202;145-164.
KING, J.R. 1980. Energetics of avian moult. *Proc. of 17th International Ornithological Congress*, pp. 312-317.
KORPIMÄKI, E. 1988. Cost of reproduction and success of manipulating broods under varying food conditions in Tengmalm's Owl. *Journal of Animal Ecology* 57: 1027-1039.
MIKKOLA, H. 1983. *Owls of Europe*. Poyser, Calton.
MOEN, C.A., A.B. FRANKLIN & R.J.GUTIERREZ 1991. Age determination of subadult Northern Spotted Owls in northwest California. *Wildlife Society Bulletin* 19: 489-493.
NEWTON, I. & M. MARQUISS 1982. Moult in the Sparrowhawk. *Ardea* 70:163-172.
PAYNE, R.B. 1972. Mechanisms and control of moult. *In* D.S. Farner & J.R. King (Eds.) *Avian Biology, Vol. 2* 103-105. Academic Press, New York.
PETTY, S.J. 1987a. Breeding of Tawny Owls *Strix aluco* in relation to their food supply in an upland forest. *In* D.J.Hill (Ed.) *Breeding and Management in Birds of Prey*, 167-179. University of Bristol, Bristol.
PETTY, S.J. 1987b. The design and use of a nestbox for Tawny Owls *Strix aluco* in upland forests. *Quarterly Journal of Forestry* 81: 103-109.
PETTY, S.J. 1989. Productivity and density of Tawny Owls *Strix aluco* in relation to the structure of a spruce forest in Britain. *Annales Zoologici Fennici* 26: 227-233.
PETTY, S.J. & S.J. THIRGOOD 1989. A radio-tracking study of post-fledging mortality of Tawny Owls in Argyll. *Ringing and Migration* 10: 75-82.
PIECHOCKI, R. 1961. Über die Großgefieder-Mauser Schleiereule und Waldkauz. *Journal of Ornithology* 102: 220-225.
PIECHOCKI, R. 1968. Die Großgefieder-Mauser des Steinkauzes (*Athene noctua*). *Journal of Ornithology* 109: 30-36.
PIETIÄINEN, H., P.SAUROLA & H. KOLUNEN 1984. The reproductive constraints on moult in the Ural Owl *Strix uralensis*. *Annales Zoologici Fennici* 21: 277-281.
SAUROLA, P. 1987. Mate and nest-site fidelity in Ural and Tawny Owls. *In* R.W. Nero *et al.* (Eds.) *Biology and Conservation of northern Forest Owls* 81-86. USDA Forest Service General Technical Report RM-142.
SOUTHERN, H.N. 1970. The natural control of a population of Tawny Owls (*Strix aluco*). *Journal of Zoology, London* 162: 197-285.
SOUTHERN.H.N., R.VAUGHAN & R.C.MUIR 1954. The behaviour of young Tawny Owls after fledging. *Bird Study* 1: 101-110.
STRESEMANN, E. & V.STRESEMANN 1966. Die Mauser der Vögel. *Journal of Ornithology* 107: 1-448.
WIJNANTS, H. 1984. Ecological energetics of the Long-eared Owl *Asio otus*. *Ardea* 72: 1-92.
WITHERBY, H.F., F.C.R.JOURDAIN, N.TICEHURST & B.W.TUCKER 1940. *The Handbook of British Birds, Vol. II*. Witherby, London.

S.J.Petty
Forestry Commission
Wildlife & Conservation Research Branch
Ardentinny, Dunoon
Argyll PA23 8TS, Scotland

Meyburg, B.-U. & R. D. Chancellor eds.1994
Raptor Conservation Today
WWGBP / The Pica Press

Reproductive Output of the Tawny Owl *Strix aluco* in relation to Small Mammal Dynamics in intensively cultivated Farmland

Jan Plesník and Miroslav Dusík

ABSTRACT

Preliminary data are presented from a population study of the Tawny Owl in lowland farmland (536km²) near Hradec Králové, east Bohemia. In 1986-1989, a total of 183 pairs of Tawny Owls nested largely in plastic nest-boxes. Although the Common Vole was the most important item in the diet and its proportion increased with increased abundance in the field (for all seasons 70.6% by numbers and 43.1% by weight), no significant differences both in clutch size and production of young were found between good and poor vole years, because when voles became scarce, Tawny Owls switched to other food (*Apodemus* mice, bank voles, birds, less shrews). Thus, the relatively high proportion of the Common Vole in the diet is considered to be a result of its availability rather than of a high degree of food specialisation (resident generalist). In view of material sample size and continuation of the research this contribution is considered to be a preliminary report.

INTRODUCTION

According to a relatively broad trophic niche, the Tawny Owl *Strix aluco* is considered to be a catholic predator (food generalist), without close specialisation for catching certain prey (Goszczynski 1977; Melde 1989). Nevertheless it has been shown that fluctuations in the density of small mammals, especially rodents, influence the reproduction of this territorial species, which is further modified by weather. These studies concentrated either on lowland broadleaved woodland (Southern 1970; Hirons 1976) or sub-urban areas such as parks (Wendland 1980, 1984), where *Apodemus* mice or bank voles were the most important prey. Tawny Owls on British farmland fed mainly on field voles (*Microtus agrestis*, Hardy 1977). The same pattern was confirmed for Tawny Owls inhabiting an upland spruce forest in Northumberland, where newly stocked sites with their grassy vegetation provided a major vole habitat (Petty 1987, 1989).

Although the composition of the Tawny Owl's diet formed part of an extensive study on predation in farmland in Poland (Ryszkowski *et al.* 1971, 1973; Goszczynski *et al.* 1981), little is known of how population fluctuations in small mammals affect reproduction output in Tawny Owls nesting or foraging in farmland. Because we have investigated predation on small mammals by aerial predators in lowland farmland since 1986, a population study on Tawny Owls has been included.

MATERIAL AND METHODS

The study was carried out between 1986-1989 in east Bohemia.

The study area covers 536km². The district of Hradec Králové, where our material was collected, is a region of intensively cultivated farmland, comprising largely arable land (65.0%) and meadows or pastures (3.4%). Especially in the south-east of the area, there are woodlands (21.3%). Water (0.9%) and built-up areas (9.4%) are dispersed throughout the farmland. Our study area lies at the confluence of two rivers, the Labe and the Orlice, at an altitude ranging between 325 and 287m.a.s.l. The crops are mainly wheat, sugar beet and barley.

To increase the population density of Tawny Owls, modified plastic 40-60 litre barrels have been used since 1984 as nest-boxes for these owls, spaced out on woodland edges or clearings, in larger islands of trees and bush in arable land or in tree-lines along streams. The numbers of nest-boxes erected are given in Table 3 (see Dusík *et al.* 1986 for additional details on nest-box production and maintenance). Data on the food of Tawny Owls, nesting in the intensively cultivated farmland were obtained by three methods:

(a) pellet analysis

(b) findings in nest-boxes

(c) analysis of nesting material after fledging of young (total 2,320 prey items). (See Plesník & Dusík 1988 for additional details on methods).

Most of the owls bred in nest-boxes. Territories were mapped by listening for hooting, using playback techniques from early February to late April. All nest sites were visited every week from the last week in February to the last in May each spring. At occupied nest sites visits were timed to obtain data on time of laying the first egg, clutch size and brood size at fledging.

We estimated the abundances of small mammals available by snap-trapping in early June (spring trapping) and in late September and early October (autumn trapping). Two sample quadrats (an alfalfa field, a mown meadow) were trapped each season and year. In each quadrat, 242 snap-traps were set over a trapping grid (10 x 10m) using two traps for each trapping point for six nights. Population densities were calculated using standard methods. Because the population dynamics of small mammals is influenced by numerous refuges in farmland, 200 traps were set in road ditches, railway cuttings, windbreaks, tree or bush islands, on waste land or on woodland edges for a 3-5 days period since 1987. The relative abundance was calculated as captured individuals/100 trap nights. A total of 1,724 specimens of 13 small mammal species were caught, of which 1,447 were Common Vole (*Microtus arvalis*). The material was treated by standard methods.

RESULTS

Comon Vole density was highest in 1988 (good vole year) and lowest in 1987 (poor vole year). From the viewpoint of vole abundance, 1986 and 1989 are intermediate vole years (see Plesník and Dusík, this volume).

Microtus voles were the most important prey group by both number and mass in the diet of the Tawny Owl (Tables 1 and 2). The proportion of Common Vole in the diet increased as its abundance increased in the landscape and ranged between 59.6% and 82.8% by numbers and 31.2% and 64.2% by weight. When Common Voles became scarce, Tawny Owls turned to other food (especially *Apodemus* mice, Bank Vole *Clethrionomys glareolus* and birds, mainly Blackbirds). Reptiles or amphibians were eaten only rarely. In a low *Microtus* vole year, insects were most numerous in the owl's diet.

Nevertheless, no significant differences both in clutch size (t=1.233, df=80, n.s.) and production of young (t=0.934, df=80, n.s., Student's t-test, two-tailed) were found between poor and good vole years. The lowest values both of clutch size and number of young fledged were found

Table 1. Proportions (%) of the most important prey species and groups by number in the diet of the Tawny Owl in 1986-1989

Prey species or groups	1986	1987	1988	1989	1986-1989
Microtus arvalis	70.1	59.6	82.8	69.2	70.6
Microtidae, tot.	74.1	66.7	83.7	80.8	76.7
Mammalia,tot.	84.9	72.5	88.7	89.4	84.1
Aves	11.9	20.6	9.9	8.3	12.5
Reptilia	0.2	0.2			0.1
Amphibia		0.2	0.7		0.2
Insecta	2.8	6.0	1.4	2.3	3.1
Nests	21	29	32	37	119
Prey animals	471	579	620	650	2320

Table 2. Proportions (%) of the most important prey species and groups by weight in the diet of the Tawny Owl in 1986-1989.

Prey species or groups	1986	1987	1988	1989	1986-1989
Microtus arvalis	44.6	31.2	64.2	41.6	43.1
Microtidae, tot.	49.5	37.2	67.2	59.2	47.8
Mammalia,tot.	73.6	60.5	89.4	85.6	68.8
Aves	25.8	38.0	10.5	14.3	28.6
Reptilia	0.3	0.3			1.5
Amphibia	0.3	1.2			1.0
Insecta	< 0.1	< 0.1	0.1	0.1	0.1

Table 3. Some features of Tawny Owl's bionomics in farmland, east Bohemia, 1986-1989.

	1986	1987	1988	1989	1986-1989
Number of breeding pairs	37	42	45	59	183
Number of nest-boxes installed (wooden/plastic)	45/95	42/113	38/133	36/132	161/473
% of nest-boxes occupied	26.4	27.1	23.4	33.9	28.9
Clutch size	2.35	3.38	3.05	2.51	2.81
(number of clutches)	(37)	(42)	(40)	(57)	(176)
Number of young fledged per laying pair	1.62	2.74	2.40	1.98	2.18
Number of fledged young per successful pairs	2.50	3.19	2.53	2.26	2.59
(number of nests)	(24)	(36)	(38)	(50)	(148)
Breeding success (young fledged/eggs laid) (in %)	69.0	81.1	78.7	78.4	77.6

in 1986 (an intermediate year for Common Vole density). Thus reproductive output in the Tawny Owl population seemed to be affected by other prey groups than Common Vole. Some environmental factors may affect the breeding performance.

DISCUSSION

Data collected in the east Bohemia lowland farmland on the variation in the diet of the Tawny Owl in relation to the density of the Common Vole are in agreement with those of Ryszkowski *et al.* (1973), who found that despite further increase in the numbers of *M. arvalis* the weight percentage of voles in the diet of *Strix aluco* remained constant, and even showed a slight drop in winter (in 1989, density of *M. arvalis* increased in cultivated fields in our study). Compared with Kestrels inhabiting the same area, Tawny Owls switched to the most abundant prey more extensively. Of the owl species examined in agrocoenoses by Goszczynski (1981), i.e. *Strix aluco, Tyto alba* and *Asio otus*, the Tawny Owl reacts the strongest to changes in the Common Vole density. During mass appearances of Common Vole, the Tawny Owl hunts primarily for this rodent. Thus the relatively high proportion of Common Vole in the Tawny Owl's diet may be considered a result of its availability rather than of a high degree of specialisation.

No differences in both clutch size and number of young produced per pair to fledging would result from the catholic nature of the Tawny Owl's diet. Its opportunistic character is connected with strong territoriality (Southern 1970). In addition, a poor vole year was not so sharply pronounced as extended low densities in some other microtine cycles, in contrast to the *Microtus agrestis* population cycle studied by Petty (1987, 1989). Population fluctuations in *Microtus* voles in field and meadow were not precisely synchronized in our study area. As shown from results of snap-trapping in 1991, no Common Voles were captured in the alfalfa quadrat in spring as well as on meadowland in autumn. For this year, the reproductive output was measured as follows: total 15 breeding pairs, mean brood size 3.08, mean number of young fledged per pair 2.15, mean number of fledged young per successful pair 2.33, breeding success 70.0% (Plesník & Dusík unpubl.). In addition, the density of *Apodemus* mice was high in the alfalfa field in 1987. Two years later, the Bank Vole population reached its peak density in refuges (see Plesník & Dusík, this volume).

In 1978-1989, the numbers of Tawny Owl breeding pairs increased almost exponentially in the study area. The owls have preferred the plastic nest-boxes to "classic" wooden ones or natural cavities or holes. Results of ringing show that the same plastic nest-box is used for several years (Plesník & Dusík unpubl.). Due to greater experience, these owls may be advantaged in foraging (see Jedrzejewska & Jedrzejewski 1989 for references). Martin (1986) showed that Tawny Owls' vision was similar to that of humans and their foraging success is related to knowledge of own home-range. In addition, reproductive output is affected by weather. For example, heavy rainfall caused damping of nests in 1986. In our study, there is some variation between territories in the number of chicks produced, as pointed out by Petty (*loc. cit.*).

To examine breeding of Tawny Owls in relation to their food supply or habitats, more extensive material is needed. Nevertheless the species' bionomics in east Bohemia intensively used farmland display features that are typical of the resident generalists (Andersson & Erlinge 1977). The importance of generalist predators in the microtine rodent cycle has been emphasised in recent years (Erlinge *et al.* 1983; Hanski *et al.* 1991).

ACKNOWLEDGEMENTS

We wish to thank Bernd-U. Meyburg, Erkki Korpimäki and Hannu Pietiänen, who gave us the chance to participate in the conference. We are very grateful to all our colleagues and students for their assistance in field work, especially Martin Fejfar, Vít Hrdoušek, Stanislav Šimek and Jirí Zajíc jr. The Czech Institute for Nature Conservation, Prague, supported J.P. financially. Our thanks are due to Miroslav Dusík jr. and Marcela Plesníková for typing the manuscript.

REFERENCES

ANDERSSON, M. & S. ERLINGE 1977: Influence of predation on rodent populations. *Oikos* 29: 591-597.

DUSÍK, M. & J. PLESNÍK 1988. Príspevek k potravní ekologii puštika obecného (*Strix aluco L.*) v zemedelsky intenzívné vyuzívané krajine (Contribution to feeding ecology of the Tawny Owl in agricultural habitat). *Sovy* 1986: 95-111 (in Czech with English summary).

DUSÍK, M., J. PLESNÍK, S. ŠIMEK & J. ZAJÍC jr. 1986. Moznosti usídlování dravcu a sov v zemedelské krajine (Management of raptors in intensively cultivated agricultural landscape). *Buteo* 1: 39-58 (in Czech with English summary).

GOSZCZYNSKI, J. 1977. Connections between predatory birds and mammals and their prey. *Acta theriol.* 22: 399-430.

GOSZCZYNSKI, J. 1981. Comparative analysis of food of owls in agrocenoses. *Ekol. pol.* 29: 431-439.

HANSKI, I., L. HANSSON & H. HENTTONEN 1991. Specialist predators, generalist predators, and the microtine rodent cycle. *J. Anim. Ecol.* 60: 353-367.

HARDY, A.R. 1977. Hunting ranges and feeding ecology of owls in farmland. Ph. D. thesis, Aberdeen University, U.K.

HIRONS, G.J.M. 1976. A population study of the Tawny Owl *Strix aluco* L. and its main prey species in woodland. Ph. D. thesis, Oxford University.

JEDRZEJEWSKA, B. & W. JEDRZEJEWSKI 1989. Wplyw ploszenia ofiar przez drapiezniki na uklad drapiezca-ofiara (Evasive response of prey and its effect on predator-prey relationships). *Wiad. ekol.* 35: 3-21 (in Polish with English summary).

MARTIN, G.R. 1986. Sensory capacity and the nocturnal habits of owls (Strigiformes). *Ibis* 128: 266-277.

MELDE, M. 1989. *Der Waldkauz.* 2nd edition. A. Ziemsen Verlag, Wittenberg Lutherstadt.

PETTY, S.J. 1987. Breeding of Tawny Owls *Strix aluco* in relation to their food supply in an upland forest. *In* D.J. Hill (Ed.): *Breeding and Management in Birds of Prey:* 167-169. University of Bristol, Bristol.

PETTY, S.J. 1989. Productivity and density of Tawny Owls *Strix aluco* in relation to the structure of a spruce forest in Britain. *Ann. Zool. Fennici* 26: 227-233.

RYSZKOWSKI, L., J. GOSZCZYNSKI & J. TRUSZKOWSKI 1973. Trophic relationships of the common vole in cultivated fields. *Acta theriol.* 18: 125-165.

RYSZKOWSKI, L., C.K. WAGNER, J. GOSZCZYNSKI & J. TRUSZKOWSKI 1971. Operations of predators in a forest and cultivated fields. *Ann. Zool. Fennici* 8: 160-168.

SOUTHERN, H.N. 1970. The natural control of population of Tawny Owls (*Strix aluco*). *J. Zool. (Lond.)* 162: 197-285.

WENDLAND, V. 1980. Der Waldkauz (*Strix aluco*) in bebauten Stadtgebiet von Berlin (West). *Beitr. Vogelkde* 26: 157-171.

WENDLAND, V. 1984. The influence of prey fluctuations on the breeding success of the Tawny Owl *Strix aluco*. *Ibis* 126: 284-295.

Jan Plesník
Czech Institue for Nature
Conservation
Slezská 9
120 2a Prague 2
Czech Republic

Miroslav Dusík
Ekostrix
503 02 Predmerice n.L. 54
Czech Republic

Tawny Owl *Strix aluco* - fledgling

Meyburg, B.-U. & R. D. Chancellor eds.1994
Raptor Conservation Today
WWGBP / The Pica Press

Feeding Ecology of Tengmalm's Owl *Aegolius funereus* in the Šumava National Park, Czechoslovakia

Jiři Pykal and Bohuslav Kloubec

ABSTRACT

The composition of Tengmalm's Owl's diet in the Šumava National Park (SW Bohemia) in a breeding season was studied from 1984-1991 through analysis of the prey remains from nest boxes. Small mammals comprised the main part of the diet. Food composition showed year-to-year fluctuation, reflecting the changes in small mammal numbers. To clarify the diet's dependence on small mammal population cycles, small mammals were trapped in two Tengmalm's Owl territories from 1988 to 1991. The results indicate that Tengmalm's Owl hunts various small mammals in proportion to their numbers at any given time. *Microtus* voles were the main source of food, but in years when their numbers were low, the most important alternative prey were *Sorex* shrews. Breeding of Tengmalm's Owl was unsuccessful in the year of minimum phase of the *Microtus agrestis* population cycle.

INTRODUCTION

The Šumava National Park in southern Bohemia contains what is probably the largest continuous population of Tengmalm's Owl in all of Czechoslovakia. Šumava is a mountainous region in SW Bohemia, the main ridge of which borders Germany to the west and Austria to the south. These are low mountains with average elevations between 700m and 1,000m and peaks reaching 1,300m. Approximately 70% of the region is covered with forest, particularly with extensive spruce monoculture. Since the 1960s a considerable amount (1,630km²) of Šumava has been protected as a Natural Park, and in 1991 the National Park which, including the transition zone, has the same area, was proclaimed. This report on the feeding ecology of Tengmalm's Owl is the outcome of research in the region conducted over the last ten years.

RESULTS

On the basis of annual spring mappings of displaying Tengmalm's Owl males, carried out since the beginning of the 1980s, it is estimated that there is approximately one Tengmalm's Owl male for every 3-5 km² of forest. The entire population in Šumava (including the promontory) is estimated at 300-500 territorial males, with 200-300 of them in the protected area. Tengmalm's Owls usually breed in natural cavities in older spruce forests of diverse spacing, often with many clearings and some new plantations. Breeding often occurs also at the forest edge, sometimes in solitary trees up to several hundred metres outside the forest proper. Nest-boxes were introduced at the beginning of the 1980s (there were 8 in 1983 and 80 in 1991), and are occupied at an average frequency of 10.8% of the 295 possibilities.

This research into the species' diet is based on analyses of prey remains taken from the nest-boxes after breeding (see Kloubec & Vacík 1990). These remains provide a representative cross-section of the nestlings' diet during the second half of their time in the nest hole (Korpimäki 1981) and were generally collected under given conditions at the turn of May/June. From one nest 64.5 prey items (SD = 43.2) were identified. The average number of individuals identified in a given year corresponds fairly well with the abundance of small mammals (Fig.1).

Figure 1. Comparison of number of prey items identified in nests of Tengmalm's Owl and spring trapping indices of small mammals abundance.

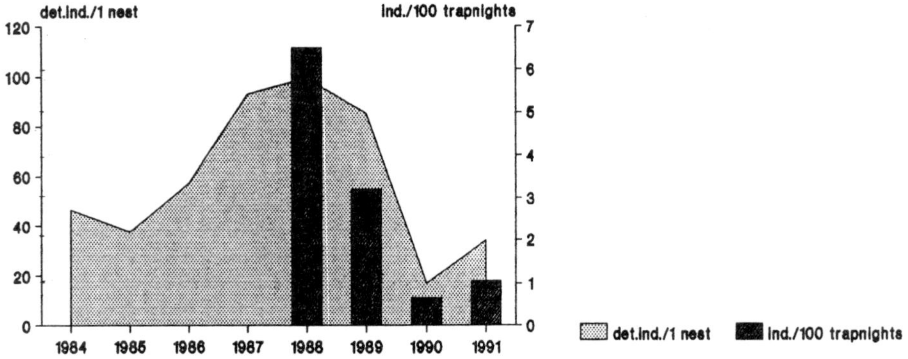

Table 1. Food composition of Tengmalm's Owl at end of the breeding season in the Šumava National Park

Species	Number ind.	Number %	Coef. var.%	Weight %	Collect %
Sorex araneus	499	27.6	91.5	12.6	100.0
Sorex minutus	41	2.3	83.0	0.4	60.7
Neomys fodiens	9	0.5	41.5	0.4	17.9
Neomys anomalus	1	0.1	-	0.0	3.6
Myotis nattereri	1	0.1	-	0.0	3.6
Clethrionomys glareolus	138	7.6	98.0	7.0	67.9
Arvicola terrestris	6	0.3	33.3	1.6	17.9
Pitymys subterraneus	44	2.4	83.9	2.2	39.3
Microtus arvalis	131	7.3	104.9	7.0	75.0
Microtus agrestis	546	30.2	101.3	42.1	96.4
Apodemus flav. + sylv.	190	10.5	93.2	13.5	78.6
Muscardinus avellanarius	79	4.4	83.8	4.3	50.0
Sicista betulina	49	2.7	102.0	1.2	46.4
Σ *Mammalia*	1,734	96.0	68.3	92.3	100.0
Small birds (to 40 g)	46	2.6	74.7	3.5	60.7
Other birds (over 40 g)	20	1.1	59.2	4.23	5.7
Σ *Aves*	66	3.7	73.2	7.7	71.4
Σ *Insecta*	6	0.3	0.0	0.0	17.9
Total %	-	100	-	100	-
Total N	1,806	1,806	1,806	39,523g	28

Table 1 indicates the composition of the owl's diet between 1983 and 1991, according to analyses of prey remains from nest-boxes after 28 breedings in 11 localities. Small mammals comprise the main part of the diet. Small passerines are seldom taken, and the greatest exception is when insects are found among the prey (*Neuroptera, Hymenoptera, Coleoptera*). Prey with an average weight of 20-35g predominate. Figure 2 shows the considerable difference in Tengmalm's Owl feeding habits from 1984 to 1991. This clearly mirrors the population cycles of small mammals in the region and illustrates the bird's dependence on them.

To clarify the pattern of this dependence we have been catching small mammals each spring and autumn since 1988 in two regularly occupied Tengmalm's Owl territories within 4km of each other. In spring, from the beginning of May to mid-June, small mammals were caught in snap-traps within a 1km radius of the nest hole, i.e. in the territory of the breeding pair (Sonerud,Solheim & Jacobsen 1986). The traps were spread in standard lines (Pelikán 1975) over a variety of terrain: meadows, clearings, young plantations, old forest. The spring captures comprised 4,662 trapnights in total. In autumn, every September or October since 1988, small mammals were caught in two stable quadrats; grassland and forest.

Figure 2. Year-to-year variation of food composition of Tengmalm's Owl at the end of the end of the breeding season in the Šumava National Park.

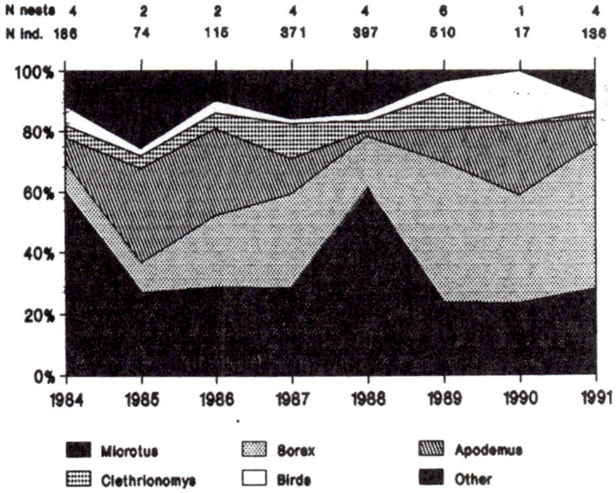

Figure 3 illustrates the frequency of the commonest genera of small mammals from 1988 to 1991, based on captures for every 100 trapnights. *Microtus agrestis* fluctuated cyclically, with its population peaking in 1988 and at a low in 1990. *Sorex* shrews were most numerous in autumn and least so in spring. *Apodemus* mice also fluctuated seasonally, although differing from year to year, while *Clethrionomys* voles remained in low numbers throughout the period. The coefficient of variation was 95.5 for *Microtus agrestis*, 27.2 for *Sorex araneus* and 15.4 for *Sorex minutus* populations.

Figure 4 shows the variation between small mammals caught in two Tengmalm's Owl territories and the prey remains examined in the same territories over the four-year period. The figures are in relative accordance. Differences between the food-base and the food consumed were not statistically significant in Territory 1 in 1988 ($\chi^2 = 3.57$, $P > 0.05$); the same was true for Territory 2 in 1989 ($\chi^2 = 6.03$, $P > 0.05$). There were higher (statistically significant) differences between food-base and food consumed in three other cases, but no species of small mammal was systematically over- or under-represented and none of the variations followed any consistent trend.

These results accordingly indicate that Tengmalm's Owl hunts different small mammals proportionately relative to their numbers in a given area at a given time; no small mammal species is given any preference. Forest species (*Apodemus, Clethrionomys*) and meadow species (*Microtus agrestis*) are also proportionately represented in the diet.

When comparing the dynamics of small mammal numbers (Fig.3) with that of the owl's food

Figure 3. Trapping indices for separate genera of small mammals in 1988 - 1991 [S = spring, A = autumn].

(Note: *M. agrestis* represents more than 90% of *Microtus* caught; captures of *M. arvalis* were rather exceptional. Captures of *sorex araneus* and *S. minutus* showed the same dynamics, therefore their indices are pooled, as well as those of *A. flavicollis* and *A. sylvaticus* for the same reason.

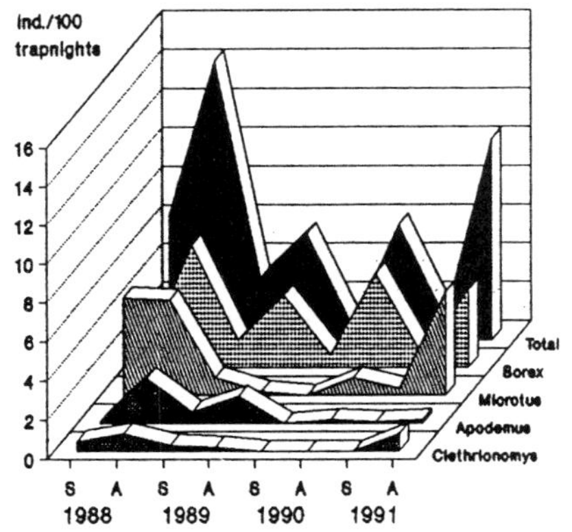

Figure 4. Comparison of the proportion of separate genera of small mammals caught in Tengmalm's Owl territory and the actual food consumed during the breeding season as identified in prey remains for two territories during a period of four years [*M - Microtus, S - Sorex, A - Apodemus, C - Clethrionomys*]

(Note: Breeding in both territories was unsuccessful in 1990.)

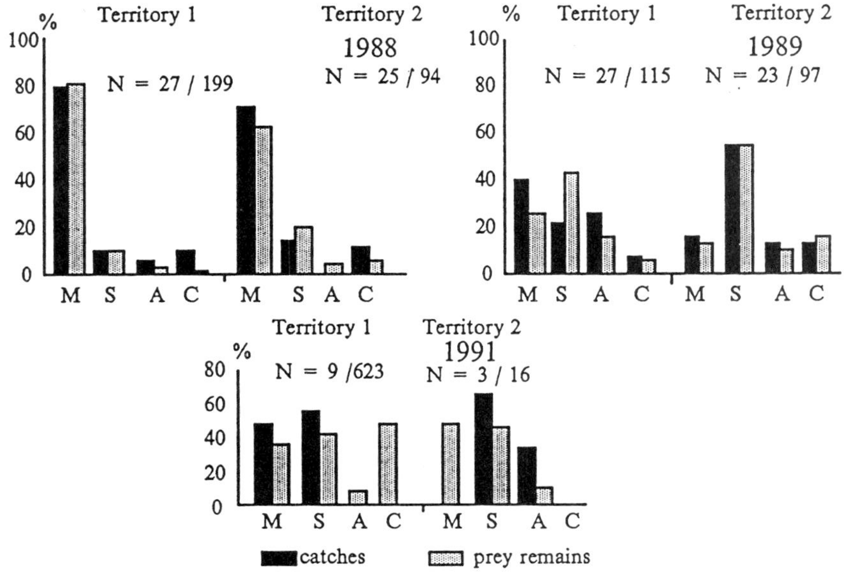

composition (Fig.2), *Microtus* voles - particularly *M. agrestis* - are clearly the main source of food in relation to their high population density. In peak vole years these comprise up to 90% of the owl's diet. In years when the voles are less numerous they range from 30% to 50%. Next are the *Sorex* shrews, whose numbers do not fluctuate so drastically, followed by a variety of small mammal species according to their availability. Birds are not a considerable alternative prey during the breeding season.

The most notable factor seems to be the number of *Microtus* voles in spring. The critical value of relative abundance is approximately 0.3 ind. per 100 trapnights. When the number of voles is lower than this, the owls breed unsuccessfully or not at all, as was the case in 1990, when no pairs bred successfully in any one of 74 nest-boxes.

The relation between food-base and diet composition of Tengmalm's Owl in the breeding season was studied by Korpimäki (1988) in western Finland and by Hörnfeldt *et al.* (1990) in northern Sweden. In both studies concerned the authors stated a considerable preference for *Microtus* voles in the diet of Tengmalm's Owl. On the other hand, *Clethrionomys* voles were taken either in proportion to their relative abundance in the field or less than expected from their relative abundance (Korpimäki *loc. cit.;* Hörnfeldt *et al., loc. cit.*). In addition, Korpimäki (*loc. cit.*) stated that birds were important alternative prey: in some poor vole years birds comprised up to 30% of the diet of Tengmalm's Owl.

The differences between these results from Scandinavia and our results from Šumava may have been caused by different availability of small mammals for Tengmalm's Owl. Ground vegetation in spruce forest in Šumava mountains is sparse, so that the availability of prey living in this forest (*Clethrionomys, Apodemus*) is consequently higher. On the contrary, *Microtus agrestis* prefers meadows, abandoned for several decades, with tall and dense vegetation cover, and consequently with lower availability of small mammals for owls. *Microtus* voles, however, are supposed to be more profitable prey than *Clethrionomys* or *Sorex*, as they are heavier (Korpimäki *loc. cit.*). Thus one can assume contradictory effects of two substantial factors, affecting the preference of prey by predator, i.e. energetic profitability (size of prey) on the one hand, and the availability of the prey on the other hand. These contradictory effects may have resulted in the situation that, under given conditions, different small mammals are hunted in proportion to their relative abundance in the field.

REFERENCES

HÖRNFELDT, B., B.-G. CARLSSON, O. LÖFGREN & U. EKLUND 1990. Effects of cyclic food supply on breeding performance in Tengmalm's Owl (*Aegolius funereus*). *Can. J. Zool.* 68: 522 - 530.

KLOUBEC, B. & R. VACÍK 1990. Outline of food ecology of Tengmalm's Owl (*Aegolius funereus L.*) in Czechoslovakia. *Tichodroma* Vol. 3: 103 - 125. Bratislava. [in Czech, with summary in English]

KORPIMÄKI, E. 1981. On the ecology and biology of Tengmalm's Owl (*Aegolius funereus*) in southern Ostrobothnia and Suomenselka, western Finland. *Acta Univ. Oul.* A 118. Biol. 13: 1 - 84.

KORPIMÄKI, E. 1988. Diet of breeding Tengmalm's Owls *Aegolius funereus*: long-term changes and year-to-year variation under cyclic food conditions. *Ornis Fennica* 65: 21 - 30.

PELIKÄN, J. 1975. On the standardization of the trapping quadrat and line for estimating the population density of small mammals in forest. *Lynx* 17: 58 - 71. Prague. [in Czech with summary in English]

SONERUD, G.A., R. SOLHEIM & B.V. JACOBSEN 1986. Home-range use and habitat selection during hunting in a male Tengmalm's Owl *Aegolius funereus. Fauna Norv., Ser. C, Cinclus* 9: 100-106.

RNDr. Jiří Pykal
Czech Institute of Nature Protection
nám. Přemysla Otakara II. 34
370 01 Ceské Budějovice
Czech Republic

Ing. Bohuslav Kloubec
Czech Institute of Nature Protection
Valy 121
379 01 Třeboň
Czech Republic

Meyburg, B.-U. & R. D. Chancellor eds.1994
Raptor Conservation Today
WWGBP / The Pica Press

The Dispersion Dynamics of Tengmalm's Owl *Aegolius funereus* in Central Europe

Ortwin Schwerdtfeger

ABSTRACT

In the course of population ecological studies on Tengmalm's Owl in the Harz mountains the species' distribution and its changes in space and time have been investigated. In an area of 200km² nearly all nests have been recorded and nearly all owls marked since 1978. In 1988 the results were summarized in a model of dispersion dynamics for the insular distributional pattern of Tengmalm's Owl as is typical for Central Europe. Further results permit the procedure of emigration and immigration in connection with reproduction and mortality-rates to now be quantified and characterized by their dependence on fluctuating food conditions. Thus we get a survey of how a population of Tengmalm's Owl consists of owls with fidelity to birth-place, fidelity to area and nomads. This is valid for both sexes and for different age groups.

Considering the long period of study, the size of the investigated population, its age structure, its reproduction as well as recapturing rates, we can assume that the results are representative for Central Europe. The phenology of dispersion dynamics differs from that of Scandinavian investigations.

INTRODUCTION

In order to take advantage of the specific resources of a bird species for its own existence and reproduction, a suitable dispersion of the individuals is very important. This applies to global dispersion in suitable habitats as well as within the local distribution of a fixed breeding area. Pattern and dynamics of a species' dispersion are determined by its system of behaviour and are regulated by environmental factors. By marking as many individuals as possible, such systems can be documented and analysed.

In the course of population ecological studies on Tengmalm's Owl in the Harz mountains nearly all broods have been recorded and nearly all owls have been marked since 1978. Thereby its distribution and changes in space and time have been investigated. The results were summarized in a model of dispersion dynamics (Schwerdtfeger 1988b). This model has been confirmed by further investigations.

Moreover, by an analysis of the age-structure of the population the mortality-rates could be estimated (Schwerdtfeger 1991). Utilising these rates it is possible to quantify the rates of emigration and immigration, and to characterise them in their dependence on fluctuating food conditions.

MATERIAL AND METHODS

The study area of 200km² situated at 51°38'N 10°33'E to 51°53'N 10°14'E, mainly consists of spruce forests and its altitude ranges from 450 to 850m a.s.l. Because of the lack of natural nest holes, nearly all broods occupy the 250 nest-boxes that are spread uniformly about the area.

The broods of the Tengmalm's Owls are frequently controlled to register the breeding data and the stored prey. Adult owls are caught at the nest-boxes: the females with a long-handled net, the males with a nylon net, while they bring in the prey, and single males with traps while investigating holes. The captured owls are aged according to the moult pattern of primaries (Schwerdtfeger 1984, 1988a, 1991).

From 1979 to 1991, 390 broods with 1,120 fledglings were systematically controlled, and 84% of the male and 98% of the female breeding birds were caught.

LOCAL DISPERSION DYNAMICS

First viewed were the dispersion dynamics in a 15km² section of the study area, where four males were resident for several years, utilizing 18 different nest-boxes for their 24 broods. Figure 1 shows the sequence and spacing of the breeding sites with 16 different females (see Schwerdtfeger 1990).

Figure 1. Shift of breeding site of four males.

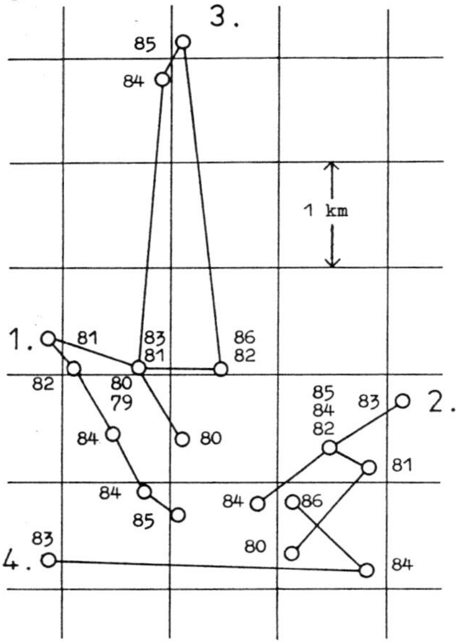

This reveals that neighbouring males shift their breeding sites from year to year, that females fluctuate more than males, and that therefore mate fidelity occurs very rarely.

These data were reconfirmed in the whole study area. Breeding-hole fidelity is rare: repeatedly caught males took an already used nesting hole in 30% out of 106 cases. With females this was only found in 5% out of 123 cases. Figure 2 depicts breeding dispersal distances. The logarithmic frequency distribution for the males results in a nearly linear decline within a few kilometres, which is considerably smaller for the females. Thus both sexes show an almost exponential distribution within about 15km. Added to that are 18 distances between 10 and 30km in the case of the females, while there is only one case of a male movement of 26km. All in all, the determined differences of the distances between males and females are significant ($p < 0.001$, U-test).

Figure 2 also shows the distribution of the dispersal distances of juveniles. With the females this distribution is nearly uniform, while for males it declines with distance.

Figure 2. Breeding and natal dispersal.

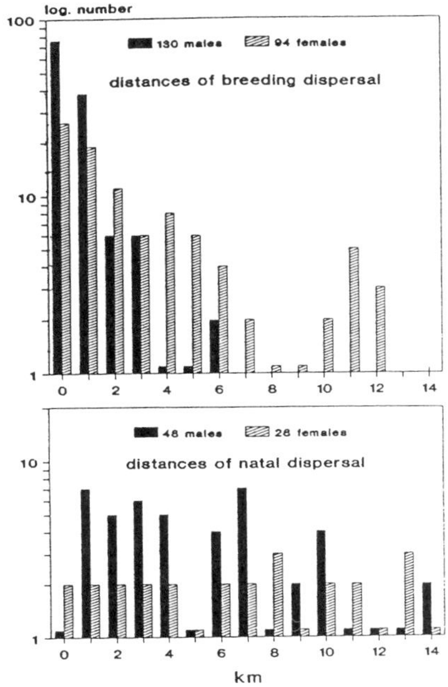

GLOBAL DISPERSION DYNAMICS

The fact that the biggest part of the captured adults had not been ringed indicates a high rate of immigration. How many owls are there with fidelity to birth area and fidelity to breeding area and how extended are the fluctuations, considering different breeding seasons?

The number of owls with fidelity to their area was determined by capture and ringing. By an analysis of the age structure, the mortality rates were estimated (Schwerdtfeger 1991) to be 30% for adult males, 36% for adult females and 75% for fledglings during their first year (assuming a sex ratio of 1:1). These parameters are concise in this study, for they make it possible to estimate the rates of emigration and immigration.

Out of 850 ringed juveniles, fledged in the study area from 1979 to 1990, only 11% of the males and 8% of the females were recaptured in the area (Fig. 3). Utilising the average mortality rate of 75%, the remaining owls, 14% of the males and 17% of the females, must have survived their first year outside the area.

Figure 3. Average fluctuation between breeding seasons.

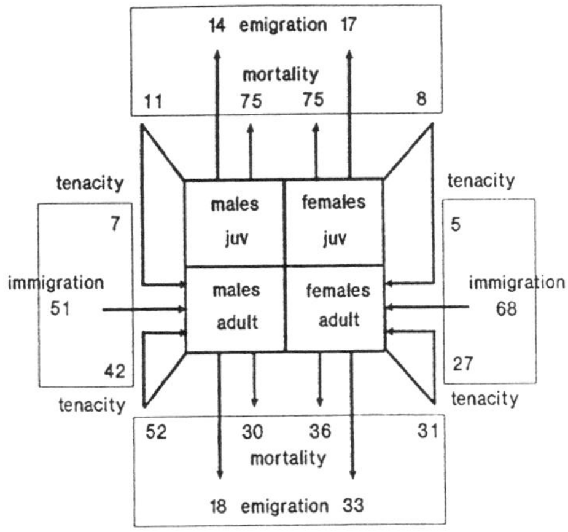

During the 12 years of investigation, on average this breeding population has been structured as follows:

Among the males 7% are juveniles fledged in the study area and 42% are adults previously caught in the area. Among the females the corresponding values are 5% and 27%. The remaining owls, that is 51% of the males and 68% of the females, must have immigrated (Fig. 3, left and right). The difference is statistically significant ($p < 0.025$, chi-square-test). How does the population change before the next breeding season? Among the captured breeding population 52% of the males and 31% of the females were captured in consecutive years, which means they were tenacious to the area.

Again, using the mortality rates as given above, 18% of the males and 33% of the females must have left the study area (Fig. 3). The difference between the sexes is significant ($p < 0.01$, chi-square-test).

Where the many dispersing owls come from and where they fly to, has been assessed by 48 recaptures and two owls found dead. Half of these recoveries suggest a continuous exchange of owls between other areas in the Harz mountains (i.e. up to 40km distant). Figure 4 depicts the other half on more distant recoveries (i.e. 50-490km). Natal and breeding dispersal are shown as thin or bold arrows respectively. Among these recovery distances just two above 195km stem from young males (Schwerdtfeger 1988b).

Figure 4. Long distances of breeding and natal dispersal.

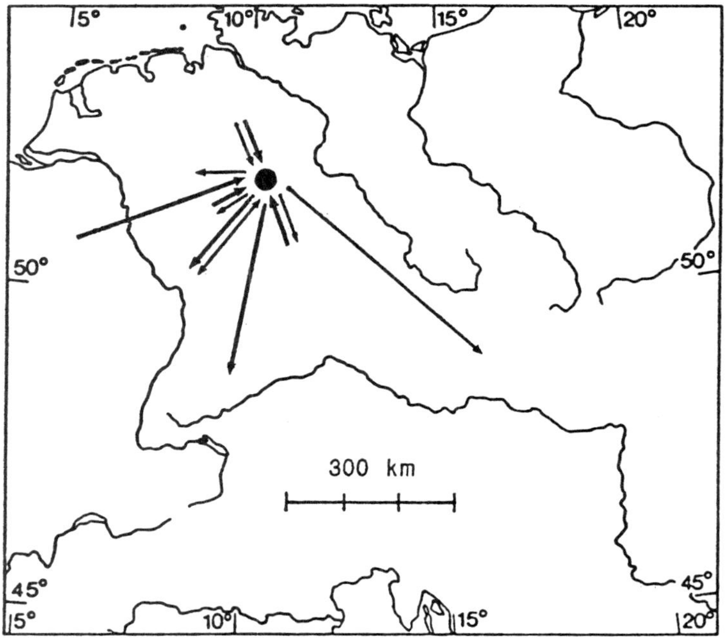

Corresponding recapture data are known between nearly all intensively investigated breeding areas of Tengmalm's Owls in Central Europe showing that a considerable exchange of individual owls takes place between those breeding areas which are geographically and ecologically fairly isolated; thus this dispersal is mainly due to juveniles and females (Schwerdtfeger 1988b).

INFLUENCE OF FOOD CONDITIONS

Having quantified all fluctuations so far, I now consider the influence of food conditions. Various factors in the breeding cycle of Tengmalm's Owl are influenced by variations of the main prey populations, i.e. *Microtus* and *Apodemus* species. In the study period from 1979 to 1991 the number of broods corresponded to the number of stored prey ($r = 0.835$, $p < 0.001$) (see Schwerdtfeger 1988a), thus suggesting that the fluctuations of owls could be influenced by food conditions.

In order to examine this, I compared the four "best" years with the highest average clutch size (1981, 84, 86, 88) and the four "worst" years with the lowest average clutch size (1982, 85, 87, 89) (see Schwerdtfeger 1991).

In Figure 5 the owls caught in these years were divided into four classes according to their capture series in the study area:

a. no further capture, neither earlier nor later
b. caught earlier, but not later
c. caught earlier and later
d. only caught later

Figure 5. Structure of recoveries between years of different food supply.

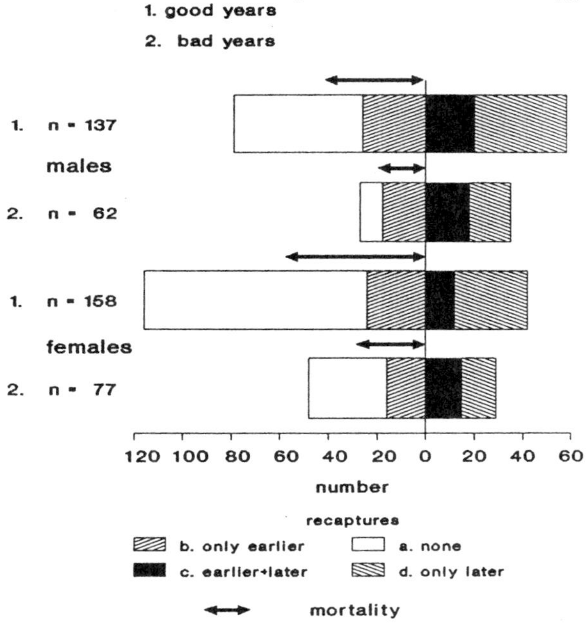

The number of owls caught earlier and later (c.) was nearly equal in good and in bad years. The numbers of owls caught only in the considered year (a.) was in good years six times and three times larger than in bad ones for males and females respectively. The number of females in this recapture class is 20% larger as compared with males.

These differences of dispersal between good and bad years are significant both for males and females ($p < 0.01$ and $p < 0.025$, chi-square-test). The same applies to differences between the sexes in good and in bad years (both $p < 0.01$).The owls of the classes (c.) and (d.) were still alive in consecutive breeding seasons. The owls not recaptured must have died or emigrated. In Figure 5 the expected mortalities in the following year are marked by arrows. The allocation of mortalities among the classes (a.) and (b.) is impossible. It is remarkable, however, that the disappearance rate is only slightly bigger than the mortality rate in bad years alone and for the males only. This suggests that all surviving males remain in the breeding area if the food conditions improve.

A dependence on the quality of food conditions was also indicated for the dispersal behaviour of juveniles fledged in this area. Within both sexes the percentage among these owls recaptured in the study area correlates to the average number of prey items deposited in the nest boxes in the year following birth ($p < 0.025$ for males and $p < 0.05$ for females, Spearman-rank-correlation). When food conditions are getting worse, of the fledged juveniles only 7.3% of the males and 6.8% of the females settled in the study area, whilst with improving food conditions the corresponding values were 37% and 32%. As these percentages are higher than the estimated average survival rates of juveniles, all surviving juveniles seem to breed in the year following their birth if the food conditions improve.

Figure 6. Age structure and recovery rates as compared to other studies.

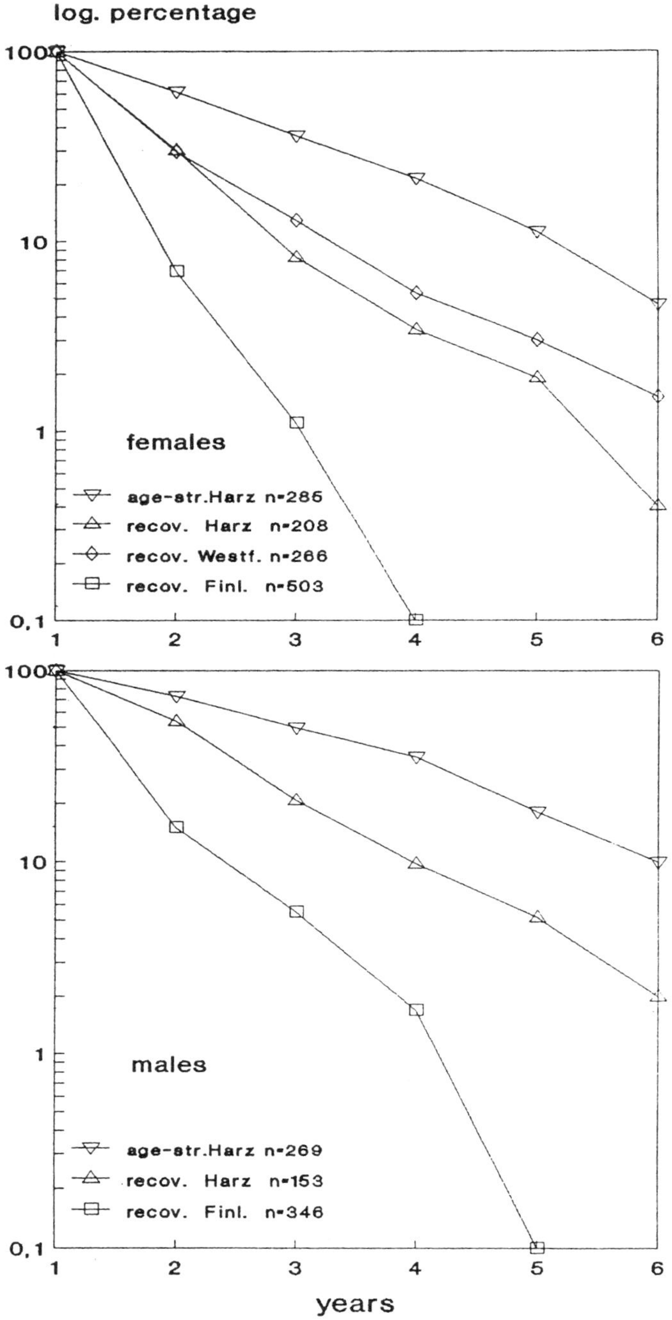

DISCUSSION

It has to be stressed that this survey on the fluctuations of the studied population is based on several assumptions. Some circumstances could not be considered sufficiently, e.g.

a. The estimated mortality rates are means over the 12 years. It is unknown how these rates vary between years as well between owls tenacious to their area and nomadic ones.

b. Data of years with good food conditions especially influence the given percentages in Figure 3, as most adults were caught in such years.

c. Non-breeding adults could not be suffciently considered: only half of the unpaired, courting males were caught, and the few caught females do not allow a conclusion as to the size of a "breeding reserve" and its yearly variation.

c. Investigation is needed into how the dispersion dynamics depend on the size of a breeding area, on its position relative to neighbouring areas and on ecological factors (Schwerdtfeger in prep.).

A summarising presentation of the fluctuations of juveniles and adults is not available from any other breeding area of Tengmalm's Owl. It is also difficult to compare basic data, as is necessary, with other breeding areas in Central Europe, due e.g. to:

1. a sufficient number of data entries, especially for males,
2. an ambitious mode of registration and
3. different ways of analysis.

Some criteria suggest, however, that the population's ecological relations, as presented here for the Western Harz, are representative for Tengmalm's Owl in Central Europe:

a. Due to the continuity of this long-term investigation, the size and location of the study area and the fact that data of nearly the entire breeding population are available, fairly accurate estimates of relevant population parameters were possible.

b. The data of the breeding biology, as well as of the annual fluctuations in the number of broods, correspond well to those published on other Central European areas (Schwerdtfeger 1988b; Korpimäki 1986).

c. The pattern of long-distance dispersal corresponds to those of other areas (e.g. Franz *et al.* 1984; Meyer 1991).

d. The age structure of my population approximately shows an exponential distribution in both sexes, as the average recapture rate follows a linear decline on a half-logarithmic scale. The total Central European population of Tengmalm's Owl should show a similar distribution (Schwerdtfeger 1991).

Comparing my results with Scandinavian investigations they show considerable differences:

a. The annual fluctuation in the number of broods determined by the coefficient of variation increases from south to north (Korpimäki 1986).

b. In Scandinavia greater distances of breeding and natal dispersal have been found than in Central Europe (e.g. Korpimäki *et al.* 1987).

c. The recapture rates there were considerably lower than in Central Europe (Löfgren *et al.* 1986; Korpimäki *et al.* 1987).

ACKNOWLEDGEMENTS

Dinah Thyerlei translated the manuscript into English. Karl Radler reviewed the manuscript and provided useful comments. I would like to thank both for their co-operation.

REFERENCES

FRANZ, A., T. MEBS & E. SEIBT 1984. Zur Populationsbiologie des Rauhfusskauzes (*Aegolius funereus*) im südlichen Westfalen und in angrenzenden Gebieten anhand von Beringungsergebnissen. *Vogelwarte* 32: 260-269.

GLUTZ VON BLOTZHEIM, U.N. & K.M. BAUER 1980. *Handbuch der Vögel Mitteleuropas,* Band 9: 533-578.

KORPIMÄKI, E. 1981. On the ecology and biology of Tengmalm's Owl (*Aegolius funereus*). Acta Universitatis Ouluensis, Series A. Scientiae Rerum Naturalium No. 118, Biologica No. 13.

KORPIMÄKI, E. 1986. Gradients in population fluctuations of Tengmalm's Owl *Aegolius feunereus* in Europe. *Oecologia* 69: 195-201.

KORPIMÄKI, E. & H. HONGELL 1986. Partial migration as an adaption to nest-site scarcity and vole cycles in Tengmalm's Owl *Aegolius funereus. Var Fagelvärld* Suppl. 11: 85-92.

KORPIMÄKI, E., M. LAGERSTRÖM & P. SAUROLA 1987. Field evidence for nomadism in Tengmalm's Owl *Aegolius funereus. Ornis Scandinavica* 18: 1-4.

KORPIMÄKI, E. 1990. Low repeatability of laying date and clutch size in Tengmalm's Owl: an adaption to fluctuating food conditions. *Ornis Scandinavica* 21: 282-286.

LÖFGREN, O., B. HÖRNFELDT & B.-G. CARLSSON 1986. Site tenacity and nomadism in Tengmalm's Owl (*Aegolius funereus*) in relation to cyclic food production. *Oecologia* 69: 321-326.

MEYER, W. & B. MEYER 1991. Erste Ergebnisse der Beringung von Rauhfusskäuzen *Aegolius funereus.* Populationsökologie Greifvogel-und Eulenarten 2. *Wiss. Beitr. Univ. Halle:* 507-518.

SCHWERDTFEGER, O. 1984. Verhalten und Populationsdynamik des Rauhfusskauzes (*Aegolius funereus*). *Vogelwelt* 32: 183-200.

SCHWERDTFEGER, O. 1988a. Analyse der Depotbeute in den Bruthöhlen des Rauhfusskauzes (*Aegolius funereus*). *Vogelwelt.* 109: 176-181.

SCHWERDTFEGER, O. 1988b. Modell zur Dispersionsdynamik des Rauhfusskauzes (*Aegolius funereus*). *In* R. Van Den Elzen, K.-L. Schuchmann & K. Schmidt-Koenig (Eds). *Proc. Int. 100. DO-G Meeting. Current Topics in Avian Biology.* Bonn 1988: 241-247.

SCHWERDTFEGER, O. 1990. Die Bedeutung populationsökologischer Kenntnisse für den Artenschutz am Beispiel des Rauhfusskauzes (*Aegolius funereus*). *Vogel und Umwelt* 6: 10-21.

SCHWERDTFEGER, O. 1991. Altersstruktur und Populationsdynamik beim Rauhfusskauz (*Aegolius funereus*). Populationsökologie Greifvogel- und Eulenarten 2. *Wiss. Beitr. Univ. Halle*: 493-506.

Ortwin Schwerdtfeger
Quellenweg 4
D3360 Osterode am Harz
Germany

Meyburg, B.-U. & R. D. Chancellor eds.1994
Raptor Conservation Today
WWGBP / The Pica Press

A silent method to record nesting events in hole-breeding Owls.

J.C. van Veen and E.M. ten Broeke

SUMMARY

Despite numerous reports on the breeding biology of Tawny Owls virtually nothing is known about breeding events and prey-provisioning (Cramp 1985). To investigate the nesting events an observation nestbox was designed, constructed and equipped for video-recording and automatic registration of nest visit activity. Whole nights could now be sampled by video-recording and the variable proportion of prey/contact visits (without prey) assessed. The automatic registration system recorded the date, time, duration and direction of nest visit activity and these data could be read directly. The event-recorder and the tunnel with two IR-sensors made it possible to distinguish between visits and incubation- or brooding breaks. The total number of nest visits and the temporal distribution of visit-activity could be accurately determined.

This silent video-recording and registration system has been applied to the Barn Owl, Little Owl and the Tawny Owl during one, two and nine successive breeding seasons respectively.

The system has proved to be a very reliable and useful method to study the species mentioned. It has several advantages over IR-photography as it is a silent method, which enables the researcher to record all the nesting events from occupation till fledging:

(1) synchronous observation by means of a video-monitor is feasible; (2) there is the possibility to choose for IR- or normal light conditions; (3) a maximum of ten hours can be recorded without interference by the researcher. The only disadvantage of the system in the field is the need for electric power (220V AC or 12V DC).

INTRODUCTION

There exist no studies about nesting behaviour and/or prey provisioning of wild owls covering the whole breeding period i.e. the (pre)oviposition, incubation and nestling periods (Cramp 1985). A few behavioural studies deal only with the nestling period with an emphasis on post brooding time (Stülcken 1961; Musarat 1980). Epple (1979) and Bühler & Epple (1980) studied the whole breeding process by means of IR-video-recording to investigate nesting behaviour and communication. Musarat (1980), however, habituated Barn Owls over a long period to light conditions and started visual observations. Later he documented his study with film and photography. There are few data on observed prey provisioning during incubation (Hirons 1980) and some concerning prey provisioning during post-brooding time exclusively (Juillard 1984; Baudvin & Dessolin 1987; De Boe 1991). For this reason we decided to investigate systematically the nesting behaviour and prey provisioning of Tawny Owls *Strix aluco* (1984-1992) and Little Owls *Athene noctua*

(1985-1987) in central Netherlands.

The purpose of this paper is to describe the functions of a specially designed nestbox, its equipment and reliability during a nine year study of nesting Tawny Owls.

RESULTS

In 1983 the basic design of a nestbox for direct observation and photography was made at the department of Animal Ecology (Z. Bruyn, technical assistant).

At first the nestboxes were placed at the gable end of haylofts in cowsheds in order to have a continuous backgroundnoise. During hatching the owls were habituated to light conditions. As soon as direct observation was possible we started to observe for three whole nights a week till the first nestling had fledged. During the first years we documented our observations with short video-recordings and several photographs. We used the Umatic videosystem which could not record longer than 30 min. without changing the cassette. This method was similar to that of Musarat (1980).

In 1987 the VHS-videosystem was introduced, enabling us to record nesting events for eight hours continuously. From this time on every year the owls were habituated to the light conditions at earlier stages of the incubation period. Ultimately it was possible (1990) to have the site lit when the owls reoccupied the nestbox without disturbing them.

During the past nine years the system was applied for two nestling periods to the Little Owl, for one to the Barn Owl and for nine years to the Tawny Owl (including three incubation periods). The behaviour of the adults and the behavioural development of the nestlings, including prey provisioning, were studied under naturally fluctuating food conditions. These observations will be published elsewhere, except for the study on nestling necrophagy presented during this conference.

The system now will be applied in the forest of Châtillon to compare the results of a small suburban-forest habitat with those of a mature beech/oak forest (Burgundy, France).

Observation nestbox

The nestbox was made of 3 cm thick softwood and consists of: (1) a tunnel with the two IR-sensors/reflectors connected with the event-recorder/printer (Fig. 1),

(2) the nest compartment (Fig. 1.) and neighbouring board (platform) for the male to transfer prey to the incubating/brooding female or for one of the parents to transfer prey to a nestling (Fig. 1.),

(3) a device (a wooden adaptor to connect the camera to the nestbox, Fig. 1) for the video-camera, which is connected to a video-recorder and a TV-monitor.

The dimensions of the nestbox are appr. 70x70 cm floor space and 65 cm height for the Tawny Owl and Barn Owl with a nest compartment itself of 30x30 cm. For a smaller owl, as for instance the Little Owl, a nest compartment itself of 23x23 cm is sufficient.

Videocamera-recording system

The nestbox has a wooden adaptor with a window for the video-or photo-camera. Through this opening the camera can monitor the nestcompartment as well as the platform where the prey is transferred. The lights neccessary for video-monitoring are on the top of the nestbox; the intensity can be regulated with a dimmer (variable transformer).

In the beginning light was provided from inside the wooden camera-adaptor and from above through a small slit (10 cm wide). This soon appeared insufficient for both photography and video-recording. Illumination from above but oblique through a complete open top of the nestbox gave the best results.

For photography it appeared that in particular the eyes of the owls were distorted by frontal illumination. Two flashes that gave a diffuse illumination from above produced the most natural photographs.

We made the observations with a common VHS video-camera, JVC GX-N7E, and two interconnected VHS recorders, JVC HR-D250. This combination enabled us to record for eight

Figure. 1. The observation nestbox, video equipment and automatic registration system.

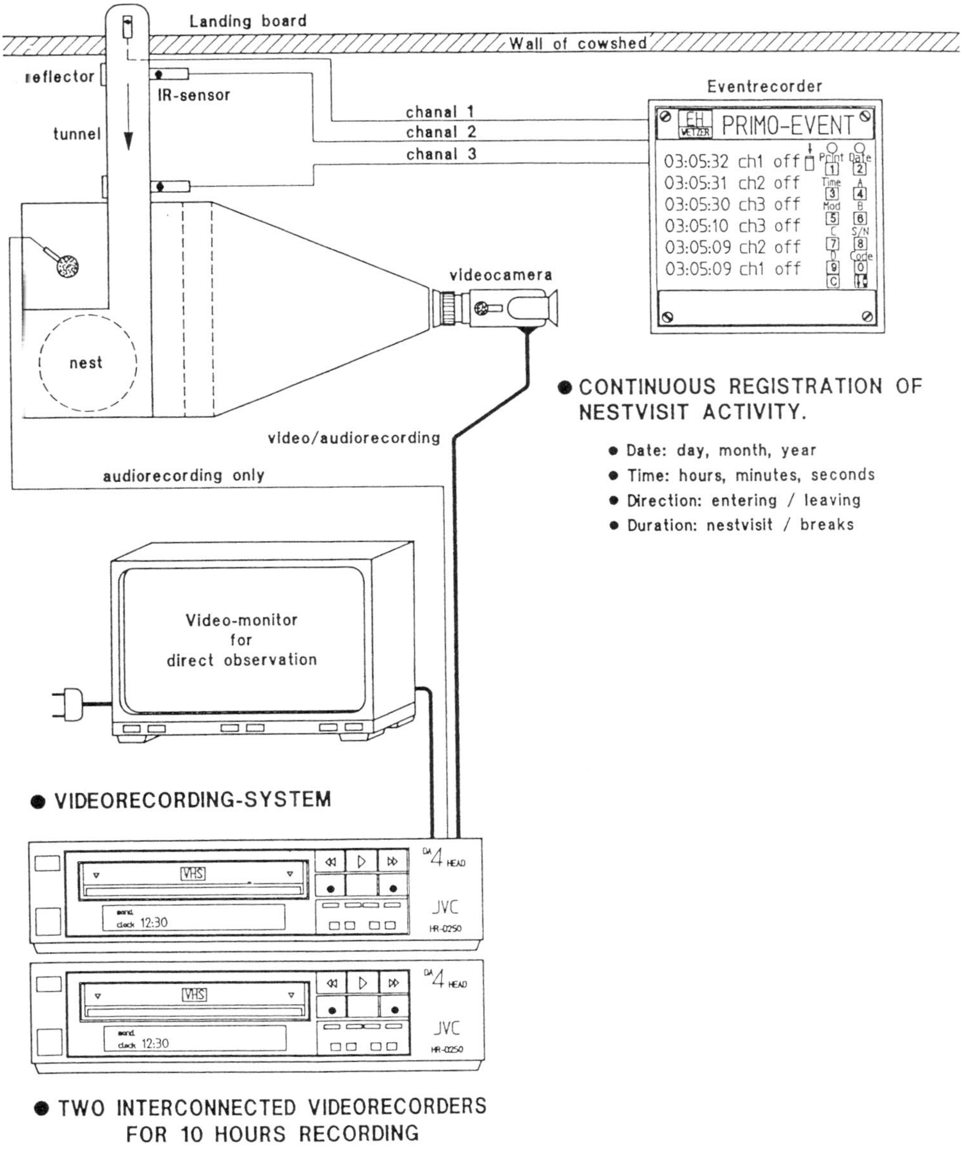

Wageningen Agricultural University

Agricultural University
Owl Research and Conservation Program
Ritzema Bosweg 32A
6703 AZ Wageningen
The Netherlands.

hours continuously (two times 4 hr video-cassette, JVC EHG-240).

From 1990 on we also used a Super VHS recorder, JVC HR-S5000E that can record for eight hours on long play mode with a common video-cassette of four hours. In 1991 the first 5 hr video-cassettes became available and ten hours continuous recording is now possible.

Nest visit registration system

At first the system was equipped with a single mechanical device triggering a pocket-calculator/printer (Casio CP-10) to register date and time of nest visit activity. This system was improved in the following years. Later a tunnel was constructed between the nestbox and the outside of about 60 cm in length. Two IR- sluices were built in the tunnel(each with an IR-sensor, Sunx beamsensor NX-22M and a reflector, Fig. 1) and connected with an event-recorder/printer. In the beginning we used a Meldedrucker (VP9250; a 7-channel recorder/printer)

and later an improved model Primo-Event (a 4 channel recorder/printer). Both instruments can be used with 220V/AC or 24V/DC power.

When an owl is visiting the nest, it passes the two IR-sluices when entering: sluice 1 is followed by sluice 2, and when leaving the sluices are passed in the reverse order. Date and time of the passages are printed. From these prints direction (entering, leaving), duration of passage and visit as well as date and time can be read directly.

DISCUSSION

Advantages video system.

There exist two types of photographic registration systems for prey provisioning. One type was applied for the first time by Southern (1971) but he did not publish any systematic study thereafter. Later Hirons (1980) applied the system to study the cause of incubation failures in Tawny Owls in the same area where Southern worked. It consists of a camera with a 400 mm telelens and a flash at a distance between 10 to 15m from the nestbox. The owls usually soon got habituated to the noise of the photographic registration system.

The other method was first applied by Juillard (1983) with the Little Owl and later by Baudvin and Dessolin (1987) and De Boe (1991) with Tawny Owls. It consists of a camera/flash system that is part of the nestbox with a wide-angle lens of usually 35 mm. This system is too noisy for adult owls and can only be applied exclusively during post-brooding time. This implies that this system cannot sample at random or at regular intervals during the whole nestling period. This is a disadvantage because during the nestling period food demand increases tremendously and often, if possible, the owls switch to larger prey.

The VHS-videosystem has several advantages over the photographic system:

(1) It is an absolutely silent method (no noises of shutters, winders and flash).

(2) Direct observation from a TV monitor in a nearby hide is feasible.

(3) It provides more information than photographic registration. Responses to calls/noises and behaviour of other individuals can be directly recorded. Besides, periods of rest and activity can be rather accurately assessed.

(4) A minimal level of light is needed for video-recording as compared to the sudden bright light of a flash.

Interesting behaviour can be analysed and kept on one videotape for comparision with similar behaviour in previous years or years to come. Cleaned videotapes can be re-used.

Usually for three whole nights a week the nesting events were video-recorded. Analysis of the video-recordings gives information about the diet, the size of the prey (juv., adult, heavy or light, decapitated or not, etc.), and the ratio of contact visits to visits with prey.

Nest visit registration system.

This automatic system can print out all nest visit activity from the first visit of the breeding season till the fledging of the last owlet. In feeding experiments adult owls even came back for laboratory mice after the fledging of their young.

In combination with whole nights, video-recording, a complete interpretation of nest visit activity can usually be given, even when both male and female visit the nestbox immediately after each other.

To quantify prey provisioning in order to assess the diet and rations of food during incubation and nestling periods separately, the total number of prey visits had to be known for any one period of time. It has appeared that Tawny Owls, like other birds, have two kinds of visits: with prey and contact visits without prey. In addition the female showed incubation and brooding breaks, which could easily be distinguished from nest visits with this method.

The duration of prey visits of the male was always shorter than his contact visits. The mean visit time of the male is shorter than that of the female. The incubation breaks last a long time at the beginning of incubation (some hours) with irregular intervals, but are scarce in the end of incubation and of a short duration (some minutes). During the nestling period brooding breaks gradually increase in duration.

With the available data printed out by the event-recorder one can easily show the temporal distribution of nest visits and breaks during incubation and nestling periods.

During the past nine years it was possible to describe the behaviour of the adults, the interactions of the adults with their offspring and the development of the nestlings under a variety of food conditions ranging from very poor years with brood reduction to peak years with maximum fledging weights. Two times the feeding of a dead nestling (nestling necrophagy) and once the handling of a dead hatchling were observed. These results were only possible thanks to this silent method.

ACKNOWLEDGEMENTS

We wish to express our appreciation to Anton Bruyn for his help in selecting the study area and the farmers Bieshaar, van Ginkel and Boersen for their hospitality. Thanks are due to the the technical assistant Zomer Bruyn (1984-1986), the Service Institute for Technical Physics in Agriculture and the Carpenters' Workshop of the Agricultural University. We also want to thank Mr. R.D. Chancellor, Hon. Secretary of the W.W.G.B.P., for his help with the correct command of English in this paper.

REFERENCES

BAUDVIN, H & J.-L. DESSOLIN 1987. A propos de la Chouette hulotte, *Strix aluco*: réponses apportées et questions posées par les "nichoirs-photos". *Nos oiseaux*, 39, 129-134.

BOE, J. de 1991. Recherche sur la régime alimentaire de la Chouette hulotte, *Strix aluco*, par la methode de photographie infrarouge. *Rapaces Nocturnes, Actes du 30e Colloque interrégional d'ornithologie Porrentruy (Suisse): 2-3-4 novembre 1990* (Réd. Michel Juillard *et al*; Ed. Nos Oiseaux), 93-108.

CRAMP, S. (Ed.) **1985.** *Handbook of the Birds of Europe the Middle East and North Africa,* Vol. 4. Oxford University Press, Oxford.

EPPLE, W. 1979. Geschwisterfütterung bei Jungen Schleiereulen *Tyto alba. Journal für Ornithologie*, 120, 226.

EPPLE, W. & P. BÜHLER (1981). Eiwenden, eirollen und Positionswechsel der brütenden Schleiereule *Tyto alba. Okologie Vögel,* 3, 203-211.

HIRONS, G.J.M. 1985. The importance of body reserves for successful reproduction in the Tawny owl *Strix aluco. Journal of Zoology, London,* 1, 1-20.

JUILLARD, M. 1983. La photographie sur pellicule infrarouge: une methode pour l'étude de régime alimentaire des oiseaux cavicole. *La Terre et la Vie*, 37, 264-285.

JUILLARD, M. 1984. *Eco-éthologie de la Chouette chevêche, Athene noctua (Scop), en Suisse.* (Dissertation) Université de Neuchâtel. - Le Pays S.A. Porrentruy, Ch.

MUSARAT, H. 1980. Beobachtungen zur Brutbiologie der Schleiereule *Tyto alba. Die Vogelwelt,* 101 (5), 175-182.

SOUTHERN, H.N. 1971. Population control in Tawny Owls. *New Scientist and Science Journal*, 19, 408-410.

STÜLCKEN, K. 1961. Zur Brut- und Aufzuchtperiode eines Waldkauzpärchens. *Falke* 8, 39-45; 79-84; 111-114.

J.C. van Veen and E.M. ten Broeke
Agricultural University Wageningen
Owl Research Project
Ritzema Bosweg 32A
6703 AZ Wageningen
The Netherlands

Short-eared Owl *Asio flammeus*

Meyburg, B.-U. & R. D. Chancellor eds.1994
Raptor Conservation Today
WWGBP / The Pica Press

Nestling Necrophagy in Tawny Owls *Strix aluco*

J.C. Van Veen

SUMMARY

The first records of nestling necrophagy were video-filmed, as well as a case of handling a dead hatchling during a systematic investigation by a videocamera-recording system to monitor the complete nesting process in Tawny Owls, including prey provisioning. This study was undertaken because there still exists a gap in the knowledge of the nesting process of Tawny Owls. Further questions of the cause of death and the fate of dead nestlings were still unanswered, because nestling mortality is rare (approx. 6%) and difficult to observe. For this purpose specially designed nestboxes for video-recording and automatic registration of nest visit activity were installed in haylofts of cowsheds in well-known Tawny Owl territories. During the longterm study death or disappearance of the youngest nestling was always preceded by a visual lag in growth and activity as compared to the next youngest sibling. Besides, it invariably happened during poor food conditions. No behaviour that might be interpreted as Cainism was ever observed, even under poor nutritional conditions with brood reduction. Neither between parents nor between parents and nestlings was any aggressive behaviour ever observed during ten breeding cases. The mechanism of competition between nestlings was based on the discrepancy in size between nestlings, determined by asynchronic hatching and enforced by poor food rates.

INTRODUCTION

In many bird species nestling mortality is not always caused by interspecific factors and bad weather conditions. Sometimes the death of nestlings is caused by intraspecific factors such as infanticide and fratricide, not necessarily followed by devouring the victims (cannibalism) (Tinbergen *et al.* 1962; O'Connor 1978; Clark & Wilson 1981; Viega 1990).

I prefer to follow McNicholl (1977) in distinguishing scavenging (i.e. the eating of a previously dead item including conspecifics, dead from other causes than infanticide/fratricide) and cannibalism (i.e. killing and subsequently eating a conspecific) rather than lumping the two instances under cannibalism, as apparently most authors do following Ingram (1959).

So far there exist no reports about infanticide among diurnal raptors and owls as for example observed in the White Stork *Ciconia ciconia* (Schüz 1984). In contrast there are numerous records about observations of fratricide in diurnal raptors, known as the "Cain and Abel battle".

However, there exist no records about firsthand observations of fratricide among owls. Reports of supposed cannibalism (infanticide/fratricide) in tytonine and strigine owls are mostly based on often meagre circumstantial evidence, as for example the disappearance of the youngest nestling. In other cases remains were found, a few times in pellets, in or near the nest.

The aim of this report is to give a complete firsthand description and analysis of the video-recorded events of nestling necrophagy and the handling of a dead hatchling by a brooding hen owl. Finally, nestling mortality and the fate of the dead nestlings in some owl species is discussed.

STUDY AREA AND METHODS

The study area is located in the middle of the Netherlands approx. 52° 02" N, 05° 25" E. A number of specially designed nestboxes for video-monitoring and automatic registration of nestvisit activity were installed at the gable end of cowsheds (Fig. 1). The selected territories have been well-known for more than 50 years; territory sizes vary between 17 and 35 ha. The territories are patches of mixed forest surrounded by vast meadow land. To achieve the best possible undisturbed breeding conditions adult owls were never caught. They were gradually habituated to light conditions.

Figure 1. Diagram of observation-nestbox, final state of improvement 1989. Tunnel (T) connects the nestbox with the wall (G) of the gable end of the cowshed. Arrow on the landing board, also provided with an infrared (Ir) detector (not visible), indicates the entrance. D1, D2 and R1, R2 are Ir-sensors and reflectors resp. The male ususally transfers its prey from the platform (P) to the female or the nestlings the nest (S). M = compartment with microphone connected with audiorecorder; A = camera-adapter; W = window and V = space necessary for videorecording, filming or photography.

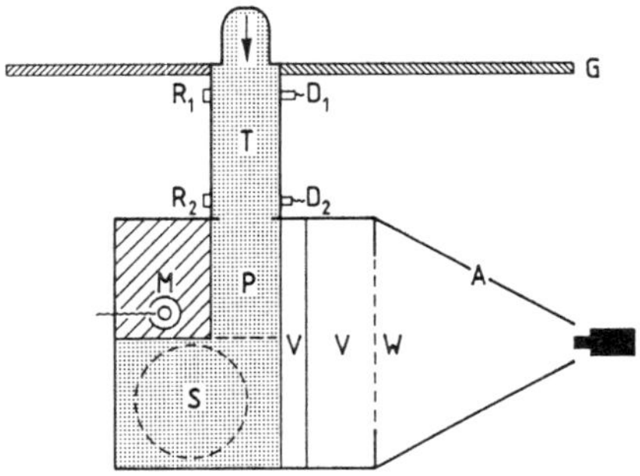

RESULTS

Events in nestling necrophagy

The following description was made from a video-recording in the night of 13/14 April 1985 at site 2 in the middle of brooding time. Five eggs were laid and five hatchlings emerged. During a temporary decrease in prey deliveries the youngest nestling starved to death. The start of the description was arbitrarily chosen approx. 4 min before the nearly dead or dead nestling was pulled out from between its nestmates.

The hen owl was brooding her chicks in the left corner of the nest. After some minutes the oldest chick, 16 days old, came into view and began to stumble around the nest, occasionally uttering begging cries and starting to nibble at the dried remains of a frog. The hen owl followed the movements of the brooded nestling, adapting her position from time to time to the gentle movements or discomfort calls of the other nestlings. One nestling, however, could be seen lying between her legs. This was quite an abnormal posture. After some time the hen owl looked down at the chicks for about 20 sec, gave a soft contact call and resumed brooding. Some 30 sec later this behaviour was repeated, but now she began to palpate the dead nestling energetically with her bill for about 5 sec and then resumed brooding. 1 min 20 sec later this behaviour was repeated but now the hen owl pulled the dead chick out from between the other ones.

The apparently dead chick hung motionless from her bill for some 7 sec and she started to nibble it. She then laid it down on the nestrim and put her right claw carefully around its body, while energetically palpating the whole body with her bill. Then her left claw was put around the body and again her right one, while she was still palpating the chick carefully. From time to time she started nibbling it. She looked about with the right claw around the body and all of a sudden plucked a tiny piece of down and skin from the hind end of the chick. She waited some seconds.

Suddenly she started to utter her feeding calls. Immediately all nestlings reacted with vigorous begging and commenced to search for food in her bill. Soon she plucked a second larger peice. The hind part was first fed in 9 plucks (1 min 21 sec), followed by the midpart, breast and wings in 10 plucks (1 min 40 sec). All nestlings got some pieces, but unequal rations. There was neither severe competition nor any aggressiveness between them. The head with the neck was fed in 19 plucks (approx. 8 min). The skull was attempted to be swallowed by two nestlings, but was regurgitated twice. The hen owl had to tear the head into pieces for feeding. Ultimately she cleaned up the plucking site and the bills of the nestlings and resumed brooding.

Analysis of the behaviour

Three distinct phases could be distinguished. (1) The brooding phase (approx. 4 min) which was considered interrupted by the perception of deviant stimuli in the dying chick. The hen owl gradually reacted to the stimuli by looking down, uttering contact calls, preening the chick, which soon turned into palpating energetically. (2) The ambivalent phase (approx. 2 min) starts with the pulling out of the chick. The hen owl showed two contrary trends, tending the chick again or handling it as a prey. It is assumed that she tried to evoke reactions of a live chick, for example discomfort cries. Then the preening gradually turned into energetically palpating the whole body of the chick, followed by the claw activity, at first carefully and later more firmly, ultimately ending in the first pluck of a tiny piece of down. (3) The last or plucking phase (approx. 12 min) is considered to be started with the uttering of the feeding calls of the hen owl.

Feeding a dead nestling

A second case of nestling necrophagy, also at site 2, was video-recorded in 1991 after brooding time. Five eggs were laid. Four eggs hatched successfully, one egg/hatchling disappeared unobserved. It was evident that the fourth nestling was developing slowly during the first seven days of its life. It showed the typical lag in growth, activity and also competitive ability at the moments of food deliveries. The nestling was weighed for the third time at the beginning (19.50 hr) of the night (April 2 1991) of its tenth and last day of life (Fig. 2). That night it must have died between 22.14 and 23.35 hr. It was moribund but still moving a little when the hen owl arrived with a Great Tit (*Parus major*) at 22.14 hr, but by the next preyvisit, a Woodmouse (*Apodemus sylvaticus*) at 23.35 hr, it was flattened against the bottom of the nest, lifeless.

The hen owl arrived with a frog (*Rana temporaria*) at 01.25 and left the nestbox immediately after. During the last two visits she appeared not to notice the dead nestling.

At 04.13 hr the hen owl arrrived with a decapitated frog, which was quickly seized by the oldest nestling and swallowed within 15 sec. At this moment it was observed that the fourth nestling was lying in the bottom of the nest, trodden under foot. Thereupon the hen owl looked down, without hesitation picked up the dead young and immediately started to pluck it.

For about 4 min 30 sec she stood with her back to the camera. During that period about 30 pluck-feeding actions could be counted. The begging frequency was high, 4.6 calls per 10 sec. The third nestling got most of the food, the first nestling got less and the second was apparently continuously begging but got nothing. Then the hen owl turned her face to the camera and picked up the remains of the fourth nestling. Only two legs and a small part of the hind end was left. Again she started to pluck and feed small pieces. After 14 plucks only the legs were left. These were presented at least 6 times and regurgitated in all instances. They were then crushed by the hen owl and swallowed by the nestlings. The begging frequency was still high. This second phase (in front of the camera) lasted about 5 min. Finally the hen owl searched with her bill for prey remains on the bottom of the nest, but did not find any. She preened the nestlings and left the nestbox.

Figure 2. Typical lag in development between the starving youngest nestling (drawn line) and its next youngest nestmate. In this case (site 2, 1991) a fourth nestling is compared with a third one.

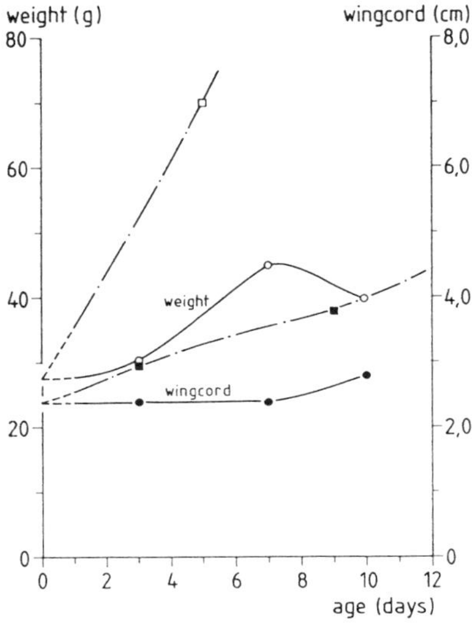

Analysis of the second case

There is no doubt that the hen owl recognized the subject on the bottom of the nest as prey at 04.13 hr. Except for the white colour, given she can distinguish a white colour, there seemed to be no stimuli to remind her of a live nestling. It is noteworthy that she plucked the victim in 47 very tiny pieces. These did not weigh more than one gram on average (weight of victim about 40 g). Besides, the handling time was very long: 9 min 30 sec as compared to the handling time of a mouse or frog prey, which could be swallowed in 15 sec to maximally 30 sec at this age.

Handling of a dead hatchling

In 1985 at site 1 a breeding attempt, five eggs, five hatchlings, soon ended in complete failure, most probably due to bad weather during hatching. It was observed, after the hen owl had left the nest, that two hatchlings had emerged and one must have died soon after. There was no prey available. After the break the hen owl resumed brooding. About 1 min before the dead hatchling was pulled out of the scrape, the hen owl had turned to the right, bowed in the direction of the dead chick and, as soon as she had touched it, began to palpate the whole body energetically and ended up with nibbling it. Then she pulled it out by its hind end. She held it head downward for some 10 sec and then laid it on the rim of the nest. Again she started to palpate the whole body and rearranged the eggs while the other hatchling was peeping. She picked up the dead hatchling again, nibbled at it shortly and laid it down. Then the right claw was carefully put round the body. She looked round for some seconds and again started to palpate it energetically. The same pattern was repeated once more and both processes lasted for in total 1 min 30 sec. Thereupon she preened it briefly, pushed it back for brooding and again further back carefully, and resumed brooding. This tending process lasted about 1 min. The whole event lasted 4 min 10 sec.

That night the hen owl handled the dead hatchling several times in a similar way. The next night it had disappeared.

Analysis of handling a dead hatchling

It is clear that a brooding hen owl continuously keeps in close contact with her young from her immediate responses to stimuli (peeping calls from the egg, discomfort cries, begging calls). In this case the hen owl must have perceived the deviant stimuli (motionless, silent, flabby, cold) from the dead hatchling and responded with typically energetic examination behaviour followed by characteristic ambivalent behaviour, which this time ended with tending a dead hatchling, repeated several times. There were no begging nestlings that forced her to feed and most probably this postponed the ultimate moment of turning into prey handling and eating the dead hatchling.

DISCUSSION

Necrophagy in Tawny Owls

Tending behaviour. Nesting activity was observed at least three whole nights a week. The pairs at site 1 and 2 were studied for two and seven breeding seasons respectively. It was obvious that the brooding hen owl was continuously in touch with her nestlings. Even during post-brooding her prey visits lasted three times longer than the male's, because they usually ended up in preening the chicks and searching for prey remains. Even after fledging she mostly uttered the alarm calls and often attacked the predator/human being approaching her fledgings (Wallin 1987 and my own observations). The behaviour of all the hen owls so far observed can be described as persistently and prudently tending her brood under all conditions. No tendencies that might be interpreted as infanticide-like were ever observed.

Mechanism of competition. During brooding competition could not be assessed, because the nestlings could not be observed. My few clear observations suggest that begging intensity is an important component of competitive capability beneath hatching order. At the sound of the arrival of a parent, the relatively larger and more agile nestmates monopolized access to the food as long as they were not satiated. Ultimately the smallest (1984, 1985, 1991) or the smallest and next smallest (1986) showed a visible lag in development (growth, weight) and activity (competition for food). Asynchronous hatching, approx. 1 day between first and second nestling and usually 2, seldom 3, between the others, determined the hierarchy of competitive capability by size and agility. No behaviour between nestmates was ever observed that might be interpreted as inter-sibling strife or Cainism.

Cause of nestling death. The mortality of Tawny Owl nestlings is low, approx. 6%, as compared to the loss of eggs, approx. 26% (my unpublished review of 14 authors: 76% of eggs laid hatched, n=256; 94% of the hatchlings fledged, n=195). These figures are comparable with the observations of Lundberg (1981) for the Ural Owl *Strix uralensis*. The death cause of the hatchling in this study was unknown.

The death of all the youngest nestlings (1984, 1985, 1991) and of the youngest and next youngest (1986) was always caused by starvation, preceded by a visible lag in development and activity.

Deviant stimuli. It was evident that in the first case described the hen owl had perceived deviant stimuli from the brood, when she responded with her uncommon behaviour. These deviant stimuli can probably be ascribed to the flabby body gradually sinking between its sturdy nestmates and the lack of activity. It is supposed that the hen owl may also have perceived differences in temperature between the dead and the other siblings. After perception of these stimuli it apparently took some time before a certain threshold was passed and she finally pulled out the dead nestling.

Ambivalent behaviour. This was characterized by a typically energetic examination of the body of the dead nestling and by a gradually stronger nibbling or claw activity, presumably in search for cues of a live chick. The longer the hen owl failed to perceive such stimuli the sooner she reached the point of recognizing it as a prey item. This process was assumed to be enhanced by her awareness of the nutritional state of the brood. Probably she herself was hungry too and was losing weight. The former supposition was in agreement with the immediate and vigorous begging response of all the nestlings, when she started to utter the first feeding calls after the second pluck. During brooding time the hen owl is continuously in touch with her nestlings and the most pronounced ambivalent behaviour was observed. During post-brooding this bond is less direct and the response to a dead nestling less immediate. Although I suppose that she must have noticed the death of the nestling, she did not respond directly. She picked it up as if she had one of her usual search actions for prey remnants. Then she dismembered the dead chick without any hesitation. I have no video-registrations of nestlings devouring or plucking a dead nestmate, but Haller (1939) reported one case.

Haller's observation. Haller (1939) gave a first hand observation of a Tawny Owl nestling devouring a dead nestmate. He observed a 4-brood at a Buzzard nest from a distance of 3 m for more than 3 hr and lit the scene if necessary with a torch. When he started the observation there were two well fed nestlings (31 and 30 days old), a third one visibly smaller (28 days) and a fourth one (26 days) with a considerable lag in growth and activity as compared to the third. Prey was delivered at 03.45 and 06.45 hr, a mouse and a large Song Thrush nestling *Turdus philomeles*. The mouse was immediately swallowed by the first or second nestling, but not by the third. the thrush was dismembered by the first and second nestling. During this activity the fourth nestling, that had lain on the floor of the nest during the whole time, was tipped over. The third owlet was attracted by the dead or moribund nestmate, now lying on its back, and started to devour it.

I have no difficulty in accepting this case as nestling necrophagy because the fourth nestling must have lain with its eyes closed for at least 3hr as can be concluded from Haller's description.

Secondly there must have been a considerable difference in size between the third nestling and its victim for it successfully to devour it. That indicates a poor season too, as was also noted by Haller. These few observations suggest that necrophagy in Tawny Owls seems to be rather the rule than the exception.

Nestling mortality in other owls

The fragmentary records suggest that there has not yet been found evidence of infanticide or fratricide in other owl species. If fresh dead nestlings were found, no injuries were observed that might have caused their death. The disappearance of owlets by supposed cannibalism in Short-eared Owls *Asio flammeus* are insufficiently investigated by Ingram (1959, 1962) to be discussed here.

In Barn Owls it is widely observed that the youngest or youngest and next youngest often disappear before fledging. Marti 1989 (North America) and Wilson *et al.* 1985 (Africa) reported that hatching order affected significantly the loss of nestlings. They found little or no evidence for Cainism in Barn Owls. In some cases they found evidence that dead nestlings had been eaten by siblings. De Jong, who studied the breeding biology of Barn Owls in the north of the Netherlands for over twenty years, could confirm these findings (pers. comm. 1991). He added that usually the chicks disappear during early nestling time (hatching to approx. 40 days) and occasionally he had evidence for nestling necrophagy. During the wandering phase (after appox. 40 days of age) they were mostly found dead near the nestsite. Such nestlings apparently died from starvation or an accident.

Preliminary conclusions

The observations about the mechanism of competition and necrophagy indicate similar processes in tytonine and strigine species. The competitive capability is determined by the size and agility of the nestling without any aggressiveness towards nestmates. Size in turn is determined by hatching order and enforced by poor food rates. During brooding the mechanisms of competition are not yet assessed because of observation difficulties. But the few accurate observations suggest that hatching order determines the begging loudness and intensity and also capability to seize the pieces fed. It is generally accepted that owls, feeding on "cyclic" fluctating small rodents, adjust their clutch size to prevailing prey abundance and profitability during prelaying time. A temporary decrease in catchability by weather when brood demand is high can cause an accidental brood reduction. Evidence for food limitation of brood size in owls as well as in diurnal raptors is rare. However when an unpredictable decrease in prey abundance occurs, brood reduction should be considered as an adjustment of brood size to prevailing prey abundance. In this sense the observations are consistent with the idea of maximization of lifetime reproductive output of the parents (Lack 1966, 1968). The mechanism of competition is consistent with diurnal raptor species with variable clutch sizes of a relatively large range, 0-6 and more eggs. Intersibling strife or Cainism only occurs in diurnal raptors with small and less variable clutch sizes: 2-3 eggs. Although Cainism is a well-known phenomenon, its selective advantage is not yet fully understood (Stinson 1979; Brown *et al.* 1977).

ACKNOWLEDGEMENTS

I thank Zomer Bruyn for his field assistance in the first years of the study (1984-1986) in particular for the video-registration of nestling necrophagy in 1985 when he was accidentally at the spot. Special thanks must go to Ellen ten Broeke and Lodewijk Koster for their field work and patience to get the second video-registration of nestling necrophagy during postbrooding in 1991 when I was studying Tawny Owls in the Châtillon Forest.

REFERENCES

BROWN, L.H. *et al.* **1977.** Breeding success in some African Eagles related to theories about sibling aggression and its effects. *Ostrich* 48: 65-71.

HALLER, W. 1939. Ueber einen Fall von Kannibalismus beim Waldkauz. *Beitr. Fortpfl. Biol. Vögel* 15: 29-31.

INGRAM, C. 1959. The importance of juvenile cannibalism in the breeding biology of certain birds of prey. *Auk* 76: 218-226.

INGRAM, C. 1962. Cannibalism by nestling Short-eared Owls. *Auk* 79: 715.

LACK, D. 1966. *Population studies of birds.* Clarendon Press, Oxford.

LACK, D. 1968. *Ecological adaptations for breeding in birds.* Methuen, London.

LUNDBERG, A. 1981. Population ecology of the Ural Owl in Central Sweden. *Ornis Scand.* 12: 111-119.

MARTI, C.D. 1989. Food sharing by sibling Common Barn Owls. *Wilson Bull.* 101: 132-134.

McNICHOLL, M.K. 1977. Usage of the term "cannibalism" and "scavenging" in ecological literature. *Canadian Field-Nat.* 91: 416.

SCHÜZ, E. 1984. Ueber Syngenophagie, besonders Kronismus, ein Beitrag zur Ethologie speziell des weiszstorchs. *Oekol. Vögel Ecol. Birds* 6: 141-158.

STINSON, CH.H. 1979. On the selective advantage of fratricide in raptors. *Evolution* 33: 1219-1225.

WALLIN, K. 1987. Defense as parental care in Tawny Owls *Strix aluco. Behaviour* 102 : 213-230.

WILSON, R.T. *et al.* **1985.** Breeding biology of the Barn Owl *Tyto alba* in central Mali. *Ibis* 128: 81-90.

J. C. Van Veen
Owl Research Project
Agricultural University
Ritzema Bosweg 32a
6703 AZ Wageningen
The Netherlands

Part 8

The Biology of Extirpated, Rare or Lesser-known Owls

Boobook Owl *Ninox novaeseelandia*

Conveners:

Dr. R. J. Clark & Dr. H. Mikkola

Meyburg, B.-U. & R. D. Chancellor eds.1994
Raptor Conservation Today
WWGBP / The Pica Press

The Distribution of Mexican Owls

Paula Enríquez-Rocha, J. Luis Rangel-Salazar
and Denver W. Holt

ABSTRACT

Mexico is rich in owl species, in spite of which knowledge about them is poor, including even their distribution. Data on 3,434 specimens in 47 national and foreign museums were compiled. Also a thorough revision of the literature was undertaken, to provide a unified picture. Twenty-eight species occur in Mexico, more than in any other country north of the equator. Four are widely distributed in the American continent. Out of the 12 tropical species, six are endangered, four are vulnerable and two maintain an apparently stable population. In Mexican law, only three are listed as endangered, one endemic and two subendemic. The Ferruginous Pygmy Owl *Glaucidium brasilianum* has been the species most collected.

The one endemic species - the Balsas Screech-owl *Otus seductus* - had only three specimens collected. Oaxaca and Michoacan were the states with greatest species richness (19) as opposed to Aguascalientes, with only two. There is controversy over the distribution range of several species, whilst another undergoes continuous taxonomic changes; these make the unification of information difficult. Important data from two principal museums have not been obtained; this might reinforce or alter our conclusions.

INTRODUCTION

Currently there are 162 known species of owls in the world (Amadon Bull 1988), 28 (17%) of which occur in Mexico, considerably more than among northern forest owls (22) (Norberg 1987) and North American species (19) (Johnsgard 1988).

Owls in Mexico have received little attention and most of the literature is old (Ridgway 1895; Kelso Kelso 1936; Moore 1937 a,b, 1941, 1947 a,b; Moore & Peters 1939; Alvarez del Toro 1949; Briggs 1954; Moore & Marshall 1959; Buchanan 1964; Northern 1965; Houston 1966). Generally, most Mexican owl species have not been fully described and their distribution is not clearly defined. Unfortunately, what is known of the latter is controversial. We present the current distribution and most up-to-date literature covering Mexican Owls.

STUDY AREA AND METHODS

Mexico (2 million km) has 32 states (Fig. 1). Its 32 different vegetation types (Rzedowski 1986), geographic location and complex topography provide a rich biological diversity of fauna and flora. More than 50% of the land mass lies 1,000m above sea level (Ramos 1985). We obtained data on specimens from 47 museums, visiting or sending questionnaires to 36 foreign and 11 national museums (Appendix 1). In addition, we reviewed the existing literature for information about Mexican owls.

Based on these data, we drew range maps for each species. Taxonomy followed that of Amadon and Bull (1988).

Figure 1. Map of México showing 32 states dividing the country.

RESULTS

Common Barn Owl **Tyto alba**

125 specimens from 30 states recorded from museum data. Friedman *et al.* (1950) also reported Barn Owls from Hidalgo and Quintana Roo. Recently, we have also recorded Barn Owls from Quintana Roo. Paynter (1955) and Hartig (1979) did not report this species from the Yucatan Peninsula. Blake (1972) and Grossman and Hamlet (1988) considered Barn Owls to be widely distributed throughout the country. This is the most widely distributed owl in Mexico. (Fig. 2,a).

Flammulated Owl **Otus flammeolus**

76 specimens from 15 states recorded. Additionally, it has been reported by Ridgway (1914), Friedman *et al.* (1950) and Blake (1972) for Distrito Federal, and A.O.U. (1983) mentioned it as occurring in Nuevo León. (Fig. 2,b).

Eastern Screech Owl **Otus asio**

150 specimens from 18 states recorded . Its distribution is restricted to north-eastern and southern Mexico, as confirmed by Marshall (1967) and Rowley (1984). However, some museum data reported its presence in western Mexico. (Fig. 2,c)

Western Screech Owl **Otus kennicottii**

117 specimens recorded from 13 states. There is much confusion about this species and its subspecific distribution due to taxonomic variations (Marshall 1967). Our data do not agree with Blake (1972), who reported this species in the states of Queretaro and Hidalgo. Its current distribution is north and south-western Mexico and Baja Peninsula. (Fig. 2,d).

Balsas Screech Owl **Otus seductus**

Only 3 specimens from the state of Michoacan recorded. Marshall (1967), Peterson and Chalif (1973) and A.O.U. (1983) also report it for Colima and Guerrero. This is the only endemic Mexican owl species, currently found only in the south-west. (Fig. 2,e).

Pacific Screech Owl ***Otus cooperi***
26 from 6 states recorded. It seems to be resident only along the Pacific slope in south-western Mexico. (Fig. 2,e).

Whiskered Screech Owl ***Otus trichopsis***
186 specimens from 20 states recorded, only from museum data. It has a wide distribution excluding both peninsulas. However, Davis (1972), A.O.U. (1983) and Eckert (1987) consider it to occur in Hidalgo and Puebla. (Fig. 2,g)

Bearded Screech Owl ***Otus barbarus***
Only 9 specimens recorded, all from Chiapas. Ridgway (1914) mentioned its occurrence south across the border in the highlands of Guatemala. It has the most restricted distribution of any Mexican owl. (Fig. 2,h).

Vermiculated Screech Owl ***Otus guatemalae***
101 specimens from 16 states recorded. Although mentioned by Friedman *et al.* (1950), Paynter (1955), Storer (1961) and Davis (1972) as occurring in Campeche, no specimens could be located there. There is the only species of genus *Otus* found in the Yucatan Peninsula. (Fig. 2,i).

Crested Owl ***Lophostrix cristata***
21 specimens from 4 states recorded. Although Grossman and Hamlet (1988) list its distribution as extending into the Yucatan Peninsula, we could not confirm this, so have not included it in the distribution maps. This species occurs in southern Mexico. (Fig. 2,j).

Spectacled Owl ***Pulsatrix perspicillata***
28 specimens from 3 states recorded. This species is also restricted to southern Mexico and its occurrence in the Yucatan Peninsula (Grossman & Hamlet 1988) is doubtful. (Fig. 2,k).

Great Horned Owl ***Bubo virginianus***
213 specimens from 26 states recorded. Brodkob (1943) mentioned it for the state of Tabasco, although no specimen exists. As its present distribution covers almost the entire country, this is quite likely to be so. (Fig. 2,l).

Mottled Owl ***Ciccaba virgata***
368 specimens from 22 states recorded. It has a wide distribution, but not as yet reported from Baja Peninsula and north-central Mexico. The museum data and the literature seem to agree on its distribution. (Fig. 2,m).

Black and White Owl ***Ciccaba nigrolineata***
45 specimens from 5 states recorded. Our museum data agree with the published literature (Ridgway 1914); Friedman *et al.* 1950; Blake 1972; Davis 1972; Peterson & Chalif 1973; A.O.U. 1983; Edwards 1989). Although Grossman and Hamlet (1988) did not report this species for the Yucatan Peninsula, Paynter (1955) cited one specimen from Quintana Roo. We also have additional data for that state. Its distribution appears to be fragmented; further surveys are needed. (Fig. 2,n).

Barred Owl ***Strix varia***
34 specimens from 8 states recorded. Some literature (Ridgway 1914; Peters 1940; Friedman *et al.* 1950; Davis 1972; A.O.U. 1983) included Puebla. However, there were no museum specimen data. Alvarez del Toro (1980) did not include Chiapas in this species' distribution , although we located 6 specimens (HMCZ No. 272862, USNM No. 193875, WFVZC No. 19724, No. 12473, No. 1247 and No. 4853). (Fig. 2,o).

Fulvous Owl ***Strix fulvescens***
Four specimens from 3 states recorded from museum data. Alvarez del Toro (1980) observed this species in the cloud forest. We located only one specimen from cloud forest, identified as *Strix varia fulvescens* (LACM-NH No. 24392). Binford (1989) did not list it in Oaxaca, where we located two specimens (COIB No. DGFS 4575, No. 4576). Friedman *et al.* (1950) reported it for the state of Mexico, but no specimens were collected. (Fig.2,p).

Spotted Owl ***Strix occidentalis***
26 specimens from 8 states recorded from museum data. Although Ridgway (1914), A.O.U.

(1983), Edwards (1989) and Peterson and Chalif (1989) report this species as occurring for Baja Peninsula, there are no specimen data. Its distribution its fragmented. (Fig. 2,q).

Northern Pygmy Owl **Glaucidium gnoma**
176 specimens from 24 states recorded. Ridgway (1914) and Friedman *et al.* (1950) reported it for Colima and Distrito Federal, but did not collect it. It has a wide distribution, but has yet to be found in the Yucatan Peninsula. (Fig.2,r).

Least Pygmy Owl **Glaucidium minutissimun**
138 from 13 states recorded. The distribution data agree with Davis (1972) and Peterson and Chalif (1989). It has yet to be reported from either peninsula, north-central or mid-central Mexico. (Fig. 2,s).

Ferruginous Pygmy Owl **Glaucidium brasilianum**
1,038 specimens from 23 states recorded. This is the highest number of specimens collected for any Mexican owl species. It has yet to be recorded from the Baja Peninsula. Although reported for Distrito Federal (Friedman *et al.* 1950) and Coahuila (A.O.U. 1983; Eckert 1987), there are no museum specimens from these areas. (Fig. 2,t).

Elf Owl **Micrathene whitneyi**
163 from 16 states recorded. Included are the Revillagigedo Island group in the Pacific Ocean. Peters (1940) and Blake (1972) reported it from the state of Mexico, and Grossman and Hamlet (1988) reported it from Tamaulipas. However, no museum specimens exist. This species does not occcur in southern Mexico or the Yucatan Peninsula. (Fig. 2,u).

Burrowing Owl **Speotyto cunicularia**
256 specimens from 26 states recorded. This species has a wide distribution and is reported to occur across the entire country (Grossman Hamlet 1988). (Fig. 2,v).

Northern Saw-Whet Owl **Aegolius acadicus**
23 specimens from 11 states recorded. It occurs in north-central and central Mexico, but in neither peninsula. Ridgway (1914), Friedman *et al.* (1950), Blake (1972) and Davis (1972) reported it from Chihuahua, Jalisco and Veracruz. (Fig. 2,w).

Unspotted Saw-Whet Owl **Aegolius ridgwayi**
Five specimens only from Chiapas. We and others (Moore 1947b; Alvarez del Toro 1980; Davis 1972; Peterson & Chalif 1973; A.O.U. 1983) have also recorded it from Chiapas. The A.O.U. (1983) reported a questionable specimen collected from Oaxaca. (Fig. 2,x).

Striped Owl **Asio clamator**
26 specimens from 3 states recorded. It occurs primarily in south-eas tern Mexico and has been reported for Veracruz and Chiapas alone by Blake (1972), Davis (1972), and Peterson and Chalif (1973). Ridgway (1914) did not report this species for Mexico. (Fig. 2,y).

Stygian Owl **Asio stygius**
17 specimens from 9 states recorded. It has been reported from Chiapas (Friedman *et al.* 1950; Davis 1972; Alvarez del Toro 1980; A.O.U. 1983) and the Yucatan Peninsula (A.O.U. 1983; Edwards 1989). However, this does not agree with our own data and those of Paynter (1955) and Hartig (1979). (Fig.2,z).

Long-Eared Owl **Asio otus**
37 specimens from 12 states recorded. The museum data and the literature are in close agreement (Ridgway 1914; Frieldman *et al.* 1950; Blake 1972; A.O.U. 1983). Its distribution is wide and there are reports of long-distance migrants from Saskatchewan, Canada (Houston 1966), Montana, USA (e.g. D. Holt, unpubl.), and Minnesota, USA (e.g. D. Evans, pers. comm.), to Mexico. (Fig. 2,aa).

Short-Eared Owl **Asio flammeus**
27 specimens from 13 states recorded. It has also been reported by Friedman *et al.* (1950), Hartig (1979), A.O.U. (1983) and Binford (1989) from the states of Distrito Federal, Jalisco, Oaxaca, Puebla, Veracruz and Yucatan. (Fig. 2,ab).

Figure 2. Delimited range maps of known owl species inhabiting Mexico. Shaded areas cover those states where the species have been recorded.

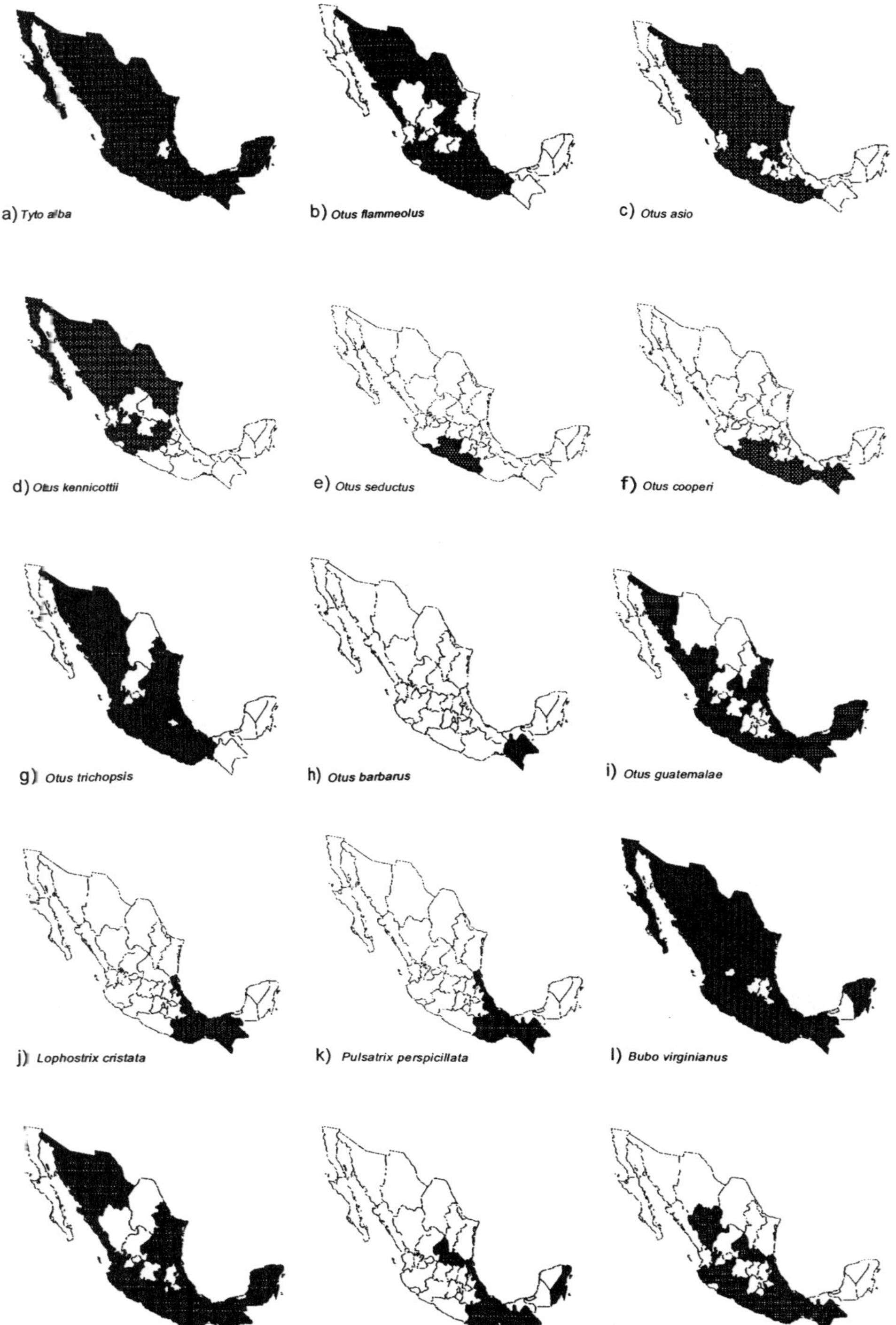

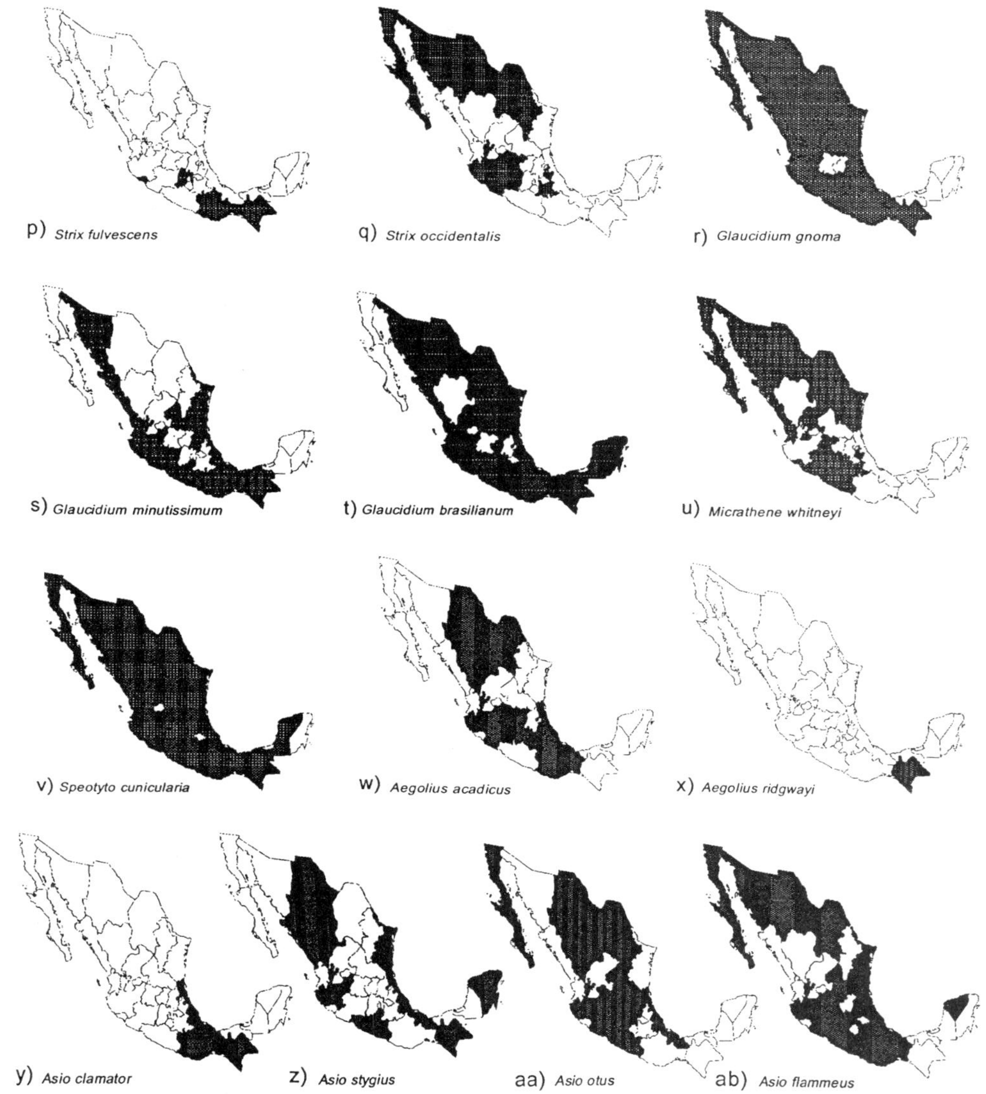

DISCUSSION

Twenty-eight Mexican owl species, both neartic and neotropical, are represented. Nineteen have neartic/neotropical affinities and nine have neotropical affinity. The Balsas Screech Owl *Otus seductus* is endemic to Mexico's Pacific slope region. The Bearded Screech Owl *Otus barbarus* and Unspotted Saw-whet Owl *Aegolius ridgwayi* are reported only from Chiapas.

The Ferruginous xygmy-Owl *Glaucidium brasilianum* provided the largest amount of data and the Balsas Screech Owl the least. The richest owl assemblage came from Oaxaca and Michoacan, with 21 and 19 species each, respectively.

The taxonomy and distribution of Mexican owls are still in question, and this is reflected in the literature. For instance, the subspecies of Screech Owl *Otus* discussed by Marshall (1967) were reported only from eastern Mexico. Our museum data also indicate the presence of some of these subspecies in western Mexico. Recently, Marshall *et al.* (1991) re-named the Vermiculated Screech Owl *Otus guatemalae* as Variable Screech Owl *O. atricapillus guatemalae.* This change was based on voice recordings.

Collection records are important to define distribution and could provide a clue as to abundance. They are important also for comparing distributional changes, both present and historically, although threatened and endangered species cannot be collected. Historic collections are important for location data. Also, lack of museum specimens may indicate rare, uncommon or easily overlooked species.

Some museum specimens and accompanying data can be only partially correct or else completely wrong. Often the date of collection and other vital information were not included. In some areas of historic distribution, habitats have been so much altered that the species concerned no longer occurs there.

We appreciate that there may be shortcomings in this manuscript. However, it is the first attempt in Mexico to draw together information on this taxonomic group.

We also hope this paper may act as a catalyst to spur further investigation into Mexican owl distribution. Then perhaps research and conservation may follows.

ACKNOWLEDGEMENTS

We are especially grateful to all people, national and foreign bird collection curators, who kindly supplied us with the information for this paper and to Joe T. Marshall for his generous help.

REFERENCES

ALVAREZ DEL TORO, M. 1949. Striped Horned Owl in southern Mexico. *Condor* 51: 232.

ALVAREZ DEL TORO, M. 1980. *Las Aves de Chiapas*. Gob. del Edo. de Chiapas. Tuxtla Gutierrez, Chis. México. 272 pp.

AMADON, D. J. BULL 1988. Hawks and Owls of the world: a distributional and taxonomic list. *Proc. West. Found. Vertebr. Zool.* 3: 295-357.

AMERICAN ORNITHOLOGIST' UNION 1983. *Check-list of North American Birds*. 6th Ed. Washington D.C. 877 pp.

BINFORD, L. 1989. A distributional survey of the birds of the Mexican state of Oaxaca. *Ornith. Mono.* 43: 418 pp.

BLAKE, E.R. 1972. *Birds of Mexico*. University of Chicago Press. Chicago Illinois. p. 208-224.

BRIGGS, M. 1954. Apparent neoteny in Saw-whet Owls of Mexico and Central America. *Proc. Biol. Soc. Wash.* 67: 179-182.

BRODKOB, P. 1943. Birds from the Gulf lowlands of southern, Mexico. *Misc. Publ. Mus. Zool. Univ. Mich.* 55:88.

BUCHANAN, M. 1964. The Mexican races of the Least Pygmy Owl. *Condor* 66: 103-112.

DAVIS, L.I. 1972. *A Field Guide to the Birds of Mexico and Central America*. Univ. of Texas Press, Austin Texas.

ECKERT, A.W. 1987. *The Owls of North America*. Weathervance Books. New York. 278 pp.

EDWARDS, E.P. 1989. *A Field Guide to the Birds of Mexico*. 2nd. ed., Ernest P. Edwards. Box A.Q. Sweet Barier. 118 pp.

FRIEDMAN, H., L. GRISCOM & R.T. MOORE 1950. *Distributional Check-list of the Birds of Mexico*. Cooper Ornithological Club, Berkeley Calif.

GROSSMAN, M. & J. HAMLET 1988. *Birds of Prey of the World*. Bonanza Books. New York 496 pp.

HARTIG, H.M. 1979 *Las Aves de Yucatán*. Fondo Edit. Yuc. Mexico. 101 pp.

HOUSTON, C. 1966. Saskatchewan Long-eared Owl recovered in Mexico. *Blue Jay* 24:178.

JOHNSGARD, P.A. 1988. *North American Owls*. Smithsonian Institution Press. 295 pp.

KELSO L. & H. KELSO 1936. A new Ciccaba from southeastern Mexico and northern Guatemala. *Auk* 53: 215-216.

MARSHALL, J.T. Jr. 1967. Parallel variation in North and Middle America Screech-owls. *Monog. West. Found Vert. Zool.* 1:72.

MARSHALL, J.T., R. BEHRSTOCK & C. KÖNIG. 1991. Voices of the New World Owls (Strigiformes: Tytonidae, Strigidae). *Wilson Bull.* 103 (2): 311-315.

MOORE, R.T. 1937a. New races of the genus *Otus* from northwestern Mexico. *Proc. Biol. Soc. Wash.* 50: 63-68.

MOORE, R.T. 1937b. Two new owls from Sinaloa, Mexico. *Proc. Biol. Soc. Wash.* 50: 103-106.

MOORE, R.T. 1941. Three new races in the genus *Otus* from central Mexico. *Proc. Biol. Soc. Wash.* 54: 151-160.

MOORE, R.T. 1947a. New owls of the genera *Otus* and *Glaucidium*.. *Proc. Biol. Soc. Wash.* 60: 141-146.

MOORE, R.T. 1947b. Two new owls, a swift and poorwill from Mexico. *Proc. Biol. Soc. Wash.* 60: 141-146.

MOORE, R.T. & J.T. MARSHALL, Jr. 1959. A new race of Screech Owls from Oaxaca. *Condor* 61: 224-

225.
MOORE, R.T. & J.L. PETERS 1939. The genus *Otus* of Mexico and Central America. *Auk* 56: 38-56.
NORBERG, A. 1987. Evolution, structure and ecology of Northern Forest Owls, pp 3-34. *In* R. Nero, R. Clark, R. Knapton & R. Hamre (eds.), *Biology and Conservation of Northern Forest Owls*. Symposium Proceedings, Manitoba. Feb 3-7.
NORTHERN, J.R. 1965. Notes on the owls of the Tres Marias Island Nayarit, Mexico. *Condor* 67: 358.
PAYNTER, R. 1955. The Ornithogeography of the Yucatan Peninsula. *Peabody Museum Nat. Hist. Yale Univ. Bull.* 9. 347 pp.
PETERS, J.L. 1940. *Check-list of Birds of the World.* Cambridge, Harvard Univ. Press.
PETERSON, R.T. & E.L. CHALIF 1973. *A Field Guide to the Mexican Birds.* Houghton Mifflin Co. Boston.
PETERSON, R. & E. CHALIF. 1989. *Aves de México.* Guía de Campo. Ed. Diana, México. 473 pp.
RAMOS, M. 1985. Endangered tropical birds in Mexico and Northern Central America. *ICBP Tech. Publ. No.* 4:305-318.
ROWLEY, J. 1984. Breeding records of land birds in Oaxaca, Mexico. *Proc. West. Found. Vert. Zool.* 3: 224.
RIDGWAY, R. 1895. On the correct subspecific names of the Texan and Mexican screech owls. *Auk* 12: 389-390.
RIDGWAY, R. 1914. The birds of North and Middle America. Part VI, *Bull. U.S. Nat. Mus.* 50: 1-882.
RZEDOWSKI, J. 1986. *Vegetación de México.* Limusa. 432p.
STORER, R. 1961. Two collections of birds from Campeche, Mexico *Univ. Mich. Mus. Occ. Papers Zool.* 621: 1-20.

Paula Enríquez-Rocha
GEB-Mex,
Ap. Postal 4-071,
06400 México,
D.F. México

Denver W. Holt
Owl Research Institute,
P.O. Box 8335,
Missoula,
Montana 59807, U.S.A.

J. Luis Rangel-Salazar
Dep. de Ecología Terrestre,
CIQRO, Ap. Postal 424,
7700 Chetumal,
Quintana Roo, México

APPENDIX 1.

List of national and foreign museums and collections consulted:

Colección Ornitológica del Instituto de Biología; Colección Ornitológica de San Nicolás de Hidalgo, Universidad de Michoacán; Escuela Nactional de Ciencias Biológicas; Instituto de Historia Natural de Chiapas; Instituto Nacional de Investigaciones Forestales y Agropecuarias-Bacalar; Instituto Nacional de Investigaciones sobre Recursos Bióticos; Laboratorio Natural de Las Joyas, Universidad de Guadalajara; Museo de Zoología de la Facultad de Ciencias; Museo de Zoología Iztacala; Salón de las Aves de Saltillo Coahuila; Universidad Autónoma de Baja California Sur; Australian Museum; Anniston Museum of Natural History; Academy of Natural Sciences of Philadelphia; Bell Museum of Natural History; Carnegie Museum of Natural History; Cornell University Collection; Zoology Collection Amsterdam Museum Netherlands; Denver Museum of Natural History; Delaware Museum of Natural History; Fort Hays Museum; Florida Museum of Natural History; Field Museum of Natural History, Chicago; Forschungsinstitut und Naturmuseum Senckenberg; Harvard Museum of Comparative Zoology; Illinois State Museum Collection; Kansas University Collection; Los Angeles California Museum of Natural History; Lousiana State University Museum of Zoology; Moore Laboratory of Zoology, Occidental College; Museo Nacional de Ciencias Naturales, Spain; Museum of Vertebrate Zoology, University of California in Berkeley; Oklahoma Museum of Natural History; Provincial Museum of Alberta; Peabody Museum Collection, Yale University; Royal Ontario Museum; Rijkmuseum Van Natuurlijke Historie, Leiden; Santa Barbara Museum of Natural History; Southwestern College Collection; San Diego Museum of Natural History; Staatliches Museum für Naturkunde, Stuttgart; Texas Cooperative Wildlife Collection; National Museum, Smithsonian Institute; University of Washington, Thomas Burke Memorial State Museum; University of Wisconsin Zoological Museum; Western Foundation of Vertebrate Zoology; Zoological Institute of the Academy of Siences, URSS.

Meyburg, B.-U. & R. D. Chancellor eds.1994
Raptor Conservation Today
WWGBP / The Pica Press

Progress of the Norfolk Island Boobook Owl *Ninox novaeseelandiae undulata* Re-establishment Programme

Penny Olsen, John Hicks, Nick Mooney and Derek Greenwood

ABSTRACT

The Norfolk Island Boobook *Ninox novaeseelandiae undulata* is confined to small, isolated Norfolk Island, an Australian territory. In 1986 it was established that one owl, a female, survived. The scarcity of large nest trees, due to past logging, and introduction of predators and competitors for tree holes, appeared to be the main conservation problems. In September 1987, two male New Zealand Moreporks *N. n. novaeseelandiae* were introduced. The female paired with one male and has produced four hybrid offspring. Two of the hybrid young appeared to have formed a pair by mid-1991 and were provided with nest boxes. A third unpaired youngster laid eggs in 1992. Islanders, the Australian National Parks and Wildlife Service and New Zealand wildlife authorities have co-operated in an attempt to re-establish an owl population. The effort is low-cost, requires little man-power, and is carried out in the wild with minimal disturbance to the sole extant female, concurrent with programmes to control introduced cats, rats, birds and plants.

INTRODUCTION

Norfolk Island is a small, isolated Australian territory: 3,450 ha in area, situated 1,367 km east of the mainland and 675 km from New Caledonia, its nearest neighbour. Two other small islands, Nepean and larger Philip Island (ca. 2km²), complete the Norfolk Island Group.

The rainforest-clad island was discovered in 1774 and later used as a penal settlement. By the early 1990s, three-quarters of the forest had been cleared and the remainder had deteriorated due to logging of prime trees, infestation by weeds and degeneration from exposure (Lane-Poole 1926; Smithers & Disney 1969; Schodde *et al.* 1983). In 1986 12% of the island was proclaimed a National Park, encompassing the two mountains (the highest reaching 318 m) and the only remaining intact fragments of original forest.

Today approximately 2,000 people populate the island. Habitat destruction, and deliberate introductions and self-introductions of exotic plants and animals have resulted in several extinctions. Since settlement, six of the island's fourteen endemic land birds have become extinct and a seventh species, the White-breasted White-eye *Zosterops albogularis*, has not been seen for several years. The Red-fronted Parakeet *Cyanoramphus novaeseelandiae cooki* numbers about 30 individuals and requires extensive management to protect the population from rats, introduced Crimson Rosellas *Platycercus elegans* and possibly domestic and feral cats.

The Norfolk Island Boobook *Ninox novaeseelandiae undulata* is thought to be a distinctive subspecies of the New Zealand Morepork, and is the only Australian owl considered to be endangered (Clarke *et al.* 1978; Garnet 1992; Collar & Andrew 1988). First recorded in the late 18th century, when it almost certainly would have occurred throughout the island, the owl is said to have largely been confined since 1909 to the gullies surrounding Mt. Pitt (Bassett-Hull 1910; Turner *et al.* 1968; Smithers & Disney 1969). However, according to the islanders it was occasionally seen in more open country. From this apparently depleted population Bell (1912-13), with a permit to remove six owls, took thirty specimens for a Sydney collector. In more recent years, visiting biologists reported hearing few, if any, owls (King 1979; Wakelin 1968; De Ravin 1975). As early as the 1960s a lack of holes for nest sites, due to logging of mature trees, was seen as a major problem (Turner *et al.* 1968; King 1981). A survey of the island's birds in 1978 located perhaps three individual owls (Schodde *et al.* 1983; Rooke 1986), yet no conservation action was taken. A search in 1985 was unsuccessful, but because islanders occasionally heard an owl it was concluded that at least one still existed (Rooke 1986).

A group of concerned ornithologists visited the island in 1986 and, assisted by Australian National Parks and Wildlife Service (ANPWS) staff and locals, were able to find only one owl, a female. She was trapped for measurement and marking, and released (Olsen 1989; Olsen *et al.* 1989). A follow-up survey in 1987 unearthed no additional owls although the female was seen on several occasions (Olsen, unpubl. report to ANPWS). Recommendations for a wild-based re-establishment programme were made, nest boxes were erected in the National Park, and in September 1987 two males of the closest extant subspecies, the New Zealand Morepork, were released (Olsen *et al.* 1989; Hicks *et al.* 1990; Olsen & Moon 1990; Hicks 1991). Olsen (1993) discusses some of the taxonomic and genetic considerations and conservation rationale behind the re-establishment attempt. Here we report on the progress of the programme.

METHODS

The capture and sexing of the original female, and recommendations for re-establishment, are described by Olsen *et al.* (1989). In 1986 fourteen nest boxes of three designs were hung in large trees in the area frequented by the female. One was an artificial hollow made from cement, the others were boxes made from marine-ply and were of two designs, one long and the other deep (donated by the Island's Flora and Fauna Society). Painted tin around the entrance protected the boxes from Black Rats *Rattus rattus* and Polynesian Rats *R. exulans*. Boxes were checked regularly and cleaned out if used by European Starling *Sturnus vulgaris* or Crimson Rosella. Once the female had settled near a nest box, an attempt was made to remove from the area all Crimson Rosellas, which are aggressive competitors for nest sites. As it became obvious that the owl did not use certain boxes these were removed to streamline nest checks. Although the locals were kept well informed of progress, to minimise the risk of disturbance the siting of the boxes was away from areas used by the public and their location was not released.

In September 1987, courtesy of the New Zealand wildlife authorities, two male New Zealand Moreporks, which had been sexed by laparoscope, were hacked from two of the nest boxes. For future identification, both were banded with an individual leg band: stainless steel over which some reflective tape had been glued. Aided by local volunteers, ANPWS staff conducted regular 'listenings' for the owls.

Disturbance of the nest boxes and the owls was limited: boxes were checked every two to three months. During the breeding season, at boxes with signs of owl activity observations were made from the ground, around dusk, and the box was inspected briefly and only after the owls had left to hunt.

About one week before fledging, the hybrid chicks were weighed, measured, individually banded (reflective tape) and a blood sample was taken for future DNA analysis.

RESULTS

Brief Summary of Breeding Attempts:

Almost immediate use of nest boxes added support to the notion that a lack of suitable holes in trees was a problem. The deeper boxes were favoured by the owl, that is, those she could not see out of when standing on the nesting substrate (290 mm long x 270 mm broad x 490 mm deep).

The Norfolk Island female paired with one of the New Zealand males almost immediately: they were seen and heard together within the area previously frequented by the female. In early October 1988 the female laid one egg which later disappeared. In 1989, two chicks hatched and were measured on 8th December. They fledged on the night of the 14th December and appeared to remain with their parents until the following winter. Similarly, in 1990 the pair raised two chicks, which were measured on the 5th December and fledged about the 15th December.

Surveys by ANPWS staff and locals in mid-1991 located the breeding pair and probably all four of their offspring, two of which (one fledged 1989 and one 1990) were together. An additional nest box was erected near to where the young pair were sighted. In 1991 the original pair laid two eggs, which broke after 2-3 weeks for unknown reasons. In 1992, the eggs broke late in incubation, almost certainly due to invasion of the box by introduced honey bees which proceeded to build a hive. The same year, one of the hybrid offspring, apparently unpaired, laid four eggs.

The Hybrid Chicks:

In both years the plumage of the chicks seemed to most resemble that of their New Zealand parent, darker than that of the Norfolk Island owls. When measured the chicks were about 4 to 4.5 weeks old and not fully grown, however their tarsus and culmen were probably close to full-sized. At that time, none was as large as the Norfolk Island female (Table 1). Similarly, none of the chicks was as heavy as the Norfolk Island female, but all were heavier than the median weight of 19 New Zealand females (mean 163 g, range 105-212; males-median 156, mean 160, range 105-195, Lex Hedley unpubl. data from museum skins). Thus we were unable to determine the sex of the chicks. However, in the 1990 brood one chick had noticeably smaller eyes than the other, perhaps indicative of a difference in sex, and the chick 'blue' later laid eggs. Survival appears to be good: all the chicks were located early in 1993.

Table 1. A comparison of weights and some measurements from the Norfolk Island Boobook female and her four hybrid chicks.

	Norfolk Island female	Hybrid Chicks 1989		Hybrid Chicks 1990	
Band Colour		Green	Blue	Yellow	Orange
Exposed culmen (mm)	15.6	14.5	14.4	14.1	13.8
Tarsal breadth (mm)	4.4	4.1	4.1	3.5	3.8
Weight (g)	213	185	179	180	195

DISCUSSION

The breeding of the owls in the wild, as opposed to the captive alternative, has meant that disturbance of the original female has been minimised and her offspring are well adjusted to the wild. Overall, monitoring of the breeding pair has not proven difficult. The programme has been low-cost (averaging > $A 2000-3000 per annum) and low effort.

Because the owls breed only once a year, and have a two-egg clutch, the recovery effort has been slow. Early in the recovery programme, removal of a clutch to an incubator (allowing the owls to re-lay) was considered to have unacceptable risks, but is an option for the future. Introduced species, Crimson Rosellas and bees, which are aggressive competitors for nest holes, cause the greatest concern. The Rosella can be controlled by removal from the area frequented by the owls; the bees are an insidious and potentially more dangerous threat.

A difficulty with a the wild-based programme has been to monitor the owls precisely, particularly the hybrid offspring once they reach independence. Future work may include radio-tracking of the juveniles. Apart from continuing management problems with the owls until they become well established, a problem which has arisen is the potential conflict between the owl recovery programme and the rat control programme, both conducted by ANPWS. Rats are significant predators of eggs and chicks of the island's smaller birds and destroy much young vegetation, hampering revegetation efforts. Control by baiting carries with it the risk of secondary poisoning of owls. The owls occasionally eat rats, but insects in particular, and small birds are more important prey. Various rat control measures have been tried, most recently an on-going programme with Quintox (dieldrin-based).

The Lord Howe Island Boobook *N.n. albaria*, another distinctive subspecies, was extinct by 1950. Had no action been taken the Norfolk Island Boobook would also have disappeared. If a viable population of hybrids can be established, then some of the genes of the original owl will be preserved. No decision has yet been reached, but it seems likely that once a viable population is established it will be left to nature to select owls most suited to existing conditions on the island.

The initial early success of the re-establishment programme must give hope to other conservation projects for very rare taxa. The extraordinary plight of the original owl, and her appeal and that of her chicks, have received wide media coverage and garnered the attention of many in positions of authority and the public at large. The project has strengthened relations between the Norfolk Islanders and ANPWS, benefiting other conservation efforts on the island. Not least, it has given a great boost to island conservation in Australia, previously much neglected.

Stop press: October 1993 - the two hybird offspring which paired in 1991 are incubating three fertile eggs

REFERENCES

BASSETT-HULL, A.F. 1910. The birds of Lord Howe and Norfolk Islands. *Proc. Linn. Soc. NSW* 34: 636-693.

BELL, R. 1912-1913. Diary on Norfolk Island. Aust. Mus., Sydney (unpubl. ms.).

CLARK, R.J., D.G SMITH & H. KELSO 1978. *Working Bibliography of Owls of the the World.* Raptor Information Centre, Nat. Wildl. Fed., Washington.

COLLAR, N.J. & P. ANDREW 1988. *Birds to Watch: The ICBP Checklist of Threatened Birds.* ICBP Tech. Bull. No. 8.

DE RAVIN, J.A. 1975. The birds of Norfolk Island. *Aust. Bird Watcher* 6:4-10.

GARNETT, S. (ed) 1992. *Threatened and Extinct Birds of Australia.* RAOU Report No. 82, 212 pp.

HICKS, J. 1991. The last owl. *Panorama* 101:46-50.

HICKS, J., P. OLSEN & D. GREENWOOD 1990. Saving the last survivor. *Birds International* 2(1): 66-73.

KING, W.B. 1979. *Endangered Birds of the World.* The ICBP Red Data Book. Smithsonian Inst., Washington.

KING, W.B. 1981. *Endangered Birds of the World.* The ICBP Red Data Book. Smithsonian Inst., Washington.

LANE-POOLE, C.E. 1926. Report on the forests of Norfolk Island. Govt. Printer of Vic., Melbourne.

OLSEN, P. 1989. The very last of the Norfolk Island Boobook. *Geo* 11(2): 70-77.

OLSEN, P. 1993 (in press). Attempted re-establishment of an endangered subspecies: the Norfolk Island Boobook *Ninox novaeseelandie undulata. In* B.D. Bell, S. Tidemann & M. Rands (Eds) *Management of Threatened Species. ICBP Bull.* (in press).

OLSEN, P. & G. MOON 1990. Of Boobooks and Moreporks. *Birds International* 2(4): 26-33.

OLSEN, P.D., N.J. MOONEY & J. OLSEN 1989. Status and conservation of the Norfolk Island Boobook *Ninox novaeseelandiae undulata.* pp. 415-422 *In* B.-U. Meyburg & R.D. Chancellor (Eds). *Raptors in the Modern World.* WWGBP Berlin & London.

ROOKE, I. 1986. Survey of the White-breasted White-eye and the Norfolk Island Boobook Owl on Norfolk Island, October-November 1985. RAOU Rep. 22.

SCHODDE, R., P. FULLAGAR & N. HERMES 1983. *A Review of Norfolk Island Birds: Past and Present.* ANPWS, Commonwealth of Australia, Canberra.

SMITHERS, C.N. & H.J. de S. DISNEY 1969. The distribution of terrestrial and freshwater birds on Norfolk Island. *Aust. Zool.* 15: 127-140.

TURNER, J.S., C.N. SMITHERS., R.D. HOOGLAND 1975. The conservation of Norfolk Island. *Aust. Cons. Found.* Spec. Publ. No. 1.

WAKELIN, H. 1968. Some notes on the birds of Norfolk Island. *Notornis* 15:175-176.

Penny Olsen
Evolutionary Ecology Group
Division of Botany and Zoology
Australian National University
Canberra, A.C.T. 0200, Australia

Nick Mooney
Department of Lands and Environment
Division of Parks and Wildlife
G.P.O. Box 44A
Hobart 7001, Australia

John Hicks
Australian Nature Conservation Agency
G.P.O. Box 636
Canberra, A.C.T. 2601
Australia

Derek Greenwood
Australian Nature Conservation Agency
P.O Box 310
Norfolk Island 2899
Australia

Meyburg, B.-U. & R. D. Chancellor eds.1994
Raptor Conservation Today
WWGBP / The Pica Press

The Distribution and Conservation of Strigiformes in Yunnan Province, China

Wen Xianji & Yang Lan

ABSTRACT

Because of its special situation and natural environment, Yunnan Province has 18 owl species which account for 62% of the total recorded in China. This paper lists the distribution, habitat, food and status of each. Threats to them are: 1) habitat destruction, 2) use of insecticides on farmland, 3) killing for medicinal purposes in remote areas. All owls are protected birds in China. More than 30 nature reserves in Yunnan Province are playing a major role in the protection of owls and their habitats. Xishuangbanna, Gaoligongshan and Ailaoshan National Nature Reserve are the three most important reserves. Since 1982, education on the protection of birds and their habitats has made most people come to understand its importance. Recommendations include: 1) provision of financial support to survey the species, their distribution and status, and to study their ecology and behaviour, 2) protection of the remaining forest and recovery of forest destroyed, 3) provision of nest-boxes in the breeding season; 4) to continue education on birds protection and promote the use of non-persistent chemicals on farmland.

INTRODUCTION

Yunnan Province, located in south-west China (21° 08'-29° 08'N, 97°31'-106°12'E), forms the main part of the Yunnan-Guizhou Plateau. Its total area is about 383,000 km², about 94% of which is mountainous plateau. It slopes downward from the north-west to the south-east. To the east of the Yuanjiang River (Red River) is the east and central Yunnan Plateau, still comparatively unimpaired. To the west of the Yuanjiang River are the Gaoligongshan, Nushan and Yunlin mountain chains, lying parallel with the Nujiang (Salween), Lancangjiang (Mekong) and Jinshajiang (Yangtze) Rivers, running from north to south and from the famous Hengduanshan Transhimalya Canyon. The average height of the ridges is over 3,000m a.s.l. The highest point is Kagebo Peak of Meli Snow Mountain, reaching 6,740m; the lowest is 76.4m at the Yuanjiang River exit, south-east of Yunnan Province.

Yunnan Province is within the monsoon belt with tropical and subtropical climates. The complex topography endows this province with climatic differences both horizontally and vertically, with frigid, temperate and torrid zones. Vegetation is mainly divided into tropical rain forest, monsoon forest, subtropical evergreen broad-leaf forest and subalpine coniferous forest.

The complex topography, climate and vegetation provide various favourable habitats for owls.

DISTRIBUTION

According to the literature and our investigations since 1958, there have been 18 owl species recorded in Yunnan Province, belonging to two families and 10 genera. The distribution of each species, its habitat, food and status are as follows: (The plotting localities are only from the collection of Kunming Institute of Zoology, Academia Sinica. Those which are first reported we marked with "*"). For each species the measurements of the first collected specimen are given in Table 1.

Tytonidae

Barn Owl ***Tyto alba***

T. a. stertens Hartert

Plotting localities: Kunming City; Jinggu county*; Jinghong County*; Menghai County.

Distribution: Kunming City, Jinggu County, Jinghong County, Menghai County (resident).

Remarks: Pan Qinghua *et al.* (1964) reported a specimen collected from Xishuangbanna (Menghai County) as *T. a. javanica.* Kuang Bangyu *et al.* (1980) considered a specimen from Kunming to be *T. a. stertens* because it differed from the specimen from Xishuangbanna by being more grey, with less orange-yellow upper parts, and silky white underparts with no orange-yellow. Cheng Tso-hsin (1987) thought all specimens from Yunnan were *T. a. javanica.*

The range of *T. a. stertens* includes India (Ali & Ripley 1969; Ripley 1982), Burma (Smythies 1986), northern, eastern and central Thailand (Deignan 1945, 1963), while the range of *T. a. javanica* includes Cochinchina, South Annam (Delacour & Jabouille 1940), South-east Asia and Java (Peters 1940). It seems that *stertens* is distributed in the north and west, while *javanica* covers the south and east.

Since the race in the area adjacent to Yunnan Province is *T. a. stertens*, our interpretation is that the specimens from Yunnan should be *T. a. stertens*, and the variation in colour is similar to the specimens from India and northern Thailand (Baker 1927; Deignan 1945).

Habitat: Hilly country and plains near cultivated lands and human habitation. Alt. 1,180-2,100m.

Food: Mainly rats and mice, occasionally large insects.

Status: Common.

2. Grass Owl ***Tyto capensis***

T. c. chinensis (Hartert)

Plotting localities: Kunming City*, Pingbian County*.

Distribution: Kunming City, Pingbian County, Mengzi County, Simao County, Pu'er County, Jinghong County, Menghai County (resident).

Habitat: Open grassland and high grass jungle. Alt. 300-2,100m.

Food: Chiefly rats and mice, sometimes lizards.

Status: Common.

3. Bay Owl ***Phodilus badius***

P.b. saturatus Robinson

Distribution: Jinghong County (resident).

Habitat: Dense evergreen forest in the submontane tracts and foothills. Alt. 620m.

Food: Not recorded in Yunnan.

Status: Very rare.

Strigidae

4. Spotted Scops Owl ***Otus spilocephalus***

O. s. latouchei (Rickett)

Plotting locality: Yanjiao, Jiangcheng County*.

Distribution: Jiangcheng County, Zhenkang County (resident).

Habitat: Submontane forests. Alt. 1,440-1,700m.
Food: Mainly insects.
Status: Rare.

5. Scops Owl ***Otus scops***
O. s. malayanus (Hay)
Plotting localities: Zhelong, Xinping County*; Niaodiao Mt., Eryuan County*
Distribution: Xinping County, Mengzi County, Eryuan County, Lushui County (resident).
Habitat: Deciduous and evergreen forest, groves of densely foliaged trees near cultivation, and orchards. Alt. 1,800-2,500m.
Food: Mainly insects.
Status: Common.

6. Collared Scops Owl ***Otus bakkamoena***
O. b. erythrocampe (Swinhoe)
Plotting localites: Xiaomengyang, Jinghong County*; Manfen and Yiwu, Mengla County*; Yongkang and Nansan, Zhenkang County*; Zhefang, Luxi County; Yingjiang County; Luobuba, Lianghe County.
Distribution: Yiliang County, Jingdong County, Mengzi County, Jinghong County, Mengla County, Zhenkang County, Luxi County, Yingjiang County, Tengchong County, Lianghe County (resident).
Remarks: The Bird Section of Kunming Institute of Zoology, Academia Sinica (1980) reported that the specimens from Luxi, Lianghe and Yingjiang Counties, western Yunnan Province, were *O. b. lettia*. Cheng Tso-hsin *et al.* (1989) adopted this view. After examining a series of almost 150 skins from nearly every part of the Asian range, Deignan (1950) thought that a specimen from the Shweli-Salween Divide, western Yunnan, was *erythrocampe*, while another from Tengchong (Tengyueh), western Yunnan, was intermediate between *erythrocampe* and *lettia* but nearer to *erythrocampe*. Because no specimen from Burma was at hand, we adopted the opinion of Deignan (1950), considering the specimen from west of Yunnan to be *erythrocampe* and that western Yunnan might be the overlap range of *erythrocame* and *lettia*.
Habitat: Forest and well-wooded hilly country near cultivation. Alt. 300-1,400m.
Food: Chiefly insects, occasionally birds and mice.
Status: Fairly common.

7. Eagle Owl ***Bubo bubo***
(1) *B. b. tibetanus* Bianchi
Plotting locality: Bapo, Gongshan County.
Distribution: Gongshan County, Deqin County (resident).
(2) *B. b. kiautschensis* Reichenow
Plotting localities: Huahongdong, Kunming City*; Dongchuan City*.
Distribution: Kunming City, Dongchuan City, Yongshan County, Tengchong County, Jinghong County, Mengzi County (resident).
Habitat: Rocky cliffs, woodland to steppes, ravines or rocky broken ground. Alt. 300-2,100m.
Food: Mainly rats and mice, sometimes rabbits and pheasants.
Status: Fairly common.

8. Forest Eagle Owl ***Bubo nipalensis***
B. n. nipalensis Hodgson
Distribution: Hekou County (resident).
Habitat: Dense evergreen and moist deciduous forest. Alt. 580m.
Food: Not recorded in Yunnan.
Status: Very rare.

9. Brown Fish Owl ***Ketupa zeylonensis***
K. z. orientalis Delacour
Plotting localities: Kunming City*; Xiaomengyang, Jinghong County*; Mengla County*;

Datang, Tengchong County.

Distribution: Kunming City, Mengzi County, Jinghong County, Mengla County, Menghai County, Shuangjiang County, Tengchong County (resident).

Remarks: The Bird Section of Kunming Institute of Zoology, Academia Sinica (1980) reported that a specimen from Tengchong, west of Yunnan, was *K. z. leschenaulti*. Cheng Tso-hsin (1987) adopted this subspecies but with a question mark. Cheng Tso-hsin *et al.* (1989) examined this specimen and found it was immature. They thought that *leschenaulti* did not occur in Yunnan. Peters (1940) and Howard & Moore (1980) recorded that the race of north-east Burma was *orientalis*. It seems to be impossible that the specimens from Tengchong, situated to the east of Burma, were *leschenaulti*. We share the opinion of Cheng Tso-hsin *et al.* (1989).

Habitat: Well-wooded country along streams, eroded ravines and steep river banks. Alt. 600-1,900m.

Food: Mainly fish, frogs.

Status: Rare.

10. Tawny Fish Owl ***Ketupa flavipes***

Plotting locality: Xiaomengyang, Jinghong County*.

Distribution: Jinghong County, Yongshan County (resident).

Habitat: Forested banks of hill streams. Alt. 620-760m.

Food: Mainly fish, frogs.

Status: Very rare.

11. Malay Fish Owl ***Ketupa ketupu***

K. k. aagaardi (Neumann)

Smythies (1986) reported one record from Yunnan, but we have never collected a specimen of this species there nor from any other area of China, and no other publication that we are aware of has reported this species being in China.

12. Collared Pigmy Owlet ***Glaucidium brodiei***

G. b. brodiei (Burton)

Plotting localities: Mangchui, Jingdong County*; Menglian County*; Mengyuan, Mengla County* Dongshan, Mile County*; Pinghe, Shuangbai County*; Jizu Mt., Binchuan County*; Biluo Snow Mt., Bijiang County*; Maku and Bapo, Gongshan County.

Distribution: Yuanjiang County, Xinping County, Mile County, Hekou County, Shuangbai County, Binchuan County, Gongshan County, Bijiang County, Jingdong County, Menglian County, Simao County, Mengla County (resident).

Habitat: Evergreen or mixed hill forests. Alt. 740-3,000m.

Food: Chiefly insects, also rats and mice, small birds.

Status: Fairly common.

13. Barred Owlet ***Glaucidium cuculoides***

(1) *G. c. whiteleyi* (Blyth)

Plotting localities: Zhenxiong County*; Ludian, Lijiang County*

Distribution: Kunming City, Lijiang County, Zhenxiong county, Yongshan County (resident).

(2) *G. c. rufescens* Stuart Baker

Plotting localities: Linjie, Chuanhe, Dongjiashan, and Huiyao, Jingdong County*; Mengmengba, Dongguo, and Xiaoheijiang, Shuangjiang County*; Matai, Lincang County*; Mangbang, Zhenkang County*; Daxueshan and Yongkang, Yongde County*; Zhefang, Luxi County.

Distribution: Luxi County, Yingjiang County, Tengchong County, Yongde County, Zhenkang County, Gengma County, Lincang County, Shuangjiang County, Jingdong County (resident).

(3) *G. c. brugeli* (Parrot)

Plotting localities: Yuanjiang County*; Mahuangbao, Hekou County*; Zongle, Menglian County*; Damenglong and Ganlanba, Jinghong County*; Menglun and Mengpeng, Mengla County*.

Distribution: Yuanjiang County, Hekou County, Menglian County, Jinghong County, Mengla

County, Menghai County (resident).

Habitat: Open forest of pine, oak, etc.; also subtropical evergreen jungle at low elevations, large tree and bamboo forest near human habitation.

Food: Mainly insects, sometimes rats and mice, frogs.

Status: Fairly common.

14. Brown Hawk Owl ***Ninox scutulata***

N. s. burmanica Hume

Plotting localities: Huiyao, Jingdong County*; Xiaomengyang, Jinghong County*; Menglun, Mengla County*; Mengzhi, Yongde County*.

Distribution: Tengchong County, Jingdong County, Gengma County, Yongde County, Mengla County, Mengzi County, Jinping County, Hekou County (resident).

Habitat: Well-wooded country, and groves of trees, often close to water. Alt. 300-1,400m.

Food: Mainly insects.

Status: Common.

15. Spotted Little Owl ***Athene brama***

A. b. pulchra HumeBaker (1927) reproted that the distribution range of *Athene brama pulchra* included Yunnan. Peters (1940) raised questions about its distribution in Yunnan. Smythies (1986) stated that *Athene brama* did not occur in Yunnan. Since a new subspecies of *Athene brama, Athene brama poikila* Yang & Li, was recorded (Yang Lan & Li Guiyuan 1989) in Baoxin and Yajiang Counties, Sichuan Province, situated to the north of Yunnan, and the range of *A. b. pulchra* is from central Burma to south-west Indochina (Howard & Moore 1980), and although we did not get a specimen of this species from Yunnan, it seems that *Athene brama* might be distributed there. But which subspecies it should be needs further study.

16. Brown Wood Owl ***Strix leptogrammica***

S. l. ticehursti Delacour

Plotting locality: Mengla County*; Datang, Tengchong County; Santai Mt., Luxi County; Danane, Yingjiang County.

Distribution: Tengchong County, Luxi County, Mengla County, Menghai County (resident).

Habitat: Deep forest. Alt. 300-2,670m.

Food: rats and mice, birds.

Status:Rare.

17. Tawny Wood Owl ***Strix aluco***

S. a. novicola (Blyth)

Plotting localities: Huahongdong, Kunming City*; Pantiange, Weixi County*; Dulongjiang, Gongshan County*; Mengwang, Luxi County; Datang, Tengchong County.

Distribution: Kunming City, Yongshan County. Lijiang County, Weixi County, Gongshan County, Tengchong County, Luxi County (resident).

Habitat: Coniferous, mixed or deciduous forests, open country with some large trees. Alt. 760-2,000m.

Food: Mainly rats and mice, sometimes frogs, birds, occasionally fish.

Status: Common.

18. Short-eared Owl ***Asio flammeus***

A. f. flammeus (Pontoppidan)

Plotting localities: Yangjie, Xundian County*; Shuangjiang County*, Simao County*.

Distribution: Xundian County, Tengchong County, Simao County, Shuangjiang County, Jinghong County (winter visitor).

Habitat: Tundra, steppes, meadows and marshes. Alt. 620-1,400m.

Food: Mainly rats and mice, sometimes small birds, large insects, occasionally plant seed.

Status: Common in winter.

Among the above 18 species, the occurrence of two in Yunnan is uncertain and needs further surveying; one is a winter visitor; 15 species are residents in Yunnan. Among these 15 residents,

Table 1. Measurements of owl specimens from Yunnan Province, China. [Note all weights in grams and linear measurements in mm]

Species	Weight	Length	Bill	Wing	Tail	Tarsus
Tyto alba stertens	485-1000	340-390	33-34	295-300	137-146	67-70
Tyto capensis chinensis	280	345	33	340	135	85
immatures	320-367	300-340	28-32	245-278	114-123	78-80
Otus spilocephalus latouchei	88	185	17-18	132	65	26
Otus scops malayanus	47-108	180-193	18-19	146-151	69-179	22-29
Otus bakkamoena erythrocampe	100-140	200-250	20-21	159-170	82-102	31-35
immatures	76-133	175-195	20	121-130	63-70	32-33
Bubo bubo kiautschensis	1000-2200	610-650	45-47	450	265-270	76-80
immatures	550-1600	380-550	37-49	270-375	136-222	68-78
Ketupa zeylonensis orientalis	1020-1359	440-545	40-48	372-390	190-206	65-73
Ketupa flavipes			44	420	194	77
Glaucidium brodiei	40-61	132-174	10-14	83-100	55-72	18-23
Glaucidium cuculoides whiteleyi	280	260	15-17	150-154	91-105	24-26
G. c. rufescens	152-240	203-257	15-17	144-164	85-94	22-29
G. c. brugeli	139-202	163-253	15-18	139-157	81-99	21-29
Ninox scutulata burmanica	184-214	297-305	19-21	212-227	145-154	27-31
immatures	174-190	255-265	19	157-193	100-110	26-30
Strix leptogrammica ticehursti	750-999	460-487	41-42	358-390	202-246	63
immatures		345	28	260	120	55
Strix aluco novicola	310-482	370-407	29-32	286-316	182-200	52-57
Asio flammeus flammeus	400	355-360	29	293-305	156-172	46-54

8 are mainly distributed in the Oriental region; two mainly in the Palearctic region; two in both Oriental and Palearctic Regions, one in both Oriental and Ethiopian Regions. One species has a worldwide distribution. The faunal characteristics of Strigiformes in Yunnan Province are the Oriental elements, mainly distributed in tropical and subtropical regions, and occupying a dominant position, while a few Palearctic elements can extend south to the province as well.

THREATS

Forest destruction is the main threat to owls. In the 1960s and 70s, the forest was logged for timber with government sanction, encroached on without plan for firewood, and illegally burnt to provide farmland. Now the primitive forest exists only inside the nature reserves. Outside the nature reserves nearly all forests have been replaced by monoculture crops, economic plants such as rubber and tea, shrubs and grassland. Many forest-dwelling species have lost their habitats, and it is difficult for many species which nest in tree hollows to find suitable nest sites. On the other hand the fact that no primitive forest remains outside nature reserves will also make it very difficult to form a network of reserves in the future. In addition, almost all buildings in the countryside are made of cement, so that wall cavities in which some species nest have decreased and it is impossible for them to nest as they used to. Another threat to owls is the use of insecticides on farm land, especially to those species inhabiting open country. In China it is said that owls can be used for medicine. Li Shizheng, who lived during the Ming Dynasty recorded this in his famous work *Compendium of Materia Medica*. But pharmacology was not then studied. In the remote countryside, some owls are still caught to-day to be used as medicine. This is the third threat.

CONSERVATION

From the analysis of their food, it is known that the large owls feed mainly on rats and mice, small owls mainly on insects, while the diet of intermediate-size species is wide, including insect, mice and rats, etc., Except for *Ketupa* which mainly feeds on fish, frogs etc., all other owls are very beneficial to agriculture and forestry, and important in maintaining the ecological balance. Furthermore, some species are rare in China, so all owls are protected according to the Wildlife Protection Law of the People's Republic of China and the List of the Protected Wildlife of National Importance in China.

Because of the special situation and natural environment of Yunnan Province, which covers only about 4% of China, 62% of all Strigiformes occurring in China have been recorded there. Among them, *Tyto alba stertens* was recorded only in Yunnan, *Glaucidium cuculoides brugeli* only in south Yunnan, *Glaucidium cuculoides rufescens* only in west Yunnan. Thus the conservation of Strigiformes in Yunnan Province is more important than any other part of China.

To protect owls, their habitats must also be protected. In Yunnan the establishment of nature reserves was begun in 1956. In 1959 24 such nature reserves were delimited, but due to lack of financial support, management organizations and staff, these reserves existed only in name. The forests in more than 10 reserves had been almost completely cut; in others hunting and logging were still rife. In 1980, the States Council approved the establishment of the first National Nature Reserve in Yunnan, in 1981 all nature reserves in Yunnan were delimited once again and more than 30 were established. They are now playing an important role in the protection of wildlife and natural habitats. The owls which live in these reserves have also been protected. The following three National Nature Reserve are of the greatest importance.

Xishuangbanna National Nature Reserve, established in 1981, is situated in the south of Yunnan Province (21°10'-22°24'N, 100°16'-101°50'E). The total area of the reserve is 241,776ha. The vegetation includes tropical rain forest, tropical monsoon forest, southern subtropical evergreen broadleaf forest, warm coniferous forest, bamboo forest, shrub forest and herbosa. Twelve owl species live in the reserves: *Tyto alba. T. capensis. Phodilus badius Otus bakkamoena. Bubo bubo. Ketupa zeylonensis. K. flavipes. Glaucidium brodiei. G. cuculoides. Ninox scutulata. Strix leptogrammica* and *Asio flammeus.*

Gaoligongshan National Nature Reserve, established in 1983, is situated in the west of Yunnan

Province (24°56'-26°09'N, 98°34'-98°50'E). The total area is 123,900ha. The vegetation mainly includes savanna shrub forest, monsoon evergreen broadleaf forest, warm coniferous forest, humid evergreen broadleaf forest, cold coniferous forest, tundra, meadows, etc. There are 10 owl species living in the reserve: *Otus scops. O. bakkamoena. Bubo bubo. Ketupa zeylonensis. Glaucidium brodiei, Glaucidium cuculoides, Ninox scutulata, Strix leptogrammica. S. aluco* and *Asio flammeus*.

Ailaoshan National Nature Reserve, established in 1986, is situated in the centre of the province (23°36'-24°44'N, 100°54'-101°30'E), with a total area of 50,360ha. The vegetation includes savanna shrub forest, cold and warm coniferous forest, dry and semi-humid evergreen broadleaf forest, humid broadleaf forest, etc. Six owl species live in this reserve: *Otus scops. O. bakkamoena. Bubo bubo. Glaucidium brodiei. G. cuculoides* and *Ninox scutulata*.

The above three National Nature Reserves, with a total area of 416,036ha, provide 14 species with ideal habitats. Some, such as Bay Owl and Tawny Fish Owl, can be observed only in these reserves. The populations of some species in the reserves are larger than in other areas.

From 1982, "Love the Birds Week" was inaugurated nation-wide every spring. During this week, citizens are educated by posters, newspapers, radio and TV. A scientific film about the beneficial role of owls has been shown across the country. In Yunnan, bird-watching competitions among middle-school students, and knowledge quizzes were held for the general public on protecting birds and their habitats. Most people have come to understand the importance of protecting birds and their habitats. Thus the conservation of owls has made great achievements in Yunnan.

RECOMMENDATIONS

The common and fairly common owls can occupy various habitats; some live in open countryside and alongside human habitations, but they need trees in which to roost and from which to spot their prey. The rare and very rare owls live almost exclusively in forest, and deforestation will make them still rarer, and even lead to their extinction in Yunnan.

The nature reserves are very important for owl protection and hold large populations of some species, but the lack of natural corridors between them makes each reserve a green island among farmland, so that genetic exchange among different populations is difficult. The population in one reserve is not large enough for some species to maintain genetic diversity, so that protection of the remaining forest not only inside reserves but also outside them, and promotion of the recovery of destroyed forest, are vital in order to form a reserve network in the future.

Fan Zhongming (1965) reported Scops Owl *(Otus scops)* breeding in nest-boxes in Liaoning Province and Li Shengde & Ruan Changwu (1988) reported Collared Scops Owl *(Otus bakkamoena)* using nest-boxes in Hubei Province. Provision of nest-boxes in the breeding season is a simple and useful method of protecting several species.Because most owls roost during the day and hunt at night, it is difficult to know the status of every species. To date it is unknown whether two species, *Ketupa ketupu* and *Athene brama*, occur in Yunnan or not. There has been little study of the ecology and behaviour of owls so far, and in order to develop suitable schemes for their conservation, we must first know their distribution, numbers, ecology and behaviour. Special financial support should be provided to carry out this research.

Education concerning the protection of these birds and their habitats must be continued, and use of non-persistent insecticides in farmland is also important.

ACKNOWLEDGEMENTS

We are particularly indebted to Dr. Richard J. Clark, a professor of biology at York College of Pennsylvania, for his valuable criticisms of the manuscript.

Wen Xianji/Yang LanKunming
Institute of Zoology
Academia Sinica
Kunming, Yunnan
People's Republic of China

Meyburg, B.-U. & R. D. Chancellor eds.1994
Raptor Conservation Today
WWGBP / The Pica Press

Mating Behaviour of Blakiston's Fish Owl *Ketupa blakistoni*

Sumio Yamamoto

ABSTRACT

Observations of mating behaviour of three pairs of Blakiston's Fish Owl for a total of 499 days were carried out annually from January 25 to April 5 between 1983 and 1990. Observation lasted from sunset to sunrise in the first two years. The frequency of mating was 18 times a season an average; 55% of the mating behaviour were observed during the 20 days prior to egg laying and most of it was concentrated around sunset on calm days. The owls, both males and females, did not display any noteworthy provocative actions. After calling to each other for 12 times (average), the female flew up first, the male immediately following. Another behaviour of the female was to turn her back to the male. These actions seemed to indicate her readiness to mate.

INTRODUCTION

Very little has been published on the mating behaviour of nocturnal owls. So far as the author knows, Mikkola's (1983) is the only report. The present paper includes the observations on the mating behaviour of three pairs of Blakiston's Fish Owl *Ketupa blakistoni* over eight years from 1983 to 1990. Fortunately, one of the pairs was not shy and their behaviour could be observed from a short distance.

STUDY AREA

Nemuro lies in the far east of Hokkaido, Japan (N43° 15', E148° 24'). The study area was located in the forests along the Bettoga River which starts in Hamanaka-cho, runs eastward through Nemuro City and flows into Lake Furen. The Bettoga is typical of the rivers of eastern Hokkaido, winding through the flat plain. It is flanked on both sides by belts of swampy land, covered mainly with birch *Betula ermani,* willow *Salix rorida* and alder *Alnus japonica*, with here and there some huge elms *Ulmus davidiana* and oaks *Quercus mongolica*. These swampy belts, 50-100m wide, connect with fir forests*Abies sachaliensis*. Up to 10km from its mouth the river is tidal and contains about 20 species of both salt and fresh water fish in abundance, From summer to autumn, 20,000 salmon, *Salmon gorbuscha* and *Onchorhynchus keta*, swim up the river. At 8km from the river's mouth, these salmon are caught for a breeding project and a salmon hatchery is located 30km higher up.

METHODS

The observations were carried out for 499 days in total from January to April for eight years, 1983 to 1990. In 1983 and 1984 surveys lasted all night, from 1½ hours before sunset to sunrise, whilst after 1985 surveys were reduced to 3½ hours. At 1½ hours before sunset, the author confirmed the owl's roost and then remained at a point from which both roosts and the surrounding area were visible. The distance from the roosts was 30m minimum and 100m maximum. The behaviour of the owl pairs was observed by using binoculars (x 8) and a telescope (x 20).

RESULTS AND DISCUSSION

Mating period

Table 1 shows the dates of the first and last copulations, the total number of copulations, as well as the dates of egg laying and annual clutch size of a pair of Blakiston's Fish Owl. The mating period, as well as the date of egg laying, varied between the years. In the 20 days prior to egg laying, usually March 1 to March 20, 50% of the copulations took place. In the year when the pair had young from the previous year, the number of copulations decreased (1986 and 1988). Although the parents did not attend to their young at this age, the latter still begged for food and sometimes occupied the same roost. In 1989 and 1990, when the first copulation was late, another individual from outside was observed in the pair's territory (10km) and was driven away. Attacks on the intruder were actively performed by the female, chasing the intruder until he, or she, left the territory. Even on a day when no intruder came, she flew to the spot and stayed there for one or two hours, after which she went hunting. Not only the pair's young but also the presence of an intruder seemed to affect copulating behaviour.

Table 1. Copulating behaviour of Blakiston's Fish Owl.

Year date	First copulation date	Last copulation date	Total number copulations	Egg deposition date	number
1983	February 8	April 1	17	March 27	1
1984	February 6	March 12	8	March 13	2
1985	February 4	March 24	25	March 25	2
1986	February 17	March 22	20	March 22	1
1987	January 29	March 21	29	March 9	2
1988	February 4	March 28	16	March 23	1
1989	February 25	March 21	12	March 20	2
1990	February 14	March 22	19	March 18	2

Figure 1. The time of copulation. Solid line indicates sunset time.

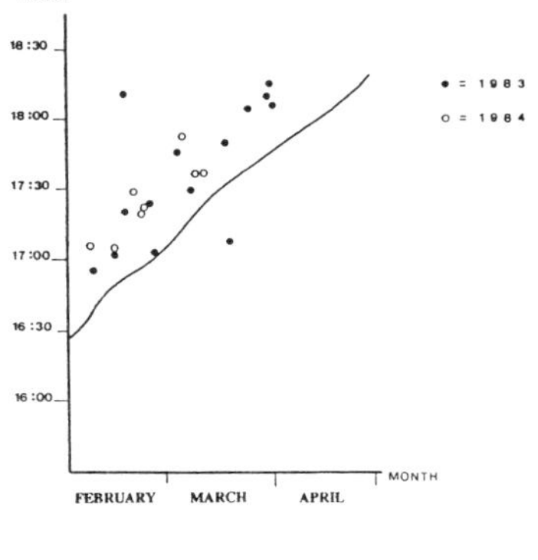

The time of copulation

In 1983 and 1984, the pair was observed always to copulate around sunset, with only three exceptions (summarized in Figure 1). From 1985 to 1990, the same tendency was shown, with copulations concentrated around a half hour after sunset.

The sites of the copulating area, roosts and nest

During the mating season, the couple change their roosts to a place nearer to the nest. There are thirty roosts within the territory, only five of them being used during the season (Fig. 2, roost site 1-5). The copulating area was 10-200m from the roosts, with an average of 96.5m, while the distance from the nest ranged from 5 to 300m (90m on average). When the pair used Nest A (Fig. 2) for the second time, the distance between the copulation area and the nest or roosts was reduced by one third of that in the first year. Use of the same nest for the third and fourth time made the distance progressively shorter. As to Nest B, the same phenomenon was observed.

The roosts used by the pair all through the year were so situated that each could confirm its partner's location. After sunset, both left together to hunt, but hunted separately until sunrise. Sometimes they came back to the roosts together, sometimes not. One instance of copulation before dawn took place when the pair were on their way to roost. The time around sunset seems the best occasion, when they stay closer to each other and copulate.

Figure 2. The territory of a pair of Blakiston's Fish Owl and the sites of nest, roosts and copulating place.
Upper figure — The broken line defines the pair's territory. The shaded area = Breeding territory.
Lower figure — A and B: Nest boxes. 2-6: Roost sites. Area within broken line = Copulating area.

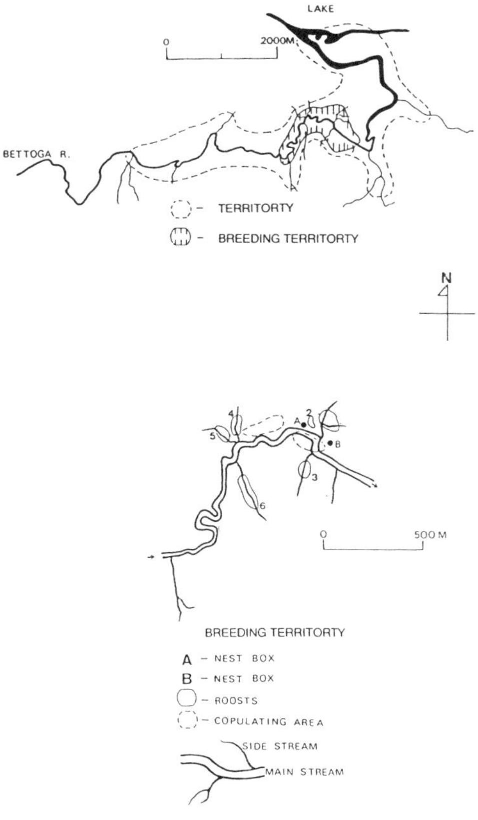

Courtship feeding

Courtship feeding usually began four days before the first copulation, though in some years it started only after the first copulation. During the mating season, courtship feeding was observed after mating, as the owls always went hunting after they finished copulating (Yamamoto 1989). From these observations, it seems that courtship feeding is not necessarily a direct factor inducing copulation.

Weather conditions for copulation

The pair copulated either on windless days or on days when the wind strength was less than 3mph, regardless of whether it was fine, cloudy, rainy, snowy or foggy. In one exceptional case when they copulated on a windy day (7mph), they chose a lower branch than usual. The wind seems to be a main factor affecting copulatory behaviour. In Nemuro district, the weather from March 1 to March 20, when copulating behaviour was most frequently observed, is comparatively calm. The temperatures at that time ranged between +7°C maximum and -2.5°C minimum. This suggests that the temperature does not affect copulatory behaviour.

Calling

When the roosts of the pair were far apart, the male would start calling earlier than usual. The female immediately reacted to her partner, and began to move. When they were less than 100m apart the female started calling in response to her mate. Most of the calls prior to copulation were made from the roosts. They lasted for about 45 minutes, while the number of calls was at most 50 with an average of 12 times. In 10 cases only one call was noted. In two instances, the pair copulated without calling. These facts suggest that the calling is generally a necessary lead up to copulation, although the birds may have some signals other than calling.

Behaviour before copulation

The female flew to the copulating site first, and the male then followed his partner, landing just beside her to copulate. The flight seems to be necessary for the female to eliminate faeces which might prevent the sperm entering her body. The female bowed her head to keep her body level. Her behaviour of showing her back to the partner seems to be a signal of willingness to copulate. The duration of mating was measured as the time of the male's riding on the female's back. Usually this was around ten seconds, with the actual copulation over in three seconds.

REFERENCES

MIKKOLA, H. 1983. *Owls of Europe.* Poyser, Calton.

YAMAMOTO, S. 1989. Courtship feeding and fledgling feeding of Blakiston's Fish Owl.*Memoirs of Preoperative Office of Nemuro Municipal Museum B.* 59-67.

Sumio Yamamoto
16 Rakuyo, Nemuro
Hokkaido 086
Japan

Part 9

The Systematics and Taxonomy of Raptors

Goshawk *Accipiter gentilis* - adult

Conveners:

Dr. C. M. White & Dr. A. Kemp

Meyburg, B.-U. & R. D. Chancellor eds. 1994
Raptor Conservation Today
WWGBP / The Pica Press

Phylogenetic relationships among Falcon species (genus *Falco*) according to DNA sequence variation of the cytochrome b gene

A. J. Helbig, I. Seibold, W. Bednarek, P. Gaucher, D. Ristow, W. Scharlau, D. Schmidl and M. Wink*

ABSTRACT

A phylogeny of 17 taxa of the genus Falco plus two Accipitrids, an owl and the domestic chicken as outgroups was reconstructed based on 300 nucleotide positions of the mitochondrial cytochrome b gene. DNA was isolated from blood, the target gene was amplified using the polymerase chain reaction and sequenced directly. The results indicate that falcons are monophyletic and more closely related to Accipitridae than to owls or galliformes. Typical kestrels (*F. tinnunculus, F. naumanni, F. punctatus*), three members of the subgenus *Hypotriorchis* (*F. eleonorae, F. concolor, F. subbuteo*) and three members of the subgenus *Hierofalco* (*F. rusticolus, F. biarmicus, F. jugger*) each form monophyletic groups. The latter subgenus, however, appears to be polyphyletic with *F. mexicanus* more closely related to the Peregrine Falcon than to the other members. In the Saker (*F. cherrug*) two very different mtDNA haplotypes were found, one almost identical to Gyrfalcon, the other one related to the Peregrine. This dichotomy can be explained by past hybridization, probably with *F. pelegrinoides*. Four taxa of the *F. peregrinus/pelegrinoides* complex were almost identical and may be conspecific. The position of *F. femoralis* and *F. columbarius* within the phylogeny is presently uncertain. The *F. rusticolus* group appears to be the oldest evolutionary lineage among the Falcon species studied. The advantages of DNA sequence data in reconstructing phylogenies and the taxonomic implications of the results are briefly discussed.

INTRODUCTION

Morphologically, the members of the genus Falco are a very homogeneous group of species, which makes it difficult to assess phylogenetic relationships within the genus (Cade 1982). Interest in resolving such relationships is more than 100 years old, as early treatments by Suschkin (1905) and Kleinschmidt (1901) demonstrate. However, most previous attempts had to rely on morphological and plumage characters (Jollie 1977; Boyce & White 1987), which are obvious adaptations

* Author for correspondence

to a certain way of life and are therefore prone to evolve convergently. Cade (1982) presented a hypothetical phylogenetic tree of the genus Falco in which the Australian Brown Falcon *F. berigora* is assumed to be closest to the common ancestor and kestrels are hypothesized to be most primitive among all other living falcons. Seven subgenera assumed to represent monophyletic groups are recognized.

Only recently have techniques become available to study directly the DNA sequences of birds and other organisms and to use these sequences, among other goals, to reconstruct phylogenies. Such data enable us to test some of the hypotheses implicit in Cade's (1982) phylogenetic tree of falcons:

1) is the grouping into subgenera correct in the sense that they do represent monophyletic groups?
2) what is the relationship among these subgenera and
3) which of them is closest to the common ancestor of all falcons?

We have determined and compared partial sequences of the mitochondrial cytochrome b gene to study the relationships of a total of 17 falcon taxa, mostly from the Palaearctic. These include four sub- or semispecies of the Peregrine Falcon complex and five species of the subgenus Hierofalco, often regarded as a superspecies (Kleinschmidt 1923-1937; Baumgart 1975).

RATIONALE OF DNA STUDIES

There are a number of features that make DNA sequences superior to any other kind of data in assessing phylogenetic relationships (cf. Hillis & Moritz 1990):

- The variability at the DNA level is much higher than at the protein level, because the genetic code is redundant, i. e. several amino acids are coded for by up to six different codons.

- Therefore, most base substitutions that occur in protein-coding regions are so-called "silent" substitutions, i.e. they do not lead to an amino acid change in the protein. Per definition, silent substitutions cannot lead to convergent evolution, i. e. similarities observed at silent positions are due either to common descent or to chance (homoplasy).

Most recent DNA studies on bird phylogeny have utilized the mitochondrial genome (rather than chromosomal genes), mainly for two reasons: mtDNA is about ten times more variable than nuclear genes in higher vertebrates; it is inherited clonally and not subject to recombination, i.e. all individuals will be homozygous with respect to the locus studied. Among mitochondrial genes the cytochrome b sequence is well characterized and is now becoming a standard reference for phylogenetic and taxonomic studies in birds (Kocher *et al.* 1989; Edwards *et al.* 1991; Richman & Price 1992). Its advantages include a moderately high rate of base substitution, availability of near-universal primer sequences for PCR (polymerase chain reaction) amplification and a relatively large published data set for comparison (ref. see above). A disadvantage of mitochondrial DNA is that it does not directly identify hybrids, because it is inherited purely maternally.

LABORATORY METHODS AND DATA ANALYSIS

Small quantities of blood (100-200 µl) were collected in EDTA-NaF preservation buffer (Arctander 1988) from captive and wild falcons in various countries (Table 1). The sampling procedure is very easy and does not harm the birds. Total DNA was isolated according to standard procedures and the cytochrome b gene was amplified using the polymerase chain reaction with primers modified from Kocher *et al.* (1989). The primary product was run and extracted from a 1 % agarose gel and reamplified asymmetrically with a primer ratio of 1:100. A portion of 300 nucleotides, i. e. about one third of the entire cytochrome b gene, was then sequenced directly with a third primer according to Sanger *et al.* (1977).

Sequences were aligned and rates of synonymous base substitutions estimated using the weighted pathway method (Li *et al.* 1985). Phylogenetic trees were constructed using the neighbour-joining procedure (Saitou & Nei 1987) of the program package PHYLIP (Felsenstein 1991) and the maximum parsimony method of PAUP 3.0 (Swofford 1991). To assess the Species

Table 1: List of species sequenced with origin and number of individuals analysed per species. F. = Falco.

Species	Origin	number
Otus choliba	Argentina	1
Buteo buteo, Common Buzzard	Germany	3
Accipiter nisus, Sparrowhawk	Germany, Israel	3
F. jugger, Lagger Falcon	India	1
F. rusticolus, Gyrfalcon	Greenland, Baltic Sea	3
F. biarmicus, Lanner	Italy, N-Africa	2
F. femoralis, Aplomado Falcon	Bolivia	1
F. columbarius, Merlin	Scandinavia	3
F. naumanni, Lesser Kestrel	Spain	3
F. tinnunculus, Eurasian Kestrel	Netherlands, Israel	4
F. punctatus, Mauritius Kestrel	Mauritius	4
F. eleonorae, Eleonora's Falcon	Greece	2
F. concolor, Sooty Falcon	Saudi Arabia	2
F. subbuteo, Eurasian Hobby	Germany	3
F. mexicanus, Prairie Falcon	USA	1
F. cherrug, Saker	Pakistan, SE-Europe, Kazakhstan	8
F. p. peregrinus, Peregrine	Scotland	1
F. p. calidus, Peregrine	Saudi Arabia	1
F. p. pelegrinoides, Barbary Falcon	Saudi Arabia	3
F. p. babylonicus, Red-naped Shahin	Pakistan, Iran	3

robustness of the various groupings within the phylogenetic tree we performed 260 parsimony bootstrap replicates with PAUP 3.0 (heuristic search, random sequence addition).

RESULTS

Excluding the primer regions, the analysis is based on a total of 300 nucleotide positions (Seibold *et al.* 1993). Of these, 119 were variable within the total set of species, 76 positions varied within the falcons. Between one and eight individuals were sequenced per species. Intraspecific sequence variation was negligible with a maximum of two nucleotide differences, but usually none (exception: Saker Falcon, see below). We used the domestic chicken (*Gallus gallus*; Desjardins & Morais 1990) and the Tropical Screech Owl (*Otus choliba*; Heidrich, Wink, König in prep.) as outgroups to root the partial phylogenetic tree of Falconiformes. Within the raptor part of the tree a Buzzard (*Buteo buteo*) and a Sparrowhawk (*Accipiter nisus*) were included as outgroups with respect to the falcons (Fig. 1). Branch lengths in the tree are proportional to genetic distances between taxa, but not neccessarily to evolutionary divergence times (due to variation of substitition rates among lineages). Numbers given for some branches show the percent frequency with which the respective groupings were found by the parsimony bootstrap test. These values indicate the level of confidence with which each clade is supported by the data.

Fig. 1: **Phylogenetic tree of falcons (genus Falco) plus two other raptors (*Buteo buteo*, *Accipiter nisus*), chicken (*Gallus domesticus*) and an owl (*Otus choliba*) as outgroups. "*F. peregrinus*" includes the subspecies peregrinus, calidus, *pelegrinoides* and *babylonicus*. The tree is based on 300 nucleotide positions of the cytochrome b gene and was constructed using the heuristic search option (informative characters only) with "closest" sequence addition (PAUP 3.0). The neighbor-joining procedure (Saitou & Nei 1987) with non-synonymous substitution rates (Li et al. 1985) produced a tree with identical topology except that the positions of *A. femoralis* and *F. columbarius* were interchanged. Numbers are parsimony bootstrap values derived from 260 replicates (only values > 50 % are shown).**

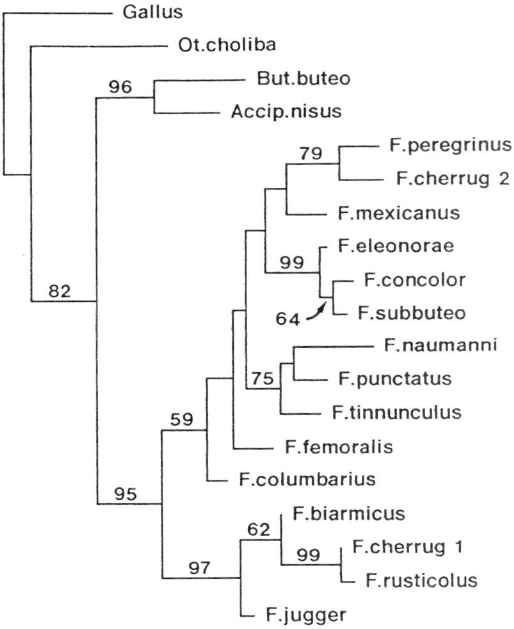

The results can be interpreted as follows: The 17 falcon taxa investigated represent a monophyletic group and are more closely related to other birds of prey (*Buteo, Accipiter*) than to owls or galliforms. Within the Genus Falco the typical kestrels (*F. tinnunculus, F. naumanni, F. punctatus*) on the one hand and all three members of the subgenus *Hypotriorchis* investigated (*F. subbuteo, F. eleonorae, F. concolor*) on the other hand are each other's closest relatives. Both these findings are in agreement with previous hypotheses, but the genetic distance between Common and Lesser Kestrels was relatively large for a species pair which is morphologically so similar. Interestingly, the Mauritius Kestrel was more similar to Lesser than to Common Kestrel, even though the latter breeds in Africa, much closer to Mauritius, than does the highly migratory, Palearctic Lesser Kestrel. The various taxa of the Peregrine complex not surprisingly fall into one clade, and among each other they are so similar that with the data available so far we are unable to resolve any species limits between them. If they are distinct species, they must be much more closely related among each other than any other species pair in this phylogeny.

The most surprising results of our study concern the subgenus Hierofalco, which according to Cade (1982) includes *F. cherrug, F. mexicanus, F. biarmicus, F. rusticolus* and *F. jugger*. Gyrfalcon, Lanner and Lagger Falcon are closely related, but Prairie Falcon clusters with the Peregrine Falcon. Two very different mtDNA haplotypes were identified in the Saker: Type I was almost identical to the Gyrfalcon, Type II differed by 12 % of the nucleotide positions from Type I and clearly resembled the Peregrine. Birds carrying one or the other type originated from the same regions (SE-Europe, Kazakhstan, Pakistan) and there was no relationship with plumage pattern (e. g. barred versus unbarred upperparts). The bootstrap values indicate a probability of less than 3 % for the possibility that the branch leading to Gyrfalcon, Lanner, Lagger and Type I Saker is an error

(Fig. 1)

Furthermore, the Gyrfalcon group seem to be the first lineage to have diverged from the ancestral Falcon stock, all other species studied were derived later. The positions of Merlin and Aplomado Falcon within the tree is rather uncertain, as indicated by the short branch-lengths; we cannot state with any degree of confidence which other species they are most closely related to, but they do seem to be similar to each other.

DISCUSSION

Our phylogenetic tree based on partial cytochrome b sequences agrees with previously suggested phylogenies in that typical kestrels, three members of the subgenus Hypotriorchis and the rusticolus-jugger-biarmicus group are each monophyletic. In the case of Hobby, Eleonora's and Sooty Falcon the obvious similarities in body proportions, colouration, hunting and migratory behaviour may actually be due to common descent and reflect the species' close evolutionary relationships (Walter 1979). It was unexpected that Hobby and Sooty Falcon clustered more closely than did Sooty and Eleonora's Falcon (although this grouping is not strongly supported, see Fig. 1). Based on distribution, morphometrics and biology, the latter two appear to be sister species (Walter 1979).

Sequence data of the large falcons of the subgenus Hierofalco provided some unexpected insights: the subgenus appears to be polyphyletic according to our data, because the Prairie Falcon is more closely related to the Peregrine than to Gyrfalcon or Lanner. The subgenus Hierofalco was defined by Kleinschmidt (1901) as a group of ecologically and morphologically similar species replacing each other in various parts of the world. They share similarities in plumage structure and pattern and body proportions (broad-based wings, long tail), which may obviously have evolved convergently as adaptations to similar hunting strategies in open terrain, where all these species live. In agreement with our findings, a chromosome study showed the Prairie Falcon to be more similar to Peregrine than to Gyrfalcon (Schmutz & Oliphant 1987). Courtship displays and vocalizations of Prairie Falcon include similarities to both Peregrine and Gyrfalcon (Wrege & Cade 1977).

Electrophoretic patterns of feather proteins (Olsen et al. 1989) and one type of mt-DNA sequence found in this study support the idea that the Saker Falcon also belongs to the subgenus Hierofalco. The fact that two very different mtDNA haplotypes occurred in Sakers, one similar to Gyrfalcon, the other to Peregrine Falcon, can be explained by past hybridization between male Sakers and female Peregrines and subsequent back-crosses with Sakers. Although very few such cases have been observed in the wild and Saker x Peregrine hybrids are sterile today (Heidenreich & Pfeffer, pers. comm.), this may not have been the case in the more distant past. The amount of sequence divergence between Peregrine and Saker Type II indicates that the hypothesized hybridization took place several million years ago. Since mitochondrial DNA is inherited clonally, the Peregrine-like haplotype may have persisted in the Saker population until today. The same scenario could potentially also account for the fairly close relationship of mtDNA sequences of Peregrine and Prairie Falcon (only 1 individual of the latter was studied), two species between which hybridization has been recorded in the wild (Oliphant 1991). If this was true, the subgenus Hierofalco may be monophyletic after all, but the hybridization must be phylogenetically very old, because the Prairie Falcon sequence differs from the Peregrine even more than the Saker Type II.

The DNA data confirm the very close relationship of the four *F. peregrinus/pelegrinoides* taxa studied. Barbary Falcon (*F. pelegrinoide*s, incl. Red-naped Shahin, *F. p. babylonicus*) and Peregrine are very similar genetically and may be conspecific (see Weick 1989). More extensive sequence data will be needed to clarify whether any consistent differences between the two forms do exist. Perhaps they have become separated very recently or are on the way to speciation. Detailed field observations are required in the small areas where their breeding ranges overlap (in Morocco and perhaps northern India) to find out whether they behave as distinct biological species.

Contrary to earlier hypotheses (Suschkin 1905; Brown & Amadon 1968; Cade 1982), Kestrels do not seem to be close living relatives of the ancestral falcon. In the mitochondrial DNA tree this position is occupied by the Gyrfalcon group. Obviously, however, our tree is incomplete and the inclusion of South American, Australian and New Zealand falcons or the African Kestrels may

may show some other species to be more primitive.

We conclude that cytochrome b sequences are sufficiently variable to untangle intrageneric relationships of falcons. Although we so far studied less than half of all living species, the DNA data allowed a more detailed resolution of relationships than a previous protein electrophoretic study (Olsen et al. 1989). The case of two highly divergent genotypes in the Saker, however, illustrates how hybridization may lead to discrepancies between gene genealogy and species phylogeny, a problem one should always be aware of when interpreting molecular phylogenies (Avise 1989). Occasional hybridization between full biological species is fairly widespread among birds (Grant & Grant 1992) and even if hybrids are sterile today, they may have been fertile in the past.

ACKNOWLEDGEMENTS

We wish to thank H. Brüning, M. Heidenreich, C. Jones, C. König, M. Pomarol, H. W. Prehn and A. Schreiber for contributing blood or DNA samples and M. Kaufmann for help in the laboratory. Special thanks are due to W. F. Martin for help with constructing the phylogenetic tree. F. Prüser and K. Mummenhoff made computer programmes available to us. W. S. Clark and C. W. White contributed valuable comments on an earlier version of the paper.

REFERENCES

ARCTANDER, P. 1988: Comparative studies of avian DNA by restriction fragment length polymorphism analysis: convenient procedures based on blood samples from live birds. *J. Ornithol.* 129: 205-216.

AVISE, J. C. 1989: Gene trees and organismal histories: a phylogenetic approach to population biology. *Evolution* 43: 1192-1208.

BAUMGART, W. 1975: Die Bedeutung funktioneller Kriterien für die Beurteilung der taxonomischen Stellung paläarktischer Großfalken. Zoolog. *Abhandl. Staatl. Museum Tierkunde Dresden* 33: 303-316.

BOYCE, D. A. & C. W. WHITE 1987: Evolutionary aspects of kestrel systematics: a scenario. In: D. M. Bird & R. Bowman (Eds.); The Ancestral Kestrel, *Raptor Research Reports* 6: 1-21. McGill Univ., Quebec.

BROWN, L. & D. AMADON 1968: *Eagles, Hawks and Falcons of the World.* Country Life Books, London.

CADE, T. J. 1982: *The Falcons of the World.* Cornell Univ. Press, Ithaca.

DESJARDINS, P. & R. MORAIS 1990: Sequence and gene organization of the chicken mitochondrial genome. *J. Mol. Biol.* 212: 599-634.

EDWARDS, S. V., P. ARCTANDER & A. C. WILSON 1991: Mitochondrial resolution of a deep branch in the genealogical tree for perching birds. *Proc. Royal Soc. London B 243:* 99-107.

FELSENSTEIN, J. 1991: PHYLIP (Phylogeny Inference Package) Version 3.4. University of California, Berkeley.

GRANT, P. R. & B. R. GRANT 1992: Hybridization of bird species. *Science* 256: 193-197.

HILLIS D. M. & C. MORITZ (EDS.) 1990: *Molecular Systematics.* Sinauer Ass., Inc., Sunderland.

JOLLIE, M. 1976-1977: A contribution to the morphology and phylogeny of the falconiformes. Evol. Theory 1: 285-298; 2: 115-300; 3: 1-142.

KLEINSCHMIDT, O. 1901: Der Formenkreis Falco Hierofalco und die Stellung des ungarischen Würgfalken in demselben. Aquila 8: 1-48.

KLEINSCHMIDT, O. 1923-37: Falco Hierofalco. Berajah, Zoographica infinita, Halle.

KOCHER, T. D., W. K. THOMAS, A. MEYER, S. V. EDWARDS, S. PÄÄBO, F. X. VILLABLANCA & A. C. WILSON 1989: Dynamics of mitochondrial DNA evolution in animals: amplification and sequencing with conserved primers. Proc. Natl. Acad. Sci. USA 86: 6196-6200.

LI, W.-H., C.-I. WU & C.-C. LUO 1985: A new method for estimating synonymous and nonsynonymous rates of nucleotide substitution considering the relative likelihood of nucleotide and codon changes. *Mol. Biol. Evol.* 2: 150-174.

OLIPHANT, L. W. 1991: Hybridization between a Peregrine Falcon and a Prairie Falcon in the wild. *J. Raptor Res.* 25: 36-39.

OLSEN, P. D., R. C. MARSHALL & A. GAAL 1989: Relationships within the genus Falco: a comparison of the electrophoretic patterns of feather proteins. *Emu* 89: 193-203.

RICHMAN, A. D. & T. PRICE 1992: Evolution of ecological differences in the Old World leaf warblers.

Nature 355: 817-821.
SAITOU, N. & M. NEI 1987: The neighbor-joining method: a new method for reconstructing phylogenetic trees. *Mol. Biol. Evol.* 4: 406-425.
SANGER, F., S. NICKLEN & A. R. COULSON 1977: DNA sequencing with chain-terminating inhibitors. *Proc. Natl. Acad. Sci. USA* 74: 5463-5467.
SCHMUTZ, S. M. & L. W. OLIPHANT 1987: Chromosome study of peregrine, prairie, and gyrfalcons with implications for hybrids. *J. Heredity* 78: 388-390.
SEIBOLD, I., A. J. HELBIG & M. WINK 1993: Molecular systematics of falcons (family Falconidae). *Naturwiss.* 80: 87-90.
SUSCHKIN, P. P. 1905: Vergleichende Osteologie der normalen Tagraubvögel (Accipitres) und die Fragen der Klassifikation. II. Die Falken und ihre nächsten Verwandten. *Nouv. Mem. Soc. Nat. Moscou* 16 (4): 1-247.
SWOFFORD, D. L. 1991: PAUP: *Phylogenetic analysis using parsimony. Version 3.0s.* Champaign, Illinois
WALTER, H. 1979: *Eleonora's Falcon - adaptations to prey and habitat in a social raptor.* University of Chicago Press, Chicago, London.
WEICK, F. 1989: Zur Taxonomie des Wanderfalken Falco peregrinus Tunstall 1771. *Ökol. Vögel, Beiheft 1*: 1-42.
WREGE, P. H. & T. J. CADE 1977: Courtship behavior of large falcons in captivity. *Raptor Res.* 11: 1-46.

Prof. Dr. M. Wink
Institut für Pharmazeutische Biologie
Universität Heidelberg
1m Neuenheim et feld
69120 Heidelberg,
Germany

Meyburg, B.-U. & R. D. Chancellor eds.1994
Raptor Conservation Today
WWGBP / The Pica Press

An Exploratory Phylogenetic Analysis of the Genera of the Accipitridae, with Notes on the Biogeography of the Family

R. N. Holdaway

ABSTRACT

An exploratory phylogenetic analysis of osteological characters for most of the genera of the Accipitridae resulted in a single tree. The Osprey *Pandion haliaetus* was as far from the main accipitrid stem as was the designated outgroup, the Secretarybird (*Sagittarius serpentarius*). The 'kites' *Elanus* and *Elanoides* were basal but separated on the tree, and the Old World vultures and serpent and snake eagles formed a clade distinct from all other accipitrids. *Geranospiza* appears to be the sister-group of *Circus* and only convergently similar to *Polyboroides*. Within the main accipitrid clade, the milvine 'kites' and sea eagles formed a major basal clade. The harpy eagles appear to be paraphyletic. *Morphnus* is placed closer to the *Accipiter/Buteo* clade than to the harpies. *Ictinia* and *Harpagus*, two genera that have been allied to other small 'kites', are shown to be part of the *Accipiter/Buteo* radiation, along with several other 'sub-buteonines'. Although there was little agreement between patterns of parasite infection and higher (above Family) level systematics among the diurnal birds of prey, the major branches of the tree were broadly consistent with the distribution of infection with species-groups in the genus *Degeeriella* (Mallophaga). A biogeographic analysis suggests a long-standing dichotomy between the evolutionary histories of Old and New World accipitrids.

INTRODUCTION

The relationships within the family Accipitridae are poorly understood (de Boer & Sinoo 1984; Jollie 1976, 1977a, 1977b, 1977c; Olson 1985). Amadon (in Stresemann & Amadon 1979: 272) declined to recognise formal divisions within the Accipitrinae, although Stresemann had recognised eleven in his original manuscript for the Checklist. Kemp & Crowe (1990) recognised two major clades within the Accipitridae, but found it difficult to resolve the relationships between genera within the major clades. Their work was unusual in being based on a variety of characters, including external morphology, behaviour, and karyology. Apart from early workers such as Milne-Edwards (1867-1871), Fürbringer (1888), and Suschkin (1899, 1900, 1905), and the selective work of Jollie (1976, 1977a, 1977b, 1977c), most classifications are based primarily on external morphology (Brown & Amadon 1968; Stresemann & Amadon 1979; Swann 1924-1945) or on biochemical characters (Sibley & Ahlquist 1972, 1990). There has been little interest in the comparative analysis of skeletal characters in the group.

Families and subfamilies within the Accipitridae have been diagnosed on external characters (e.g., Witherby *et al.* 1939). Osteological diagnoses of subfamilial groups in the Accipitridae often do not allow different groups to be distinguished. Friedmann (1950) gave identical osteological diagnoses for several of his subfamilial groups. Osteological characters continued to be omitted from most recent diagnoses and systematic treatments (Amadon 1953, 1964, 1978, 1982a, 1982b; Brown & Amadon 1968; Friedmann 1950; Stresemann & Amadon 1979), despite their potential (Jollie 1976, 177a, 1977b, 1977c). It is not surprising, therefore, that it is difficult to incorporate fossil accipitrids into these classifications (Olson 1985). Even when the fossil material is copious and well-preserved, the paucity of knowledge of skeletal characters within the Accipitridae has hampered progress in determining relationships (Ballmann 1969, 1973). Haast's Eagle (*Harpagornis moorei*), a huge extinct accipitrid from the late Quaternary of New Zealand, is represented by material comparable to that held for living taxa. The relationships of Haast's Eagle have, however, remained obscure since Haast described it in 1872 (Haast 1872; Oliver 1930, 1945, 1955; Owen 1879; Shufeldt 1896).

The phylogenetic analysis reported here was undertaken as part of research on the roles that phylogeny, ecology, and historical constraints (Seilacher 1979) played in the evolution of structural traits and functional morphology in this eagle. It was part of a wider study whose prime emphasis was the palaeobiology of the eagle. The limitations in the treatment must be seen in this light.

Level of treatment

The history of the taxonomy and systematics of the Falconiformes [=Accipitriformes] has been reviewed at length by Sibley & Ahlquist (1972, 1990) and Jollie (1976, 1977a, 1977b, 1977c), and summarised by Kemp & Crowe (1990). The reviews include extensive literature citations and comparisons of previous classifications, and only a brief summary of recent views pertinent to the scope of the present study is presented here.

Problems remain with identifying the higher taxonomic levels within the diurnal birds of prey. The main problem until recently has been of what groups to include within the traditional order Falconiformes. As generally conceived (e.g., Brown & Amadon 1968; Stresemann & Amadon 1979), the Order Falconiformes includes diverse groups whose major features in common are a hooked beak and a generally carnivorous diet. Stresemann & Amadon (1979) accepted four suborders: Cathartae (Vulturidae [Cathartidae *auct.*]; the 'New World' vultures); Accipitres (Accipitridae; hawks, eagles, kites, and Old World vultures); Sagittarii (Sagittariidae; *Sagittarius serpentarius*); and Falcones (Falconidae: falcons and caracaras). They listed two subfamilies in the Accipitridae: the Pandioninae (containing only the osprey (*Pandion haliaetus*); and the Accipitrinae (Stresemann & Amadon 1979).

The profound differences between the major groups have been appreciated for many years (Beddard 1898; Hudson 1948; Friedmann 1950). Jollie (1953) countered Clay's (1951) suggestion that the order was monophyletic - based on the distribution of several genera of bird lice (Mallophaga) on hosts in the different bird families - with strong evidence for polyphyly.

Recent work supports Jollie's contention. Of the four suborders recognised by Stresemann & Amadon, there is now compelling osteological (Emslie 1988; Jollie 1976, 1977a, 1977b, 1977c; Ligon 1967; pers. obs.), karyological (de Boer 1976), behavioural (König 1982), and biochemical (Sibley & Ahlquist 1990) evidence that the Vulturidae are related to the storks (Ciconiidae) and do not belong with the accipitrids. The evidence was acknowledged by Friedmann (1950), Brown & Amadon (1968), and Amadon (in Stresemann & Amadon 1979), but was not followed in the classifications of any of these workers.

Sagittarius differs from the Accipitridae in several ways, including its gross karyotype (de Boer 1975) and thigh muscle formula (BXY as against A, Beddard (1898)). It has been accorded various ranks, up to subordinal level (Brown & Amadon 1968), and even excluded from the Falconiformes altogether (Jollie 1977c).

The falconid karyotype differs greatly from that of the Accipitridae (de Boer 1976), and Jollie (1976, 1977a, 1977b, 1977c) concluded on osteological, pterylogical, and other morphological grounds that the Falconidae are not related to the accipitrids.

Despite the differences in detail between the karyotypes of the Falconidae, Sagittariidae, and Accipitridae, Kemp & Crowe (1990) pointed out that the families are the only ones lacking large macrochromosomes. This is apparently a derived character (de Boer & Sinoo 1984; Ryttman *et al.* 1987). Other characters used by Kemp & Crowe (1990) to support monophyly of the three groups are variable within the groups.

Whatever the higher relationships of the Accipitridae, de Boer (1975, 1976) and de Boer & Sinoo (1984) have stressed the uniqueness of the accipitrid karyotype. The peculiarity of the karyotype strongly suggests that the group is monophyletic and does not include *Pandion* or *Sagittarius*.

The object of the present study was to determine the relationships between as many genera of the Accipitridae as possible, using osteological characters, so that fossil taxa could be incorporated into the phylogeny. The sister group of *Harpagornis moorei* could then be established amongst the apparently homogeneous assemblage of about 60 genera currently recognised in the family.

My use of the genus as the basic OTU assumed that generic level systematics of the Accipitridae were well founded. This is probably not a valid assumption because the limits of several genera are blurred by frequent changes in taxonomy, particularly in *Spizaetus* and African forest eagles (e.g., Amadon 1982a). However, my sample represented most of the major variation amongst c 220 species in the family (Stresemann & Amadon 1979).

Phylogenetic analysis

There have been three recent attempts to produce a non-linear arrangement of species within the Accipitridae. Two of these left open the connections between major branches (Brown & Amadon 1968; Jollie 1977c). Although he examined osteological features in his systematic work on the Accipitridae, Jollie (1976, 1977a, 1977b, 1977c) rejected the use of phylogenetic (cladistic) techniques as inappropriate. In the most recent study, however, Kemp & Crowe (1990) analysed a variety of behavioural, karyological, anatomical, and skin characters, using a computer-aided cladistic approach.

I used phylogenetic analysis because it is based on the assumption that shared derived characteristics are the best indicators of common ancestry (Hennig 1966; Wiley 1981). The use of derived characters reduces the effects of shared primitive features (symplesiomorphies) and of convergent features (homoplasies) (Wiley 1981). The development of several computer programs (e.g., HENNIG, MACCLADE, PAUP, PHYLIP) have simplified the analysis of large character suites for many operational taxonomic units (OTUs).

I rejected the phenetic approach of seeking a measure of overall similarity as inappropriate because there was strong evidence for convergence (e.g., between *Ictinia* and the *Elanus* kites (Shufeldt 1896)) in the Accipitridae. Like Raikow (1985), I believe that the traditional eclectic systematic method, as used by Amadon, Brown, Jollie, and Stresemann cannot generate a classification based on phylogeny (Amadon 1953, 1964, 1977, 1978, 1982a, 1982b, Brown 1982, Brown & Amadon 1968, Jollie 1976, 1977a, 1977b, 1977c, Stresemann & Amadon 1979).

Only those genera generally accepted as belonging in the Accipitridae were included in my analysis. Neither the falcons nor the New World vultures are considered further here, for the reasons outlined above. However, I included *Sagittarius* as an outgroup for analysis of the relationships within Stresemann & Amadon's (1979) Accipitrinae. *Pandion* was also included because of its subfamilial rank within the Accipitridae in Stresemann & Amadon (1979), although other authors have accorded it familial (Brown & Amadon 1968) or even subordinal rank (Hudson 1948). The phylogenetic hypothesis for the Accipitridae represented by the tree reported here is further interpreted by means of a formal, unambiguous (Raikow 1985) classification.

Biogeography of the Accipitridae

The most recent discussion of the biogeography of diurnal raptors is that of Kemp & Crowe (1990). They concluded, in part, that the biogeography of clades "offers little insight to their areas of origin." I report here also the results of an analysis of the global distribution of species of Accipitridae. Species density was analysed cladistically (Brooks 1985), to see if any patterns congruent with phylogenetic patterns could be discerned.

METHODS

Taxa and specimens

A full survey of all species in the Accipitridae was not attempted. Instead, each monotypic genus and up to three species from polytypic genera were studied. Some genera of Accipitridae are not well-defined, for example there is considerable discussion as to the limits of *Aquila, Accipiter,* and *Gyps* (Amadon & Brown 1968; Amadon, in Amadon & Stresemann 1979: Amadon 1978, 1982a), so species unequivocally assigned to those genera were used.

I examined skeletal material of *Pandion haliaetus*, *Sagittarius serpentarius*, and 66 species representing 51 of the approximately 60 genera and 215-220 species presently included in the Accipitridae (Appendix 1). Eight genera were represented by two species, and one genus by three species.

Several taxa were represented in collections only by part skeletons, or a few bones removed from study skins. Material of others (*Dryotriorchis, Megatriorchis, Harpyopsis, Eutriorchis, Oroaetus, Hamirostra, Lophoictinia, Henicopernis*) was either not available in the collections visited, or was not held in collections at the time (e.g., Blandamer & Burton 1979). *Sarcogyps* and *Torgos* are sometimes recognised as monotypic genera, but were included in *Aegypius* by Amadon (1977) and Stresemann & Amadon (1979). Only *Aegypius* was examined in this study.

South-east Asian species of *Spizaetus* were poorly represented in collections, so that genus, as presently understood (Stresemann & Amadon 1979), was represented by the American *Spizaetus ornatus*. The absence of south-east Asian taxa is unfortunate, because they are geographically one of the closest groups of forest eagles to *Harpagornis moorei*, and have been suggested as possibly being similar to it morphologically (Brathwaite & Holdaway 1987).

Analysis of characters

I used only qualitative, multi-state osteological characters so that *Harpagornis moorei* could be scored for all characters used in the analysis. Most characters were defined after examination of series of homologous elements from as full a range of taxa as possible. Other characters had already been defined or illustrated, primarily by Jollie (1976, 1977a, 1977b, 1977c) and Olson (1982, 1987).

Of 273 characters assessed, 188 were used in the analysis of 45 taxa, including the outgroup (mean 4.2 features per OTU). The other characters either could not be assessed for sufficient taxa, or their different states could not be surveyed adequately. The unused characters are here included as a basis for future work (Appendix 2).

All skeletal characters were discrete features having at least two definable states. Character states were tabulated for each OTU. Characters were assumed to be homologous if they involved similar structures in corresponding positions on the same elements. Most could be described using standard terminology (Ballmann 1969; Baumel 1979; Howard 1929), and are therefore subject to the least possible error in assumed homology as present knowledge of avian osteology permits. Most difficulty was experienced in reconciling some characters, especially of the pelvis, femora, and tibiotarsi of *Sagittarius* and *Pandion* with those in similar anatomical positions in accipitrids.

Whenever possible, characters were checked for intraspecific and interspecific variation; where this was found, the feature was reassessed or omitted if the variation was considered to be too great.

Characters were weighted equally because there was no reliable information on the conservativeness of any particular feature. Characters were coded as missing if no material was available, or if an element was damaged and the state was difficult to determine.

Characters are listed and described in Appendix 2. The OTU-character state matrix is available from the author.

Trees

I used the program PAUP (Swofford 1985) to generate phylogenetic trees for 42 living genera, *Harpagornis*, *Pandion* and *Sagittarius*. PAUP uses parsimony to produce one or more shortest trees; those in which fewest changes of character state are required. The MULPARS (multiple parsimony) option was invoked, in which all equal length trees are kept until a shorter tree is found. This procedure avoids the possibility that one tree may be accepted from several trees of different topology and the same length. It also helps to reduce the possibility that searching may be limited when rearrangement of a single tree does not result in a shorter tree. If several trees are kept in the computer's memory, it is possible that another equal-length tree will be found from which a shorter tree can be derived (Swofford 1985).

To maximise the chance of finding the shortest tree, the GLOBAL branch swapping option was used. Global swapping involves removing every possible subtree and inserting it at all other positions in search of a shorter tree.

The Accipitridae is apparently so isolated phylogenetically that it is difficult to determine the higher taxon with which it shares its most recent common ancestor (Olson 1985). In alternative recent classifications, *Sagittarius* is considered to be a subclade of either the major clade Order Falconiformes (Stresemann & Amadon 1979) or the Parvorder Accipitrida (Sibley & Ahlquist 1988). I did not use the Falconidae as an outgroup because it was more difficult to assess the homology of characters between the Accipitridae and Falconidae than between the accipitrids and *Sagittarius*. The outgroup was chosen from within the small group of postulated closest relatives, because it was not an object of this study to investigate the relationships of the accipitrids with other families.

Polarities of character state changes were not assumed, and I did not attempt to derive transformation series for the character states. With the data unordered option in effect, PAUP algorithms develop transformation series for the features, and do not assume that transformation series were known. Primitive and derived states were generated by PAUP by outgroup comparison, using *Sagittarius* as the outgroup. Examination of the characters used suggests that it should be possible to derive transformation series for them on outgroup and ontological criteria when a full analysis of the Accipitridae is undertaken.

Pandion was tried as the outgroup, and the trees produced were similar, but not identical, in topology to those produced using *Sagittarius*. *Sagittarius* was the preferred outgroup because its separation from the Accipitridae is supported by a range of evidence (de Boer & Sinoo 1984; Jollie 1976, 1977a, 1977b, 1977c). On the other hand, there is some support for the hypothesis that *Pandion* and the accipitrids share a most recent common ancestor (Sibley & Ahlquist 1972; Tyler 1966).

No ontogenetic information was available for most characters used and as a consequence developmental data could not be used to determine character state polarities. I did not use the criterion of wide representation of a character indicating plesiomorphy (primitiveness), because of the apparent homogeneity of morphology and the high level of plesiomorphy within the family suggested by karyological data (de Boer & Sinoo 1984).

All taxa compared were taken as belonging to a single, natural clade because all species in the family that have been studied so far share the derived condition, apparently unique within Aves, of having only 6-12 microchromosomes (de Boer & Sinoo 1984).

Comparisons with other data

Trees were assessed by making comparisons with published classifications, and with morphological and other data available in the literature. Trees were also compared with information on host-parasite relationships of bird lice (Mallophaga) and results of a biogeographic analysis (see below). It was not possible to use data from fossils (Olson 1985), but the presence of Vulturidae in Europe during the Tertiary (Cracraft & Rich 1972), and of accipitrid vultures in North America until the late Pleistocene (Rich 1980), was taken into account.

Biogeography of the Accipitridae

Patterns of distribution of living accipitrids were analysed by using genera as characters, and numbers of species in each genus as character states. This is a modification of the method discussed by Brooks (1985). OTUs were geographic regions that usually coincided with boundaries and sub-boundaries of biogeographic regions. Numbers of species in each genus in each of 18 areas were compiled from distributional data and maps provided by Brown & Amadon (1968) and Stresemann & Amadon (1979). Numbers of species were arrayed against area (Appendix 3) and trees produced using PAUP (Swofford 1985), with MULPARS and GLOBAL branch swapping options selected, and character states unordered. The tree topologies were then compared with those obtained from the phylogenetic study.

RESULTS AND DISCUSSION

General

Two shortest trees were found with almost identical topologies (consistency index 0.217). They differed only in the position of *Gypaetus* in the accipitrid vulture clade (see below). The main branches of the second tree are shown in Fig. 1, and details of its branches are shown in Figs 2-13.

The results confirmed the monophyly of several groups that have been recognised at various taxonomic levels in different classifications.

Basal branches

Sagittarius was separated from the other taxa by changes in 59 of 188 characters, including 11 unambiguous autapomorphies. My results supported karyological evidence that *Sagittarius* is not close to the Accipitridae (de Boer 1976).

Pandion branched off first in the main sequence, and was almost as far from the accipitrids as was the outgroup (*Sagittarius*). Forty-six characters, including 13 autapomorphies, supported its distinction. Ten characters were unique to *Pandion* (Fig. 2). The separation of *Pandion* from the Accipitridae agreed with conclusions based on pterylosis (Compton 1938), karyology (Ryttman *et al.* 1987), and osteology (Jollie 1976, 1977a, 1977b, 1977c), but some degree of relationship is indicated by eggshell structure (Tyler 1966).

My results confirmed the polyphyly of the 'kites' *sensu* Brown & Amadon (1968). *Elanus* and *Elanoides* were separate clades (Fig. 1, 2). *Elanoides* was defined by 23 characters, but no autapomorphies. *Elanus*, however, had five autapomorphies among 31 characters. Osteological characters confirmed the separation of these genera; Friedmann (1950) and Brown & Amadon (1968) also separated them on claw morphology.

I had insufficient data to test whether *Gampsonyx* and *Chelictinia* are sister groups of *Elanus* as is implied by Friedmann's (1950) grouping of the three genera in the subfamily Elaninae. *Gampsonyx* was long included in the Falconidae, as it superficially resembles small falcons. Osteologically, however, it is clearly an accipitrid (Brodkorb 1960).

Accipitrid vultures and the serpent eagles

Monophyly of the accipitrid vultures and the so-called 'serpent eagles' was supported by 17 characters, including two autapomorphies, within the Accipitridae as accepted here (one was shared with *Pandion*, Fig. 2).

The clade included two major branches, with 14 characters defining the vultures, and nine the serpent eagles (Fig. 3, 4, 5). The vultures (Fig. 4, 5) included three genera (*Gypaetus, Neophron*, and *Gypohierax*), whose proximity to the typical vultures has been questioned (Brown & Amadon 1968; Jollie 1977c), and one (*Pernis*) which has usually been included with the elanoidid kites (Jollie 1977c). The serpent eagle branch included *Polyboroides* (African Harrier-Hawk) and *Terathopius* (Bateleur Eagle), in addition to *Spilornis* (Asiatic Serpent Eagles) and *Circaetus* (Snake Eagles of Eurasia and Africa).

Inclusion of *Polyboroides* with the serpent eagles was based on 29 characters (Fig. 3). Three of 17 convergences were with *Geranospiza* (South American Crane Hawk), whose relationship to *Polyboroides* has been debated for many years (Burton 1978; Brown & Amadon 1968; Friedmann 1950; Jollie 1977c).

Friedmann (1950) thought that they were closely related, whereas Brown & Amadon (1968: 21) stated that *Polyboroides* is "definitely related to the snake-eagles and might be regarded as only a specialised member of that group". They based this view partly on the similarity of the plumage of the young to that of *Spilornis*. Burton (1978) concluded that the shared derived characters of the intertarsal joint seemed to support a relationship but could not exclude the possibility of convergence of these characters. He noted, however, that if the intertarsal joint criterion was omitted, then there was little evidence for a close relationship between the two taxa. Jollie (1977c) placed *Polyboroides* with the accipitrid vultures and serpent eagles, and *Geranospiza* grouped them with South American '*sub*-Buteos'. Beddard (1889) noted that *Polyboroides* was similar in its myology to *Gypohierax*.

My data confirmed a relationship between *Polyboroides* and the serpent eagles, but as a plesiomorphic taxon within the group rather than a highly specialised (derived) one as suggested by Brown & Amadon (1968). Nevertheless, it did exhibit four autapomorphies.

Terathopius did not possess any autapomorphies, but was defined by a suite of 24 characters, including 17 convergences, 6 reversals, and one complex character. The inclusion of *Terathopius* with the serpent eagles supports Brown & Amadon's (1968) interpretation. Jollie (1977c) concluded that it was intermediate between the serpent eagles and the accipitrid vultures.

The clade of serpent eagles was defined by 17 characters (Fig. 3). *Spilornis* lacked an autapomorphy among a suite of 30 distinguishing characters. *Circaetus*, however, had one autapomorphic character among the 25 that separated it from *Spilornis*. Brown & Amadon (1968) and Jollie (1977c) considered the two genera were closely related.

de Boer & Sinoo (1984) found that *Circaetus gallicus* had a karyotype identical to that of the accipitrid vultures, and only slightly different from that of *Pernis*. The karyological data provide some support for the branching pattern found here.

In the vulturine branch, the separation of *Gypohierax* (Palmnut Vulture) was supported by 28 characters, but no autapomorphies (Fig. 4). *Gypohierax* was included with the vultures by Brown & Amadon (1968), who suggested that it linked them to the sea eagles (*Haliaeetus*). Brown & Amadon (1968) also suggested that it most resembled *Neophron* (Egyptian Vulture) amongst the other vultures, a view also held by Jollie (1977c) and Suschkin (1899), but not confirmed here.

The monophyly of a group consisting of *Pernis* (honey buzzards) and *Neophron* was supported by 13 characters, but none of these was an unambiguous autapomorphy (Fig. 4). As noted above, *Pernis* has usually been placed near *Elanoides* (Brown & Amadon 1968; Jollie 1977c) and not with the accipitrid vultures. However, Brown & Amadon (1968) implied that there was at least a distant relationship by suggesting that the vultures had evolved from kites, and Jollie (1977c) noted that *Neophron* is " 'kite-like' in many respects", although it superficially resembles *Necrosyrtes*. *Pernis* was characterised by four autapomorphies, and *Neophron* by three and another character shared with *Pandion* (Fig. 4).

The position of the Bearded Vulture, *Gypaetus*, in the branching sequence of the accipitrid vultures was the only difference between the two shortest trees. In the first tree, *Gypaetus* was the sister group of a clade containing *Necrosyrtes* (African Hooded Vulture), *Gyps* (Griffon Vultures), and *Aegypius* (Black and Lappet-faced Vultures of Africa and Eurasia) (Fig. 5). In the second tree (Fig. 4), *Gypaetus* was the sister group of all the vultures except *Gypohierax*.

de Boer (1976) concluded that the differences between the karyotypes of *Gypaetus* and the other vultures did not support a close relationship between the former and the vultures, and more recently de Boer & Sinoo (1984) also rejected the relationship. Instead, they proposed that *Gypaetus* was near *Circus* (harriers), *Pernis*, and the so-called booted eagles (including *Aquila* and *Spizaetus* (de Boer & Sinoo 1984)). However, they also noted that the condition in *Gypaetus*, *Pernis*, and the booted eagles could have evolved independently from an 'original' condition, namely that found in *Circaetus*. Such thinking is more in line with my second tree than my first.

Clay (1951) proposed that the Accipitridae and the Vulturidae constitute a monophyletic group because they share the same taxa of bird lice (Mallophaga). However, in 1951 it was not clear that accipitrid ('Old World') and vulturid ('New World') vultures had been sympatric in Europe and North America for millions of years, and until as recently as the late Pleistocene in North America (Cracraft & Rich 1972; Howard 1932; Olson 1985; Rich 1980). There was ample time for lice to have colonised new hosts, particularly when both host groups probably fed at the same carcases, and their presence on both cannot be considered indicative of a close relationship between the hosts.

Monophyly of the remaining three genera (*Necrosyrtes, Gyps*, and *Aegypius* was supported by 26 characters (19 convergences, 6 reversals, 1 synapomorphy) (Fig. 5). *Gyps* and *Aegypius* were linked by 21 characters; *Gyps* was characterised by three autapomorphies. Jollie (1977c) recognised a similar grouping of these three genera, as did Brown & Amadon (1968).

Circus* and *Geranospiza

Circus was found to be the sister group of *Geranospiza* (Fig. 6), and not a sub-buteonine (Amadon 1982b). Nor was it close to *Accipiter* as suggested by Jollie (1977c), despite the apparent close resemblance of its postcranial anatomy (Olson & James 1991). The monophyly of the clade consisting of *Geranospiza* and *Circus* was supported by two synapomorphies. As noted above, *Geranospiza* was not close to *Polyboroides*. The karyotype of *Geranospiza* (Williams & Benirschke 1976) differs from the unique *Circus* karyotype (de Boer & Sinoo 1984). This feature supports the likelihood of an early separation of the two genera.

Sibley & Ahlquist (1972) found that the egg white proteins of *Circus* were similar to those of *Elanus*. The similarity is probably plesiomorphic, because the egg white proteins of these genera were similar to those of *Pandion*.

Machaerhamphus

Brown & Amadon (1968) regarded the bat kite *Machaerhamphus* as an aberrant elanoidid kite. However, Jollie concluded that the skeletal evidence was equivocal and suggested that it is "an extreme type without close relatives ... [that had] ... a long and independent history" (Jollie 1977c: 121(321)).

My phylogenetic reconstruction indicated that it represented a separate clade, whose monophyly was supported by two autapomorphies, one of which was, however, shared with the outgroups (Fig. 1). It was linked to other 'kites' only by symplesiomorphies.

Milvine kites and sea eagles

The data support a sister group relationship between the milvine 'kites' (*Milvus* and *Haliastur*) and the sea and fishing eagles (*Haliaeetus* and *Ichthyophaga*) (Fig. 7). However, *Buteogallus* (the South American black hawks) was an unexpected member of the clade. Jollie (1977c) placed it with *Heterospizias* and *Busarellus* in the same clade as the Harpies, whereas Brown & Amadon (1968) included it with *Heterospizias* and *Leucopternis*. Jollie (1977c: 117-118) grouped *Buteogallus* with *Heterospizias* and summed up the problems of relationships among the Accipitridae when he pointed out that "the Central and South American species of the buteogallin supergenus appear to retain more of the primitive features, a statement that is more of a hope than a defensible hypothesis".

Monophyly of the whole clade was supported by one synapomorphy, the shape of the notch for the *peronaeus* nerve in the proximal tarsometatarsus, among 10 defining characters.

Monophyly of the milvines and haliaeetines is supported by 13 characters, including the fusion of the first two phalanges of the second pedal digit. Olson (1982) surveyed the distribution of this derived character in the Accipitridae and reported it in *Ictinia*, *Busarellus*, *Haliastur*, *Milvus*, *Haliaeetus*, and *Ichthyophaga*. These genera occurred in three distinct groups on the trees found here (Fig. 1), and the character did not define a small, monophyletic group as proposed by Olson (1982).

It is unclear what functional advantage, if any, is associated with the phalangeal fusion, but at least some members of all three groups take fish, although Olson (1982) rejected any connection with diet or habits. However, he regarded *Ictinia* as a kite, whereas my results indicated that it is related to *Buteo* and *Accipiter* as suggested by Shufeldt (1891) (see below). The absence of fused phalanges in *Pandion*, an obligate fish predator, weakens the argument for their evolution principally for fishing.

As Olson (1982) pointed out, the sequence *Milvus-Haliastur-Haliaeetus-Ichthyophaga* parallels an increasing association with aquatic environments and reliance on a diet of fish. *Buteogallus* is mainly a crab-eater that lives in swampy habitats, and this accords to some extent with its basal position in the clade. The specialised fishing behaviours exhibited by *Busarellus* are, according to my results, convergent on those of the milvine-haliaeetine clade.

Geranoaetus and *Heterospizias*

The isolation of *Geranoaetus* (Grey Eagle-buzzard) as a separate clade is supported by 23 characters, including one autapomorphy (Fig. 8). Despite the 'identity' of its karyotype with that of *Buteo* (de Boer & Sinoo 1984), *Geranoaetus* appears to be an early offshoot from the buteonine-accipitrine lineage rather than a sub-buteonine as concluded by Amadon (1982b). Its resemblance to the buteonines is probably symplesiomorphic.

Heterospizias (Savannah Hawk) is another isolated South American form (Fig. 9) symplesiomorphically similar to the buteonine groups with which it has been linked (Brown & Amadon 1968; Jollie 1977c). It is not close to *Buteogallus*, with which it was synonymised by Amadon (1982b). Following an examination of osteological characters, Plótnick (1956) concluded that *Heterospizias* was similar to *Buteo* and relatively distant from *Accipiter*, a conclusion which is supported by my results if the resemblance to *Buteo* is considered to be plesiomorphic.

Aquila, *Spizaetus*, and *Harpagornis*

Aquila (Golden Eagle group) and *Spizaetus* (South American Hawk Eagles) were independently derived, but adjacent on both trees. Monophyly of the aquiline genera, *Aquila* and *Harpagornis*, was supported by one synapomorphy (Fig. 9). The placement of *Harpagornis* as the sister group of *Aquila* was the major finding of this study, with respect to the primary objective of my thesis research. The proximity of the aquilines to the spizaetines makes an examination of the African and south-east Asian taxa presently placed in *Spizaetus* all the more urgent. Brown & Amadon (1968) suggested that the Asian forms may be a separate group, and Jollie (1977c) showed the genus had two parts, which he thought resembled each other "as much through convergence, as through common ancestry" (Jollie 1977c: 117(317).

Harpagornis itself was separated from *Aquila* by two autapomorphies within the Accipitridae as accepted here, although both character states were shared with *Pandion*. One character of the femur was convergent with *Ictinia*, another (of the tibiotarsus) was shared with *Elanus*, and a tibiotarsal character was shared with the *Gyps-Aegypius* clade.

Oliver (1930) concluded that *Harpagornis* was most closely related to *Aquila*, but later (Oliver 1945, 1955) changed his mind and suggested that it was related to *Haliaeetus*: "By the form of the skull, however, it should be placed nearer to *Haliæëtus*. In fact, it is further from *Aquila* than is *Haliæëtus*" (Oliver 1945: 137).

Shufeldt (1896) noted similarities to both *Haliaeetus* and *Aquila*, and placed *Harpagornis* "between" them. My results indicate that resemblances to *Haliaeetus* are symplesiomorphic, and that the bird is an aquiline. However, the closeness of the branch point of the clade to that of the South American *Spizaetus*, and the absence of data on Asian *Spizaetus* indicate that further research will be necessary before the group can be understood.

It has been assumed, without substantiation, that *Harpagornis* is most closely to the Australian Wedge-tailed Eagle (*Aquila audax*) (e.g., Duff 1949). Without a detailed study of the relationships within and between *Aquila* and *Haliaeetus*, however, the sister taxon cannot be identified. Insufficient material of some of the rarer taxa precluded my examining this question.

Busarellus, *Hieraaetus*, and *Polemaetus*

The inclusion of *Busarellus* (Fishing Buzzard) in a clade with a group of African and Eurasian eagles (Fig. 10) was unexpected, in view of its present position in the sub-buteonines (Brown & Amadon 1968). The clade is supported by 18 characters, none of which is an unambiguous synapomorphy, however. The clade consisting of *Busarellus* alone is based on 21 characters, of which one is an autapomorphy (Fig. 10), and one the apparently convergent fusion of the pedal phalanges discussed above with respect to the milvine-haliaeetine clade. *Hieraaetus* and *Polemaetus* are linked by nine character state changes (Fig. 10).

Brown & Amadon (1968) noted that Ridgway (1873) thought that *Busarellus* was isolated, and perhaps close to *Hamirostra* (Australian Black-breasted Buzzard). However, they concluded that "the resemblance to that genus is superficial and the resemblance to the neo-tropical genera just mentioned [*Heterospizias, Buteogallus*, and *Parabuteo*] is real" (Brown & Amadon 1968: 565). Olson (1982) believed that Ridgway's 1873 and 1876 papers were the "last opinion on the matter to be founded on anything other than tradition", and that later works relied on the sequence of genera in Ridgway's publications rather than his stated conclusions. Olson (1982) also pointed out that no characters had been published that justified the linking of *Busarellus* with the sub-buteonines.

The position of *Hieraaetus*, the genus of Eurasian and African Hawk Eagles, has been debated, including whether it should be recognised at all or whether the constituent species should be included in *Aquila* (Brown & Amadon 1968). Its position in my scheme as the sister group of *Polemaetus* is supported by nine characters, including four examples of convergence (Fig. 10). Brown & Amadon (1968) concluded that *Polemaetus* was not close to *Spizaetus* or any other genus, but Amadon (1982a) merged the two under *Hieraaetus*, citing behavioural similarities in evidence. *Polemaetus* was distinguished by a single unambiguous autapomorphy among 20 characters (Fig. 10).

The "booted eagles"

Nine genera of large eagles with feathered legs have been recognised as a monophyletic group, but the inclusion of taxa such as *Ictinaetus* has been questioned (Amadon 1982a). Amadon (1982a) submerged one genus in *Hieraaetus* and three in *Spizaetus*.

My results suggest that the "booted eagles" is a paraphyletic grouping of taxa, based on a single character that has been demonstrated to vary even within genera (Amadon 1982a). The submergence of *Stephanoaetus* and *Lophaetus* in *Spizaetus* is not supported by the topology of the tree described here.

Harpies

Recognition of *Stephanoaetus* (African Crowned Eagle) as a sister group of *Harpia* (South American Harpy Eagle) is based on 11 characters, but no unambiguous synapomorphies (Fig. 11). *Harpia* exhibited three autapomorphies, but *Stephanoaetus* none.

As noted above, the placement of *Stephanoaetus* in the harpy clade does not support its submergence in *Spizaetus* (Amadon 1982a; Voous & Wijsman 1964) or even a close relationship with *Spizaetus* as suggested by Brown & Amadon (1968). Brown (1982) resurrected *Stephanoaetus*. However, Amadon (1982a) pointed out some similarities between *Harpia* and *Stephanoaetus* in proportions, habits, a two-year breeding cycle, and immature plumage.

Jollie (1977c) grouped *Stephanoaetus* with *Polemaetus* and *Spizaetus*, and apparently separated these and other "aquilins" from the harpies. However, his diagrams are somewhat ambiguous and the aquilins appear as a sister group of the harpies in one that details relationships among the accipitrin and buteonine genera.

Lophaetus, Pithecophaga and *Morphnus*

Similarities between these geographically widely separated taxa are apparently symplesiomorphic, because all formed separate clades in my tree (Fig. 1, 11).

My results do not support Amadon's (1982a) lumping of *Lophaetus* and *Spizaetus*. *Lophaetus* (mis-spelled *Lophoaetus* in Brown & Amadon 1968, and in Amadon 1982), the African Long-crested Eagle, was considered to be the sister group of *Spizaetus*, *Polemaetus*, and *Stephanoaetus* by Jollie (1977c).

Pithecophaga forms another monotypic clade. Its karyotype is similar to that of the aegypiines (de Boer & Sinoo 1984), but its position on my tree suggests that the resemblances may be symplesiomorphic. Shufeldt (1919) concluded that it was related to *Harpia*. Brown & Amadon (1968: 22) also placed it near *Harpia*, although they noted "We do not claim that the New and Old World genera placed in this group [*Pithecophaga, Harpyopsis, Harpia, Morphnus*] have any special or close relationship, but viewed on a worldwide basis they all represent the climax of one line of raptorial evolution". This comment suggests that Brown & Amadon (1968) viewed the harpies as a grade rather than a phylogenetic group. Jollie (1977c) placed *Pithecophaga* near the gypaetins, but left the proximity of the connection unresolved.

Morphnus (Guianan Crested Eagle) also constitutes a separate lineage on my tree, but it is not particularly close to the harpies, with which it was grouped by Brown & Amadon (1968) and Jollie (1977c). It differs from *Harpia* in having short, broad wings, and a long tail, which give it the proportions of an *Accipiter*. The karyotype is normal for an accipitrid (Williams & Benirschke 1976).

Kaupifalco

Kaupifalco (African Lizard Buzzard) branches off at the base of the accipitrine/buteonine group (Fig. 12). Jollie (1977c) placed it beside *Buteo* and *Butastur* (not dealt with here) which, together with *Leucopternis* and *Parabuteo*, formed his paraphyletic 'buteonin core'. Brown & Amadon (1968) thought it near *Buteo*, and that it resembled 'fortuitous[ly]' some species of *Leucopternis*.

Harpagus and *Ictinia*

Harpagus (Double-toothed Kite) and *Ictinia* (Mississippi Kites) formed a clade supported by 16 characters, including two unambiguous synapomorphies (Fig. 12). Shufeldt (1891) pointed out that the skeleton of *Ictinia* is similar to that of *Buteo*, but Jollie (1977c) included *Ictinia* with the elanin kites, and Brown & Amadon (1968: 20) placed it between the elanin and milvine kites, commenting that it is "like *Milvus* and *Elanus* a classic kite in form". The fused phalanges of the second pedal digit are apparently convergent with those of *Busarellus* and the milvines and haliaeetines (see above).

L Miller (1937) pointed out that *Harpagus bidentatus* has been placed in both the Falconidae (by Carriker and Bowdler Sharpe) and the Accipitridae (by Peters). Suschkin (1905) rejected a relationship with the Falconidae, a contention based mainly on the denticulate bill, and Miller (1937) pointed out several osteological features that support its being an accipitrid resembling *Accipiter* more than *Elanus*. He placed it "between" *Elanus leucurus* and *Accipiter cooperii.*

Amadon (1961), however, argued that *Harpagus* is a kite, and he rejected similarities to *Accipiter* as coincidental or the result of mimicry. Later he suggested that, despite reports that the bird hunts like an *Accipiter*, it is probably 'kite-like' in the way it hunts lizards and large insects (Amadon 1964). However, he also pointed out that it resembles *Accipiter* in being strongly sexually dimorphic in size.

Harpagus was separated from *Ictinia* by two autapomorphies among 31 character state changes.

Melierax, accipiters, and the buteos

Melierax (African Chanting Goshawks) and the accipiters and buteos are supported as a monophyletic clade by 10 characters, including one unambiguous synapomorphy (Fig. 12, 13). Brown & Amadon (1968) placed *Melierax* between *Circus* and the accipiters, but noted that its relationships are not obvious.

Buteo (Buzzards) and *Accipiter* (Sparrowhawks and Goshawks) are the most speciose genera in the family (Stresemann & Amadon 1979). Their close relationship was pointed out by Brown & Amadon (1968). Jollie (1977c) also placed them near each other, and included *Leucopternis* (American White Hawks) and *Erythrotriorchis* (Australian Red 'Goshawk') in the group. Both he and Brown & Amadon (1968), however, linked *Erythrotriorchis* with *Accipiter.*

On my tree *Leucopternis* is the sister group of a clade composed of *Buteo*, and *Parabuteo* (American Bay-winged Hawk), and so shares a most recent common ancestor with the clade containing *Accipiter* and *Buteo*. Brown & Amadon (1968) concluded that *Leucopternis* is related to *Buteo*. Jollie (1977c) made it a sister group of *Parabuteo*, judging from his diagram, and together with *Geranospiza*, he linked them with *Buteo* on one side and *Accipiter* on the other.

Parabuteo is the sister group of *Buteo* (Fig. 13). Brown & Amadon (1968) concluded that it was very close to *Buteo*. However, they also raised the possibility of a relationship with *Heterospizias* and *Buteogallus*. Later, Amadon (1982b) chose to ally *Parabuteo* with *Heterospizias*, and he synonymised in turn *Heterospizias* with *Buteogallus*. These genera are widely separated in the tree found here, and their synonymy is not supported.

Olson (1987) discussed the distribution of the procoracoid foramen in the Accipitridae. He found it to be invariably absent in *Accipiter*, nearly or completely absent in some individuals of *Harpagus* and *Circus*, but present in others. Examination of a specimen in the British Museum

(Natural History) labelled as *Erythrotriorchis* and listed as such in Blandamer & Burton (1979) revealed a fully developed procoracoid foramen. This specimen is actually referable to *Haliastur sphenurus* (pers. obs.).

DNA-DNA hybridisation

Sibley & Ahlquist (1990) presented a phylogenetic tree for the class Aves, based on DNA-DNA hybridisation data. The tree included one species of each of seven genera of Accipitridae (*Gyps, Aegypius, Neophron, Gypaetus, Harpagus, Accipiter*), two species of an eighth (*Buteo*), four of a ninth (*Circus*), *Pandion* and *Sagittarius*. The topology of their tree is very similar to mine, except for the position of *Circus* (put as the sister group of *Harpagus* as against a near-basal clade in mine), and details of the branching within the vultures.

Sagittarius is basal in the Sibley & Ahlquist tree, separated from *Pandion* by 2.6 $_*T_{50}$ units[1]. *Pandion* itself is separated from the accipitrids by 2.6 units. The vultures are then 1.2 units, and the other accipitrids 0.6 units, from the common node with *Pandion*.

In the vultures, the distance between *Gyps* and *Aegypius* is not resolved, and *Neophron* and *Gypaetus* are sister groups. In the other major clade, *Accipiter* is the sister group of the two *Buteo* species as in my tree, and *Harpagus* is a sister group of *Circus*. Given the few taxa involved, the correspondence between the two trees is understandable.

Mallophaga

Clay (1951) used the distribution of taxa of Mallophaga (bird lice) to argue that the Falconiformes is a monophyletic group. Other evidence suggests that this is not correct. The distribution of genera such as *Laemobothrion*, which occurs on both accipitrid and vulturid vultures (Nelson & Price 1965) probably results from the long sympatry of the two vulture groups in North America and Europe (Cracraft & Rich 1972; Rich 1980).

Within the Accipitridae as understood here, however, the distribution of species in the genus *Degeeriella* has been used to elucidate intrafamilial relationships (Clay 1958). Although most genera of Accipitridae appear to have their own species or subspecies of *Degeeriella*, the presence of particular species groups of Mallophaga may indeed reflect major groupings in the Accipitridae (Fig. 14A). This may be so even though it is difficult to relate character differences in the lice to separation times of the host taxa (Clay 1958).

The elanid and elanoidid kites share species of the *D. elani* species group (Clay 1958). Members of this group are also found on *Chelictinia* (African Swallow-tailed Kite) and *Aviceda* (Crested Hawks), which are not included in my phylogenetic tree because of insufficient data, although the *Degeeriella* on *Aviceda* is less certainly related to others of the *elani* group (Clay 1958). A species of the *elani* group also occurs on *Gampsonyx* (American Pearl Kite), which Clay incorrectly included in the Falconidae; *Gampsonyx* was later shown to be an accipitrid (Brodkorb 1960).

Pernis, traditionally placed with the kites, hosts lice of a different species group (*phlyctopygus*) and members of the *elani* species group are absent (Clay 1958). The *phlyctopygus* group apparently shows affinities to the *regalis* species group taxa characteristic of the milvine kites, and *Haliaeetus* (Clay 1958). *Ichthyophaga* and *Buteogallus* have species of the *fulva* group instead, possibly a plesiomorphic condition, as the *fulva* group is the only one known on most genera of the sister clade to the milvines (Fig. 14A). The only exceptions are the presence of lice of the *discocephalus* species group on *Aquila* and one species of *Haliaeetus*, and the *regalis* group on two species of *Buteo* (Clay 1958) (Fig. 14A). The presence of *discocephalus* lice on two northern species of *Haliaeetus* may be the result of contact between *Aquila* and *Haliaeetus* at feeding sites in winter when food supplies are restricted.

Members of the *fulva* group are also found on species of the Serpent Eagle clade (Fig. 14B). The presence of the distinctive *punctifer* group on both *Gyps* and *Gypaetus* (Clay 1958) is a derived character supporting their relationship as depicted in Fig. 4 and 5. However, the presence of a *regalis* louse on *Gypohierax* (Fig. 14C) is apparently either a plesiomorphic feature, or the result of host transfer.

In general, the distribution of the species groups of *Degeeriella* provides independent support

---

1 $_*T_{50}$ is the difference between the temperature at which all DNA is single chain, and the temperature at which 50% of the DNA has formed duplexes.

for the topology of my phylogenetic trees based on osteological data. Species of the *elani* group seem to be associated with taxa isolated by the initial radiation of accipitrids and represented today by the elanin and elanoidin kites and the Crested Hawks.

Possession of the *fulva* group is a plesiomorphic feature of accipitrid genera, and the presence of *regalis*, *discocephalus*, and *punctifer* groups are derived features of the milvins, aquilins, and gypaetins, respectively. The *phlyctopyga* group appears to be autapomorphic for *Pernis*. Its presence on *Neophron* would provide strong supporting evidence for the branching pattern of the tree presented here.

Biogeography

The Accipitridae is a cosmopolitan family, absent only from Antarctica and some remote oceanic islands (Brown & Amadon 1968). An inspection of the species distributions given by Stresemann & Amadon (1979) shows, however, that there is considerable heterogeneity in the representation of different genera in different regions. A tree of the relationships among operational geographic units (OGUs) derived from the taxon distribution matrix (Appendix 3) using PAUP, and South America as the designated ancestor, is shown in Fig. 15. The geographic areas used are shown in Fig. 16.

The tree can be viewed as indicating either that South America and Africa have been the scene of separate radiations of accipitrids, or that formerly more widespread diverse faunas had been disrupted by Tertiary and Quaternary climatic changes, leaving remnant faunas. The inclusion of accipitrid vultures in North American deposits and vulturids in Europe (Olson 1985) tends to support this view, but the high degrees of endemicity and low proportion of shared taxa argue strongly against it.

Intermediate areas exhibited mixes of taxa in proportion both to their distance from each centre, and to the relative vagility of the taxa. The second factor is exemplified by the accipitrid faunas of New Zealand, Greenland, and Oceania. The major, or only, groups in these areas are the *Haliaeetus* eagles, *Circus*, and the occasional *Aquila*-type (New Zealand), *Buteo* (Galapagos and Hawaii), and *Accipiter* (Fiji). Fiji is linked by islands to Melanesia and there are no major water crossings involved in reaching the archipelago. *Accipiter* apparently reached at least as far east as Tonga until humans arrived (Olson 1991 - pers. comm. from Steadman), but this record is not included in the present analysis. These are the only genera whose species seem to be able, or willing, to cross large water gaps, and they are the most cosmopolitan of the accipitrids.

South-east Asia and the Indo-Philippine islands are 'sister groups', whose accipitrid faunas are linked to Australia and to Asia north of the Himalayas and from there to Europe, and Africa; but they have little in common with the North American fauna (Fig. 15). The distribution of apparently relict taxa across the now widely separated land masses of the southern hemisphere, and the inability of most accipitrids to cross large water gaps suggest that these taxa have been isolated by movement of land masses during the birds' evolutionary history. A corollary is that the taxa are old. The oldest accipitrids known are late Eocene to early Oligocene in age, but buteonine hawks do not appear in the fossil record until the middle Miocene of Europe (Olson 1985).

If the accipitrids radiated during the Oligocene, then the position and movement of continental blocks from the Oligocene to the present may have influenced or helped drive the evolution of the group. Sea gaps between Australia and Antarctica and Antarctica and South America were very much narrower during the Oligocene than they are today, according to Owen's (1983, map 66) map of continental positions 29 million years BP.[2] Antarctica and the Falkland Islands had extensive forests at that time (Birnie & Roberts 1986; Rich 1975), and the environment would have favoured the spread of birds from South America to Australia or vice versa. Antarctica itself may have been the site of much bird evolution, of which there is presently no known fossil record apart from that of penguins (Fordyce 1991; Rich 1991).

Africa had separated from both South America and Antarctica millions of years before they separated from each other (Owen 1983), and the faunal links between Africa and the others are much more distant. It was effectively isolated from both South America and Antarctica-Australia by wide oceans or long distances by land during the Oligocene.

---

2 Owen's reconstructions were rejected by Cox (1990), but Owen (1990) argued strongly that the objections were based on poor cartographic techniques.

Figure 1. Phylogenetic tree of genera of the Accipitridae, based on analysis of 188 osteological characters. Aegypiine clade is shown in Fig. 4 and 5. See Appendix 1 for taxa representing genera and Appendix 2 for characters.

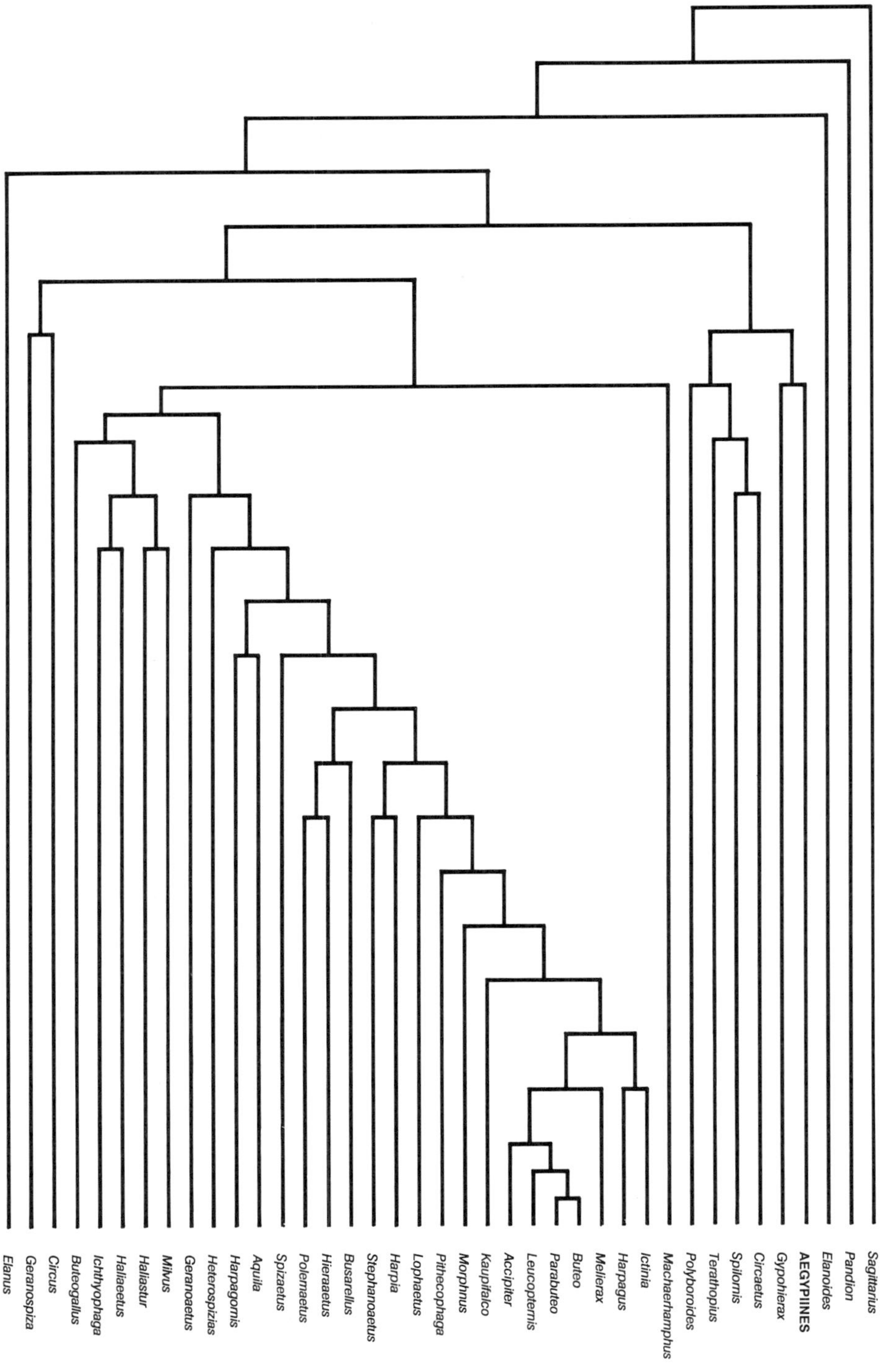

Figure 2. Basal branches of phylogenetic tree of the Accipitridae, including the outgroup (*Sagittarius*) and *Pandion*. The 'kites' *Elanoides* and *Elanus* share symplesiomorphic resemblances. Character state changes are shown on each branch. See Appendix 2 for characters.

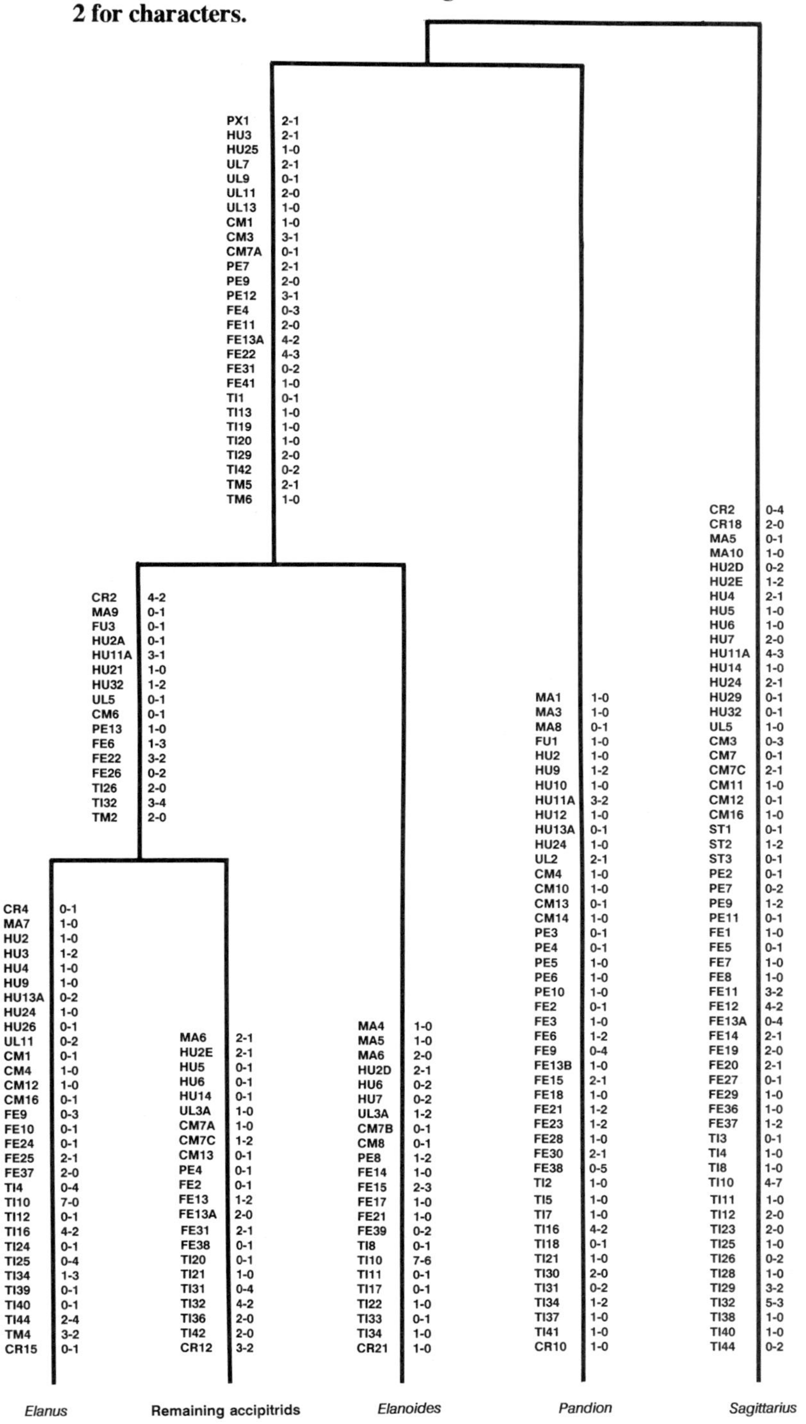

Figure 3. **'Serpent' (*Spilornis*) and 'snake' (*Circaetus*) eagle, and African Harrier-Hawk (*Polyboroides*) and Bateleur (*Terathopius*) clades, and their relationship to the basal branches of the vulturine clade (including *Gypohierax*). Conventions as in Figure 2.**

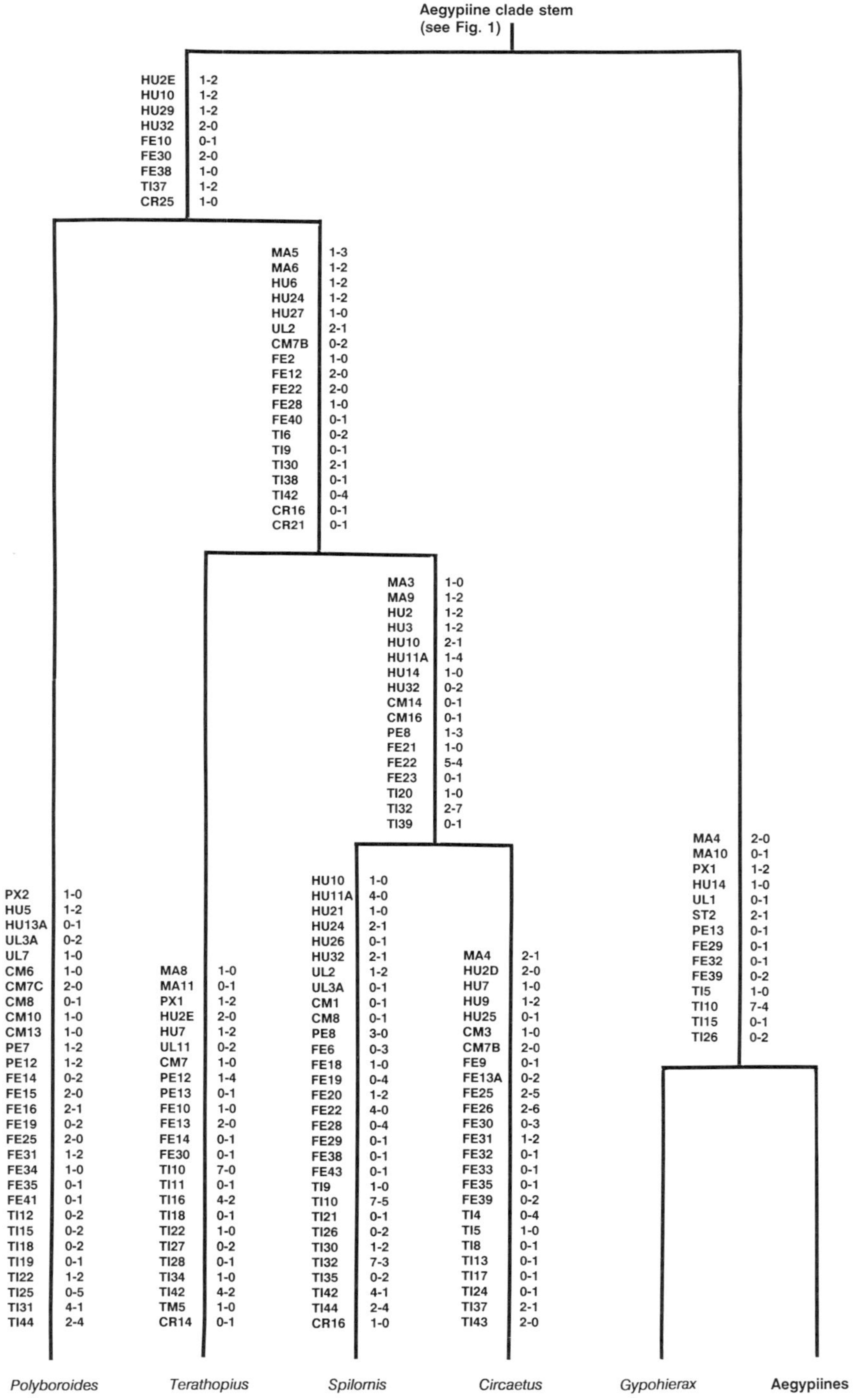

Figure 4. Basal clades of the large vulturines, including the Palm-nut Vulture *Gypohierax*, the Bearded Vulture *Gypaetus*, and the Egyptian Vulture *Neophron*. Note the position of the Honey Buzzard *Pernis* as sister-group of *Neophron* and the that these share a most recent ancestor with the 'core' aegypiines. See Figure 5 for relationships within the 'core' clade. Conventions as in Figure 2.

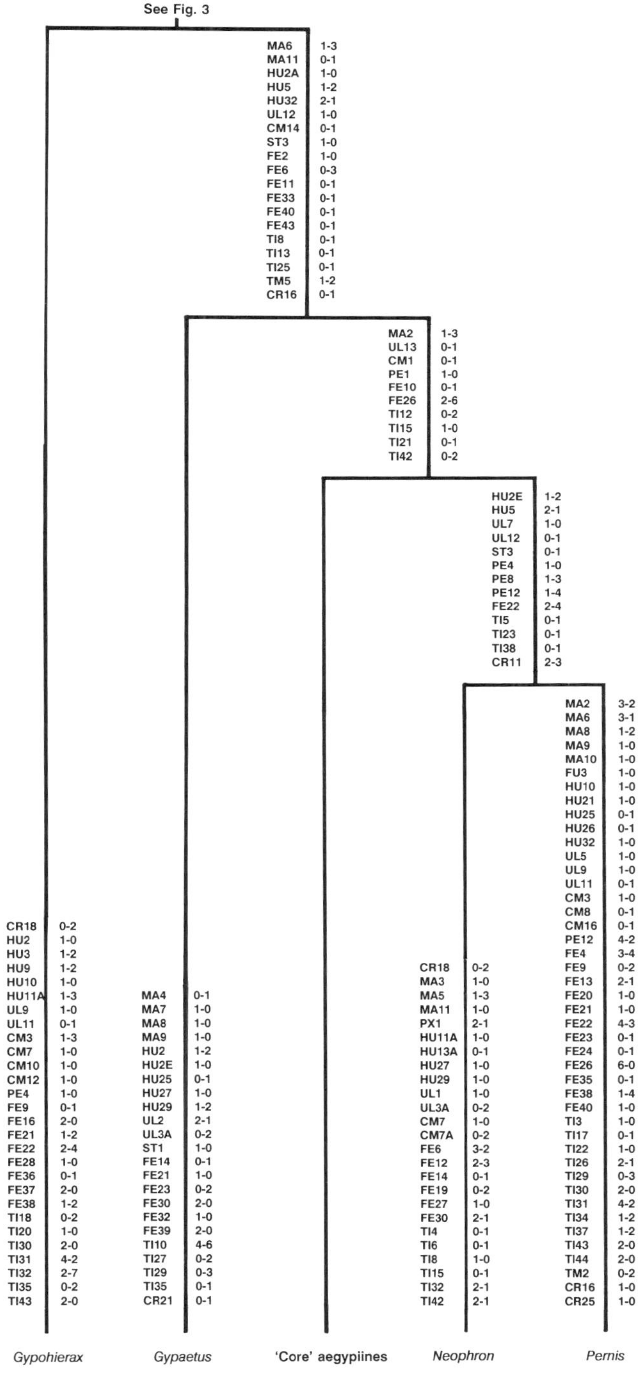

Figure 5. Relationships of the Old World vultures. See Figure 4 for basal branches of the vulturine clade. Conventions as in Figure 2.

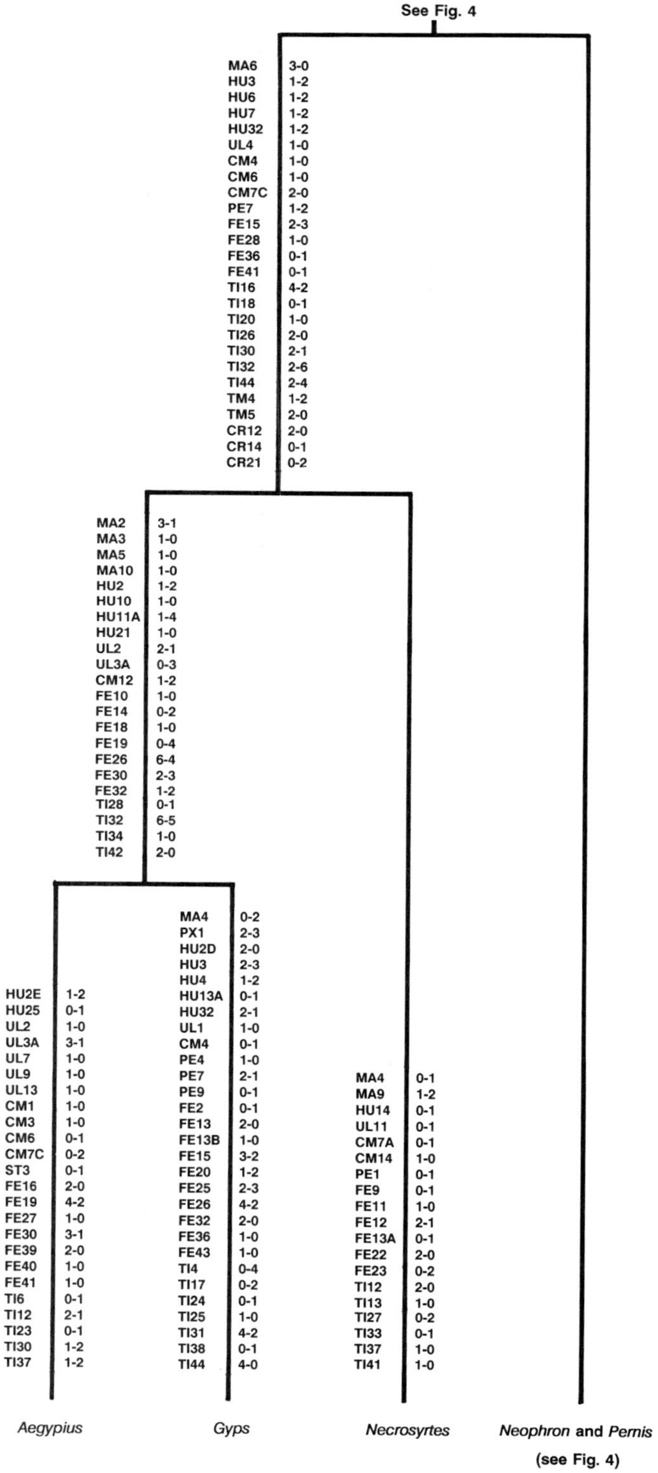

Figure 6. Basal branches of the main accipitrid clade. The Crane Hawk (*Geranospiza*) and the harriers (*Circus*) are sister-groups, and the Bat Hawk (*Machaerhamphus*) is the sister-group of all remaining accipitrids. Conventions as in Figure 2.

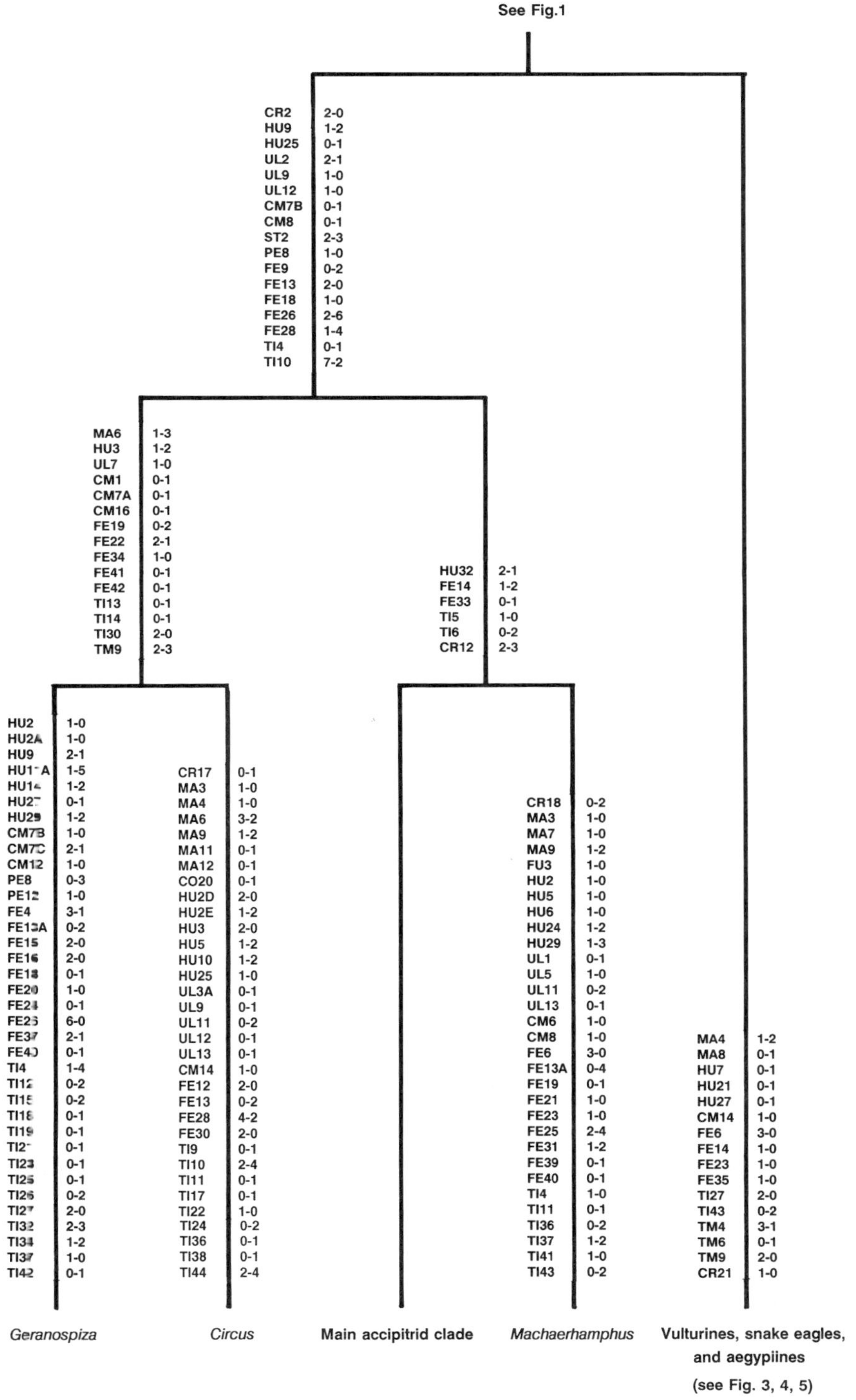

Figure 7. The fish eagles (*Haliaeetus* and *Ichthyophaga*) and milvine kites (*Haliastur* and *Milvus*) clades, showing their sister-group relationship. See Figure 8 for their relationship to *Buteogallus* and the 'core' taxa. Conventions as in Figure 2.

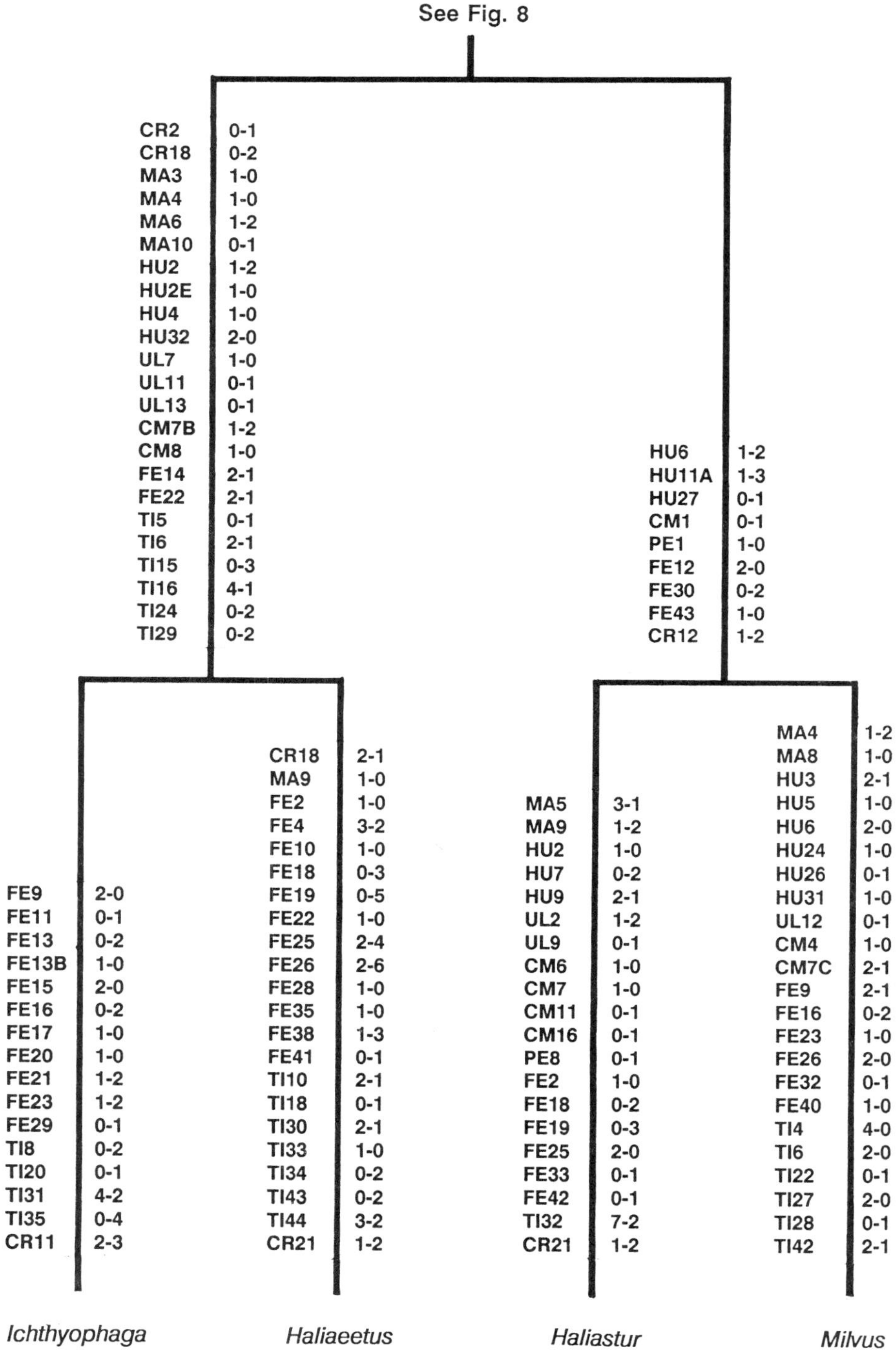

Figure 8. Relationships of the American Black Hawk (*Buteogallus*) and Buzzard Eagle (*Geranoaetus*) to the milvine-haliaeetine clade, and to the accipitrine 'core' taxa. Conventions as in Figure 2.

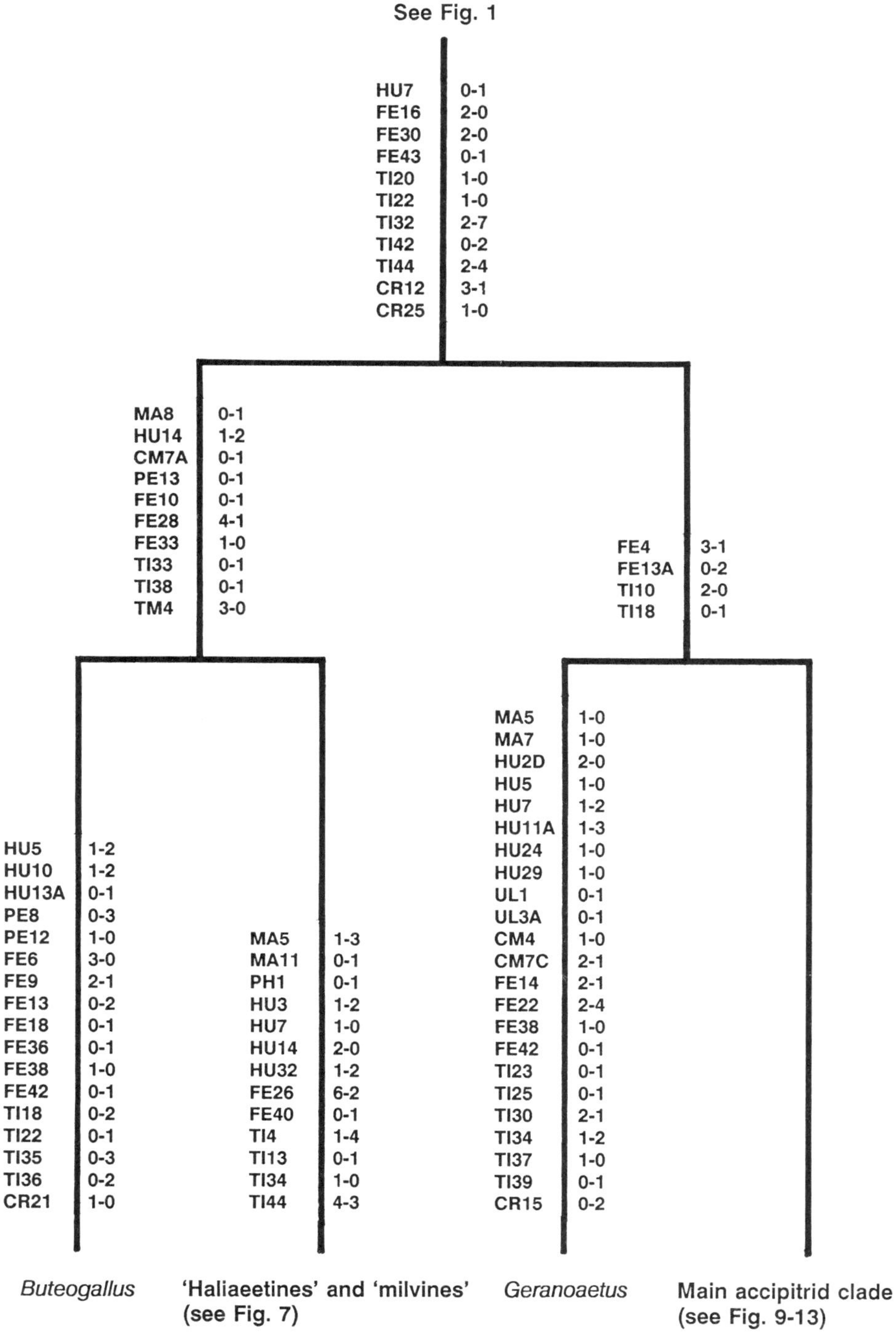

Figure 9. Relationships of the Savannah Hawk (*Heterospizias*) to the aquilines and the accipitrid 'core'. *Harpagornis* is sister-group to *Aquila*. Conventions as in Figure 2.

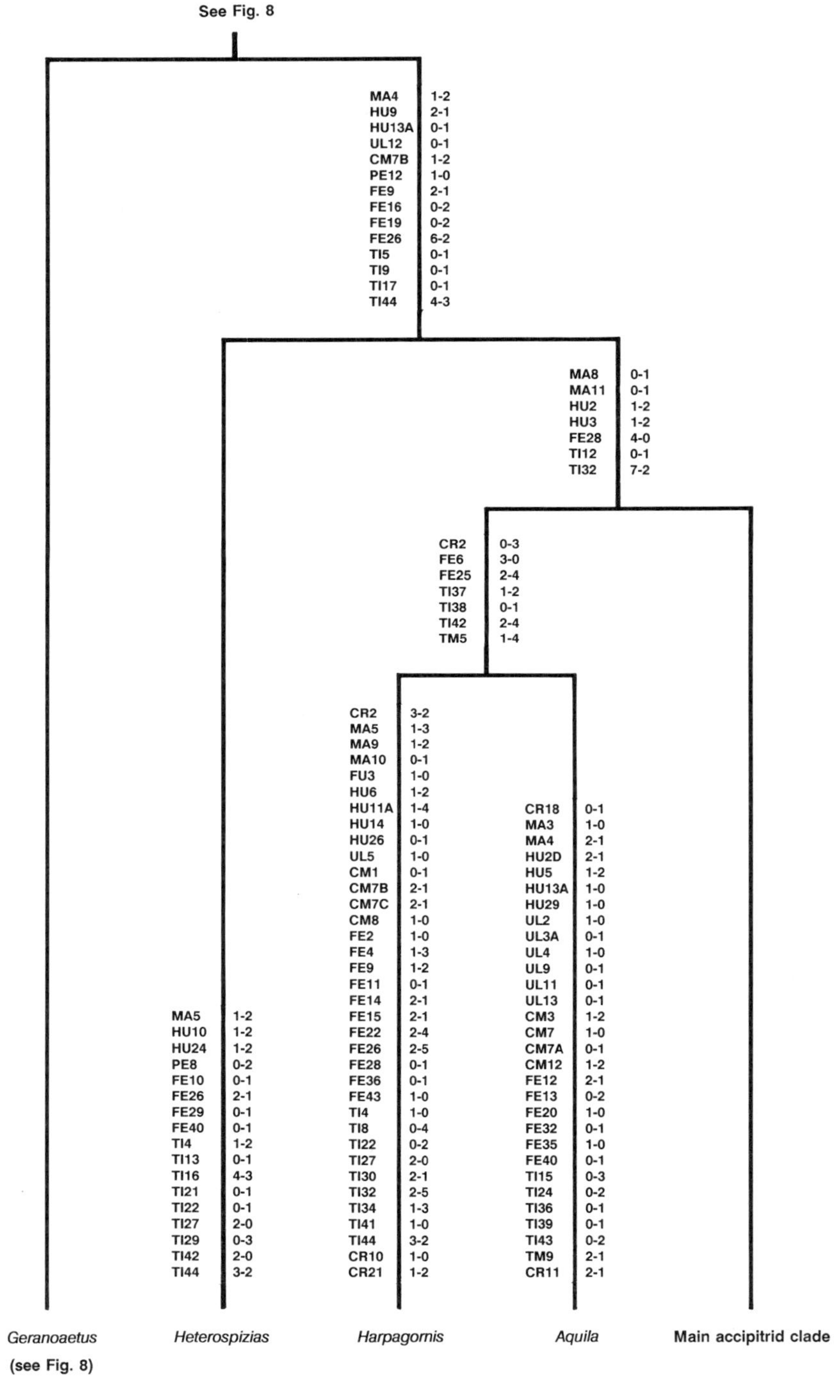

Figure 10. Relationships of the 'hawk eagles' of the genera *Spizaetus* and *Hieraaetus*. The African Martial Eagle is sister-group to *Hieraaetus*, and the Black-collared, or Fishing, Hawk (*Busarellus*) shares a most recent ancestor with the Old World hawk eagles. Conventions as in Figure 2.

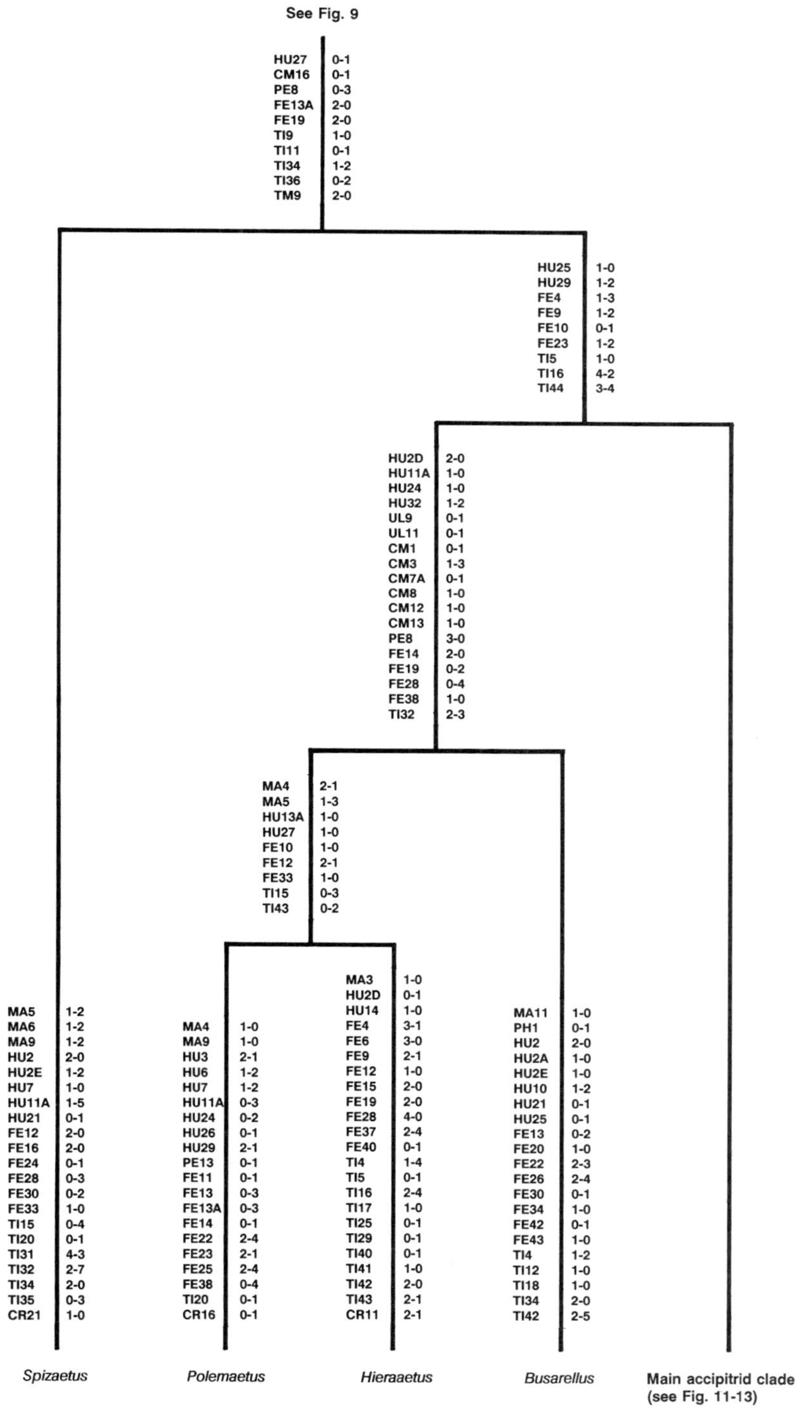

Figure 11. The 'Harpy' eagles, showing the sister-group relationship of the African Crowned Eagle (*Stephanoaetus*) and the Neotropical Harpy (*Harpia*), but the paraphyly of the other great forest eagles. In particular, the Guianan Crested Eagle (*Morphnus*) shares a most recent ancestor with the accipitrid 'core' taxa (see Figure 12 and 13). Conventions as in Figure 2.

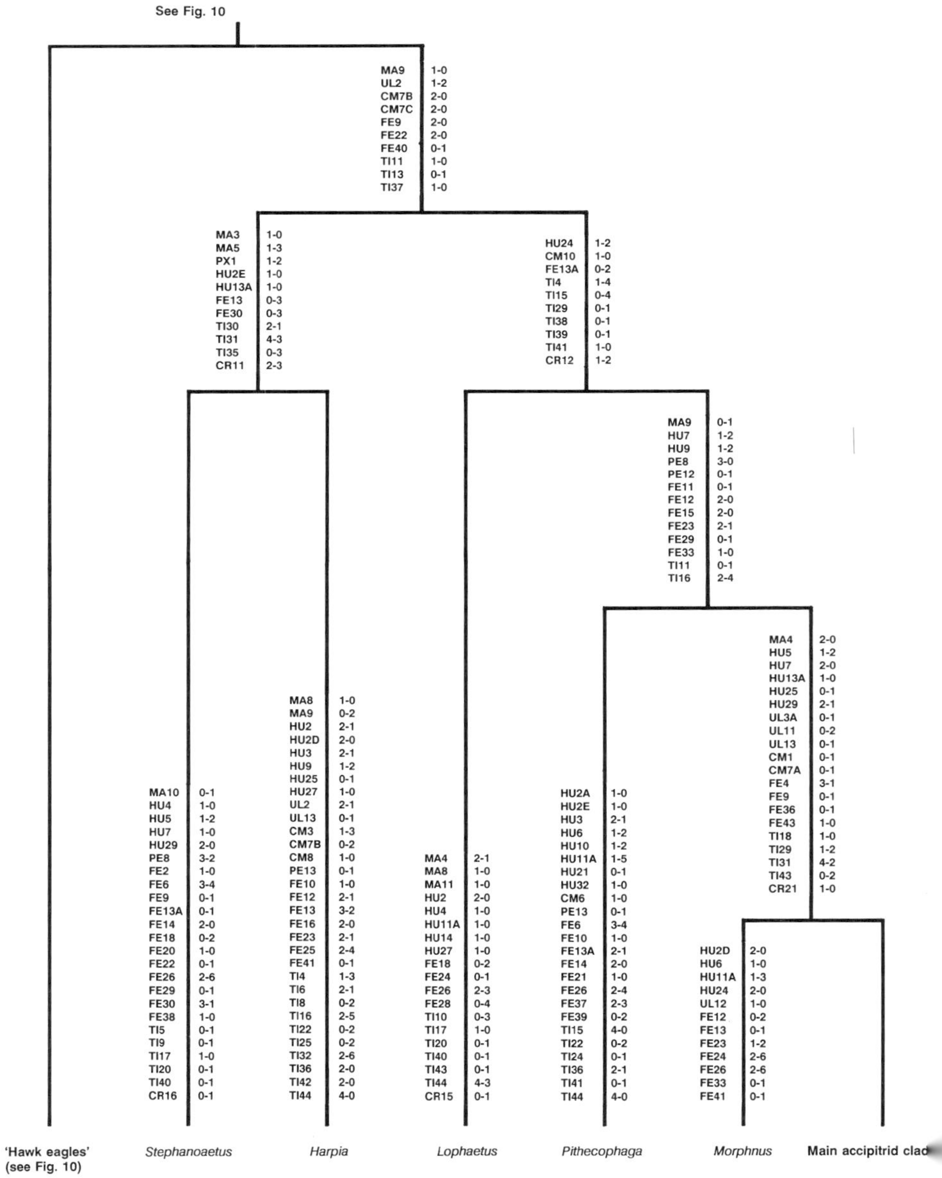

Figure 12. Basal branches of the accipitrid 'core'. The Tooth-billed Kite (*Harpagus*) and Mississippi Kite (*Ictinia*) are accipitrids near *Accipiter* and *Buteo* and are not 'elanids'. Conventions as in Figure 2.

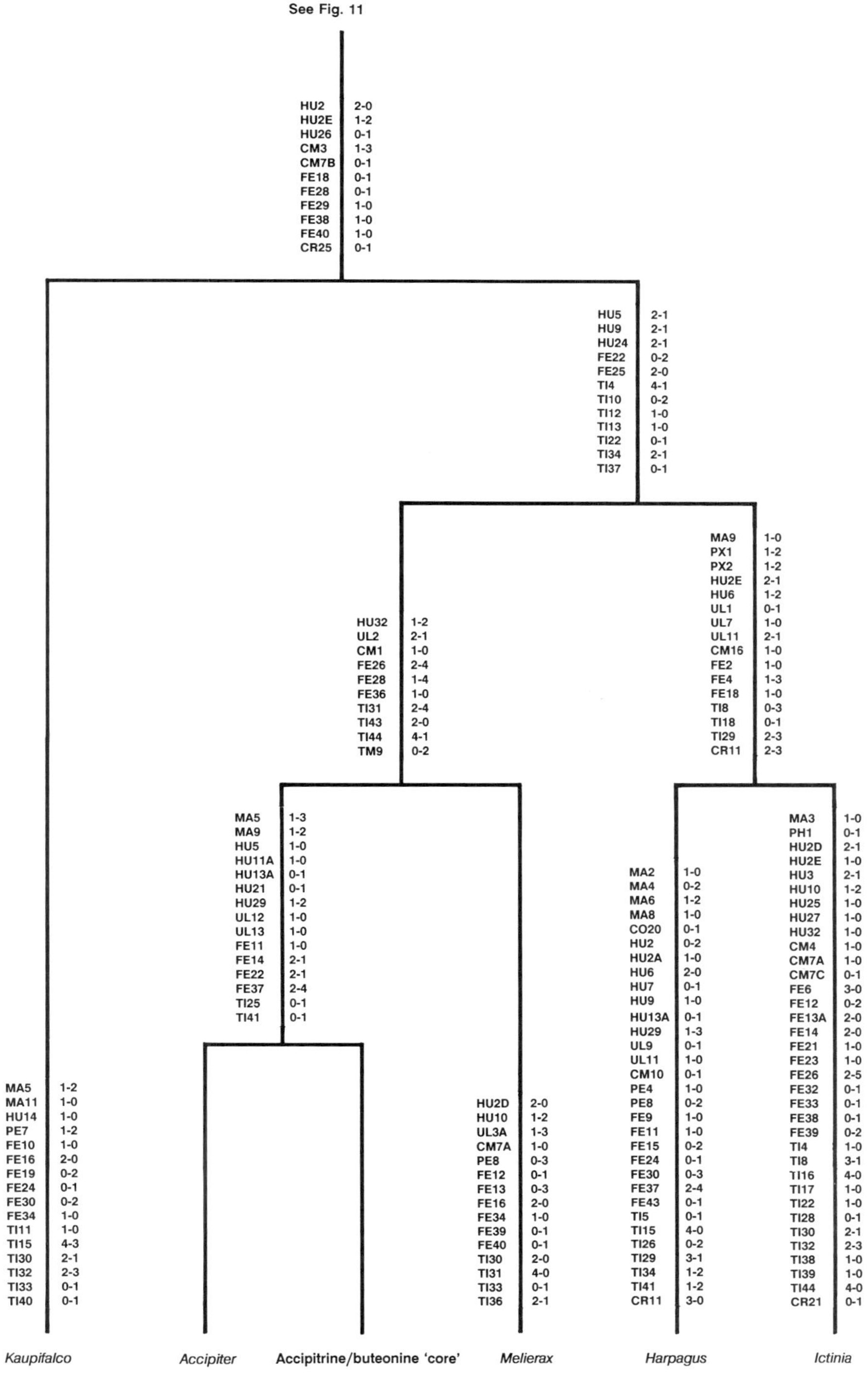

Figure 13. **The 'accipitrid core', comprising the 'sub-buteos' (American White Hawk *Leucopternis* and Harris's Hawk *Parabuteo*) and the goshawks (*Accipiter*) and buzzards (*Buteo*). *Accipiter* is sister-group to the clade containing the other taxa. Conventions as in Figure 2.**

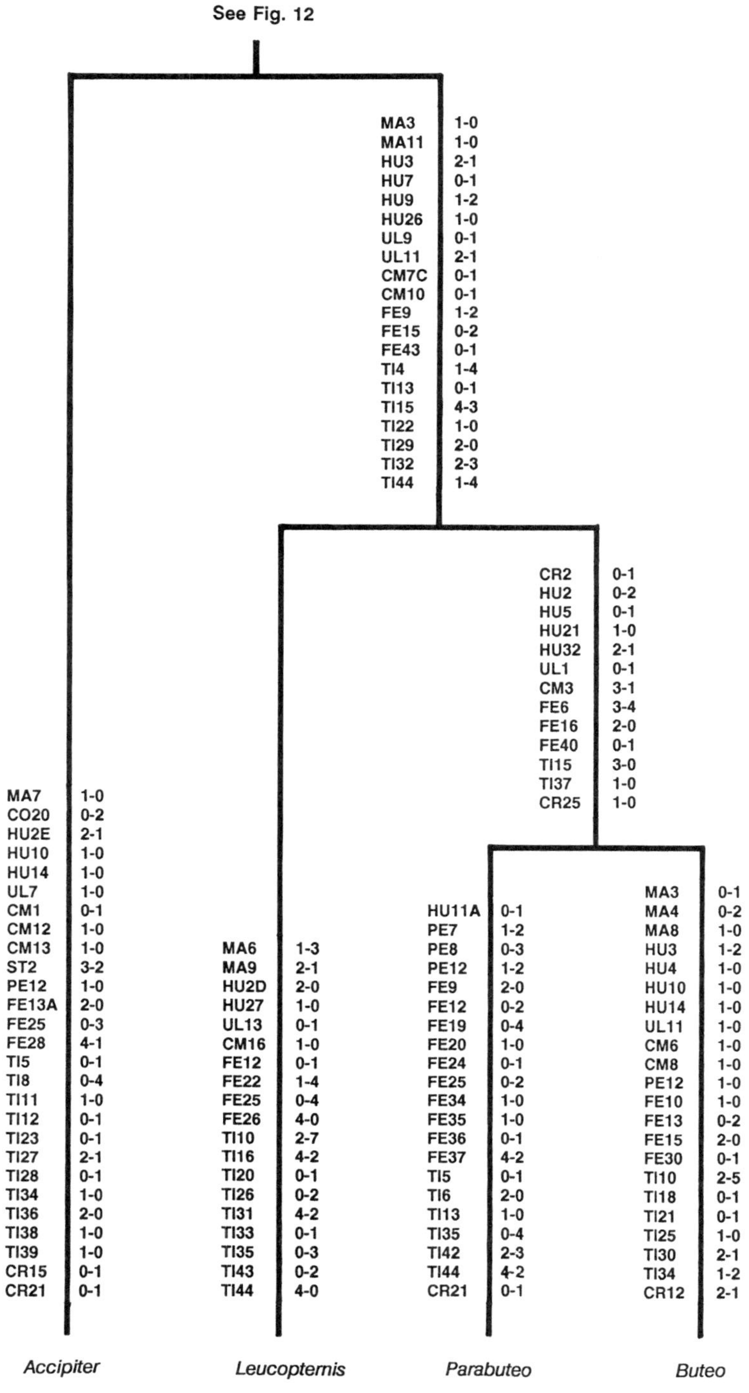

Figure 14A. **Phylogenetic tree of the genera of the Accipitridae, showing the species groups (e.g., *elani*) of the feather louse genus *Degeeriella* (Insecta: Mallophaga) to which each genus is known to be host (from Clay 1958). See Figures 1-13 for detailed relationships within the Accipitridae, and Figure 14B and 14C for distribution of louse species-groups within the gypaetiines.**

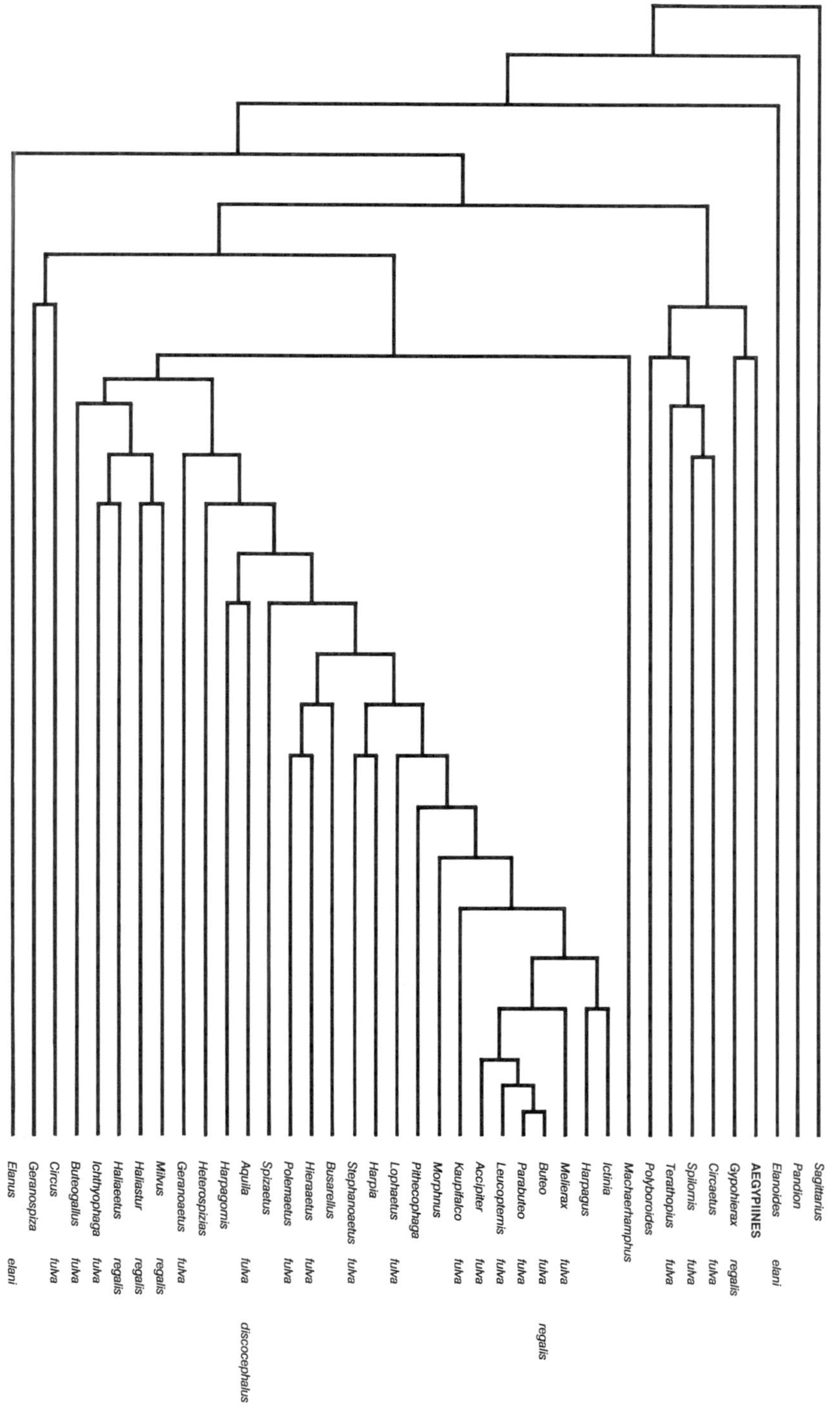

Figure 14B. Phylogenetic tree of the gypaetiines and snake eagles, showing the species groups of the feather louse genus *Degeeriella* (Insecta: Mallophaga) to which each genus is known to be host (from Clay 1958).

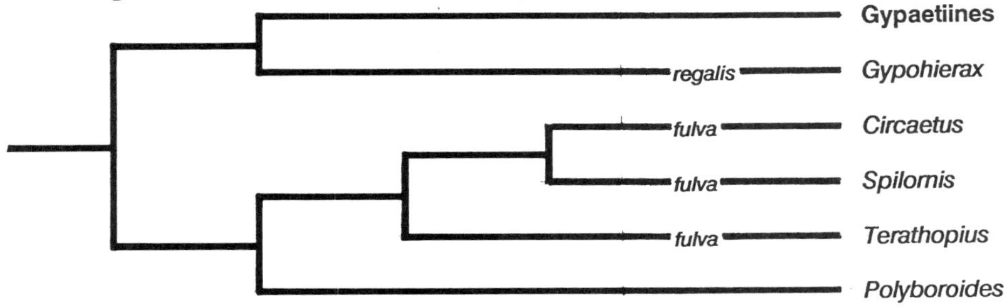

Figure 14C. Phylogenetic tree of the gypaetiines/aegypiines, showing the species groups of the feather louse genus *Degeeriella* (Insecta: Mallophaga) to which each genus is known to be host (from Clay 1958).

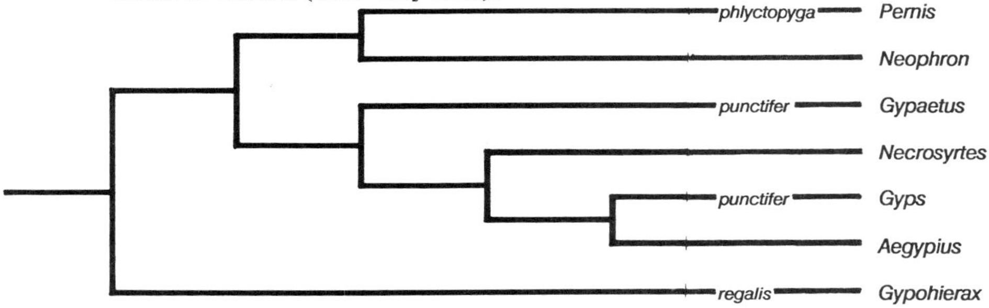

Figure 15. Biogeographic tree of the Accipitridae, using areas as taxa, genera as characters, and number of species in an area as character states. See Appendix 3 for matrix of taxa and areas, and Figure 16 for location of areas used in analysis.

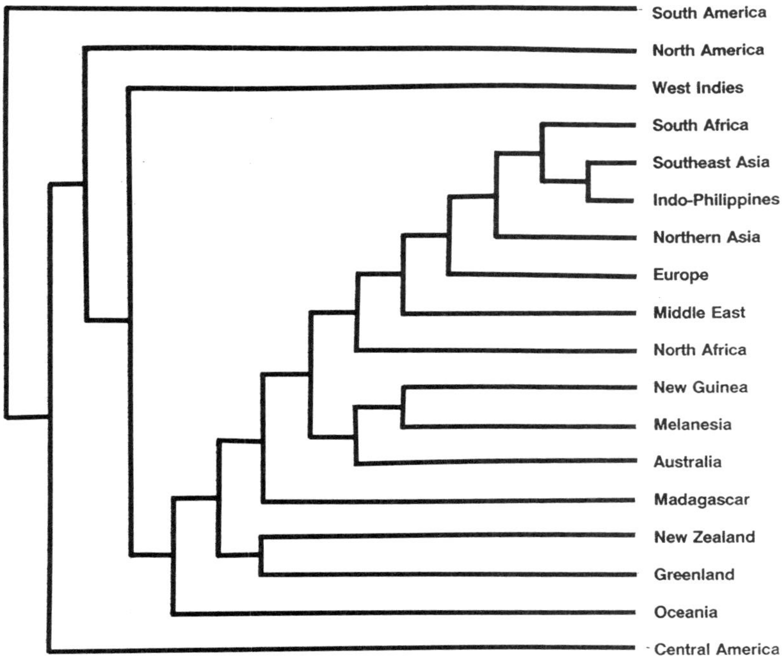

Figure 16 Location of areas used in analysis, Numbers are numbers of genera/number of species. Data from Brown & Amadon (1968). Although the Old World has about twice the land area of the new, the ratio of endemic genera is about 1.7:1

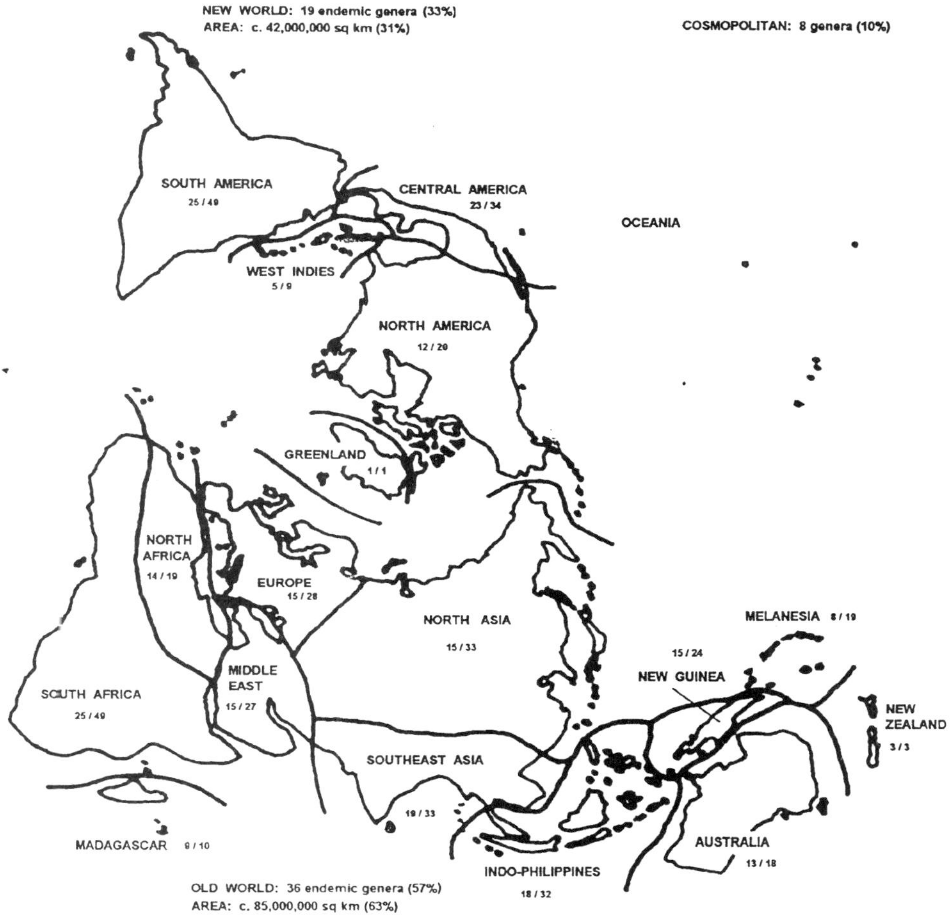

	NW	OW
Genera	1	1.7
Species	1	2

Note: 8 / 19 denotes genera / species

The long-held view that birds colonised Australia from the north (e.g., Mayr 1944) has been refuted by systematic work showing that an independent radiation of the passerines produced groups convergent on Palaearctic families (Sibley & Ahlquist 1985). Much of the evolutionary history of the Accipitridae may have occurred on southern land masses, including Antarctica. The presence of endemic taxa such as *Lophoictinia*, *Hamirostra*, and *Erythrotriorchis* suggests that not all accipitrids have colonised Australia from elsewhere.

The Australian fossil record includes several accipitrids of up to mid-Miocene age (Rich & Baird 1986), but these, including a supposed gypaetin vulture, are of uncertain relationships (Rich & van Tets 1982).

Large accipitrids are known from the Australian Quaternary (Rich & van Tets 1982; Rich & Baird 1986), but the association Rich & Baird (1986) make between large size and scavenging habits is unproven.

Australia had extensive rain forests until the late Quaternary (Rich 1975), and the barriers to forest birds formed by the hot desert of Australia and the cold desert of Antarctica are relatively new. Present forest areas in New Guinea, Southeast Asia, and South America were linked by others in the geologically recent past. Links between isolated forest taxa such as *Harpyopsis* of New Guinea and *Pithecophaga* of the Philippines may be better sought to the south rather than the north. Indeed, Rich & van Tets (1982) reported that a small fossil eagle (*Necrastur alacer*) from the Australian Pleistocene resembled *Harpyopsis*.

The poor pre-Quaternary fossil record of accipitrids in Australia (Rich & Baird 1986), and present total absence of such a record in New Zealand (Fordyce 1991) makes a definitive statement on the origin of Haast's Eagle impossible. Its sister group relationship with *Aquila* suggests that it may be a relatively recent immigrant from Australia, but little is known about the time of radiation or dispersal of the *Aquila* eagles, or even how long *Aquila audax* has been in Australia. One of the large Quaternary accipitrids may have been larger than *Aquila audax* (Rich 1991) and perhaps similar in size to Haast's Eagle. Another species, smaller than *"Harpagornis assimilis"*, had bones of similar shape to those of Haast's Eagle (Rich & van Tets 1982). This material warrants further study.

The ancestor of Haast's Eagle may have arrived as early as the Early Miocene, when the New Zealand forests were similar to those in highland New Guinea today (Pocknall 1989), and the Tasman Sea was somewhat narrower (Owen 1983).

Relationships of Haast's Eagle

The principal result of my analysis is the placement of Haast's Eagle as sister group of *Aquila*, the genus containing the Golden and Wedge-tailed Eagles (*Aquila chrysaetos* and *A. audax*) (Stresemann & Amadon 1979). A relationship with *Aquila* conflicts with Oliver's (1945, 1955) conclusions, but is in accordance with one popularly held view of the relationships of Haast's Eagle (e.g., Duff 1949). Brathwaite & Holdaway's (1987) suggestion that Haast's Eagle was similar to *Spizaetus* could not be refuted or supported because of the paucity of material of South-east Asian *Spizaetus*. However, a South American *Spizaetus* is close to *Harpagornis* on my phylogenetic tree.

The phylogenetic tree

I did not expect to derive a single principal tree topology from the array of qualitative osteological characters used. Livezey (1986) found 50 equal-length trees for the Anseriformes, using 120 characters that for the most part were established, and ordered transition series. However, Siegel-Causey (1988) obtained one tree from 137 characters for 30 species.

The overall consistency indices for both these studies were much higher than found here. This could have resulted from my characters being less well defined, the complexity of the variation within the group (Jollie 1976, 1977a, 1977b, 1977c), and the short time available to me to assess character states over more species within each genus, and of the large number of taxa. It was less easy to 'mine' the literature for characters, because previous studies (e.g., Amadon 1953, 1978, 1982a, 1982b; Brown 1982; Brown & Amadon 1968; Friedmann 1950) concentrated on details of bill, legs, and wing and tail proportions.

Archie (1989) questioned the value of consistency indices (Kluge & Farris 1969) as measures of the efficiency of the analysis, who emphasised the inverse relationship between the number of taxa studied and the consistency index, and between the consistency index and the number of characters.

The consistency index obtained here (0.217), although low, is at a level to be expected in analyses of more than 40 taxa, using well over 100 characters (Archie 1989, fig. 5a). The number of steps per character (8.9) was above those given for missing value data, but less than for 2-state data. However, if Archie's (1989) fig. 1 plots are extrapolated to 45 taxa (as used here), there is closer agreement in number of steps per character.

While the low consistency index may result largely from intrinsic properties of large data sets (Archie 1989), examination of the character state changes suggests that evolution within the group has been by changes in suites of minor features within historical, phylogenetic, and broad functional constraints (Seilacher 1979).

Homoplasies and character-state reversals rather than absolute synapomorphies characterise most clades within the Accipitridae. Superficial resemblances in external characters have often formed the basis of classifications within and between genera (Amadon 1982b - sub-buteonines; Wattel 1973 - accipiters), but these were shown to reflect adaptation to a limited range of niches available for raptors. An indication of the ability of different lineages to give rise to ecological correlates is the strong external resemblance of *Ictinia* to the *Elanus* kites in colour pattern, proportions, and behaviour. In its skeleton, as Shufeldt (1891) noted long ago and was confirmed here, *Ictinia* is very close to *Buteo*.

External resemblances of phylogenetically distinct lines have resulted in the complex and fluid higher taxonomy of the Accipitridae (reviewed by Sibley & Ahlquist (1972)). A feature of the tree presented here is the association of groups of species long thought to be related on general resemblances, such as the milvine kites and sea eagles and the accipitrid vultures and serpent eagles.

Although it is comforting that the tree topology incorporates existing arrangements, this is not a valid test of the hypothesised relationships presented here. Indeed, Panchen (1982) has argued that parsimony, the basic assumption of the techniques used here, is inconsistent with the hypothetico-deductive model of science, as championed by Popper (1959) and there is no satisfactory test of such trees. My results, however, support the view of Kemp & Crowe (1990) that a cladistic approach is useful in resolving some of the more controversial aspects of accipitrid relationships, despite Jollie's (1976) doubts. With our present profound ignorance of the relationships within and without the family (Olson 1985), no approach should be dismissed completely. Results of this and Kemp & Crowe's (1990) can now be tested against information from other sources, such as DNA studies.

Choice of characters

The features chosen for this study tended to be those that described the shape and structure of individual elements, so that they could be of maximum use for analysis of fossil taxa. Some were more 'descriptive' than is usual in comparative morphology. All features used displayed recognisable variation within the group, or between the group and the outgroups used and therefore can be considered as characters suitable for analysis by maximum parsimony techniques.

That the analysis converged on two closely similar trees (differing only on the position of a single taxon within a major clade) without a priori or a posteriori weighting of features suggests that noise from 'poorer' characters was overcome by the use of large numbers of features. For an exploratory study such as this, use of many characters can not only result in the discovery of basic pattern as a guide to forming hypotheses on smaller subsets more amenable to analysis, but also allows an evaluation of the variability of new characters.

Raptor ecology and homoplasy

The results revealed the complex nature of the variation in characters among different clades within the family. This was apparent in the few osteological characters such as the procoracoid foramen and fused pedal phalanges whose distribution and taxonomic value have been discussed previously (Olson 1982, 1987), as well as in less well defined characters identified in my examination of the material. The frequent reversals reflect the limited variance in structure within the group, and the way morphologies have been mixed and matched in different lineages.

Symplesiomorphies were found to be a major source of confusion in discerning intrafamilial relationships.

Methodological limitations

Most of the problems with assessing character states for taxa resulted from the state and availability of specimens. Apart from the taxa that were not available in any institution, others were represented by incomplete specimens or sometimes a few bones. Others were incompletely prepared, and characters were obscured. Many taxa, especially of large eagles and vultures, were represented by captive specimens that had evidence of damage or disease associated with captivity. Some had osteoarthritic lesions that obscured characters of the lower leg bones, and several had healed broken wings.

Taxonomic conclusions

Some more general conclusions on the classification within the Accipitridae may be drawn. *Sagittarius* and *Pandion* were found to be sufficiently distinct in their osteology to warrant maintaining them as at least families. My study did not include other non-accipitrids so the proximity of *Sagittarius* to the accipitrids could not be assessed. From the profound differences in osteology, it is likely to be a distant relationship.

As has been suspected, the 'kites' proved to polyphyletic (e.g., Shufeldt 1891) within the family, representing a grade rather than a clade. *Elanus*, *Elanoides*, and *Ictinia* demonstrate how closely convergent external morphologies can be in different clades, through homoplasy and plesiomorphic traits associated with an insectivorous and lower vertebrate diet.

My phylogenetic tree provides at least partial support for Brown & Amadon's (1968) suggestion that omnivorous and scavenging kites and *Pernis*-like species are the least advanced members of the family. Brown & Amadon's 1968) hypothesis that the adaptive radiation of the Accipitridae reached various 'culmination points' in, for example, the accipitrid vultures, the harriers (*Circus*) of open country, bird-catching *Accipiter*s, and swift eagles (such as *Spizaetus*), and other large eagles (such as *Harpia*) is supported in that each of these groups represents a clade on my phylogenetic tree. However, the relationships within the *Buteo-Accipiter* clade are more complex, so all the eagles, *Buteo*s and *Accipiter* cannot be separated in this way.

To summarise the information in my preferred phylogenetic tree, I include a tentative classification of the Accipitridae. The conventions of Wiley (1981) were followed, so that the order of the branching is reflected by the list, with the earlier major clades recognised by Linnaean-style inclusive group names to tribal level. This classification goes to a much lower taxonomic level (tribe) than other recent treatments to emphasise what I see as potentially the most fruitful areas for future research.

CLASSIFICATION OF THE ACCIPITRIDAE - BASED ON THE PHYLOGENETIC TREE PRESENTED HERE
(using conventions suggested by Wiley (1981)

Order Ciconiiformes (sensu Sibley & Ahlquist 1990)

Family Pandionidae (Sclater & Salvin, 1873)
Family Accipitridae (Vieillot, 1816)
    Subfamily Elanoidinae Shufeldt, 1891
        Elanoides
    Subfamily Elaninae Blyth, 1849
        Elanus
        Gampsonyx (incertae sedis)
        Chelictinia (incertae sedis)
    Subfamily Gypaetinae Vieillot, 1816
        Tribe Gypaetini Vieillot, 1816

Gypohierax
Pernis
Neophron
Gypaetus
Necrosyrtes
Aegypius
Gyps
Tribe Circaetini Blyth, 1849
Polyboroides
Terathopius
Spilornis
Circaetus
Subfamily Circinae Bonaparte, 1838
Circus
Geranospiza
Subfamily Machaerhamphinae **new name**
Machaerhamphus
Subfamily Milvinae Vigors, 1824
Tribe Buteogallini new name
Buteogallus
Tribe Milvinae Vigors, 1824
Milvus
Haliastur
Haliaeetus
Ichthyophaga
Subfamily Accipitrinae (Vieillot, 1816)
Geranoaetus
Heterospizias
Aquila
Harpagornis†
Spizaetus
Busarellus
Hieraaetus
Polemaetus
Harpia
Stephanoaetus
Lophaetus
Pithecophaga
Morphnus
Kaupifalco
Ictinia
Harpagus
Melierax
Accipiter
Leucopternis
Parabuteo
Buteo

The higher classification of Haast's Eagle therefore becomes:

Order Ciconiiformes
Family Accipitridae
Subfamily Accipitrinae
Genus *Harpagornis* Haast, 1872
Harpagornis moorei Haast, 1872

If the higher classification of Sibley & Ahlquist (1990) is not fol*lowed, the ordinal name should* be Accipitriformes (Vieillot), as listed by Brodkorb (1964).

Further progress in morphological studies of the evolutionary history of the accipitrids will involve refining the set of osteological characters and integrating data from other sources such as cytology, as has been done by Kemp & Crowe (1990). Results of biochemical analyses, should be especially illuminating.

ACKNOWLEDGEMENTS

I thank Storrs Olson (NMNH), Dick Zusi (NMNH), Phil Angle (NMNH), Philip Burton (BMNH), Graham Cowles (BMNH), Jo Bailey (BMNH), John Darby (OMNZ), Bev McCulloch (CMNZ), and Phil Millener (NMNZ) for access to collections in their care and assistance with specimens. The work benefited from discussions with Alan Kemp (Transvaal Museum), Mike Winterbourn, and Ewan Fordyce. Ricardo Palma provided much-needed assistance with the literature of Mallophaga. Mike Winterbourn constructively criticised various drafts of the MS. I thank especially Phil and Jennie Burton, Jane Kestner, and Mike and Kerri Beardsell for hospitality above and beyond the call of duty on various study trips. Maureen and Scott provided essential moral and physical support for the duration.

I gratefully acknowledge financial support from several funding agencies. The research was completed while I was in receipt of a New Zealand University Grants Committee Post-Graduate Scholarship. Research at the British Museum (Natural History) and in the United States was made possible by a Prince and Princess of Wales Science Scholarship of The Royal Society of New Zealand. A Short-Term Visitor Travel Grant from the Office of Fellowships and Grants, Smithsonian Institution allowed me to examine material at the National Museum of Natural History. Basic support was provided throughout by the Main South Road Voluntary Scientific Support Foundation.

REFERENCES

AMADON, D. 1953. Remarks on the Asiatic Hawk-eagles of the genus *Spizaetus*. *Ibis* ***95***: 492-500.

AMADON, D. 1961. Remarks on the genus *Buteogallus*. *Novedades Colombianus* ***1(6)***: 358-360.

AMADON, D. 1964. Taxonomic notes on birds of prey. *American Museum novitates* ***2166***: 1-24.

AMADON, D. 1977. Notes on the taxonomy of vultures. *Condor* ***79***: 413-416.

AMADON, D. 1978. Remarks on the taxonomy of some Australian raptors. *Emu* ***78***: 115-118.

AMADON, D. 1982a. A revision of the sub-buteonine hawks (Accipitridae, Aves). *American Museum novitates* ***2741***: 1-20.

AMADON, D. 1982b. The genera of booted eagles: *Aquila* and relatives. *Journal of the Yamashina Institute of Ornithology* ***14***: 108-121.

ARCHIE, J.W. 1989. Homoplasy excess ratios: new indices for measuring levels of homoplasy in phylogenetic systematics and a critique of the consistency index. *Systematic zoology* ***38(3)***: 253-269.

BALLMANN, P. 1969. Die Vögel aus der altburdigalen Spaltenfüllung von Wintershof (West) bei Eichstätt in Bayern. *Zitteliana* ***1***: 5-60.

BALLMANN, P. 1973. Fossile Vogel aus dem Neogen der Halbinsel Gargano (Italien). *Scripta geologica* ***17***: 1-75.

BAUMEL, J.J. 1979. Osteologia. *In*: Baumel, J.J.; King, A.S.; Lucas, A.M.; Breazile, J.E.; Evans, H.E. (*ed.*) *Nomina anatomica avium: an annotated anatomical dictionary of birds*: 53-119. Academic Press, London.

BEDDARD, F.E. 1889. On certain points in the anatomy of the Accipitres, with reference to the affinities of *Polyboroides*. *Proceedings of the Zoological Society of London* ***59***: 77-82.

BEDDARD, F.E. 1898. *The structure and classification of birds*. Longmans, Green, London.

BIRNIE, J.F. & ROBERTS, D.E. 1986. Evidence of Tertiary forest in the Falkland Islands (Islas Malvinas). *Paleogeography, paleoclimatology, paleoecology* ***55***: 45-53.

BLANDAMER, J.S. & BURTON, P.J.K. 1979. Anatomical specimens of birds in the collections of the British Museum (Natural History). *Bulletin of the British Museum (Natural History) (Zoology)* ***34(4)***: 125-180.

BRATHWAITE, D.H. & HOLDAWAY, R.N. 1987. A preliminary reconstruction of *Harpagornis moorei*: top predator in the moa's world [Abstract]. *New Zealand journal of ecology* ***10***: 162.
BRODKORB, P. 1960. The skeleton and systematic position of *Gampsonyx*. *Auk* ***77***: 88-89.
BRODKORB, P. 1964. Catalogue of fossil birds Part 2 (Anseriformes through Galliformes). *Bulletin of the Florida State Museum, Biological sciences* ***8***: 195-335.
BROOKS, D.R. 1985. Historical ecology: a new approach to studying the evolution of ecological associations. *Annals of the Missouri Botanical Garden* ***72***: 660-680.
BROWN, L.H. 1982. Genus *Stephanoaetus*. *In:* Brown, L.H., Urban, E.K. & Newman, K. (ed.) *The birds of Africa, vol. 1:* 429-433. Academic Press, London.
BROWN, L.H. & AMADON, D. 1968. *Eagles, hawks and falcons of the World.* Country Life Books, London. 2 vol.
BURTON, P.J.K. 1978. The intertarsal joint of the harrier-hawks *Polyboroides* spp and the Crane Hawk *Geranospiza caerulescens*. *Ibis* ***120***: 171-177.
CLAY, T. 1951. The Mallophaga and relationships within the Falconiformes. *Ibis* ***93***: 628.
CLAY, T. 1958. Revisions of Mallophaga genera. *Degeeriella* from the Falconiformes. *Bulletin of the British Museum (Natural History) (Entomology)* ***7(4)***: 121-207.
COMPTON, L.V. 1938. The pterylosis of the Falconiformes with special attention to the taxonomic position of the osprey. *University of California publications in zoology* ***42***: 173-211.
COX, C.B. 1990. New geological theories and old biogeographical problems. *Journal of biogeography* ***17***: 117-130.
CRACRAFT, J. & RICH, P.V. 1972. The systematics and evolution of the Cathartidae in the Old World Tertiary. *Condor* ***74***: 272-283.
de BOER, L.E.M. 1975. Karyological heterogeneity in the Falconiformes (Aves). *Experientia* ***31/10*** *(15.10.1975)*: 1138-1139.
de BOER, L.E.M. 1976. The somatic chromosome complements of 16 species of Falconiformes (Aves) and the karyological relationships of the order. *Genetica* ***46***: 77-113.
de BOER, L.E.M. & SINOO, R.P. 1984. A karyological study of Accipitridae (Aves: Falconiformes), with karyotypic descriptions of 16 species new to cytology. *Genetica* ***65***: 89-107.
DUFF, R. 1949. *Pyramid Valley*. Friends of the Canterbury Museum, Christchurch. 48 p.
EMSLIE, S.D. 1988. The fossil history and phylogenetic relationships of condors (Ciconiiformes: Vulturidae) in the New World. *Journal of vertebrate paleontology* ***8(2)***: 212-228.
FORDYCE, R.E. 1991. A new look at the fossil vertebrate record of New Zealand. *In*: Rich, P.V.; Monaghan, V.M.; Baird, R.F. Rich, T.H. (*ed.*) *Vertebrate palaeontology of Australasia*. pp. 1191-1316. Pioneer Design Studio and Monash University, Melbourne.
FRIEDMANN, H. 1950. The birds of North and Middle America. Part XI Order Falconiformes: Diurnal birds of prey. *Bulletin of the United States National Museum* ***50***: 1-527.
FÜRBRINGER, M. 1888. *Untersuchungen zur Morphologie und Systematik der Vögel, zugleich ein Beitrag zur Anatomie der Stutz- und Bewegungsorgane*. van Holkema, Amsterdam. 2 vol. 1751 p.
HAAST, J. 1872. On *Harpagornis*, an extinct gigantic bird of prey, containing description of femur, ungual phalanges, and rib. *Transactions and proceedings of the New Zealand Institute 4 [1871]*: 192-196.
HENNIG, W. 1966. *Phylogenetic systematics*. University of Illinois Press, Urbana.
HOWARD, H. 1929. The avifauna of Emeryville shellmound. *University of California publications in zoology* ***32(2)***: 301-394.
HOWARD, H. 1932. Eagles and eagle-like vultures of the Pleistocene of Rancho La Brea. *Carnegie Institute of Washington publication* ***429*** *[Contributions to palaeontology]*: 1-111.
HUDSON, G.E. 1948. Studies on the muscles of the pelvic appendage in birds II. The heterogeneous Order Falconiformes. *American midland naturalist* ***39(1)***: 102-127.
JOLLIE, M. 1953. Are the Falconiformes a monophyletic group? *Ibis* ***95***: 369-371.
JOLLIE, M. 1976. A contribution to the morphology and phylogeny of the Falconiformes, part 1. *Evolutionary theory* ***1***: 285-298.
JOLLIE, M. 1977a. A contribution to the morphology and phylogeny of the Falconiformes, part 1. *Evolutionary theory* ***2(4)***: 285-298.
JOLLIE, M. 1977b. A contribution to the morphology and phylogeny of the Falconiformes, part 2. *Evolutionary theory* ***2(5)***: 285-298.
JOLLIE, M. 1977c. A contribution to the morphology and phylogeny of the Falconiformes, part 3. *Evolutionary theory* ***3(1)***: 285-298.

KEMP, A.C. & CROWE, T.M. 1990. A preliminary phylogenetic and biogeographic analysis of the genera of diurnal raptors. *In:* Peters, G. & Hutterer, R. (ed.) *Vertebrates in the tropics:* 161-175.
KLUGE, A.G. & J.S. FARRIS 1969. Quantitative phyletics and the evolution of anurans. *Systematic zoology* ***18***: 1-32.
KÖNIG, C. 1982. Zur systematische Stellung der Neuweltgeier (Cathartidae). *Journal für Ornithologie* ***123(3)***: 259-267.
LIGON, J.D. 1967. Relationships of the cathartid vultures. *Occasional papers of the Museum of Zoology, University of Michigan* ***651***: 1-26.
LIVEZEY, B.C. 1986. A phylogenetic analysis of recent anseriform genera using morphological characters. *Auk* ***103***: 73-754.
MAYR, E. 1944. Timor and the colonization of Australia by birds. *Emu* ***46***: 113-130.
MILLER, L.H. 1937. Skeletal studies of the tropical hawk *Harpagus*. *Condor* ***39***: 219-221.
MILNE-EDWARDS, A. 1867-1871. *Recherches anatomiques et paléontologiques pour servir à l'histoire des oiseaux fossiles de la France*. 4 vol. V. Masson et Fils, Paris.
NELSON, R.C. & PRICE, R.D. 1965. The *Laemobothrion* (Mallophaga: Laemobothriidae) of the Falconiformes. *Journal of medical entomology* ***2(3)***: 249-257.
OLIVER, W.R.B. 1930. *New Zealand birds*. Fine Arts, Wellington..
OLIVER, W.R.B. 1945. Avian evolution in New Zealand and Australia. *Emu* ***45***: 55-77, 119-152.
OLIVER, W.R.B. 1955. *New Zealand birds, 2nd ed.* A.H. & A.W. Reed, Wellington.
OLSON, S.L. 1982. The distribution of fused phalanges of the inner toe in the Accipitridae. *Bulletin of the British Ornithologists' Club* ***102(1)***: 8-12.
OLSON, S.L. 1985. The fossil record of birds. *In:* Farner, D.S., King, J.R. & Parkes, K.C. (ed.) *Avian biology, vol. VIII:* 79-252. Academic Press, London.
OLSON, S.L. 1987. Variation in the procoracoid foramen in the Accipitridae. *Rivista Italiana ornitologia, Milano* ***57(3-4)***: 1-4.
OLSON, S.L. 1991. Patterns of avian diversity and radiation in the Pacific as seen through the fossil record. *In*: Dudley, E.C. (*ed.*) *The unity of evolutionary biology. Vol. 1*: 314-318. Dioscorides Press, Portland Oregon.
OLSON, S.L. & H.F. JAMES 1991. Descriptions of thirty-two new species of birds from the Hawaiian Islands. Part I. Non-Passeriformes. *Ornithological monographs* ***45***: 1-88.
OWEN, H.G. 1983. *Atlas of continental displacement, 200 million years to the present.* Cambridge University Press, New York. 159 p.
OWEN, H.G. 1990. [Letter] Of gaps and globes. Comments on the Guest Essay 'New geological theories and old biogeographical problems' by C.B. Cox (1990). *Journal of biogeography* ***17***: 693-695.
OWEN, R. 1879. Memoir on the trunk and limbs of a gigantic bird of prey (*Harpagornis moorei*, von Haast). *In*: *Memoirs on the extinct wingless birds of New Zealand; with an appendix on those of England, Australia, Newfoundland, Mauritius, Rodriguez.* J van Voorst, London.
PANCHEN, A.L. 1982. The use of parsimony in testing phylogenetic hypotheses. *Zoological journal of the Linnaean Society* ***74***: 305-328.
POCKNALL, D.T. 1989. Late Eocene to Early Miocene vegetation and climate history of New Zealand. *Journal of the Royal Society of New Zealand* ***19(1)***: 1-18.
POPPER, K.R. 1959. *The logic of scientific discovery*. Hutchinson, London. 479 p.
RAIKOW, R.J. 1985. Problems in avian classification. *Current ornithology* ***2***: 187-212.
RICH, P.V. 1975. Antarctic dispersal routes, wandering continents, and the origin of Australia's non-passerine avifauna. *Memoirs of the National Museum of Victoria* ***36***: 63-125.
RICH, P.V. 1980. 'New World vultures' with Old World affinities? *Contributions to vertebrate evolution* ***5***: 1-115.
RICH, P.V. 1991. The Mesozoic and Tertiary history of birds of the Australian plate. *In*: Rich, P.V.; Monaghan, V.M.; Baird, R.F. & Rich, T.H. (*ed.*) *Vertebrate palaeontology of Australasia*: 721-808. Pioneer Design Studio and Monash University, Melbourne.
RICH, P.V. & R.F. BAIRD 1986. History of the Australian avifauna. *Current ornithology* ***4***: 97-139.
RICH, P.V. & G.F. van TETS 1982. Fossil birds of Australia and New Guinea: their biogeographic, phylogenetic and biostratigraphic input. *In*: Rich, P.V.; Thompson, E.M. (*ed.*) *The fossil vertebrate record of Australasia*. pp. 235-384. Monash University, Melbourne.
RIDGWAY, R. 1873. Catalogue of the ornithological collection of the Boston Society of Natural History. Part II. Falconidae. *Proceedings of the Boston Society of Natural History* ***16***: 43-106.
RYTTMAN, H.; H. TEGELSTROM; K. FREDGA & J. SONDELL 1987. The karyotype of the osprey,

Pandion haliaetus (Aves: Falconiformes). *Genetica* ***74***: 143-147.
SEILACHER, A. 1979. Constructional morphology of sand dollars. *Paleobiology* ***5***: 191-221.
SHUFELDT, R.W. 1891. Some comparative osteological notes on the North-American kites. *Ibis* ***6*** *series 3*: 228-232.
SHUFELDT, R.W. 1896. On the affinities of *Harpagornis*: a letter dated 25th January, 1895 to Professor T. Jeffery Parker by R.W. Shufeldt, M.D., Smithsonian Institution, Washington. *Transactions and proceedings of the New Zealand Institute* ***28 (1895)***: 665.
SHUFELDT, R.W. 1919. Osteological and other notes on the Monkey-eating Eagle of the Philippines, *Pithecophaga jefferyi* Grant. *Philippine journal of science* ***15(1)***: 33-58.
SIBLEY, C.G. & J.E. AHLQUIST 1972. A comparative study of the egg white proteins of non-passerine birds. *Peabody Museum of Natural History bulletin 39.*
SIBLEY, C.G. & J.E. AHLQUIST 1985. The phylogeny and classification of the Australo-Papuan passerine birds. *Emu* ***85(1)***: 1-14.
SIBLEY, C.G. & J.E. AHLQUIST, 1990. *Phylogeny and classification of birds.* Yale University Press, New Haven & London.
SIEGEL-CAUSEY, D. 1988. Phylogeny of the Phalacrocoracidae. Condor **90**: 885-905.
STRESEMANN, E. & D. AMADON 1979. Falconiformes. *In:* Mayr, E. & Cottrell, G.W. (ed.) *Checklist of the birds of the world, vol. 1, 2nd ed:* 271-425.
SUSCHKIN, P. 1899. Beiträge zur Classification der Tagraubvögel mit Zugrundelegung der osteologischen Merkmale. *Zoologischer Anzeiger* ***22***: 500-518.
SUSCHKIN, P. 1900. Systematische Ergebnisse osteologischer Untersuchungen einiger Tagraubvögel. *Zoologischer Anzeiger* ***23***: 269-277.
SUSCHKIN, P. 1905. Zur Morphologie des Vögelskeletets. Vergleichende Osteologie der Normalen Tagraubvögel (Accipitres) und die Fragen der Classification. Teil I. Grundeinteilung der Accipitres. *Nouvelle mémoires Société Naturaliste, Moscou* ***16***: 1-65.
SWANN, H.K. 1924-1945. *A monograph of the birds of prey (order Accipitres).* 16 pts. (6-16 edited by A. Wetmore). Weldon & Wesley, London.
SWOFFORD, D.L. 1985. *PAUP: phylogenetic analysis using parsimony. Version 2.4.* Illinois Natural History Survey, Champaign. 67 p.
TYLER, C. 1966. A study of the eggshells of the Falconiformes. *Journal of zoology, London* ***150***: 413-425.
VOOUS, K.H. & H.J.W. WIJSMAN 1964. Notes on the African Hawk-eagles. *Biologischer Jaarbucher: Dodonaea, Ghent* ***32***: 151-163.
WATTEL, J. 1973. Geographical differentiation in the genus *Accipiter. Publications of the Nuttall Ornithological Club, no. 13.* 231 p.
WILEY, E.O. 1981. *Phylogenetics: the theory and practice of phylogenetic systematics.* Wiley-Interscience, New York.
WILLIAMS, R.M. & R.J. BENIRSCHKE 1976. The chromosomes of four species of Falconiformes. *Experientia* ***32/3***: 310-311.
WITHERBY, H.F., F.C.R. JOURDAIN, N.F. TICEHURST & B.W. TUCKER 1939. *Handbook of British birds, vol. III.* H.G. & F. Witherby, London.

R. N. Holdaway
Dept. of Zoology
University of Canterbury
Private Bag, Christchurch
New Zealand

APPENDIX 1

Material examined for phylogenetic study of the Accipitridae, listed alphabetically within families.

Institutions: BMNH, Sub-department of Ornithology, British Museum (Natural History) - now Natural History Museum - Tring, England (no prefix to specimen number); NMNH, National Museum of Natural History, Smithsonian Institution, Washington, D.C., U.S.A. (all numbers prefixed USNM); NMNZ, National Museum of New Zealand, Wellington, New Zealand (numbers prefixed S).

SPECIMENS

Pandionidae

Pandion haliaetus, 1851.11.10.65, incomplete; *Pandion haliaetus carolinensis*, ✝,USNM 18466, Chesapeake Bay, **captivity**, 3 Jan 1969; *Pandion haliaetus carolinensis*, USNM 851, Carlisle, Pennsylvania.

Sagittariidae

Sagittarius serpentarius, S/1952.3.198, South Africa; USNM 321578, Cape of Good Hope, South Africa, Sep 1865.

Accipitridae

Accipiter nisus, ✝, S/1987.31.1, Witley, Surrey, England, 9 Aug 1987; ✏, immature, 1910.10.2.1, 12 Oct 1910; /, USNM 554271, Assen, Holland, 15 Feb 1979; *Aegypius monachus*, 1872.10.25.5; ✏, USNM 428040, captivity, 29 Aug 1949; *Aquila audax*, ✏, 1898.5.7.6, Sydney; *Aquila chrysaetos*, S/1973.66.57, captivity; ✝, adult, USNM 491476, Alaska, 1973(?); *Aviceda leuphotes*, 1845.1.12.30, Nepal; *Aviceda subcristata rufa*, ✏, Obi Besar, Moluccas, Indonesia, 29 Jul 1982; *Busarellus nigricollis*, ✝, 1895.3.10.7, 6 Sep 1895 [first identified as *Heterospizias meridionalis*: note by P Suschkin in box, changing identification]; USNM 345773, between Caceres and Concepcion, 6 Oct 1940; *Butastur liventer*, 1850.8.15.79, Java; *Butastur indicus*, USNM 223986, Cavite, Philippines, Feb 13 1916, skull; *Buteo buteo*, S/1952.1.173, Llwyngwair, N. Pembrokeshire, 1916; USNM 556291, Ede, Holland, 16 Apr 1981; *Hypomorphnus [=Buteogallus] urubitinga*, 1858.5.26.12; *Buteogallus urubitinga urubitinga*, ✝, USNM 319433, Caimancito, Argentina, Jun 1930; *Chelictinia riocourii*, 1904.4.28.3, Gambia; ✏, USNM 569279, Kelam, Ethiopia, 15 Mar 1975, leg bones removed from skin; *Chondrohierax uncinatus uncinatus*, USNM 289784, Santa Marta region, Colombia; *Circaetus gallicus*, 1930.3.24.261; ✏, USNM 430827, Essex Vale, Southern Rhodesia [Zimbabwe], 15 Sep 1958; *Circus aeruginosus aeruginosus*, 1924.5.31.234, captivity, Apr 1897; ✝, USNM 557495, Kyzyl-Agach, Azerbaijan, USSR, Jan 1977; *Elanoides forficatus*, 1902.2.2.25, Texas; ✝, USNM 289686, Holopaw, Florida, 27 Apr 1925; *Elanus caeruleus*, ✝, 1898.5.7.10, South Africa, 27 Sep 1894; *Elanus caeruleus caeruleus*, ✏, USNM 558447, 23 km north of Capetown, Cape Province, Republic of South Africa, 12 Mar 1981; *Erythrotriorchis radiatus*, 1872.10.22.9, Cape York [Australia] [=*Haliastur sphenurus*]; *Gampsonyx swainsonii*, ✏, USNM 345789, Tres Barras, Brazil, 2 Jul 1941; *Geranoaetus melanoleucos*, ✏, S/1954.10.3, southwest South America, captivity, 6 May 1954; USNM 318388, Cachapol River, Chile; *Geranospiza caerulescens*, 1903.12.20, Serra da Chapada, central Brazil, Jun 1902; *Geranospiza caerulescens nigra*, USNM 18450, Orizaba, Mexico; *Gypaetus barbatus*, 1911.2.9.2; USNM 17834, Algeria, 1842; *Gypohierax angolensis*, 1850.11.13.14; ✝, USNM 291316, Efulan, Cameroun, West Africa, 7 Apr 1927; *Gyps africanus*, S/1983.19.6, Karoi, 1647S, 2935E, 1983; *Gyps fulvus*, 1861.2.26.6, captivity, 30+ years; *Gyps ruepelli*, ✝, USNM 430014, captivity, 2 Feb 1958; *Haliaeetus albicilla*, 1851.11.10.46✝; *Haliaeetus leucocephalus*, 1930.3.24.262, May 1911; ✝, USNM 431884, Yakutat, Alaska, Jan 1961; *Haliastur indicus*, USNM 556985, Jailolo District, Halmahera Is, Moluccas, Indonesia, 2 Apr 1981; *Haliastur sphenurus*, S/1964.1.14, Harrow, Victoria, Australia, 24 Jan 1963; *Harpagornis moorei*, ✏✝, NMNZ S 27773, Mount

Owen, Nelson, New Zealand, Jan 1990; *Harpagus dentatus*, USNM 559320, 10 miles up Cuyuni River, Guyana, 8 Jan 1984; *Harpia harpyja*, 1872.10.25.1; ✏, USNM 429223, captivity, Nov 2 1949; ✏, USNM 429223, captivity, 2 Nov 1949; *Harpyhaliaetus solitarius*, USNM 49656, San Geronimo, Guatemala, 2 leg bones ex skin same number; *Heterospizias meridionalis*, ✏, 1903.12.20.1, Serra da Chapada, central Brazil; *Heterospizias meridionalis meridionalis*, USNM 227378, Puerto Pinasco, Paraguay, 8 Sep 1920; *Hieraaetus fasciatus*, 1847.10.21.50; *Hieraaetus fasciatus spilogaster*, †, USNM 430796, Mphoengs, Southern Rhodesia [Zimbabwe], 18 Aug 1958; *Ichthyophaga ichthyaetus*, 1845.1.12.20; USNM 468555, captivity, 7 Jan 1958; *Ichthyophaga humilis [=nana]*, †, USNM 224807, Toli Toli, Celebes [Sulawesi], Indonesia, 8 Dec 1914; *Ictinaetus malayensis*, ✏, S/1969.1.1, Gunong Benom, Malaya; *Ictinia plumbea*, †, 1903.12.20.253, Serra da Chapada, Brazil, 29 Oct 1902; *Kaupifalco monogrammicus*, †, 1869.10.19.28, Africa; †, USNM 322456, Cameroun, West Africa, 10 Apr 1931; *Leptodon cayenensis*, ✏, USNM 32973, Central America, feet only; *Leucopternis (albicollis†) polionota*, 1846.4.21.18; *Leucopternis melanops*, ✏, USNM 432181, captivity, 23 Jul 1963; *Lophaetus occipitalis*, 1861.1.19.6; †, USNM 291451, Temkaka, Sudan, Africa, 28 Feb 1928; *Machaerhamphus alcinus*, ✏, adult, S/1956.20.1, Gomantong, North Borneo, 16 Apr 1956; USNM 559816, Gomantong Caves, 35 km south of Sandakan, Sabah, Malaysia, Dec 1982; *Melierax musicus* (*M. canorus*), 1903.1.6.13, Deelfontein; *Melierax gabar*, †, USNM 290384, Africa, Oct 28 1926; *Milvus milvus milvus*, †, 1940.7.6.1, Wales; *Milvus migrans lineatus*, ✏, USNM 319228, Szechwan, China, 21 Jul 1930; *Morphnus guianensis*, 1851.12.2.10; †, USNM 432243, captivity, 4 Aug 1963, trunk skeleton; USNM 18468, skull; *Necrosyrtes monachus*, 1860.1.19.8, Natal; USNM 18894, Cunga, Angola, West Africa; *Neophron percnopterus*, 1847.10.21.25, South Africa; USNM 17835, North Africa; *Parabuteo unicinctus harrisi*, ✏, 1900.11.30.30, Brownsville, Texas, 6 May 1900; †, USNM 343414, Starr County, Texas, Jul 25 1936; *Pernis apivorus*, 1871.12.29.3; *Pernis apivorus gurneyi*, USNM 343983; Chiengmai, northern Siam [Thailand], 20 Jan 1937; *Pithecophaga jefferyi*, S/1961.23.1, captivity, Nov 1961; †, captivity, 30 Jun 1970; *Polyboroides radiatus*, 1860.12.31.1, Natal; *Polyboroides typus*, ✏, USNM 291787, Efulan, Cameroun, West Africa, 4 Feb 1928; *Polemaetus bellicosus*, S/1957.9.1, Africa, captivity, 20 May 1957; †, USNM 430533, Syringa, Southern Rhodesia [Zimbabwe], 30 Nov 1957; *Rostrhamus sociabilis*, †, USNM 553612, Buenos Aires, Argentina, 4 Mar 1966, captivity; *Spilornis cheela bassus*, 1850.8.15.14, India; *Spilornis cheela*, 1845.1.12.12, Nepal; *Spilornis cheela burmanicus*, †, USNM 343985, San Sai Luang (near Chiengmai), northern Siam [Thailand], 27 Feb 1936; *Spizaetus ornatus*, S/1952.1.177; †, USNM 430495, captivity, 15 Mar 1958; *Spizastur melanoleucos*, USNM 321507, Velhas River, Brazil, 1866; *Stephanoaetus coronatus*, ✏, S/1954.30.42; †, USNM 346652, captivity, 15 May 1943; *Terathopius ecaudatus*, 1853.1.21.2, South Africa; †, USNM 431431, Norton, Southern Rhodesia [Zimbabwe], 3 Jul 1961; *Urotriorchis macrourus batesi*, †, USNM 292398, Efulan, Cameroun, West Africa, Aug 6 1928.

APPENDIX 2

Features evaluated for and used (bold type) in preliminary and final runs of PAUP (Swofford 1984).

No	Code	Feature [codes for feature states and intermediates]
1	CR1	Median ridge of palatal surface of rostrum: a, obliterating median groove; b, not obliterating groove [a/0 b/1]
2	**CR2**	Palatal processes of premaxilla: a, fused together; b, free; c, bony septal bar; d, in contact, not fused; e, in contact anteriorly, fused posteriorly [a/0 a-b/1 b/2 c/3 d/4 e/5]
3	CR3	Tip of vomer: a, not bridging gap between palatine processes of premaxilla; b, bridging gap [a/0 b/1]
4	**CR4**	Maxillo-palatines and palatines: a, not widely separated or with strong rostral bar; b, widely separated, with strong rostral bar [a/0 b/1]
5	CR5	Posterolateral angle of palatine: a, square, long parallel margin; b, tapered to pterygoid

		process; c, evenly rounded; d, rounded and notched [a/0 b/1 c/2 d/3]
6	CR6	Palatine fossa: a, not excavated, no choanal ridge; b, well excavated, strong choanal ridge medially [a/0 b/0]
7	CR7	Vomer: a, absent; b, thin, laterally compressed splint; c, slender, with anterior knob; d, nearly tubular, inflated [a/0 b/1 c/2 d/3]
8	CR8	Posteropterygoids: a, clasping parasphenoid rostrum; b, not clasping rostrum [a/0 b/0]
9	CR9	Dorsal surface of maxillopalatine processes: a, fused with ventral wall of vestibule; b, free, forming lateral part of vestibule floor [a/0 b/1]
10	**CR10**	Prefrontal: a, free; b, in contact with frontal and with lateral ethmoid but not fused; c, fused with frontal and with lateral ethmoid [a/0 b/1 c/2]
11	**CR11**	Orbital process of prefrontal: a, curved posteriad; b, flat, spatulate; c, curved rostrad; d, straight [a/0 b/1 c/2 d/3]
12	**CR12**	Posterior margin of supraorbital process of prefrontal: a, pointed to attenuated; b, squared off or notched; c, inflated [a/0 b/1 c/2]
13	CR13	Superciliary: a, present, well-developed; b, absent or rudimentary [a/0 b/1]
14	**CR14**	Lateral wall of nasal vestibule: a, not, or poorly, ossified; b, ossified [a/0 b/1]
15	**CR15**	Zygomatic process of squamosal: a, well-developed; b, absent or rudimentary; c, present but reduced [a/0 b/1 c/2]
16	**CR16**	Articular process of squamosal: a, well-developed; b, absent or rudimentary [a/0 b/1]
17	**CR17**	Tympanic margin: a, not flared; b, flared laterally into a more or less rectangular plate; c, flared into curved plate; d, straight, rostrad [a/0 b/1 c/2 d/3]
18	**CR18**	Basipterygoid processes: a, usually present in adults; b, absent; c, rudimentary [a/0 a-b/1 b/2 c/3]
19	CR19	Posterior tympanic process: a, present, simple; b, absent; c, forming 'cup' around quadrate articulation [a/0 b/1 c/2]
20	CR20	Median basiparasphenoid process: a, absent; b, median tubercle at caudal end of a median ridge; c, several, separated, tubercles; d, irregular transverse ridge [a/0 b/1 c/2 d/3]
21	CR20A	Lateral basiparasphenoid process: a, absent; b, a ridge; c, a prominent swelling [a/0 b/1 c/2]
22	**CR21**	Interorbital septum: a, perforate; b, small perforation; c, imperforate [a/0 b/1 c/2]
23	CR22	Constriction of nasal vestibule towards middle naris: a, nil; b, slight; c, distinct [a/0 b/1 c/2]
24	CR23	Quadrate articular surface: a, 'normal'; b, smoothly rounded, blending with ventral surface; medial articular surface narrow, extending along caudal margin nearly to caudal angle [a/0 b/1]
25	CR24	Small notch in quadrate: a, absent; b, present [a/0 b/1]
25A	**CR25**	Postorbital process: a, broad, flat in lateral view; b, pointed, attenuated to a spike [a/0 b/1]
26	**MA1**	Median articular processes: a, concave ventrally; b, convex ventrally [a/0 b/1]
27	**MA2**	Mandibular rami: a, bent ventrad then rostrad near distal end; b, curving ventrad, then rostrad in symphysis; c, curved evenly ventrad from at least half-way to tip [a/0 b/1 b-c/2 c/3]
28	**MA3**	Median articular process: a, with ventrocaudal flange; b, no flange [a/0 b/1]
29	**MA4**	Small tubercle (continuation of linear muscle scar running dorsoventrad across internal angle of ramus at articulation): a, present; b, absent; c, ridge [a/0 b/1 c/2]
30	**MA5**	Tubercle on median proximal face of ramus, at dorsal edge of angular: a, absent; b, small; c, large [a/0 b/1 b-c/2 c/3]
31	**MA6**	Tubercle in MA5: a, so far caudal as to be on dorsal edge, giving extra tubercle there; b, in line with coronoid process; c, between coronoid and surarticular processes; d, caudal to coronoid process [a/0 b/1 c/2 d/3]
32	**MA7**	Mandibular symphysis: a, very short; b, not short [a/0 b/1]
33	**MA8**	Rami, in dorsal view: a, bowed laterad, then sharply mediad rostrally; b, straight; c, with definite angle [a/0 b/1 c/2]
34	**MA9**	Retroarticular process: a, absent; b, small; c, large [a/0 b/1 c/2]
35	**MA10**	Dorsal edge of rami: a, turned over laterally to form a flange; b, no flange [a/0 b/1]
36	**MA11**	Tip: a, pointed; b, blunt or rounded [a/0 b/1]
37	**MA12**	Symphysis: a, excavated into U-shape; b, filled to a flat surface [a/0 b/1]
38	**FU1**	Head of clavicle: a, attenuated, pointed caudally; b, terminating more or less acutely, but not

		pointed [a/0 b/1]
39	FU2	Coracoid articular surface: a, raised from blade dorsally and ventrally; b, not raised; c, raised ventrally; d, raised dorsally
40	**FU3**	Hypocleidium: a, present; b, absent [a/0 b/1]
41	FU4	Axis of coracoidal articulation: a, in line with caudal margin of furcula at ventral end of articulation: b, at angle of less than 90°; c, at c.90° [a/0 b/1 c/2]
42	FU5	Length of coracoid articular facet: a, about equal to ramal width; b, up to two-thirds ramal width [a/0 b/1]
43	FU6	Rami bent: a, once, near dorsal end; b, once, near the centre; c, twice, dorsally and ventrally [a/0 b/1 c/2]
44	FU7	Pneumatic foramina in lateral fossa with: a, absent; b, present [a/0 b/1]
45	FU8	Dorsocaudal tip of furcula: a, in contact with acromion; b, not in contact [a/0 b/1]
46	**ST1**	Coracoidal sulci: a, separated at manubrial spine; b, closely adjacent; c, overlapping [a/0 b/1 c/2]
47	**ST2**	Number of rib articulations on costal margin: a, 4; b, 5; c, 6; d, 7 [a/0 b/1 c/2 d/3]
48	**ST3**	Sternocoracoidal impression: a, with pneumatic foramen; b, without foramen [a/0 b/1]
49	ST4	Tubercle for brace ligament: a, present; b, absent [a/0 b/1]
50	ST5	Caudal margin: a, thickened, triangular in outline; b, bluntly pointed; c, almost square, slightly indented, or notched; d, deeply square-notched, leaving acute triangle medially [a/0 b/1 c/2 d/3]
51	ST6	Sternocoracoidal fossa extending caudally to: a, 2nd costal articulation; b, 3rd articulation; c, 4th articulation; d, 5th articulation; e, 6th or 7th [a/0 b/1 c/2 d/3 e/4]
52	ST7	Sternocoracoidal process: a, with anteromedial projection; b, with no projection [a/0 b/1]
53	ST8	Lateral processes: a, present; b, rudimentary; c, absent [a/0 b/1 c/2]
54	ST9	Ventral margin of sternocoracoidal fossa: a, adjacent to *M. supracoracoideus* scar; b, well separated from scar [a/0 b/1]
55	ST10	Manubrial spine: a, short, blunt; b, long, thin [a/0 b/1]
56	ST11	Scar of *M. supracoracoideus*: a, lobed; b, with smoothly curved outline [a/0 b/1]
57	ST12	Cranial end of sternal carina: below base of manubrial spine; b, caudal to base of manubrial spine; c, well cranial to base of spine (below spine tip) [a/0 b/1 c/2]
58	ST12A	Deepest point of sternal carina: a, at cranial end; b, displaced caudad [a/0 b/1]
59	CO1	Clavicular facet in medial view: a, divided into cranial and caudal sections by shallow depression; b, a single, well-defined facet ending ventrally in sharp, projecting line; c, a separate facet on the ventrolateral surface [a/0 b/1 c/2]
60	CO2	Distinct facet on dorsal surface between lateral margin and sternocoracoidal impression: a, present; b, absent [a/0 b/1]
61	CO3	Sternocoracoidal tuberosity (posterior ligament scar): a, prominent; b, obscure; c, absent [a/0 b/1 c/2]
62	CO4	Oval or circular impression on dorsolateral surface opposite coracoidal fenestra: a, distinct; b, obscure; c, absent; d, present, proximal to coracoidal fenestra [a/0 b/1 c/2 d/3]
63	CO4A	(**CO20**) Coracoidal fenestra: a, always present; b, variable; c, absent [a/0 b/1 c/2]
64	CO5	Dorsolateral surface of head: a, with distinct fossa; b, without fossa [a/0 b/1]
65	CO6	Subclavicular fossa: a, with pneumatic foramen (-ina); without foramen (-ina) [a/0 b/1]
66	CO7	Tip of procoracoid: a, deflected ventrad; b, not deflected [a/0 b/1]
67	CO8	Sternocoracoidal process: a, short, with parallel sides [a/0 b/1 c/2 d/3]
68	CO9	Insertion of posterior ligament: a, lateral; b, near sternocoracoidal impression; c, medial; d, on coracoid shaft [a/0 b/1 c/2 d/3]
69	CO10	Sternocoracoidal impression: a, without pneumatic foramina; b, without foramina [a/0 b/1]
70	**HU1**	Brachial impression: a, extending as deep pit between proximal edges of internal and external condyles; b, not extending between condyles as pit [a/0 b/1]
71	**HU2**	Outline of proximal margin of deltoid crest: a, concave; b, straight; c, convex [a/0 b/1 c/2]
72	**HU2A**	Distal end of deltoid crest: a, running smoothly into line of shaft (except for pectoral attachment tubercle); b, with a distinct step to shaft [a/0 b/1]
73	HU2B	Apical 'crestlet' on deltoid crest: a, present; b, absent [a/0 b/1]

74	HU2C	External tuberosity: a, on line between deltoid crest and head; b, cranial to axis of head [a/0 b/1]
75	**HU2D**	Proportions of deltoid crest: a, proximal section shorter than distal; b, proximal section longer than distal; c, sections of equal length [a/0 b/1 c/2]
76	**HU2E**	Outline of distal margin of deltoid crest: a, concave; b, straight; c, convex [a/0 b/1 c/2]
77	**HU3**	Position of nutrient foramen with respect to distal end of bicipital crest: a, opposite; b, distal to; c, well distal to; d, at c. 50 % of shaft [a/0 b/1 c/2 d/3]
78	**HU4**	Position of nutrient foramen with respect to distal end of deltoid crest: a, opposite; b, proximal to; c, distal to crest [a/0 b/1 c/2]
79	**HU5**	Ligamental groove: a, entire, deep, cutting off bicipital surface; b, shallow, rectangular [a/0 b/1]
80	**HU6**	Bicipital furrow: a, deep, narrow; b, broad; c, obscure to obsolete [a/0 b/1 c/2]
81	**HU7**	Shape of bicipital surface in internal view: a, convex, evenly rounded from bicipital crest; b, flat, with small radius curve from bicipital crest; c, concave [a/0 b/1 c/2]
82	HU8	Orientation of proximal margin of internal tuberosity: a, proximad; b, distad [a/0 b/1]
83	**HU9**	Distal extension of median crest: a, running into margo caudalis (caudal margin); b, parallel to caudal margin; c, parallel to caudal margin, but with deep fossa between [a/0 b/1 c/2]
84	**HU10**	Orientation of bicipital crest to shaft, at distal end of crest: a, meeting shaft at ± 90°; b, at acute angle; c, running into line of shaft [a/0 b/1 c/2]
85	**HU11A**	Outline of internal margin of bicipital crest viewed normal to shaft: a, with definite angle proximally and distally, ± parallel to shaft between; b, ± evenly curved; c, with definite proximal and distal angles and internal margin diverging internally proximally; d, with angle to shaft distally, parallel to shaft on to internal tuberosity proximally; e, as in d but angled towards shaft proximally; f, a single angle [a/0 b/1 c/2 d/3 e/4 f/5]
86	HU12	Proportion of pneumatic fossa occupied by pneumatic foramen: a, most (>2/3); b, part (<2/3) [a/0 b/1]
87	HU13	Internal tricipital groove: a, deep, with sharp external ridge; b, shallow to obscure [a/0 b/1]
88	**HU13A**	Distal anconal fossa: a, triangular section, with internal side deepest; b, rectangular section; c, divided by strong external margin to inner tricipital groove [a/0 b/1 c/2]
89	**HU14**	Distal end of bicipital crest: a, a wide shelf; b, narrow shelf; c, no shelf [a/0 b/1 c/2]
90	HU15	Attachment of *M. infraspinatus* on proximal bicipital crest: a, elongate; b, short, rounded [a/0 b/1]
91	HU16	Attachment of *M. supraspinatus*: a, clear, raised; b, inconspicuous [a/0 b/1]
92	HU17	Extent of external tuberosity in palmar view: a, prominent; b, in line from head to deltoid crest [a/0 b/1]
93	HU18	Impression of *M. brachialis anticus* in brachial depression: a, an extended pit; b, a raised scar; c, extending proximally from brachial depression [a/0 b/1 c/2]
94	HU19	Bicipital crest: a, thick; b, thin [a/0 b/1]
95	HU20	Shaft anconal to ectepicondylar prominence: a, with fossa; b, without fossa, shaft smoothly convex [a/0 b/1]
96	**HU21**	Shape of apex of deltoid crest: a, angular, 'sharp'; b, smoothly rounded [a/0 b/1]
97	HU22	Ectepicondylar prominence: a, blunt, with or without distinct pit; b, pointed [a/0 b/1]
98	HU23	Position of deltoid crest apex: a, opposite distal end of bicipital crest; b, distal to distal end of bicipital crest [a/0 b/1]
99	**HU24**	Bicipital crest terminating as: a, sharp ridge along internal margin; b, ridge cranial to internal margin; c, very short ridge [a/0 b/1 c/2]
100	**HU25**	Distal end of median crest: a, proximal to distal end of bicipital crest; b, opposite distal end of bicipital crest [a/0 b/1]
101	**HU26**	Brachial depression: a, deep; b, shallow [a/0 b/1]
102	**HU27**	Lateral extent of ectepicondylar prominence in anconal view: a, projecting beyond external margin as strong ridge; b, not projecting beyond margin as ridge [a/0 b/1]
103	HU28	Impressions of *Mm. latissimus dorsi*: a, in shallow groove; b, not in groove [a/0 b/1]
104	**HU29**	Distal margin of bicipital surface delimited by: a, wide notch; b, faint groove, no notch; c, definite groove, but no notch; d, step [a/0 b/1 c/2 d/3]
105	HU30	'Swelling' below head, at distal end of capital groove: a, present to well-developed; b, absent;

		c, pit, not a swelling [a/0 b/1 c/2]
106	**HU31**	Shape of external tricipital groove: a, shallow or indistinct; b, deep, with raised internal border [a/0 b/1]
107	**HU32**	Caudal margin: a, rounded; b, an angle defined by planes above and below; c, as in b, but sharp angle of c. 90° [a/0 b/1 c/2]
108	**UL1**	Shape of distal end of brachialis anticus impression: a, acute; b, rounded [a/0 b/1]
109	**UL2**	Shaft proximal to trochlea: a, trochlea undercut by fossa; b, deep fossa, but not undercutting trochlea; c, fossa shallow or obscure [a/0 b/1 c/2]
110	UL3	Intermuscular line past nutrient foramen: a, sharp; b, obscure or absent [a/0 b/1]
111	**UL3A**	'Double' intermuscular line: a, reaching, or nearly so, nutrient foramen; b, merging well proximal to foramen; c, merging distal to foramen; d, single throughout length [a/0 b/1 c/2 d/3]
112	**UL4**	Proximal end of *M. brachialis anticus* impression: a, with pneumatic foramina; b, not pneumatic [a/0 b/1]
113	**UL5**	Junction between internal margin of shaft and external condyle: a, smooth; b, with pronounced step [a/0 b/1]
114	UL6	Carpal tuberosity: a, bluntly pointed; b, 'squared off' [a/0 b/1]
115	**UL7**	Proximal end of *M. brachialis anticus* impression: a, broad, shallow; b, deep groove, with internal border extended as thin shelf; c, narrow; prominence for anterior articular ligament broad [a/0 b/1 c/2]
116	UL8	Olecranon: a, acutely pointed; b, blunt [[a/0 b/1]
117	**UL9**	Outline of external condyle: a, evenly rounded; b, with distal angle = 'squared' [a/0 b/1]
118	UL10	Process beside distal tendinal pit: a, prominent; b, obscure [a/0 b/1]
119	**UL11**	Position of nutrient foramen relative to brachialis anticus impression: a, less than length of impression distal to impression; b, about length of impression distal to impression; c, further distal to impression than length of impression [a/0 b/1 c/2]
120	**UL12**	Proximal surface of carpal tuberosity: a, undercut by fossa; b, not undercut [a/0 b/1]
121	**UL13**	Proximal margin of trochlea: a, angular, with sharp internal angle at junction with internal condyle; b, smooth curve [a/0 b/1]
122	UL14	Orientation of axis of carpal tuberosity: a, proximad; b, distad [a/0 b/1]
123	**CM1**	Proximal internal edge of minor metacarpal: a, with prominent, flat-ended tubercle; b, no tubercle, perhaps a rounded swelling [a/0 b/1]
124	CM2	Pisiform process: a, thin, rounded in section; b, long, oval or rectangular in section; c, robust, round [a/0 b/1 c/2]
125	**CM3**	Pollical facet: a, rounded; b, proximal and distal notches dividing surface into two segments; c, surfaces separated; d, notched, internal surface reduced [a/0 b/1 c/2 d/3]
126	**CM4**	Depressio metacarpi interna: a, shallow; b, deep [a/0 b/1]
127	CM5	Sulcus internus: a, deep, internal surface of major metacarpal rounded, distal symphysis projecting internally; b, broad and shallow, internal surface of major metacarpal flattened, symphysis not projecting [a/0 b/1]
128	**CM6**	Depressio metacarpi externa: a, deep; b, shallow [a/0 b/1]
129	**CM7**	Shape of carpal trochlea in proximal view: a, internal condyle concave internally; b, concave externally [a/0 b/1]
130	**CM7A**	Shape of carpal trochlea in proximal view: a, external condyle concave internally; b, external condyle concave externally; c, straight [a/0 b/1 c/2]
131	**CM7B**	Junction of proximal end of external margin of minor metacarpal: a, in line with external condyle; b, in line with internal condyle; c, between condyles [a/0 b/1 c/2]
132	**CM7C**	Proximal end of minor metacarpal: a, with deep fossa; b, with no fossa; c, with shallow groove [a/0 b/1 c/2]
133	**CM8**	Posterior carpal fossa: a, deep; b, shallow [a/0 b/1]
134	CM9	Ligamental attachment of pisiform process: a, prominent swelling, with or without pit; b, small or obscure [a/0 b/1]
135	**CM10**	Position of pollical facet: a, less than or equal to 50% of distance from internal condyle to distal end of proximal symphysis; b, more than 50% to distal end of proximal symphysis [a/0 b/1]
136	**CM11**	Length of distal symphysis: a, less than or equal to distal width of major metacarpal; b, greater

		than width of major metacarpal [a/0 b/1]
137	**CM12**	Anterior carpal fossa: a, shallow; b, deep pit; c, pit, with pneumatic foramen or foramina [a/0 b/1 c/2]
138	**CM13**	Internal ligamental fossa: a, shallow; b, deep [a/0 b/1]
139	**CM14**	Junction of distal end of internal of condyle with shaft: a, smooth; b, stepped [a/0 b/1]
140	CM15	Shape of end of major metacarpal in distal view: a, approximately rectangular; b, more or less triangular, anteroexternal side convex [a/0 b/1]
141	**CM16**	Facet for digit of minor metacarpal: a, set off from major metacarpal by deep pit; b, no deep pit [a/0 b/1]
142	**PE1**	Dorsal fenestrae: a, large, conspicuous; b, absent or small [a/0 b/1]
143	**PE2**	Postacetabular ilium and synsacral plate: a, fused, with no obvious suture; b, not fused [a/0 b/1]
144	**PE3**	Cranial ends of iliac plates: a, rounded in dorsal view; b, straight or inclined anterolaterally [a/0 b/1]
145	**PE4**	Posterior iliac crests: a, more or less straight and parallel; b, bowed outward [a/0 b/1]
146	**PE5**	Width across posterior iliac crests in dorsal view: a, about equal to pelvis length; b, less than two-thirds pelvis length [[a/0 b/1]
147	**PE6**	Anterior iliac crests: a, separated from synsacral plate by large fenestrae; b, not separated [a/0 b/1]
148	**PE7**	Posterior iliac crests: a, produced as square process above acetabulum; b, produced above acetabulum, but not forming square process; c, not produced above acetabulum [a/0 b/1 c/2]
149	**PE8**	Shape of posterior end of ilioischiadic plate: a, tapering to rounded point; b, notched; c, abruptly arrowing before posterior extremity; d, knickpoint in posterior iliac crest [a/0 b/1 c/2 d/3]
150	**PE9**	Pubis: a, rodlike, not expanded; b, slight expansion; c, with broad expansion [a/0 b/1 c/2]
151	**PE10**	Shape and direction of anterior synsacral caudal vertebrae: a, long, slender, parallel, or diverging towards acetabulum; b, relatively short, broadly converging [a/0 b/1]
152	**PE11**	Posterior synsacral caudal vertebrae: coalescing with broad, medially projecting plate; b, free, articulating with mesial iliac edge (Note: In Sagittarius there is a broad plate enclosing the posterior ilioischiatic space ventrally) [a/0 b/1]
153	**PE12**	Number and arrangement of caudal synsacral vertebrae (anterior, posterior): a, 2+2; b, 2+3; c, 2+2+1; d, 3+3; e, 2+3+1 [a/0 b/1 c/2 d/3 e/4]
154	**PE13**	Posterior iliac crests above ilioischiatic fossa: a, shelf-like; b, not produced as a shelf [a/0 b/1]
155	PE14	Mesial protuberance at posterior ilio-ischiatic suture: present, forming ‘constriction’ of cauadal space; b, absent [a/0 b/1]
156	**FE1**	Rotular groove: a, in line with shaft; b, at angle to shaft [a/0 b/1]
157	**FE2**	Rotular groove: a, short; b, long [a/0 b/1]
158	**FE3**	Pneumatic foramen: a, absent; b, present [a/0 b/1]
159	**FE4**	Cranial outline of shaft: a, straight in lateral view; b, curved in lateral view; b, bent caudad near distal end; c, bent caudad near midpoint of shaft [a/0 b/1 b-c/2 c/3 c-a/4]
160	**FE5**	Trochanteral ridge: a, short cranially, but extending proximoplantad as strong ridge; b, not so [a/0 b/1]
161	**FE6**	Cranial intermuscular line(s): a, medial; b, lateral;, c, along centre-line [a/0 a-b/1 b/2 c/3 c-a/4]
162	**FE7**	Number of cranial intermuscular lines: a, 1; b, 2 [a/0 b/1]
163	**FE8**	Medial condyle: a, projecting in line with shaft; b, projecting cranially [a/0 b/1]
164	**FE9**	Popliteal fossa: a, deep; b, shallow and broad; c, shallow, with deep pit; d, narrow, aligned with shaft; e, undercutting condyles [a/0 b/1 c/2 d/3 e/4]
165	**FE10**	Popliteal fossa: a, with pneumatic foramen; b, without [a/0 b/1]
166	**FE11**	Caudal intermuscular line: a, single, weakly defined; b, forked; c, strongly defined, central on shaft; d, multiple [a/0 b/1 c/2 d/3]
167	**FE12**	Rotular groove section: a, rectangular; b, U-shaped; c, approximately V-shaped [a/0 a-b/1 b/2 b-c/3 c/4]

168 **FE13** Large muscle scar proximal to popliteal fossa: a, a line; b, more or less oval; c, divided into 2 separate scars [a/0 a-b/1 b/2 c/3]

169 **FE13A** Large muscle scar proximal to popliteal fossa: a, central on caudal surface; b, lateral; c, medial [a/0 a-b/1 b/2 b-c/3 c/4]

170 **FE13B** Large muscle scar proximal to popliteal fossa: a, a pit; b, a tubercle [a/0 b/1]

171 **FE14** Caudal intercondylar notch: a, V-shaped; b, deep U-section completely separating surfaces so that inner face of condyle is equal to outer face height; c, shallow U-section [a/0 b/1 c/2]

172 **FE15** Proximal caudal fossa: a, deep; b, shallow; c, shaft convex [a/0 a-b/1 b/2 c/3]

173 **FE16** Caudal edge of iliac surface: a, smoothly curved; b, with distinct angle [a/0 a-b/1 b/2]

174 **FE17** Shallow secondary fossa proximal to popliteal fossa: a, present; b, absent [a/0 b/1]

175 **FE18** Median face of median condyle: a, with fossa; b, without fossa (perhaps small pit); c, with large tubercle [a/0 b/1 c/2 a-c/3]

176 **FE19** Transition of proximal cranial end of median condyle with shaft: a, stepped; b, smooth; c, a high step [a/0 a-b/1 b/2 b-c/3 c/4 a-c/5]

177 **FE20** Cranial ridge of median condyle: a, extending further proximally than lateral ridge; b, equal; c, lateral extending further proximally [a/0 b/1 c/2]

178 **FE21** Fibular condyle: a, narrow; b, shelf-like; c, with deep pit proximally [a/0 b/1 c/2]

179 **FE22** Proximal edge of fibular condyle: a, with muscle insertion pit running distally as large notch, so that outline of condyle is a blunt projection; b, partly notched; c, square; d, not notched, rounded; e, not notched, but with a large pit; f, not notched, with the proximal outline square [a/0 b/1 c/2 d/3 e/4 f/5]

180 **FE23** Prominent tubercle on medial margin distal to femur head: a, present; b, absent; c, a raised linear scar [a/0 b/1 c/2]

181 **FE24** Trochanteral ridge: a, high, so that proximal outline of bone nearly triangular; b, low, outline of bone ± rectangular [a/0 b/1]

182 **FE25** Median condyle: a, ± flat in distal view, from intercondylar notch to median margin; b, curved; c, with definite angle; d, concave [a/0 a-b/1 b/2 b-c/3 c/4 d/5 a-d/6]

183 **FE26** Proximo-lateral extension of fibular condyle: a, absent; b, pointed; c, ± square; d, rounded; e, double [a/0 a-b/1 b/2 b-c/3 c/4 a-c/5 d/6 e/7]

184 **FE25** Median condyle: a, square; d, rounded; e, double [a/0 a-b/1 b/2 b-c/3 c/4 a-c/5 d/6 e/7]

184 **FE27** Prominent tubercle medial to popliteal fossa: a, present; b, absent [a/0 b/1]

185 **FE28** Proximal trochanteral ridge turned medially to overhang and form fossa on and above iliac surface: a, present; b, absent; c, with second fossa [a/o b/1 a-c/2 b-c/3 c/4]

185 **FE29** Cranial intermuscular line: a, nearly straight; b, directed toward lateral margin, then straight down shaft, forming clear angle [a/0 b/1]

187 **FE30** Caudal junction of medial condyle with shaft: a, with tubercle; b, tubercle extending laterally as ridge (forming pit); c, tubercle small to absent; d, tubercle extending proximo-laterally as line towards scar of FE13 [a/0 b/1 c/2 d/3]

188 **FE31** Proximal outline of trochanteral ridge in lateral view: a, angular, with distal limb returned; b, rounded; c, angular [a/0 b/1 c/2]

189 **FE32** Cranial edge of iliac facet: a, a slight crest; b, not a crest [a/0 a-b/1 b/2]

190 **FE33** Proximal end of lateral condyle; muscle insertion at proximal end of ridge: a, at junction with shaft (termination coincides with shaft margin); b, displaced laterally [a/0 b/1]

191 **FE34** Bone proportions: a, long and slender; b, of ‘normal’ proportions [a/0 b/1]

192 **FE35** Prominent muscle attachment across popliteal fossa: a, a line; b, absent [a/0 b/1]

193 **FE36** Muscle scar of 13A and B: a, distal to or ± in popliteal fossa; proximal to fossa [a/0 b/1]

194 **FE37** Depth of rotular groove: a, equal to depth; b, less than width; c, much less than width [a/0 a-b/1 b/2 b-c/3 c/4]

195 **FE38** Trochanteral ridge: a, ± smoothly curved over pneumatic foramen in lateral view; b, arched over foramen; c, with a large swelling distal to foramen; d, with a very large muscle scar distally [a/0 a-b/1 b/2 b-c/3 a-c/4 c/5 d/6]

196 **FE39** Area proximal to pneumatic foramen: a, with no ridge; b, with strong transverse ridge; c, with trochanter medial enough for intermuscular line to run distad down medial side of foramen directly from it [a/0 b/1 c/2]

197 **FE40** Distal part of external face of fibular condyle: a, impressed so that proximo-lateral process stands proud of lateral surface; b, not impressed [a/0 b/1]

198	**FE41**	Proximo-caudal median protuberance: a, absent; b, present [a/0 b/1]
199	**FE42**	Trochanteral ridge and lateral margin of iliac facet: a, merged cranially; b, separated [a/0 b/ 1]
200	**FE43**	Proximal cranial end of lateral condyle: a, with no step; with obvious step [a/0 b/1]
201	**TI1**	Distal condyles: a, extending as far caudally as cranially; b, ± in line with posterior surface of shaft [a/0 b/1]
202	**TI2**	Trochleal groove and sulcus: a, very deep; b, shallow [a/0 b/1]
203	**TI3**	Sulcus: a, caudal to line of shaft; b, running into caudal surface [a/0 b/1]
204	**TI4**	Fibula insertion: a, near distal end of shaft; b, 0.5-0.67 distance down shaft [a/0 a-c/1 b/2 b-c/3 c/4]
205	**TI5**	Lateral cnemial crest: a, long (> width); b, short (= width) [a/0 b/1]
206	**TI6**	Medial proximal ligaments: a, inserting on shaft midline; b, inserting at distal end of medial crest [a/0 a-b/1 b/2]
207	**TI7**	Lateral proximal articular surface: a, deeply excavated; b, not deeply excavated, or pit laterally [a/0 b/1]
208	**TI8**	Proximal plantar surface: a, strongly keeled (with lateral and/or medial fossae); b, rounded; c, low keel or ridge, not defined by fossae [a/0 a-c/1 b/2 b-c/3 c/4]
209	**TI9**	Lateral cranial fossa: a, open to head; b, filled to distal edge of ridge running from lateral crest [a/0 b/1]
210	**TI10**	Median cnemial crest: a, notched; b, smoothly convex; c, short, lateral length, with sharp angle separating proximal from distal sections; d, stepped at distal end [a/0 a-b/1 a-c/3 b/4 b-d/5 c/6 d/7]
211	**TI11**	Sulcus extending: a, ± equally up cranial and caudal surfaces; b, 50% higher up caudal surface [a/0 b/1]
212	**TI12**	Condyles: a, equal in width; b, medial condyle wider; c, lateral wider [a/0 b/1 c/2]
213	**TI13**	Lateral condyle caudal limb: a, entire; b, notched [a/0 b/1]
214	**TI14**	Distal margins of shaft: a, diverging abruptly to width over condyles; b, subparallel near condyles [a/0 b/1]
215	**TI15**	Supratendinal bridge: a, 30-60° to shaft axis; b, ± at right angles to axis; c, ± parallel to axis [a/0 a-b/1 a-c/2 b/3 c/4]
216	**TI16**	Muscle scar: a, at proximal end of supratendinal bridge; b, proximal to proximal end; c, well proximal to end; d, on medial margin [a/0 a-b/1 b/2 b-c/3 c/4 d/5]
217	**TI17**	Muscle scar: a, a surface roughening; b, a prominent tubercle; c, a pit [a/0 b/1 c/2]
218	**TI18**	Intercondylar groove: a, narrow; b, broad; c, shallow or obscure [a/0 b/1 c/2]
219	**TI19**	Tibial cartilage sulcus: a, tapering; b, ± parallel-sided [a/0 b/1]
220	**TI20**	Caudal arm of medial condyle: a, entire; b, notched [a/0 b/1]
221	**TI21**	Cranial proximal sulcus: a, excavated; b, obscure [a/0 b/1]
222	**TI22**	Medial shaft margin opposite supratendinal bridge: a, convex; b, concave; c, straight [a/0 b/ 1 c/2]
223	**TI23**	Supratendinal bridge: a, narrow (length > width); b, broad (length width); c, length >> width [a/0 b/1 c/2]
224	**TI24**	Supratendinal bridge: a, flat; b, twisted; c, round; d, bent [a/0 b/1 d/2]
225	**TI25**	Supratendinal bridge: a, narrowing distally; b, parallel-sided; c, narrowing proximally; d, narrowing proximally and distally; e, narrowing centrally, pinched [a/0 a-c/1 b/2 c/3 d/4 e/ 5]
226	**TI26**	Supratendinal bridge arising: a, away from medial margin; b, from medial margin [a/0 a-b/ 1 b/2]
227	**TI27**	Distal tendinal bridge orifice: a, circular; b, subtriangular [a/0 a-b/1 b/2]
228	**TI28**	Lateral condyle: a, squared off proximally; b, tapering proximally [a/0 b/1]
229	**TI29**	Proximal cranial end of medial condyle: a, squared off; b, extending laterally to partly obscure distal orifice of tendinal canal; c, tapering proximally [a/0 a-b/1 b/2 c/3]
230	**TI30**	Nutrient foramen: a, proximal to distal end of fibular crest; b, opposite end of crest; c, distal to end of crest [a/0 b/1 c/2]
231	**TI31**	Entepicondylar prominence: a, very small to absent; b, small; c, large [a/0 a-b/1 b/2 b-c/3 c/ 4]

232	**TI32**	External ligamental attachment: a, very small to absent; b, triangular; c, shelf-like; d, on lateral condyle; e, a lateral tubercle; f, a ridge [a/0 a-b/1 b/2 c/3 c-f/4 d/5 e/6 f/7]
233	**TI33**	Surface distolateral to tendinal canal: a, broad; b, narrow [a/0 b/1]
234	**TI34**	Surface distolateral to tendinal canal: a, without prominence or pit; b, with prominence; c, with pit; d, with deep, narrow pit [a/0 b/1 b-c/2 c/3]
235	**TI35**	Tendinal canal: a, central on shaft; b, confined to medial side of centre line; c, extending across most of shaft, deep and sunken [a/0 a-b/1 a-c/2 b/3 c/4]
236	**TI36**	Medial margin at tendinal canal: a, broad; b, a thin plate [a/0 a-b/1 b/2]
237	**TI37**	Median condyle: a, recurved proximo-cranially; b, not recurved; c, with no sharp angle, running smoothly from shaft [a/0 b/1 c/2]
238	**TI38**	Medial distal caudal groove: a, convex or flat, edge not extending medially; b, deeply concave, edge extending medially [a/0 b/1]
239	**TI39**	Medial distal caudal groove: a, without proximal pit; b, with proximal pit [a/0 b/1]
240	**TI40**	Cranial surface of median condyle: a, not inflated; b, inflated [a/0 b/1]
241	**TI41**	Proximal cranial sulcus: a, narrow (50% of cranial surface); b, wide [a/0 b/1] (refers to position of lateral crest)
242	**TI42**	Ectepicondylar prominence: a, absent; b, small; c, large; d, linear [a/0 a-b/1 b/2 b-c/3 b-d/4 c/5 d/6]
243	**TI43**	Medial condyle: a, entire in distal view; b, notched [a/0 a-b/1 b/2]
244	**TI44**	Intercondylar space: a, narrow (< condyle width); b, wide (> condyle width); c, equal to condyle width [a/0 a-c/1 b/2 b-c/3 c/4]
245	TM1	Calcaneal processes: a, widely separated; b, close-set
246	**TM2**	Tendinal canal: a, open; b, almost closed; c, closed [a/0 b/1 c/2]
247	TM3	Outer calcaneal process: a, produced, almost as large as inner; b, displaced laterally and flattened; c, otherwise
248	**TM4**	Notch for *N. peronaeus*: a, absent; b, indistinct; c, wide-mouthed; d, almost closed (270° closure) [a/0 b/1 c/2 d/3]
249	**TM5**	Lateral calcaneal ridge: a, extending distally, fading into lateral posterior margin; b, delineated medially by fossa of *M. abductor digiti IV*; c, lateral ridge displaced medially and fused with medial ridge; d, displaced medially but not fused; e, lacking, posterior aspect ± flat, ridge a line marking margins of *M. abductor digiti IV* and *M. adductor digiti II* impressions [a/3 b/4 c/0 d/1 e/2]
250	**TM6**	Median calcaneal process: a, pillar-like; b, an elongated plate; c, otherwise [a/0 b/1]
251	TM7	Proximal and posterior margins of median calcaneal process: a, bent medially; b, not bent medially
252	TM8	Medial calcaneal process: a, separated from medial margin by fossa of *M. flexor hallucis brevis*; b, lacking distinct fossa medial to process, which arises almost from margin of bone
253	**TM9**	Medial proximal vascular foramen: a, medial and proximal to distal margin of medial process; b, medial to distal margin or on ridge below distal margin; c, lateral to ridge; d, on ridge below distal margin to just lateral to margin [a/0 a-b/1 b/2 b-c/3]
254	TM10	Tubercle for *M. tibialis anticus*: a, lateral to midline; b, just medial to midline
255	TM11	Lateral proximal vascular foramen: a, on medial side of lateral ridge; b, on lateral side or on lateral slope of hypotarsal ridge
256	TM12	Lateral condylar surface: a, higher than medial; b, surfaces at equal level, or medial higher
257	TM13	*M. tibialis anticus* tubercle: a, near proximal foramina; b, not near foramina
258	TM14	Lateral metatarsal prominence: a, hardly discernible; b, well-defined
259	TM15	Frenula: a, completely ossified; b, present; c, absent [It should be possible to sub-divide b: scars project, narrowly separated, near medial margin; broad lateral scar nearly on mid-line; scars at different levels, medial higher than lateral; lateral higher than medial; at same level]
260	TM16	Posterior flexor groove: a, hollowed out and unmarked; b, relatively flat, with a series of shallow impressions for 3 posterior muscles
261	TM17	Scar of first metatarsal: a, directed ± medially; b, directed posteriorly
262	TM18	Proximal edge of metatarsal facet: a, raised, separated from projecting line of medial tarsal edge by notch; b, not separated by notch
263	TM19	Openings at distal end end of tendinal groove: a, two; b, one

264	TM20	*M. extensor digiti III* origin's upper and medial margins: a, indicated by scar; b, not indicated by scar
265	TM21	Cranial surface proximal to middle trochlea: a, with pit; b, no pit; c, indistinct pit
266	TM22	Origin of *M. abductor digiti II*: a, fairly distinct, roughened, extending from tibilalis anticus to upper and lateral margins of first metatarsal articulation; b, not so
267	TM23	Inner trochlea (digit II) posteromedial process: a, bent toward tarsal midline; b, not bent
268	TM24	Posterolateral process of digit II trochlea: a, short, thick, separated from articular surface by groove; b, not so
269	TM25	Digit IV trochlea posterolateral projection margin: a, truncated, pointed at ventroposterior angle; b, rounded posteriorly
270	TM26	Groove for *M. abductor digiti IV* tendon on posterolateral margin of shaft: a, wide, clearly marked; b, narrow, shallow
270	TM27	Proximal anterior fossa: a, deep; b, shallow
271	**PH1**	Phalanges 1 and 2 on pedal digit 2: a, free; b, fused in most or all specimens [a/0 b/1]
272	**PX1**	Number of cervical vertebrae: a, 13; b, 14; c, 15; d, 17 [a/0 b/1 c/2 d/3]
273	**PX2**	Number of cervical ribs: a, 1; b, 2; c, 3 [a/0 b/1 c/2]

APPENDIX 3

Number of species in each genus of Accipitridae in each of 18 geographical areas (Fig. 16).

Node	PANDI	AVIC	LEPT	CHON	PERN	HENI	GAMP	ELANO	MACH	ELANU	ROST	ICTINIA	HARPAGU	HAMI	LOPHOI	MILV	HALIAS	HALIAA	ICHTH	GYPO	NEOP	NECRO	GYPAE	GYPS	AEGYP	CIRCAE	TERA	SPIL	DRYO	EUTR	GERAN	POLY	CIRCUS	MELIE	UROTE	MEGA	ERYTH	KACC	AUP
1 NORTHAM	1	0	0	0	0	0	0	1	0	1	1	1	0	0	0	0	0	1	0	0	0	0	0	0	0	0	0	0	0	0	0	0	1	0	0	0	0	3	0
2 CENTRAM	0	0	1	1	0	0	1	1	0	1	1	1	1	0	0	0	0	0	0	0	0	0	0	0	0	0	0	0	0	0	1	0	0	0	0	0	0	4	0
3 WINDIES	1	0	1	0	0	0	0	0	0	0	1	0	0	0	0	0	0	0	0	0	0	0	0	0	0	0	0	0	0	0	0	0	0	0	0	0	0	2	0
4 SOUTHAM	0	0	1	1	0	0	1	1	0	1	2	1	2	0	0	0	0	0	0	0	0	0	0	0	0	0	0	0	0	0	1	0	2	0	0	0	0	5	0
5 SOUTHAF	1	1	0	0	0	0	0	0	1	1	0	0	0	0	0	1	0	1	0	1	1	1	1	3	2	4	1	0	1	0	0	1	2	3	1	0	0	8	1
6 NORTHAF	1	0	0	0	0	0	0	0	0	1	0	0	0	0	0	2	0	0	0	0	1	0	1	2	1	1	0	0	0	0	0	0	2	1	0	0	0	1	0
7 MADAGAS	0	0	0	0	0	0	0	0	1	1	0	0	0	0	0	1	0	1	0	0	0	0	0	0	0	0	0	0	0	1	0	1	2	0	0	0	0	1	0
8 EUROPE	1	0	0	0	1	0	0	0	0	1	0	0	0	0	0	2	0	1	0	0	1	0	1	1	1	1	0	0	0	0	0	0	4	0	0	0	0	3	0
9 MIDEAST	1	0	0	0	0	0	0	0	0	1	0	0	0	0	0	2	0	1	0	0	1	0	1	1	2	1	0	0	0	0	0	0	4	1	0	0	0	4	0
10 NORTHAS	1	0	0	0	1	0	0	0	0	0	0	0	0	0	0	1	0	3	0	0	0	0	1	2	1	1	0	0	0	0	0	0	5	0	0	0	0	5	0
11 SEASIA	1	2	0	0	1	0	0	0	0	1	0	0	0	0	0	1	1	2	2	0	1	0	0	3	1	1	0	3	0	0	0	0	0	0	0	0	0	4	0
12 INDOPHI	1	1	0	0	2	0	0	0	1	1	0	0	0	0	0	1	1	1	2	0	0	0	0	2	1	0	0	3	0	0	0	0	0	0	0	0	0	6	0
13 NEWGUIN	1	1	0	0	0	1	0	0	1	1	0	0	0	0	0	1	2	1	0	0	0	0	0	0	0	0	0	0	0	0	0	0	1	0	0	1	0	9	0
14 MELANES	1	1	0	0	0	1	0	0	0	0	0	0	0	0	0	1	2	2	0	0	0	0	0	0	0	0	0	0	0	0	0	0	1	0	0	0	0	A	0
15 AUSTRAL	1	1	0	0	0	0	0	0	0	2	0	0	0	1	1	1	2	1	0	0	0	0	0	0	0	0	0	0	0	0	0	0	2	0	0	0	1	3	0
16 NEWZEAL	0	0	0	0	0	0	0	0	0	0	0	0	0	0	0	0	0	1	0	0	0	0	0	0	0	0	0	0	0	0	0	0	1	0	0	0	0	1	0
17 OCEANIA	0	0	0	0	0	0	0	0	0	0	0	0	0	0	0	0	0	1	0	0	0	0	0	0	0	0	0	0	0	0	0	0	1	0	0	0	0	0	0
18 GREENLA	0	0	0	0	0	0	0	0	0	0	0	0	0	0	0	0	0	1	0	0	0	0	0	0	0	0	0	0	0	0	0	0	0	0	0	0	0	0	0

	Node	BUTAS	LEUCO	BUTEOG	HETER	HARPYH	BUSAR	PARA	GERANO	BUTEO	MORPH	HARPIA	ICTINA	HARPYO	PITHE	HIERAA	AQUILA	SPIZAS	SPIZAE	LOPHAE	OROAE	POLEM	STEPH	SAG	HARPA	CHELIC
1	NORTHAM	0	0	1	0	0	0	1	0	7	0	0	0	0	0	0	1	0	0	0	0	0	0	0	0	0
2	CENTRAM	0	2	3	1	1	1	1	0	6	1	1	0	0	0	0	1	1	2	0	0	0	0	0	0	0
3	WINDIES	0	0	0	0	0	0	0	0	4	0	0	0	0	0	0	0	0	0	0	0	0	0	0	0	0
4	SOUTHAM	0	8	3	1	2	1	1	1	8	1	1	0	0	0	0	0	1	2	0	1	0	0	0	0	0
5	SOUTHAF	1	0	0	0	0	0	0	0	3	0	0	0	0	0	2	3	0	1	1	0	1	1	1	0	0
6	NORTHAF	0	0	0	0	0	0	0	0	1	0	0	0	0	0	1	3	0	0	0	0	0	0	0	0	1
7	MADAGAS	0	0	0	0	0	0	0	0	1	0	0	0	0	0	0	0	0	0	0	0	0	0	0	0	0
8	EUROPE	0	0	0	0	0	0	0	0	3	0	0	0	0	0	2	5	0	0	0	0	0	0	0	0	0
9	MIDEAST	0	0	0	0	0	0	0	0	2	0	0	0	0	0	2	3	0	0	0	0	0	0	0	0	0
10	NORTHAS	1	0	0	0	0	0	0	0	4	0	0	0	0	0	2	4	0	1	0	0	0	0	0	0	0
11	SEASIA	2	0	0	0	0	0	0	0	0	0	0	1	0	0	2	2	0	2	0	0	0	0	0	0	0
12	INDOPHI	2	0	0	0	0	0	0	0	0	0	0	1	0	1	2	0	0	3	0	0	0	0	0	0	0
13	NEWGUIN	0	0	0	0	0	0	0	0	0	0	0	1	1	0	1	1	0	0	0	0	0	0	0	0	0
14	MELANES	0	0	0	0	0	0	0	0	0	0	0	0	0	0	0	0	0	0	0	0	0	0	0	0	0
15	AUSTRAL	0	0	0	0	0	0	0	0	0	0	0	0	0	0	1	1	0	0	0	0	0	0	0	0	0
16	NEWZEAL	0	0	0	0	0	0	0	0	0	0	0	0	0	0	0	0	0	0	0	0	0	0	0	1	0
17	OCEANIA	0	0	0	0	0	0	0	0	2	0	0	0	0	0	0	0	0	0	0	0	0	0	0	0	0
18	GREENLA	0	0	0	0	0	0	0	0	0	0	0	0	0	0	0	0	0	0	0	0	0	0	0	0	0

Saw-whet Owl *Aegolius a. acadicus*

Meyburg, B.-U. & R. D. Chancellor eds.1994
Raptor Conservation Today
WWGBP / The Pica Press

A Morphometric Analysis of *Accipiter* Species

Alan Kemp and Tim Crowe

ABSTRACT

Samples of up to 10 study skins for 45 of the 48 species in the genus *Accipiter* were measured for 24 dimensions of the head, wings, tail and feet. For each species and each sex within a species, the logged values of the means of each measurement were analysed by cluster and factor analysis. Two clusters were identified, large goshawks together with larger females of a few other species and the remaining smaller species. *A ovampensis,* with its rather falcon-like proportions, was the most aberrant species. Morphometric similarities between species and subspecies were compared with their known biogeography. Similar species were allopatric or ecologically separated, but there was considerable convergence between species in different areas and between the individual sexes of different species.

INTRODUCTION

The genus *Accipiter* is the largest and one of the most homogeneous within the avian order Falconiformes, comprising 22% of the 223 species in the family Accipitridae (Amadon & Bull 1988). It was reviewed in detail by Wattel in 1973, when 43 species were recognised, but subsequent studies suggest that it consists of 48 species, including those previously in the genera *Megatriorchis* and *Erythrotriorchis* (Amadon & Bull 1988). Wattel (1973) examined patterns of geographical differentiation within the genus, based partly on traditional measurements of the bill, wing, tail and tarsus, together with dimensions of the middle toe and hind claw. The measurements were compared by univariate statistics and by transforming them to relative proportions of the wing length to minimize effects of body size. This study provided one of the first extensive morphometric analyses of an entire avian genus (Wattel 1973).

The present study is part of a series examining the systematics and morphometrics of raptors (Kemp & Crowe 1990, 1991, in press). It attempts to define morphometric similarities between species to assess the extent that phenetic characters have been used in deciding systematic relationships and may be used to define ecological similarity. A morphometric analysis of 280 of the 291 species of diurnal birds of prey (Falconiformes) indicated that smaller *Accipiter* species were most similar to *Micrastur buckleyi, M. ruficollis, M. gilvicollis,* male *Falco novaeseelandiae* and *Micronisus (Melierax) gabar*, while larger ones resembled males of *Spizaetus* spp., *Hieraaetus ayresii, H. kienerii* and *Spizastur melanoleucus*, both sexes of *Parabuteo unicinctus* and females of *Circus maillardi* (Kemp & Crowe 1991). Although at least two groups can be recognised within the genus *Accipiter* based on morphological characters (Kemp & Crowe 1990), previous assessment of systematic relationships have been based mainly on phenetic, not necessarily phylogenetic similarities.

MATERIALS AND METHODS

Twenty-four measurements of the head (8), wing (4), legs (2), feet (8) and tail (2) (Biggs *et al.* 1978) were taken on samples of up to 10 study skins of 45 of the 48 species of *Accipiter* (Amadon & Bull 1988) and 5 distinctive subspecies. No specimens were available for *A. princeps, A. nanus* and *A. brachyurus*, all Australasian island endemics with restricted ranges. The distribution of measurements was bimodal for all species and subspecies (except *A. imitator, A. luteoschistaceus, A. doriae* and *A. collaris* where only one sex was represented). Larger specimens were taken to be female, smaller to be male and the samples for each sex were analysed separately.

The mean for each measurement was calculated for each sample (Table 1) and the logged values of the 96 sets of means, for all species, subspecies and sexes, were compared by centroid cluster analysis and factor analysis (Bio-Medical Data Package, BMDP). Details of the samples taken are available from A.C.K. and of the analyses from T.M.C. It should be noted that the measurements are not absolute values of the dimensions for the species concerned; rather they are indices of those dimensions as recorded from dry museum specimens by one recorder (A.C.K.).

RESULTS

The cluster analysis joined morphometrically similar species at low euclidean amalgamation distances but separated dissimilar species by their higher amalgamation distances (Fig. 1). There are two major clusters, one incorporating both sexes of the larger goshawks (11 species) together with the larger females of some smaller species (7 species), the other comprising the remaining smaller species. The most aberrant species, morphometrically, is *A. ovampensis.* The smaller species also formed two groups, one mainly males and the other larger females, although each sex of less dimorphic species occurred in the same cluster and of more dimorphic species in separate clusters.

Only one factor, out of the five specified for the analysis, was necessary to record the patterns of correlation within the data. In the orthogonally rotated factor loadings, this factor accounted for 21.7% of the variance explained. The sorted and rotated loadings for Factor 1 (Table 2) indicate that measurements of the wing, feet and bill contributed most to this factor. Gape width, an index of swallowing capacity, contributed least to the factor analysis. The list in sequence of the factor scores indicates morphometric similarities between species and sexes (Table 3). Since all members of the genus appear to be sexually dimorphic in size, the standard index of dimorphism using wing length can be compared with one derived from the factor scores (Table 4). These two measures of dimorphism are strongly correlated ($r = -0.86$, S.E. = 0.11, $P<0.001$) although the exact sequence of species is not the same for each index of dimorphism.

DISCUSSION

The principal separation within the genus is on overall size, despite log transformation of the means to reduce this effect. That the genus is rather homogeneous is indicated by only one factor accounting for correlation of the variation. The most clearly separated clusters are females of the large goshawks (*A. gentilis, A. meyerianus, A. melanoleucus, A. henstii* and *A. buergersii*), males of the smallest sparrowhawks (*A. superciliosus, A. collaris, A. minullus* and *A. erythropus*) and the aberrant *A. ovampensis*. The latter has long been known for its relatively long wings, short tail and short tarsus within the genus (Wattel 1973), which may be related to more frequent falcon-like stooping than in other species (Kemp & Kemp 1975). Many of the other clusters of species or subspecies are consistent with previous analyses of the genus, such as the "gentilis" group of large goshawks and the "nisus" group of long-toed sparrowhawks (Wattel 1973).

The extent of morphometric similarity (Fig. 1, Table 3) can also be compared to the biogeographical distribution for each species (Table 1). Similar species occur allopatrically, at least when breeding, or are separated ecologically in the few instances where sympatric. This applies even to the most diverse radiation of *Accipiter* species, within the Australasian region (including Wallacea), where 20 species (42% of the genus) occur. It confirms the Gaussian pattern established by Wattel (1973), which has also been found for the genus *Falco* (Kemp & Crowe in

Table 1. **Scientific names, common names and biogeographical realm of Accipiter species (after Amadon & Bull 1988) and subspecies (after Weick 1980) that were measured. Sample sizes and mean measurements used in cluster and factor analyses are presented, with the sexes separated on bimodality of the samples.**

Species of Accipiter	Sex	n	Measurement																							
			BL	BD	SL	JL	JB	GL	BW	GW	SW	WL	SECL	AL	UL	TLC	TLO	TARL	HT	IT	CT	OT	HC	IC	CC	OC
A. albogularis, Pied Sparrowhawk, Australasian (Solomons)																										
	f	7	29.4	16.2	60	43	30	25	13.4	21	36	246	166	105	83	187	171	68	24	23	38	30	21.5	21.1	16.5	14.2
	m	5	27.0	15.1	54	37	25	22	12.1	20	32	217	147	91	71	166	157	64	22	21	36	27	19.3	18.4	15.2	12.7
A. b. badius, Shikra, Afrotropical																										
	f	5	20.0	12.3	45	32	24	17	10.2	16	27	189	115	74	59	146	137	48	15	14	25	19	12.9	12.5	11.0	9.2
	m	5	17.9	11.1	41	29	22	15	8.8	14	26	174	106	71	54	132	124	44	14	13	23	17	11.4	11.0	10.0	8.4
A. b. dussumieri, Shikra, Indomalayan																										
	f	5	22.4	13.0	50	35	25	19	10.1	17	29	208	143	90	71	169	158	54	19	18	32	23	16.4	15.7	12.4	10.8
	m	4	20.3	12.3	46	31	21	18	10.4	16	26	187	125	77	65	148	141	52	18	17	29	21	14.5	13.9	11.7	10.1
A. bicolor, Bicoloured Hawk, Neotropical																										
	f	5	27.8	16.1	57	41	30	22	12.1	19	33	241	178	107	86	199	187	69	27	25	42	29	21.2	20.7	15.5	12.6
	m	5	23.9	13.7	49	35	25	19	10.5	16	29	212	153	94	74	168	166	59	21	20	37	25	17.1	16.5	12.6	10.6
A. brachyurus, New Britain Collared Sparrowhawk, Australasian (New Britain)																										
A. brevipes, Levant Sparrowhawk, Palaearctic																										
	f	5	22.8	13.0	49	37	27	19	10.6	19	29	235	143	94	76	176	164	51	18	16	30	23	14.6	14.3	11.2	9.6
	m	5	21.0	12.5	46	32	24	17	10.5	16	28	217	132	87	71	160	153	50	16	16	29	22	13.5	13.2	11.4	9.8
A. buergersii, Chestnut-mantled Goshawk, Australasian (New Guinea)																										
	f	2	36.1	20.8	73	56	41	30	14.1	25	41	324	216	132	119	242	225	77	39	36	59	39	33.6	32.5	23.8	17.1
	m	3	32.5	19.6	67	48	36	28	13.6	24	38	295	192	115	106	215	207	72	32	31	53	34	29.2	28.4	21.5	14.9
A. butleri, Nicobar Sparrowhawk, Indomalayan (Nicobars)																										
	f	1	22.3	12.6	48	34	24	20	10.9	16	32	183	133	84	63	155	141	50	20	16	28	21	14.7	13.4	11.1	9.7
	m	3	21.4	12.2	47	31	23	19	8.7	16	26	169	125	74	51	147	142	49	16	15	26	19	13.7	13.1	11.6	9.3

Species of Accipiter	Sex	n	BL	BD	SL	JL	JB	GL	BW	GW	SW	WL	SECL	AL	UL	TLC	TLO	TARL	HT	IT	CT	OT	HC	IC	CC	OC
A. castanilius, Chestnut-flanked Sparrowhawk, Afrotropical																										
	f	4	22.7	13.1	51	33	25	18	10.5	18	29	182	145	82	64	165	152	58	20	18	31	22	16.6	15.8	11.2	9.6
	m	5	19.5	11.5	43	29	22	16	8.9	15	26	156	121	71	57	137	123	53	14	15	26	18	13.0	12.6	9.3	8.0
A. cirrocephalus, Australian Collared Sparrowhawk, Australasian																										
	f	5	21.3	12.5	46	32	23	17	9.9	15	26	238	150	101	77	173	176	66	19	19	37	27	16.6	16.5	12.4	10.4
	m	5	18.3	11.3	41	28	20	13	9.4	13	24	206	133	87	67	145	154	57	16	15	32	22	13.1	13.2	10.0	8.4
A. collaris, Semi-collared Hawk, Neotropical																										
	m	3	21.8	13.2	48	33	25	17	10.3	16	29	174	124	79	60	137	134	49	19	18	34	25	17.6	16.8	12.6	10.8
A. cooperi, Cooper's Hawk, Nearctic																										
	f	5	28.6	16.4	59	45	33	25	12.7	21	35	263	181	116	88	222	205	71	26	24	42	30	23.2	21.6	15.0	12.8
	m	5	23.7	14.4	54	38	27	20	11.5	18	32	235	159	102	78	198	184	63	22	21	37	25	18.8	17.8	13.4	11.0
A. doriae, Doria's Goshawk, Australasian (New Guinea)																										
	m	2	32.7	19.0	66	48	34	27	12.7	25	39	296	213	124	111	264	241	82	31	27	46	30	28.1	26.4	19.8	15.5
A. erythrauchen, Gray Moluccan Collared Sparrowhawk, Australasian (Moluccas)																										
	f	7	23.3	13.5	49	35	25	18	10.9	15	28	207	147	92	72	160	156	62	23	22	41	29	17.7	18.2	13.9	11.8
	m	2	22.3	13.2	48	35	25	18	10.8	15	30	200	132	88	72	149	148	64	21	20	39	27	17.2	16.8	12.7	10.9
A. erythropus, Red-thighed Sparrowhawk, Afrotropical																										
	f	5	19.2	11.3	42	29	20	15	9.2	13	25	171	121	75	62	127	130	47	17	15	28	21	12.9	12.9	10.5	9.1
	m	5	16.3	9.9	36	26	20	12	7.7	12	23	147	107	64	51	112	113	44	15	14	26	19	11.3	11.4	9.1	7.9
A. f. fasciatus, Brown Goshawk, Australasian																										
	f	5	30.5	17.0	65	46	34	26	13.9	23	38	304	191	124	96	242	216	82	27	25	43	31	23.8	22.1	17.2	14.6
	m	5	28.1	16.0	61	44	32	25	11.9	21	36	288	180	121	93	229	210	80	26	24	40	29	22.3	21.3	17.9	14.9
A. f. francesii, Malagasy Sparrowhawk, Madagascan																										
	f	6	22.6	13.1	50	36	26	20	10.9	18	29	171	126	77	64	153	144	53	16	16	27	21	14.6	14.0	12.2	10.5
	m	6	20.3	12.0	45	32	22	16	9.6	16	27	159	119	69	59	136	131	50	14	14	24	18	12.8	12.6	11.0	9.5

Species Accipiter	Sex of	n	BL	BD	SL	JL	JB	GL	BW	GW	SW	WL	SECL	AL	UL	TLC	TLO	TARL	HT	IT	CT	OT	HC	IC	CC	OC
A. f. brutus/griveaudi, Malagasy Sparrowhawk, Madagascan (Comores)																										
	f	5	22.3	12.3	49	43	24	18	10.8	17	29	164	119	73	58	137	134	53	17	17	28	21	14.6	14.1	12.0	10.3
	m	5	19.5	11.1	46	32	23	18	9.7	15	27	144	108	64	53	115	112	47	15	14	25	18	12.5	11.8	10.4	8.5
A. gentilis, Northern Goshawk, Palaearctic & Nearctic																										
	f	5	37.7	21.7	78	58	42	33	15.8	29	46	357	237	155	124	266	243	84	35	32	51	37	32.5	30.3	21.2	17.6
	m	5	33.8	19.1	71	52	38	28	13.4	25	42	318	203	136	113	231	215	76	28	27	45	33	27.2	26.1	18.0	14.9
A. griseiceps, Celebes Crested Goshawk, Australasian (Sulawesi)																										
	f	3	25.9	14.7	56	41	30	22	11.1	19	35	197	144	86	72	164	154	56	21	21	31	24	20.9	19.6	14.6	12.3
	m	3	24.0	13.6	53	37	27	23	9.9	16	33	181	137	77	66	147	143	52	19	19	28	22	18.4	17.2	13.4	10.5
A. gularis, Japanese Sparrowhawk, Palaearctic																										
	f	5	20.4	12.3	44	32	23	16	10.1	15	26	194	128	80	64	140	137	52	17	16	31	22	14.3	14.2	11.1	9.5
	m	5	17.1	10.3	39	27	20	13	9.1	13	25	168	112	73	57	120	121	49	14	14	27	20	11.9	12.1	9.1	7.8
A. gundlachi, Cuban Hawk, Nearctic (Cuba)																										
	f	1	31.0	17.2	61	47	33	28	14.1	25	41	280	200	108	83	245	218	72	36	34	50	38	28.2	26.1	18.2	15.9
	m	1	25.9	15.2	59	41	31	22	13.3	22	32	237	172	107	78	213	188	68	24	23	42	30	20.6	19.5	15.3	10.7
A. haplochrous, New Caledonian Sparrowhawk, Australasian (New Caledonia)																										
	f	6	27.0	15.7	57	39	28	22	13.0	20	34	237	159	102	77	180	174	66	21	21	35	26	18.6	18.5	15.0	12.4
	m	6	24.3	13.8	52	37	27	20	11.6	18	31	205	140	93	70	157	152	60	20	18	32	23	15.7	15.7	12.4	10.5
A. hennicogrammus, Moluccan Barred Sparrowhawk, Australasian (Moluccas)																										
	f	5	30.0	16.8	60	42	30	23	12.4	19	36	247	174	106	84	215	184	74	20	20	32	25	16.7	16.5	14.3	12.2
	m	5	27.1	15.5	55	38	28	20	10.9	17	33	215	152	92	71	190	173	62	17	18	30	23	15.0	14.9	12.9	11.0
A. henstii, Madagacar Goshawk, Madagascan																										
	f	4	38.7	22.5	76	57	42	33	14.2	26	41	322	246	147	115	281	263	96	37	33	53	38	33.3	30.3	22.6	19.0
	m	4	40.1	19.1	67	48	36	27	13.0	23	38	282	208	124	101	239	220	83	30	25	46	32	26.4	24.5	17.6	15.8

Species Accipiter	Sex of	n	BL	BD	SL	JL	JB	GL	BW	GW	SW	WL	SECL	AL	UL	TLC	TLO	TARL	HT	IT	CT	OT	HC	IC	CC	OC
A. imitator, Imitator Sparrowhawk, Australasian (Solomons)																										
	f	1	27.2	14.1	48	32	21	20	12.0	19	28	209	155	83	61	169	155	59	17	18	27	22	14.1	14.1	13.0	11.3
A. luteoschistaceus, Blue and Gray Sparrowhawk, Australasian (New Britain)																										
	m	1	23.0	13.3	59	37	27	19	11.3	19	30	193	138	80	70	148	138	59	17	18	27	19	13.3	13.1	12.5	10.1
A. madagascariensis, Madagascar Sparrowhawk, Madagascan																										
	f	7	22.6	13.4	50	34	25	18	10.6	17	29	218	160	99	75	183	180	64	22	21	38	27	17.6	18.0	13.6	11.2
	m	3	18.0	10.6	41	27	19	14	8.7	14	24	173	126	76	61	140	145	54	17	16	31	21	12.3	13.0	9.7	8.0
A. melanochlamys, Black-mantled Goshawk, Australasian (New Guinea)																										
	f	5	29.0	16.7	59	42	30	23	13.5	22	35	251	177	104	80	195	177	68	22	22	37	28	20.6	20.0	15.5	13.3
	m	6	25.7	15.5	53	38	28	21	12.3	19	32	220	155	94	72	169	158	64	20	19	31	24	17.2	16.2	12.7	11.2
A. melanoleucus, Black and White Goshawk, Afrotropical																										
	f	5	36.3	21.2	70	55	40	33	14.1	24	41	337	234	146	120	256	233	84	36	31	55	38	28.5	27.4	20.4	17.0
	m	3	30.9	18.3	64	46	33	28	12.2	20	39	280	188	120	105	213	196	75	29	26	43	30	24.3	22.5	17.2	14.2
A.meyerianus, Papuan Goshawk, Australasian (except Australia)																										
	f	2	39.0	22.7	72	56	46	33	14.6	28	42	326	229	150	120	247	229	78	33	32	50	38	29.9	28.4	20.3	17.7
	m	2	35.7	20.9	72	51	38	30	14.2	24	40	295	200	128	103	208	198	72	29	27	45	31	27.2	25.7	18.1	15.4
A. minullus, Little Sparrowhawk, Afrotropical																										
	f	5	19.4	12.0	40	29	21	15	9.5	15	25	158	115	70	55	121	122	45	17	15	28	21	12.7	12.6	9.6	8.3
	m	5	16.3	10.6	36	25	19	13	7.8	12	22	140	103	60	50	105	106	39	14	13	24	17	10.6	10.5	8.5	7.4
A. nanus, Dwarf Sparrowhawk, Australasian (Sulawesi)																										
A. nisus, Eurasian Sparrowhawk, Palaearctic																										
	f	5	22.5	12.8	50	35	26	18	10.4	17	29	230	149	100	78	181	174	60	20	20	39	26	16.7	17.3	12.8	10.8
	m	5	18.7	11.0	44	29	23	16	9.2	15	26	202	131	85	66	150	154	54	16	15	33	21	12.6	13.0	10.2	8.0
A. n. novaehollandiae, Variable Goshawk, Australasian																										
	f	5	35.9	20.6	71	52	38	30	13.0	25	39	311	222	134	96	241	230	84	31	30	49	36	29.7	27.5	20.9	18.0
	m	5	30.4	17.5	62	45	33	25	11.7	21	36	261	184	112	94	196	191	72	27	25	40	29	23.8	22.0	16.8	14.1

Species Accipiter	Sex of	n	BL	BD	SL	JL	JD	GL	DW	GW	SW	WL	SECL	AL	UL	TLC	TLO	TARL	HT	IT	CT	OT	HC	IC	CC	OC
A. n. griseogularis, Variable Goshawk, Australasian (Moluccas)																										
	f	6	32.9	18.3	63	47	33	26	12.1	21	37	261	186	118	87	207	194	72	27	25	40	30	23.2	21.4	16.1	13.5
	m	4	27.4	15.6	56	41	29	23	10.8	19	34	222	159	95	72	171	162	60	23	22	34	25	18.7	17.5	13.5	11.1
A. n. hiogaster, Variable Goshawk, Australasian (Sundas)																										
	f	5	28.8	16.0	56	41	29	22	11.7	18	34	214	149	93	75	166	157	60	21	20	32	24	17.6	16.9	14.3	12.3
	m	4	24.9	14.8	50	36	26	19	10.4	15	32	184	128	80	65	146	141	53	17	17	27	21	14.8	14.5	12.2	10.2
A. ovampensis, Ovambo Sparrowhawk, Afrotropical																										
	f	5	22.7	13.2	49	34	25	18	11.4	17	27	254	161	106	87	185	185	50	22	21	41	27	18.1	18.7	12.1	9.6
	m	5	19.3	11.3	43	30	22	15	9.5	14	24	221	138	84	73	157	160	45	18	18	35	23	15.1	15.3	10.3	8.5
A. poliocephalus, Gray-headed Sparrowhawk, Australasian (New Guinea)																										
	f	5	28.2	16.3	58	41	29	23	12.1	21	34	228	158	99	83	189	171	66	21	19	32	25	17.0	16.9	14.6	12.4
	m	5	25.6	14.7	53	38	27	21	10.6	17	32	198	138	89	70	160	148	60	18	18	29	22	15.4	15.4	13.0	10.9
A. poliogaster, Gray-bellied Hawk, Neotropical																										
	f	4	29.8	16.7	65	45	31	27	13.2	20	36	273	198	124	101	205	198	64	28	25	41	29	22.2	22.2	15.4	12.3
	m	4	25.1	14.3	54	39	29	23	10.5	18	32	227	161	98	82	169	161	50	21	20	33	23	16.4	17.3	12.2	9.7
A. princeps, Gray-headed Goshawk, Australasian (New Britain)																										
A. radiatus, Red Goshawk, Australasian																										
	f	5	38.4	22.1	78	56	41	33	15.5	28	43	420	249	167	143	270	264	82	41	39	67	43	37.7	35.4	23.6	18.1
	m	4	31.3	17.8	66	47	33	27	12.3	23	37	362	207	140	122	220	221	74	33	32	55	35	29.4	28.4	19.7	14.8
A. rhodogaster, Vinous-breasted Sparrowhawk, Australasian (Sulawesi)																										
	f	5	23.9	13.7	50	34	25	18	10.9	16	29	195	140	92	72	148	144	60	23	21	39	29	17.9	18.0	13.8	11.8
	m	5	18.8	11.9	41	29	21	15	9.2	14	25	166	117	74	60	122	129	52	17	16	32	22	13.9	14.1	10.6	9.2
A. rufitorques, Fiji Goshawk, Australasian (Fiji)																										
	f	5	28.6	15.6	57	42	29	22	12.8	19	33	234	159	100	81	176	170	65	21	22	37	27	19.6	18.6	14.5	12.4
	m	5	24.6	14.0	50	35	26	20	10.8	17	31	201	137	83	66	149	144	56	18	18	30	23	16.3	15.6	12.8	10.9

Species of Accipiter	Sex	n	Measurement																							
			BL	BD	SL	JL	JB	GL	BW	GW	SW	WL	SECL	AL	UL	TLC	TLO	TARL	HT	IT	CT	OT	HC	IC	CC	OC
A. rufiventris, Rufous-breasted Sparrowhawk, Afrotropical																										
	f	5	22.1	13.1	48	35	24	19	11.3	17	28	234	151	100	78	184	178	56	19	19	40	26	15.9	16.2	11.8	9.9
	m	5	19.4	11.6	43	31	22	15	10.0	15	26	202	129	84	66	151	154	52	17	15	43	22	13.2	13.3	10.1	8.6
A. soloensis, Gray Frog Hawk, Palaearctic																										
	f	5	20.2	11.5	44	33	24	16	10.9	16	26	198	121	75	61	143	133	43	15	14	25	18	12.2	11.8	10.5	8.6
	m	5	19.8	11.3	44	31	22	16	10.0	15	25	186	111	73	60	135	127	43	14	13	24	18	11.6	11.3	10.1	8.5
A. striatus, Sharp-shinned Hawk, Nearctic & Neotropical																										
	f	5	20.6	12.0	44	32	23	16	9.8	15	25	208	142	90	70	165	168	57	17	17	35	23	14.2	14.4	10.4	9.0
	m	5	17.6	10.6	37	27	20	13	8.4	14	23	178	122	75	57	137	140	50	13	14	30	20	11.5	12.2	8.6	7.4
A. superciliosus, Tiny Hawk, Neotropical																										
	f	5	20.9	12.5	46	31	23	15	10.4	15	27	160	114	70	60	117	117	48	19	18	32	24	16.6	15.9	12.1	10.2
	m	5	17.8	10.9	41	29	22	13	8.7	13	24	134	95	59	48	96	96	42	14	14	25	20	13.0	12.7	9.8	8.2
A. t. tachiro, African Goshawk, Afrotropical																										
	f	5	29.0	16.4	59	44	32	26	11.7	21	34	239	180	107	83	213	196	67	26	23	36	26	24.7	22.4	15.2	13.2
	m	5	25.1	14.9	54	40	29	21	11.1	18	32	222	159	90	71	176	168	59	20	18	32	23	19.2	17.5	13.1	11.2
A. t. macroscelides, African Goshawk, Afrotropical (rainforest)																										
	f	5	26.7	14.7	56	40	29	23	10.8	19	33	218	165	97	77	196	179	63	21	20	33	24	19.9	18.1	12.9	11.7
	m	5	22.0	12.7	50	34	25	19	10.2	17	30	189	143	83	67	160	146	60	16	16	28	20	15.0	14.3	10.5	8.9
A. trinotatus, Spot-tailed Sparrowhawk, Australasian (Sulawesi)																										
	f	6	21.1	11.8	46	34	25	17	9.8	15	29	164	123	72	56	143	128	53	17	16	25	19	13.2	12.6	11.1	9.7
	m	5	20.0	11.4	46	33	24	16	9.2	16	29	155	115	67	53	136	122	53	15	15	24	18	12.1	11.8	10.4	9.2
A. trivirgatus, Asian Crested Goshawk, Indomalayan																										
	f	5	29.9	16.8	66	49	36	27	12.4	22	40	264	200	119	95	217	205	72	27	26	40	30	28.2	25.0	16.4	14.4
	m	5	26.5	15.4	60	43	32	25	11.2	20	37	229	171	100	82	192	179	66	23	23	35	27	23.7	21.4	14.5	12.6

Species of Accipiter	Sex	n	Measurement																						
			BL	BD	SL	JL	JB	GL	BW	GW	SW	WL	SECL	AL	UL	TLC	TLO	TARL	HT	IT	CT	OT	HC	IC	CC	OC
A. virgatus, Besra Sparrowhawk, Indomalayan																										
	f	5	22.7	13.1	48	34	25	18	11.0	16	28	207	150	95	73	168	165	60	21	20	39	28	17.7	17.2	12.7	10.8
	m	5	18.2	10.9	41	28	20	14	9.1	13	25	154	121	75	60	133	134	53	16	16	31	22	13.4	13.0	9.6	8.0

Measurements (see Biggs *et al.* 1978 for details):

Head measurements: BL = bill chord, BD = bill depth, SL = skull length, JL = jaw length, GL = gape length, BW = bill width, GW = gape width, SW = skull width.

Wing measurements: WL = wing length, SECL = secondary length, AL = alula length, UL = ulna length.

Tail measurements: TLC = centre tail length, TLO = outer tail length.

Leg measurements: TARL = tarsus length, HT = hind toe length, IT = inner toe length, CT = centre toe length, OT = outer toe length, HC = hind claw chord, IC = inner claw chord, CC = centre claw chord, OC = outer claw chord.

Table 2. Matrix of factor loadings for each measurement taken (as in Biggs *et al.* 1978), orthogonally rotated and sorted in order of variance explained within each factor.

Measurement	Contribution to Factor 1
Secondary length	0.980
Inner claw chord	0.976
Hind claw chord	0.974
Inner toe length	0.974
Centre claw chord	0.973
Bill depth	0.971
Jaw length	0.971
Alula length	0.967
Hind toe length	0.967
Skull length	0.966
Outer claw chord	0.966
Bill chord	0.965
Ulna length	0.960
Jaw-bill length	0.957
Centre tail length	0.953
Gape length	0.950
Outer tail length	0.950
Wing length	0.949
Skull width	0.945
Outer toe length	0.938
Bill width	0.930
Tarsus length	0.927
Centre toe length	0.902
Gape width	0.793

Table 3. Order of estimated factor score for each species and sex.

Species	Sex	Estimated factor score
A. minullus	m	-1.902
A. erythropus	m	-1.711
A. superciliosus	m	-1.616
A. gularis	m	-1.419
A. b. badius	m	-1.375
A. striatus	m	-1.370
A. f. brutus/griveaudi	m	-1.252
A. minullus	f	-1.221
A. soloensis	m	-1.195
A. castanilius	m	-1.181
A. virgatus	m	-1.163
A. madagascariensis	m	-1.142
A. erythropus	f	-1.118
A. trinotatus	m	-1.105
A. f. francesii	m	-1.076
A. rhodogaster	m	-1.030
A. soloensis	f	-1.009
A. cirrocephalus	m	-0.955
A. butleri	m	-0.932
A. b. badius	f	-0.931
A. trinotatus	f	-0.884
A. nisus	m	-0.881
A. rufiventris	m	-0.818
A. superciliosus	f	-0.803
A. gularis	f	-0.759
A. b. dussumieri	m	-0.742
A. f. brutus/griveaudi	f	-0.690
A. brevipes	m	-0.625
A. ovampensis	m	-0.611
A. striatus	f	-0.609
A. butleri	f	-0.565
A. f. francesii	f	-0.564
A. t. macroscelides	m	-0.555
A. collaris	m	-0.540
A. n. hiogaster	m	-0.502
A. luteoschistaceus	m	-0.413
A. castanilius	f	-0.412
A. imitator	m	-0.345
A. rufitorques	m	-0.323
A. griseiceps	m	-0.319
A. brevipes	f	-0.316
A. b. dussumieri	f	-0.295
A. cirrocephalus	f	-0.250
A. erythrauchen	m	-0.239
A. poliocephalus	m	-0.223
A. haplochrous	m	-0.176
A. bicolor	m	-0.148
A. virgatus	f	-0.139
A. rufiventris	f	-0.132
A. rhodogaster	f	-0.112
A. nisus	f	-0.067
A. hennicogrammus	m	-0.062
A. erythrauchen	f	-0.050
A. poliogaster	m	-0.014

Species	Sex	Estimated factor score
A. madagascariensis	f	0.005
A. t. tachiro	m	0.017
A. melanochlamys	m	0.037
A. griseiceps	f	0.117
A. ovampensis	f	0.144
A. cooperi	m	0.174
A. albogularis	m	0.186
A. n. griseogularis	m	0.188
A. n. hiogaster	f	0.198
A. t. macroscelides	f	0.215
A. poliocephalus	f	0.335
A. haplochrous	f	0.363
A. rufitorques	f	0.397
A. hennicogrammus	f	0.462
A. trivirgatus	m	0.551
A. gundlachi	m	0.572
A. bicolor	f	0.620
A. melanochlamys	f	0.622
A. t. tachiro	f	0.708
A. albogularis	f	0.709
A. cooperi	f	0.852
A. n. novaehollandiae	m	0.902
A. poliogaster	f	0.916
A. f. fasciatus	m	0.949
A. n. griseogularis	f	0.958
A. melanoleucus	m	1.101
A. trivirgatus	f	1.120
A. f. fasciatus	f	1.199
A. henstii	m	1.383
A. gundlachi	f	1.392
A. meyerianus	m	1.421
A. buergersii	m	1.454
A. doriae	m	1.454
A. radiatus	m	1.492
A. gentilis	m	1.494
A. n. novaehollandiae	f	1.689
A. melanoleucus	f	1.901
A. buergersii	f	1.952
A. meyerianus	f	1.957
A. gentilis	f	2.132
A. henstii	f	2.136
A. radiatus	f	2.412

Table 4. Comparison of indices of sexual size dimorphism based on mean wing length (m/f x 100, Table 1) and difference in factor scores (Table 3).

Species	Sexual dimorphism index	
	Wing length	Difference in factor score
A. soloensis	93.9	0.186
A. erythrauchen	96.6	0.189
A. trinotatus	94.5	0.221
A. f. fasciatus	94.7	0.250
A. brevipes	92.3	0.309
A. butleri	92.3	0.367
A. griseiceps	91.9	0.436
A. b. badius	92.1	0.444
A. b. dussumieri	89.9	0.447
A. buergersii	91.0	0.498
A. f. francesii	93.0	0.512
A. albogularis	88.2	0.523
A. hennicogrammus	87.0	0.524
A. meyerianus	90.5	0.536
A. haplochrous	86.5	0.539
A. poliocephalus	86.8	0.558
A. f. brutus/griveaudi	87.8	0.562
A. trivirgatus	86.7	0.569
A. melanochlamys	87.6	0.585
A. erythropus	85.9	0.593
A. gentilis	89.0	0.638
A. gularis	86.6	0.660
A. cooperi	89.4	0.678
A. minullus	88.6	0.681
A. rufiventris	86.3	0.686
A. t. tachiro	92.3	0.691
A. n. griseogularis	85.1	0.700
A. cirrocephalus	86.5	0.705
A. rufitorques	85.9	0.720
A. henstii	87.6	0.753
A. ovampensis	87.0	0.755
A. striatus	85.6	0.761
A. bicolor	88.0	0.768
A. castanilius	85.7	0.769
A. n. novaehollandiae	83.9	0.770
A. t. macroscelides	86.7	0.770
A. n. hiogaster	86.0	0.787
A. melanoleucus	83.1	0.800
A. superciliosus	83.8	0.813
A. nisus	87.8	0.814
A. gundlachi	84.6	0.820
A. rhodogaster	85.1	0.918
A. radiatus	86.2	0.920
A. poliogaster	83.2	0.930
A. virgatus	74.4	1.024
A. madagascariensis	79.4	1.147

Figure 1. Centroid cluster analysis of logged mean values of 24 dimensions for 45 species of *Accipiter* and five subspecies (from Table 1) using the programme BMDP. The euclidean amalgamation distance of each cluster is indicated by the scale down the side of the phenogram.

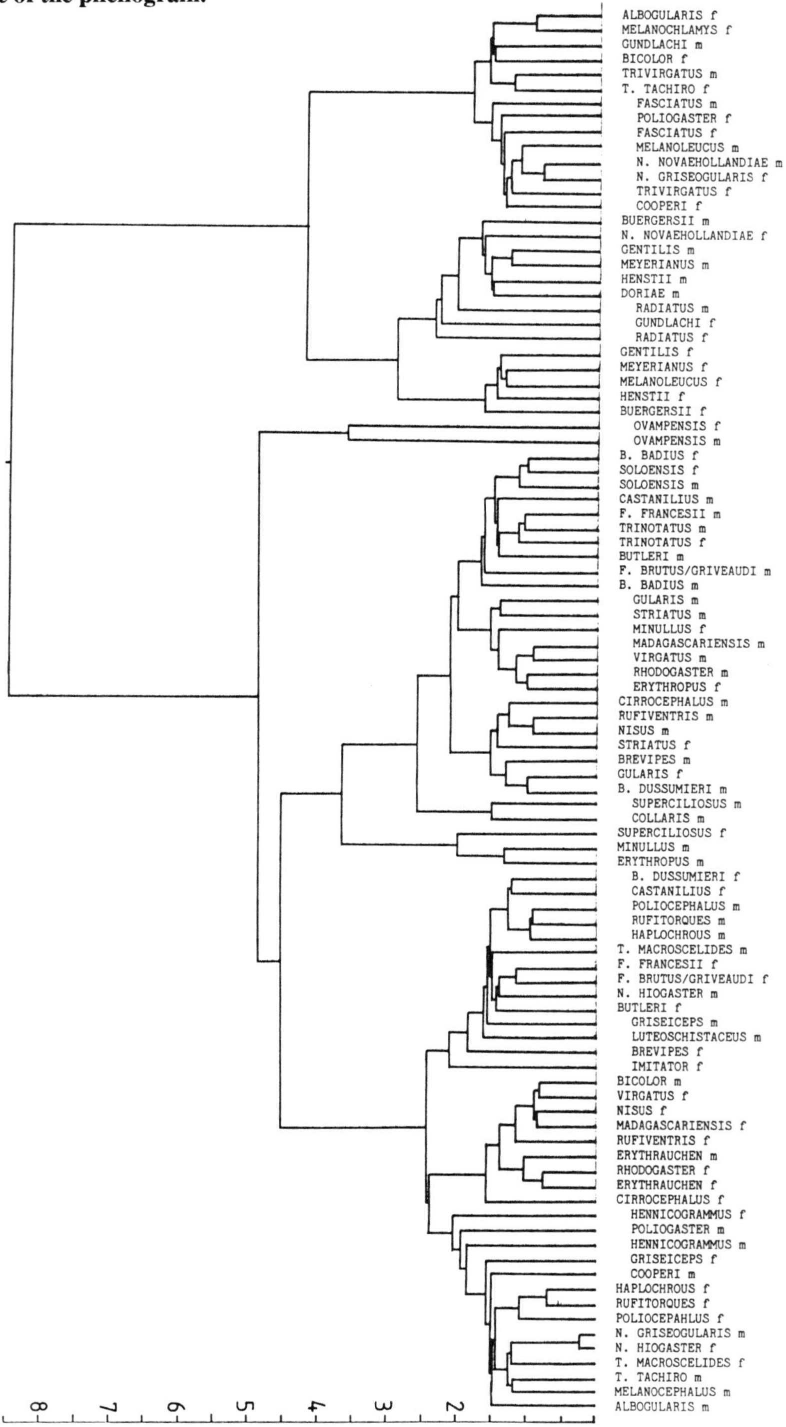

press) and which may apply to most raptorial species. However, there are no cosmopolitan or widespread *Accipiter* species that overlap geographically with many other species, as is found in the genus *Falco*.

Not all subspecies of a species cluster with the same group of species, indicating the validity of considering them as separate populations both ecologically and systematically. Furthermore, in most clusters one sex may be more similar to the opposite rather than the same sex of another species. However, each sex is not always clustered with the same set of species, suggesting that the sexes may either both be similar to their replacement species, or one may be more similar to another species-group.

This indicates the necessity to consider each sex as separate morphometric and ecological units and the problem of trying to compare the ecology of species with dimorphic sexes. Previous studies of sexual dimorphism in raptors have used either body mass or wing length as their indices of dimorphism, whereas it is well known that the sexes may also differ in proportions of various body parts, such as the head and feet. It is suggested that the factor index may be a more comprehensive reflection of sexual differences than one based only on a single dimension, such as wing length, which is itself only a correlate of body size.

ACKNOWLEDGEMENTS

We thank Dean Amadon, Peter Colston, Meg Kemp, John Mendelsohn, the American Museum of Natural History, Frank Chapman Memorial Fund, British Museum (Natural History, Sub-department of Ornithology), Transvaal Museum, Foundation for Research Development, Council for Scientific and Industrial Research and University of Cape Town for their support.

REFERENCES

AMADON, D. & J. BULL 1988. Hawks and owls of the world: a distributional and taxonomic list, with the genus *Otus* by Joe T. Marshall and Ben F. King. *Proceeding of the Western Foundation for Vertebrate Zoology* 3(4) : 295-357.

BIGGS, H. C., R. BIGGS & A. C. KEMP 1978. Measurements of raptors. Pp. 77-82 *in* A.C. Kemp (Ed.). *Proceedings of a Symposium on African Predatory Birds*. Pretoria. Northern Transvaal Ornithological Society.

KEMP, A.C. & T.M. CROWE 1990. A preliminary phylogenetic and biogeographical analysis of the genera of diurnal raptors. *In*: G. Peters & R. Hutterer (Eds.) *Vertebrates in the Tropics*. Bonn : Museum Alexander Koenig.

KEMP, A.C. & T.M. CROWE 1991. Morphometrics of the Falconiformes : an overview. *Acta XX Congressus Internationalis Ornithologici*, Vol. 1 : 483-490.

KEMP, A.C. & T.M. CROWE 1993 A morphometric analysis of *Falco* species. *In*: M. Nicholls (Ed.) *The Biology and Conservation of Small Falcons*. Canterbury: The Hawk Trust.

KEMP, A.C. & M.I. KEMP 1975. Observations on the breeding biology of the Ovambo Sparrowhawk, *Accipiter ovampensis* Gurney (Aves: Accipitridae). *Annals of the Transvaal Museum* 29: 185-190.

WATTEL, J. 1973. Geographical differentation in the genus *Accipiter*. *Nuttall Ornithological Club* 13: 1-231.

WEICK, F. 1980. *Die Greifvögel der Welt*. Berlin: Verlag Paul Parey.

Dr. Alan Kemp
Department of Birds
Transvaal Museum
P.O. Box 413
Pretoria, 0001
South Africa

Prof. Tim Crowe
Percy FitzPatrick Institute
University of Cape Town
Rondebosch, 7700
South Africa

African Pygmy Falcon *Polihierax semitorquatus*

Meyburg, B.-U. & R. D. Chancellor eds.1994
Raptor Conservation Today
WWGBP / The Pica Press

Possible Effect of Anthropogenic Environmental changes on Morphological Variation of some European Birds of Prey

V.I. Pererva and A.V. Grazhdankin

INTRODUCTION

Problems of animal adaptation to human activity have attracted increasing attention in recent years. Behavioural reactions are normally the quickest form of organism response to anthropogenic factors of varying intensity. Changes in ecology and quantity of species are also of much interest. Moreover there are few investigations into basic transformations of animal morpho-physiology, which concern vital aspects of their biology and influence heredity.

Correlation has been confirmed of changes in morpho-physiological traits of certain mammals under the influence of anthropogenic factors (primarily towards diminution and deformation of the skull as well as the skeleton as a whole) in Aurochs (Zalkin 1962; Paaver 1965; Werestschagin & Rusakov 1979; Kobrynczuk 1985), Saiga Antelope (Zhirnov 1982; Pronjaev 1986) and Przhewalski's Horse (Klimov 1990). Few such changes are known in birds. However, at the beginning of the 1970s Wladishevsky (1973) noted certain differences between "agricultural" and "urban" populations of House Sparrows *Passer domesticus* in the Carpathian Mountains region, such as diminution in size of body parts (stomach, limbs). Tomialojc's (1995) research on European House Sparrows concluded that modern western forms adapted to new environments more quickly than eastern ones. There is no doubt that the natural environments in Europe have been substantially transformed through human activity.

Our hypothesis is that during the last century western Palaearctic populations of birds of prey evolved more than eastern ones. In our opinion this is due to more intensive western anthropogenic factors which influence natural trends in evolutional development of intraspecific forms. For birds of prey, one criterion for such a mode of evolution is, we suggest, intensification of sexual dimorphism in dimensions. We follow the conclusions of Hill (1944) and K.A. Judin (1958) that sexual size dimorphism in primitive members of the Falconiformes is expressed to a lesser degree than in more developed ones. Accordingly our second hypothesis is that decrease in the degree of sexual dimorphism within an intraspecific form of birds of prey indicates its inhibition in evolutional development.

The influence of anthropogenic factors can lead to an imbalance of genetic and phenotypic structure of a species as a whole and of interspecific forms in particular. Wladishevsky (1973, 1975) concluded that "synanthropic" forms are more variable in body dimensions than "wild populations", connected with different directions of selection. One way of producing such an imbalance of traits and increase in their coefficients of variance is by "infusion of blood" of domestic animals into wild ones, as with boars in Poland (Zurowski *et al.* 1970).

Thus we offer a third hypothesis: changes in traits through time, expressed as cofficients of variance, indicate the influence of factors (in this case anthropogenic) on a population of animals.

Our criteria for evaluating trait transformation in some birds of prey under the influence of anthropogenic factors are organ dimensions and their coefficient of variance, degree of sexual dimorphism and period of time when morphological changes could have taken place, based on the material available. The period (1824-1987) can be divided into three stages: first - 1824-1900, second - 1901-1930 and third - 1931-1987. These correspond with periods of varying degrees of intensity of anthropogenic influence on European fauna. The strongest impact was during the 1930s and beginnning of the 1940s in connection with the Second World War, use of toxic chemicals and appearance of synanthropic populations of Rock Doves as a new prey-base.

MATERIALS AND METHODS

Investigations were carried out on four species of raptor widespread in the Palaearctic: Saker Falcon *Falco cherrug*, Goshawk *Accipiter gentilis*, Steppe Eagle *Aquila nipalensis* and Imperial Eagle *A.heliaca*. We used study collections in museums (Zool. Inst. of Russia, St. Petersburg; Moscow State University, Moscow; Ukrainian A. Sc., Kiev) and eagles discovered dead below electric power lines in Kazakhstan and Kalmikia in 1981-1986. Subspecies differentiation (except of birds found under power lines) was done according to distribution of intraspecific populations (Dementiev 1951). Only adult birds collected in their nesting period (April-August) and with labels defining sites were analysed.

We measured lengths of wing (Lw), tail (Lt), first claw (L1c), bill at cere (Lb), and height of bill at cere (Hb), taking bill and claw measurements as previously stated (Grazhdankin & Pererva 1986). A total of 261 Goshawks (135 f., 126 m.), 161 Saker Falcons (82 f., 79 m.) 91 Steppe Eagles (34 f., 57 m.) and 61 Imperial Eagles (39 f., 22 m.) were measured. Results were analysed for arithmetical mean, mean error, quadratic deviation, significance by t-test and coefficient of variation. Degree of sexual dimorphism (r) was determined according to the formula of Hill (1944): $r = A/B \times 100\%$ where A is arithmetical mean value of male traits and B of corresponding female traits. A decrease in the "r" value corresponds to an increase in sexual dimorphism, and increase to the contrary.

RESULTS

Saker Falcon

A widespread polymorphic species inhabiting natural zones of forest, steppe, forest-steppe and semi-desert from Central Europe in the west to Manchuria and China in the east. Saker Falcon subspecific structure is not yet defined: some authors distinguish 6 subspecies (Dementiev 1951; Weick 1980), while others 4 subspecies (Stepanian 1975) or 3 (Kozlove 1969).

We made a preliminary attempt to revise subspecies on the basis of the coefficient of differences (CD) (Mayr 1970). The following subspecies according to Dementiev (1951) were evaluated: *danubialis, cherrug, saceroides, coatsi, milvipes* and *hendersoni*, taken from west to east. For each of the five traits studied no difference of more than 0.74 was found (Fig. 1), whereas according to the "rule of 75%" a population is considered as an independent subspecies when CD = 1.28 (Mayr 1970).

Earlier, based on statistical analysis of colouration intensity in various forms of Saker Falcon, a distinct difference between *danubialis* and *milvipes* was shown (Grazhdankin 1988). Based on our analysis of metric traits of Saker Falcon subspecies, we concluded that no distinct differences exist at the subspecific level. Therefore we analysed the whole species as a monophyletic taxon. We expect the largest anthropogenic pressure to be on the western populations of Saker Falcon, sometimes united under the name *danubialis,* which inhabit Europe west of the River Volga.

During the last 100 years there was a marked diminution in all body parts of females in this population (Table 1, Fig. 1). Shortening of wing, tail and bill was almost significant (t = 1.3-1.9)

Figure 1. Changeability of length of wing (Lw), tail (Lt), and first claw (L1c) in subspecies (A-F) of Sacer Falcon ($\bar{X}$ ± SD)
1, 2, 3 - traits changeability in *F. ch. danubialis* at time intervals: 1 - 1824-1900, 2 - 1901-1930, 3 - 1931-1987.
A - *F. ch. danubialis*, B - *F. ch. cherrug*, C - *F. ch. saceroides*, D - *F. ch. coatsi*, E - *F. ch. milvipes*, F - *F. ch. hendersoni*.

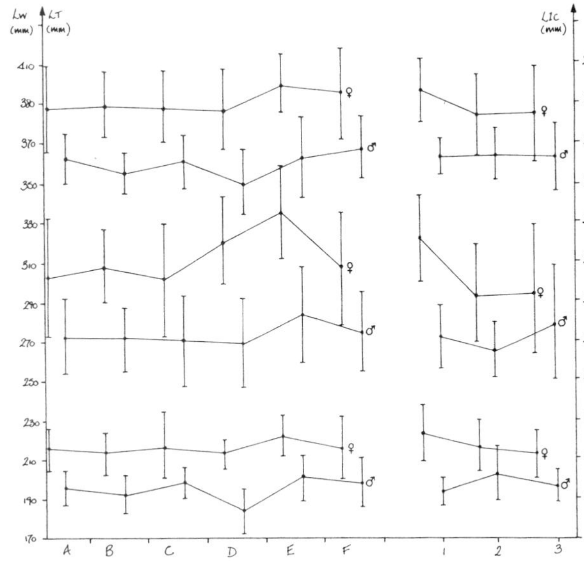

and height of the bill and the length of claw 1 were significant (t = 2.9-2.3). At the same time, over the whole area females had a lesser tendency to diminution. Males of the western population group *danubialis* changed quite differently (Table 2). There was a significant enlargement in the dimensions of wing, tail, claw and bill. The same tendencies in claw and bill were noted for the species as a whole, but length of tail and bill decreased somewhat during the last century.

There was a markedly wider variation of traits in females of the "*danubialis*" group (Fig. 1). Variation of traits through time was also greater than variation recorded between subspecies by Dementiev (1951). Besides, during the past century, variability in the range of dimensional traits as expressed by the coefficient of variation (CV) tended to increase, especially in western forms. This is in contrast to the decline in coefficient of variation for females as a whole. Thus, within the last decades, the species has been stable in dimensional traits but western populations tend to destabilisation with wide variation (Tables 1 & 2). There is also a marked diminution in sexual dimorphism in birds of the western "*danubialis*" population (Table 3).

Goshawk

In the Palaearctic a variable number of subspecies is distinguished: 10 (Dementiev 1951), 8 (Gladkov 1941), 6 (Stepanian 1975; Weick 1980) and even one (Wattel 1981). We followed Dementiev and analysed 8 subspecies; *gallinarum, buteoides, gentilis, caucasicus, suschkini, schvedowi, albidus* and *fujiyamae*. To define deformation in metric traits it is sufficient to examine only data on nominal subspecies (Tables 1 & 2). There are trends towards diminution of wing and bill in both sexes and claw 1 in females. There is also a significant increase in tail length in both sexes. Simultaneously we found an increase in variation: in the last century coefficients of variation in wing, tail and bill in males and in tail and claw in females increased (Tables 1 & 2). Sexual dimorphism in the "*gentilis*" population decreased in height of bill and claw length and, as for other metric traits, there were unsteady modulations in time (Table 3).

Steppe Eagle

In the Palaearctic there are two subspecies (Dementiev 1951) but differences between males are not sufficient for separation of given taxa with a differentiation coefficient (by Mayr 1970) of less than 1.28 (Grazhdankin & Pererva 1986). Steppe Eagles that perished from electrocution in 1981-1992 had smaller bills and claws than those in museums from the 19th and early 20th centuries (Grazhdankin & Pererva 1986). This was established for the species as a whole, whereas differential analysis of birds within the subspecies *orientalis* and *nipalensis* shows various trends. For "*nipalensis*" inhabiting Central Asia there is a decrease of traits in both sexes (Tables 1 & 2). Over the same time period there was some shortening of bill and claws in males of the western subspecies "*orientalis*", whereas in females there was some enlargement. Variation in degree of sexual dimorphism in these subspecies also developed differently (Table 3): this index was almost unchanged during the whole period in the eastern subspecies, whereas in the western one the tendency to stability of sexual dimorphism degree was marked only during the first three decades of the 20th century (second period).

Imperial Eagle

There are two separate, geographically isolated subspecies. In Russian territory the nominate *Aquila heliaca* showed a trend towards diminution (Tables 1 & 2), especially in males. Enlargement of the bill in females was noted at the same time, as for females of Steppe Eagles.

DISCUSSION

Variations in features of animals under anthropogenic impact has not been previously discussed in biology, due to the common view that evolutionary transformations require a long time process. Compared to the millions of years necessary for even insignificant differences to appear, similar effects within a decade do not seem probable, even though the cause of such changes may be considered evolutionary.

At present it is still impossible to give a full scientific description of anthropogenic factors. Hence it is reasonable to use such a term as "complex anthropogenic impact" and, when possible, to divide this into separate kinds of human activity. This report identifies two causes and accordingly two separate mechanisms for external metric trait transformation in birds of prey.

It would be simple to think that anthropogenic impact produces a unidimensional transformation, for example only diminution, but the collected data show a more complicated pattern. This is due, in our opinion, to a compromise between the natural evolutionary transformation of the species and new anthropogenic tendencies in wildlife.

The following two factors most affected Palaearctic birds of prey during the last decades:

1. A change in diet due to the disappearance of large prey species and appearance of new food sources.

2. A change in age structure of the population, due to extermination of adults and early breeding of young.

The effect of the first factor can be seen in Goshawks. At the turn of the century this species fed mainly on gallinaceous birds and hares (Kalchreuter 1981). From the 1930s the number of pigeons (wild and domestic) in Europe rose steeply (Thissen 1981) and in recent decades passerine birds also began to play an important role as food for Goshawks (Pererva 1988).

Birds of prey capture more small than large prey to feed nestlings and for their own nourishment. The catching of smaller prey requires a higher expenditure of energy. Goshawks of both sexes, now forced to capture small and medium-sized prey in comparison to their own size, show wing-shortening (as the general diminution equivalent) and simultaneous tail-lengthening, both of which are important for the successful pursuit of passerines and pigeons.

In the early 20th century, the diet and the dispersion of the Steppe Eagle were closely linked to suslik (Osmolovskaja 1953; Warshawski *et al.* 1983). Moreover, due to a steep rise in saiga numbers from the beginning of the 1950s as a result of successful protection (Zhirnov 1982), large birds of prey obtained a new source of food in saiga carcases and younger animals. Such food is accessible at any season and Steppe Eagles began actively to consume it (Korelov 1962; Fadeev 1986).

Such interconnections between raptors and their prey can be seen increasingly often during the

Table 1. Changes of metric traits in different forms (sub-species) of female birds of prey in sequential time periods (1 - 1824-1900, 2 - 1901-1930, 3 - 1931-1987).

Subspecies	Trait	1824-1900 N	Size	CV	N	Periods 1901-1930 Size	CV	N	1931-1987 Size	CV	t
A. gentilis	Lw	11	369,8±2,4	2,0	16	364,9±1,5	1,6	9	367,0±2,5	2,0	-0,8
	Lt	11	233,8±3,0	4,1	16	256,8±4,1	6,2	9	265,9±1,9	2,0	+9,0
	Lb	11	26,4±0,3	4,2	16	26,2±0,2	3,1	9	26,3±0,2	1,9	-0,3
	Hb	11	15,7±0,3	5,7	16	15,4±0,1	3,2	9	15,2±0,2	3,9	-1,6
	L1c	11	34,2±0,2	1,8	16	33,3±0,2	2,7	9	33,7±0,4	3,6	-1,0
F. cherrug danubialis	Lw	15	395,4±4,3	4,2	15	383,5±5,6	5,4	11	384,4±7,6	6,3	-1,3
	Lt	15	223,1±3,9	6,5	15	216,5±3,6	6,2	11	213,0±3,9	5,8	-1,8
	Lb	15	23,8±0,3	5,0	15	23,1±0,3	5,6	10	23,0±0,3	4,3	-1,9
	Hb	15	14,6±0,2	4,8	15	13,9±0,2	5,0	11	13,8±0,2	4,3	-2,9
	L1c	15	23,6±0,3	4,7	15	22,2±0,3	5,8	11	22,3±0,5	7,2	-2,3
F. cherrug cherrug	Lw	6	384,0±8,8	5,1	11	392,9±4,8	3,9	11	389,5±4,6	3,7	+0,6
	Lt	6	214,0±3,9	4,1	11	212,7±4,2	6,3	11	212,7±3,1	4,7	-0,3
	Lb	6	23,6±0,5	4,2	10	22,9±0,5	6,1	11	23,7±0,4	5,1	+0,2
	Hb	6	14,1±0,2	3,5	10	14,1±0,3	7,1	11	13,9±0,2	5,0	-0,7
	L1c	6	23,1±0,3	2,6	11	22,7±0,3	3,5	11	23,3±0,3	3,9	±0,5
F. cherrug (Sum)	Lw	32	393,1±3,6	5,1	75	388,7±2,5	5,6	94	389,1±1,9	4,7	-1,0
	Lt	32	217,4±2,0	5,2	75	216,4±1,8	7,0	94	215,0±1,3	5,8	-1,0
	Lb	32	23,5±0,2	6,0	72	23,2±1,2	6,0	89	23,4±0,1	5,1	-0,4
	Hb	32	14,2±0,2	5,6	74	14,0±0,1	6,4	92	13,9±0,1	5,0	-1,8
	L1c	32	23,3±0,2	5,2	75	23,0±0,2	7,0	94	23,3±0,1	5,6	0
Aquila n. orientals	Lb	6	39,6±0,9	4,8	10	39,1±0,5	4,1	51	41,1±0,7	4,8	+1,3
	Hb	7	20,5±0,4	5,4	10	19,8±0,4	5,6	53	20,1±0,7	3,8	-0,5
	L1c	7	34,3±1,2	8,6	10	35,9±0,9	7,5	50	35,6±2,1	7,8	+0,5
	L2c	7	33,6±0,2	5,7	10	34,5±0,8	6,7	-	-	-	+1,1
Aquila n. nipalensis	Lb	3	42,8±1,3	4,2	7	41,7±0,8	5,0	4	41,4±0,5	2,2	-1,0
	Hb	4	21,5±1,0	8,4	7	21,7±0,4	4,6	4	21,3±0,4	3,3	-0,2
	L1c	4	38,9±1,2	5,1	7	38,2±0,9	6,0	4	37,7±0,9	4,0	-0,8
	L2c	4	35,2±0,9	4,3	7	35,8±0,8	5,6	4	35,5±0,9	4,2	+0,2
Aquila heliaca	Lb	16	44,0±0,6	5,7	7	44,7±0,5	2,7	13	45,3±0,7	5,5	+1,4
	Hb	14	23,7±0,2	3,4	7	24,0±0,2	2,5	14	23,7±0,3	4,2	0
	L1c	14	39,8±0,8	7,0	8	39,2±0,6	4,1	15	39,6±0,7	6,8	-0,2
	L2c	14	36,7±0,6	6,3	8	36,3±0,5	3,6	14	36,4±0,6	6,0	-0,4

Table 2. Changes of metric traits in different forms (subspecies) of male birds of prey in sequential time periods (see Table 1).

Subspecies	Trait	1824-1900 N	1824-1900 Size	1824-1900 CV	1901-1930 N	1901-1930 Size	1901-1930 CV	1931-1987 N	1931-1987 Size	1931-1987 CV	t
A.g.gentilis	Lw	7	321,6±1,5	1,2	15	325,±1,6	1,8	16	318,5±3,0	3,6	-0,9
	Lt	7	200,0±4,5	5,5	15	215,0±3,6	6,2	16	222,8±4,6	8,1	+3,5
	Lb	7	22,2±0,2	2,3	15	22,2±0,2	3,6	16	21,8±0,2	4,1	-1,4
	Hb	7	13,6±0,2	3,7	15	13,6±0,1	2,2	16	13,5±0,1	3,0	-0,4
	L1c	7	26,8±0,4	3,7	15	27,9±0,2	2,5	16	27,9±0,3	3,6	+2,2
F.ch.danubialis	Lw	22	361,7±2,0	2,5	10	363,0±4,1	3,4	8	362,3±6,5	4,7	+0,1
	Lt	22	192,8±1,5	3,5	10	203,7±3,9	5,7	8	197,0±3,1	4,2	+1,2
	Lb	22	21,3±0,2	4,2	10	21,5±0,3	5,1	8	21,8±0,3	3,7	+1,4
	Hb	22	12,9±0,1	4,7	10	13,2±0,2	4,5	8	13,1±0,2	5,0	+0,9
	L1c	22	21,2±0,2	3,8	10	20,8±0,2	3,4	8	21,5±0,5	6,5	+0,6
F.ch.cherrug	Lw	6	353,7±3,8	2,4	10	354,8±3,7	3,2	10	354,3±3,5	3,0	+0,1
	Lt	6	194,8±2,1	2,4	10	190,3±2,4	3,7	10	191,8±3,8	5,9	-0,7
	Lb	6	21,2±0,4	4,7	10	21,4±0,3	3,7	10	21,5±0,3	4,2	+0,6
	Hb	6	13,2±0,3	4,5	10	13,3±0,1	2,3	10	12,9±0,2	4,7	-0,8
	L1c	6	20,8±0,4	3,8	10	21,5±0,2	2,8	10	21,1±0,2	3,3	+0,7
F.cherrug (sum)	Lw	37	361,5±2,2	3,7	75	362,3±1,8	4,1	82	360,2±2,0	5,0	-0,4
	Lt	36	194,4±1,4	4,4	80	198,3±1,4	6,4	80	195,8±1,5	6,7	+0,7
	Lb	36	21,4±0,2	6,1	83	21,4±0,1	6,1	83	21,2±0,2	10,4	-0,7
	Hb	36	13,0±0,1	5,4	76	13,2±0,1	4,5	82	13,1±0,1	9,2	+0,7
	L1c	37	21,2±0,1	4,2	75	21,5±0,1	5,6	84	21,5±0,1	5,6	+2,1
A.n.orientalis	Lb	17	37,9±0,5	5,5	14	38,4±0,7	6,8	51	37,4±1,4	4,2	-0,3
	Hb	18	19,3±0,2	4,7	15	19,8±0,2	4,0	51	19,1±0,7	3,9	-0,3
	L1c	18	32,5±0,4	5,2	15	33,0±0,7	8,2	35	32,2±1,2	4,9	-0,2
	L2c	18	31,7±0,4	4,7	15	31,8±0,6	7,2	-	-	-	+0,1
A.n.nipalensis	Lb	2	40,4±2,0	5,0	14	39,3±0,5	5,1	4	39,2±0,7	2,8	-0,6
	Hb	2	21,2±0,6	2,8	15	20,9±0,2	3,8	5	20,7±0,3	2,4	-1,3
	L1c	3	33,8±1,5	5,9	15	33,4±0,8	9,0	4	32,3±0,7	3,4	-0,9
	L2c	3	33,3±1,6	6,9	15	32,6±0,6	6,7	4	32,0±0,8	4,1	-0,7
Aquila heliaca	Lb	12	42,1±0,6	4,5	-	-	-	8	41,4±0,7	4,8	-0,8
	Hb	12	22,6±0,3	4,9	-	-	-	8	22,4±0,3	3,6	-0,5
	L1c	12	35,0±0,6	6,3	2	34,4±0,3	-	7	34,7±1,1	7,8	-0,2
	L2c	12	33,5±0,6	5,7	2	33,1±0,2	-	7	33,9±1,2	8,6	+0,3

Table 3. Sexual dimorphism indices (r) in different sub-species of birds of prey in the Palaearctic (1824 - 1987)

Subspecies / Trait	*F. ch.danubialis*					*F. ch. cherrug*					*F. cherrug* (sum)				
	Lw	Lt	Lb	Hb	L1c	Lw	Lt	Lb	Hb	L1c	Lw	Lt	Lb	Hb	L1c
1. 1824-1900	91.5	86.4	89.5	88.4	89.8	92.1	91.0	89.8	93.6	90.0	92.0	89.4	91.1	91.5	91.0
2. 1901-1930	94.7	94.1	93.1	95.0	93.7	90.3	89.5	93.5	94.3	94.7	93.2	91.6	92.2	94.3	93.5
3. 1931-1987	94.3	92.5	94.8	94.9	96.4	91.0	90.2	90.7	92.8	90.6	92.6	91.1	90.6	94.2	92.3
trend in time 1-2	-	-	-	-	-	+	+	-	-	-	-	-	-	-	-
intervals 2-3	+	+	-	+	-	-	-	+	+	+	+	+	+	-	+

Subspecies / Trait	*A. gentilis gentilis*					*A. n. orientalis*				*A. n. nipalensis*				*A. heliaca*			
	Lw	Lt	Lb	Hb	L1c	Lb	Hb	L1c	L2c	Lb	Hb	L1c	L2c	Lb	Hb	L1c	L2c
1. 1824-1900	87.0	85.5	84.1	86.5	78.4	95.7	94.1	94.8	94.3	94.4	98.6	86.9	94.6	94.3	95.4	87.9	91.3
2. 1901-1930	89.2	83.7	84.7	88.2	84.0	98.0	100	91.9	92.2	94.2	96.3	87.4	91.1	-	-	-	-
3. 1931-1987	86.8	83.8	82.8	88.8	82.8	91.0	95.0	90.4	-	94.7	97.2	85.7	90.1	91.4	94.5	87.6	93.1
trend in time 1-2	-	+	-	-	-	-	-	+	+	+	+	+					
intervals 2-3	+	-	+	-	+	+	+	+		-	-	+	+ +	-	+	+	-

comment: + tend to increase (r)
- tend to decrease (r)

last decades, leading to the direct correlation of many events in the eagle's life to the migratory status and time schedule of cattle and other ecological parameters of saiga (Zhirnov 1992; Fadeev 1986).

We believe that further *nipalensis* specialisation for rodent capture (marmots, susliks and mice) is mainly responsible for the progressive diminution of the species. That this process is natural is suggested by the constant degree of sexual dimorphism in nominal subspecies (Table 3), even against the background of simultaneous diminution of males and females. *Orientalis,* inhabiting the region of densest saiga population (Kalmikia, Kazakhstan), had changes in degree of sexual dimorphism with differently directed trends between the three periods.

The second cause is the change in age structure of the populations of raptors. If this process is due to extermination of the adults, the nesting places are liberated for the young and this alters the general appearance of the population. For Goshawks from Denmark, such a process of replacing adult breeding females by younger ones was described in detail by Thissen (1981). Young Goshawks have different body proportions from the adults. For example, young North American *Accipiter gentilis atricapillus* have shorter wings and longer tails than adults (Mueller *et al.* 1976). This, in additon to other changes in body structure such as wingloading, is suggested to aid flight for the young.

Such selection would promote the process of wing shortening and tail lengthening in the eastern European populations of Goshawks in two ways: first, by larger breeding participation of birds with extreme proportions, and secondly by the gain in power expenditure while hunting numerous small and medium-size prey.

Therefore the anthropogenic changes observed in 20th century Europe and during the last decades on the Asian continent lead to transformation of behaviour, ecology and numerical decrease of birds of prey. They also affect profound biological peculiarities of the species. This is alarming because the direction of the changes does not coincide with the natural evolutionary processes in wildlife. Natural selection is replaced by an artificial one.

It is impossible to neglect these changes because they violate one of the fundamental principles of nature protection strategy - the conservation of natural biodiversity.

REFERENCES

DEMENTIEV, G.P. 1951. Ptizi Sovetskogo Sojuza, t.1. Chistsnie ptizi. M., Izdatelstvo AN SSSR. 652

FADEEV, V.A. 1986. Svjaz stepnich orlov s saigakami v Kazakstane. V kn.: Redkie zhivotnie Kazakstana. Alma-Ata, *Nauka:* 125-126.

GLADKOV, N.A. 1941. Taxonomy of Palaearctic Goshawks. *Auk*, v.58, N1: 80-90.

GRAZHDANKIN, A.V. 1988. Kolichestvennaja ozenka okraski po otrazhatelnoj sposobnosti operenia i vozmozhnosti ejo primenenija pri issledovanijah izmentschivosti ptiz. *Zool.J.*, t.67, 7: 1066-1072.

GRAZHDANKIN, A.V. & V.I. PERERVA 1986. Priznaki polovogo dimorphizma u stepnogo orla (*Aquila nipalensis)* i mogilnika (*A.heliaca*). *J.Obstschei biologii*, t. 47, 2: 268-273.

HILL, N.P. 1944. Sexual dimorphism in the Falconiformes. *Auk,* v.61, N2: 228 - 234.

JUDIN, K.A. 1953. Morphologitscheskie adaptatsii sem. Falconidae v svjazi s voprosami sistematiki. - V kn.: Pamjati akad. P.P. Suschkina, M. - L: Izdatelstvo AN SSSR: 135-208.

KALCHREUTER, H. 1981. The Goshawk in Western Europe. In *Understanding the Goshawk*. pp. 18-27.

KLIMOV, V.V. 1990. Loschadj Przhevalskogo. M.: Agropromizdat: 253.

KOBRYNZUK, F. 1985. The influence of inbreeding on the shape and size of the skeleton of the European bison. *Acta theriol.* v.30,n 21-31: 379-422.

KORELOV, M.N. 1962. Ptitsi Kazakhstana. t.2. Otrjad chistsnie ptizi. Alma-Ata, Izdatelstvo AN Kaz.SSR: 488-707.

KOZLOVA, E.V. 1969. Rodstvennije svjazi sokolov-balobanov i kretscheta i verojatnaja istorija ih rasselenija.-*Zool.zh.*,t.48, v.12: 1838-1851.

MAYR, E. 1970. Printsipi zoologitscheskoii systematiki. M.,Mir, 454.

MUELLER, H.C., D.D. BERGER & G. ALLEZ 1976. Age and sex variation in the size of Goshawks. *Bird-Band.*, v.47.N4: 310-318.

OSMOLOVSKAJA, V.I. 1953. Geographitscheskoje raspredelenije Chistjih ptits ravninnogo Kazakhstana i ich znatschenije v istrebleniji vrediteljei. *Tr. Inst., geogr.* Mat. po biogeogr SSSR, v.54, 219-307.

PAAVER, K.L. 1965. Formirovanije teriofauniji i izmentschivost mlekopitajuschich Pribaltiki v holotsene. Tartu,493.

PERERVA, V.I. 1988. Soprjazhennost geographitscheskoji izmentschi vosti pitanija i podvidovoji structurji khitschnich ptiz.-V kn.: Ekologija i povedenije ptits. M.: *Nauka,*54-64.

PRONJAEV, A.V. 1986. Phenotypitscheskaja charakteristika populjatsciji saigaka.- Tes.dokl. 4 sjiezda Vsesojuzn. teriol. obtschestva, t.3, M.,*Nauka*, 163-164.

STEPANIAN, L.S. 1975. Sostav I raspredelenije ptits fauni SSSR: Nevorobjinije. M.:*Nauka*, 370.

THISSEN, J., MÜSKENS G. 1981. Trends in the Dutch goshawk population.- in *Understanding the Goshawk.*28-42.

TOMIALOJ, L. 1985. Urbanization as a test of adaptive potentials in birds.- Acta XVIII Congressus Internat. ornithol., August 16-24. 1982. Moscow. *Nauka*,v.2: 608-614.

WARSCHAVSKIJI, S.N., R.S. WARSCHAVSKIJI, V.K. GARBUZOV, P.I. KAMNEV A.V. POPOV, M.N. SCHILOV & N.V. TSCHEPOTJIEV 1983. Osobennosti razmetschenija i tschislennosti populatsiji stepnogo orla v zapadnoji tschasti areala v svjazi s tschislennostjiu malogo suslika. V kn.: Vid i ego produktivnost v areale.M.: *Nauka*: 48-53.

WATTEL, J. 1981. The goshawk and its relatives.- *In Understanding the Goshawk.*6-15.

WAICK, F. 1980. *Die Greifvögel der Welt.* Hamburg, Berlin: P.Parey. pp.159.

WERESTSCHAGIN, N.K. & O.S. RUSAKOV 1979. Kopjitnije severo-zapada SSSR, L.: *Nauka,* 308.

WLADJISCHEVSKIJ, D.V. 1973. Morphologitscheskije reaktscii ptits izmenenije usloviji suschestvovanija v anthropogennom landschafte.- V Kn.:Problemi evolutscii. Novosybirsk,:*Nauka*, t.3.242-248.

WLADJISCHEVSKIJ, D.V. 1975. Ptitsi v anthropogennom landschafte. Novosybirsk,: *Nauka*: 198.

ZHIRNOV, LV. 1982. Vozvraschtsenije k zhizni: Lesnaja promischlennost, 223.

ZALKIN, V.I. 1962. K istorii zhivotnovodstva i ochti v vostotschnoji Europe.- Mat. issledov. po archeologii SSSR, N 107: 5-129.

ZUROWSKI, W. H.SIUDOWA & B.GALKA 1970. Effect of single pig's blood addition on the local wild bear (*Sus scrofa*) population. *Transactions of IX Internat. Congr. of Game Biologists* (Moscow, September 1969) Moscow: 253-238.

Dr. Victor I. Pererva / A.V. Grazhdankin
Research Institute of Nature Conservation
VNII Priroda p/o Vilar
Sadki-Znamenskoje
113628 Moscow
Russia

Spotted Owl *Strix occidentalis*

Meyburg, B.-U. & R. D. Chancellor eds.1994
Raptor Conservation Today
WWGBP / The Pica Press

DNA-Fingerprinting of Eleonora´s Falcon *Falco eleonorae**

I. Swatschek, F. Feldmann, D. Ristow,
W. Scharlau, C. Wink & M. Wink

INTRODUCTION

Although many bird species seem to be monogamous according to observations and ringing recoveries, there is increasing evidence that extra-pair copulations (EPC) are not exceptional but occur at a certain rate in many populations. The study of pairing systems and the question of EPC became possible with the introduction of techniques which employ methods of molecular biology.

Especially the technique of DNA-fingerprinting is a powerful means to analyse close relationships within populations, e.g. pedigree analysis. Several protocols are available. They differ in the choice of a specific DNA-probe and/or the method of detecting hybridized DNA. Jeffreys *et al.* 1985; Ali *et al.* 1986; Nakamura *et al.* 1987; Georges *et al.* 1988; Zischler *et al.* 1989; Gyllensten *et al.* 1989). In this study we used synthetic oligonucleotide probes [$(GAA)_5$, L18] and as a detection method, immunological procedures that avoid the use of radioactivity.

Eleonora´s Falcon *Falco eleonorae* breeds on isolated islands of the Mediterranean and winters in Madagascar. This species lives colonially and up to 400 breeding pairs can be found on rather small rocky islands. Eleonora´s Falcon is territorial. Since space is limited on these islands, a breeding territory usually is small, with a radius of 10-50 m. As a consequence, breeding pairs nest in close proximity and usually have visual contact with each other. With respect to the known incidence of EPC in other bird species, our working hypothesis was that, although Eleonora´s Falcon is a monogamous bird (Ristow *et al.* 1979) EPC should occur. To test this hypothesis we studied seventeen families of Eleonora´s Falcon from an Aegean colony by DNA-fingerprinting.

MATERIAL AND METHODS

Collection of Blood

In 1991 we captured 78 adult female and 28 male falcons on an Aegean island (Ristow *et al.* 1991). Venous blood (c. 100 ml) was taken and stored in DNA-buffer (Arctander 1988). Blood was also collected from young falcons of which parent birds had been captured. Blood was stored at ambient temperature up to four weeks, then transferred to Heidelberg and stored at - 20°C.

Extraction of DNA

0.5 ml of the blood samples were mixed with 5 ml lysis-buffer (25 mM EDTA, 75 mM NaCl,

* *Part 20 of a series on the biology of Eleonora´s Falcon.*

10 mM Tris, pH 7.5, 1% SDS) containing 1 mg proteinase K. After overnight incubation at 37°C, proteins were removed by precipitation with 2.5 ml of saturated NaCl solution. By adding 16 ml of 100% ethanol to the supernatant the DNA precipitated and was collected with a glass rod. The DNA was washed with 70% ethanol to remove salts, then airdried and dissolved in 1 ml H_2O.

Cleavage by Restriction Enzymes

30 µg DNA per sample were digested overnight with 25 units Hinf I (Pharmacia). Completeness of digestion was controlled by agarose gel-electrophoresis of 3 µg of the digested DNA.

Preparation of Oligonucleotide Probes

Ologonucleotide probe L18 was constructed synthetically according to the core sequence of a minisatellite fo the Willow Warbler (*Phylloscopus trochilus*) (Gyllensten *et al.* 1989), $(GAA)_5$ was purchased from Fresenius (Oberursel, FRG). The oligonucleotide probes were labelled with digoxigenin by using Dig-11-dUTP and terminal transferase. Internal standards and molecular weight markers were coupled with digoxigenin using a UV-sensitive digoxigenin derivate (Boehringer).

Electrophoresis

Genomic DNA which was treated with restriction enzyme was separated by agarose gel-electrophoresis: 0.7% agarose gels were run in 1xTAE-buffer at 4°C, 42V for 65 hours. The length of the gels was 30 cm.

Transfer of DNA from Agarosegels onto Nylon Membranes

When gel-electrophoresis was completed DNA was transferred from the gel to nylon membrane (Biodyne B) by capillary transfer as outlined by Maniatis *et al.* (1989). Nylon membranes were kept at 80°C for two hours to immobilize the DNA.

Hybridization and Detection

Detection employed immunological methods: DNA/DNA-hybrids were detected by an antibody which was raised against digoxigenin. This antibody was coupled to a phosphatase which in turn produced a coloured product at the sites of hybridization (Boehringer). After colour reactions were completed, nylon membranes were documented and processed by the Bioprofil system.

RESULTS AND DISCUSSION

We obtained blood samples of 106 breeding adult falcons. Some of them lost their clutch due to rat predation (Wink *et al.* 1985), so that no young became available. The chicks of other falcons were too young to obtain blood samples at the time we had to finish our field survey. So the final DNA-fingerprint analysis could only be performed on seventeen families of Eleonora´s Falcon.

In four families, the DNA of both male and female and their respective young was analysed (Fig. 1). Considering the bandsharing between females and their respective young it is obvious that the female was the real mother in all cases (see bands indicated by arrows in Fig. 1). The same conclusion can be obtained for the corresponding males, i.e. the male was the natural father in these families. In thirteen further families, DNA was available only from either the male or the female (Table 1). In all these cases the parentage of the parent whose DNA was available could be assessed unequivocally. Again, no evidence for EPC or extra-pair fertilization (EPF) could be detected.

More difficult was assessment of the parentage of the other parent bird, whose DNA was not available. However, we found in most cases that two to four bands which were not present in the profile of the known parent occurred concomitantly in those of the young. This is clear evidence that the unknown parent was identical for all the respective chicks. We cannot rule out, however, the unlikely case that a close relative of the unknown parent might have interfered. Therefore, we

Figure 1. Examples for DNA-fingerprinting of Eleonora´s falcons
a) DNA-profiles of 10 unrelated adult males
b) DNA-profile of a family with 2 young
c) DNA-profiles of a female with her 2 young

Arrows indicate significant bands

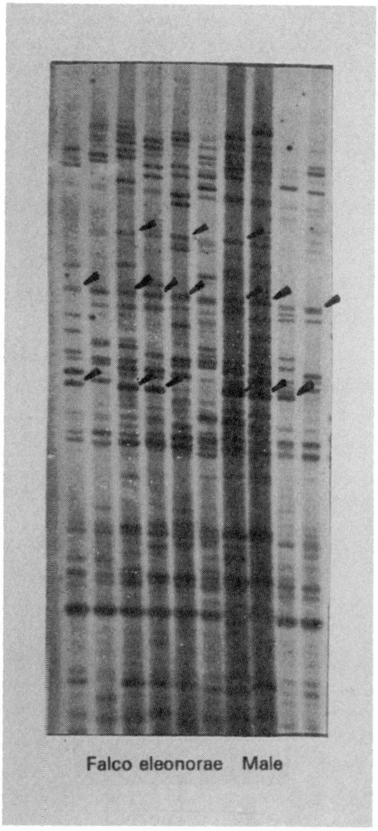

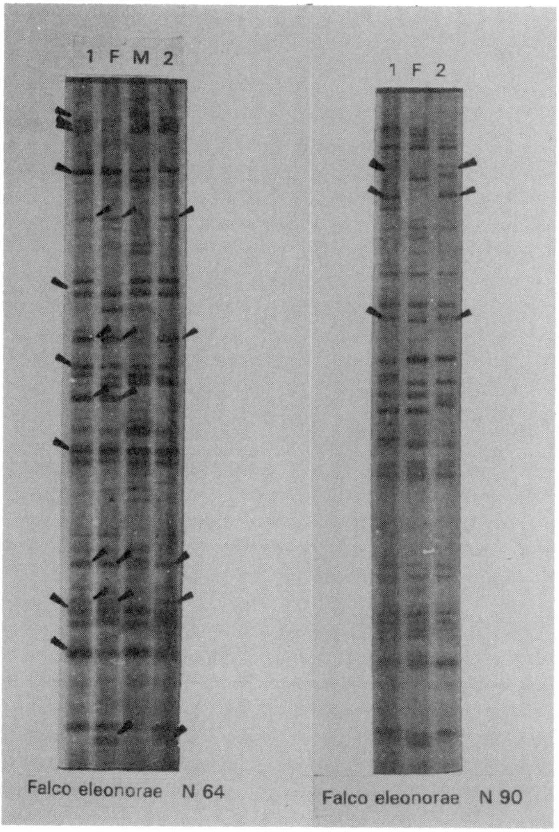

Table 1: Pedigree analysis in 17 families of *Falco eleonorae*

Nest	Parentage Young A		B		C	
	M	F	M	F	M	F
DNA of both parents available						
64	+	+	+	+		
83	+	+	+	+		
56	+	+	+	+		
11	n.d.		+	+	+	+
DNA of male available						
30	+	*	+	*		
85	+					
DNA of female available						
22	*	+	*	+		
26	*	+	*	+		
31	?	+	?	+		
45		+				
47		+				
90	*	+	*	+		
91	*	+	*	+		
101	*	+	*	+		
110	*	+	*	+	*	+
121		+				
125	*	+	*	+		

+ = *parentage certain*
* = *parentage "very likely"*
? = *gels could not be read with certainty*

Table 2. Summary of parentage assessments

	Number of young		
	certain	very likely	??
Female is the mother	27	3	1
Male is the father	11	15	5
Evidence for EPC	none	none	none

have classified these findings only as "very likely" (Tables 1 and 2). We could not make an unequivocal assessment because not all bands were clearly visible. However, these cases provide no evidence for EPC either.

Summarizing this analysis, we thus found no evidence for EPC. Also the incidence of egg-dumping by an unrelated female must be a rare event, which nevertheless occurs. In 1979 we found a clutch of four eggs and their measurements indicated that this clutch was produced by two females contributing two eggs each (Wink & Ristow, unpublished).

Our DNA-fingerprint analysis clearly indicates, that parent birds seen at a nest of Eleonora´s Falcon are usually the natural fathers and mothers of the respective young. This result shows that a general statement on the abundance of EPF in birds of prey cannot be given. Even in likely candidates for EPF, such as the colonially breeding Eleonora´s Falcon, strictly monogamous behaviour was determined. The analysis by DNA-fingerprinting thus confirms our previous results obtained by observation and ringing recoveries.

Figure 1 reveals another phenomenon. A number of bands are shared by both male, female and the young of one nest. In a population in which all adults are genetically unrelated, the number of these bands shared should be rather low whereas it is higher when animals are related. For example, in colonies of the eusocial naked Mole-rat (*Heterocephalus glaber*), DNA-fingerprints show an extremely high level of bandsharing indicating the close relationship of the animals (Reeve *et al.* 1990). Following a similar argument, we preliminarily assume, that the adult Eleonora´s Falcons of the breeding colony studied are genetically related because of the relatively high degree of bandsharing (see markings in Fig. 1).

ACKNOWLEDGEMENTS

Our research was supported by grants of the Deutsche Forschungsgeminschaft (We 719/7-1). We thank Ch. Langlotz for technical assistance, and the Greek government for permission to do research on Eleonora´s Falcon.

SUMMARY

Seventeen families of Eleonora´s Falcon were analysed by DNA-fingerprinting using oligonucleotide probes. Although the birds breed colonially and in close proximity, no evidence was obtained for EPF, indicating that male and female seen at a falcon´s nest are usually the natural parents of the respective young.

REFERENCES

ALI S. D., R. MÜLLER, & J. T. EPPLEN, 1986. DNA fingerprinting by oligonucleotide probes specific for simple repeats. *Hum. Genet.* 74: 239-243.

ARCTANDER, P. 1988. Comparative studies of avian DNA by restriction fragment length polymorphism analysis: Convenient procedures based on blood samples form live birds. *J. Orn.* 129: 205-216.

GEORGES, M., A.-S. LEQUARRE, M. CASTELLI, R. HANSET & G. VASSART 1988. DNA fingerprinting in domestic animals using four different minisatellite probes. *Cytogenet. Cell. Genet.* 47: 127-132.

GYLLENSTEN, U. B., S. JAKOBSSON, H. TEMRIN & A. C. WILSON 1989. Nucleotide sequence and genomic organization of bird minisatellites. *Nucleic Acids Research* 17: 2203-2214.

JEFFREYS, A. J., V. WILSON & S. L. THEIN 1985. Hyperveriable minisatellite regions in human DNA. *Nature* 314: 67-73.

MANIATIS, T., J. SAMBROOK & E. F. FRITSCH 1989. *Molecular cloning: A laboratory manual.* Cold Spring Harbor Laboratory Press, Cold Spring Harbor (1989).

NAKAMURA Y., M. LEPPERT, P. O'CONELL, R. WOLFF, T. HOLM, M. CULVER, C. MARTIN, E. FUJIMOTO, M. HOPF, E. KUMLIN & R. WHITE. 1987. Variable number of tandem repeat (VNTR) markers for human gene mapping. *Science* 235: 1616-1622.

REEVE, H. K., D. F. WESTNEAT, W. A. NOON, P. W. SHERMAN, C. & F. AQUADRO 1990. DNA "fingerprinting" reveals high levels of inbreeding in colonies of the eusocial naked molerat. *Proc. Natl. Acad. Sci. USA*. 87: 2496-2500.

RISTOW, D., C. WINK & M. WINK 1979. Site tenacity and pair bond of the Eleonora´s Falcon. *Il-Merill* 20, 16-18.

RISTOW, D., F. FELDMANN, W. SCHARLAU, C. WINK & M. WINK 1991. Population dynamics of Cory´s Shearwater (*Calonectris diomedea*) and Elonora´s Falcon (*Falco eleonorae*) in the Eastern Mediterranean. *In* A. Seitz & V. Loeschke (eds). *Species conservation: A population-biological approach*, p. 199-212, Birkhäuser Verlag, Basel.

WINK, M., D. RISTOW & C. WINK 1985. Biology of Eleonora´s Falcon: 7. Variability of clutch size, egg dimensions and egg coloring. *Raptor Research* 19: 8-14.

ZISCHLER, H., I. NANDA, R. SCHÄFER, M. SCHMID & J. T. EPPLEN 1989. Digoxigenated oligonucleotide probes specific for simple repeats in DNA fingerprinting and hybridization in situ. *Hum. Genet.* 82: 227-233.

Prof. Dr. M. Wink
Institut für Pharmazeutische Biologie
Universität Heidelberg
Im Neuenheimer Feld 364
D-6900 Heidelberg

Part 10

Environmental Contaminants and Raptors

Swallow-tailed Kite *Elanoides forficatus*

Convener:

Dr. R. W. Risebrough

Meyburg, B.-U. & R. D. Chancellor eds.1994
Raptor Conservation Today
WWGBP / The Pica Press

Toxic Chemicals and Birds of Prey: Discussions in Berlin in 1992

R.W. Risebrough

The structure of the Contaminants Session at the Ivth World Conference on Birds of Prey in Berlin, as well as of this overview paper, has followed with one major exception that of the IIIrd World Conference in Eilat and of its summary chapter (Risebrough 1989). The exception has derived from a need to incorporate a discussion of current research on the PCBs and of their current ecological relevance to birds of prey.

The principal contaminant issues of concern for the protection of birds of prey appeared in 1987 to fall within six principal considerations: 1) A re-interpretation of past events, in the light of recently acquired knowledge and understanding. This is of evident scientific interest, and responds to a continuing need to provide a technically sound basis for conservation policies that would protect birds of prey from adverse effects of the use of biocidal chemicals in all parts of the world; 2) Documentation of now-familiar effects of toxic chemicals on birds of prey, such as eggshell thinning and depressed productivity, in areas of the world that have hitherto received relatively little attention; 3) Priorities for future research and projects; 4) New chemicals or new uses of chemicals; 5) Re-introduction of raptors into polluted environments; 6) Implementation of national and international strategies for reducing harmful effects of toxic chemicals on birds of prey.

Although the papers presented in Berlin provided a very uneven coverage of these topics, the same format is followed in this overview chapter, except that the sixth topic is not discussed in the absence of any suggested new approaches. The review of current relevance of the PCBs is included with an assessment of their role in contributing to the population declines of the past. To reduce the demands on space, all references for the papers in the Contaminants Session are combined into a common bibliography.

One editorial inconsistency deserves mention. The name "White-tailed Eagle" is used for *Haliaeetus albicilla* in the papers by North American authors, but there appears to be no justifiable reason to apply the dictates of the Committee on Classification and Nomenclature of the American Ornithologists Union to the papers of European authors, in which the traditional name "White-tailed Sea Eagle" continues to be used.

1. RE-INTERPRETATION OF THE PAST

At the Eilat Conference in 1987 a major effort was made to sort out the relative contributions of DDE and of dieldrin in contaminant-induced population declines of several raptor species, particularly the Peregrine Falcon, *Falco peregrinus*. The need for this had become apparent at the Second World Conference in Thessaloniki in 1982: the British contingent was unanimous in believing that adult mortalities caused by dieldrin had been the major factor in the declines of Peregrine Falcons and Sparrowhawks, *Accipiter nisus*, in Britain; most of the North Americans considered that depressed productivity associated with DDE-induced shell thinning was the major factor in the disappearance of the Peregrine from eastern North America and the population declines of other species such as the Osprey, *Pandion haliaetus*, and Bald Eagle, *Haliaeetus leucocephalus*. A mixed message indicating a fundamental uncertainty about the real cause(s) of the population declines was coming from the community with the greatest interest in protecting birds of prey. Academically, this situation was unacceptable, inconsistent with the need to establish an historical accuracy. Moreover, an uncontested argument from either side could be used to justify continuing use of these or comparable biocidal chemicals in several parts of the world.

In the discussions of dieldrin-DDE effects, nothing, or almost nothing, was said about the PCBs and their possible role in population declines. Over the past five years there have been major advances in the understanding of the physiological and biochemical mechanisms of action of PCBs. It is clearly time to assess the role of PCBs in the population declines of raptor populations in the past, and their current role in causing or contributing to the depressed productivity in the several raptor populations still experiencing such difficulties. This was the principal theme of the Contaminants Session, and is the principal focus of this overview chapter.

Dieldrin-DDE

My own conclusions from the discussions in Eilat, which followed those on the same theme in the proceedings of The Peregrine Fund Conference in Sacramento (Cade *et al.* 1988; Nisbet 1988; Risebrough & Peakall 1988) are that depressed productivity caused by DDE could have caused the disappearance of the Peregrine from eastern North America over a 20-year period and that adult mortalities caused by the DDT compounds without any contribution from other contaminants made extinction inevitable; adult mortalities caused by dieldrin and other organochlorine biocides undoubtedly had a major additional impact on the population, or would have had if Peregrines were still surviving. In Britain, the use of dieldrin came at a time when the Peregrine population had been stressed by DDE-induced low productivity over a decade. The number of non-breeding birds without territories is therefore expected to have been abnormally low. Normally, a bird without a territory would quickly replace a member of a pair that has died such that an increase in the adult mortality rate might not be immediately detected; any increase in mortality rate, even a relatively small one, would much more likely be detected if the floating population without territories was depressed in its numbers (Risebrough & Peakall 1988; Risebrough 1989). This factor could explain why the decline of breeding Peregrines in Britain coincided more closely with the use pattern of dieldrin rather than that of DDT.

Newton *et al.* (1992) have compiled data on the percentages of mortalities of Sparrowhawks and Kestrels, *Falco tinnunculus*, that were caused by dieldrin in Britain over the period 1963-90. Population changes were correlated with the changes in dieldrin-induced mortalities. Incorporation of these data, together with productivity data, into a population model might provide further insight into the importance of adult mortalities vs. depressed productivity as causes of the population declines in these and other species affected by organochlorines. Mentioned in the discussion of the papers at the Eilat symposium (Risebrough 1989) but not adequately developed was the importance in assessing the relative importance of dieldrin (principally adult mortalities) and DDE (principally depressed productivity) of applying population parameters on a species-by-species basis to population models such as those developed by Grier (1979, 1980, 1991). A model applied at this symposium to Bald Eagles in northern California (Jenkins, this volume) was based on population parameters of adult survival, juvenile mortality and productivity compiled over a ten-year period in a sub-population. Over the period 1966-1972, autopsies of 145 Bald Eagles found dead in the U.S. indicated that 12.4 % had died of dieldrin poisoning (Mulhern *et al.* 1970; Belisle *et al.* 1972; Cromartie *et al.* 1975. A comparable 11% increase of adult mortality, without any depression of productivity, would have only a small effect in the northern California population; yearly adult survival would be reduced from 94.6% to 94%.

The uncompleted task is to compile the best available current estimates of the relevant natural population parameters of all species that have been affected by contaminants, and from a model predict the effects of increases in adult and juvenile mortalities and depressions in productivities, taking into account the existence of a non-breeding component without territories, density-dependent factors, age-dependent mortality factors, etc. This is therefore proposed as the priority topic for the Contaminants Session at the Vth World Conference in 1997.

Moreover, further clarification of the dieldrin-DDE and the increased mortality-depressed productivity factors will be a pre-requisite in resolving a new controversy that is developing - on the relevance and importance of past and present impacts of PCBs.

The Avian Toxicology of PCBs

When PCBs were first recognized as global contaminants, similar to the DDT compounds in their environmental behavior and whose local abundance was frequently as high or higher than that of the DDTs, a role in the population declines of birds of prey appeared likely (Jensen *et al.* 1969; Koeman *et al.* 1969; Risebrough *et al.* 1968). David Peakall's experiments showed that PCBs, like DDT, DDE, and dieldrin, induced mixed-function oxidase enzymes in the liver that degraded the female sex hormone and other steroid hormones into polar metabolites (Peakall 1967; Risebrough *et al.* 1968; Lincer & Peakall 1970). Estrogen was known to be linked with the deposition of medullary bone, the principal source of eggshell calcium (Simkiss 1967), and a link with shell thinning appeared plausible. This hypothesis was soon disproved: PCBs were found not to be the major cause of shell thinning (Peakall 1971; Heath *et al.* 1972; McLane & Hughes 1980), and the absence of adverse effects except in the oviduct in populations highly contaminated with DDE such as the California Brown Pelicans, *Pelecanus occidentalis*, that were laying very thin-shelled eggs, pointed to a mechanism of action that was local and confined to the oviduct (Risebrough *et al.* 1970).

PCBs have a relatively low acute toxicity to most avian species (Stickel *et al.* 1984) and only in those cases when body burdens were particularly high would they be expected to have contributed to adult mortalities (e.g. Koeman *et al.* 1973). The domestic chicken is an exception and is particularly sensitive to PCB toxicity (e.g. Flick *et al.* 1965; Vos & Koeman 1970; Bush *et al.* 1974), just as the mink, *Mustela vison*, is among mammals (Aulerich & Ringer 1977).

A number of experimental studies have demonstrated PCB effects on behavior (e.g. Peakall & Peakall 1973; Kreitzer & Heinz 1974; Tori & Peterle 1983; Koval *et al.* 1987). Comparable effects have been shown to be caused by DDE (Haegele & Hudson 1973, 1977; Richie & Peterle 1979) dieldrin (Gesell *et al.* 1979; Kreitzer & Heinz 1974), toxaphene (Kreitzer 1980), endrin (Kreitzer & Heinz 1974; Kreitzer 1980), and chlordane (Kreitzer & Heinz 1974), suggesting a common mechanism of action. In the field a lower intensity of nest defense behavior by Merlins, *Falco columbarius*, was associated with higher concentrations in the eggs of DDE and PCBs and with shell thinning (Fyfe *et al.* 1976; Fox & Donald 1980) Nest defense and other behavior patterns of Herring Gulls, *Larus argentatus*, was altered in colonies with higher levels or organochlorine contamination (Fox *et al.* 1978). A mixture of DDE, PCBs, mirex and photomirex in the proportions encountered in the Lake Ontario ecosystem produced alterations in the behavior of Ringed Turtle-Doves, *Streptopelia risoria,* under experimental conditions (McArthur *et al.* 1983). Ratcliffe's earlier observations of apparent abnormal behavior of Peregrines (i.e. Ratcliffe 1970) are recalled. The bulk of the evidence indicates therefore that PCBs, and the other organochlorines, had a significant role in depressing productivity through modifications of behavior.

Although induction of the mixed-function oxidase enzymes results in degradation of steroid hormones, feed-back mechanisms maintained levels of plasma progesterone in Mourning Doves, *Zenaida maroura* (Koval *et al.* 1987), Ringed Turtle-Doves (McArthur *et al.* 1983) and Japanese Quail, *Coturnix* (Biessmann 1982). In each of these studies, however, significant deviations in the timing of hormone response resulted in effects that would cause a general decrease in reproductive efficiency with ecological significance. The corrective action worked, but did not provide the fine-tuning necessary to maintain reproductive efficiency.

Another mechanism whereby PCBs can affect behavior has its most dramatic example in a depression of learning ability by human children exposed to PCBs in the womb (Jacobson *et al.* 1985, 1990a, 1990b). The effect has been confirmed experimentally with monkeys (Schantz *et al.* 1991) and may be related to a reduction of brain levels of dopamine (Seegal *et al.* 1990, 1991a). In birds, depression of both dopamine and norepinephrine in the brains of Ringed Turtle-Doves followed feeding of 10 or 100 ppm Aroclor 1254, 20 or 200 ppm DDE, or 4 or 16 ppm dieldrin, but not by 1 ppm Aroclor 1254, 2 ppm DDE, or 1 ppm dieldrin (Heinz *et al.* 1980). The effect has been associated in monkeys with lightly-chlorinated congeners with a chlorine in the *ortho* position (Seegal *et al.* 1990, 1991b; Shain *et al.* 1991).

Very different kind of PCB effects provide the background for the papers by Henny *et al.* and

Falandysz *et al.* (this volume). Unlike the effects on behavior, these do not share a common mechanism of action with the organochlorine biocides; rather, biochemical effects are shared with the chlorinated dibenzofurans and dioxins. The history of this fascinating chapter in Pollution Ecology has recently been summarized by Gilbertson *et al.* (1991). Briefly, a disease in chickens that first appeared in 1957 and that was characterized by edemas (Schmittle *et al.* 1958) was traced to contamination of the feed fats by a chlorinated dioxin (Cantrell *et al.* 1969). Among the dioxins, the 2,3,7,8-tetrachlorodibenzo-*p*-dioxin (TCDD) had the highest capability to cause the disease (Higginbotham *et al.* 1968). PCBs produced comparable effects at higher doses; symptoms included abnormalities of both the bill and the feet (Flick *et al.* 1965; Kohanawa *et al.* 1969; Bush *et al.* 1974). The finding of comparable abnormalities in chicks of Common Terns, *Sterna hirundo,* and Roseate Terns, *S. dougallii*, in Long Island Sound (Hays & Risebrough 1972) and in several species of water-birds in the Great Lakes (Gilbertson *et al.* 1976) prompted concern that dioxin-like compounds were present in the environment.

Initially, the dioxin-type effect of PCBs was attributed to the presence as contaminants in commercial PCB mixtures of chlorinated dibenzofurans, structurally similar to the dioxins but somewhat less toxic (Vos *et al.* 1970; Bowes *et al.* 1975). Experiments with Mallards, *Anas platyrhynchos*, fed PCBs with a known dibenzofuran composition indicated, however, that the dibenzofurans were accumulated to a much lower extent than the PCBs (Norstrom *et al.* 1976), indicating a low potential for ecological effects. A major achievement in PCB research over the past several years has been the identification of several PCB congeners, those that resemble the dioxins in their structure, as the cause of the majority of the dioxin-type effects observed in the environment, including among birds embryonic mortalities and deformities (Kubiak *et al.* 1989; Gilbertson *et al.* 1991; Tillitt *et al.* 1992) similar to those produced by PCBs in chickens (Cecil *et al.* 1974). These PCB congeners have been termed "coplanars" because the absence of chlorines in the *ortho* positions permits a planar configuration resembling that of the dioxins and benzofurans (see the papers by Henny *et al.* and Falandysz *et al.* in this volume).

In assessing the relative importance of these effects in relation to other contaminant-induced effects on raptors both in the present time and in the past, this session was particularly fortunate in receiving contributions from two laboratories that have made major contributions in the development of analytical techniques for the identification and measurement of the coplanars in environmental samples, the laboratories of Drs. Yamashita, Tanabe, and Tatsukawa in Japan, and that of the U.S. Fish and Wildlife Service in Columbia, Missouri.

Ecological Relevance of Dioxin-type Effects

Several investigators of the distribution of PCBs in Great Lakes ecosystems (e.g. Heinz *et al.* 1984) have remarked that if fish-eating birds were as sensitive to PCBs as are chickens, many Great Lakes populations would long ago have been decimated. One of the coplanars, PCB-77, had no effects on embryos of several duck species, Herring Gulls, and Black-headed Gulls, *Larus ridibundus*, at doses 1-3 orders of magnitude higher than the LD_{50} to chick embryos; turkeys and pheasants are also less sensitive to the effects of coplanar PCBs than are chickens (Brunström 1988; Brunström & Reutergårdh 1986). This high magnitude of interspecific variation precludes any rigorous comparison of effects between raptors and other groups or among raptor species based on concentrations of the coplanars, or of their toxicities expressed as equivalencies (TEQs) to the toxicity of TCDD, the most toxic of the dioxins.

The recovery of raptor populations, described in many papers presented at the Sacramento conference in 1986 (Cade *et al.* 1988) has continued. Relatively few populations still experience depressed productivity in North America and Europe, and only in these can current effects of the coplanar PCBs be looked for.

Productivity of the Bald Eagles has generally improved (i.e. Jenkins *et al.* this volume) but the sub-population breeding in the Columbia River Estuary in north-western US continues to have poor reproductive success; levels of TCDD in five eggs were "elevated", with a mean concentration of 32 pg/g (Anthony *et al.* 1993). This value, expressed as a Toxic Equivalent, is less than 1% of the geometric mean of TEQs derived from coplanars in breast muscle of adult female White-tailed Eagles in north-west Poland (Falandysz *et al.* this volume). Other studies have reported that TCDD usually accounts for only a small fraction of the total TEQs (Kubiak *et al.* 1989; Jarman *et al.* in press; Henny *et al.* this volume) such that without data on the other active compounds it is not possible to evaluate the potential for a dioxin-type effect in this population. The mean of estimated total PCBs (13 ppm) measured in the eggs was higher than the mean DDE concentration (10 ppm). Since depressed productivity was related to shell thinning in this population (Anthony *et al.* 1993), DDE alone would appear to be sufficient to account for the low productivity (Wiemeyer *et al.* 1984, 1993; Nisbet & Risebrough this volume).

Depressed productivity of Bald Eagles breeding on the shores of several of the Great Lakes is discussed in the papers by Best *et al.* and Bowerman *et al.* (this volume). A coplanar contribution is suggested from observations of chicks with beak abnormalities. The DDE alone, however, in the eggs from Lake Michigan and Huron (Bowerman *et al.* this volume) could account here also for the depressed productivity without a contribution from a coplanar effect or other PCB effects. Since concentrations of PCBs are highly correlated with those of DDE, it would be difficult to demonstrate conclusively, as in previous studies (Wiemeyer *et al.* 1984, 1993; Nisbet 1988) a separate contribution of the PCBs. Other local species such as the Double-crested Cormorant, *Phalacrocorax auritus*, almost disappeared during the years of high DDE contamination (Anderson & Hamerstrom 1967) but numbers have greatly increased with the decline in environmental levels of DDE (e.g. Sharf & Shugart 1981; Price & Weseloh 1986). PCB effects can now be distinguished from those of DDE (i.e. Tillitt *et al.* 1992). A further decline in DDE levels might therefore be necessary before a separate PCB effect on the local Bald Eagles can be distinguished in the Great Lakes area. Needed are analyses of the causes of failure (natural or non-contaminant causes, embryonic mortality not explained by non-contaminant events, infertility or very early embryonic mortality, etc.) and correlations with levels of total PCBs, the coplanars, and DDE.

In a sample of 85 unhatched eggs of White-tailed Eagles obtained in 1965-1978, infertile addled eggs contained significantly higher levels of both DDE and PCBs than fertile unsuccessful eggs (Helander *et al.* 1982). Unless the addled eggs had contained small decomposed embryos, such a pattern is unlike that observed in the fertility and hatchability of eggs of chickens on PCB diets. In these, fertility was not affected, but embryonic mortality occurred earlier in the more contaminated eggs (Tumasonis *et al.* 1973; Bush *et al.* 1974). The Sea Eagle pattern is also unlike that observed a colony of Double-crested Cormorants in which embryonic mortality was correlated with coplanar concentrations (Tillitt *et al.* 1992). Helander's observations are consistent with a combined DDE/PCB effect on fertility or behavior being a significant factor in depressing productivity; an association between higher total PCB levels and embryonic mortality would be expected if the coplanar PCBs were a major factor in causing depressed productivity in the Sea Eagles.

Coplanar contamination of the White-tailed Eagles from coastal areas of Poland is high, accounting for geometric mean TEQs from 3,500 to 11,600 pg/g in breast muscle, depending on the method of estimation (Falandysz *et al.* this volume). Helander (1983) found abnormal toes in a White-tailed Eagle chick that died after pipping and beak abnormalities in 2 of 115 nestlings examined live on the Baltic coast of Sweden, but none in 60 examined in Lapland. Analyses of fish, cod-liver oils, eggs of the Common Murre, *Uria aalge*, and eggs of the White-tailed Eagle have shown no change in PCB levels in the Baltic since the early 1970s but a significant decline in DDE (Olsson 1978; Schneider 1978; Luckas *et al.* 1980a,b; Koivusaari *et al.* 1980; Kannan *et al.* 1992; Helander this volume); simultaneously, productivity of the White-tailed Eagles has increased over the region (Oehme 1990; Oehme & Manowsky 1991; Mizera 1990; Mizera & Szymkiewicz 1991; Koivusarri *et al.* 1980; Helander this volume. These data and observations indicate that DDE, or a combined DDE-PCB effect, was primarily responsible for depressed productivity and that a PCB effect independent of DDE, such as that of the coplanars, has had only a minor role. The minimum estimate of a threshold level for dioxin-type effects at the population level in White-tailed Eagles would therefore be in the range of 4-12 ng/g, higher by 1-2 orders of magnitude than that determined by Tillitt *et al.* (1992) for Double-crested Cormorants.

The Peregrines of central and southern California have been increasing, in part or entirely as a result of an intensive program of manipulation and management (Walton and Thelander 1988). Productivity of many pairs, however, would be low or zero in the absence of a management program (Linthicum *et al.* this volume; Walton this volume). Jarman *et al.* (in press) determined a mean total TEQ of 120 pg/g from dioxins, benzofurans and coplanar PCBs in 7 eggs from 5 sites in 1983-1988 based on the toxic equivalency factors (TEFs) of Kutz *et al.* (1990) and Safe (1990). This is a level at which an increase in embryonic mortality in Double-crested Cormorant eggs can be detected (Tillitt *et al.* 1992); the total TEQs were determined by bioassay rather than application of TEFs to measured concentrations of active compounds. Peregrines, however, can not be assumed to be as sensitive as chickens or cormorants, or as insensitive as ducks, to the dioxin-like effects. Henny *et al.* (this volume) report much higher levels of total TEQs in eggs of 6 Peregrine clutches from arctic Russia from which a geometric mean of 890 pg/g can be calculated. About half of the TEQs, however, derive from PCB-118, a congener that contains one chlorine in an *ortho* position, with significant contributions from other *ortho* PCBs. Jarman *et al.* included only the 4 coplanar congeners (#s 37, 77, 126 & 169) in their estimate of PCB contributions to a potential dioxin-like effect. Including congeners 118 and 105 in the analysis would increase the estimate of total TEQs in the California eggs by a factor of about 4 to around 500 TEQs; other AHH-active congeners, if present in the California peregrines in about the same relative amounts as in the arctic eggs, would increase the estimate to no more than about 600, a level still below that of Henny *et al.* for a population in arctic Russia that has been increasing. The 890 pg/g mean in the Russian eggs would therefore appear to be a minimum threshold level of effect of dioxin-like compounds for Peregrines. If the eggs with higher TEQ levels in the Russian sample had dead embryos, a coplanar effect might be indicated; an absence of development would suggest other kinds of PCB/DDE effects.

A TEF derived for one species may not, however, apply to another; those used by Henny *et al.*, from Safe (1990), would indicate that PCB-118 is 100x less toxic than PCB-126; Brunström (1989) has reported that the toxicity of PCB-118 is 8000 times less toxic than PCB-126 when injected into chick embryos.

No evidence can be found therefore for a dioxin-type effect at the present time in a raptor population that is ecologically relevant, in the sense that a threat to the population exists. Fish-eating birds in contaminated areas of the Great Lakes that are experiencing dioxin-type effects such as the Caspian Tern, *Hydroprogne caspia*, and Double-crested Cormorants have been increasing with the decline in DDE residues; the incidence of bill abnormalities in the highly-contaminated Cormorant colony of Green Bay, Lake Michigan, has been about 0.5 % (Environment Canada 1991). Although there is a high incidence of local embryonic mortality associated with the coplanars (Tillitt *et al.* 1992), and however deplorable this may be, the population is not affected.

Certainly, continuation of PCB use on a global scale at the rate of increase in production of the late 1960s would have created a disastrous situation for many species, particularly for our own. The efforts in the late 1960s and early 1970s to end the uses of PCBs and the organochlorine biocides were well worth the time. That the eagles and peregrines have come back is our response, after 23 years, to the Editor of NATURE who wrote in 1969 "The fact that many professional scientists have recently been contributing to this misguided assessment of the risks of modern life is reprehensible" (*Nature* 224:1242).

Synergistic Effects of DDE and PCBs?

Jeffrey Lincer's Ph.D. thesis (Lincer 1972) is frequently cited in the literature but is not generally available. We publish here critical data from his thesis that suggest a synergistic effect of PCBs and DDE (Lincer, this volume). The results, however, are not conclusive since the small sample size precludes assignment of statistical significance; incubator technology has since improved. None of the eggs of the group fed DDE and PCBs hatched (Table 2, Lincer this volume). In the only other comparable feeding study we are aware of, Mallards, *Anas platyrhynchos*, fed a combination of DDE and Aroclor 1254 produced fewer eggs and showed a higher incidence of egg-eating than ducks on control, DDE, or PCB diets (Risebrough & Anderson 1975).

Clearly, Lincer's experiment should be repeated, with several dose levels; also, other unanswered questions remain to be answered (see below).

A synergistic DDE-PCB effect would also explain why productive Bald Eagle pairs in California and Arizona frequently produce eggs with higher DDE levels than the 3-5 ppm threshold determined by Wiemeyer *et al.* (1984) and Nisbet (1989) (Jenkins *et al.* this volume; Nisbet & Risebrough this volume). PCB levels in the earlier data set were generally higher. Here also sample sizes as yet preclude assignment of statistical significance.

Water Loss from Thin-Shelled Eggs

One of the unresolved apparent inconsistencies mentioned in Eilat derived from reports in the literature that thin-shelled eggs lost water less rapidly than normal eggs, while observations at the

Santa Cruz Predatory Bird facility indicated that thin-shelled eggs lost water more rapidly. We publish here a report from Santa Cruz (Linthicum *et al.* this volume) that clearly demonstrates that most thinner-shelled eggs brought in from the wild lose water more rapidly than normal; in the absence of corrective action by incubation at higher humidities, the embryos die. Some of the thinner-shelled eggs, however, lose water at the normal rates (Figure 2, Linthicum *et al.*). The Santa Cruz eggs differ from those in the experiments of Peakall *et al.* (1973) and Cooke (1979) in that initially at least they contain living embryos but why the other thin-shelled eggs should have decreased functional pore areas is not explained. Is there a link with the observations (i.e. B.J. Walton, pers. comm.) that egg survival and hatchability is much improved after several days of natural incubation but otherwise might be low? Is the high rate of water loss in some thin-shelled eggs due to the presence of structural abnormalities of the kind recently observed in eggs of Bald Eagles (Bland 1990)?

Unresolved questions remain; these also might be answered if the experiments of Lincer (above) could be repeated and expanded in scope to address questions of water loss, embryo survival, and changes in eggshell structure.

The water loss data from Santa Cruz indicate the importance of water balance to hatchability and could explain why species such as the Prairie Falcon, *Falco mexicanus*, experience DDE-related reproductive failures at a low level of thinning (Risebrough 1989).

Effects of Metals?

Falandysz and Mizera (this volume) provide additional data that feathers are useful monitoring media for heavy metals in local environments. There is no established link, however, with effects on individual birds or on populations. Helander *et al.* (1982) have clearly shown that mercury was not a factor in the population decline of White-tailed Eagles in the Baltic. This is a species, however, that has evolved in an environment in which a principal food source contains relatively high mercury levels. At the Eilat Conference, Furness *et al.* (1989) demonstrated a link, whether causal or incidental, between mercury levels and depressed productivity of Golden Eagles, *Aquila chrysaetos*, breeding on the island of Rhum in western Scotland. This species evolved in an environment with low mercury levels in the food sources. Is it now more sensitive than White-tailed Eagles to dietary mercury?

2. FAMILIAR EFFECTS IN NEW PLACES

Unfortunately we have only one contribution from an area of the world where biocide effects on raptors had not yet been investigated, that of Basili *et al.* from Venezuela. The preliminary data do not suggest an organochlorine problem. Observations of unregulated unrestricted use of other biocides indicate, however, the potential for other kinds of ecological disruptions.

Needed are studies in Asia, including India and China where DDT and HCH (hexachlorocyclohexanes, including lindane) and probably other organochlorines continue in widespread use.

3. PRIORITIES FOR FUTURE RESEARCH AND PROJECTS

There remain many unanswered questions on the immediate reasons for the reproductive failures and of their relative importance, - egg breakage, abnormal gas exchange, embryonic mortalities caused by toxins, behavioral abnormalities, etc., and of their physiological and biochemical basis. Even the mechanism of eggshell thinning is not adequately explained (i.e. Bland 1990; Lowe & Stendell 1991). Although no longer as relevant as they once were to a conservation policy, these questions nevertheless retain their scientific interest and importance.

As indicated above, in those areas of the world where DDT and other organochlorine biocides are still being used, particularly India, China, South-east Asia and areas of Africa and Latin America, studies of the status of those species potentially at risk, combined with laboratory analyses of unhatched eggs and other available samples, remain a priority.

Of equal immediate priority and of much greater longer-term priority would appear to be studies that determine effects of biocide use on local biodiversity and the abundance of prey species at all levels of the food webs. Many papers in the late 1950s and 1960s, e.g. Hickey & Hunt (1960a,

1860b), documented massive avian mortalities following applications of DDT, but evidence for longer-term population changes is generally lacking, e.g. Henny (1972). A longer-term field study of White-headed Black Chats, *Thamnolaea arnoti,* has shown, however, population reductions in areas of recurring DDT use in NW Zimbabwe (Douthwaite 1992). A report from Spain indicates depressed productivity of Blue Tits, *Parus caeruleus,* resulting from a shortage of prey following sprayings with a synthetic pyrethroid (Pascual & Peris 1992). Applications of any biocide will inevitably reduce populations of some components of food webs at least temporarily; continued applications could reduce the prey base of local raptors.

Population declines of frogs and other amphibians are occurring on a massive scale (e.g. Wake 1991; Pechmann *et al.* 1991); there is an analogy with the raptor declines of the 1960s, except that there appear to be no or few common factors that would explain the majority of the reported local disappearances or population reductions of the amphibians. How many other species are disappearing with them, and in the context of this symposium, how would such changes affect raptors? More than ever before is there a need for long-term, in-depth, ecological investigations.

4. NEW CHEMICALS; NEW USES OF OLD CHEMICALS

In their discussion of the potential hazards of the organophosphate fenthion, Lacombe *et al.* (this volume) review also effects of other less persistent biocides on raptors and their prey base. Additional support is therefore provided for the recommendations for the long-term research programs proposed above. Similarly, the observations of Peeters (this volume) indicate the need for field monitoring of the effects of rodenticide applications.

5. RE-INTRODUCTION OF RAPTORS TO POLLUTED ENVIRONMENTS

At the Eilat meeting, Garcelon *et al.* (1989) discussed problems arising from the re-introduction of Bald Eagles to Santa Catalina Island in Southern California; eggs with weak shells broke in the nest or failed to hatch during artificial incubation (Jenkins *et al.* this volume). The principal cause of their disappearance about 30 years ago, environmental contamination by DDE, was still active.

Three of the last California Condors, *Gymnogyps californianus*, in the wild died after ingesting lethal levels of lead (Janssen *et al.* 1986). Lead poisoning from bullet fragments was therefore probably a significant factor in the population decline of the species over the past century. Lead bullets are still widely used in the areas where captive-reared condors are now being released, and pose a potential hazard once the reintroduced birds begin to range more widely. The introduction to the market of all-copper bullets with superior ballistic properties is a possible solution of this problem. But nothing is known about the toxicity of copper to condors; the hypothesis that copper poisoning from ingested bullet fragments contributed to the earlier deaths of condors can not be excluded. Waterfowl deaths from copper poisoning have been documented (Henderson & Winterfield 1975; Kobayashi *et al.* 1991). Feeding experiments with a surrogate species such as the Turkey Vulture, *Cathartes aura,* would likely yield information useful for a future conservation strategy.

ACKNOWLEDGEMENTS

I thank my colleague Daniel Anderson for his assistance in reviewing and editing the manuscripts submitted in the Contaminants session. Pablo Cardinale Pizani, Wally Jarman and Alison Gee assisted in editing and transcribing manuscripts. Stanley N. Wiemeyer provided valuable comments. Financial assistance in preparations for the Conference and in editing of the manuscripts in this session was provided by the Bodega Bay Institute.

R.W. Risebrough
2711 Piedmont Avenue
Berkeley, CA 94705, USA

Meyburg, B.-U. & R. D. Chancellor eds.1994
Raptor Conservation Today
WWGBP / The Pica Press

Organochlorines in Venezuelan Raptor Eggs

Gianfranco Basili,
Pablo Cardinale-Pizani & Robert W. Risebrough

As in most countries in Latin America and elsewhere in the Developing World, biocide use in Venezuela is largely unregulated; through advertising and publicity the international manufacturing companies have major impacts on amounts and patterns of use. Applications are frequently excessive, resulting in human mortality and sickness, as well as deleterious effects on wildlife that remain largely undocumented.

Although Venezuela had a large biocide-producing industry in the past, most biocides are now imported (Burton & Philogène 1986). Many regulations governing biocide use have been promulgated (República de Venezuela 1979). In 1984 uses of the principal organochlorine biocides, - DDT, aldrin, dieldrin, heptachlor, toxaphene and chlordane were ended by decree (República de Venezuela 1983); mirex uses were ended a year later (República de Venezuela 1985). DDT, however, is still widely used in the anti-malarial campaigns in the Amazonian regions, and other regulations are not generally enforced.

The present study was undertaken in 1989 to obtain a preliminary data set on levels of organochlorines in eggs of several species of the local raptors.

MATERIALS AND METHODS

Raptor eggs were collected from three different areas of the Venezuelan central flatlands (Figure 1), known locally as *Los Llanos*, which lie between the Orinoco River and the Andean Coastal Highlands: (A) *Acarigua*, the vicinity of a wealthy city about 400 km southwest of Caracas. Rice, sugar-cane, and sorghum are the dominant crops, but tobacco, tomatoes, cotton, sesame and sunflower are also cultivated; (B) *Calabozo*, the vicinity of an agricultural town south of Caracas. Rice is the only crop cultivated on a large scale, with approximate yields of 3,000 kilos/hectare; (C) *Mantecal*, a cattle ranching area, with very little other agriculture. Most eggs were collected in the vicinity of *El Hato El Frío*, a ranch well-known for ecotourism and ecological research.

The species sampled were: Savanna Hawk, *Buteogallus meridionalis*, Black-shouldered Kite, *Elanus caeruleus*, Roadside Hawk, *Buteo magnirostris*, Yellow-headed Caracara, *Milvago chimachima*, and American Kestrel, *Falco sparverius*.

Because refrigeration, ice or dry ice were usually not available, eggs were hard-boiled in the field. This worked well, the principal disadvantage being the difficulty in obtaining dry-weight determinations of residue concentrations in the laboratory. Lipid weights are reported in this paper; division by 20 converts the values to approximate wet weight concentrations. Analytical methods were largely those of Risebrough *et al.* (1986).

Figure 1. Collection areas in Venezuela: A) Acarigua; B) Calabozo; C) Mantecal

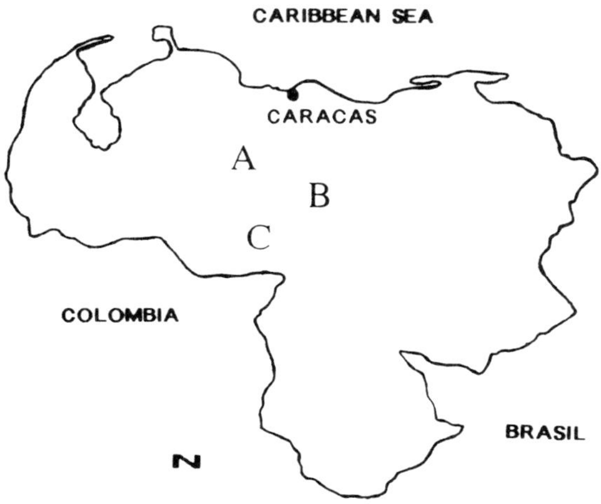

RESULTS AND DISCUSSION

The five species sampled feed primarily on insects, small reptiles, and small mammals; the residue levels are expected to be lower than in bird-eating species. The highest concentration recorded, 12,000 g^{-9}/g (12 ppm) is less than a part per million on a wet-weight basis, a concentration that is generally below thresholds of harm.

The relative high amounts of the parent DDT compound, *p,p'*-DDT, and of the other principal compound in technical DDT, *o,p'*-DDT, in a Savanna Hawk egg from Calabozo indicates recent DDT use in that area. Mirex is frequently found in many samples of South American wildlife, a result of its intensive local use in the control of leaf-cutting ants (R.W. Risebrough & A.M. Springer, unpublished). The few data we present here do not suggest a problem with mirex use in Venezuela, since concentrations were generally low. Chlordane compounds (*t*-nonachlor and oxychlordane) are derived from mixtures used both in agriculture and termite control. Heptachlor epoxide derives in part from technical chlordane, and in part from heptachlor, a potent insecticide. The use of all of these compounds has been ended in North America and in many other countries, because of risks to human health. Wildlife has benefitted from these actions.

The two eggs of the Savanna Hawk from Mantecal, the cattle ranch area, contained much lower concentrations of the DDT compounds reported than the single egg from the rice-growing area of Calabozo. Concentrations of the other compounds were also lower, but differences were generally less.

PCBs were detected, also in low concentrations, in all of the samples. These data will be presented in a more comprehensive report to be published later.

A United Nations report more than a decade ago (Maltby 1980) predicted decreasing uses in Venezuela of the organochlorines in the 1980s, with or without restrictions on their use, and increasing uses of several of the organophosphate and carbamate insecticides. The 1978 use of DDT was estimated to be 730,000 kg, about 1/7 that of Mexico at that time, with a projected 50% decrease over the next decade.

We have not been able to confirm such predictions or to obtain better data. More field studies on the impacts of biocides on the environment are needed in Venezuela. Although less persistent than the organochlorines, the more toxic organophosphates and carbamates may nevertheless affect the composition and abundance of raptor populations through their effects on the food webs. We observed many uses of the highly toxic organophosphate biocide parathion, frequently a cause of accidental human deaths. The carbamate carbofuran (Furadan) is listed in the brochures we have obtained as one of the biocides imported to Venezuela. Used primarily as a soil insecticide, it is highly toxic to birds (Flickinger *et al.* 1980; Balcomb *et al.* 1984; Eisler 1985); careless use would greatly increase the mortalities of seed-eating birds and the raptors that prey on them.

Table 1. Organochlorine biocides in the eggs of Venezuelan raptors. ng/g lipid.

Species	Locality	*p,p'*-DDE	*p,p'*-DDT	*o,p'*-DDT	*p,p'*-DDD	Mirex	*t*-nonachlor	Oxychlor	Hept Epox
Savanna Hawk	B	12,000	8,600	590	2,900	73	530	180	88
	C	110	34	4	1	29	30	49	49
	C	140	< 1	< 1	< 1	20	21	< 5	< 5
Roadside Hawk	A	2,000	280	nm	nm	nm	nm	nm	nm
	A	900	21	34	17	70	190	1,400	2,800
Black-shouldered Kite	A	1,400	27	nm	nm	nm	nm	nm	nm
	A	1,200	14	nm	nm	nm	nm	nm	nm
	A	440	< 1	13	< 1	38	74	640	370
	A	12,000	74	140	160	40	630	700	700
	A	1,400	< 1	< 1	< 1	26	9	54	27
Yellow-headed Caracara	A	1,800	5	nm	nm	nm	nm	nm	nm
American Kestrel	A	1,500	19	17	22	44	44	200	110

nm, not measured; *t*-nonachlor, *trans*-nonachlor; oxychlor, oxychlordane; hept epox, heptachlor epoxide

ACKNOWLEDGEMENTS

Financial support was provided by Wildlife Conservation International, now NYZS The Wildlife Conservation Society; we wish to give particular thanks to Stuart Strahl for his support of the project. Professor Gonzalo Morales of the Universidad Central de Venezuela, Sr. Philip Desenne, Sr. Peter Bichier, and Allison Basili provided invaluable assistance and support in undertaking the field studies in Venezuela. Facilities of the University of California, Santa Cruz, and of the Bodega Bay Institute, Berkeley, were used in the analysis of the samples.

Gianfranco Basili
Department of Wildlife Ecology
1630 Linden Drive
University of Wisconsin
Madison, WI 53706
U.S.A.
Pablo Cardinale-Pizani
Environmental Engineering and Health Sciences Laboratory
Richmond Field Station, Building 112
University of California
1301 S. 46th Street
Richmond, CA 94804 U.S.A.

Robert W. Risebrough
The Bodega Bay Institute
2711 Piedmont Ave
Berkeley, CA 94705
U.S.A.

Meyburg, B.-U. & R. D. Chancellor eds.1994
Raptor Conservation Today
WWGBP / The Pica Press

Reproductive Impairment of Bald Eagles *Haliaeetus leucocephalus* along the Great Lakes Shorelines of Michigan an Ohio

David A. Best, William W. Bowerman IV, Timothy J. Kubiak, Scott R. Winterstein, Sergej Postupalsky, Mark C. Shieldcastle & John P. Giesy, Jr.

ABSTRACT

The Bald Eagle, *Haliaeetus leucocephalus*, population of the Great Lakes and adjacent interior areas has rebounded since the early 1960s. In the states of Michigan and Ohio, the number of breeding pairs on the Great Lakes increased from 17 to 57 in 1981-1990 and from 93 to 141 in adjacent interior regions. Reproduction, however, is still impaired along the Great Lakes shorelines of Michigan and Ohio and at inland sites accessible to runs of anadromous Great Lakes fish. Mean productivity in these areas, respectively, in 1981-1990 was 0.68 (N = 342) and 0.66 (N = 53), significantly lower than the productivity in interior regions of 1.00 (N = 1,040). Inexperienced, newly-established pairs have significantly lower reproductive success than experienced, established pairs, but experienced Great Lakes breeding pairs reproduce at levels similar to those of inexperienced pairs, significantly lower than those of experienced pairs in inland breeding areas. The data indicate that the increase in the coastal breeding population is a result of immigration of young birds from inland areas.

INTRODUCTION

Bald Eagles were nearly extirpated along the Great Lakes shorelines in the 1950s and early 1960s and along with the Peregrine Falcons, *Falco peregrinus*, were the early sentinels of *p,p'*-DDE reproductive effects. After the ending of DDT use in the early 1970s in the United States and Canada, eagle populations began to recover (Postupalsky 1978). Productivity of these reestablished populations, however, does not appear to be uniform. In order to understand the recovery of Bald Eagles in the Great Lakes Basin, we examined the current population trends, the effects of the length of site occupancy on productivity, and the influence of inexperienced breeding pairs of eagles breeding on the shorelines of the Great Lakes and in interior regions of Michigan and Ohio.

METHODS

Productivity Analysis

We analyzed Bald Eagle productivity data for all breeding areas within Michigan and Ohio, 1981-90. Breeding areas were assigned three categories: *Great Lakes*, those breeding areas within 8.0 km of a Great Lake shoreline; *interior*, those breeding areas 8.0 km or further from a Great Lakes shoreline; and *anadromous*, those inland breeding areas accessible to runs of anadromous Great Lakes fish. Productivity for each category was determined by dividing the total number of young by the number of occupied breeding areas for each year (Postupalsky 1974).

Occupancy Analysis

Productivity as a function of occupancy was analyzed by comparing breeding attempts for each breeding area sequentially from year of initiation (Year 1) through Year 9 of breeding. We analyzed productivity data of all new or re-established breeding areas within Michigan and Ohio, 1975-90. Breeding areas were assigned three categories: *interior; Lakes Michigan/Huron*, Great Lakes and anadromous breeding areas within those watersheds; and *Lakes Superior/Erie,* Great Lakes and anadromous breeding areas within those watersheds. Great Lakes breeding areas were grouped based on no significant differences in addled egg residues and previous reproductive outcomes (Kubiak & Best 1991).

Experience Analysis

The effect of breeding pair experience was analyzed by comparing breeding attempts for each breeding area on a time sequence analysis, 1981-90. Breeding areas were assigned two categories: *experienced breeding pairs,* those occupying a breeding area 3 or more years; and *inexperienced breeding pairs*, those occupying a breeding area less than 3 years, including those breeding areas reoccupied after a 4 year or greater abandonment. A paired *t*-test was used to compare productivity between experienced and inexperienced pairs among years. Experienced breeding pairs were then split into two categories for comparison against inexperienced pairs: *experienced interior pairs*, interior pairs occupying a breeding area 3 or more years; and *experienced Great Lakes pairs*, Great Lakes and anadromous pairs occupying a breeding area 3 or more years.

Statistical Analysis

Data analysis were performed by ANOVA using SAS/STAT 6.03 for microcomputers (SAS Institute Inc. 1988). Differences between categories were determined using Tukey's (HSD) Studentized Range Test (Tukey 1951).

RESULTS

The Bald Eagle population has continued to grow during the 1980s; in the states of Michigan and Ohio, the number of breeding pairs on the Great Lakes increased from 17 to 57 in 1981-1990 and from 93 to 141 in adjacent interior regions (Table 1). Productivity, however, has varied among breeding areas, with interior breeding areas having significantly greater productivity (Anova, $F_{2,27}$ = 8.2, P 0.0017) than Great Lakes and anadromous breeding areas (Table 1). No changes in productivity were found between 1981 and 1990 ($F_{9,20} = 0.55$, $P = 0.82$).

Productivity increased between the first and third-fourth year of occupancy in inland areas and on the shores of Lakes Superior and Erie (Figure 1); this is attributed to experience (see below). Productivity on the shores of Lakes Michigan and Huron remained low during the first four years of occupancy and thereafter (Figure 1). Among the regions, the interior breeding areas had significantly greater productivity ($F_{1,18} = 36$, P 0.0001); nest locations explained 66.7% of the variation in productivity.

Table 1. Number of nests, fledged young, and productivity[1] of Bald Eagles in Michigan and Ohio, 1981-90.

Area	Total	1981	1982	1983	1984	1985	1986	1987	1988	1989	1990
Nests											
Interior	1,040	87	86	93	93	100	96	105	124	124	132
Great Lakes	342	17	17	22	22	29	35	46	51	46	57
Anadromous	53	6	4	5	5	5	4	4	3	8	9
Young											
Interior	1,041	96	81	90	90	105	89	113	125	127	125
Great Lakes	234	14	14	14	12	14	22	41	37	24	42
Anadromous	35	3	0	1	3	3	3	4	1	9	8
Productivity[1]											
Interior	1.00[a]	1.10	0.94	0.97	0.97	1.05	0.93	1.08	1.01	1.02	0.95
Great Lakes	0.68[b]	0.82	0.82	0.64	0.55	0.48	0.63	0.89	0.73	0.52	0.74
Anadromous	0.66[b]	0.50	0.00	0.20	0.60	0.60	0.75	1.00	0.33	1.13	0.89

[1] Productivity measured as young per occupied nest. Letters signify significant differences between means ($P < 0.002$).

Figure 1. Productivity of Bald Eagles in two shoreline regions of the Great Lakes and in the interior region of Michigan and Ohio vs. year of nest occupancy.

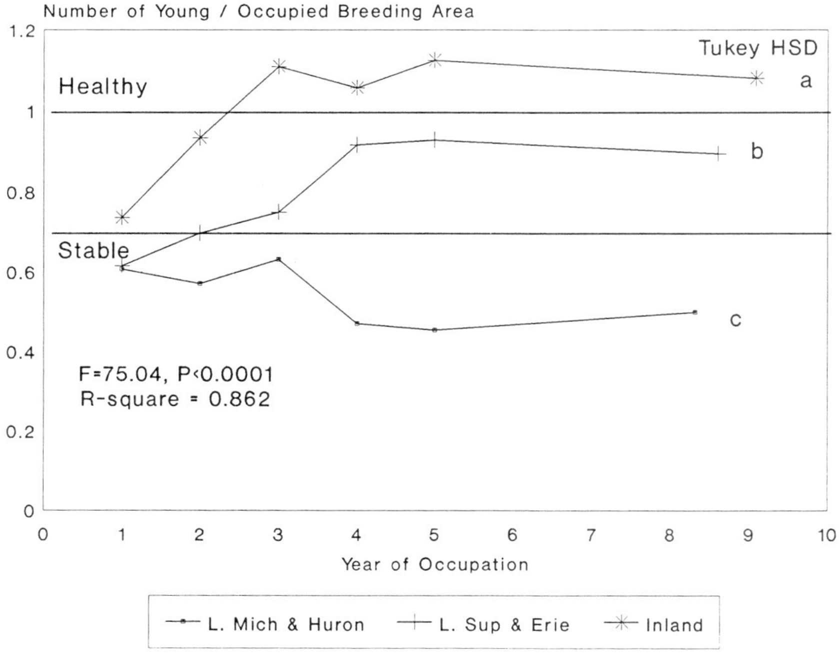

Figure 2. Productivities of Interior and Great Lakes experienced pairs of Bald Eagles and of all inexperienced breeding pairs in Michigan and Ohio, 1981-90.

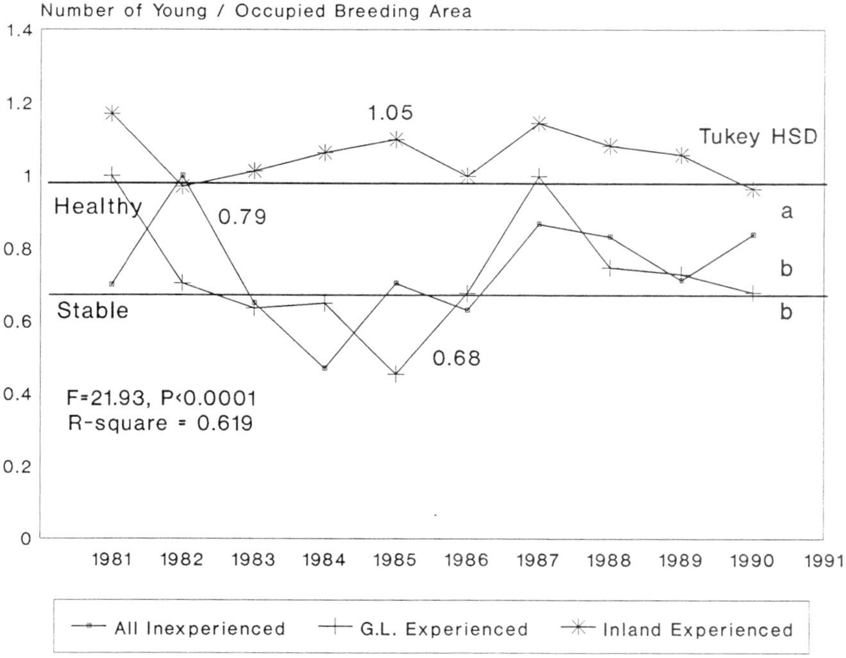

Interior experienced pairs had higher productivity than either the Great Lakes experienced pairs or all inexperienced pairs (Figure 2; $F_{2,27} = 21.9$, P 0.0001). No significant differences were found between all inexperienced pairs and Great Lakes experienced pairs ($F_{9,10} = 0.26$, $P = 0.97$), nor were there any detectable trends over time ($F_{9,10} = 0.26$, $P = 0.97$).

DISCUSSION

Bald Eagles nesting along the Great Lakes shorelines and interior areas accessible to runs of Great Lakes anadromous fish have higher organochlorine contaminant concentrations in blood plasma and addled eggs than those eagles from more interior sites (Bowerman *et al.* 1990; Kubiak & Best 1991; Bowerman *et al.* this volume); these data provide additional confirmation of the link between the observed depressed productivity and organochlorine contamination.

The mean productivities of 0.68 of the Great Lakes pairs over 1981-1990 (N = 342) and 0.66 of the "anadromous" pairs (N = 53) are considered barely marginal to maintain a population, let alone to permit an increase (Sprunt *et al.* 1973). The number of breeding pairs on the Great Lakes increased from 17 in 1981 to 57 in 1990 (Table 1). We attribute this growth to the relatively high productivity of the interior-nesting birds of 1.0 (N = 1,040 over 1981-1990), which has provided not only enough young to produce an increase in numbers of interior-breeding pairs from 86-87 in 1981-1982 to 132 in 1990, but to repopulate historic and other available habitat on the Great Lakes shorelines.

A visual examination of Figure 1 indicates that productivity does not change with years of occupancy, i.e. that after year 4 continued exposure to contaminants does not further depress productivity. Our definition of "experienced" pairs would include pairs in which one member has been replaced; the maintenance of mean productivity might therefore be due at least in part to a high incidence of young, relatively uncontaminated birds in the breeding population. Whether productivity decreases over the life-time of individual highly-contaminated individuals will be determined only by continuing research. Whether the shore-nesting birds experience higher mortalities as a result of feeding on Great Lakes fish, as has been suggested (Kozie 1985; Bowerman 1991), is also the subject of continuing investigations.

ACKNOWLEDGEMENTS

We would like to thank A. Bath, D. Case, J. Holt, J. Papp, L. Schumann, and G. Tori, for their assistance with logistics and in the field. R. Aldrich, R. Bowerman, J. Edde, D. Elsing, K.R. Ennis, J. Hammill, T. Havard, J. Hendrickson, R. Hill, W. Irvine, N. Johnson, J. Johnston, R. Lou, C. Taylor, W. Taylor, T. Weise, and J. Wienrich assisted with Bald Eagle productivity surveys in Michigan. Funding was provided by USDI-Fish and Wildlife Service, Michigan Department of Natural Resources: Natural Heritage Program-Nongame Wildlife Fund, Ohio Department of Natural Resources: Division of Wildlife-Nongame Fund, USDA-Forest Service, and Earthwatch.

David A. Best & Timothy J. Kubiak
USDI-Fish and Wildlife Service,
East Lansing Field Office
1405 S. Harrison Rd.,
East Lansing, Michigan 48823 USA

William W. Bowerman IV & J.P. Giesy, Jr.
Department of Fisheries and Wildlife, Pesticide Research Center
Institute for Environmental Toxicology,
Michigan State University
East Lansing, Michigan 48824 USA

Scott R. Winterstein
Department of Fisheries and Wildlife,
Michigan State University
East Lansing, Michigan 48824 USA

Sergej Postupalsky
1817 Simpson Street, Apartment 201
Madison, Wisconsin 53713 USA

Mark C. Shieldcastle
Ohio Department of Natural Resources
Crane Creek Wildlife Research Station
13229 West State Route 2,
Oak Harbor, Ohio 43449 USA

Steller's Sea Eagle *Haliaeetus pelagicus*

Meyburg, B.-U. & R. D. Chancellor eds.1994
Raptor Conservation Today
WWGBP / The Pica Press

The Influence of Environmental Contaminants on Bald Eagle *Haliaeetus leucocephalus* Populations in the Laurentian Great Lakes, North America

William W. Bowerman IV, David A. Best,
John P. Giesy, Jr., Timothy J. Kubiak & James G. Sikarskie

ABSTRACT

Concentrations of PCBs and *p,p'*-DDE in blood plasma of nestling Bald Eagles, *Haliaeetus leucocephalus*, were higher in areas near the Great Lakes, where productivity was depressed, than in interior areas where productivity was higher. Residues in addled eggs were highest in samples from Lakes Michigan and Huron; although productivities were lowest in these areas, they were higher than those that would be predicted from previous studies that have related DDE levels to productivity. The productivity estimates may, however, be biased if the breeding sites were experiencing a high rate of turn-over of adult eagles. Fresh, wet-weight concentrations of PCBs, *p,p'*-DDE, and dieldrin in addled eggs were significantly and inversely correlated with productivity, but the three residues were highly correlated among themselves, precluding any assessment of their relative contributions to depressed productivities.

INTRODUCTION

Bald Eagle populations in North America declined during the 1950s and early 1960s, primarily due to the effects of *p,p'*-DDE, a degradation product of DDT (Wiemeyer *et al.* 1984). Bald Eagles nesting along the coasts and islands of the Laurentian Great Lakes were nearly extirpated by the mid 1960s. Since 1977, eagle populations have been increasing; in 1981-1990 the Great Lakes sub-population tripled, and a 50 % increase was recorded in inland areas in Michigan and Ohio (Best *et al.* this volume). Reproduction, however, is not uniform among locations; in areas where nesting eagles feed on the Great Lakes food chain, productivity is significantly lower (Best *et al.* this volume). We collected addled eggs and nestling blood plasma from throughout the Great Lakes Basin to relate measured concentrations of organochlorine pesticides and PCBs to adverse reproductive effects.

METHODS

Blood collection and analysis

Blood was collected from 46 nestling Bald Eagles in Michigan during 1987 and 1988, and from 121 nestlings in Michigan, Minnesota, Ohio, Ontario, and Wisconsin in 1989 (Bowerman *et al.* 1990). Blood was collected from the brachialus vein using sterile techniques with heparinized glass syringes fitted with 22- or 24-gauge needles. The syringes had previously been washed with hexane and acetone. Samples of whole blood were transferred to heparinized vacuum tubes, kept on ice in coolers, and centrifuged within 48 h of collection. Plasma was decanted and transferred to vacuum tubes and frozen (Morizot *et al.* 1985). Concentrations of PCBs and organochlorine pesticides were determined using gas chromatography and confirmed using GC/MS (Price *et al.* 1986; MDPH 1987). The reported limits of quantification were 5 ppb for *p,p'*-DDE and 10 ppb for total PCBs.

Addled egg collection and analysis

Forty-one addled or abandoned eggs were collected from 31 Bald Eagle breeding areas in Michigan and Ohio between 1986 and 1990. Five fresh eggs were collected from five breeding areas in Alaska in 1990 to determine background concentrations in eagle eggs from a control area. Eggs were archived using techniques developed by the Richter Museum of Natural History, University of Wisconsin-Green Bay (T. Erdmann, pers. corr.). Egg contents were stored in chemically-clean jars and frozen prior to shipment for chemical analyses. Eggs were measured, weighed, and eggshell thicknesses determined. Concentrations of PCBs and organochlorine pesticides were determined using gas chromatography and confirmed using GC/MS (Mississippi State University 1985). The reported limits of quantification, uncorrected for egg content moisture loss, were 0.10 ppm for *p,p'*-DDE and dieldrin, and 0.50 ppm for total PCBs. Fresh, wet-weight concentrations of organochlorine pesticides and PCBs were then determined using equations to adjust for moisture loss (Stickel *et al.* 1973).

Ambrose *et al.* (1988a) have shown no differences in residue concentrations between addled eggs and eggs collected at random earlier in the season from the same clutch of Peregrine Falcons, *Falco peregrinus*. In this case therefore the addled eggs did not constitute a biased sample. Helander *et al.* (1982), however, demonstrated higher levels of DDE and PCBs in addled eggs than in other eggs; the addled eggs were not unbiased samples of the egg population, but represented rather a subset of the eagle population with higher contaminant levels. In this study we relate residue levels in addled eggs with productivity of the sampled sites; in this context therefore they are unbiased samples. See below, for a discussion of possible bias in the productivity estimates.

Productivity estimates

Reproduction was determined for eight geographic realms where eggs were collected for all breeding attempts between 1986-1990. Productivity of each realm was derived by dividing the total number of fledged young by the total number of occupied breeding areas (Postupalsky 1974).

Since the sample size of nests conforming to criteria previously used (i.e. Wiemeyer *et al.* 1984) was small, productivity of individual nests was estimated on a case-by-case basis. The population is rapidly expanding, and many nests where eggs were collected had fewer than 3 years of productivity data available between 1982-1990.

As in earlier studies, the site rather than the female was the sampling unit. Unlike this rapidly expanding population with a large number of non-territorial younger birds, populations in the 1960s and 70s were declining or stable, and can be expected to have had lower numbers of non-territorial birds. Productivity estimates may therefore be influenced by turnover rates.

Statistical analysis

Concentrations of *p,p'*-DDE, total PCBs, and dieldrin in blood plasma from nestling eagles were contrasted among geographic regions with the Kruskal-Wallis ^{2} approximation using SAS/STAT© NPAR1WAY (SAS Institute Inc. 1988). Differences among groups were determined using the Kruskal-Wallis simultaneous rank test (Miller 1981). Fresh, wet-weight concentrations of *p,p'*-DDE, total PCBs, and dieldrin in addled eggs from eight geographic realms were correlated with productivity using the Spearman's rank correlation test.

Definitions

Breeding areas were subdivided into two groups, Great Lakes and interior. *Great Lakes* breeding areas were those breeding areas located within 8.0 km of a Great Lakes shoreline or along a riverine reach with Great Lakes runs of anadromous fish. *Interior* breeding areas were those breeding areas located greater than 8.0 km from a Great Lakes shoreline and were not on an anadromous accessible riverine reach.

RESULTS

Mean concentrations of PCBs and *p,p'*-DDE in plasma from nestling eagles from Great Lakes breeding areas were significantly higher than those in plasma from interior areas (P 0.0001; Kruskal-Wallis ^{2} 28.6, PCBs; 21.8 *p,p'*-DDE; Table 1).

Eggs collected from Lake Michigan and Huron shorelines contained the highest mean concentrations of PCBs, *p,p'*-DDE, and dieldrin; these areas had the lowest productivity (Table 2). Eggs collected from Alaska contained the lowest concentrations of PCBs, *p,p'*-DDE, and dieldrin, and this area had the highest productivity. Productivity was significantly and inversely correlated with fresh, wet-weight mean concentrations of PCBs ($r_s = -0.78$), *p,p'*-DDE ($r_s = -0.73$), and dieldrin ($r_s = -0.64$) in addled eggs, but the residues were also significantly correlated with each other (Spearman's rank correlation test, N = 36; P 0.0001).

Table 1. Arithmetic mean concentrations and ranges of *p,p'*-DDE and total PCBs in plasma of nestling Bald Eagles, Great Lakes Basin.

Region	n	*p,p'*-DDE	Total PCBs
Great Lakes	42	61 (13-306)	183 (33-520)
Interior	79	20 (2-193)	24 (5-200)

µg/l, wet weight. Kruskal-Wallis ^{2}: PCBs, 28.6; *p,p'*-DDE, 21.8; P 0.0001.

DISCUSSION

Blood plasma of nestling bald eagles has been correlated with concentrations of organochlorine pesticides and PCBs representative of the eagles' prey base within roughly 8 km of the nest site for the first 6-9 weeks post-hatch (Bowerman *et al.* 1990). Nestlings are thereby appropriate biosentinels of the general contamination of their immediate environment. Concentrations of PCBs in plasma from nestlings from Great Lakes breeding areas were 6 times greater than those from interior breeding areas, while *p,p'*-DDE concentrations were 3 times greater.

Addled eagle eggs were used to determine concentrations of organochlorine pesticides and PCBs associated with reproductive impairment. Sprunt *et al.* (1973) recorded productivities of about 1.0 in two stable populations and about 0.7 in a third stable population in Florida. We follow Wiemeyer *et al.* (1984) in using a productivity of 1.0 as indicative of a healthy population unaffected by contaminants. In our sample (Table 2), mean productivities in the Great Lakes and in interior areas were 0.63 for Lakes Michigan and Huron, 0.78 for Lakes Erie and Superior, and 0.94 for the interior regions (Table 2). In a much larger sample Best *et al.* (this volume) determined a mean productivity of 0.68 for all Great Lakes sites in 1981-1990 and 1.00 for the interior.

In this data set, like those previously examined for the relationships between productivity and

Table 2. Productivity within the Great Lakes Basin and Alaska (Kubiak & Best 1991) and geometric mean concentrations, with the range, of *p,p'*-DDE, total PCBs, and dieldrin in addled Bald Eagle eggs.

Realm	n	*p,p'*-DDE[1]	Total PCBs[1]	Dieldrin[1]	Productivity[2]
Alaska	5	0.5	1.3	0.01	1.29
		(0.3-0.7)	(0.8-2.1)	(0.01-0.02)	
Interior Breeding Areas					
Michigan Lower Penin.	4	2.2	6.2	0.09	1.14
		(1.0-5.7)	(1.9-14)	(0.06-0.25)	
Michigan Upper Penin.	9	1.7	5.0	0.13	0.93
		(0.5-16)	(1.8-29)	(0.02-0.91)	
Interior Ohio	3	1.8	9.0	0.13	0.71
		(1.3-3.1)	(5.7-20)	(0.07-0.42)	
Great Lakes Breeding Areas					
Lake Superior	3	3.2	8.5	0.19	0.84
		(1.5-9.5)	(3.4-14)	(0.08-0.51)	
Lake Erie	7	2.8	20	0.45	0.75
		(1.9-10)	(8.6-44)	(0.25-0.69)	
Lake Michigan	2	17	38	1.1	0.68
		(10-30)	(27-55)	(0.60-2.0)	
Lake Huron	3	16	73	0.88	0.59
		(8.5-41)	(50-110)	(0.39-2.3)	

1 Fresh wet weight, ppm.

2 Total number of fledged young divided by the total number of occupied breeding areas (Postupalsky 1974).

contaminant residues (Wiemeyer *et al.* 1984, 1993; Nisbet 1989) the high correlation between DDE and PCB residues precludes any attempt to sort out their relative contributions to the depressed productivity. The previous analyses, however, would predict almost zero productivity at the DDE residue levels we measured in the eggs from Lakes Michigan and Huron. A possible bias in the productivity estimates, discussed above, might explain at least in part this apparent inconsistency between our data and those previously published.

DDE has been associated with the thin eggshell syndrome of Bald Eagles (Wiemeyer *et al.* 1984). Approximately 25 percent of the eggs represented in this paper have shells that are 15% thin (Best, unpublished). A DDE effect on reproduction is therefore indicated.

We have no evidence that links the observed levels of dieldrin with reproductive failures.

PCBs produce teratogenic effects, such as bill defects (Gilbertson *et al.* 1991). Bill defects in six nestling eagles have been observed from areas in the Great Lakes region (Ontario, Michigan, Wisconsin, and Minnesota) between 1968 and 1989 (Grier 1968; Bowerman *et al.* in prep.). In Sweden, nestling White-tailed Eagles, *Haliaeetus albicilla*, with bill defects were believed to be related to PCBs (Helander 1983). In an examination of chicken feeding studies, Aroclor and dioxin-like PCB congener concentrations in hen's feed explained toxic, egg-intrinsic reproductive effects (Kubiak *et al.* 1989). PCB concentrations in Bald Eagle eggs are far greater than known effect levels in poultry experiments, as measured by either total PCB or by certain individual, dioxin-like, PCB congener concentrations (Kubiak 1988; Britton & Huston 1973; Brunström & Andersson 1988).

An assessment of the role of the PCB congeners producing dioxin-type effects in Bald Eagles of the Great Lakes region is nearing completion. This analysis should refine our understanding of the relative contributions of the dioxin-like effects of these congeners, of other effects of PCBs, and of DDE-induced eggshell deficiencies to the present reproductive failures of Bald Eagles in the Laurentian Great Lakes.

ACKNOWLEDGEMENTS

D. Baird, J. Bruce, D. Case, H. Davis, G. Dawson, R. Doepker, K. Doran, R. Eckstein, J. Edde, D. Elsing, D. Evans, J. Hammill, J. Hendrickson, M. Hodgkins, J. Holt, P. Hunter, J. Kesel, K. Kozie, M. Martell, J. Papp, L. Pfanmueller, S. Postupalsky, M. Schieldcastle, J. Soehnel, J. Weinrich, T. Weise, and many other people assisted us in the field. E. Evans, R. Scheel, and R. Welch assisted in chemical analysis of plasma samples. This study was funded by the USDI-Fish and Wildlife Service, Consumers Power Company, USDA-Forest Service, Michigan Department of Natural Resources-Nongame Wildlife Program, Michigan Department of Public Health, Minnesota Pollution Control Agency, Miller Brewing Company, Michigan Audubon Society, The Eagle Foundation, and EARTHWATCH.

William W. Bowerman IV & John P. Giesy, Jr.
Department of Fisheries and Wildlife
Pesticide Research Center Institute for Environmental Toxicology
Michigan State University, East Lansing, Michigan 48824 USA.

David A. Best & Timothy J. Kubiak
USDI-Fish and Wildlife Service, East Lansing Field Office
1405 S. Harrison Rd., East Lansing, Michigan 48823 USA.

James G. Sikarskie
Department of Small Animal Clinical Sciences
College of Veterinary Medicine, Michigan State University
East Lansing, Michigan 48824 USA.

Meyburg, B.-U. & R. D. Chancellor eds.1994
Raptor Conservation Today
WWGBP / The Pica Press

Organochlorines and Eggshell Thinning in Peregrine Falcon *Falco peregrinus* Eggs from the Eastern United States, 1986 - 1988

S.A. Burns, W.M. Jarman, T.J. Cade, L.F. Kiff & B.J. Walton

ABSTRACT

Comparisons of DDE and PCB concentrations (n=37) and shell thicknesses (n=112) of addled Peregrine Falcon, *Falco peregrinus*, eggs collected from the East Coast of the United States in 1986-1988 with earlier data indicated no detectable changes in residue levels or shell thickness over the decade. Geometric means of *p,p'*-DDE and the sum of the PCB congeners in the eggs, 7.8 and 8.9 mg/kg (wet weight) respectively, and the geometric mean shell thickness of all eggs collected between 1985 and 1988 (0.32 mm, or 11% thinning) were below and above, respectively, threshold levels considered critical for reproductive success. Although local variations in contamination patterns were detected, concentrations of the organochlorines measured over the region were significantly correlated with each other, indicating that a general contamination pattern exists over the region.

INTRODUCTION

In 1976, 12 years after Berger *et al.* (1969) had failed to find any active eyries of Peregrine Falcons in eastern North America, and 4 years after DDT use ended in the United States, personnel from The Peregrine Fund Inc. began an intensive effort to re-establish the Peregrine Falcon in North America using captive breeding and other management techniques (Barclay & Cade 1983). Gilroy & Barclay (1988) have presented data on DDE and PCB residues and on shell thicknesses of addled eggs produced by the introduced population in the early 1980s. In this paper we present data on levels of these and other organochlorine contaminants in eggs of Eastern Peregrines obtained in 1986-1988, and on shell thicknesses, in part to determine whether detectable changes in environmental levels have occurred over the decade, and in part to determine the present contamination patterns in this population.

MATERIALS AND METHODS

Collection

The eggs and shell fragments were collected by personnel from The Peregrine Fund, Inc. as part of the long-term Peregrine Falcon management program in the eastern US. Only eggs that failed to hatch were used for the organochlorine analysis in this study. The collection areas (Figure 1) consisted of four historic inland cliff nest sites (Northern Region), and 22 sites in the mid-Atlantic region, one of which, the Delaware Memorial Bridge, had two eyries. The state of New Jersey contained two subregions: Delaware Bay and River (n=5), and the New Jersey coast (n=8). The eggs were collected from Peregrine nests on cliffs, bridges, buildings, towers erected for release purposes, and a water tower.

Extraction and Analysis

The contents of 37 addled eggs collected between 1986 and 1988 were analyzed for organochlorine compounds at the University of California Santa Cruz, Long Marine Laboratory. When more than one addled egg was collected from a nest, one egg was randomly chosen and analyzed. For a detailed account of the method see Jarman *et al.* (1993a). Briefly, a homogenized aliquot was extracted with dichloromethane in a soxhlet apparatus, lipid was then applied to a florisil column, and the extracts were analyzed using a gas chromatograph (GC/ECD) equipped with two columns.

Eggshell thickness measurements

Eggshells (n=112) were measured at the Western Foundation of Vertebrate Zoology, Camarillo, California. The measurements were made with a model 35 PS Federal bench comparator thickness gauge. Whole eggs were measured on the equator through the blow-hole near the middle of one side. If no membrane was attached to the shell, a compensation factor of 0.063 mm was added, which was the mean thickness of the eggshell membranes of 20 pre-1947 Peregrine eggs.

RESULTS AND DISCUSSION

Eggshell thickness

The log DDE residue values were negatively correlated with shell thickness ($r = -0.387$, $P < 0.05$; Pearson's Correlation Coefficient), consistent with the results of earlier studies (Cade *et al.* 1971; Peakall & Kiff 1988; Gilroy & Barclay 1988). The geometric mean thickness over the time period 1981-1988 did not change significantly (Anova, $P > 0.05$). The geometric mean of all eggs was 0.32 mm, or 11% thinner than the historical pre-1947 mean thickness of 0.36 mm (Anderson & Hickey 1972). Only seven shells collected between 1981 and 1988 were thicker than the historical mean level (Figure 2a). The amount of eggshell thinning found in this study is well below the 17% threshold level above which population declines in Peregrines are expected (Peakall & Kiff 1988).

Organochlorines: Trends over Time

DDE and PCB concentrations were compared to data from an earlier study of eastern Peregrine eggs collected between 1981 and 1984, reported as clutch means (Gilroy & Barclay 1988). No change in DDE and PCB levels over the period 1981-1988 could be detected (Anova, ($P > 0.05$) (Figures 2b, 2c). The PCB values of samples collected between 1981 and 1984 were quantified as Aroclor® mixtures; this method may produce estimates of total PCBs that are higher by a factor of two or more than the values generated using individual PCB congeners (Turle *et al.* 1991). This bias, however, while affecting any conclusion about whether levels have increased, would not affect our conclusion that there was no detectable decrease in PCB contamination levels over the decade.

Several data sets have indicated that DDE levels dropped sharply in eastern North America during the 1970s, i.e. the data from the monitoring program using wing muscles of Mallards, *Anas*

Figure 1. Location of egg collection sites for organochlorine analysis.

MID ATLANTIC REGION SITES:

1. Egg Island (Is), N.J. (DBR)
2. Heislerville, N.J. (DBR)
3. Sea Isle City, N.J. (NJC)
4. Atlantic City, N.J. (NJC)
5. Brigantine, N.J. (NJC)
6. Swan Bay, N.J. (NJC)
7. Tuckerton, N.J. (NJC)
8. Manahawkin, N.J. (NJC)
9. Sedge Is., N.J. (NJC)
10. Ocean Gate, N.J. (NJC)
11. Delaware Memorial Bridge, N.J. (DBR)
12. Walt Whitman Br (Br.), N.J. (DBR)
13. Betsy Ross Br., N.J. (DMR)
14. Baltimore, MD.
15. Smith Is., MD.
16. South Marsh Is., MD.
17. Francis Scott Key Br., MD.
18. Cobb Is., VA.
19. Chincoteague, VA
20. Verrazano Br., N.Y.
21. Throgs Neck Br. N.Y.
22. Cornell Medical School, N.Y.

NORTHERN REGION SITES:

23. Hurricane Mountain, N.Y.
24. Mount Pisgah, VT.
25. Bristol, VT.
26. Franconia Notch, N.H.

(DBR) Delaware Bay and River subregion
(NJC) New Jersey Coast subregion

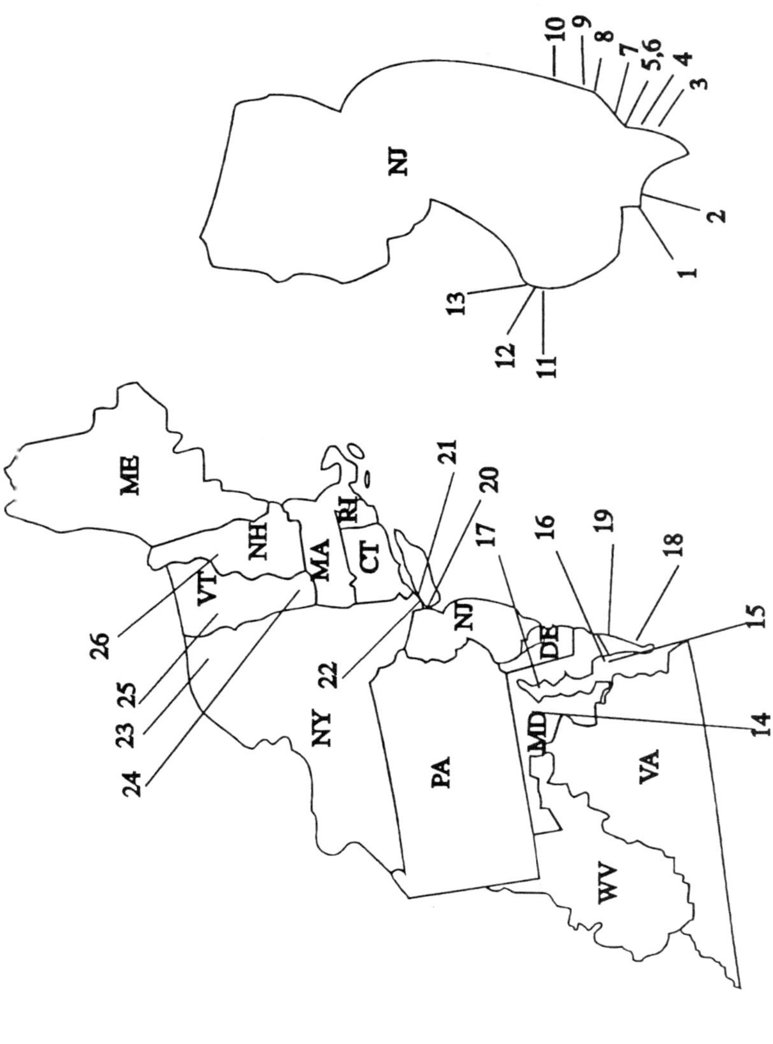

Figure 2. Scatterplots and geometric mean concentrations of eggshell thickness (mm, top) *p,p'*-DDE (middle), and PCBs (bottom, both mg/kg, wet weight) in East Coast Peregrine Falcon eggs, 1981-1988. DDE and PCB data from eggs collected between 1981-1984 are from Gilroy & Barclay (1988).

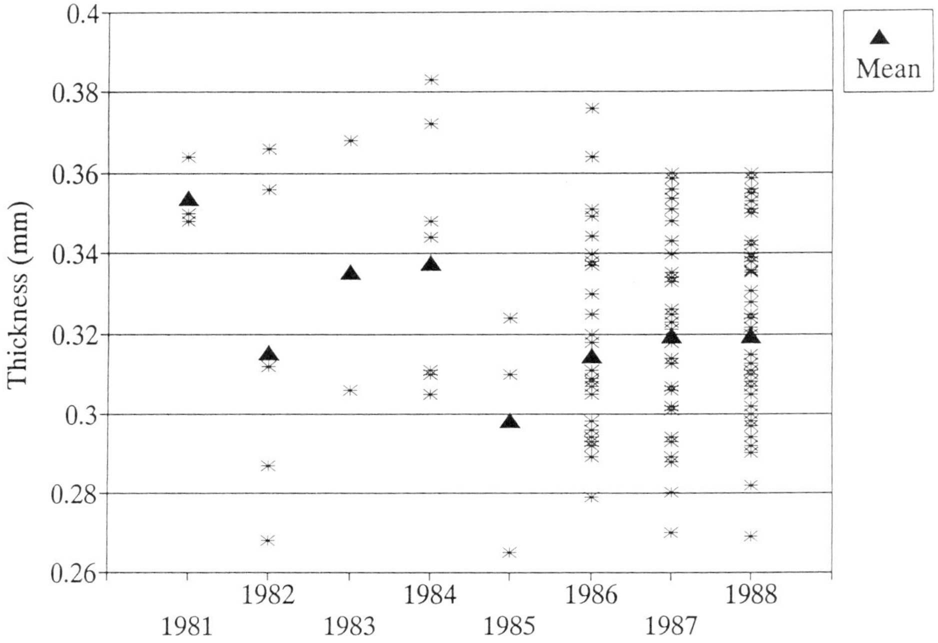

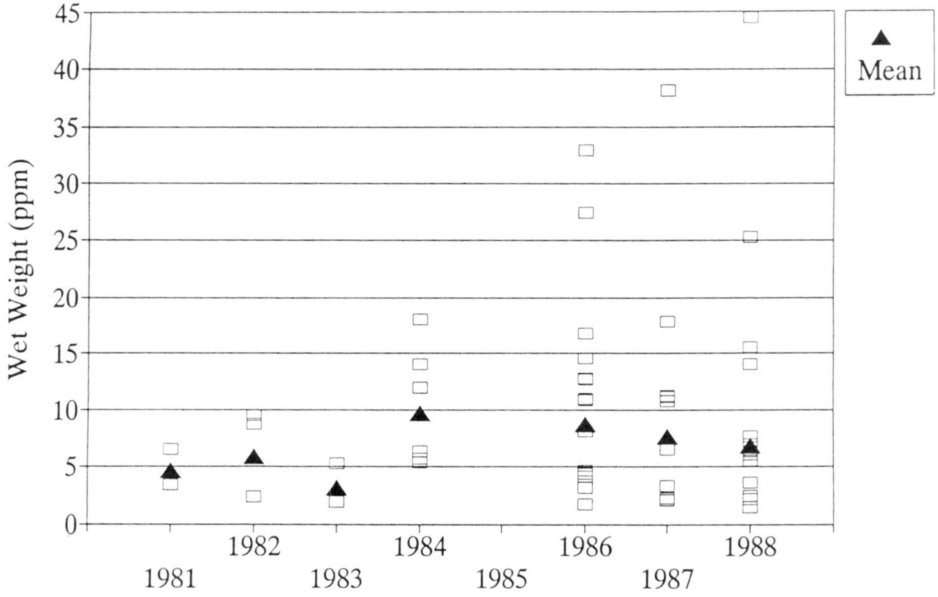

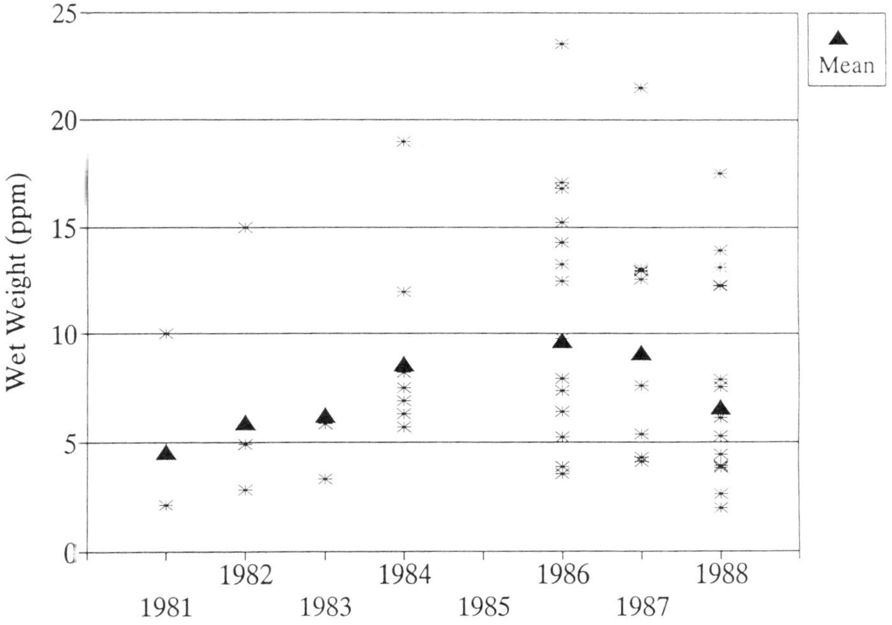

platyrhynchos, and Black Ducks, *A. rubripes* (Heath 1969; Heath & Hill 1974; Prouty & Bunck 1986). DDE and other DDT contamination also declined in coastal marine waters (Elliott *et al.* 1988) In the Great Lakes, levels of DDE, PCBs and several other organochlorines dropped sharply in the mid-1970s, but levelled off during the 1980s with few detectable trends (Weseloh *et al.* 1979; Mineau *et al.* 1984; Environment Canada *et al.* 1991b). Our data suggest a comparable pattern for DDE and PCBs in the northeastern states during the 1980s.

Organochlorines: A Regional Contamination Pattern

No differences in levels of any of the contaminants among the regions (Table 1) could be detected (Northern vs. Mid-Atlantic; among Northern, Chesapeake, New Jersey coast and Delaware Bay; New Jersey coast vs. Delaware Bay; Anova, $P > 0.05$). Moreover, with the exception of HCB which shows variable recoveries in the analyses, and of a barely non-significant correlation between PCBs and Heptachlor epoxide ($r_s = 0.34$, $df = 30$, $P = 0.05$) all contaminants were significantly correlated with each other ($r_s > 0.39$, $df = 30$, $P < 0.05$; Spearman's Rank Correlation Analysis). A region-wide contamination pattern is indicated. Visual examination indicated that the profiles of the individual PCB congeners were similar between the northern and mid-Atlantic regions.

Dieldrin levels in the eggs ranged from 91 to 810 µg/kg (ppb), with a geometric mean value of 270 µg/kg (n=33). The geometric mean value of dieldrin in Peregrine eggs collected from Great Britain between 1961 - 1977 was calculated to be 200 µg/kg (n=146) by Nisbet (1988) from data of Ratcliffe (1980) and Cooke *et al.* (1982).

Local Variation

New Jersey Atlantic Coast sites

There were a total of eight Peregrine sites along the New Jersey coast. Although these sites are close geographically, the levels of organochlorine residues in eggs vary greatly. An example of this is the difference between the Brigantine and Atlantic City sites, which are less than 8 km apart. Brigantine is approximately 5 km inland in a coastal marsh, and the Atlantic City site is located on a casino overlooking a marsh directly on the coast. The Brigantine site had the highest ratio of DDE:PCB, 3.1, whereas the Atlantic City site had the lowest DDE:PCB ratio of all the sites, 0.36. The contaminant levels between these sites also varied between 1986 and 1988. The mean of the Brigantine DDE levels (n=3) was higher than the mean of the Atlantic City levels (n=2) by a factor of 5.8 (38 mg/kg versus 6.5 mg/kg). The PCB residue levels of the Atlantic City site were higher than the Brigantine site by a factor of 1.5 (18 vs 12 mg/kg). The fact that these two nests are geographically close and yet have different levels of organochlorines indicates that these females may be feeding on different prey sources. The birds from the Atlantic City site have been observed taking rails as their primary prey.

The productivity of active nests on the New Jersey coast was higher than the Delaware Bay and River sites from 1979-1988 (Steidl *et al.* 1991). The means of the New Jersey PCB and DDE residue levels during 1986-1988 are approximately 1.5 times higher than those from the Delaware Bay region (Table 1). This suggests that the low productivity of the Delaware region may be due to causes other than the organochlorine residues reported in this study.

Bridge sites

Seven collection sites were from Peregrine nests located on bridges. Four of the bridge sites are on the Delaware River, two of these on the same bridge, east and west Delaware Memorial Bridge (DMB). These four sites are located within 50 km of each other. The largest difference in residue levels is between DMB west and DMB east: the DDE level of the first clutch DMB west was five times higher than the DMB east level (17 vs 3.4 mg/kg) and the PCB value was six times higher (18 vs 2.8 mg/kg). Second clutch DMB west DDE value was 1.8 times higher (6.1 vs. 3.4 mg/kg), and the PCB value was 2.9 times higher (8.3 vs 2.8 mg/kg). The levels in the egg from Betsy Ross Bridge were approximately three times lower than those from the Walt Whitman Bridge for both DDE and PCB (5.3 vs 18, and 4.3 vs 14 mg/kg respectively). These differences indicate either that the females are feeding on different prey sources, or that the ingestion of occasional "hot" prey items results in a different contaminant profile in the eggs.

Two bridge sites are in the New York City area, Verrazano Narrows Bridge and Throgs Neck Bridge, and have almost identical levels of DDE and PCB (2.0 vs 2.1, and 4.4 vs 4.7 mg/kg respectively).

Building Sites

Eggs were collected from three Peregrine nests located on buildings in metropolitan cities: Atlantic City, New Jersey (Atlantic); Cornell Medical School, New York (Cornell); and Baltimore, Maryland (Balt). In the eggs collected in 1988, all three sites had similar DDE levels but the Atlantic City site had three times the PCB level of Baltimore and two times more than the Cornell site.

CONCLUSION

The levels of organochlorine compounds and of eggshell thinning measured in this study were generally below those associated with population declines (Peakall & Kiff 1988); there are, however, areas of concern (*i.e.* the New Jersey coast and the Delaware River and Bay area) where the combined DDE and PCB levels are possibly high enough to affect reproduction. According to Steidl *et al.* (1991), the Delaware River and Bay area has lower productivity than the New Jersey coast region, but we found that the DDE and PCB values were similar between the regions. Therefore, there may be a factor in addition to DDE or PCB that might account for the depressed productivity in the Delaware River and Bay area.

The overall levels of DDE were similar to levels found in both Rocky Mountain and California Peregrine eggs, but the PCB levels were higher in the East Coast eggs (Jarman *et al.* 1992a). The possibility that the higher PCB levels could have a negative effect warrants further research.

Table 1. Organochlorine levels (geometric means, ± 1 std. dev., µg/kg, wet weight) in unhatched Peregrine Falcon eggs collected from the eastern United States, 1986-1988.

	All Sites	North	Mid Atlantic			
			All Mid At.	Chesapeake Bay	New Jersey Coast	Delaware River & Bay
Parameter	n=37	n=4	n=33	n=5	n=14	n=7
% Lipid	6.5 (4.9-8.6)	6.4 (5.3-7.9)	6.5 (4.8-8.6)	7.3 (6.1-8.6)	6.3 (4.7-8.4)	6.9 (4.9-9.7)
% H_2O	83 (78-88)	83 (81-86)	83 (78-88)	79 (75-83)	84 (80-88)	81 (75-88)
p,p'-DDE	7,800 (3,200-19,000)	5,000 (2,500-10,000)	8,200 (3,000-20,000)	4,900 (2,600-9,000)	12,000 (5,500-25,000)	9,900 (5,200-19,000)
HCB	23 (11-47)	26 (12-53)	22 (11-46)	29 (14-59)	25 (15-42)	22 (11-42)
trans-nonachlor	200 (86-470)	190 (120-290)	200 (84-490)	160 (65-410)	280 (150-550)	210 (90-480)
Hept epox	170 (72-400)	94 (37-240)	170 (76-400)	200 (120-320)	190 (120-300)	170 (61-490)
Oxychlor	400 (150-1,100)	140 (16-1,200)	460 (260-820)	370 (259-530)	460 (230-910)	580 (360-930)
Mirex	190 (77-460)	170 (81-380)	190 (77-470)	180 (69-470)	230 (150-350)	200 (89-440)
β-HCH	7.8 (2.9-21)	3.6 (0.70-19)	8.6 (3.7-20)	5.9 (3.0-11)	10 (3.5-29)	11 (5.4-22)
Dieldrin	270 (91-810)	100 (21-500)	270 (96-780)	170 (30-950)	340 (133-650)	340 (170-680)
Σ PCB	8,900 (4,800-17,000)	6,100 (3,000-12,000)	9,400 (5,200-17,000)	6,800 (3,900-12,000)	14,000 (10,000-18,000)	9,100 (4,900-17,000)
DDE/PCB	0.87 (0.47-1.6)	0.83 (0.80-0.87)	1.0 (0.45-1.7)	0.7 (0.51-1.0)	0.73 (0.36-1.4)	1.1 (0.40-0.81)

HCB, hexachlorobenzene; Hept epox, heptachlor epoxide; Oxychlor, oxychlordane

ACKNOWLEDGEMENTS

We would like to thank Marty Gilroy and Jim Weaver for collecting the eggs, Clark Sumida for his work on the eggshell measurements, and John Barclay for sharing with us his invaluable knowledge on East Coast Peregrine biology. Funding was provided by The Peregrine Fund, Inc., the Santa Cruz Predatory Bird Research Group, and the Institute of Marine Sciences, University of California Santa Cruz.

S.A. Burns & W.M. Jarman
Institute of Marine Sciences
University of California Santa Cruz
Santa Cruz, CA 95064 USA

T.J. Cade
The Peregrine Fund Inc.
World Center for Birds of Prey
5666 West Flying Hawk Ln., Boise, ID 83709 USA

L.F. Kiff
Western Foundation of Vertebrate Zoology
439 Calle San Pablo, Camarillo CA 93010 USA

B.J. Walton
Santa Cruz Predatory Bird Research Group
University of California Santa Cruz
Santa Cruz CA 95064 USA

Meyburg, B.-U. & R. D. Chancellor eds.1994
Raptor Conservation Today
WWGBP / The Pica Press

Trace Element Concentrations in Feathers of White-Tailed Sea Eagles *Haliaeetus albicilla* Collected Recently in Poland

Jerzy Falandysz & Tadeusz Mizera

INTRODUCTION

Bird feathers contain relatively high concentrations of trace metals (Berg *et al.* 1966; Doi & Fukuyama 1983; Szefer & Falandysz 1983; Goede & Bruin 1984; Wiemeyer *et al.* 1986). Due to the ease with which feather samples can be taken without injuring birds, as well as the relative stability of feather keratin, feathers have served in many programs as a monitoring medium for environmental pollution and contamination by heavy metals and trace elements (Berg *et al.* 1966; Lindberg & Odsjö 1983; Fiuczynski 1983; Doi *et al.* 1984; Appelquist *et al.* 1985; Wiemeyer *et al.* 1986; Szefer & Falandysz 1987; Thompson *et al.* 1990).

Metals are deposited in feathers during their formation and growth; concentrations appear to reflect both the nutritional status of the bird and the trace metal content of recently consumed food.

Mercury, primarily in the form of methylmercury, seems to be very firmly bound to keratin (Appelquist *et al.* 1984). Feathers are thus an excellent material for studies of temporal trends of this toxic element in both terrestrial and marine environments (Berg *et al.* 1966; Appelquist *et al.* 1985).

When discussing metal content in feathers, however, mechanisms other than internal deposition during formation and growth must be considered. Even after feather growth has stopped, metabolism has ceased, and the feather is dead, external adsorption or leaching can take place. Due to its high total surface to weight ratio, the vane of the feather is suspected to be much more susceptible to alterations in metal content than the shaft.

An external deposition of selenium, lead and arsenic from secretion products of both preen and salt glands has been observed in feather vanes of Dunlin, *Calidris alpina* (Goede & Bruin 1984; 1986). It has also been shown that feathers may take up various metals externally (copper, iron, nickel and zinc) from direct contact with environmental media such as air, water, mud, etc. (Kelsall & Burton 1979; Rose & Parker 1982; Goede & Bruin 1984; 1986).

The purpose of this study is to investigate the degree and possible exposure of White-tailed Sea Eagles breeding in the western part of inland Poland to mercury, lead, cadmium, zinc, copper, manganese, and iron, using feathers as a monitoring tissue. The present communication is a preliminary result.

MATERIALS AND METHODS

Sample collection and preparation

Most of the different types of feather samples were collected at various nesting grounds of White-tailed Sea Eagles in the western part of Poland between 1986 and 1988 (forest inspectorates Bogdaniec, D bno, K odawa and Sulechów; Fig. 1). Some of the feathers were also taken from lead-poisoned birds collected in the same areas from 1986 to 1987 (forest inspectorates D bno and Skwierzyna), and from an immature male electrocuted in the northern part of Poland in 1984. The feathers were dried at ambient laboratory temperature, placed individually in clean polyethylene bags, tagged and stored until analysis.

Figure 1: Sites from which feather samples of White-tailed Sea Eagle collected 1986-1988 in western Poland

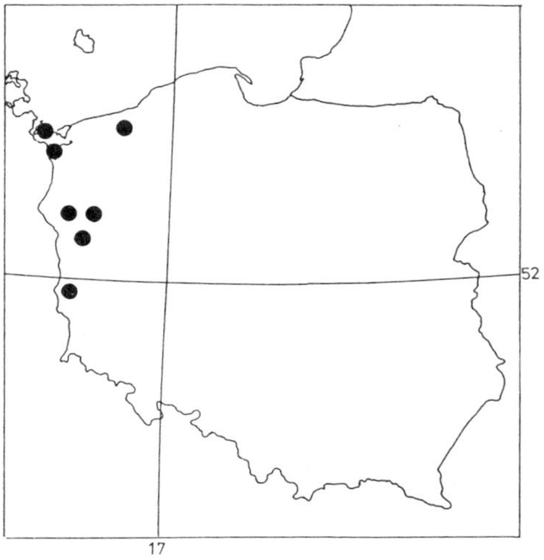

Chemical analysis

The feathers were measured and then dried at 60°C for 24 hours.

For determination of mercury the upper parts (1/3 of the total length) of the feathers were wet-digested with concentrated nitric acid in an all-glass apparatus consisting of a round-bottomed flask, partial condenser and a reflux water cooler. The digest was diluted with redistilled water. Excess oxidizing substances were removed by adding hydroxylamine hydrochloride. Mercury (II) was reduced to metallic mercury by tin chloride solution (20%) in sulfuric acid. Mercury was evaporated by passing a stream of nitrogen through the solution and was determined by cold vapor atomic absorption using a UV Mercury Monitor LDC/Milton Roy, at a setting of 253.7 nm.

For determination of lead, cadmium, manganese, copper, zinc, and iron, the lower parts (2/3 of the total length) of the feathers were placed in silica vessels, and dry-ashed at 420°C. A few drops of concentrated nitric acid were added to whiten the ash. The resulting residue was dissolved in 5-10 ml of 1 M nitric acid and aspirated into the air-acetylene flame of the Pye Unicam SP 9 atomic absorption spectrophotometer.

Most of the analyses were conducted on single feathers, but in the case of small feathers (plumae and some of the tectrices), pooled samples of whole feathers were prepared. Altogether 33 samples were analyzed for mercury and 28 for the other trace elements.

Table 1. Concentrations of trace metals in feathers of White-tailed Sea Eagles (µg/g on a dry weight basis).

Sampling details (location, month, year and feather type)	No.	Lead	Cadmium	Copper	Zinc	Manganese	Iron	Mercury
Forest Inspectorate: Sulechów								
Location: Przetocznica								
May & June 1987; remiges (33 & 37cm)	2	5.6	0.24	6.7	100	7.3	200	4.8
		3.9-8.1	*0.14-0.33*	*6.1-7.3*	*100-100*	*5.3-9.2*	*200-200*	*1.7-7.9*
March 1988; remiges	1	12	1.2	8.9	63	8.2	230	5.7
June 1987; tectrices (16 & 18cm)	2	NA	NA	NA	NA	NA	NA	8.5
June 1987; rectrices (28cm)	1	1.1	0.27	1.4	46	1.2	110	2.6
Location: Nietkowice								
October 1986; tectrices (23-30cm)	3	6.4±2.9	0.19±0.13	8.7±0.6	120±16	9.5±6.5	120±90	8.3±2.6[a]
October 1986; remiges (39cm)	1	10	0.24	11	60	14	450	2.7
May 1987; remiges (48cm)	1	7.6	0.13	7.2	73	5.2	140	3.2
May 1987; rectrices (30cm)	2	5.7	0.29	7.7	100	5.1	240	4.3
		5.3-6.1	*0.28-0.29*	*7.1-8.3*	*97-110*	*4.6-5.6*	*230-250*	*3.3-5.3*
May 1987; tectrices (30cm)	1	6.8	0.17	8.4	120	11	250	18
Location: Bialków (Division 7 & 219)								
June 1986; remiges I (46-48cm)	3	7.5 ±1.7	0.16±0.04	7.8±0.9	88±13	6.2±1.8	140±30	10±3
		6.5-9.4	*0.13-0.20*	*7.0-8.7*	*73-96*	*4.6-8.1*	*130-170*	*6.1-17*
June 1986; rectrices (32cm)	1	6.0	0.16	7.4	120	4.2	250	10
June 1986; tectrices (31cm)	1	5.2	0.086	7.8	140	6.8	130	12

Sampling details (location, month, year and feather type)	No.	Lead	Cadmium	Copper	Zinc	Manganese	Iron	Mercury
(Division 30d)								
May 1987; remiges I (49cm)	1	8.1	0.16	7.9	87	7.3	150	7.6
May 1987; remiges II (33cm)	1	4.4	0.044	6.5	91	3.3	140	2.8
May 1987; rectrices (31cm)	1	4.0	0.14	5.0	76	5.5	220	4.3
Location: Province of Koszalin (electrocuted male)[b]								
1984; remiges I (39-43cm)	6	3.3±0.4	0.10±0.07	6.2±0.7	110±20	4.7±1.0	85±24	4.3±11
		2.7-3.8	*0.06-0.23*	*5.1-7.4*	*95-140*	*3.7-5.9*	*54-120*	*2.9-5.6*
tectrices (21-25cm)	3(5)[c]	4.5±3.1	0.17±0.27	6.2±3.2	160±75	6.9±2.2	180±35	7.8±3.4
		2.2-8.0	*<0.006-0.48*	*2.5-8.3*	*120-250*	*4.4-8.2*	*160-220*	*3.2-11*
Forest Inspectorate:Klodawa(Division 90)								
1986; remiges II (36cm)	1	4.3	0.15	6.7	80	4.5	130	2.8
Location: Lubsko								
remiges I (No.9; left,43.5cm)	1	3.7	0.10	4.8	110	5.8	140	0.66
remiges I (No.9; right,50cm)	1	4.0	0.052	5.0	100	5.9	150	2.8
tectrices[d]	1(5)	11	0.38	9.5	360	7.0	590	41
tectrices (vexilum)	1(9)	NA	NA	NA	NA	NA	NA	19
plumae[d]	-	23	0.41	21	300	22	750	37

Sampling details (location, month, year and feather type)	No.	Lead	Cadmium	Copper	Zinc	Manganese	Iron	Mercury
Forest Inspectorate: Skwierzyna								
Location: Lubieniewice, January 1987[e]								
remiges (vexilum)	2	5.9	0.15	7.1	110	5.8	170	2.7
		5.6-6.1	*0.11-0.19*	*6.7-7.4*	*100-110*	*5.1-6.4*	*170-170*	*1.6-3.8*
rectrices	1	4.3	0.11	6.8	120	5.8	250	2.4
tectrices (9cm)	1	NA	NA	NA	NA	NA	NA	NA
plumae[d]	-	NA	NA	NA	NA	NA	NA	NA
Forest Inspectorate: Debno								
Location: Baranówka								
June 1986; remiges (45cm)	1	3.1	0.063	6.7	90	2.5	65	5.3
Location: Debno, February 1987[e]								
remiges II	2	5.1	0.29	5.9	120	8.5	180	4.5
		4.2-6.0	*0.21-0.36*	*5.0-6.7*	*120-120*	*7.0-10*	*180-180*	*4.4-5.2*
tectrices	1	NA	NA	NA	NA	NA	NA	6.1
tectrices	1	16	0.92	10	280	36	830	11
plumae[d]	1	9.7	0.61	16	210	14	240	5.8
Forest Inspectorate: Bogdaniec								
Location: Zacisze								
remiges (30 & 33cm)	2	3.1	0.53	6.5	100	3.6	110	8.7
		2.7-3.4	*0.044-0.062*	*6.1-6.8*	*90-100*	*3.5-3.6*	*91-130*	*5.4-12*

[a] For mercury No. = 4.
[b] Immature bird.
[c] Pooled samples (number of feathers in brackets).
[d] Determined in the whole feather, otherwise in the upper (1/3 of the total length) or the lower part (2/3 of the total length) for mercury and other trace metals, respectively.
[e] Lead-poisoned bird.

RESULTS AND DISCUSSION

Concentrations of trace elements determined in feathers of White-tailed Sea Eagles are presented in Table 1.

Mercury

The mean mercury concentration in the feathers examined was 8.5±8.9 μg/g on a dry-weight basis (range 0.66-41). In three feather samples from Lubsko (Forest Inspectorate Kodawa) and one from Nietkowice (Sulechów) the concentration of mercury ranged from 18 to 41 μg/g (29±12). This is much higher than mercury concentrations determined in the 29 other feather samples, which ranged from 0.66 to 17μg/g (5.7±3.0).

Berg *et al.* (1966) detected mercury in feathers of White-tailed Sea Eagles collected in different regions of Sweden from 1893 to 1949 in the range of 2.7 to 16 μg/g, with a mean for 12 central tail feathers and 5 inner primaries of 6.6 and 9.8 μg/g, respectively. These data seem to reflect a "background level" of mercury in White-tailed Sea Eagles from the Swedish environment not contaminated with this metal from anthropogenic sources. Much higher concentrations of mercury, *i.e.* 49 μg/g (38-64) have been reported by the authors cited above in 5 central tail feathers of birds collected between 1952 and 1965 in a region of Sweden close to the Baltic Sea. In a similar study feathers of four birds collected from the Archipelago of Stockholm in 1965 and 1966 contained mercury in the range of 23 to 51 μg/g (40±13; Jensen *et al.* 1972).

Lead and cadmium

Lead concentrations determined in the feather samples ranged from 1.1 to 23 μg/g, with a mean of 6.8±4.5 μg/g. In four samples lead concentrations were above 10 μg/g, ranging from 11 to 23μg/g, with a mean of 16±5. In the remaining samples the mean was 5.4±2.1 μg/g. One of two lead-poisoned White-tailed Sea Eagles (from D bno) contained apparently higher concentrations of that metal in two feather samples - 9.7 and 16 μg/g (Table 1).

Raptors breeding in the vicinity of Berlin contained lead in their feathers in concentrations ranging from 11 to 24 μg/g (Fiuczynski 1983), generally higher than the concentrations determined in White-tailed Sea Eagle feathers in our study (Table 1). Lead concentrations similar to those found in this study in feathers of California Condors, *Gymnogyps californianus*, ranged from 1.9 to 14 μg/g (Wiemeyer *et al.* 1986).

The mean concentration of cadmium in the feathers examined was 0.25±0.26 μg/g on a dry weight basis (range <0.006-1.2). Highest concentrations were in the four samples with the highest mercury concentrations (see above), 0.73±0.40 μg/g. Mean cadmium concentration in the remaining 24 samples was 0.17±0.12.

White-tailed Sea Eagle feathers examined previously contained cadmium in concentrations from 0.83 to 1.2 μg/g (Falandysz 1986; Falandysz *et al.* 1988).

Copper, zinc, manganese and iron

The feathers examined contained 7.9±3.6 μg/g (1.4-21) of copper, 130±70 μg/g (46-360) of zinc, 8.1±6.9 μg/g (1.2-36) of manganese, and 240±190 μg/g (91-590) of iron. The concentrations of these essential trace metals are within the ranges found in feathers of potential prey species of White-tailed Sea Eagles, including Long-tailed Ducks, *Clangula hyemalis*, and Scaup Ducks, *Aythya marila* (Szefer & Falandysz 1983; 1987), and appear typical.

Inter-metallic relationships

Linear correlation coefficients (r) between the concentrations of elements determined in feathers of White-tailed Sea Eagles show a lack of significant correlation between pairs Cd-Hg (0.19), Cd-Zn (0.35) and Hg-Mn (0.35). All other pairs of metals showed a significant positive correlation, with highest values of the determination coefficients (r^2) for the pairs Cu-Pb, Mn-Pb, Fe-Pb, Fe-Zn, Fe-Mn and Zn-Hg (0.61-0.74; Table 2).

Table 2. Inter-metallic correlation coefficients, r^a, in feathers of White-tailed Sea Eagles.

	Cd	Cu	Zn	Mn	Fe	Hg
Pb	0.62	0.86	0.67	0.79	0.85	0.65
Cd	-	0.41	0.35	0.60	0.53	0.19
Cu		-	0.62	0.63	0.65	0.68
Zn			-	0.61	0.78	0.82
Mn				-	0.84	0.35
Fe					-	0.65

[a] Critical values at 0.05 and 0.01 levels are 0.38 and 0.49, respectively.

Jerzy Falandysz
Environmental and Toxicological Chemistry Research Group
Department of Chemistry, University of Gdańsk
ul. Sobieskiego 18, PL 80-952
Gdańsk, Poland

Tadeusz Mizera
Department of Zoology, Agricultural University
ul. Wojska Polskiego 7 i C, PL 60-625
Poznan, Poland

Meyburg, B.-U. & R. D. Chancellor eds.1994
Raptor Conservation Today
WWGBP / The Pica Press

Highly Toxic Non-Ortho-Chlorine substituted Coplanar PCBS in White-Tailed Sea Eagles *Haliaeetus albicilla* from Poland

Jerzy Falandysz, Nobuyoshi Yamashita, Shinsuke Tanabe, Ryo Tatsukawa, Tadeusz Mizera & Bogdan Jakuczun

INTRODUCTION

The Baltic Sea continues to be highly contaminated by polychlorinated biphenyls (PCBs) and other persistent organochlorine compounds, prompting concern for the welfare of marine predators at the higher trophic levels, including mammals and eagles (Melvasalo *et al.* 1981, Baltic Marine Environment Protection Commission 1990). Particularly high levels of total PCBs and *p,p'*-DDE have been reported in the tissues of White-Tailed Sea Eagles, *Haliaeetus albicilla*, found dead in locations around the Baltic Sea, *i.e.* in the Archipelago of Stockholm in Sweden (Jensen *et al.* 1972) and in the Finnish Archipelago (Paasivirta *et al.* 1983).

Our recent findings have indicated a steady-state of contamination by PCBs in the southern part of the Baltic proper over the last two decades (Kannan *et al.* 1992). Among the PCB congeners, No. 77 (3,3',4,4'-tetrachlorobiphenyl), No. 126 (3,3',4,4',5-pentachlorobiphenyl) and No. 169 (3,3',4,4',5,5'-hexachlorobiphenyl) are the most active inducers of microsomal aryl hydrocarbon hydroxylase (AHH) and ethoxyresorufin *o*-diethylase (EROD) enzymes and therefore pose the greatest threat of dioxin-type effects. Due to the absence of chlorines in the *ortho* positions of the biphenyl rings, these PCB congeners attain coplanarity, making them structurally similar to the dioxins (Tanabe *et al.* 1987, Voogt *et al.* 1990). In this paper we report the concentrations of these non-*ortho*-chlorine coplanar PCB isomers in White-Tailed Sea Eagles found dead in the breeding areas of coastal and inland Poland between 1982 and 1990, and evaluate the toxicology of these residues.

MATERIALS AND METHODS

Sample Preparation

Autopsy material consisted of specimens of White-Tailed Sea Eagles collected since 1982 from two breeding areas of Poland (Figure 1). Six of the birds examined originated from the southwestern coast of the Baltic Sea (an area of the Wolinski National Park and its surroundings), and three were from a woodland area of the western part of Poland (Province of Gorzów). A single

Figure 1: Breeding areas of the White-tailed Sea Eagle from which sample specimens collected for autopsy since 1982 a) in NE Poland, b) N Poland

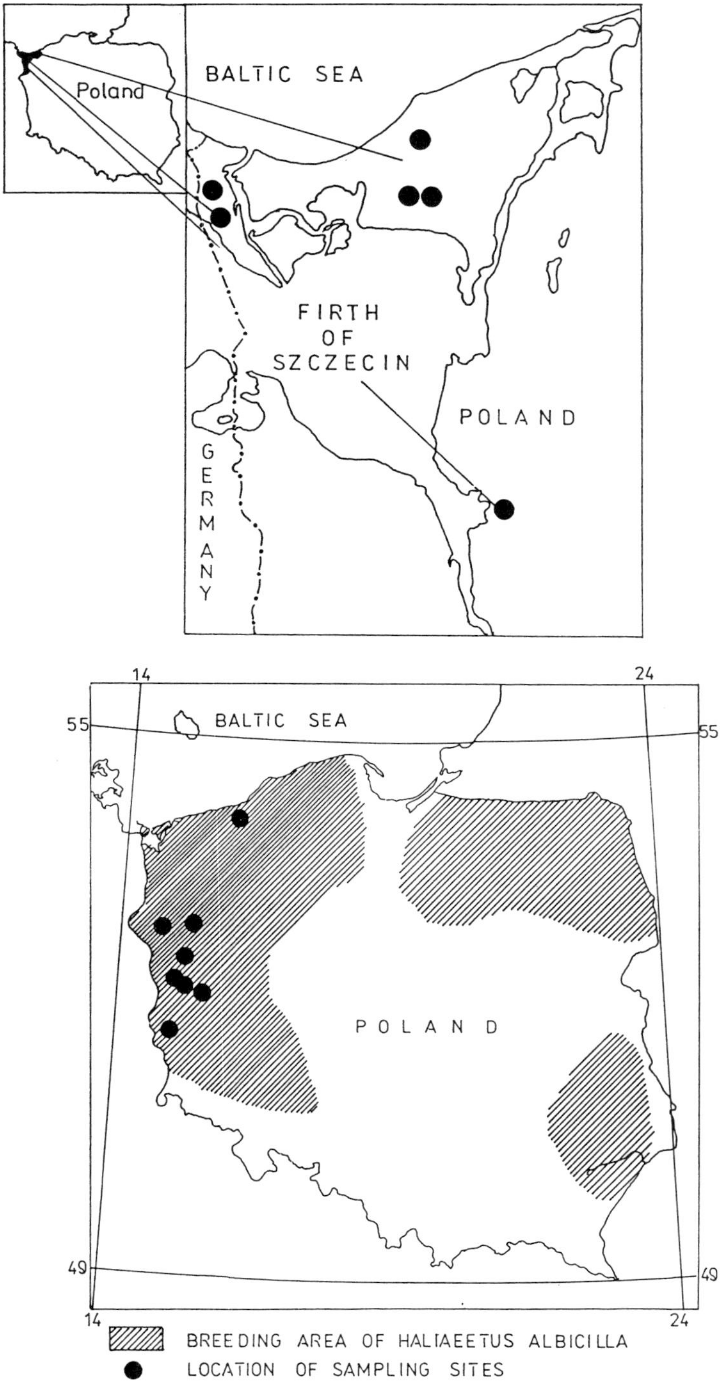

immature male was a bird that was electrocuted in the northern part of the country (Table 1). Breast muscle was selected for determination of the PCBs. The samples were stored frozen (-20°C), with the exception of the carcass collected in 1982; a lipid extract was prepared (with light petroleum in a Soxhlet apparatus) and kept in a sealed vial until analysis.

Chemical analysis

About 10 g of breast muscle were digested with alkaline-alcohol, re-extracted with hexane, and cleaned-up using silica gel (Wako gel S-1) column chromatography and 5% fuming sulfuric acid treatment. Non-*ortho* coplanar PCBs (IUPAC Nos. 77, 126 and 169) were separated from other isomers and congeners using carbon column chromatography (Tanabe *et al.* 1989).

A gas chromatograph/mass spectrometer (Hewlett-Packard 5890 GC with 5970 mass selective detector) in electron impact (EI) mode at 70 ev was equipped with a fused silica capillary column (30 m x 0.25 mm i.d., film thickness 0.25 µm, DB-1701 for the coplanar congeners and an analogous DB-1 column for the other PCB congeners). The operating conditions were as follows: injection port 260°C; transfer line 280°C; initial temperature for analysis of coplanar PCBs 180°, rate 2°C/min, final temperature 250°C; initial column temperature for other PCBs 140°C, rate 2.5°C/min, final temperature 250°C, hold time 10 min.

For the confirmation/quantification of the coplanar PCBs, M+ and (M+2)+ cluster ions were monitored at m/z 290 and 292 for No. 77, m/z 324 and 326 for No. 126, and m/z 358 and 360 for No. 169. The other PCB isomers and congeners were quantified by selective ion monitoring (SIM) at m/z 222, 256, 292, 326, 360, 394, 428 and 464 for di-, tri-, tetra-, penta-, hexa-, hepta-, octa- and nonachlorobiphenyls, respectively. Authentic standards of PCBs 77, 126, and 169 were of 98-100% purity. A mixture of Kanechlors 300, 400, 500 and 600, equal amounts of each, with known PCB composition was used as a standard for the quantification of total PCBs by GC-MS.

RESULTS AND DISCUSSION

With the exception of the specimen taken from the outskirts of the Firth of Szczecin, eagles from the coastal region of the Baltic Sea contained strikingly high concentrations of total and non-*ortho* coplanar PCBs in their breast muscle, ranging from 66,000 to 480,000 ng/g and from 16 to 340 ng/g, respectively, on a wet weight basis. Birds from the interior were relatively much less contaminated (Table 1).

Comparably high concentrations of total PCBs have been reported in tissues of White-tailed Sea Eagles found dead elsewhere in the Baltic Sea, *i.e.* in the Archipelago of Stockholm in Sweden (Jensen et al. 1972) and in the Finnish Archipelago (Paasivirta *et al.* 1983).

Data on total PCBs (Table 1) are in very good agreement with those reported earlier that were obtained with conventional packed glass columns (Falandysz 1984, 1986; Falandysz *et al.* 1988).

The concentrations of non-*ortho* coplanar PCBs in eagles collected in 1982 and 1987 in the Woliński National Park appear to be the highest so far reported in wildlife tissue; on a lipid basis concentrations are 34 and 47 times higher, respectively.

Concentrations of non-*ortho* coplanar PCBs have been reported recently in tissues and eggs of White-tailed Sea Eagles from different regions of Finland (Paasivirta *et al.* 1989; Tarhanen *et al.* 1989; Paasivirta & Rantio 1991). Two of the five Sea Eagles examined by Tarhanen *et al.* (1989) were adult females and originated from the Finnish coastal area of the Baltic Sea. Total concentrations of the 3 coplanar PCBs and of total PCBs in their muscles were 18 and 140 ng/g, and 17,000 and 250,000 ng/g on a wet-weight basis, respectively. The reports by Paasivirta *et al.* (1989) and Paasivirta & Rantio (1991) present data on the 3 coplanar PCBs in muscles of three White-tailed Sea Eagles on a lipid-weight basis (240, 260 and 620 ng/g).

The eagles from the interior contained not only considerably lower concentrations of PCBs but also differed in their isomer and congener composition - with a higher content of lower-chlorinated PCB 77 and lower contents of the penta- and hexachloro coplanars (Figure 2). This difference in congener composition between coastal and interior regions may result from a combination of different principal sources and differences in the environmental half-lives among the congeners.

An immature male collected after electrocution in Northern Poland in 1984 contained a very different pattern of coplanar contamination, with PCB 77 accounting for 90% and PCB 169 only

1.5% (Figure 2). A similar composition, 90% of PCB 77, 8.7% of PCB 126, and 1.3% of PCB 169, was reported in breast muscle of a four-months old juvenile White-tailed Sea Eagle from the Quarken Area of the Gulf of Bothnia, Baltic Sea (Tarhanen *et al.* 1989).

Figure 2. Composition (%) of non-*ortho* coplanar PCBs in breast muscles of White-tailed Sea Eagles from different breeding sites in Poland. ■ Coastal area (Wolinski National Park) (n=5), ▩ Coastal area (Firth of Szczecin) (n=1), ▤ Northern Poland (Immature Male) (n=1), ▨ Inland Poland (Province of Gorzów) (n=3)

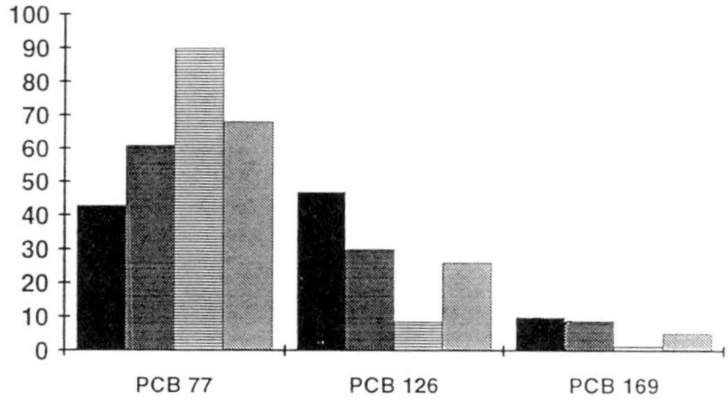

Since immature White-tailed Sea Eagles frequently undertake long-range movements, their contamination patterns may not reflect that of the areas of collection.

Toxicities of the planar chlorinated aromatic compound are currently expressed in units of equivalent toxicities of the most toxic compound, 2,3,7,8-TCDD (TEQs); on the basis of their ability to induce the microsomal aryl hydrocarbon hydroxylase (AHH) and ethoxyresorufin *o*-diethylase (EROD) enzymes, the toxicities of the coplanars in the Baltic coast female eagles are estimated to range from 3,000 to 64,000 pg/g of dioxin equivalents in the AHH test and from 2,400 to 51,000 pg/g in the EROD test (Table 1). For comparison with data in other papers of this symposium, the estimated toxicities based on the factors derived by Safe (1990) are also presented.

PCB 126 clearly accounts for most of the dioxin-type toxicity in these samples (Table 1); it, and the other coplanar congeners are currently the most hazardous among the dioxin-type compounds in the Baltic (Paasivirta & Rantio 1991).

At present it seems rather difficult to relate accurately the concentrations of coplanar and total PCBs in breast muscles of female White-tailed Sea Eagles to suspected critical concentrations in eggs of 800,000-900,000 ng/g of total PCBs on a lipid weight basis (Helander *et al.* 1982) that are associated with depressed reproduction. The White-tailed Sea Eagle is a long-lived species; pairs breeding on the Baltic coast are exposed over their life-times to high contaminant levels in the food web (Jensen *et al.* 1969; Borg *et al.* 1969; Koivusaari 1976; Oehme 1980; Falandysz 1980; Falandysz *et al.* 1988; Kannan *et al.* 1992). Productivity has been depressed (Helander *et al.* 1982; Helander 1985) and higher contaminant burdens (Falandysz & Szefer 1983; Falandysz *et al.* 1988; Tarhanen *et al.* 1989) may affect the survival of adult birds.

The relatively large number of pairs breeding in interior Poland since 1981 have produced a surplus of young that have colonized the coastal areas, replacing birds that may have succumbed to contaminants. Recently, young and probably relatively uncontaminated eagles from interior Poland have been breeding in the Firth of Szczecin area (Figure 1). The number of pairs in the coastal area of the southwestern Baltic has increased from six in 1977-78 to twelve in 1982, and to seventeen in 1988; productivity has increased from 0.17 to 0.42, and to 0.88, respectively (Mizera and Szymkiewicz 1991).

No ecotoxicological studies have so far been undertaken of diverse toxic effects on White-tailed Sea Eagles in the Woli ski National Park and adjacent areas. This region of the Baltic coast is a nesting area for only about 10-15 % of the Polish population of Sea Eagles, but Pomeranian Bay and the Lower Odra and Lower Wis a Rivers are the most important wintering quarters for Sea Eagles from interior Poland and probably also from Scandinavia. During the season 1990-91 about 100 White-tailed Sea Eagles wintered in Pomeranian Bay (Czeraszkiewicz - personal communication). Studies of contamination sources, particularly of continuing sources of PCBs, and their effects on eagles clearly deserve continued attention.

Table 1. Non-*ortho* coplanar PCBs and their calculated 2,3,7,8-TCDD toxic equivalents, and total PCBs in fresh breast muscle of White-tailed Sea Eagles.

Sampling site, year, sex and cause of death	Concentration, ng/g PCB 77	PCB 126	PCB 169	Total PCBs	Total toxic equivalents pg/g, (% from PCB No. 126) AHH[a]	EROD[b]	Safe (90)[c]
Wolinski National Park							
1982; adult female, unknown	140	160	38	480,000	64,000 (99)	51,000 (99)	19,000 (83)
1984; adult female, unknown	6.3	7.5	1.9	66,000	3,000 (99)	2,400 (99)	910 (83)
1986; adult female, unknown	29	20	3.5	140,000	8,100 (99)	5,400 (99)	2,500 (81)
1987; adult female, unknown	45	53	11	340,000	21,000 (99)	17,000 (100)	6,300 (84)
1989; adult female, unknown	13	16	2.7	68,000	6,400 (99)	5,100 (100)	1,900 (86)
Firth of Szczecin							
1990; adult male, unknown	4.9	2.4	0.66	17,000	970 (99)	780 (99)	320 (75)
Northern Poland							
1984; immature male, electrocuted	18	1.7	0.35	7,000	730 (93)	560 (96)	370 (46)
Inland Poland							
1987; adult female, lead poisoning	9.5	3.0	0.55	32,000	1,200 (98)	970 (99)	420 (71)
1987; adult female, lead poisoning	2.9	1.2	0.15	12,000	490 (98)	380 (100)	160 (77)
1988; adult male, unknown	4.9	2.4	0.66	4,600	970 (99)	770 (100)	320 (75)

Conversion factors for 2,3,7,8-TCDD equivalents:	PCB IUPAC No. 77	PCB IUPAC No. 126	PCB IUPAC No. 169
[a] AAH: Smith *et al.* 1990	2.70E-03	4.00E-01	1.60E-03
[b] EROD: Smith *et al.* 1990	9.00E-04	3.20E-01	3.30E-03
[c] Safe (1990)	1.00E-02	1.00E-01	5.00E-02

ACKNOWLEDGEMENTS

This study was conducted in the Faculty of Agriculture, Ehime University, Japan, and was supported by the Japanese Society for the Promotion of Science (JSPS) under a long-term Visiting Professor fellowship awarded to Dr. J. Falandysz.

Jerzy Falandysz
Environmental and Toxicological Chemistry Research Group,
Department of Chemistry, University of Gdańsk,
ul. Sobieskiego 18,
PL 80-952 Gdańsk, Poland

Nobuyoshi Yamashita,
Shinsuke Tanabe & Ryo Tatsukawa
Department of Environment Conservation
Ehime University, 3-5-7 Tarumi, Matsuyama 790, Japan

Tadeusz Mizera
Department of Zoology,
Agricultural University,
ul. Wojska Polskiego 71 C,
PL 60-625 Poznań , Poland

Bogdan Jakuczun
Museum of Wolinski National Park,
Al. Niepodleglo ci 3,
PL 72-610 Midzyzdroje, Poland

Meyburg, B.-U. & R. D. Chancellor eds.1994
Raptor Conservation Today
WWGBP / The Pica Press

Pre-1954 Breeding Success and Producktivity of White-Tailed Sea Eagles *Haliaeetus albicilla* in Sweden

Björn Helander

INTRODUCTION

Depressed reproductive ability caused by one or more environmental contaminants has been a common feature among several raptor species in recent decades. Typically, reduced hatchability of the eggs results in both a decrease in the proportion of successfully breeding pairs and a decrease in the number of young reared per successfully breeding pair. The product of these parameters gives the overall productivity of the population, or of the individual pair over a number of years.

In evaluating the status of a species, it is essential to know what these parameters are in a healthy population. Since differences in climate, food supply, etc., may change these parameters within the same species among areas, comparisons should preferably be made using data from the same or an ecologically similar area.

In this note, data given by Helander (1985) on the breeding success of White-tailed Sea Eagles on the Baltic Sea coast in Sweden in the first half of this century are scrutinized and used in combination with historical brood size data to produce an estimate of the average productivity of the population at that time.

MATERIALS AND METHODS

Data on the breeding success of individual pairs before 1954 and of brood sizes were taken from Helander (1985). The data on breeding success were obtained from banders and other ornithologists and from the literature. Only data which could be combined into sets of 3 or more consecutive years for each locality were used. This is important; scattered data from single years would almost certainly give an overrepresentation of successful breeding attempts.

The 91 brood size records used to estimate the average brood size included 63 obtained mainly from ornithologists' notes made upon the inspection of nests and 28 from banding records (Swedish Bird Ringing Office). In those days, it was not the routine in Sweden to include in the banding records data on the total number of nestlings and eggs - only the banded birds were recorded. By interviewing the banders I know that in at least two cases nests contained one nestling in addition to the ones banded (one was too small to band, the other was inaccessible). For this reason, a possible difference between the brood records obtained from the banding records and those obtained directly from ornithologists was investigated.

RESULTS AND DISCUSSION

The distribution of broods containing 1, 2, and 3 young was not significantly different between the banding records and the ornithologists' notes (chisquare = 0.683, d.f. = 2, $P > 0.70$). The brood size distribution of the whole sample was 24 x 1, 58 x 2, and 9 x 3 young. The average brood size was 1.84.

The sets of breeding success data, comprising between 3 and 10 years in succession, are given in Table 1. Of 43 recorded breeding attempts within these sets of data, 31 were successful and 12 unsuccessful, producing an estimate of the average breeding success of the Swedish Baltic Sea eagles before 1954 of 72%.

These data sets comprise a total of 53 potential breeding years; thus, for most of the sets, data were lacking for one or a few years. Such lack of data may or may not have an influence on the estimated average breeding success, depending on whether the areas were actually visited or not by the observers during those years. Eagles that fail early in the breeding season, especially if they have also built a new nest in the area, would be much more likely to have been overlooked at the time when these areas were usually checked, which was during the nestling period, than would a successful pair. Theoretically, in a study like this based on assembled material from other observers, a failure by an observer to locate his eagles in a certain year could easily lead to a „lack of data“ for that year. This would tend to produce an underestimate of the number of unsuccessful breeding attempts. On the other hand, if the areas were actually not checked by the observer during those years, there would be no reason to assume that the breeding success would have been different (on average) during the years for which data are lacking, as compared to the others.

The lack of data for some years in this study was mostly due to the fact that the areas were not visited by the observers during those years. In some cases, however, it was not possible to assess whether this was the case or whether no young were found. This factor provides a small positive bias to the estimate of breeding success, for the reasons given above.

Since the purpose of this investigation is to obtain a good estimate of the natural reproduction of sea eagles in this area, another factor that must be considered is the possible impact of human interference. Persecution of the eagles was more common during the first half of this century than it is today. The cases of nest sabotage that are known to have affected the pairs in this study occurred during the nestling period and were easily recognized. The possibility of sabotage of some nests earlier in the breeding cycle cannot, however, be excluded. Such cases would then tend to bias the estimate of natural breeding success downwards, working in the opposite direction from the factor discussed above.

From an estimated average breeding success of 72% and a mean brood size of 1.84, the average productivity is estimated to be 1.32 young per pair for the pre DDT-era in this population.

The range in estimated average breeding success, calculated for all 53 years within the sets of data by assuming that all „lack of data“-years represented either all unsuccessful or all successful breeding attempts is 58 - 77%. The corresponding range in productivity is 1.07-1.42.

It should be noted that the figures given here represent a non-saturated population, which increased from the mid 1920s to the early 1950s (Helander 1988). Thus, no density-dependent, negative influence on the breeding success would be expected in this case. In a saturated population, the overall breeding success might be lower due to more frequent aggressive encounters between individuals in competition for nest-sites and food.

Björn Helander
Swedish Society for Nature Conservation
Box 4625,
S-116 91, Stockholm, Sweden

Table 1. **Number of years with successful and unsuccessful breeding attempts among 9 pairs of White-tailed Sea Eagles, recorded before 1954 on the Swedish Baltic coast. Data from Helander (1985).**

Territory	Period	Successful	Unsuccessful	No-data
1	1936-1938	2	1	0
2	1943-1952	7	2	1
3	1946-1950	3	1	1
4	1915-1924	6	3	1
5	1944-1948	1	3	1
6	1938-1947	5	2	3
7	1945-1950	4	0	2
8	1950-1953	3	0	1
		31	12	10

Meyburg, B.-U. & R. D. Chancellor eds.1994
Raptor Conservation Today
WWGBP / The Pica Press

Productivity in Relation to Residue Levels of DDE in the Eggs of White-Tailed Sea Eagles *Haliaeetus albicilla* in Sweden

Björn Helander

The reproductive ability of the White-tailed Sea Eagle on the Swedish coast of the Baltic Sea began to deteriorate during the 1950s and reached its bottom level during the 1970s (Helander 1985). Sea Eagle populations on the Finnish and Estonian coasts of the Baltic demonstrated similar poor reproductive results during the 1970s (Stjernberg *et al.* 1990, Randla 1976), indicating a common cause connected with the Baltic ecosystem. Since the Baltic is heavily polluted, it has been important to assess the possible influence of chemical compounds on the reproductive ability of the Sea Eagle in this region.

Koivusaari *et al.* (1980) reported a significant decrease of DDE in Sea Eagle eggs from the northern Baltic in 1972-1978 and an (insignificant) increase in productivity in this population in 1974-1978 as compared to 1969-1973. PCB and mercury levels in the eggs did not change during this period and it was suggested that the decrease in DDE was the most obvious reason for the increasing productivity. Studying populations on the central and southern Baltic coast, Helander *et al.* (1982) found significantly lower levels of DDE and PCBs in fertile as compared to infertile clutches and in eggs from productive as compared to unproductive pairs; the lowest levels occurred in eggs from successful breeding attempts. Mercury levels were equal in all the groups. The correlation between the levels of DDTs and PCBs in the eggs made it difficult to separate their effects on reproduction within the population. A comparative study based on data from different Sea Eagle and Bald Eagle, *Haliaeetus leucocephalus*, populations indicated a stronger correlation for DDE with reduced productivity than for PCBs. Attempting to study whether interannual variations in residue levels could explain breeding failures of otherwise successful pairs, Helander (1983) compared Sea Eagle eggs from: 1) successful nests, 2) otherwise productive nests that failed due to human disturbance, and 3) otherwise productive nests that failed without any indication of disturbance. There was no significant difference among the groups in PCB or mercury levels, and between the first and second group in DDE levels, but the DDE levels were significantly higher in the latter group. These investigations all indicated that DDE had the strongest influence on Sea Eagle reproduction.

Wiemeyer *et al.* (1984) found that the reproductive ability of Bald Eagles in 14 states in the USA was most closely correlated with DDE in the eggs, and that reproductive failure approached 100% where DDE levels in the eggs exceeded 15 ppm (wet weight). This suggests that there is a difference in sensitivity to DDE between Bald Eagles and Sea Eagles, for which Helander *et al.* (1982) reported an average of 26 ppm DDE in eggs from successful nests.

This paper presents data on productivity in relation to residue levels of DDE in the eggs of White-tailed Sea Eagles on the Swedish Baltic coast to complement similar data for the Bald Eagle presented by Jenkins *et al.* (this volume).

MATERIALS AND METHODS

The breeding success of the Swedish Baltic Sea Eagle population has been surveyed annually since 1964. Nests were inspected about 4 weeks after normal hatching time to determine the outcome of breeding attempts and to collect unhatched eggs and shell fragments for investigations. Eggs were collected only occasionally in 1964-1970 (8 clutches) but systematically in 1971-1992 (123 clutches). Individual eggs were analyzed for residue levels of organochlorines according to Jensen *et al.* (1979), at the Swedish Museum of Natural History and the National Swedish Environment Protection Agency Special Analytical Laboratory. The sum of DDTs consisted almost exclusively of DDE (*p,p'*-DDT was not found in any of the samples and *p,p'*-DDD averaged less than 1% of the analyzed DDT components) and is further denoted as DDE. When more than 1 egg was analyzed from a clutch, the arithmetic mean level was used.

Productivity, defined as the average number of young produced per year (yr) was calculated for each territory from all breeding attempts with known outcome during a 5-yr period consisting of the egg-sampling yrs ± 2 yrs. Breeding attempts that failed after strong disturbance at the nest were excluded, as were those yrs when subadults occurred in the mated pairs, resulting in no egg production; yrs when adult pairs produced no eggs were included in the productivity calculations. From some territories, eggs obtained within a 5-yr period represented the same female. When 5-yr periods around a sampling year overlapped, a longer period including 2 or more sampling yrs ± 2 yrs was designated and the arithmetic mean level of DDE from the clutches included was related to the average productivity for the whole period. This was done in order to avoid an over-representation of some females; it restricted the material to a total of 78 sets of data.

RESULTS AND DISCUSSION

There is an obvious decline in productivity with increasing levels of DDE in the eggs (Figure 1). To simplify comparison with other investigations, the scale in the figure indicates both lipid weight (lw) and the approximate corresponding wet weight (ww) values, assuming an average fat content in the eggs of about 5% (from calculations of original fat contents by Helander *et al.* (1982) based on total egg volume, here adjusted upwards to compensate for the airsac).

With one exception, productivity was lower than 1.0 when DDE reached 500 ppm lw (25 ppm ww) and virtually no reproduction occurred (again with one exception) when DDE concentrations exceeded 900 ppm lw (45 ppm ww). At DDE concentrations of 300-400 ppm lw (15-20 ppm ww), several pairs demonstrated a productivity between 1.0 and 1.75, which is in the range considered normal for the species in this region before the appearance of DDE (Helander, this volume).

The four numbered circles (Figure 1), representing higher productivity at high levels of DDE, deserve some comments. No. 1 represents one single egg from a successful breeding attempt; the productivity figure is based on 4 broods (a 5th brood was destroyed by human disturbance soon after hatching and was excluded from the calculations). This case indicates either that some females are able to reproduce normally at DDE levels close to 600 ppm lw (about 30 ppm ww), or the collected egg was not representative of the female. Helander et al. (1982) found that the intra-clutch variation in DDE levels in 15 Sea Eagle clutches averaged only about 10% from the clutch mean; thus, single eggs can in most cases be considered representative of the clutch. However, the range in deviation from the mean was up to 29%; some clutches therefore would contain one egg with almost twice the DDE level of the other. From the DDE-productivity relationship, it is likely that the more contaminated egg in such clutches would not hatch. It cannot be excluded that No. 1 is such an "outlier".

Figure 1. **Residue levels of DDE (ppm, mg/kg) in White-tailed Sea Eagle eggs and the corresponding productivity (average number of young produced per yr during a 5 yr period; yr of egg sampling ± 2 yrs or longer; for details, see Material and Methods). Residue levels are given on a lipid weight basis with the corresponding approximate wet weight levels in brackets (based on an average original lipid content of 5% in the eggs). Filled circles, eggs collected during the 1960s and 1970s; unfilled circles, eggs collected during the 1980s and 1990s.**

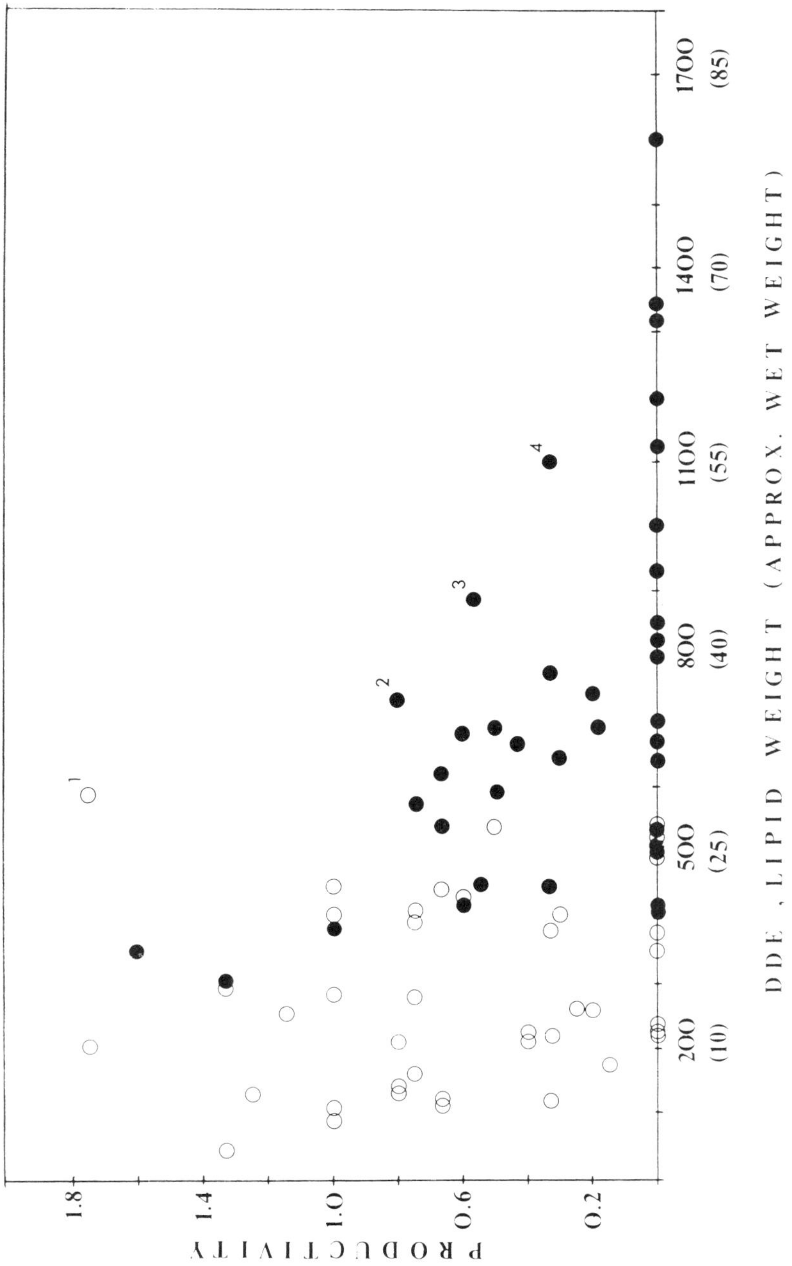

No. 2 represents the average DDE level in eggs from 3 successful breeding attempts over a 7 yr period and the productivity over a 10 yr period, all representing the same female. The range in DDE levels between the clutches was fairly small (650-860 ppm lw). Unless all 3 eggs represent "outliers" as discussed above it appears safe to conclude that some Sea Eagle females can keep up a productivity at DDE levels of about 700 ppm lw (about 35 ppm ww), although this is obviously rare. No. 3 represents the average DDE level in 2 eggs from unsuccessful breeding attempts 2 yrs apart and the productivity over a 7 yr period for the same female; the DDE levels were 900 and 870 ppm lw, respectively. No. 4, on the other hand, is based on weaker data: a single egg from the last, unsuccessful breeding attempt of a female and productivity for only a 3 yr period.

The approximate ww values corresponding to the lw values as given in Figure 1 should be treated with some caution, since they are based on an average fat content in Sea Eagle eggs. Fat contents in the eggs vary, however, and for eggs with fat contents deviating considerably from the mean the DDE levels on a lipid weight basis are not actually corresponding to the ww values as suggested in the figure. As an example, the egg in set No. 4 contained only about 4.1% lipids and thus had a true DDE level of "only" about 45 ppm on a ww basis, as compared to a derived level of 55 ppm based on an assumed fat content of 5%.

The distribution in Figure 1 of filled circles, representing eggs from the 1960s and 70s, and of unfilled circles, representing the 1980s and 90s, clearly demonstrates an improvement during the latter period with regard to the contamination with DDE. The levels have not exceeded 600 ppm in the eggs from the 1980s and 90s, whereas 2/3 of the eggs exceeded that level during the 1960s and 70s, reaching as high as 1800-1900 ppm (lw) in some clutches (disguised in averages in the figure). A corresponding improvement in productivity has taken place: only 8% of the data sets from the 1960s and 70s represented a productivity of 1.0, as compared to 27% in more recent years.

Björn Helander
Swedish Society for Nature Conservation
Box 4625,
S-116 91 Stockholm, Sweden

Meyburg, B.-U. & R. D. Chancellor eds.1994
Raptor Conservation Today
WWGBP / The Pica Press

Organochlorine Pesticides, Chlorinated Dioxins and Furans, and PCBs in Peregrine Falcon *Falco peregrinus* Eggs from the Kola Peninsula, Russia

Charles J. Henny, Sergei A. Ganusevich,
F. Prescott Ward, & Ted R. Schwartz

ABSTRACT

Nesting of a bog-associated population of migratory Peregrine Falcons, *Falco peregrinus*, along the Ponoy River depression, Kola Peninsula, Russia, has been studied since 1977. In 1987-91 production rates averaged 1.94 young per active nest and the number of breeding pairs increased from 4 to 10. In 1991, most eyrie sites were visited during the egg stage and a "sample" egg was collected for contaminant analysis. Eight Peregrine Falcon eggs contained relatively low concentrations of *p,p'*-DDE (DDE) (geometric mean 3.5 µg/g) and of other organochlorine pesticides. These DDE concentrations are similar to those reported in Peregrine Falcon eggs from an Alaskan population that had also showed a recent population increase. Eggshell thinning (11.4%) was similar to that found in Alaska. Concentrations of polychlorinated biphenyls (PCBs) were higher than DDE concentrations, comparable to the contamination profile shown by Peregrine Falcon populations in Fennoscandia, and were higher than those found in Alaskan birds. Before this study, no Peregrine Falcon eggs from Russia had been analyzed for PCB congeners, polychlorinated dibenzo-*p*-dioxins (PCDDs), or polychlorinated dibenzofurans (PCDFs). Conversions of analytical concentrations of 2,3,7,8-tetrachlorodibenzo-*p*-dioxin (TCDD), other PCDDs, PCDFs and PCB congeners based on relative aryl hydrocarbon hydroxylase induction potencies allowed the estimation of total 2,3,7,8-TCDD equivalents (TEQs). The TEQs are in the range that is associated with embryonic mortality in other species. Even though the Peregrine Falcon population now seems to be released from decades of a DDT problem, exposure to other contaminants continues. There is an obvious need to assess further the sources and longer-term trends of the PCBs. We also report residue concentrations from one White-tailed Eagle, *Haliaeetus albicilla*, egg.

INTRODUCTION

At the First World Conference on Birds of Prey, Galushin (1977) noted a rapid and continuous decline of the Peregrine Falcon in the Soviet Union. Unfortunately chemical residue levels were unavailable for pesticides or other poisons in eggs or carcasses, but taking into consideration some indirect evidence, he suggested pesticides were at least partly responsible for the decline. Peakall and Kiff (1979) measured eggshells at the Zoological Museum, Moscow, and reported significant shell thinning (25%) in eggs of Peregrine Falcons from Siberia in 1961-66. They also reported the presence of DDE in shell membranes of the eggs measured. Because of this background and the general understanding that DDE residues in Peregrine Falcon eggs decreased widely following DDT bans in the early 1970s (Cade *et al.* 1988), Henny and Ward travelled to the study area of Ganusevich on the Kola Peninsula in 1991 to collect Peregrine Falcon eggs. The eggs were brought to the United States for analyses of eggshell thickness and chemical residues.

STUDY AREA

Ganusevich (1988) provided a review of raptors nesting on the Kola Peninsula of extreme northwestern Russia (near the Finland border), including Osprey, *Pandion haliaetus*, White-tailed Eagle, *Haliaeetus albicilla*, Northern Goshawk, *Accipiter gentilis*, Eurasian Sparrowhawk, *Accipiter nisus*, Rough-legged Buzzard, *Buteo lagopus*, Golden Eagle, *Aquila chrysaetos*, Hen Harrier, *Circus cyaneus*, Merlin, *Falco columbarius*, Gyrfalcon, *Falco rusticolus*, and Peregrine Falcon. Ganusevich began studying the Peregrine Falcon population on the Kola Peninsula in 1977. Its known territories have been monitored annually with additional searches for new territories. Aerial, boat, and foot surveys of selected areas of the peninsula suggest a local distribution of the Peregrine Falcon population in the basin of the upper and middle course of the Ponoy River. The Ponoy depression is characterized by large bogs, many small and large lakes, rivers, and hills with parcels of land elevated (above the bogs) with forests, rocks, and cliffs. An abundance of prey (primarily shorebirds associated with the bogs and lakes), suitable nesting sites, and the absence of human activities define optimum conditions for breeding of the Peregrine Falcon. The territories are constant from year to year, although the actual eyrie site may change annually. An easy access to many eyries by predatory animals sometimes causes nest failure.

As part of a general survey for environmental contaminants from the Kola Peninsula, we elected to evaluate chemical residue levels of organochlorine (OC) pesticides and selected chlorinated aromatic compounds in the eggs of Peregrine Falcons. Our concern about DDT, other OC pesticides, polychlorinated biphenyls (PCBs), polychlorinated dibenzo-*p*-dioxins (PCDDs), and polychlorinated dibenzofurans (PCDFs) centers on their toxicity, persistent nature, and propensity for bioaccumulation. Our analysis of PCB congeners focused on those congeners with zero or one chlorine substituted in the ortho position of the phenyl rings. They are particularly toxic to sensitive species and are potent inducers of hepatic aryl hydrocarbon hydroxylase (AHH) (Safe 1987). These planar non-ortho-C1 PCB congeners are approximate isostereomers of 2,3,7,8-tetrachlorodibenzo-*p*-dioxin (TCDD) and their ability to induce AHH activity is similar to that of TCDD (Safe 1990). The group of PCBs, PCDDs, and PCDFs that induce AHH activity will be collectively referred to as planar halogenated hydrocarbons (PHHs).

ANALYTICAL METHODS

Sample extraction, lipid determination, cleanup and fractionation procedures have been described in detail (Schmitt *et al.* 1985; Schmitt *et al.* 1990). The fraction of the sample extract containing PCBs and PHHs was quantitatively divided into 2 portions, one for determination of specific congeners by the method of Schwartz and Stalling (1991), and one for enrichment and determination of PHHs by the method of Smith *et al.* (1990).

Organochlorine residues were determined by gas chromatographic separation using DB-1 and OV-17 fused silica capillary columns with electron-capture detection as described previously (Schmitt *et al.* 1985, 1990; Smith *et al.* 1990; Schwartz and Stalling 1991). Extracts containing dioxins and furans were separated by gas chromatography in a DB-5 capillary column and quantified with a Finnigan mass spectrometer. Calibration provided the relative response factors of the native (analytes) and C^{13}-labelled congeners (recovery standards) within each homologue series, from which concentrations of the dioxin and furan analytes were calculated. The non-ortho-Cl PCB congener concentrations were determined with a DB-1 capillary column in a HP 5890A gas chromatograph interfaced to a VG70-250S high-resolution mass spectrometer. Calibration provided the relative response factors of the native and C^{13}-labelled PCB congeners, from which concentrations of the non-ortho-Cl PCB analytes were calculated. For all analytes, extraction efficiencies (recoveries) were measured using the relative responses of internal reference (added to extracts before gas chromatography) and recovery standards.

Method and procedure blanks were processed with the samples to verify that solvents, reagents, apparatuses and instrumentation did not add detectable positive biases to the residue concentrations. For statistical treatment, the method lower limits of detection (MLLDs) and method lower limits of quantitation (MLLQs) for each contaminant were determined according to the method of Keith *et al.* (1983). In general the MLLDs and MLLQs were similar to those reported previously (Schmitt *et al.* 1990). Residue concentrations in eggs were corrected to an approximate fresh wet weight (Stickel *et al.* 1973) and expressed on a wet-weight basis.

RESULTS

Peregrine Population

The number of known Peregrine Falcon nesting territories has increased during the early years of investigations by Ganusevich (1988) because of increased detection from better understanding of the region and habitat requirements. A complete annual survey of all 15 known nesting territories has been made since 1987 in the 1,000 km^2 study area (Table 1).

Table 1. The breeding success of Peregrine Falcons on the Kola Peninsula in Russia, 1987-91 (Ganusevich, unpublished data).

Category	1987	1988	1989	1990	1991	TOTAL
Active Nests	4	5	5	8	10	32
No. of Nestlings	9	10	12	12	19	62
Young/Active Nest	2.25	2.00	2.40	1.50	1.90	1.94

Prey Species

Food remains from the eyries and vicinity were used to evaluate prey species eaten by the Peregrine Falcons. Ganusevich collected 269 prey items over the years, all but 1 of which were birds, including 30 prey species: Ruff, *Philomachus pygnax*, 52.0%, Common Snipe, *Gallinago gallinago*, 8.6%, Jack Snipe, *Lymnocryptes minima*, 4.8%, Wood Sandpiper, *Tringa glareola*, 4.5%, and Arctic Tern, *Sterna paradisaea*, 3.4%; other species comprised not more than 3% of prey items.

Egg Contaminant Residues and Eggshell Thickness

Intact eggs were obtained from 6 different clutches in 1991, and large eggshells were obtained from 2 additional clutches. At Trophim Hill where a 3-day-old young was present, we collected 3 addled eggs. Eyries with eggshells only included 1 destroyed by a predator (probably a fox) and another (2 young produced) where a broken eggshell was found below the nest ledge. Therefore, egg residues were obtained from 6 nest sites and eggshell thicknesses from 8 nest sites (Table 2). Viable eggs were collected at only 3 nests (Devichy Hill, Okunjevy Hill and Palnik Lake); the other 5 eggs were already dead at the time of collection.

Table 2. Clutch size, young produced and eggshell thickness for Peregrine Falcons on the Kola Peninsula, Russia, 1991.

Nest Site	Clutch Size	No. of Young	Eggshell Thickness (mm)
Devichy Hill	4[a]	3	0.289
Okunjevy Hill	4[a]	3	0.310
Trophim Hill	4[b]	1	0.311[c]
Palnik Lake	3[a]	2	0.283
Vuljavr Lake	3[b]	2	0.306
Maloe Vasiljevskoe Lake	NA	0	0.325[d]
Verhnekamenskoe Lake	3	2	0.323[d]
Tebek Rus	4[b]	3	0.333
El River	3	3	--
Veha	NA	0	--
Mean	3.50	1.90	0.310

NA = Not Available.
[a] Viable egg was collected from the clutch for residue analyses.
[b] Addled egg(s) collected from clutch.
[c] Mean of 3 addled eggs (0.310, 0.311, and 0.312 mm)
[d] Large eggshell that was not intact.

Mean clutch size was 3.50 eggs with an equal number of 3-egg and 4-egg clutches. An average of 1.90 young was produced per nesting attempt, and if all 3 viable eggs collected had yielded young, the production rate would have been 2.20 young in 1991. Mean eggshell thickness (and SD) in 1991 was 0.310 (0.017) mm, compared with 0.350 mm for pre-DDT era Swedish Peregrines between 1861 and 1946 (Lindberg 1975); this represents a reduction of 11.4%. The pre-DDT era Swedish shell thickness information was the geographically closest data available. Other indices to thickness, such as those from Finland (Lindén *et al.* 1984), were not directly comparable to our thickness measurements. The 3 eggs from the same clutch (Trophim Hill) showed nearly identical shell thicknesses. The mean for the 3 Trophim Hill eggs was used to calculate the overall mean for the 8 clutches sampled.

The *p,p'*-DDE concentrations were judged low; the geometric mean was 3500 ng/g or 3.5 μg/g (fresh wet weight) with no concentrations above 5 μg/g (Table 3). Total PCBs were higher (geometric mean 7.3 μg/g), with values from some eggs about triple the mean. The Trophim Hill clutch had 3 addled eggs (with no development) and contained the highest PCB and PHH levels (Tables 3 - 6). All residues from the 3 eggs are shown to document the remarkable consistency in contaminant concentrations among eggs within the same clutch.

The study area also contained a number of White-tailed Eagle nests. We had the opportunity to sample one of these nests. An addled egg was obtained from a nest with a large young nearly ready to fledge. Although one egg is inadequate to reach many conclusions, the eggshell thickness was 0.611 mm, with residue concentrations presented in Tables 3 - 6. Koivusaari *et al.* (1980) reported a pre-DDT era shell thickness [mean (SE)] of 0.620 (0.010) mm from nearby Finland (1884-1935).

The relative biologic potencies of a suite of PCDD, PCDF and PCB congeners to induce microsomal AHH in the H4IIE rat hepatoma cell line have been summarized by Safe (1990). Transforming our Peregrine Falcon egg concentrations (Tables 4-6), on the basis of each PHH's induction capability relative to 2,3,7,8-TCDD, permits the reporting of relative contributions in a common unit of measure, TCDD-equivalents (TEQs, Table 7). The equation used to obtain relative induction potencies is identical to that published by Sawyer *et al.* (1984). Conversion factors were

Table 3. Organochlorine pesticides and total polychlorinated biphenyls (PCBs) (ng/g, fresh wet weight) in Peregrine Falcon eggs and one White-tailed Eagle egg from the Kola Peninsula, Russia, 1991.

Nest Site	%Lipid	TOXA	DDE	DDD	DDT	MIREX	PCBs	HCB	LIND	βHCH	OXY	HE	*t*NON	*c*CHL	DIEL	*c*NON
Devichy Hill	3.5	200	4,100	30	88	25	18,000	43	150	74	36	49	6	0	76	7
Okunjevy Hill	3.3	90	3,900	5	7	11	5,000	30	2	270	47	45	6	0	26	1
Trophim Hill[a]	4.0	200	3,000	18	19	110	18,000	37	22	83	48	62	20	0	160	9
	4.2	200	3,400	17	25	110	21,000	37	19	84	48	66	20	0	170	8
	3.9	200	3,200	18	17	130	21,000	39	16	88	57	63	15	0	170	8
Palnik Lake	2.1	90	4,400	5	18	6	3,000	39	1	61	25	24	4	0	39	1
Vuljavr Lake	4.9	60	4,600	7	30	10	4,000	26	140	99	21	27	2	0	58	1
Tebek Rus	3.3	100	1,900	6	17	26	7,000	24	50	39	29	36	5	0	53	3
Geometric Mean[b]	--	110	3,500	9	22	19	7,300	33	18	86	33	39	5	0	59	2
White-tailed Eagle	4.1	90	700	24	0	2	2,000	4	0	12	4	3	12	8	14	4

Note: TOXA = Toxaphene, PCBs = Total Polychlorinated Biphenyls, HCB = Hexachlorobenzene, LIND = Lindane, OXY = Oxychlordane, HE = Heptachlor Epoxide, *t*NON = *trans*-Nonachlor, *c*CHL = *cis*-Chlordane, DIEL = Dieldrin, DDE = *p,p'*-DDE, *c*NON = *cis*-Nonachlor, DDD = *p,p'*-DDD, DDT = *p,p'*-DDT. No Dacthal, *o,p'*-DDE, *o,p'*-DDD, *o,p'*DDT, Endrin or Methoxychlor were detected.

[a] Three eggs from the same clutch.

[b] Arithmetic mean of 3 eggs from Trophim Hill was used to calculate overall geometric mean for the six Peregrine Falcon clutches sampled.

Table 4. Polychlorinated Dibenzo-*p*-Dioxins (pg/g, wet weight) in Peregrine Falcon eggs and one White-tailed Eagle egg from the Kola Penninsula, 1991, and their Toxic Equivalency Factors (TEFs)[a].

	Tetra	Penta		Hexa			Hepta	Octa
	2,3,7,8	1,2,3,7,8	1,2,4,7,8	1,2,3,4,7,8	1,2,3,6,7,8	1,2,3,7,8,9	1,2,3,4,6,7,8	--
TEF	1.0	0.5	0.005	0.1	0.1	0.1	0.01	--
Nest Site								
Devichy Hill	30	18	<0.4(ND)	5.2	10	0.7	0.8(NQ)	1.6
Okunjevy Hill	5.2	8.0	<0.2(NQ)	2.7	3.7	<0.2(NQ)	0.6	2.1
Trophim Hill[b]	37	27	<0.1(NQ)	7.2	16	1.0	1.6	4.9
	38	28	<0.1(NQ)	7.3	17	1.1	1.6	4.8
	37	28	<0.2(NQ)	7.8	17	1.0	1.7	5.1
Palnik Lake	5.3	9.6	<0.3(ND)	1.8	9.0	0.3	0.8	1.6
Vuljavr Lake	4.0	3.8	<0.3(NQ)	1.4	3.3	<0.3(NQ)	0.6	4.6
Tebek Rus	11	14	<0.2(ND)	5.2	7.4	0.4	0.8	2.6
Geometric Mean[c]	11	11	(ND,NQ)	3.3	7.2	0.3	0.7	2.6
White-tailed Eagle[d]	1.2	1.6	<0.2(ND)	0.3	0.8	<0.1(ND)	<0.3(NQ)	1.8

[a] TEFs from Kutz *et al.* (1990).
[b] Three eggs from the same clutch.
[c] Arithmetic mean of 3 eggs from Trophim Hill was used to calculate overall geometric mean for the six Peregrine Falcon clutches sampled.
[d] Arithmetic mean of two samples from the same egg.
(ND) Not Detected -- Primary and/or secondary ions for the analyte cluster were not detected.
(NQ) Not Quantifiable -- Secondary/Primary ion ratio exceeds QC limit or cluster incomplete.

Table 5. Polychlorinated Dibenzofurans (pg/g, wet weight) in Peregrine Falcon eggs and one White-tailed egg from the Kola Penninsula, 1991, and their Toxic Equivalency Factors (TEFs)[a].

	Tetra	Penta		Hexa				Hepta		Octa
	2,3,7,8	1,2,3,7,8	2,3,4,7,8	1,2,3,4,7,8	1,2,3,6,7,8	1,2,3,7,8,9	2,3,4,6,7,8	1,2,3,4,6,7,8	1,2,3,4,7,8,9	--
TEF	0.1	0.05	0.5	0.1	0.1	0.1	0.1	0.01	0.01	--
Nest Site										
Devichy Hill	55	9.2	49	5.5	3.0	0.5	1.8	<0.3(NQ)	<1(NQ)	3.8
Okunjevy Hill	31	3.0	15	2.0	0.8	<0.2(NQ)	0.5	<0.3(NQ)	<0.4(NQ)	1.0
Trophim Hill	49	10	62	14	5.2	0.8	2.7	1.0	<2(NQ)	4.2
	52	11	65	14	5.8	0.7	2.8	0.8	1.7	3.4
	50	11	63	15	5.7	0.8	2.8	<1(NQ)	<2(NQ)	3.6
Palnik Lake	12	1.3	22	1.9	1.6	<0.3(ND)	0.6	<0.4(ND)	<0.4(ND)	0.6
Vuljavr Lake	18	1.3	9.9	0.9	0.6	<0.2(NQ)	0.3	<0.3(NQ)	<0.3(NQ)	0.8
Tebek Rus	41	7.7	38	4.3	2.5	<0.2(NQ)	1.2	<0.3(NQ)	<0.4(NQ)	1.1
Geometric Mean	30	4.0	27	3.2	1.8	0.2	0.9	0.2	0.3	1.4
White-tailed Eagle	1.6	0.6	5.1	0.6	0.4	<0.1(NQ)	0.4	<0.1(NQ)	<0.1(NQ	<0.3(NQ)

[a] TEFs from Kutz *et al.* (1990).

Table 6. AAH-active PCB congeners (ng/g, wet weight) in Peregrine Falcon eggs and one White-tailed Eagle egg from the Kola Penninsula, Russia, 1991, and their Toxic Equivalency Factors (TEFs)[a]

	Tetra		Penta					Hexa				Hepta
	77	81	105	114	118	123	126	156	157	167	169	189
TEF	0.01	---	0.001	0.001	0.001	0.001	0.1	0.001	0.001	0.001	0.05	0.001
Nest Site												
Devichy Hill	3.0	0.27	180	18	1,300	6.1	2.8	160	24	120	0.44	21
Okunjevy Hill	2.2	0.18	54	4.9	320	1.8	1.2	53	11	37	0.21	7.7
Trophim Hill	2.6	0.28	210	18	1,200	6.0	3.8	230	32	130	1.2	39
	2.7	0.31	210	18	1,300	6.1	3.8	240	33	130	1.3	39
	2.5	0.29	220	19	1,300	7.3	3.6	250	35	140	1.2	42
Palnik Lake	0.51	0.05	39	3.0	200	<0.43 (ND)	0.61	43	6.0	20	0.14	5.0
Vuljavr Lake	0.85	0.07	33	3.2	210	0.9	0.46	43	4.7	26	0.16	6.3
Tebek Rus	1.6	0.13	54	6.1	410	1.7	1.1	78	9.1	59	0.33	14
Geometric Mean	1.5	0.14	72	6.7	450	1.7	1.3	82	12	51	0.31	12
White-tailed Eagle	0.14	0.03	17	2.0	93	<0.43 (ND)	0.19	16	2.0	10	0.05	1.6

[a] TEFs from Safe (1990).

Table 7. Calculated 2,3,7,8-TCDD equivalences (TEQs) for Polychlorinated dibenzo-*p*-dioxins and dibenzofurans, and AHH-active PCB congeners (pg/g) in Peregrine Falcon eggs, and one White-tailed Eagle egg from the Kola Penninsula, Russia, 1991.

	Dioxins		Furans			PCBs						TEQs
	2,3,7,8	Total	2,3,7,8	2,3,4,7,8	Total	77	105	118	126	169	Total	Total
<u>Nest Site</u>												
Devichy Hill	30	41	5.5	25	32	30	180	1,300	280	22	2,100	2,200
Okunjevy Hill	5.2	9.8	3.1	8	26	22	54	320	120	11	640	680
Trophim Hill	37	53	4.9	31	39	26	210	1,200	380	61	2,400	2,400
	38	55	5.2	32	40	27	210	1,300	380	64	2,400	2,500
	37	54	5	32	40	25	220	1,300	360	62	2,500	2,600
Palnik Lake	5.3	11	1.2	11	13	5.1	39	200	61	7	390	410
Vuljavr Lake	4.0	6.4	1.8	5	7.1	8.5	33	210	46	8	390	410
Tebek Rus	11	19	4.1	19	24	16	54	410	110	17	770	810
White-tailed Eagle	1.2	2.1	0.16	2.6	2.9	1.4	17	93	19	2.5	170	170

Note: Total TEQs for dioxins, furans, and PCBs are the summation of all calculated values (see all concentrations used and TEFs in Tables 4-6.

obtained from literature values by Safe (1990). Certain PHHs were not included because of their low computed TEQs (<0.01 pg/g in any egg), as noted in Table 7.

As can be readily seen, the AHH-active PCB congeners dominate the biological potency and thus the estimated toxic potency of the chlorinated PHH isosteres that we report. In all samples, PCB congeners account for more than 94% of the estimated TEQs. The marked difference in total estimated TEQs between the White-tailed Eagle egg and falcon eggs from the clutch with 3 addled eggs (170 TEQ/g egg for eagle egg compared with about 2,500 TEQ/g egg for falcon eggs) is striking. These differences most likely reflect variation in dietary contamination of the two species.

DISCUSSION AND CONCLUSIONS

The limited region of the Ponoy River depression that is surrounded by bogs now supports an increasing population of nesting Peregrine Falcons. Earlier population estimates are not available, but the adjacent Fennoscandian Peregrine Falcon population declined during the 1950s and 1960s and probably reached its lowest level at the beginning of the 1970s (Lindberg 1985). During the late 1970s both productivity and the number of breeding pairs increased in Finland and Norway, but not in Sweden. The 1975-81 production in northern Finland (above 66° N. Latitude) was much better (1.91 young/pair) than in southern Finland (1.16 young/pair) (Wikman 1985). Thinner-shelled eggs were also reported in southern Finland (Lindén *et al.* 1984).

Reproductive success in northern Finland increased to 2.1 young per breeding attempt in 1981-85 (Lindberg *et al.* 1988). Although the data from Finland were collected about 6 years before ours, the production rates from northern Finland and the recent rates from the Kola Peninsula (study area is above 66° N. Latitude) were similar. The eggshells from the Kola Peninsula still show thinning, but the relationship of DDE to eggshell thickness, as discussed by Blus *et al.* (1972) is typically manifested by a much more rapid improvement in shell thickness as DDE concentrations decrease below those observed in these eggs. In Alaska, in 1979-84, DDE egg residues were higher (geometric mean 10.1 μg/g) and eggshell thinning was more severe (13.1 to 13.6%, depending on subspecies), but the DDE apparently had a minimal effect on productivity as the population at that time was increasing (Ambrose *et al.* 1988a, 1988b). The populations have continued to increase in recent years and DDE residues have continued to decline (Ambrose and Henny, unpublished data). Reported PCB concentrations are now much lower in Alaska (geometric mean, 2.0 to 2.7 μg/g, depending on subspecies; Ambrose *et al.* 1988a) than in western Russia.

Prey species have not been analyzed for contaminants in the Kola Peninsula; prey species, however, have been identified. We found that 5 key species, all associated with bogs, accounted for 73.3% of the diet. Lindén *et al.* (1984), in their earlier work in Finland, noted large variation in DDE levels in Peregrine Falcon eggs and suggested that chemical contamination in the population was not uniform. The relatively low DDE contamination in Kola Peninsula Peregrine Falcon eggs now appears quite uniform; higher PCB concentrations are more variable. Lindberg *et al.* (1983) noted that chemical residue concentrations in some important prey species on the breeding grounds in Sweden were not high enough to account for the levels found in Peregrine Falcons, suggesting either that residues were accumulated outside the breeding grounds or that bioaccumulation factors for Peregrine Falcons were higher than expected. Wintering-grounds accumulation of DDE was documented for Arctic Peregrine Falcons in North America (Henny *et al.* 1982), and may occur in the Kola Peninsula population. This may explain the higher variability in PCB concentrations. Unfortunately, little is known about the wintering localities of Peregrine Falcons that nest in the Kola Peninsula. Young have been ringed in recent years, but no recoveries have been recorded. The Ruff (52% of the prey on the breeding grounds) rests and molts along the coast of western Europe, the Mediterranean Sea, the Black Sea, the Caspian Sea, and the Nile Valley; most winter in Africa (Van Rhijn 1991).

We were surprised by the relative concentrations of PCBs and TEQs in these Peregrine Falcon eggs compared with those reported in studies of other species. Forster's Terns, *Sterna forsteri*, with about the same concentrations of PHHs experienced reduced reproductive success (Kubiak *et al.* 1989). An unhatched Bald Eagle, *Haliaeetus leucocephalus,* egg, with concentrations approximately twice that of Peregrine Falcon eggs in this study, died at day 19 or 20 and exhibited beak deformity (Schwartz *et al.* pers. comm.). The high PCB and PHH concentrations in the 3 addled eggs at Trophim Hill are of special concern. Hatchability was reduced when PCB residues in chicken eggs ranged from 3 to 14 µg/g (wet weight) (Cecil *et al.* 1974) and 16 µg/g in Ringed Turtle-Dove, *Streptopelia risoria,* eggs (Peakall & Peakall 1973). When Forster's Tern eggs from Green Bay, Wisconsin, USA contained a median concentration of 22.5 µg/g PCBs, hatching success was 52% of that of controls (Hoffman *et al.* 1987). However, at Green Bay the eggs also contained a number of other potentially critical contaminants (Kubiak *et al.* 1989). Although no toxicological data exist for Peregrine Falcon sensitivity to these PHHs, there is cause for concern based on similar PHH concentrations in other species.

The TEQ approach needs to be interpreted with some caution. We do not suggest that the TEQs estimated by our procedure are in fact the actual equivalents that could be present in each egg. Unknown compounds which are AHH active could increase equivalents; others may even reduce the estimated equivalents by antagonism. Regardless, subsequent studies could achieve a more realistic biologically-determined estimate, based on the work of Tillitt *et al.* (1991a). Tillitt *et al.* (1991b) measured the relative biological activity of colonial fish-eating water bird egg extracts by an AHH induction *in vitro* bioassay using the same rat hepatoma H4IIE cell line that was the basis of our equivalents calculations. The bioassay-derived TEQs in the waterbird eggs concurred with residue analyses and biological data from other studies, although the absolute values measured in the bioassay were less than the calculated TEQs.

ACKNOWLEDGEMENTS

We are grateful to Vladimir Flint and Alexander Sorokin (Russian Ministry of Ecology and Natural Resources) and Steven Kohl (Office of International Affairs, U.S. Fish and Wildlife Service) for supporting this project. We also acknowledge the support of William Seegar and Mark Fuller toward the initiation and conduct of this study. We are also grateful to Paul Peterman, John Meadows, James Zajicek, and Robert Gale (National Fisheries Contaminant Research Center) for their assistance in the determination of chemical residues. The manuscript was improved by the comments of Gary Heinz, David Hoffman, and Grey Pendleton of the Patuxent Wildlife Research Center. The study was carried out under Area V of the U.S.-Russia Environmental Agreement.

Charles J. Henny
U. S. Fish and Wildlife Service
Patuxent Wildlife Research Center
3080 SE Clearwater Drive
Corvallis, Oregon 97333 U.S.A.

Sergei A. Ganusevich
Russian Ministry of Ecology and Natural Resources
Znamenskoye-Sadki, P. O., Vilar
Moscow 113628 Russia

F. Prescott Ward
U. S. Army Chemical Research,
Development, and Engineering Center
Aberdeen Proving Ground, Maryland 21010 U.S.A.

Ted R. Schwartz
U. S. Fish and Wildlife Service
National Fisheries Contaminant Research Center
4200 New Haven Road
Columbia, Missouri 65201 U.S.A.

Meyburg, B.-U. & R. D. Chancellor eds.1994
Raptor Conservation Today
WWGBP / The Pica Press

DDE Contamination and Population Parameters of Bald Eagles *Haliaeetus leucocephalus* in California and Arizona, USA

J. Mark Jenkins, Ronald M. Jurek, David K. Garcelon, Robert Mesta, W. Grainger Hunt, Ronald E. Jackman, Daniel E. Driscoll & Robert W. Risebrough

ABSTRACT

Eggs laid by Bald Eagles reintroduced to Santa Catalina Island in southern California have continued to experience breakage in the field and embryonic death during artificial incubation; DDE levels have remained high since the first egg was laid in 1987. In northern California, however, the population is expanding with an annual increase of 6.7 %, a rate predicted by the population parameters measured in a 10-year study of 10 nesting pairs on the Pit River in Shasta County. The relatively isolated population of approximately 25 pairs in Arizona also maintains a high level of productivity, in the order of 0.9 young fledged per occupied nest. This paper summarizes the population and DDE residue data available at this time. DDE concentrations in excess of 3-5 ppm wet weight, previously determined to be the threshold level of effects on productivity in this species, were recorded in unhatched eggs from sites where mean productivity was high, suggesting a lower sensitivity to DDE than predicted from previous data.

At the Third World Conference, Garcelon *et al.* (1989) described the reintroduction of Bald Eagles, *Haliaeetus leucocephalus*, to Santa Catalina Island in southern California. The species had been common on the southern California islands in the early years of the century, with a minimum population size of 24 pairs, but the last known breeding was recorded in 1949 (Kiff 1980). The excessively high contamination of the area by DDT compounds, derived from the wastes discharged by the world's largest manufacturer of DDT in Los Angeles, was considered the most plausible cause of this local extinction (Garcelon *et al.* 1989). The recovery of the productivity of local Brown Pelicans, *Pelecanus occidentalis*, from near zero in 1969-71 to near-normal levels in 1974, parallel with a steep decline of DDE residues in a principal prey species, the Northern Anchovy, *Engraulis mordax*, (Anderson *et al.* 1975) prompted the recovery program for the eagles. Unfortunately, the first egg laid by a reintroduced bird, in 1987, broke in the nest; DDE levels of 470 ppm in the yolk lipid (Garcelon *et al.* 1989) were several times higher than the threshold of sensitivity to DDE previously determined by Wiemeyer *et al.* (1984) and Nisbet (1989). In this paper we summarize the breeding activities of the Santa Catalina eagles through 1991 and the population status of the species elsewhere in California and the adjacent state of Arizona, and present data on DDE residues in unhatched eggs throughout these areas.

Methods for the analysis of DDE have been described by Risebrough *et al.* (1986). Two eggs obtained in 1984 from Packer's Bay were analyzed in the laboratory of the California Department of Fish and Game. Unhatched eggs were collected toward or after the end of the breeding season and preserved frozen or refrigerated until analysis. Wet weights of the samples consisting of yolk lipids were estimated from the mean lipid content of 11 eggs showing no visible embryonic development, 7.32% ± 1.13 (SD). Wet weight concentrations (Table 1) were not corrected for water loss; percent moisture is included among the data of Table 1.

In California, the breeding population has been monitored annually since 1970 by the California Department of Fish and Game in cooperation with other agencies and private individuals. Current procedures include a request that participants check each territory three times during the breeding season to determine occupancy, breeding activity, and productivity. The population has shown a continuing increase since the late 1970s (Figure 1; Jurek, 1990; Jurek, unpublished). Mean productivity, young fledged per active nest, in 1977-91 was 1.01.

Figure 1. Occupied territories of Bald Eagles in California, 1977-1992. Circles show predicted number of territories extrapolated from 1990 based on population parameters measured on the Pit River. Details in text.

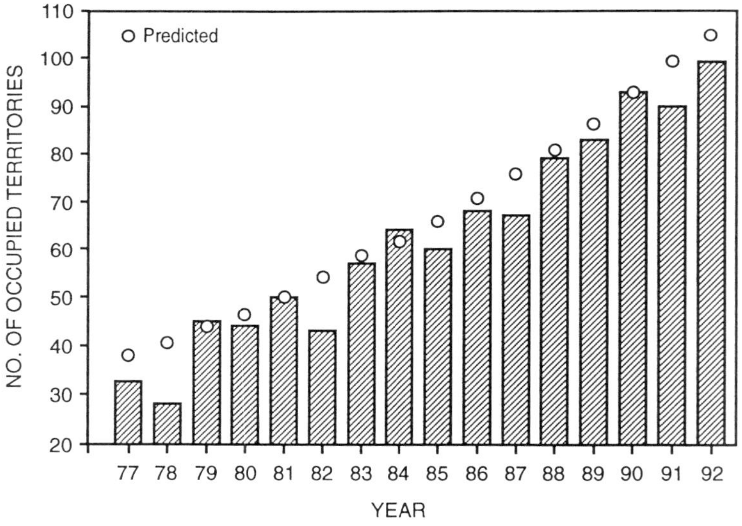

Population parameters of 10 pairs breeding along the Pit River in Shasta County have been determined by Jenkins (this volume): adult survivorship, 94.6%; first-year survival, 76.9%; productivity, 0.81 young/occupied site. These parameters predict a yearly increase of 6.7 %. Application of this rate of yearly increase to the 1990 value of the breeding population yields a curve that closely matches the observed population increase in northern California in the 1980s (Figure 1). In the northern California population as a whole, survivorship, shown to be more important than productivity in affecting population change (Jenkins, this volume), is therefore similar to that determined for the Pit River group.

Breeding in southern California was observed in 1989 and 1990 on Lake Cachuma in Santa Barbara County (1 and 2 young fledged) and in 1990 on Lake Arrowhead east of Los Angeles (unsuccessful).

Table 1. Productivity of Bald Eagles in Arizona, northern California, and Santa Catalina Island in territories where unhatched or broken eggs were obtained for organochlorine analyses; DDE, parts per million.

Site	Year	Fledged	DDE lipid	DDE wet	Est. Prod.	Comments
ARIZONA						
Cedar Basin	1986	0				
	1987	0				
	1988	0	31	2.3	0.0	No visible development;
	1989	0				77.8% H_2O
	1990	0				
Chino	1985	2				No visible development;
	1986	0(2)	110	8.9	1.0	64.3% H_2O; two young
	1987	--				fostered into nest;
						new female in 1987.
McDowell	1986	2				
	1987	1				
	1988	0	94	8.0	1.25	No visible development;
	1989	2				77.1% H_2O
Cliff	1988	2				
	1989	0	120	7.7	0.67	No visible development;
	1990	0				78.0% H_2O
Horseshoe	1987	3				
	1988	1				
	1989	0	74	3.4	1.50	No visible development;
	1990	2				78.5% H_2O
Alamo	1988	1				
	1989	1	130	5.3	1.33	Embryo, 1/3 development;
	1990	2				80.0% H_2O
Horse Mesa	1985	0				
	1986	2	100	4.7	1.33	Embryo, 3/4 developed
	1987	2		(est.)		65.9% H_2O; 5.9% lipid
SANTA CATALINA IS.						
Twin Rocks	1987	0	470			One egg, broke in nest;
Female „Chator“				25	0.0	yolk remnants analyzed
				(est)		Early embryo died,
	1989	--	210			artifical incubation
Seal Rocks	1988	0	740			One egg, broke in nest;
Female „Shasta“				67	0.0	yolk remnants analyzed
				(est)		Early embryo died,
	1990	--	1,100			artificial incubation
Pinnacle Rock	1991	--	600	44	0.0	Early embryo died,
Female „Bray“				(est)		artificial incubation

Site	Year	Fledged	DDE lipid	DDE wet	Est. Prod.	Comments
Lands End Female „Wray“	1991	(1)				Two eggs laid, artificial incubation; one hatched, second died at pipping.
NORTHERN CALIFORNIA						
Pit River, Shasta Co						
Dusty	1985	0				
	1986	0	41	2.5		No development; 81.6 %H_2O
	1987	0				
	1988	0	26	2.5	0.6	No development; 76.0 %H_2O
	1989	2				
	1990	2				
South Shore	1982	0				
	1983	0	120	--		Crushed egg
	1984	0				
	1985	--	61	4.7	0.0	3 eggs removed, artifical incubation, no development
	1986	0				
	1987	0				
North Shore	1982	0				
	1983	2				
	1984	0	150			Crushed egg
	1985	0				
	1986	--	53	4.1	0.25	2 eggs removed, artifical incub., 78.4% H_2O (mean); small embryos died
	1987	1				
	1988	0				
Pit 3	1988	2				
	1989	2				
	1990	0	26	1.3	1.0	2 large embryos, died near hatching after death of female; 83.6% H_2O
	1991	0				
Pit 6	1988	0				
	1989	0	24	0.50	0.25	Embryo near hatching
	1990	1				
	1991	0				
O'Brien, Shasta Co.	1984	1				
	1985	0				
	1986	--	280 (est)	8	1.0	Artificially incubated, chick near hatch;5.5% lipid, 79.7% H_2O
	1987	2				
	1988	1				

Site	Year	Fledged	DDE lipid	DDE wet	Est. Prod.	Comments
Packer's Bay,	1982,83	1				
Shasta Co.	1984	0	--	9.5	0.4	Means of 2 eggs; analysis CDFG, small embryos
	1985,86	0				
	1987	0				
	1988	2				
	1989	0				
	1990	1				
	1991	0	19	1.3	0.5	Embryo 1/2 developed;
	1992	0				80.3% H_2O
Hirz Bay,	1982	1				
Shasta Co.	1983	0				
	1984	0	175	10	0.8	No develop., 82.7% H_2O
	1985	1				
	1986	2				
Lake Pillsbury,	1982	2				
Lake Co.	1983	0				
	1984	0	90	5.6	1.0	No develop., 80.0% H_2O
	1985	2				
	1986	1				
Mountain Meadows	1984,85	NO				
West, Lassen Co.	1986	0	34	2.5	0.67	No develop., 77.6% H_2O
	1987	2				
	1988	0				
Cool Springs,	1984	2				
Plumas Co.	1985	1				
	1986	0	110	8.5	1.4	No develop., 79.8% H_2O
	1987	2				
	1988	2				
Rocky Point,	1984,85	0				
Lake Almanor	1986	0	300	22	0.0	No develop., 66.3% H_2O
	1987	NO	(est)			12.3% lipid
	1988	0				
Mud Creek Rim,	1984	0	75	2.6	0.67	Early embryo; 83.7% H_2O
Lake Almanor	1985	2				
	1986	0				

NO: not occupied

Among the northern California sites from which one or more unhatched eggs were obtained, two had zero productivity over the period of observation (Table 1). The female of South Shore was found dead in April 1992 with injuries probably inflicted by another eagle; a stricture in the lower oviduct accounted for the reproductive failures (National Wildlife Health Research Center, Madison, Wisconsin). The egg from the other site, Rocky Point, contained 300 ppm DDE in the lipid, estimated from the mean lipid determination to be equivalent to about 22 ppm wet weight. This is in the range where the data presented by Wiemeyer *et al.* (1984) would predict a very low level of reproductive success. Eggs from 5 of the remaining 12 sites (2 values from Packer's Bay) had DDE levels above 5 ppm, in the higher range of the estimated threshold interval, suggesting potential effects on productivity. Productivity of the more contaminated group, however, was higher (0.92 vs 0.56).

The Arizona population of approximately 25 pairs appears to be stable; reported productivities have ranged from 0.80 young/occupied territory in 1975-81, 1.13 in 1982-86, to 0.87, 1.04, and 0.52 in 1987-89 (Forbis 1988; Grubb *et al.* 1990; Hunt *et al.* 1992). A review of all of the available data, however, has shown that productivity and nest success rates have remained stable over the past two decades at levels comparable to those reported in other populations in North America considered healthy. Overall, the mean young per occupied site was 0.9 eaglets; nest success averaged 57%. A nest occupancy rate of 85% was 14% higher than the average for other populations as reported by Stalmaster (1987); the 15% nestling mortality rate in Arizona equals that in other populations (Hunt *et al.* 1992).

Unhatched eggs were obtained in 1986-89. Two of the sites had been sampled previously by Grubb *et al.* (1990). Two eggs from Horseshoe contained a mean DDE concentration of 8 ppm in 1977; the 1989 egg contained 3.4 ppm. Horse Mesa eggs contained 4.4 and 4.7 ppm in 1983 and 1986, respectively (Grubb *et al.* 1990; Table 1). Geometric mean DDE concentration in the earlier eggs was 3.3 ppm; 4 of the 7 eggs from the later collection contained DDE levels above 5 ppm; correction for water loss would decrease these values by no more than 20% (Table 1); corrected values would remain above 5 ppm. These higher values of DDE do not appear to be associated with depressed productivity (Table 1).

In contrast, all but one of the eggs laid by the reintroduced birds on Santa Catalina Island in 1987-1991 broke in the nest or the embryo died during artificial incubation (Table 1). After the second egg laid, by female 'Shasta' in 1988, broke in the nest, the decision was made to remove eggs for artificial incubation at the Predatory Bird Research Group facilities in Santa Cruz. Female 'Chator', who laid the 1987 egg, produced 2 eggs in 1989: the first disappeared within 48 hours; the embryo of the second died at an early stage, the egg showing an abnormally high rate of water loss (J. Linthicum and B.J. Walton, unpublished). High water loss and early embryonic death also occurred in the egg produced by 'Shasta' in 1990. In 1991, three eggs were produced by two pairs; one of these hatched after artificial incubation and the young bird was fledged in the wild. All of the eggs analyzed contained exceptionally high levels of DDE (Table 1). Management of this population by artificial incubation and/or the importation of healthy eggs from other areas will evidently be necessary for years to come.

The present data set from California/Arizona therefore supports the conclusions reached from the set compiled by Wiemeyer *et al.* (1984) from eggs laid in 1969-1979, mostly in eastern North America, that depressed productivity is associated with higher levels of DDE; the apparent threshold of sensitivity appears, however, to be higher in California/Arizona. This question is explored in the companion paper by Nisbet and Risebrough (this volume).

ACKNOWLEDGEMENTS

Research was supported by the Pacific Gas and Electric Company, the California Department of Fish & Game, the Catalina Island Conservancy, the U.S. Bureau of Reclamation, and the Bodega Bay Institute.

J. Mark Jenkins
Technical and Ecological Services
Pacific Gas and Electric Company
3400 Crow Canyon Road
San Ramon, CA 94583, USA

Ronald M. Jurek
California Department of Fish and Game
1416 Ninth Street
Sacramento CA 95814

David K. Garcelon
Institute for Wildlife Studies
P.O. Box 127
Arcata, CA 95521, USA

Robert W. Risebrough
The Bodega Bay Institute
2711 Piedmont Avenue
Berkeley, CA 94705, USA

W. Grainger Hunt, Ronald E. Jackman
& Daniel E. Driscoll
BioSystems Analysis, Inc.
303 Potrero St., Suite 29-203
Santa Cruz, CA 95060

Robert Mesta
U.S. Fish and Wildlife Service
Ventura Field Office
2140 Eastman Avenue, Suite 100
Ventura, CA 93003, USA

Meyburg, B.-U. & R. D. Chancellor eds.1994
Raptor Conservation Today
WWGBP / The Pica Press

The Impact of Fenthion on Birds of Prey

D. Lacombe, D.M. Bird,
K.A. Hunt & P. Mineau

Fenthion is an organophosphate insecticide (OP) registered worldwide. It is widely used in mosquito control (Grue 1982) and is frequently applied to livestock (Smith 1987), domestic pets and various crops. It is also used as a contact avicide to control birds (Thomsett 1987; Bruggers *et al.* 1989; Wiemeyer 1991). Fenthion has been frequently involved in wildlife mortality including several thousand passerines (Seabloom *et al.* 1973), Black-billed Magpies, *Pica pica,* (Hanson & Howell 1981), and raptors (Henny *et al.* 1987; Wiemeyer 1991). Several cases of secondary poisoning of raptors by contaminated target bird species have been reported with fenthion used as an avicide and as an insecticide (Seabloom *et al.* 1973; Hanson & Howell 1981; Zinkl *et al.* 1981; DeWeese *et al.* 1983; Wenneborg 1986; Thomsett 1987; Bruggers *et al.* 1989; Dominick *et al.* 1989).

The toxicity of fenthion results from its oxidation in the body to several potent secondary metabolites (Francis & Barnes 1963). Fenthion inhibits acetylcholinesterase (AChE), the enzyme that breaks down the neurotransmitter acetylcholine, causing its accumulation at nerve synapses and consequent disruption of nerve function (O'Brien 1967:55).

In American Kestrels, *Falco sparverius* and fenthion-exposed House Sparrows, *Passer domesticus*, fenthion intoxication was characterized by coughing and sneezing, body tremors, overall weakness, ataxia, loss of balance, partial paralysis of the wings, excessive salivation, and finally complete paralysis of the legs (Hunt *et al.* 1991; Hunt *et al.* in press). These observations are in agreement with fenthion intoxication symptoms reported elsewhere for both orally dosed and dermally exposed birds (Besser & DeCino 1963; Hudson *et al.* 1984).

Birds are highly sensitive to fenthion as indicated by low oral LD_{50} values ranging from 2.5 to 25.9 mg/kg (Tucker & Crabtree 1970; Schafer *et al.* 1983; Smith 1987) and low LC_{50} values ranging from 30 to 231 ppm in the diet (Hill *et al.* 1975). Dietary toxicity of fenthion appears to vary between families and species of birds (Hill 1972; Hill *et al.* 1975). Among species studied, raptors are more sensitive to the toxic effects of this OP than some of the potential target species. For example, the acute oral LD_{50} values of fenthion were 1.0 mg/kg of body weight for the American Kestrel and 5.6 mg/kg of body weight for the House Sparrow, a target bird species (Schafer *et al.* 1964; Schafer *et al.* 1969). American Kestrels were also found to be susceptible to other OPs and carbamates relative to other avian species. Similarly, Eastern Screech-owls, *Otus asio*, were found to be sensitive to fenthion (LD_{50} value=4.6 mg/kg) and other ChE inhibitors (Wiemeyer & Sparling 1991).

Secondary poisoning has not generally been considered to be an important route of exposure to OPs. However, the ingestion of OP poisoned vertebrates (birds and small mammals) has resulted in mortality in raptors under field conditions (Mendelsshon & Paz 1977; Wilson *et al.* 1991).

Traditionally, an inhibition of total brain ChE level of 20% has been determined to be diagnostic of exposure. Inhibition of 50% is associated with mortality as well as with a number of severe sublethal effects (Grue *et al.* 1991). Prior to our work (Hunt *et al.* 1991; Hunt *et al.* in press), no one had systematically investigated the secondary poisoning hazard of fenthion to birds of prey under realistic conditions when used as an avicide dispensed through a toxic perch system.

Toxic hazard of fenthion to raptors in field situations has been demonstrated by observations of sick or dead birds in association with fenthion treatments (Beard 1969; Elder & Henderson 1969; Seabloom *et al.* 1973; Stickel 1973; Zinkl *et al.* 1981). External contamination on target birds is a contributing factor in the secondary poisoning of raptors (Schafer *et al.* 1964; Hunt *et al.* 1991; Hunt *et al.* in press). Our studies have shown that American Kestrels have no aversion to eating, on a daily basis, House Sparrows that had come into contact with the fenthion perches (Hunt *et al.* 1991; Hunt *et al.* in press). Moreover, kestrels captured fenthion-exposed sparrows 12 times more often than normal, unexposed sparrows in the same flocks. Fenthion-exposed sparrows displayed aberrant behavior at the time of capture (Hunt *et al.* in press). Similarly, following spraying of the avicide Queletox® (60% fenthion) in Kenya, the flapping moribund Red-billed Quelea, *Quelea quelea*, were very conspicuous to passing raptors and were quickly eaten (Thomsett 1987).

Under aviary conditions where kestrels were allowed to hunt, most (11/14) died within one day after killing and at least partially consuming 1 House Sparrow exposed to fenthion. The inhibition of ChE activity in the brain of these birds was 81% and 97% in the plasma as compared to controls (Hunt *et al.* 1991). Another study has shown that the average depression of brain ChE activity for birds that died 8 hours after dosing with fenthion was 88.0% for the American Kestrels and 92.0% for Eastern Screech-owls (Wiemeyer & Sparling 1991). The capture behavior of American Kestrels treated with 50 mg/kg of acephate (corresponding inhibition of brain ChE activity = 25% and ChE plasma activity = 40%) was not affected when using an artificial moving prey model (Rudolph *et al.* 1984). In our laboratory, we are conducting a series of experiments on American Kestrels treated with another ChE inhibitor, Physostigmine. Doses of this carbamate ChE inhibitor were selected to span 25-50% inhibition of brain ChE activity and kestrels had to catch a living wild mouse, *Mus musculus*. These results will increase our knowledge on the general effect of sublethal doses of ChE inhibitors on the hunting behavior of the kestrel, a behavior that is necessary for survival of adults and their offspring.

The significance of OP-related mortality to wildlife populations is not known. However, the mortality of about 400 raptors (species with reproductive potentials lower than those of most birds) following the misuse of the OP monocrotophos on a 8 km² area (Mendelsshon & Paz 1977) indicates that the potential for population effects exists (Grue *et al.* 1983). Moreover, sublethal exposures to fenthion and other ChE inhibitors are suspected to have detrimental effects on survival and reproduction (Grue *et al.* 1991; Patnode & White 1991).

Sublethal exposure of birds of prey to OPs may result in loss of body weight due to pesticide-induced anorexia as observed in other bird species (Costa & Murphy 1982; Grue 1982). Lowered food consumption may reduce egg production (Stromborg 1977; 1981) in raptors and this effect on reproduction may be more severe with the alteration of hormone concentrations due to OP exposure (Rattner *et al.* 1982a,b). Growth of nestlings and particularly growth of altricial nestlings may be depressed following OP exposure resulting in lower weights at fledging (Pearce & Busby 1980; Powell & Gray 1980). Lower body weight at fledging is associated with decrease in post-fledging survival in non-treated birds (Perrins 1965; Smith 1967; Loman 1977). Also survival of adult raptors and that of their offspring depends on their ability to hunt. Since OPs can reduce visual acuity (Plestina & Pivkovic-Plestina 1978), vigilance (Levin & Rodnitzky 1976), and food-seeking behavior (Adams 1977), raptors may become less efficient in providing food to their young, their mate, or themselves.

Where fenthion is used as a contact avicide, secondary poisoning hazard is expected to be greater for raptors feeding on one of the nuisance species targeted by fenthion (i.e., Rock Dove (*Columba livia*), European Starling, *Sturnus vulgaris*, House Sparrow, and Red-billed Quelea), and on other nuisance species as the Red-winged Blackbird, *Agelaius phoeniceus*, the Brown-headed Cowbird, *Molothrus ater*, and the Common Grackle, *Quiscalus quiscula*, which may have access to fenthion perches in agricultural areas in North America. In urban areas, non-target species such as the Chimney Swift, *Chaetura pelagica*, and the Cliff Swallow, *Hirundo pyrrhonota*, may also be contaminated with fenthion since they are nesting on structures where fenthion perches are used (chimneys and bridges respectively). Raptors susceptible to fenthion poisoning include the opportunistic American Kestrel (Bildstein & Collopy 1987; Mueller 1987; Hunt *et al.* in press), and several Buteo and Accipiter species (Storer 1966; Palmer 1988). Moreover, several species of falcons (American Kestrel, Peregrine Falcon, *F. peregrinus*, and Merlin, *F. columbarius*, are becoming increasingly common in urban areas. Fenthion has been suspected as a cause of mortality in Saskatoon Merlins (L. Oliphant, pers. comm.) and approximately 90% of the prey species of urban Merlins in Saskatoon consisted of House Sparrows (Oliphant 1974). Rock Doves are captured by Merlins only on few occasions (Warkentin & Oliphant 1988). These species along with the European Starling are prey taken by Peregrine Falcons (Can. Wildl. Serv. 1988; Palmer 1988). Consumption of fenthion-contaminated birds could have severe implications for recovery programs (Cade *et al.* 1988). Falcons are released in urban areas where fenthion is used as a perch avicide and the risk of secondary poisoning extends to rural areas where they are also used (Weber 1979; Wenneborg 1986).

Fenthion used as an insecticide in terrestrial and aquatic environment is relatively non persistent but it can be acutely toxic to birds (U.S. Environmental Protection Agency 1988). When used as an avicide, fenthion is a clear hazard to nontargeted birds of prey.

D. Lacombe & D.M. Bird
Avian Science and Conservation Centre of McGill University
21111 Lakeshore Road, Ste. Anne de Bellevue
Quebec, Canada H9X 3V9.

K.A. Hunt
The Institute of Wildlife and Environmental Toxicology
Clemson University
P.O. Box 2278, Clemson,
South Carolina, U.S.A. 29632-2278.

P. Mineau
National Wildlife Research Centre
Canadian Wildlife Service,
Environment Canada
100 Gamelin Blvd,
Hull, Quebec, Canada K1A 0H3.

Meyburg B.-U. & R. D. Chancellor eds.1994
Raptor Conservation Today
WWGBP / The Pica Press

Weight loss during artificial incubation vs. Eggshell thinning of California Pergrine Falcon *Falco peregrinus* Eggs brought from the Wild

Janet L. Linthicum, Walter M. Jarman,
Brian J. Walton, Robert W. Risebrough,
Lloyd F. Kiff & Jason S. Minton

ABSTRACT

Our data on water loss from Peregrine Falcon eggs brought from the wild for artificial incubation at facilities of the Santa Cruz Predatory Bird Research Group appear to be inconsistent with several published reports that water loss is depressed in thin-shelled eggs, whether the thinning has been induced experimentally by DDE or is associated with DDE in the eggs of wild birds. Water loss increased with decreasing thickness in our samples, but variance in the rate of water loss was much higher in the thinner-shelled eggs. Although we have not resolved the discrepancies we suggest that patterns of water loss may be different in eggs with living, developing embryos and eggs with dead embryos or eggs preserved in museums. A contaminant effect on the metabolism of embryos and the possible presence of structural abnormalities in eggs with higher rates of water loss are other factors that might explain, in part, these observations.

INTRODUCTION

Among the unresolved problems mentioned at the Third World Conference (Risebrough 1989) was an apparent discrepancy between observations at the Predatory Bird Research Group of the University of California, Santa Cruz (SCPBRG), and the data of several published papers. Peakall *et al.* (1973) reported that dietary DDE thinned the shells, decreased breaking strength and unexpectedly, decreased water loss in three species of birds, white Peking ducks, *Anas platyrhynchos*, American Kestrels, *Falco sparverius*, and Ringed Turtle-Doves, *Streptopelia risoria*. This was attributed to a reduction in the number of pores through the eggshell that are the pathways of exchange of water vapor and other gases. Eggs of Common Terns, *Sterna hirundo*, that failed to hatch after natural incubation in an Alberta colony also showed a lower rate of water loss that was correlated with abnormalities of shell structure, including a reduction in the number of pores and of mammillae (Fox 1976). Cooke (1979) measured water loss from museum eggs of Peregrine

Falcons, *Falco peregrinus*, and found that the functional pore area was decreased in the modern, thinner-shelled eggs. In contrast, we measured higher rates of water loss in thinner-shelled Peregrine eggs. We present our data in an initial attempt to resolve this apparent discrepancy.

MATERIAL AND METHODS

Collection and incubation

The eggs in this study (N = 136) were collected from wild eyries between 1985 and 1990 for artificial incubation by the SCPBRG as part of a long-term Peregrine Falcon recovery program in California. In most cases, wild eggs were collected from nest sites deemed unlikely to fledge young on their own, based upon a prior history of failure, in order to prevent breakage and egg loss. Eggs were transported from the field in portable incubators held at a temperature of 37°C.

The incubation technique used at the SCPBRG follows closely that of Burnham (1983). After candling to determine approximate age of the embryo, the eggs are weighed and measured. Because none of the eggs in this study were collected fresh, the theoretical fresh weight was calculated from the egg dimensions (Burnham 1983). We assumed a natural total weight loss of 15% during incubation until pipping (Rahn & Ar 1974, Rahn *et al.* 1979, Burnham 1983). This loss in weight is attributable to a loss of water vapor through the pores of the eggshell as the embryo develops (Rahn *et al.* 1979). The eggs were then placed in an incubator at 35% humidity, and the weight loss was monitored for 48 hours. Eggs weighing more than expected, - on the basis of their estimated weights when fresh and of their predicted water loss during early incubation, - and that showed a low rate of loss during the 48-hour incubation at 35% humidity, were transferred to a „dry" incubator (roughly 20% humidity, with no water added to the incubator; Figure 1A). Eggs weighing less than expected and that had high rates of water loss were transferred to a higher-humidity incubator (60 or 75%) in an attempt to minimize the excessive water loss (Figure 1B). Weight loss was then monitored daily and the egg was treated accordingly. The contents of eggs that do not hatch were placed in solvent-washed jars for future chemical analysis; eggshells were sent to the Western Foundation of Vertebrate Zoology (WFVZ) for thickness measurements and archiving.

In an attempt to standardize our samples as much as possible, only eggs that were alive during the initial 48 hour period, and only those that were showing development (*i.e.*, had at least five days of incubation prior to arrival) were included in this analysis. Not included were eggs with obvious structural damage such as dents or cracks. Nor were eggs included that contained visible pock marks that are routinely covered with glue to retard excessive rates of water loss.

Eggshell thickness measurements

The eggshell fragments were measured at the WFVZ using a model 35 PS Federal bench comparator thickness gauge. If no membranes were attached to the shell a compensation factor of 0.063 mm was added, the mean thickness of the eggshell membranes of 20 pre-1947 Peregrine eggs. Eggshell thickness was then compared to the estimated thickness of the pre-1947 Peregrine eggs from California, previously determined to be 0.369 mm, to calculate the percent thinning.

Statistics

Statistical operations were performed with the software "Minitab" (Ryan *et al.* 1985).

RESULTS AND DISCUSSION

Water loss in our sample (N = 136) increased with thinning: Spearman's rank correlation coefficient = - 0.401, ($P < 0.01$). The relationship, however, does not appear to be linear; eggs with shell thickness less than 0.32 mm, about 13% thin, showed a much higher variance of water loss during the first two days of incubation at 35% relative humidity (Figure 2).

One consistent difference between our sample and those described above in the cited papers

Figure 1. **Egg weight loss during artificial incubation at the Santa Cruz Predatory Bird Research Group facilities. The solid lines show the predicted weight loss (15%) during incubation, beginning at the calculated initial fresh weight. Weight loss during the first 48 hours of incubation at 35% humidity determines the humidity of the next stage of incubation. 1A: Site SC-2, egg 87-15. Transferred to a "dry" incubator at approximately 20 % humidity. 6.5% thin; 1B: Site MC-6, egg 90-127. Transferred to 75% humidity. 18.4% thin. Both eggs hatched.**

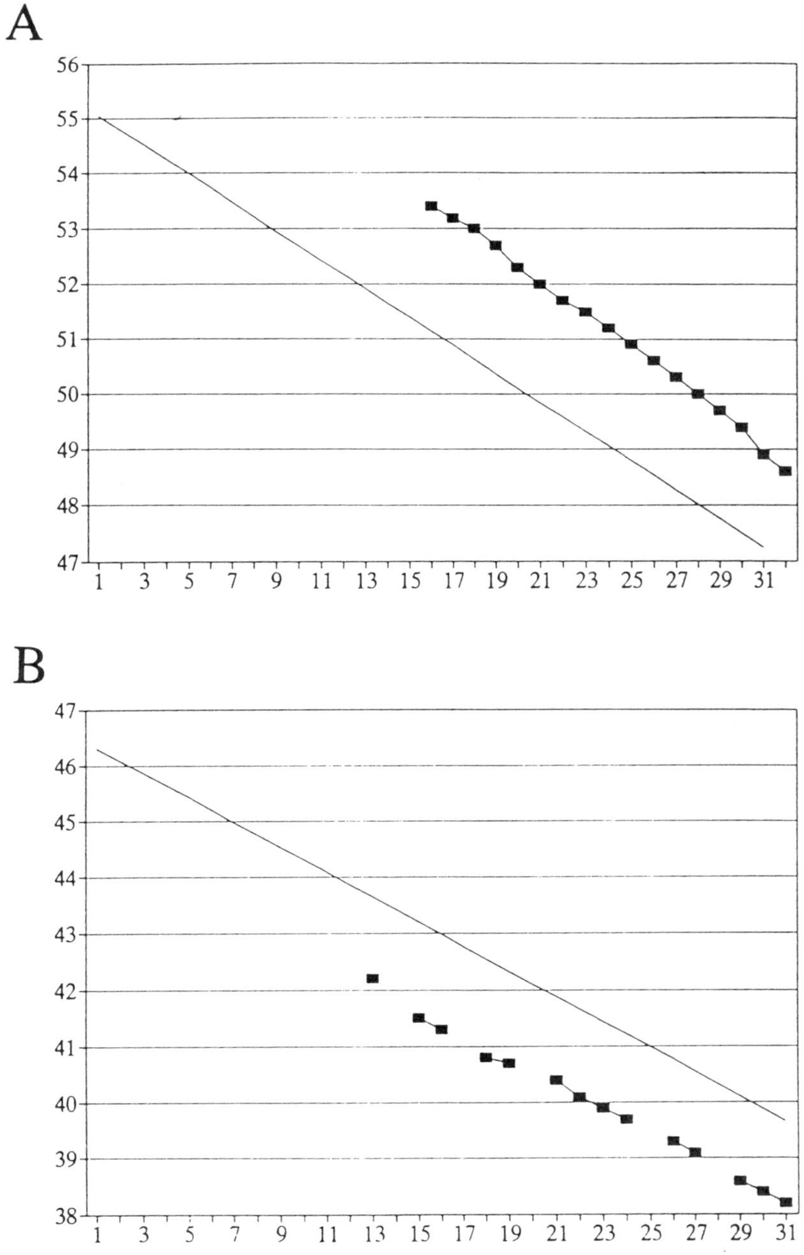

Figure 2. Weight loss (grams per day) over the first 48 hours of artificial incubation at 35% humidity versus eggshell thickness of Peregrine Falcon eggs brought from the wild in 1985-1990. N = 136. The normal range of weight loss of Peregrine eggs is 0.20-0.28 g per day, depending on egg size.

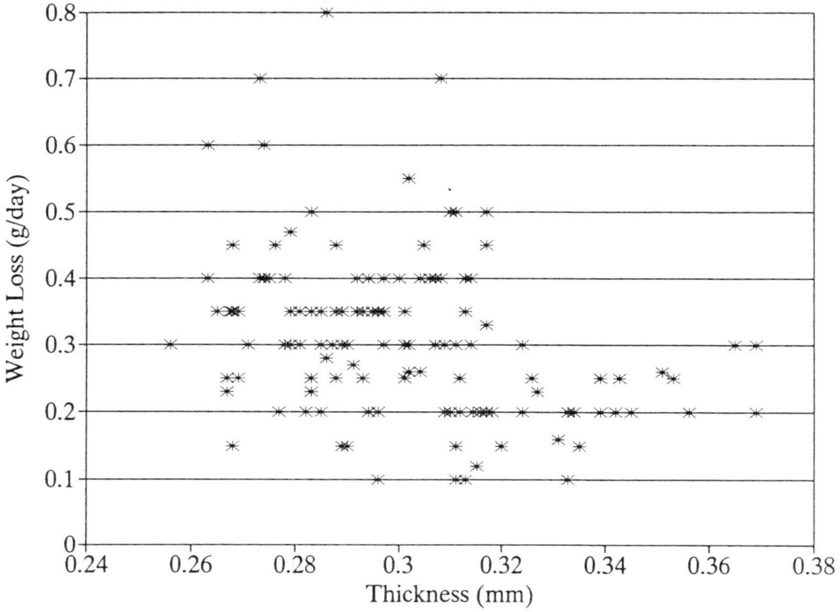

is that our data were derived from living eggs whereas the other data derived principally from eggs without living, developing embryos. Peakall *et al.* (1973) determined water loss by placing the eggs in a desiccator and weighing them daily. Although some eggs may initially have been fertile, it is unlikely that there would have been any development before death of the embryos. In Fox's study (1976), water loss was determined by weighing the wild eggs during incubation. Of the 26 eggs in the study that failed to hatch, 61% were addled (no discernable embryonic development), 17% died during the first week, 4% during the second, and 18% during the third week, including 11% that died during pipping; water loss from these eggs was less than in the eggs that hatched (Fox 1976). Cooke (1979) determined water loss in the museum eggs of Peregrines by filling the eggshells with distilled water, sealing any holes, placing them in a desiccator, and weighing them daily. Water loss from the modern eggs was decreased at temperatures of 20°C and 40°C, but the diference in water content was statistically significant only at 20°C. Both Fox (1976) and Peakall *et al.* (1973) had concluded that the number of pores was reduced in their thin-shelled eggs, but Cooke (1979) considered this unlikely. He found no reduction in the numbers of pores in the thinner-shelled eggs, measuring them by dyeing the inside of the shell, and counting the number of red spots that appeared on the outer shell. He did find, however, that the reduction in water vapor conductance was associated with an increase in the ratio of mammillae height to mammillary layer, and suggested that structural disruptions in the inner layer of the eggshell were responsible for the lower rate of water loss. No organochlorine levels were reported in this manuscript.

Lindén *et al.* (1984) measured weight loss during the natural incubation of Peregrine eggs in Finland; three of the four clutches of thinner-shelled eggs disappeared before the second weighing and a slight negative correlation between water loss and thickness was not statistically significant. Unpublished observations were quoted, however, of high rates of water loss during artificial incubation of Peregrine eggs unless humidity was increased.

During the metabolic burning of fat, water is generated, increasing the difference in water vapor pressures between the egg interior and the external environment. Although the passage of gases through the membrane and shell is passive, the net flux is determined by the difference in vapor pressure (Rahn *et al.* 1979). This factor could therefore account for the higher rates of weight loss in the viable Common Tern eggs measured by Fox (1976), but would not explain the observed differences among the eggs of our study, nor the observations of Peakall *et al.* (1973) and of Cooke (1979).

Organochlorines may increase the rate of basic metabolic processes (Matsumura 1975), and produce an excitatory syndrome in the central nervous system (Cohn *et al.* 1981). Such an effect could account for some of the differences observed in our sample, but its significance awaits experimental verification; an increase in rate-of-loss might be expected as the embryo matures.

Particularly to be explained is why some of the thinnest-shelled eggs, 0.26-0.28 mm or 26-30% thin, have normal rates of water loss, whereas other eggs showing 13-30% thinning have rates of water loss 3-4 times higher under the standard conditions of 35% humidity (Figure 2).

ACKNOWLEDGEMENTS

Funding for this study was provided by the SCPBRG, The Peregrine Fund, Inc., and the Institute of Marine Sciences, University of California, Santa Cruz. The authors wish to thank Nancy Clum of The Peregrine Fund, Inc. for her valuable comments on the manuscript.

Janet L. Linthicum, Brian J. Walton & Jason S. Minton
Santa Cruz Predatory Bird Research Group
University of California
Santa Cruz, CA 95064, USA

Walter M. Jarman
Institute of Marine Sciences
University of California
Santa Cruz, CA 95064, USA

Robert W. Risebrough
The Bodega Bay Institute
2711 Piedmont Ave.
Berkeley, CA 94705, USA

Lloyd F. Kiff
Western Foundation of Vertebrate Zoology
439 Calle San Pablo
Camarillo, CA 93010, USA

Meyburg, B.-U. & R. D. Chancellor eds.1994
Raptor Conservation Today
WWGBP / The Pica Press

A Suggestion of Synergistic effects of DDE and Aroclor 1254 on Reproduction of the American Kestrel *Falco sparverius*

Jeffrey L. Lincer

ABSTRACT

Most laboratory toxicological studies have been undertaken with only one compound, administered at several doses. Environmental studies routinely report mixtures of contaminants in food webs, but synergistic effects have rarely been looked for. American Kestrels fed a combination of DDE and PCBs had a higher rate of egg breakage and a lower rate of pipping and hatching than did Kestrels exposed to DDE or PCBs alone. Although small sample sizes preclude rigorous statistical analysis, these results provide support for the hypothesis that PCBs also had a significant role in the population declines of several species of birds of prey.

METHODS

American Kestrels, *Falco sparverius*, were obtained from nest-boxes in the Ithaca, New York, area and by trapping during fall migration. Individual juxtaposed cages, with plywood walls between, measured approximately 3 m x 6 m, with a sloping roof providing a height of 4-5.5 m. Each cage contained one male and one female. Day-old cockerels were provided once a day. Eggs were collected five days after the last egg of a clutch was laid. For artificial incubation, eggs were transferred to a still-air incubator (Schano 1969); temperature at the top of the eggs was maintained between 35.5° and 36.3° C. Eggs were turned approximately 180 degrees once every six hours. Concentrated mixtures of DDE, Aroclor 1254, or a combination were made up in a small volume of acetone to which sesame oil was added. These solutions were gently heated to evaporate the acetone and then brought up to the desired volumes. Dead cockerels were injected in the breast region with 0.2 ml of the oil, providing dietary concentrations of 3 ppm DDE, 10 ppm Aroclor, or 3 ppm DDE + 10 ppm Aroclor 1254. Feeding on the dosed food began in March and was continued until late August. Eggs and eggshells were weighed on a Mettler balance to the nearest 0.001 g. Shells were measured for breadth and length to the nearest 0.1 mm with a Mitutoyo No. 505-633 caliper. After careful washing and draining, shell thickness was measured to the nearest 0.005 mm at the equator (four locations) with an Ames No. 255 ME thickness gauge. Determinations of Ratcliffe's index were made by dividing the weight of the dried eggshell (mg) by the length and breadth in millimeters (Ratcliffe 1970).

RESULTS

Eggshell Thickness. Ratcliffe's index was 13% and 16% lower in the groups fed DDE and DDE+PCB, respectively, than the index of the control group (Table 1; $P < 0.001$; '*t*' test); the difference between the two treatment groups was not significant ($P > 0.1$, 2-sided '*t*' test). Thickness index of the PCB group was 6.2% higher than that of the controls but the requirement of the '*t*' test for equal variances appears not to be met; $F = 2.56$, $P < 0.05$, (Table 1). The higher mean thickness of the PCB group may not therefore be significant.

Table 1. Changes in Ratcliffe's thickness index and shell thickness in eggs of Kestrels fed 3 ppm DDE, 10 ppm PCBs, 3 ppm DDE + 10 ppm PCBs, and a control diet.

	Control	DDE	PCBs	DDE+PCBs
Ratcliffe's index				
N	15	17	18	12
Mean, S.D.	0.920	0.799*	0.977	0.770*
	.050	.054	.080	.045
Thickness				
N	15	18	14	15
Mean, S.D.	0.171	0.145*	0.176	0.139*
	.013	.009	.015	.008

* Significantly different from control, $P < 0.001$

Breakage. No egg breakage occurred in the control (N=3), DDE (N=5), PCB (N=5; one nest had breakage attributable to other causes), but broken eggs were found in each of the DDE+PCB nests (N=5). This distribution has a very low probability (< 0.005) from a Chi-square analysis, but the low number of samples in the control group precludes a rigorous application of this test.

Artificial Incubation. Incubation conditions were imperfect, as indicated by the low rate of pipping and hatching of the control eggs (Table 2). However, none of the eggs of the DDE+PCB group hatched. No statistical significance can be attached to this observation because of the low hatching rate of the controls and the relatively small sample sizes, but a synergistic effect of DDE and PCB on hatchability is suggested.

Table 2. Pipping and hatching rates of artificially-incubated Kestrel eggs.

Diet	Eggs incubated	Eggs pipped	Eggs hatched
Control	11	6	4
DDE	20	6	5
PCBs	11	2	2
DDE+PCBs	7	0	–

DISCUSSION

In wild raptors, PCBs have almost always been associated with DDE and with lesser amounts of other organochlorines (i.e. Lincer 1972; Lincer & Clark 1978; Risebrough *et al.* 1968; Fiuczynski & Wendland 1968; Prestt *et al.* 1970; Peakall & Lincer 1970). Most laboratory studies of effects of PCBs on avian reproduction, however, have not addressed synergistic effects with other environmental chemicals. Risebrough & Anderson (1975) found that Mallards, *Anas platyrhynchos,* fed a combination of DDE and Aroclor 1254 produced fewer eggs than ducks on control, DDE, or PCB diets and also showed a higher incidence of egg eating. Thickness index of eggs of the DDE+PCB group was lower than that of the DDE group, but the differences were not statistically significant.

It is apparent that the role synergistic effects of DDE and PCBs may have had in the population declines of several raptor species in the 1950s-1970s has not been adequately addressed with the appropriate follow-up experiments; the data presented here suggest that it may have been significant.

ACKNOWLEDGEMENTS

The studies were undertaken in partial fulfillment of a doctoral program at Cornell University (Lincer 1972) under the direction of Professor T.J. Cade. I thank Dr. Cade for his encouragement and assistance, and Dr. David P. Peakall for helpful comments on this manuscript.

Jeffrey L. Lincer
BioSystems Analysis, Inc.
5355 Mira Sorrento Place, #100
San Diego, CA 92121, USA

Meyburg, B.-U. & R. D. Chancellor eds.1994
Raptor Conservation Today
WWGBP / The Pica Press

Relationship of DDE to Productivity of Bald Eagles *Haliaeetus leucocephalus* in California and Arizona, USA

I.C.T. Nisbet & R.W. Risebrough

ABSTRACT

Analysis of the relationships between the DDE concentrations in unhatched eggs of Bald Eagles in California/Arizona in 1984-1991 and estimated productivities showed a significant S-shaped dose response. Productivity was not affected by DDE concentrations below 9-12 ppm wet weight, but declined sharply above 12 ppm. This critical level of sensitivity to DDE is higher than that (5.8 ppm) found in an earlier analysis of Bald Eagles from other parts of the USA in 1969-79, but statistical significance could not be shown with the available sample size. The difference, however, suggests that an additional factor may have been operating in the earlier period.

INTRODUCTION

Wiemeyer *et al.* (1984) and Nisbet (1989) analyzed the relationships between productivity in Bald Eagles *Haliaeetus leucocephalus* and organochlorine contaminants, using data compiled by Wiemeyer *et al.* (1984) for eight regions of North America between 1969 and 1979. They found that reduced productivity in this species was most closely associated with egg residues of DDE. However, they were unable to exclude the possibility that other contaminants may have contributed to reproductive failure in this species, in part because of intercorrelations among the residue levels of the various contaminants.

One approach to resolving this issue is to examine other sets of data on the same species. By analyzing data from other geographical areas or later periods, it may be possible to find data sets with different patterns of residue levels of the various contaminants. This paper reports on productivity and egg residue levels of DDE in Bald Eagles nesting in California and Arizona between 1984 and 1991. The specific hypothesis tested is whether the relationship between productivity and DDE in this area and in this time period is the same as that found in the data of Wiemeyer *et al.* 10-15 years earlier and in different parts of North America. If not, the difference will suggest that other factor(s) were operating in one or both of the populations.

MATERIALS AND METHODS

We used the data set compiled by Jenkins *et al.* (this volume). Included in Table 1 of that paper are all of the productivity data used to derive the estimate of mean productivity for each nesting area. The three critical samples from Santa Catalina Island were assigned productivity estimates of zero, since eggs either broke in the nest or embryos died during artificial incubation. When more than one egg was obtained from a site, DDE, water, and lipid contents were averaged. Samples from Horse Mesa, Pit 3 and Pit 6, containing advanced embryos or chicks near hatch, were not used in the final analysis. The two samples from Packer's Bay, separated by 7 years, were considered as two values. The O'Brien sample, a chick near hatch, contained 280 ppm DDE lipid weight, 15.4 ppm wet weight. Although lipid content was relatively high (5.5%), DDE was estimated conservatively as 8 ppm to account for changes during incubation. The Almanor egg contained 37 ppm wet weight, but water content was low. The estimated wet weight was derived from the mean percent lipid, 7.3 % (Jenkins *et al.*, this volume). No correction was made for water loss in the remaining samples; water content was greater than 75% in all but one, the egg from Chino. The sample selected consisted therefore of 6 territories in Arizona, 12 territories in northern California, and 3 on Santa Catalina Island (Figure 1).

We fitted the data to the linear regression model

$$P^K = a + b(1 + DDE^n/c^n)^{-1},$$

where P = mean productivity, DDE is the concentration of DDE in the sample egg, a and b are regression parameters to be determined, and k, c and n are parameters defining the S-shaped dose-response function. Values of k, c and n were explored systematically until the explained variance R^2 was maximized. This procedure is the same as that used by Nisbet (1989) for the 1969-79 data set; the parameter values obtained by Nisbet for this data set were k = 1.4, c = 3.8, n = 20. The resulting curve, shown in Figure 1, drops sharply in the DDE range around 3.8 ppm.

Figure 1. Productivity of Bald Eagles in California/Arizona in 1984-91 vs. the DDE concentrations in egg contents. Dashed line: California-Arizona data set of this paper; solid line: derived by Nisbet (1989) for data set of Wiemeyer *et al.* (1984).

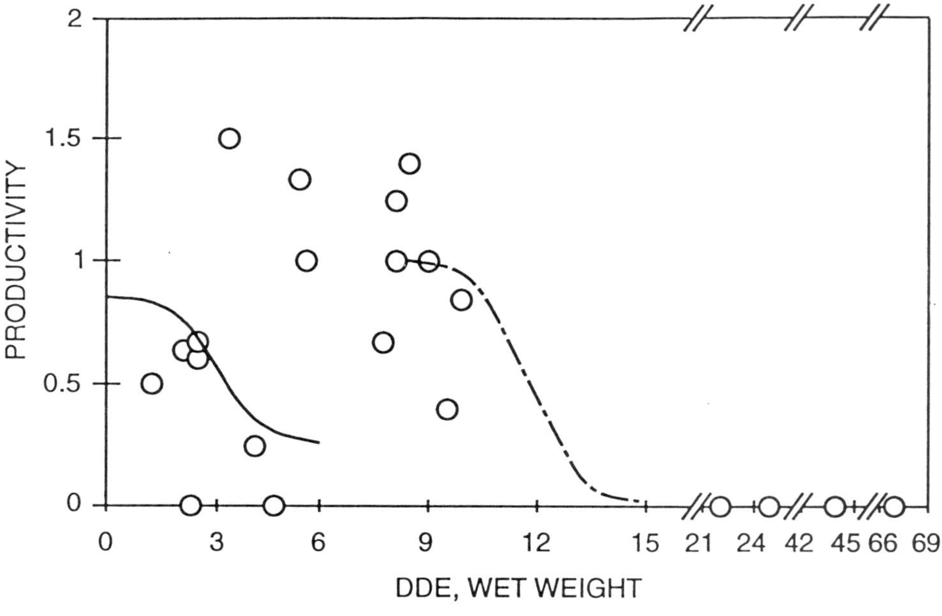

RESULTS AND DISCUSSION

Our analysis of the 1984-91 California/Arizona data set fixed a value of k = 1; this parameter has the greatest influence on the predicted productivity at DDE = 0. The best fit to the regression model was obtained with c = 12, n = 18 (R^2 = 0.362, P = 0.004). Lower values of k increased values of R^2. This result is consistent with earlier findings (Nisbet 1989) that reduced productivity in Bald Eagles is significantly associated with egg residues of DDE, and that the dose-response relationship is S-shaped (Figure 1).

Our curve for the 1984-91 data set has an inflection point at DDE = 12 ppm, whereas that for the 1969-79 set has an inflection point at DDE = 3.8 ppm. On the null hypothesis that there is no difference in distribution between the California/Arizona data and the 1969-79 data, there is an equal probability that the points corresponding to these eggs would fall above or below the 1969-79 regression line. Seven of the points fall below this line, 14 above (or have DDE > 14 ppm). The null hypothesis for this sample size can not be rejected ($P > 0.10$, chi-square test). A larger sample size would be needed to provide a critical test of the hypothesis.

The difference between the two critical values suggests that an additional factor (either independent of or correlated with DDE) contributed to reduced productivity in the 1969-79 data set. Possible candidates for such a factor include another contaminant (e.g., PCBs or oxychlordane), an interaction between DDE and another contaminant, or a residual effect of the birds' exposure to higher DDE levels in the years before 1969. Oxychlordane was the contaminant most strongly associated (after DDE) with reduced productivity in the 1969-79 data set (Nisbet 1989). However, data on oxychlordane levels, as well as of PCBs and the other organochlorines, in the California/Arizona eggs are not yet available. PCBs were highly correlated with DDE in the 1969-1979 data set (Wiemeyer *et al.*, 1984) such that a PCB effect, or a synergistic DDE-PCB effect, may not have been detectable. The residual effect hypothesis might be testable if data were available for an identifiable pair during a period of DDE decline.

In spite of our failure to demonstrate statistical significance, the data nevertheless provide support for a hypothesis that DDE was not the only contributor to the reproductive failures experienced by Bald Eagles in earlier years.

ACKNOWLEDGEMENTS

We wish to acknowledge J.M. Jenkins, R.M. Jurek, D.K. Garcelon, R. Mesta, W.G. Hunt and D.E. Driscoll as co-workers in this project, and thank them for their assistance.

Ian C.T. Nisbet
I.C.T. Nisbet & Company
72 Codman Road
Lincoln MA 01773, USA

Robert W. Risebrough
The Bodega Bay Institute
2711 Piedmont Avenue
Berkeley, CA 94705, USA

Meyburg, B.-U. & R. D. Chancellor eds.1994
Raptor Conservation Today
WWGBP / The Pica Press

Suspected poisoning of Golden Eagles *Aquila chrysaetos* by Chlorophacinone

H. J. Peeters

Eight pairs of Golden Eagles, *Aquila chrysaetos*, are resident in a 35 km^2 area in Southern Alameda County, California, that is part of the watershed of the San Francisco Water Department. They feed primarily on ground squirrels *Spermophilus beecheyi,* perceived by cattle ranchers as agricultural pests. The author has studied the population since 1984.

In early June, 1990, chlorophacinone, an anticoagulant rodenticide, was applied in the form of poison-coated oat groat by ranchers and County personnel in an effort to reduce the squirrel population. During the following week, numerous squirrel carcasses as well as occasional staggering or crawling moribund individuals were found on the grassy slopes of the treated range. Deer Mice, *Peromyscus maniculatus*, a non-target species, were also found dead; several were found partially consumed in squirrel burrows.

On June 19, 1990, an eagle pair was observed leading two recently fledged young, a male and a female, into the treated area. The adult eagles were seen carrying dead squirrels to the fledgling young. Partially consumed squirrels under a roosting tree, some with bait kernels adhering to their flesh, showed evidence of poisoning. Tissues, particularly subdermal fat, had a bright blue coloration derived from a tracer pigment added to the poison bait; the muscles of dead animals had a characteristic pale appearance.

On June 25, the young female eagle was found sitting on the ground, appearing unwell; her feathers were fluffed up despite the warm weather, and her wings drooped. She flew with difficulty from a hilltop to a bluff about 75 yards away and there lay down exposed to a strong wind and intense sunlight. On June 27, the young male was found dead, as was the fledgling female on June 28. The crop of the female showed extensive hemorrhaging; the pectoral muscles, deficient in blood, were extremely pallid. The male was not examined. The adult male eagle was last seen on June 25 and is presumed to have died also. The old female was still alive and apparently well on August 30, but disappeared from the territory in late fall.

With the appearance of dead and dying ground squirrels, 20-30 Turkey Vultures, *Cathartes aura*, moved into the area and fed on poisoned squirrel carcasses over a two-week period without apparent ill effect; no carcasses were found during frequent searches. Likewise, Red-tailed Hawks, *Buteo jamaicensis*, both adults and fledglings, fed on the carcasses and appeared unharmed three weeks later.

In a study of the effects of chlorophacinone on captive American Kestrels, *Falco sparverius*, Radvanyi *et al.* (1988) reported that juvenile kestrels were more severely affected than adults by directly administered chlorophacinone, and that kestrels fed poisoned mice hemorrhaged in one or more organs. Other physical and behavioral changes in treated birds included loss of balance, decreased flying ability, diarrhea, loss of appetite and conspicuous wing-drooping. In these kestrels, chlorophacinone dosages as small as one-third that required to kill a meadow vole *Microtus sp.* sufficed to bring on behavioral and gross pathological changes and death. The authors suggested that wild kestrels would suffer sublethal secondary poisoning or death if they consumed one poisoned mouse daily for three weeks.

Reporting on secondary poisoning of owls by anticoagulant biocides, Mendenhall and Pank (1980) found that the related rodenticide diphacinone was toxic to Great-horned, *Bubo virginianus*, and Saw-whet Owls, *Aegolius acadicus*, but not to Barn Owls, *Tyto alba*, and that owls fed on chlorophacinone showed "no abnormalities". Consumption of diphacinone-laced mutton caused sublethal hemorrhaging in Golden Eagles, producing weakness and increased prothrombin (Savarie *et al.* 1979). At the University of California at Santa Cruz, during two-week periods following squirrel-poisoning campaigns in 1979 that used both chlorophacinone and diphacinone, non-target species that were found dead included seven Great-horned Owls, one Barn Owl, one Red-tailed Hawk, one Coyote, *Canis latrans*, two Badgers, *Taxidea taxus*, one Striped Skunk, *M. mephitis*, and one Bobcat, *Lynx rufa* (B.J. Walton, pers. comm.).

These observations indicate that laboratory feeding experiments may not necessarily predict effects in the wild; they suggest that chlorophacinone and diphacinone can have profoundly different effects not only on different taxa but even on different age groups within a species. Even closely related genera, such as *Aquila* and *Buteo*, may show totally different effects after ingestion of poisoned animals. The apparent lack of toxicity of chlorophacinone to Turkey vultures thus does not guarantee, for example, that chlorophacinone will be equally harmless to the California Condor, *Gymnogyps californianus*, which is currently being re-introduced into a ground squirrel-rich environment.

Any program using these anticoagulant rodenticides should therefore be considered potentially hazardous to local raptors.

Clearly, application procedures should be strictly controlled and the local raptor populations closely monitored for deleterious effects. The observations of the present study suggest that any carcass found be examined for evidence of hemorrhaging and for abnormally pale musculature that would indicate a blood deficiency.

ACKNOWLEDGEMENTS

I thank E. Stewart, G. Lester, and F. Marino of the San Francisco Water Department for their assistance throughout the project.

H.J. Peeters
Department of Biology, Chabot College
Hayward, CA 94549-5001

Meyburg, B.-U. & R. D. Chancellor eds.1994
Raptor Conservation Today
WWGBP / The Pica Press

The Peregrines *Falco peregrinus* of Morro Rock

Brian J. Walton

Dr. Hickey's symposium in Madison in 1965 (Hickey 1969) both documented population declines of several raptor species and stimulated a generation of research activities devoted to finding out the causes of these unprecedented events. In California and Baja California studies of Peregrine Falcons, *Falco peregrinus,* lead to the detection of PCBs in the North American environment (Risebrough *et al.* 1968) and documented a population decline that exceeded 90% (Herman *et al.* 1970). The peregrines of California appeared to be following the populations in eastern North America into extinction.

One site that was consistently active in those years was Morro Rock on the south central coast. This high offshore rock adjacent to an estuary is a magnet for peregrines. As at a number of other sites in southern California, the peregrines of Morro Rock continue to show a high level of shell thinning and of DDE contamination. This year, 1992, will be the last year in which eggs will be removed for artificial incubation to be replaced by captive-reared young (Walton & Thelander 1988; Linthicum *et al.* this volume). These and other peregrines in Southern California will be the principal indicator of continuing environmental contamination. I have therefore assembled available data on productivity, both before and after manipulation, shell thinning, DDE residues, and turnover of the breeding birds to document the historical record and to provide the baseline for continuing monitoring activities.

The data (Table 1) indicate: 1) continuing severe shell thinning; 2) a surprisingly high variation in thinning between first and second clutch in two years (11.0 vs 22.8, 25.2 vs 11.4); 3) continuing high DDE contamination through the 1980s; 4) beginning in 1970, occupancies for females of 6, 11, and 5 years; 5) beginning in 1969 occupancies for males of 4 (minimum), 5, 9, 2, and 4 (minimum) years.

Lloyd Kiff, Sam Sumida, Robert Risebrough, Walter Jarman, Stephanie Burns and Janet Linthicum provided unpublished data. I thank them and all of my other colleagues who have worked to ensure that peregrines will continue to be a part of the California environment.

Brian J. Walton
Santa Cruz Predatory Bird Research Group
University of California
Santa Cruz, CA 95064, USA

Table 1. The Peregrine Falcons of Morro Rock, California, 1967-1992.

Year	(m,d)[a]	Eggs Laid	Young Fostered	Young Fledged	Eggs at PBRG[b] Incub.	Eggs at PBRG[b] Hatch	Thinning[c] 1st	Thinning[c] 2nd	DDE ppm dry	Notes
1967		Unkn	--	1+	--	--				
1968		Unkn	--	3	--	--				
1969		0	--	0	--	--			130[d]	Female died at egg laying
1970		0	--	0	--	--				New female
1971		Unkn	--	3	--	--				
1972		Unkn	--	0	--	--				
1973		0	--	0	--	--				New male
1974		Unkn	--	4	--	--				
1975		3	--	2	--	--				Female hit wire after breeding
1976		3	--	2	--	--	11.7	63		New female
1977	(m)	Unkn	2	1	0	--	17.1	130		Male shot after breeding season
1978	(m)	3	1	1	0	--	16.5	140		New male
1979	(m,d)	6	2	2	6	3	22.8	11.0	160	
1980	(m,d)	7	2	2	4	2	28.2	30.9	160	
1981	(m,d)	8	2	2	7	4	29.3	30.6	91	
1982	(m,d)	7	2	2	6	5	26.3	27.1		
1983	(m)	4	3	2	3	0	25.2	160		
1984	(m,d)	6	2	2	3	2	22.0	27.4		
1985	(m)	3	2	2	2	0	19.5			
1986	(m)	3	2	2	3	1	25.5			
1987	(m)	4	2	2	1	0	23.0			New male, new female
1988	(m)	5	2	2	4	2	11.4	25.2	61,150	
1989	(m)	3	2	2	2	0	26.3			
1990	(m)	4	1	1	3	1	24.7			
1991	(m)	1	2	2	1	0				
1992	(m)	4	2	2	4	0				New female

[a] m, manipulated; d, double-clutched
[b] Eggs brought to Santa Cruz for incubation included some that were later found to be dead
[c] Means of first and second clutches
[d] Estimated from concentration of yolk lipid of egg recovered from oviduct

REFERENCES

ADAMS, P.M. 1977. Effects of anticholinergic and cholinesterase blocking drugs on appetitive behavior under different deprivation conditions. *Life Sci.* 21:129-136.

AMBROSE, R.E., C.J. HENNY, R.E. HUNTER & J.A. CRAWFORD 1988a. Organochlorines in Alaskan Peregrine Falcon Eggs and their current impact on productivity. Pages 385-393 *in* T.J. Cade, J.H. Enderson, C.G. Thelander & C.M. White, eds. *Peregrine Falcon Populations: Their Management and Recovery.* The Peregrine Fund, Inc., Boise, Idaho.

AMBROSE, R.E., R.J. RITCHIE, C.M. WHITE, P.F. SCHEMPF, T. SWEM & R. DITTRICK 1988b. Changes in the status of Peregrine Falcon populations in Alaska. Pages 73-82 *in* T.J. Cade, J.H. Enderson, C.G. Thelander & C.M. White, eds. *Peregrine Falcon Populations: Their Management and Recovery.* The Peregrine Fund, Inc., Boise, Idaho.

ANDERSON, D.W. & F. HAMERSTROM 1967. The recent status of Wisconsin cormorants. *Passenger Pigeon* 29:3-15.

ANDERSON, D.W. & J.J. HICKEY 1972. Eggshell changes in certain North American birds. *Proc. Internat. Ornithol. Congr.* 15:514-540.

ANDERSON, D.W., J.R. JEHL, R.W. RISEBROUGH, L.A. WOODS, JR., L.R. DeWEESE & W.G. EDGECOMB 1975. Brown pelicans: improved reproduction off the southern California coast. *Science* 190:806-808.

ANTHONY, R.G., M.G. GARRETT & C.A. SCHULER 1993. Environmental contaminants in Bald Eagles in the Columbia River Estuary. *J. Wildl. Manage.* 57:10-19.

APPELQUIST, H., S. ASBIRK & I. DRABAEK 1984. Mercury monitoring: mercury stability in bird feathers. *Mar. Pollut. Bull.* 15:22-24.

APPELQUIST, H., I. DRABAEK & S. ASBIRK 1985. Variation in mercury content of guillemot feathers over 150 years. *Mar. Pollut. Bull.* 16:244-248.

AULERICH, R.J. & R.K. RINGER 1977. Current status of PCB toxicity to mink and effect on their young. *Arch. Environ. Contam. Toxicol.* 6:279-292.

BALCOMB, R., C.A. BOWEN, D. WRIGHT & M. LAW 1984. Effects on wildlife of at-planting corn applications of granular carbofuran. *J. Wildl. Manage.* 48:1353-1359.

BALTIC MARINE ENVIRONMENT PROTECTION COMMISSION 1990. *Second Periodic Assessment of the State of the Marine Environment of the Baltic Sea, 1984-1988.* Balt. Sea Environ. Proc. No. 35B. 432 pp.

BARCLAY, J.H. & T.J. CADE 1983. Restoration of the Peregrine Falcon in the eastern United States. *Bird Conserv.* 1:3-37.

BEARD, J. 1969. Massachusetts bird kill. *Smithsonian Event Report* 87-69. Smithsonian Institution. Washington, D.C., USA.

BELISLE, A.A., W.L. REICHEL, L.N. LOCKE, T.G. LAMONT, B.M. MULHERN, R.M. PROUTY, R.B. DEWOLF & E. CROMARTIE 1972. Residues of organochlorine pesticides, polychlorinated biphenyls, and mercury and autopsy data for Bald Eagles, 1969 and 1970. *Pestic. Monit. J.* 6:133-138.

BERG, W., A. JOHNELS, B. SJÖJSTRAND & T. WESTERMARK 1966. Mercury content in feathers of Swedish birds from the past 100 years. *Oikos* 17:71-83.

BERGER, D.D., C.R. SINDELAR, JR. & K.E. GAMBLE. 1969. The status of the breeding Peregrines of the eastern United States. Pages 165-173 *in* J.J. Hickey, ed. *Peregrine Falcon Populations: Their Biology and Decline.* Madison, Univ. of Wisconsin Press. 596 pp.

BESSER, J.F. & T.J. DeCINO 1963. *Progress Report in Laboratory and Field Tests with Bayer 29493 (DRC-632) for the Control of Urban Pest Birds.* U.S. Dept. Interior. Bureau Sport Fisheries & Wildlife. Denver, CO, USA.

BIESSMANN, A. 1982. Effects of PCBs on gonads, sex hormone balance and reproductive processes of Japanese quail *Coturnix coturnix japonica* after ingestion during sexual maturation. *Environ. Pollut.* (Ser. A) 27:15-30.

BILDSTEIN, K.L. & M.W. COLLOPY 1987. Hunting behavior of Eurasian (*Falco tinnunculus*) and American Kestrels (*F. sparverius*): a review. Pages 66-81 *in* D.M.Bird & R.Bowman, eds. *The Ancestral Kestrel.* Raptor Research Foundation, Inc. and Macdonald Raptor Research Centre of McGill University, Ste. Anne de Bellevue, Quebec, Canada.

BLAND, D. 1990. *The Relationship of Organic and Inorganic Components of Eggshells to DDE Content in Eggs of California Brown Pelicans and Bald Eagles.* M.Sc. Thesis. University of California Santa Cruz. 43 pp.

BLUS, L.J., C.D. GISH, A.A. BELISLE & R.M. PROUTY 1972. Logarithmic relationship of DDE residues to eggshell thinning. *Nature* 235:376-377.
BORG, K., H. WANNTORP, K. ERNE & E. HANKO 1969. Alkyl mercury poisoning in terrestrial Swedish wildlife. *Viltrevy* 6:301-379.
BOWERMAN, W.W., IV. 1991. *Factors Influencing Breeding Success of Bald Eagles in Upper Michigan.* M.A. Thesis, N. Mich. Univ., Marquette. 113 pp.
BOWERMAN IV, W.W., D.A. BEST, E.D. EVANS, S. POSTUPALSKY, M.S. MARTELL, K.D. KOZIE, R.L. WELCH, R.H. SCHEEL, K.F. DURLING, J.C. ROGERS, T.J. KUBIAK, D.E. TILLITT, T.R. SCHWARTZ, P.D. JONES & J.P. GIESY 1990. PCB concentrations in plasma of nestling Bald Eagles from the Great Lakes Basin, North America. Pages 212-216 *in* H. Fiedler & O. Hutzinger, eds. *10th Intl. Conf. on Organohalogen Compounds, Bayreuth, Germany*, Vol. IV.
BOWES, G.W., M.J. MULVIHILL, B.R. SIMONEIT, A.L. BURLINGAME & R.W. RISEBROUGH 1975. Identification of chlorinated dibenzofurans in American polychlorinated biphenyls. *Nature* 256:305-307.
BRITTON, W.M. & T.M. HUSTON 1973. Influence of polychlorinated biphenyls in the laying hen. *Poultry Sci.* 52:1620-1624.
BRUGGERS, R.L., M.M. JAEGGER, J.O. KEITH, P.L. HEGDAL, J.B. BOURASSA, A.A. LATIGO & J.N. GILLIS 1989. Impact of fenthion on nontarget birds during Quelea control in Kenya. *Wildl. Soc. Bull.* 17:149-160.
BRUNSTRÖM, B. 1988. Sensitivity of embryos from duck, goose, Herring Gull, and various chicken breeds to 3,3',4,4'-tetrachlorobiphenyl. *Poultry Science* 67:52-57.
BRUNSTRÖM, B. 1989. Toxicity of coplanar polychlorinated biphenyls in avian embryos. *Chemosphere* 19:765-768.
BRUNSTRÖM, B. & L. REUTERGÅRDH 1986. Differences in sensitivity of some avian species to the embryotoxicity of a PCB, 3,3',4,4'- tetrachlorobiphenyl, injected into the eggs. *Environ. Pollut. Ser.* A. 42:37-45.
BRUNSTRÖM, B. & L. ANDERSSON 1988. Toxicity and 7-ethoxyresorufin-o-deethylase-inducing potency of coplanar polychlorinated biphenyls in chick embryos. *Arch. Toxicol.* 62:263-266.
BURNHAM, W.A. 1983. Artificial incubation of falcon eggs. *J. Wildl. Manage.* 47:158-168.
BURTON, D.K. & B.J.R. PHILOGÈNE 1986. *An Overview of Pesticide Usage in Latin America.* Canadian Wildlife Service Latin American Program; Report on Contract OST85-00181 Canadian Wildlife Service, Ottawa.
BUSH, B., C.F. TUMASONIS & F.D. BAKER 1974. Toxicity and persistence of PCB homologs and isomers in the avian system. *Arch. Environ. Contam. Toxicol.* 2:195-212.
CADE, T.J., J.L. LINCER, C.M. WHITE, D.G. ROSENEAU & L.G. SWARTZ. 1971. DDE residues and eggshell changes in Alaskan falcons and hawks. *Science* 172:955-957.
CADE, T.J., J.H. ENDERSON, C.G. THELANDER & C.M. WHITE, eds. 1988. *Peregrine Falcon Populations: Their Management and Recovery*. The Peregrine Fund, Inc., Boise, Idaho. 949 pp.
CANADIAN WILDLIFE SERVICE 1988. *Anatum Peregrine Falcon Recovery Plan.* Department of the Environment. Ottawa, Canada.
CANTRELL, J.S., N.C. WEBB & A.J. MABIS 1969. The identification and crystal structure of a hydropericardium-producing factor: 1,2,3,7,8,9,-hexachloro-dibenzo-p-dioxin. *Acta Cryst* 25:150-154.
CECIL, H.C., J. BITMAN, R.J. LILLIE, G.F. FRIES & J. VERRETT 1974. Embryotoxic and teratogenic effects in unhatched fertile eggs from hens fed polychlorinated biphenyls (PCBs). *Bull. Environ. Contam. Toxicol.* 11:489-495.
COHN, M.L., N. VENKATESAN & S.J. COHN 1981. Neurological effects of chlorinated hydrocarbons. Pages 243-256 *in* M.A.Q. Khan & R.H. Stanton, eds. *Toxicology of Halogenated Hydrocarbons: Health and Ecological Effects*. Pergamon, New York.
COOKE, A.S. 1979. Changes in egg shell characteristics of the Sparrowhawk (*Accipiter nisus*) and Peregrine (*Falco peregrinus*) associated with exposure to environmental pollutants during recent decades. *J. Zool., Lond.* 187:245-263.
COOKE, A.S., A.A. BELL & M.B. HAAS 1982. *Predatory birds, Pesticides and Pollution.* NERC, Swindon. 74 pp.
COSTA, L.G. & S.D. MURPHY 1982. Passive avoidance retention in mice tolerant to the organophosphorus insecticide disulfoton. *Toxicol. Appl. Pharmacol.* 65:451-458.
CROMARTIE, E., W.L. REICHEL, L.N. LOCKE, A.A. BELISLE, T.E. KAISER, T.G. LAMONT,

B.M. MULHERN, R.M. PROUTY & D.M. SWINEFORD 1975. Residues of organochlorine pesticides and polychlorinated biphenyls and autopsy data for bald eagles, 1971-72. *Pestic. Monit.* J. 9:11-14.

DeWEESE, L.R., L.C. McEWEN, L.A. SETTINI & R.D. BLINGER 1983. Effects on birds of fenthion aerial applications for mosquito control. *J. Econ. Entomol.* 76:906-911.

DOI, R. & Y. FUKUYAMA 1983. Metal content in feathers of wild and zoo-kept birds from Hokkaido, 1976-78. *Bull. Environ. Contam. Toxicol.* 31:1-8.

DOI, R., H. OHNO & M. HARADA 1984. Mercury in feathers of wild birds from the mercury-polluted area along the shore of the Shiranai Sea. Japan. *Sci. Total Environ.* 40:155-167.

DOMINICK, H.J., T.F. LONG, C.C. MUDGETT, F.L. RIECKS & M.C. VASSMER 1989. *Four Episodes of Apparent Poisoning of Raptors* by an Avicide, Fenthion, in Illinois. Illinois Department of Public Health, Springfield, IL.

DOUTHWAITE, R.J. 1992. Effects of DDT treatments applied for tsetse fly control on White-headed Black Chat (*Thamnolaea arnoti*) populations in Zimbabwe. Part I: population changes. *Ecotoxicology* 1:17-30.

EISLER, R 1985. Carbofuran Hazards to Fish, Wildlife, and Invertebrates: a Synoptic Review. *U.S. Fish Wildl. Serv. Biol. Rep.* 85(1.3). 36 pp.

ELDER, J.B. & C. HENDERSON 1969. *Pesticide Field Appraisal. Field Appraisal of ULV Baytex Mosquito Control Applications on Fish and Wildlife.* US Bur. Sport Fish Wildl., Ohio Dep. Nat. Res. Spec. Rep. 71 pp.

ELLIOTT, J.E., R.J. NORSTROM, & J.A. KEITH 1988. Organochlorines and eggshell thinning in Northern Gannets (*Sula bassanus*). *Environ. Pollut.* 52:81-102.

ENVIRONMENT CANADA, DEPARTMENT OF FISHERIES AND OCEANS & HEALTH AND WELFARE CANADA 1991a. Effects of Contaminants on Wildlife species. Pages 555-637 in *Toxic Chemicals in the Great Lakes and Associated Effects. Volume II: Effects.* Minister of Supply and Services Canada. Ottawa.

ENVIRONMENT CANADA, DEPARTMENT OF FISHERIES AND OCEANS & HEALTH AND WELFARE CANADA 1991b. Concentrations of Contaminants in Wildlife Species. Pages 311-392 in *Toxic Chemicals in the Great Lakes and Associated Effects. Volume I: Contaminant Levels and Trends.* Minister of Supply and Services Canada. Ottawa.

FALANDYSZ, J. 1980. Chlorinated hydrocarbons in gulls from the Baltic south coast. *Mar. Pollut. Bull.* 11:75-80.

FALANDYSZ, J. 1984. Metals and organochlorines in a female White-tailed Eagle from Uznam Island, southwestern Baltic Sea. *Environ. Conserv.* 11:262-263.

FALANDYSZ, J. 1986. Metals and organochlorines in adult and immature males of White-tailed Eagle. *Environ. Conserv.* 13:69-70.

FALANDYSZ, J. & P. SZEFER 1983. Metals and organochlorines in a specimen of White-tailed Eagle. *Environ. Conserv.* 10:256-258.

FALANDYSZ, J., B. JAKUCZUN & T. MIZERA 1988. Metals and organochlorines in four female White-tailed Eagles. *Mar. Pollut. Bull.* 19:521-526.

FIUCZYNSKI, D. 1983. Heavy metals in Berlin raptors (*Aves: Falconiformes*) and their food. Pages 827-829 *in* Vol. 2, *Intern. Conf. Heavy Metals in the Environment.* CEP Consultants, Inc. Edinburgh.

FIUCZYNSKI, V.D. & V. WENDLAND 1968. Zur Populationsdynamik des Schwarzen Milans (*Milvus migrans*) in Berlin Beobachtungen 1952-1967. *J. Ornithologie* 109:462-471.

FLICK, D.F., R.G. O'DELL & V.A. CHILDS 1965. Studies of the chick edema disease. 3. Similarity of symptoms produced by feeding chlorinated biphenyl. *Poultry Science* 44:1460-1465.

FLICKINGER, E.L., KING K.A, W.F. STOUT & M.M. MOHN 1980. Wildlife hazards from Furadan 3G applications to rice in Texas. *J. Wildl. Manage.* 44:190-197.

FORBIS, L.A. 1988. Status and trends of Bald Eagles breeding in Arizona, 1975-1986. Pages 282-288 *in* R.L. Glinski *et al.*, eds. *Proceedings of the Southwest Raptor Management Symposium and Workshop.* National Wildlife Federation, Washington, D.C. 395 pp.

FOX, G. 1976. Eggshell quality: Its ecological and physiological significance in a DDE-contaminated tern population. *Wilson Bull.* 88:459-477.

FOX, G.A. & T. DONALD 1980. Organochorine pollutants, nest defense behavior and reproductive success in Merlins. *Condor* 82:81-84.

FOX, G.A., A.P. GILMAN, D.B. PEAKALL & F.W. ANDERKA 1978. Behavioral abnormalities of nesting Lake Ontario Herring Gulls. *J. Wildl. Manage.* 42:477-483.

FRANCIS, J.I. & J.M. BARNES 1963. Studies on the mammalian toxicity of fenthion. *Bull. WHO* 29:205-212.

FURNESS, R.W., J.L. JOHNSTON, J.A. LOVE & D.R. THOMPSON 1989. Pollutant burdens and reproductive success of Golden Eagles *Aquila chrysaetos* exploiting marine and terrestrial food webs in Scotland. Pages 495-500 *in* B.-U. Meyburg & R.D. Chancellor, eds. *Raptors in the Modern World.* World Working Group on Birds of Prey. Berlin, London & Paris.

FYFE, R.W., R.W. RISEBROUGH & W. WALKER II 1976. Pollutant effects on the reproduction of the Prairie Falcons and Merlins of the Canadian prairies. *Can. Field-Nat.* 90:346-355.

GALUSHIN, V. M. 1977. Recent changes in the actual and legislative status of birds of prey in the U.S.S.R. Pages 152-159 *in* R.D. Chancellor, ed. *World Conference on Birds of Prey, Vienna, 1-3 October, 1975:* Report of Proceedings. International Council for Bird Preservation. London. xii, 442 pp.

GANUSEVICH, S. A. 1988. Raptors on the Kolsky Peninsula. *Ornitologiya* 23:73-80.

GARCELON, D.K., R.W. RISEBROUGH, W.M. JARMAN, A.B. CHARTRAND & E.E. LITTRELL 1989. Accumulation of DDE by Bald Eagles *Haliaeetus leucocephalus* reintroduced to Santa Catalina Island in southern California. Pages 491-494 *in* B.-U. Meyburg and R.D. Chancellor, eds., *Raptors in the Modern World.* Proceedings of the III World Conference on Birds of Prey and Owls. World Working Group on Birds of Prey and Owls. Berlin, London and Paris. 611 pp.

GESELL, G.G., R.J. ROBEL, A.D. DAYTON & J. FRIEMAN 1979. Effects of dieldrin on operant behavior of Bobwhites. *J. Environ. Sci. Health* B14:153-170.

GILBERTSON, M., R.D. MORRIS & R.A. HUNTER 1976. Abnormal chicks and PCB residue levels in eggs of colonial birds on the lower Great Lakes (1971-73). *Auk* 93:434-442.

GILBERTSON, M., T.J. KUBIAK, J.P. LUDWIG & G.A. Fox 1991. Great Lakes embryo mortality, edema, and deformities syndrome (GLEMEDS) in colonial fish-eating birds: Similarity to chick-edema disease. *J. Tox. Environ. Health.* 33:455-520.

GILROY, M.J. & J.H. BARCLAY 1988. DDE residues and eggshell characteristics of reestablished Peregrines in the eastern United States. Pages 403-411 *in* T.J. Cade, J.H. Enderson, C.G. Thelander & C.M. White, eds. *Peregrine Falcon Populations: Their Management and Recovery.* The Peregrine Fund, Inc., Boise, ID. 949 pp.

GOEDE, A.A. & M. de BRUIN 1984. The use of bird feather parts as a monitor for metal pollution. *Environ. Pollut.* (Ser. B) 8:281-298.

GOEDE, A.A. & M. de BRUIN 1986. The use of bird feathers for indicating heavy metal pollution. *Environ. Monit. Assess.* 7:249-256.

GRIER, J.W. 1968. Immature Bald Eagle with an abnormal beak. *Bird Banding* 39:58-59.

GRIER, J.W. 1979. Caution on using productivity or age ratios alone for population inferences. *Raptor Res.* 13:20-24.

GRIER, J.W. 1980. Modeling approaches to Bald Eagle population dynamics. *Wildl. Soc. Bull.* 8:316-322.

GRIER, J.W. 1991. Population modeling: An introduction and overview. Pages 134-157 *in Proc. Midwest Raptor Manage. Symp. and Workshop. National Wildl. Federation Scientific and Technical Series No. 15.* Washington DC.

GRUBB, T.G., S.N. WIEMEYER & L.F. KIFF 1990. Eggshell thinning and contaminant levels in Bald Eagle eggs from Arizona, 1977 to 1985. *Southwestern Naturalist* 35:298-301.

GRUE, C.E. 1982. Response of Common Grackles to dietary concentrations of four organophosphate pesticides. *Arch. Environ. Contam. Toxicol.* 11:617-626.

GRUE, C.E., W.J. FLEMING, D.G. BUSBY & E.F. HILL 1983. Assessing hazards of organophosphate pesticides to wildlife. *Trans. North Am. Wildl. Nat. Res. Conf.* 48:200-220.

GRUE, C.E., A.D.M. HART & P. MINEAU 1991. Biological consequences of depressed brain cholinesterase activity in wildlife. Pages 151-209 *in* P. Mineau, ed. *Cholinesterase-inhibiting Insecticides: Their impact on Wildlife and the Environment. Chemicals in Agriculture, Vol. 2.* Elsevier, New York.

HAEGELE, M.A. & R.H. HUDSON 1973. DDE effects on reproduction of ring doves. *Environ. Pollut.* 4:53-57.

HAEGELE, M.A. & R.H. HUDSON 1977. Reduction of courtship behavior induced by DDE in male Ringed Turtle Doves. *Wilson Bull.* 89:593-601.

HANSON, J. & J. HOWELL 1981. Possible fenthion toxicity in magpies (*Pica pica*). *Can. Vet. J.* 22:18-19.

HAYS, H. & R.W. RISEBROUGH 1972. Pollutant concentrations in abnormal young terns from Long Island Sound. *Auk* 89: 19-35.

HEATH, R.G. 1969. Nationwide residues of organochlorine pesticides in wings of Mallards and Black Ducks. *Pestic. Monit. J.* 3:115-123.

HEATH, R.G. & S.A. HILL 1974. Nationwide organochlorine and mercury residues in wings of adult Mallards and Black Ducks during the 1969-70 hunting season. *Pestic. Monit. J.* 7:153-164.

HEATH, R.G., J.W. SPANN, J.F. KREITZER & C. VANCE 1972. Effects of polychlorinated biphenyls on birds. *Proc. Intern. Ornithol. Congr.* 15:475-481.

HEINZ, G.H., E.F. HILL & J.F. CONTRERA 1980. Dopamine and norepinephrine depletion in ring doves fed DDE, dieldrin, and Aroclor 1254. *Toxicol. Appl. Pharmacol.* 53:75-82.

HEINZ, G.H., D.M. SWINEFORD & D.E. KATSMA 1984. High PCB residues in birds from the Sheboygan River, Wisconsin. *Environ. Monit. Assess.* 4:155-161.

HELANDER, B. 1983. *Reproduction of the White-tailed Sea Eagle Haliaeetus albicilla (L.) in Sweden, in Relation to Food and Residue Levels of Organochlorine and Mercury Compounds in the Eggs.* Ph.D. Dissertation, University of Stockholm.

HELANDER, B. 1983. *Sea Eagle -- Experimental Studies: Artificial Incubation of White-tailed Sea Eagle Eggs 1978-1980 and the Rearing and Introduction to the Wild of an Eaglet.* Report snv pm 1386. Nat. Swedish Environ. Protection Board. Solna.

HELANDER, B. 1985. Reproduction of the White-tailed Sea Eagle *Haliaeetus albicilla* in Sweden. *Holarctic Ecol.* 8:211-227.

HELANDER, B. 1988. Den svenska havsörnsstammens utveckling - en tillbakablick. Pages 86-91 *in* P. Gerdhag & B. Helander *Havsörn.* Bonniers. Stockholm. (in Swedish)

HELANDER, B., M. OLSSON & L. REUTERGÄRDH 1982. Residue levels of organochlorine and mercury compounds in unhatched eggs and the relationships to breeding success in White-tailed Sea Eagles *Haliaeetus albicilla* in Sweden. *Holarctic Ecol.* 5:349-366.

HENDERSON, B.M. & R.W. WINTERFIELD 1975. Acute copper toxicosis in the Canada Goose. *Avian Diseases* 19:385-387.

HENNY, C.J. 1972. *An Analysis of the Population Dynamics of Selected Avian Species.* Wildl. Res. Rpt. 1., U.S. Bureau of Sport Fisheries and Wildlife.. Washington D.C. 99 pp.

HENNY, C.J., F.P. WARD, K.E. RIDDLE & R.M. PROUTY 1982. Migratory Peregrine Falcons, *Falco peregrinus*, accumulate pesticides in Latin America during winter. *Can. Field-Nat.* 96:333-338.

HENNY, C.J., E.J. KOLBE, E.F. HILL & L.J. BLUS 1987. Case histories of Bald Eagle and other raptors killed by organophosphorous insecticides topically applied to livestock. *J. Wildl. Dis.* 23:292-295.

HERMAN, S.G., M.N. KIRVEN & R.W. RISEBROUGH 1970. The Peregrine Falcon decline in California: I. A preliminary review. *Aud. Field Notes* 24:609-613.

HICKEY, J.J. (Ed.) 1969. *Peregrine Falcon Populations: Their Biology and Decline.* Madison, Univ. of Wisconsin Press., 596 pp.

HICKEY, J.J. & L.B. HUNT 1960a. Initial song bird mortality following Dutch elm disease control program. *J. Wildl. Manage.* 24:259-265.

HICKEY, J.J. & L.B. HUNT 1960b. Songbird mortality following annual programs to control Dutch elm disease. *Atl. Nat.* 15:87-92.

HIGGINBOTHAM, G.R., A. HUANG, D. FIRESTONE, J. VERRETT, J. RESS & A.D. CAMPBELL 1968. Chemical and toxicological evaluations of isolated and synthetic chloroderivatives of dibenzo-*p*-dioxins. *Nature* 220:702-703.

HILL, E.F. 1972. Avoidance of lethal dietary concentrations of insecticides by House Sparrows. *J. Wildl. Manage.* 36:635-639.

HILL, E.F., R.G. HEATH, J.W. SPANN & J.D. WILLIAMS 1975. *Lethal Dietary Toxicities of Environmental Pollutants to Birds.* US Fish Wildl. Serv. Spec. Sci. Rep. Wildl. No. 191. 61 pp. Washington, D.C.

HOFFMAN, D.J., B.A. RATTNER, L. SILEO, D. DOCHERTY & T.J. KUBIAK 1987. Embryotoxicity, teratogenicity, and aryl hydrocarbon hydroxylase activity in Forster's Terns on Green Bay, Lake Michigan. *Environ. Res.* 42:176-184.

HUDSON, R.H., R.K. TUCKER & M.A. HAEGELE 1984. *Handbook of Toxicity of Pesticides to Wildlife.* 2nd ed. US Fish and Wildl. Serv. Resour. Publ. 153.

HUNT, K.A., D.M. BIRD, P. MINEAU & L. SHUTT 1991. Secondary poisoning hazard of fenthion to American Kestrels. *Arch. Environ. Contam. Toxicol.* 21:84-90.

HUNT, K.A., D.M. BIRD, P. MINEAU & L. SHUTT. Selective predation of organophosphate-exposed prey by American Kestrels. *Anim. Behav.* (in press).

HUNT, W.G., D.E. DRISCOLL, E.W. BIANCHI & R.E. JACKMAN 1992. *Ecology of Bald Eagles in Arizona.* Volumes I-IV. Report to U.S. Bureau of Reclamation. Contract 6-CS-30-04470. Biosystems Analysis, Inc., Santa Cruz CA 95060.

JACOBSON, S.W., G.G. FEIN, J.L. JACOBSON, P.M. SCHWARTZ & J.K. DOWLER 1985. The effect of intrauterine PCB exposure on visual recognition memory. *Child Dev.* 56:853-860.

JACOBSON, J.L., S.W. JACOBSON & H.E.B. HUMPHREY 1990a. Effects of exposure to PCBs and related compounds on growth and activity in children. *Neurotoxicol. Teratol.* 12:319-326.

JACOBSON, J.L., S.W. JACOBSON & H.E.B. HUMPHREY 1990b. Effects of *in utero* exposure to polychlorinated biphenyls and related contaminants on cognitive functioning in young children. *J. Pediatr.* 116:38-45.

JANSSEN, D.L., J.E. OOSTERHUIS, J.L. ALLEN, M.P. ANDERSON, D.G. KELTS & S.N. WIEMEYER 1986. Lead poisoning in free-ranging California Condors. *J. Amer. Veter. Med. Assoc.* 189:1115-1117.

JARMAN, W.M., R.J. NORSTROM, M. SIMON, S.A. BURNS, C.A. BACON & B.R.T. SIMONEIT 1993a. Organochlorines, including chlordane compounds and their metabolites in Peregrine Falcon, Prairie Falcon, and Clapper Rail eggs from the U.S.A. *Environ. Pollut.*, (in press).

JARMAN, W.M., S.A. BURNS, R.R. CHANG, R.D. STEPHENS, R.J. NORSTROM, M. SIMON & J. LINTHICUM 1993b. Determination of PCDDs, PCDFs, and PCBs in California Peregrine Falcons (*Falco peregrinus*) and their eggs. *Environ. Toxicol. Chem.*, (in press).

JENKINS, J.M. Modeling of a resident Bald Eagle population using empirical life table parameters. This volume.

JENSEN, S., A.G. JOHNELS, M. OLSSON & G. OTTERLIND 1969. DDT and PCB in marine animals from Swedish waters. *Nature* (London) 224:247-250.

JENSEN, S., A.G. JOHNELS, M. OLSSON & T. WESTERMARK 1972. The avifauna of Sweden as indicators of environmental contamination with mercury and chlorinated hydrocarbons. *Proc. Int. Ornithol. Congr.* 15:455-465. Leiden.

JENSEN, S., L. REUTERGÅRDH & B. JANSSON 1979. Analytical methods for measuring organochlorines and methylmercury by gas chromatography. *Seventh FAO-SIDA Workshop on Aquatic Pollution in Relation to Protection of Living Resources.* FAO Tech. Paper No. FIR: TPLR/79/4. 15 pp.

JUREK, R.M. 1990. *California Bald Eagle Breeding Population Survey and Trend, 1970-90.* State of California, Department of Fish and Game. Nongame Bird and Mammal Section Report. Sacramento. 16 pp., appendices.

KANNAN, K., J. FALANDYSZ, N. YAMASHITA, S. TANABE & R. TATSUKAWA 1992. Temporal trends of organochlorine concentrations in cod-liver oil from the southern Baltic proper, 1971-1989. *Mar. Pollut. Bull.* 24:358-363.

KEITH, L.H., W. CRUMMETT, J. EGAN Jr., R.A. LIBBY, J.K. TAYLOR & G. WENTLER 1983. Principles of environmental analysis. *Anal. Chem.* 55:2210-2218.

KELSALL, J.P. & R. BURTON 1979. Some problems in identification or origins of Lesser Snow Geese by chemical profiles. *Can. J. Zool.* 57:2292-2302.

KIFF, L.F. 1980. Historical changes in resident populations of California Islands raptors. Pages 651-673 *in* D.M. Power, ed. *The California Islands: Proceedings of a Multidisciplinary Symposium.* Santa Barbara Museum of Natural History. Santa Barbara.

KOBAYASHI, Y., A. SHIMADA, T. UMEMURA & T. NAGAI 1992. An outbreak of copper poisoning in Mute Swans (*Cygnus olor*). *J. Vet. Med. Sci.* 54:229-233.

KOEMAN, J.H., M.C. TEN NOEVER DE BRAUW & R.H. DE VOS 1969. Chlorinated biphenyls in fish, mussels and birds from the river Rhine and the Netherlands coastal area. *Nature* (London) 221:1126-1128.

KOEMAN, J.H., H.C.W. VAN VELZEN-BLAD, R. DE VRIES & J.G. VOS 1973. Effects of PCB and DDE in cormorants and evaluation of PCB residues from an experimental study. *J. Reprod. Fert.*, Suppl. 19:353-364.

KOHANAWA, M., S. SHOYA, T. YONEMURA, K. NISHIMURA & Y. TSUSHIO 1969. Poisoning due to an oily by-product of rice-bran similar to chick-edema disease. II. Tetrachlorobiphenyl as a toxic substance. *Nat. Inst. Anim. Health* 9:220-228.

KOIVUSAARI, J. 1976. Chlorinated hydrocarbons and total mercury in the prey of the White-tailed Eagle (*Haliaeetus albicilla* L.) in the Quarken Straits of the Gulf of Bothnia Finland. *Bull. Environ. Contam. Toxicol.* 15:235-241.

KOIVUSAARI, J., I. NUUJA, R. PALOKANGAS & M. FINNLUND 1980. Relationships between productivity, eggshell thickness and pollutant contents of addled eggs in the population of White-tailed Eagles *Haliaeetus albicilla* L. in Finland during 1969-1978. *Environ. Pollut.* (Series A) 23:41-52.

KOVAL, P.J., T.J. PETERLE & J.D. HARDER 1987. Effects of polychlorinated biphenyls on Mourning Dove reproduction and circulating progesterone levels. *Bull. Environ. Contam. Toxicol.* 39:663-670.

KOZIE, K.D. 1985. *Breeding and feeding ecology of Bald Eagles in the Apostle Islands National Lakeshore.* M.S. Thesis. University of Wisconsin. Stevens Point.

KREITZER, J.F. 1980. Effects of toxaphene and endrin at very low dietary concentrations on discrimination acquisition and reversal in Bobwhite quail, *Colinus virginianus. Environ. Pollut.* (Ser. A) 23:217-230.

KREITZER, J.F. & G.H. HEINZ 1974. The effect of sublethal dosages of five pesticides and a polychlorinated biphenyl on the avoidance response of *Coturnix* quail chicks. *Environ. Pollut.* 6:21-29.

KUBIAK, T.J. 1988. Testimony before U.S. House of Representatives Subcommittee on Investigations and Oversight of the Committee on Public Works and Transportation, *U.S. Congressional Record*, 14 April 1988, pp. 72-81.

KUBIAK, T.J. & D.A. BEST 1991. *Wildlife Risks Associated with Passage of Contaminated Anadromous Fish at Federal Energy Regulatory Commission Licensed Dams in Michigan.* USDI-Fish and Wildl. Serv., E. Lansing, Mich., 48 pp.

KUBIAK, T.J., H.J. HARRIS, L.M. SMITH, T.R. SCHWARTZ, D. L. STALLING, J.A. TRICK, L. SILEO, D.E. DOCHERTY & T.C. ERDMAN 1989. Microcontaminants and reproductive impairment of the Forster's Tern on Green Bay, Lake Michigan - 1983. *Arch. Environ. Contam. Toxicol.* 18:706-727.

KUTZ, F.W., D.G. BARNES, D.P. BOTTIMORE, H. GREIM & E.W. BRETTHAUER 1990. The international toxicity equivalency factor (I-TEF) method of risk assessment for complex mixtures of dioxins and related compounds. *Chemosphere* 20:751-757.

LEVIN, H.S. & R.L. RODNITZKY 1976. Behavioral effects of organophosphate pesticides in man. *Clin. Toxicol.* 9:391-405.

LINCER, J.L. 1972. *The Effects of Organochlorines on the American Kestrel (Falco sparverius Linn.).* Ph.D. dissertation, Cornell Univ. Ithaca. 95 pp.

LINCER, J.L. & D.B. PEAKALL 1970. Metabolic effects of polychlorinated biphenyls in the American Kestrel. *Nature* (London) 228:783-784.

LINCER, J.L. & R. CLARK 1978. Organochlorines in raptor eggs in the Cayuga Lake Basin. *N.Y. Fish & Game J.* 25:121-128.

LINDBERG, P. 1975. Pilgrimsfalken i Sverige. *Svenska Naturskyddsföreningen.* Stockholm.

LINDBERG, P. 1985. Population status, pesticide impact and conservation efforts for the Peregrine (*Falco peregrinus*) in Sweden, with some comparative data from Norway and Finland. Pages 343-351 *in* I. Newton and R.D. Chancellor, eds. *Conservation Studies of Raptors.* ICBP Tech. Publication No. 5. Cambridge, England.

LINDBERG, P. & T. ODSJÖ 1983. Mercury levels in feathers of Peregrine Falcon, *Falco peregrinus*, compared with total mercury content in some of its prey species in Sweden. *Environ. Pollut.* (Ser. B) 5:297-318.

LINDBERG, P., T. ODSJÖ & L. REUTERGÅRDH 1983. Residue levels of polychlorobiphenyls, DDT, and mercury in bird species commonly preyed upon by the Peregrine Falcon (*Falco peregrinus* Tunst.) in Sweden. *Arch. Environ. Contam. Toxicol.* 14:203-212.

LINDBERG, P., P.J. SCHEI & M. WIKMAN 1988. The Peregrine Falcons in Fennoscandia. Pages 159-172 *in* T.J. Cade, J.H. Enderson, C.G. Thelander & C.M. White, eds. *Peregrine Falcon Populations: Their Management and Recovery.* The Peregrine Fund, Inc., Boise, Idaho. 949 pp.

LINDÉN, H., T. NYGÄRD & M. WIKMAN 1984. On the eggshell thickness and reproduction of the Peregrine Falcon (*Falco peregrinus*) in Finland. *Ornis Fennica* 61:116-120.

LOMAN, J. 1977. Factors affecting clutch and brood size in the Crow, *Corvus cornix. Oikos* 29:294-301.

LOWE, T.P. & R.C. STENDELL 1991. Eggshell modifications in captive American Kestrels resulting from Aroclor® 1248 in the diet. *Arch. Environ. Contam. Toxicol.* 20:519-522.

LUCKAS, B., H. WETZEL & O. RECHLIN 1980a. Zur Kontamination von Ostseefischen mit polychlorierten Biphenylen. *Nahrung* 24:405-411.

LUCKAS, B., H. WETZEL & O. RECHLIN 1980b. Ergebnisse der Trend- Untersuchungen von Ostseefischen in Bezug auf ihren Gehalt an DDT und seinen Metaboliten. *Acta Hydrochim. Hydrobiol.* 8:157-173.

MALTBY, C. 1980. Report on the use of pesticides in Latin America. *United Nations Industrial Development Organization.* UNIDO/IOD 353 (19 May 1980). 139 pp.

MATSUMURA, F. 1985. *Toxicology of Insecticides.* Plenum Press, New York.

McARTHUR, M.L.B., G.A. FOX, D.B. PEAKALL & B.J.R. PHILOGÈNE 1983. Ecological significance of behavioral and hormonal abnormalities in breeding Ring Doves fed an organochlorine chemical mixture. *Arch. Environ. Contam. Toxicol.* 12:343-353.

McLANE, M.A.R. & D.L. HUGHES 1980. Reproductive success of Screech Owls fed Aroclor 1248. *Arch. Environ. Contam. Toxicol.* 9:661-665.

MELVASALO, T., J. PAWLAK, K. GRASSHOFF, L. THORELL & A. TSIBAN (eds.) 1981. Assessment of the Effects of Pollution on the Natural Resources of the Baltic Sea, 1980. *Balt. Sea Environ. Proc* No. 5B, 426 pp.

MENDELSSHON, H. & U. PAZ 1977. Mass mortality of birds of prey caused by azodrin, an organophosphorus insecticide. *Biol. Conserv.* 11:163-170.

MENDENHALL, V.M. & L.F. PANK 1980. Secondary poisoning of owls by anticoagulant rodenticides. *Wildl. Soc. Bull.* 8:311-315.

MICHIGAN DEPARTMENT OF PUBLIC HEALTH. 1987. *Analytical method No. 7.* Center of Environ. Hlth. Sci., Epidemol. Studies Lab., Lansing, Mich.

MILLER, R.G. 1981. *Simultaneous Statistical Inference.* Springer-Verlag Inc., New York.

MINEAU, P., G.A. FOX, R.J. NORSTROM, D.V. WESELOH, D.J. HALLETT & J.A. ELLENTON. 1984. Using the Herring Gull to monitor levels and effects of organochlorine contaminants in the Canadian Great Lakes. Pages 425-452 *in* J.O. Nriagu & N.S. Simmons, Eds. *Toxic Contamination in the Great Lakes.* Wiley. New York.

MISSISSIPPI STATE UNIVERSITY. 1985. *Method 1: Analysis for Chlorinated Hydrocarbon Pesticides and Related Compounds.* Mississippi State Chemical Laboratory, Mississippi State, Mississippi.

MIZERA, T.L. 1990. The White-tailed Sea Eagle *Haliaeetus albicilla* in Poland: The present status and prospects. *Baltic Birds* 5:17-23.

MIZERA T. & M. SZYMKIEWICZ 1991. Trends, status and management of the White-tailed Sea Eagle *Haliaeetus albicilla* in Poland. *Birds of Prey Bulletin* 4:1-10.

MORIZOT, D.C., R.G. ANTHONY, T.G. GRUBB, S.W. HOFFMAN, M.E. SCHMIDT & R.E. FERRELL 1985. Clinal genetic variation at enzyme loci in bald eagles (*Haliaeetus leucocephalus*) from the western United States. *Biochem. Gen.* 23:337-345.

MUELLER, H.C. 1987. Prey selection by kestrels: a review. Pages 83-106 *in* D.M. Bird & R. Bowman, eds. *The Ancestral Kestrel.* Raptor Research Foundation, Inc. and Macdonald Raptor Research Centre of McGill University, Ste. Anne de Bellevue, Quebec.

MULHERN, B.M., W.L. REICHEL, L.N. LOCKE, T.H. LAMONT, A. BELISLE, E. CROMARTIE, G.F. BAGLEY & R.M. PROUTY 1970. Organochlorine residues and autopsy data from Bald Eagles 1966-1968. *Pestic. Monit. J.* 4:141-144.

NEWTON, I., I. WYLLIE & A. ASHER 1992. Mortality from the pesticides aldrin and dieldrin in British Sparrowhawks and Kestrels. *Ecotoxicology* 1:31-44.

NISBET, I.C.T. 1988. The relative importance of DDE and dieldrin in the decline of Peregrine Falcon populations. *Pages 351-375 in* T. J. Cade, J. H. Enderson, C. G. Thelander & C. M. White, eds. *Peregrine Falcon Populations: Their Management and Recovery.* The Peregrine Fund, Inc., Boise, ID. 949 pp.

NISBET, I.C.T. 1989. Organochlorines, reproductive impairment, and declines in Bald Eagle *Haliaeetus leucocephalus* populations: Mechanisms and dose-response relationships. Pages 483-489 *in* B.-U. Meyburg & R.D. Chancellor, eds. *Raptors in the Modern World.* World Working Group on Birds of Prey and Owls. Berlin, London, and Paris. 611 pp.

NORSTROM, R.J., R.W. RISEBROUGH & D.J. CARTWRIGHT 1976. Elimination of chlorinated dibenzofurans associated with polychlorinated biphenyls fed to Mallards (*Anas platyrhynchos*). *Toxicol. Appl. Pharmacol.* 37: 217-228.

O'BRIEN, R.D. 1967. *Insecticides: Action and Metabolism.* Academic Press, New York.

OEHME, G. 1980. Der Seeadler, *Haliaeetus albicilla* (L.) als biologischer Spitzenindikator für das vorhandensein persistenter Biozide in der Biosphäre. Pages 81-89 *in* R. Schubert & J. Schuh, eds. *Bioindikation auf der Ebene der Individuen.* Wiss. Beitr. 1980/26 (P10), Martin-Luther-Universität. Halle-Wittenberg.

OEHME, G. 1990. Population status and reproduction of the White-tailed Sea Eagle, *Haliaeetus albicilla* (L.), and their trends in the German Democratic Republic (GDR), 1971 - 1986. *Baltic Birds* 5:59-63.

OEHME, G. & O. MANOWSKY 1991. Entwicklung und Reproduktion des Seeadlerbestandes im ehemaligen Bezirk Frankfurt/O unter besonderer Berücksichtigung der Schorfheide. *Populationsökologie Greifvogel- u. Eulenarten* 2:167-182. Wiss. Beitr. Univ. Halle 1991/4.
OLIPHANT, L.W. 1974. Merlins-the Saskatoon falcons. *Blue Jay* 32:140-147.
OLSSON, M. 1978. Bioaccumulating substances - mainly DDT and PCB - in biota in the Gulf of Bothnia. *Finnish Mar. Res.* 224:227-237.
PAASIVIRTA J. & T. RANTIO 1991. Chloroterpenes and other organochlorines in Baltic, Finnish and Arctic wildlife. *Chemosphere* 22:47-55.
PAASIVIRTA J., R. PAUKKU, H. SURMA-AHO, J. TARHANEN & I. WELLING 1983. Analyses of xenobiotics in birds. *Report of the Ministry of Environment, Finland* (In Finnish).
PAASIVIRTA J., K. MÄNTYKOSKI, J. KOISTINEN, T. KUOKKANEN, E. MANNILA & K. RISSANEN 1989. Structure analysis of planar polychloroaromatic compounds in environment. *Chemosphere* 19:149-154.
PALMER, R.S. 1988. *Handbook of North American Birds.* Volumes 4 & 5. Yale University Press, New Haven.
PASCUAL, J.A. & S.J. PERIS 1992. Effects of forest spraying with two application rates of cypermethrin on food supply and on breeding success of the Blue Tit (*Parus caeruleus*). *Environ. Toxicol. Chem.* 11:1271-1280.
PATNODE, K.A. & D.H. WHITE 1991. Effects of pesticides on songbird productivity in conjunction with pecan cultivation in southern Georgia: a multiple-exposure experimental design. *Environ. Toxicol. Chem.* 10:1479-1486.
PEAKALL, D.B. 1967. Pesticide-induced enzyme breakdown of steroids in birds. *Nature* 216:505-506.
PEAKALL, D.B. 1971. Effect of polychlorinated biphenyls (PCBs) on the egg shells of Ring Doves. *Bull. Environ. Contam. Toxicol.* 6:100-101.
PEAKALL, D.B. & L.F. KIFF 1979. Eggshell thinning and DDE residue levels among Peregrine Falcons *Falco peregrinus*: a global perspective. *Ibis* 121:200-204.
PEAKALL, D.B. & L.F. KIFF 1988. DDE contamination in Peregrines and American Kestrels and its effect on reproduction. Pages 337-350 *in* T.J. Cade, J.H. Enderson, C.G. Thelander & C.M. White, eds. *Peregrine Falcon Populations: Their Management and Recovery.* The Peregrine Fund Inc., Boise, ID. 949 pp.
PEAKALL, D.B. & J.L. LINCER 1970. Polychlorinated biphenyls: another long-life widespread chemical in the environment. *BioScience* 20:958-964.
PEAKALL, D.B. & M.L. PEAKALL 1973. Effects of a polychlorinated biphenyl on the reproduction of artificially and naturally incubated dove eggs. *J. Appl. Ecol.* 10:863-868.
PEAKALL, D.B., J.L. LINCER, R.W. RISEBROUGH, J.B. PRITCHARD & W.B. KINTER 1973. DDE-induced egg-shell thinning: structural and physiological effects in three species. *Comp. Gen. Pharmac.* 4:305-313.
PEARCE, P.A. & D.G. BUSBY 1980. Research on the effects of fenitrothion on the White-throated Sparrow. Pages 24-27 *in* I.W. Varty (compiler) *Environmental Surveillance in New Brunswick, 1978-1979. Effects of Spray Operations for Forest Protection Against Spruce Budworm.* Committee for Environmental Monitoring of Forest Insect Control Operations, Dep. For Res. Univ. of New Brunswick, Fredericton.
PECHMANN, J.H.K., D.E. SCOTT, R.D. SEMLITSCH, J.P. CALDWELL, L.J. VITT & J.W. GIBBONS 1991. Declining amphibian populations: The problem of separating human impacts from natural fluctuations. *Science* 253:892-895.
PERRINS, C.M. 1965. Population fluctuations and clutch size in the great tit, *Parus major* L. *J. Anim. Ecol.* 34:601-647.
PLESTINA, R. & M. PIVKOVIC-PLESTINA 1978. Effect of anticholinesterase pesticides on the eye and vision. *CRC Critical Rev. Toxicol.* 6:1-23.
POSTUPALSKY, S. 1974. Raptor reproductive success: Some problems with methods, criteria, and terminology. Pages 21-31 *in* F.N. Hamerstrom Jr., B.E. Harrell & R.R. Ohlendorff, eds. *Management of Raptors.* Raptor Res. Report No. 2.
POSTUPALSKY, S. 1978. The Bald Eagles return. *Natural History* 7:62-63.
POWELL, G.V.N. & D.C. GRAY 1980. Dosing free-living nestling starlings with an organophosphate pesticide, famphur. *Can. J. Zool.* 60:2233-2235.
PRESTT, I., D.J. JEFFRIES & J.W. MACDONALD 1968. Post-mortem examinations of four rough-legged buzzards. *Brit. Birds* 61:457-465.

PRICE, I.M. & D.V. WESELOH 1986. Increased numbers and productivity of Double-crested Cormorants, *Phalacrocorax auritus*, on Lake Ontario. *Can. Field-Nat.* 100:474-482.

PRICE, H.A., R.L. WELCH, R.H. SCHEEL & L.A. WARREN 1986. Modified multiresidue method for chlordane, toxaphene, and polychlorinated biphenyls in fish. *Bull. Environ. Contam. Toxicol.* 37:1-9.

PROUTY, R.M. & C.M. BUNCK. 1986. Organochlorine residues in adult Mallard and Black Duck wings, 1981-82. *Environ. Monit. Assess.* 6:49-57.

RADVANYI, A., P. WEAVER, C. MASSARI, D. BIRD & E. BROUGHTON 1988. Effects of chlorophacinone on captive kestrels. *Bull. Environ. Contam. Toxicol.* 41:441-448.

RANDLA, T. 1976. White-tailed Eagle *Haliaeetus albicilla* and Golden Eagle *Aquila chrysaëtos* in Estonia. *Ornis Fennica* 53:125-127.

RAHN, H. & A. AR 1974. The avian egg: Incubation time and water loss. *Condor* 76:147-152.

RAHN, H., A. AMOS & C.V. PAGANELLI 1979. How bird eggs breath. Pages 208-217 in *Birds*. W.H. Freeman and Company, San Francisco, CA.

RATCLIFFE, D.A. 1970. Changes attributable to pesticides in egg breakage frequency and eggshell thickness in some British birds. *J. Appl. Ecol.* 7:67-115.

RATCLIFFE, D.A. 1980. *The Peregrine Falcon.* Vermillion, South Dakota, Buteo Books.

RATTNER, B.A., L. SILEO & C.G. SCANES 1982a. Hormonal responses and tolerance to cold of female quail following parathion ingestion. *Pestic. Biochem. Physiol.* 18:132-138.

RATTNER, B.A., L. SILEO & C.G. SCANES 1982b. Oviposition and the plasma concentrations of LH, progesterone and corticosterone in bobwhite quail (*Colinus virginianus*) fed parathion. *J. Reprod. Fertil.* 66:147-155.

REPÚBLICA DE VENEZUELA 1979. *Recomendaciones para el combate de plagas.* Serie 2. 18 pp.

REPÚBLICA DE VENEZUELA 1983. *Gaceta Oficial de la República de Venezuela.* Ministerios de Sanidad y Asistencia Social y Agricultura y Cría.

REPÚBLICA DE VENEZUELA 1985. *Indice de Productos Químicos Registrados.* Ministerio de Agricultura y Cría, Caracas. 25 pp.

RICHIE, P.J. & T.J. PETERLE. 1979. Effect of DDE on luteinizing hormone levels in the ring doves during courtship and nesting. *Bull. Environ. Contam. Toxicol.* 23:220-226.

RISEBROUGH, R.W. 1989. Toxic Chemicals and Birds of Prey: Discussions at Eilat in 1987. Pages 515-525 *in* B.-U. Meyburg & R.D. Chancellor, eds. *Raptors in the Modern World*, Proceedings of the III World Conference on Birds of Prey and Owls. World Working Group on Birds of Prey and Owls. Berlin, London and Paris. 611 pp.

RISEBROUGH, R.W. & D.W. ANDERSON 1975. Some effects of DDE and PCB on Mallards and their eggs. *J. Wildl. Manage.* 39:509-513.

RISEBROUGH, R.W. & D.B. PEAKALL 1988. The importance of various organochlorines in the decline of Peregrine Falcon populations. Pages 449-462 *in* T.J. Cade, J.H. Enderson, C.G. Thelander & C.M. White, eds. *Peregrine Falcon Populations: Their Management and Recovery.* The Peregrine Fund, Boise. 949 pp.

RISEBROUGH, R.W., P. REICHE, D.B. PEAKALL, S.G. HERMAN & M.N. KIRVEN 1968. Polychlorinated biphenyls in the global ecosystem. *Nature* (London) 220:1098-1102.

RISEBROUGH, R.W., J.D. DAVIS & D.W. ANDERSON 1970. Effects of various chlorinated hydrocarbons. Pages 40-53 *in* J. W. Gillett, ed. *The Biological Impact of Pesticides in the Environment.* Environmental Health Sciences Series 1, Oregon State University, Corvallis.

RISEBROUGH, R.W., W.M. JARMAN, A.M. SPRINGER, W. WALKER II & W.G. HUNT 1986. A metabolic derivation of DDE from Kelthane. *Environ. Toxicol. Chem.* 5:13-19.

ROSE, G.A. & G.H. PARKER 1982. Effects of smelter emissions on metal levels in the plumage of Ruffed Grouse near Sudbury, Ontario, Canada. *Can. J. Zool.* 60:2659-2667.

RUDOLPH, S.G., J.G. ZINKL, D.W. ANDERSON & P.J. SHEA 1984. Prey-capturing ability of American Kestrels fed DDE and acephate or acephate alone. *Arch. Environ. Contam. Toxicol.* 13:367-372.

RYAN, B. F., B. L. JOINER, & T. A. RYAN, Jr. 1985. *Minitab Handbook*, 2nd Edition. PWS-Kent, Boston.

SAFE, S. 1987. Determination of 2,3,7,8-TCDD toxic equivalent factors (TEFs): Support for the use of the *in vitro* AHH induction assay. *Chemosphere* 16:791-802.

SAFE, S. 1990. Polychlorinated Biphenyls (PCBs), Dibenzo-*p*-dioxins (PCDDs), Dibenzofurans (PCDFs), and related compounds: Environmental and mechanistic considerations which support the development of toxic equivalency factors (TEFs). *Crit. Rev. Toxicol.* 21:51-88.

SAS INSTITUTE, Inc. 1988. *SAS/STAT User's Guide*, Release 6.03 Edition. Cary, N.C., 1028 pp.
SAVARIE, P.J., D.J. HAYES, R.T. MCBRICE & J.D. ROBERTS 1979. Efficiency and safety of diphacinone as a pesticide. Pages 69-79 *in* E.E. Kenaga, ed. *Avian and Mammalian Wildlife Toxicology*. Am. Soc. for Testing and Materials Spec. Tech. Publ. 693.
SAWYER, T.W., A.D. VATCHER & S. SAFE 1984. Comparative aryl hydrocarbon hydroxylase induction activities of commerical PCBs in Wistar rats and rat hepatoma H4IIE cells in culture. *Chemosphere* 13:695-701.
SCHAFER Jr.,E.W., R.B. BRUNTON, T.J. DeCINO & D.J. CUNNINGHAM 1964. *Acute Oral Toxicity of DRC-632 to Sparrow Hawks.* US Dep. Inter., Bur. Sport Fish Wildl., Denver, CO.
SCHAFER Jr.,E.W., R.R. WEST & D.J. CUNNINGHAM 1969. New Starling toxicant: DRC-1347. *Pest Control* 37:22-30.
SCHAFER Jr.,E.W., W.A. BOWLES, JR. & J. HURLBUT 1983. The acute oral toxicity, repellency, and hazard potential of 998 chemicals to one or more species of wild and domestic birds. *Arch. Environ. Contam. Toxicol.* 12:355-382.
SCHANO, E.A. 1969. *How to Make a Still-Air incubator.* Extension Publication L-8-1a. New York State College of Agriculture. Cornell University. Ithaca, N.Y.
SCHANTZ, S.L., E.D. LEVIN & R.E. BOWMAN 1991. Long-term neurobehavioral effects of perinatal polychlorinated biphenyl (PCB) exposure in monkeys. *Environ. Toxicol. Chem.* 10:747-756.
SCHARF, W.C. & G.W. SHUGART 1981. Recent increases in Double-crested Cormorants in the U.S. Great Lakes. *Amer. Birds* 35:910-911.
SCHMITT, C.J., J.L. ZAJICEK & M.A. RIBICK 1985. National Pesticide Monitoring Program: Residues of organochlorine chemicals in freshwater fish, 1980-1981. *Arch. Environ. Contam. Toxicol.* 14:225-260.
SCHMITT, C.J., J.L. ZAJICEK & P.H. PETERMAN 1990. National Contaminant Biomonitoring Program: Residues of organochlorine chemicals in U.S. freshwater fish, 1976-1984. *Arch. Environ. Contam. Toxicol.* 19:748-781.
SCHMITTLE, S.C., H.M. EDWARDS & D. MORRIS 1958. A disorder of chickens probably due to a toxic feed—Preliminary report. *J. Am. Vet. Med. Ass.* 132:216-219.
SCHNEIDER, R. 1978. Concentrations of PCB in cod tissues from the western Baltic: food chain accumulation or partioning between surrounding water and body lipids? *Int. Council for the Exploration of the Sea.* C.M. 1978/E:10. Marine Environmental Quality Committee. Copenhagen. 11 p.
SCHWARTZ, T.R. & D.L. STALLING 1991. Chemometric comparison of polychlorinated biphenyl residues and toxicologically active polychlorinated biphenyl congeners in the eggs of Forster's Terns (*Sterna fosteri*)(sic). *Arch. Environ. Contam. Toxicol.* 20:183-199.
SEABLOOM, R.W., G.L. PEARSON, L.W. ORING & J.R. REILLY 1973. An incident of fenthion mosquito control and subsequent avian mortality. *J. Wildl. Dis.* 9:18-20.
SEEGAL, R.F., B. BUSH & W. SHAIN 1990. Lightly chlorinated *ortho*-substituted PCB congeners decrease dopamine in nonhuman primate brain and in tissue culture. *Toxicol. Appl. Pharmacol.* 106:136-144.
SEEGAL, R.F., B. BUSH & K.O. BROSCH 1991a. Sub-chronic exposure of the adult rat to Aroclor 1254 yields regionally-specific changes in central dopaminergic function. *NeuroToxicol.* 12:55-66.
SEEGAL, R.F., B. BUSH & W. SHAIN 1991b. Neurotoxicology of *ortho*-substituted polychlorinated biphenyls. *Chemosphere* 23:1941-1949.
SHAIN, W., B. BUSH & R. SEEGAL 1991. Neurotoxicity of polychlorinated biphenyls: Structure-activity relationship of individual congeners. *Toxicol. Appl. Pharmacol.* 111:33-42.
SIMKISS, K. 1967. *Calcium in Reproductive Physiology.* Reinhold Publ. Co. New York.
SMITH, G.J. 1987. *Pesticide Use and Toxicology in Relation to Wildlife: Organophosphorus and Carbamate Compounds.* Fish and Wildl. Ser. Res. Pub. 170. Washington, DC.
SMITH, L.M., T.R. SCHWARTZ, K. FELTZ & T.J. KUBIAK 1990. Determination and occurrence of AHH-active polychlorinated biphenyls, 2,3,7,8-tetrachloro-*p*-dioxin and 2,3,7,8- tetrachlorodibenzofuran in Lake Michigan sediment and biota. The question of their relative toxicological significance. *Chemosphere* 21:1063-1085.
SMITH, S.M. 1967. An ecological study of winter flocks of Black-capped and Chestnut-backed Chickadees. *Wilson Bull.* 79:200-207.
SPRUNT IV, A., W.B. ROBERTSON, Jr., S. POSTUPALSKY, R.J. HENSEL, C.E. KNODER & F.J. LIGAS 1973. Comparative productivity of six Bald Eagle populations. *Trans. North Am. Wildl. Nat. Res. Conf.* 38:96-106.

STALMASTER, M.V. 1987. *The Bald Eagle*. Universe Books. New York, N.Y. 227 pp.
STEIDL, R.J., C.R. GRIFFIN, L.J. NILES, & K. E. CLARK 1991. Reproductive success and eggshell thinning of a reestablished Peregrine Falcon population. *J. Wildl. Manage.* 55:294-299.
STICKEL, L.F., S.N. WIEMEYER & L.J. BLUS 1973. Pesticide residues in eggs of wild birds: adjustment for loss of moisture and lipid. *Bull. Environ. Contam. Toxicol.* 9:193-196.
STICKEL, W.H. 1973. Effects on wildlife of newer pesticides and other pollutants. *Proc. West. Assoc. State Game Fish Comm.* 53:484-491.
STICKEL, W.H., L.F. STICKEL, R.A. DRYLAND & D.L. HUGHES 1984. Aroclor 1254 residues in birds: lethal levels and loss rates. *Arch. Environ. Contam. Toxicol.* 13:7-13.
STJERNBERG, T., J. KOIVUSAARI & I. NUUJA 1990. Population trends and nesting success of the White-tailed Eagle in Finland 1970-1989. (Summary of a report in Finnish). *Lintumies* 25:65-75.
STORER, R. 1966. Sexual dimorphism and food habits in three North American accipiters. *Auk* 83:423-436.
STROMBORG, K.L. 1977. Seed treatment pesticide effects on pheasant reproduction at sublethal doses. *J. Wildl. Manage.* 41:632-642.
STROMBORG, K.L. 1981. Reproductive tests of diazinon on bobwhite quail. Pages 19-30 *in* D.W. Lamb & E.E. Kenaga, eds. *Avian and Mammalian Toxicology: Second Conference.* ASTM STP 757. American Society for Testing and Materials, Philadelphia, PA.
SZEFER, P. & J. FALANDYSZ 1983. Investigations of trace metals in long-tailed duck (*Clangula hyemalis* L.) from the Gdansk Bay. *Sci. Total Environ.* 29:269-276.
SZEFER, P. & J. FALANDYSZ 1987. Trace metals in the soft tissues of scaup ducks (*Aytha marila* L.) wintering in Gdansk Bay, Baltic Sea. *Sci. Total Environ.* 65:203-213.
TANABE S., N. KANNAN, A.N. SUBRAMANIAN, S. WATANABE & R. TATSUKAWA 1987. Highly toxic coplanar PCBs: occurrence, source, persistency and toxic implications to wildlife and humans. *Environ. Pollut.* 47:147- 163.
TANABE S., N. KANNAN, T. WAKIMOTO, R. TATSUKAWA, T. OKAMANO & Y. MATSUDA 1989. Isomer-specific determination and toxic evaluation of potentially hazardous coplanar PCBs, dibenzofurans and dioxins in the tissues of "Yusho" PCB poisoning victim and in the causal oil. *Toxicol. Environ. Chem.* 24:215-231.
TARHANEN J., J. KOISTINEN, J. PAASIVIRTA, P.J. VUORINEN., J. KOIVUSAARI, I. NUUJA, N. KANNAN & R. TATSUKAWA 1989. Toxic significance of planar aromatic compounds in Baltic ecosystem - new studies on extremely toxic coplanar PCBs. *Chemosphere* 18:1067-1077.
THOMPSON, D.R., F.M. STEWART & R.W. FURNESS 1990. Using seabirds to monitor mercury in marine environments. The validity of conservation ratios for tissue comparisons. *Mar. Pollut. Bull.* 21:339-312.
THOMSETT, S. 1987. Raptor deaths as a result of poisoning Quelea in Kenya. *Gabar* 2:33-38.
TILLITT, D.E., J.P. GIESY & G.T. ANKLEY 1991a. Charterization of the H4IIE rat hepatoma cell bioassay as a tool for assessing toxic potency of planar halogenated hydrocarbons in environmental samples. *Environ. Sci. Technol.* 25:87-92.
TILLITT, D.E., G.T. ANKLEY, D.A. VERBRUGGE, J.P. GIESY, J.P. LUDWIG & T.J. KUBIAK 1991b. H4IIE rat hepatoma cell bioassay-derived 2,3,7,8-tetrachlorodibenzo-*p*-dioxin equivalents in colonial fish-eating waterbird eggs from the Great Lakes. *Arch. Environ. Contamin. Toxicol.* 21:91-101.
TILLITT, D.E., G.T. ANKLEY, J.P. GIESY, J.P. LUDWIG, H. KURITA-MATSUBA, D.V. WESELOH, P.S. ROSS, C.A. BISHOP, L. SILEO, K.L. STROMBORG, J. LARSON & T.J. KUBIAK 1992. Polychlorinated biphenyl residues and egg mortality in Double-crested Cormorants. *Environ. Toxicol. Chem.* 11:1281-1288.
TORI, G.M. & T.J. PETERLE 1983. Effects of PCBs on Mourning Dove courtship behavior. *Bull. Environ. Contam. Toxicol.* 30:44-49.
TUCKER, R.G. & D.G. CRABTREE 1970. *Handbook of Toxicity of Pesticides to Wildlife.* Denver Wildl. Res. Center, Res. Publ. No. 84.
TUKEY, J.W. 1951. Quick and Dirty Methods in Statistics, Part II: Simple Analyses for Standard Designs, *Proc. 5th Annu. Conf. Am. Soc. for Qual. Control*, 189-197.
TUMASONIS, C.F., B. BUSH & F.D. BAKER 1973. PCB levels in egg yolks associated with embryonic mortality and deformity of hatched chicks. *Arch. Environ. Contam. Toxicol.* 1:312-324.
TURLE, R., R.J. NORSTROM, & B. COLLINS 1991. Comparison of PCB quantitation methods: re-analysis of archived specimens of Herring Gull eggs from the Great Lakes. *Chemosphere* 22:201-213.

U.S. ENVIRONMENTAL PROTECTION AGENCY 1988. *Guidance for the Reregistration of Pesticide Products Containing Fenthion as the Active Ingredient.* United States Environmental Protection Agency, Office of Pesticides and Toxic Substances, Washington D.C.
VAN RHIJN, J.G. 1991. *The Ruff.* T. & A.D. Poyser Ltd., London 209 pp.
deVOOGT P., D.E. WELLS, L. REUTERGÅRDH & U.A.T. BRINKMAN 1990. Biological activity, determination and occurrence of planar, mono- and di-*ortho* PCBs. *Inter. J. Environ. Anal. Chem.* 40:1-46.
VOS, J.G. & J.H. KOEMAN 1970. Comparative toxicologic study with polychlorinated biphenyls in chickens with special reference to porphyria, edema formation, liver necrosis and tissue residues. *Toxic. Appl. Pharmac.* 17:656-668.
VOS, J.G., J.H. KOEMAN, H.L. VAN DER MAAS, M.C. TEN NOEVER DE BRAUW & R.H. DE VOS 1970. Identification and toxicological evaluation of chlorinated dibenzofuran and chlorinated naphthalene in two commercial polychlorinated biphenyls. *Food Cosmet. Toxicol.* 8:625-633.
WAKE, D. 1991. Declining amphibian populations. *Science* 253:860.
WALTON, B.J., & C.G. THELANDER 1988. Peregrine Falcon management efforts in California, Oregon, Washington, and Nevada. Pages 587-597 *in* T.J. Cade, J.H. Enderson, C.G. Thelander & C.M. White, eds. *Peregrine Falcon Populations: Their Management and Recovery.* The Peregrine Fund, Inc. Boise. 949 pp.
WARKENTIN, I.G. & L.W. OLIPHANT 1988. Seasonal predation of large prey by merlins. *Wilson Bull.* 100:137-139.
WEBER, W.J. 1979. *Health Hazards from Pigeons, Starlings and English Sparrows.* Thomson Publications. Fresno, CA, USA.
WENNEBORG, R. 1986. Rid-A-Bird. *Hawk Chalk* 25:47-48.
WESELOH, D.V., P. MINEAU & D.J. HALLETT. 1979. Organochlorine contaminants and trends in reproduction in Great Lakes Herring Gulls, 1974-1978. *Trans. North Am. Wildl. Nat. Res. Conf.* 44:543-557.
WIEMEYER, S.N. 1991. Effects of environmental contaminants on raptors in the Midwest. Pages 168-181 *in Proc. Midwest Raptor Manage. Symp. and Workshop. National Wildl. Federation Scientific and Technical Series No. 15.* Washington DC.
WIEMEYER, S.N. & D.W. SPARLING 1991. Acute toxicity of four anticholinesterase insecticides to American Kestrels, Eastern Screech-owls and Northern Bobwhites. *Environ. Toxicol. Chem.* 10:1139-1148.
WIEMEYER, S.N., T.G. LAMONT, C.M. BUNCK, C.R. SINLAR, F.J. GRAMLICH, J.D. FRASER & M. BYRD 1984. Organochlorine pesticides, polychlorinated biphenyl, and mercury residues in Bald Eagle eggs -- 1969-79 -- and their relationships to shell thinning and their relationships to shell thinning and reproduction. *Arch. Environ. Contam. Toxicol.* 13:529-549.
WIEMEYER, S.N., R.M. JUREK & J.F. MOORE 1986. Environmental contaminants in surrogates, foods, and feathers of California condors (*Gymnogyps californianus*). *Environ. Monit. Ass.* 6:91-111.
WIEMEYER, S.N., C.M. BUNCK & C.J. STAFFORD 1993. Environmental contaminants in Bald Eagle eggs - 1980-84 - and further interpretations of relationships to productivity and shell thickness. *Arch. Environ. Contam. Toxicol.* 24:213-227.
WIKMAN, M. 1985. The Peregrine population in Finland. Pages 353-358 *in* I. Newton & R.D. Chancellor, eds. *Conservation Studies of Raptors.* ICBP Tech. Publication No. 5. Cambridge, England.
WILSON, B.A., M.J. HOOPER, E.E. LITTRELL, P.J. DIETRICH, M.E. HANSEN, C.P. WEISSKOPF & J.N. SEIBER 1991. Orchard dormant sprays and exposure of red-tailed hawks to organophosphates. *Bull. Environ. Contam. Toxicol.* 47:717-724.
ZINKL, J.G., D.A. JESSUP, A.I. BISHCOFF, T.E. LEW & E.B. WHEELDON 1981. Fenthion poisoning of wading birds. *J. Wildl. Dis.* 17:117-119.

Resolutions

Martial Eagle *Polemaetus bellicosus*

IV WORLD CONFERENCE ON BIRDS OF PREY AND OWLS

Berlin, Germany, 10-17 May 1992

RESOLUTION 1

RECOGNISING	that many of the conservation problems concerning birds of prey are due to worldwide over-population by human beings
URGES	the United Nations and governments of all countries to make greater efforts to promote family planning and birth control

RESOLUTION 2

WHEREAS	large-scale impacts are often a consequence of Regional Development plans supported by EEC Structural Funds throughout Southern Europe and
WHEREAS	internal and external environmental control mechanisms, namely Environmental Impact Assessments, are largely ineffective in preventing or minimising those impacts,
URGES	the EEC and the national governments of Southern Europe to enforce the control mechanisms upon such plans.

RESOLUTION 3

WHEREAS	the survival of several raptor species depends largely on the conservation of some non-breeding (juvenile or immature) individuals concentrating in certain areas
RECOMMENDS	that such areas of concentration be included among the criteria established for assessment and declaration as Special Important Bird Areas as set out in the EEC Directive on Birds.

RESOLUTION 4

WHEREAS	Fenthion is being sold under various trade names as a contact avicide to control pest species in Africa (primarily *Quelea*) and in North America (primarily House Sparrows, Starlings and Pigeons), and
WHEREAS	field and laboratory research has shown that Fenthion in its present use constitutes a serious secondary poisoning hazard to birds of prey,
URGES	the responsible government agencies in the countries where Fenthion is used to take appropriate and immediate action to halt the further use of Fenthion as a contact avicide until research has been undertaken to find ways and means of its safe application.

RESOLUTION 5

NOTING	that in the Federal Republic of Germany research into the protection of birds of prey is affected in various ways by the right of individual hunters to take raptors into possession, and
CONSIDERING	that these species are of importance as environmental indicators and
CONSIDERING	that attitudes towards utilisation of the environment have changed so that this right is no longer justifiable
URGES	the German Parliament to take the decision to change the law in order that the situation of these species may be improved by deleting all birds of prey without exception from Paragraph 2 of the Federal Hunting Law.

RESOLUTION 6

CONCERNED for the effective and long-term protection of breeding places, surface waters and hunting areas for the Sea Eagle and Osprey in all German states with breeding pairs and

CONSIDERING the sensitivity of the Sea Eagle and Osprey to human disturbance of various kinds as well as the increasing threat to their habitat and

NOTING that a certain increase in the Sea Eagle and Osprey population has been achieved only through intensive protection measures, providing a necessary reserve as regards present and future negative factors

URGES the German Section of ICBP and the DDA (umbrella organisation of German avifaunists), as well as other state and social organisations concerned to determine that the Sea Eagle and Osprey should remain on the Red List of the Federal Republic of Germany in the highest category of endangerment, since only further effective protection measures, including research into the species' population dynamics, can secure the population and make possible a re-colonisation of former breeding areas.

RESOLUTION 7

NOTING that the Lesser Spotted Eagle, being the rarest and most endangered of all eagle species regularly breeding in Germany, has already disappeared from large areas as a breeding species during the last decades, and

WHEREAS the present area of distribution within Brandenburg is confined to a small part of the state in the north-east, which is at the same time the southern and eastern limit of the species' distribution,

CONGRATULATES the new Government of this state on having established the largest Biosphere Reserve in Germany, which is also an important breeding area for the species, and

RECOMMENDS that the Government of Brandenburg, the appropriate Federal Government bodies and nature conservation organisations support a project soon to be initiated to study and protect the present population of the Lesser Spotted Eagle in this state.

RESOLUTION 8

NOTING that the Eagle Owl *Bubo bubo* became extinct as a breeding bird in Brandenburg in 1885 and

CONSIDERING that, for the first time since that date, a pair of Eagle Owls once again bred successfully in Kreis Zossen in 1991 and also in 1992 and

CONCERNED over plans to develop this area as a research centre and golf course

URGES the Environment Minister for Brandenburg to preserve the forest in which the Owl breeds and its environs by establishing a protected zone around it, forbidding the use of pesticides and rodenticides, preserving the trees and other vegetation together with the meadows and ponds, in collaboration with local naturalists.

RESOLUTION 9

RECOGNISING that the nature reserve "Nonnenhof mit Lieps" near Neubrandenburg is one of the most important areas in Mecklenburg-Vorpommern for endangered raptors like the White-tailed Eagle and the Osprey and other species and

CONSIDERING that the International Council for Bird Preservation has included this area in the list of Important Bird Areas (IBA) in Europe and

NOTING that close to this nature reserve, in the landscape reserve (Landschaftsschutzgebiet) "Tollensebecken", a big holiday park, golf course and riding place is planned and already authorised by the Minister of Economy of Mecklenburg-Vorpommern and

WHEREAS these plans are an infringement of the EC directives concerning nature conservation

URGES the European Parliament and the Parliament of Mecklenburg-Vorpommern to prevent development of the project at this ecologically sensitive place and to ensure that the Important Bird Area with its surroundings is effectively protected.

RESOLUTION 10

NOTING that a research project regarding protection of the Lesser Spotted Eagle has been in progress for some time in Mecklenburg-Vorpommern, where 80% of the German population occurs,

URGES the government of the state of Mecklenburg-Vorpommern to implement the project recommendations regarding habitat protection by the leaders of this project, e.g. that the breeding areas must be prevented from development by road-building and tourism and conserved in the long term through contracts with the relevant land-owners whereby exploitation of the territory shall be diminished, and

RECOMMENDS that the government of Mecklenburg-Vorpommern, the Federal Ministry of the Environment, the German Research Council and any other appropriate body support this project.

RESOLUTION 11

NOTING that the recent political developments in the former USSR have resulted in the formation of independent states which now lack adequate legal control over the conservation of raptors and owls and

CONCERNED over increasing illegal trapping and exporting of rare and endangered species, particularly falcons

URGES the governments of the independent states and administrations of autonomous regions and districts within the territory of the former USSR to establish wildlife conservation legislation, to protect all raptor species (*Falconiformes* and *Strigiformes*) and to become signatories to CITES

RESOLUTION 12

WHEREAS birds of prey and owls are an important part of biodiversity, particularly in the territory of the former USSR,

URGES political leaders of the new independent states within the former USSR who are attending the forthcoming "Earth Summit" in Brazil to seek support from other governmental representatives and international organisations to strengthen the environmental policy and legislative control of conservation within these states.

RESOLUTION 13

RECOGNISING that the United States of America's Endangered Species Act of 1972 has served as a model piece of legislation for the provision of legal status for endangered and threatened species of birds of prey and numerous other species of fauna and flora in various parts of the world and

WHEREAS the current authorisation of this Endangered Species Act is due to expire on 30 September 1992

URGES the US Government to effect the passage of re-authorisation of this legislation so that there may be continuity of protection of those species of wildlife presently considered to be endangered or threatened.

RESOLUTION 14

CONCERNED at the lack of enforcement of the bird protection laws in Malta, which results in the shooting of thousands of migrating raptors each year and

CONSIDERING the efforts being made throughout Europe to protect these birds and

NOTING that Malta has applied for membership in the European Community

URGES the Maltese Government to take immediate action to bring legislation up to the standard required by the European Community and to properly enforce it.

RESOLUTION 15

RECOGNISING that many species of birds of prey are endangered worldwide and that, in addition to conservation of their breeding and wintering areas, protection of their migration routes is one of the most important tasks for the international community and

CONSIDERING that the Republic of Syria is an area of vital importance for migration and wintering of a number of Palearctic species, some of which are endangered

NOTING that the increasing number of tourists includes numbers of conservationists who are shocked to witness the mass killing of birds of prey and their commercial exploitation, both alive and stuffed, as typified by the hunting and taxidermists' shops in Damascus and other towns, regularly supplied from collecting centres in Qariatyn, Palmyra and other desert localities, as well as the falcon-trading village of Ruhaybe and

CONSIDERING that thousands of birds of prey are shot annually and live Saker Falcons trapped or imported for sale from neighbouring countries and

WHEREAS the breeding populations of these species are protected in other countries at considerable expense and

CONSIDERING that as a result of persecution several native Syrian species have been greatly reduced or extirpated

URGES the President of the Syrian Republic to exercise his full authority to protect all birds of prey breeding in or migrating through his country and to promote the concept amongst the people of his country that birds of prey should not be killed but should be regarded as a valuable cultural asset, the safe migration of which through Syria must in future be ensured.

RESOLUTION 16

CONSIDERING the poor state of the Philippine Eagle *Pithecophaga jefferyi*, with 14 eagles in captivity and only 23 known in the wild, and its risk of extinction

SUPPORTS the Philippine Eagle Conservation Program Inc. in its efforts to preserve the Philippine Eagle and its environment and

URGES the Government of the Philippines and all national and international organisations to lend their full support to this endeavour.

RESOLUTION 17

RECOGNISING the continuing efforts to conserve the Mauritius Kestrel *Falco punctatus*,

CONGRATULATES the Government of the Republic of Mauritius on the success of its multi-disciplinary project which has resulted in an increase of the number of Kestrels from four known wild birds in 1974 to a free-living population of about 170 birds to-day, and

URGES the Government of the Republic of Mauritius to continue its efforts to restore the Kestrel population and to ratify the Black River Gorges National Park, including the forests around Bassin Blanc, which will provide secure habitat for the Kestrel and for the other endangered wild land birds of the island.

RESOLUTION 18

CONSIDERING that the international sectors of the Douro/Duero and Tejo/Tajo rivers represent important areas for cliff-nesting raptors at an international level,

URGES	the governments of Spain and Portugal to co-ordinate efforts to create protected areas in these regions.

RESOLUTION 19

RECOGNISING	that with regard to the reintroduction of the Bearded Vulture a certain number of rules have been laid down and
NOTING	with pleasure that in Spain steps are being taken to re-establish the Bearded Vulture in areas outside the Pyrenees, and
CONCERNED	that this project be internationally recognised and accepted
URGES	that the rules governing such a project should be adhered to and that intentions to remove eggs from the wild population should in no case be implemented.

RESOLUTION 20

NOTING	that in Austria there formerly occurred 34 breeding species of birds of prey and owls, of which to-day only 23 remain, 19 of which are in the Red List,
URGES	the Austrian authorities to bring their legislation up to the level required by CITES and the Bern Convention.

RESOLUTION 21

AWARE	that human activities have reduced many populations of birds of prey to dangerously low numbers and, in some areas to extinction
RECOMMENDS	reintroductions to Mt. Carmel in Israel

RESOLUTION 22

CONCERNED	about the possible impact on migrating birds of prey and other species of the Voice of America relay station projected for construction in the Aravah Valley in Israel and
FEARING	that this may have the following effects on these migrating birds: collisions with high towers, net antennas and mazes of cables, and the possible influence of micro-wave radiation on approaching and roosting birds and on the orientation, navigation and behaviour of migrating birds,
URGES	the governments of Israel and the United States of America to cancel this project.

RESOLUTION 23

APPRECIATING	the generosity of the Berlin Senate and the German Research Council in sponsoring the IV World Conference on Birds of Prey and Owls, its participants would like to express their profound gratitude for their support and express the hope that, in order to complete the success and significance of this Conference, sympathetic consideration will be given towards similarly supporting publication of the Proceedings.

RESOLUTION 24

THANKS	the staff of the Conference Centre at Gosen for their great efforts under difficult conditions and for contributing so much towards the success of this conference and
URGES	the Governments of Berlin and Brandenburg and all those concerned to keep this Centre open for future scientific and cultural meetings, for which it is so admirably suited.